The *Contract With God* Trilogy

The Will Eisner Library

Hardcover Compilations

Will Eisner's New York
Life in Pictures

Paperbacks

A Contract With God
A Life Force
New York: The Big City
City People Notebook
Will Eisner Reader
The Dreamer
Invisible People
To the Heart of the Storm
Dropsie Avenue
Life on Another Planet
Family Matter
Minor Miracles
Name of the Game
The Building
The Plot: The Secret Story of the Protocols of the Elders of Zion

Other Books by Will Eisner

Fagin the Jew

The *Contract With God* Trilogy

Life on Dropsie Avenue

A Contract With God • A Life Force • Dropsie Avenue

Will Eisner

W. W. Norton & Company
New York • London

Printed in the United State of America
First Edition

For information about permission to reproduce selections from this book, write to Permissions, W. W. Norton & Company, Inc., 500 Fifth Avenue, New York, NY 10110

Manufacturing by R. R. Donnelley, Willard Division
Production: Julia Druskin and Sue Carlson

Library of Congress Cataloging-in-Publication Data

Eisner, Will.
The contract with God trilogy : life on Dropsie Avenue / Will Eisner.
p. cm.
Contents: A contract with God—A life force—Dropsie Avenue.
ISBN 0-393-06105-1
1. Graphic novels. I. Title: Life on Dropsie Avenue. II. Eisner, Will. Contract with God.
III. Eisner, Will. Life force. IV. Eisner, Will. Dropsie Avenue. V. Title.

PN6727.E4A6 2005
741.5'973—dc22

2005053944

W. W. Norton & Company, Inc., 500 Fifth Avenue, New York, NY 10110
www.wwnorton.com

W. W. Norton & Company Ltd., Castle House, 75/76 Wells Street, London W1T 3QT

4 5 6 7 8 9 0

To Ann

Contents

List of New Illustrations

The following twelve illustrations were created by the author especially for this edition.

Preface

This book contains stories drawn from the endless flow of happenings characteristic of city life. Some are true. Some could be true.

Born and brought up in New York City and having survived and thrived there, I carry with me a cargo of memories, some painful and some pleasant, which have remained locked in the hold of my mind. I have an ancient mariner's need to share my accumulation of experience and observations. Call me, if you will, a graphic witness reporting on life, death, heartbreak and the never-ending struggle to prevail . . . or at least to survive.

In 1978, encouraged by the work of the experimental graphic artists Otto Nückel, Franz Masareel and Lynd Ward, who in the

1930s published serious novels told in art without text, I attempted a major work in a similar form. In a futile effort to entice the patronage of a mainstream publisher, I called it a "graphic novel." It was a collection of four related stories, drawn from memory, which took place in a single tenement in the Bronx. The title of the book, named for the lead story, became *A Contract With God*. Though no major publisher would touch it at the time, this novel has remained in print for twenty-seven years, and has been published in eleven different languages. I followed this first effort with other more ambitiously constructed graphic novels. Two of them, closely related to the struggle for survival in the urban environment, are included with *A Contract With God* in this trilogy. All are anchored on a single street in the borough of the Bronx in New York City. The street is Dropsie Avenue, a caricature of a neighborhood that is nevertheless very real to me.

As the story unfolds, it is at 55 Dropsie Avenue where Frimme Hersh deals with God; where the street singer fails to grasp his chance for glory. It is on Dropsie Avenue where a diminutive enemy defeats the super, and Willie comes of age. It is in an alley on Dropsie Avenue where Jacob Shtarkah tries to find the meaning of life. It is also on Dropsie Avenue, finally, where I undertake the biography of the street

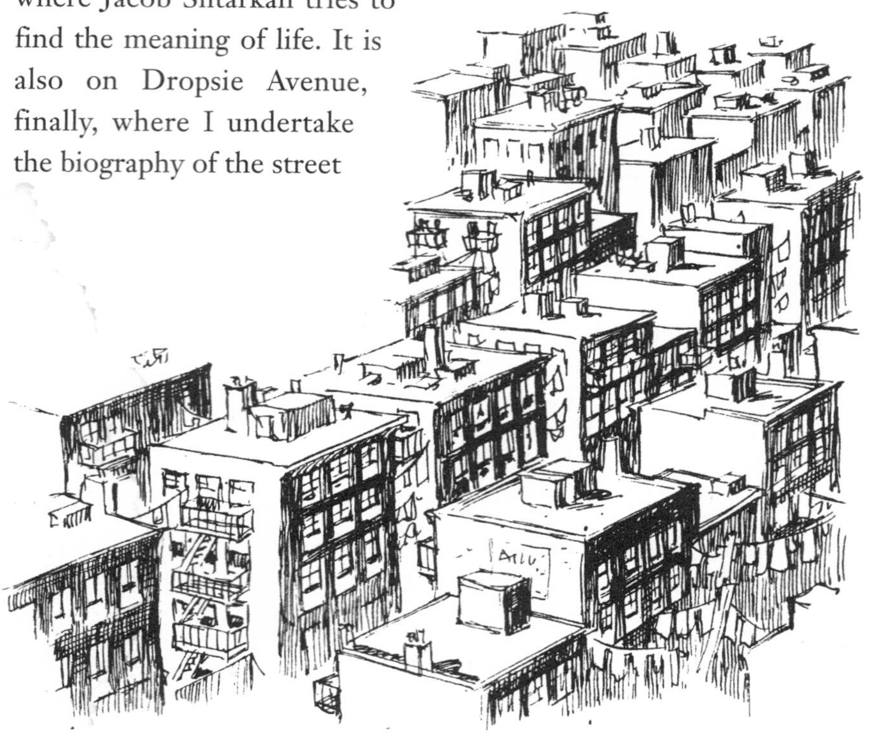

itself, through the physical evolution of the block, the rise and fall of the tenement building at No. 55 and the ethnic and social changes of its stream of occupants.

The tenement—the name derives from a fifteenth-century legal term for a multiple dwelling—always seemed to me a "ship afloat in concrete." After all, didn't the building carry its passengers on a voyage through life? No. 55 sat at the corner of Dropsie Avenue near the elevated train, or the elevated as we called it in those days. It was a treasure house of stories that illustrated tenement life as I remembered it, stories that needed to be told before they faded from memory. Within its "railroad flats," with rooms strung together train-like, lived low-paid city employees or laborers and their turbulent families. Most were recent immigrants, intent on their own survival. They kept busy raising children and dreaming of the better life they knew existed "uptown." Hallways were filled with a rich stew of cooking aromas, sounds of arguments, and the tinny wail from Victrolas. What community spirit there was stemmed from the common hostility of tenants toward the landlord or his surrogate superintendent. Typically, the building's tenants came and went with regularity, depending on the vagaries of their fortunes. But many remained for a lifetime, imprisoned there by poverty or old age. Within its walls great dramas played out. There was no real privacy or anonymity. Everybody knew about everybody. Human dramas, both good and bad, instantly gathered witnesses like ants swarming around a piece of dropped food. From window to window or on the stoop below, the tenants analyzed, evaluated and critiqued each happening, following an obligatory admission that it was really none of their business.

"A Contract With God," the first part of this book, examines the subject of man's relationship with his God. This very basic human preoccupation stems from the primal concern with survival. We are told early on that God will either punish us or reward us, depending on our behavior, in accordance with a compact. The clergy provides the terms, edicts, and conditions, and our parents enforce this contract.

The creation of this story was an exercise in personal agony. My only daughter, Alice, had died of leukemia eight years before the publication of this book. My grief was still raw. My heart still bled. In fact, I could not even then bring myself to discuss the loss. I made Frimme Hersh's daughter an "adopted child." But his anguish was mine. His argument with God was also mine. I exorcised my rage at a deity that I believed violated my faith and deprived my lovely 16-year-old child of her life at the very flowering of it. This is the first time in thirty-four years that I have openly discussed it.

"The Street Singer," which appeared as the second vignette in the original *A Contract With God*, was a creature of the Depression years. These were desperate times when no device to earn some money was beyond reproach. The street singers were men who appeared in the narrow space between the tenements to provide impromptu concerts. As a boy I often tossed a penny down into our back alley for the man who regularly appeared there to sing, in a wine-soaked voice, popular songs or off-key operatic arias. Mothers seemed charmed by this seedy romantic troubadour. Fathers were sure he was a spy for robbers, and the meaner kids sometimes threw down a button wrapped in paper to see how angry the man would get when he opened it. To me, however, he brought a bit of theatrical glamour to the grim alley. The mystery about who he was has remained with me over the years. Finally, with this book about tenement life, I was able to immortalize his story.

"The Super" is a story built around the mysterious but threatening custodian of the Bronx apartment house where I lived as a young boy. Since we never had contact with or even knew the landlord, the superintendent was the person we dealt with on the day-to-day matters of habitation. He lived in the cellar, was unmarried, and seemed perpetually cranky, probably because he was constantly being annoyed by tenants who demanded repairs, better heat in the winter, or complained about poor maintenance. Generally the super was feared and avoided, and blamed for any unusual happening, real or imagined.

"Cookalein," the final story in the first book, is a Yiddish-English word, which means "cook alone." It describes a summer resort on a farm where the guests cooked their own meals. Each summer, in the Catskill Mountains about 150 miles from New York City, not far from the more upscale resorts that catered to the urban middle class, farmers made some extra money by opening their farms to vacationers. Many farmers built small "bungalows," forerunners to the motels of the '40s, on their properties. They opened their kitchens in the "main house" for mothers to cook meals for their families. A rental was very cheap. No maid service or food was included, and guests brought their own linens. The countryside excursion was a welcome experience, particularly for the young, who

had a chance to help with farm chores, watch the process of animal life, drink milk from cows' udders and, most crucially, enjoy the freedom of living away from the prison-like environment of the city. In this brief exposure to a bucolic atmosphere, a young boy, amid the drama of his parents' lives, could have his first romance and a first real sexual experience—an ethereal event—in the clear air and wholesomeness of a mountain farm. Glamour and excitement, which wafted down from the great hotels only a few miles away, added to the theatrics of the summer holiday. "Cookalein" is a combination of invention and recall. It is an honest account of my coming of age.

In 1983, five years after the publication of the first novel, I began work on *A Life Force*, placing this graphic novel at the same address as *A Contract With God*. The debate over Darwinism and Creationism continues over the decades, but the meaning of life remains scientifically unanswerable. It is one thing to deal with How we got here. It is another to deal with Why. I undertook this book after my 65th birthday, a hallmark that seemed to arrive too soon. For someone who has always felt caught in a mortal struggle with time and who has an enormous number of yet undone projects ahead, this was a sobering event. Suddenly, enduring memories that were accumulations of the detritus of living seemed more ephemeral.

We measure time as a ratio based on how long we've lived. Of course, at 65, a year seems more ephemeral: it is 1/65 of one's life. The more I ruminated on this, the harder it was to quell my preoccupation with it. The only way to deal with this thought was to address it head on. For me, it would be the writing of a novel on aging, a subject I was sure everyone must encounter sooner or later. At the time, the graphic medium was still rather young for this kind of probing. But graphic narrative is a language that can provide visual metaphors appropriate to such a heavy theme. To the indifferent youngster, I promise that this story will be waiting for you when you reach sixty-five.

Because I was dealing with a personal concern, I made Jacob Shtarkah, the protagonist in *A Life Force*, me in disguise, a character through whom I could play out the story. And while none of the events in Jacob's life occurred in mine, they were drawn from neighborhood stories that I could knowingly display as examples. During my formative years in the city, my family moved from borough to borough, each time to a different ethnic environment. To reinforce reality, I set the events during the Great Depression—a time when life and living were more marginal and precarious, yet the reason for it all seemed as unattainable as ever. And while Jacob is a fictional stand-in for my mature self, the character Willie, along with his counterpart in "Cookalein," directly represents the youthful me. Willie's story in both instances is essentially autobiographical.

In 1995 I couldn't restrain myself and I returned again to my familiar setting with *Dropsie Avenue: The Neighborhood*, the third element of this trilogy. To anyone growing up in any large city, the immediate neighborhood becomes the world. The street on which one lives provides a kid with local identification somewhat similar to being branded by national origin. Streets have a status. They grow, get old and change in character. In large coastal cities, immigration has an effect on the profile of a street, altering it as each new group enters, stays awhile, assimilates and then moves away. Streets seem to have a discernible life. Some start out ostentatiously and gradually descend into slums while others begin as poor and disreputable neighborhoods and rise to ostentation through what city planners call gentrification. Dropsie Avenue, this fictitious stage where my past and my imagination collided, has a history similar to real streets in the Bronx. Like its inhabitants, it has a turbulent existence but an unquenchable instinct for survival. *Dropsie Avenue* is a story of life, death and resurrection.

I've spent a long career—spanning eight decades—combining and refining words and pictures. My early work in newspaper comics and comic books allowed me to entertain millions of readers weekly, but I always felt there was more to say. I pioneered the use of comics for instructional manuals for American soldiers, covering three major wars, and later used comics to educate grade school children. Both were heady responsibilities that I took very seriously. But I yearned to do still more with the medium. At an age when I could have "retired," I chose instead to create literary comics, then a decidedly oxymoronic term. Acceptance has not always been easy, but I have seen it arrive in my lifetime. It has been most gratifying to see the graphic novel and many of its exceptional creators gradually become an accepted part of the book world. I couldn't find a major publisher to take *A Contract With God* only a quarter century ago, and now graphic novels represent the book industry's fastest growing genre.

The three graphic novels collected herein represent a vital part of my *oeuvre*. It brings great satisfaction to know that they now reach a new generation of readers.

Will Eisner

Tamarac, Florida
December 2004

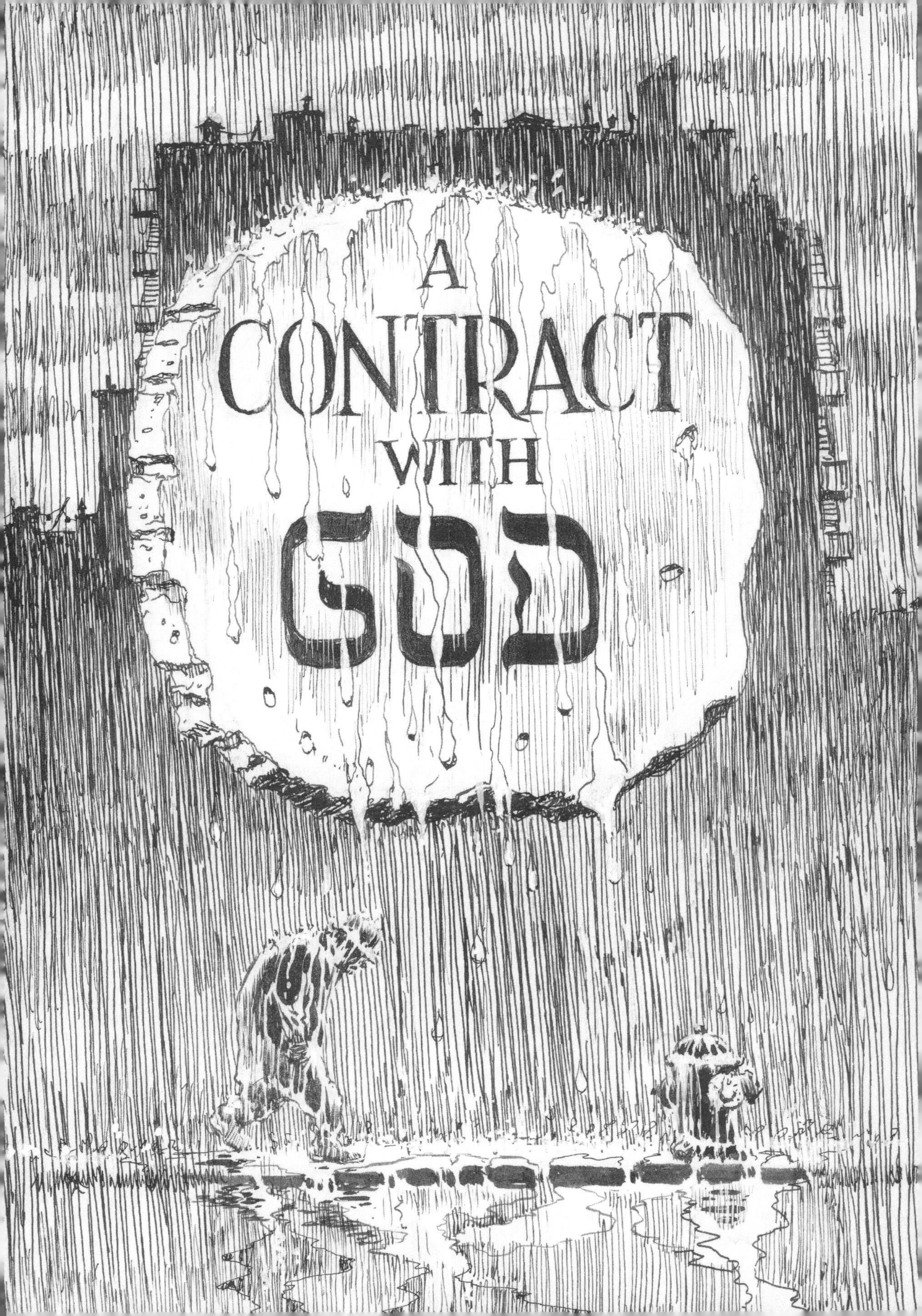
A
CONTRACT
WITH
GOD

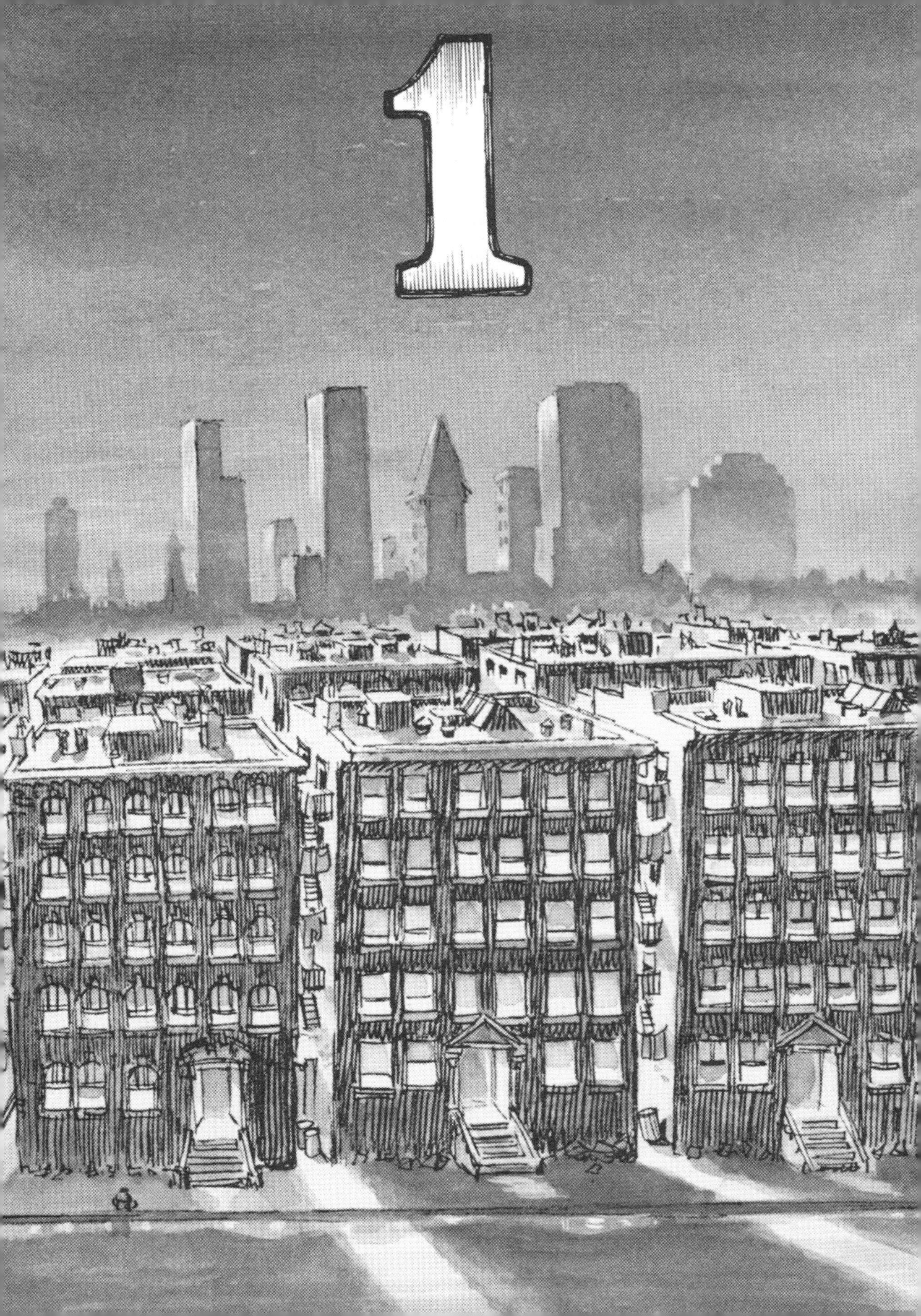
1

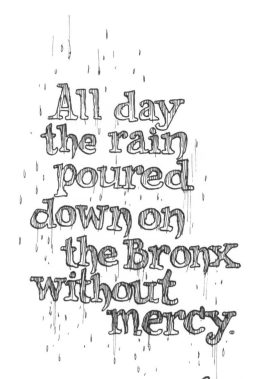

All day
the rain
poured
down on
the Bronx
without
mercy.

The sewers overflowed
and the waters rose
over the curbs of the street.

The tenement at No.55 Dropsie Avenue seemed ready to rise and float away on the swirling tide! "Like the ark of Noah," it seemed to Frimme Hersh as he sloshed homeward.

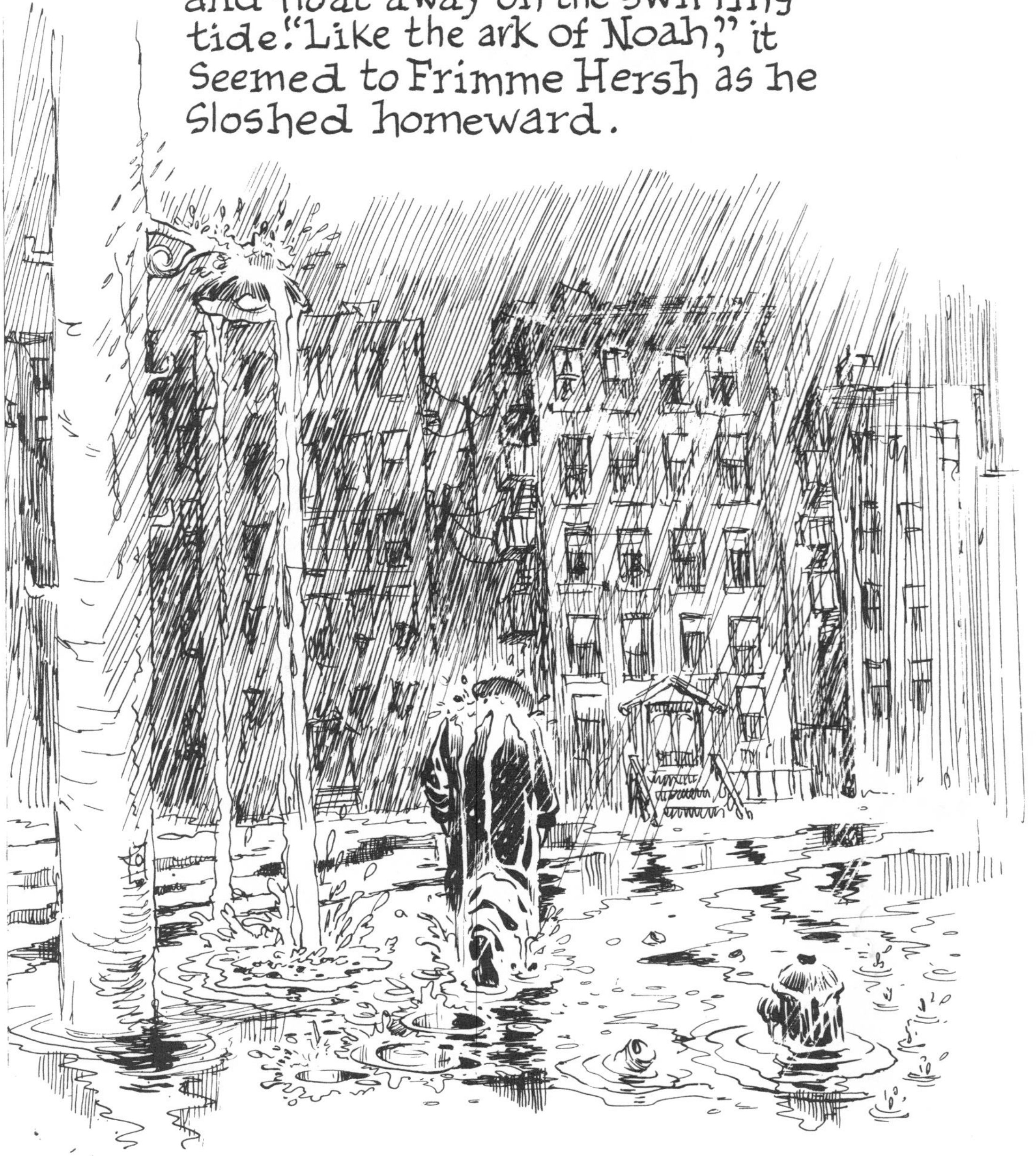

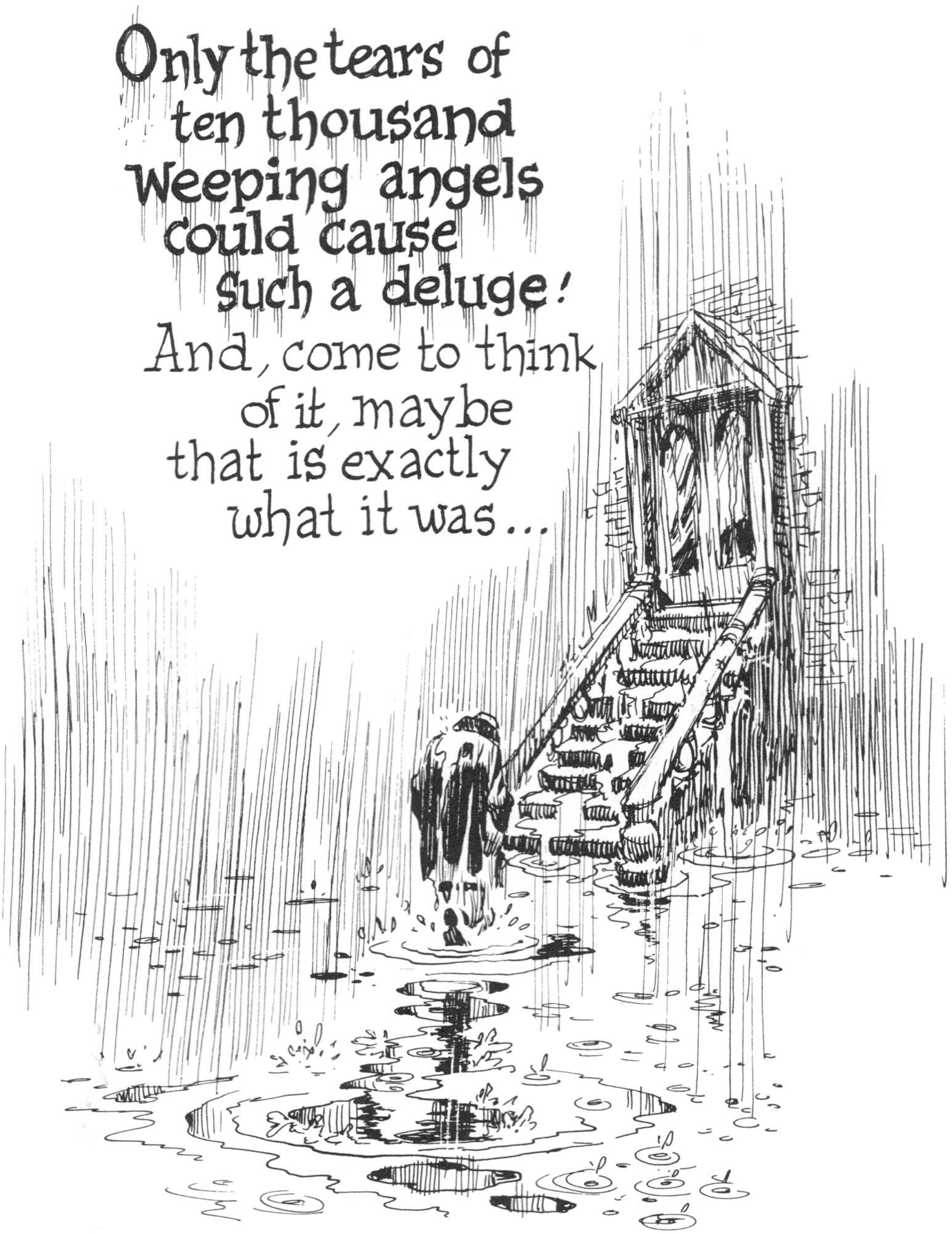
Only the tears of ten thousand weeping angels could cause such a deluge!
And, come to think of it, maybe that is exactly what it was...

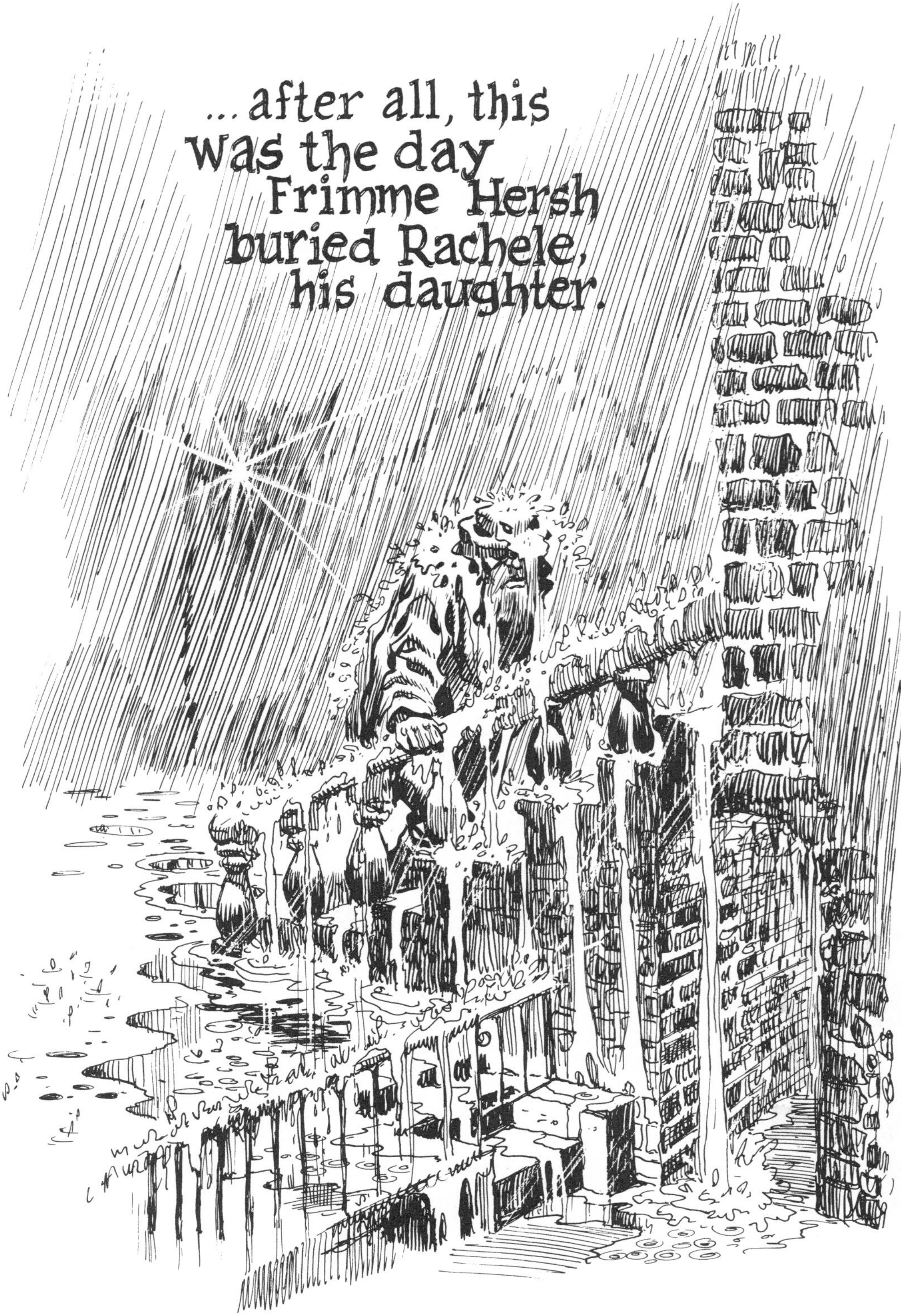
...after all, this
was the day
Frimme Hersh
buried Rachele,
his daughter.

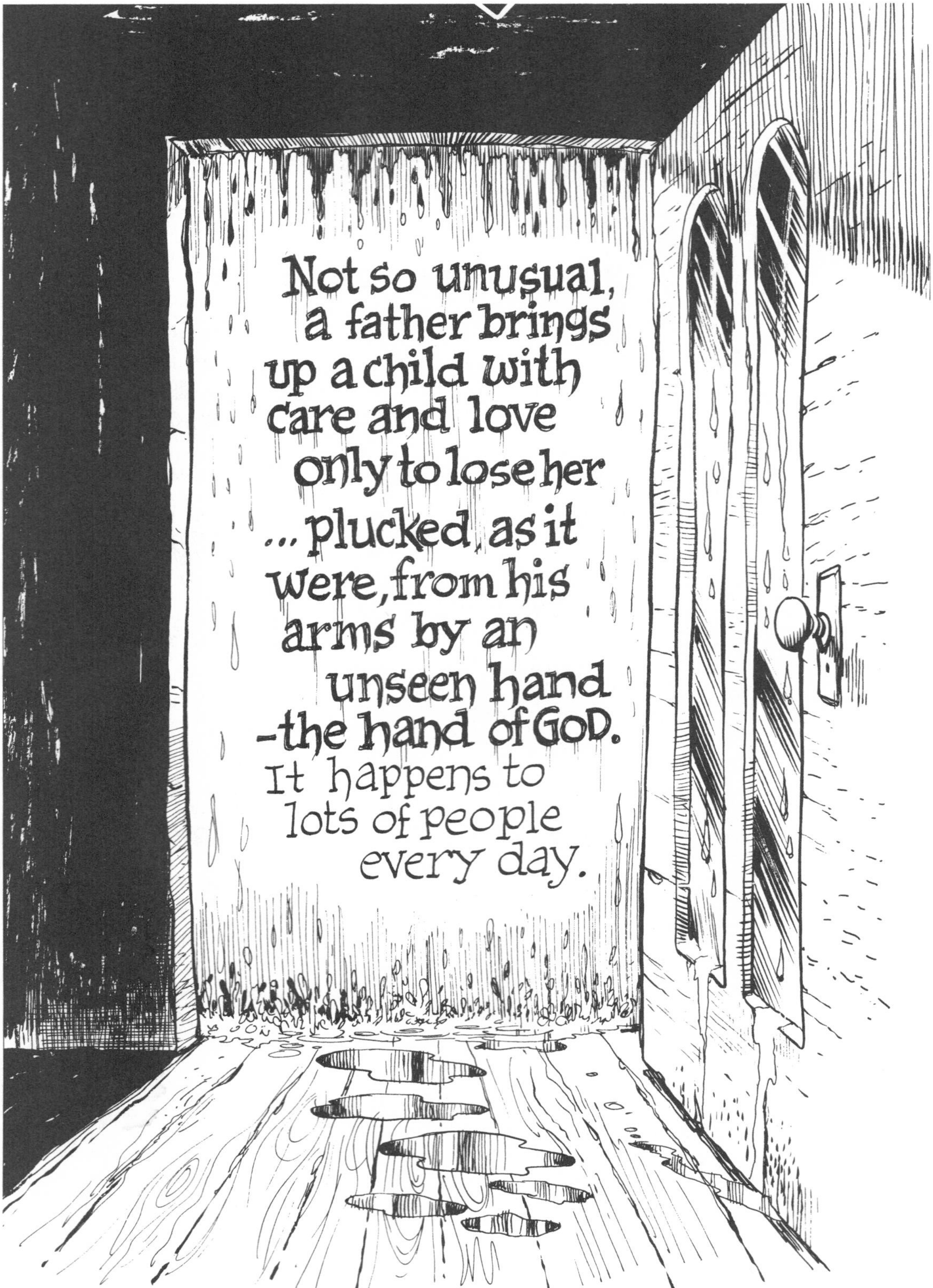
Not so unusual, a father brings up a child with care and love only to lose her ... plucked, as it were, from his arms by an unseen hand - the hand of GOD.
It happens to lots of people every day.

...to others, maybe.

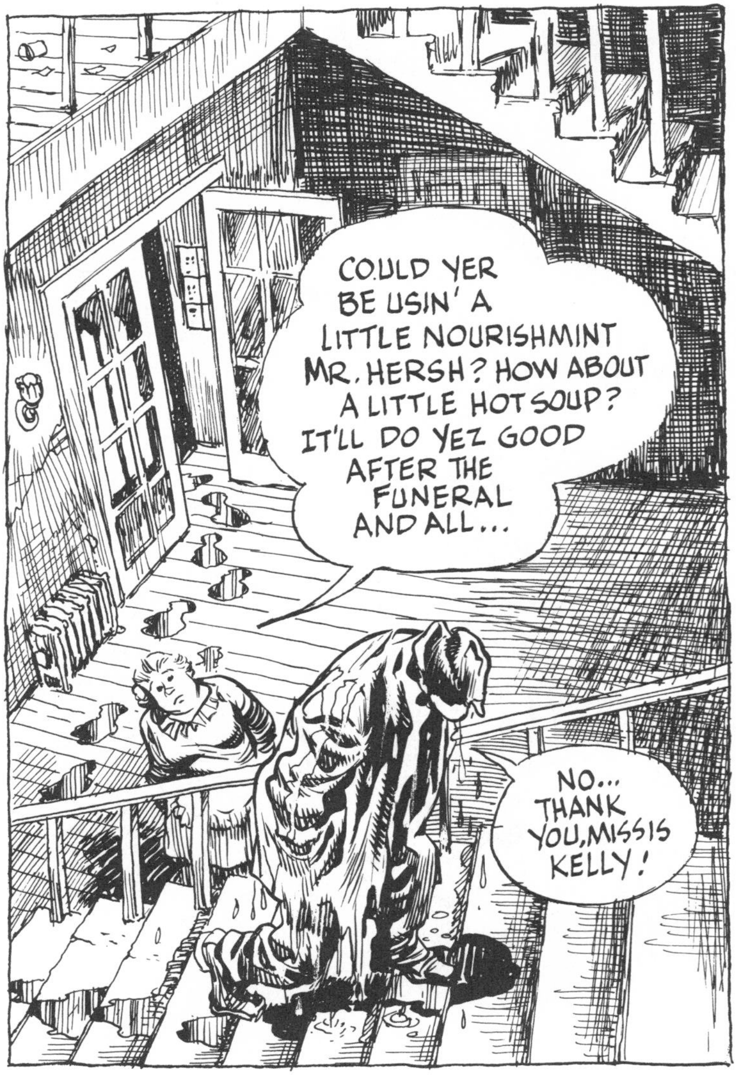
COULD YER BE USIN' A LITTLE NOURISHMINT MR. HERSH? HOW ABOUT A LITTLE HOT SOUP? IT'LL DO YEZ GOOD AFTER THE FUNERAL AND ALL...
NO... THANK YOU, MISSIS KELLY!

... but not to Frimme Hersh.

And why not to Frimme Hersh ??

That's a fair question!

It should not have happened
to Frimme Hersh

BECAUSE FRIMME HERSH HAD A CONTRACT WITH GOD!

And a contract is a contract!

It was, after all, a solemn agreement of many years.

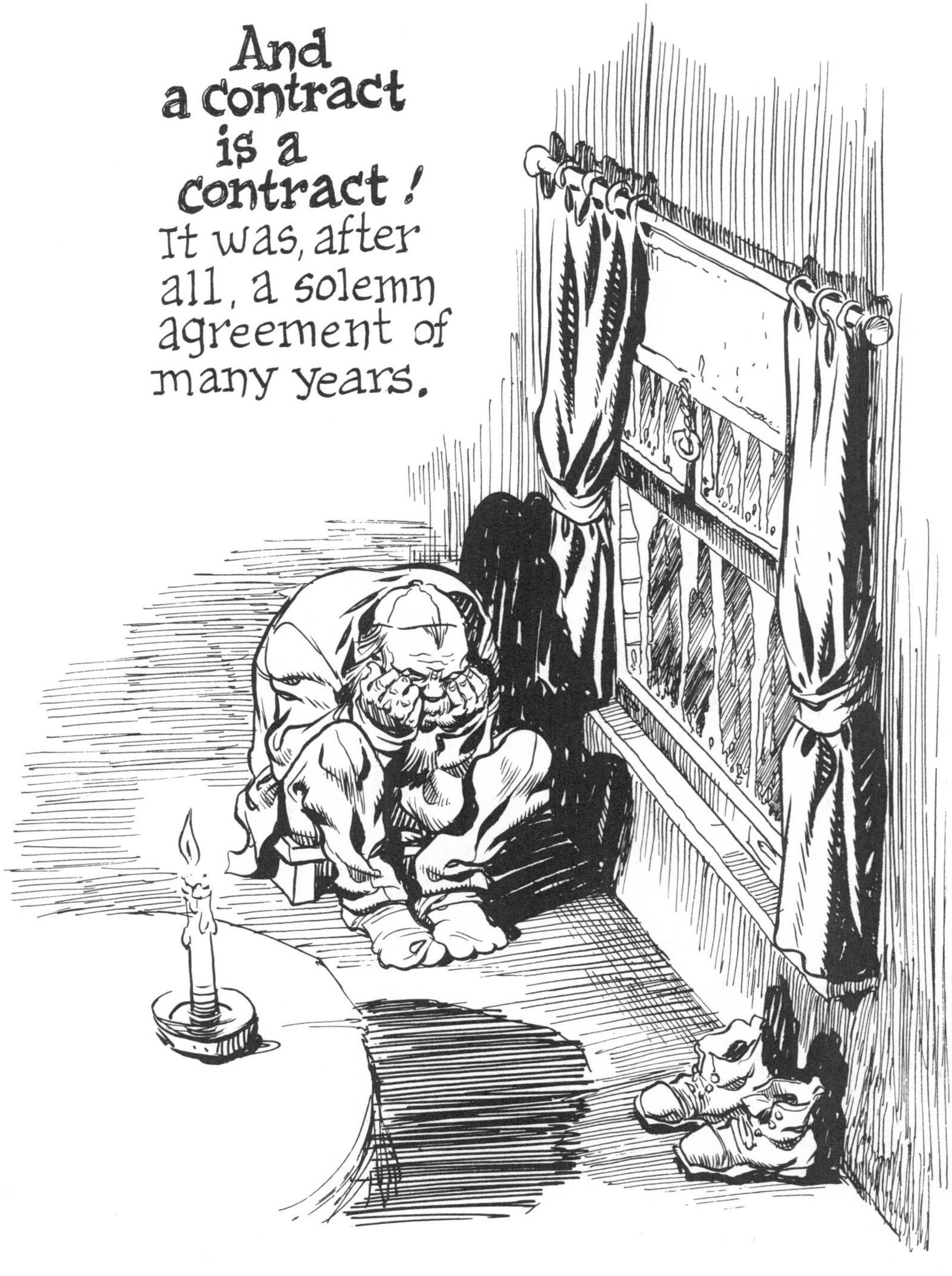

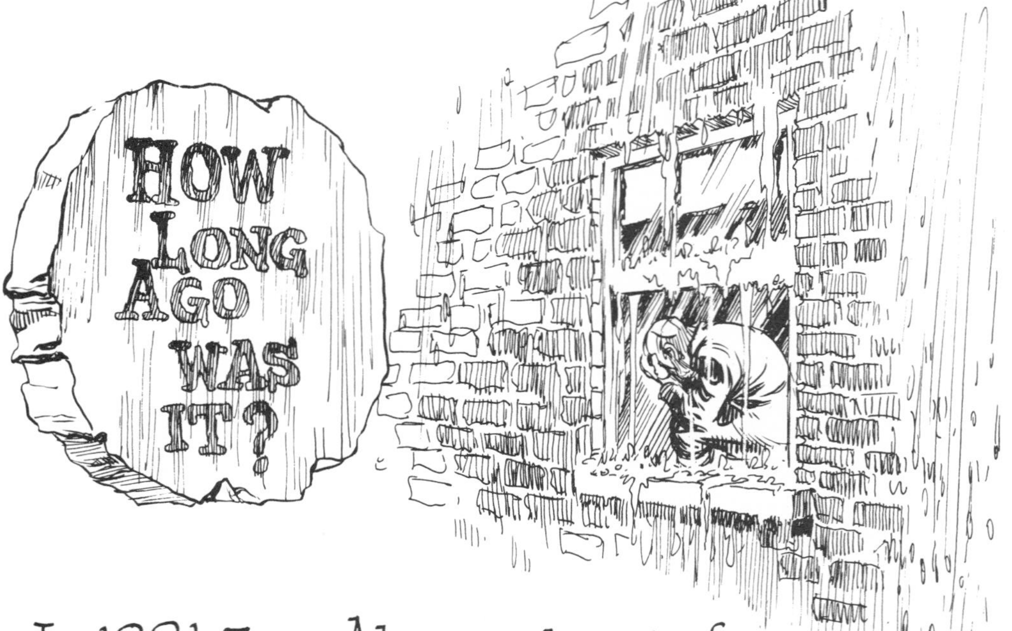
HOW LONG AGO WAS IT?

In 1881 Tsar Alexander II of Russia was assassinated and a wave of terrible anti-semitic pogroms swept the country.

In that year also, Frimme Hersh was born in a little village near Tiflis, named Piske.

Somehow his family survived the massacre and Frimmehleh, as he was lovingly called, grew up.

By the time he was ten, it became clear that this boy was special. He was brilliant and seemed to acquire knowledge from the air. In a poor shtetl like Piske, where survival was the main concern, how else?

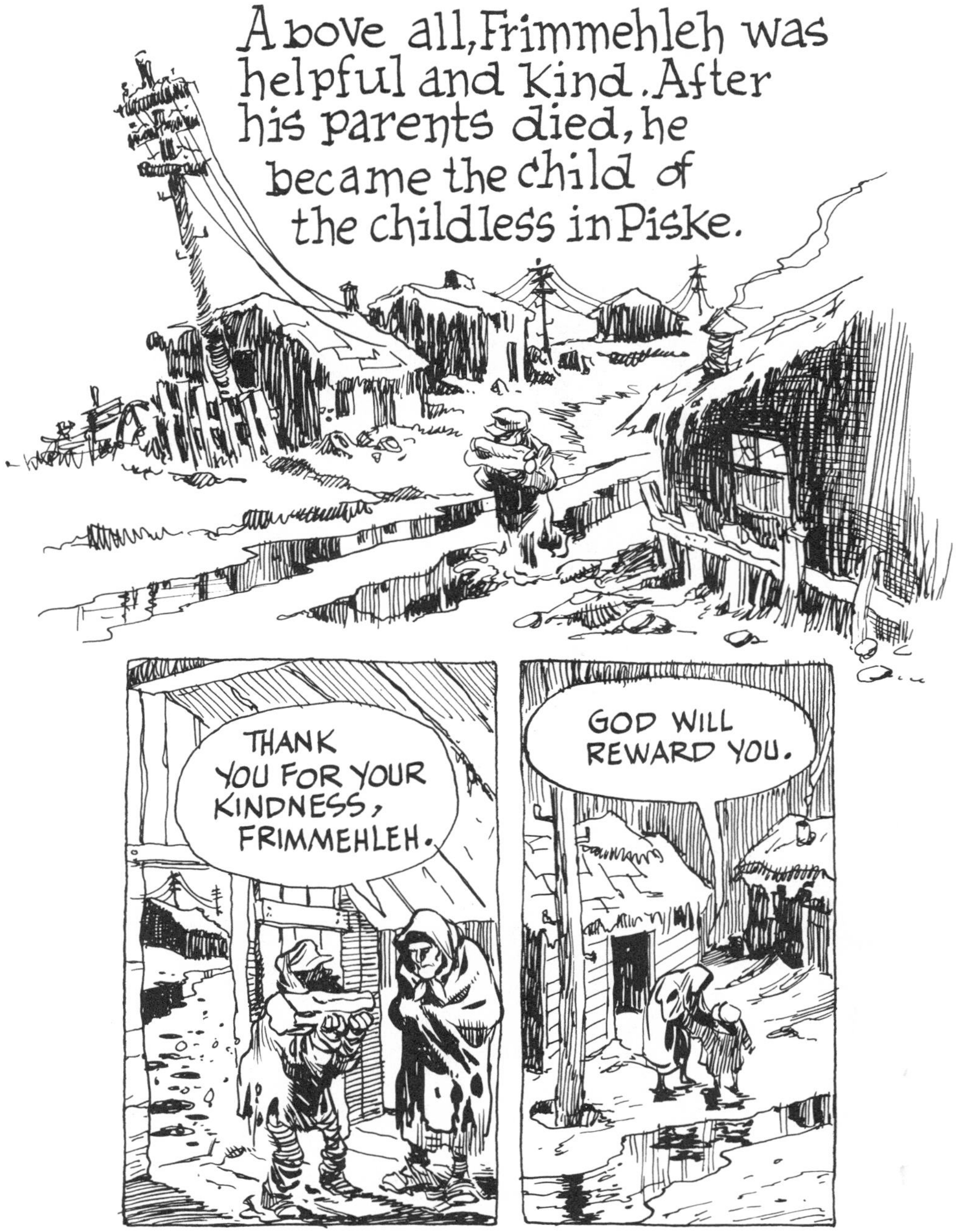
Above all, Frimmehleh was helpful and kind. After his parents died, he became the child of the childless in Piske.
THANK YOU FOR YOUR KINDNESS, FRIMMEHLEH.
GOD WILL REWARD YOU.

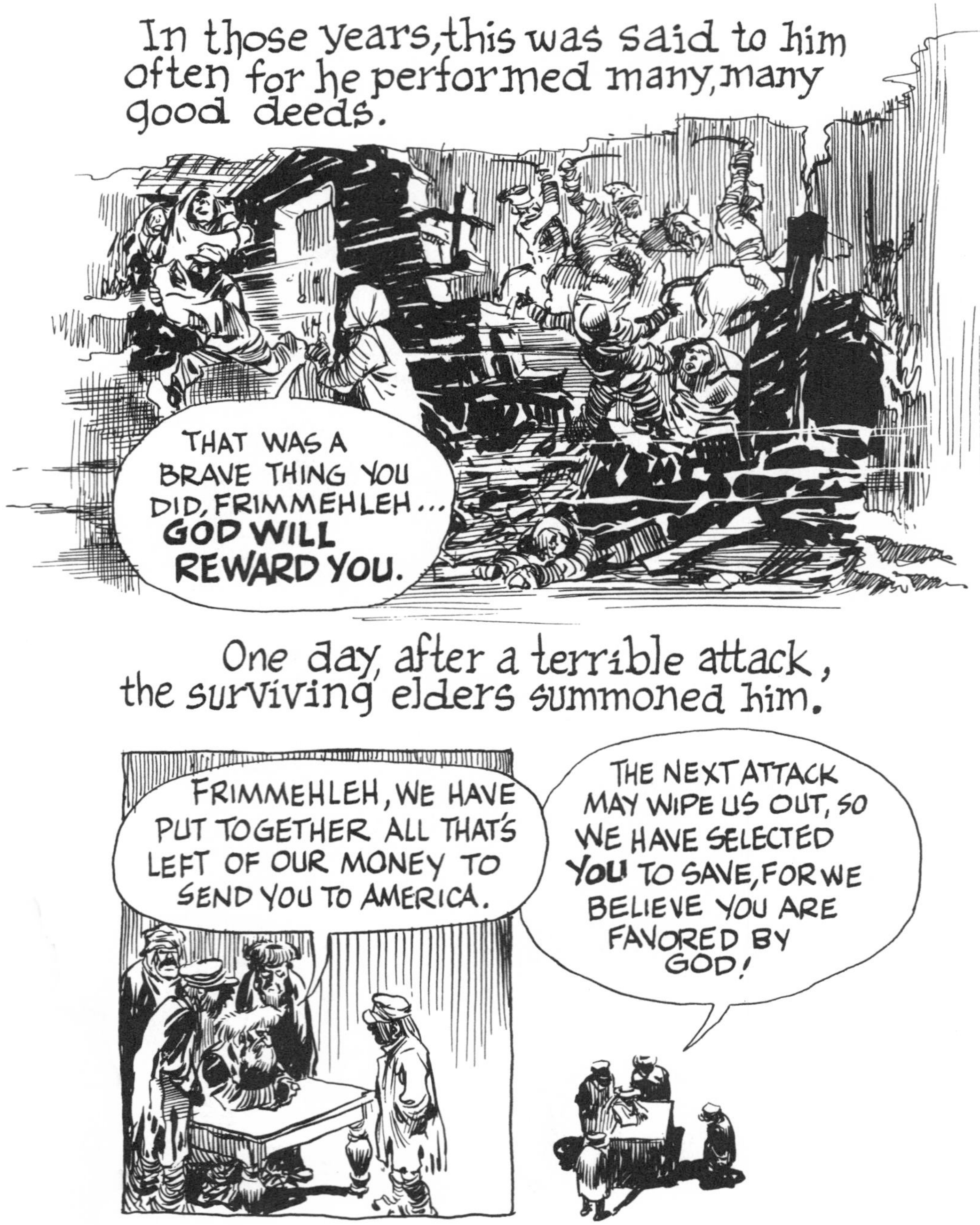
In those years, this was said to him often for he performed many, many good deeds.
THAT WAS A BRAVE THING YOU DID, FRIMMEHLEH... GOD WILL REWARD YOU.
One day, after a terrible attack, the surviving elders summoned him.
FRIMMEHLEH, WE HAVE PUT TOGETHER ALL THAT'S LEFT OF OUR MONEY TO SEND YOU TO AMERICA.
THE NEXT ATTACK MAY WIPE US OUT, SO WE HAVE SELECTED YOU TO SAVE, FOR WE BELIEVE YOU ARE FAVORED BY GOD!

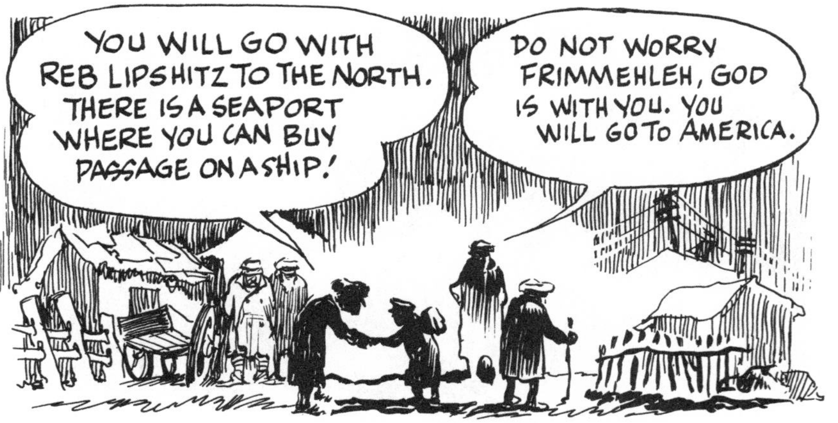
YOU WILL GO WITH REB LIPSHITZ TO THE NORTH. THERE IS A SEAPORT WHERE YOU CAN BUY PASSAGE ON A SHIP!
DO NOT WORRY FRIMMEHLEH, GOD IS WITH YOU. YOU WILL GO TO AMERICA.

...And so Hersh obeyed. Two nights later on the trail deep in the forest...

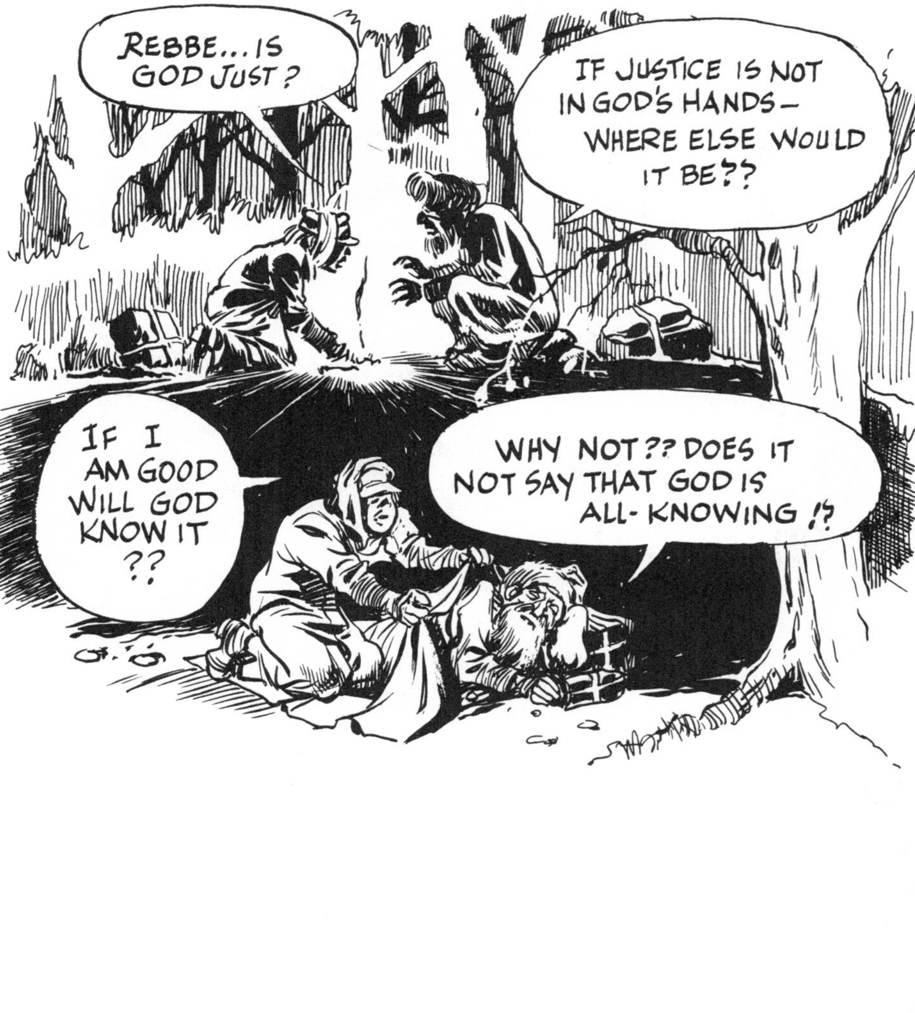
REBBE... IS GOD JUST?
IF JUSTICE IS NOT IN GOD'S HANDS— WHERE ELSE WOULD IT BE??
IF I AM GOOD WILL GOD KNOW IT ??
WHY NOT?? DOES IT NOT SAY THAT GOD IS ALL-KNOWING !?

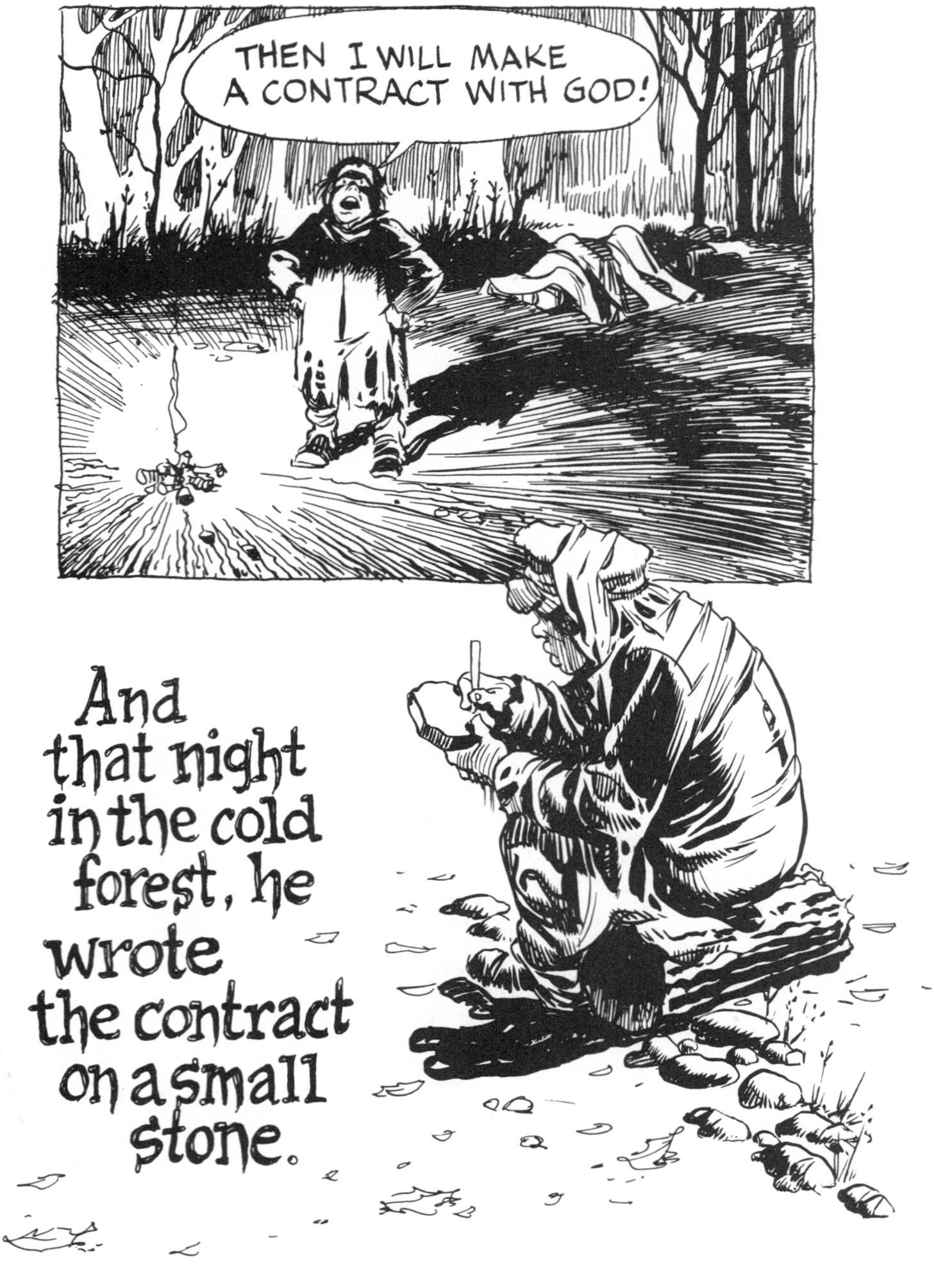
THEN I WILL MAKE A CONTRACT WITH GOD!
And that night in the cold forest, he wrote the contract on a small stone.

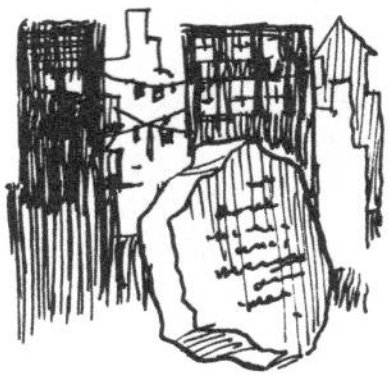

And with the little stone tablet in his pocket, Frimme Hersh settled in New York City where he found shelter in the Hassidic community. There he took religious instruction and devoted himself to good works.

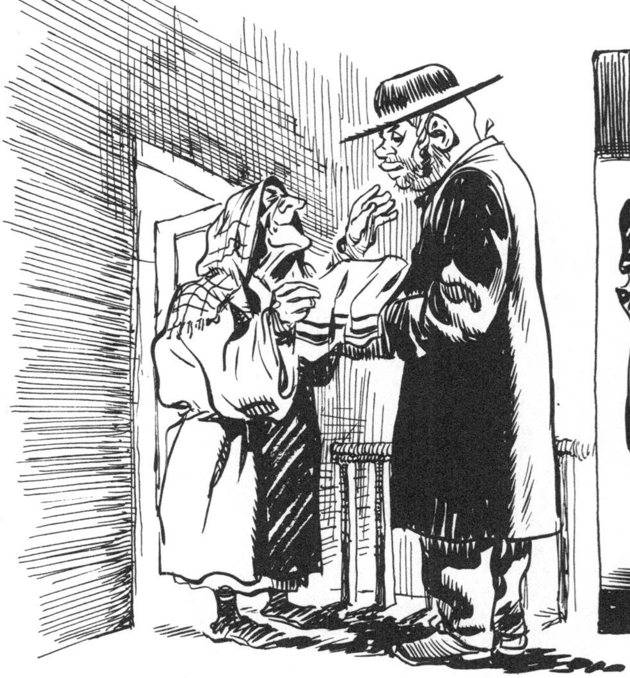

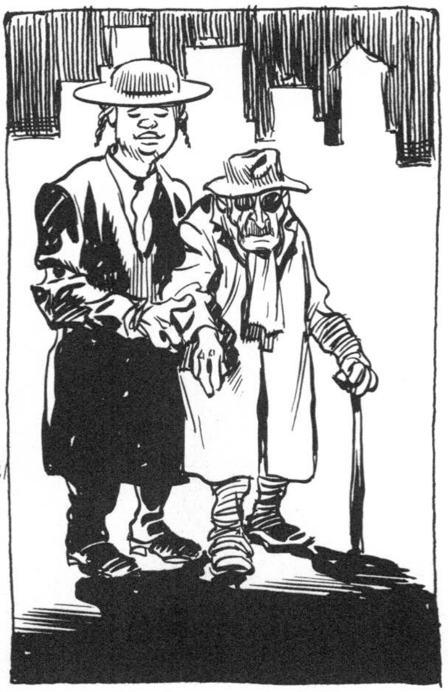

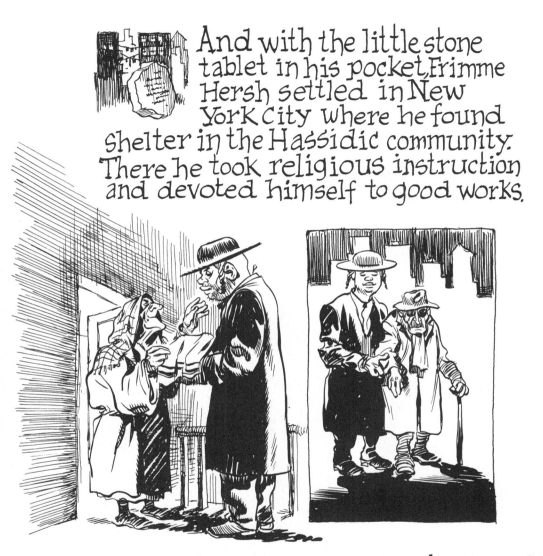

Faithfully and piously, he adhered to the terms of his contract with GOD.

In time he became a respected member of the Synagogue, trusted with money and social matters.
So it was not surprising that it was on Hersh's doorstep that an anonymous mother abandoned her infant girl. What could be clearer? To Frimme, this was part of his pact with GOD.

Since no one wanted a child born of GOD-Knows-What Kind of parents, Frimme Hersh adopted the baby himself.

He named her Rachele, after his mother, and devoted himself to her with all his love.

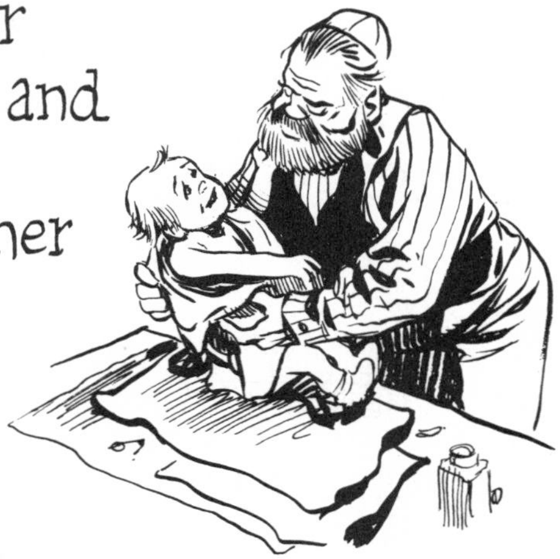

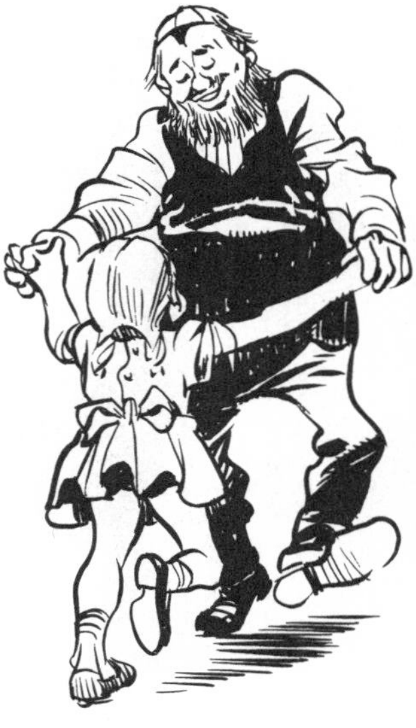

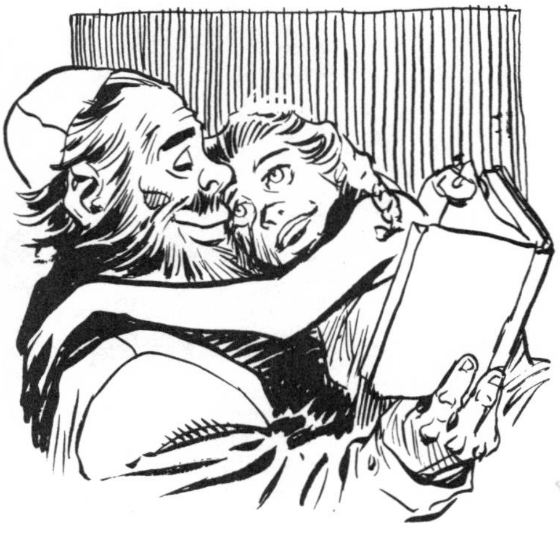

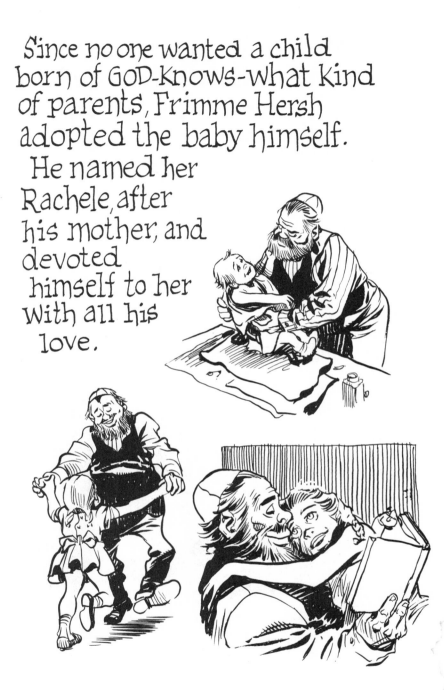

So, she grew up blossoming in the warmth and nourishment of Frimme's gentle heart and pious ways. She was indeed his child and the joy of his years. Then one day - in the springtime of her life - Rachele fell ill.

Suddenly and fatally.

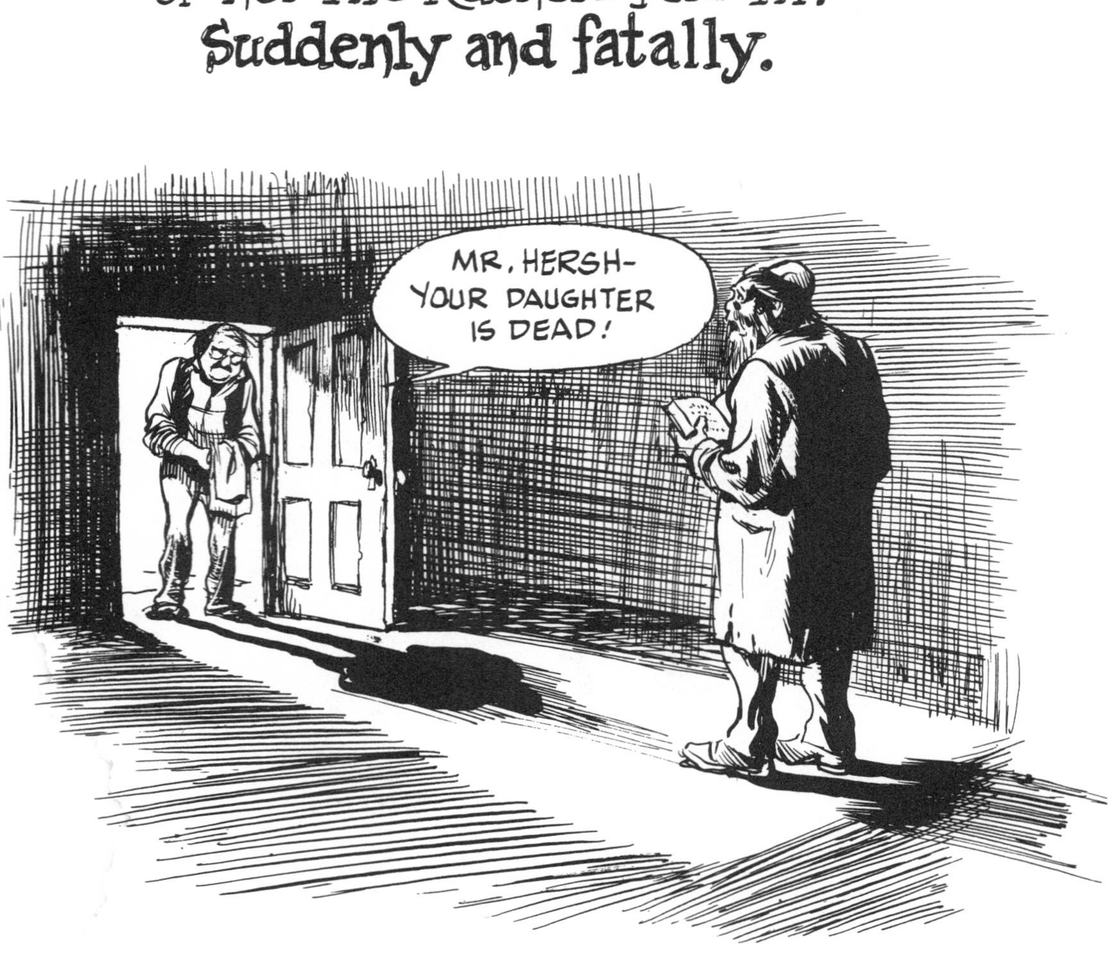
MR. HERSH- YOUR DAUGHTER IS DEAD!

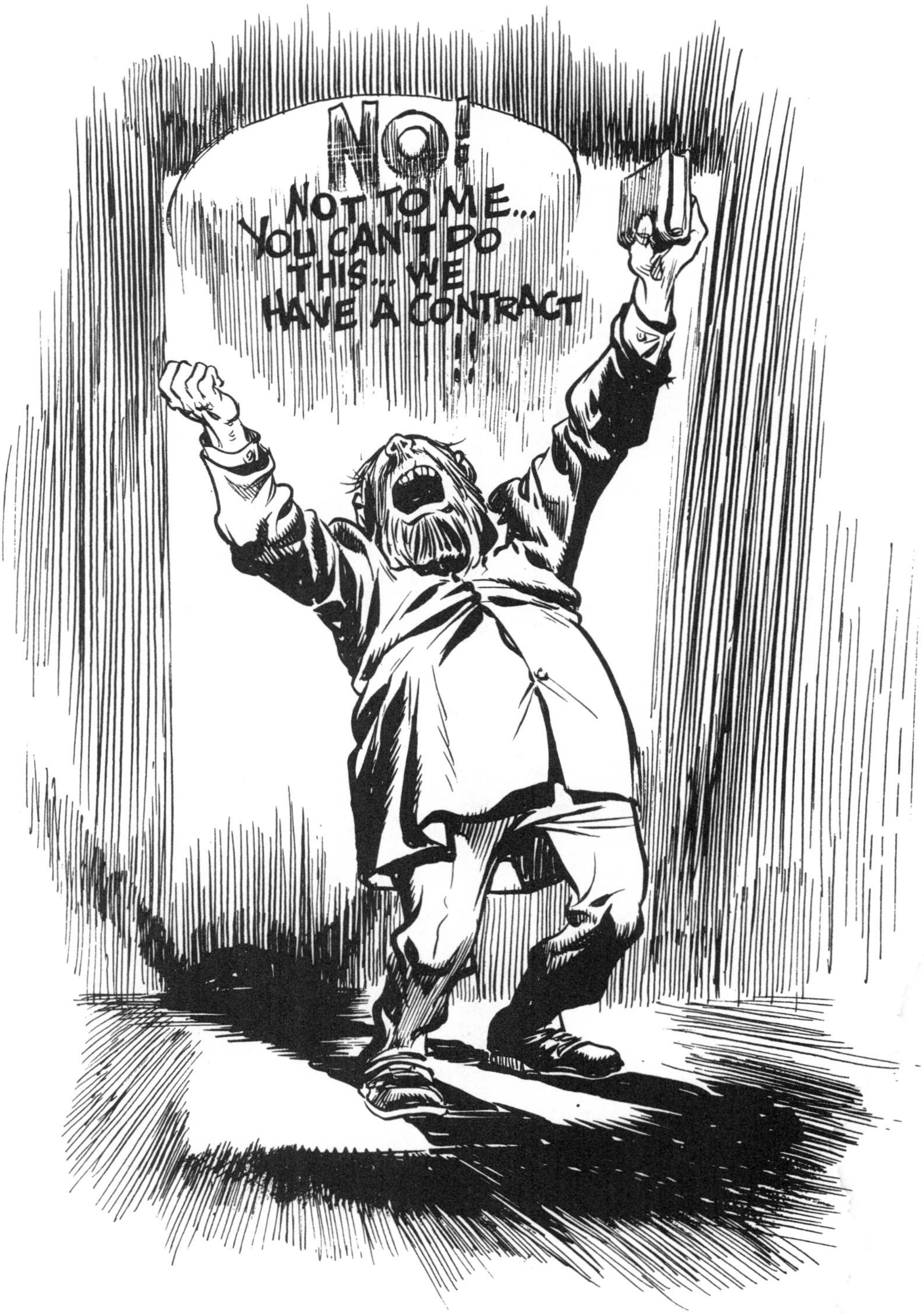
NO!
NOT TO ME...
YOU CAN'T DO
THIS... WE
HAVE A CONTRACT
!!

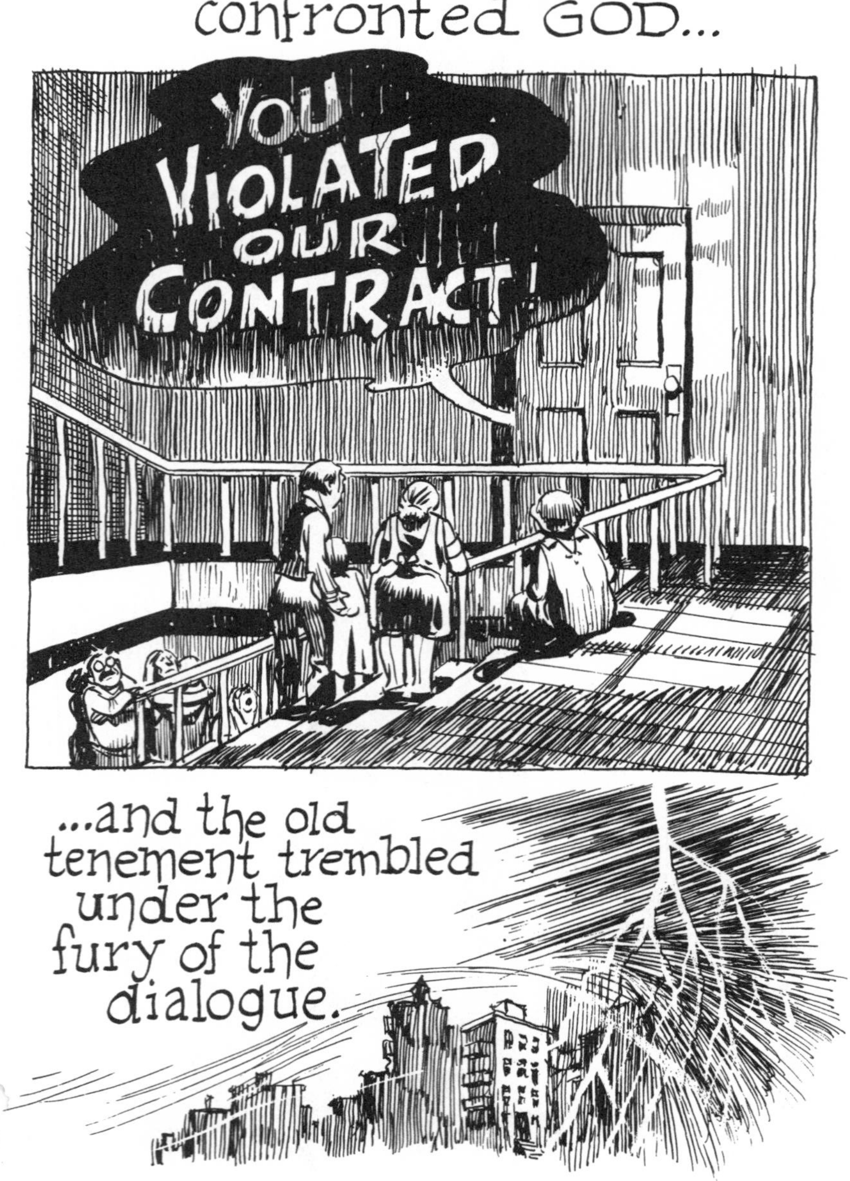
That night Frimme Hersh confronted GOD...
YOU VIOLATED OUR CONTRACT!
...and the old tenement trembled under the fury of the dialogue.

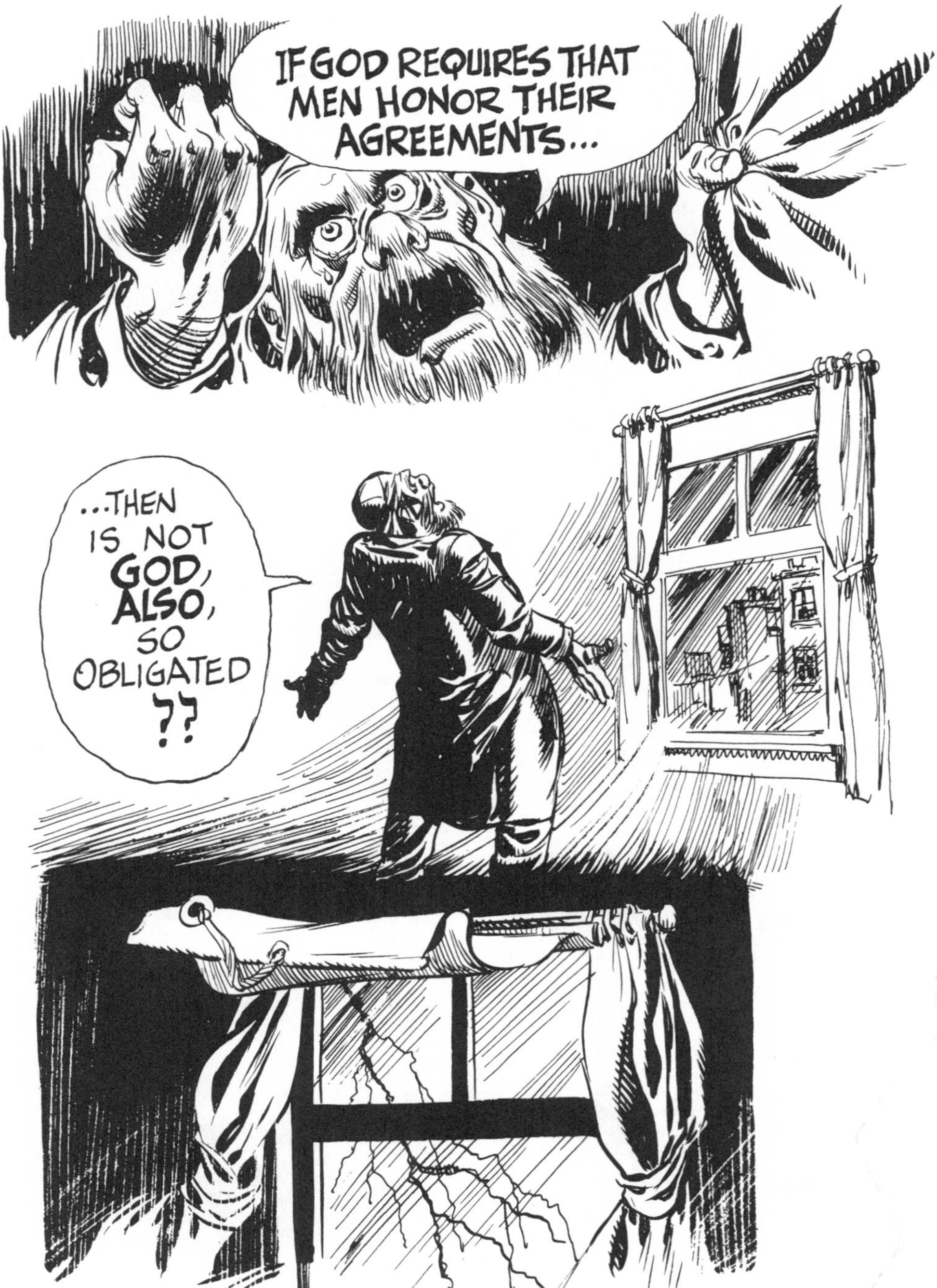
IF GOD REQUIRES THAT MEN HONOR THEIR AGREEMENTS...
...THEN IS NOT GOD, ALSO, SO OBLIGATED ??

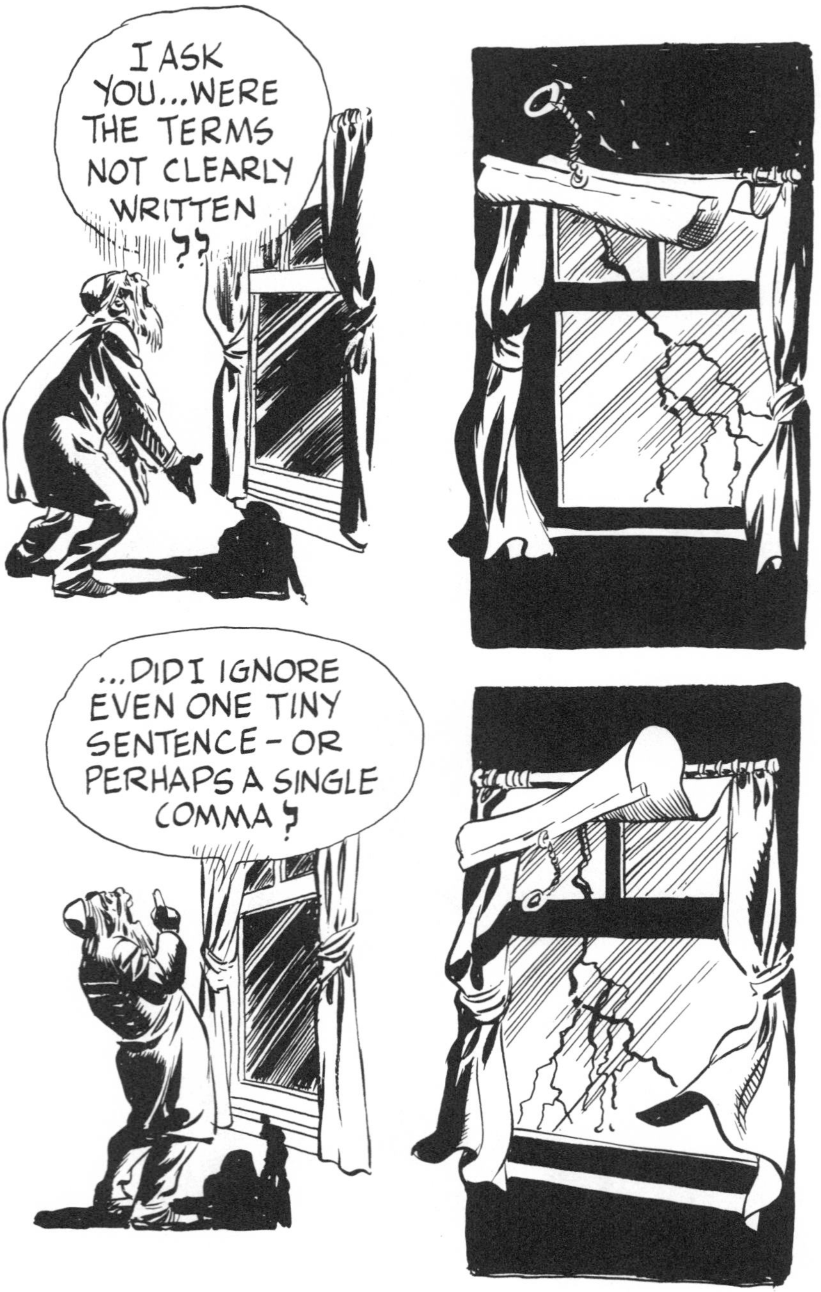
I ASK YOU...WERE THE TERMS NOT CLEARLY WRITTEN ?
...DID I IGNORE EVEN ONE TINY SENTENCE - OR PERHAPS A SINGLE COMMA ?

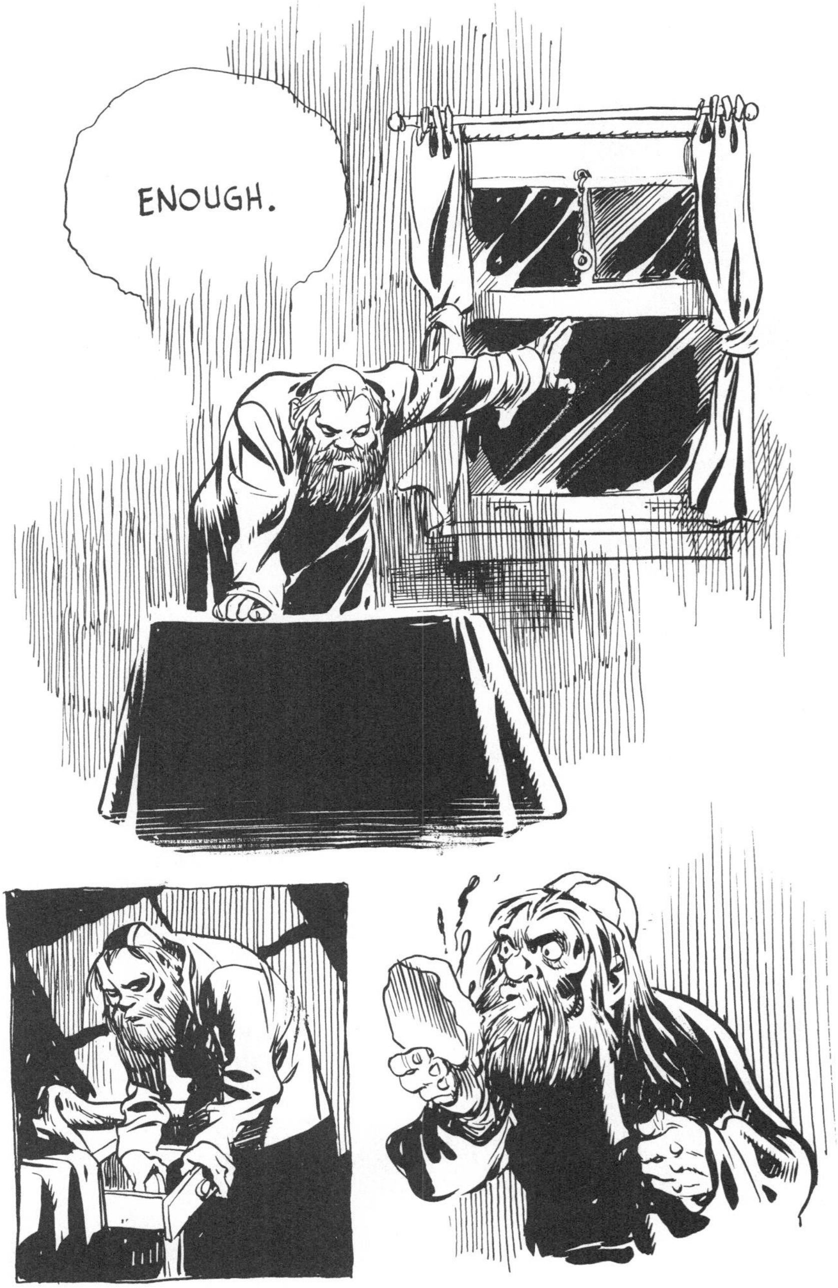
ENOUGH.

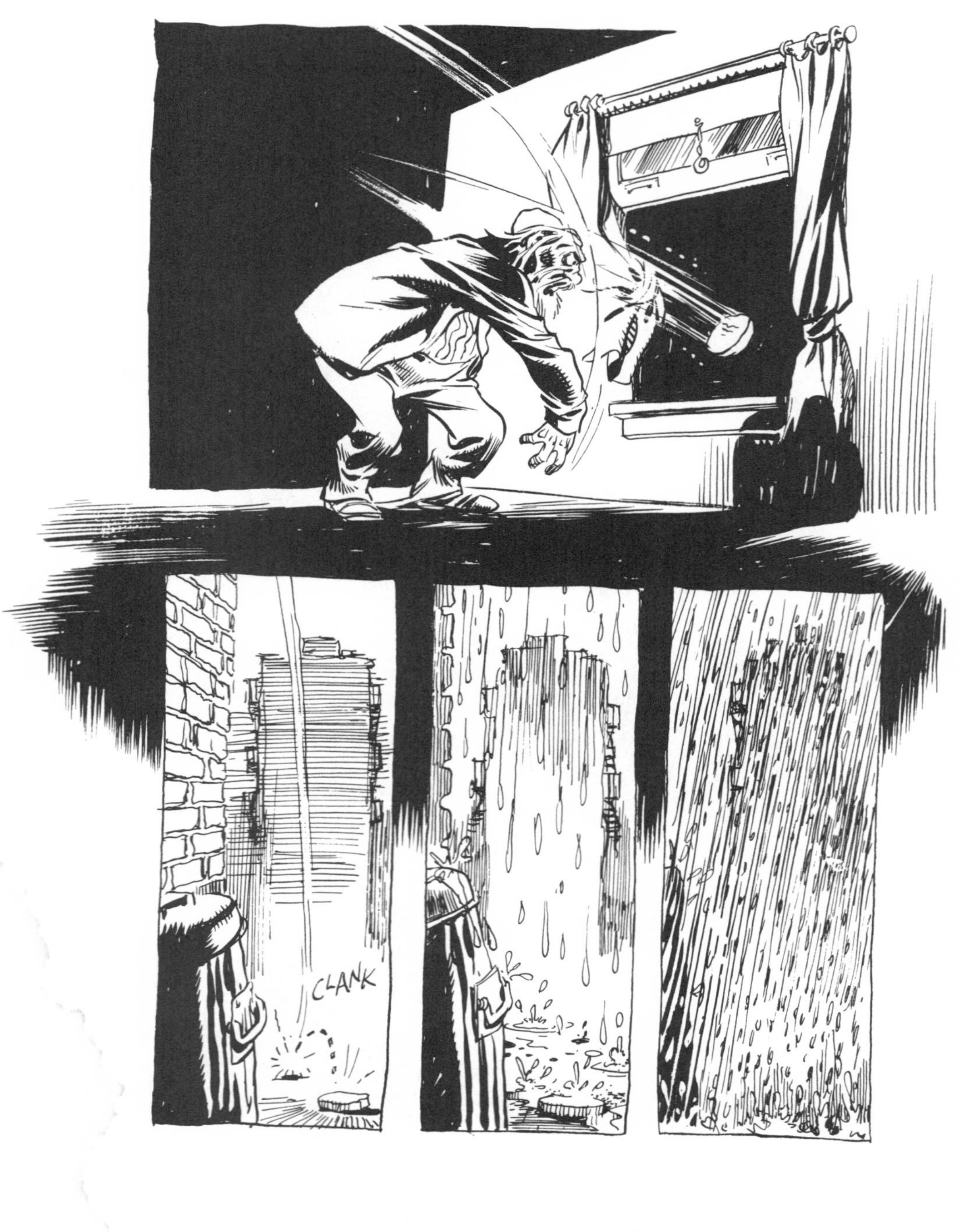
CLANK

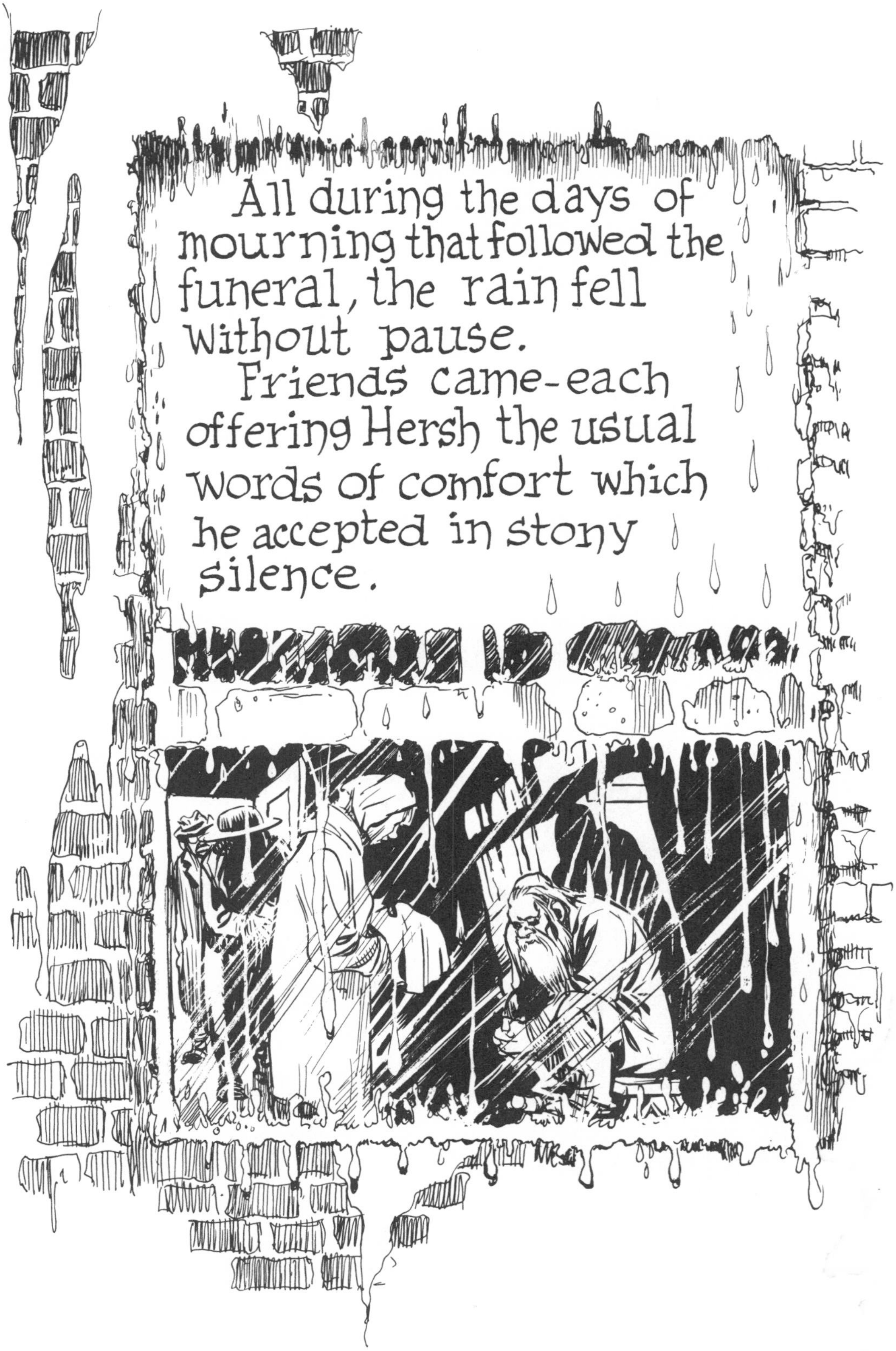
All during the days of mourning that followed the funeral, the rain fell without pause.
Friends came-each offering Hersh the usual words of comfort which he accepted in stony silence.

At the end of the days
of Shiva in the dawn of the
eighth day, the sun rose in a
clear sky and Frimme Hersh
said the morning prayer...for
the last time.

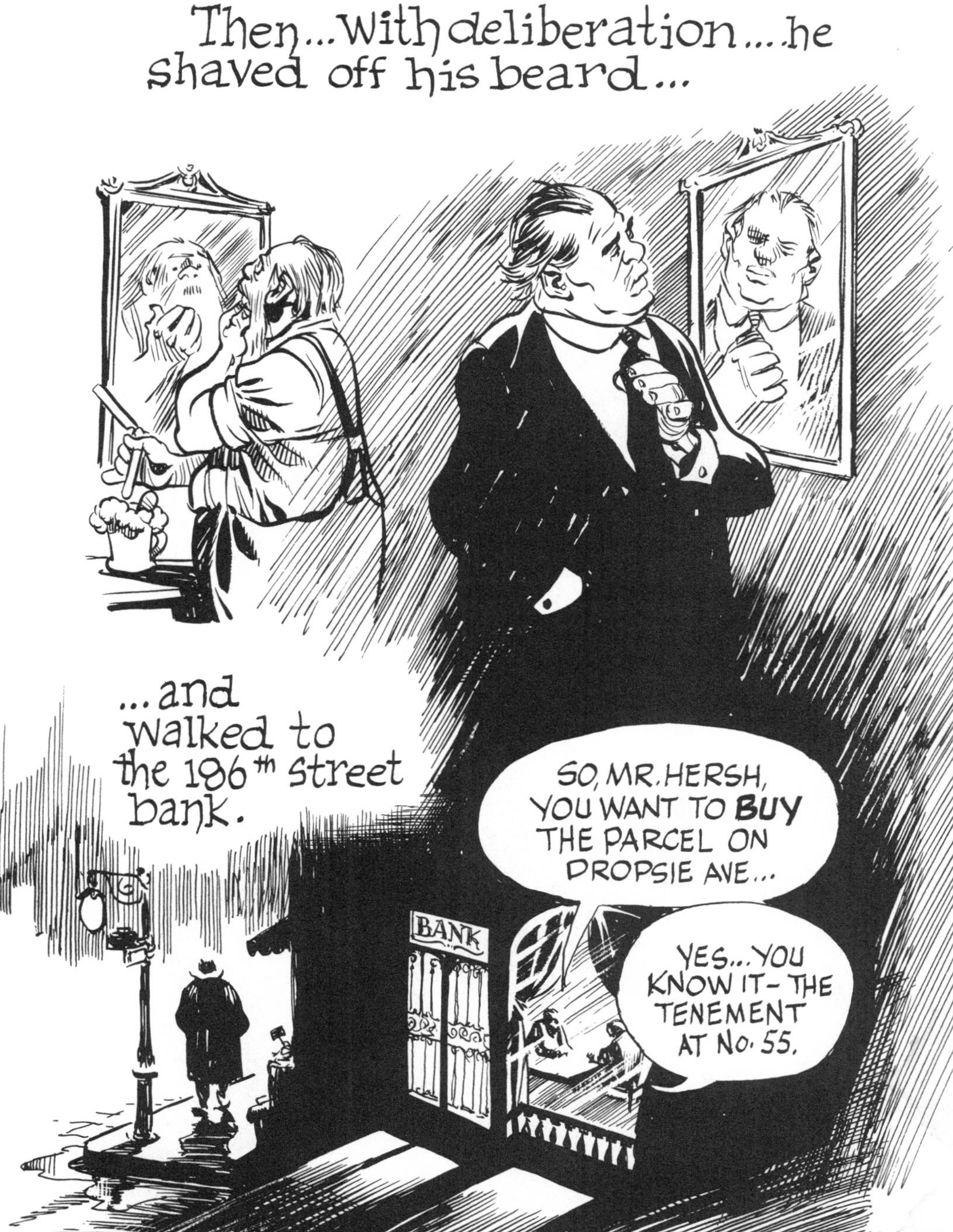
Then... with deliberation.... he shaved off his beard...
...and walked to the 186th street bank.
BANK
SO, MR. HERSH, YOU WANT TO BUY THE PARCEL ON DROPSIE AVE...
YES... YOU KNOW IT- THE TENEMENT AT No. 55.

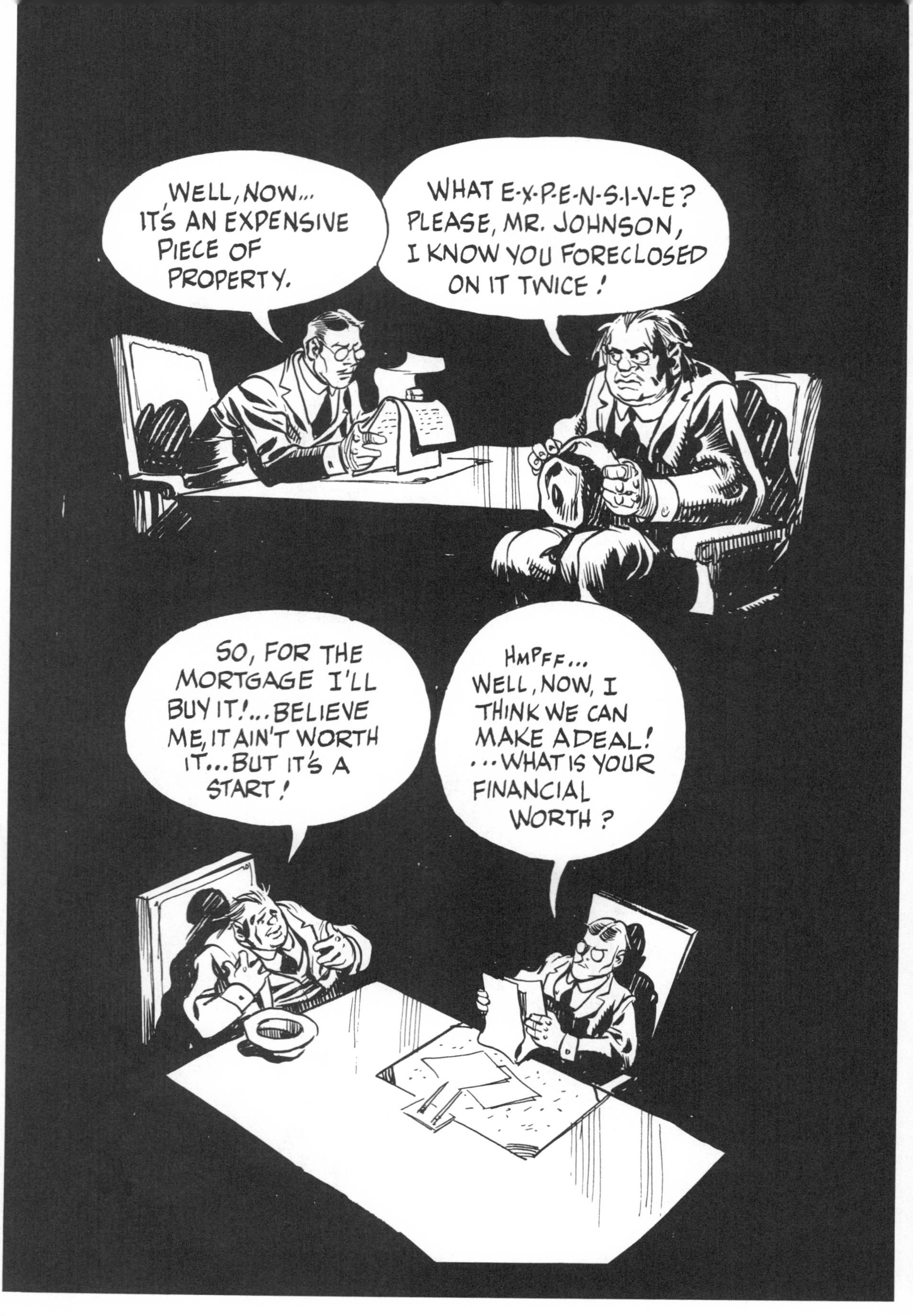
WELL, NOW... IT'S AN EXPENSIVE PIECE OF PROPERTY.
WHAT E-X-P-E-N-S-I-V-E? PLEASE, MR. JOHNSON, I KNOW YOU FORECLOSED ON IT TWICE!
SO, FOR THE MORTGAGE I'LL BUY IT!... BELIEVE ME, IT AIN'T WORTH IT... BUT IT'S A START!
HMPFF... WELL, NOW, I THINK WE CAN MAKE A DEAL! ...WHAT IS YOUR FINANCIAL WORTH?

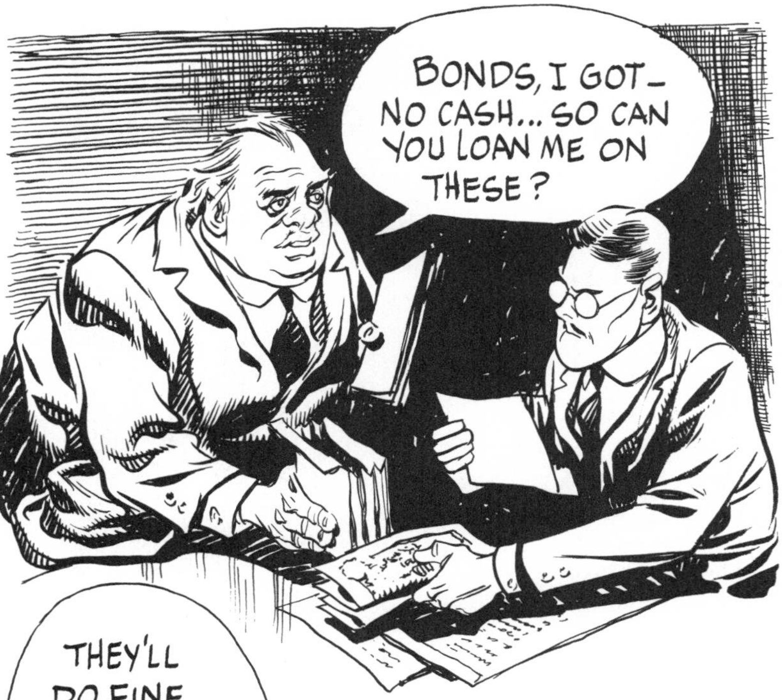
BONDS, I GOT– NO CASH... SO CAN YOU LOAN ME ON THESE?

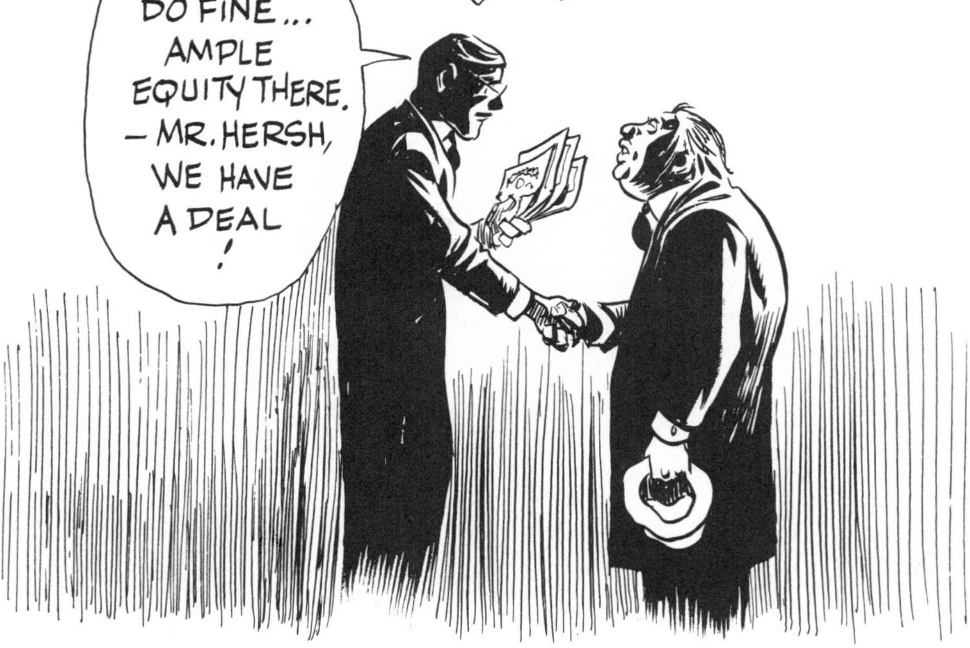
THEY'LL DO FINE... AMPLE EQUITY THERE. – MR. HERSH, WE HAVE A DEAL!

For the first time, Frimme HersH lied. For the first time, he committed an act which formerly was unthinkable. The bonds were not his- they had only been entrusted to him for safekeeping by the synagogue.

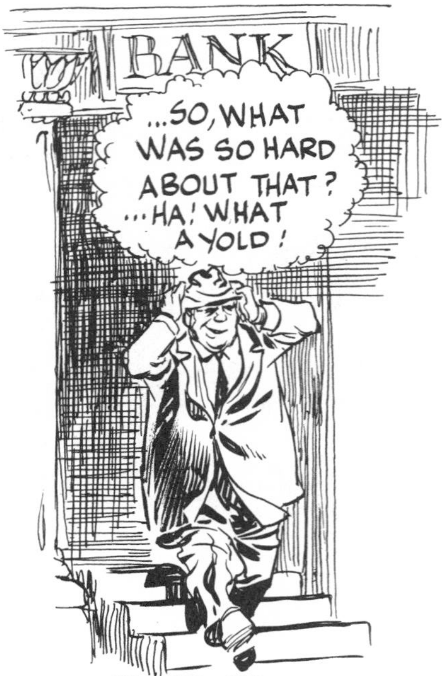
BANK
...SO, WHAT WAS SO HARD ABOUT THAT? ...HA! WHAT A YOLD!

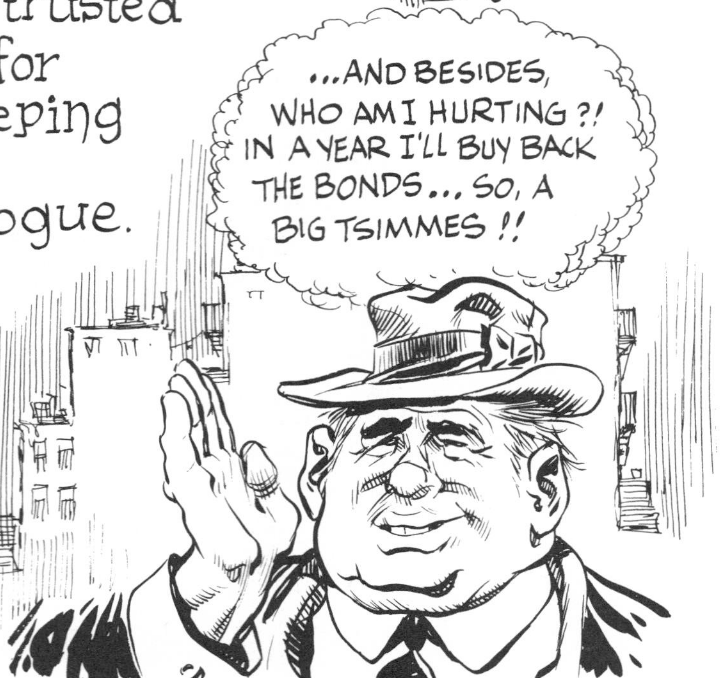
...AND BESIDES, WHO AM I HURTING?! IN A YEAR I'LL BUY BACK THE BONDS... SO, A BIG TSIMMES!!

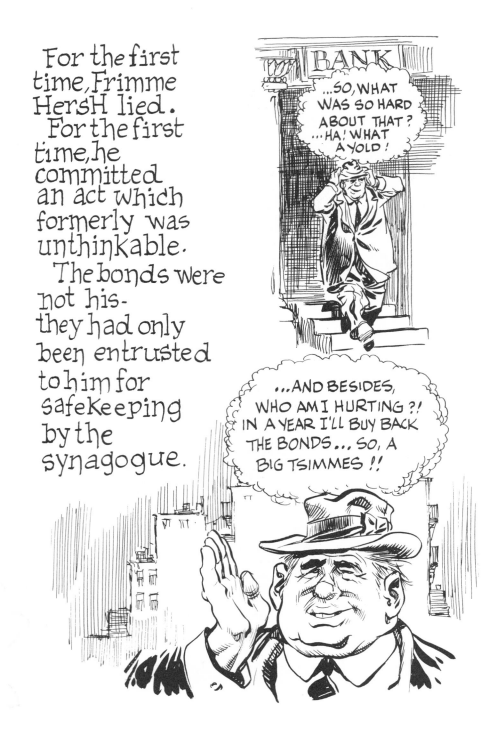

So, Frimme Hersh became the new owner of 55 Dropsie Avenue.

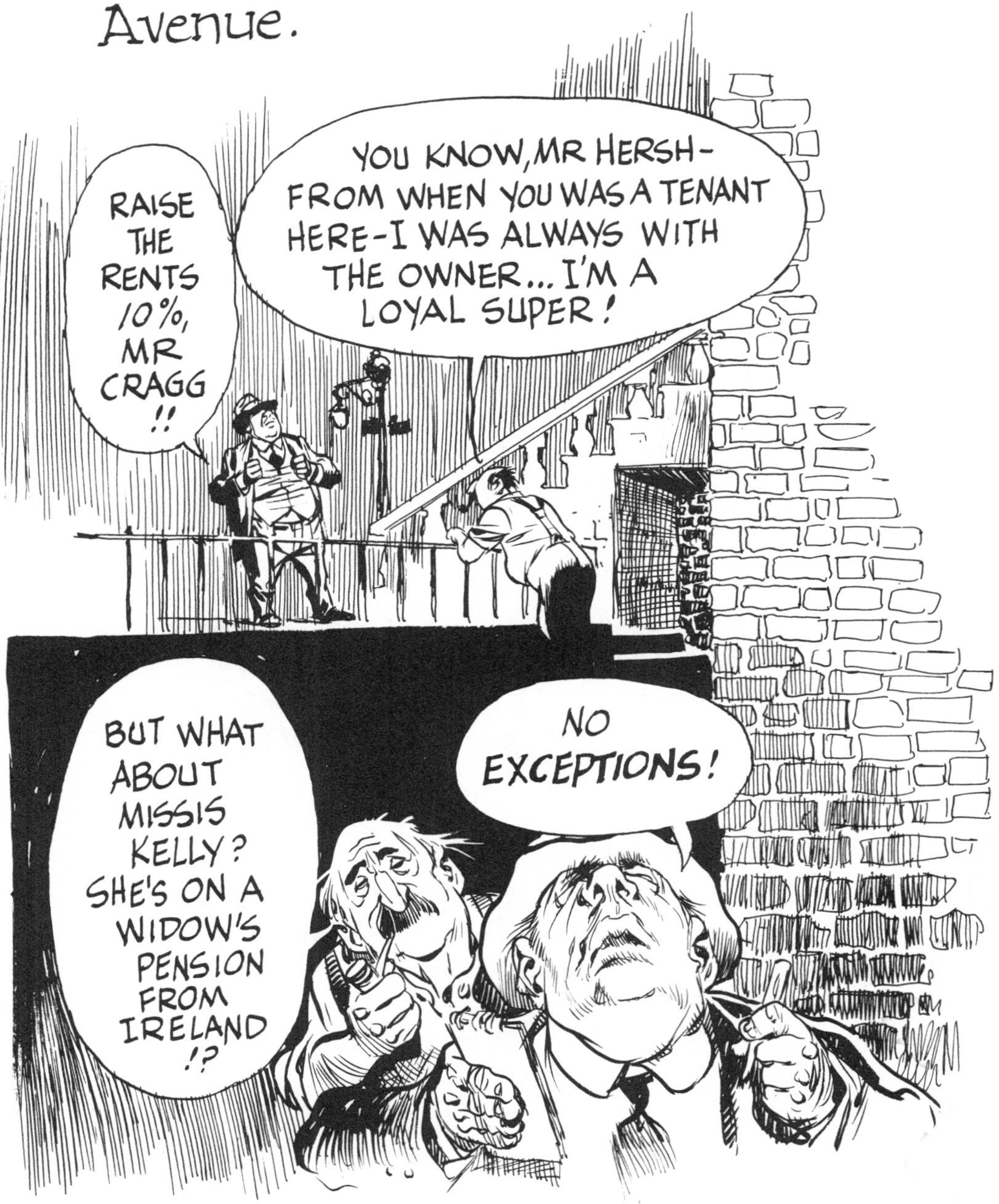
RAISE THE RENTS 10%, MR CRAGG !!
YOU KNOW, MR HERSH- FROM WHEN YOU WAS A TENANT HERE-I WAS ALWAYS WITH THE OWNER... I'M A LOYAL SUPER!
BUT WHAT ABOUT MISSIS KELLY? SHE'S ON A WIDOW'S PENSION FROM IRELAND !?
NO EXCEPTIONS!

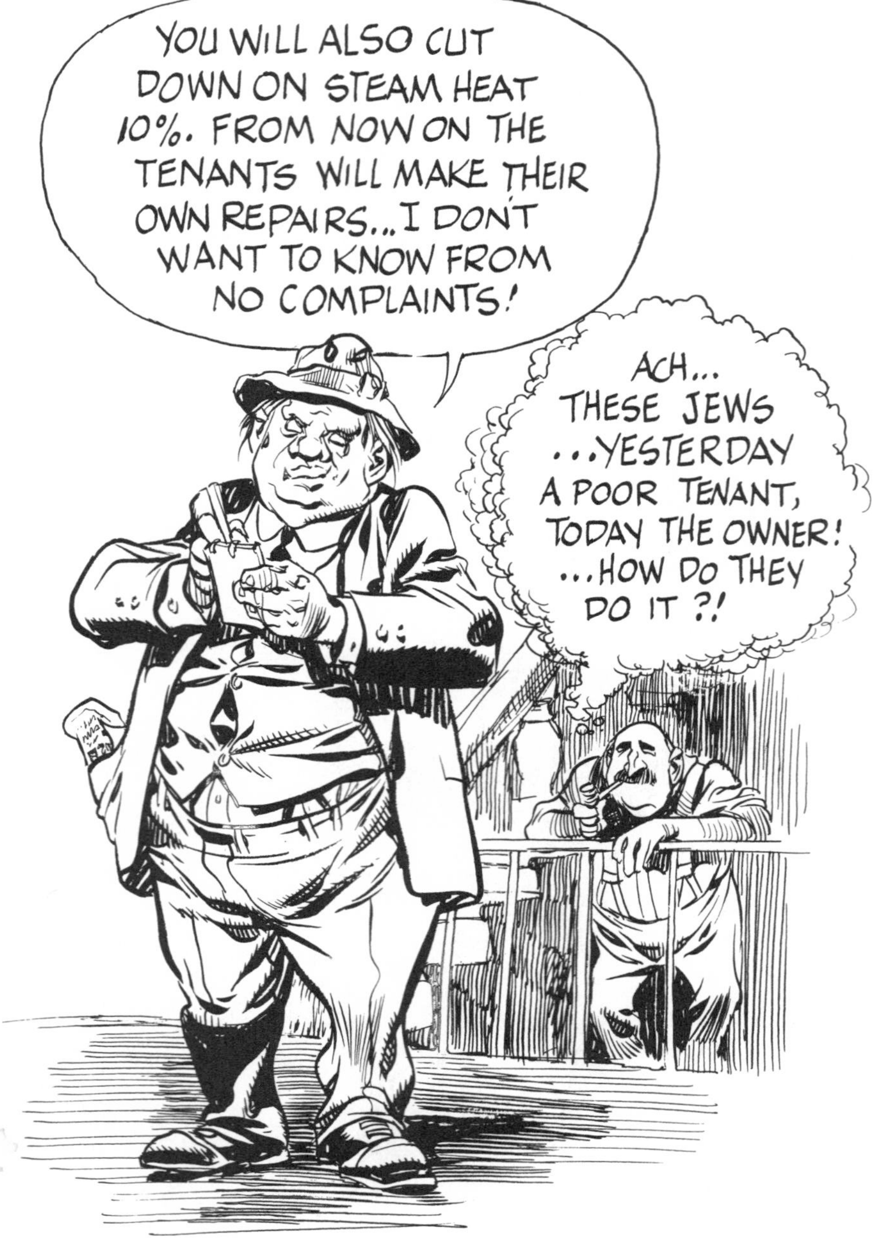
YOU WILL ALSO CUT DOWN ON STEAM HEAT 10%. FROM NOW ON THE TENANTS WILL MAKE THEIR OWN REPAIRS... I DON'T WANT TO KNOW FROM NO COMPLAINTS!
ACH... THESE JEWS ...YESTERDAY A POOR TENANT, TODAY THE OWNER! ...HOW DO THEY DO IT ?!

Within a year, Frimme Hersh gleaned enough out of the property to acquire the one next door. Within the next three years, he accumulated the beginning of a real estate empire.

His success appeared to be as much the result of uncanny luck as anything else.

THEY'RE GOING TO PULL DOWN THE EL. NOW YOUR PROPERTY WILL TRIPLE IN VALUE.

REMEMBER THAT GARBAGE DUMP YOU WERE STUCK WITH LAST YEAR... NOW THE CITY WANTS IT FOR A GARAGE...THEY'LL PAY WELL!

Before long he took a mistress,
a 'shikseh' from Scranton, Pa.,
and took up a lifestyle he
felt more appropriate to his
new station.
   He traded buildings like toys.
   But one building he never
sold-the tenement on Dropsie Ave.
At least once every week he would
come there...just to look at it.

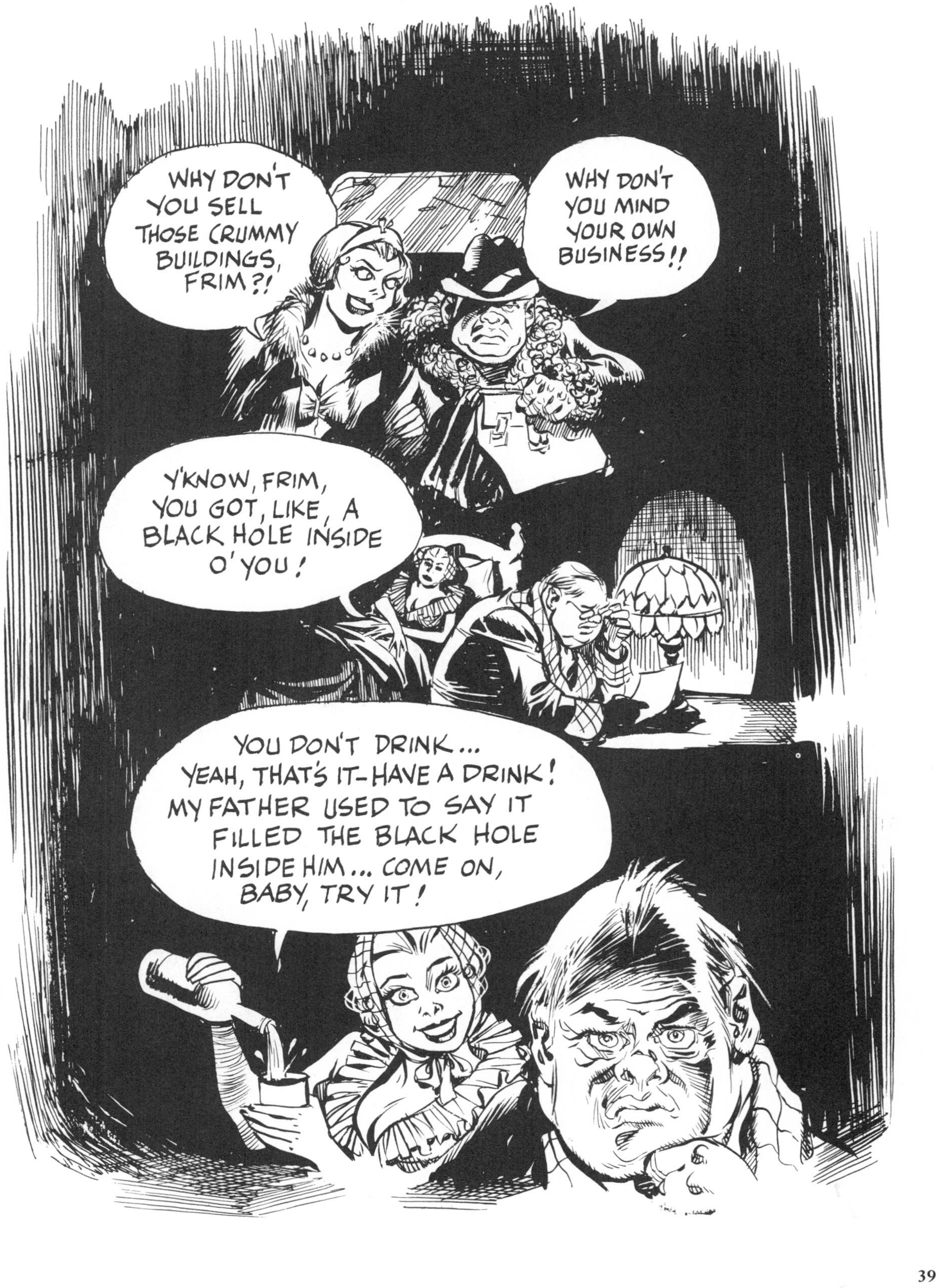
WHY DON'T YOU SELL THOSE CRUMMY BUILDINGS, FRIM?!
WHY DON'T YOU MIND YOUR OWN BUSINESS!!
Y'KNOW, FRIM, YOU GOT, LIKE, A BLACK HOLE INSIDE O' YOU!
YOU DON'T DRINK... YEAH, THAT'S IT-HAVE A DRINK! MY FATHER USED TO SAY IT FILLED THE BLACK HOLE INSIDE HIM... COME ON, BABY, TRY IT!

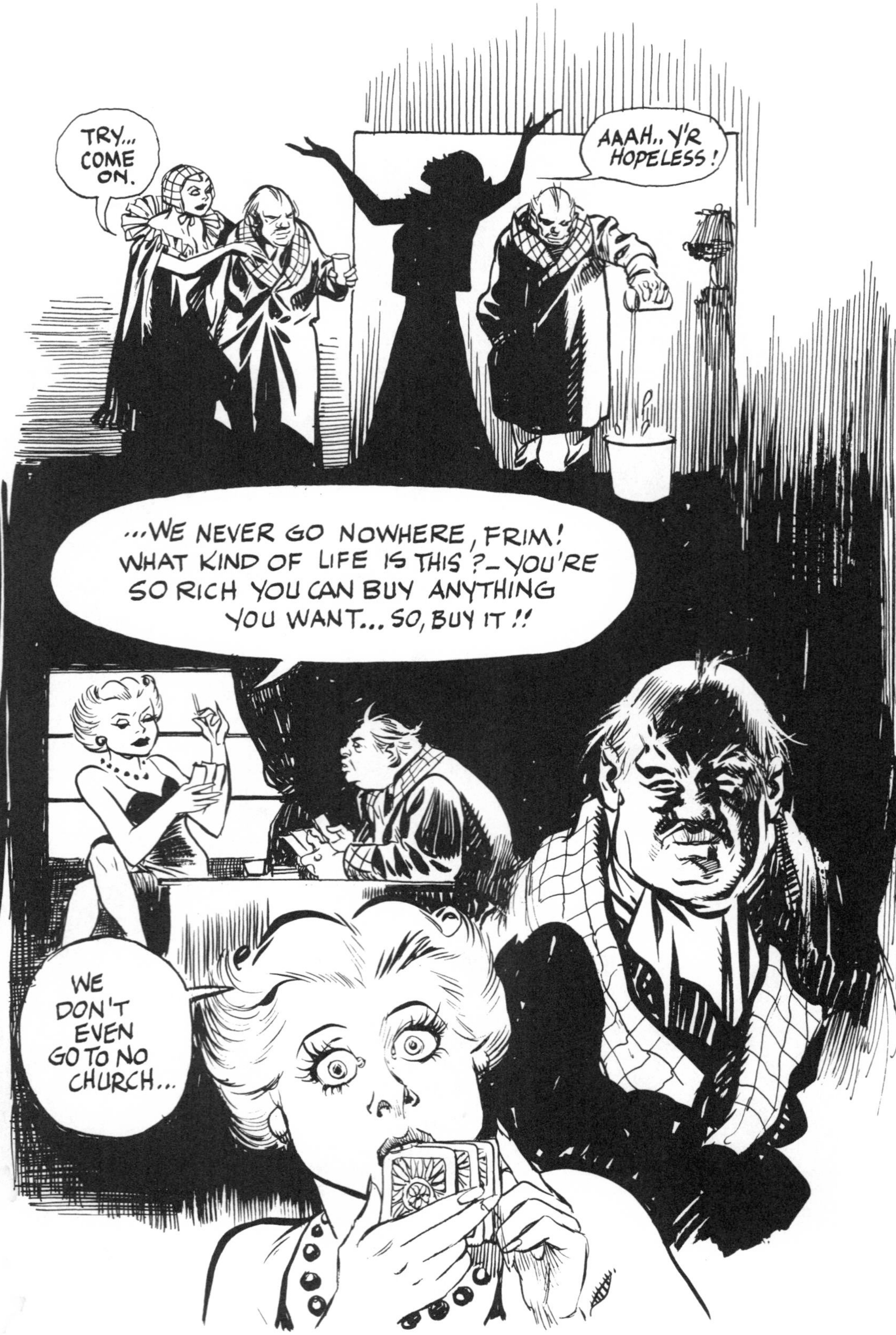
TRY... COME ON.
AAAH.. Y'R HOPELESS!
...WE NEVER GO NOWHERE, FRIM! WHAT KIND OF LIFE IS THIS?– YOU'RE SO RICH YOU CAN BUY ANYTHING YOU WANT... SO, BUY IT!!
WE DON'T EVEN GO TO NO CHURCH...

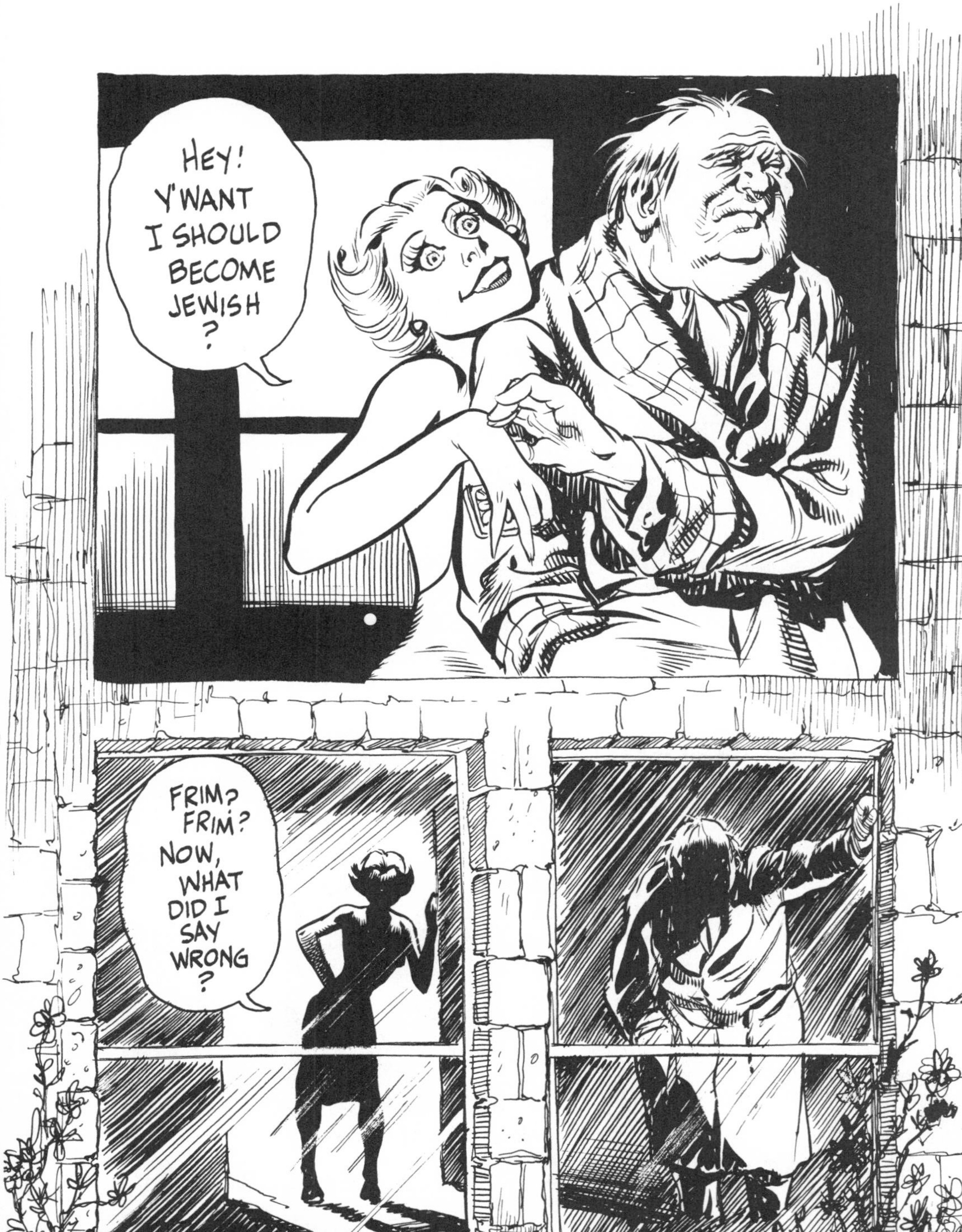
HEY! Y'WANT I SHOULD BECOME JEWISH ?
FRIM? FRIM? NOW, WHAT DID I SAY WRONG ?

One evening Frimme Hersh
walked from his penthouse
uptown all the way to
the old synagogue.

There he
called on
the wisest of
the elders.

DO YOU REMEMBER ME?... I'M FRIMME HERSH.

WE REMEMBER YOU.

I AM VERY RICH NOW. EVERYTHING I TOUCH TURNS TO GOLD— AS THEY SAY.

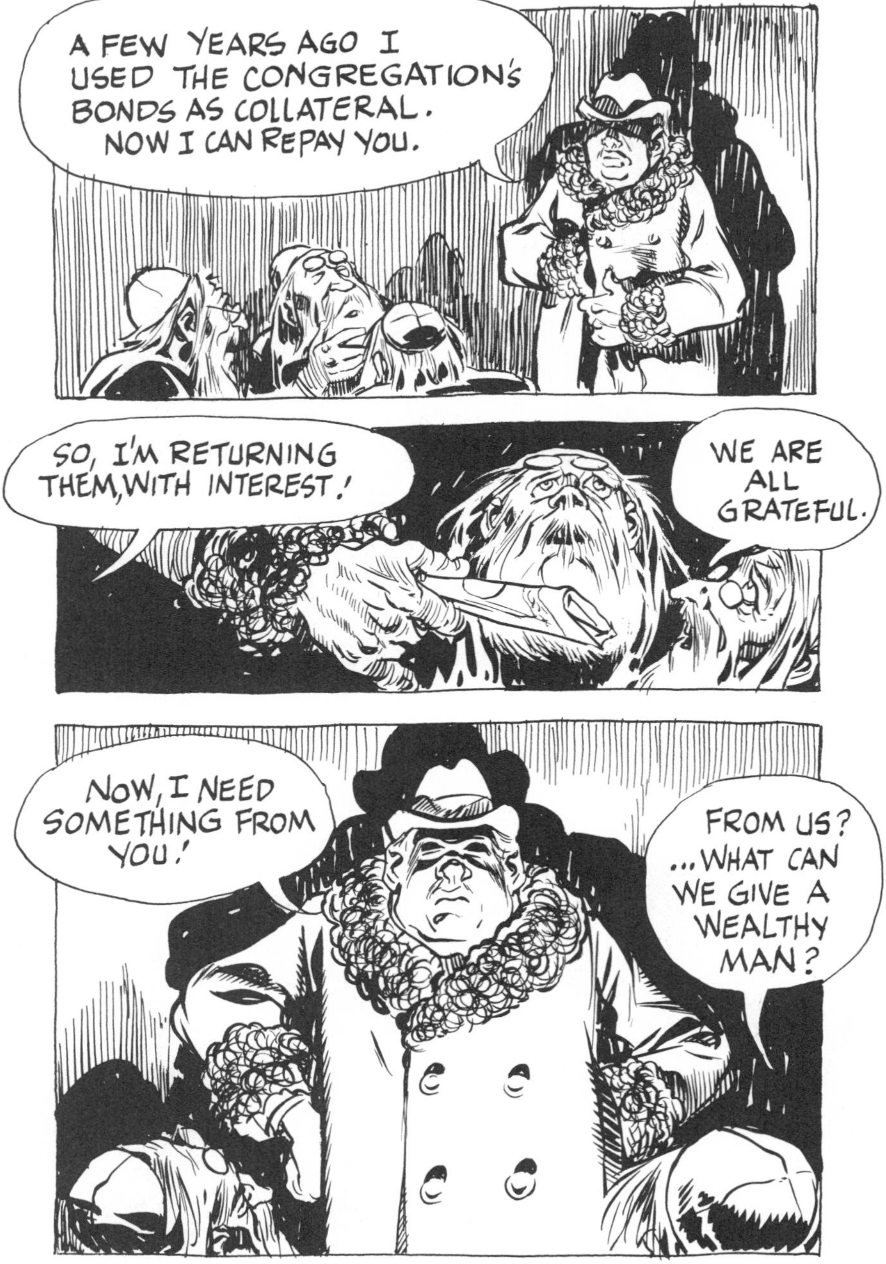
A FEW YEARS AGO I USED THE CONGREGATION'S BONDS AS COLLATERAL. NOW I CAN REPAY YOU.
SO, I'M RETURNING THEM, WITH INTEREST!
WE ARE ALL GRATEFUL.
NOW, I NEED SOMETHING FROM YOU!
FROM US? ...WHAT CAN WE GIVE A WEALTHY MAN?

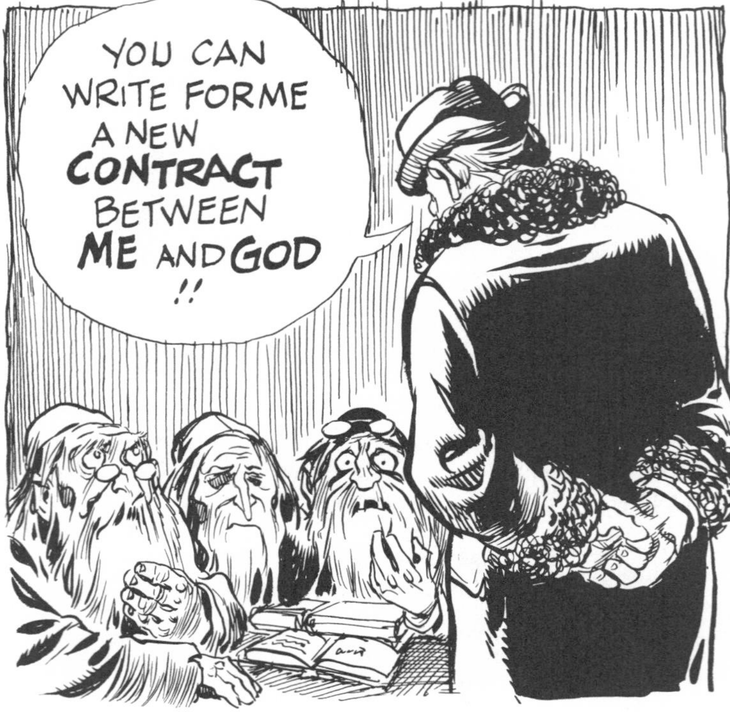
YOU CAN WRITE FORME A NEW CONTRACT BETWEEN ME AND GOD !!

Carefully, Hersh recounted the history of his former contract.

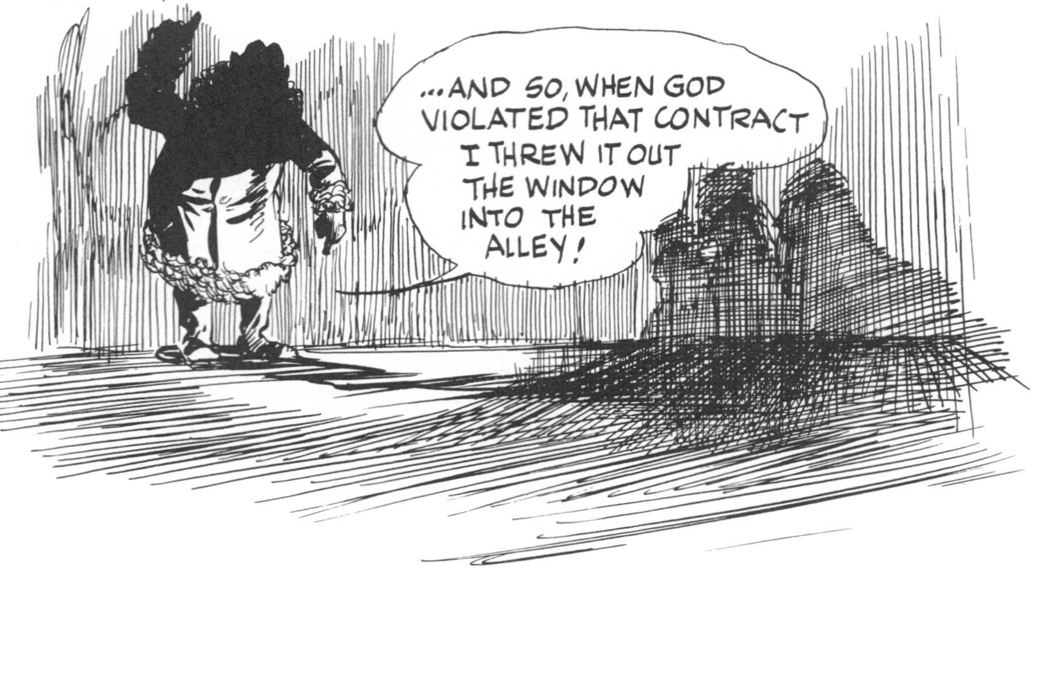
...AND SO, WHEN GOD VIOLATED THAT CONTRACT I THREW IT OUT THE WINDOW INTO THE ALLEY!

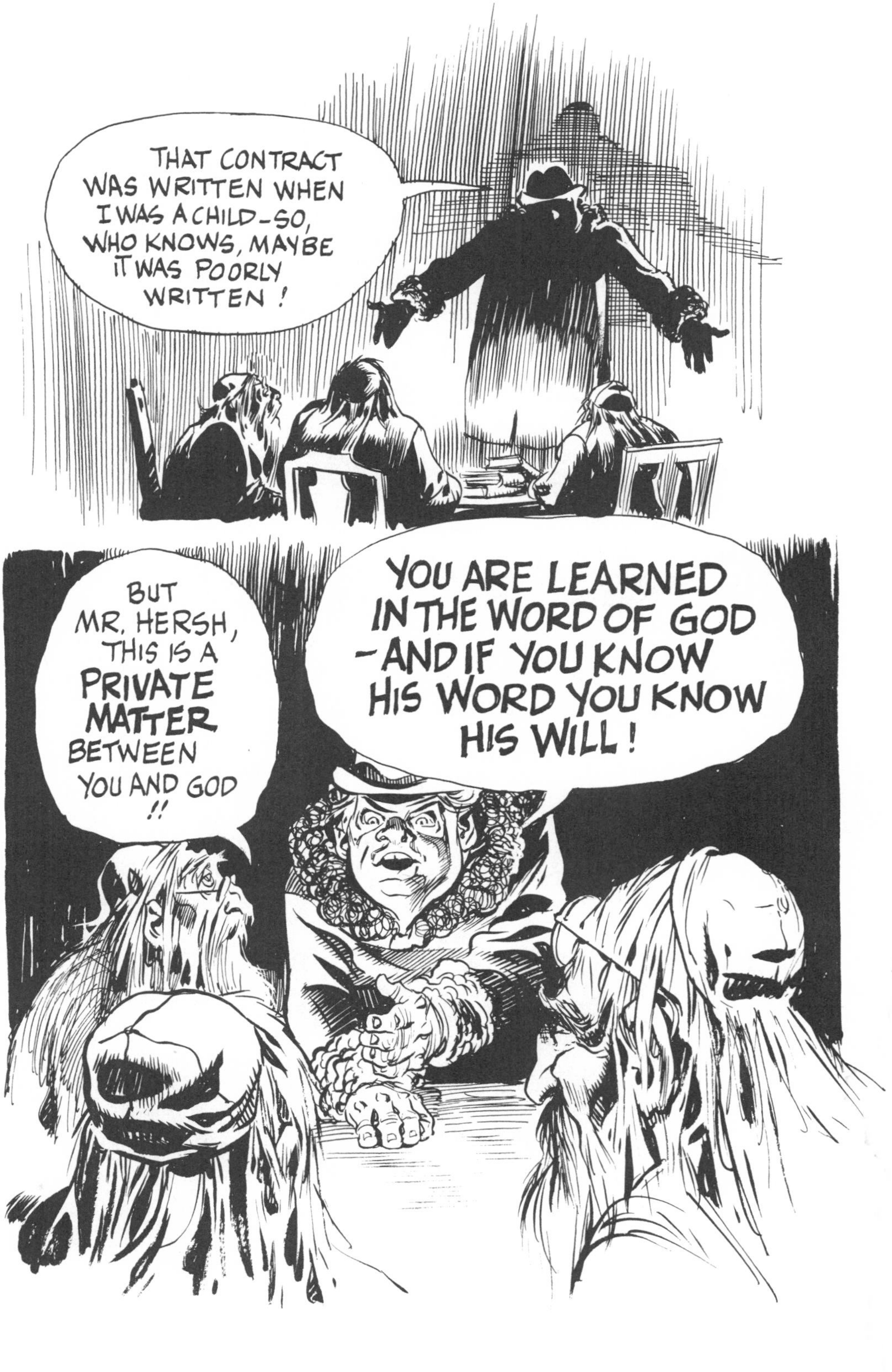

THAT CONTRACT WAS WRITTEN WHEN I WAS A CHILD-SO, WHO KNOWS, MAYBE IT WAS POORLY WRITTEN!
BUT MR. HERSH, THIS IS A PRIVATE MATTER BETWEEN YOU AND GOD!!
YOU ARE LEARNED IN THE WORD OF GOD -AND IF YOU KNOW HIS WORD YOU KNOW HIS WILL!

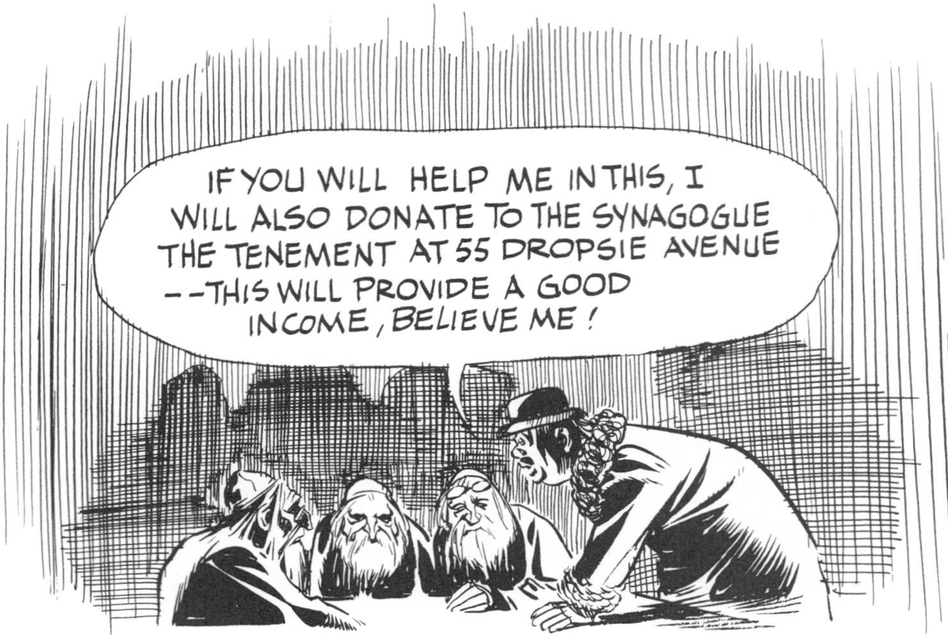
IF YOU WILL HELP ME IN THIS, I WILL ALSO DONATE TO THE SYNAGOGUE THE TENEMENT AT 55 DROPSIE AVENUE --THIS WILL PROVIDE A GOOD INCOME, BELIEVE ME!

And so the three old men pondered the request.

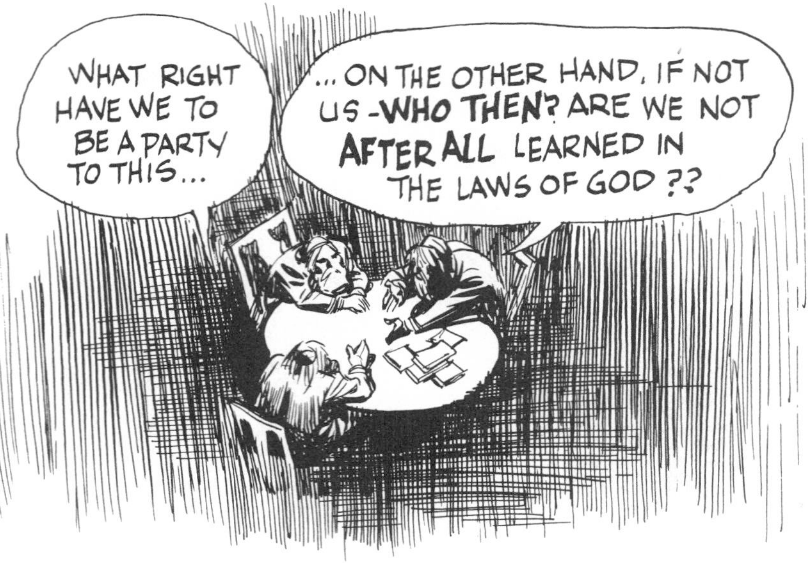
WHAT RIGHT HAVE WE TO BE A PARTY TO THIS...
...ON THE OTHER HAND, IF NOT US -WHO THEN? ARE WE NOT AFTER ALL LEARNED IN THE LAWS OF GOD??

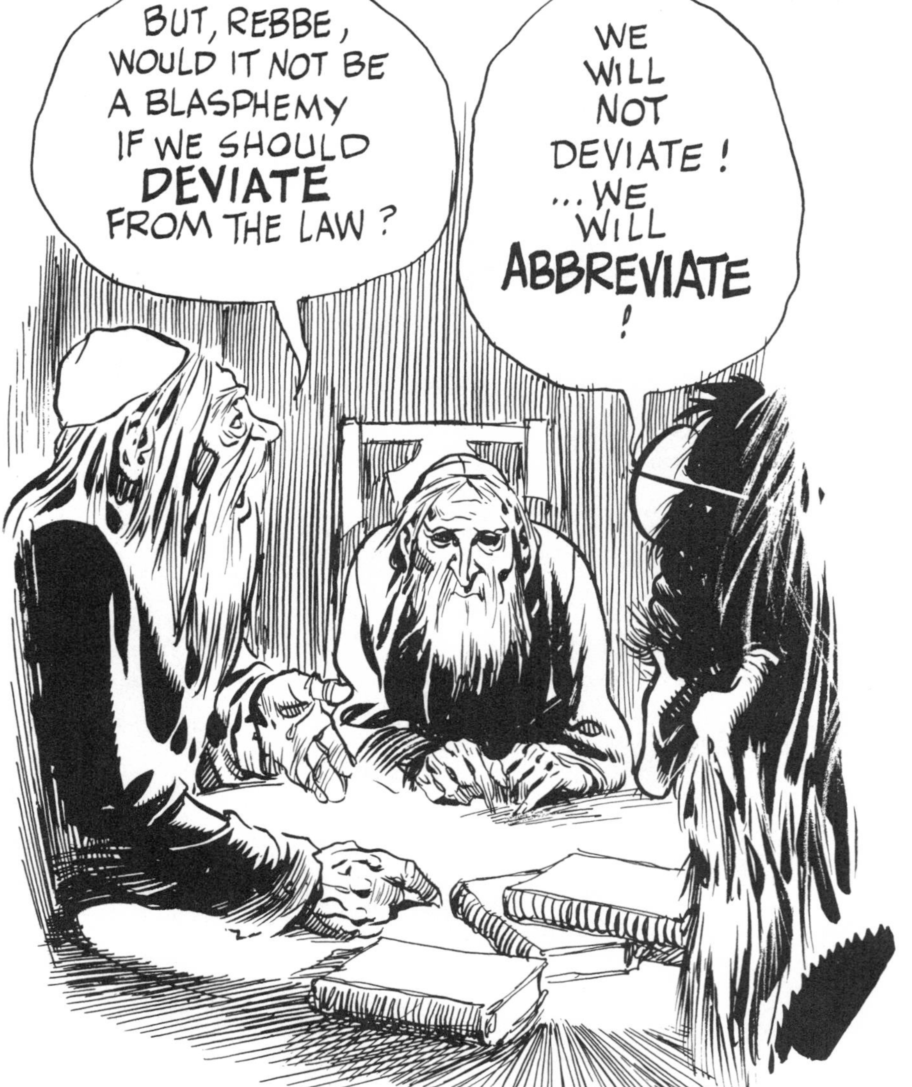
BUT, REBBE, WOULD IT NOT BE A BLASPHEMY IF WE SHOULD **DEVIATE** FROM THE LAW?
WE WILL NOT DEVIATE! ...WE WILL **ABBREVIATE**!

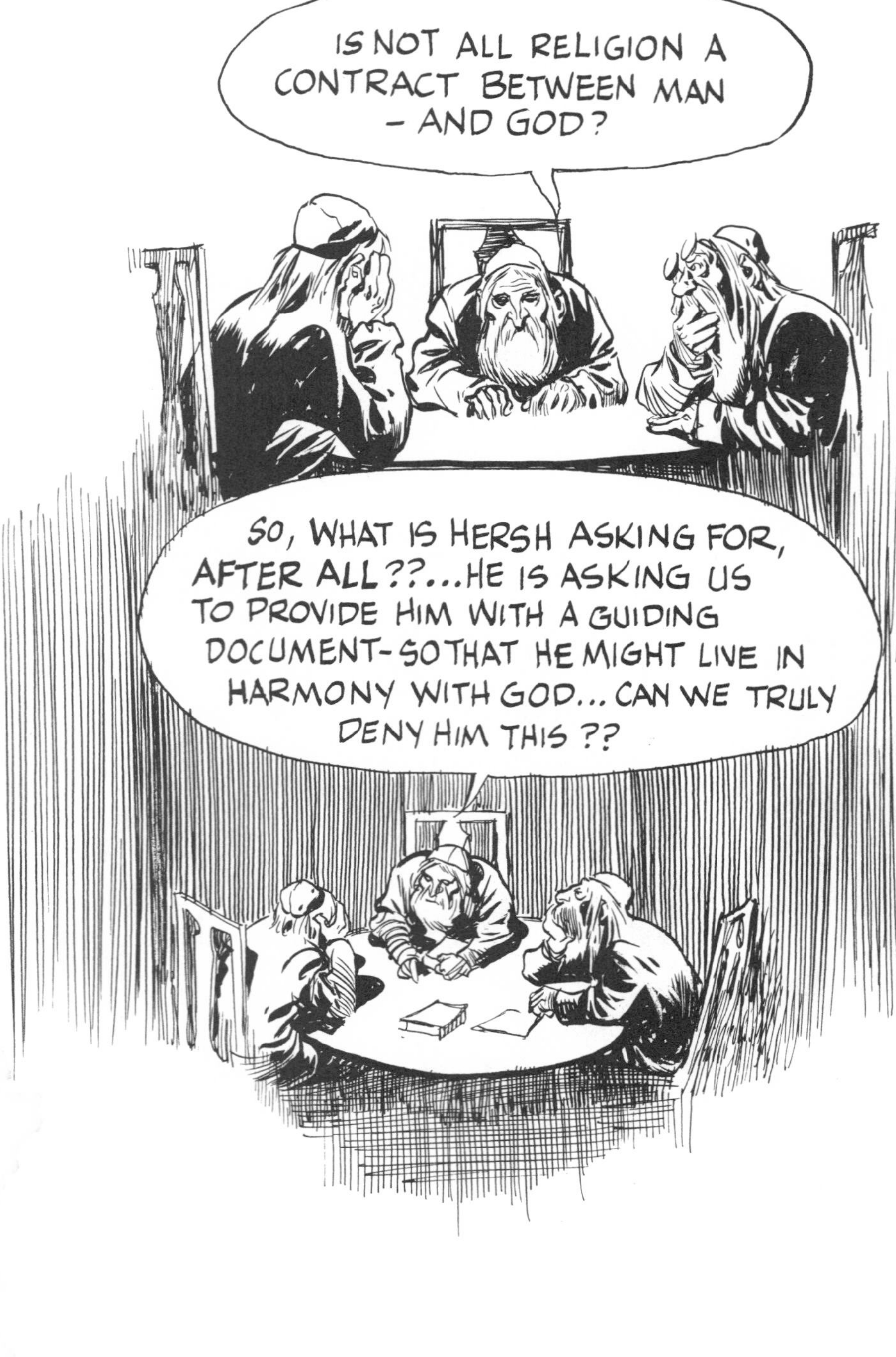
IS NOT ALL RELIGION A CONTRACT BETWEEN MAN – AND GOD?
SO, WHAT IS HERSH ASKING FOR, AFTER ALL??...HE IS ASKING US TO PROVIDE HIM WITH A GUIDING DOCUMENT-SO THAT HE MIGHT LIVE IN HARMONY WITH GOD... CAN WE TRULY DENY HIM THIS??

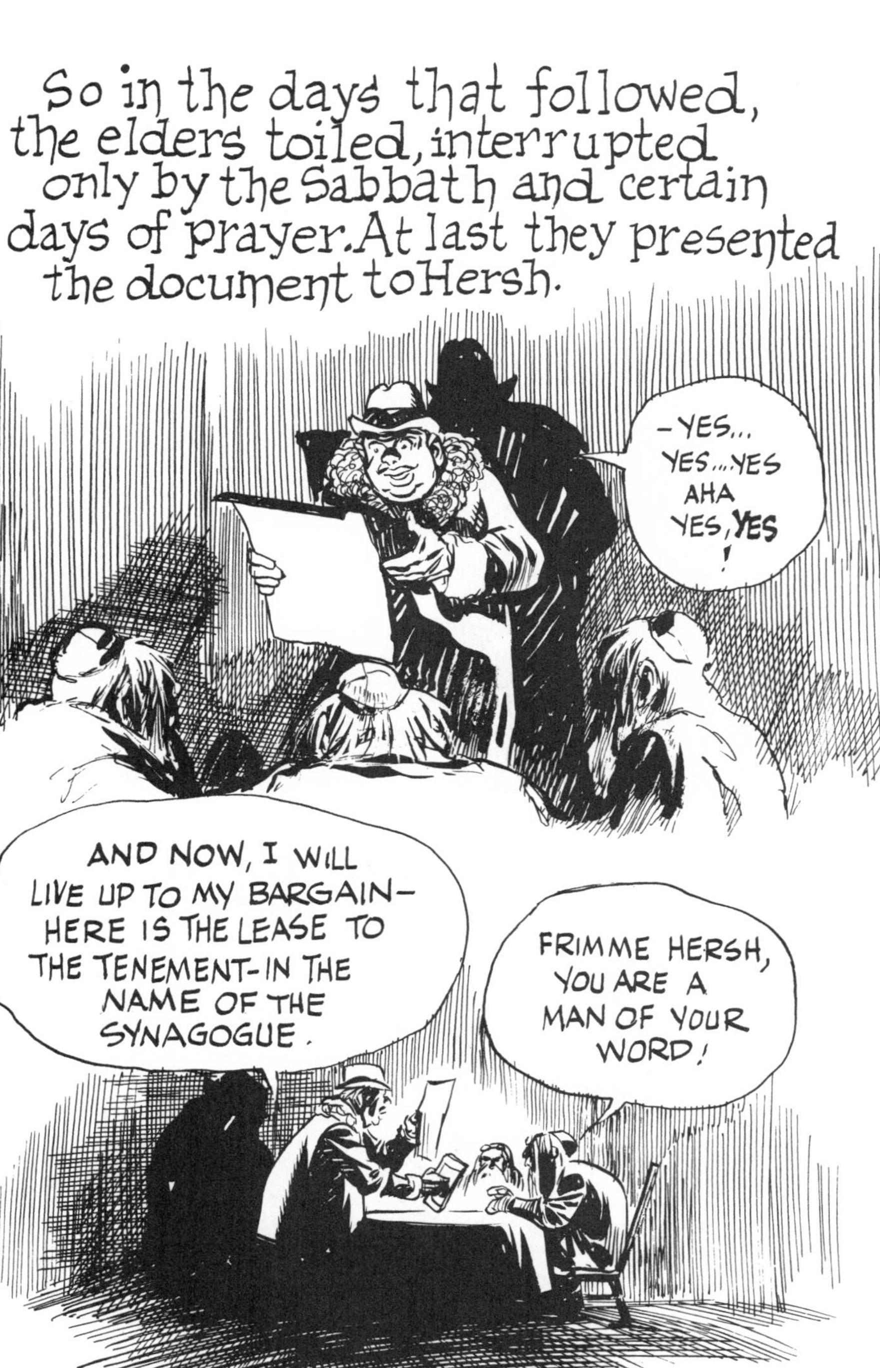
So in the days that followed, the elders toiled, interrupted only by the Sabbath and certain days of prayer. At last they presented the document to Hersh.
-YES... YES...YES AHA YES, YES!
AND NOW, I WILL LIVE UP TO MY BARGAIN- HERE IS THE LEASE TO THE TENEMENT- IN THE NAME OF THE SYNAGOGUE.
FRIMME HERSH, YOU ARE A MAN OF YOUR WORD!

All that night Hersh sat reading the contract. Again and again...he studied every word with great care.

It was bona-fide without question!

AT LAST-I HAVE A GENUINE CONTRACT WITH GOD!

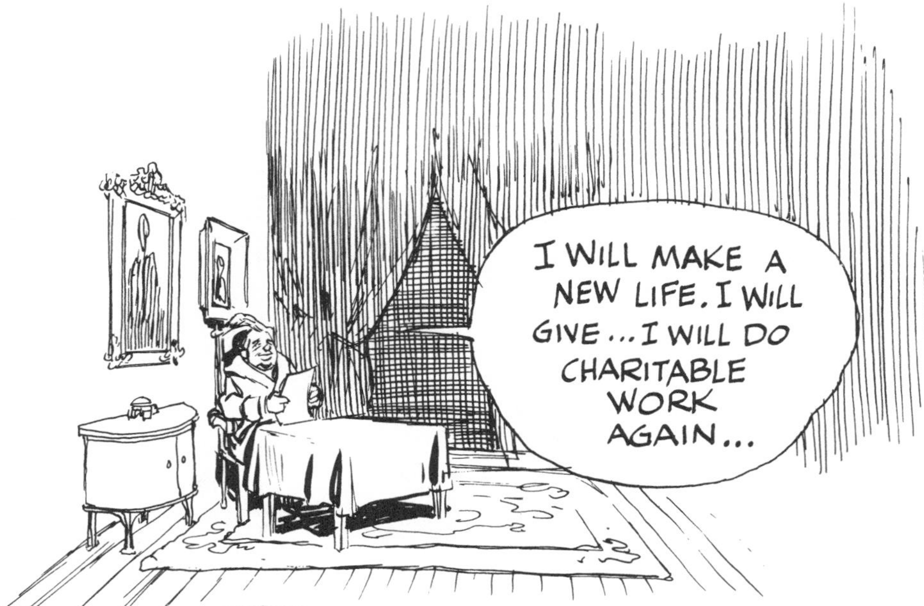
I WILL MAKE A NEW LIFE. I WILL GIVE ... I WILL DO CHARITABLE WORK AGAIN ...

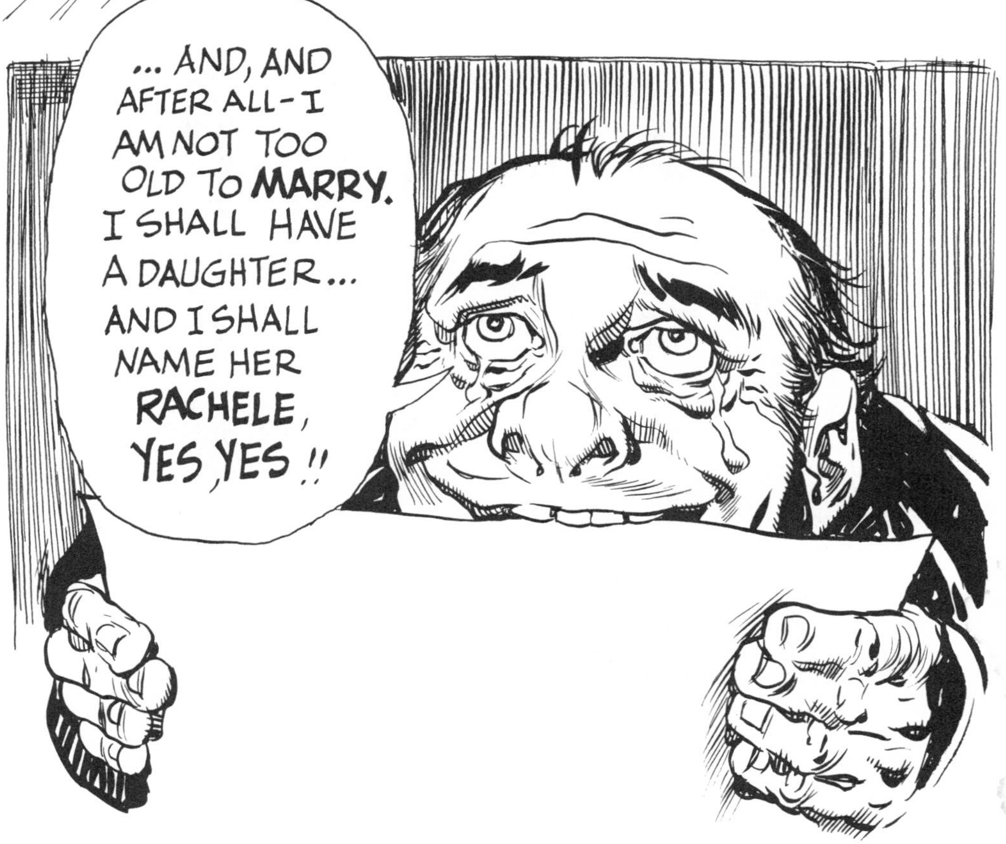
... AND, AND AFTER ALL - I AM NOT TOO OLD TO **MARRY.** I SHALL HAVE A DAUGHTER ... AND I SHALL NAME HER **RACHELE, YES, YES** !!

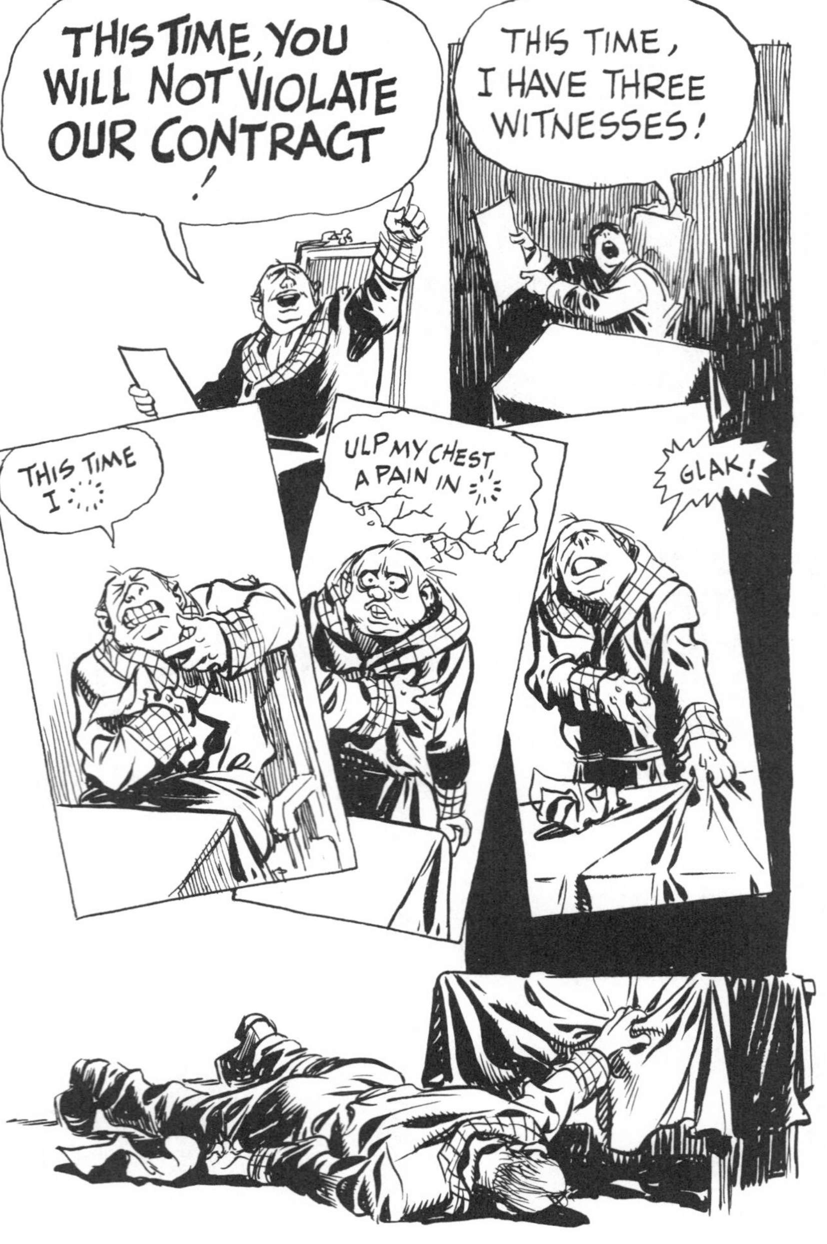
THIS TIME, YOU WILL NOT VIOLATE OUR CONTRACT!
THIS TIME, I HAVE THREE WITNESSES!
THIS TIME I
ULP MY CHEST A PAIN IN
GLAK!

At the exact moment of Hersh's last earthly breath... a mighty bolt of lightning struck the city... Not a drop of rain fell.... Only an angry wind swirled about the tenements.

On Dropsie Avenue the old
tenements seemed to tremble
in the storm. It reminded the
tenants of that day, years ago,
when Frimme Hersh argued
with GOD and terminated
their contract.

REAL ESTATE
TYCOON DIES
HEAD OF
REALTY CO
EMPIRE D

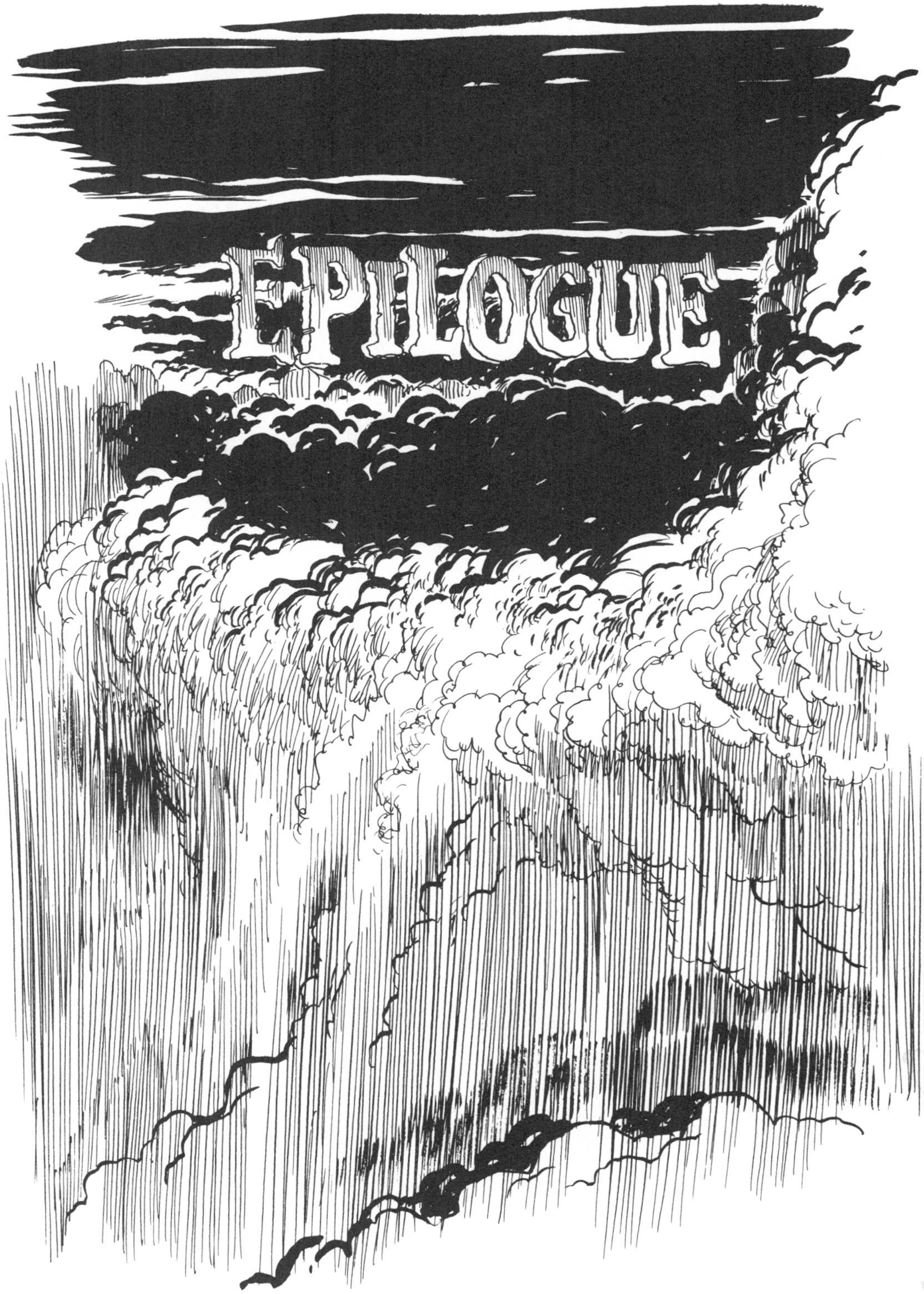
EPILOGUE

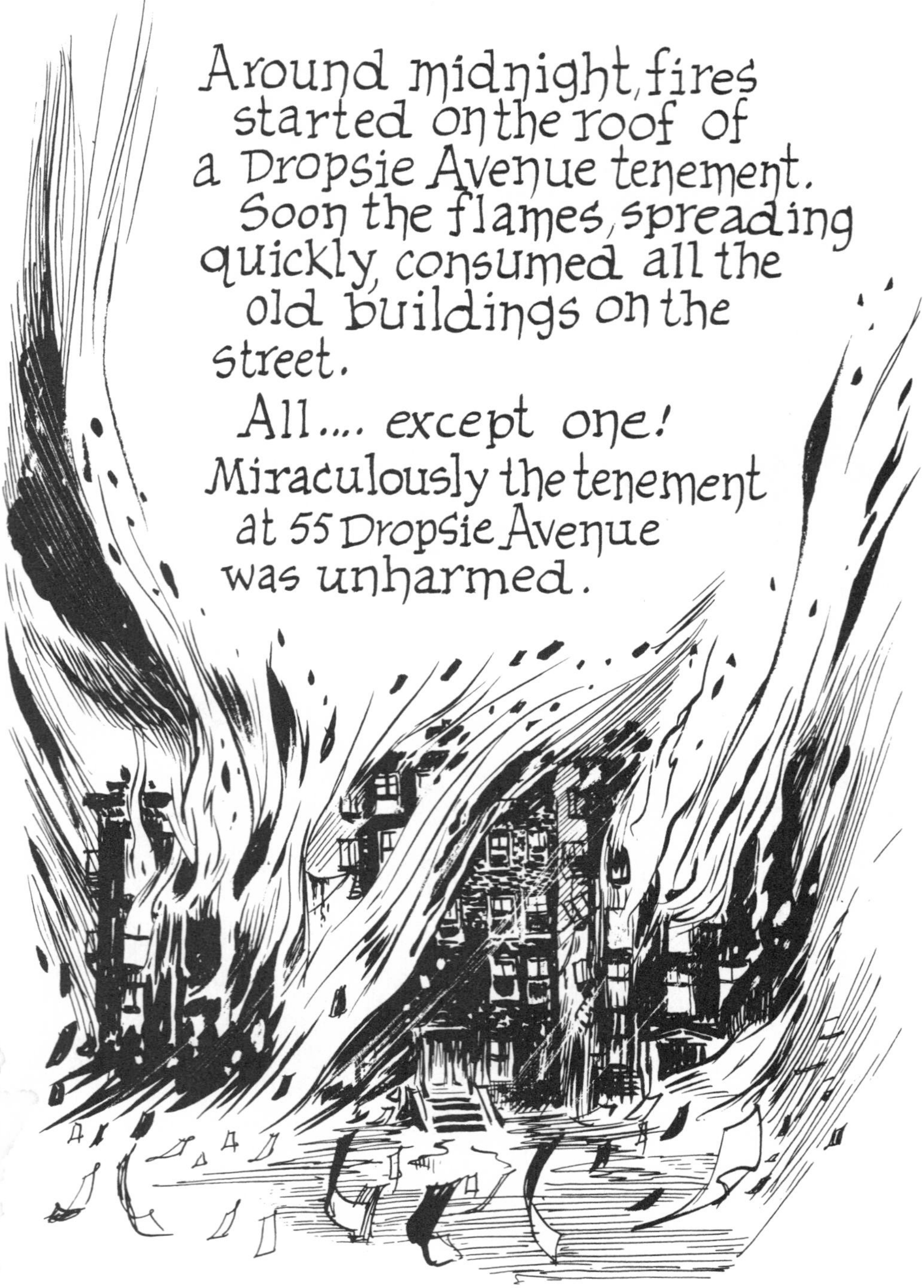
Around midnight, fires started on the roof of a Dropsie Avenue tenement. Soon the flames, spreading quickly, consumed all the old buildings on the street.
All.... except one!
Miraculously the tenement at 55 Dropsie Avenue was unharmed.

And it happened that a boy,
Shloime Khreks, was
the hero of the day.

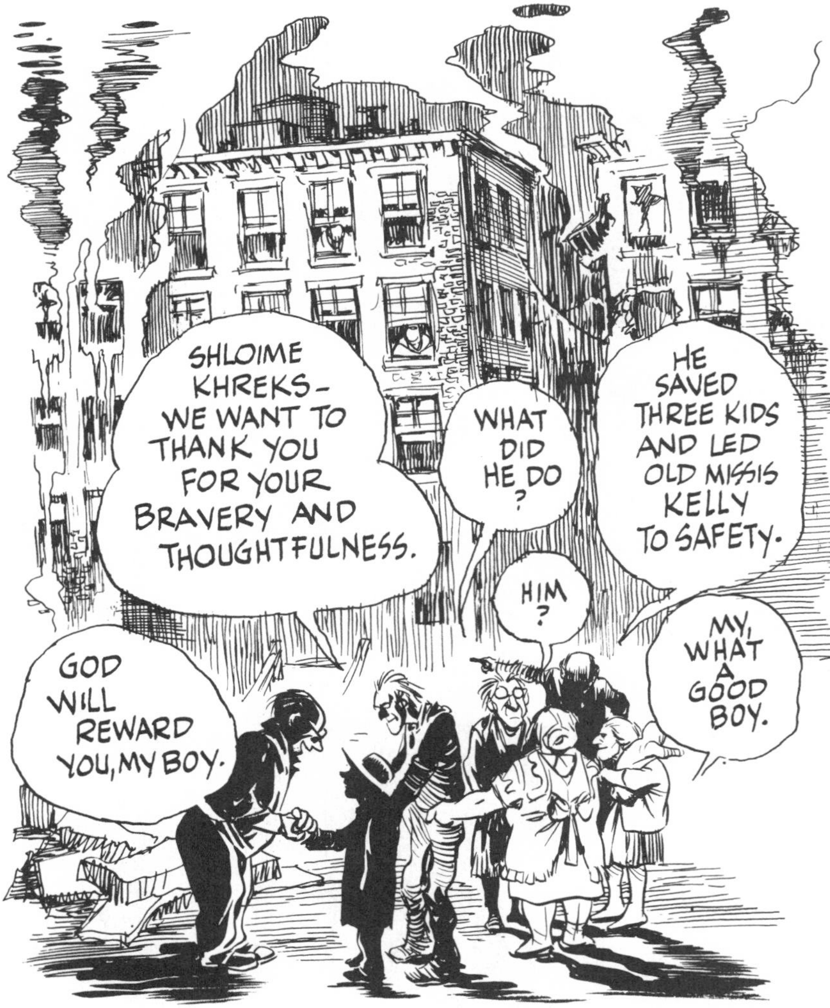
SHLOIME KHREKS- WE WANT TO THANK YOU FOR YOUR BRAVERY AND THOUGHTFULNESS.
WHAT DID HE DO ?
HE SAVED THREE KIDS AND LED OLD MISSIS KELLY TO SAFETY.
HIM ?
MY, WHAT A GOOD BOY.
GOD WILL REWARD YOU, MY BOY.

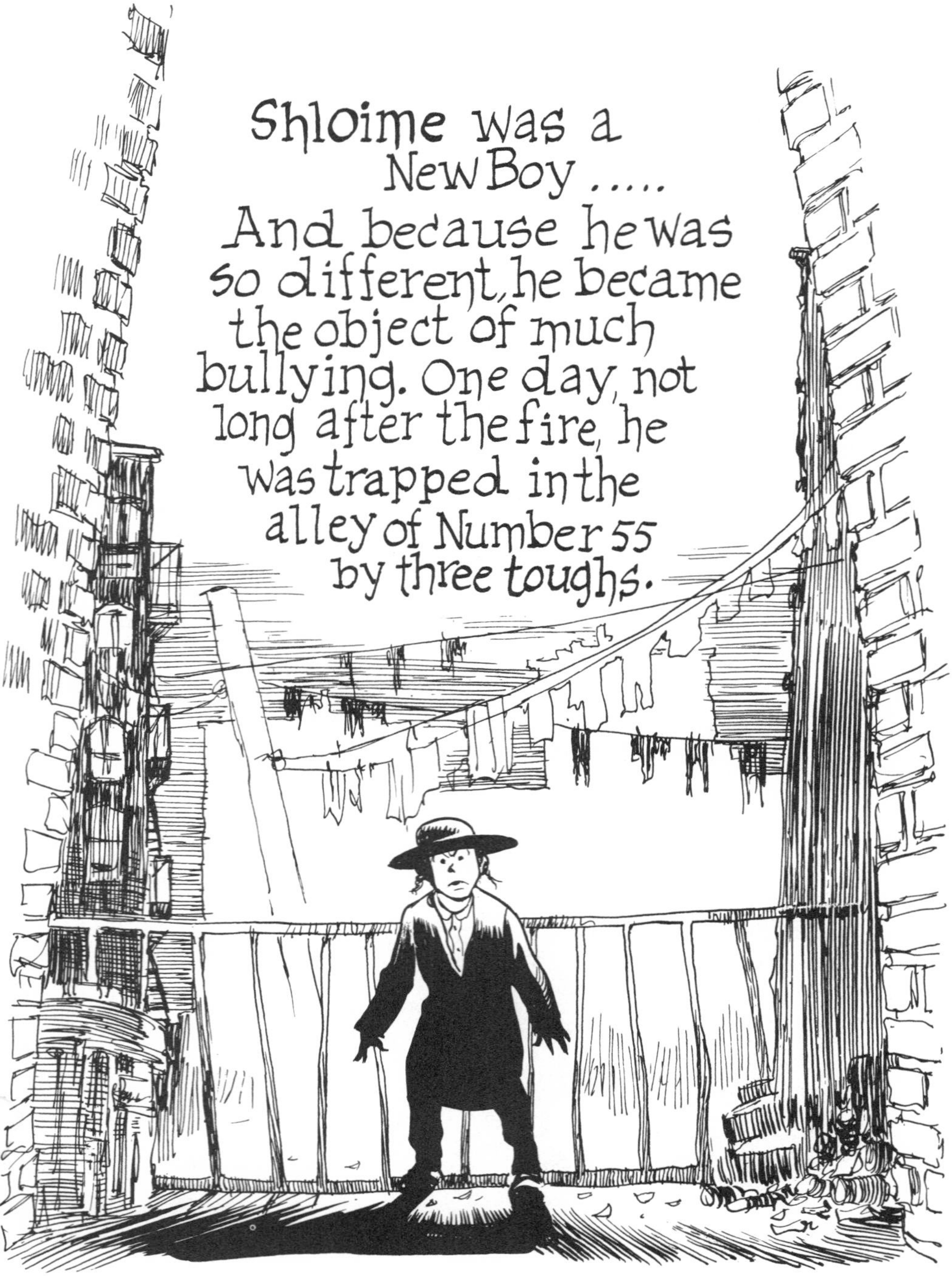
Shloime was a New Boy ..... And because he was so different, he became the object of much bullying. One day, not long after the fire, he was trapped in the alley of Number 55 by three toughs.

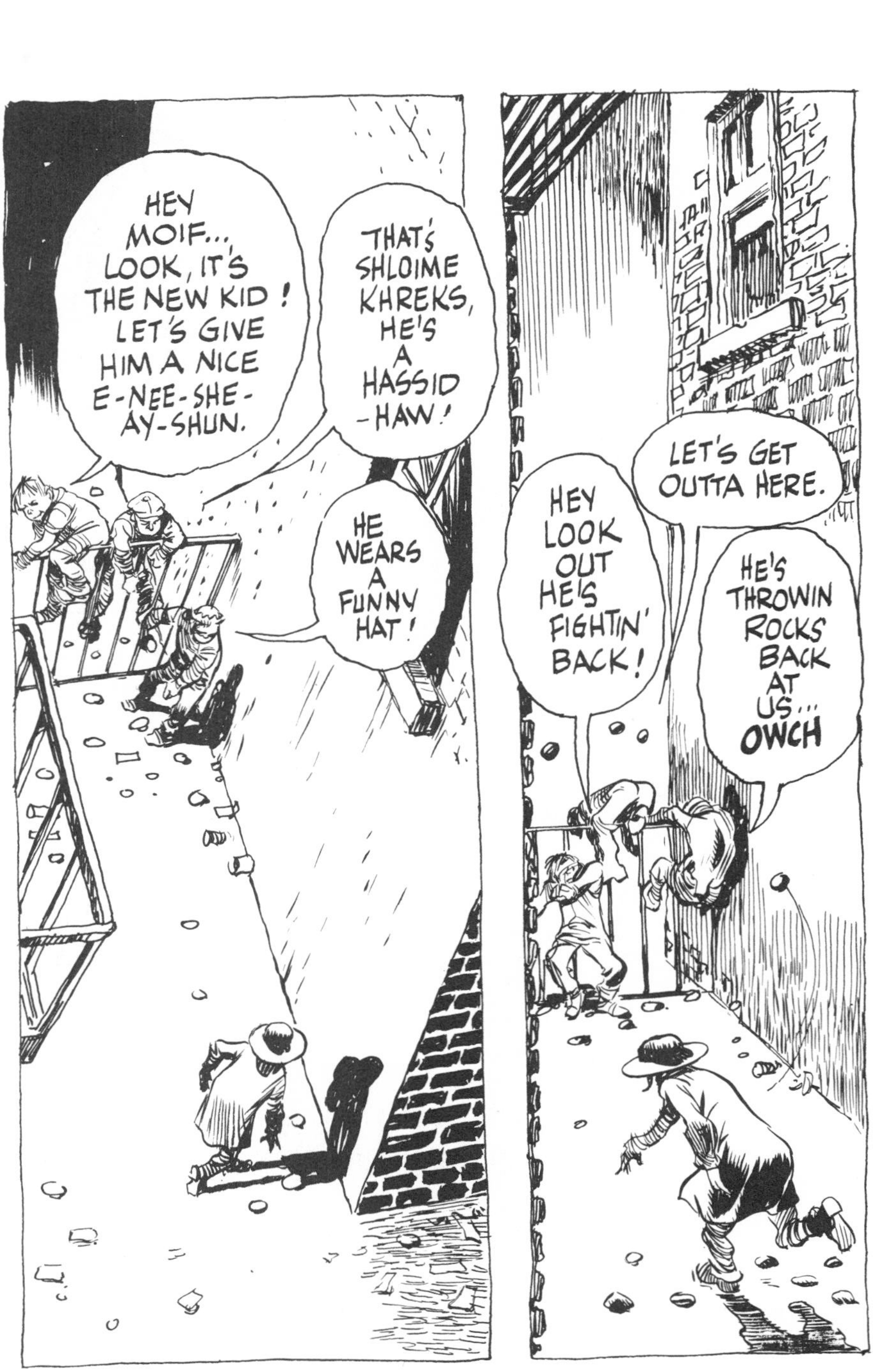
HEY MOIF..., LOOK, IT'S THE NEW KID! LET'S GIVE HIM A NICE E-NEE-SHE-AY-SHUN.
THAT'S SHLOIME KHREKS, HE'S A HASSID-HAW!
HE WEARS A FUNNY HAT!
HEY LOOK OUT HE'S FIGHTIN' BACK!
LET'S GET OUTTA HERE.
HE'S THROWIN ROCKS BACK AT US... OWCH

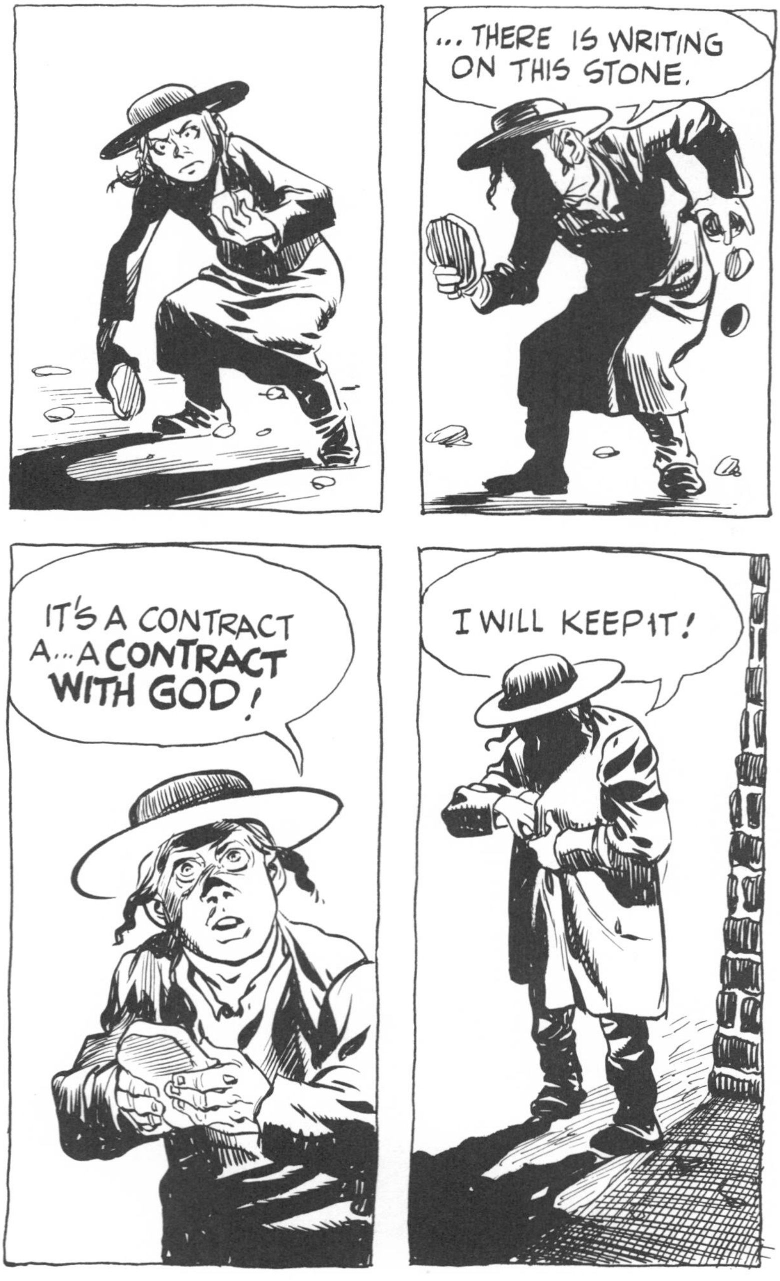
...THERE IS WRITING ON THIS STONE.
IT'S A CONTRACT A...A CONTRACT WITH GOD!
I WILL KEEP IT!

...And that evening on the stoop of the tenement, Shloime Khreks signed his name below that of Frimme Hersh... thereby entering into a contract with GOD.

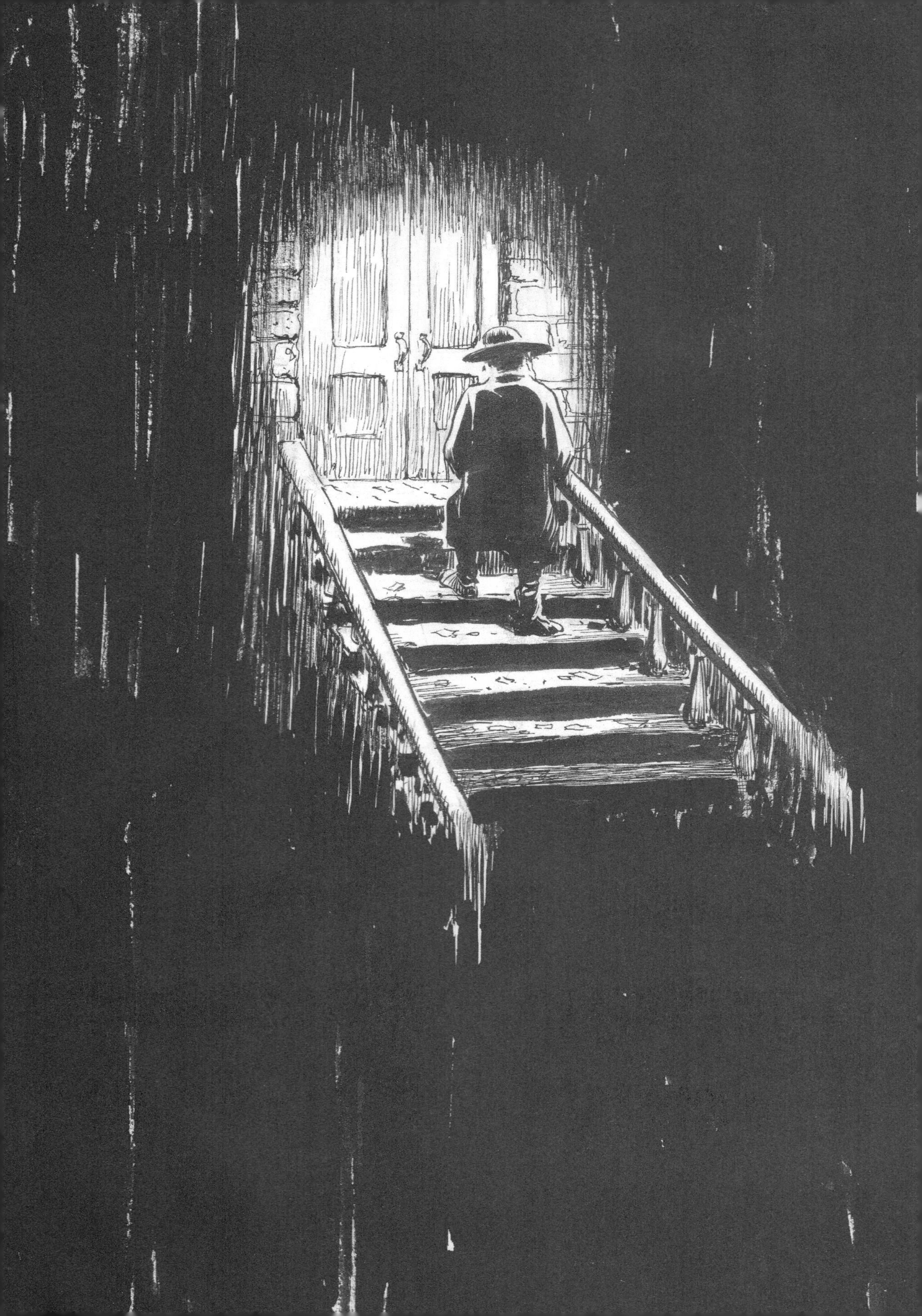

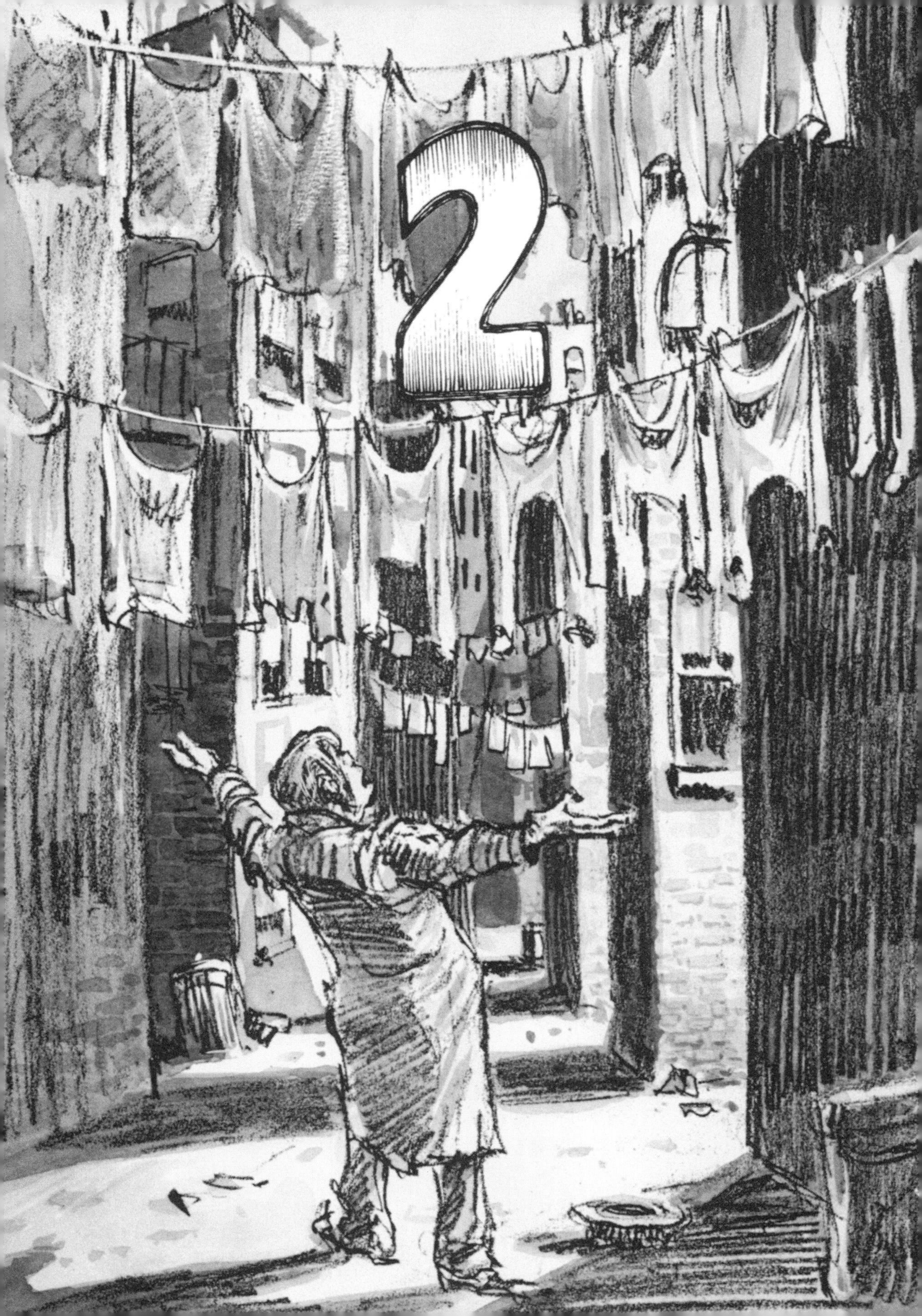
2

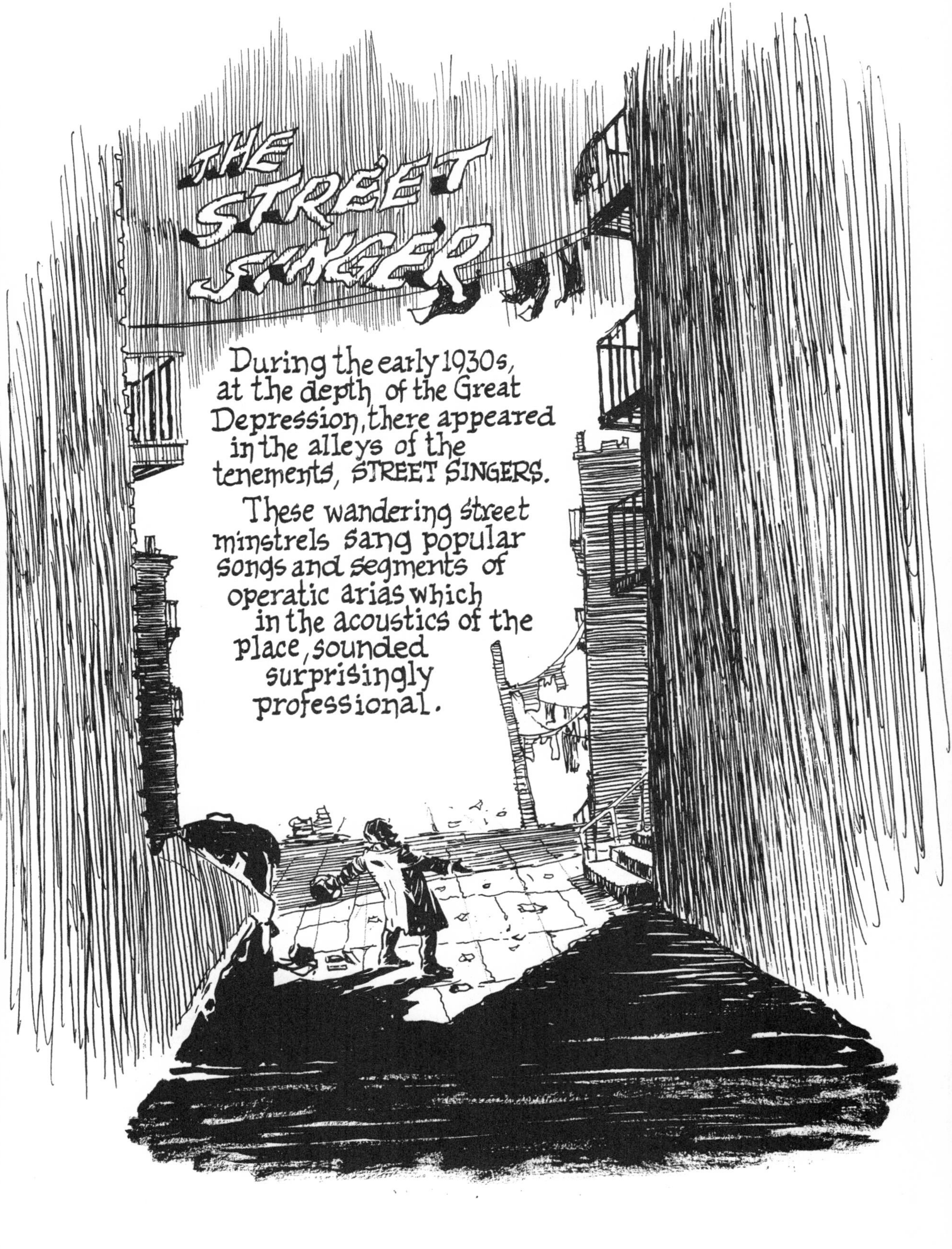
THE STREET SINGER
During the early 1930s, at the depth of the Great Depression, there appeared in the alleys of the tenements, STREET SINGERS.
These wandering street minstrels sang popular songs and segments of operatic arias which in the acoustics of the place, sounded surprisingly professional.

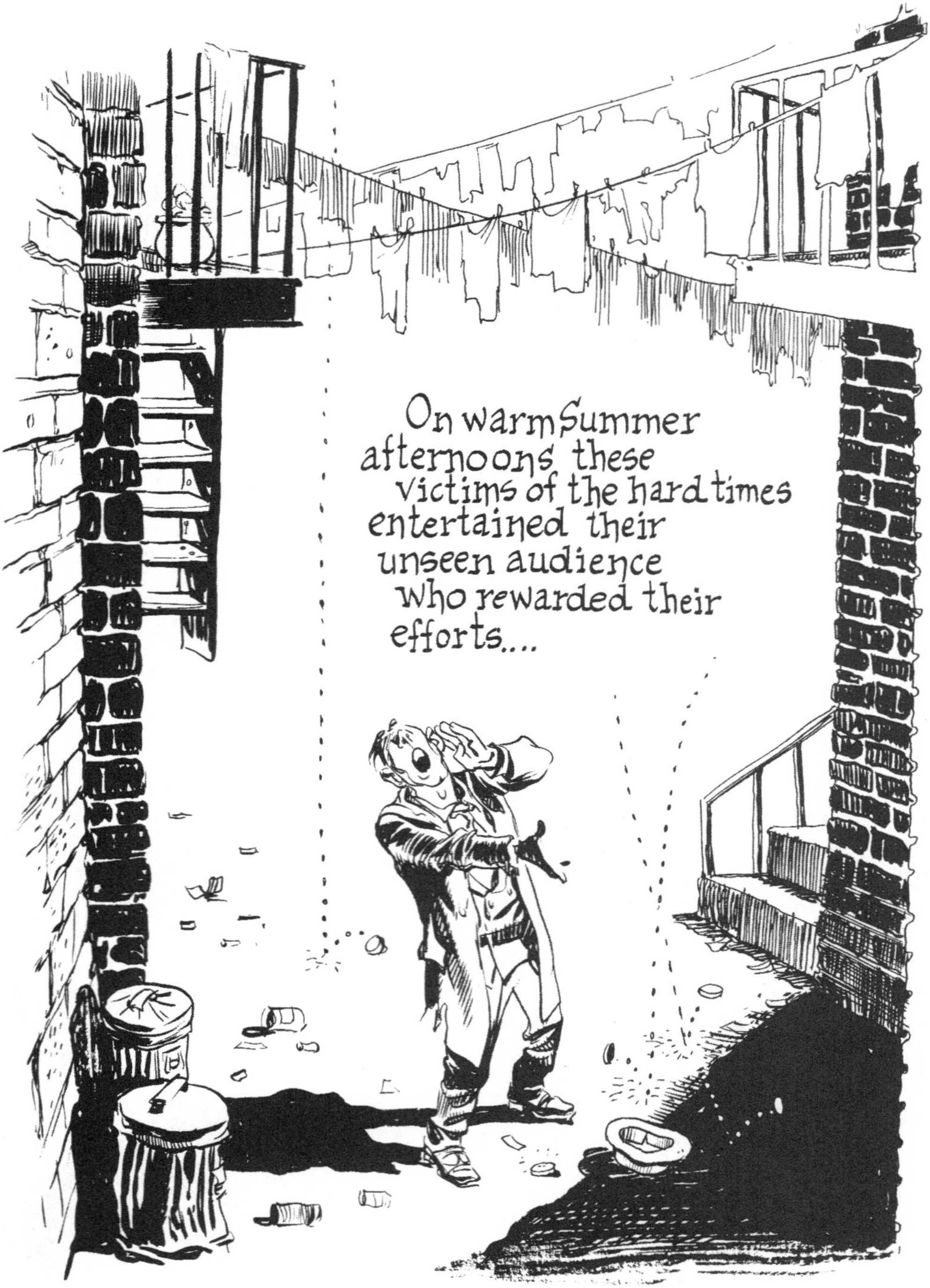
On warm Summer afternoons these victims of the hard times entertained their unseen audience who rewarded their efforts....

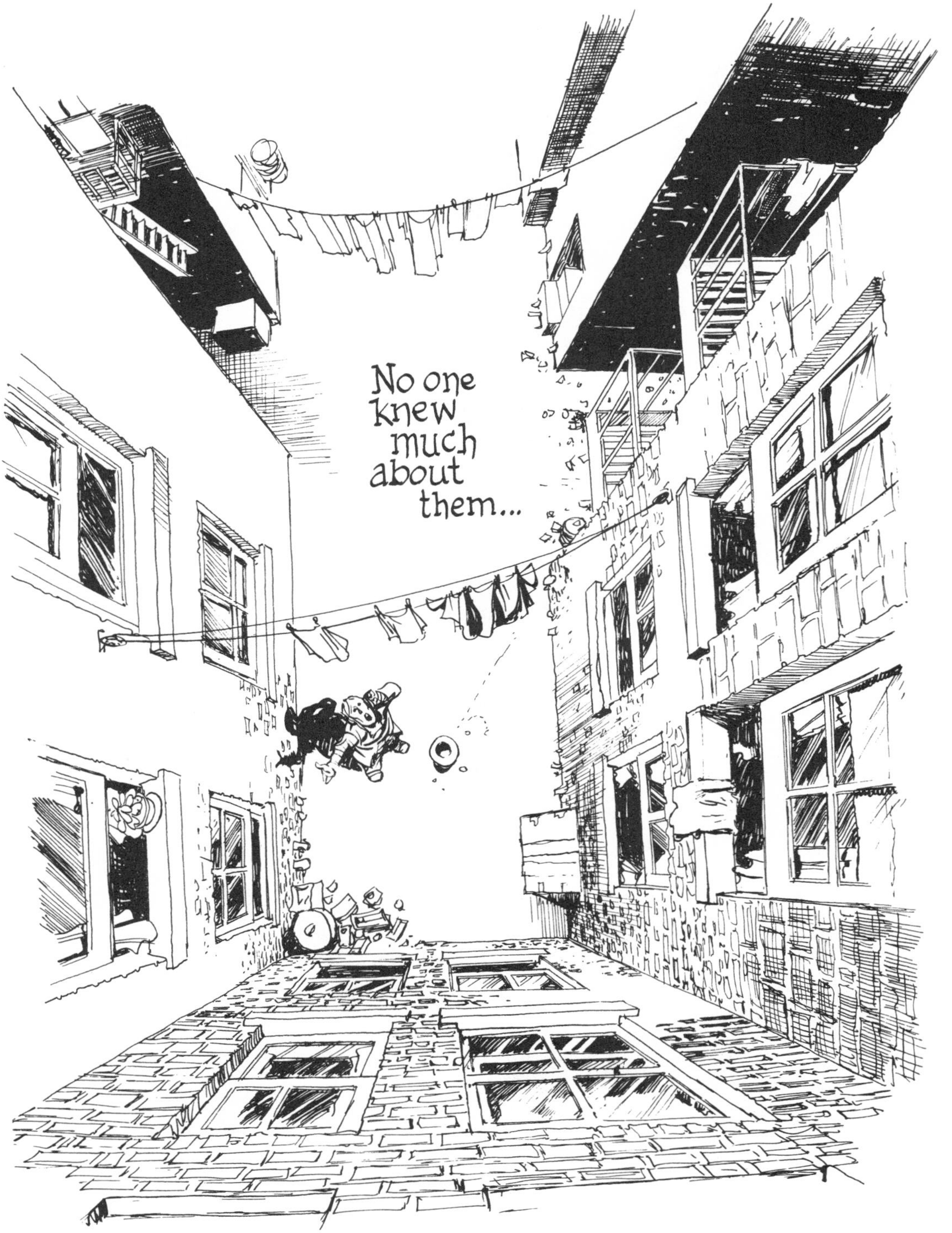
No one knew much about them...

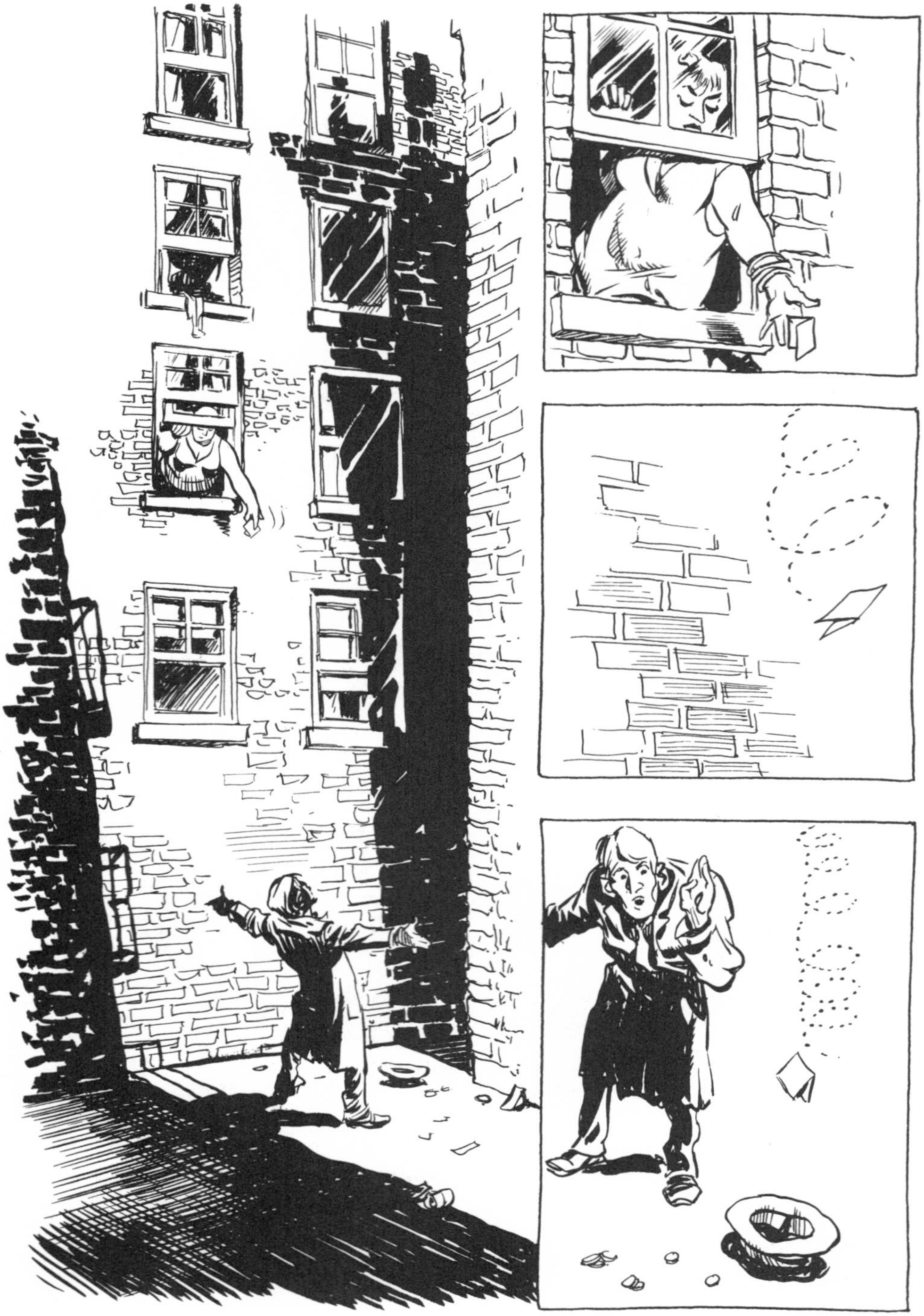

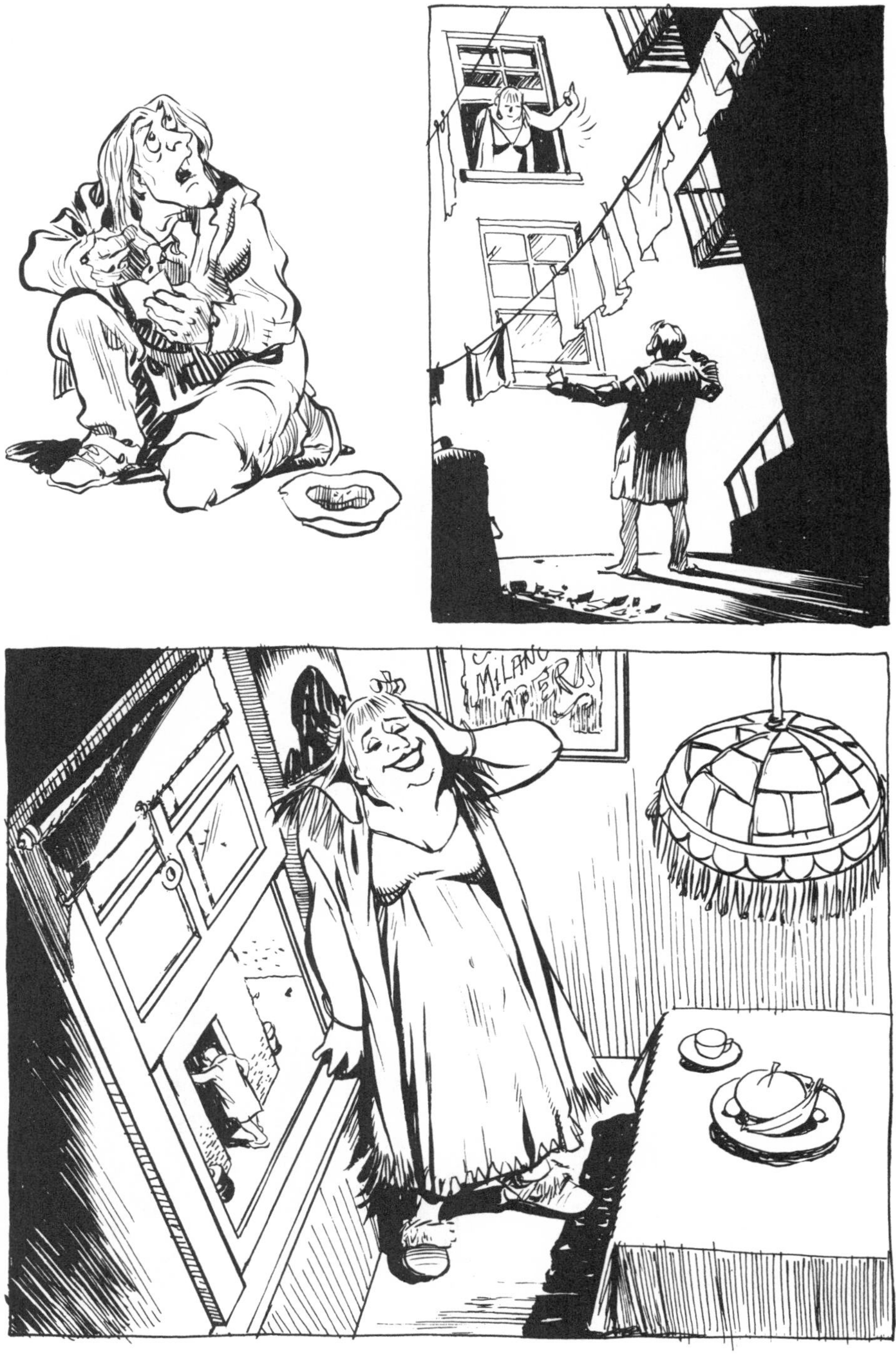

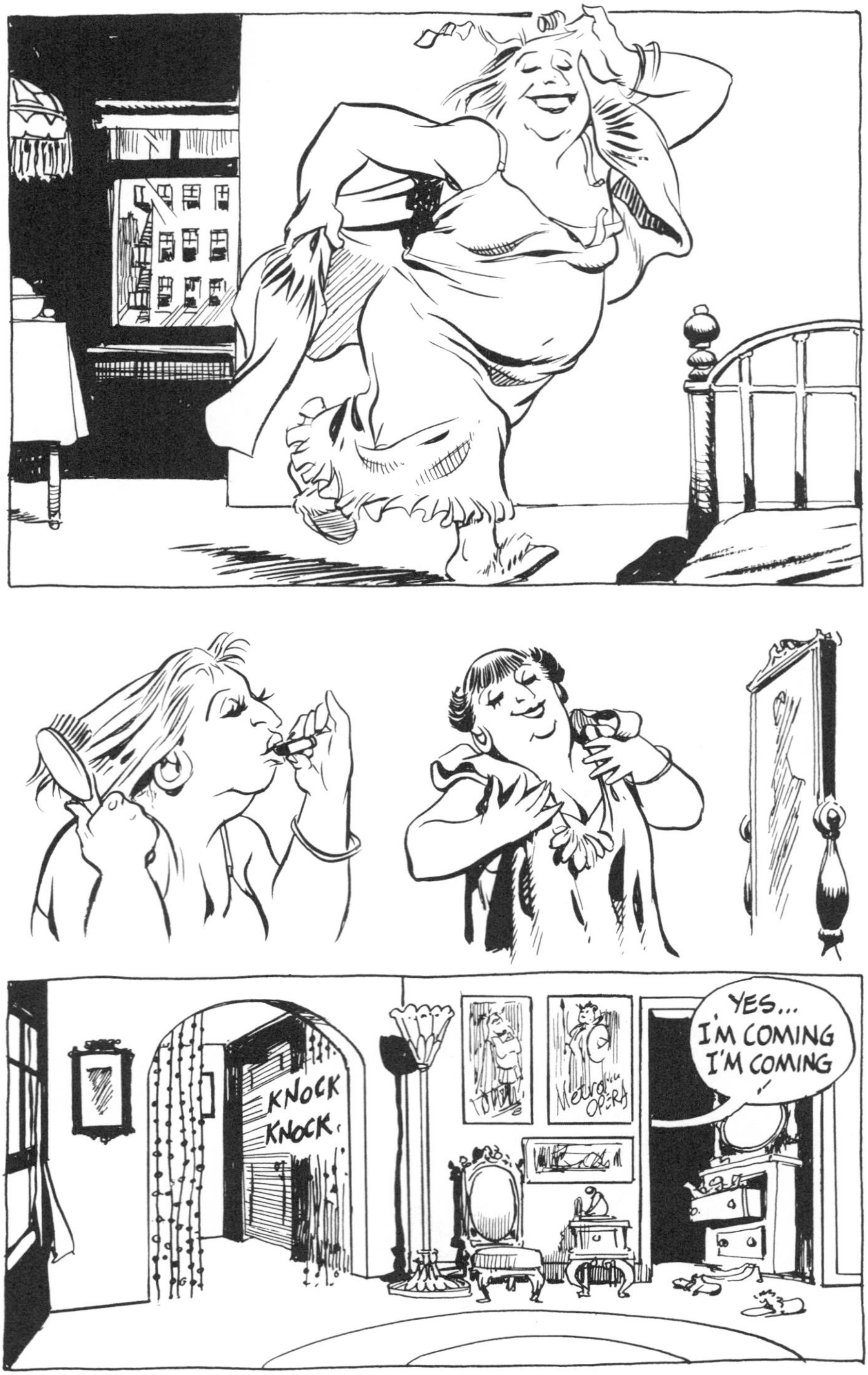
KNOCK
KNOCK
YES...
I'M COMING
I'M COMING

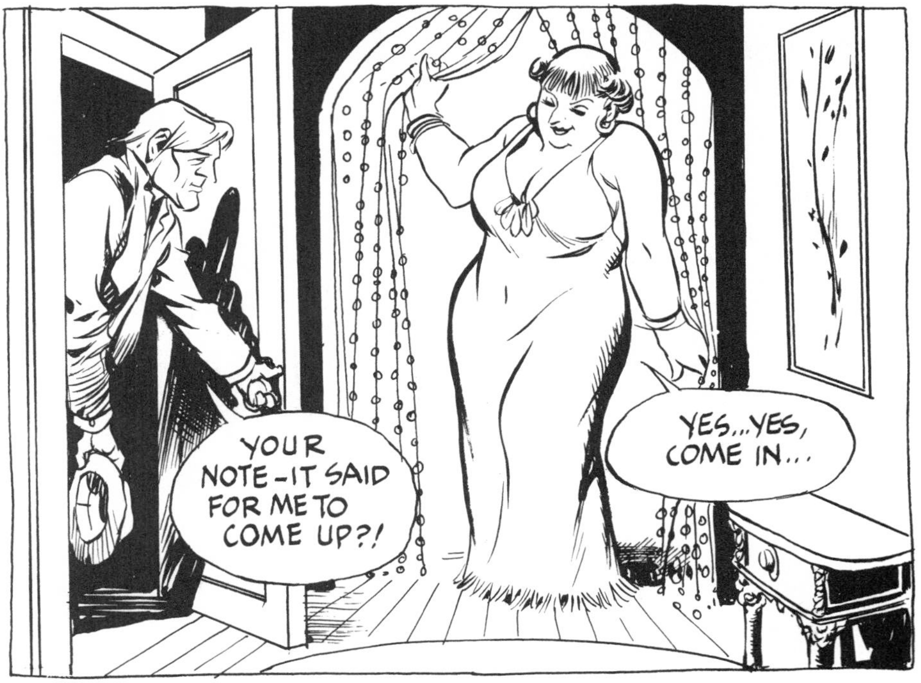
YOUR NOTE-IT SAID FOR ME TO COME UP?!
YES...YES, COME IN...

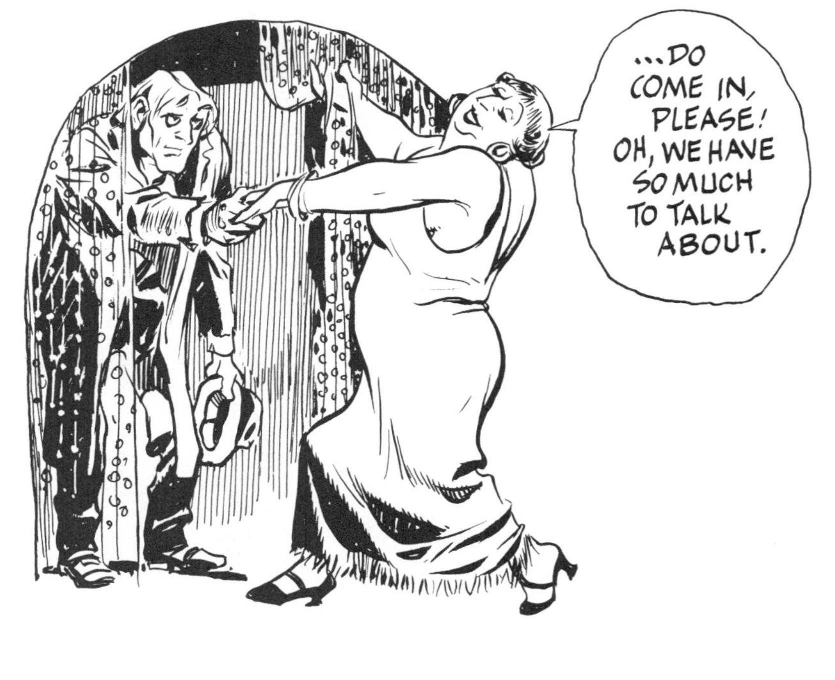
...DO COME IN, PLEASE! OH, WE HAVE SO MUCH TO TALK ABOUT.

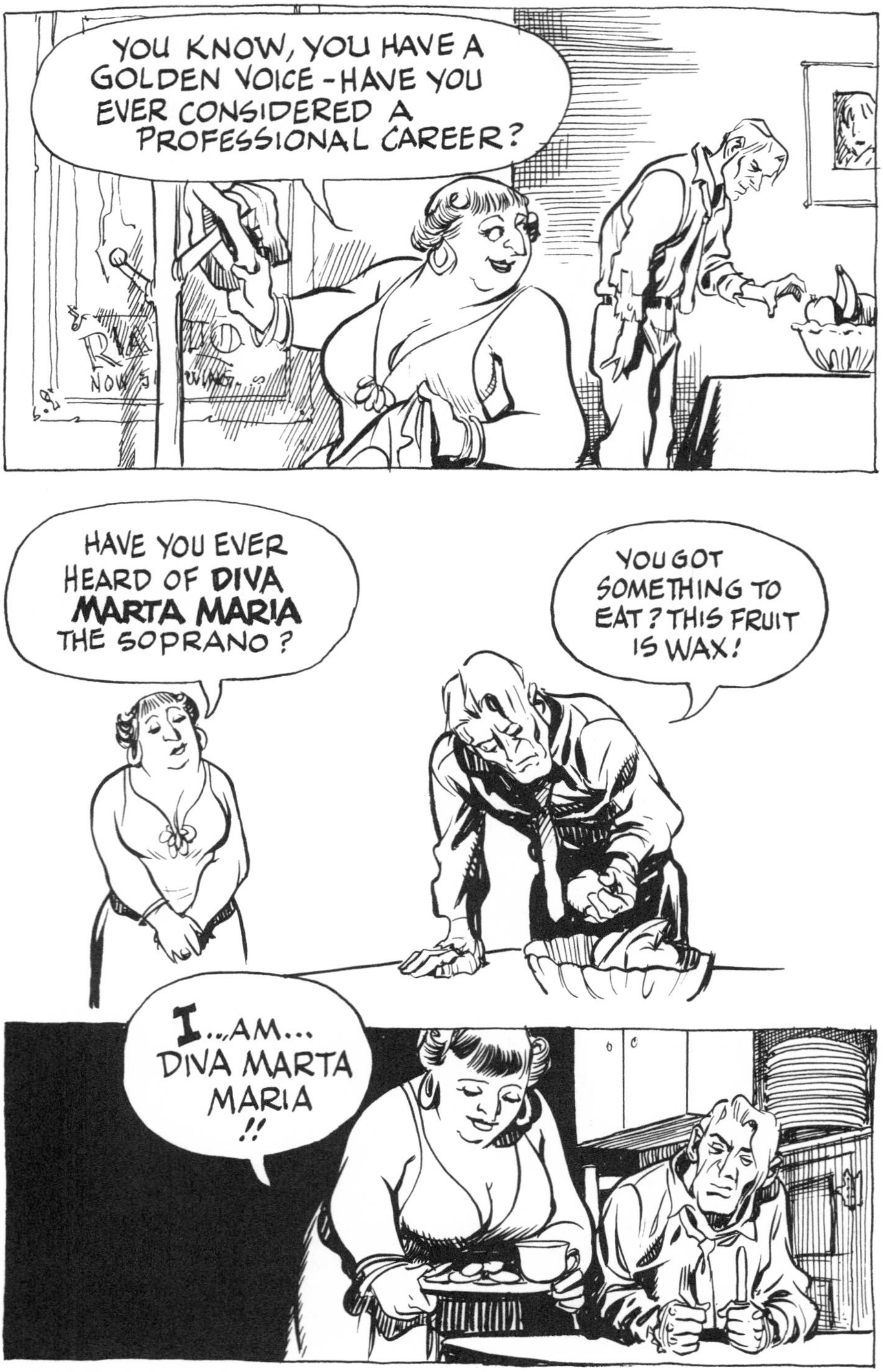
YOU KNOW, YOU HAVE A GOLDEN VOICE - HAVE YOU EVER CONSIDERED A PROFESSIONAL CAREER?
HAVE YOU EVER HEARD OF **DIVA MARTA MARIA** THE SOPRANO?
YOU GOT SOMETHING TO EAT? THIS FRUIT IS WAX!
I...AM... DIVA MARTA MARIA !!

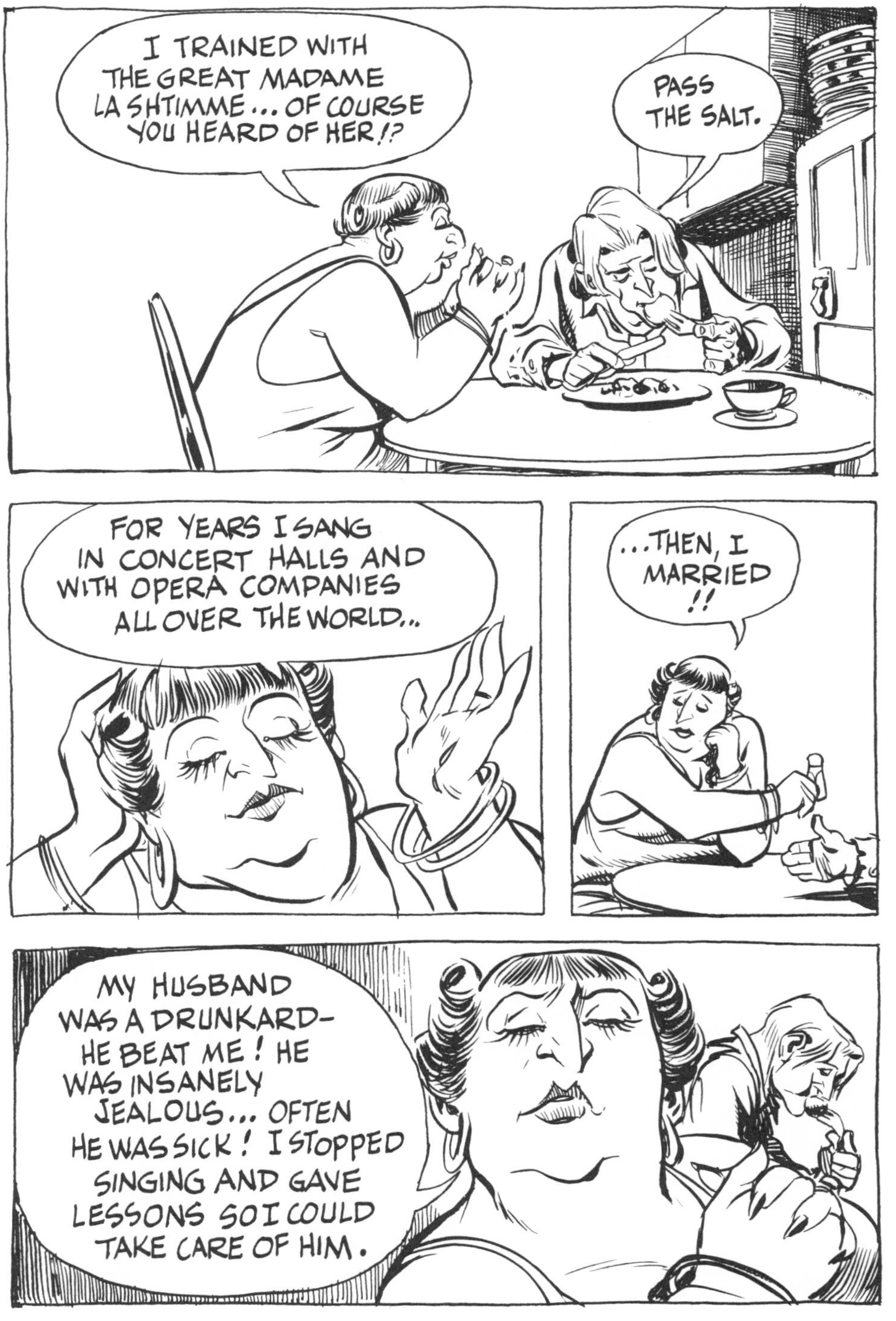
I TRAINED WITH THE GREAT MADAME LA SHTIMME... OF COURSE YOU HEARD OF HER!?
PASS THE SALT.
FOR YEARS I SANG IN CONCERT HALLS AND WITH OPERA COMPANIES ALL OVER THE WORLD...
...THEN, I MARRIED !!
MY HUSBAND WAS A DRUNKARD- HE BEAT ME! HE WAS INSANELY JEALOUS... OFTEN HE WAS SICK! I STOPPED SINGING AND GAVE LESSONS SO I COULD TAKE CARE OF HIM.

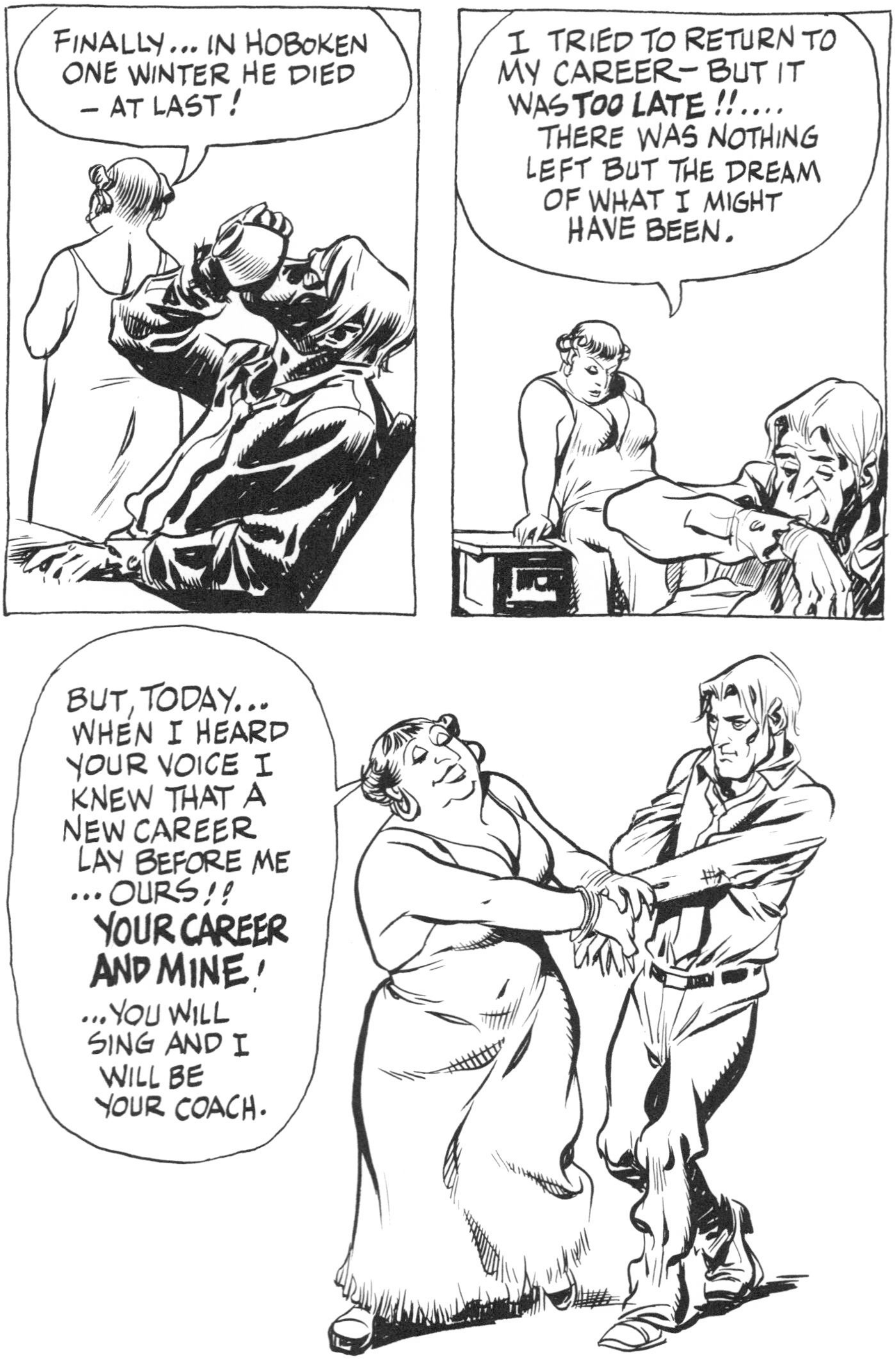
FINALLY... IN HOBOKEN ONE WINTER HE DIED – AT LAST!
I TRIED TO RETURN TO MY CAREER– BUT IT WAS TOO LATE!!.... THERE WAS NOTHING LEFT BUT THE DREAM OF WHAT I MIGHT HAVE BEEN.
BUT, TODAY... WHEN I HEARD YOUR VOICE I KNEW THAT A NEW CAREER LAY BEFORE ME ...OURS!! YOUR CAREER AND MINE! ...YOU WILL SING AND I WILL BE YOUR COACH.

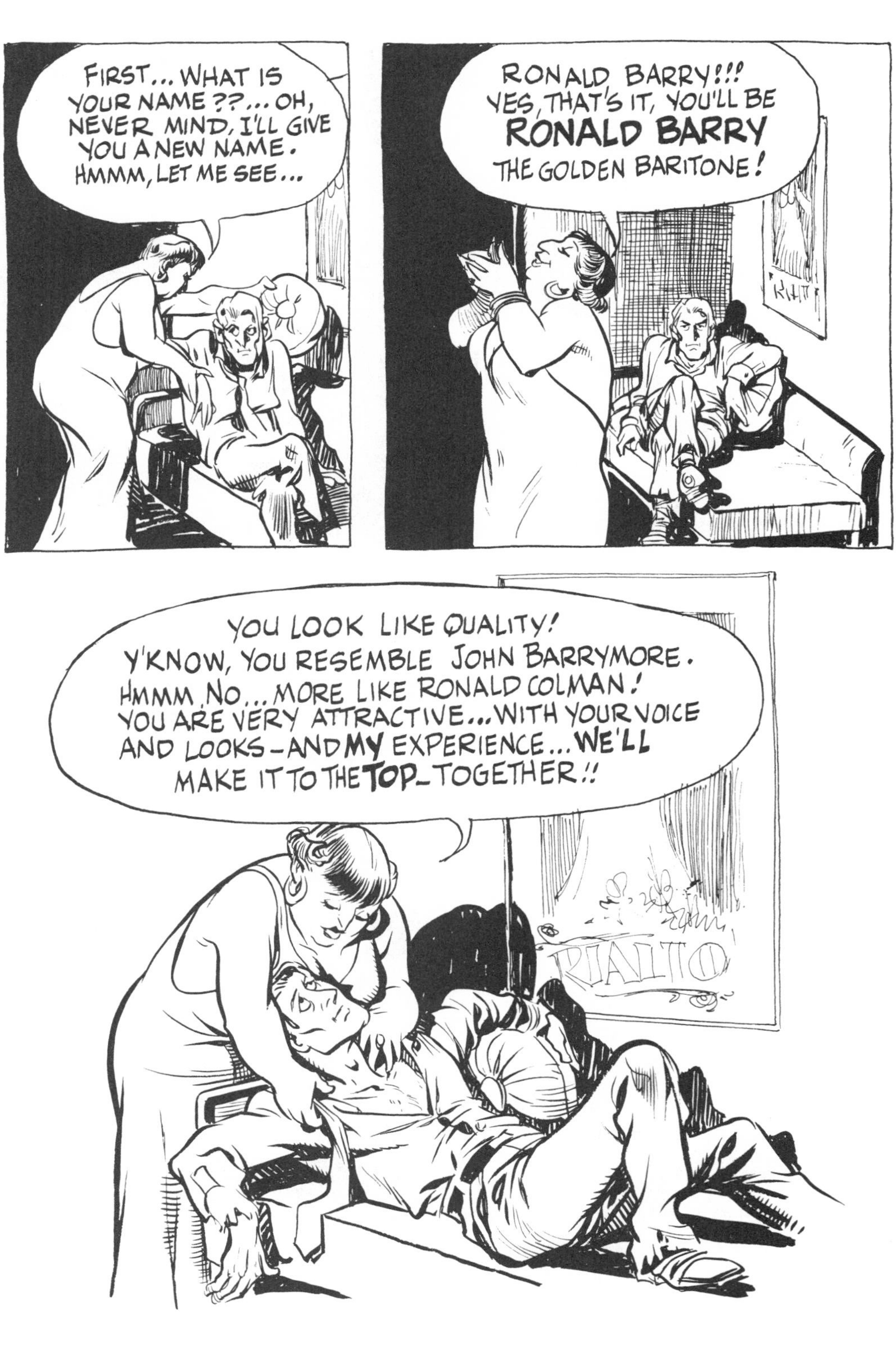
FIRST... WHAT IS YOUR NAME ??... OH, NEVER MIND, I'LL GIVE YOU A NEW NAME. HMMM, LET ME SEE...
RONALD BARRY!!! YES, THAT'S IT, YOU'LL BE **RONALD BARRY** THE GOLDEN BARITONE!
YOU LOOK LIKE QUALITY! Y'KNOW, YOU RESEMBLE JOHN BARRYMORE. HMMM NO... MORE LIKE RONALD COLMAN! YOU ARE VERY ATTRACTIVE... WITH YOUR VOICE AND LOOKS - AND **MY** EXPERIENCE... **WE'LL** MAKE IT TO THE **TOP** - TOGETHER!!
RIALTO

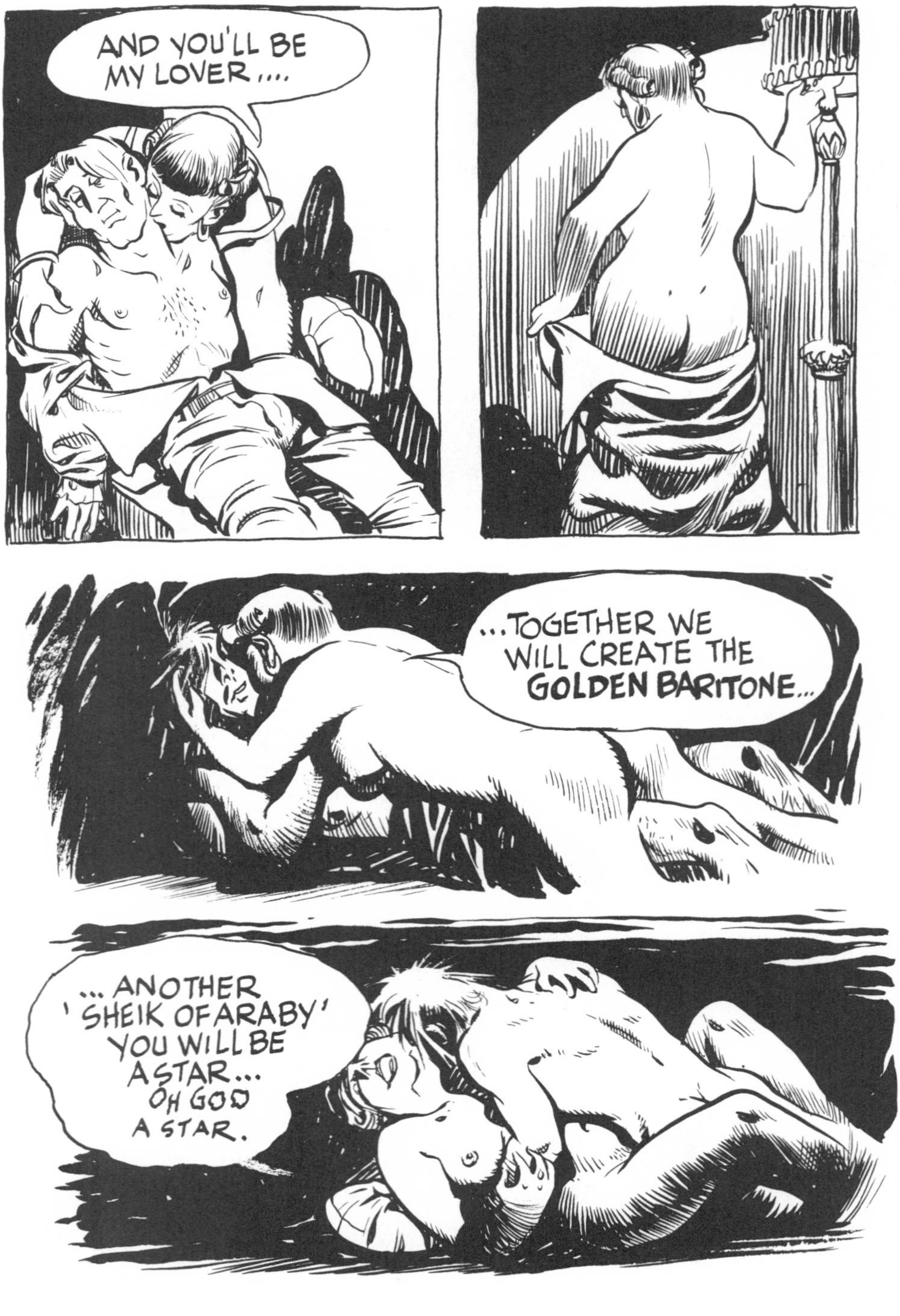
AND YOU'LL BE MY LOVER....
...TOGETHER WE WILL CREATE THE GOLDEN BARITONE...
...ANOTHER 'SHEIK OF ARABY' YOU WILL BE A STAR... OH GOD A STAR.

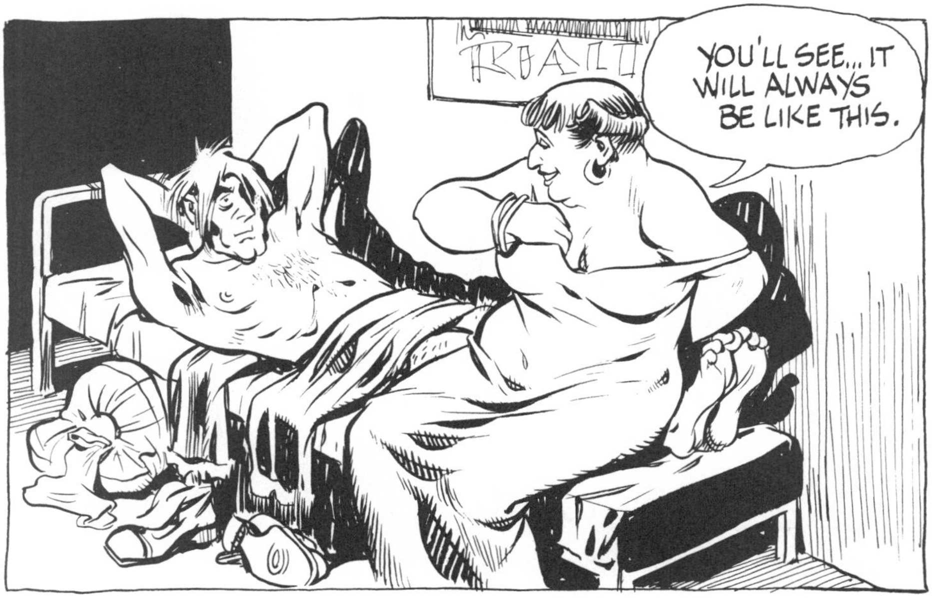
YOU'LL SEE... IT WILL ALWAYS BE LIKE THIS.

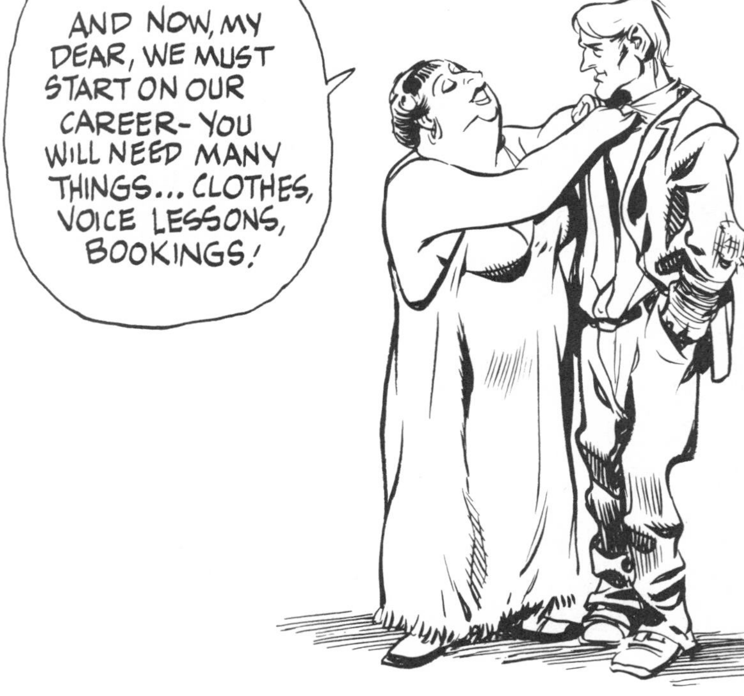
AND NOW, MY DEAR, WE MUST START ON OUR CAREER- YOU WILL NEED MANY THINGS... CLOTHES, VOICE LESSONS, BOOKINGS!

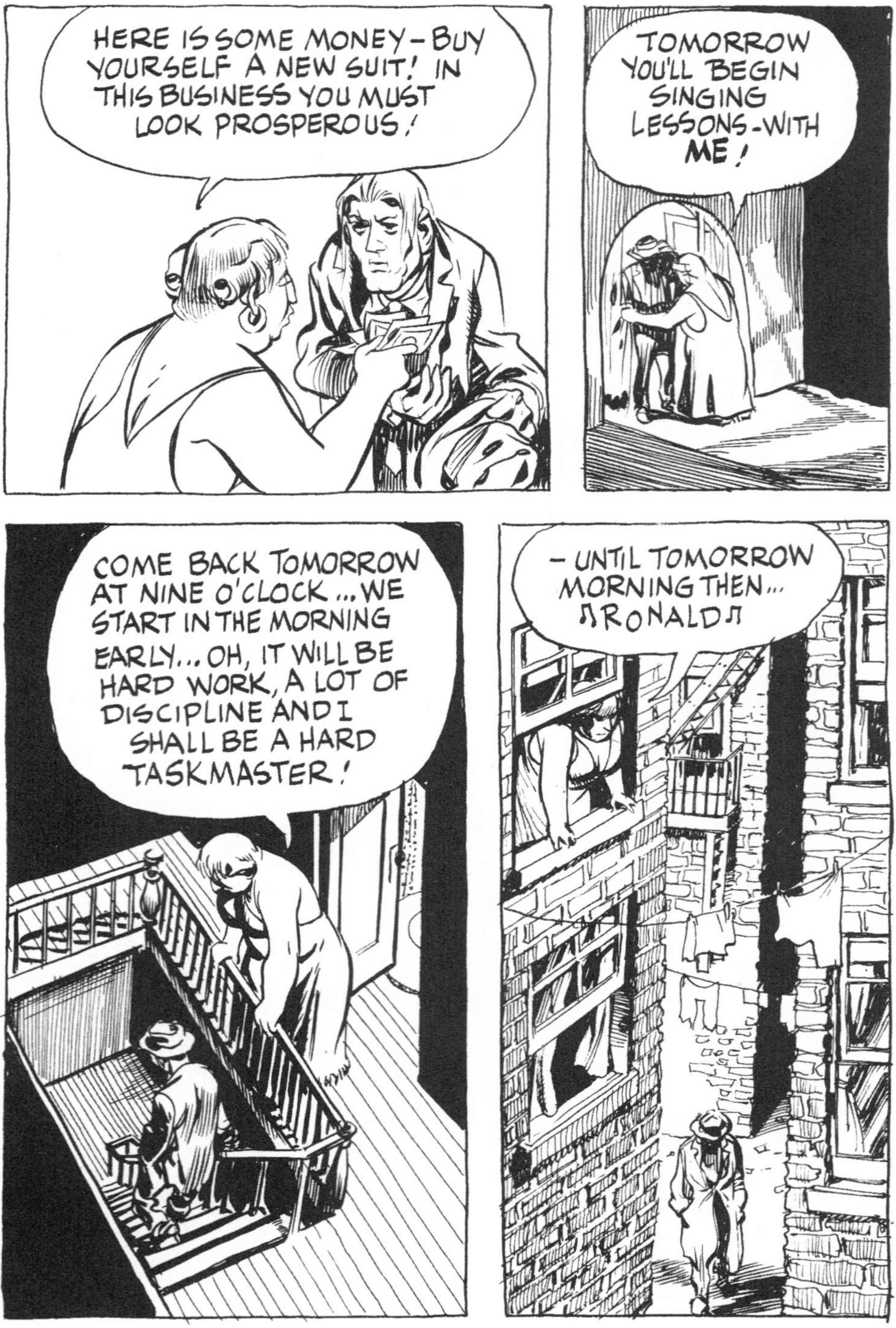
HERE IS SOME MONEY – BUY YOURSELF A NEW SUIT! IN THIS BUSINESS YOU MUST LOOK PROSPEROUS!
TOMORROW YOU'LL BEGIN SINGING LESSONS – WITH ME!
COME BACK TOMORROW AT NINE O'CLOCK ... WE START IN THE MORNING EARLY... OH, IT WILL BE HARD WORK, A LOT OF DISCIPLINE AND I SHALL BE A HARD TASKMASTER!
– UNTIL TOMORROW MORNING THEN... ♫RONALD♫

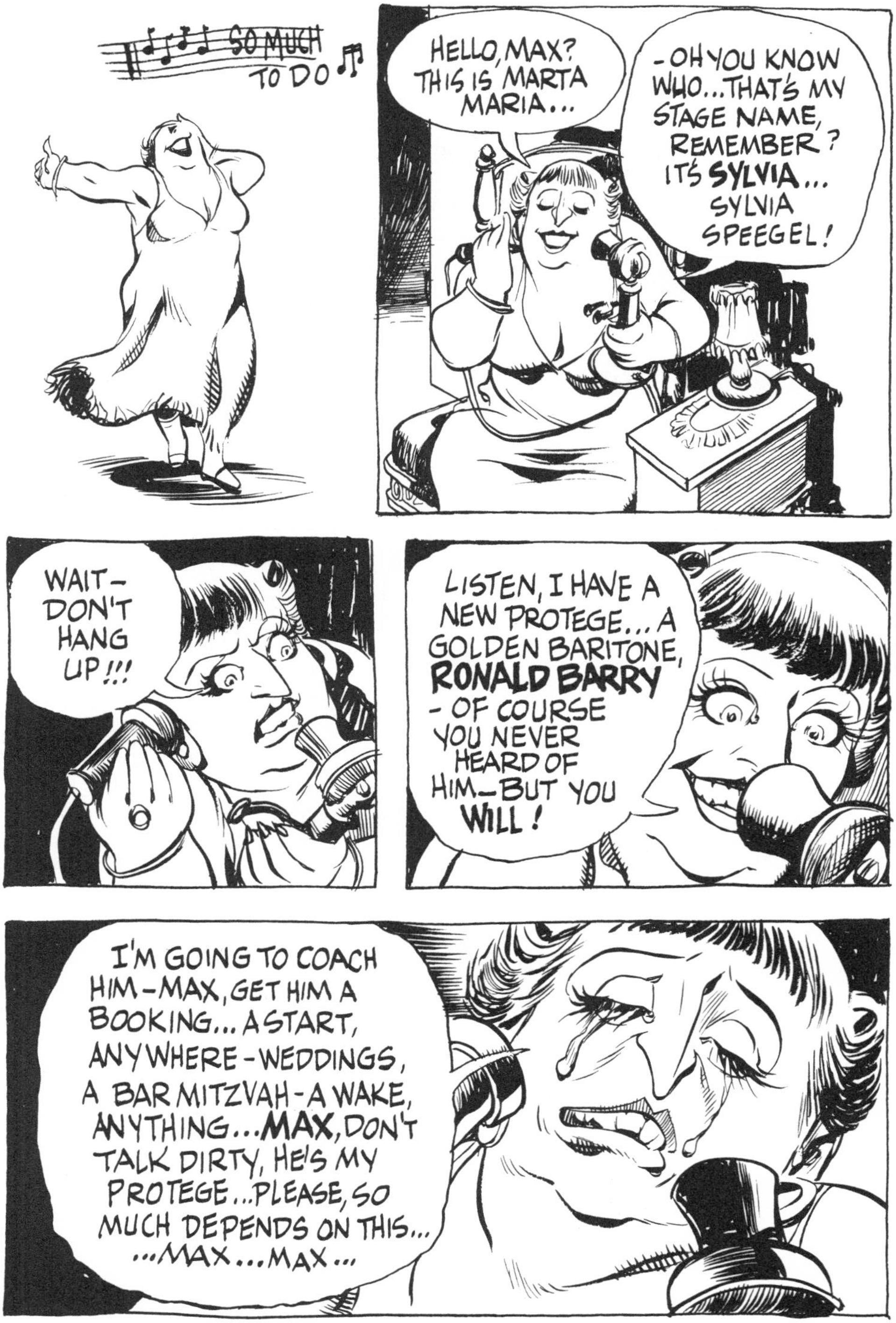
SO MUCH TO DO
HELLO, MAX? THIS IS MARTA MARIA...
-OH YOU KNOW WHO...THAT'S MY STAGE NAME, REMEMBER? IT'S SYLVIA... SYLVIA SPEEGEL!
WAIT- DON'T HANG UP!!!
LISTEN, I HAVE A NEW PROTEGE... A GOLDEN BARITONE, RONALD BARRY - OF COURSE YOU NEVER HEARD OF HIM- BUT YOU WILL!
I'M GOING TO COACH HIM-MAX, GET HIM A BOOKING... A START, ANYWHERE-WEDDINGS, A BAR MITZVAH-A WAKE, ANYTHING...MAX, DON'T TALK DIRTY, HE'S MY PROTEGE...PLEASE, SO MUCH DEPENDS ON THIS... ...MAX...MAX...

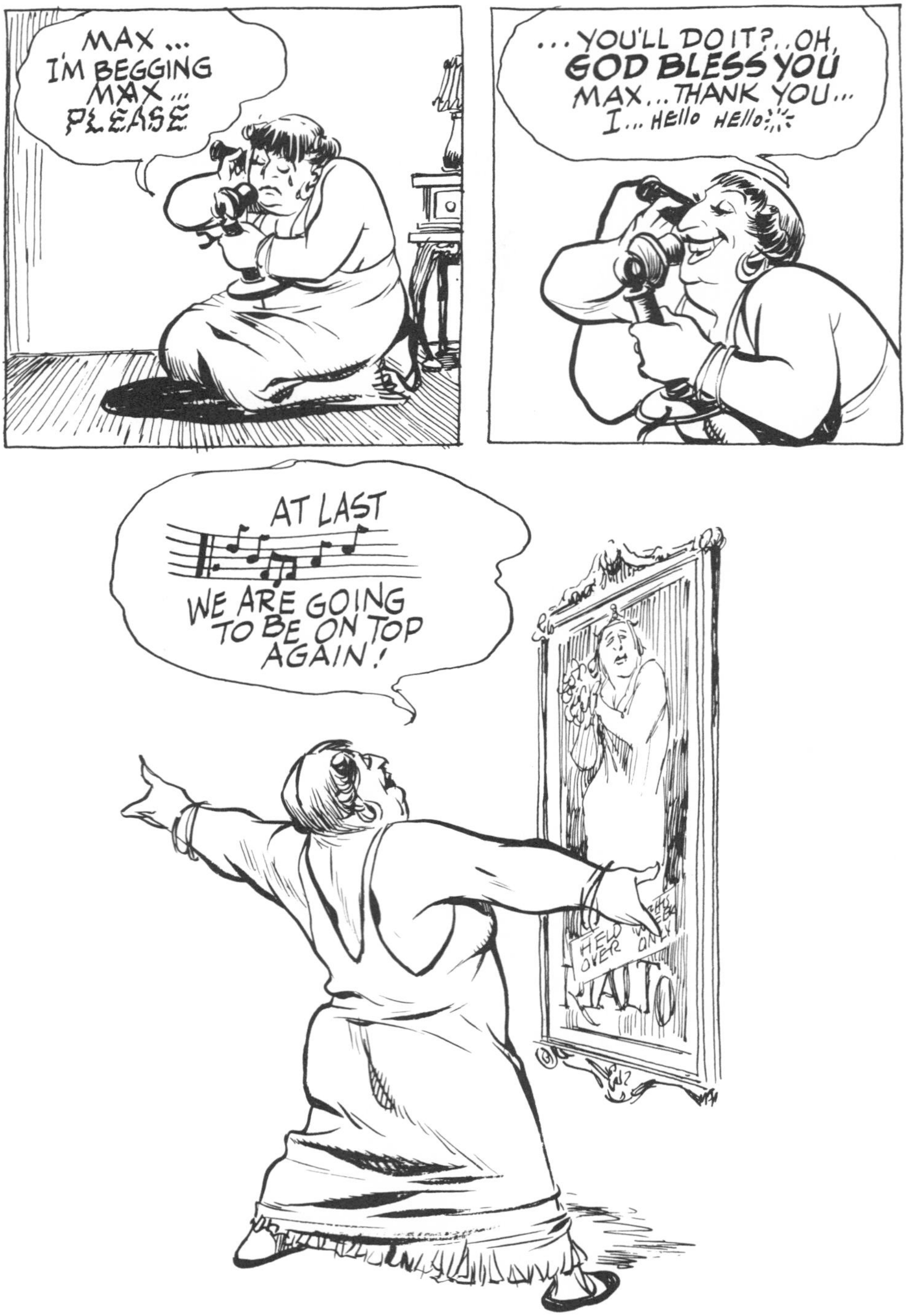
MAX ... I'M BEGGING MAX ... PLEASE
... YOU'LL DO IT? .. OH, GOD BLESS YOU MAX ... THANK YOU ... I ... Hello Hello
AT LAST WE ARE GOING TO BE ON TOP AGAIN!
HELD OVER

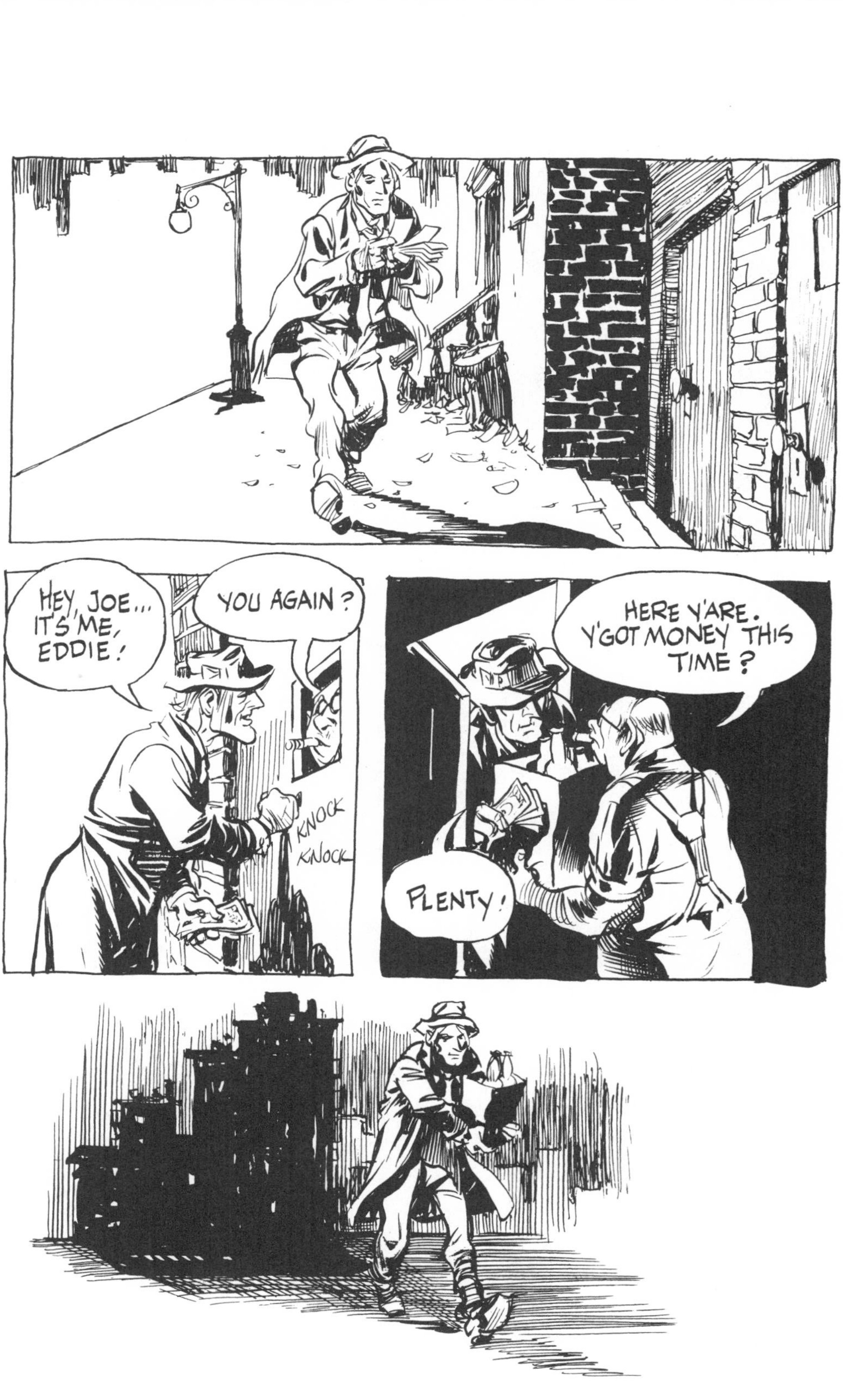
HEY, JOE... IT'S ME, EDDIE!
YOU AGAIN?
KNOCK
KNOCK
HERE Y'ARE. Y'GOT MONEY THIS TIME?
PLENTY!

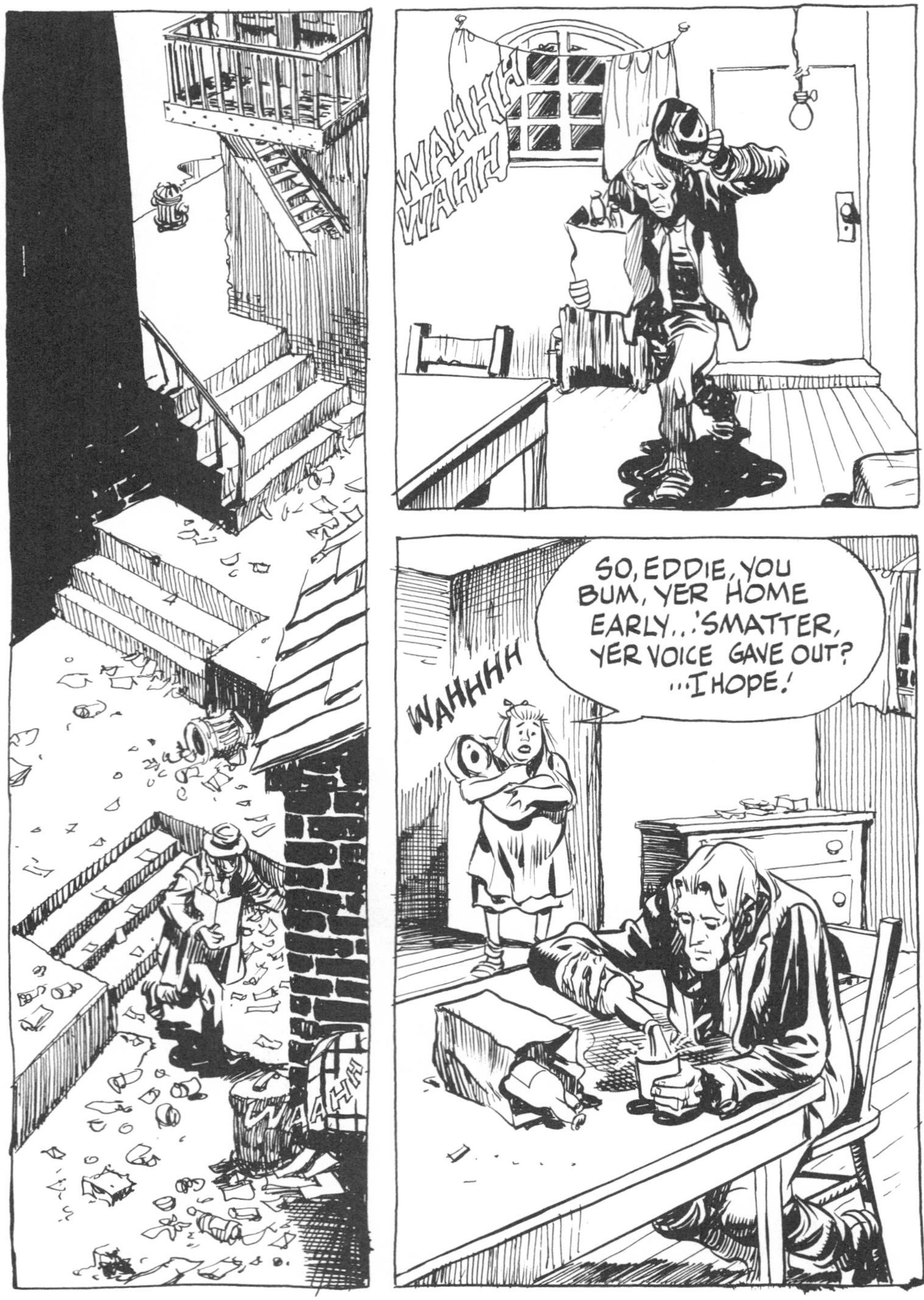
WAAHH
WAHHH
WAHHH
SO, EDDIE, YOU BUM, YER HOME EARLY...'SMATTER, YER VOICE GAVE OUT? ...I HOPE!
WAHHHH

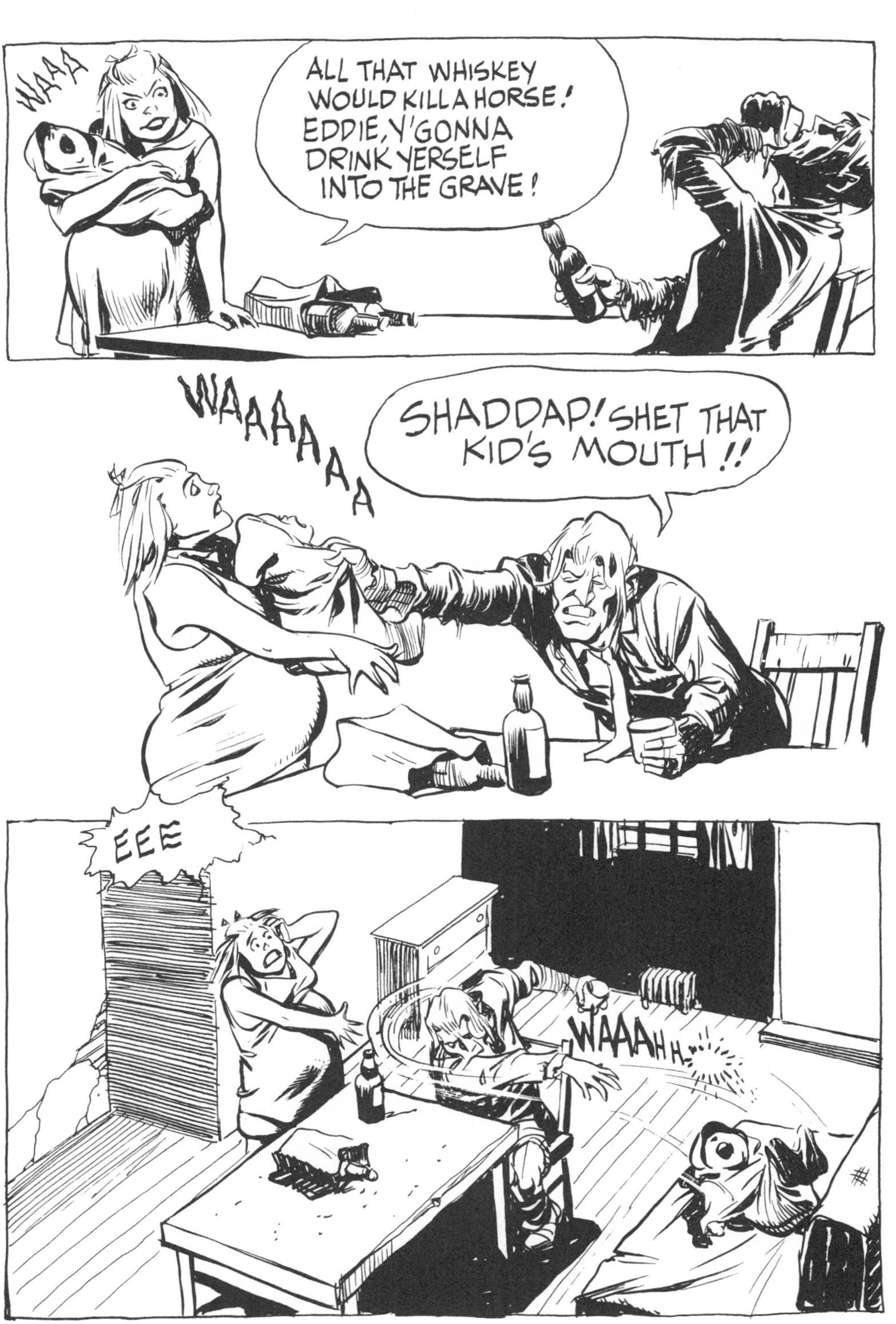
WAAA
ALL THAT WHISKEY WOULD KILL A HORSE! EDDIE, Y'GONNA DRINK YERSELF INTO THE GRAVE!
WAAAAAAA
SHADDAP! SHET THAT KID'S MOUTH !!
EEE
WAAAHH

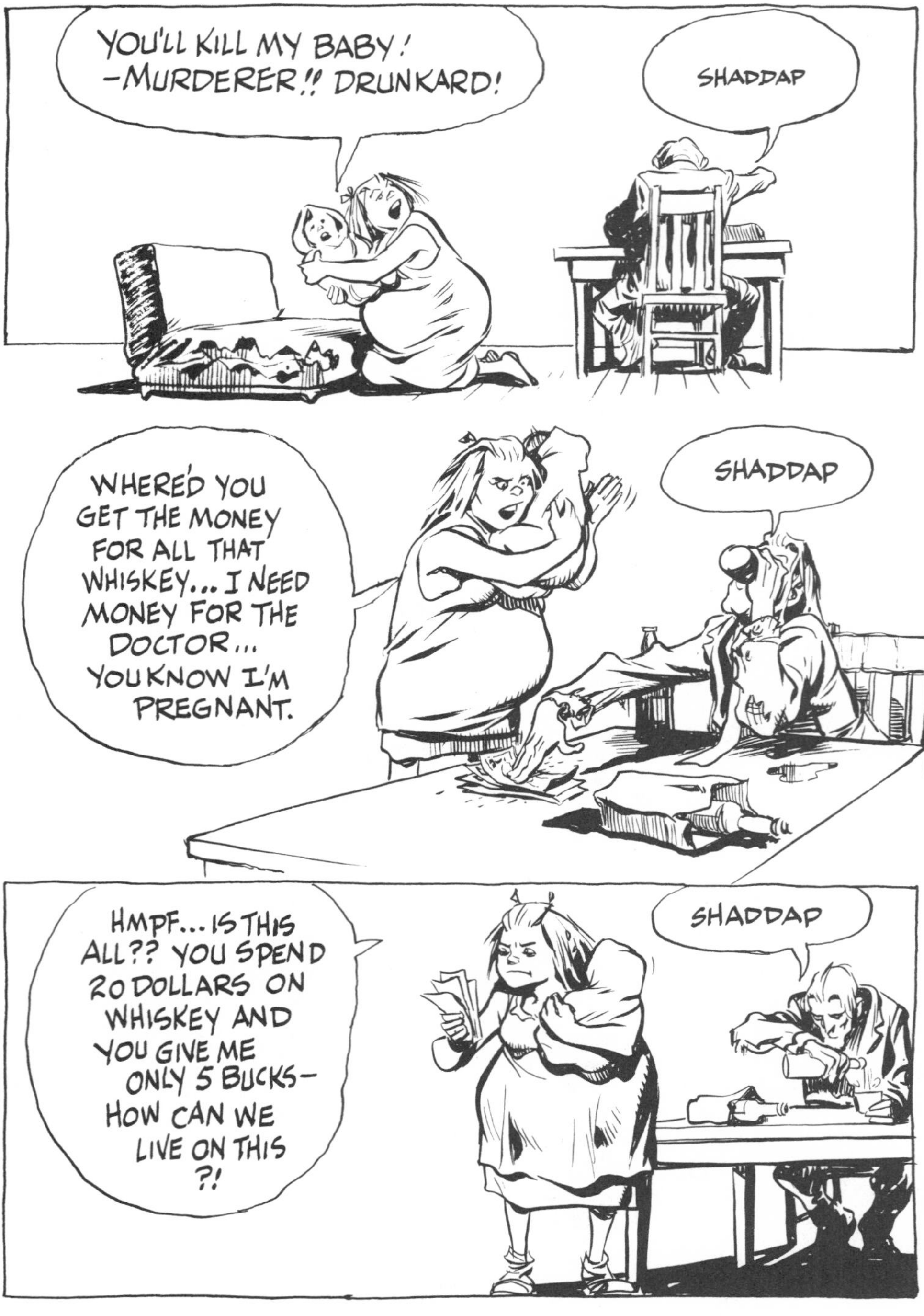
YOU'LL KILL MY BABY! -MURDERER!! DRUNKARD!
SHADDAP
WHERE'D YOU GET THE MONEY FOR ALL THAT WHISKEY... I NEED MONEY FOR THE DOCTOR... YOU KNOW I'M PREGNANT.
SHADDAP
HMPF... IS THIS ALL?? YOU SPEND 20 DOLLARS ON WHISKEY AND YOU GIVE ME ONLY 5 BUCKS- HOW CAN WE LIVE ON THIS ?!
SHADDAP

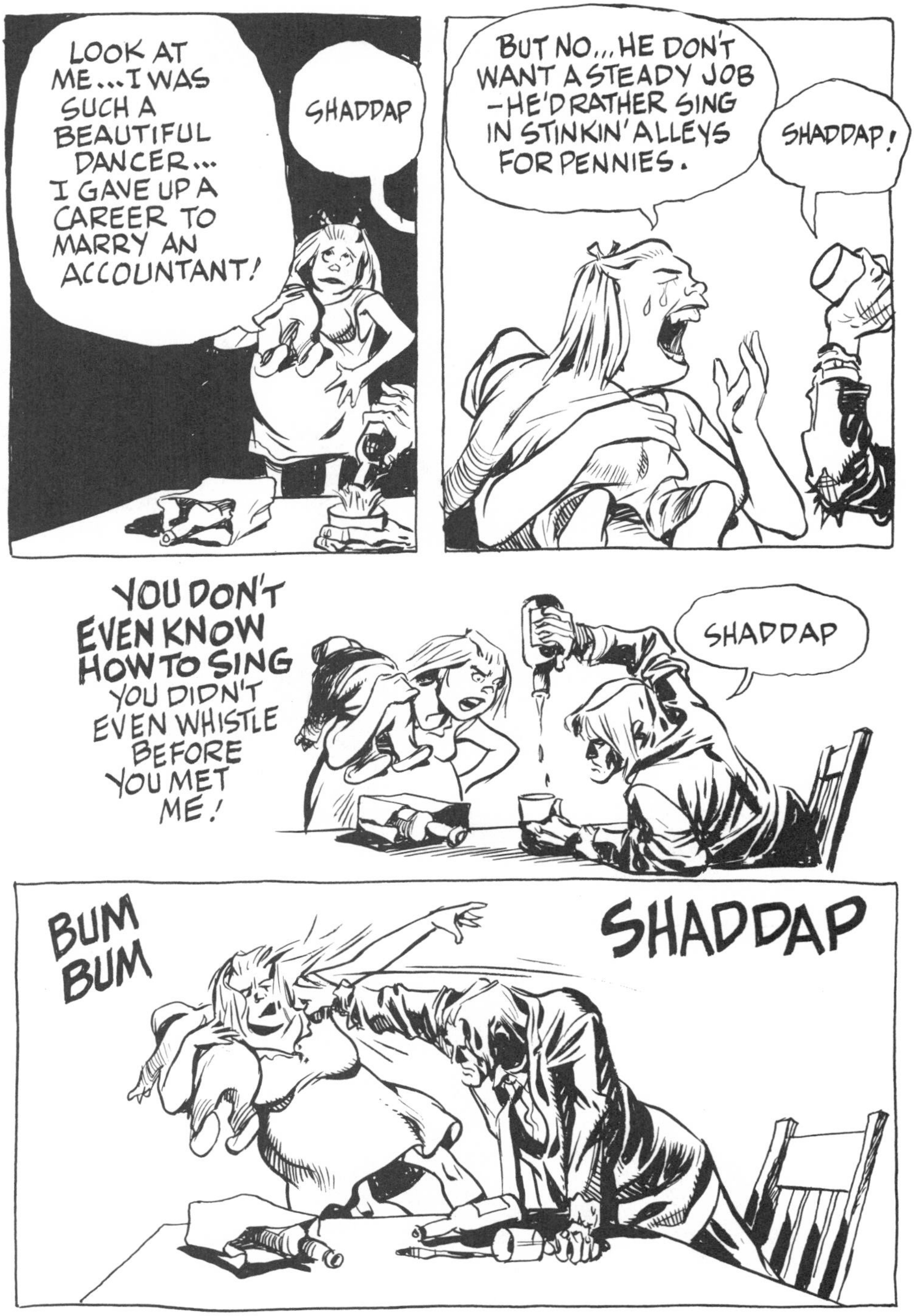
LOOK AT ME...I WAS SUCH A BEAUTIFUL DANCER... I GAVE UP A CAREER TO MARRY AN ACCOUNTANT!
SHADDAP
BUT NO,,, HE DON'T WANT A STEADY JOB -HE'D RATHER SING IN STINKIN' ALLEYS FOR PENNIES.
SHADDAP!
YOU DON'T EVEN KNOW HOW TO SING YOU DIDN'T EVEN WHISTLE BEFORE YOU MET ME!
SHADDAP
BUM BUM
SHADDAP

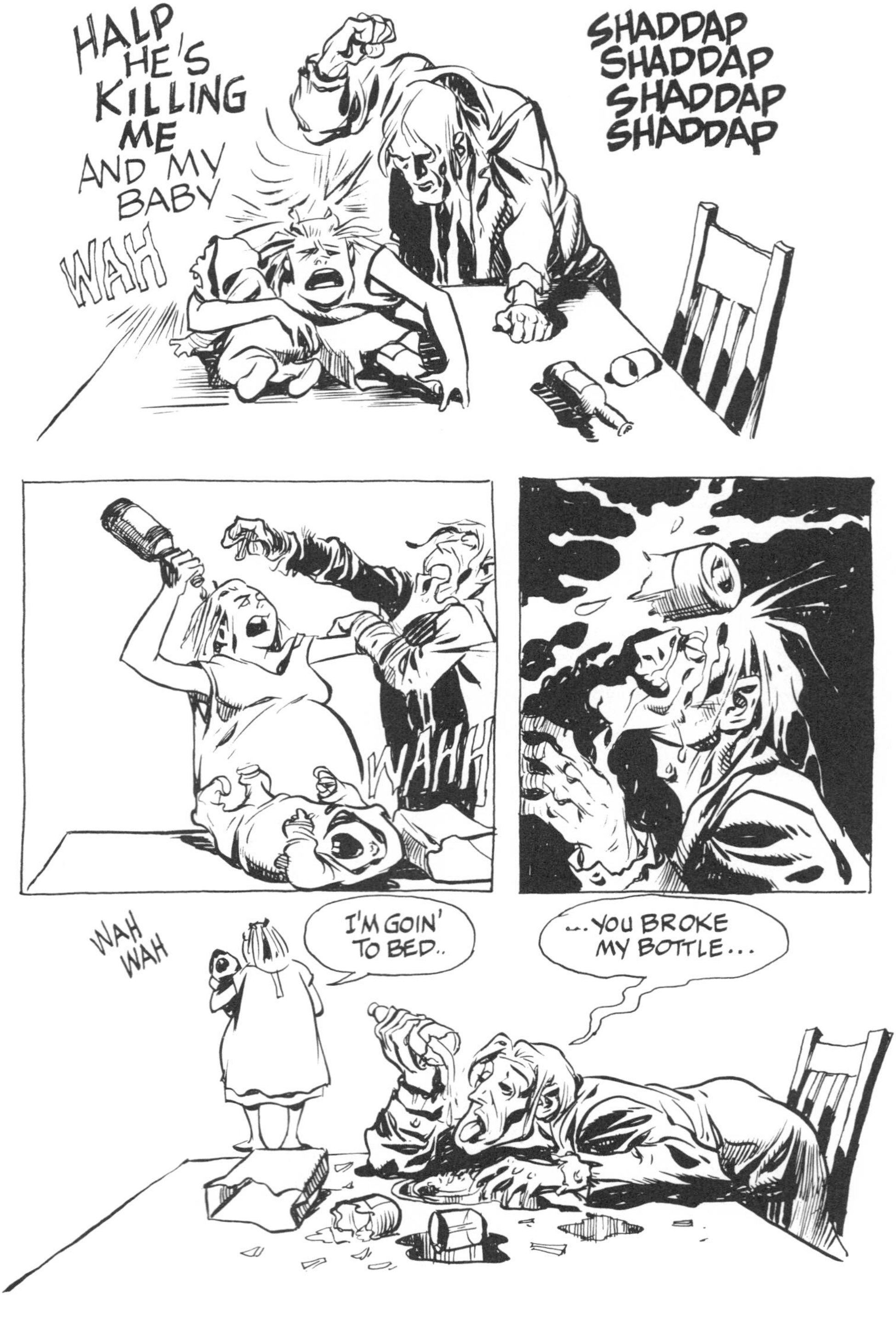
HALP HE'S KILLING ME AND MY BABY
WAH
SHADDAP SHADDAP SHADDAP SHADDAP
WAHH
WAH WAH
I'M GOIN' TO BED..
...YOU BROKE MY BOTTLE...

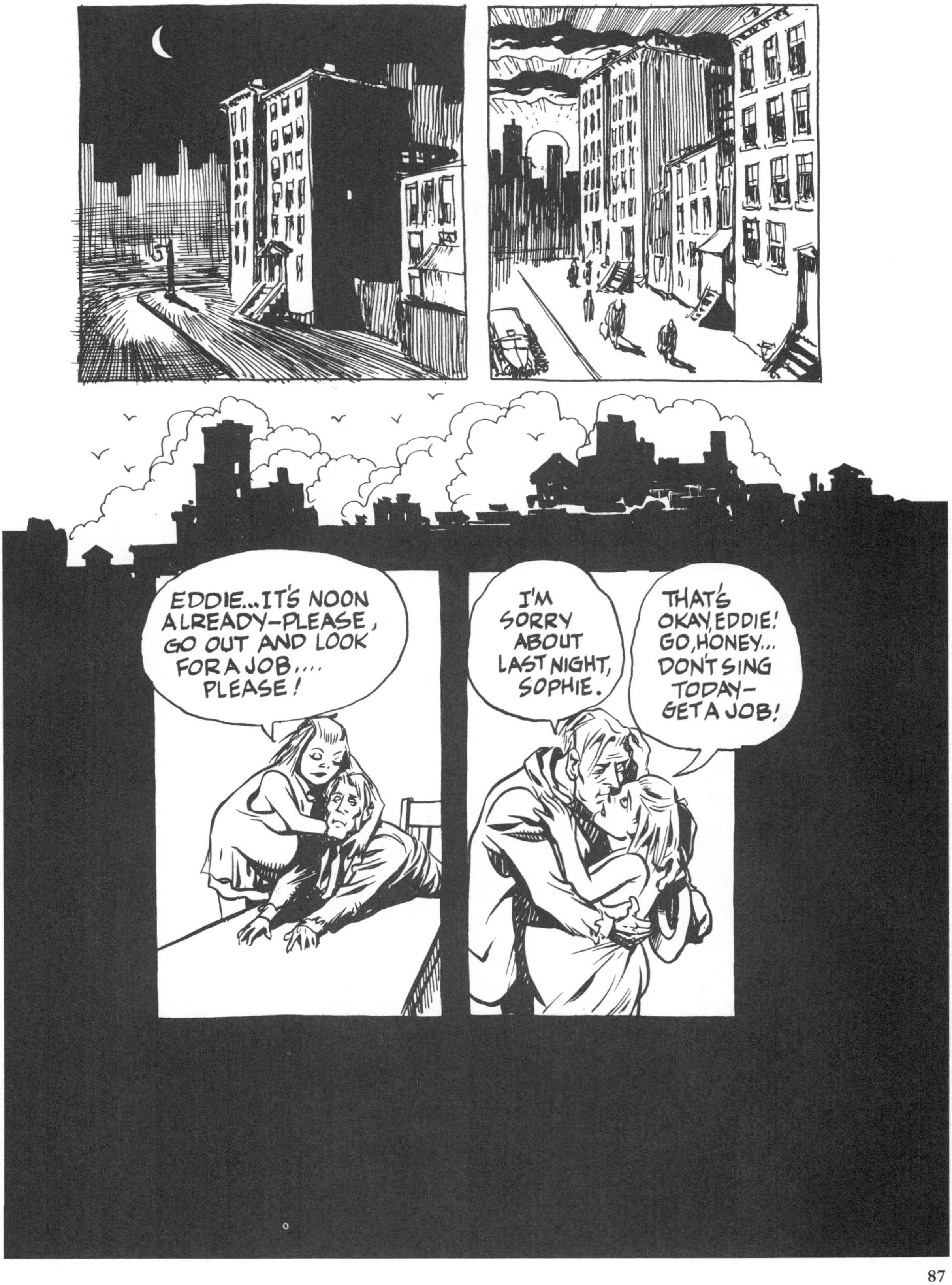
EDDIE...IT'S NOON ALREADY—PLEASE, GO OUT AND LOOK FOR A JOB.... PLEASE!
I'M SORRY ABOUT LAST NIGHT, SOPHIE.
THAT'S OKAY, EDDIE! GO, HONEY... DON'T SING TODAY— GET A JOB!

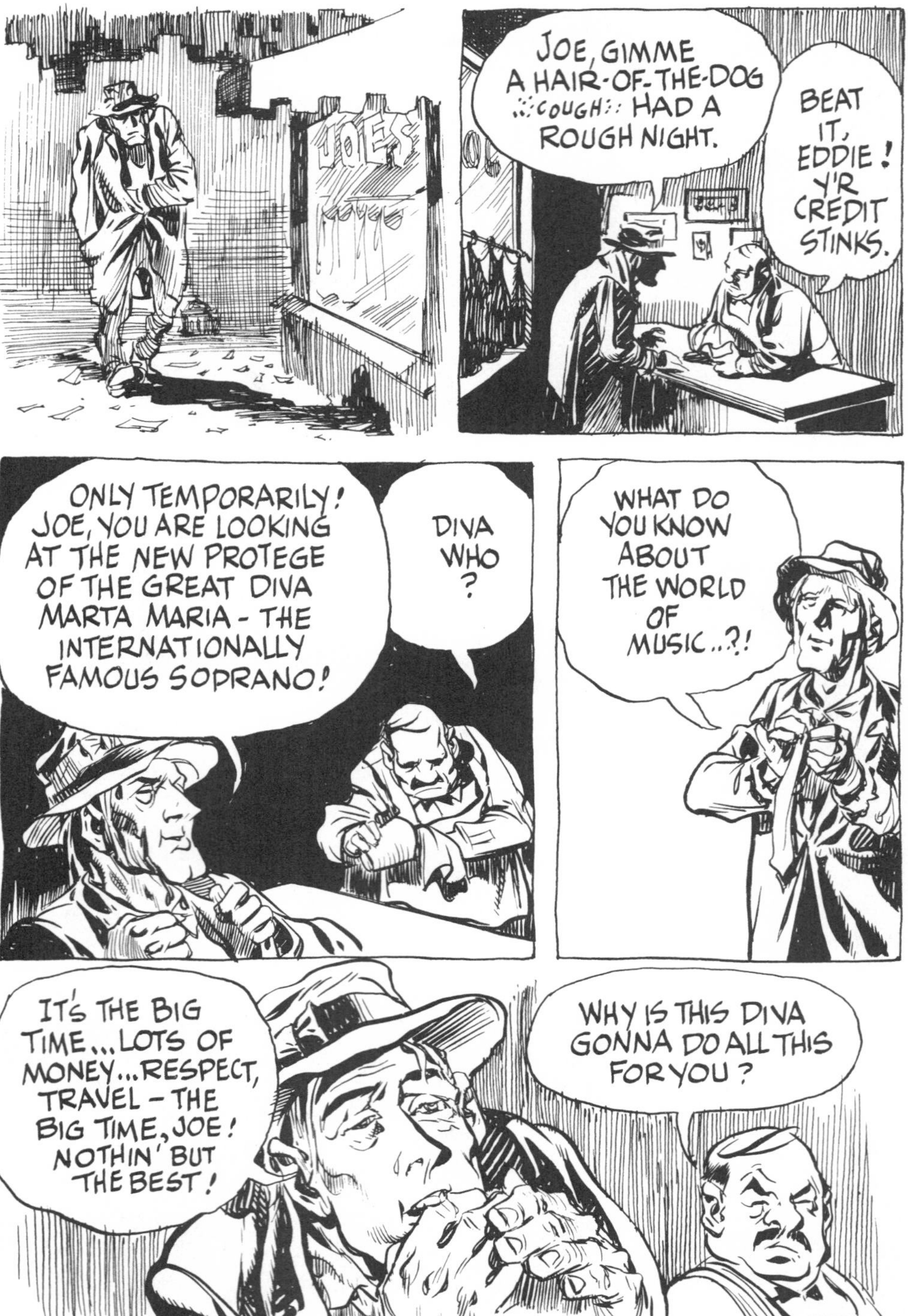
JOES
JOE, GIMME A HAIR-OF-THE-DOG ::COUGH:: HAD A ROUGH NIGHT.
BEAT IT, EDDIE! Y'R CREDIT STINKS.
ONLY TEMPORARILY! JOE, YOU ARE LOOKING AT THE NEW PROTEGE OF THE GREAT DIVA MARTA MARIA - THE INTERNATIONALLY FAMOUS SOPRANO!
DIVA WHO?
WHAT DO YOU KNOW ABOUT THE WORLD OF MUSIC..?!
IT'S THE BIG TIME... LOTS OF MONEY... RESPECT, TRAVEL - THE BIG TIME, JOE! NOTHIN' BUT THE BEST!
WHY IS THIS DIVA GONNA DO ALL THIS FOR YOU?

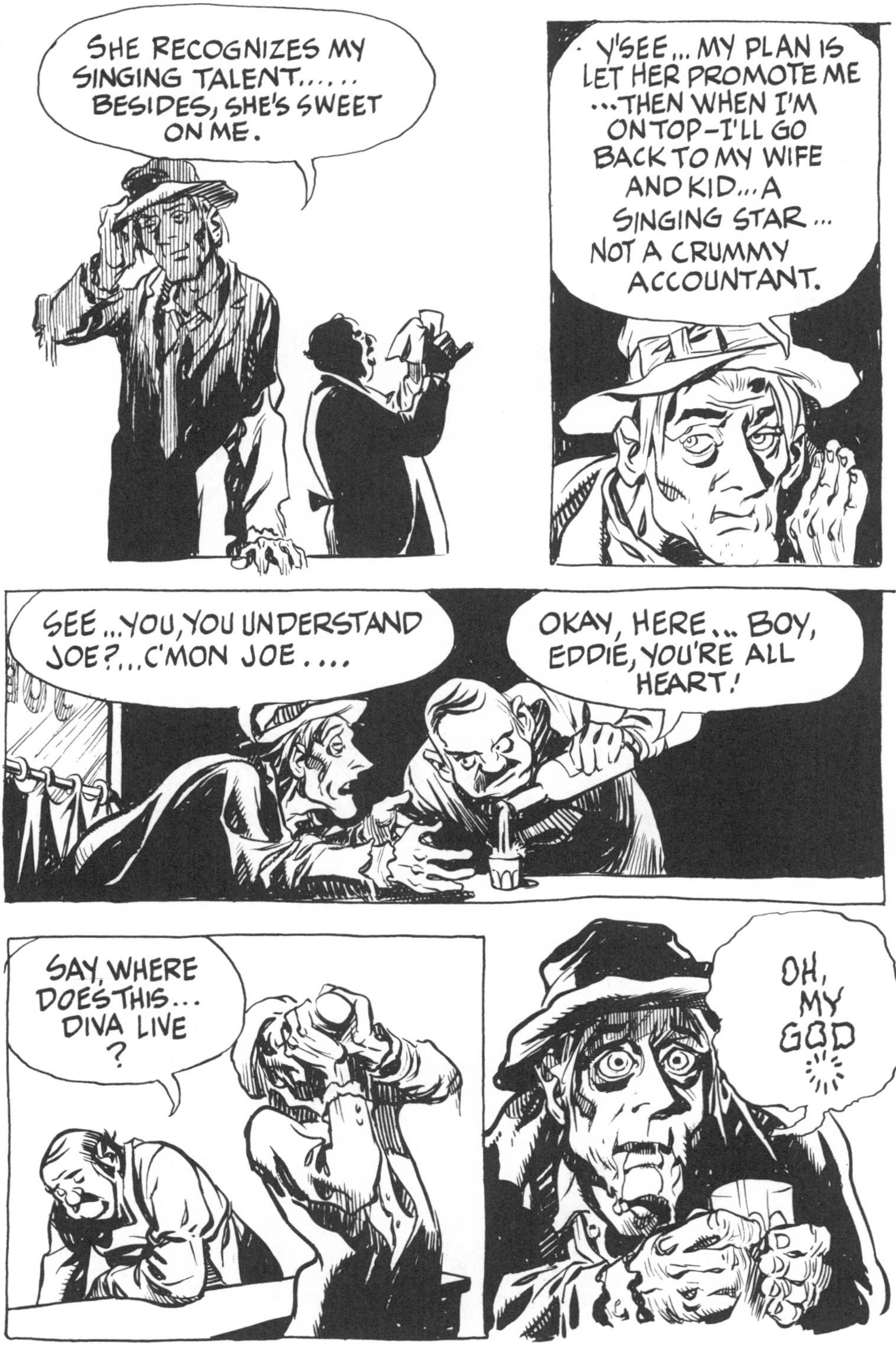
SHE RECOGNIZES MY SINGING TALENT...... BESIDES, SHE'S SWEET ON ME.
Y'SEE... MY PLAN IS LET HER PROMOTE ME ...THEN WHEN I'M ON TOP-I'LL GO BACK TO MY WIFE AND KID... A SINGING STAR... NOT A CRUMMY ACCOUNTANT.
SEE...YOU, YOU UNDERSTAND JOE?...C'MON JOE....
OKAY, HERE... BOY, EDDIE, YOU'RE ALL HEART!
SAY, WHERE DOES THIS... DIVA LIVE ?
OH, MY GOD

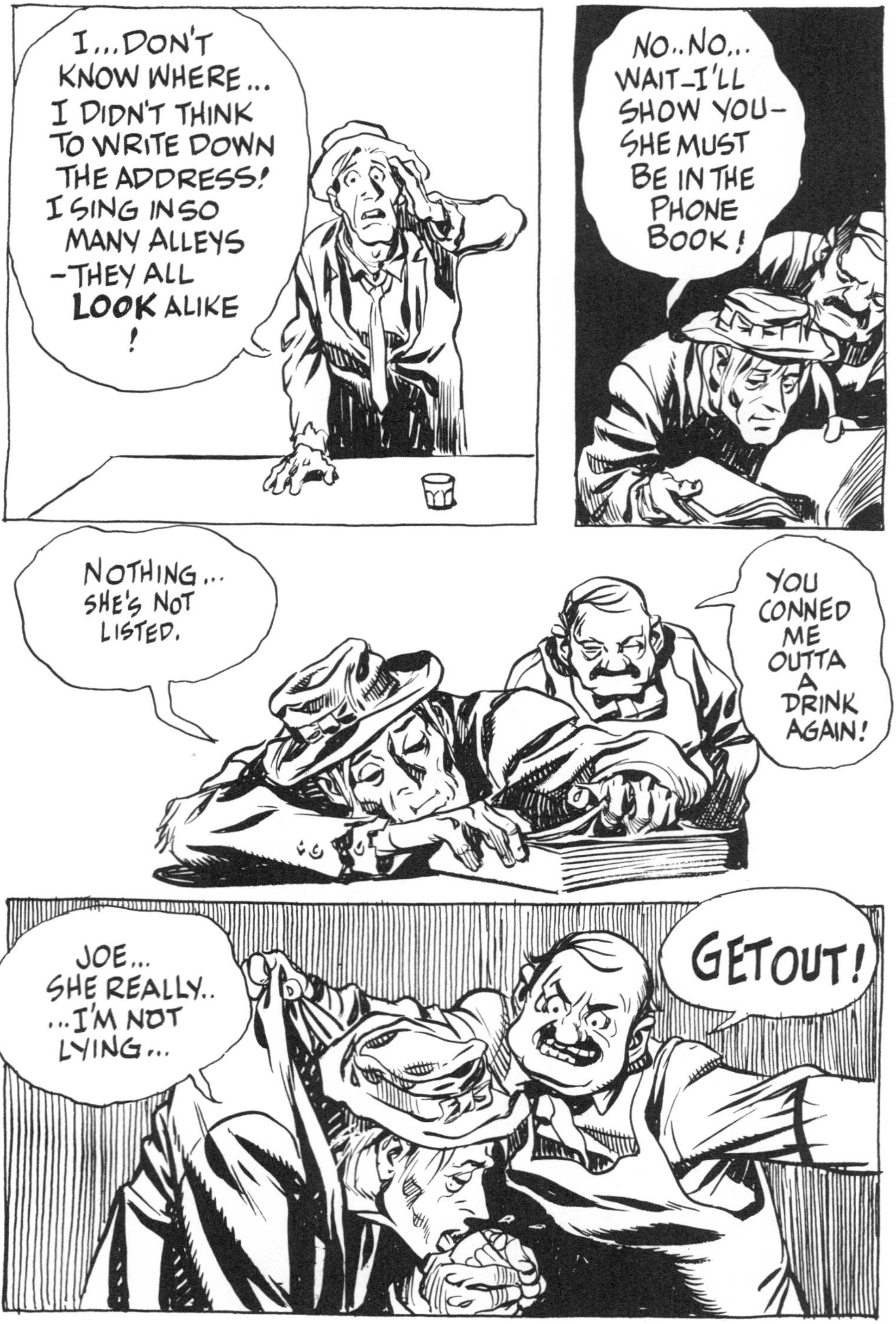
I...DON'T KNOW WHERE... I DIDN'T THINK TO WRITE DOWN THE ADDRESS! I SING IN SO MANY ALLEYS –THEY ALL **LOOK** ALIKE !
NO..NO... WAIT–I'LL SHOW YOU– SHE MUST BE IN THE PHONE BOOK!
NOTHING... SHE'S NOT LISTED.
YOU CONNED ME OUTTA A DRINK AGAIN!
JOE... SHE REALLY.. ...I'M NOT LYING...
GETOUT!

OUT!
JOE'S

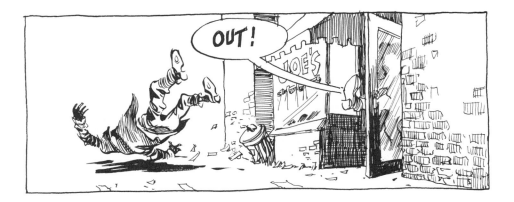

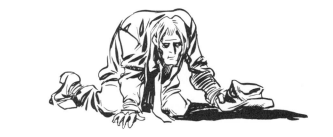

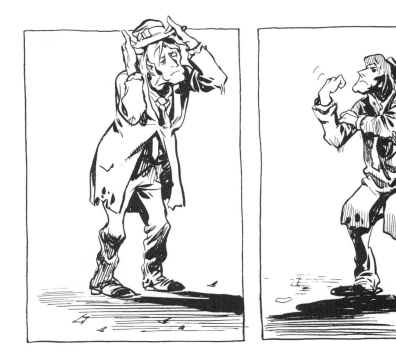

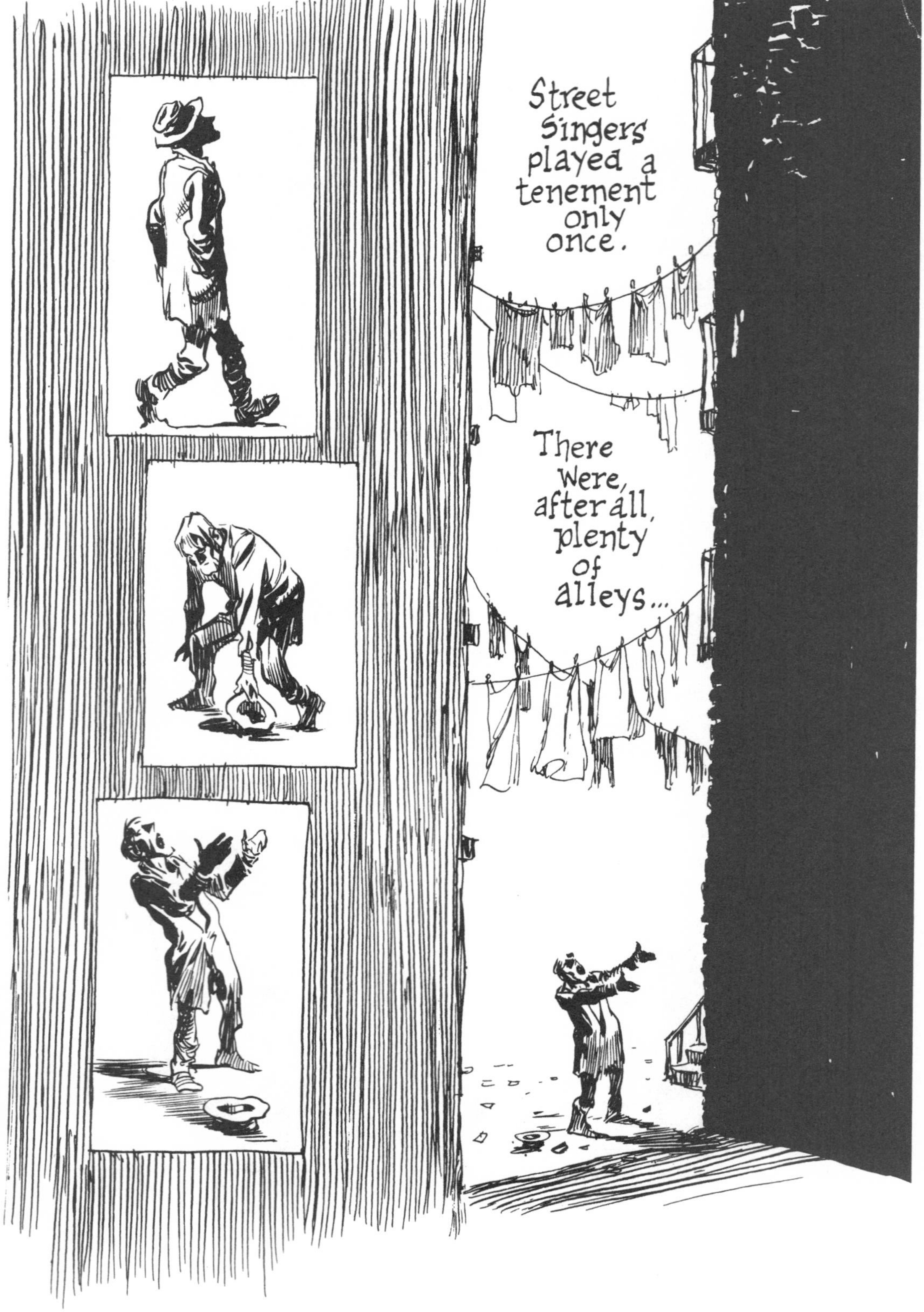
Street Singers played a tenement only once.
There were, after all, plenty of alleys...

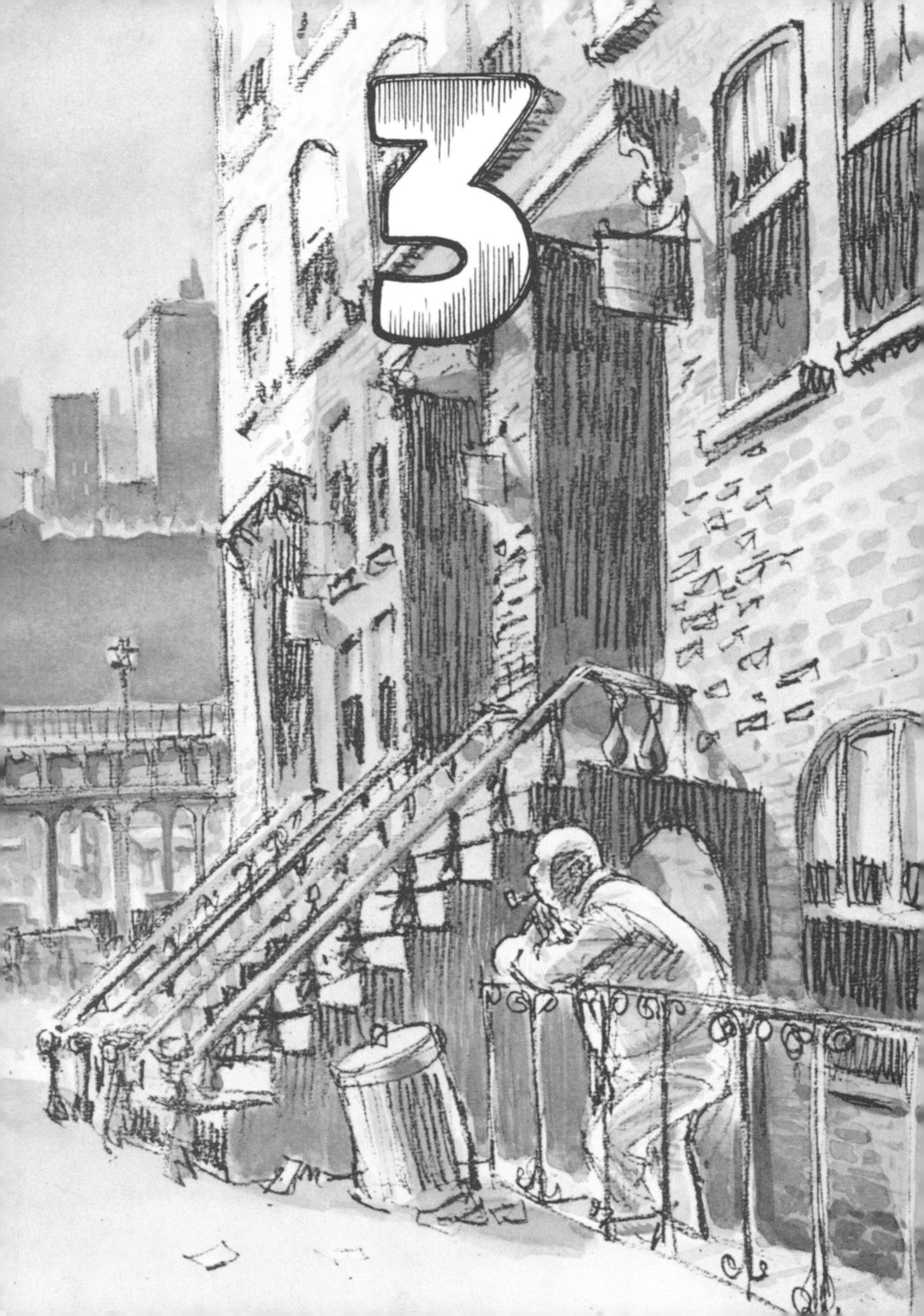
3

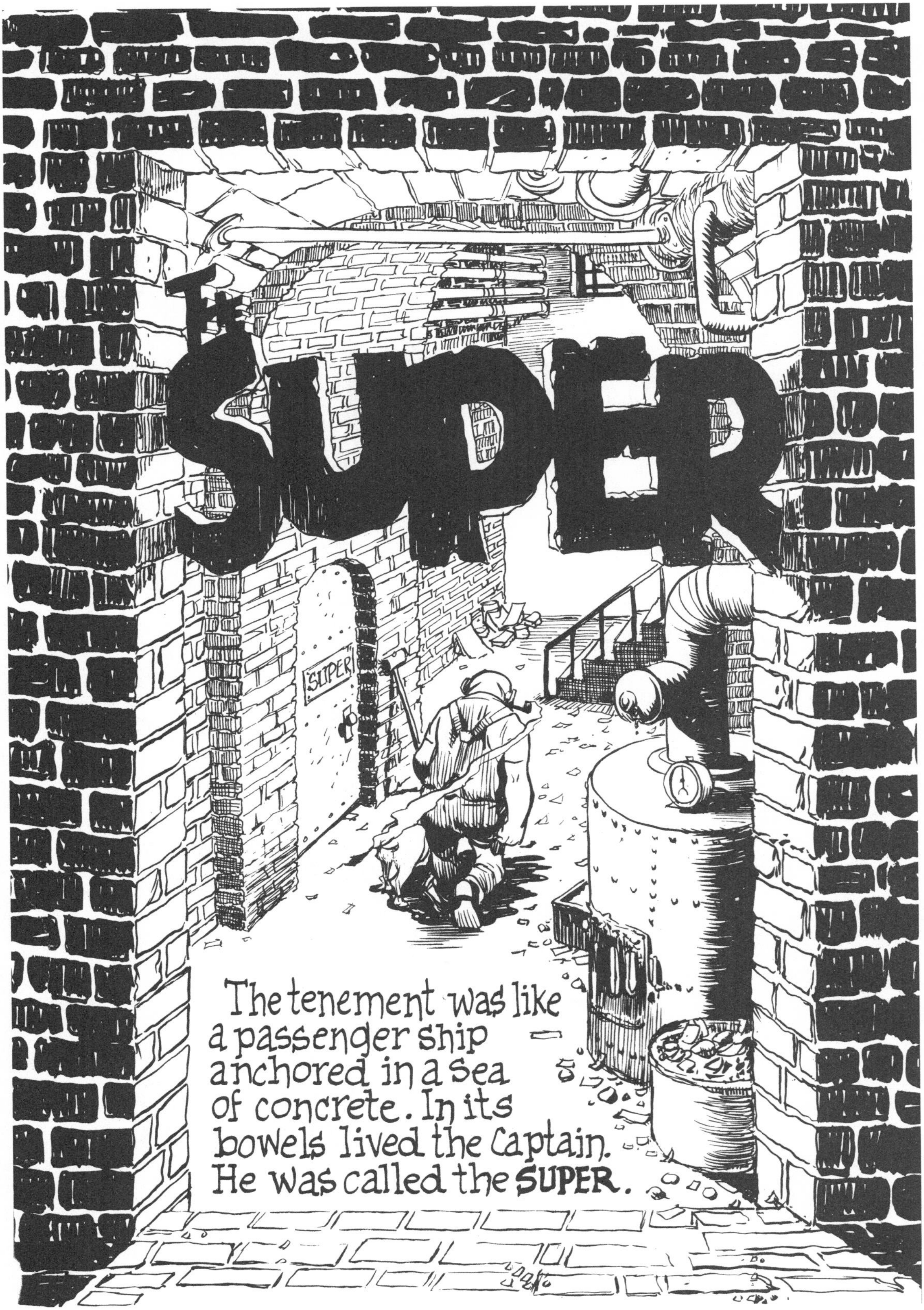
The SUPER
SUPER
The tenement was like a passenger ship anchored in a sea of concrete. In its bowels lived the Captain. He was called the SUPER.

The super at 55 Dropsie was Mr. Scuggs.

MISTER SCUGGS, WHEN YOU GONNA FIX THE HALL STEPS? WHAT KINDA BUILDING YOU RUNNIN' HA??

Nobody really liked Mr. Scuggs.

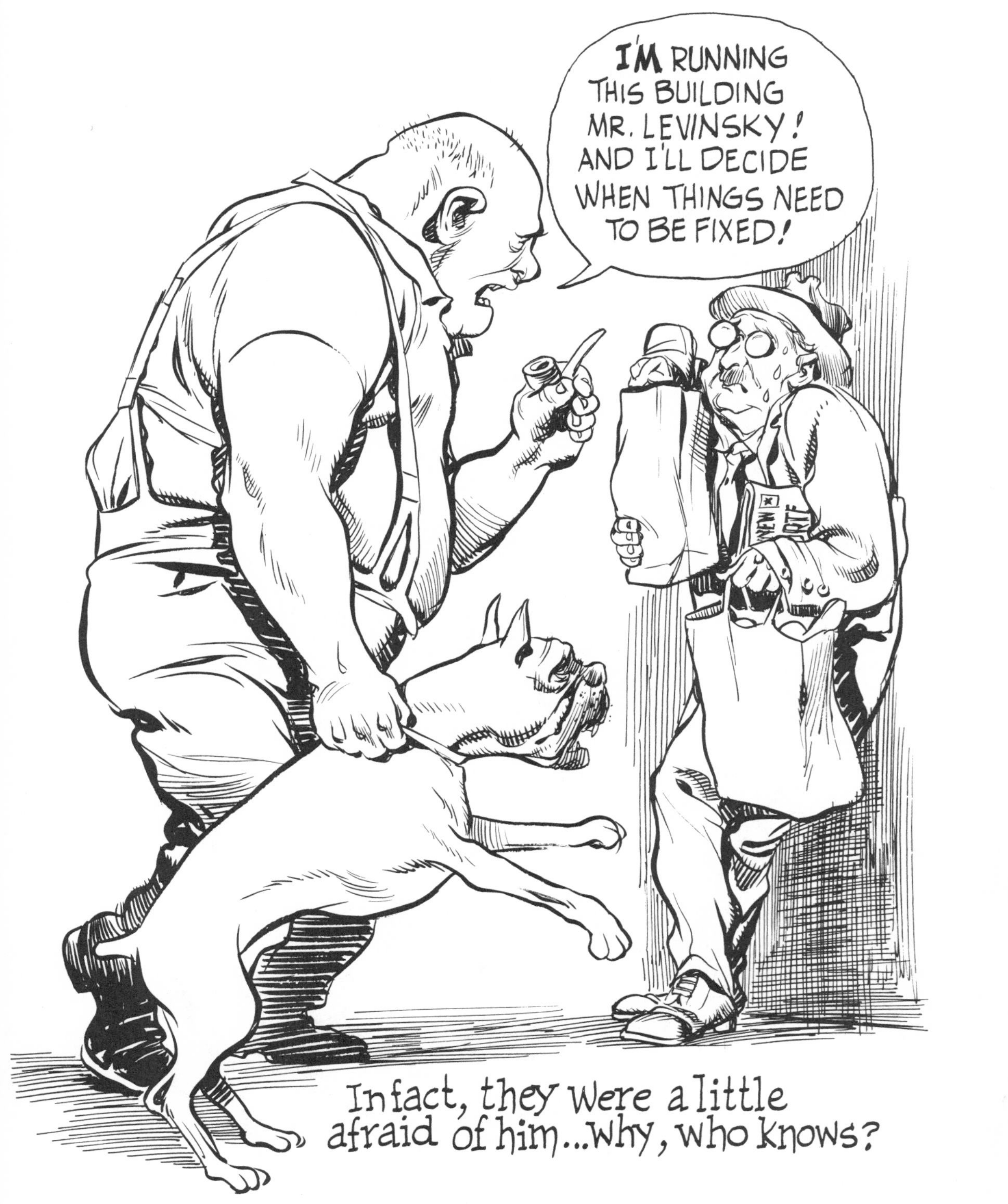
I'M RUNNING THIS BUILDING MR. LEVINSKY! AND I'LL DECIDE WHEN THINGS NEED TO BE FIXED!
In fact, they were a little afraid of him...why, who knows?

Perhaps it was what they **didn't** know that fed the fear.

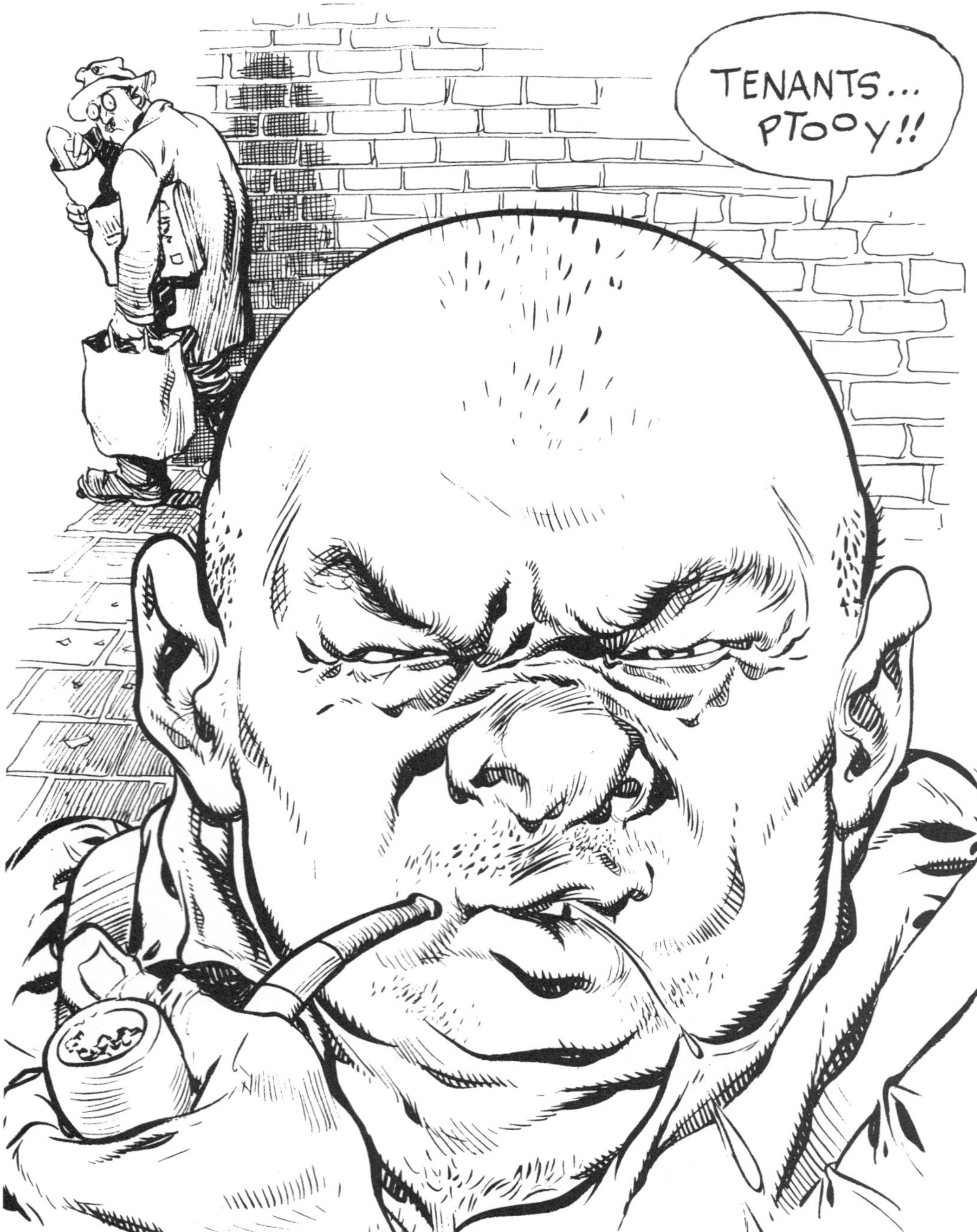
TENANTS... PTOOY!!

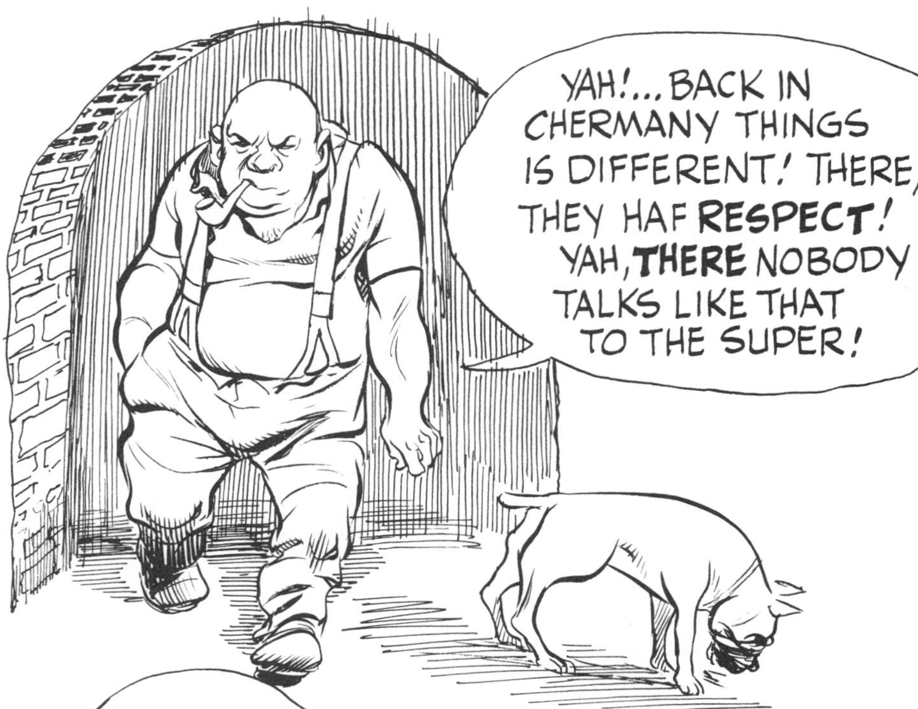
YAH!... BACK IN CHERMANY THINGS IS DIFFERENT! THERE, THEY HAF **RESPECT**! YAH, **THERE** NOBODY TALKS LIKE THAT TO THE SUPER!

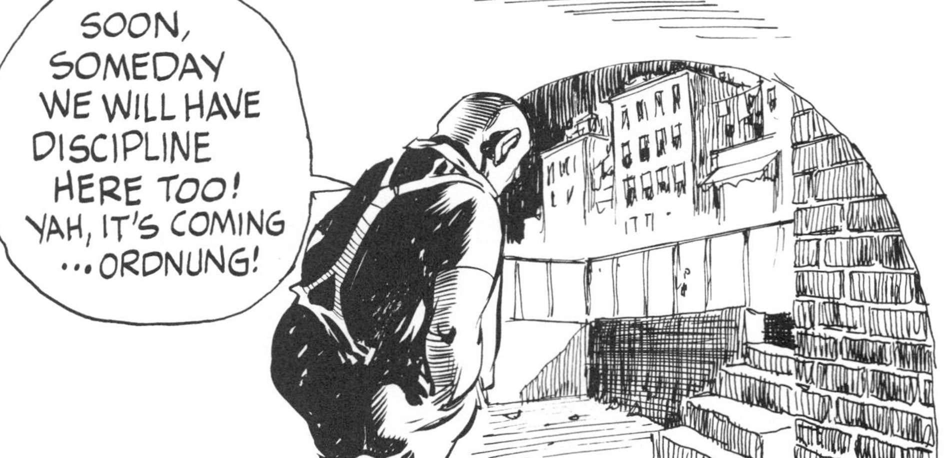
SOON, SOMEDAY WE WILL HAVE DISCIPLINE HERE TOO! YAH, IT'S COMING ...ORDNUNG!

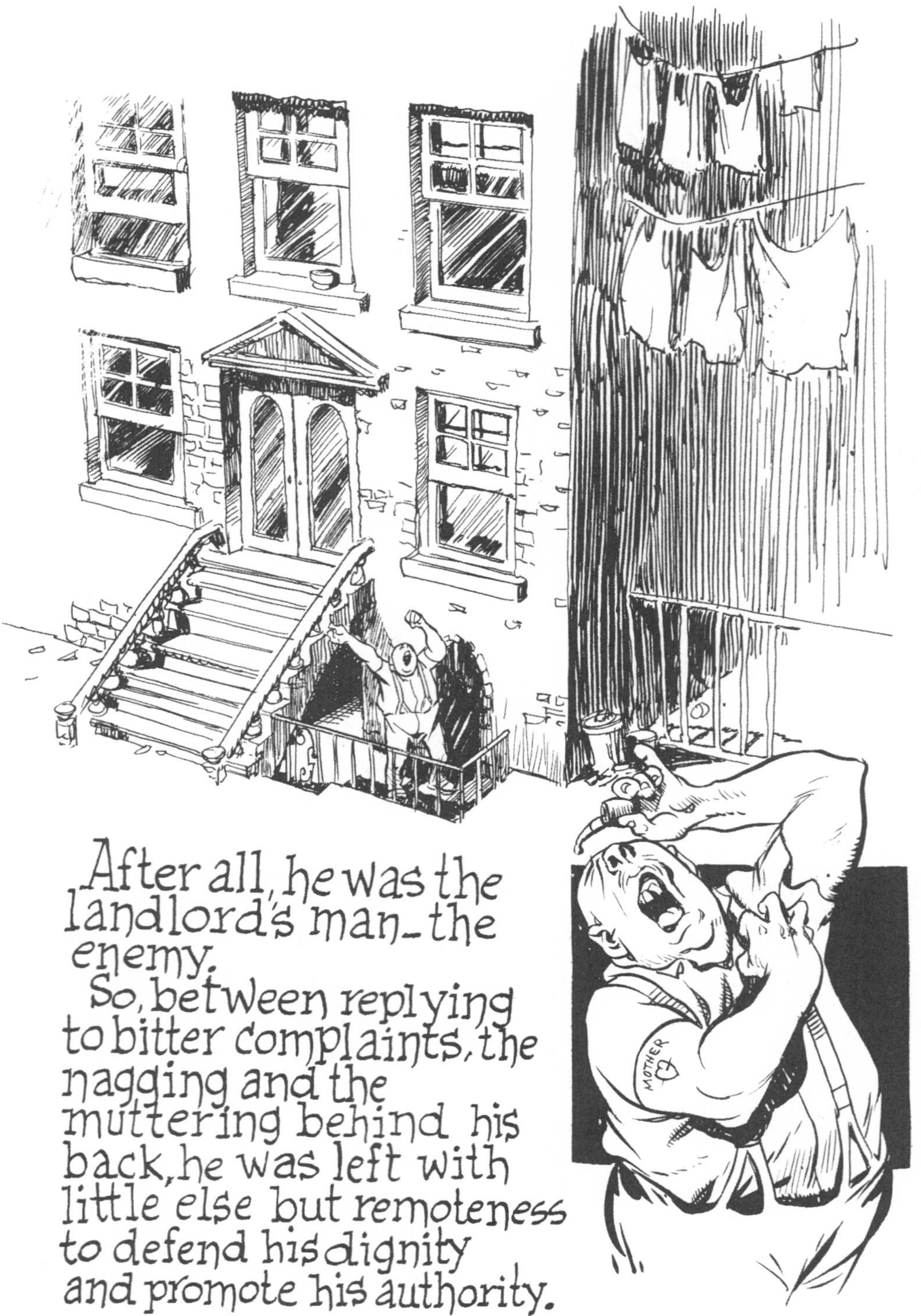
After all, he was the landlord's man–the enemy.
So, between replying to bitter complaints, the nagging and the muttering behind his back, he was left with little else but remoteness to defend his dignity and promote his authority.
MOTHER

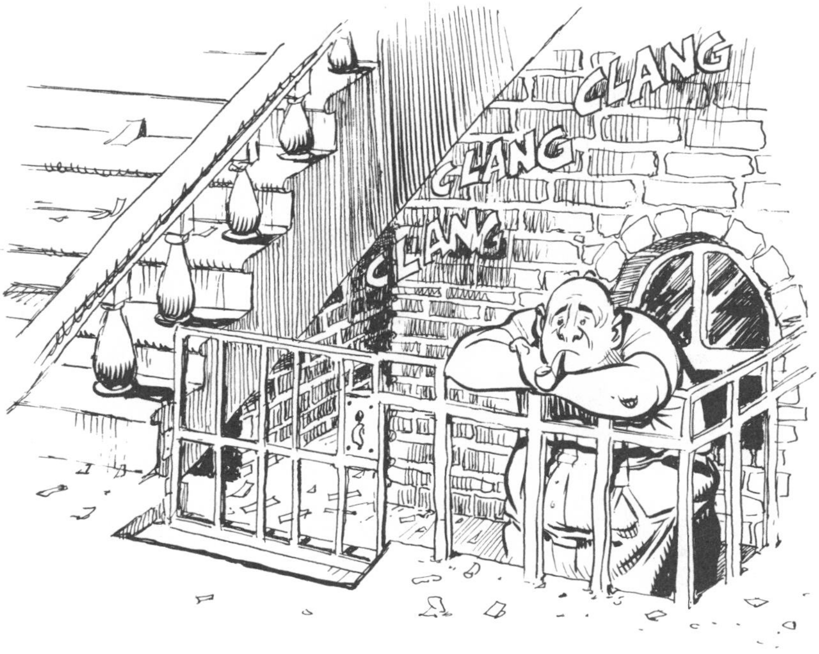
CLANG
CLANG
CLANG

His job was
not an easy one.

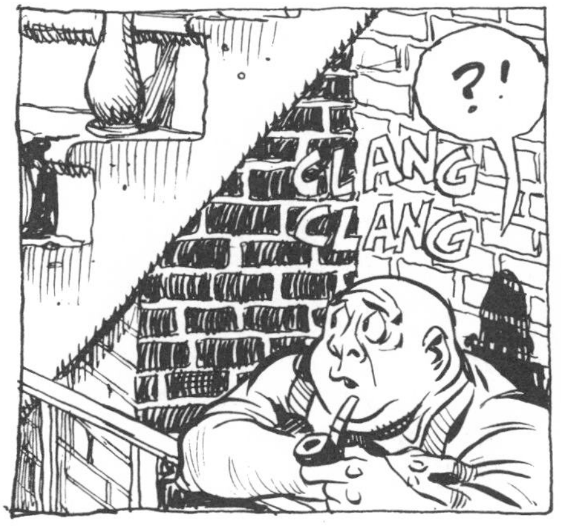
?!
CLANG
CLANG

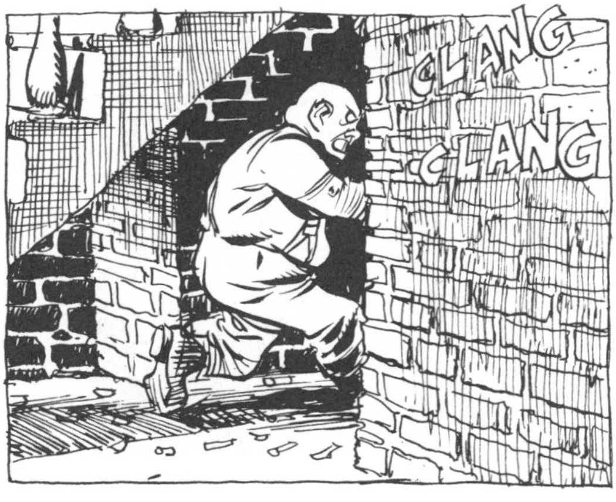
CLANG
CLANG

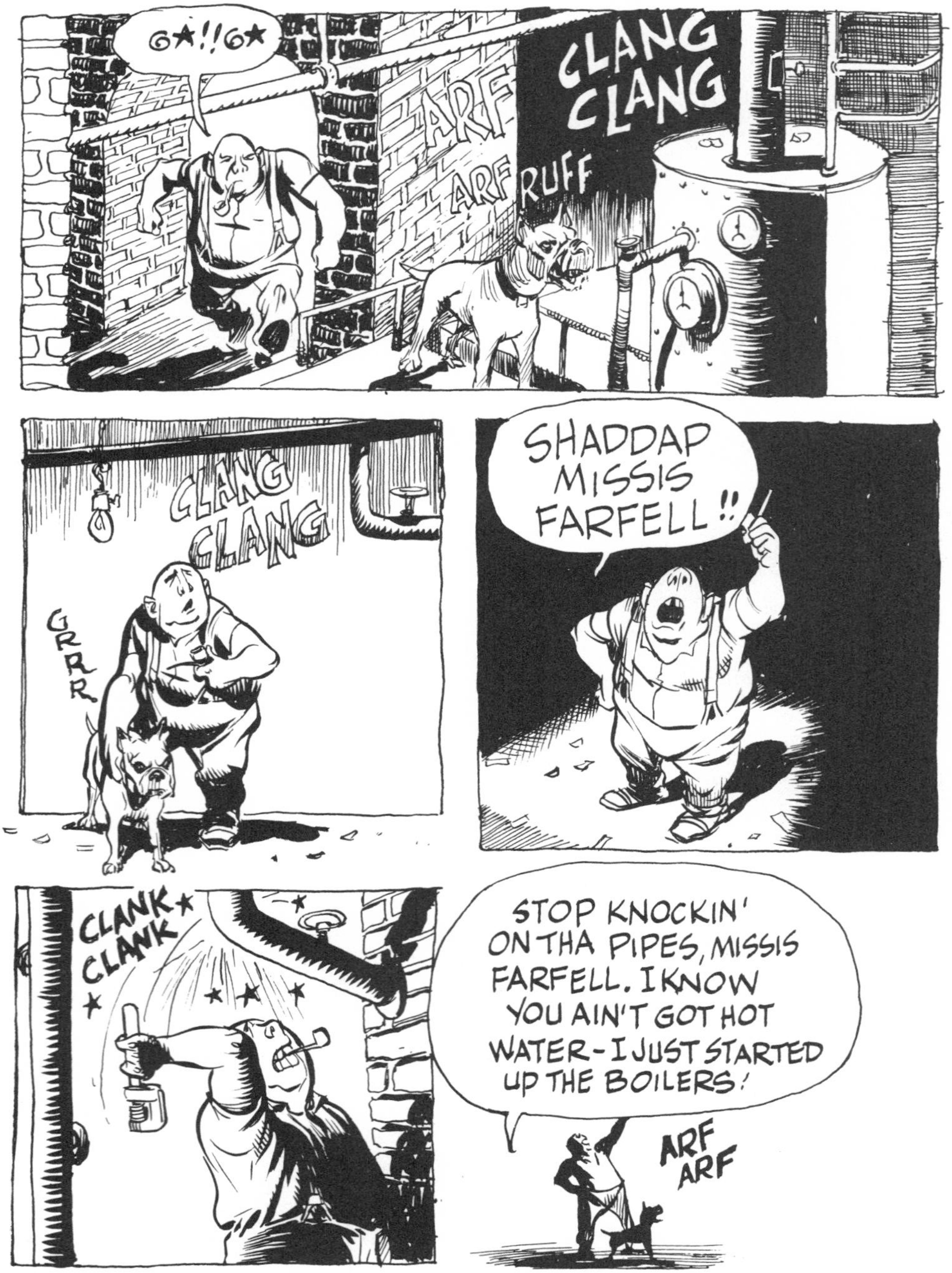
G★!!G★
CLANG
CLANG
ARF
ARF
RUFF
CLANG
CLANG
GRRR
SHADDAP MISSIS FARFELL!!
CLANK★
CLANK
STOP KNOCKIN' ON THA PIPES, MISSIS FARFELL. I KNOW YOU AIN'T GOT HOT WATER - I JUST STARTED UP THE BOILERS!
ARF
ARF

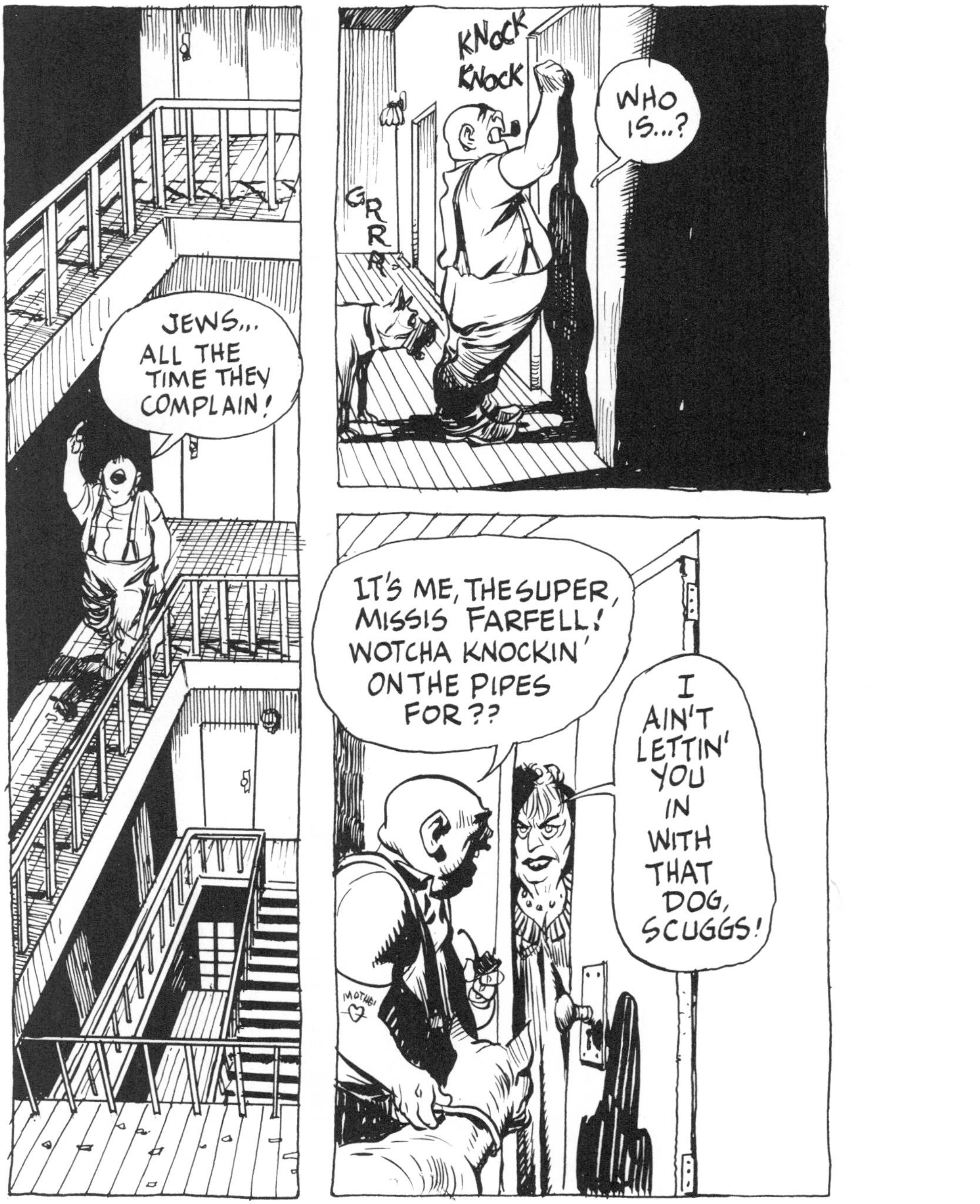
JEWS... ALL THE TIME THEY COMPLAIN!
KNOCK KNOCK
GRRR
WHO IS...?
IT'S ME, THE SUPER, MISSIS FARFELL! WOTCHA KNOCKIN' ON THE PIPES FOR??
I AIN'T LETTIN' YOU IN WITH THAT DOG, SCUGGS!

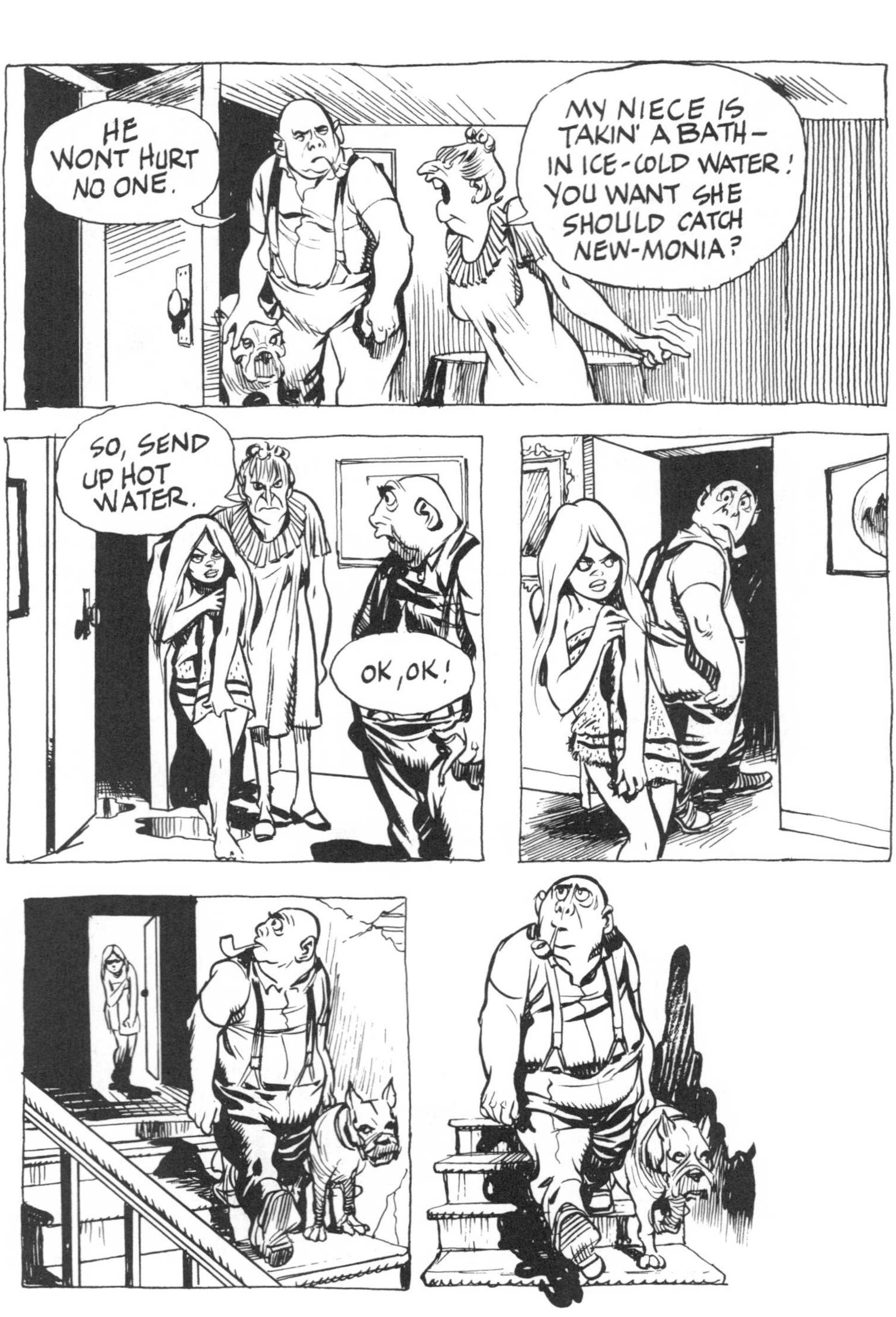
HE WONT HURT NO ONE.
MY NIECE IS TAKIN' A BATH– IN ICE-COLD WATER! YOU WANT SHE SHOULD CATCH NEW-MONIA?
SO, SEND UP HOT WATER.
OK, OK!

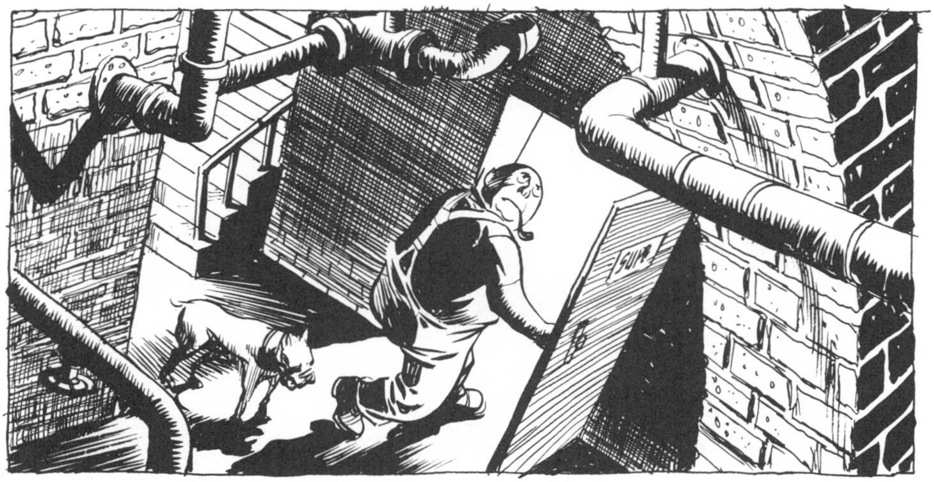
SUPR.

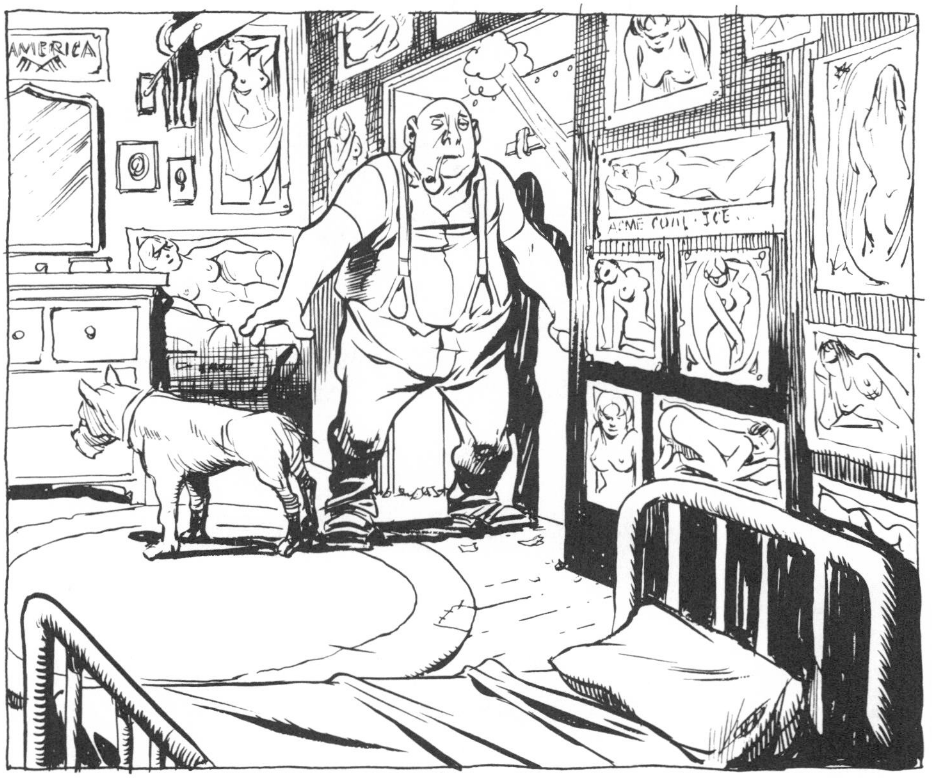
AMERICA
ACME COAL · ICE

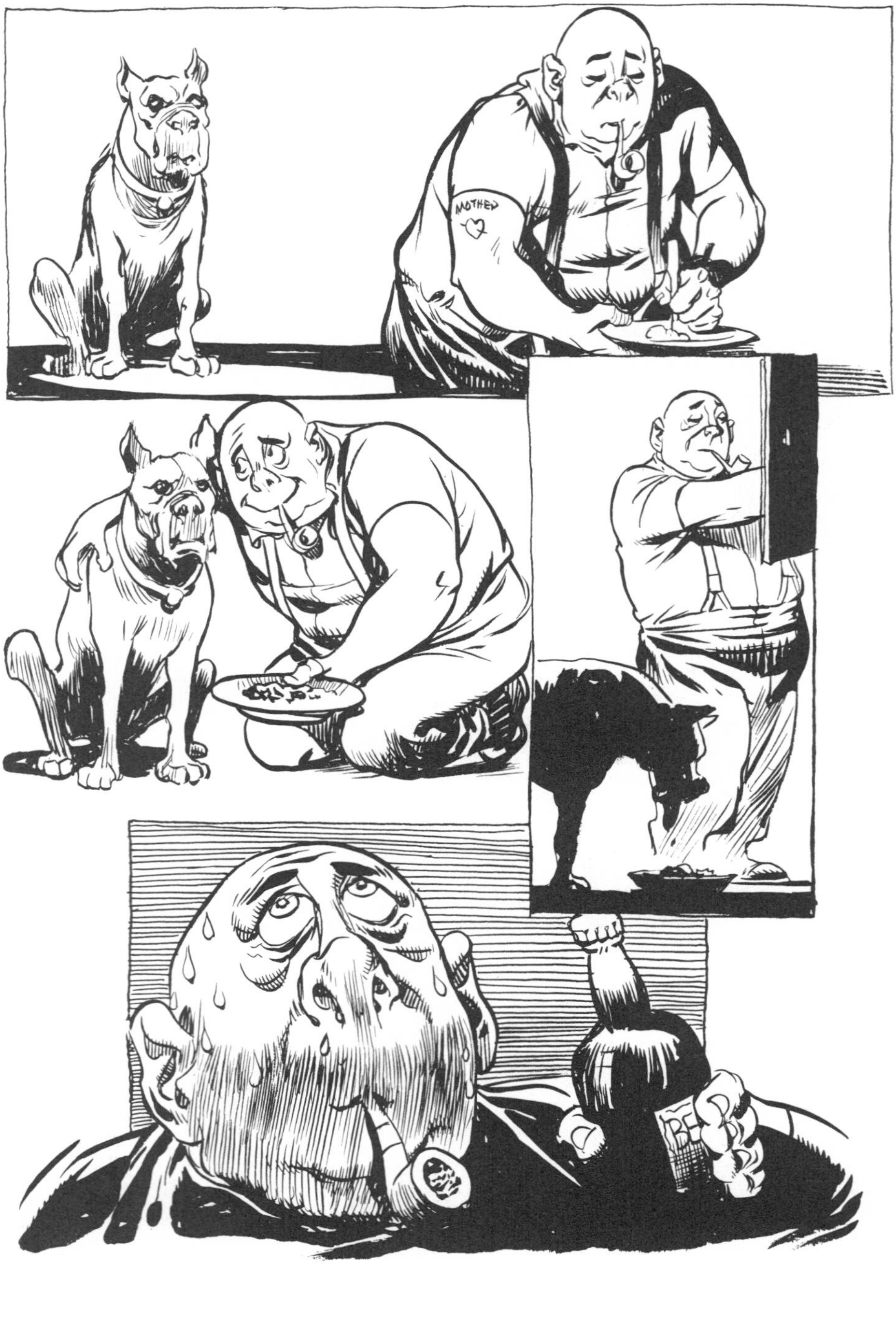
MOTHER

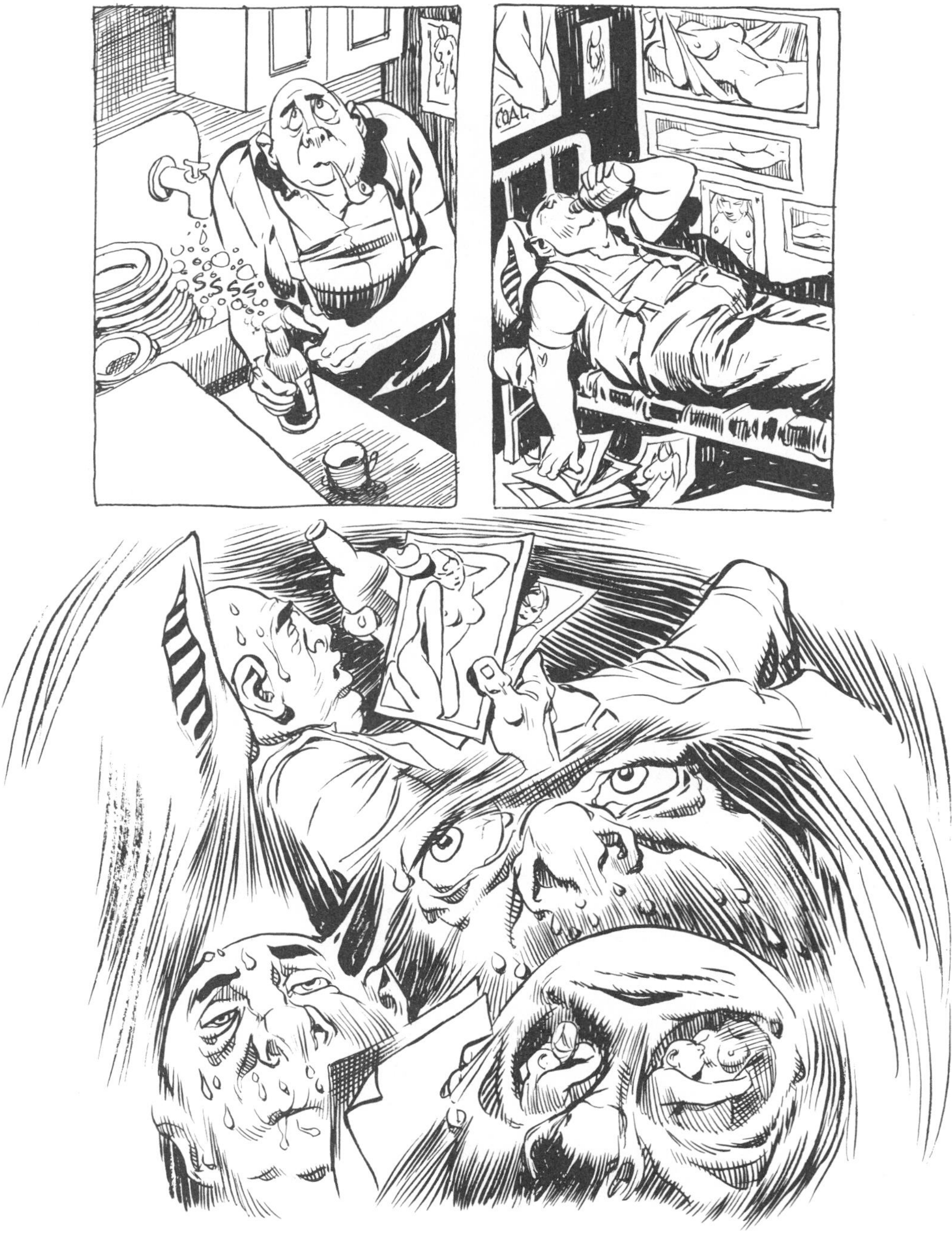
SSSS
COAL

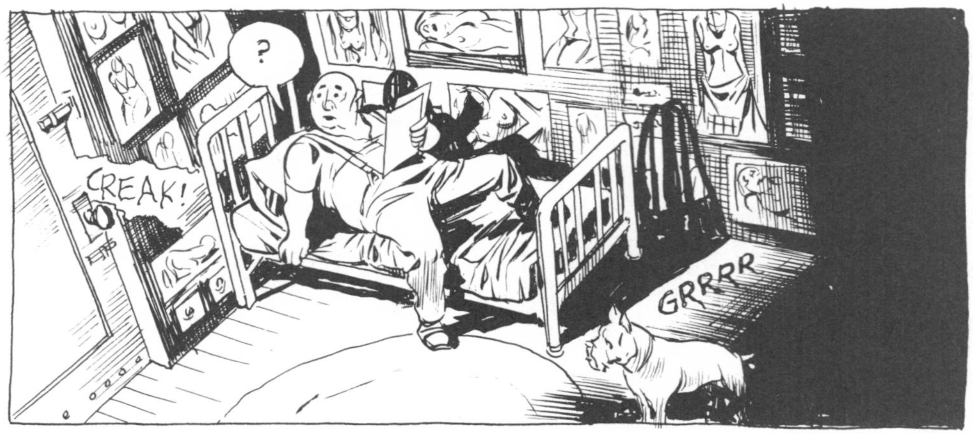
?
CREAK!
GRRRR

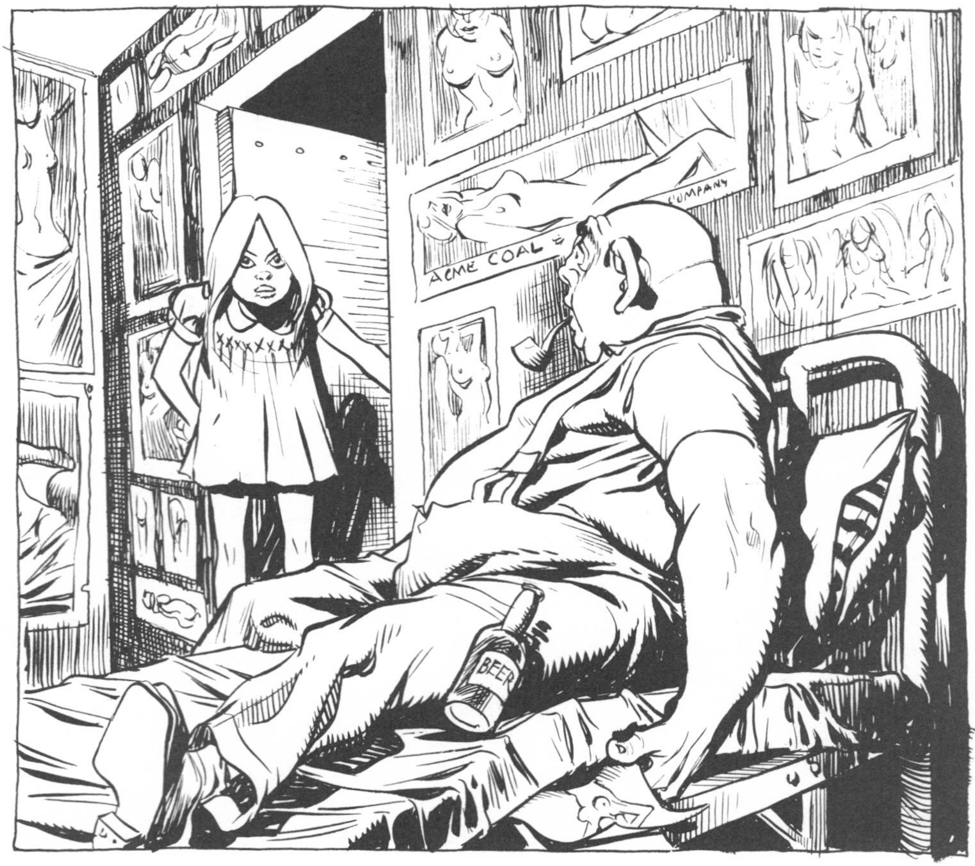
ACME COAL &
COMPANY
BEER

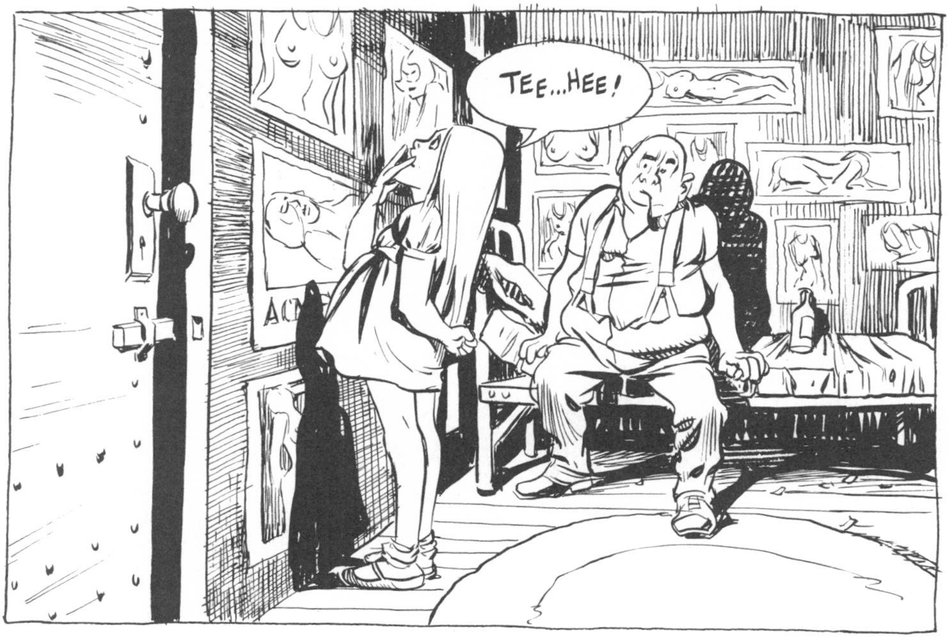
TEE...HEE!

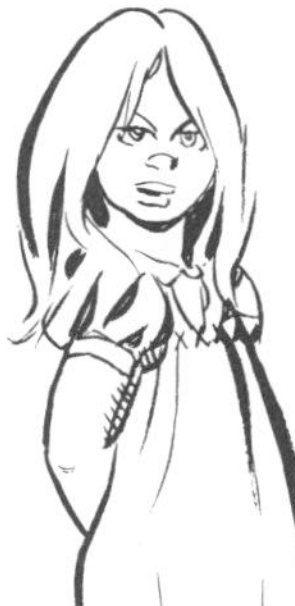

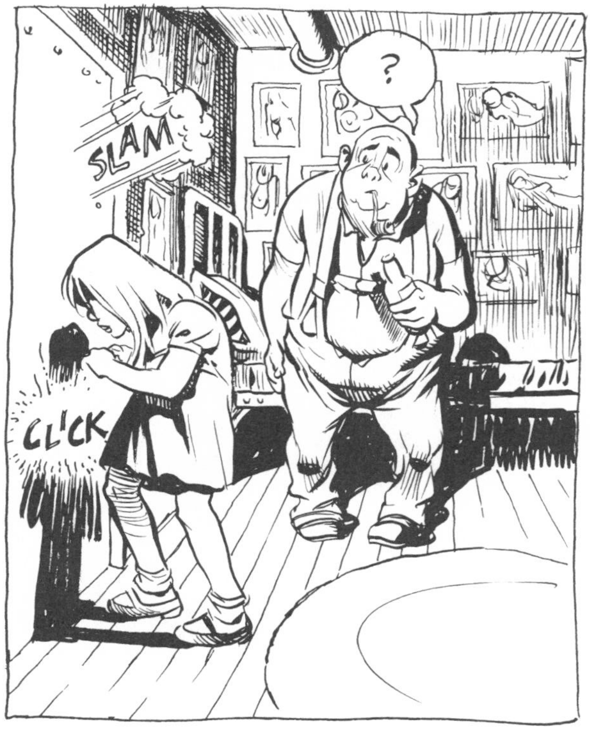
?
SLAM
CLICK

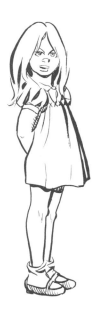

YOU WANNA ??

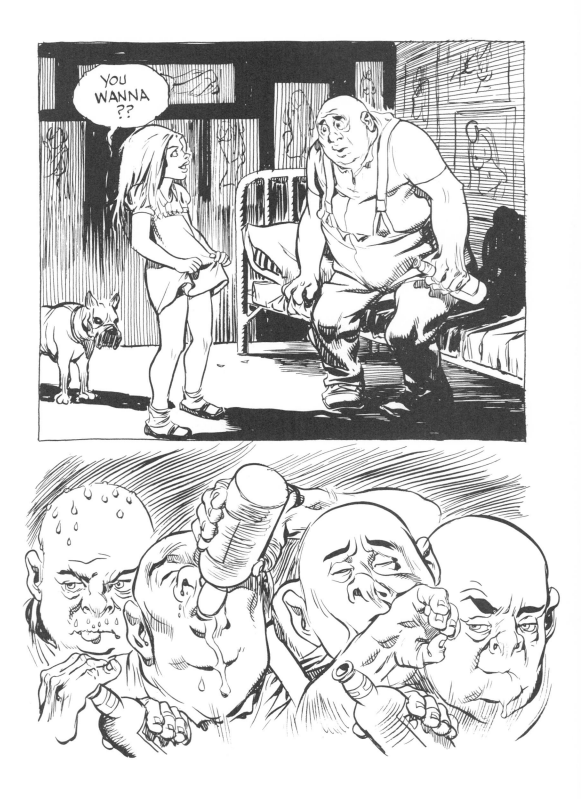

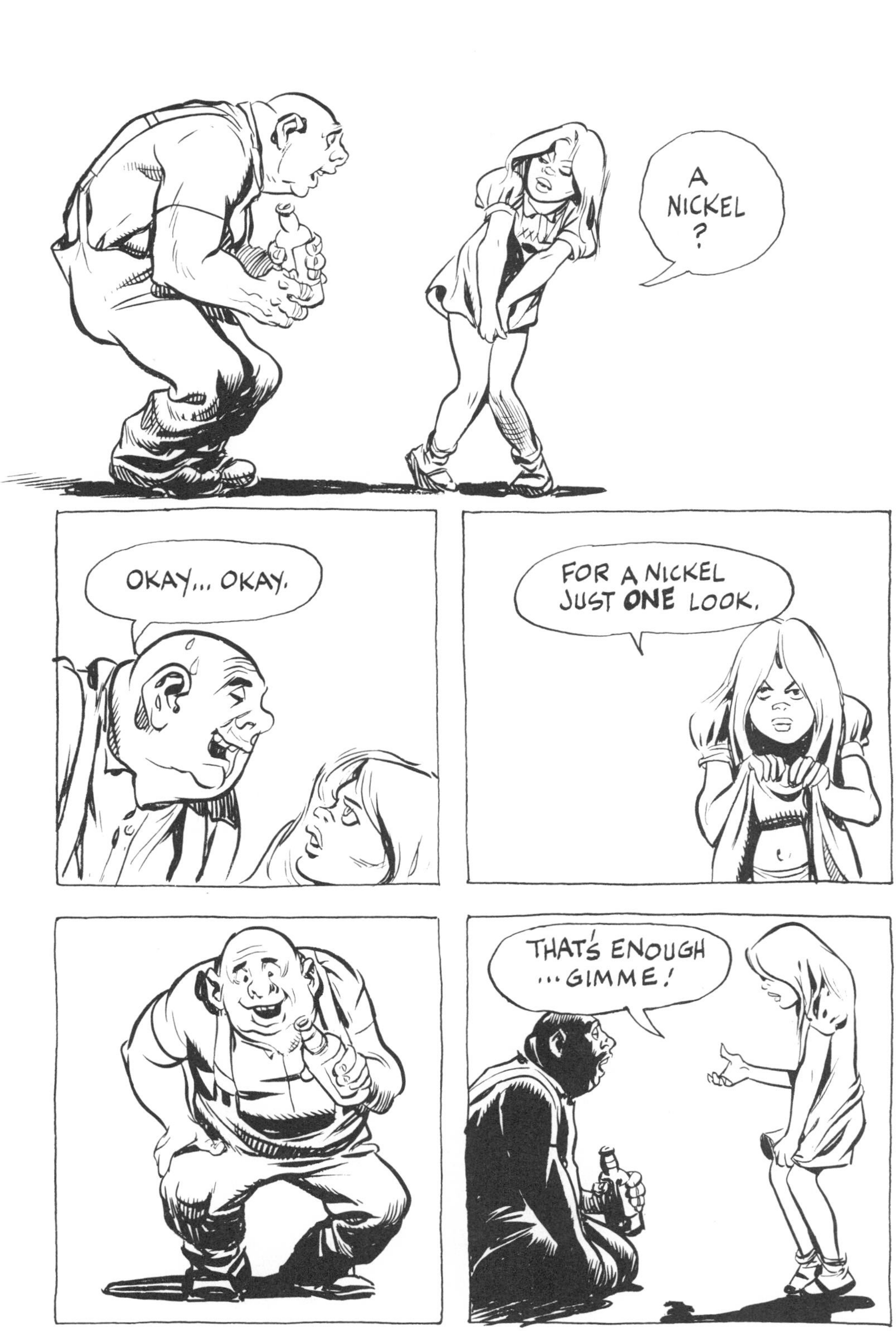

A NICKEL ?
OKAY... OKAY.
FOR A NICKEL JUST ONE LOOK.
THAT'S ENOUGH ...GIMME!

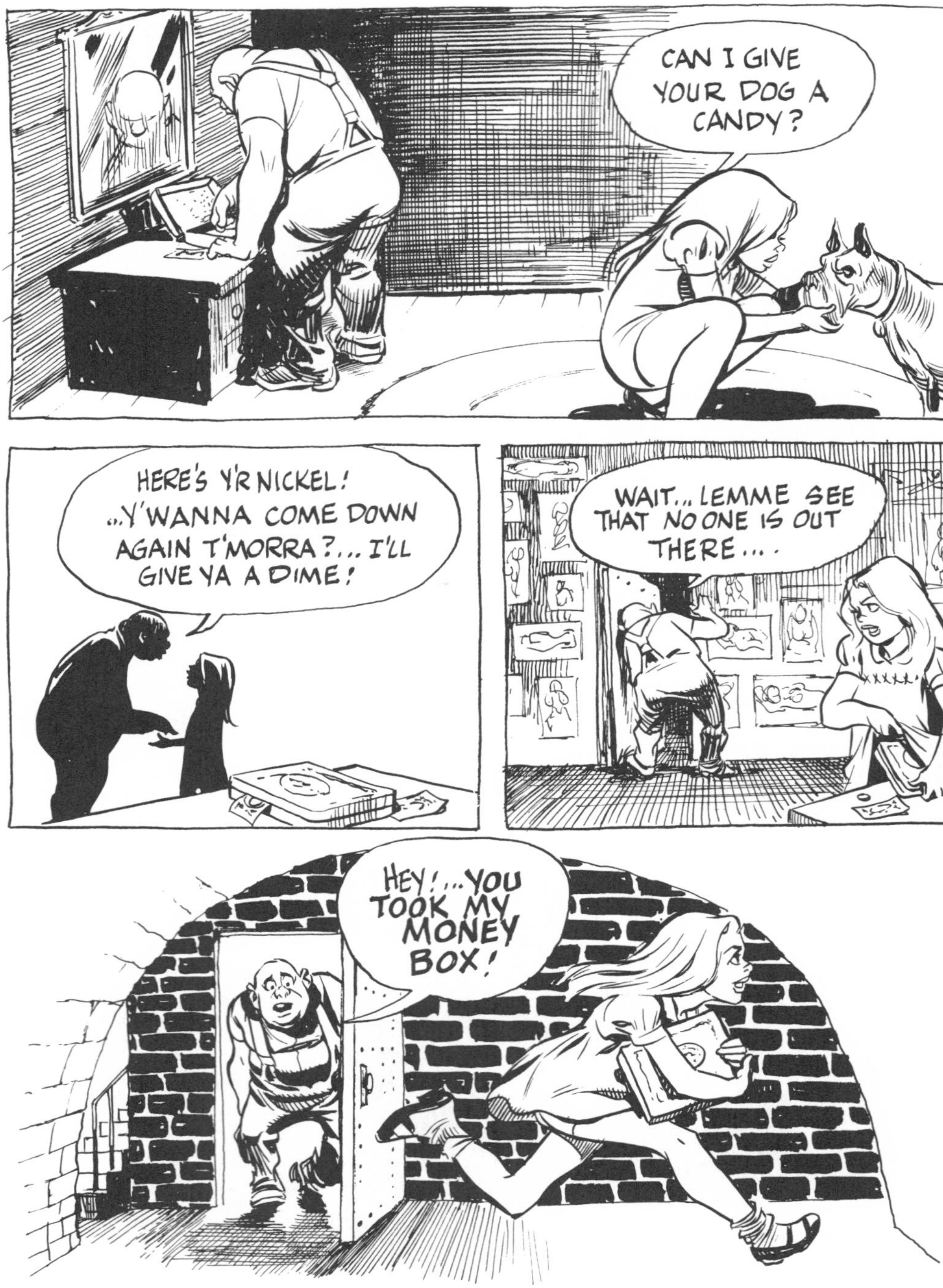
CAN I GIVE YOUR DOG A CANDY?
HERE'S Y'R NICKEL! ..Y'WANNA COME DOWN AGAIN T'MORRA?... I'LL GIVE YA A DIME!
WAIT... LEMME SEE THAT NO ONE IS OUT THERE....
HEY!...YOU TOOK MY MONEY BOX!

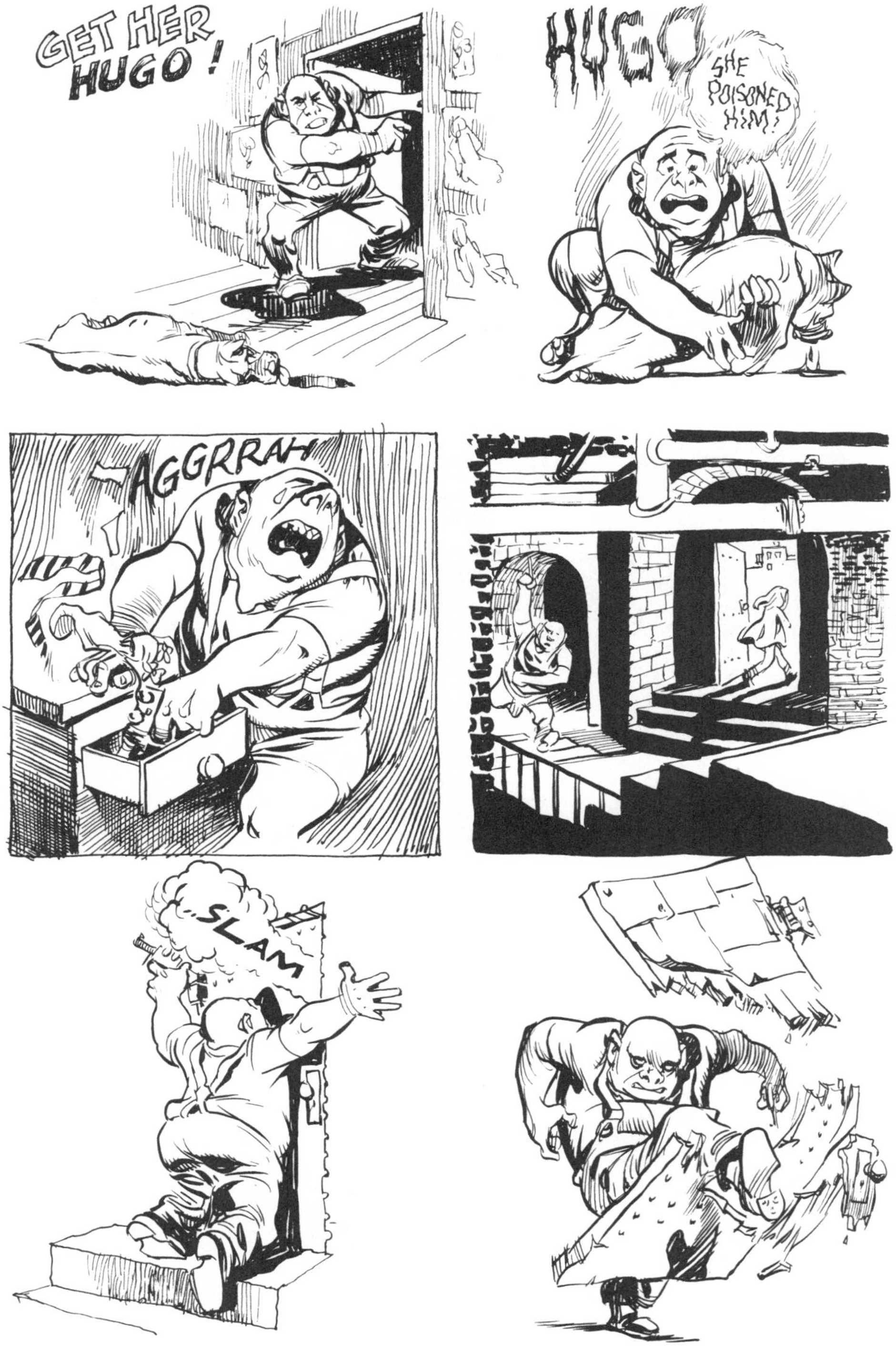
GET HER HUGO!
HUGO
SHE POISONED HIM!
AGGRRAH
SLAM

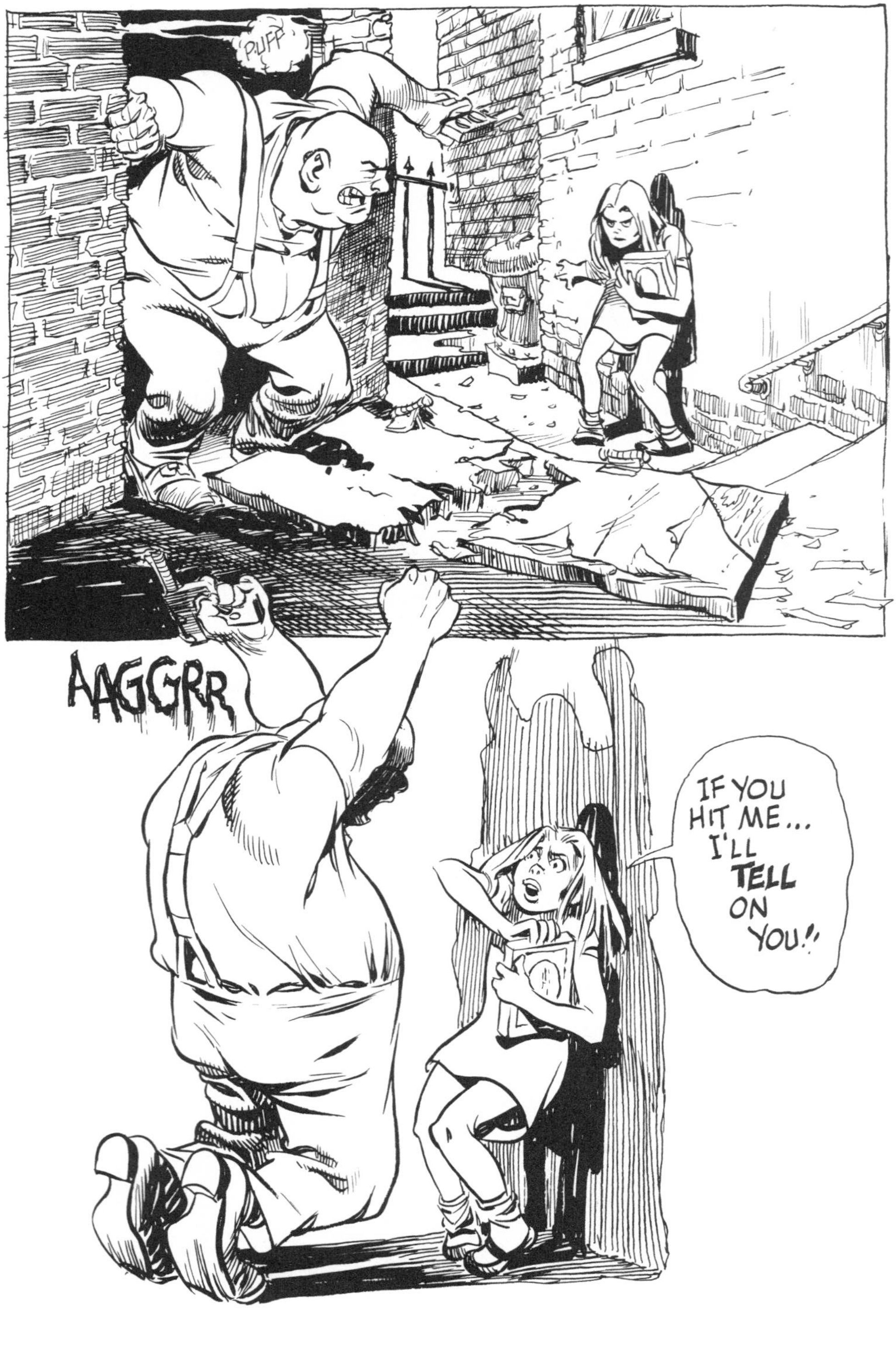
PUFF
AAGGRR
IF YOU HIT ME... I'LL TELL ON YOU!!

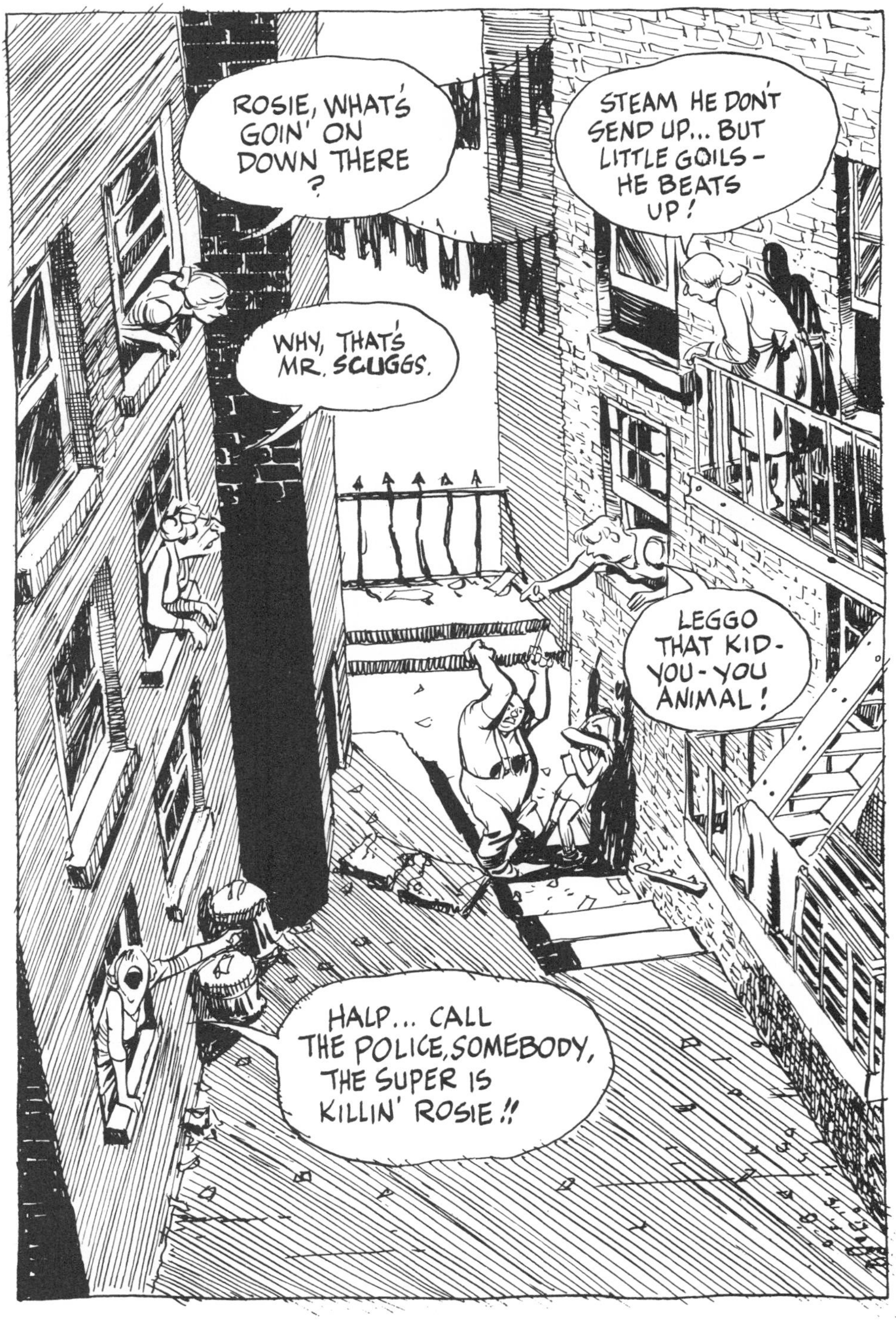
ROSIE, WHAT'S GOIN' ON DOWN THERE ?
STEAM HE DON'T SEND UP... BUT LITTLE GOILS - HE BEATS UP!
WHY, THAT'S MR. SCUGGS.
LEGGO THAT KID- YOU- YOU ANIMAL!
HALP... CALL THE POLICE, SOMEBODY, THE SUPER IS KILLIN' ROSIE!!

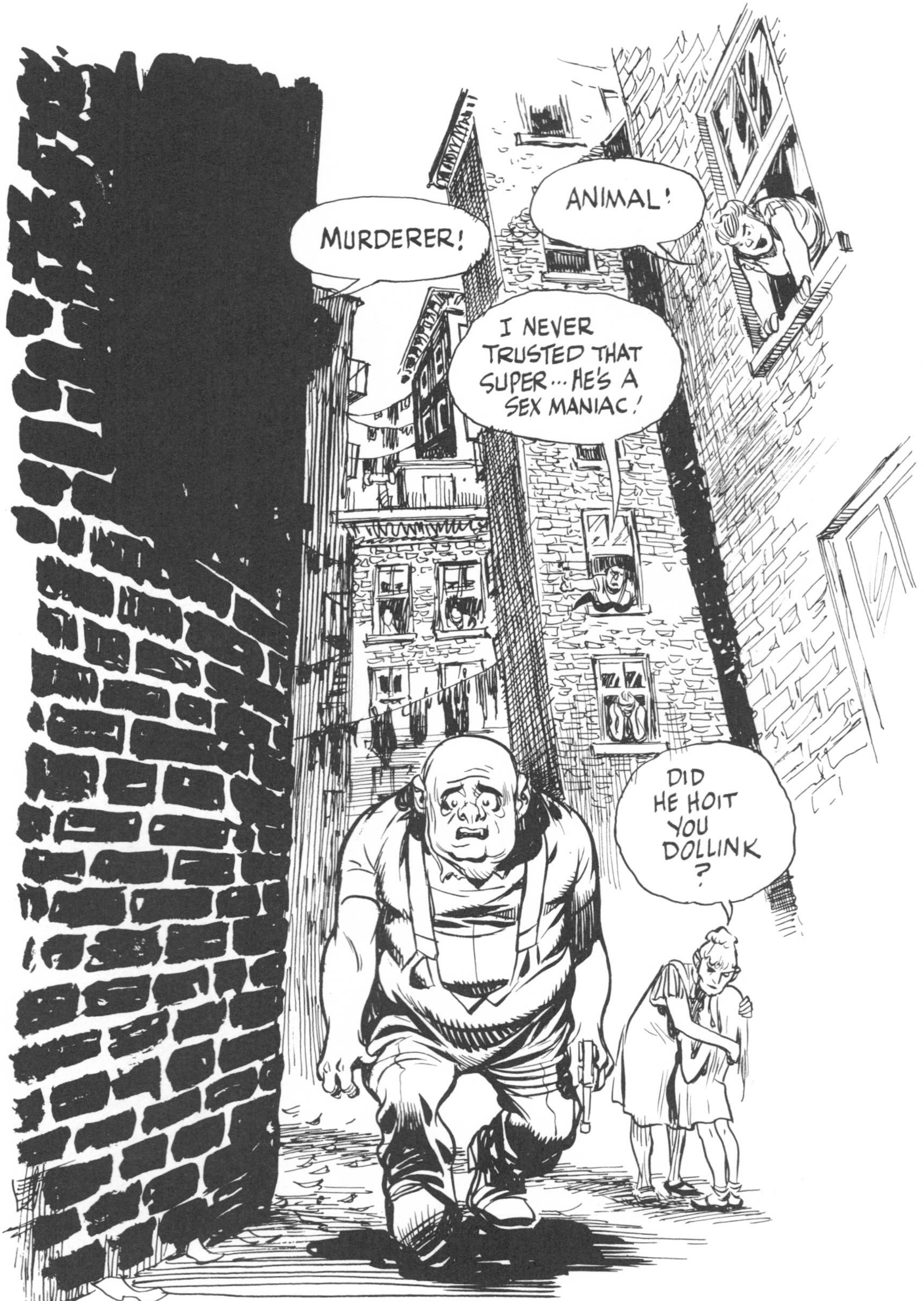
MURDERER!
ANIMAL!
I NEVER TRUSTED THAT SUPER... HE'S A SEX MANIAC!
DID HE HOIT YOU DOLLINK ?

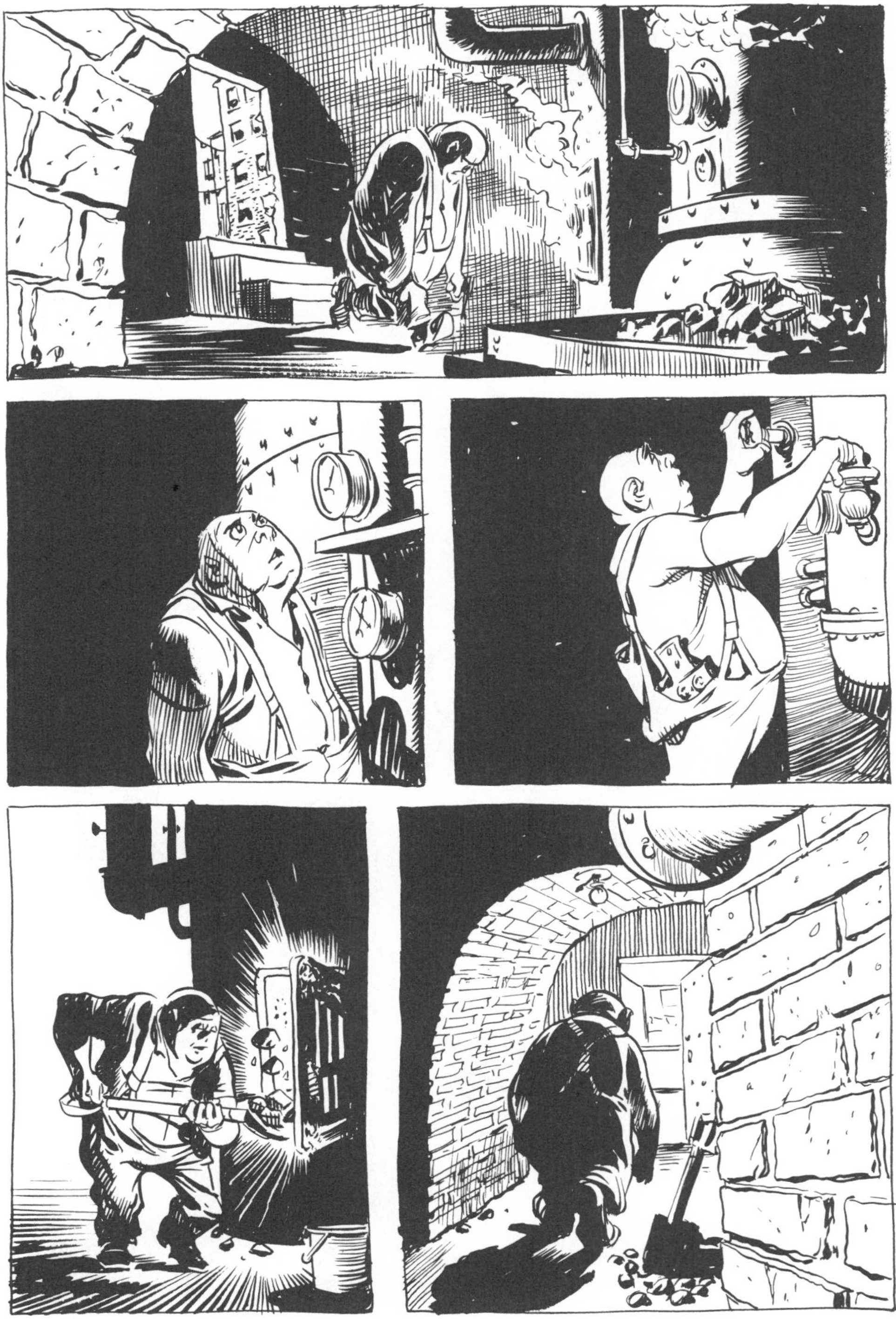

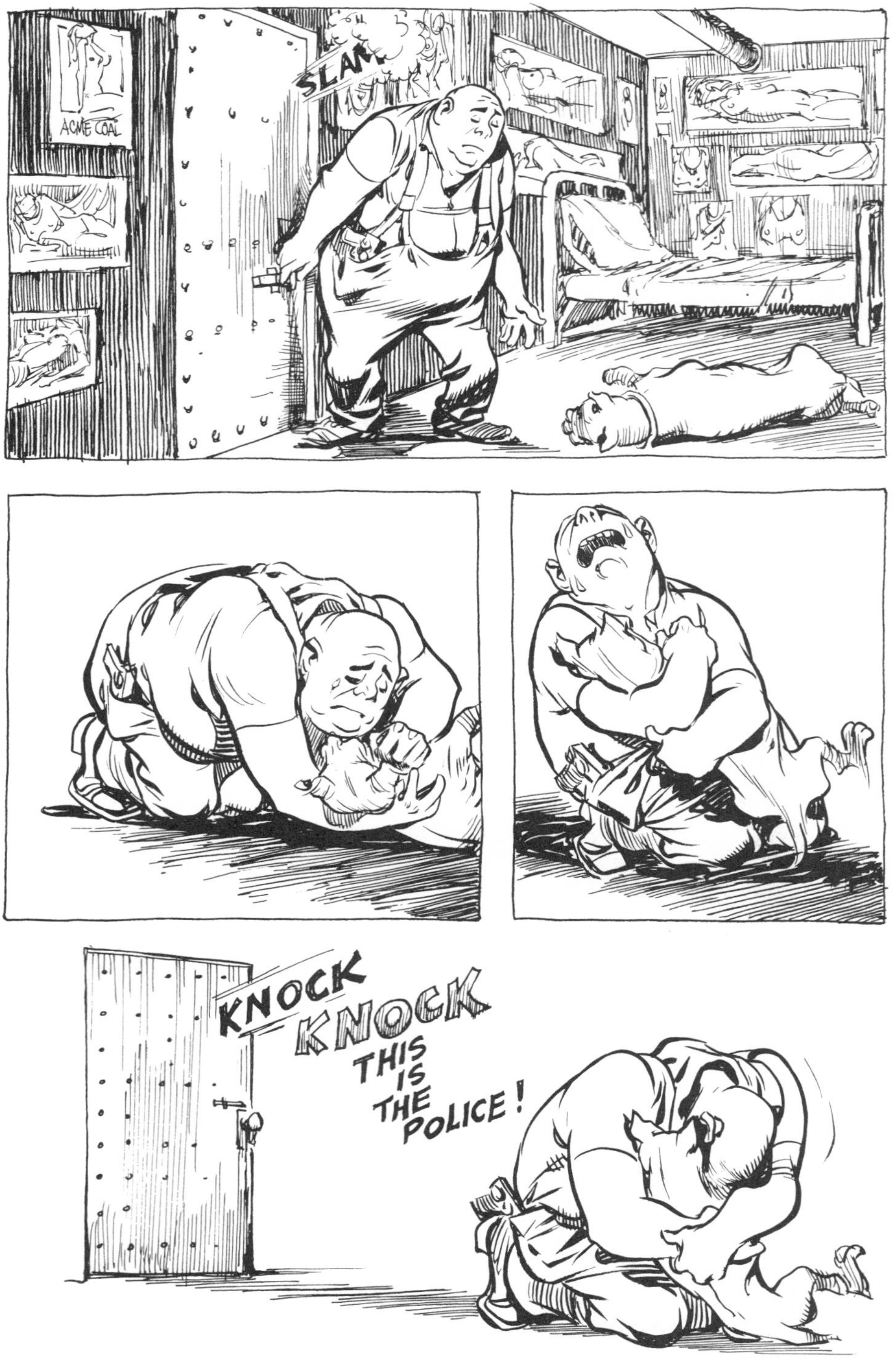
SLAM
ACME COAL
KNOCK
KNOCK
THIS IS THE POLICE!

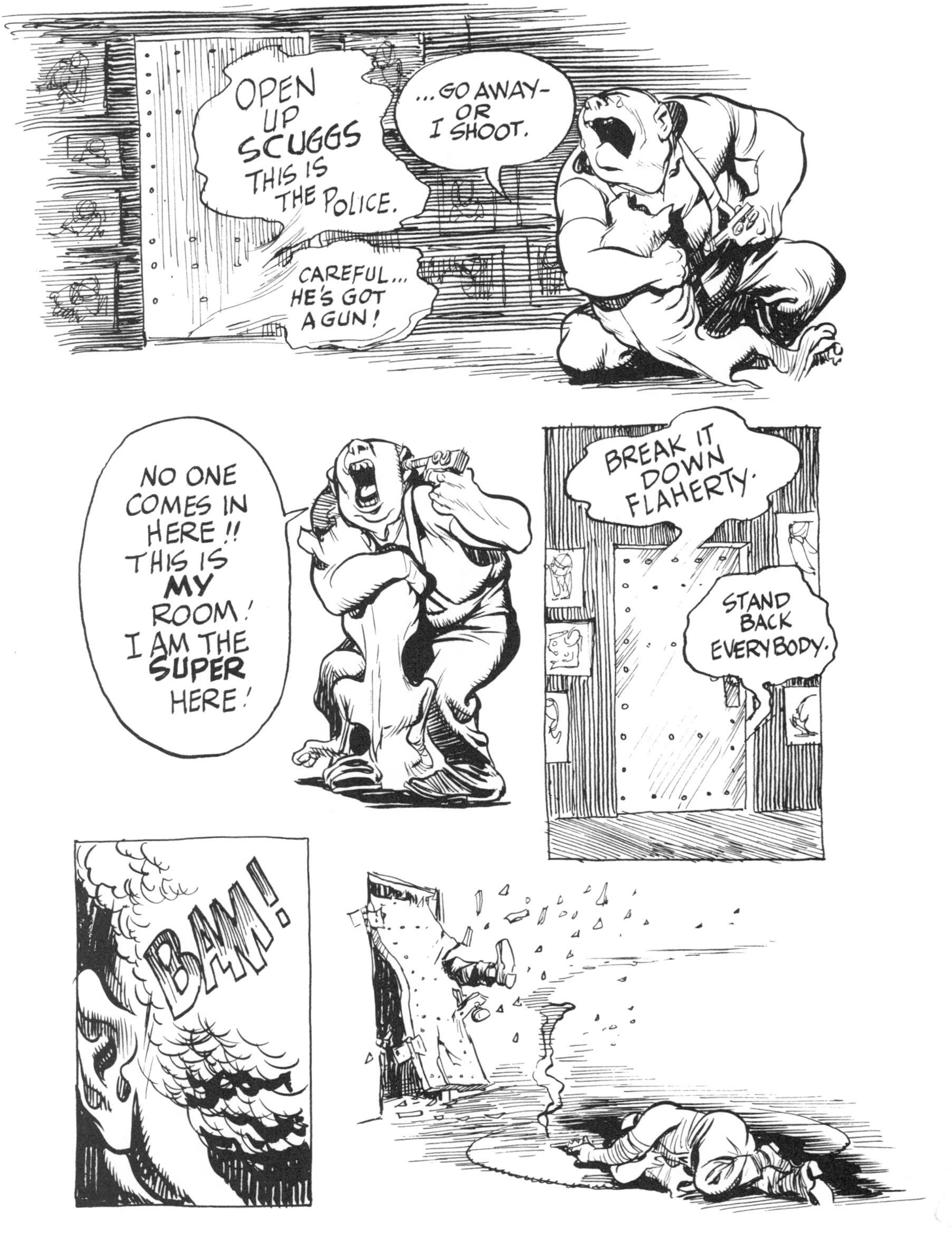
OPEN UP SCUGGS THIS IS THE POLICE.
...GO AWAY- OR I SHOOT.
CAREFUL... HE'S GOT A GUN!
NO ONE COMES IN HERE!! THIS IS MY ROOM! I AM THE SUPER HERE!
BREAK IT DOWN FLAHERTY.
STAND BACK EVERYBODY.
BAM!

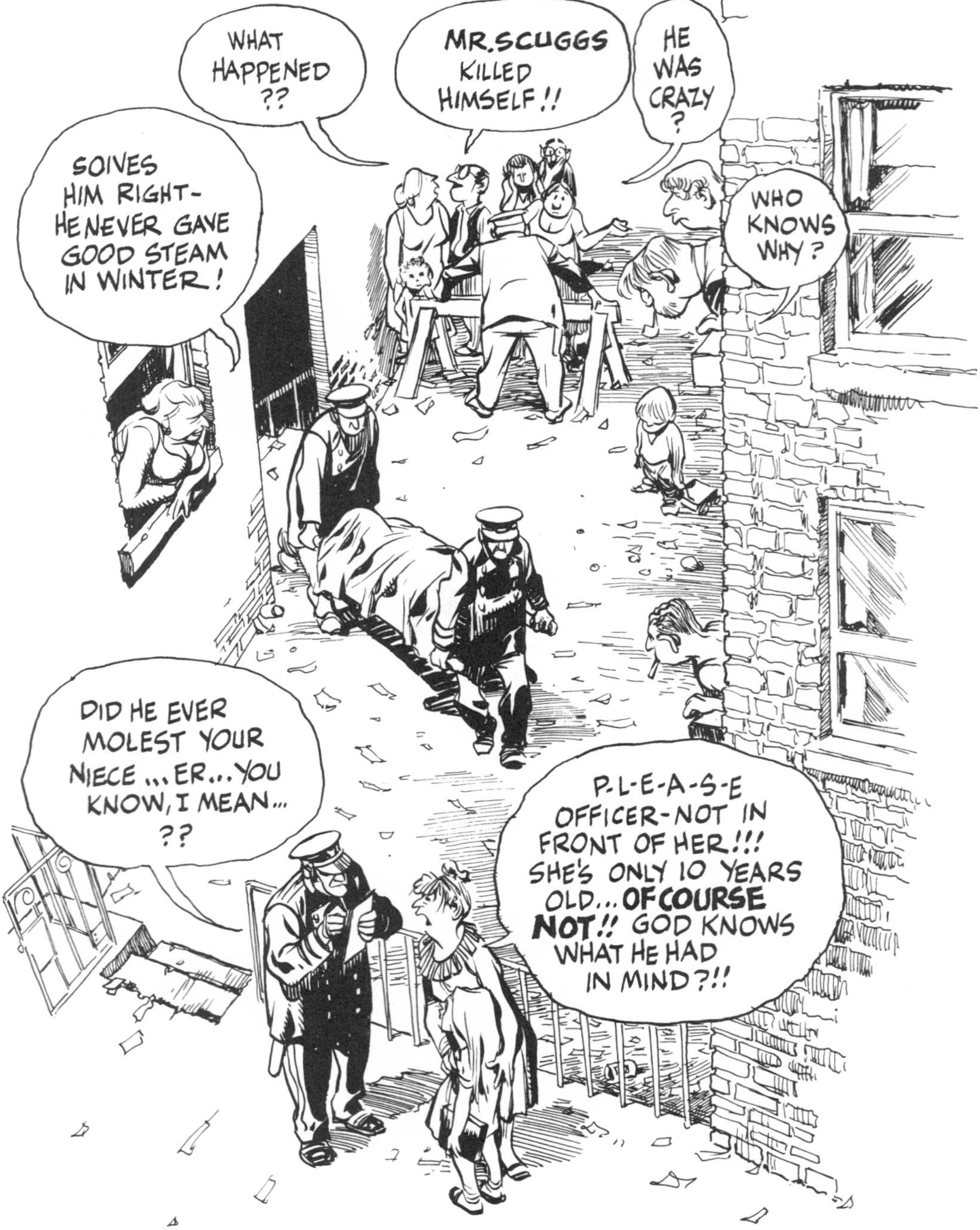
SOIVES HIM RIGHT- HE NEVER GAVE GOOD STEAM IN WINTER!
WHAT HAPPENED ??
MR. SCUGGS KILLED HIMSELF!!
HE WAS CRAZY ?
WHO KNOWS WHY?
DID HE EVER MOLEST YOUR NIECE ... ER ... YOU KNOW, I MEAN... ??
P-L-E-A-S-E OFFICER-NOT IN FRONT OF HER!!! SHE'S ONLY 10 YEARS OLD... OF COURSE NOT!! GOD KNOWS WHAT HE HAD IN MIND?!!

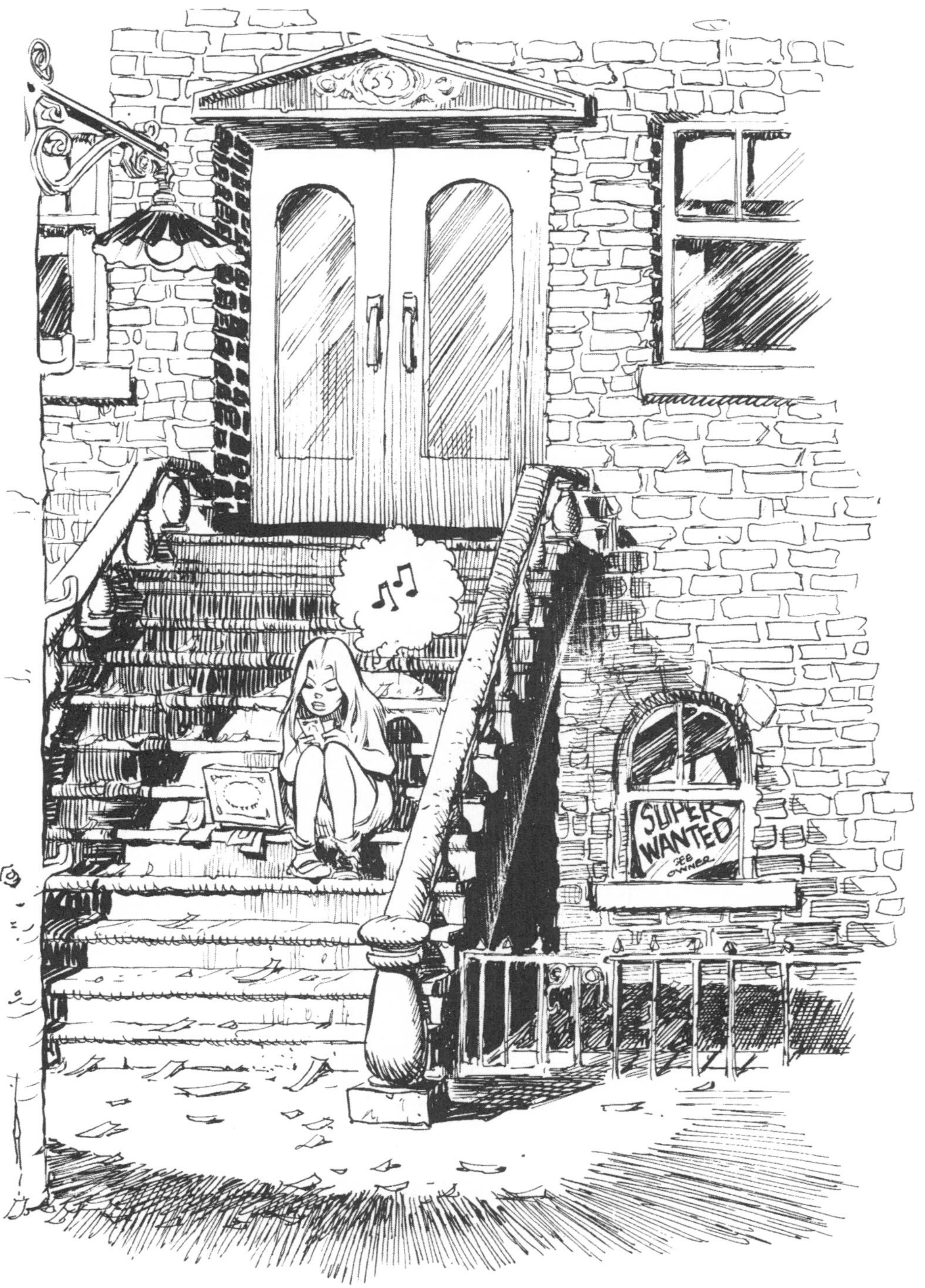
SUPER
WANTED
SEE OWNER

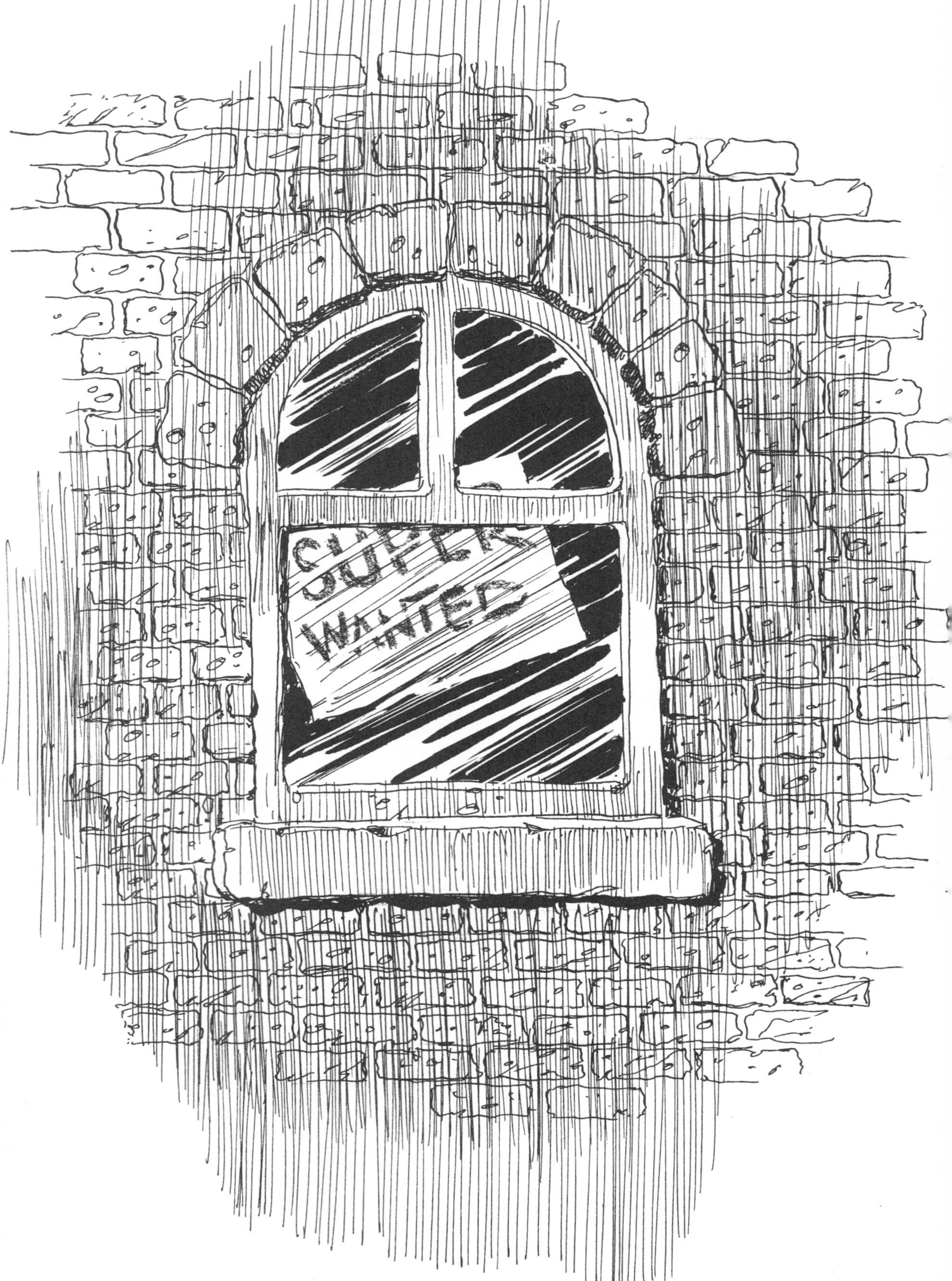
SUPER
WANTED

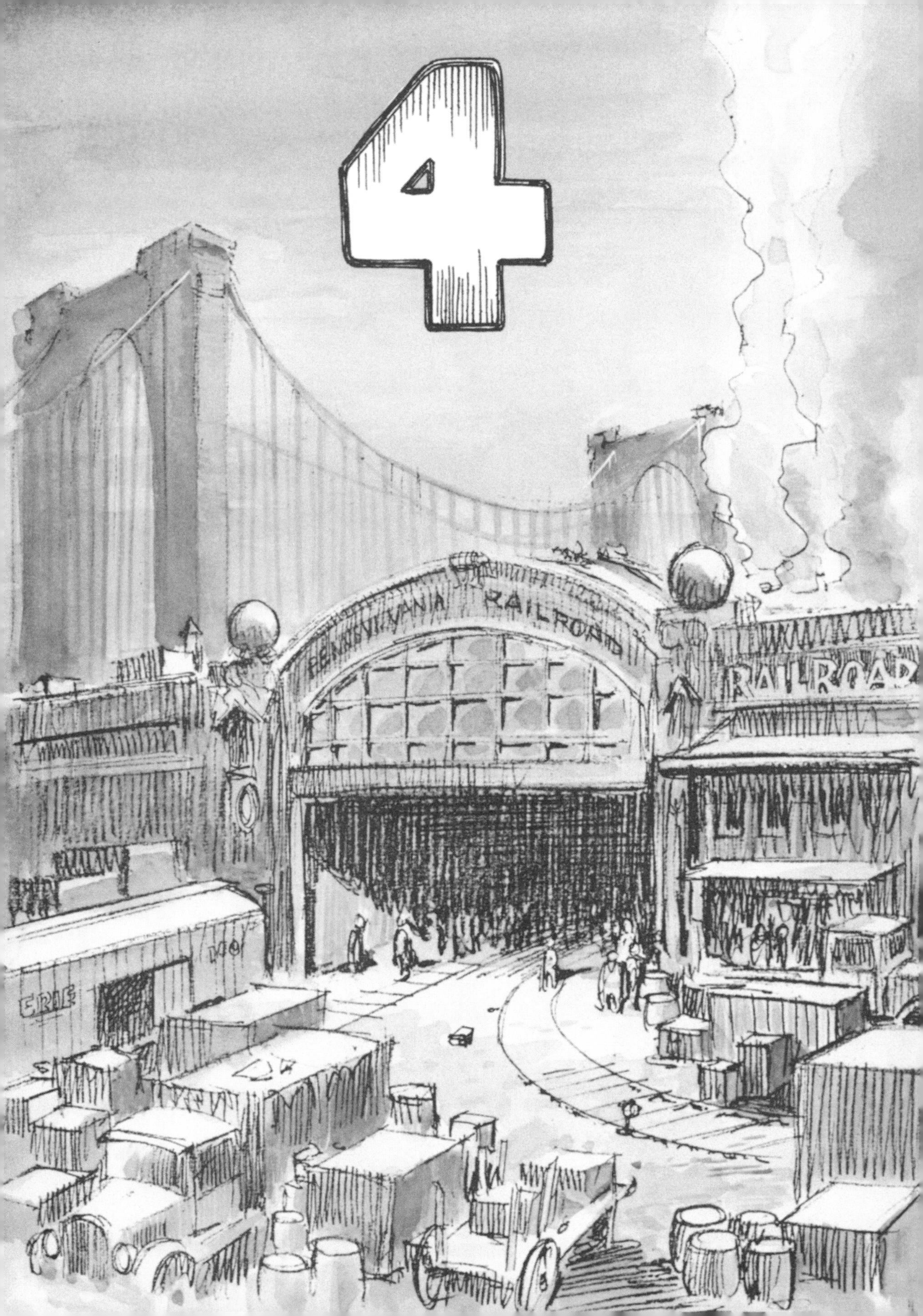
4
PENNSYLVANIA RAILROAD
ERIE

COOKALEIN

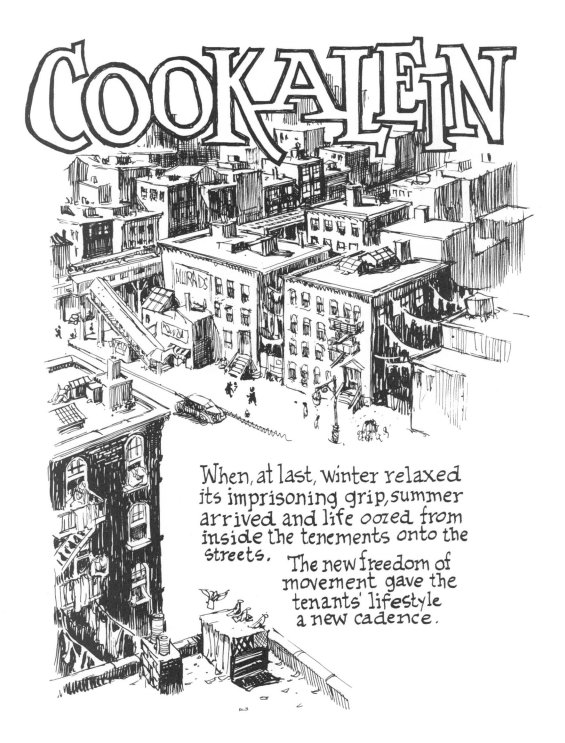

When, at last, winter relaxed its imprisoning grip, summer arrived and life oozed from inside the tenements onto the streets. The new freedom of movement gave the tenants' lifestyle a new cadence.

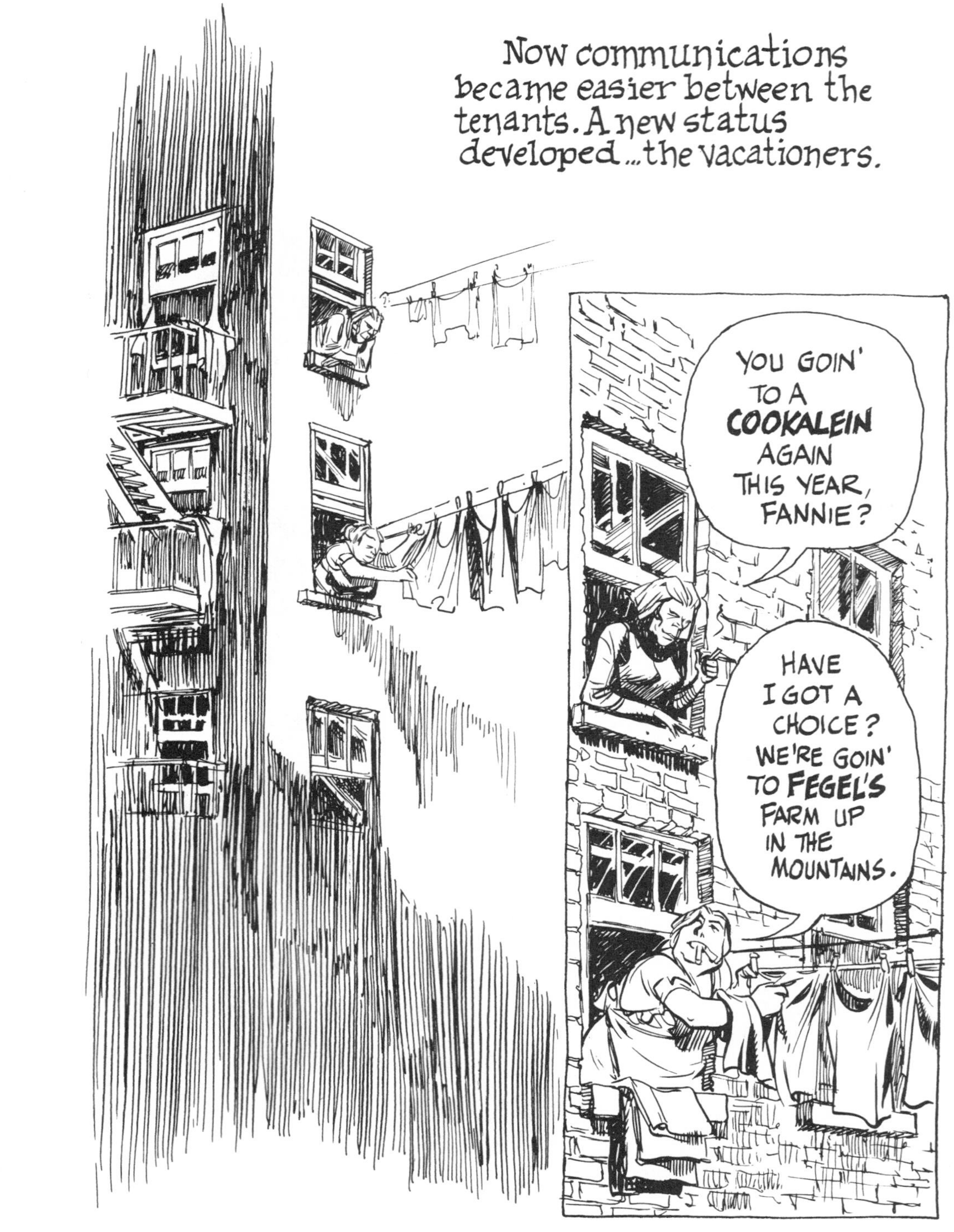
Now communications became easier between the tenants. A new status developed...the vacationers.
YOU GOIN' TO A **COOKALEIN** AGAIN THIS YEAR, FANNIE?
HAVE I GOT A CHOICE? WE'RE GOIN' TO **FEGEL'S** FARM UP IN THE MOUNTAINS.

For some tenants it was
time to harvest the yield
from a year of doing without.

FANNIE ... YOU'RE A WONDER! HOW'D YOU PUT TOGETHER $75 ON WHAT I BRING IN?

HOW ELSE? 2-DAY-OLD BREAD, YESTERDAY'S MILK AND HAND-ME-DOWN CLOTHES FROM MY SISTER'S KIDS...IF I LEFT IT TO YOU WE'D HAVE NOTHING!

WHAT ARE WE GONNA DO THIS SUMMER, MA?

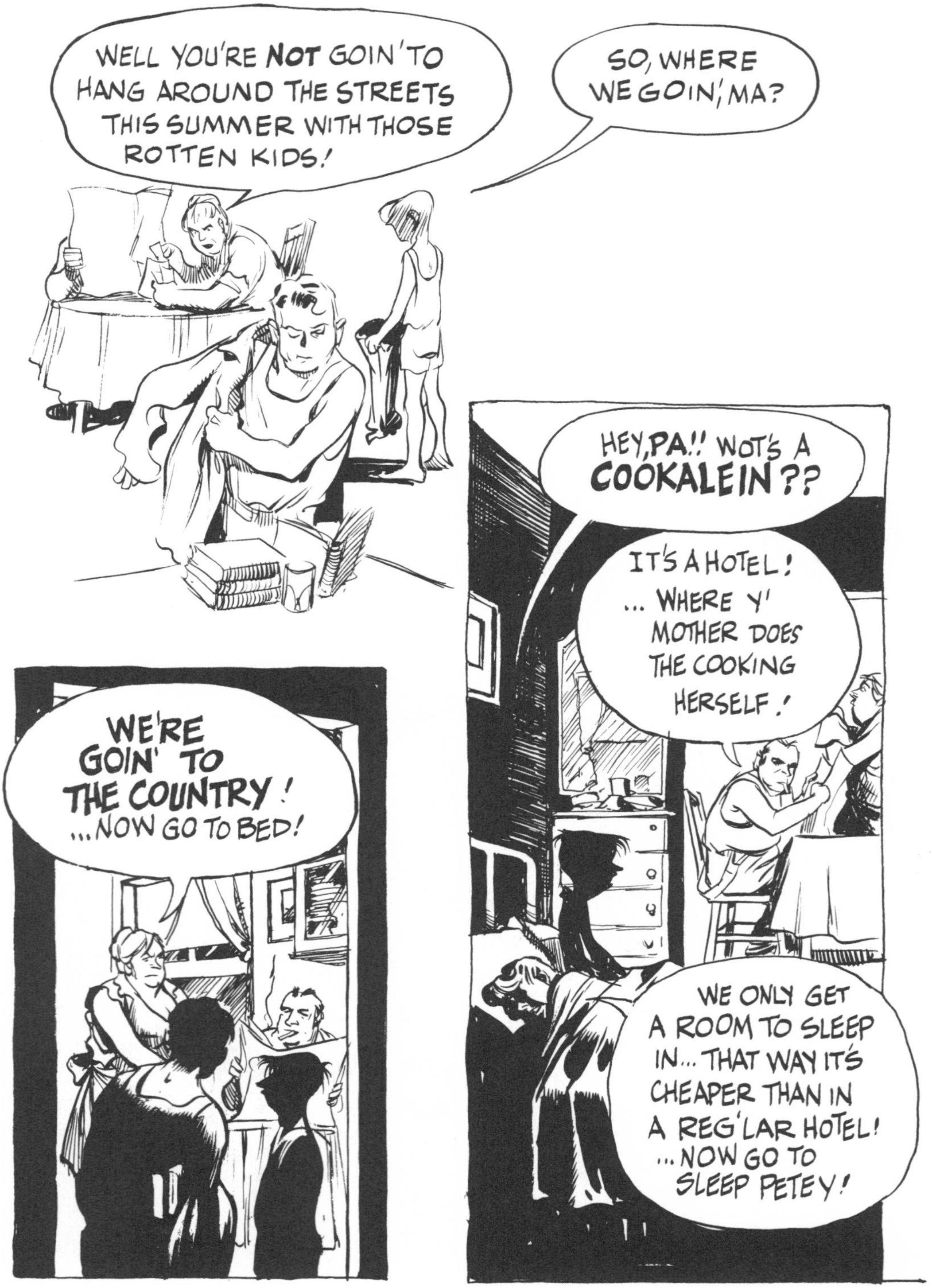
WELL YOU'RE NOT GOIN' TO HANG AROUND THE STREETS THIS SUMMER WITH THOSE ROTTEN KIDS!
SO, WHERE WE GOIN', MA?
WE'RE GOIN' TO THE COUNTRY! ...NOW GO TO BED!
HEY, PA!! WOT'S A COOKALEIN??
IT'S A HOTEL! ... WHERE Y' MOTHER DOES THE COOKING HERSELF!
WE ONLY GET A ROOM TO SLEEP IN... THAT WAY IT'S CHEAPER THAN IN A REG'LAR HOTEL! ...NOW GO TO SLEEP PETEY!

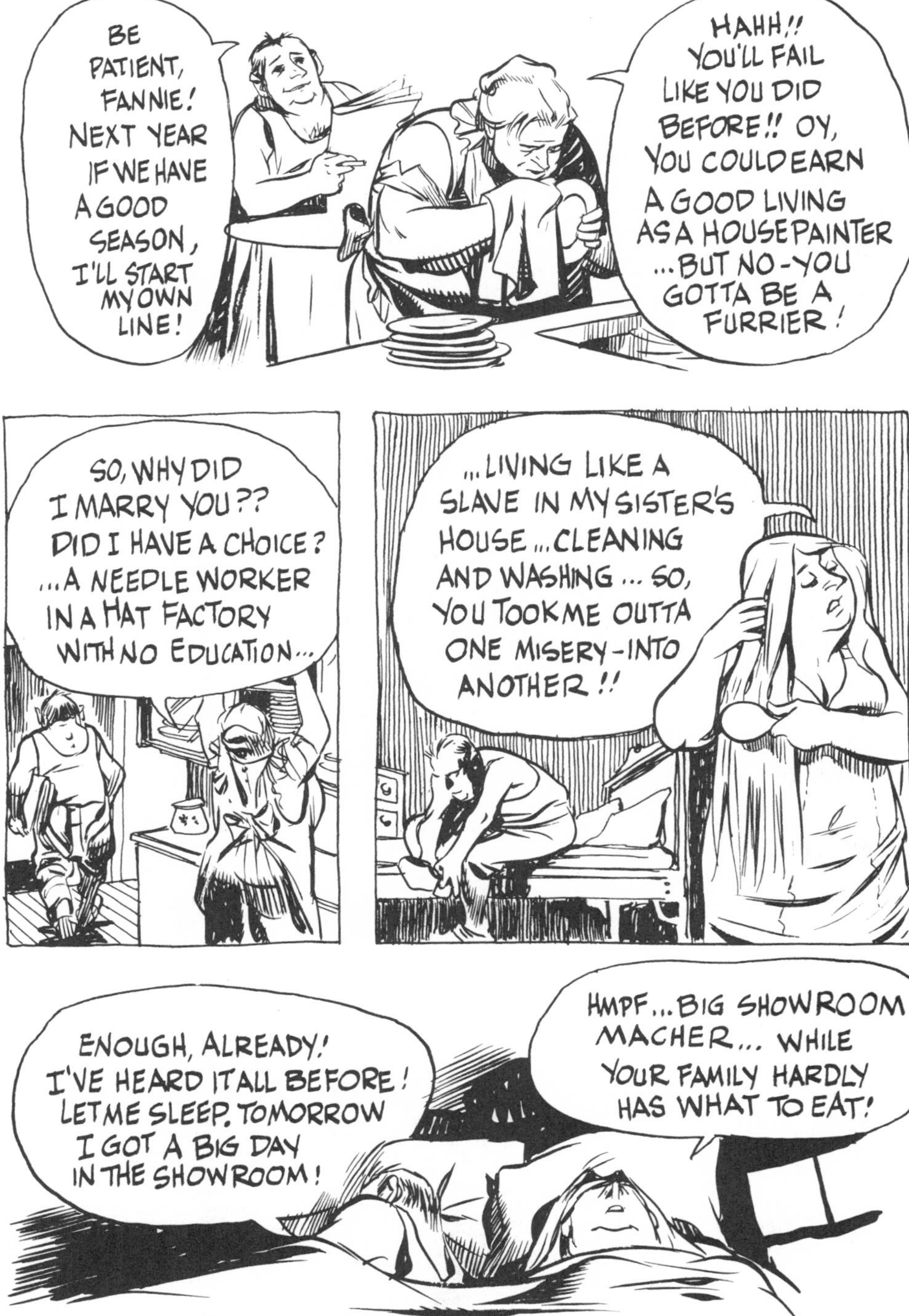
BE PATIENT, FANNIE! NEXT YEAR IF WE HAVE A GOOD SEASON, I'LL START MY OWN LINE!
HAHH!! YOU'LL FAIL LIKE YOU DID BEFORE!! OY, YOU COULD EARN A GOOD LIVING AS A HOUSEPAINTER ...BUT NO-YOU GOTTA BE A FURRIER!
SO, WHY DID I MARRY YOU?? DID I HAVE A CHOICE? ...A NEEDLE WORKER IN A HAT FACTORY WITH NO EDUCATION...
...LIVING LIKE A SLAVE IN MY SISTER'S HOUSE...CLEANING AND WASHING ... SO, YOU TOOK ME OUTTA ONE MISERY-INTO ANOTHER!!
ENOUGH, ALREADY! I'VE HEARD IT ALL BEFORE! LET ME SLEEP. TOMORROW I GOT A BIG DAY IN THE SHOWROOM!
HMPF... BIG SHOWROOM MACHER... WHILE YOUR FAMILY HARDLY HAS WHAT TO EAT!

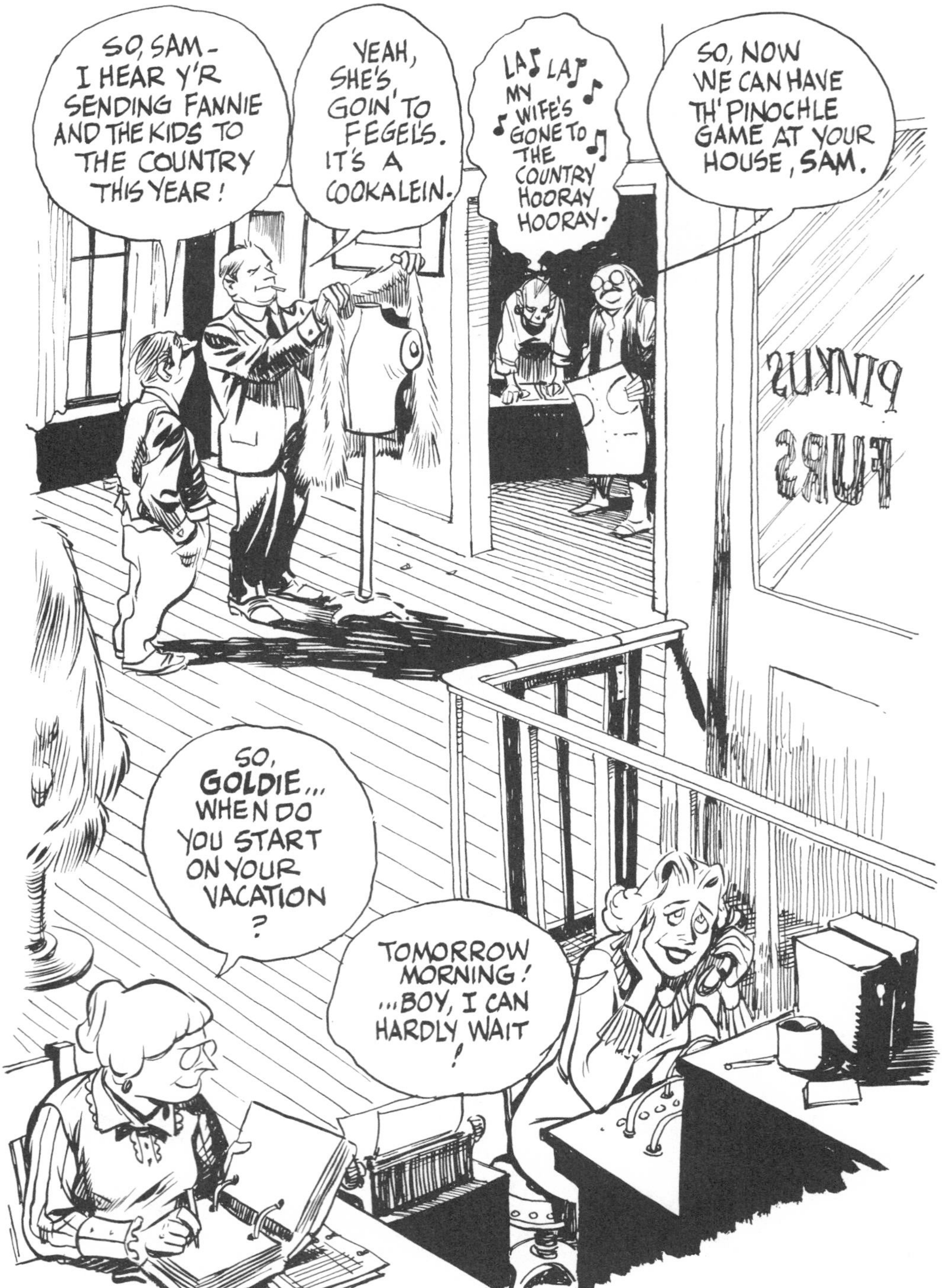
SO, SAM - I HEAR Y'R SENDING FANNIE AND THE KIDS TO THE COUNTRY THIS YEAR!
YEAH, SHE'S GOIN' TO FEGEL'S. IT'S A COOKALEIN.
LA LA MY WIFE'S GONE TO THE COUNTRY HOORAY HOORAY.
SO, NOW WE CAN HAVE TH' PINOCHLE GAME AT YOUR HOUSE, SAM.
PINKUS FURS
SO, GOLDIE... WHEN DO YOU START ON YOUR VACATION?
TOMORROW MORNING! ...BOY, I CAN HARDLY WAIT!

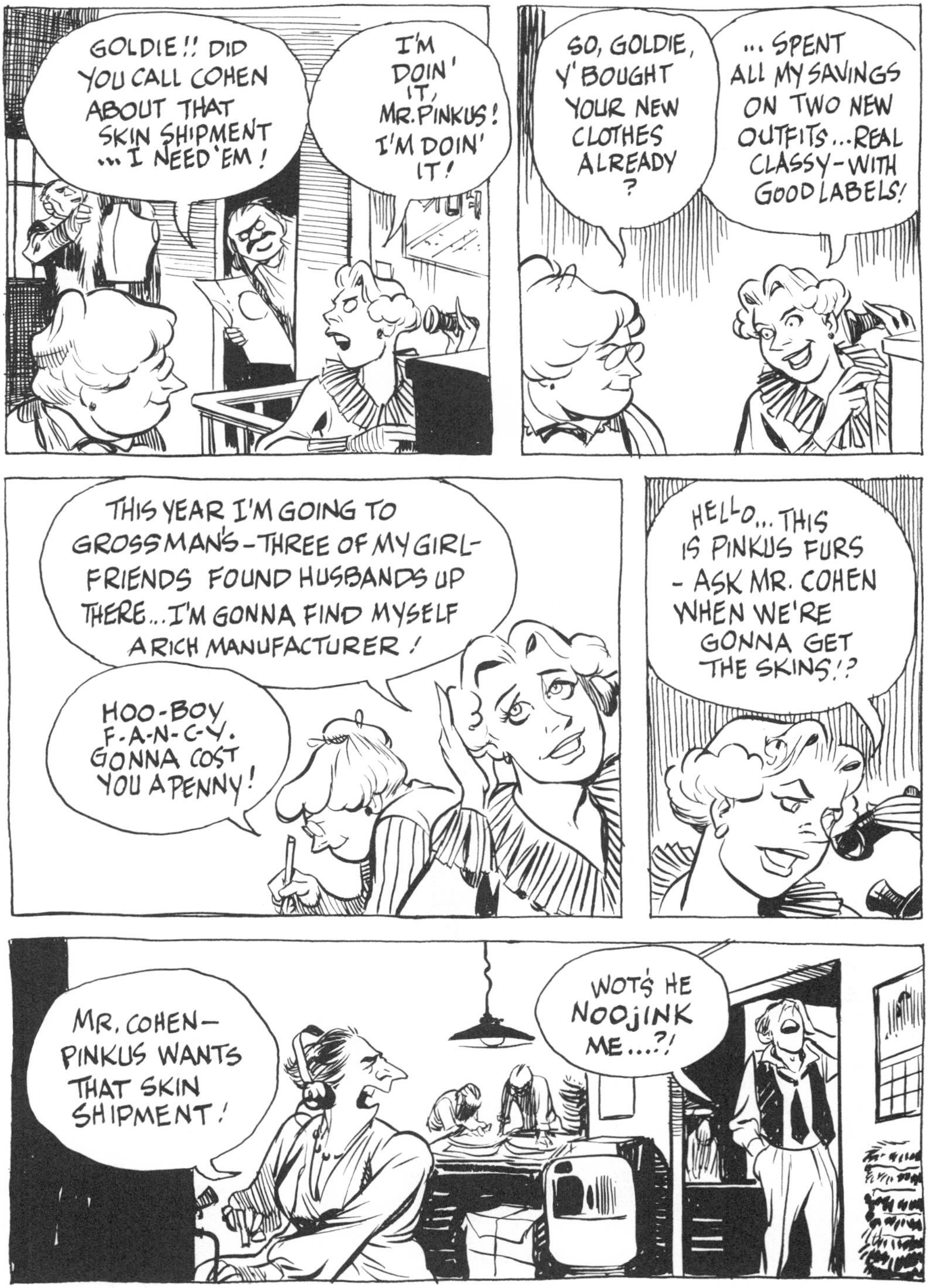
GOLDIE!! DID YOU CALL COHEN ABOUT THAT SKIN SHIPMENT ... I NEED 'EM!
I'M DOIN' IT, MR. PINKUS! I'M DOIN' IT!
SO, GOLDIE, Y' BOUGHT YOUR NEW CLOTHES ALREADY?
... SPENT ALL MY SAVINGS ON TWO NEW OUTFITS ... REAL CLASSY-WITH GOOD LABELS!
THIS YEAR I'M GOING TO GROSSMAN'S - THREE OF MY GIRL-FRIENDS FOUND HUSBANDS UP THERE ... I'M GONNA FIND MYSELF A RICH MANUFACTURER!
HOO-BOY F-A-N-C-Y. GONNA COST YOU A PENNY!
HELLO... THIS IS PINKUS FURS - ASK MR. COHEN WHEN WE'RE GONNA GET THE SKINS!?
MR. COHEN - PINKUS WANTS THAT SKIN SHIPMENT!
WOT'S HE NOOJINK ME...?!

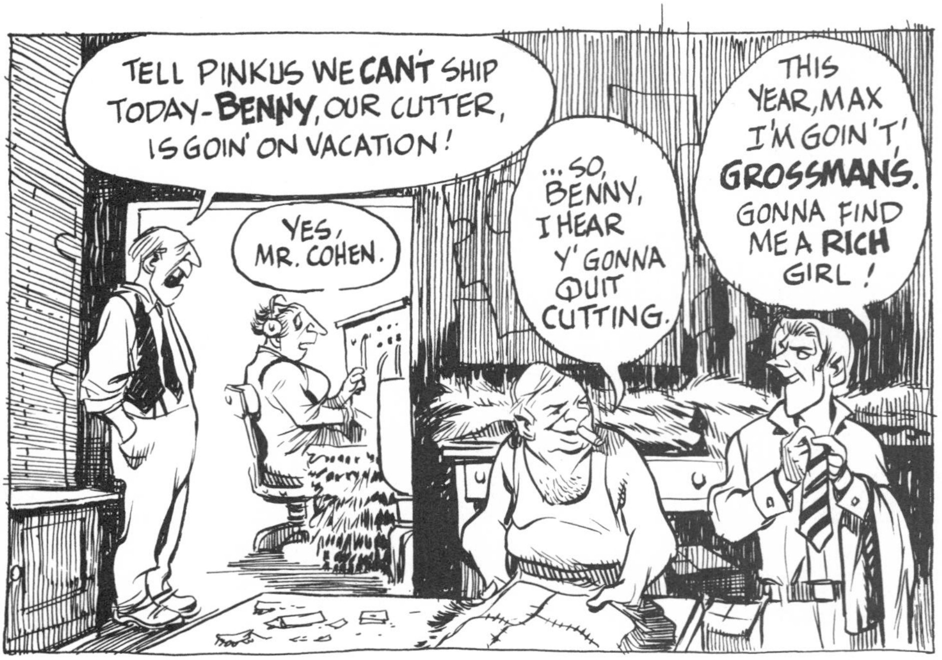
TELL PINKUS WE CAN'T SHIP TODAY-BENNY, OUR CUTTER, IS GOIN' ON VACATION!
YES, MR. COHEN.
...SO, BENNY, I HEAR Y' GONNA QUIT CUTTING.
THIS YEAR, MAX I'M GOIN 'T' GROSSMAN'S. GONNA FIND ME A RICH GIRL!

It was a time to come to a reckoning with dreams-time to climb over the invisible walls and escape.

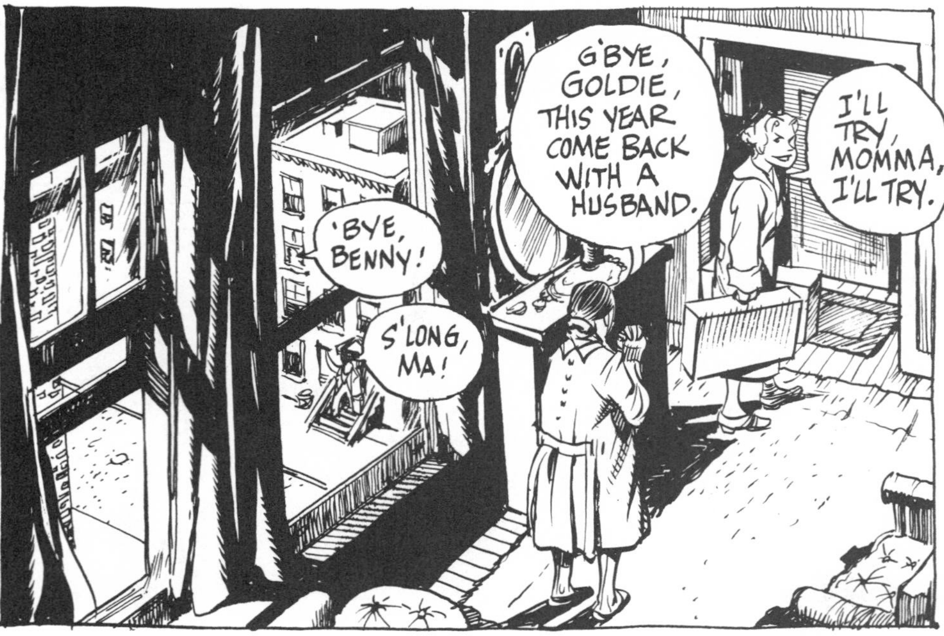
'BYE, BENNY!
S'LONG, MA!
G'BYE, GOLDIE, THIS YEAR COME BACK WITH A HUSBAND.
I'LL TRY, MOMMA, I'LL TRY.

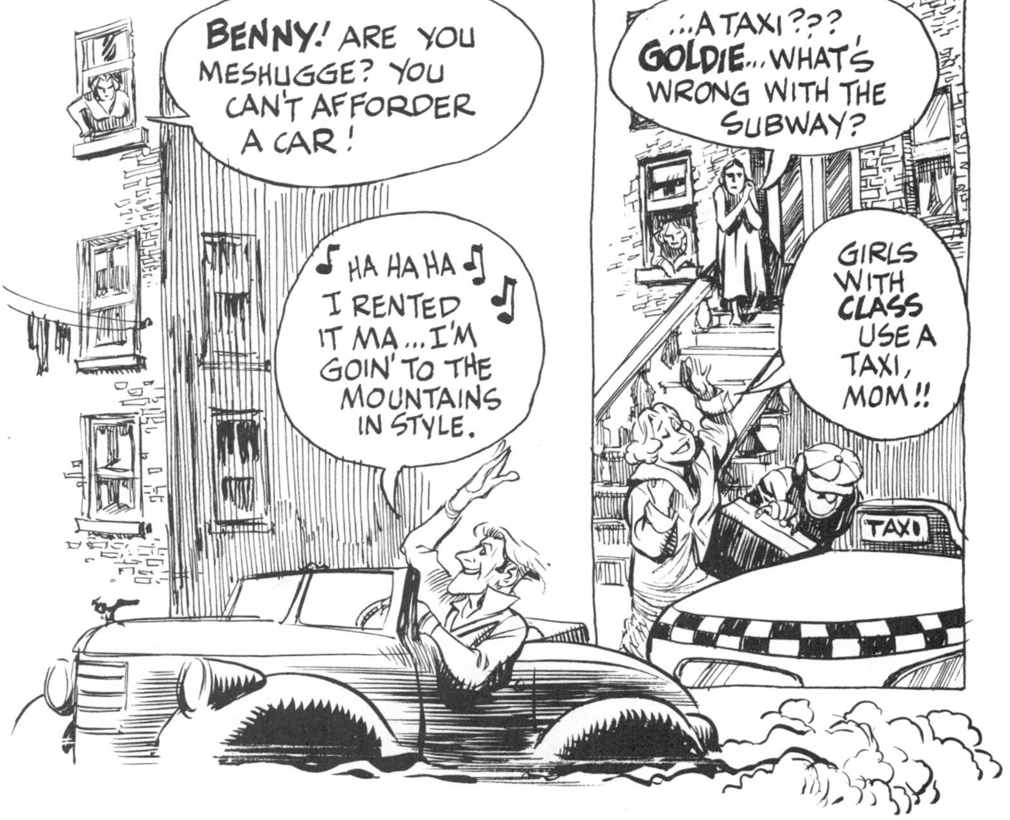
BENNY! ARE YOU MESHUGGE? YOU CAN'T AFFORDER A CAR!
HA HA HA I RENTED IT MA... I'M GOIN' TO THE MOUNTAINS IN STYLE.
...A TAXI??? GOLDIE... WHAT'S WRONG WITH THE SUBWAY?
GIRLS WITH CLASS USE A TAXI, MOM!!
TAXI

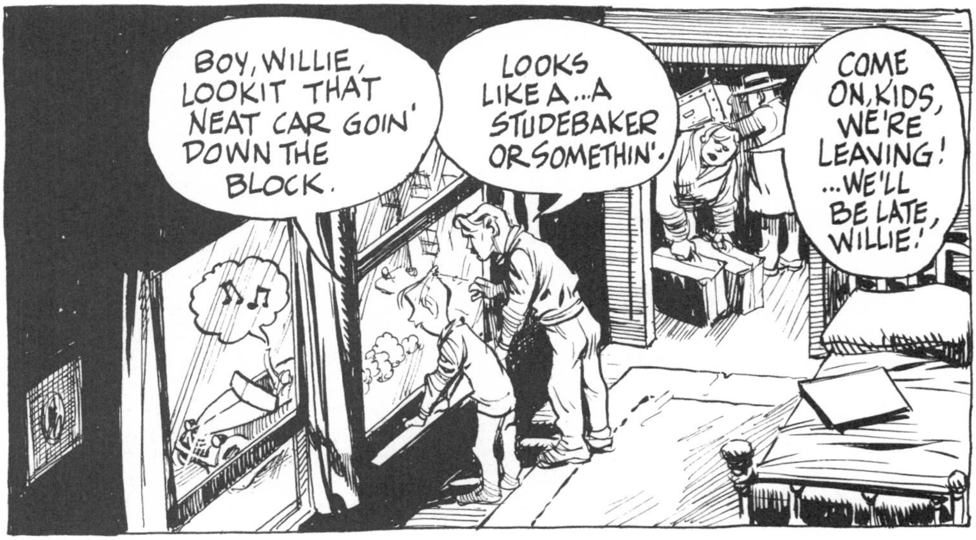
BOY, WILLIE, LOOKIT THAT NEAT CAR GOIN' DOWN THE BLOCK.
LOOKS LIKE A...A STUDEBAKER OR SOMETHIN'.
COME ON, KIDS, WE'RE LEAVING! ...WE'LL BE LATE, WILLIE!

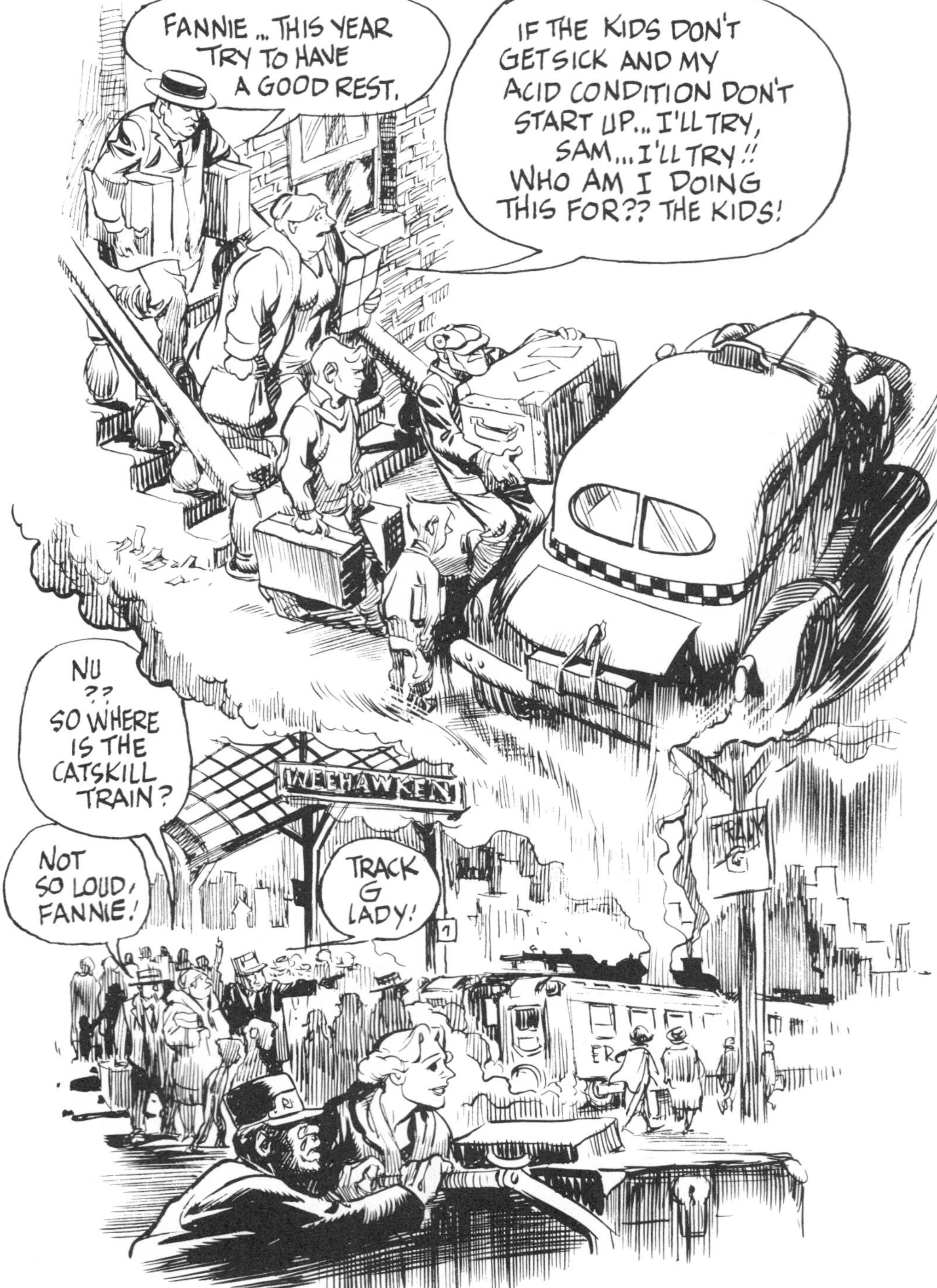
FANNIE ... THIS YEAR TRY TO HAVE A GOOD REST.
IF THE KIDS DON'T GETSICK AND MY ACID CONDITION DON'T START UP... I'LL TRY, SAM... I'LL TRY!! WHO AM I DOING THIS FOR?? THE KIDS!
NU ?? SO WHERE IS THE CATSKILL TRAIN?
WEEHAWKEN
NOT SO LOUD, FANNIE!
TRACK G LADY!
TRAIN G

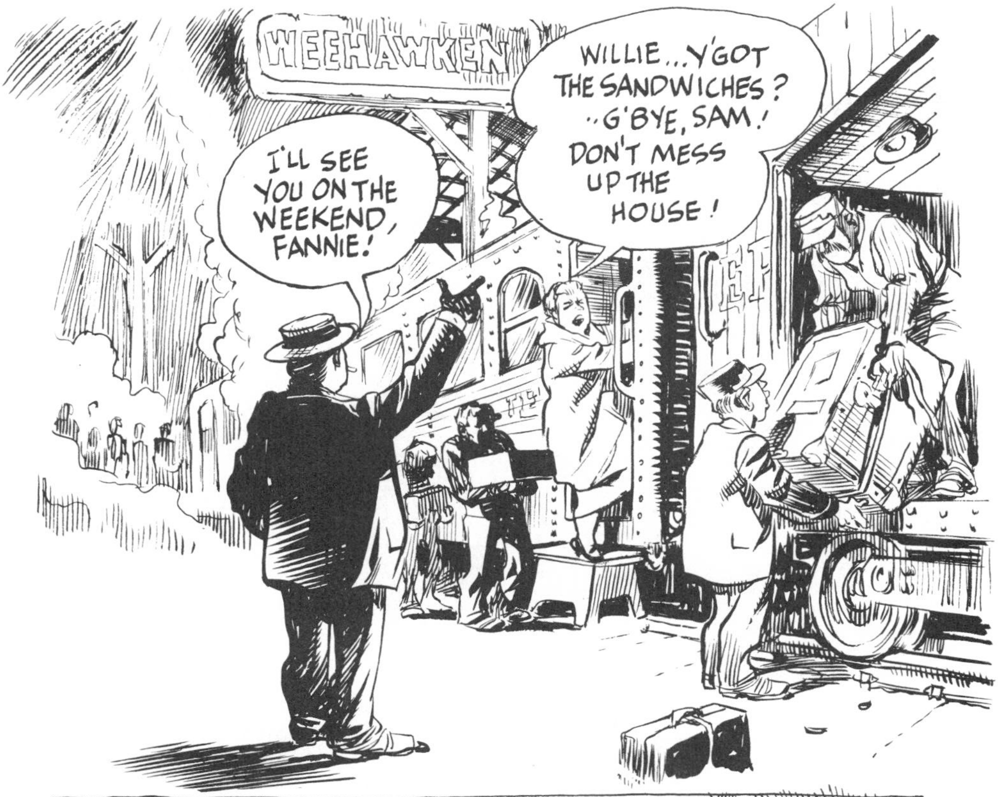
WEEHAWKEN
I'LL SEE YOU ON THE WEEKEND, FANNIE!
WILLIE...Y'GOT THE SANDWICHES? ..G'BYE, SAM! DON'T MESS UP THE HOUSE!

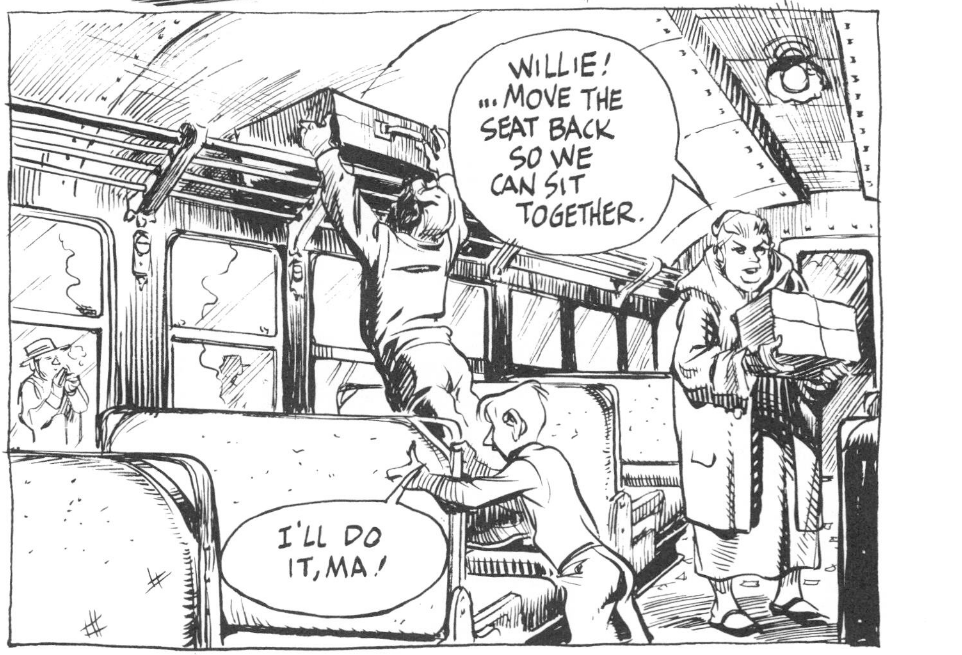
WILLIE! ...MOVE THE SEAT BACK SO WE CAN SIT TOGETHER.
I'LL DO IT, MA!

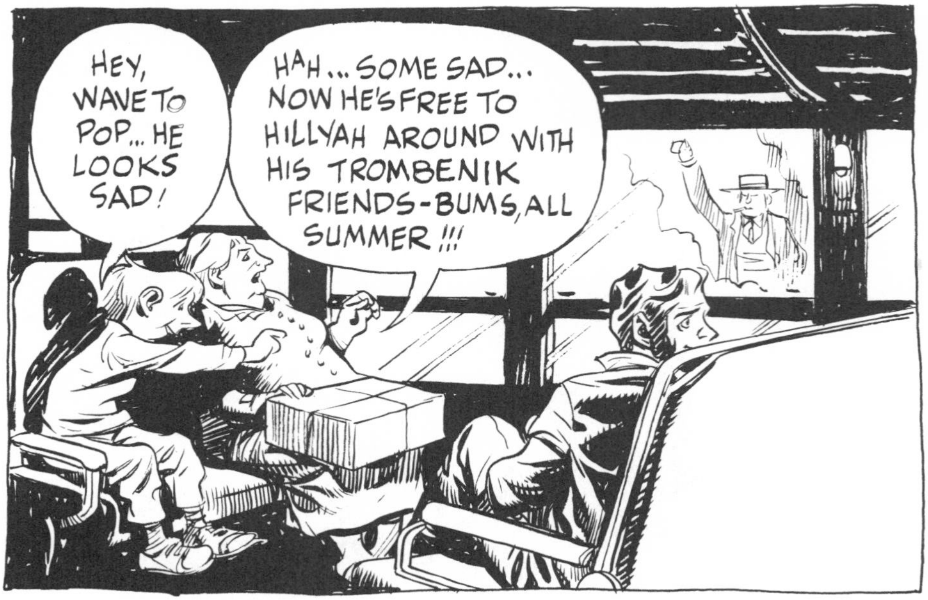
HEY, WAVE TO POP... HE LOOKS SAD!
HAH... SOME SAD... NOW HE'S FREE TO HILLYAH AROUND WITH HIS TROMBENIK FRIENDS-BUMS, ALL SUMMER!!!

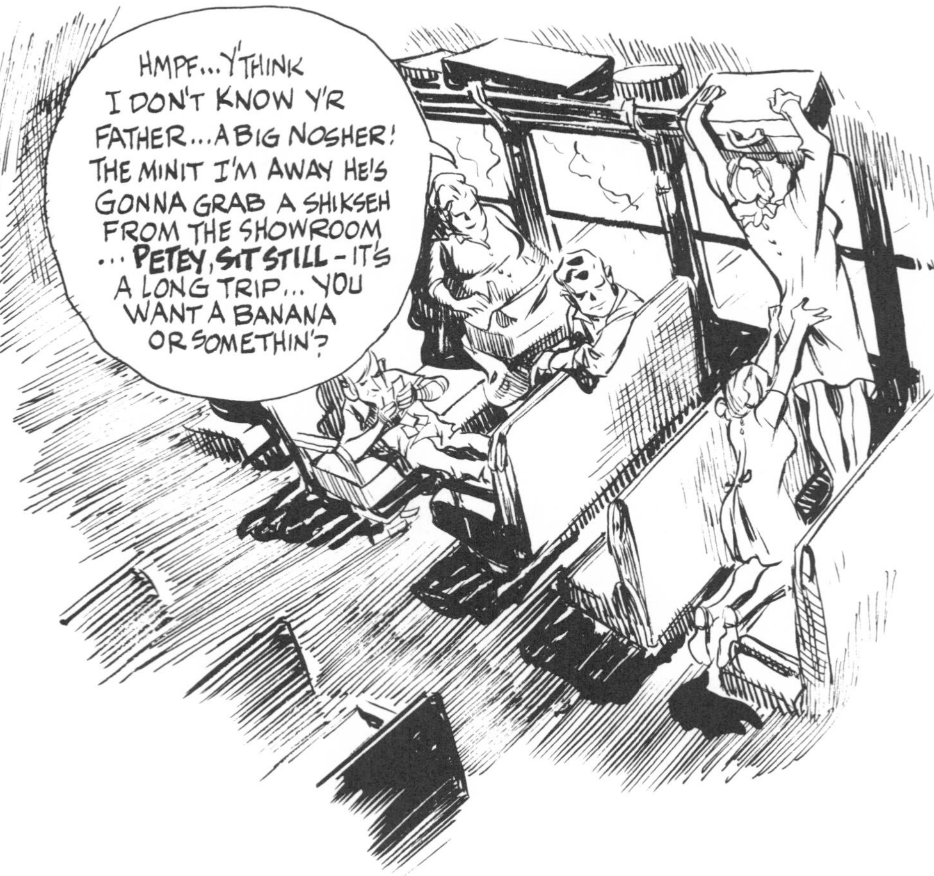
HMPF... Y'THINK I DON'T KNOW Y'R FATHER... A BIG NOSHER! THE MINIT I'M AWAY HE'S GONNA GRAB A SHIKSEH FROM THE SHOWROOM ... **PETEY, SIT STILL** - IT'S A LONG TRIP... YOU WANT A BANANA OR SOMETHIN'?

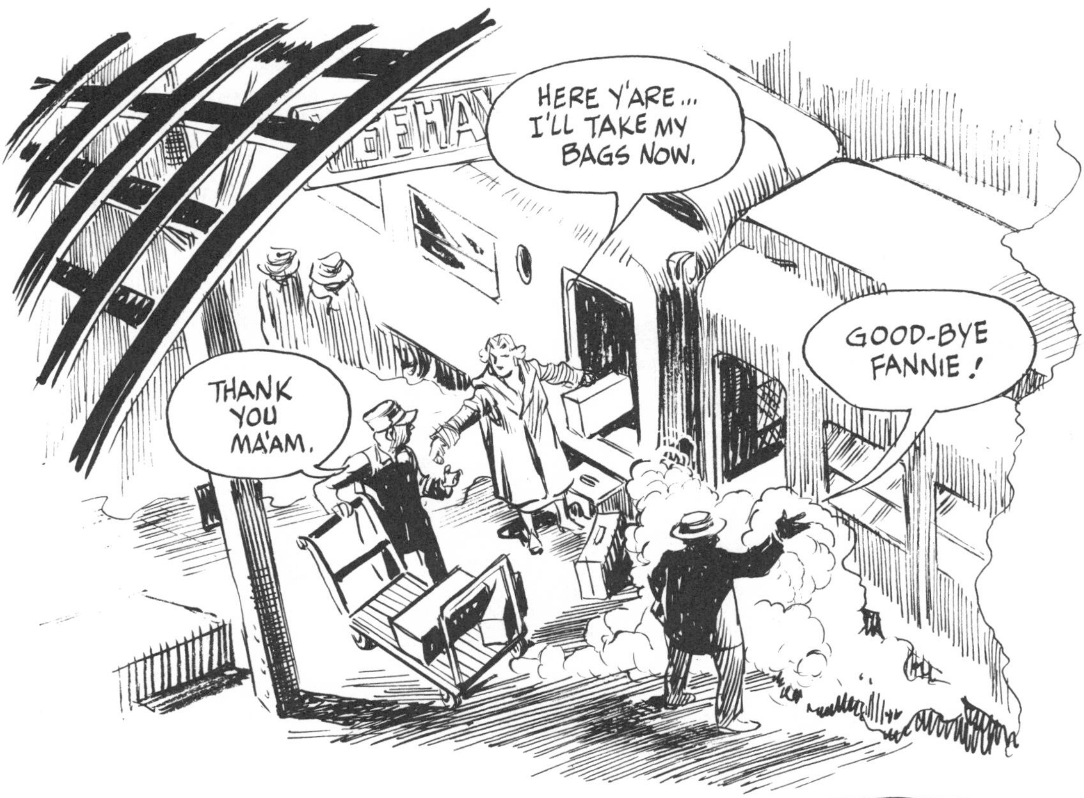
HERE Y'ARE...
I'LL TAKE MY
BAGS NOW.
THANK
YOU
MA'AM.
GOOD-BYE
FANNIE!

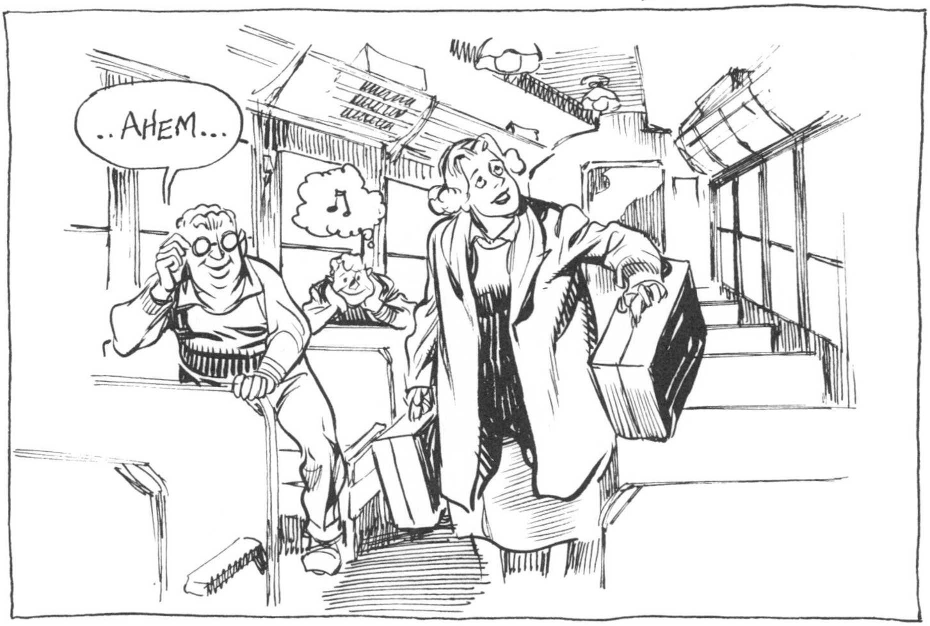
..AHEM...

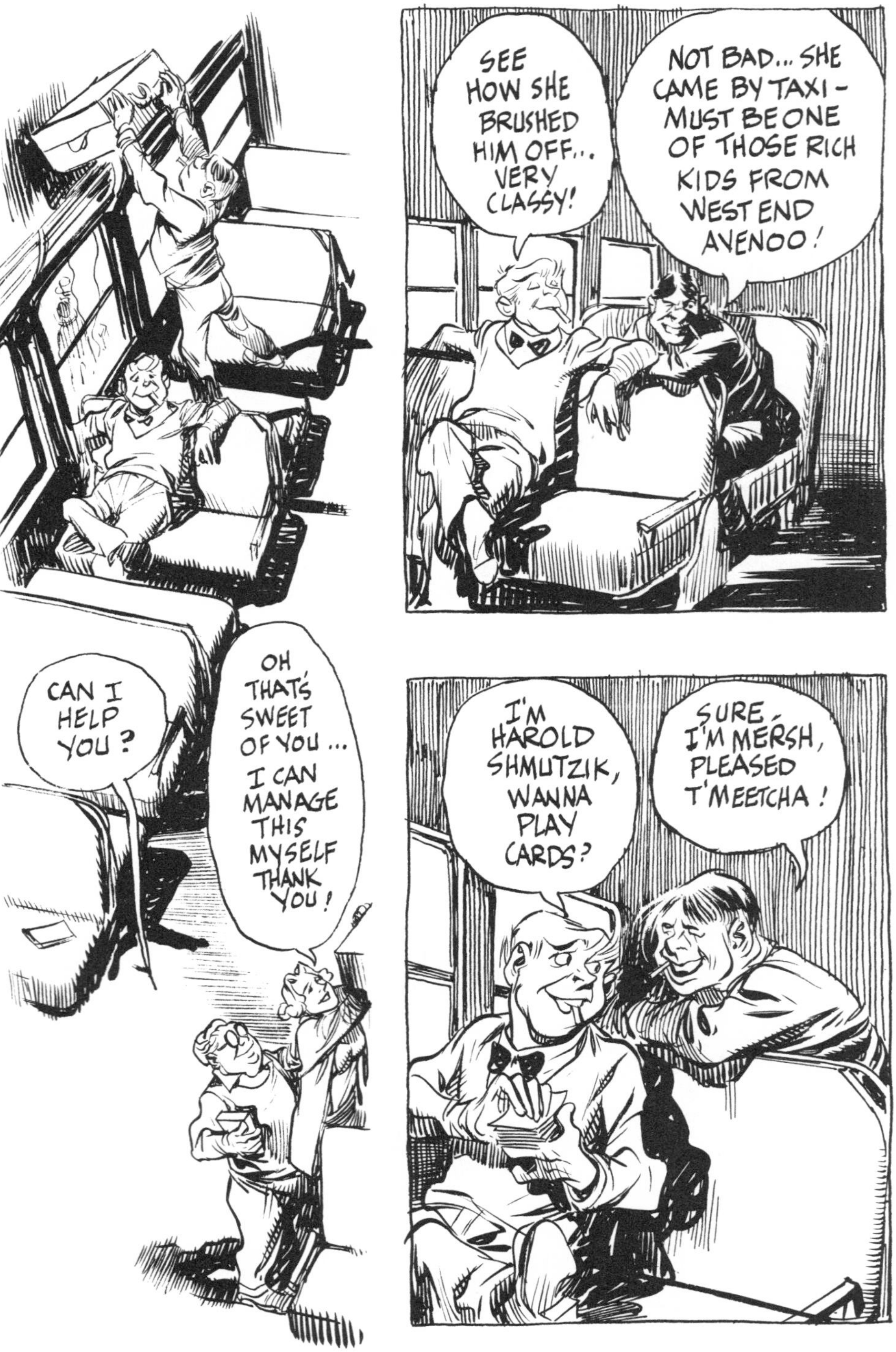
SEE HOW SHE BRUSHED HIM OFF... VERY CLASSY!
NOT BAD... SHE CAME BY TAXI - MUST BE ONE OF THOSE RICH KIDS FROM WEST END AVENOO!
CAN I HELP YOU?
OH THAT'S SWEET OF YOU... I CAN MANAGE THIS MYSELF THANK YOU!
I'M HAROLD SHMUTZIK, WANNA PLAY CARDS?
SURE, I'M MERSH, PLEASED T'MEETCHA!

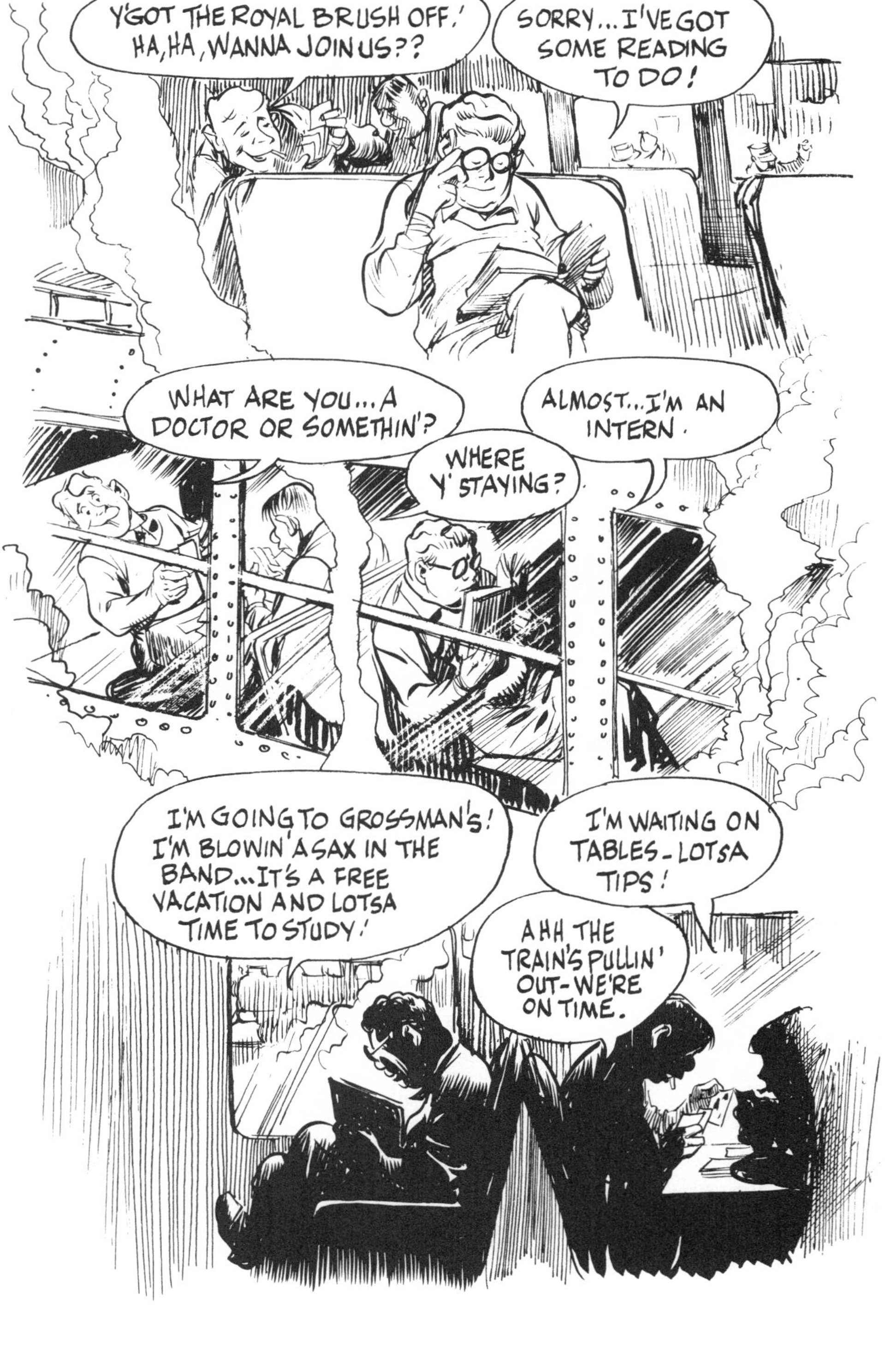
Y'GOT THE ROYAL BRUSH OFF.' HA, HA, WANNA JOIN US??
SORRY... I'VE GOT SOME READING TO DO!
WHAT ARE YOU... A DOCTOR OR SOMETHIN'?
ALMOST... I'M AN INTERN.
WHERE Y' STAYING?
I'M GOING TO GROSSMAN'S! I'M BLOWIN' A SAX IN THE BAND... IT'S A FREE VACATION AND LOTSA TIME TO STUDY!
I'M WAITING ON TABLES - LOTSA TIPS!
AHH THE TRAIN'S PULLIN' OUT - WE'RE ON TIME.

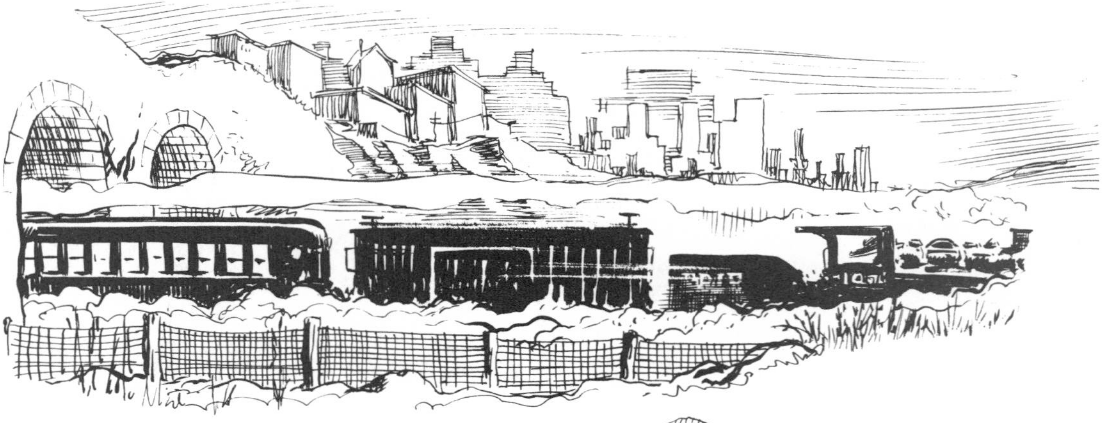

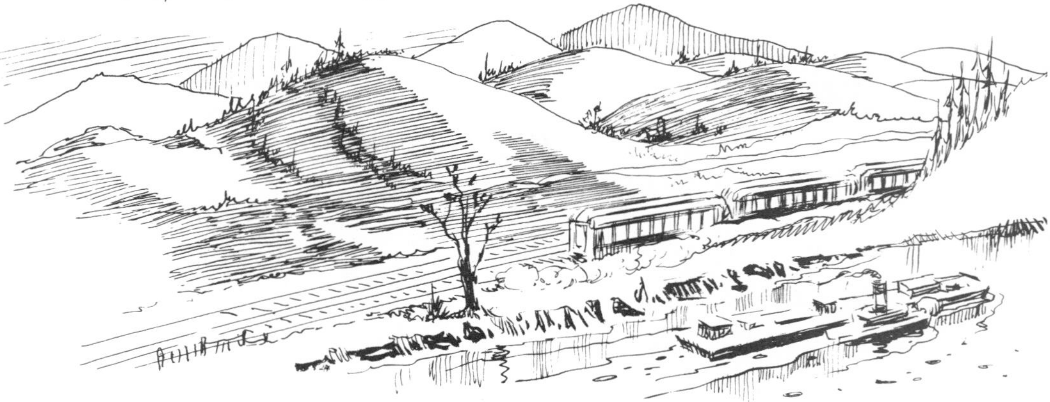

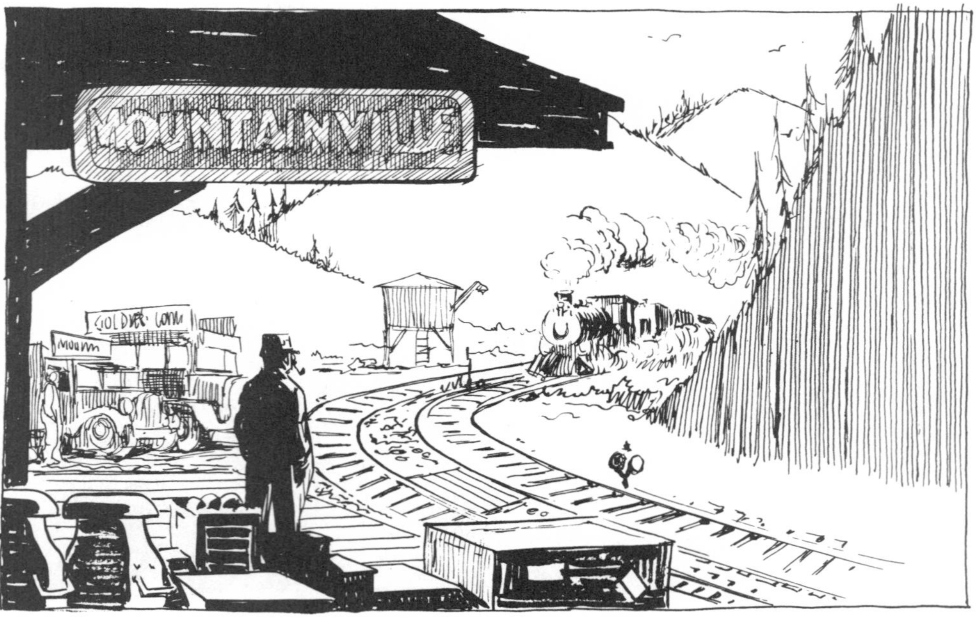

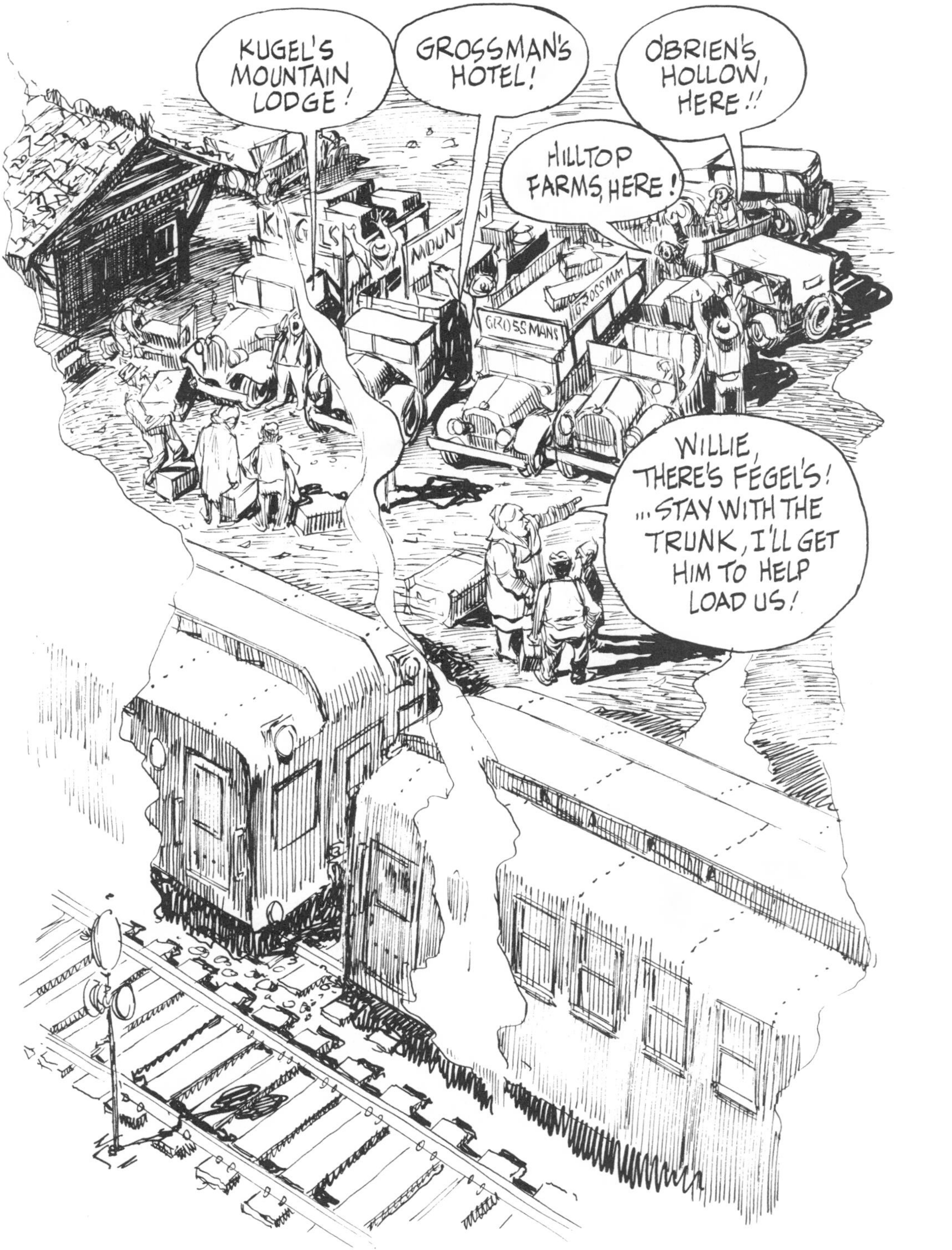
KUGEL'S MOUNTAIN LODGE!
GROSSMAN'S HOTEL!
O'BRIEN'S HOLLOW, HERE!!
HILLTOP FARMS, HERE!
GROSSMAN'S
GROSSMAN
WILLIE, THERE'S FEGEL'S! ...STAY WITH THE TRUNK, I'LL GET HIM TO HELP LOAD US!

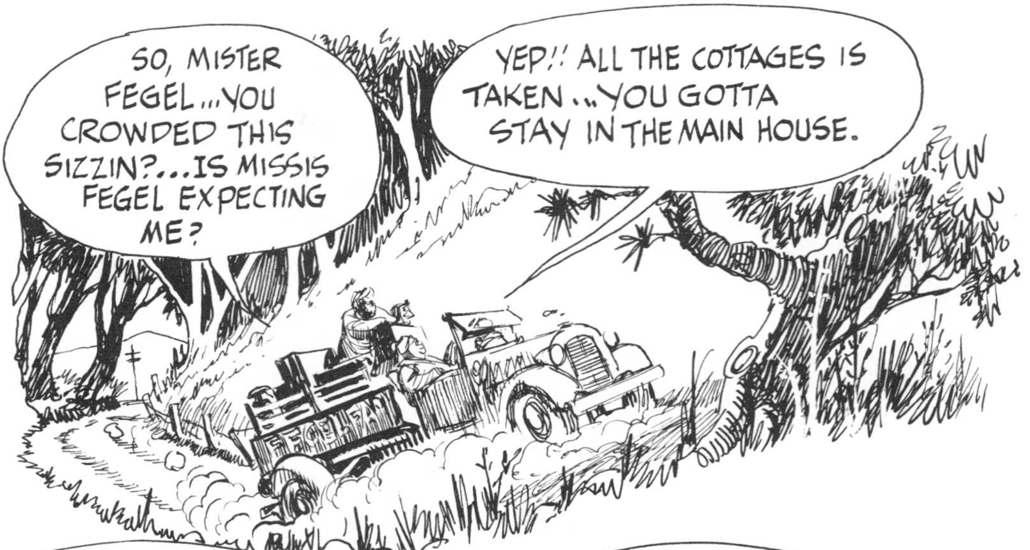
SO, MISTER FEGEL...YOU CROWDED THIS SIZZIN?...IS MISSIS FEGEL EXPECTING ME?
YEP!! ALL THE COTTAGES IS TAKEN...YOU GOTTA STAY IN THE MAIN HOUSE.

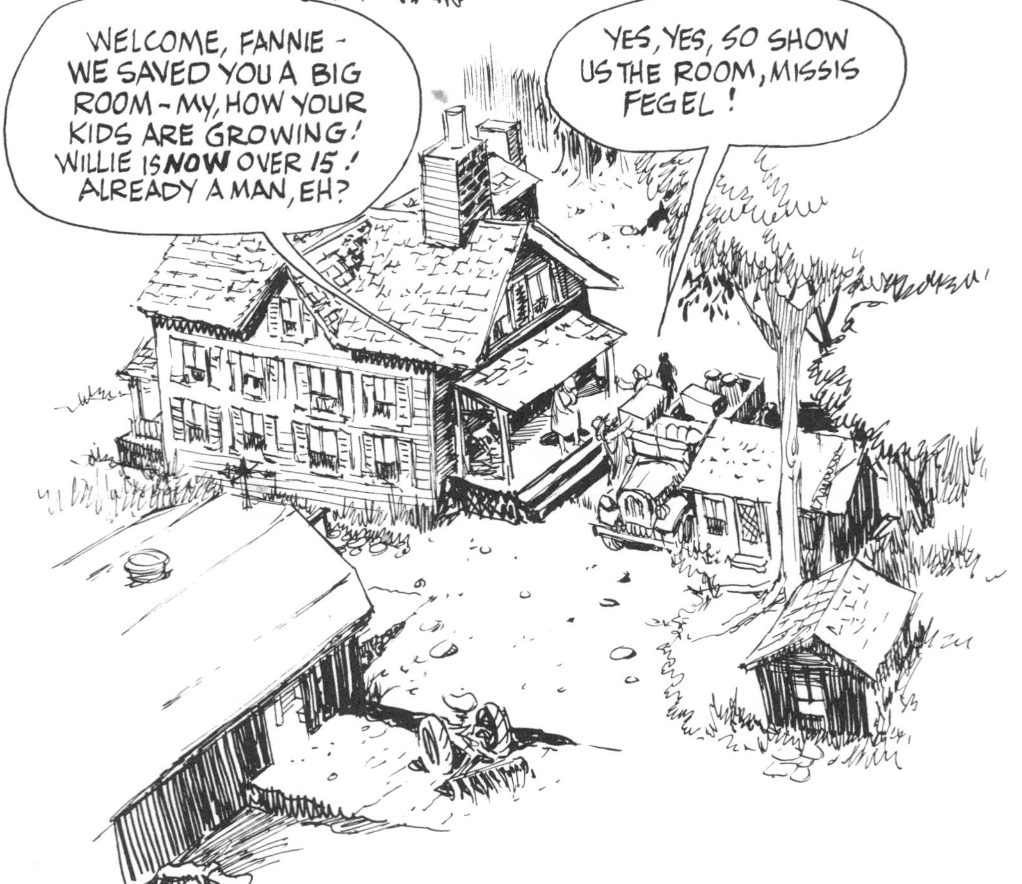
WELCOME, FANNIE - WE SAVED YOU A BIG ROOM - MY, HOW YOUR KIDS ARE GROWING! WILLIE IS **NOW** OVER 15! ALREADY A MAN, EH?
YES, YES, SO SHOW US THE ROOM, MISSIS FEGEL!

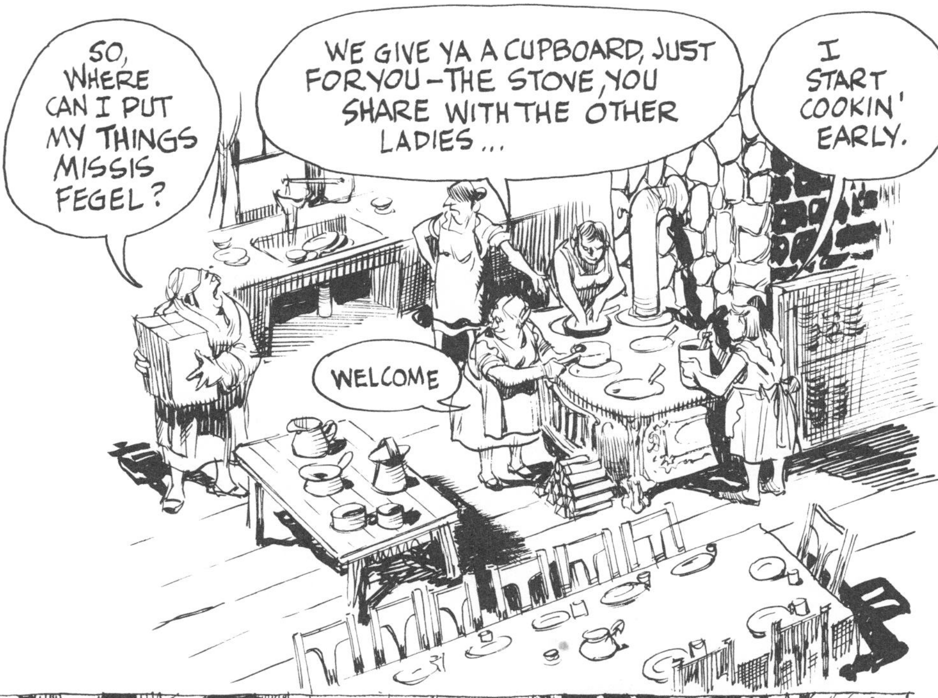
SO, WHERE CAN I PUT MY THINGS MISSIS FEGEL?
WE GIVE YA A CUPBOARD, JUST FOR YOU – THE STOVE, YOU SHARE WITH THE OTHER LADIES...
I START COOKIN' EARLY.
WELCOME

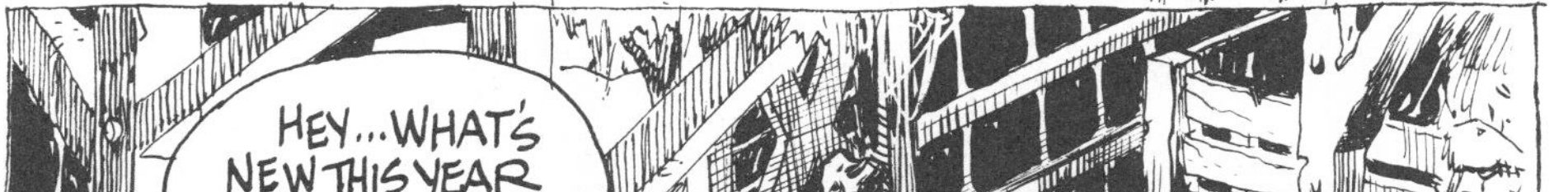
HEY...WHAT'S NEW THIS YEAR AROUND HERE MR. FEGEL??
WAL...THIS YEAR WE GOT ENTERTAINMENT ...I BUILT A CASINO OUTTA THE OLD BARN...Y'CAN DANCE WITH THE OLD LADIES..HAHA...SO, WE AIN'T GROSSMAN'S!

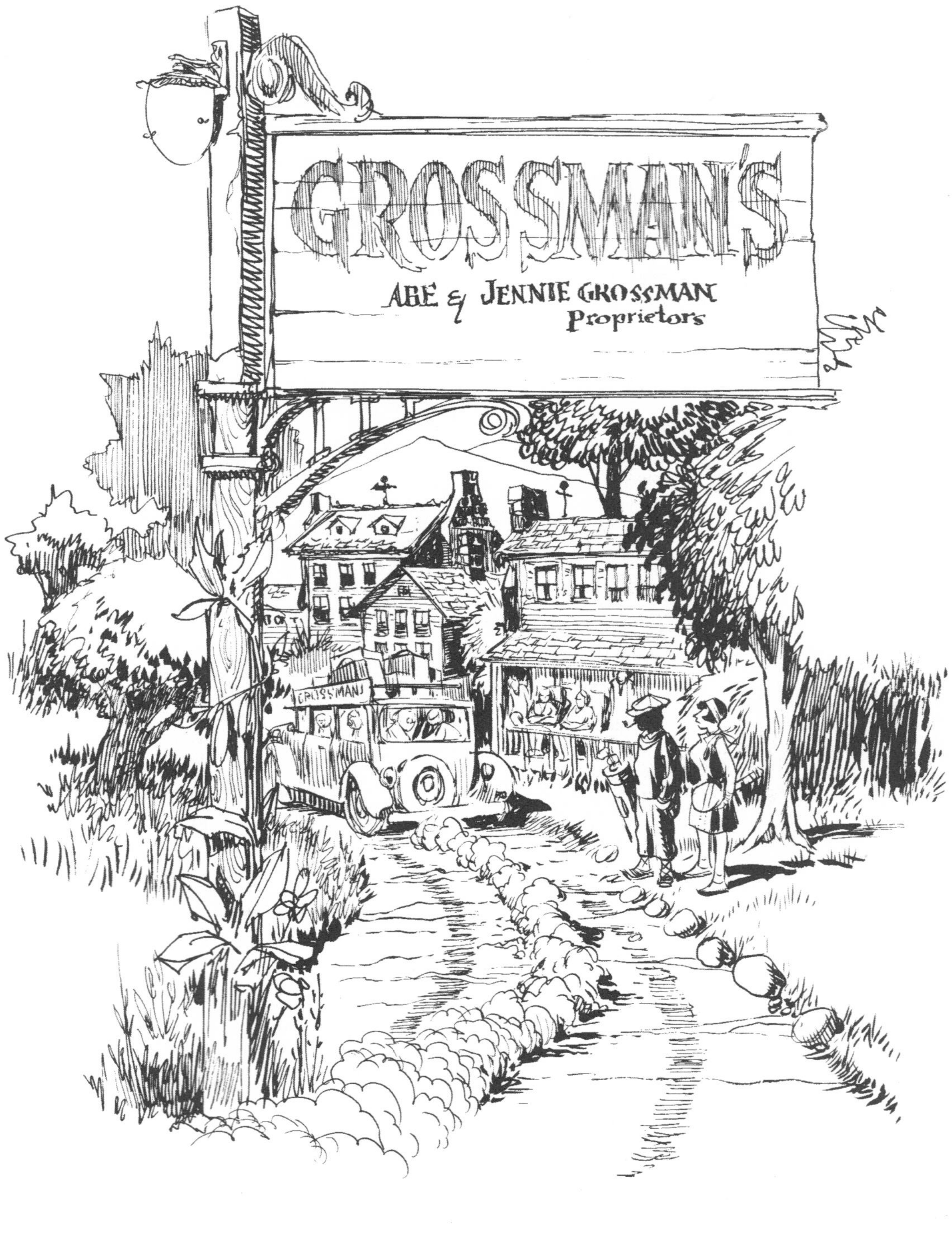

GROSSMAN'S
ABE & JENNIE GROSSMAN
Proprietors
GROSSMAN'S

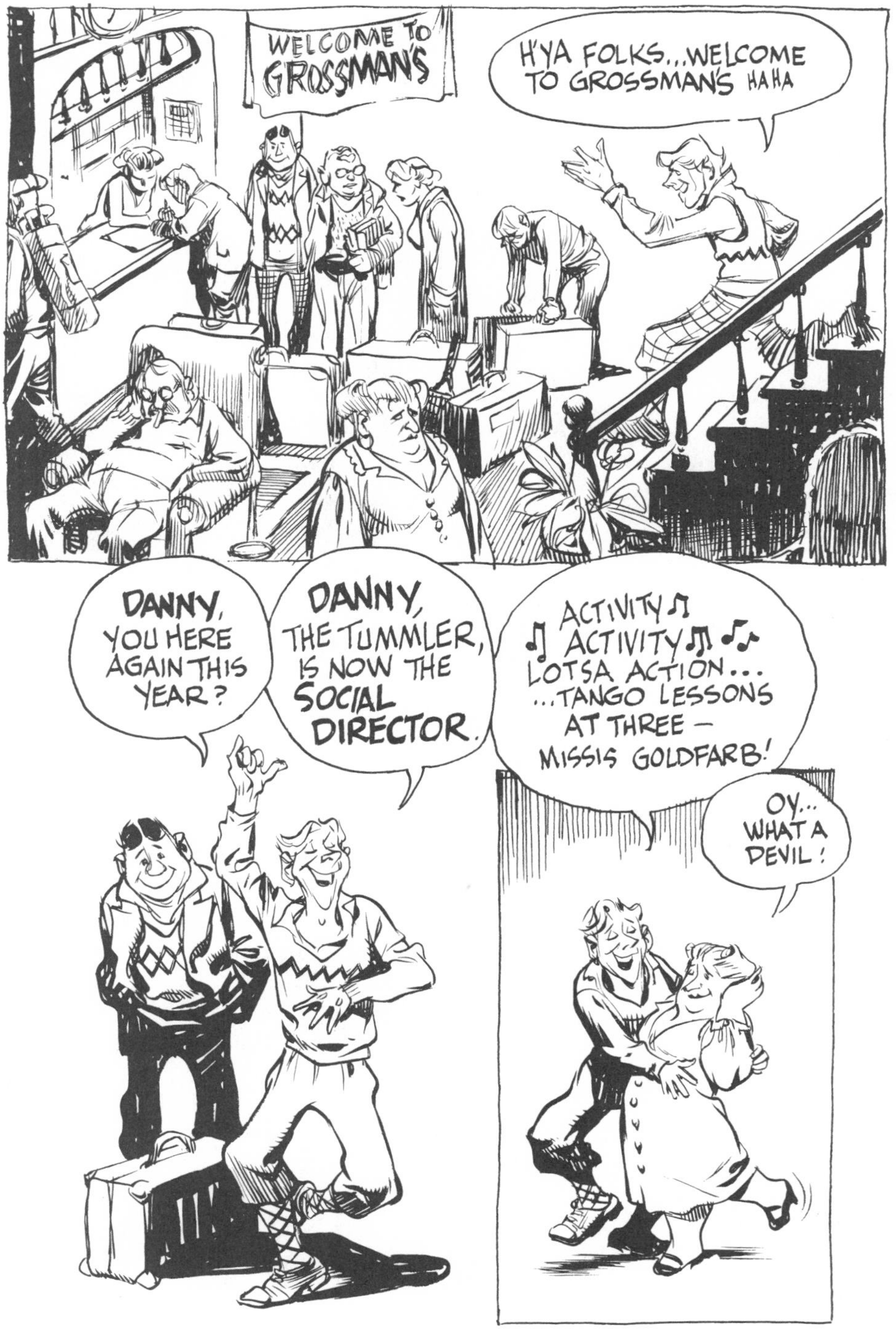
WELCOME TO GROSSMAN'S
H'YA FOLKS...WELCOME TO GROSSMAN'S HAHA
DANNY, YOU HERE AGAIN THIS YEAR?
DANNY, THE TUMMLER, IS NOW THE SOCIAL DIRECTOR.
ACTIVITY ♫ ACTIVITY ♫ LOTSA ACTION... ...TANGO LESSONS AT THREE – MISSIS GOLDFARB!
OY... WHAT A DEVIL!

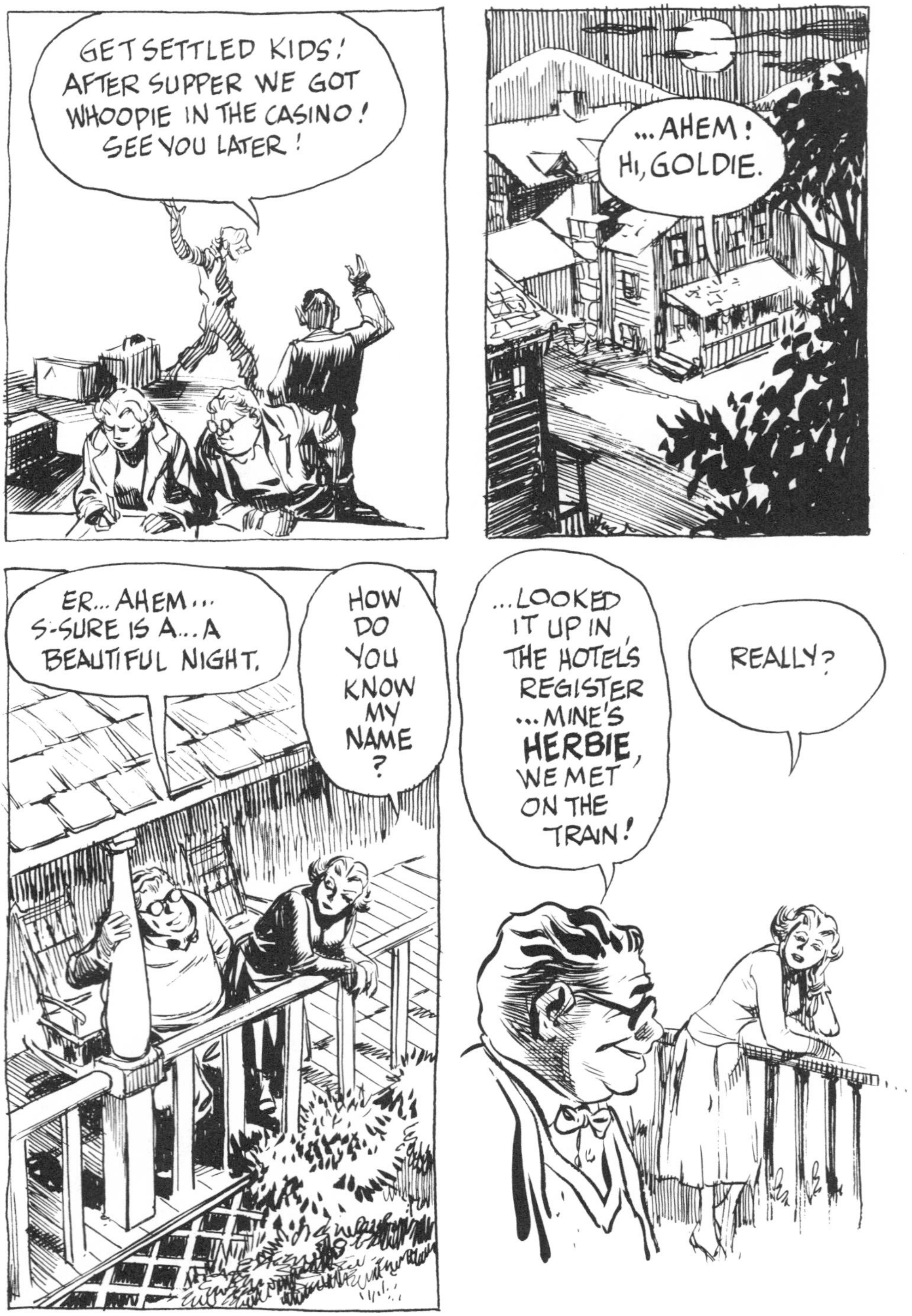
GET SETTLED KIDS! AFTER SUPPER WE GOT WHOOPIE IN THE CASINO! SEE YOU LATER!
...AHEM! HI, GOLDIE.
ER...AHEM... S-SURE IS A...A BEAUTIFUL NIGHT.
HOW DO YOU KNOW MY NAME?
...LOOKED IT UP IN THE HOTEL'S REGISTER ...MINE'S HERBIE, WE MET ON THE TRAIN!
REALLY?

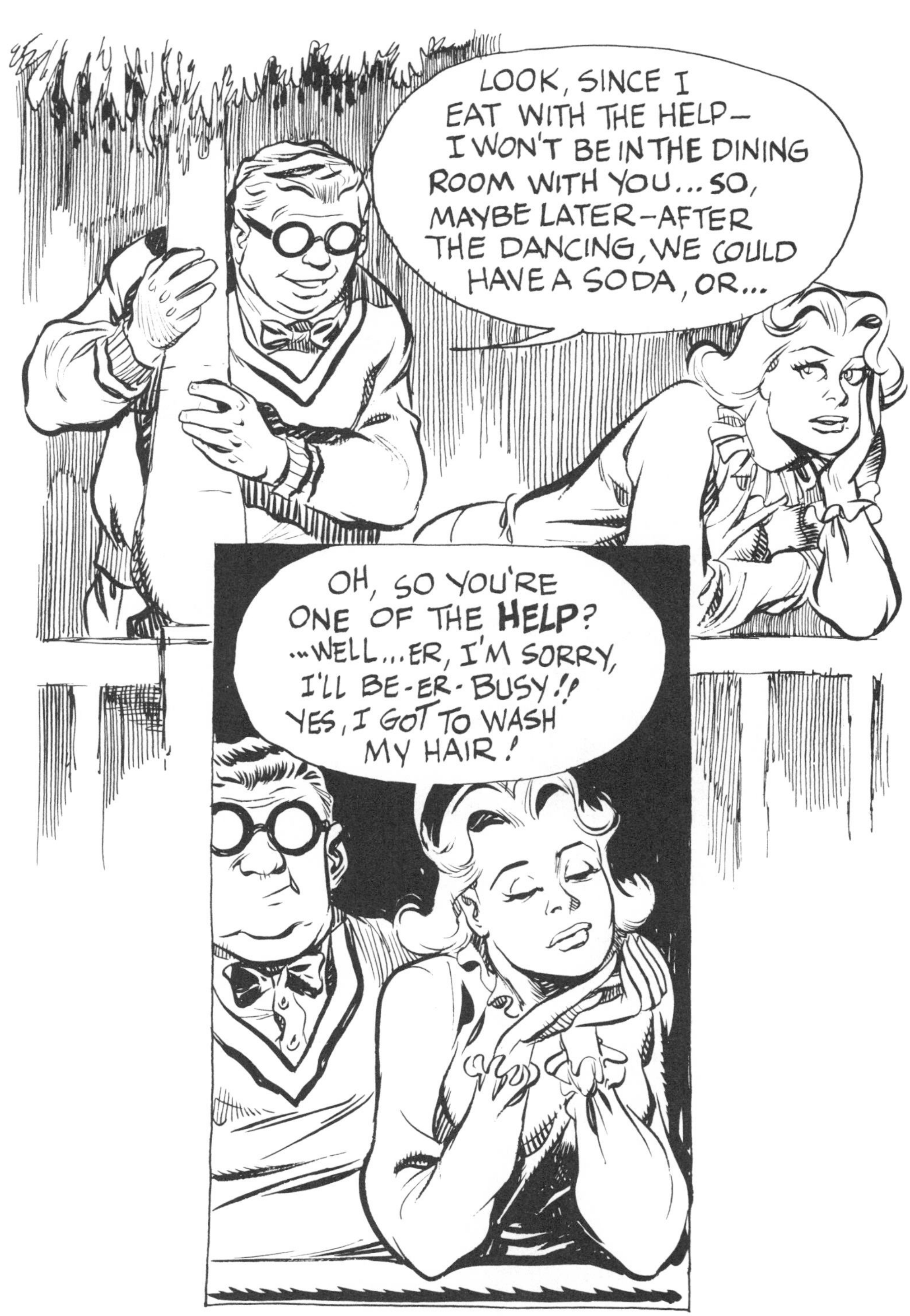
LOOK, SINCE I EAT WITH THE HELP— I WON'T BE IN THE DINING ROOM WITH YOU... SO, MAYBE LATER—AFTER THE DANCING, WE COULD HAVE A SODA, OR...
OH, SO YOU'RE ONE OF THE HELP? ...WELL... ER, I'M SORRY, I'LL BE-ER-BUSY!! YES, I GOT TO WASH MY HAIR!

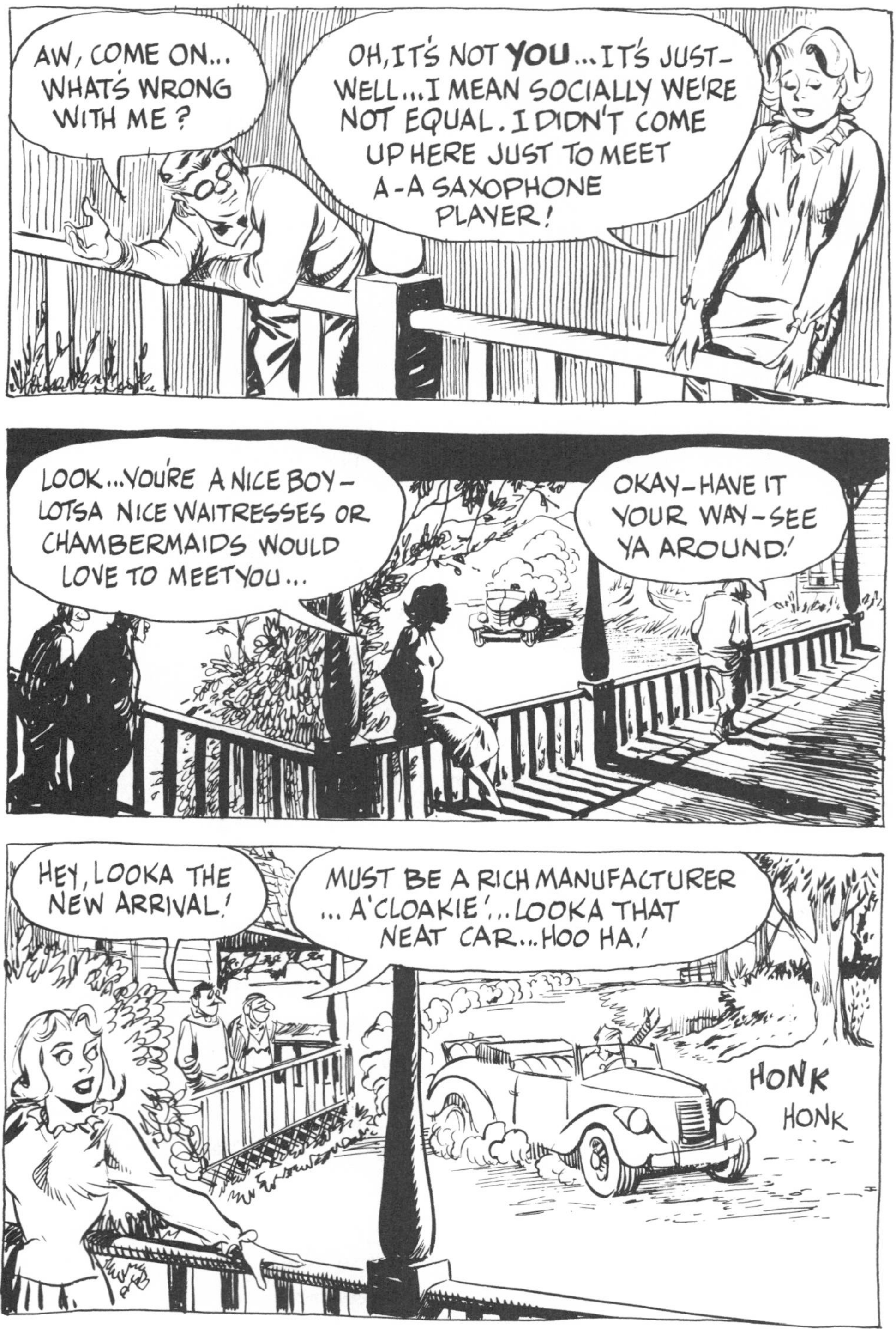
AW, COME ON... WHAT'S WRONG WITH ME ?
OH, IT'S NOT **YOU**... IT'S JUST- WELL... I MEAN SOCIALLY WE'RE NOT EQUAL. I DIDN'T COME UP HERE JUST TO MEET A-A SAXOPHONE PLAYER!
LOOK... YOU'RE A NICE BOY- LOTSA NICE WAITRESSES OR CHAMBERMAIDS WOULD LOVE TO MEET YOU...
OKAY-HAVE IT YOUR WAY-SEE YA AROUND!
HEY, LOOKA THE NEW ARRIVAL!
MUST BE A RICH MANUFACTURER ... A 'CLOAKIE'... LOOKA THAT NEAT CAR... HOO HA!
HONK
HONK

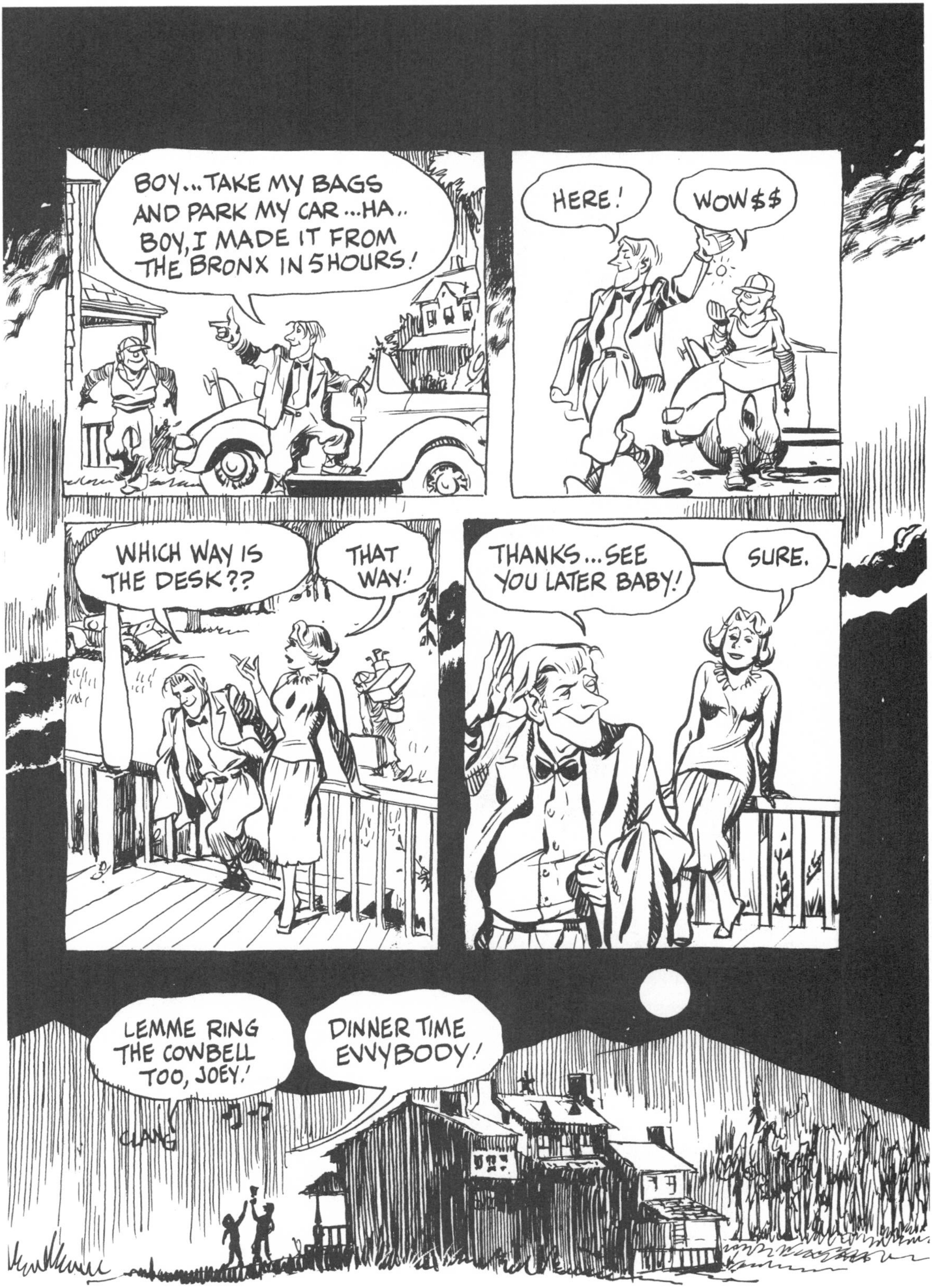
BOY... TAKE MY BAGS AND PARK MY CAR ...HA.. BOY, I MADE IT FROM THE BRONX IN 5 HOURS!
HERE!
WOW$$
WHICH WAY IS THE DESK??
THAT WAY!
THANKS... SEE YOU LATER BABY!
SURE.
LEMME RING THE COWBELL TOO, JOEY!
DINNER TIME EVVYBODY!
CLANG

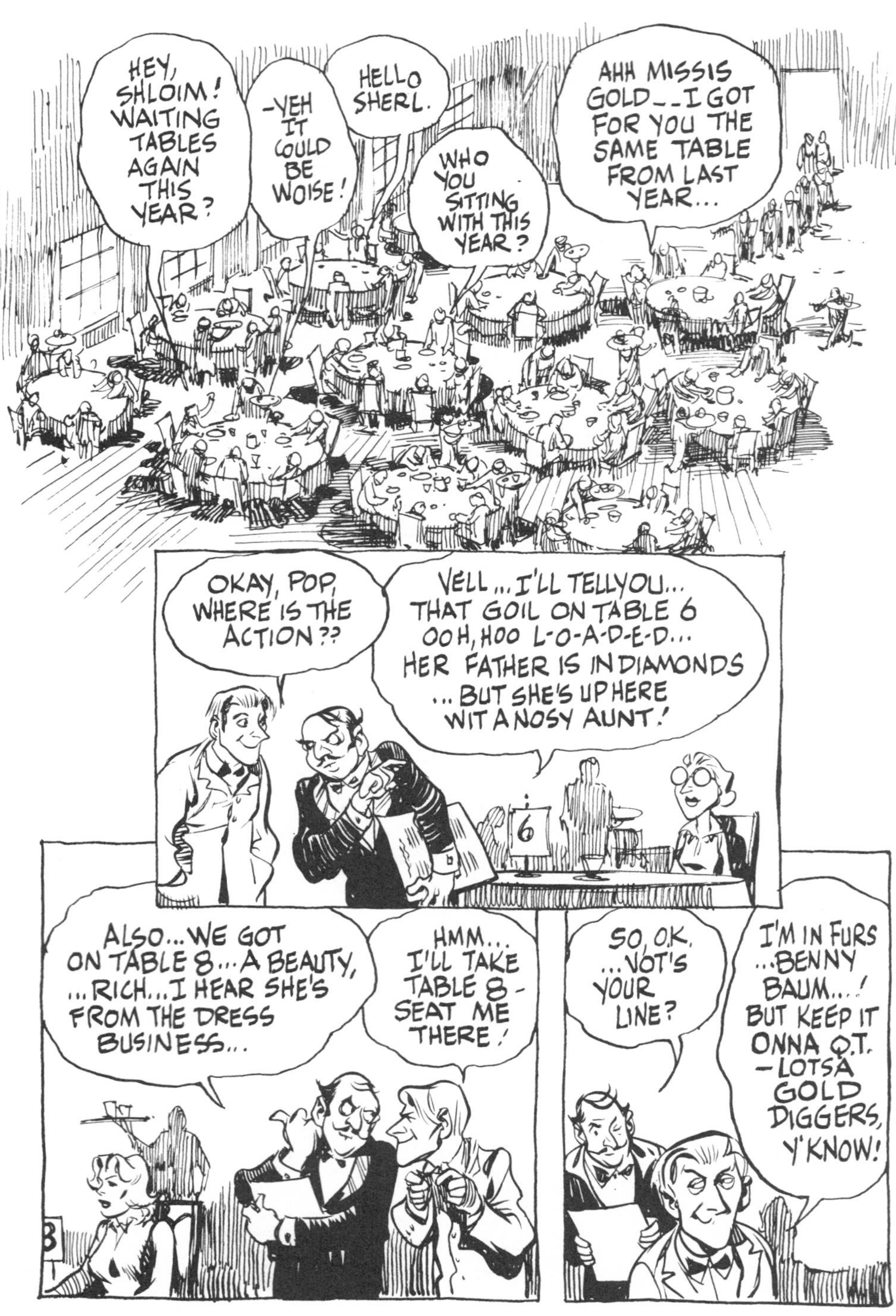
HEY, SHLOIM! WAITING TABLES AGAIN THIS YEAR?
-YEH IT COULD BE WOISE!
HELLO SHERL.
WHO YOU SITTING WITH THIS YEAR?
AHH MISSIS GOLD--I GOT FOR YOU THE SAME TABLE FROM LAST YEAR...
OKAY, POP, WHERE IS THE ACTION??
VELL... I'LL TELLYOU... THAT GOIL ON TABLE 6 OOH, HOO L-O-A-D-E-D... HER FATHER IS IN DIAMONDS ...BUT SHE'S UP HERE WIT A NOSY AUNT!
6
ALSO... WE GOT ON TABLE 8... A BEAUTY, ...RICH... I HEAR SHE'S FROM THE DRESS BUSINESS...
HMM... I'LL TAKE TABLE 8 - SEAT ME THERE!
8
SO, O.K. ...VOT'S YOUR LINE?
I'M IN FURS ...BENNY BAUM...! BUT KEEP IT ONNA Q.T. -LOTSA GOLD DIGGERS, Y'KNOW!

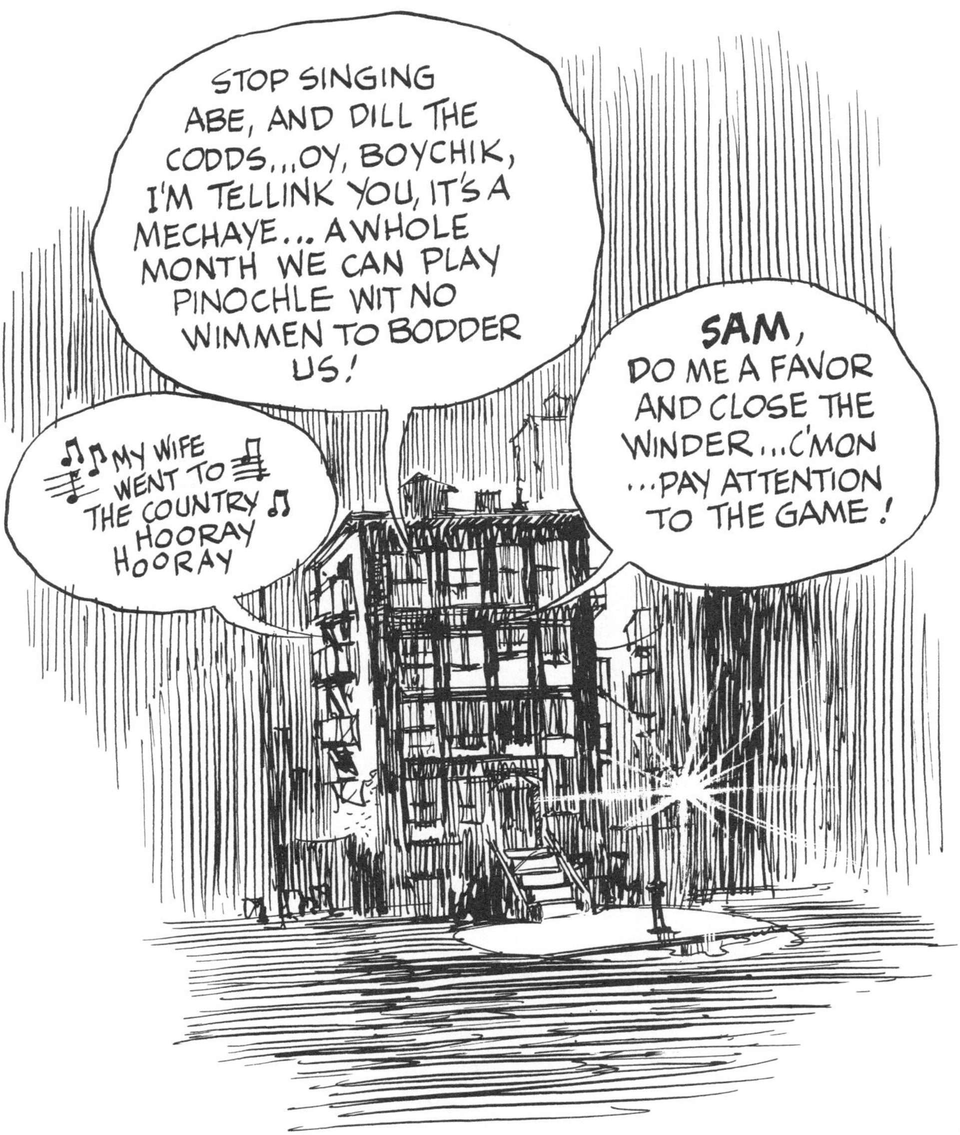
STOP SINGING ABE, AND DILL THE CODDS,,,OY, BOYCHIK, I'M TELLINK YOU, IT'S A MECHAYE... A WHOLE MONTH WE CAN PLAY PINOCHLE WIT NO WIMMEN TO BODDER US!
MY WIFE WENT TO THE COUNTRY HOORAY HOORAY
SAM, DO ME A FAVOR AND CLOSE THE WINDER...C'MON ...PAY ATTENTION TO THE GAME!

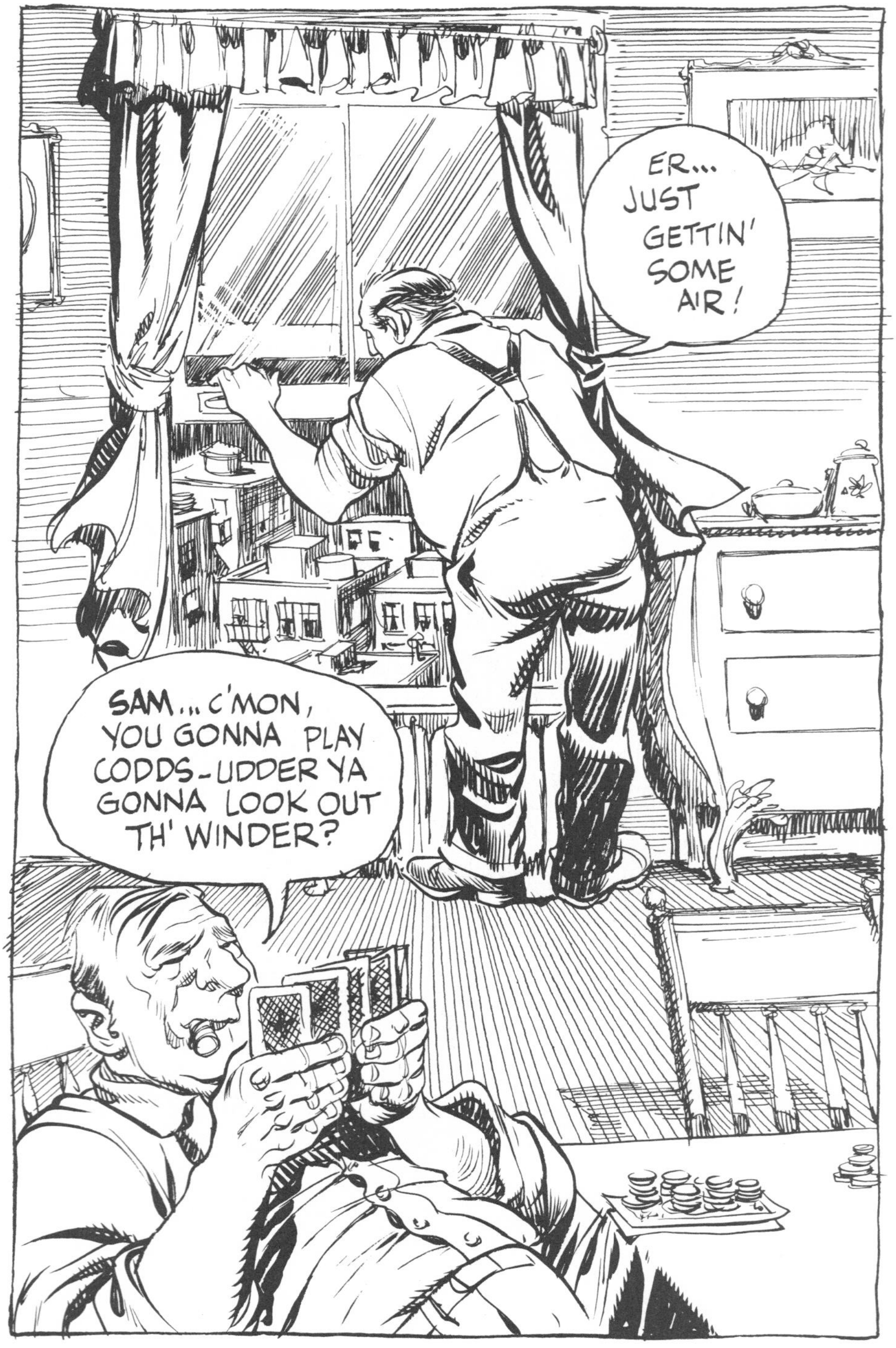
ER... JUST GETTIN' SOME AIR!
SAM... C'MON, YOU GONNA PLAY CODDS-UDDER YA GONNA LOOK OUT TH' WINDER?

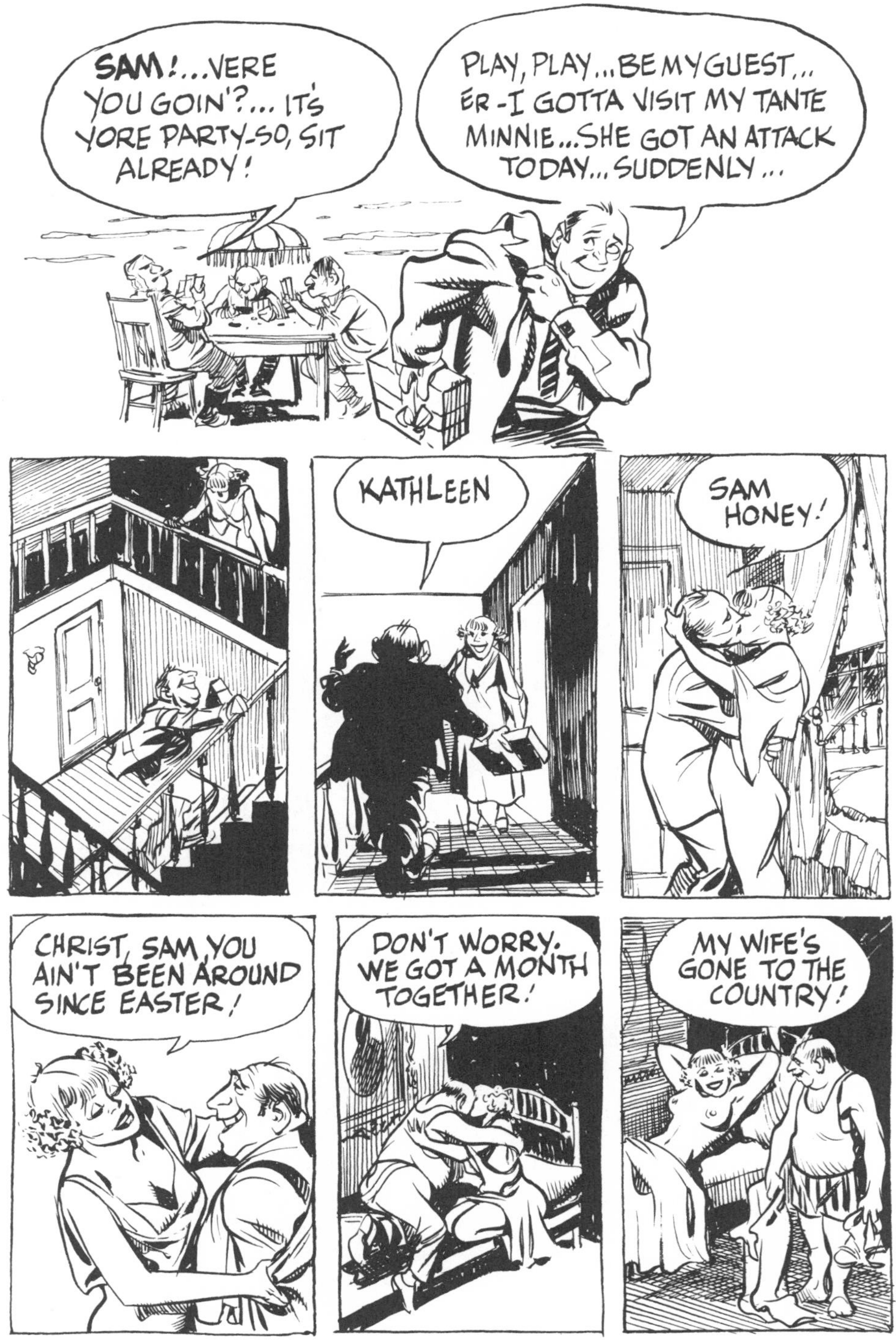
SAM!...VERE YOU GOIN'?... IT'S YORE PARTY-SO, SIT ALREADY!
PLAY, PLAY...BE MY GUEST... ER-I GOTTA VISIT MY TANTE MINNIE...SHE GOT AN ATTACK TODAY... SUDDENLY...
KATHLEEN
SAM HONEY!
CHRIST, SAM YOU AIN'T BEEN AROUND SINCE EASTER!
DON'T WORRY. WE GOT A MONTH TOGETHER!
MY WIFE'S GONE TO THE COUNTRY!

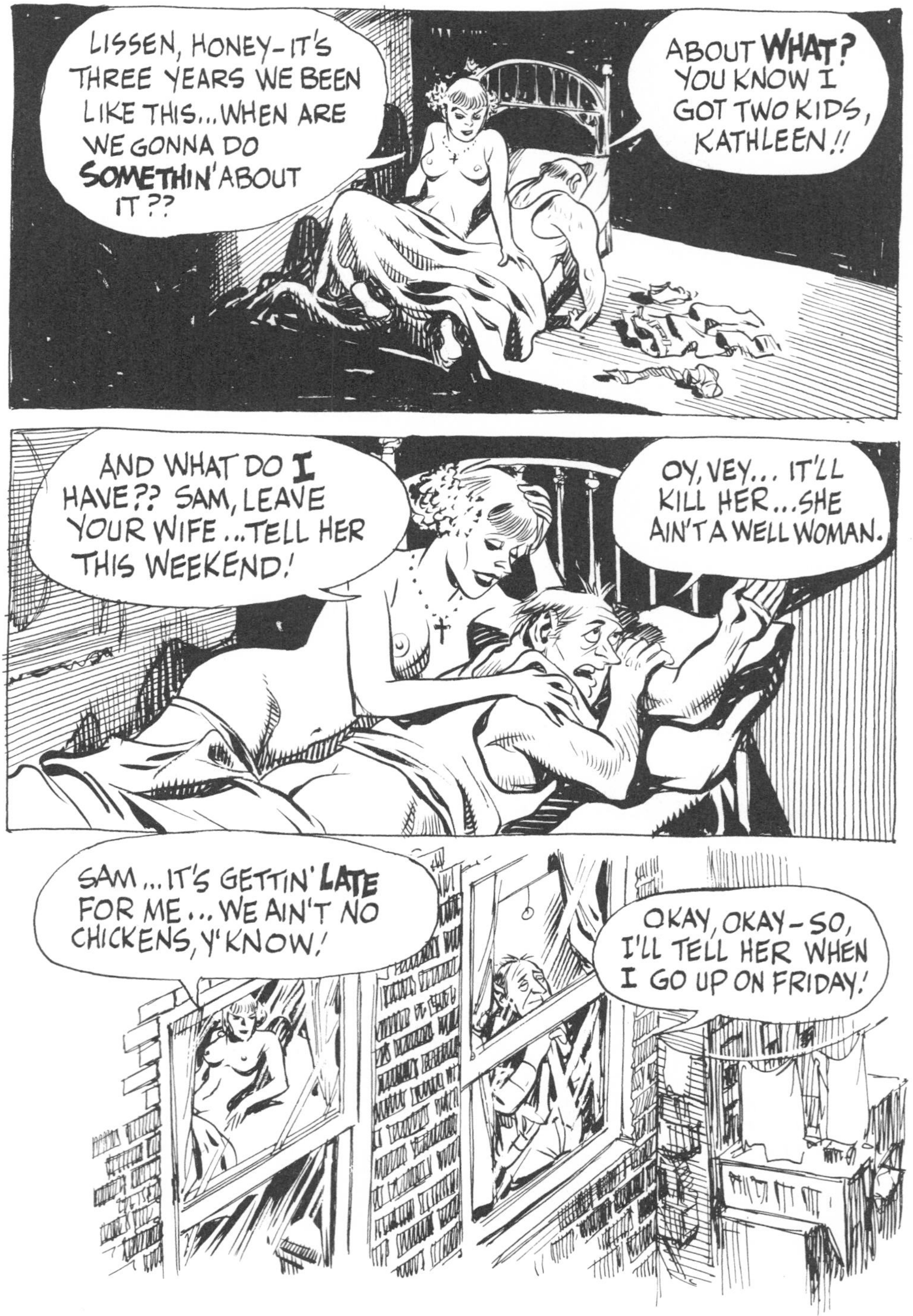
LISSEN, HONEY-IT'S THREE YEARS WE BEEN LIKE THIS...WHEN ARE WE GONNA DO SOMETHIN' ABOUT IT??
ABOUT WHAT? YOU KNOW I GOT TWO KIDS, KATHLEEN!!
AND WHAT DO I HAVE?? SAM, LEAVE YOUR WIFE...TELL HER THIS WEEKEND!
OY, VEY... IT'LL KILL HER...SHE AIN'T A WELL WOMAN.
SAM...IT'S GETTIN' LATE FOR ME...WE AIN'T NO CHICKENS, Y'KNOW!
OKAY, OKAY-SO, I'LL TELL HER WHEN I GO UP ON FRIDAY!

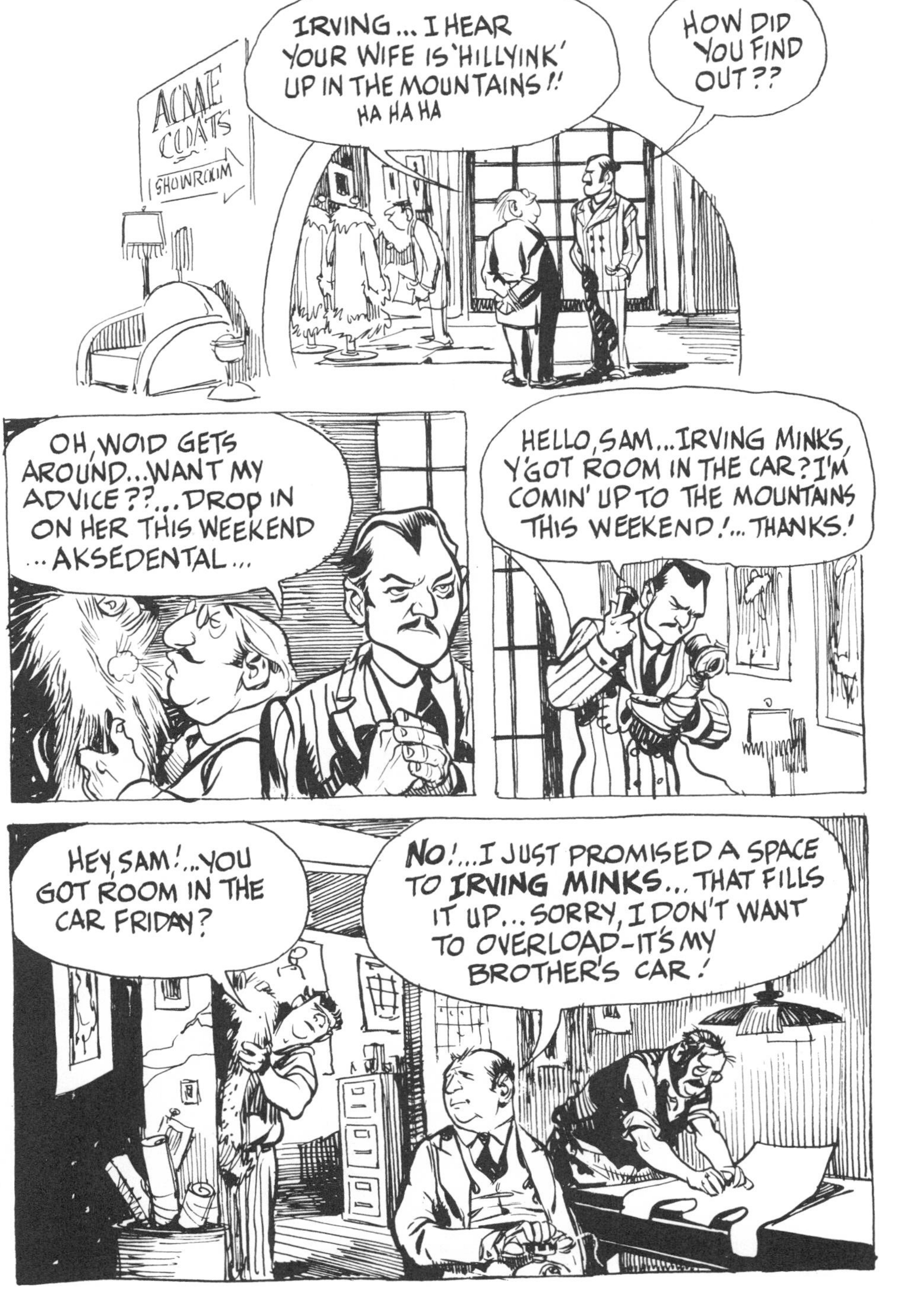

ACME COATS
SHOWROOM
IRVING... I HEAR YOUR WIFE IS 'HILLYINK' UP IN THE MOUNTAINS!! HA HA HA
HOW DID YOU FIND OUT??
OH, WOID GETS AROUND...WANT MY ADVICE??...DROP IN ON HER THIS WEEKEND ...AKSEDENTAL...
HELLO, SAM...IRVING MINKS, Y'GOT ROOM IN THE CAR? I'M COMIN' UP TO THE MOUNTAINS THIS WEEKEND!...THANKS!
HEY, SAM!...YOU GOT ROOM IN THE CAR FRIDAY?
NO!...I JUST PROMISED A SPACE TO IRVING MINKS...THAT FILLS IT UP...SORRY, I DON'T WANT TO OVERLOAD-IT'S MY BROTHER'S CAR!

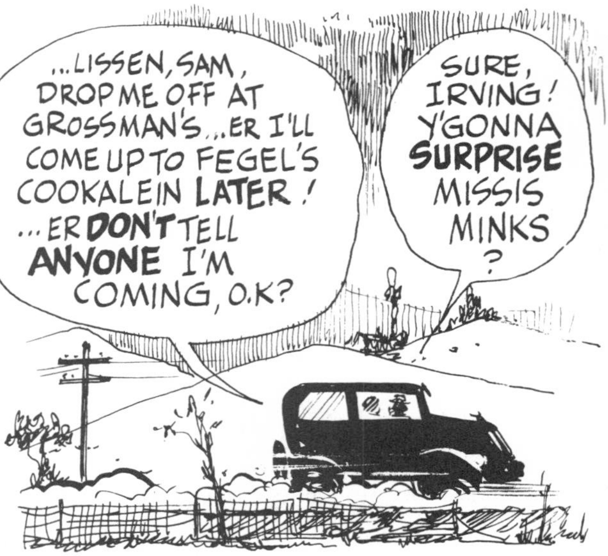
...LISSEN, SAM, DROP ME OFF AT GROSSMAN'S...ER I'LL COME UP TO FEGEL'S COOKALEIN **LATER**! ...ER **DON'T** TELL **ANYONE** I'M COMING, O.K?
SURE, IRVING! Y'GONNA **SURPRISE** MISSIS MINKS?

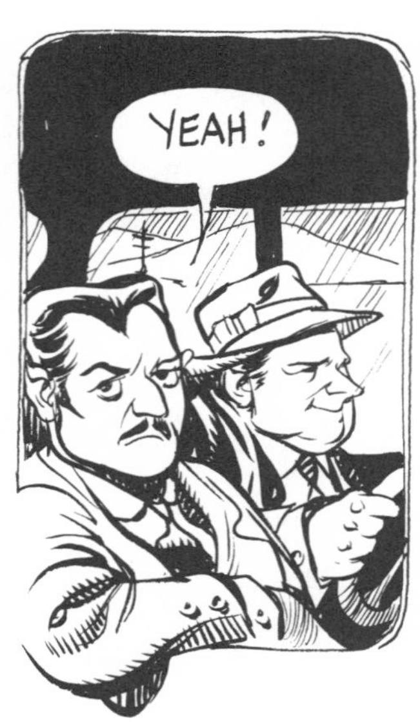
YEAH!

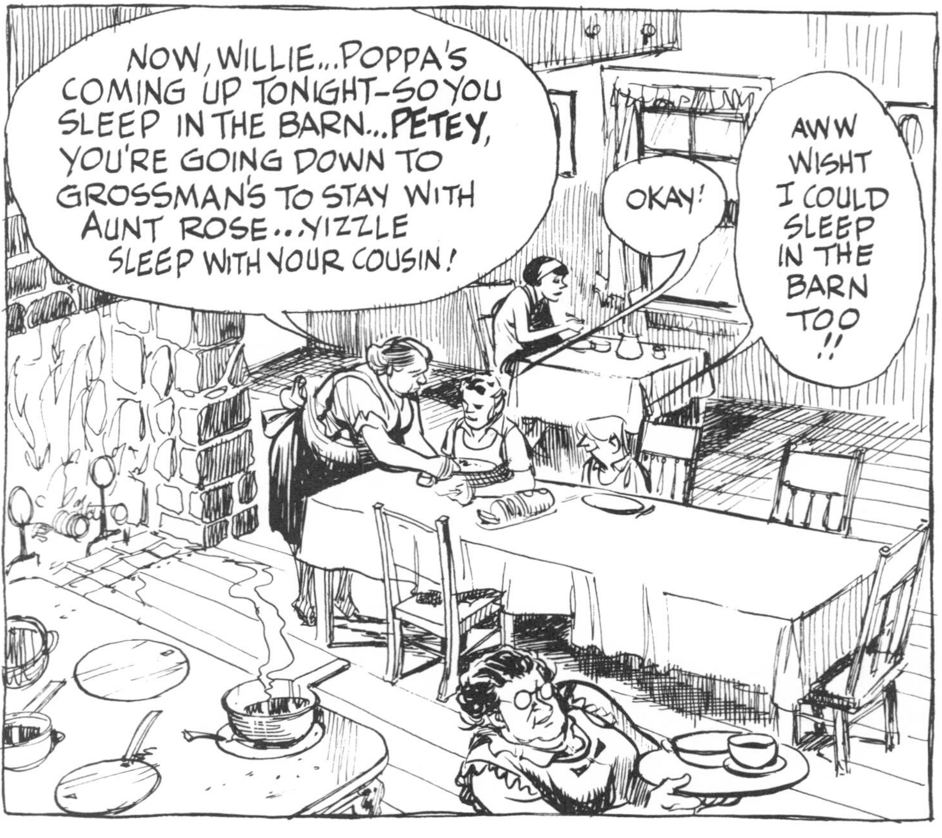
NOW, WILLIE...POPPA'S COMING UP TONIGHT-SO YOU SLEEP IN THE BARN...**PETEY**, YOU'RE GOING DOWN TO GROSSMAN'S TO STAY WITH AUNT ROSE...YIZZLE SLEEP WITH YOUR COUSIN!
OKAY!
AWW WISHT I COULD SLEEP IN THE BARN TOO!!

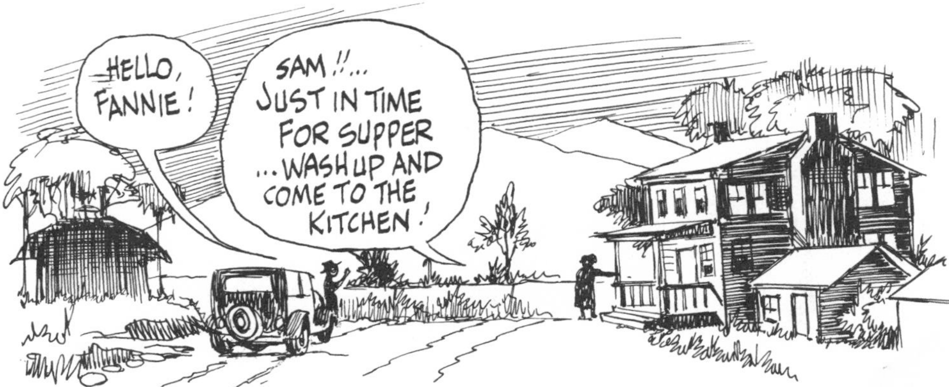
HELLO, FANNIE!
SAM!!... JUST IN TIME FOR SUPPER ...WASH UP AND COME TO THE KITCHEN!

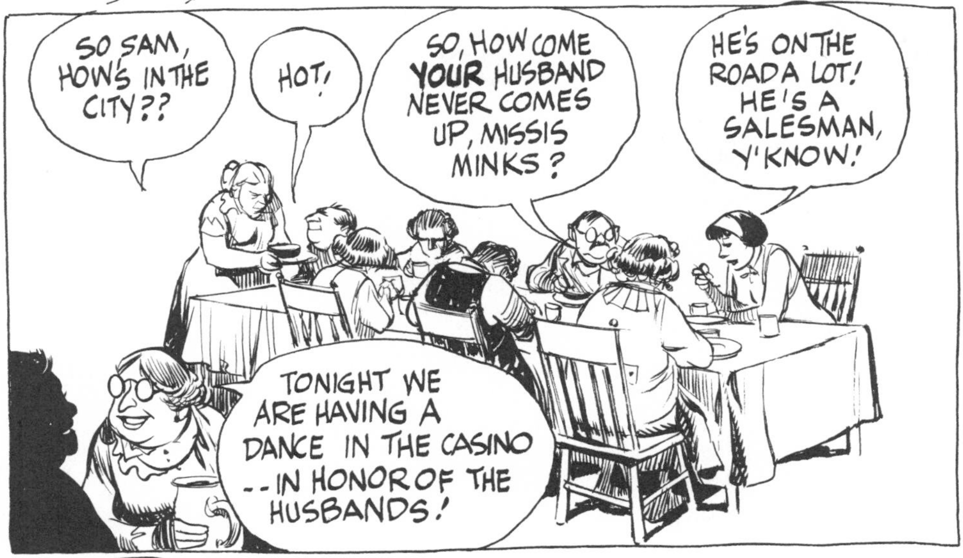
SO SAM, HOW'S IN THE CITY??
HOT!
SO, HOW COME **YOUR** HUSBAND NEVER COMES UP, MISSIS MINKS?
HE'S ON THE ROADA LOT! HE'S A SALESMAN, Y'KNOW!
TONIGHT WE ARE HAVING A DANCE IN THE CASINO --IN HONOR OF THE HUSBANDS!

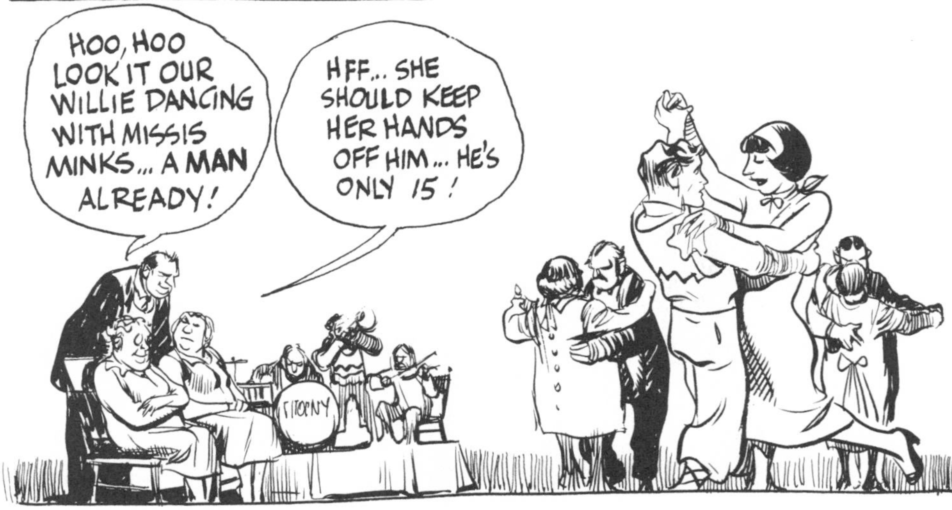
HOO, HOO LOOK IT OUR WILLIE DANCING WITH MISSIS MINKS... A **MAN** ALREADY!
HFF... SHE SHOULD KEEP HER HANDS OFF HIM... HE'S ONLY 15!

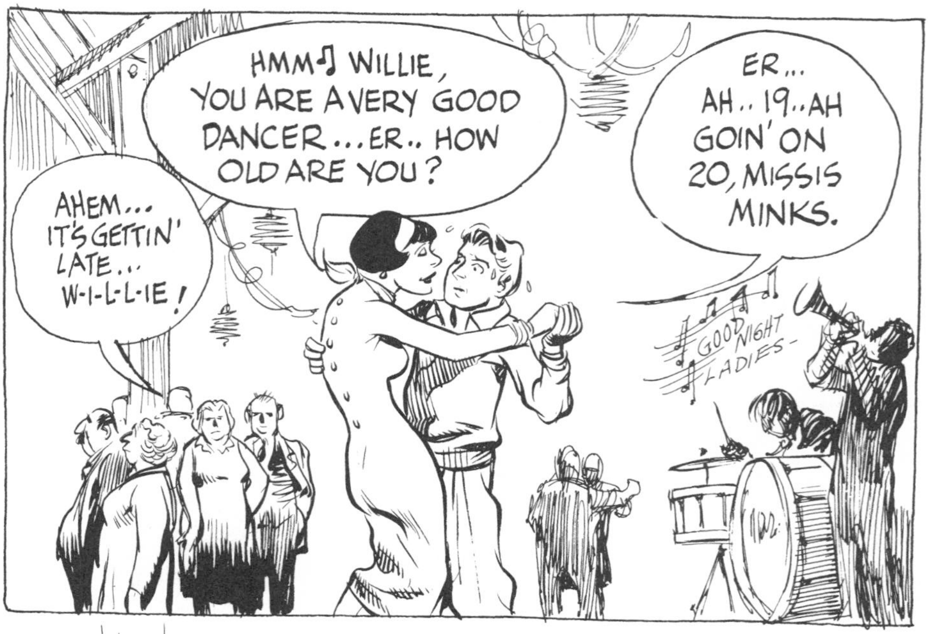
HMM♫ WILLIE, YOU ARE A VERY GOOD DANCER... ER.. HOW OLD ARE YOU?
ER... AH.. 19.. AH GOIN' ON 20, MISSIS MINKS.
AHEM... IT'S GETTIN' LATE... W-I-L-L-IE!
GOOD NIGHT LADIES-

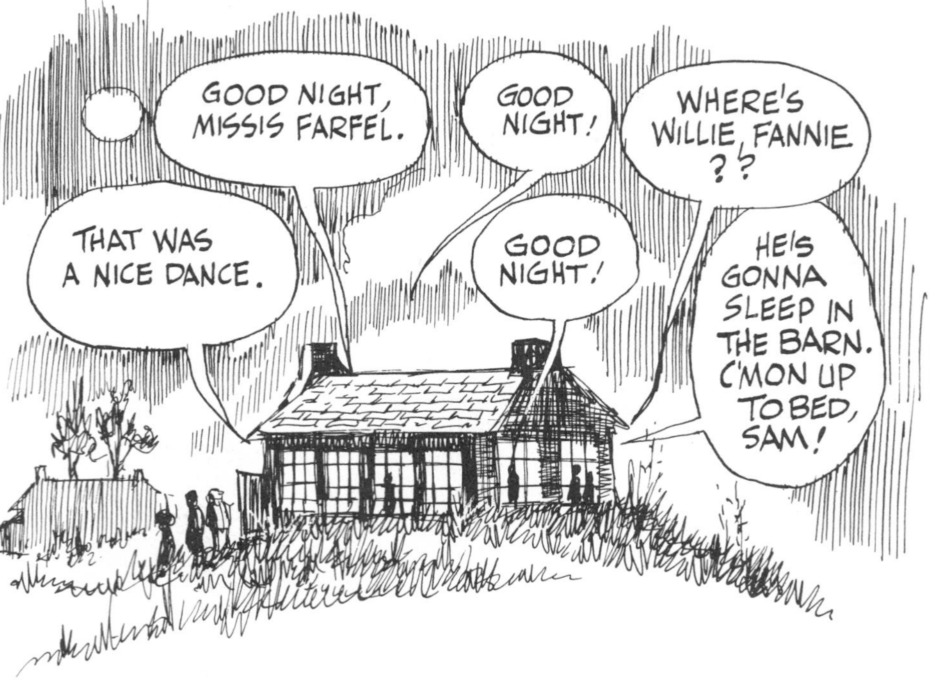
GOOD NIGHT, MISSIS FARFEL.
GOOD NIGHT!
WHERE'S WILLIE, FANNIE ??
THAT WAS A NICE DANCE.
GOOD NIGHT!
HE'S GONNA SLEEP IN THE BARN. C'MON UP TO BED, SAM!

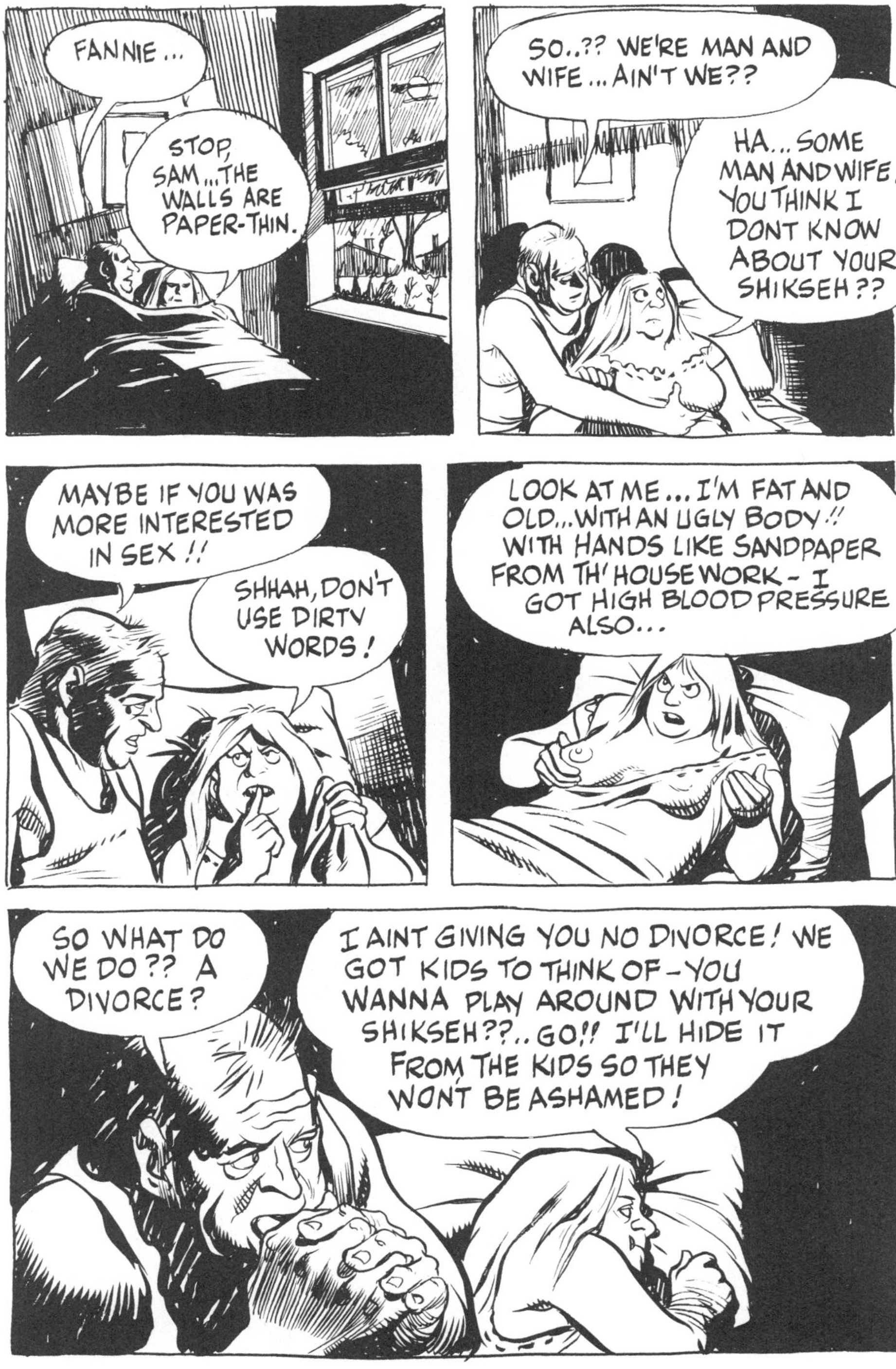
FANNIE...
STOP, SAM...THE WALLS ARE PAPER-THIN.
SO..?? WE'RE MAN AND WIFE...AIN'T WE??
HA...SOME MAN AND WIFE! YOU THINK I DONT KNOW ABOUT YOUR SHIKSEH??
MAYBE IF YOU WAS MORE INTERESTED IN SEX!!
SHHAH, DON'T USE DIRTY WORDS!
LOOK AT ME...I'M FAT AND OLD...WITH AN UGLY BODY!! WITH HANDS LIKE SANDPAPER FROM TH' HOUSEWORK - I GOT HIGH BLOOD PRESSURE ALSO...
SO WHAT DO WE DO?? A DIVORCE?
I AINT GIVING YOU NO DIVORCE! WE GOT KIDS TO THINK OF - YOU WANNA PLAY AROUND WITH YOUR SHIKSEH??..GO!! I'LL HIDE IT FROM THE KIDS SO THEY WONT BE ASHAMED!

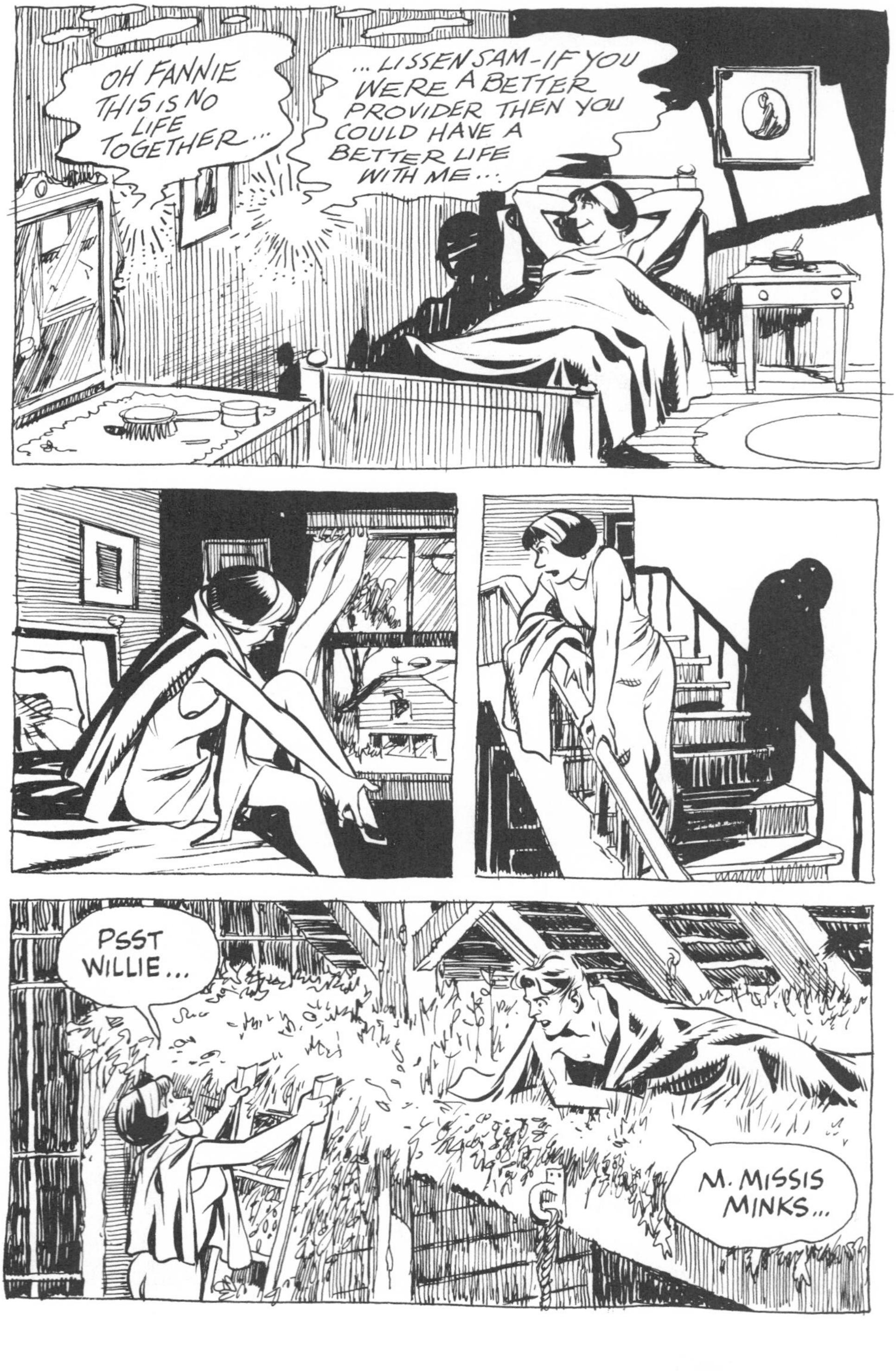
OH FANNIE THIS IS NO LIFE TOGETHER...
...LISSEN SAM-IF YOU WERE A BETTER PROVIDER THEN YOU COULD HAVE A BETTER LIFE WITH ME...
PSST WILLIE...
M. MISSIS MINKS...

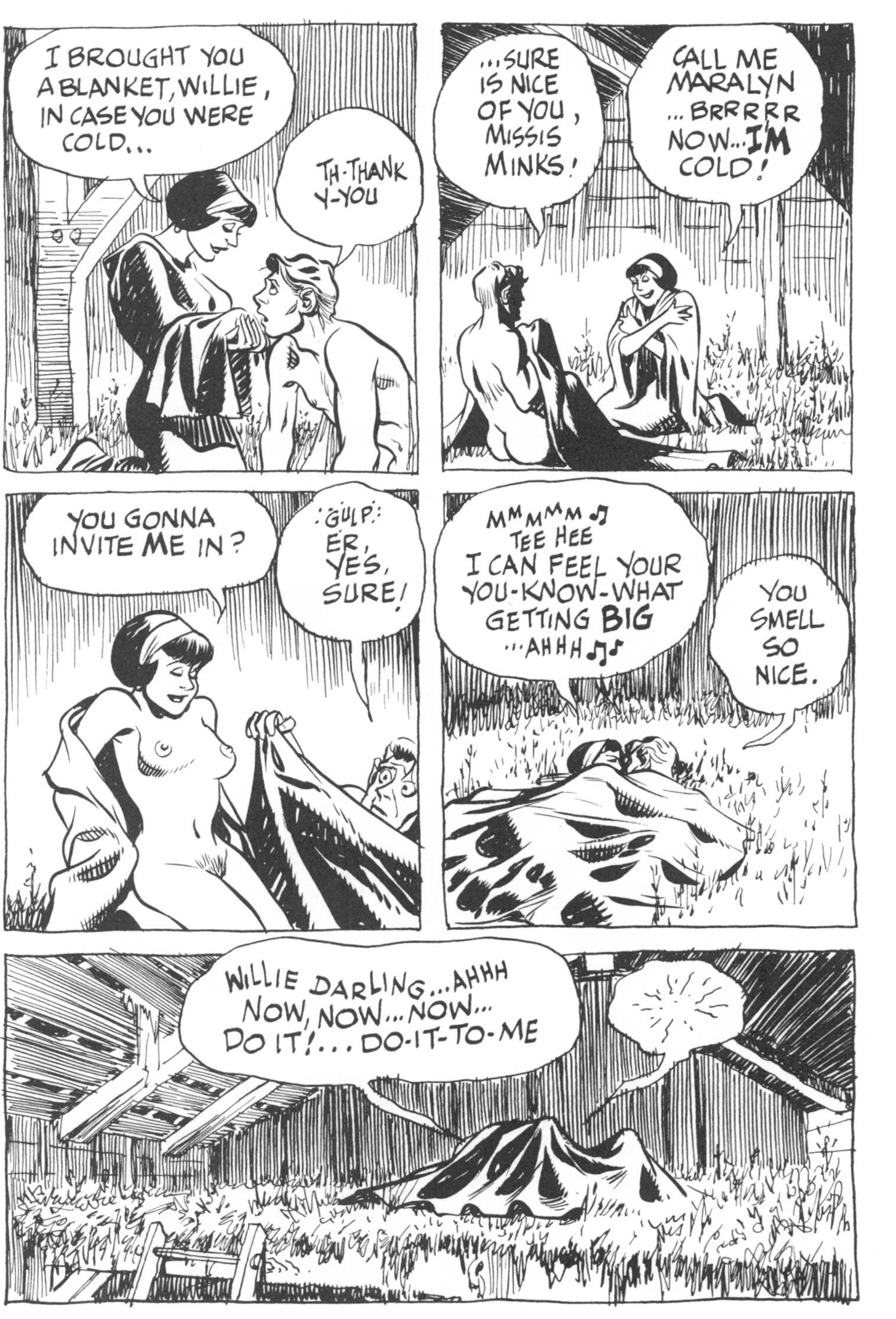
I BROUGHT YOU A BLANKET, WILLIE, IN CASE YOU WERE COLD...
TH-THANK Y-YOU
...SURE IS NICE OF YOU, MISSIS MINKS!
CALL ME MARALYN ...BRRRRR NOW...I'M COLD!
YOU GONNA INVITE ME IN?
:GULP: ER, YES, SURE!
MMMMM ♫ TEE HEE I CAN FEEL YOUR YOU-KNOW-WHAT GETTING BIG ...AHHH ♫♪
YOU SMELL SO NICE.
WILLIE DARLING...AHHH NOW, NOW...NOW... DO IT!... DO-IT-TO-ME

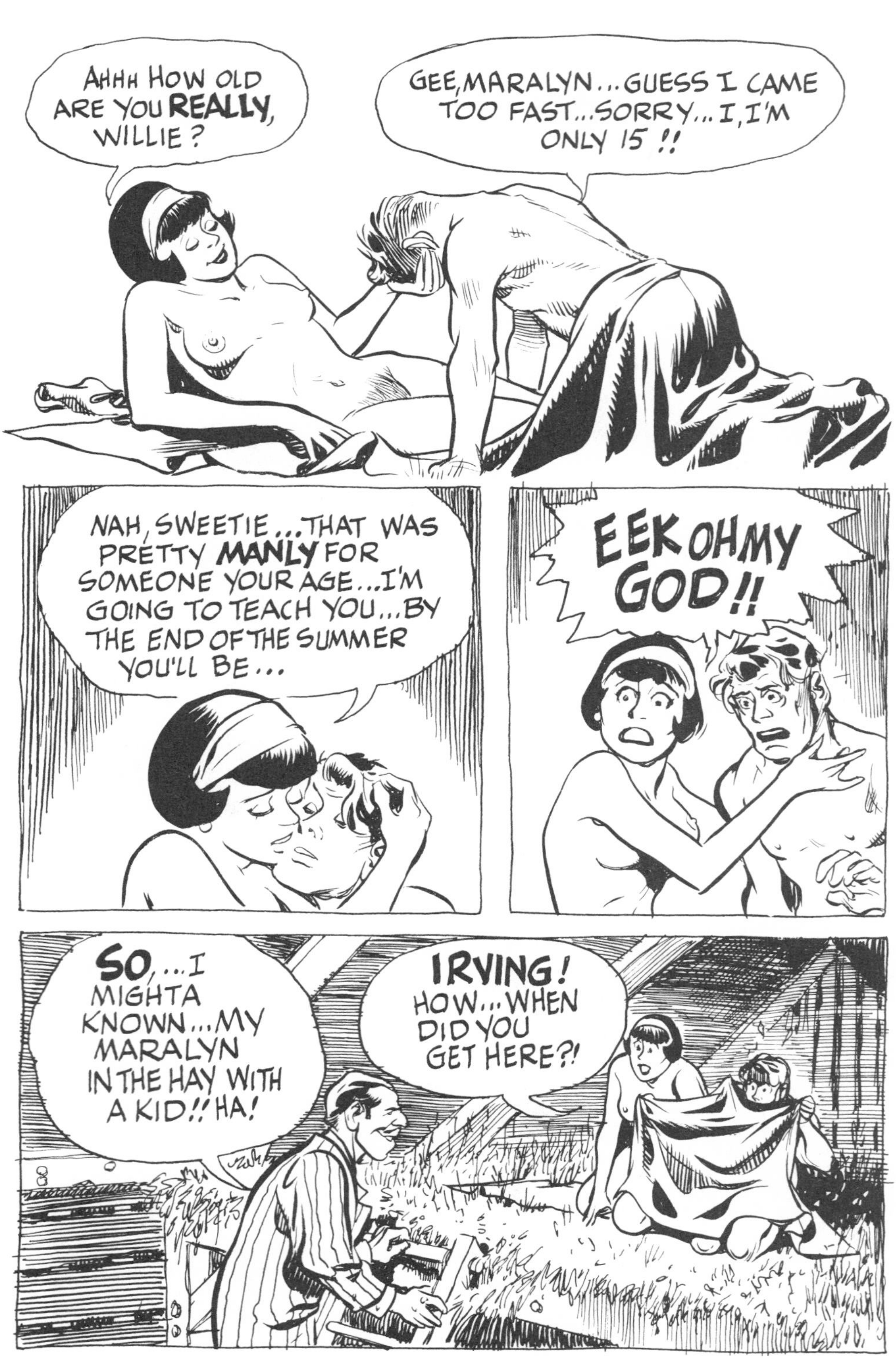
AHHH HOW OLD ARE YOU REALLY, WILLIE?
GEE, MARALYN... GUESS I CAME TOO FAST... SORRY... I, I'M ONLY 15 !!
NAH, SWEETIE... THAT WAS PRETTY MANLY FOR SOMEONE YOUR AGE... I'M GOING TO TEACH YOU... BY THE END OF THE SUMMER YOU'LL BE...
EEK OHMY GOD!!
SO, ...I MIGHTA KNOWN... MY MARALYN IN THE HAY WITH A KID!! HA!
IRVING! HOW... WHEN DID YOU GET HERE?!

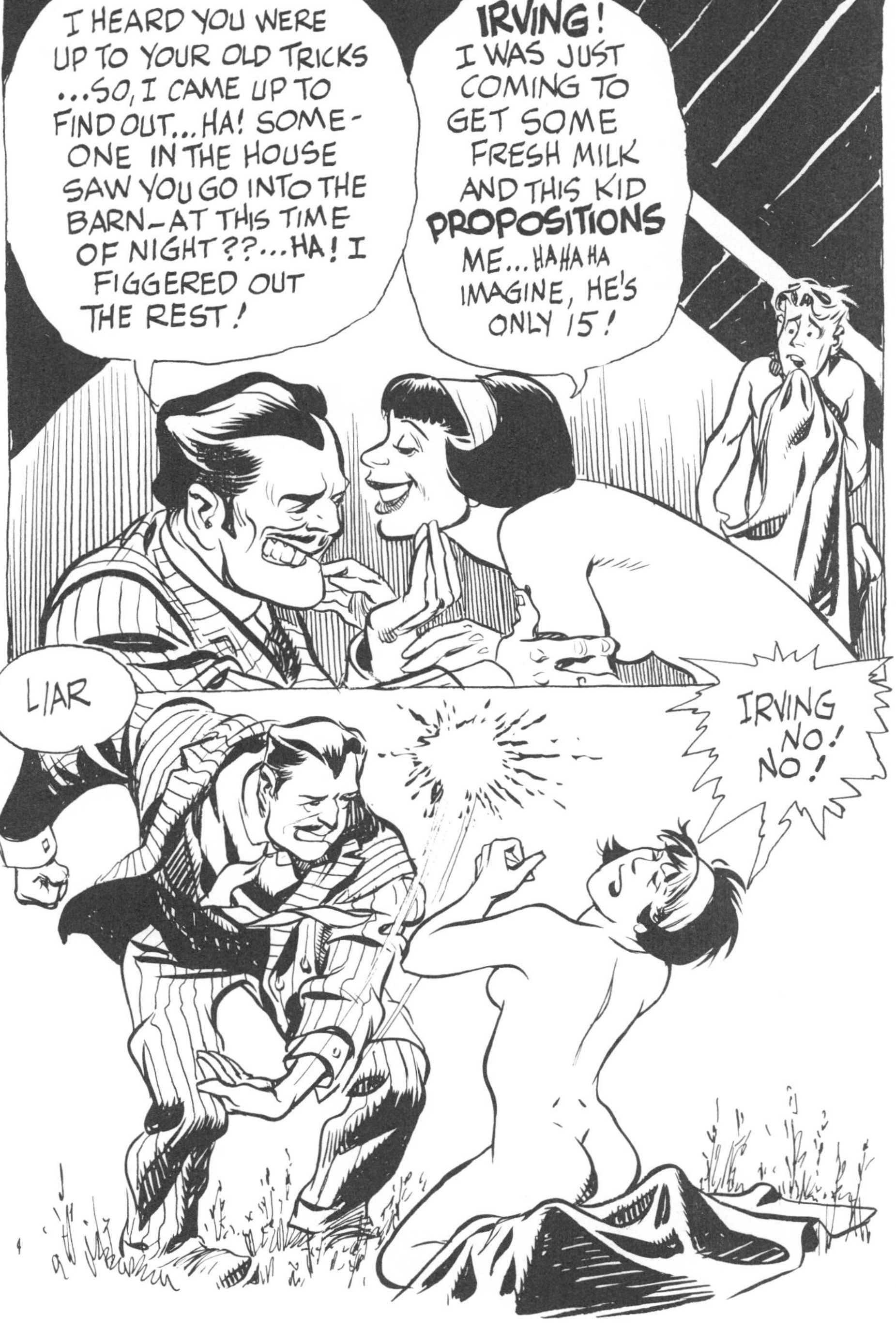
I HEARD YOU WERE UP TO YOUR OLD TRICKS ...SO, I CAME UP TO FIND OUT...HA! SOME-ONE IN THE HOUSE SAW YOU GO INTO THE BARN—AT THIS TIME OF NIGHT??...HA! I FIGGERED OUT THE REST!
IRVING! I WAS JUST COMING TO GET SOME FRESH MILK AND THIS KID PROPOSITIONS ME...HAHAHA IMAGINE, HE'S ONLY 15!
LIAR
IRVING NO! NO!

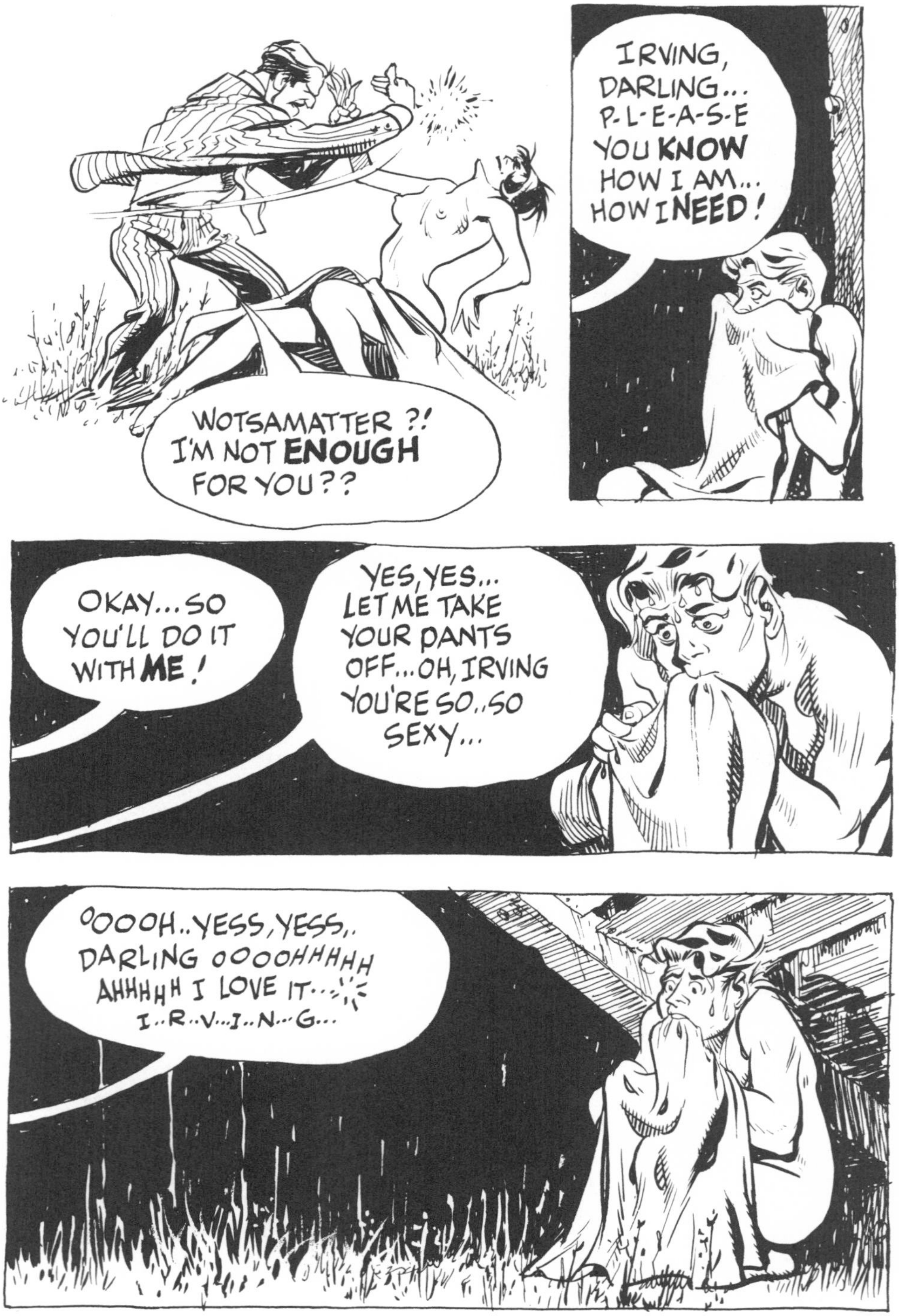
WOTSAMATTER ?! I'M NOT ENOUGH FOR YOU??
IRVING, DARLING... P-L-E-A-S-E YOU KNOW HOW I AM... HOW I NEED!
OKAY...SO YOU'LL DO IT WITH ME!
YES, YES... LET ME TAKE YOUR PANTS OFF...OH, IRVING YOU'RE SO..SO SEXY...
OOOOH..YESS, YESS,. DARLING OOOOHHHHH AHHHHH I LOVE IT...
I..R..V..I..N..G...

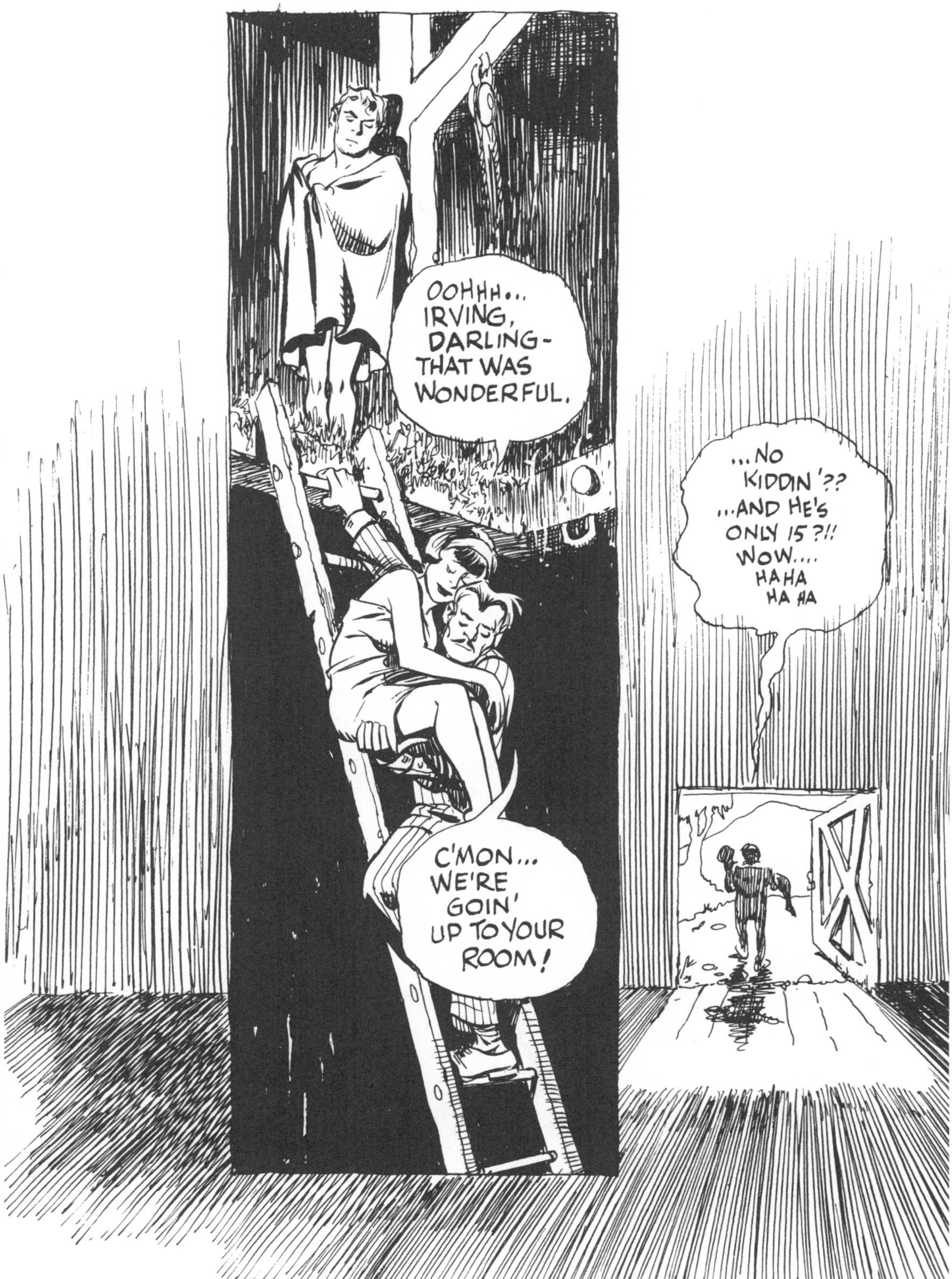
OOHHH... IRVING, DARLING- THAT WAS WONDERFUL.
C'MON... WE'RE GOIN' UP TO YOUR ROOM!
...NO KIDDIN'?? ...AND HE'S ONLY 15?!! WOW.... HA HA HA HA

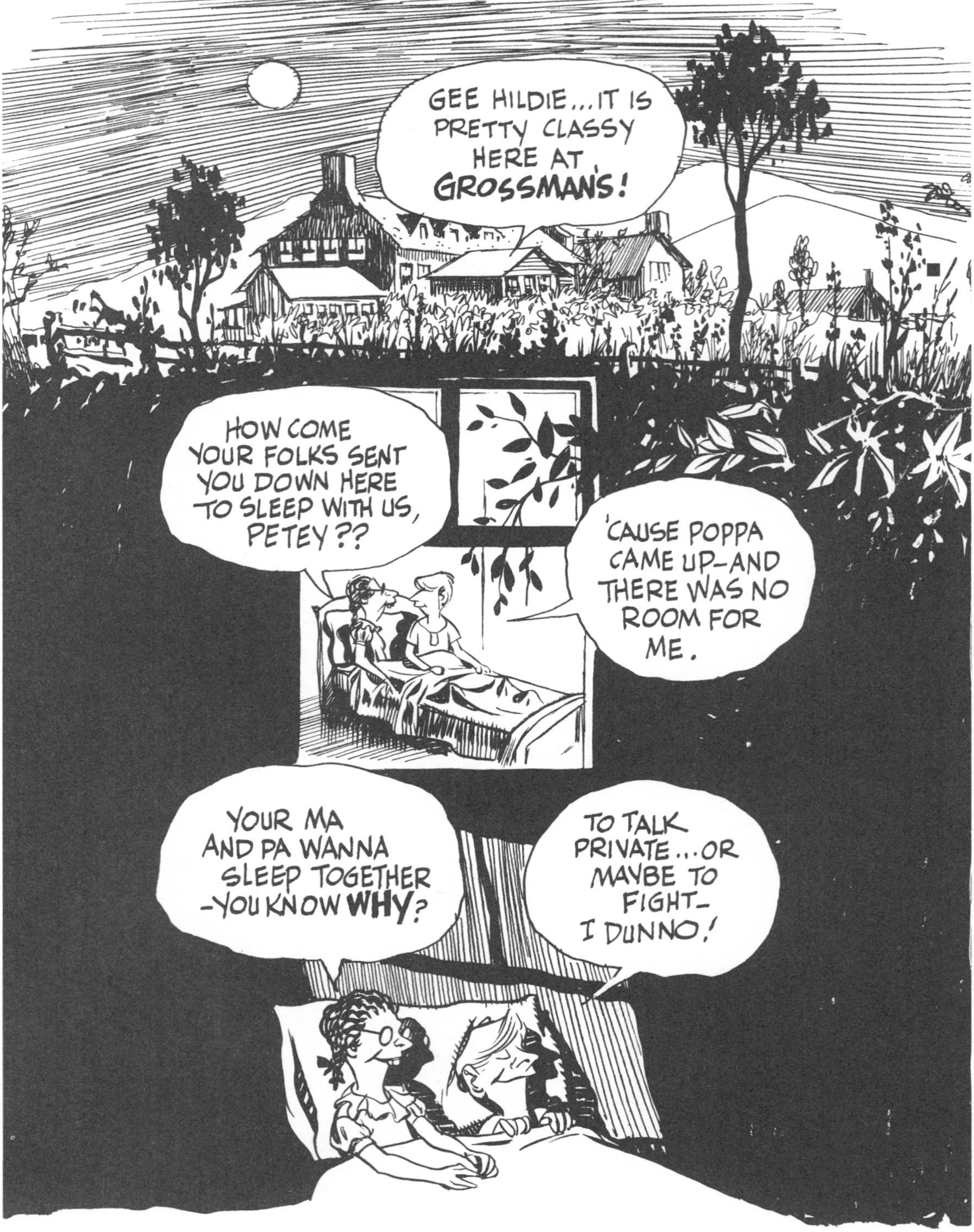
GEE HILDIE... IT IS PRETTY CLASSY HERE AT GROSSMAN'S!
HOW COME YOUR FOLKS SENT YOU DOWN HERE TO SLEEP WITH US, PETEY??
'CAUSE POPPA CAME UP–AND THERE WAS NO ROOM FOR ME.
YOUR MA AND PA WANNA SLEEP TOGETHER -YOU KNOW WHY?
TO TALK PRIVATE... OR MAYBE TO FIGHT– I DUNNO!

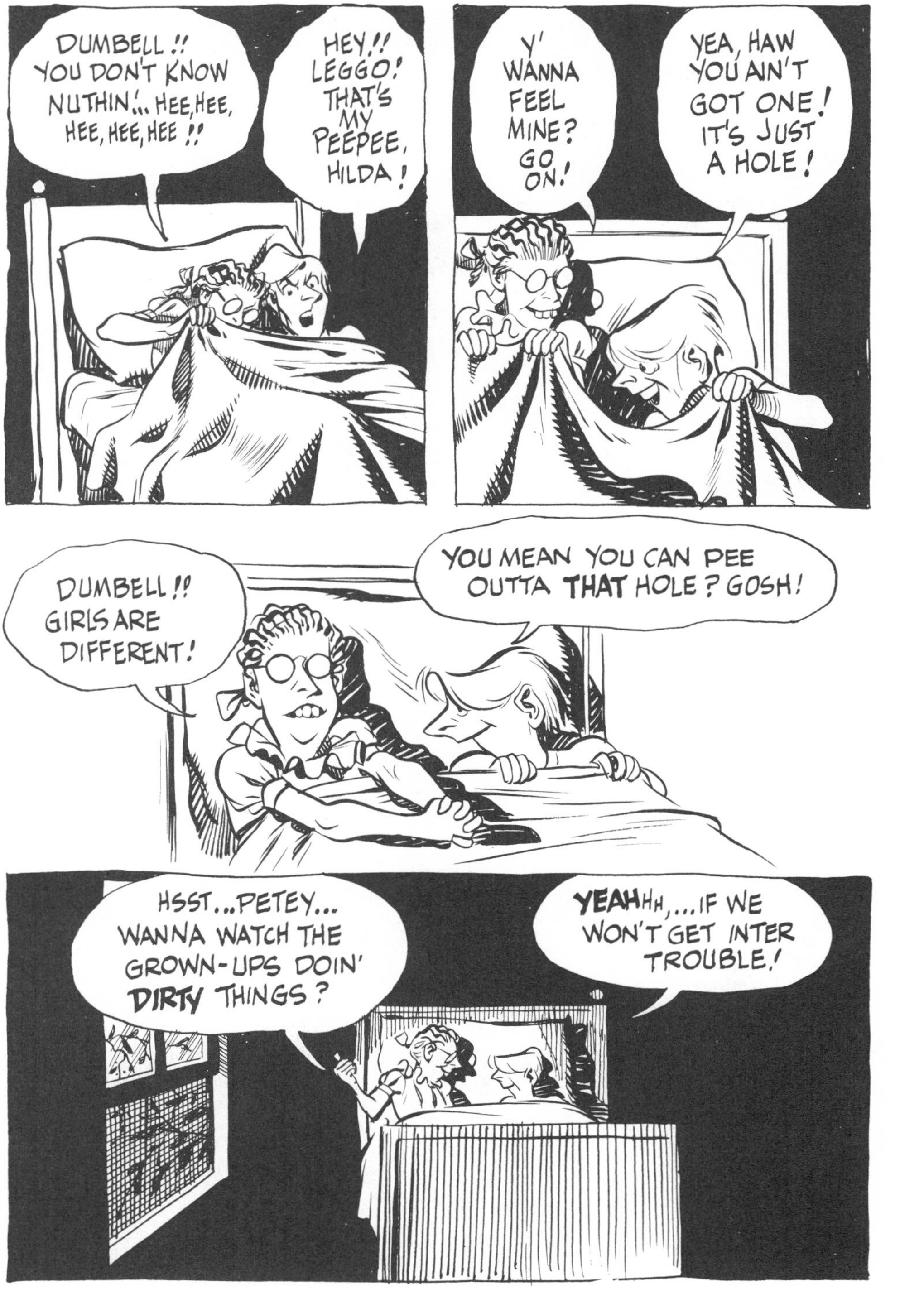
DUMBELL !! YOU DON'T KNOW NUTHIN'... HEE, HEE, HEE, HEE, HEE !!
HEY !! LEGGO! THAT'S MY PEEPEE, HILDA!
Y' WANNA FEEL MINE? GO ON!
YEA, HAW YOU AIN'T GOT ONE! IT'S JUST A HOLE!
DUMBELL !! GIRLS ARE DIFFERENT!
YOU MEAN YOU CAN PEE OUTTA THAT HOLE? GOSH!
HSST...PETEY... WANNA WATCH THE GROWN-UPS DOIN' DIRTY THINGS?
YEAHHH,...IF WE WON'T GET INTER TROUBLE!

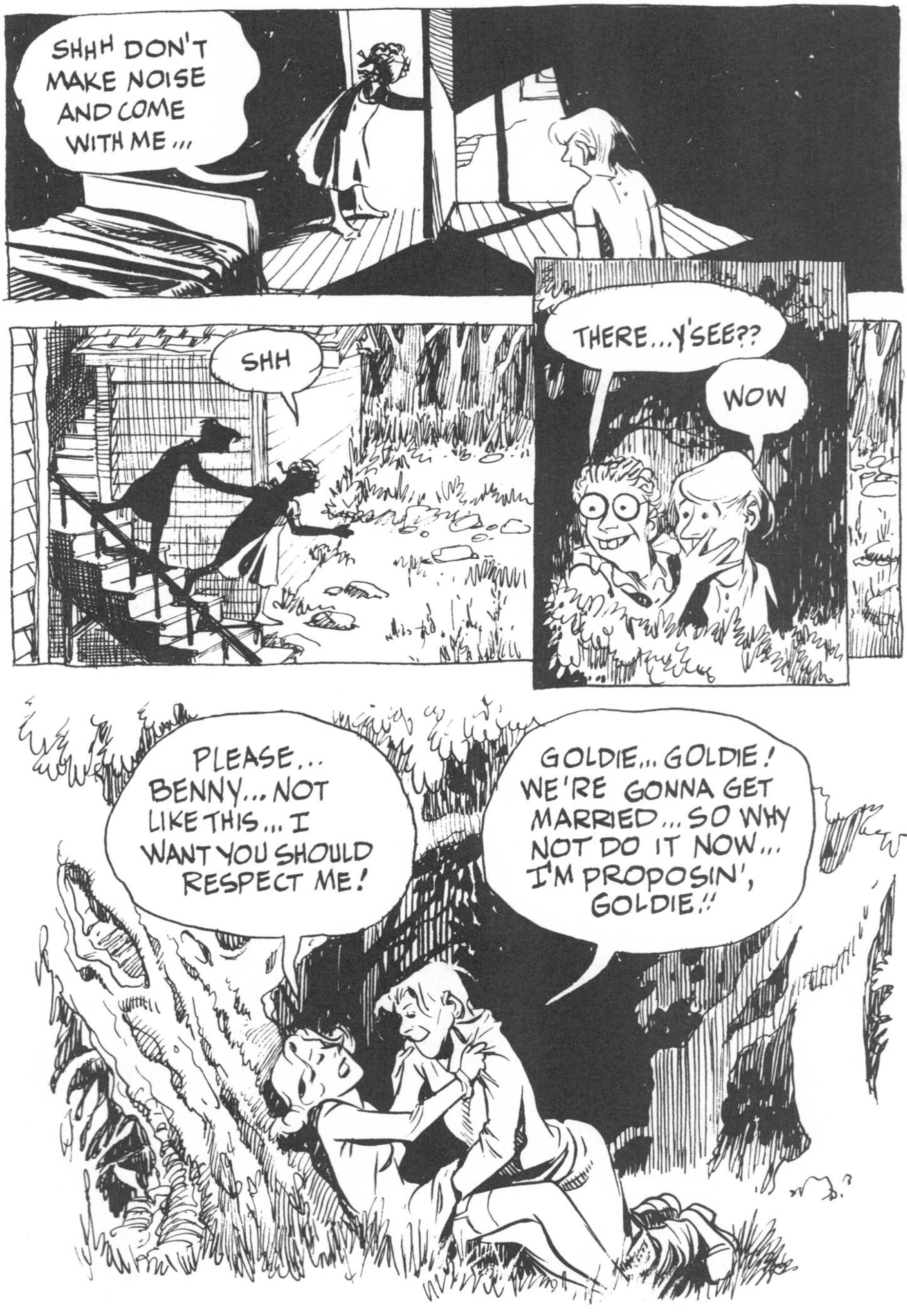

SHHH DON'T MAKE NOISE AND COME WITH ME ...
SHH
THERE...Y'SEE??
WOW
PLEASE... BENNY... NOT LIKE THIS... I WANT YOU SHOULD RESPECT ME!
GOLDIE... GOLDIE! WE'RE GONNA GET MARRIED... SO WHY NOT DO IT NOW... I'M PROPOSIN', GOLDIE!!

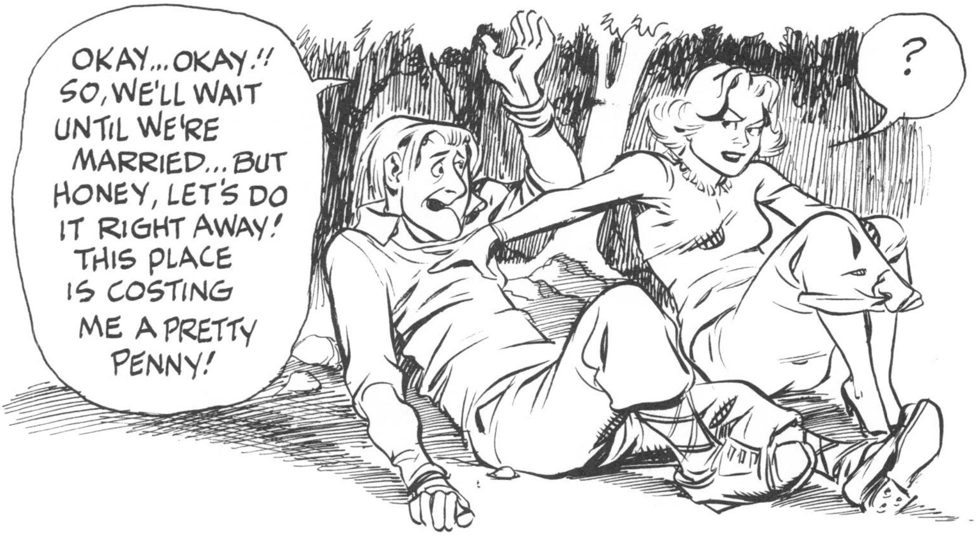
OKAY... OKAY!! SO, WE'LL WAIT UNTIL WE'RE MARRIED... BUT HONEY, LET'S DO IT RIGHT AWAY! THIS PLACE IS COSTING ME A PRETTY PENNY!
?

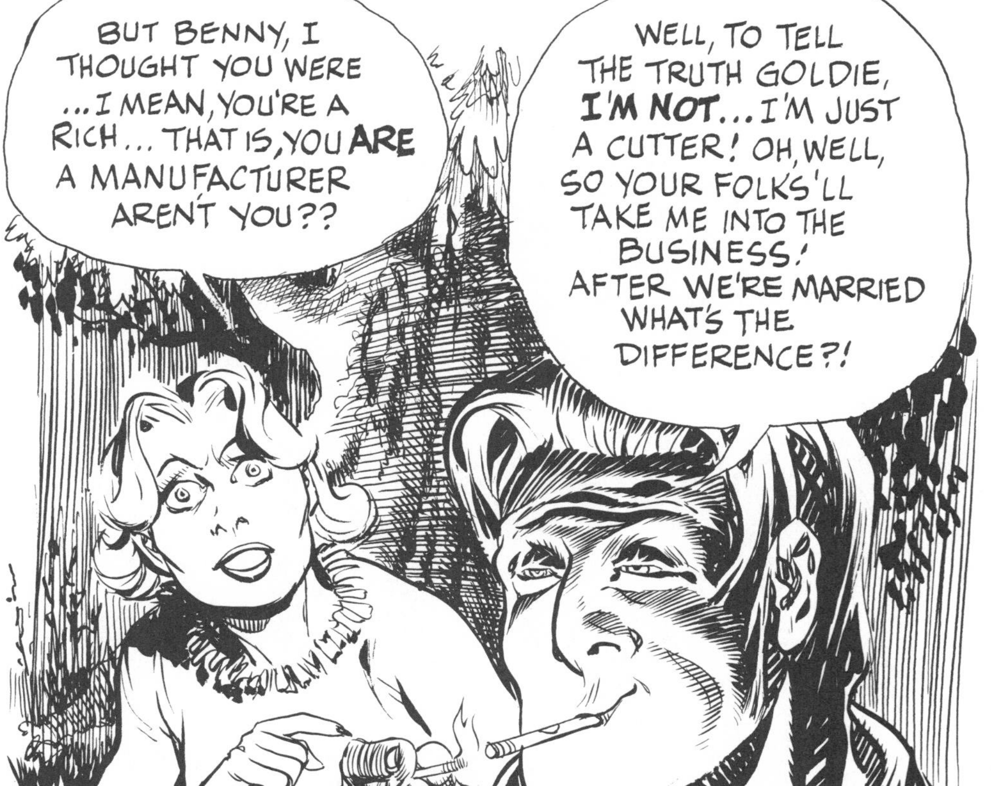
BUT BENNY, I THOUGHT YOU WERE ...I MEAN, YOU'RE A RICH... THAT IS, YOU ARE A MANUFACTURER AREN'T YOU??
WELL, TO TELL THE TRUTH GOLDIE, I'M NOT... I'M JUST A CUTTER! OH, WELL, SO YOUR FOLKS'LL TAKE ME INTO THE BUSINESS! AFTER WE'RE MARRIED WHAT'S THE DIFFERENCE?!

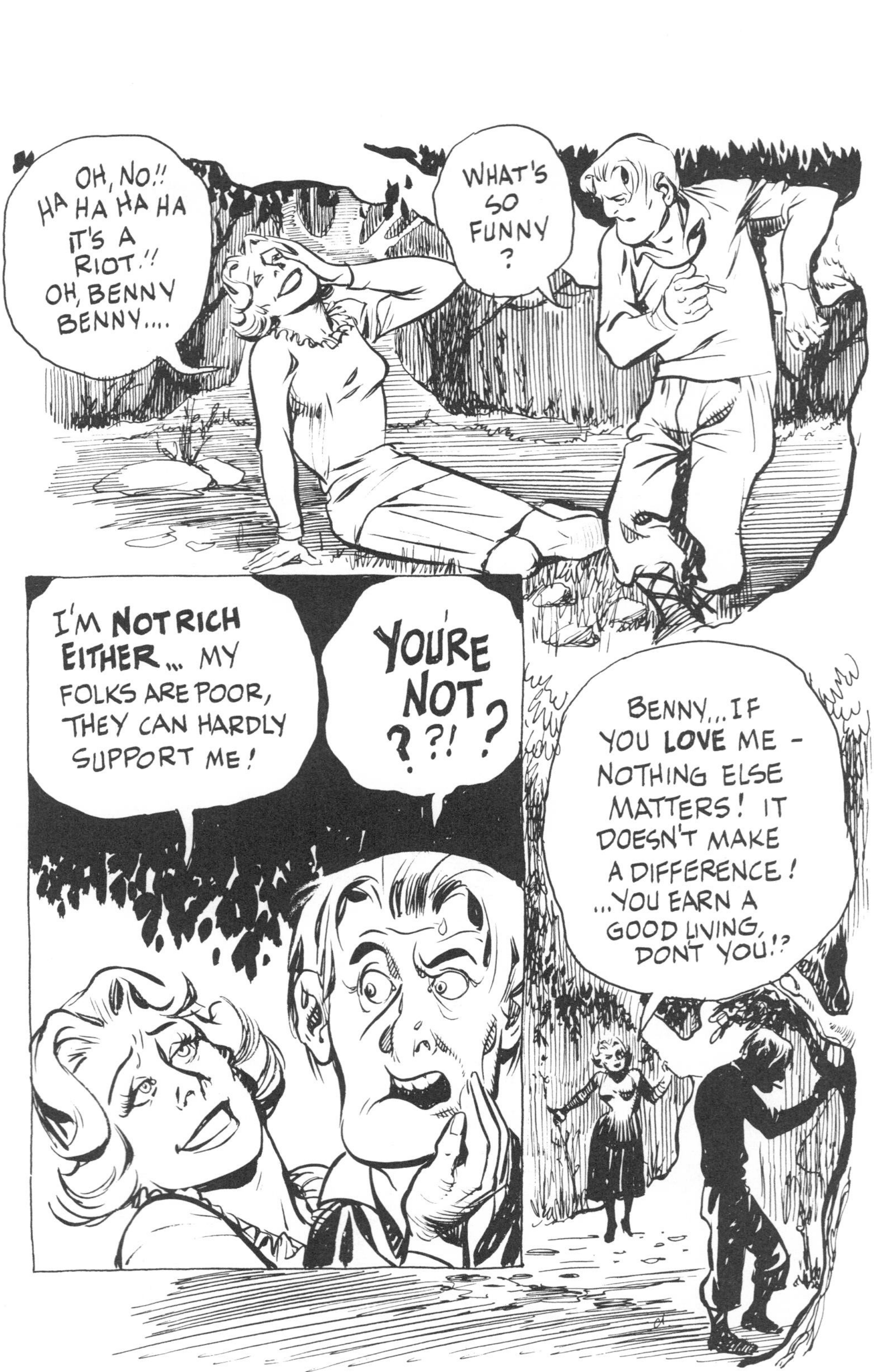
OH, NO!! HA HA HA HA IT'S A RIOT!! OH, BENNY BENNY....
WHAT'S SO FUNNY ?
I'M NOT RICH EITHER... MY FOLKS ARE POOR, THEY CAN HARDLY SUPPORT ME!
YOU'RE NOT ??! ?
BENNY... IF YOU LOVE ME - NOTHING ELSE MATTERS! IT DOESN'T MAKE A DIFFERENCE! ...YOU EARN A GOOD LIVING, DONT YOU!?

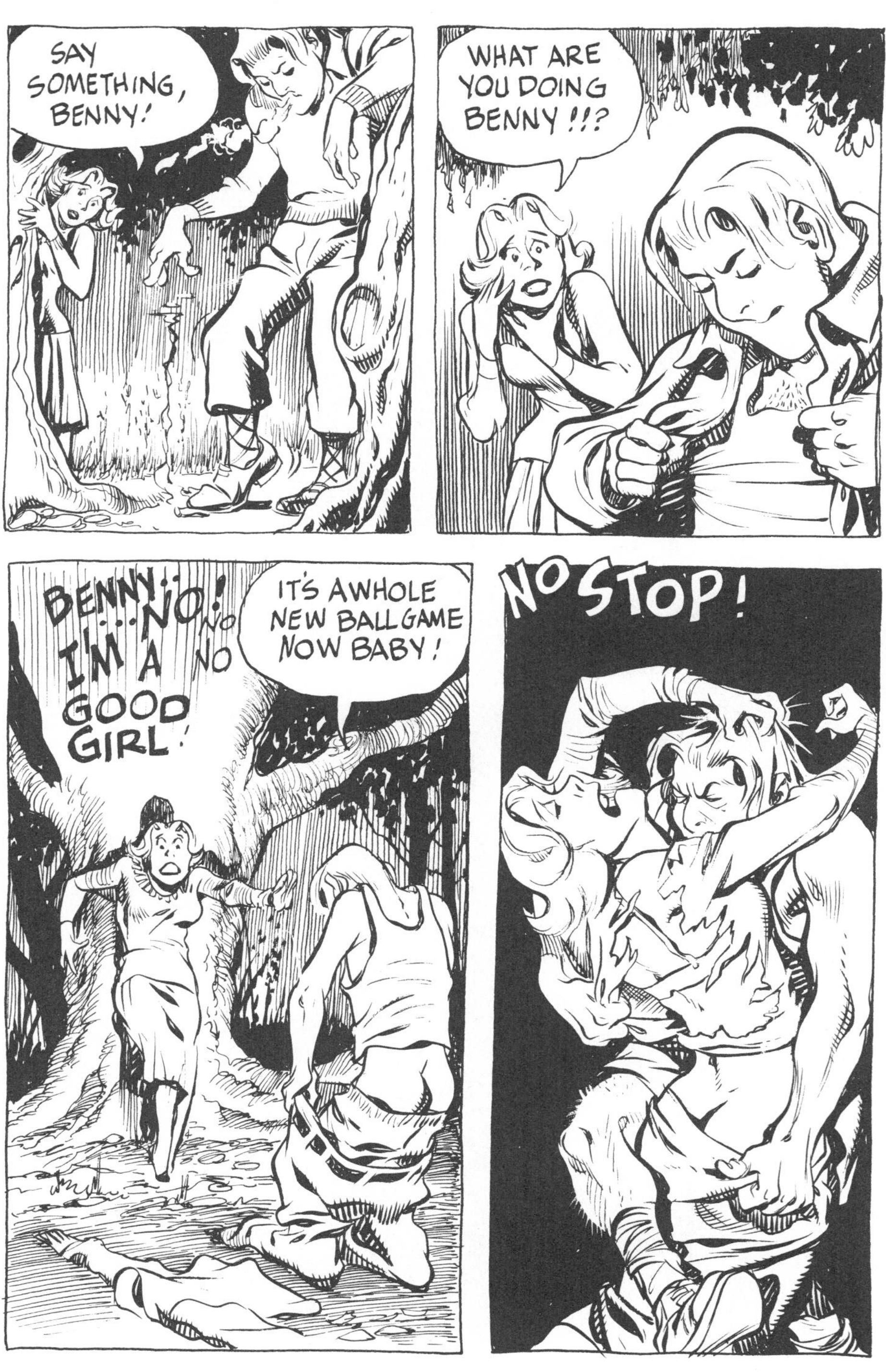
SAY SOMETHING, BENNY!
WHAT ARE YOU DOING BENNY !!?
BENNY... ...NO! I'M A GOOD GIRL!
NO NO
IT'S A WHOLE NEW BALL GAME NOW BABY!
NO STOP!

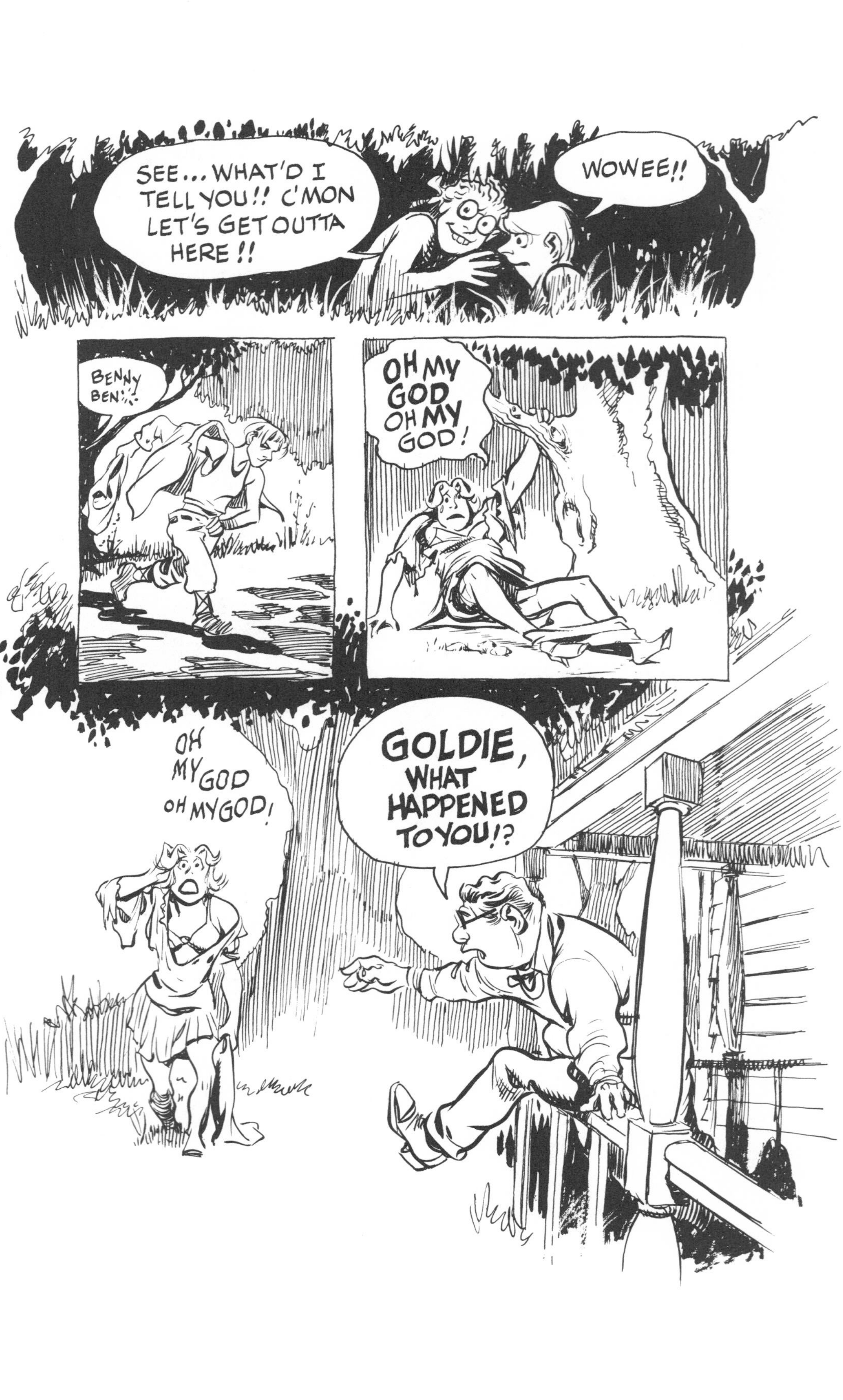
SEE... WHAT'D I TELL YOU!! C'MON LET'S GET OUTTA HERE!!
WOWEE!!
BENNY BEN!
OH MY GOD OH MY GOD!
OH MY GOD OH MY GOD!
GOLDIE, WHAT HAPPENED TO YOU!?

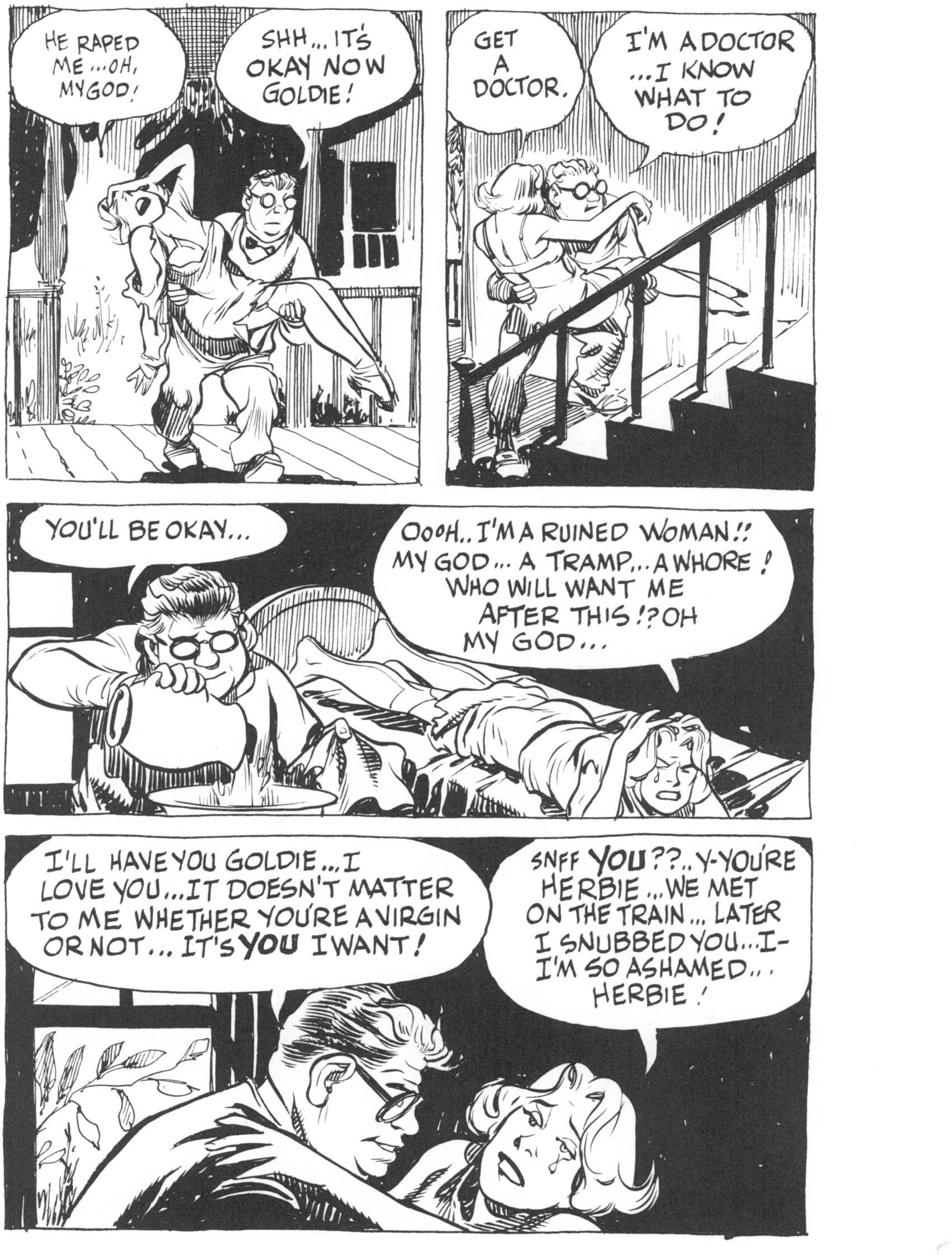
HE RAPED ME ...OH, MY GOD!
SHH... IT'S OKAY NOW GOLDIE!
GET A DOCTOR.
I'M A DOCTOR ...I KNOW WHAT TO DO!
YOU'LL BE OKAY...
OOOH.. I'M A RUINED WOMAN!! MY GOD... A TRAMP... A WHORE! WHO WILL WANT ME AFTER THIS!? OH MY GOD...
I'LL HAVE YOU GOLDIE... I LOVE YOU... IT DOESN'T MATTER TO ME WHETHER YOU'RE A VIRGIN OR NOT... IT'S **YOU** I WANT!
SNFF **YOU**??.. Y-YOU'RE HERBIE... WE MET ON THE TRAIN... LATER I SNUBBED YOU... I- I'M SO ASHAMED... HERBIE!

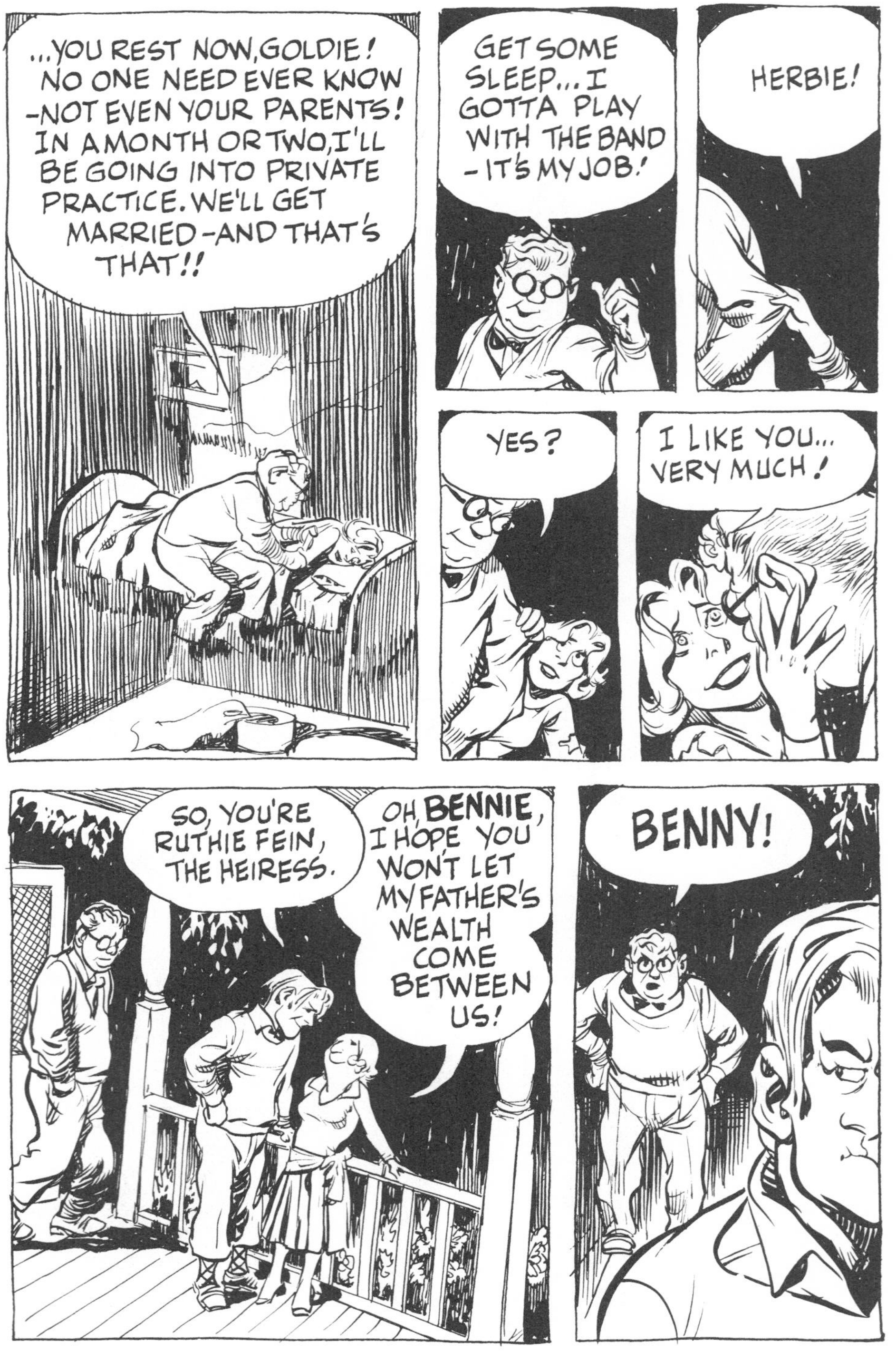
...YOU REST NOW, GOLDIE! NO ONE NEED EVER KNOW -NOT EVEN YOUR PARENTS! IN A MONTH OR TWO, I'LL BE GOING INTO PRIVATE PRACTICE. WE'LL GET MARRIED-AND THAT'S THAT!!
GET SOME SLEEP...I GOTTA PLAY WITH THE BAND -IT'S MY JOB!
HERBIE!
YES?
I LIKE YOU... VERY MUCH!
SO, YOU'RE RUTHIE FEIN, THE HEIRESS.
OH, BENNIE, I HOPE YOU WON'T LET MY FATHER'S WEALTH COME BETWEEN US!
BENNY!

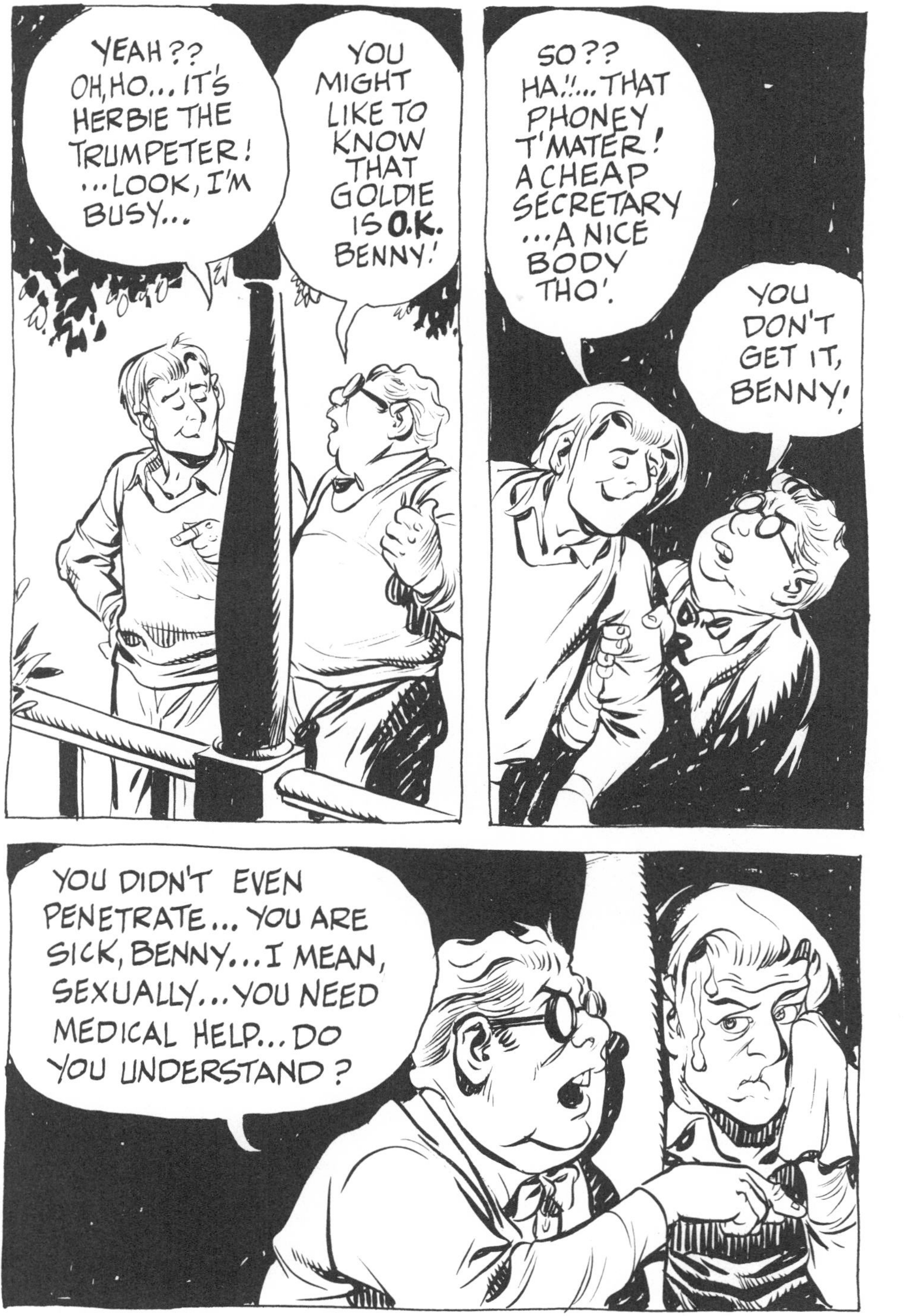
YEAH?? OH, HO... IT'S HERBIE THE TRUMPETER! ...LOOK, I'M BUSY...
YOU MIGHT LIKE TO KNOW THAT GOLDIE IS O.K. BENNY!
SO?? HA!!... THAT PHONEY T'MATER! A CHEAP SECRETARY ...A NICE BODY THO'.
YOU DON'T GET IT, BENNY!
YOU DIDN'T EVEN PENETRATE... YOU ARE SICK, BENNY... I MEAN, SEXUALLY... YOU NEED MEDICAL HELP... DO YOU UNDERSTAND?

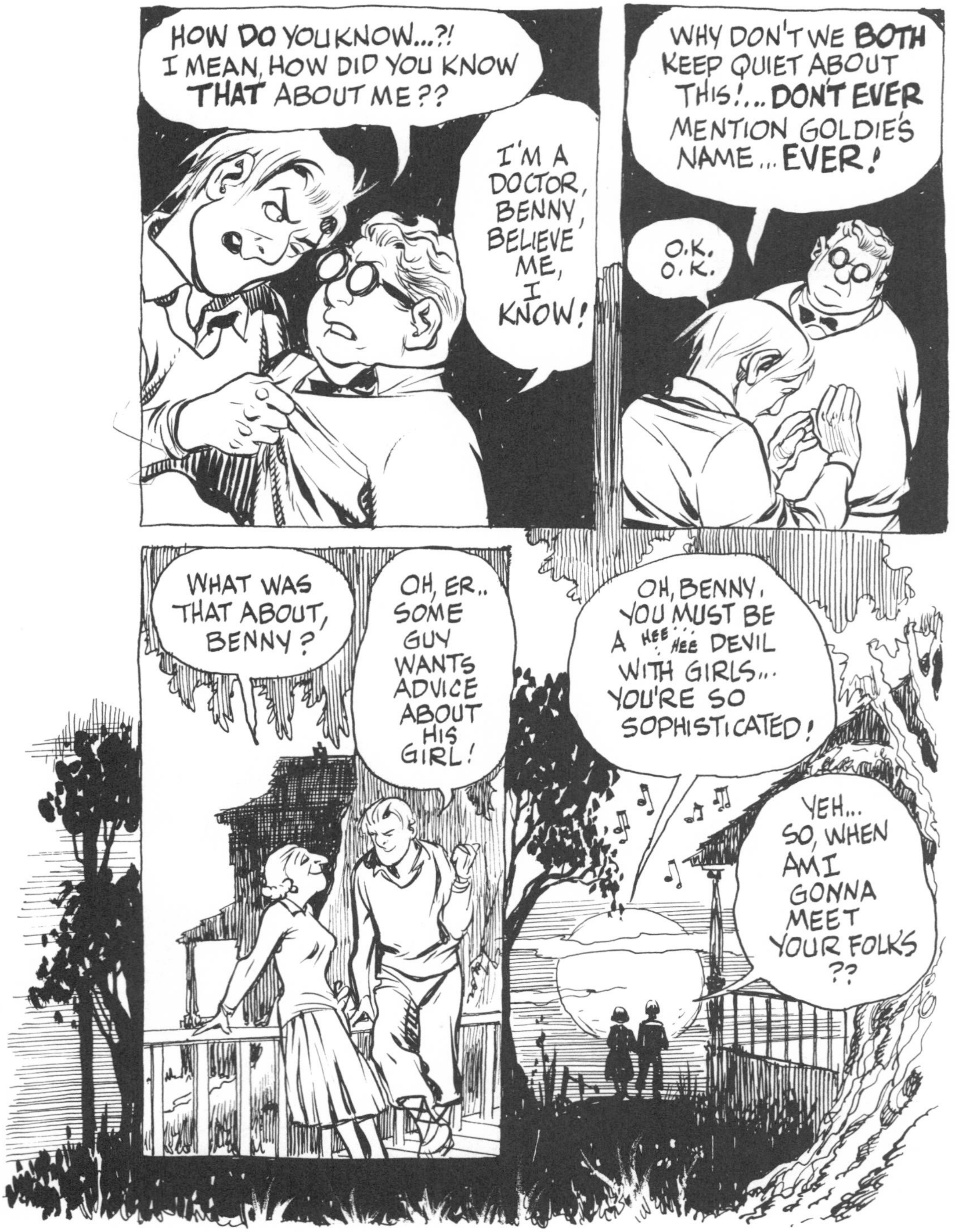
HOW DO YOU KNOW...?! I MEAN, HOW DID YOU KNOW THAT ABOUT ME??
I'M A DOCTOR, BENNY, BELIEVE ME, I KNOW!
WHY DON'T WE BOTH KEEP QUIET ABOUT THIS!... DON'T EVER MENTION GOLDIE'S NAME... EVER!
O.K. O.K.
WHAT WAS THAT ABOUT, BENNY?
OH, ER.. SOME GUY WANTS ADVICE ABOUT HIS GIRL!
OH, BENNY, YOU MUST BE A HEE HEE DEVIL WITH GIRLS... YOU'RE SO SOPHISTICATED!
YEH... SO, WHEN AM I GONNA MEET YOUR FOLKS??

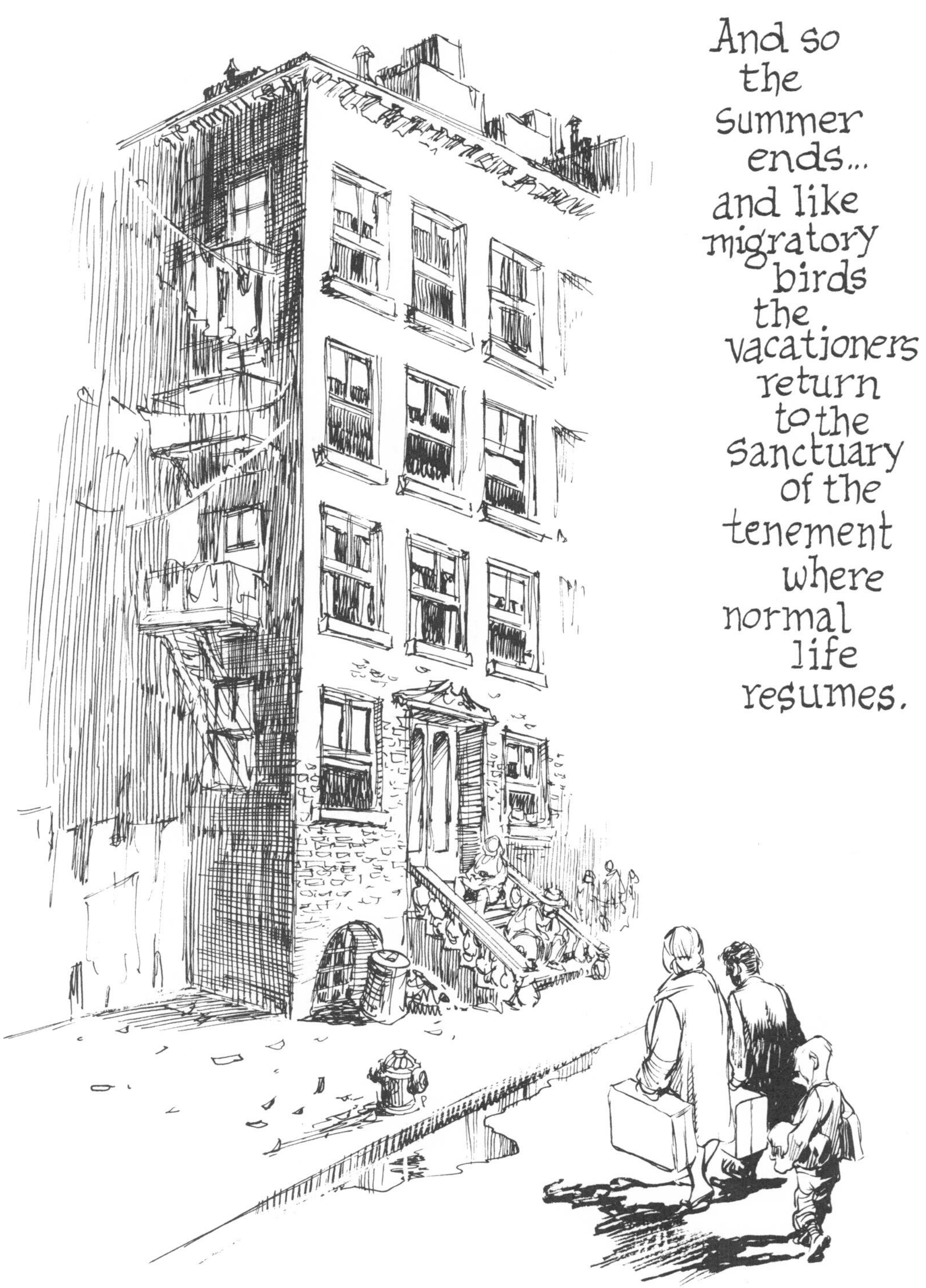
And so the summer ends... and like migratory birds the vacationers return to the sanctuary of the tenement where normal life resumes.

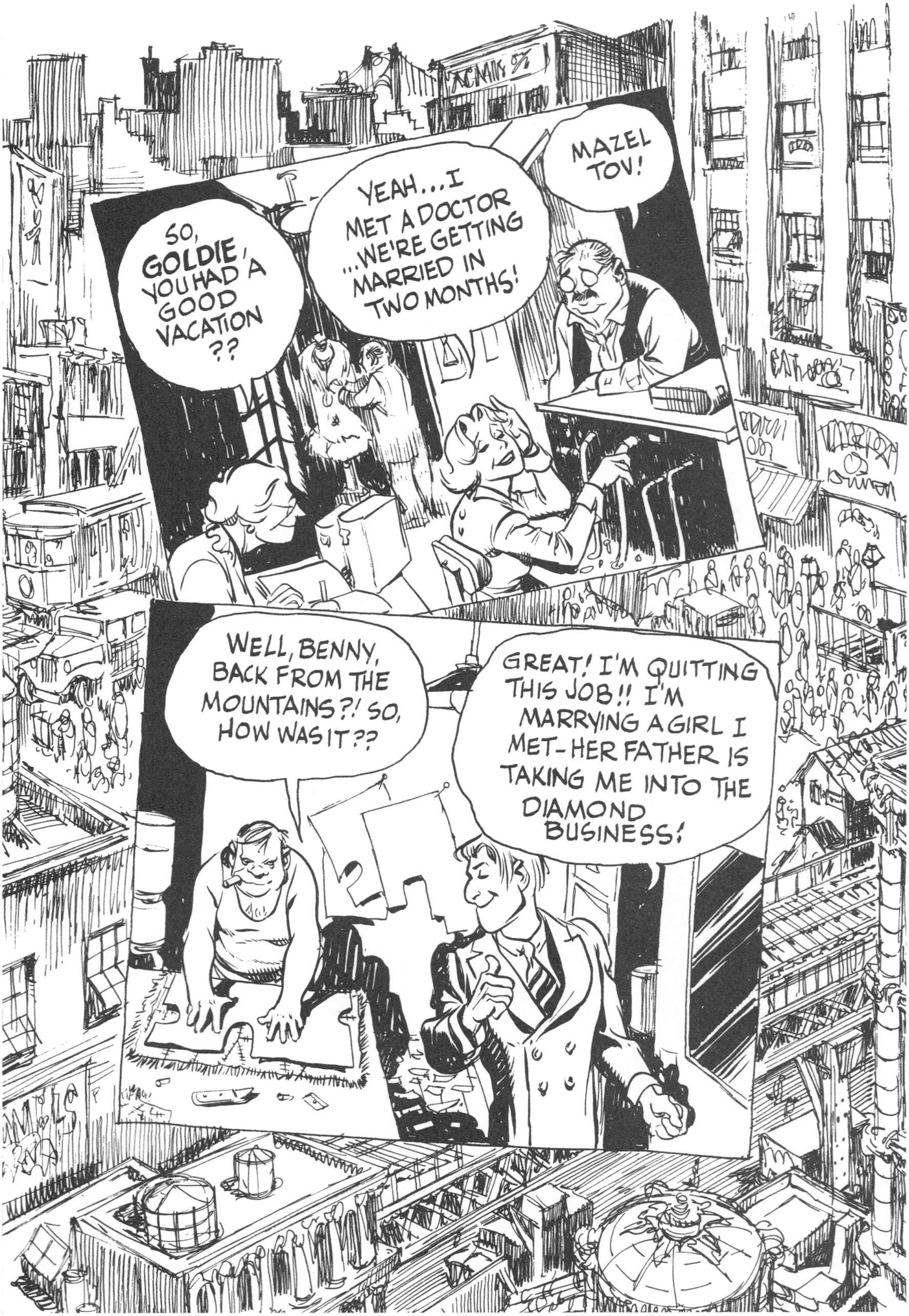
SO, GOLDIE, YOU HAD A GOOD VACATION ??
YEAH...I MET A DOCTOR ...WE'RE GETTING MARRIED IN TWO MONTHS!
MAZEL TOV!
WELL, BENNY, BACK FROM THE MOUNTAINS?! SO, HOW WAS IT??
GREAT! I'M QUITTING THIS JOB!! I'M MARRYING A GIRL I MET-HER FATHER IS TAKING ME INTO THE DIAMOND BUSINESS!

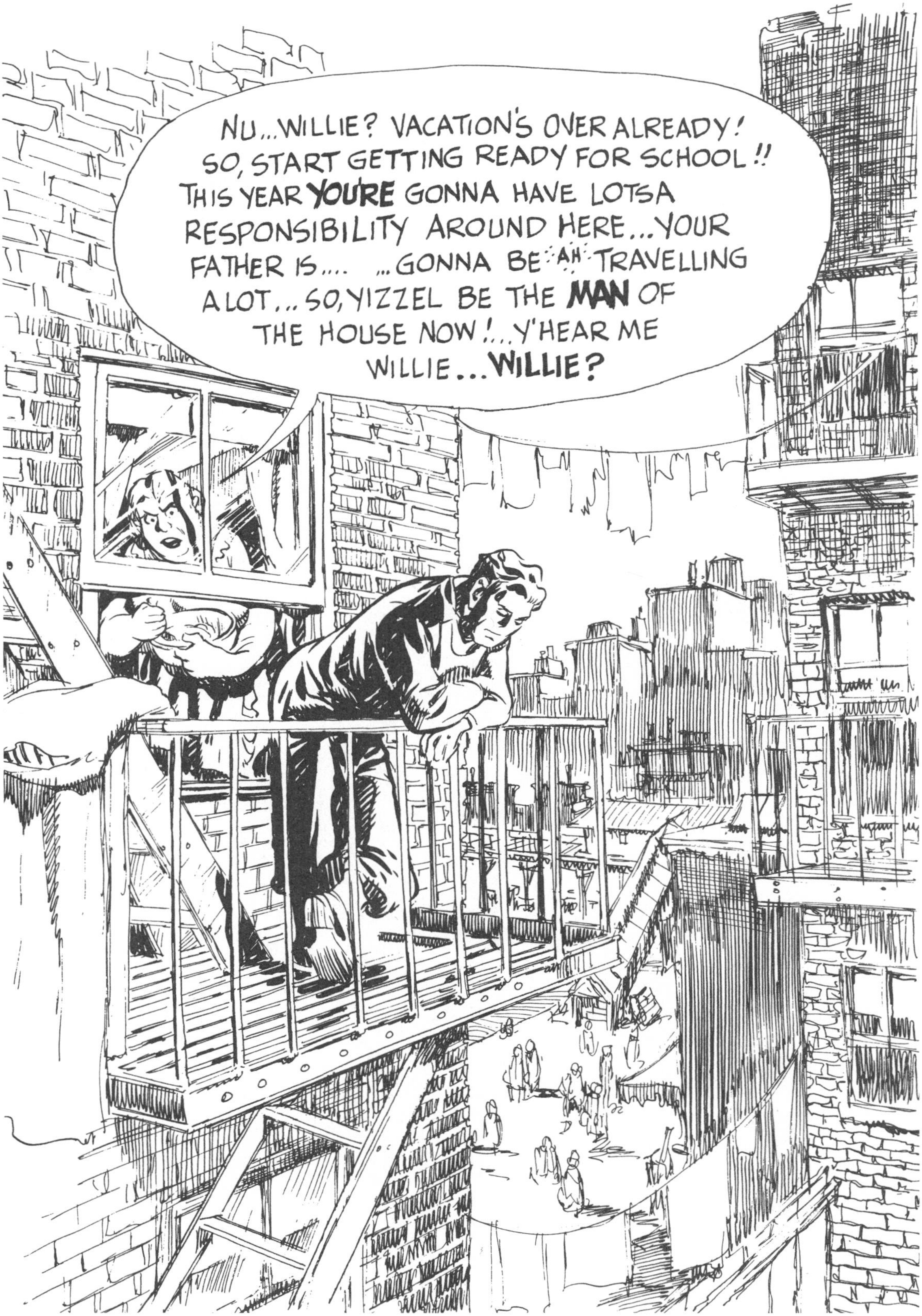
NU...WILLIE? VACATION'S OVER ALREADY! SO, START GETTING READY FOR SCHOOL!! THIS YEAR YOU'RE GONNA HAVE LOTSA RESPONSIBILITY AROUND HERE...YOUR FATHER IS.... ...GONNA BE AH TRAVELLING A LOT...SO, YIZZEL BE THE MAN OF THE HOUSE NOW!...Y'HEAR ME WILLIE...WILLIE?

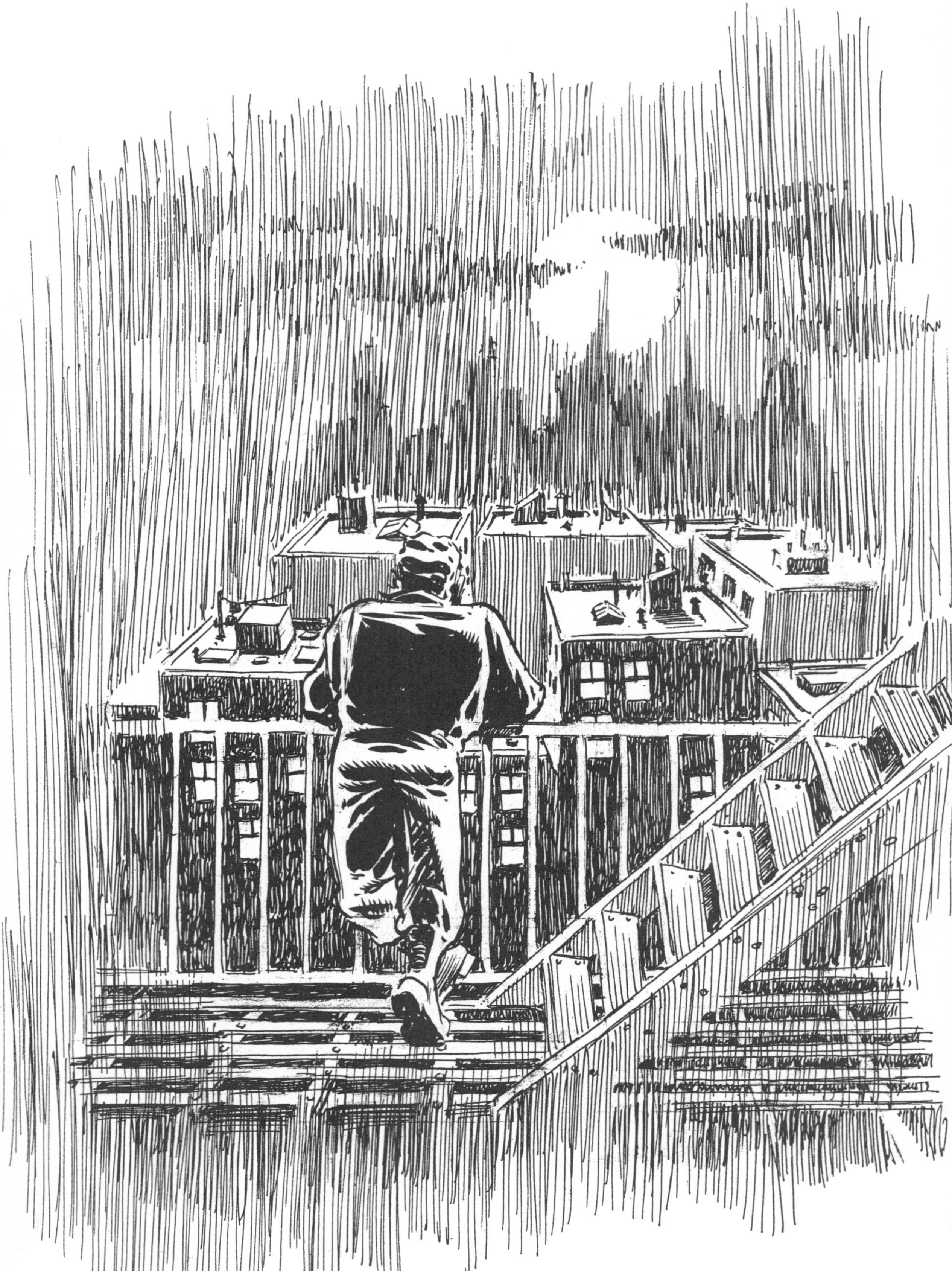

A LIFE FORCE

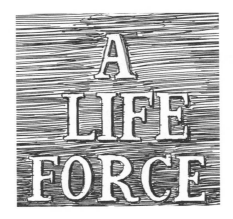

A LIFE FORCE

Who Knows...who Knows,
why all the creatures of earth
struggle so to live.
Why they scurry about, run from
danger and continue to live
out a natural span,
seemingly in response to
a mysterious Life Force.

So, the question is
WHY? WHAT FOR?
Ask the insects...
Maybe they know!

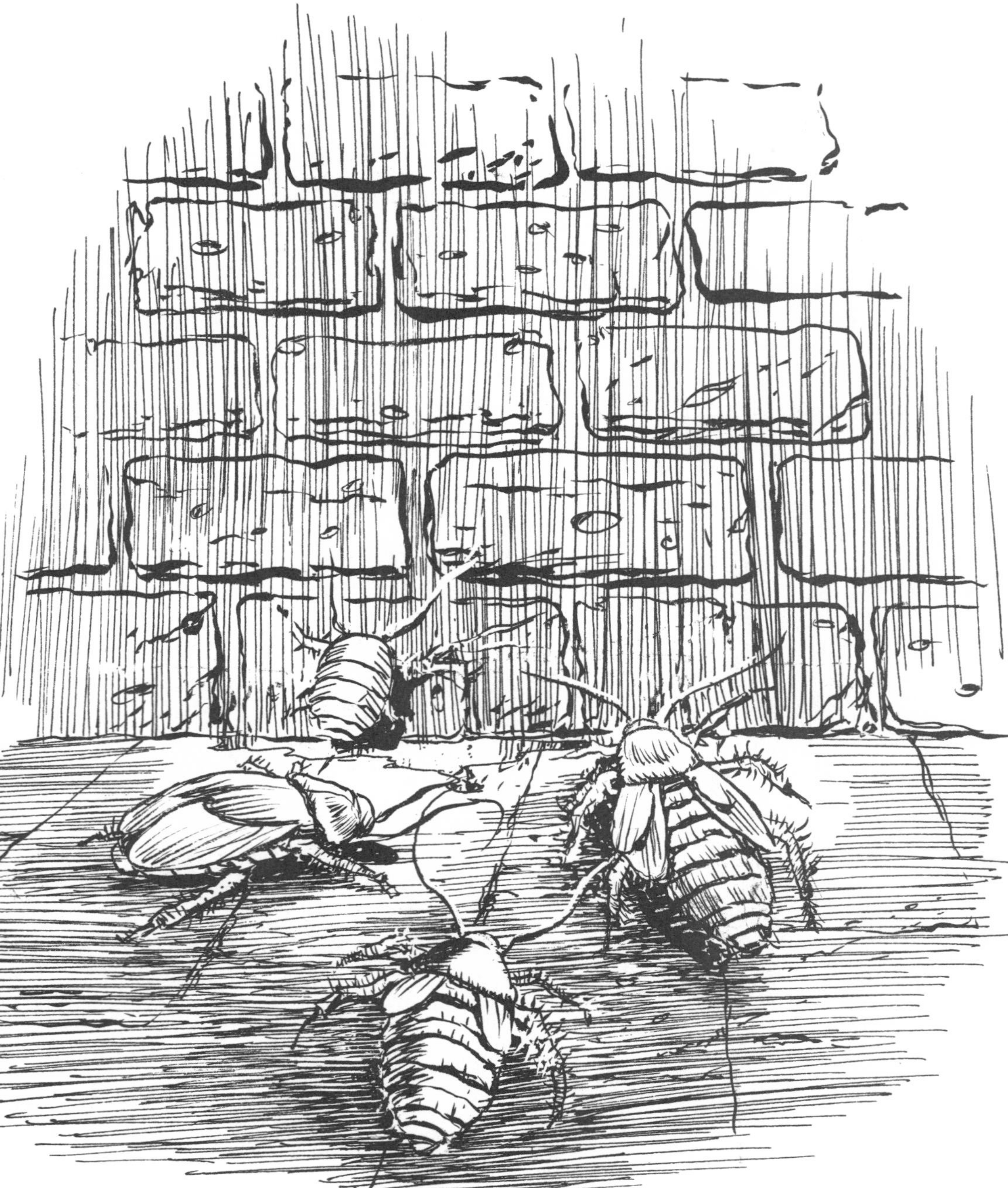

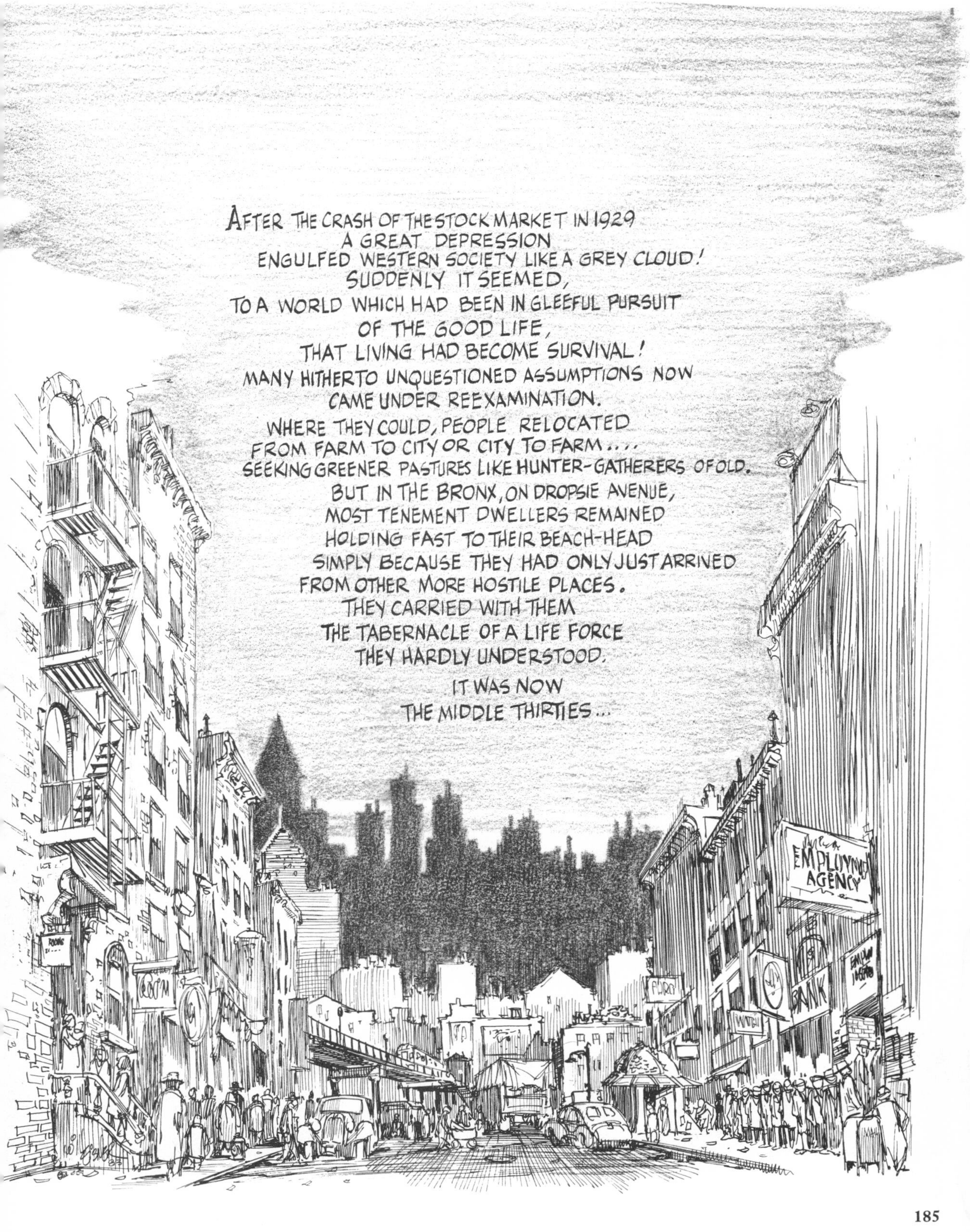
AFTER THE CRASH OF THE STOCK MARKET IN 1929
A GREAT DEPRESSION
ENGULFED WESTERN SOCIETY LIKE A GREY CLOUD!
SUDDENLY IT SEEMED,
TO A WORLD WHICH HAD BEEN IN GLEEFUL PURSUIT
OF THE GOOD LIFE,
THAT LIVING HAD BECOME SURVIVAL!
MANY HITHERTO UNQUESTIONED ASSUMPTIONS NOW
CAME UNDER REEXAMINATION.
WHERE THEY COULD, PEOPLE RELOCATED
FROM FARM TO CITY OR CITY TO FARM....
SEEKING GREENER PASTURES LIKE HUNTER-GATHERERS OF OLD.
BUT IN THE BRONX, ON DROPSIE AVENUE,
MOST TENEMENT DWELLERS REMAINED
HOLDING FAST TO THEIR BEACH-HEAD
SIMPLY BECAUSE THEY HAD ONLY JUST ARRIVED
FROM OTHER MORE HOSTILE PLACES.
THEY CARRIED WITH THEM
THE TABERNACLE OF A LIFE FORCE
THEY HARDLY UNDERSTOOD.
IT WAS NOW
THE MIDDLE THIRTIES...
AGENCY
BANK

1934

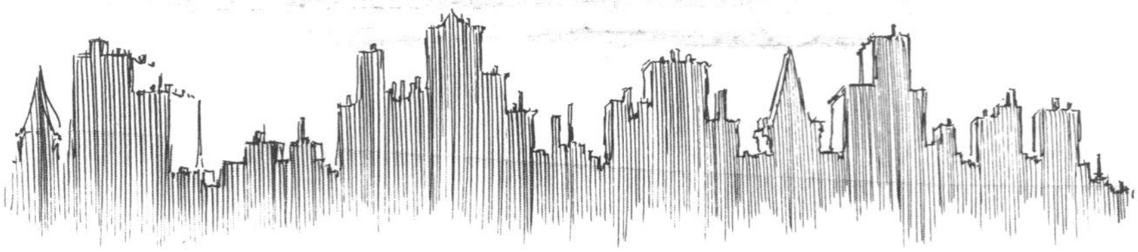

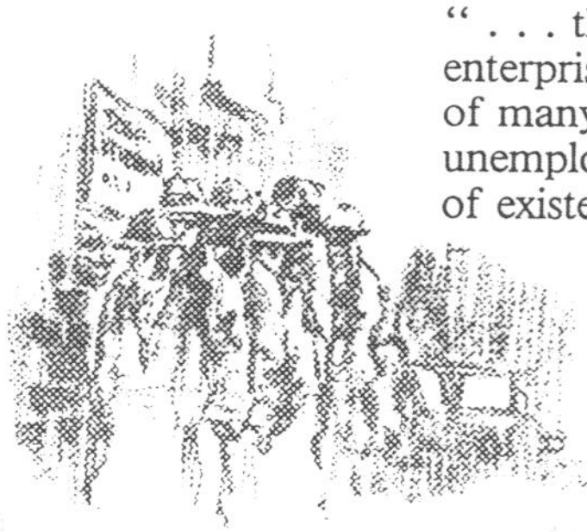

" . . . the withered leaves of industrial enterprise lie on every side . . . the savings of many thousands of families are gone . . . unemployed citizens face the grim problem of existence. . . ."

FRANKLIN D. ROOSEVELT
From his first Inaugural Address

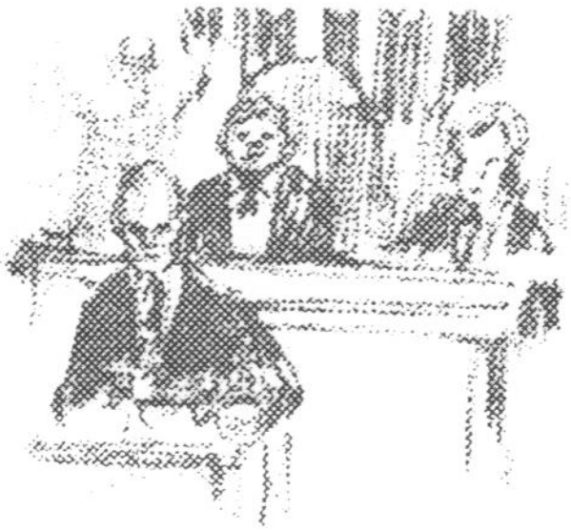

ITEMS FROM
THE NEW YORK PRESS

1500 HOMELESS LIVE IN ARMORY

69th REGIMENT HOUSES POOR

FEB. 7, 1934

Sheltered from the cold, over 1500 homeless people have found at least temporary refuge in the 69th Regiment Armory at Lexington Avenue and Twenty-Sixth Street in New York.

These victims of the depression, poorly clothed and dispirited, have been pouring into the huge building filling the drill floor and the mezzanine. Coming from the inclement pavements and wet doorways or dank subway kiosks, they encamp on the polished wooden floors.

SIMPLE GAMES OCCUPY THEIR TIME

In an effort to keep up morale,the men play checkers, jigsaw puzzles and hang around a piano played by a volunteer of surprising talent.

SLUMP CAN AFFECT PEOPLE'S HEALTH

INCREASE IN ILLNESS AND REDUCTION OF INCOME EFFECT.

In an article published on Jan. 14 by the *New York Times,* it was reported that the average annual income of a representative group of American wage-earners dropped from $1700 in 1929 to $900 this year.

The significance of the statistic is that historically an economic depression usually results in sickness and impaired vitality.

RATE OF DEATH SINCE 1929 HAS REDUCED

Strangely enough, the U.S. death rate has fallen despite the drop in living standards.

TWO MEN FAINT OF HUNGER IN CITY HALL WHILE WOMAN SCREAMS

MAYOR LA GUARDIA HALTS CONFERENCE

MARCH 2, 1934

According to the *New York Times,* two men in a group of twenty-two unemployed people besieged City Hall in the belief that the mayor would give them jobs in snow removal work, collapsed in the hall outside the Mayor's Office.

Both men, exhausted from lack of food, were immediately taken to the Beekman Street Hospital at Mayor Fiorello La Guardia's orders.

"WANT JOBS, NOT FOOD"

The men had worked the day before at snow clearing for the Sanitation Department until they were laid off for lack of work.

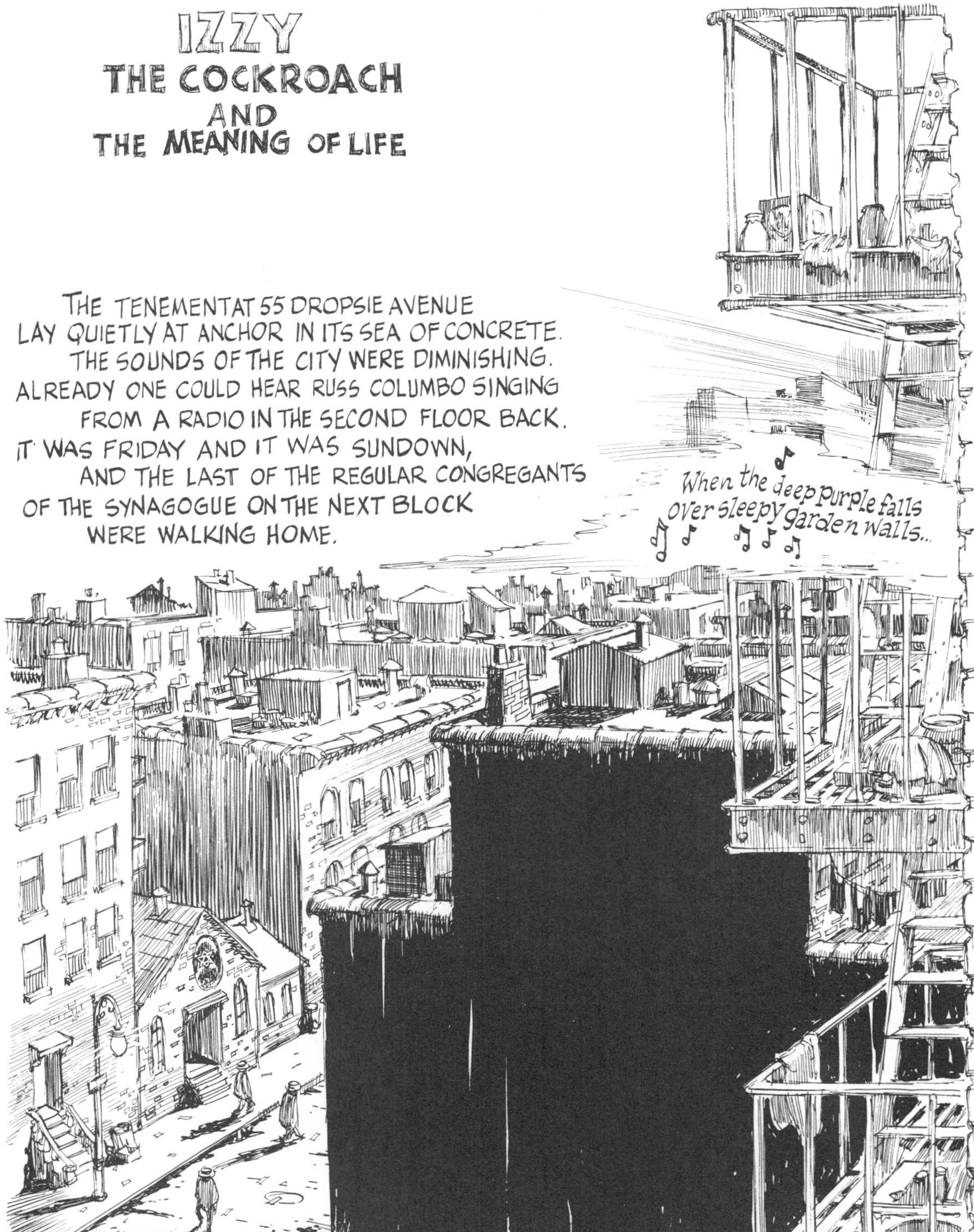
IZZY
THE COCKROACH
AND
THE MEANING OF LIFE
THE TENEMENT AT 55 DROPSIE AVENUE LAY QUIETLY AT ANCHOR IN ITS SEA OF CONCRETE. THE SOUNDS OF THE CITY WERE DIMINISHING. ALREADY ONE COULD HEAR RUSS COLUMBO SINGING FROM A RADIO IN THE SECOND FLOOR BACK. IT WAS FRIDAY AND IT WAS SUNDOWN, AND THE LAST OF THE REGULAR CONGREGANTS OF THE SYNAGOGUE ON THE NEXT BLOCK WERE WALKING HOME.
When the deep purple falls over sleepy garden walls...

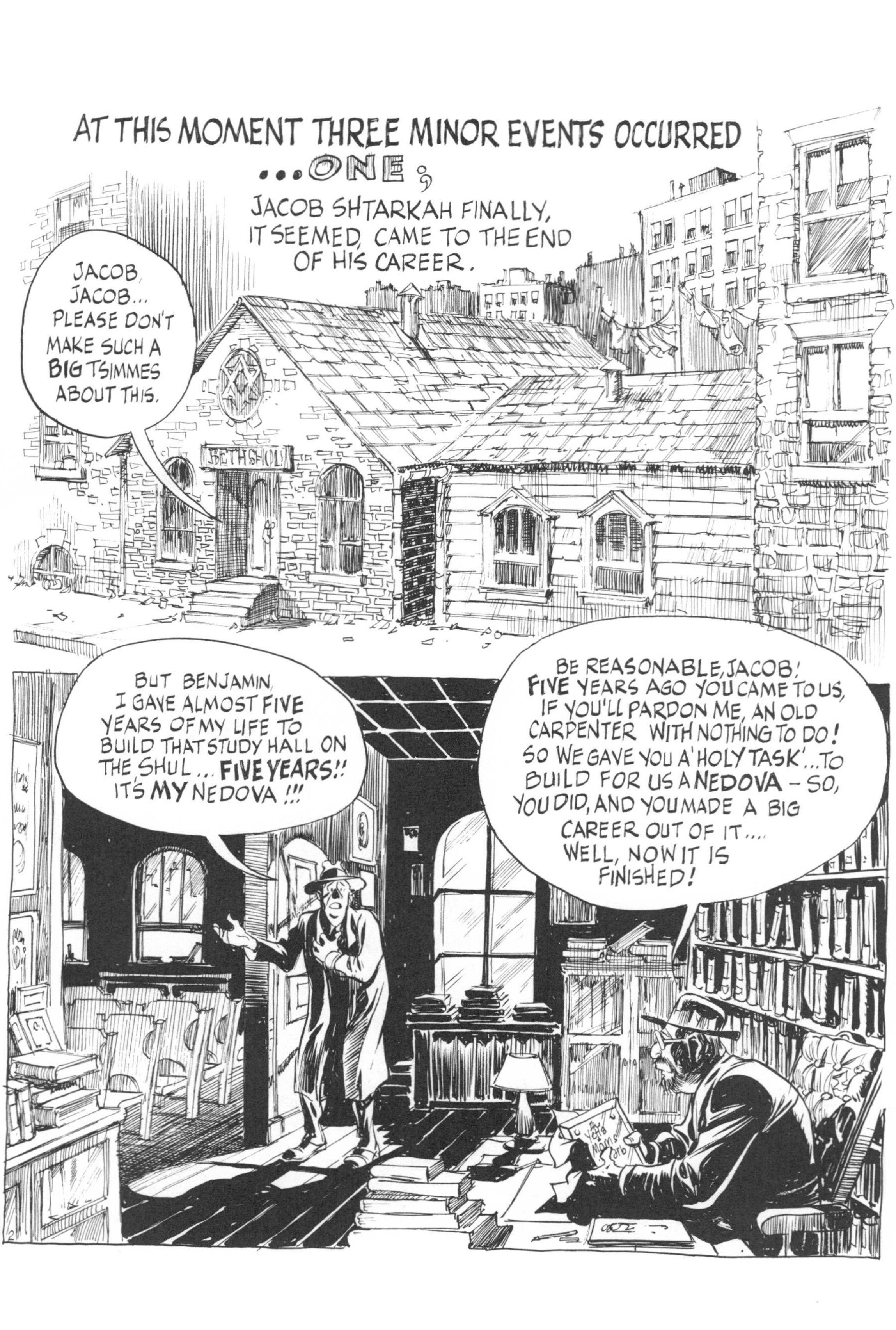
AT THIS MOMENT THREE MINOR EVENTS OCCURRED
...ONE;
JACOB SHTARKAH FINALLY, IT SEEMED, CAME TO THE END OF HIS CAREER.
JACOB, JACOB... PLEASE DON'T MAKE SUCH A BIG TSIMMES ABOUT THIS.
BETH SHOLOM
BUT BENJAMIN, I GAVE ALMOST FIVE YEARS OF MY LIFE TO BUILD THAT STUDY HALL ON THE SHUL... FIVE YEARS!! IT'S MY NEDOVA!!!
BE REASONABLE, JACOB! FIVE YEARS AGO YOU CAME TO US, IF YOU'LL PARDON ME, AN OLD CARPENTER WITH NOTHING TO DO! SO WE GAVE YOU A 'HOLY TASK'...TO BUILD FOR US A NEDOVA – SO, YOU DID, AND YOU MADE A BIG CAREER OUT OF IT.... WELL, NOW IT IS FINISHED!

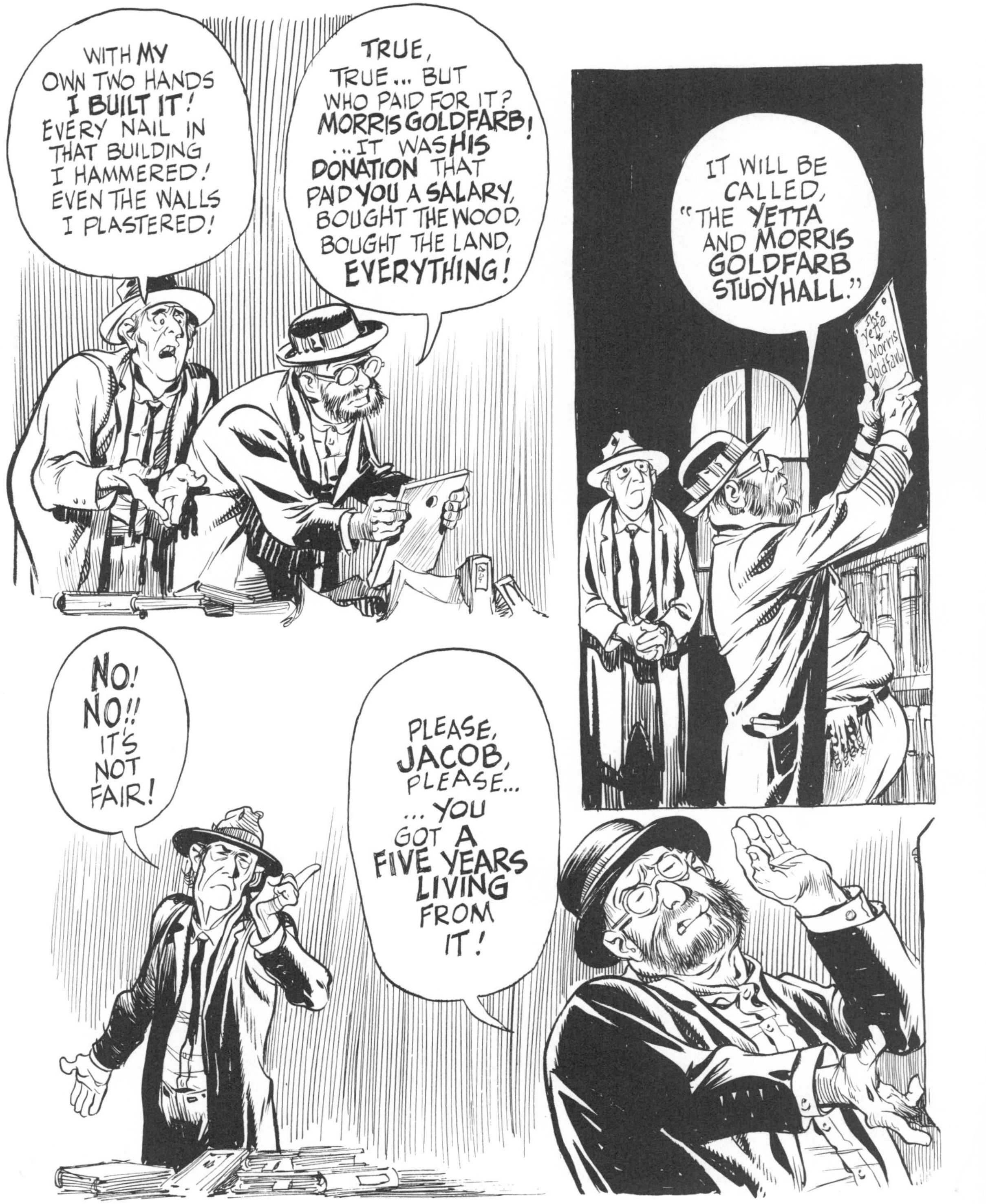
WITH MY OWN TWO HANDS I BUILT IT! EVERY NAIL IN THAT BUILDING I HAMMERED! EVEN THE WALLS I PLASTERED!
TRUE, TRUE... BUT WHO PAID FOR IT? MORRIS GOLDFARB! ...IT WAS HIS DONATION THAT PAID YOU A SALARY, BOUGHT THE WOOD, BOUGHT THE LAND, EVERYTHING!
IT WILL BE CALLED, "THE YETTA AND MORRIS GOLDFARB STUDY HALL."
NO! NO!! IT'S NOT FAIR!
PLEASE, JACOB, PLEASE... ...YOU GOT A FIVE YEARS LIVING FROM IT!

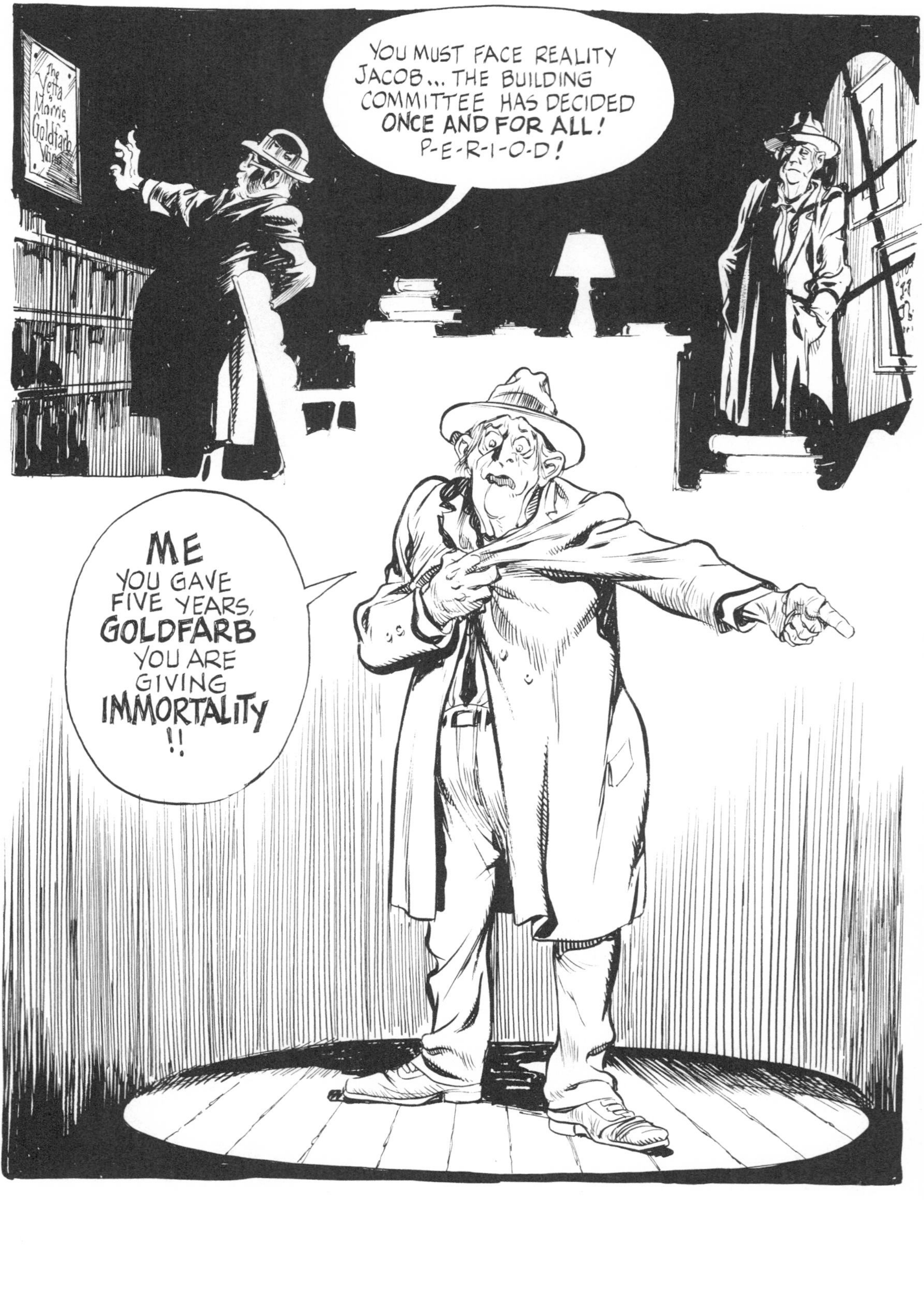
YOU MUST FACE REALITY JACOB... THE BUILDING COMMITTEE HAS DECIDED ONCE AND FOR ALL! P-E-R-I-O-D!
ME YOU GAVE FIVE YEARS, GOLDFARB YOU ARE GIVING IMMORTALITY !!

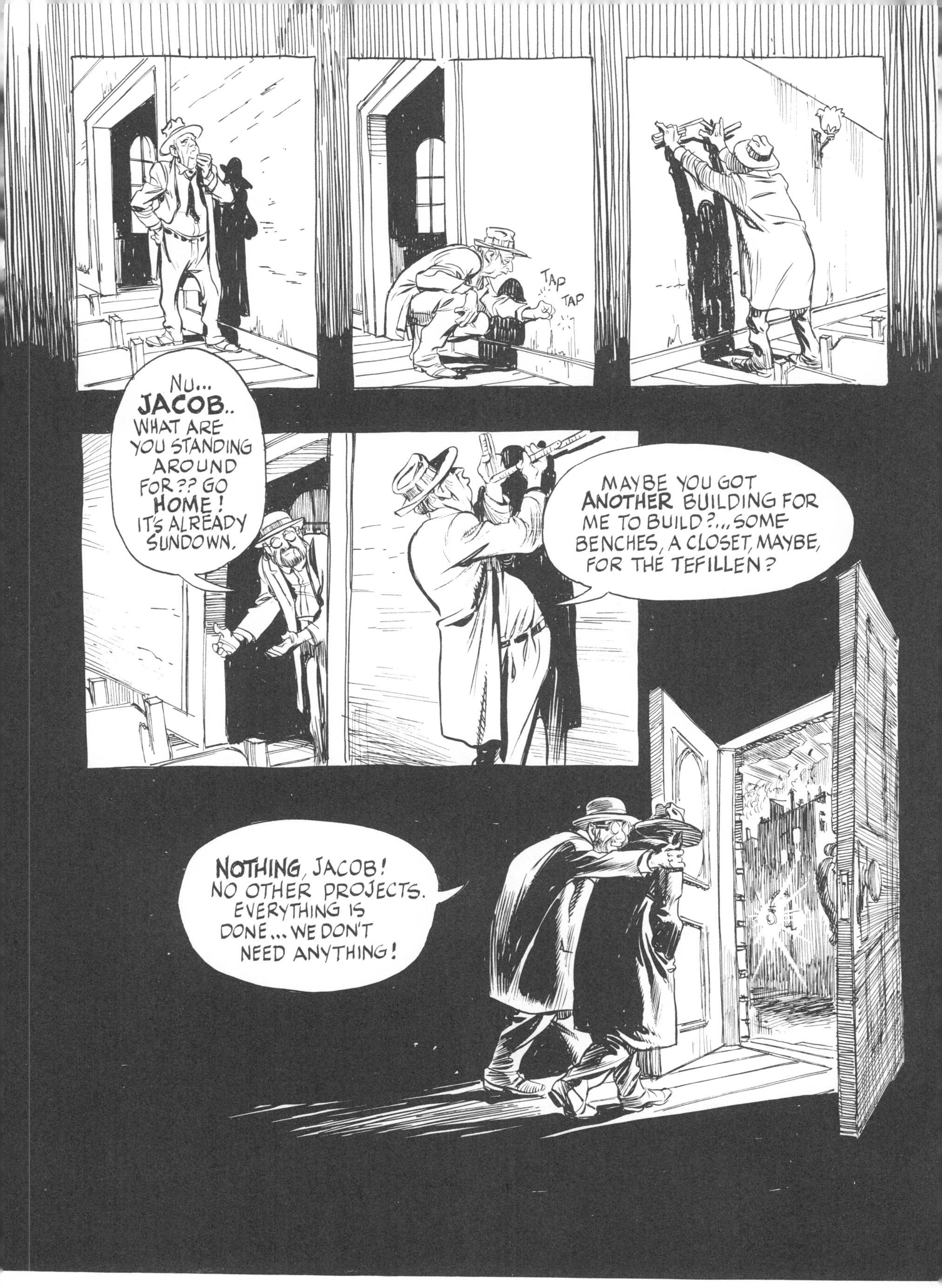
TAP TAP
NU... JACOB.. WHAT ARE YOU STANDING AROUND FOR?? GO HOME! IT'S ALREADY SUNDOWN.
MAYBE YOU GOT ANOTHER BUILDING FOR ME TO BUILD?.., SOME BENCHES, A CLOSET, MAYBE, FOR THE TEFILLEN?
NOTHING, JACOB! NO OTHER PROJECTS. EVERYTHING IS DONE... WE DON'T NEED ANYTHING!

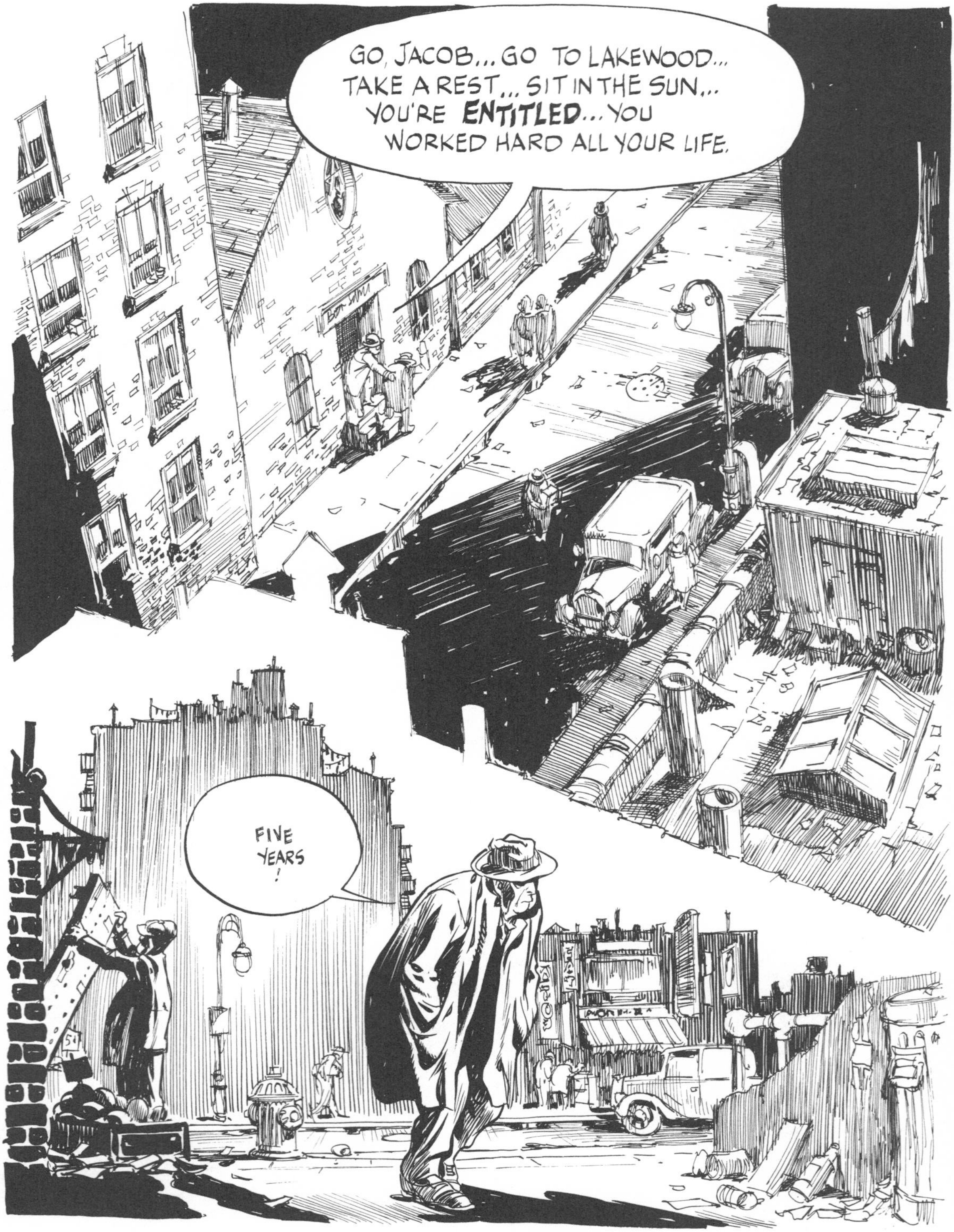
GO, JACOB... GO TO LAKEWOOD... TAKE A REST... SIT IN THE SUN... YOU'RE ENTITLED... YOU WORKED HARD ALL YOUR LIFE.
FIVE YEARS!

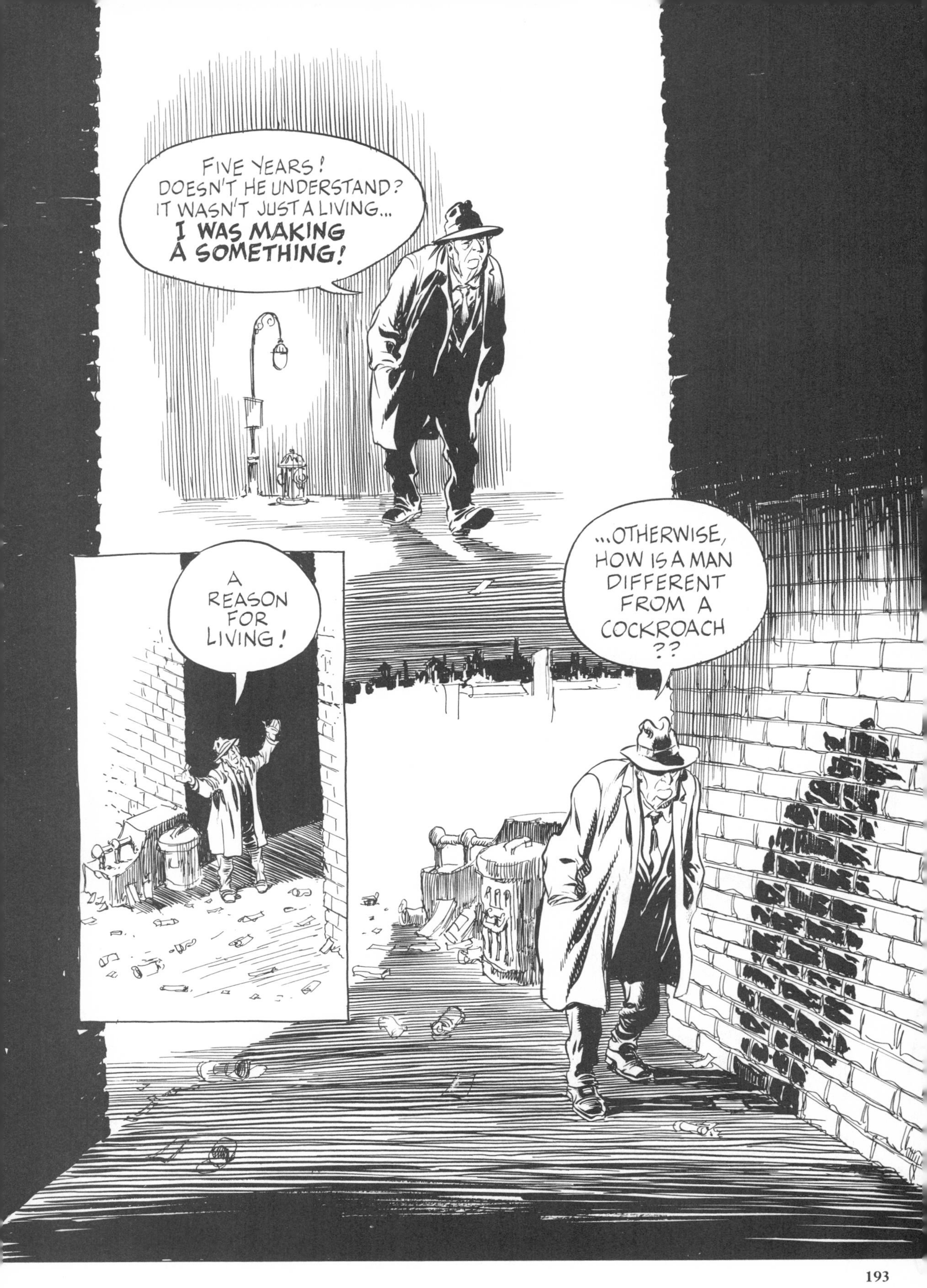
FIVE YEARS! DOESN'T HE UNDERSTAND? IT WASN'T JUST A LIVING... **I WAS MAKING A SOMETHING!**
A REASON FOR LIVING!
...OTHERWISE, HOW IS A MAN DIFFERENT FROM A COCKROACH ??

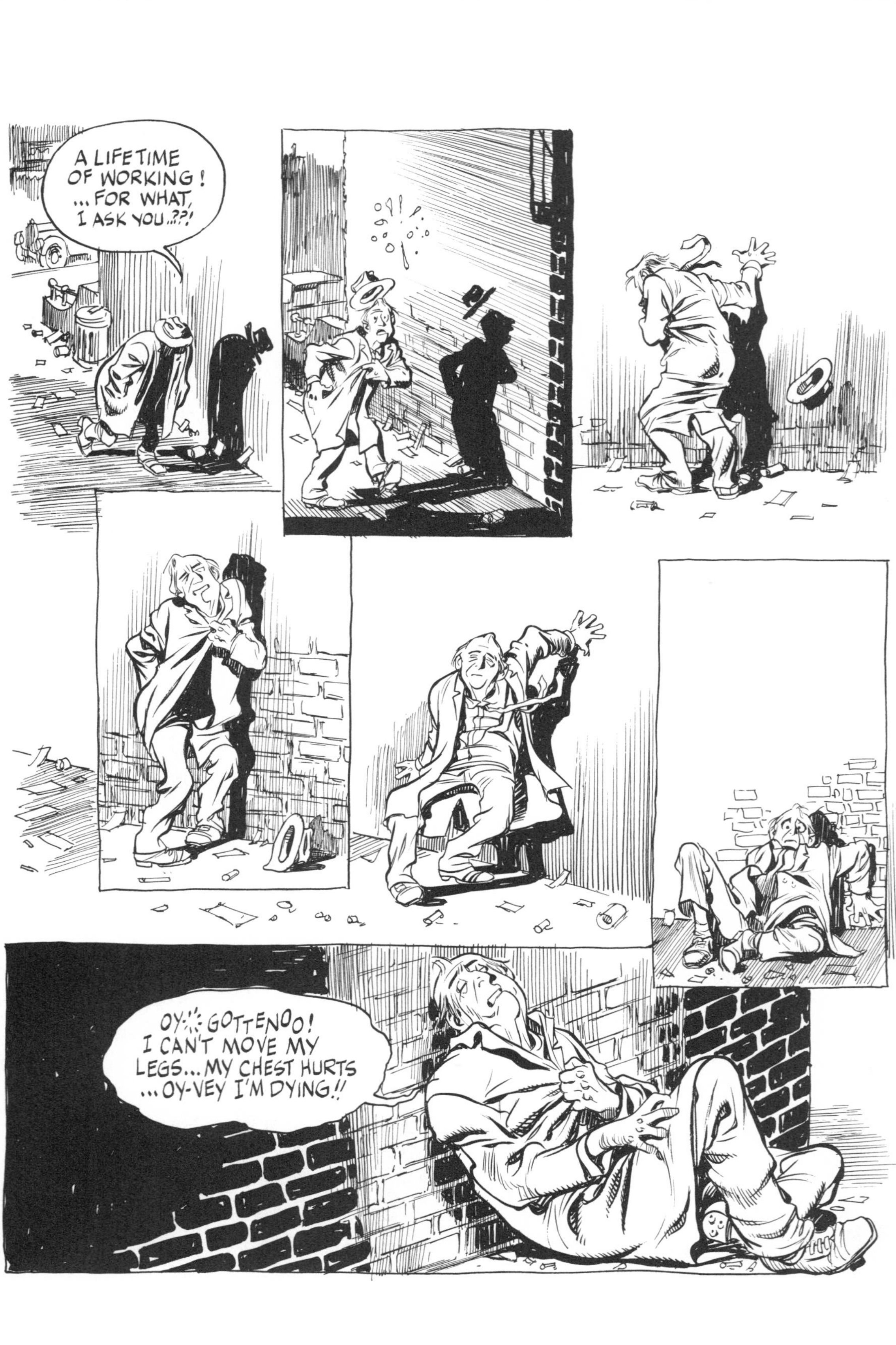
A LIFETIME OF WORKING! ...FOR WHAT, I ASK YOU..??!
OY! GOTTENOO! I CAN'T MOVE MY LEGS... MY CHEST HURTS ...OY-VEY I'M DYING!!

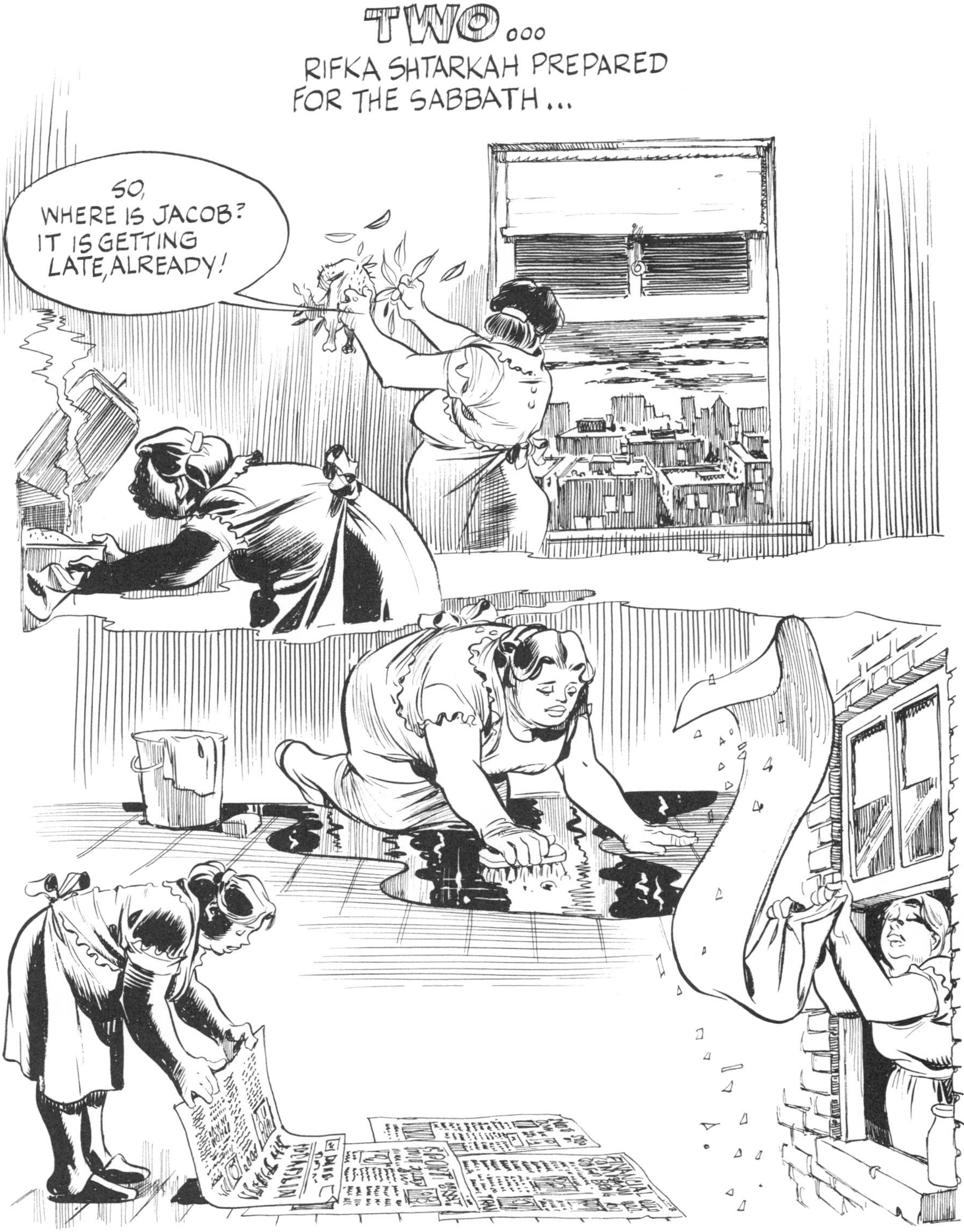
TWO...
RIFKA SHTARKAH PREPARED FOR THE SABBATH...
SO, WHERE IS JACOB? IT IS GETTING LATE, ALREADY!

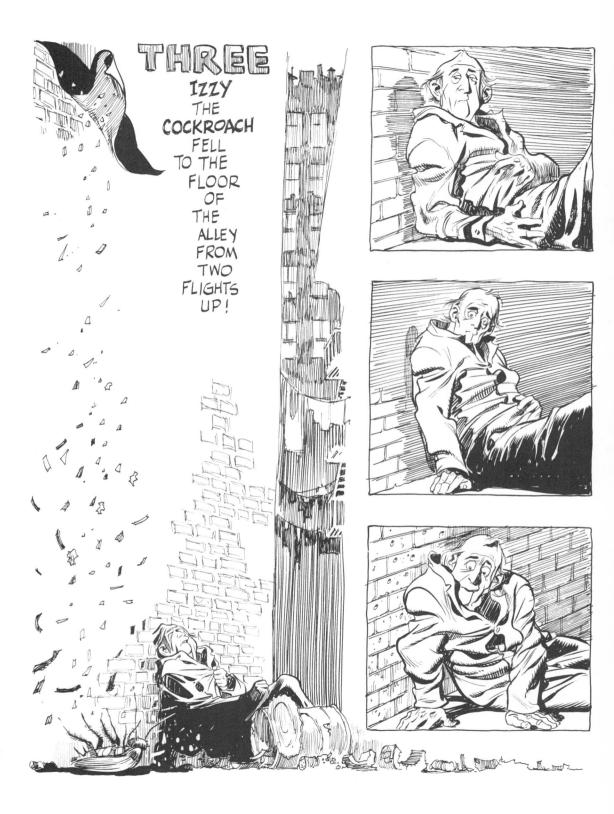

THREE

IZZY THE COCKROACH FELL TO THE FLOOR OF THE ALLEY FROM TWO FLIGHTS UP!

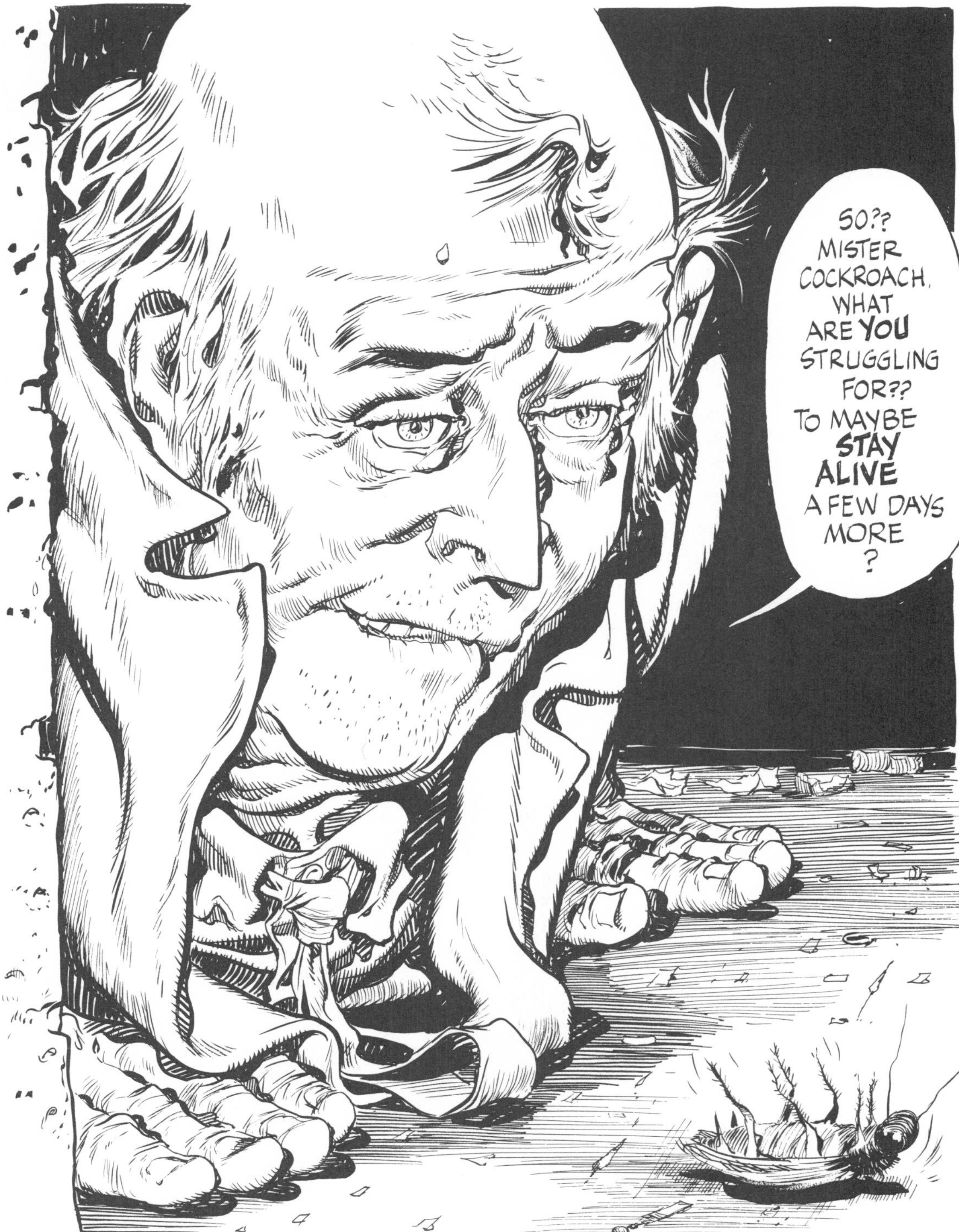
SO?? MISTER COCKROACH. WHAT ARE YOU STRUGGLING FOR?? TO MAYBE STAY ALIVE A FEW DAYS MORE ?

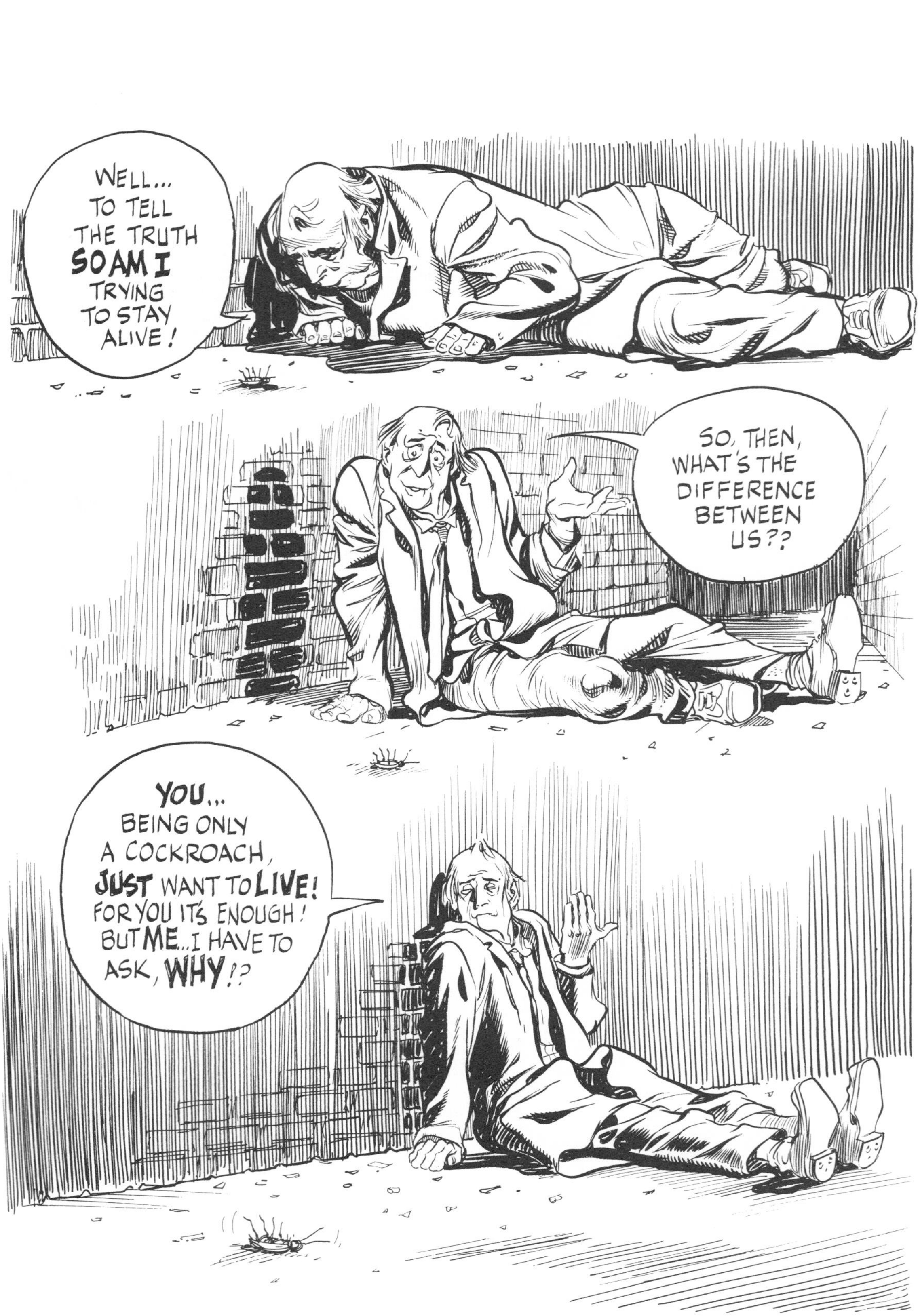
WELL... TO TELL THE TRUTH SO AM I TRYING TO STAY ALIVE!
SO, THEN, WHAT'S THE DIFFERENCE BETWEEN US??
YOU... BEING ONLY A COCKROACH, JUST WANT TO LIVE! FOR YOU IT'S ENOUGH! BUT ME... I HAVE TO ASK, WHY!?

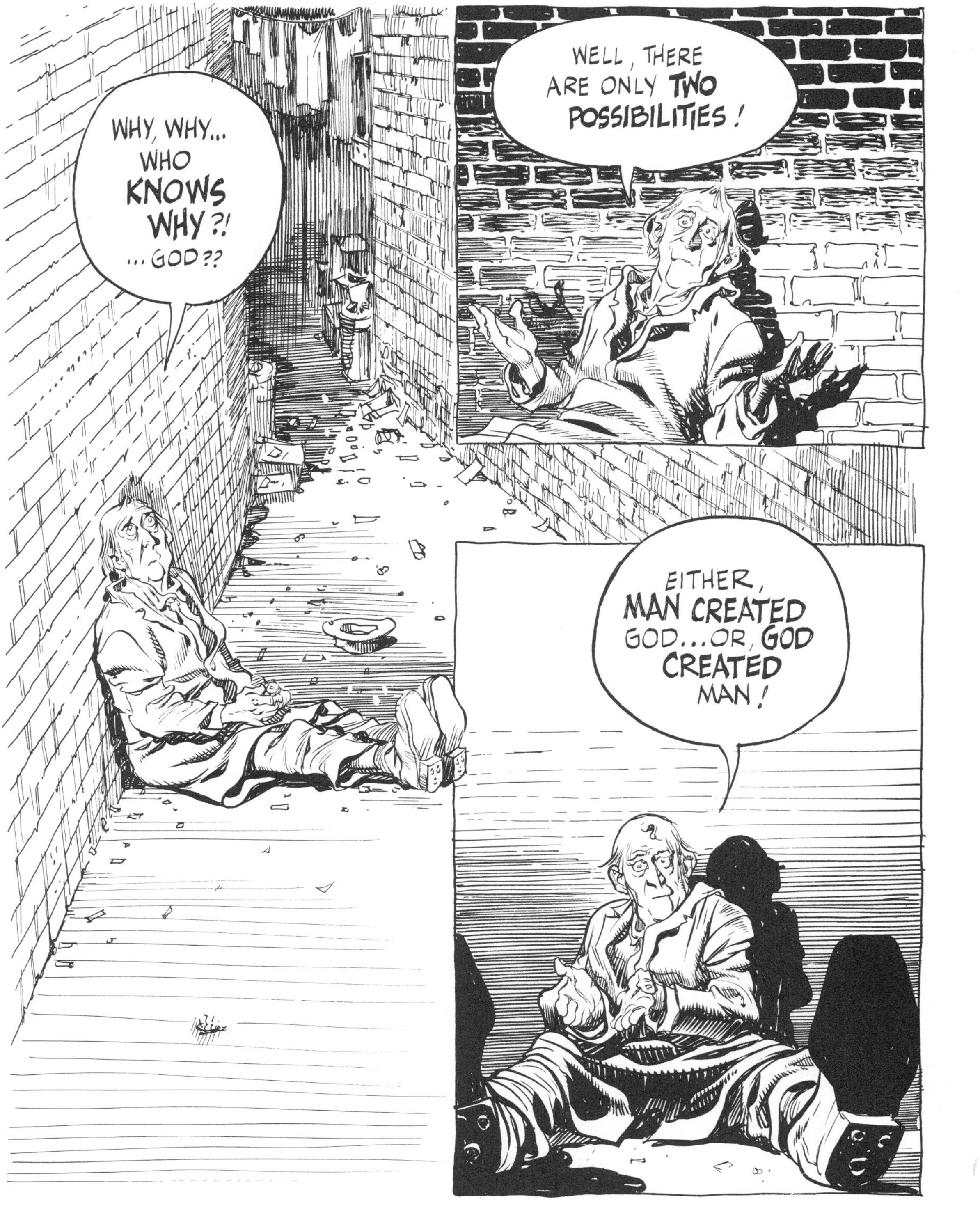
WHY, WHY... WHO KNOWS WHY ?! ...GOD ??
WELL, THERE ARE ONLY TWO POSSIBILITIES !
EITHER, MAN CREATED GOD...OR, GOD CREATED MAN !

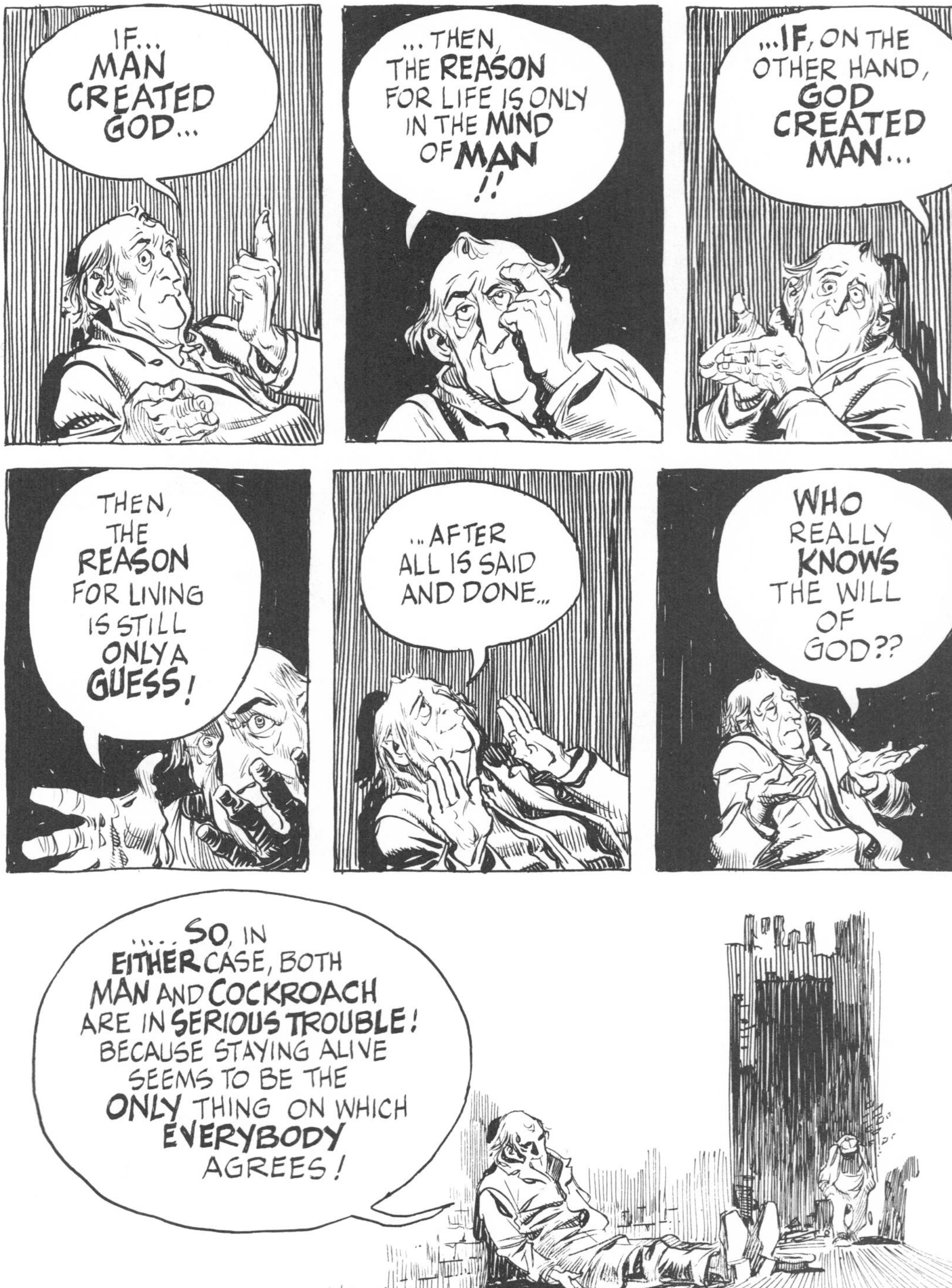
IF... MAN CREATED GOD...
...THEN, THE REASON FOR LIFE IS ONLY IN THE MIND OF MAN !!
...IF, ON THE OTHER HAND, GOD CREATED MAN...
THEN, THE REASON FOR LIVING IS STILL ONLY A GUESS!
...AFTER ALL IS SAID AND DONE...
WHO REALLY KNOWS THE WILL OF GOD??
.....SO, IN EITHER CASE, BOTH MAN AND COCKROACH ARE IN SERIOUS TROUBLE! BECAUSE STAYING ALIVE SEEMS TO BE THE ONLY THING ON WHICH EVERYBODY AGREES!

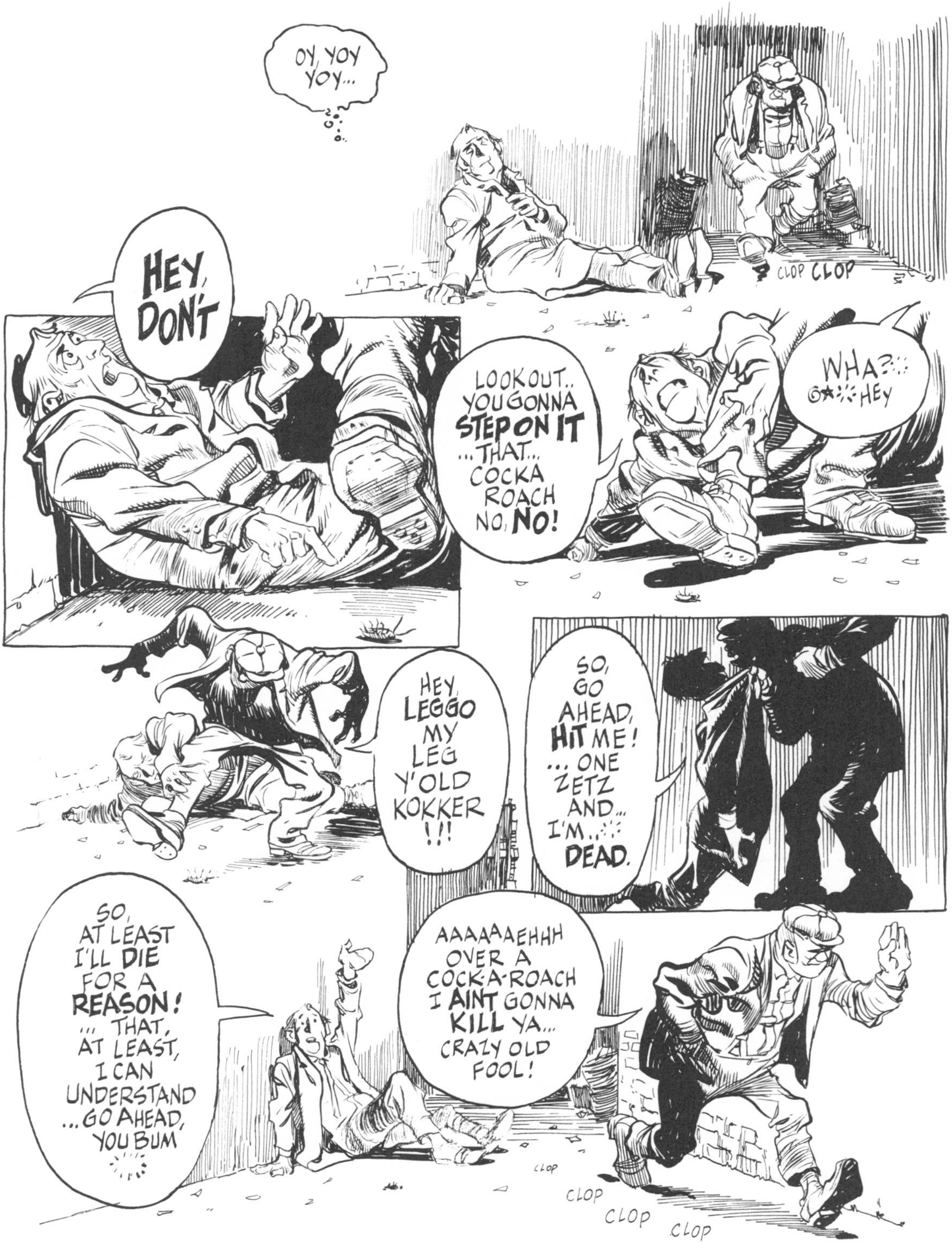
OY, YOY YOY...
CLOP CLOP
HEY, DON'T
LOOKOUT.. YOU GONNA STEP ON IT ...THAT... COCKA ROACH NO, NO!
WHA?... ...HEY
HEY, LEGGO MY LEG Y'OLD KOKKER !!!
SO, GO AHEAD, HIT ME! ... ONE ZETZ AND... I'M... DEAD.
SO, AT LEAST I'LL DIE FOR A REASON! ... THAT, AT LEAST, I CAN UNDERSTAND ...GO AHEAD, YOU BUM
AAAAAAEHHH OVER A COCK-A-ROACH I AINT GONNA KILL YA... CRAZY OLD FOOL!
CLOP
CLOP
CLOP
CLOP

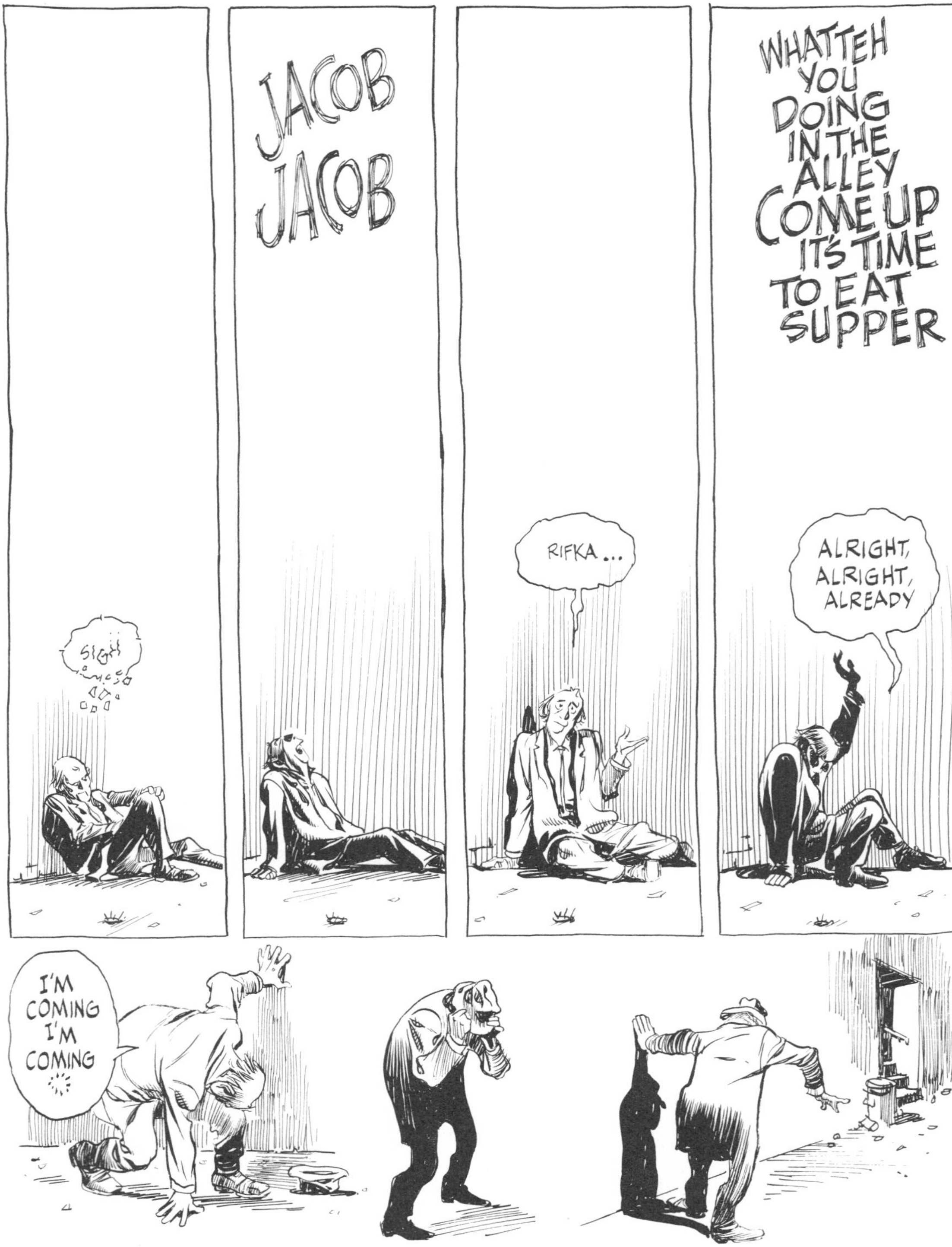
SIGH
JACOB
JACOB
RIFKA...
WHATTEH YOU DOING IN THE ALLEY COME UP IT'S TIME TO EAT SUPPER
ALRIGHT, ALRIGHT, ALREADY
I'M COMING I'M COMING

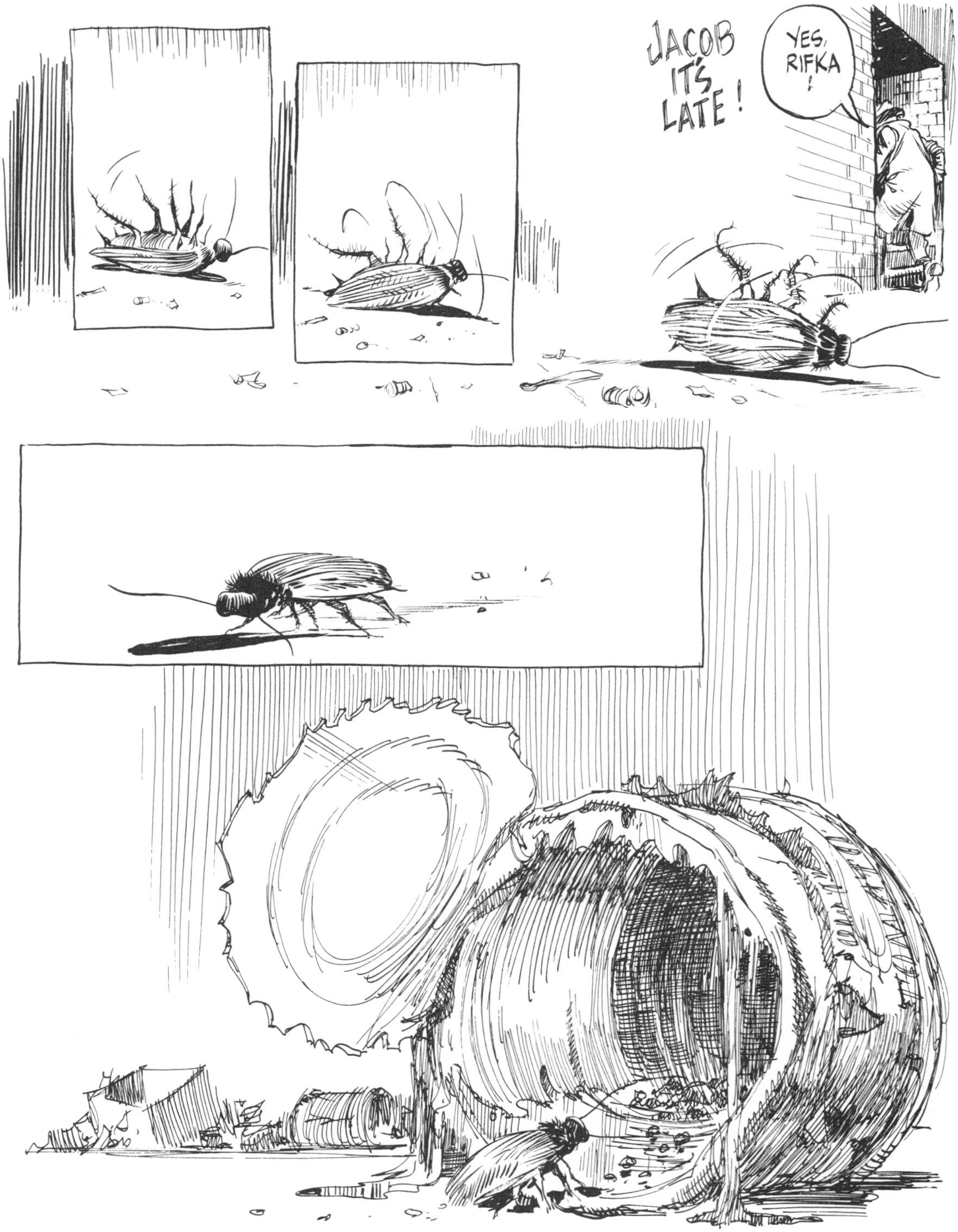
JACOB IT'S LATE!
YES, RIFKA!

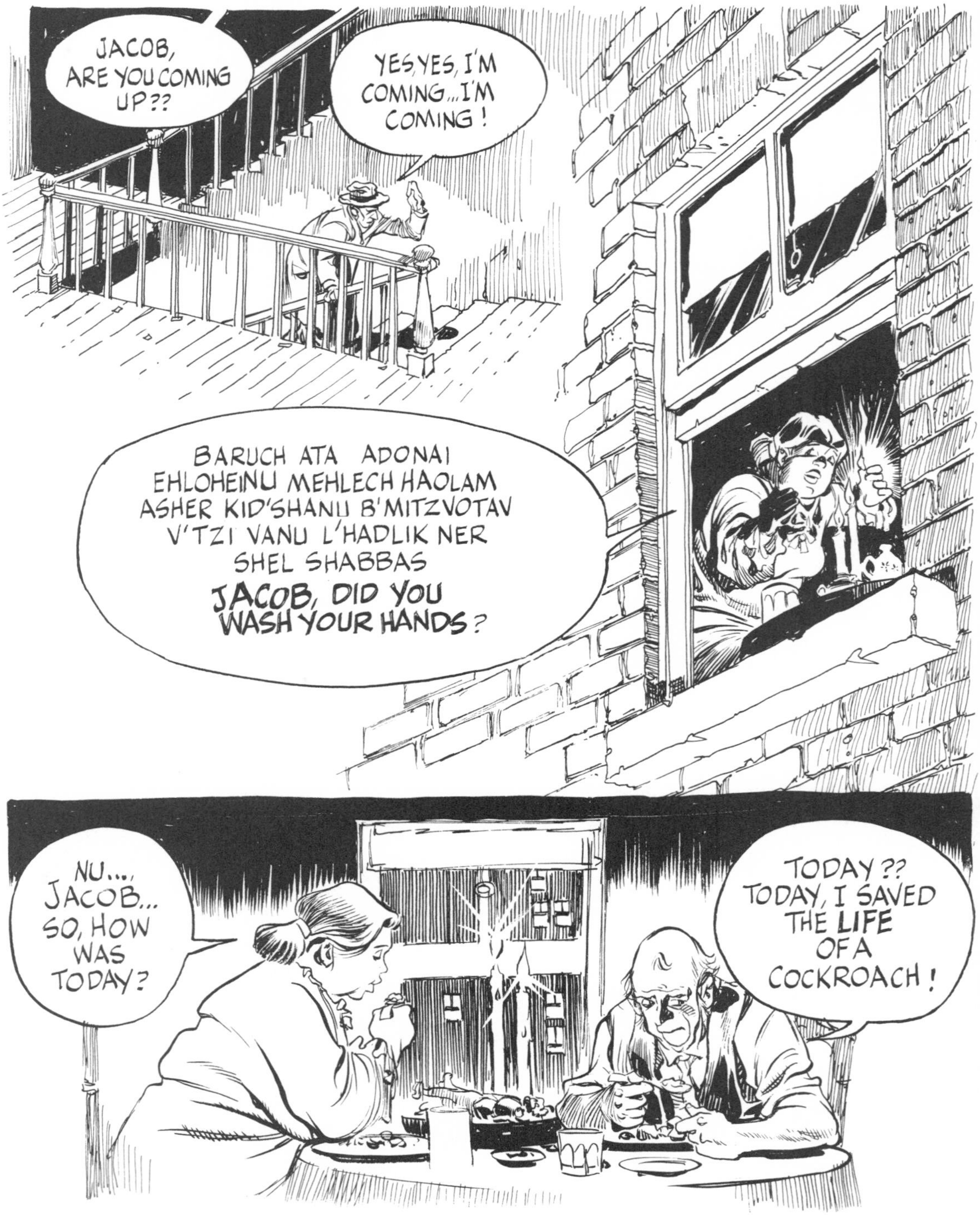
JACOB, ARE YOU COMING UP??
YES,YES, I'M COMING...I'M COMING!
BARUCH ATA ADONAI EHLOHEINU MEHLECH HAOLAM ASHER KID'SHANU B'MITZVOTAV V'TZI VANU L'HADLIK NER SHEL SHABBAS
JACOB, DID YOU WASH YOUR HANDS?
NU..., JACOB... SO, HOW WAS TODAY?
TODAY?? TODAY, I SAVED THE LIFE OF A COCKROACH!

ESCAPEE

SOUTH, SOUTHWEST– ACROSS THE HARLEM RIVER
WHERE THE BRONX ENDS, IS MANHATTAN ISLAND.
THERE...IS THE LAND OF PROMISE.

DANIEL, SON OF JACOB,
MADE IT FROM DROPSIE AVENUE.
VIA NIGHT SCHOOL,
MEDICAL SCHOOL BY DAY
(DRIVING A TAXI BY NIGHT)
AND FINALLY
AN INTERN
AT MT. HEBRON HOSPITAL
MANHATTAN EAST SIDE.
DANIEL HAD **ESCAPED**...
INTO THE MAINSTREAM.

HELLO, MOMMA ... THIS IS DANIEL.

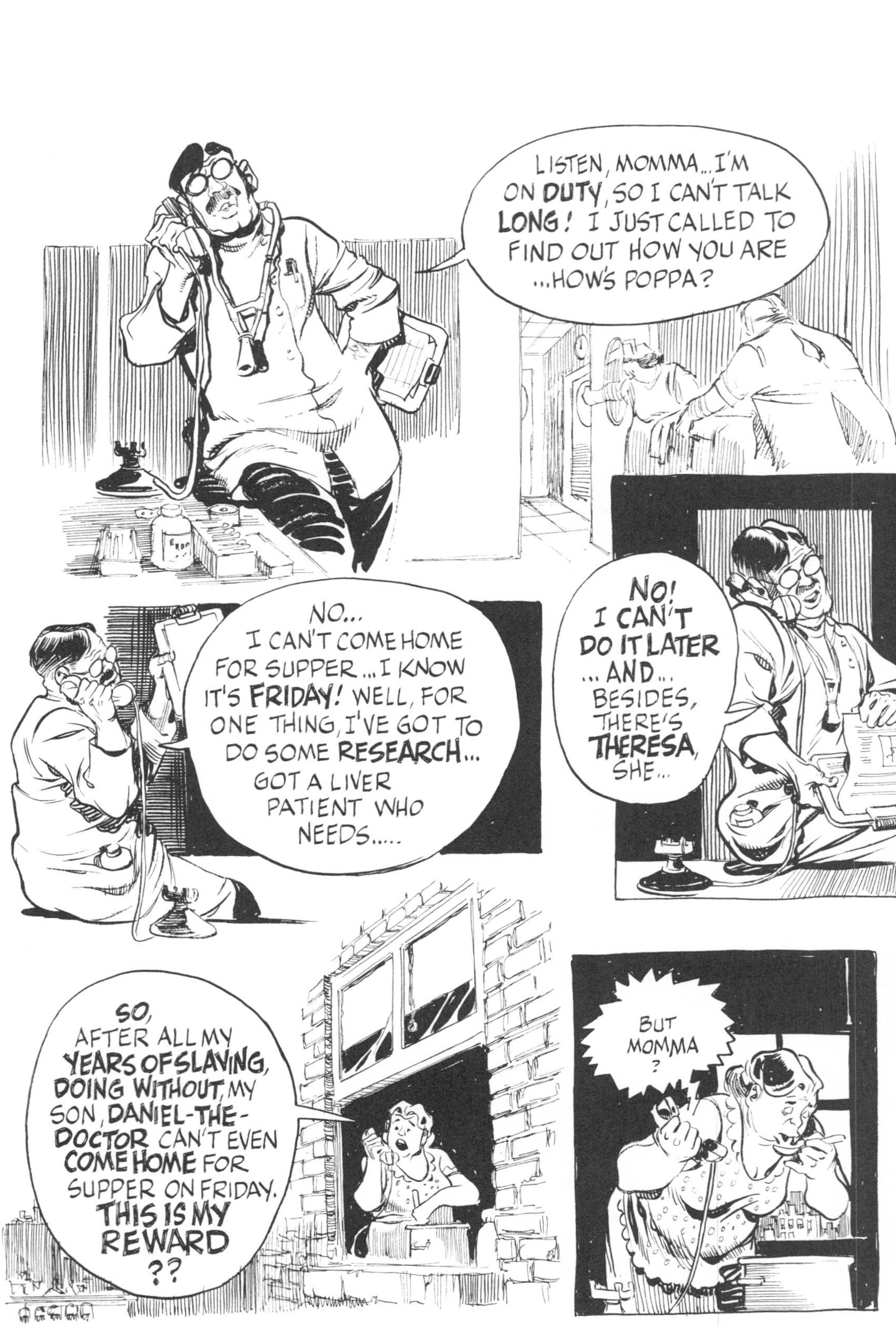
LISTEN, MOMMA...I'M ON DUTY, SO I CAN'T TALK LONG! I JUST CALLED TO FIND OUT HOW YOU ARE ...HOW'S POPPA?
NO... I CAN'T COME HOME FOR SUPPER...I KNOW IT'S FRIDAY! WELL, FOR ONE THING, I'VE GOT TO DO SOME RESEARCH... GOT A LIVER PATIENT WHO NEEDS.....
NO! I CAN'T DO IT LATER ...AND... BESIDES, THERE'S THERESA, SHE...
SO, AFTER ALL MY YEARS OF SLAVING, DOING WITHOUT, MY SON, DANIEL-THE-DOCTOR CAN'T EVEN COME HOME FOR SUPPER ON FRIDAY. THIS IS MY REWARD ??
BUT MOMMA ?

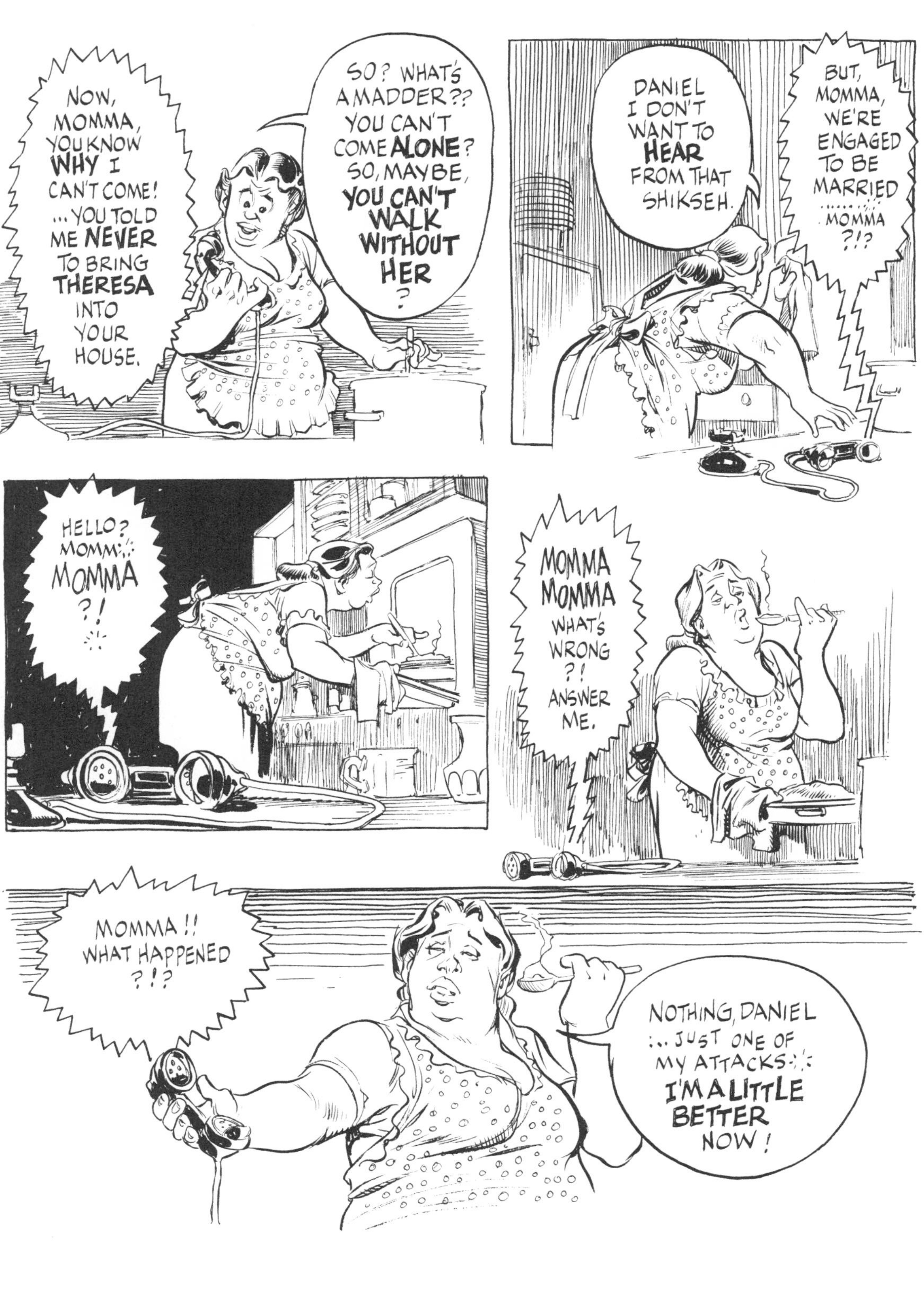

NOW, MOMMA, YOU KNOW WHY I CAN'T COME! ...YOU TOLD ME NEVER TO BRING THERESA INTO YOUR HOUSE.
SO? WHAT'S AMADDER?? YOU CAN'T COME ALONE? SO, MAYBE, YOU CAN'T WALK WITHOUT HER?
DANIEL I DON'T WANT TO HEAR FROM THAT SHIKSEH.
BUT, MOMMA, WE'RE ENGAGED TO BE MARRIED ...... MOMMA ?!?
HELLO? MOMM... MOMMA ?!
MOMMA MOMMA WHAT'S WRONG ?! ANSWER ME.
MOMMA!! WHAT HAPPENED ?!?
NOTHING, DANIEL ... JUST ONE OF MY ATTACKS... I'M A LITTLE BETTER NOW!

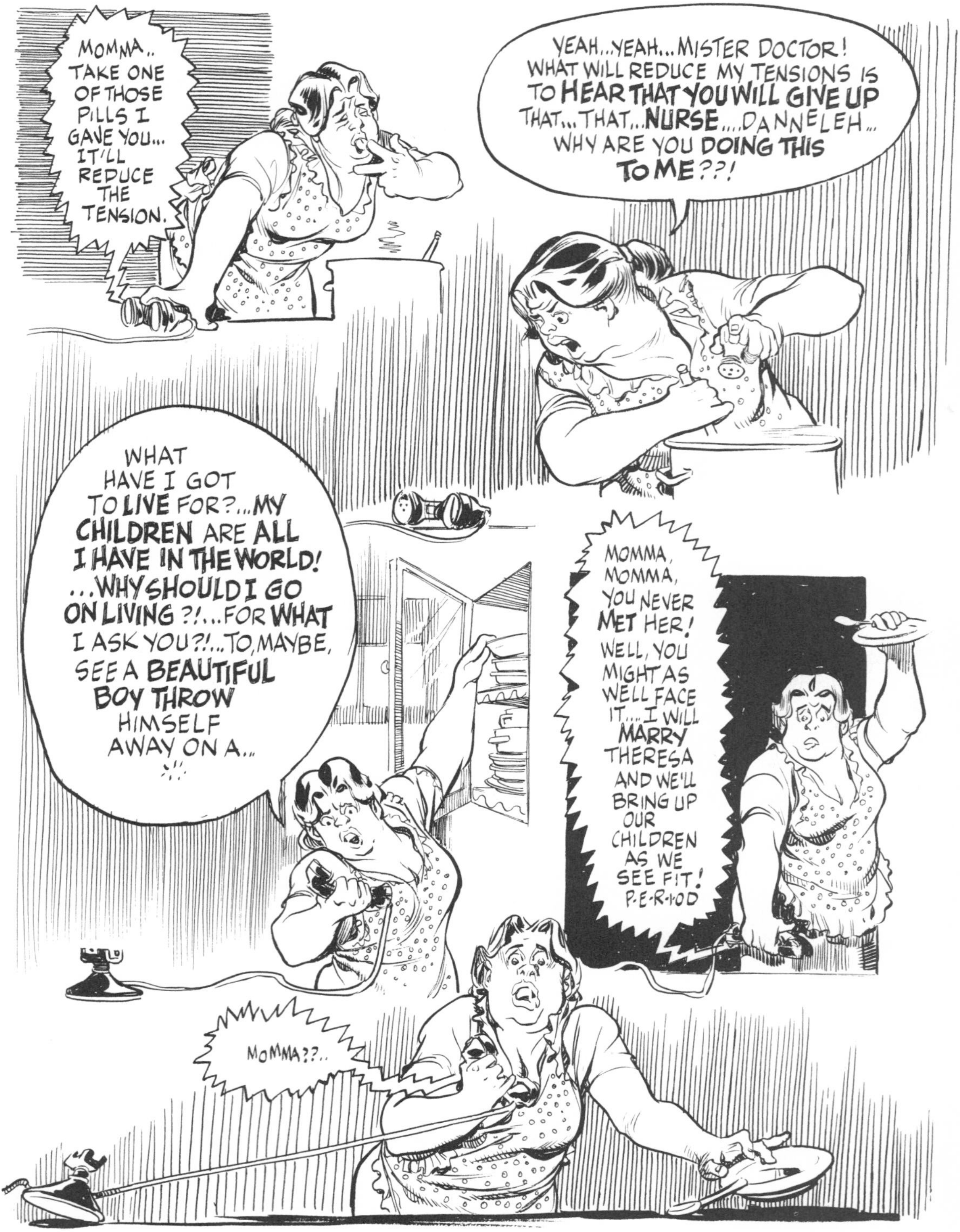
MOMMA.. TAKE ONE OF THOSE PILLS I GAVE YOU... IT'LL REDUCE THE TENSION.
YEAH...YEAH...MISTER DOCTOR! WHAT WILL REDUCE MY TENSIONS IS TO HEAR THAT YOU WILL GIVE UP THAT...THAT...NURSE...DANNELEH... WHY ARE YOU DOING THIS TO ME??!
WHAT HAVE I GOT TO LIVE FOR?...MY CHILDREN ARE ALL I HAVE IN THE WORLD! ...WHY SHOULD I GO ON LIVING?!...FOR WHAT I ASK YOU?!...TO, MAYBE, SEE A BEAUTIFUL BOY THROW HIMSELF AWAY ON A...
MOMMA, MOMMA, YOU NEVER MET HER! WELL, YOU MIGHT AS WELL FACE IT...I WILL MARRY THERESA AND WE'LL BRING UP OUR CHILDREN AS WE SEE FIT! P-E-R-I-OD
MOMMA??..

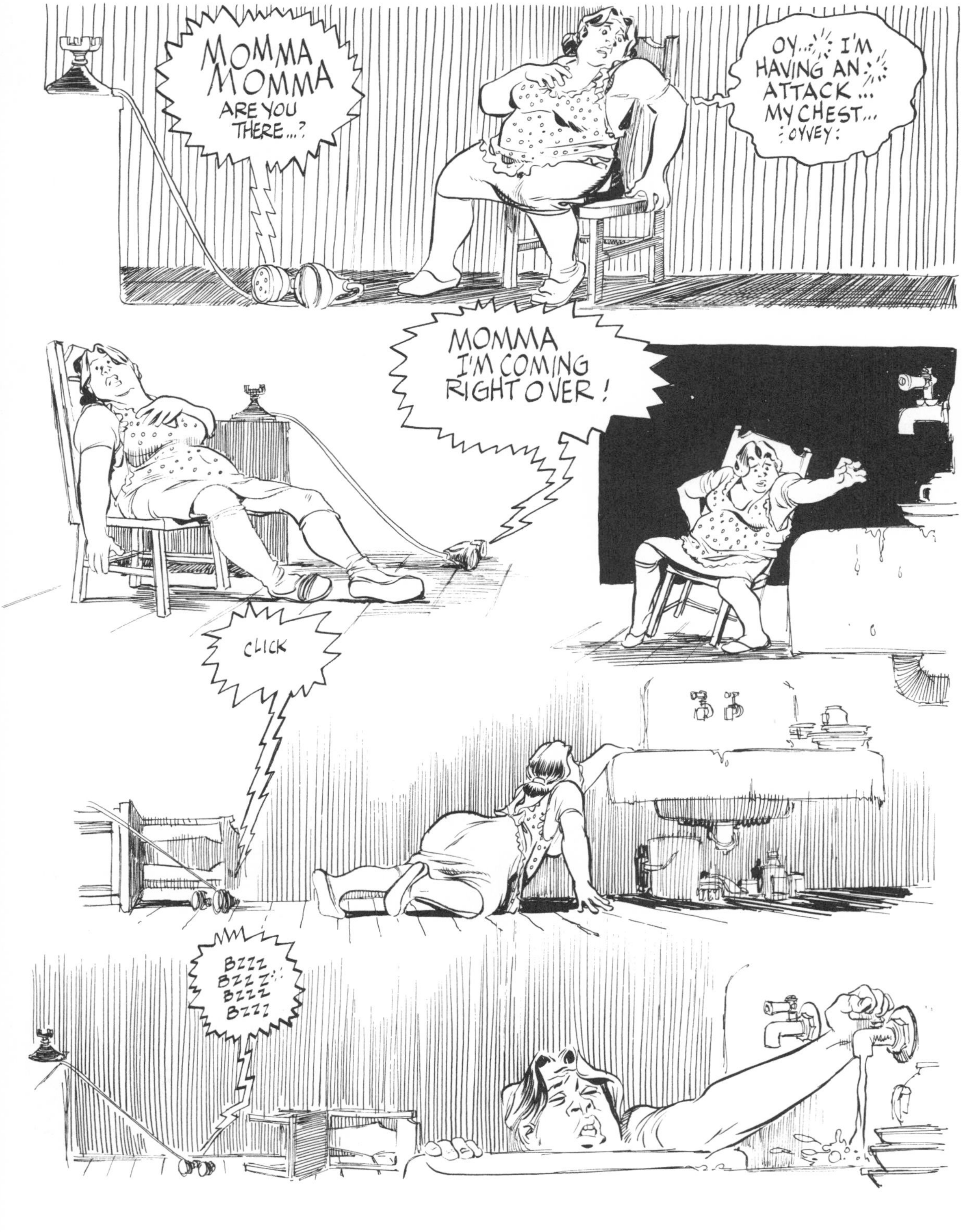
MOMMA MOMMA ARE YOU THERE...?
OY..! I'M HAVING AN ATTACK... MY CHEST... OYVEY
MOMMA I'M COMING RIGHT OVER!
CLICK
BZZZ BZZZ BZZZ BZZZ

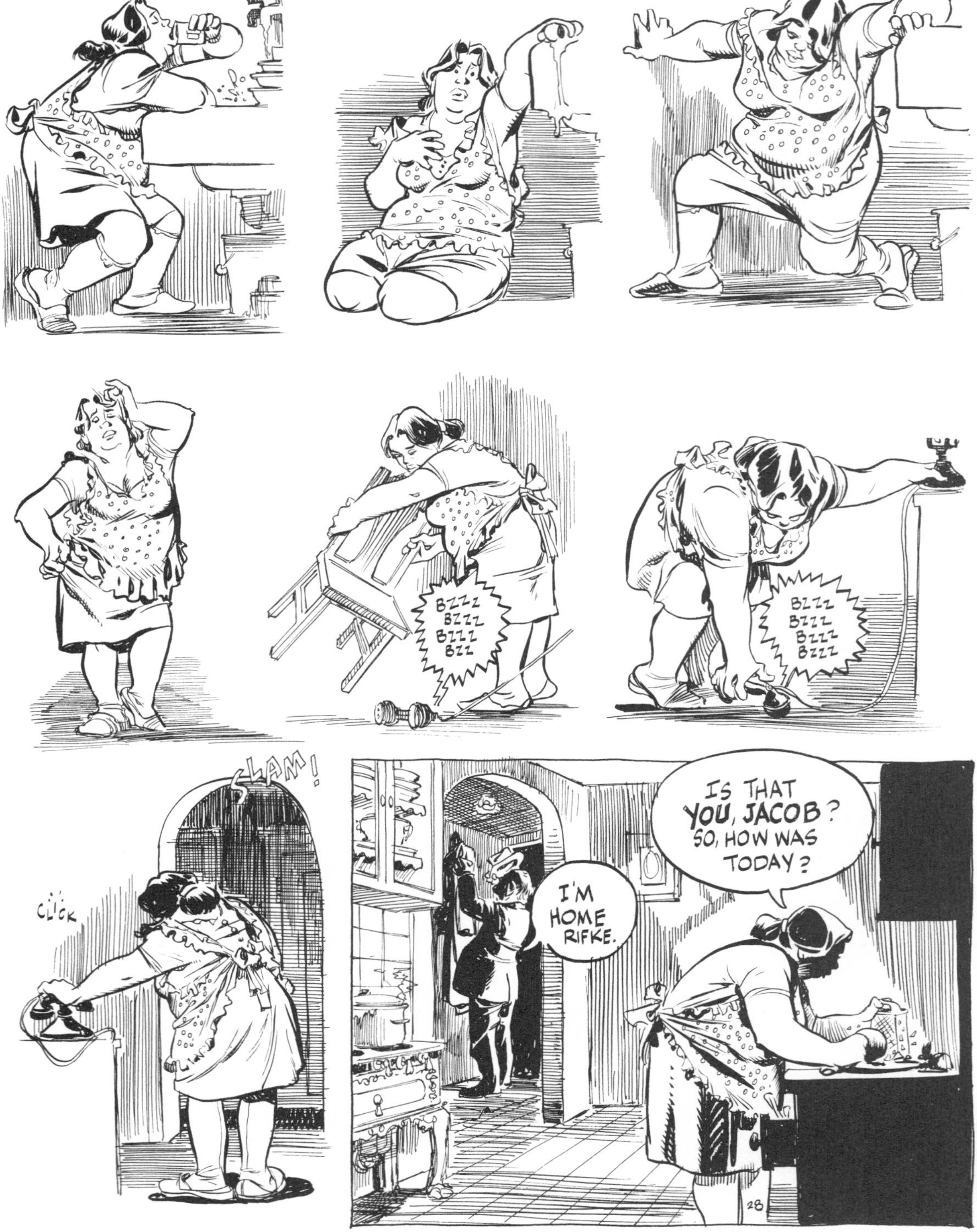
BZZZ BZZZ BZZZ BZZ
BZZZ BZZZ BZZZ BZZZ
SLAM!
CLICK
I'M HOME RIFKE.
IS THAT **YOU, JACOB**? SO, HOW WAS TODAY?

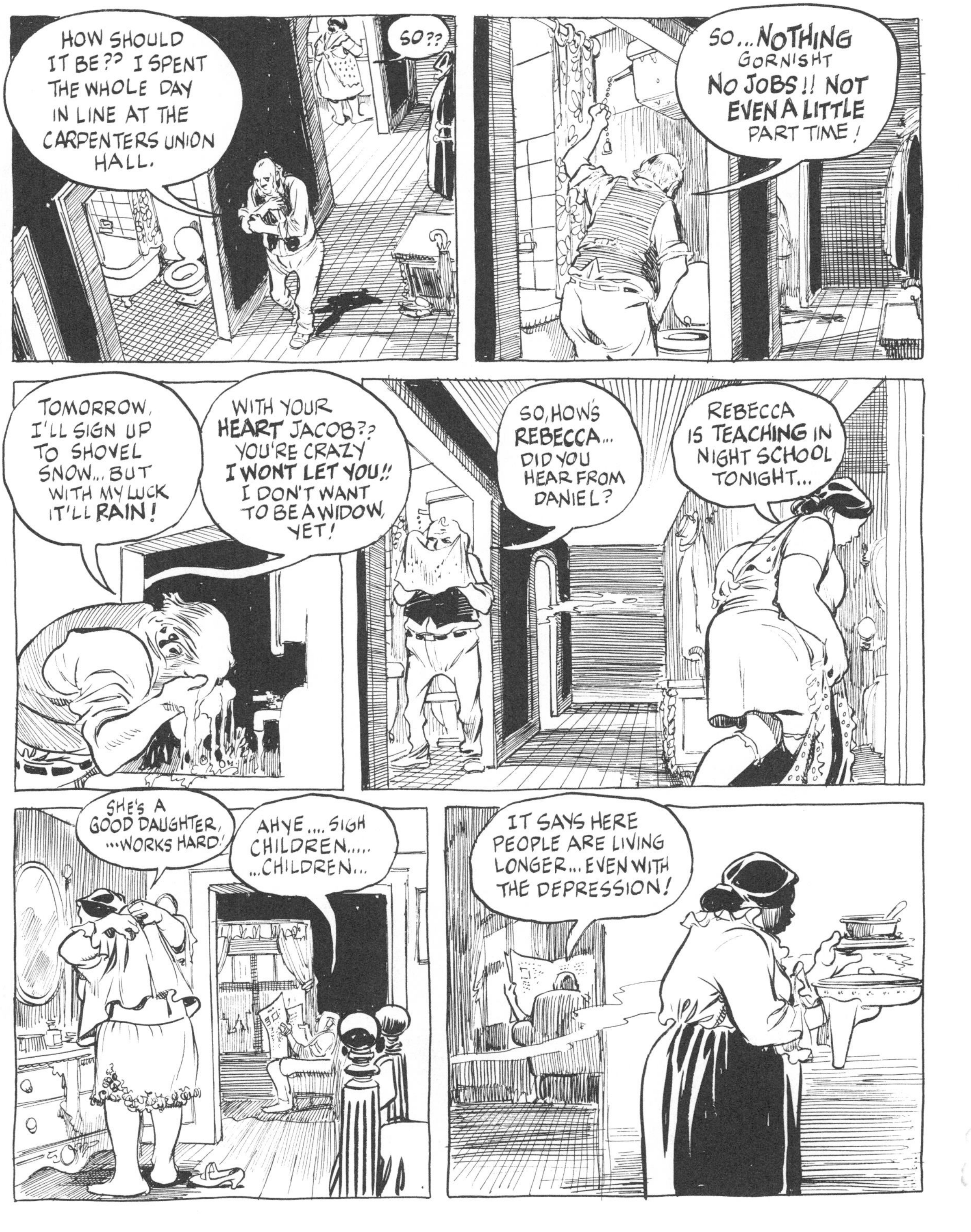

HOW SHOULD IT BE?? I SPENT THE WHOLE DAY IN LINE AT THE CARPENTERS UNION HALL.
SO??
SO... NOTHING GORNISHT NO JOBS!! NOT EVEN A LITTLE PART TIME!
TOMORROW, I'LL SIGN UP TO SHOVEL SNOW... BUT WITH MY LUCK IT'LL RAIN!
WITH YOUR HEART JACOB?? YOU'RE CRAZY I WONT LET YOU!! I DON'T WANT TO BE A WIDOW, YET!
SO, HOW'S REBECCA... DID YOU HEAR FROM DANIEL?
REBECCA IS TEACHING IN NIGHT SCHOOL TONIGHT...
SHE'S A GOOD DAUGHTER, ...WORKS HARD!
AHYE.... SIGH CHILDREN..... ...CHILDREN...
IT SAYS HERE PEOPLE ARE LIVING LONGER... EVEN WITH THE DEPRESSION!

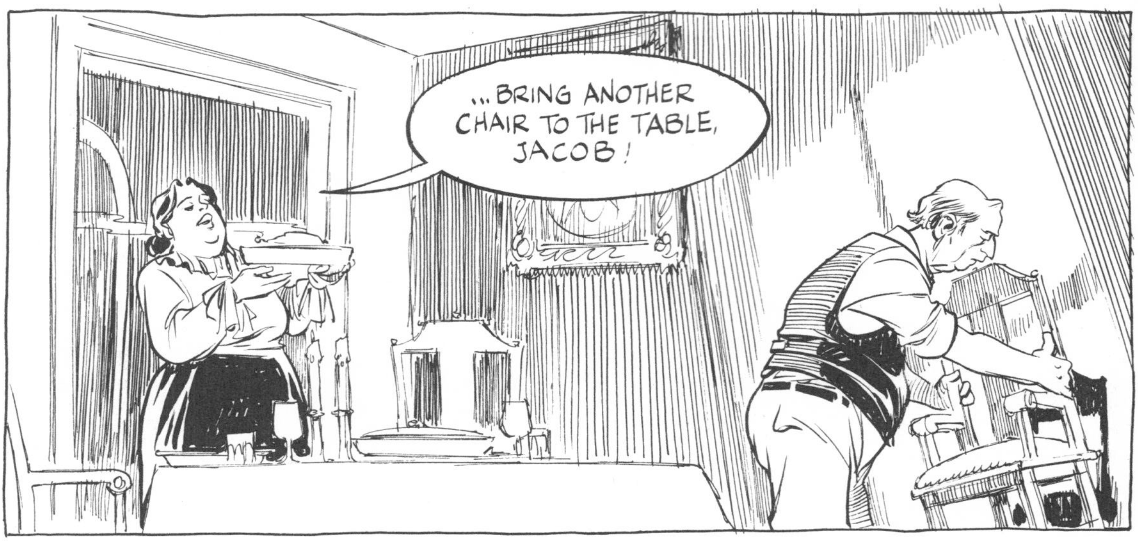
...BRING ANOTHER CHAIR TO THE TABLE, JACOB!

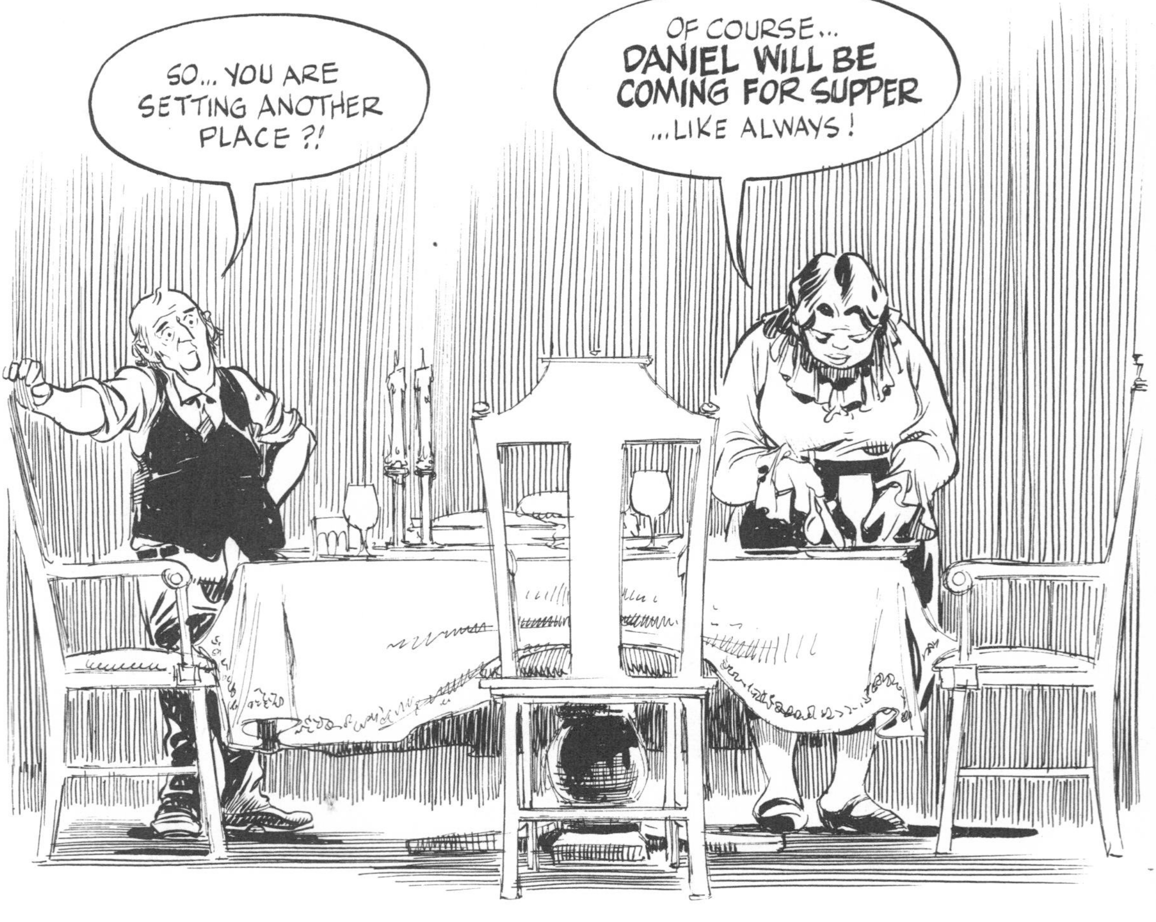
SO... YOU ARE SETTING ANOTHER PLACE ?!
OF COURSE... **DANIEL WILL BE COMING FOR SUPPER** ...LIKE ALWAYS!

ON THE TOP FLOOR, BACK, LIVED GOD

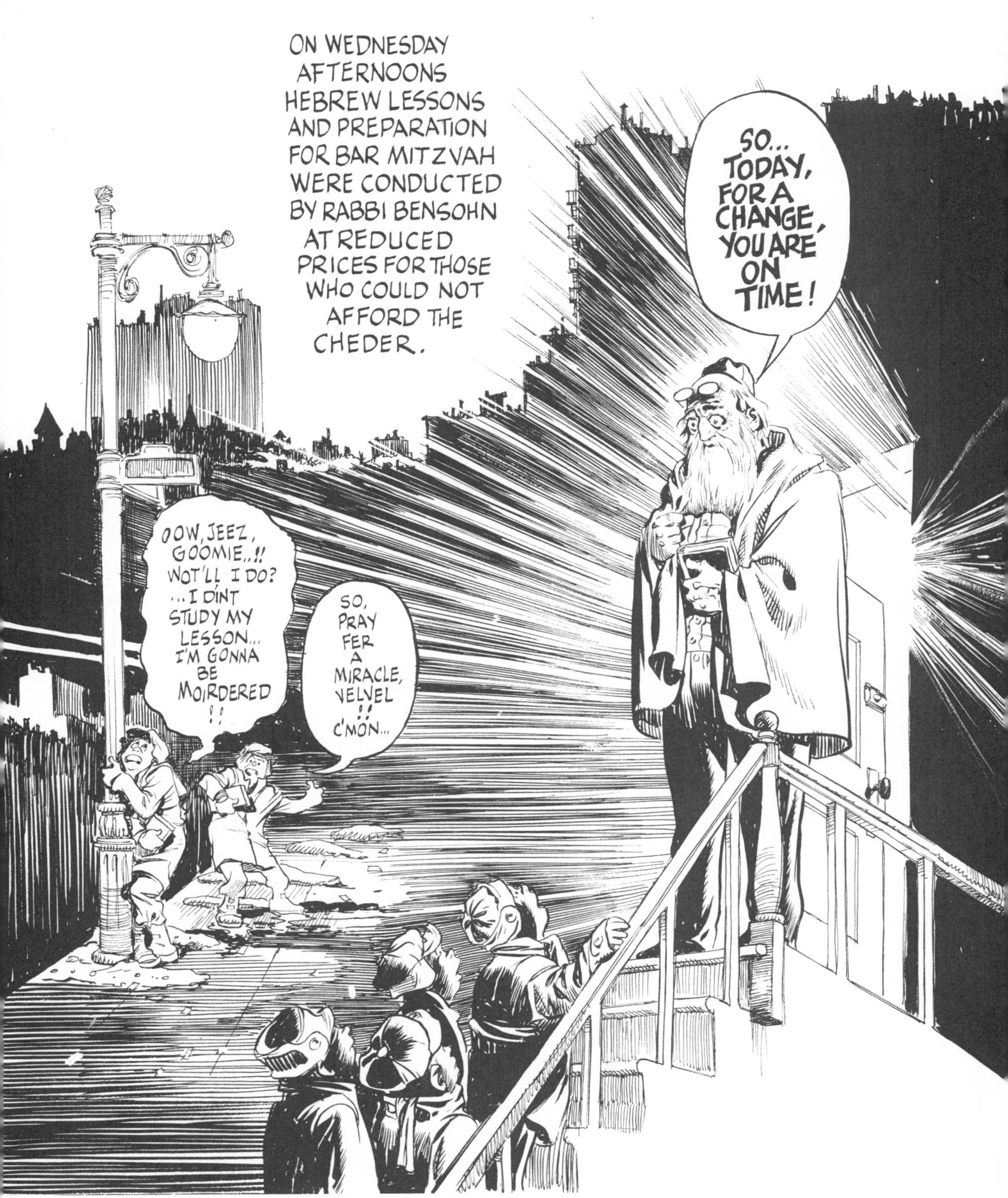
ON WEDNESDAY AFTERNOONS HEBREW LESSONS AND PREPARATION FOR BAR MITZVAH WERE CONDUCTED BY RABBI BENSOHN AT REDUCED PRICES FOR THOSE WHO COULD NOT AFFORD THE CHEDER.
SO... TODAY, FOR A CHANGE, YOU ARE ON TIME!
OOW, JEEZ, GOOMIE..!! WOT'LL I DO? ...I DINT STUDY MY LESSON... I'M GONNA BE MOIRDERED !!
SO, PRAY FER A MIRACLE, VELVEL !! C'MON...

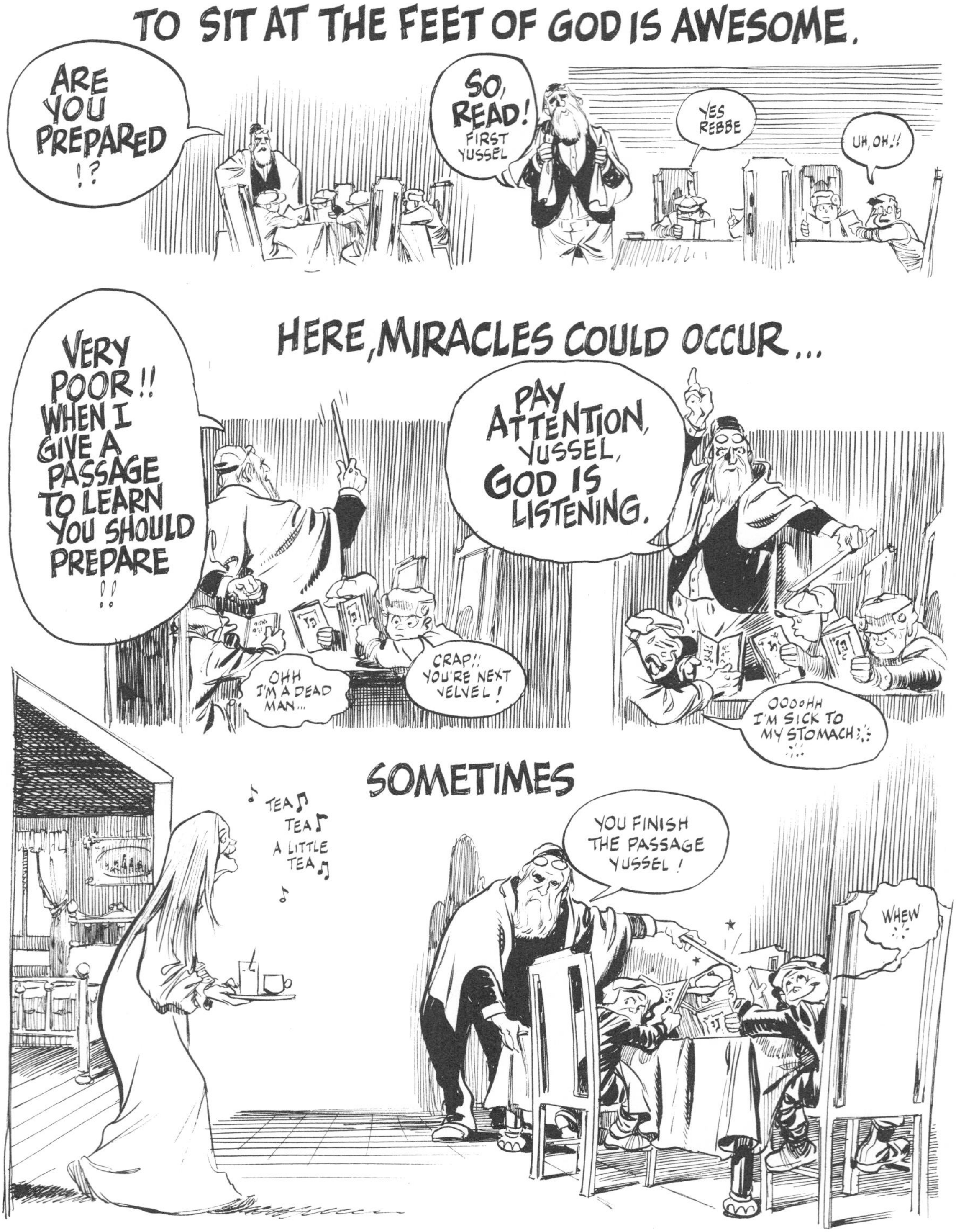
TO SIT AT THE FEET OF GOD IS AWESOME.
ARE YOU PREPARED !?
SO, READ! FIRST YUSSEL
YES REBBE
UH, OH!!
HERE, MIRACLES COULD OCCUR...
VERY POOR!! WHEN I GIVE A PASSAGE TO LEARN YOU SHOULD PREPARE !!
OHH I'M A DEAD MAN...
CRAP!! YOU'RE NEXT VELVEL!
PAY ATTENTION, YUSSEL, GOD IS LISTENING.
OOOoHH I'M SICK TO MY STOMACH
SOMETIMES
TEA
TEA
A LITTLE TEA
YOU FINISH THE PASSAGE YUSSEL!
WHEW

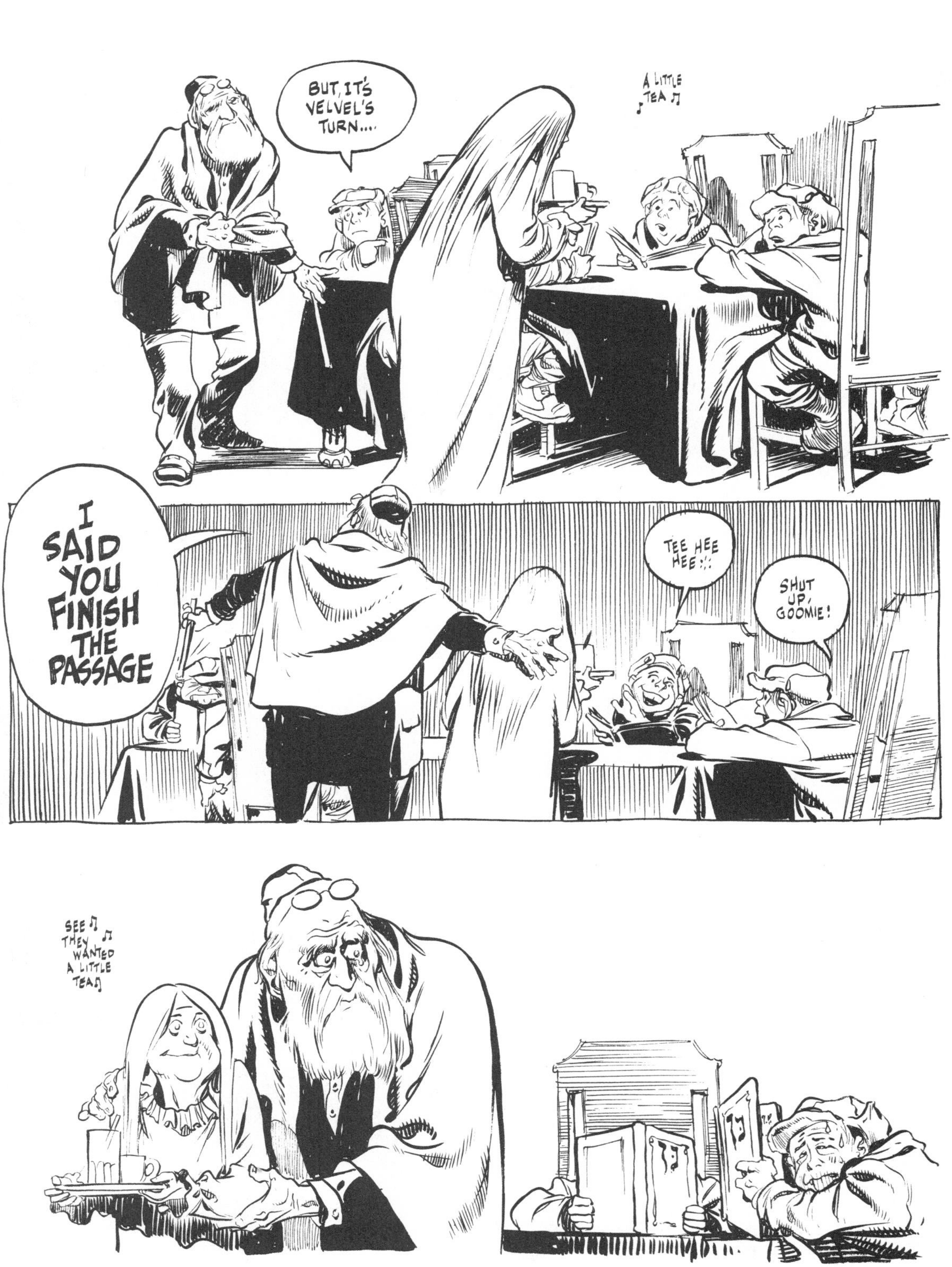

BUT, IT'S VELVEL'S TURN....
A LITTLE TEA ♫
I SAID YOU FINISH THE PASSAGE
TEE HEE HEE
SHUT UP, GOOMIE!
SEE ♫ THEY ♫ WANTED A LITTLE TEA ♫

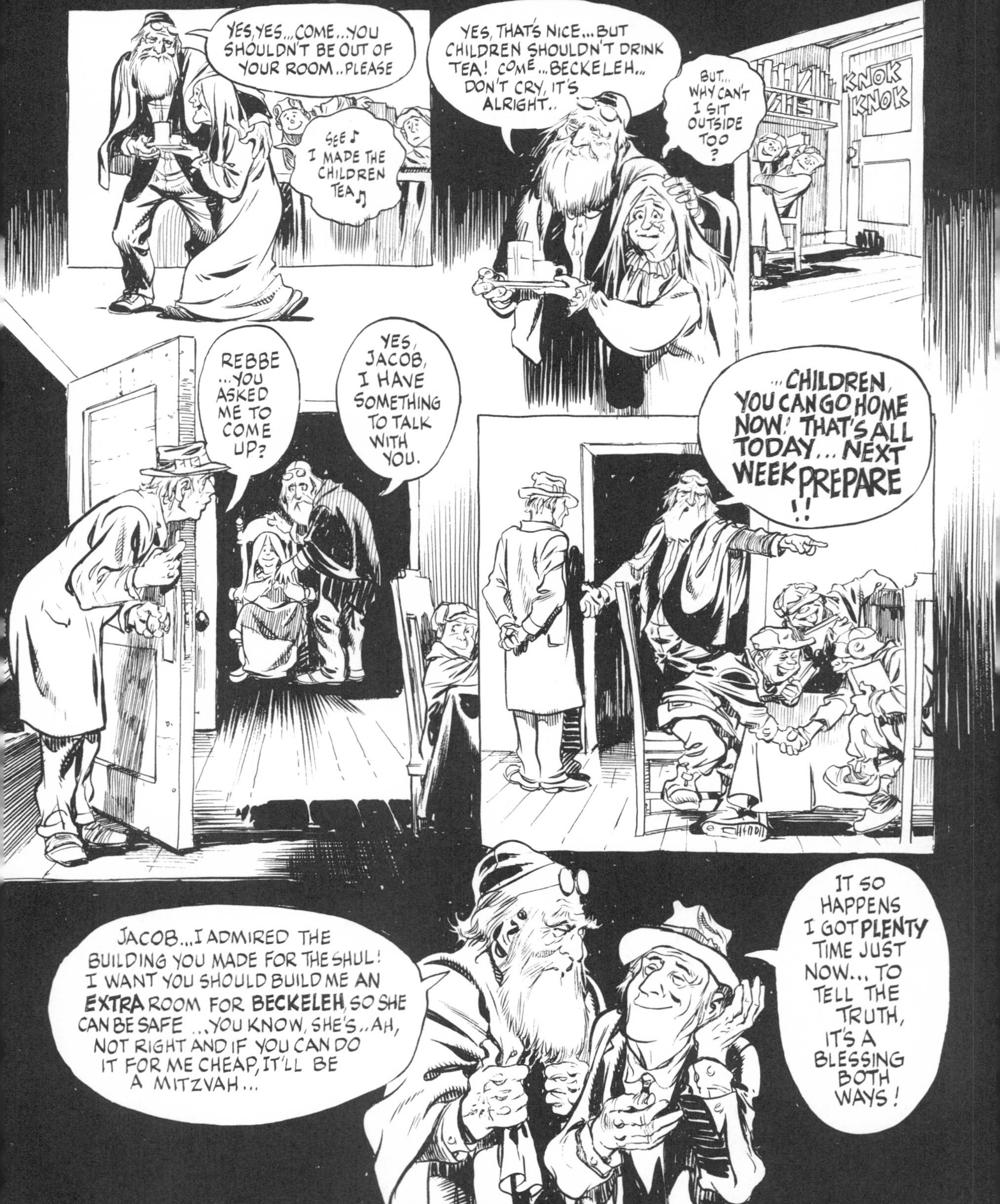
YES, YES... COME... YOU SHOULDN'T BE OUT OF YOUR ROOM.. PLEASE
SEE ♪ I MADE THE CHILDREN TEA ♫
YES, THAT'S NICE... BUT CHILDREN SHOULDN'T DRINK TEA! COME... BECKELEH... DON'T CRY, IT'S ALRIGHT..
BUT... WHY CAN'T I SIT OUTSIDE TOO ?
KNOK KNOK
REBBE ...YOU ASKED ME TO COME UP?
YES, JACOB, I HAVE SOMETHING TO TALK WITH YOU.
...CHILDREN, YOU CAN GO HOME NOW! THAT'S ALL TODAY... NEXT WEEK PREPARE !!
JACOB... I ADMIRED THE BUILDING YOU MADE FOR THE SHUL! I WANT YOU SHOULD BUILD ME AN EXTRA ROOM FOR BECKELEH, SO SHE CAN BE SAFE ...YOU KNOW, SHE'S.. AH, NOT RIGHT AND IF YOU CAN DO IT FOR ME CHEAP, IT'LL BE A MITZVAH...
IT SO HAPPENS I GOT PLENTY TIME JUST NOW... TO TELL THE TRUTH, IT'S A BLESSING BOTH WAYS!

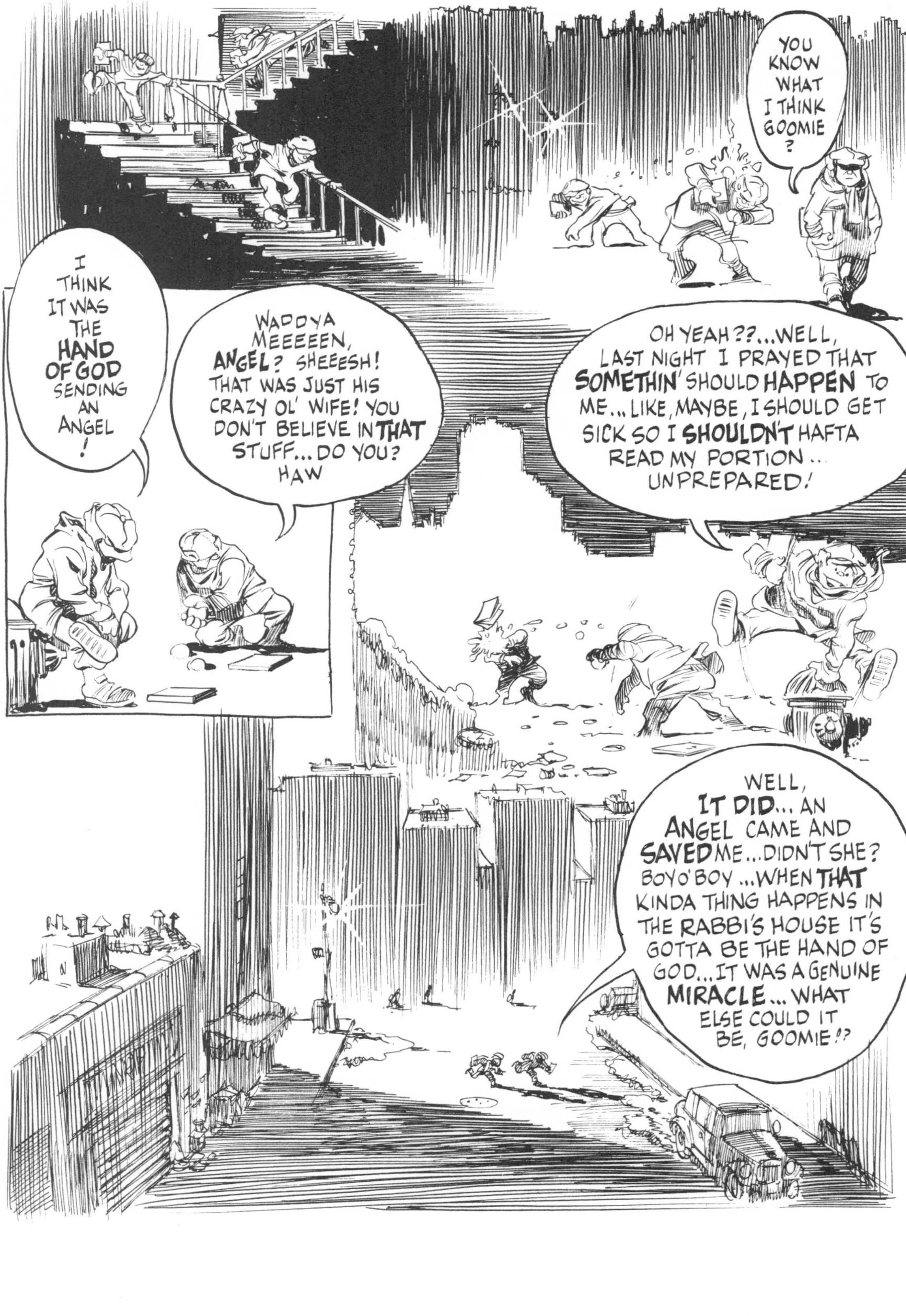
YOU KNOW WHAT I THINK GOOMIE ?
I THINK IT WAS THE HAND OF GOD SENDING AN ANGEL !
WADDYA MEEEEEN, ANGEL? SHEEESH! THAT WAS JUST HIS CRAZY OL' WIFE! YOU DON'T BELIEVE IN THAT STUFF... DO YOU? HAW
OH YEAH??...WELL, LAST NIGHT I PRAYED THAT SOMETHIN' SHOULD HAPPEN TO ME... LIKE, MAYBE, I SHOULD GET SICK SO I SHOULDN'T HAFTA READ MY PORTION .. UNPREPARED!
WELL, IT DID... AN ANGEL CAME AND SAVED ME...DIDN'T SHE? BOY O' BOY ...WHEN THAT KINDA THING HAPPENS IN THE RABBI'S HOUSE IT'S GOTTA BE THE HAND OF GOD...IT WAS A GENUINE MIRACLE... WHAT ELSE COULD IT BE, GOOMIE !?

HOWEVER MANKIND DEALT WITH ITS SURVIVAL, THERE REMAINED YET ANOTHER FORCE, MIGHTY AND IMPLACABLE... THE WEATHER!

JANUARY, 1934, ARRIVED TO A SLUSHY NEW YORK. It began mildly. A warm wave thawed the accumulation of snow that was deposited on the city in the month before. Firemen had to be called out to deal with floods caused by suddenly-thawed sprinklers in over 200 buildings. Meanwhile, 40,000 were given work to clear the snow. In the New York Harbor, fog, resulting from the sudden warmth, delayed ship traffic.

JANUARY ENDED IN SUDDEN COLD! The mercury dropped 52 degrees in one day and the thermometers of the city stood at 5 degrees above zero with icy winds and snow flurries swirling around the buildings.

FEBRUARY BEGAN AFTER THREE DAYS OF BITTER COLD. Warm winds brought relief, just briefly, for a heavy snowfall buried the city! While 2000 worked at shovelling streets and 20,000 out-of-work people eagerly awaited a chance for a job, bad news came from the Bronx! At the Bronx Zoo the groundhogs failed to come out! Those who counted on these creatures to predict spring were bitterly disappointed. Then the temperature dropped to 15 degrees and a pile-up of 9.6 inches of snow, giving employment to the 20,000 jobless at snow removal.

ON FEBRUARY 2, THERE WAS OTHER GOOD NEWS! Up in the Bronx Zoo the groundhog finally came out, saw his shadow, and promptly scurried back to his nest. It was clearly a portent of an early spring. But by the day's end the mercury dropped to 4 degrees . . . a record for this date.

ON FEBRUARY 3RD ICE FLOES RAMPANT ON THE HUDSON RIVER! Propelled by the currents they dragged three ships for twenty blocks from their anchorage.

ON FEBRUARY 13 THE CITY WAS LASHED BY A BITTER GALE FOLLOWED BY A HEAVY SNOWFALL! Within eleven hours the mercury dropped 20 degrees. On the rivers the Coast Guard struggled to save men on barges adrift on the icy waters. But the snowfall gave work to 6000 jobless men hired to clean streets.

ON FEBRUARY 15, N.Y. BRACED FOR ANOTHER COLD. The New York Times reported that a cold wave was coming from the Rocky Mountains and that an unemployed man was found dead of the cold alongside a bunkmate who was unconscious. The following day the paper reported that the first half of February was the coldest in the 63 years of the New York City Weather Bureau's records.

ON FEBRUARY 20, THE CITY WAS HIT AGAIN! After almost a week of wavering the mercury dropped to 9 degrees above zero and a 9-inch snowfall immobilized the city. For hours the suburbs were cut off. Suburbanites in snow shoes and skis were also using horses and sleds to get around.

ON FEBRUARY 22, N.Y. WAS PINIONED BY SNOW! The city's newspapers carried stories of milk being delivered to the suburbs by plane. In the city itself 50,000 people were at work digging out. Slowly, commuters were able to get back to work. In the New York Times an expert, Mr. Raubenheimer, called the storm ". . . a carbon copy of the Blizzard of 1888."

BY FEBRUARY 27, THE CITY TRIED TO FREE ITSELF! After a day or two of rising and falling temperature which caused icy streets that were soon covered by a 9-inch snowfall, the papers carried reports that some Long Island and New Jersey communities were cut off from the city. In Manhattan hotels were jammed with snowbound commuters. Only the busses were running. Nine storm-related injuries were reported. The following day the total fatalities related to the thermometer rose to 14. Stores announced that skis and earmuffs sold out! The mercury dropped to 9 degrees above zero but the city somehow averted a coal and food shortage and fed its park animals, while in Westchester County the roads were cleared.

MARCH CAME IN LIKE A LAMB THIS YEAR. With a 15 degree rise in temperature which caused a thaw that melted the accumulated ice, water flooded the streets of the city.

ON APRIL 24, THE CITY FELT THE FIRST THUNDERSTORM OF THE YEAR!

BY MAY 21, THE CITY SWELTERED! A record heat of 88 degrees Fahrenheit roasted the city and left one heat prostration case. This was followed by hail, rain and lightning which caused damage and resulted in 3 prostrations within 72 hours.

JULY ARRIVED WITH THE MERCURY AT 91 DEGREES. Within the next three days 13 more heat prostrations and 5 deaths were reported in the press before a rainstorm finally brought a short relief. But the mercury hovered at over 92 degrees for the next eight days leaving about 12 overcome and 3 dead.

ST. SWITHEN'S DAY WAS SULTRY and ended in showers.

JULY ENDED WITH THE MERCURY AT 89 DEGREES. A count of the heat-related casualties which the New York Times reported for the month came to 29 prostrations and 11 deaths. Two heat records were set, they said.

AUGUST BEGAN, RECORDING THE COOLEST AUGUST 6 IN HISTORY. At the end of the month, after zooming up to 95 degrees, the month ended with the coolest day in August's history.

FINALLY, BY DECEMBER   New York returned to a seasonal norm and a light snow powdered the rooftops.

* * * *

NEVERTHELESS, THE COCKROACHES IN THE TENEMENTS ON DROPSIE AVENUE, RESPONDING TO A LIFE FORCE EQUAL TO THE ENVIRONMENT, CONTINUED THEIR PROLIFERATION AS THEY HAD FOR OVER FOUR MILLION YEARS!

SHABBASGOY

The Shaftsburys emigrated to New England in 1850. There they founded an axe-handle factory which flourished. It remained in the family's hands until the death of Elton Josiah Shaftsbury around 1927.

His son, Elton Shaftsbury II, his only heir, then took over the operation of the Shaftsbury Wood Products Company.

Actually, young Elton had little interest in running a business. He had been reared in comfort and security. With an unquestioned confidence in his survival that came from the certainty of his social position, he expected his world to go on, as it was, forever. His skills were mainly centered in the art of being accepted and the maintenance of the shallow relationships that were normal for his set.

What Elton Shaftsbury II really wanted was freedom to pursue his social life.

So, upon the death of his father, Elton sold the factory and put the proceeds into the stock market.

This enabled him to engage in a more 'gentlemanly' vocation. He joined a main-line Wall Street brokerage house and occupied himself with being a 'customer's-man'. Here his social contacts and rich friends were an asset that allowed him to make money in a 'nice way'!

In the fall of 1929, the stock market collapsed, and within months his holdings were wiped out. The brokerage house, like so many others, collapsed and his circle of friends suffered similarly... they soon dispersed.

Elton's last savings were demolished in the failure of the notorious Bank of U.S.

By the winter of 1933 Elton Shaftsbury II, broke and unemployed, was reduced to selling apples on the corner of Wall and William Streets.

219

1929

BYRD IN SAFE FLIGHT OVER SOUTH POLE

The N.Y. Times on Nov. 30 reported that Admiral Byrd, the first to conquer the North Pole, succeeded in flying over the South Pole as well.

President Herbert Hoover sent the aviator and his crew a congratulatory message that said in part ". . . we are glad of proof that the spirit of great adventure still lives."

Mayor Jimmy Walker, of New York said, ". . . the American flag will look great down there."

SOCIAL NOTE

BERLIN, OCT. 29

Fritz Von Opel, the first man to fly a rocket plane, revealed today, he would wed Frau Selnik who is one of Germany's six women pilots. They will come to New York in November.

STOCK MARKET DROPS 15 BILLION OCT. 29 SELL OFF WORST IN HISTORY 16,410,030 SHARES TRADED

EMBEZZLER GIVES UP $47,000 NAVY LOOT

BURIED IN D.C. CHICKEN YARD

OCT. 30, 1929

Lt. Charles Musil, U.S. Navy Paymaster surrendered to the authorities and led them to the cache in a chicken yard. However, $6,100 is still missing and the embezzler admits that he bought some stock before he became penitent and gave up.

BANKS OPTIMISTIC BUT SUPPORT FAILS

On Wednesday, Oct. 30, the New York press reported a major sell off of panic proportions on the previous day. By the end of trading, however, leading issues recovered as much as 14 points in 15 minutes to momentarily, at least, assuage the pall of gloom that overhung the financial centers.

RALLY BRIEF

Organized support from the leading financial houses is gathering to help offset the "mob psychology" that is blamed for the plunge.

1930

MURDER OF GAMBLER STILL UNSOLVED

FEB. 4, 1930

The New York Times in a special report revealed that the killing of Arnold Rothstein on Nov. 4, 1928 has precipitated an inquiry into the affairs of the city's magistrates courts, police department, and possibly fire department. Governor Franklin D. Roosevelt, when asked whether he would or would not veto an investigation, laughed, and said he would wait until he saw the legislation before deciding.

LINDBERGH SETS RECORD CROSSES U.S. IN 14½ HRS.

APRIL 20, 1930

Col. Charles A. Lindbergh added another first to his laurels by flying coast to coast, 14,000 feet at 180 mph. His wife served as navigator.

UNEMPLOYMENT ATTACKED IN SENATE

DEMOCRATS BLAME HOOVER'S POLICIES

MARCH 3, 1930

A major New York paper in an exclusive article reported that the Senate's Democratic leaders accused the Hoover Administration of diverting attention from the increase in unemployment. He questioned administration statistics.

"RECOVERY NEAR" DEPRESSION PEAK OVER SAYS HOOVER

"STOCK MARKET CRASH DUE TO SPECULATION ORGY BY PUBLIC"

MAY 1930

President Herbert Hoover in a statement to the press, said today that the programs he instituted succeeded in maintaining courage and confidence. The worst is over, he feels.

CONDITIONS GROWING DAILY WORSE SAYS SENATOR LA FOLLETTE.

The Republican Senator from Wisconsin denounced attempts to label demonstrations by the unemployed as a movement by "The Reds." Another Republican guessed that unemployment stood at 6 million despite the questionably lower statistics from federal agencies.

300 N.Y. UNION LOCALS MEET IN MOVE TO COMBAT ACUTE UNEMPLOYMENT

MARCH 8, 1930

A meeting of major union locals in New York's Beethoven Hall will be held on March 19th.

1931

STOCK MARKET UP

FEB. 17, 1931

The Stock Market rose 2-8 points yesterday on accumulating evidence of a business pickup. This followed a flurry of buying activity the week earlier when on Feb. 11, a rally from public buying sent the list up.

HOOVER WILL VETO BONUS BILL DESPITE SENATE PASSAGE

FEB. 20, 1931

The President, despite a vote in the Senate of 72-2 in favor of a loan bill for veterans' payments, warned that it would cause a weakening of the government's financial structure.

400,000 DEPOSITORS OF NY BANK OF U.S. FATE NOW IN DOUBT

REAL VALUE OF BANK'S ASSETS UNACCOUNTED

FEB. 2, 1931

The NY State Banking Dept. report issued yesterday was without a satisfactory account of the actual condition of the failed bank's assets. After weeks of liquidation, the books of the bank remain as cloudy as they were on the day it closed.

$75,000,000 of the closed bank's assets are apparently lost or at least cannot be accounted for.

HUNGER RIOTS FAIL AS BRONX MARCH IS BROKEN UP BY COPS

JANUARY 9, 1931

In a demonstration that was reportedly staged by Communists in Manhattan, Brooklyn and the Bronx, police succeeded in easily dispersing what was termed as a "sparse" turnout.

At the Salvation Army's bread line on the Bowery at 4th Street, Manhattan, a policeman's jaw was broken.

HOUSEPAINTERS MAY USE NARROWER BRUSH TO CREATE MORE JOBS

FEB. 20, 1931

The New York Times carried a story today of a threat by the Painters Union of Long Island to go from the normal 6-inch paint brush to a smaller 3-inch brush so as to double the employment of housepainters in the city.

1932

F.D. ROOSEVELT WINS IN A LANDSLIDE ANTI-PROHIBITION CONGRESS NOW IN O'BRIEN BECOMES NEW YORK'S MAYOR

N.Y. CITY ASKS BANKS AID MAY DEFAULT CITY WAGE CUT $20,000,000

DEC. 7, 1932

The city faced an inevitable default on its obligations. Local bankers called on to rescue New York said that the cut in city payrolls was not enough and urged that another $25,000,000 be cut in city spending before credit could be restored to permit their loan.

Meanwhile, members of the Patrolmen's Benevolent Assn. launched a drive to enlist public support against their pay cut.

SWARMS OF MOTHS BLANKET THE BRONX

JULY 9, 1932

By midnight last night, a blizzard of fluttering moths engulfed the Bronx and then headed on to include Manhattan, Queens and Brooklyn. According to the New York Times, these were a gypsy moth specie and in such great numbers that they halted auto traffic on Jerome Avenue and Pelham Parkway. The police, deluged with phone calls, said that they were at a loss as to just what they were expected to do about it.

DEMOCRATS CONTROL CONGRESS IN RECORD NATIONAL VOTE

ONLY SIX STATES VOTED FOR HERBERT HOOVER

NOV. 9, 1932

In his lead article in the New York Times, Arthur Krock said "... a political cataclysm unprecedented in the nation's history and produced by three years of Depression" elected Franklin Delano Roosevelt, President of the United States.

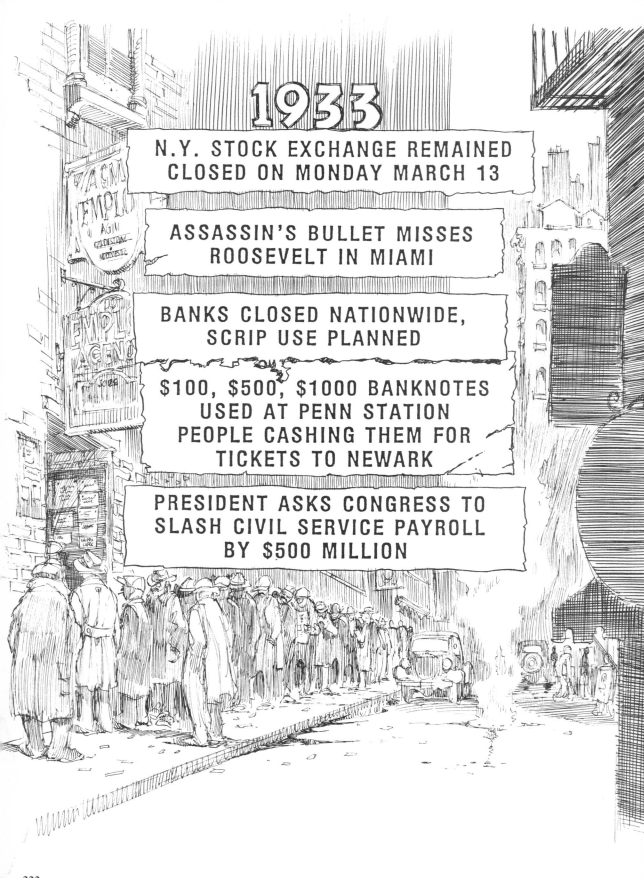

1933

N.Y. STOCK EXCHANGE REMAINED CLOSED ON MONDAY MARCH 13

ASSASSIN'S BULLET MISSES ROOSEVELT IN MIAMI

BANKS CLOSED NATIONWIDE, SCRIP USE PLANNED

$100, $500, $1000 BANKNOTES USED AT PENN STATION PEOPLE CASHING THEM FOR TICKETS TO NEWARK

PRESIDENT ASKS CONGRESS TO SLASH CIVIL SERVICE PAYROLL BY $500 MILLION

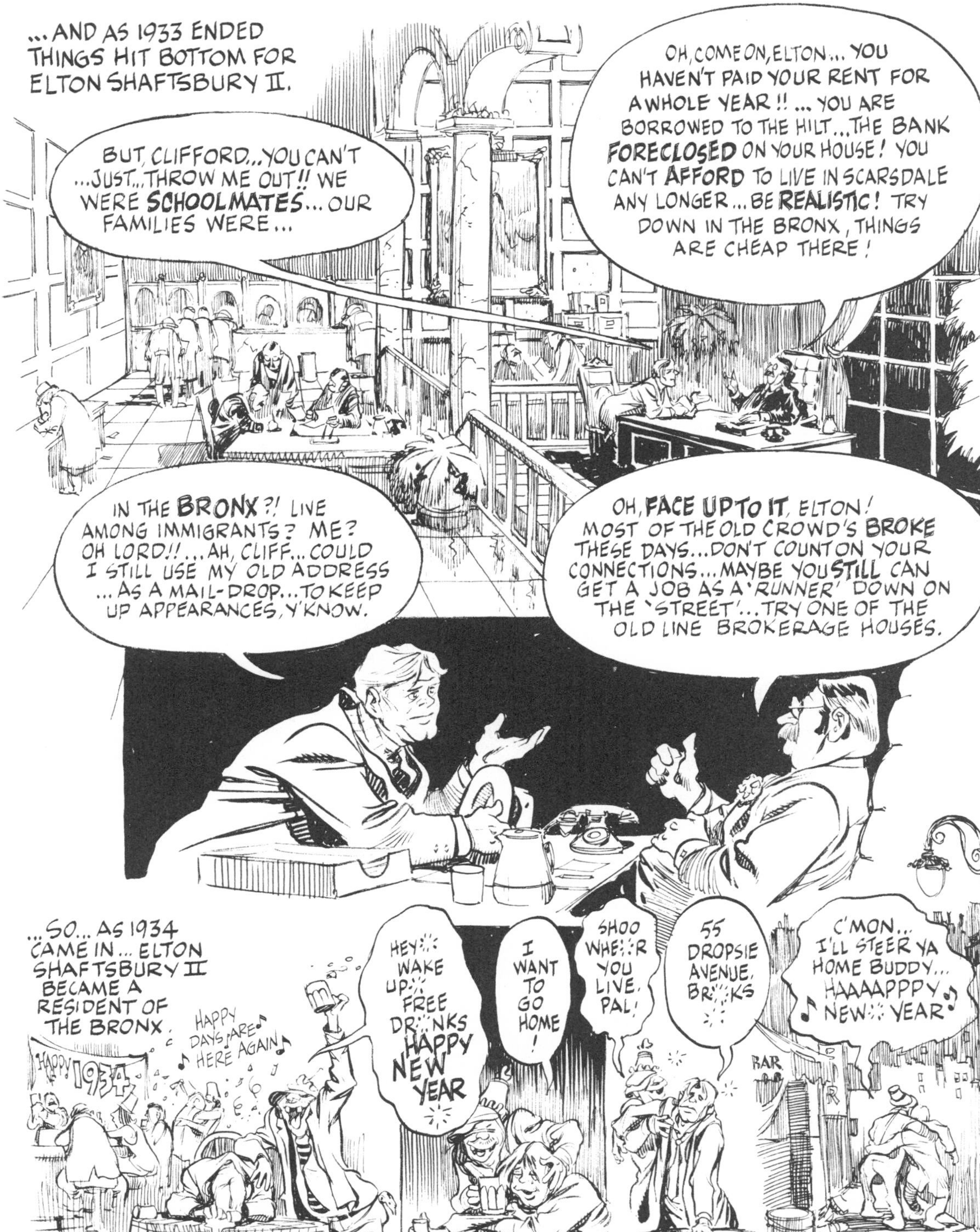
...AND AS 1933 ENDED THINGS HIT BOTTOM FOR ELTON SHAFTSBURY II.
BUT, CLIFFORD...YOU CAN'T ...JUST...THROW ME OUT!! WE WERE SCHOOLMATES... OUR FAMILIES WERE...
OH, COME ON, ELTON... YOU HAVEN'T PAID YOUR RENT FOR A WHOLE YEAR!! ... YOU ARE BORROWED TO THE HILT...THE BANK FORECLOSED ON YOUR HOUSE! YOU CAN'T AFFORD TO LIVE IN SCARSDALE ANY LONGER... BE REALISTIC! TRY DOWN IN THE BRONX, THINGS ARE CHEAP THERE!
IN THE BRONX?! LIVE AMONG IMMIGRANTS? ME? OH LORD!!...AH, CLIFF... COULD I STILL USE MY OLD ADDRESS ...AS A MAIL-DROP...TO KEEP UP APPEARANCES, Y'KNOW.
OH, FACE UP TO IT, ELTON! MOST OF THE OLD CROWD'S BROKE THESE DAYS...DON'T COUNT ON YOUR CONNECTIONS...MAYBE YOU STILL CAN GET A JOB AS A 'RUNNER' DOWN ON THE 'STREET'...TRY ONE OF THE OLD LINE BROKERAGE HOUSES.
...SO... AS 1934 CAME IN... ELTON SHAFTSBURY II BECAME A RESIDENT OF THE BRONX.
HAPPY DAYS ARE HERE AGAIN
HAPPY 1934
HEY WAKE UP FREE DR NKS HAPPY NEW YEAR
I WANT TO GO HOME!
SHOO WHE R YOU LIVE, PAL!
55 DROPSIE AVENUE, BR KS
C'MON... I'LL STEER YA HOME BUDDY... HAAAAPPPY NEW YEAR
BAR

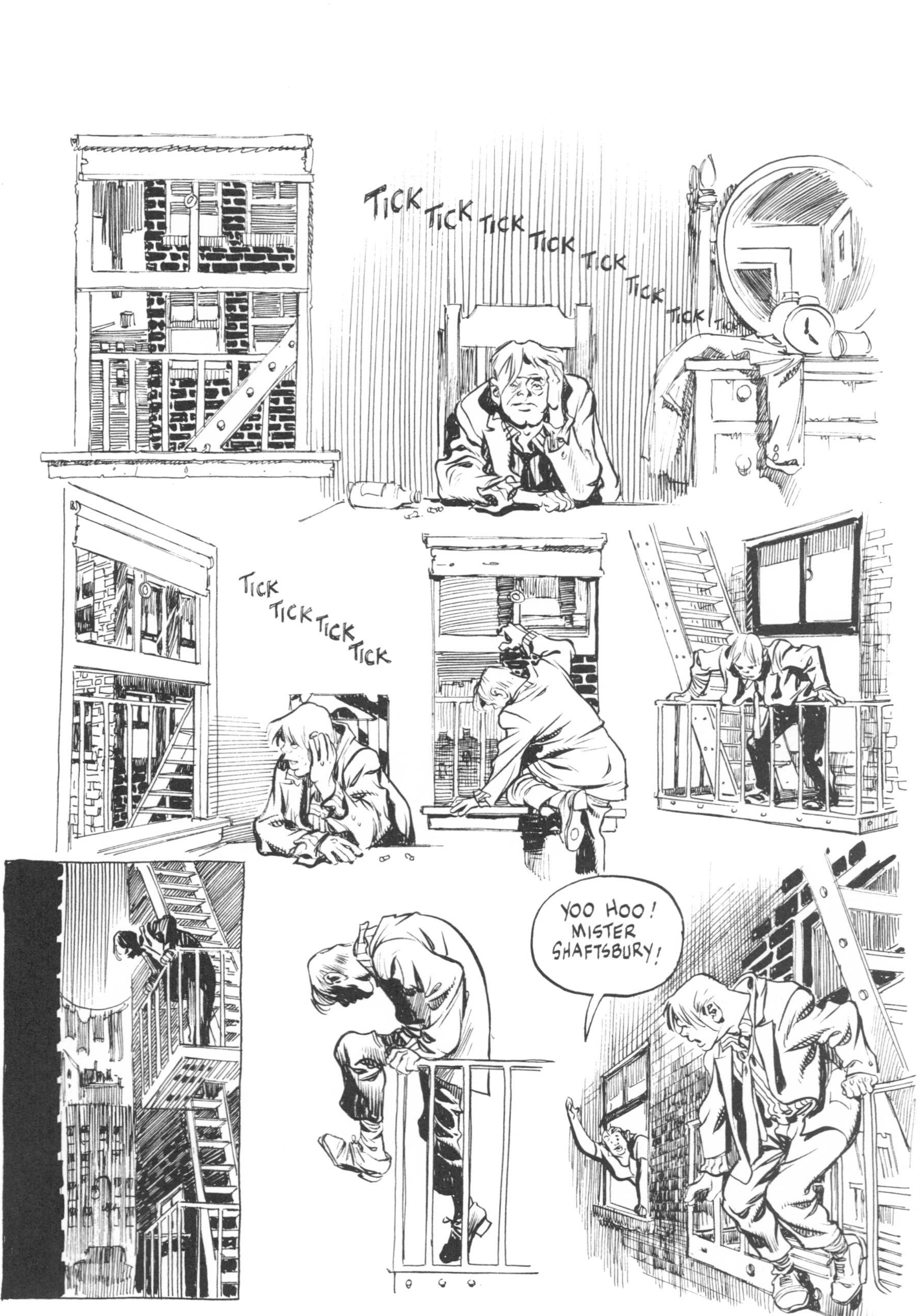
TICK TICK TICK TICK TICK TICK TICK TICK
TICK TICK TICK TICK
YOO HOO! MISTER SHAFTSBURY!

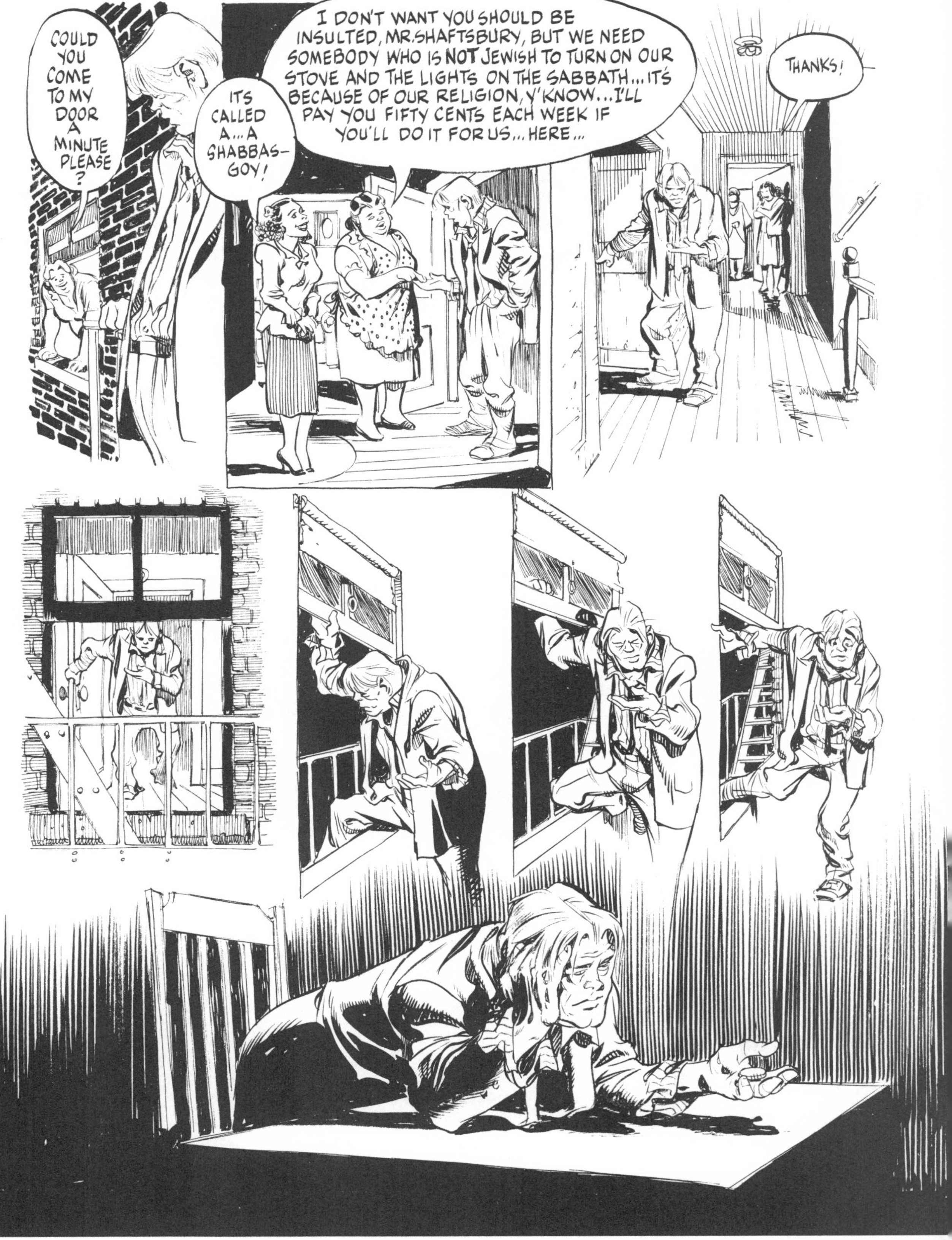

COULD YOU COME TO MY DOOR A MINUTE PLEASE?
ITS CALLED A... A SHABBAS-GOY!
I DON'T WANT YOU SHOULD BE INSULTED, MR. SHAFTSBURY, BUT WE NEED SOMEBODY WHO IS NOT JEWISH TO TURN ON OUR STOVE AND THE LIGHTS ON THE SABBATH... IT'S BECAUSE OF OUR RELIGION, Y'KNOW... I'LL PAY YOU FIFTY CENTS EACH WEEK IF YOU'LL DO IT FOR US... HERE...
THANKS!

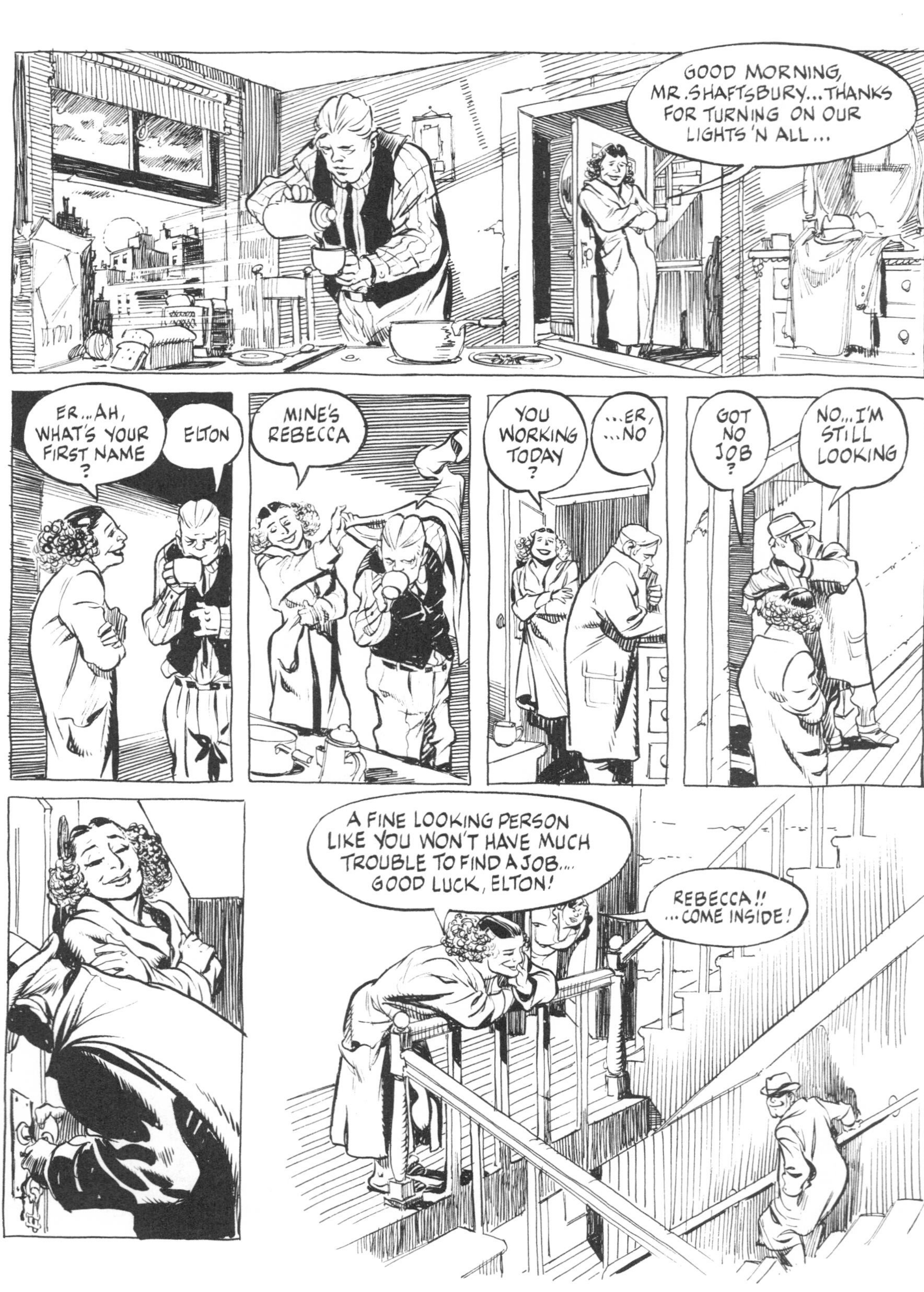
GOOD MORNING, MR. SHAFTSBURY... THANKS FOR TURNING ON OUR LIGHTS 'N ALL...
ER... AH, WHAT'S YOUR FIRST NAME ?
ELTON
MINE'S REBECCA
YOU WORKING TODAY ?
...ER, ...NO
GOT NO JOB ?
NO... I'M STILL LOOKING
A FINE LOOKING PERSON LIKE YOU WON'T HAVE MUCH TROUBLE TO FIND A JOB.... GOOD LUCK, ELTON!
REBECCA!! ...COME INSIDE!

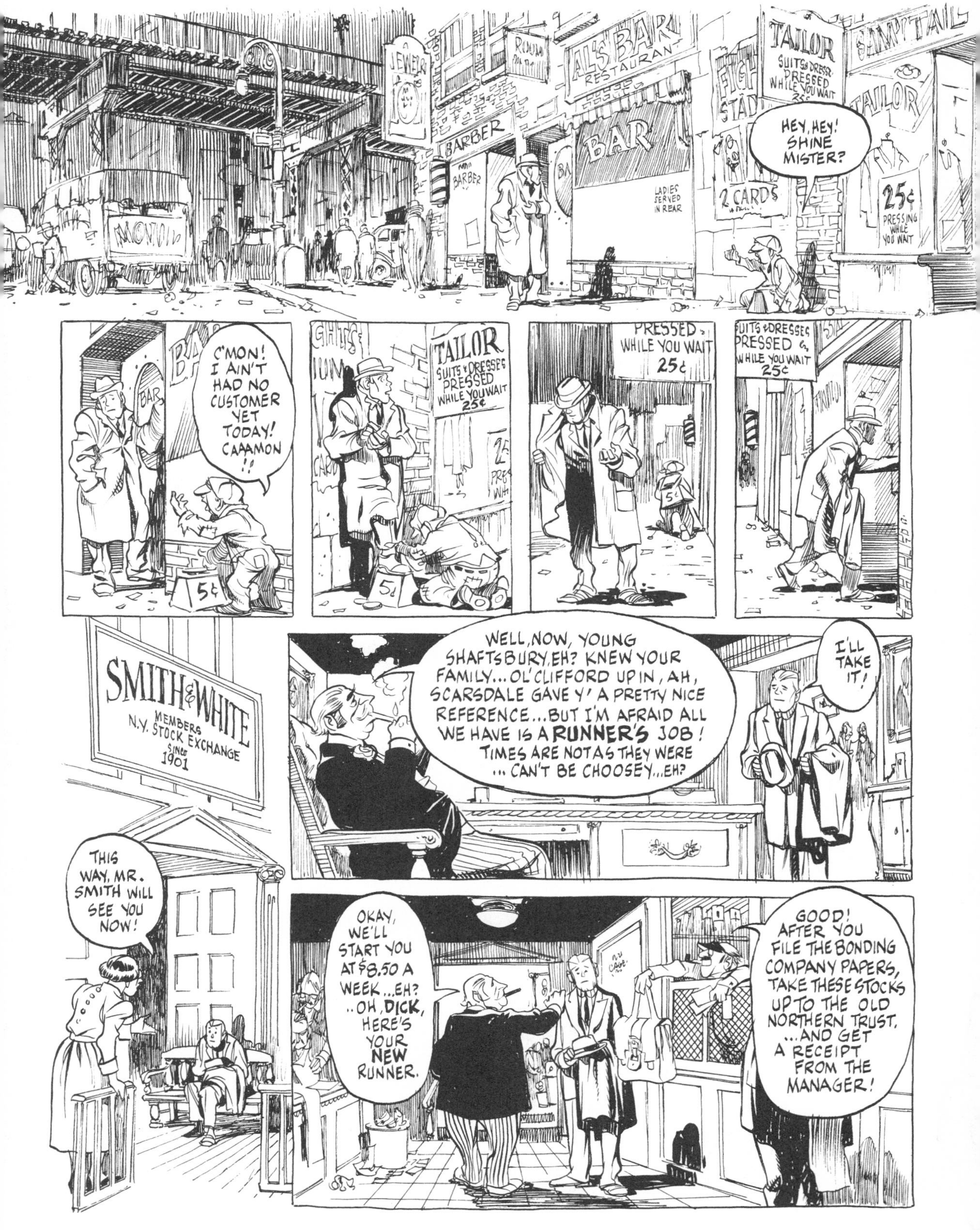

JEWELRY
AL'S BAR RESTAURANT
BARBER
BAR
LADIES SERVED IN REAR
2 CARDS
TAILOR SUITS & DRESSES PRESSED WHILE YOU WAIT
TAILOR
25¢ PRESSING WHILE YOU WAIT
HEY, HEY! SHINE MISTER?
BAR
C'MON! I AIN'T HAD NO CUSTOMER YET TODAY! CAAAMON!!
5¢
TAILOR SUITS & DRESSES PRESSED WHILE YOU WAIT 25¢
5¢
PRESSED WHILE YOU WAIT 25¢
5¢
SUITS & DRESSES PRESSED WHILE YOU WAIT 25¢
SMITH & WHITE MEMBERS N.Y. STOCK EXCHANGE SINCE 1901
WELL, NOW, YOUNG SHAFTSBURY, EH? KNEW YOUR FAMILY... OL' CLIFFORD UP IN, AH, SCARSDALE GAVE Y' A PRETTY NICE REFERENCE... BUT I'M AFRAID ALL WE HAVE IS A RUNNER'S JOB! TIMES ARE NOT AS THEY WERE ... CAN'T BE CHOOSEY... EH?
I'LL TAKE IT!
THIS WAY, MR. SMITH WILL SEE YOU NOW!
OKAY, WE'LL START YOU AT $8.50 A WEEK... EH? ..OH, DICK, HERE'S YOUR NEW RUNNER.
GOOD! AFTER YOU FILE THE BONDING COMPANY PAPERS, TAKE THESE STOCKS UP TO THE OLD NORTHERN TRUST. ...AND GET A RECEIPT FROM THE MANAGER!

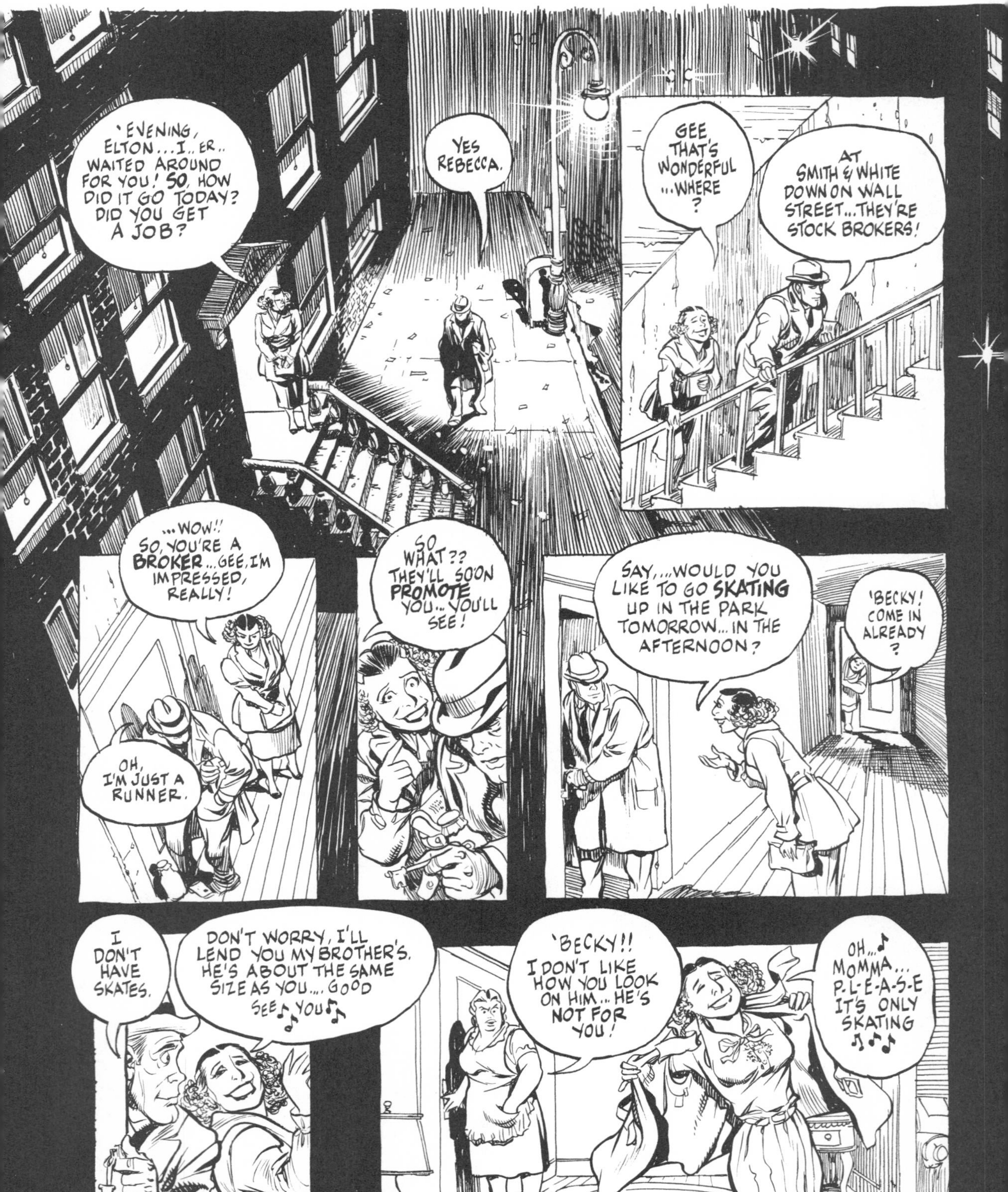

'EVENING, ELTON... I.. ER.. WAITED AROUND FOR YOU! SO, HOW DID IT GO TODAY? DID YOU GET A JOB?
YES REBECCA.
GEE THAT'S WONDERFUL ...WHERE ?
AT SMITH & WHITE DOWN ON WALL STREET... THEY'RE STOCK BROKERS!
...WOW!! SO, YOU'RE A BROKER... GEE, I'M IMPRESSED, REALLY!
OH, I'M JUST A RUNNER.
SO WHAT?? THEY'LL SOON PROMOTE YOU... YOU'LL SEE!
SAY,... WOULD YOU LIKE TO GO SKATING UP IN THE PARK TOMORROW... IN THE AFTERNOON?
'BECKY! COME IN ALREADY ?
I DON'T HAVE SKATES.
DON'T WORRY, I'LL LEND YOU MY BROTHER'S. HE'S ABOUT THE SAME SIZE AS YOU.... GOOD SEE YOU
'BECKY!! I DON'T LIKE HOW YOU LOOK ON HIM... HE'S NOT FOR YOU!
OH... MOMMA... P.L.E.A.S.E IT'S ONLY SKATING

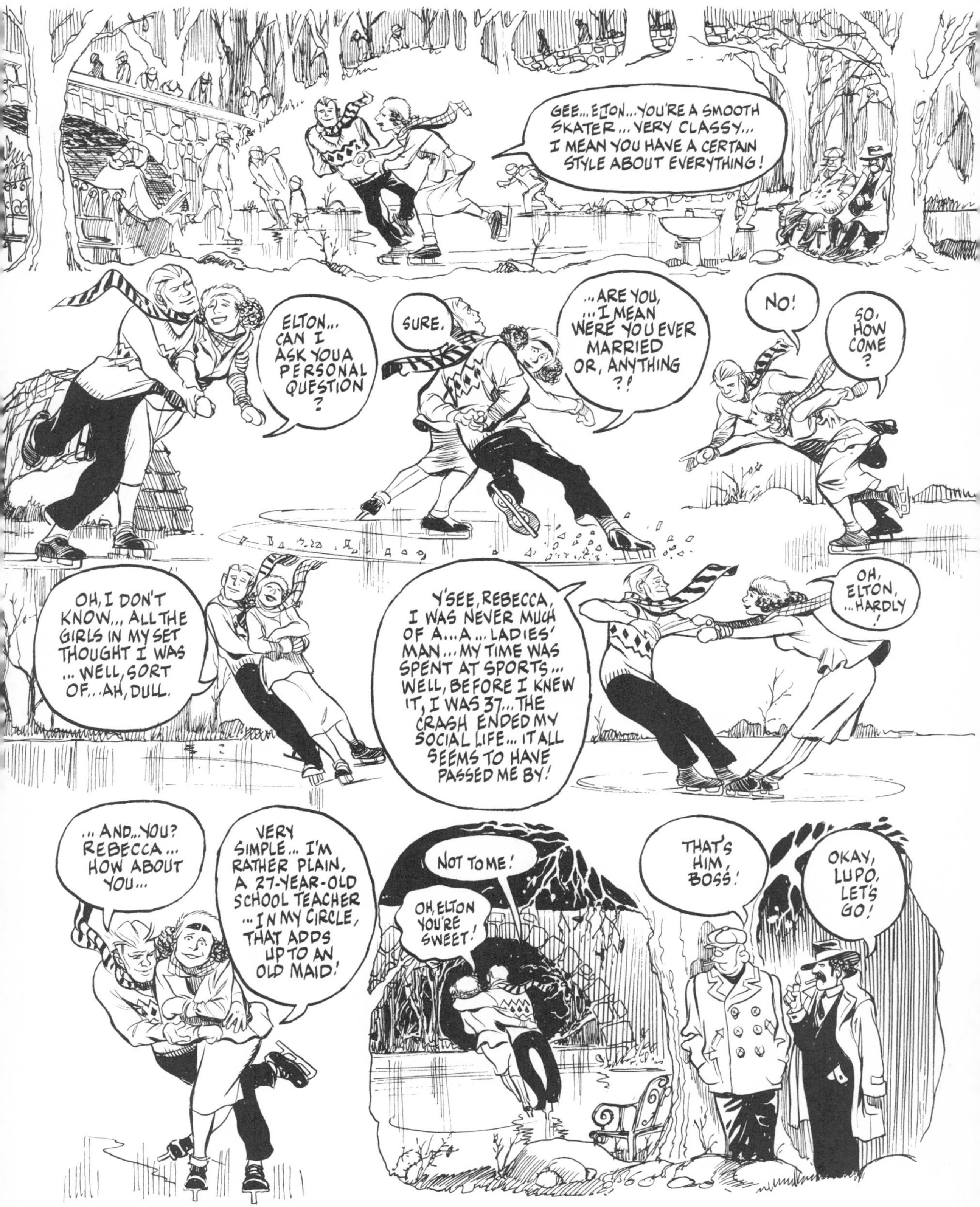
GEE... ELTON... YOU'RE A SMOOTH SKATER... VERY CLASSY... I MEAN YOU HAVE A CERTAIN STYLE ABOUT EVERYTHING!
ELTON... CAN I ASK YOU A PERSONAL QUESTION?
SURE.
...ARE YOU, ...I MEAN WERE YOU EVER MARRIED OR, ANYTHING ?!
NO!
SO, HOW COME?
OH, I DON'T KNOW... ALL THE GIRLS IN MY SET THOUGHT I WAS ... WELL, SORT OF... AH, DULL.
Y'SEE, REBECCA, I WAS NEVER MUCH OF A... A... LADIES' MAN... MY TIME WAS SPENT AT SPORTS... WELL, BEFORE I KNEW IT, I WAS 37... THE CRASH ENDED MY SOCIAL LIFE... IT ALL SEEMS TO HAVE PASSED ME BY!
OH, ELTON ...HARDLY!
... AND... YOU? REBECCA... HOW ABOUT YOU...
VERY SIMPLE... I'M RATHER PLAIN, A 27-YEAR-OLD SCHOOL TEACHER ...IN MY CIRCLE, THAT ADDS UP TO AN OLD MAID!
NOT TO ME!
OH, ELTON YOU'RE SWEET!
THAT'S HIM, BOSS!
OKAY, LUPO, LET'S GO!

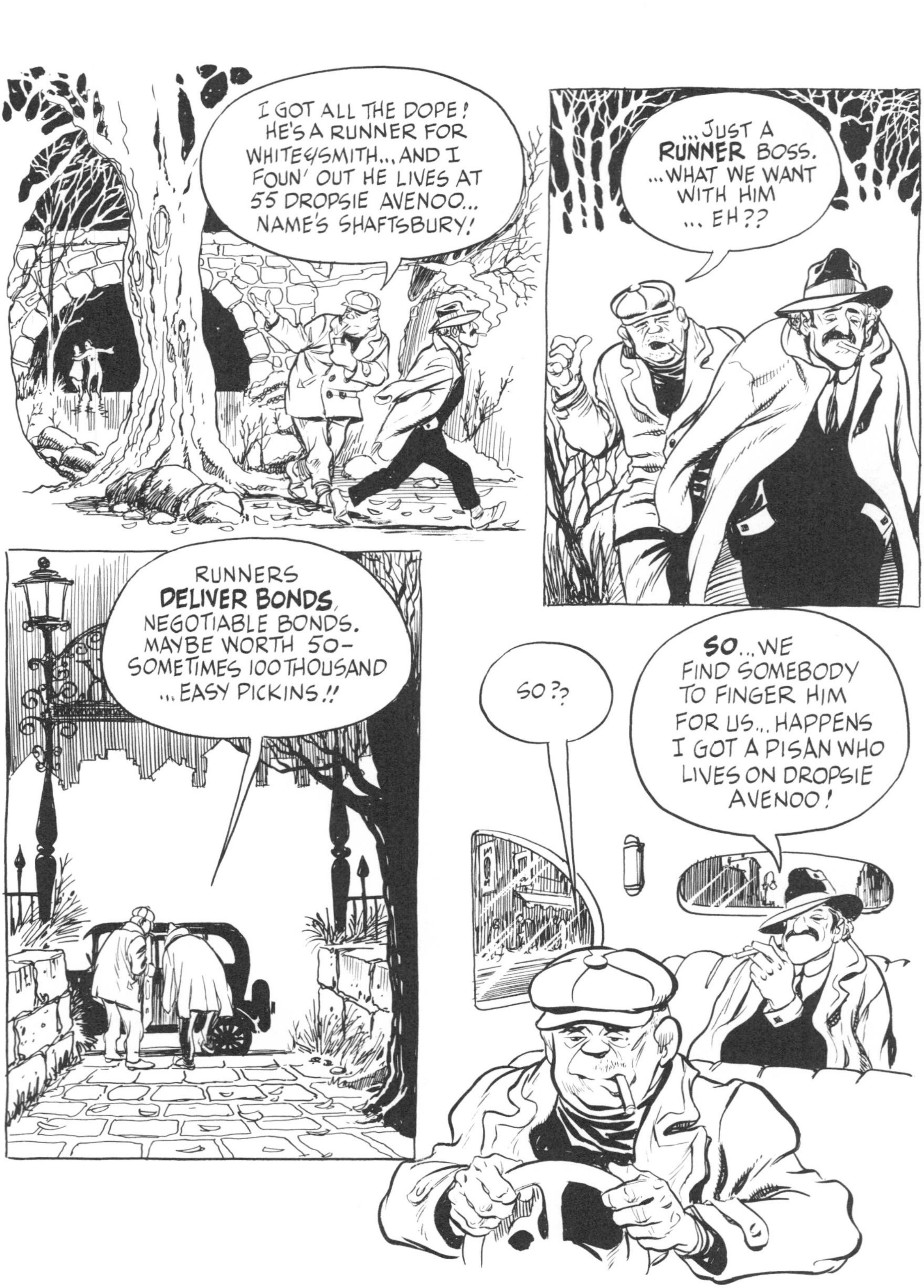
I GOT ALL THE DOPE! HE'S A RUNNER FOR WHITE&SMITH... AND I FOUN' OUT HE LIVES AT 55 DROPSIE AVENOO... NAME'S SHAFTSBURY!
...JUST A RUNNER BOSS. ...WHAT WE WANT WITH HIM ... EH??
RUNNERS DELIVER BONDS, NEGOTIABLE BONDS. MAYBE WORTH 50-SOMETIMES 100 THOUSAND ...EASY PICKINS!!
SO??
SO...WE FIND SOMEBODY TO FINGER HIM FOR US... HAPPENS I GOT A PISAN WHO LIVES ON DROPSIE AVENOO!

THE BLACK HAND

BETWEEN 1861 AND 1934 THE POPULATION OF ITALY HAD A NATURAL INCREASE OF ABOUT 400,000 A YEAR. THE DENSITY OF ITS POPULATION AVERAGED ABOUT 359 PERSONS PER SQUARE MILE.

DURING THE YEARS AFTER WORLD WAR I, THE ECONOMY, ESPECIALLY IN SOUTHERN ITALY AND SICILY, COULD BARELY SUPPORT ITS POPULATION. EMPLOYMENT WAS SO SCARCE THAT ONLY 150 DAYS OF WORK PER YEAR WAS THE AVERAGE. IN THE SOUTHERN FARM LANDS, MALARIA AND OTHER POVERTY-RELATED DISEASES KEPT PRODUCTIVITY LOW.

THE STRONG CENTRAL GOVERNMENT SET UP IN 1870 HAD LONG BEEN BESET BY LOCAL GROUPS THAT GREW OUT OF STRONG 'FAMILIES' WHO CONTROLLED REGIONS. SMUGGLING, PETTY CRIME AND CORRUPTION WAS RIFE. LOYALTY TO A 'FAMILY' OR A SECRET SOCIETY WAS A WAY OF LIFE.

SO, BETWEEN 1919 AND 1924 EMIGRATION SOARED... WITH AMERICA AS THE FAVORED DESTINATION.

IN 1920, ALONE, OVER 300,000 ITALIAN IMMIGRANTS ENTERED THE UNITED STATES.

FINALLY, IN 1924, THE U.S. IMMIGRATION ACT CUT THE TORRENT AND ESTABLISHED A QUOTA OF ONLY 3,845 ITALIAN IMMIGRANTS PER YEAR.

THEREAFTER, ABETTED BY THE POLICIES OF THE FASCIST GOVERNMENT, IMMIGRATION TO THE U.S. DWINDLED TO A TRICKLE. NOW, GETTING TO AMERICA BECAME A MATTER OF SOME SKILL AND CONNECTION.

HERE, THE OLD WORLD 'FAMILY' GROUPS AND SECRET SOCIETIES CAME INTO IMPORTANCE. FOR A FEE, THEY WANGLED VISAS, BRIBED OFFICIALS... OR ACTUALLY SMUGGLED MANY IMMIGRANTS INTO THE COUNTRY.

ONCE HERE, THEY WERE OFTEN INDENTURED TO THE SMUGGLING 'FAMILIES'... OR AT LEAST IN HEAVY DEBT FOR THEIR PASSAGE FEE. THESE FEES WERE INVARIABLY COLLECTED.

ONE OF THE GROUPS, WITH SICILIAN ROOTS WAS **THE BLACK HAND**. THEY, LIKE THE MAFIA, WERE OLD HANDS AT DISCIPLINE AND ENFORCEMENT.

A BLACK HAND IMPRINT ON ONE'S DOOR OR ON A LETTER WAS A NOTICE THAT WAS NOT TAKEN LIGHTLY.

HEY, KID!! THIS 55 DROPSIE AVENOO??

YUP!

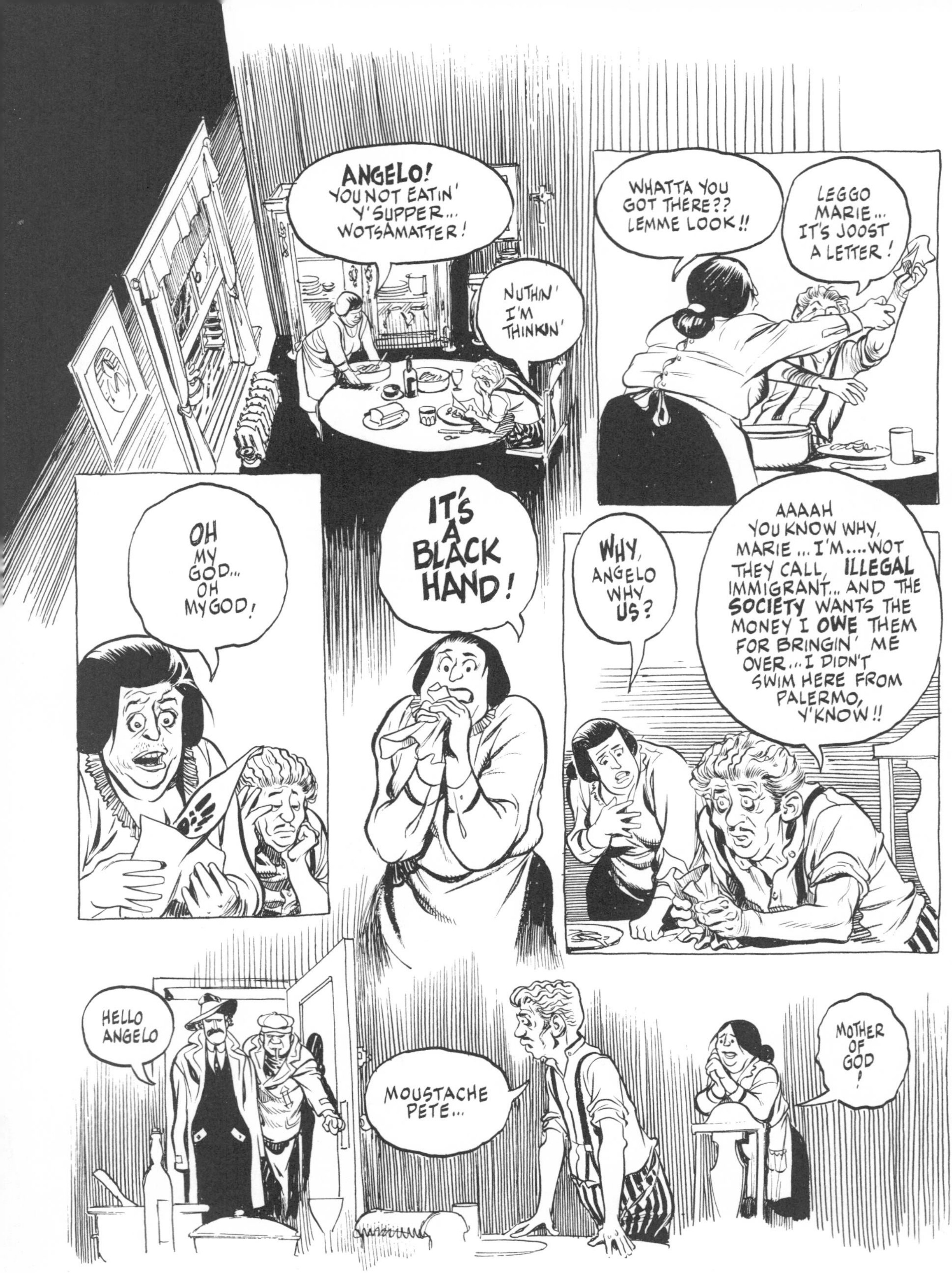

ANGELO! YOU NOT EATIN' Y'SUPPER... WOTSAMATTER!
NUTHIN' I'M THINKIN'
WHATTA YOU GOT THERE?? LEMME LOOK!!
LEGGO MARIE... IT'S JOOST A LETTER!
OH MY GOD... OH MY GOD!
IT'S A BLACK HAND!
WHY, ANGELO WHY US?
AAAAH YOU KNOW WHY, MARIE... I'M.... WOT THEY CALL, ILLEGAL IMMIGRANT... AND THE SOCIETY WANTS THE MONEY I OWE THEM FOR BRINGIN' ME OVER... I DIDN'T SWIM HERE FROM PALERMO, Y'KNOW!!
HELLO ANGELO
MOUSTACHE PETE...
MOTHER OF GOD!

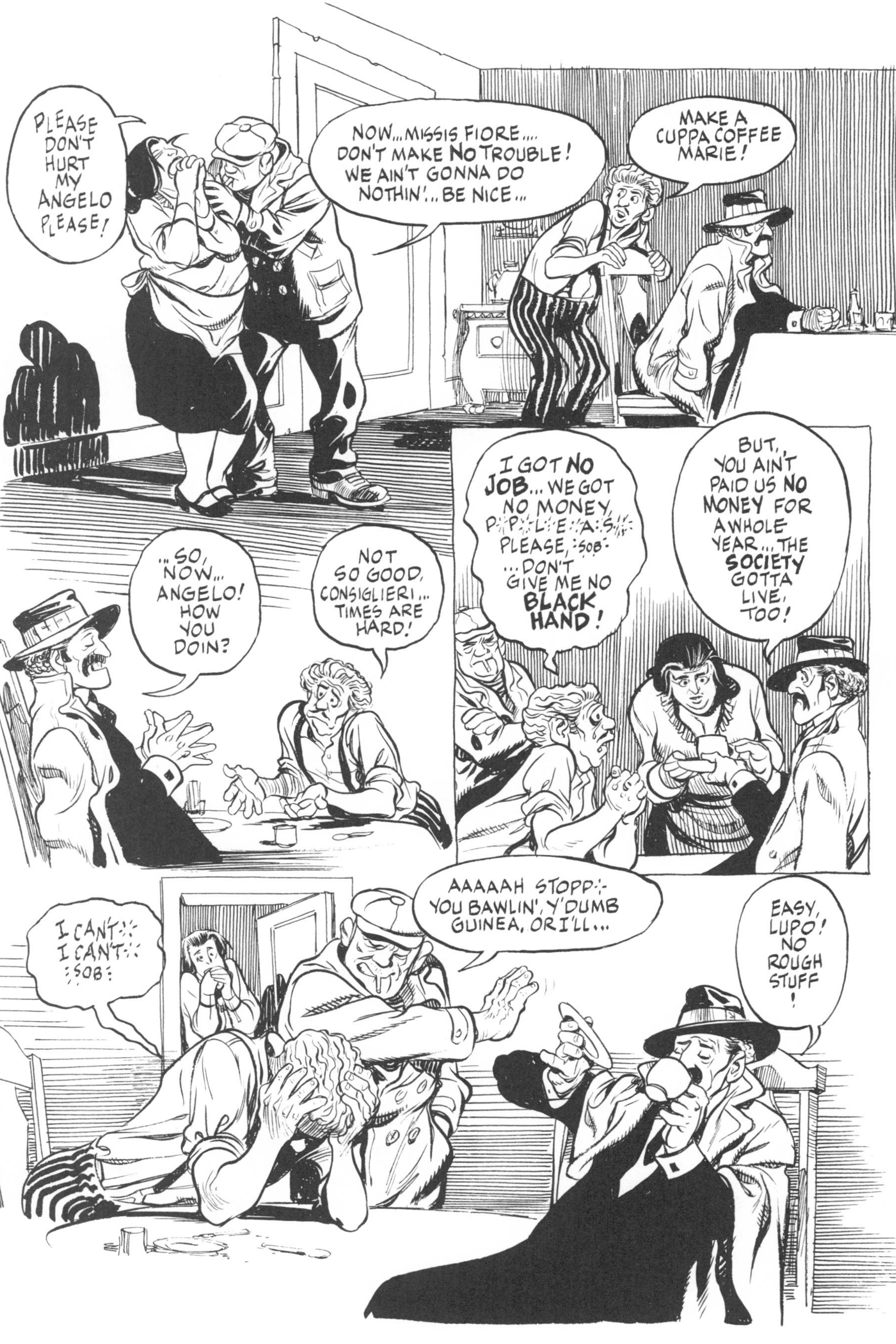
PLEASE DON'T HURT MY ANGELO PLEASE!
NOW... MISSIS FIORE.... DON'T MAKE NO TROUBLE! WE AIN'T GONNA DO NOTHIN'... BE NICE...
MAKE A CUPPA COFFEE MARIE!
...SO, NOW... ANGELO! HOW YOU DOIN?
NOT SO GOOD, CONSIGLIERI... TIMES ARE HARD!
I GOT NO JOB... WE GOT NO MONEY, P-P-L-E-A-S- PLEASE, SOB ...DON'T GIVE ME NO BLACK HAND!
BUT, YOU AIN'T PAID US NO MONEY FOR A WHOLE YEAR... THE SOCIETY GOTTA LIVE, TOO!
I CAN'T I CAN'T SOB
AAAAAH STOPP- YOU BAWLIN', Y'DUMB GUINEA, OR I'LL...
EASY, LUPO! NO ROUGH STUFF!

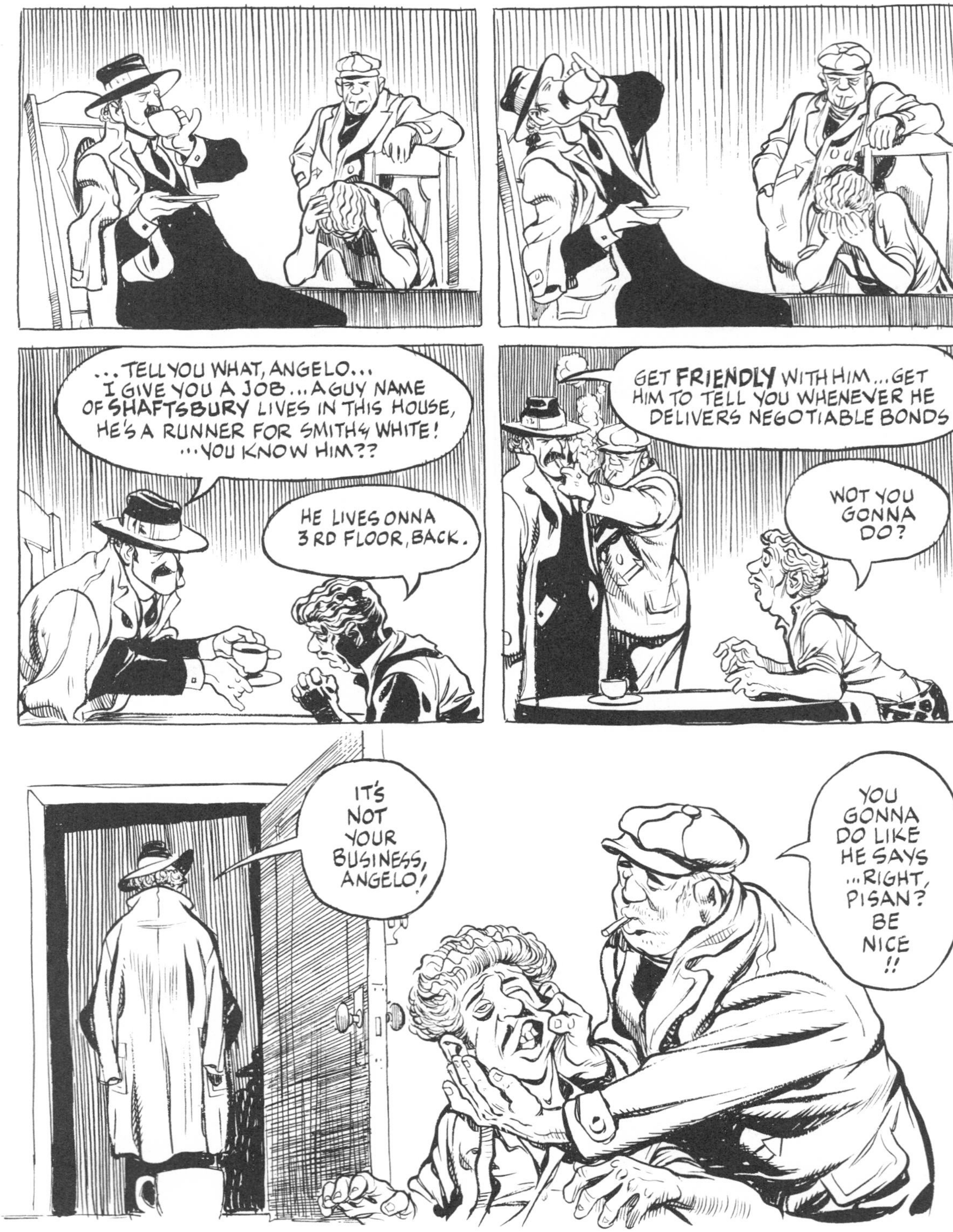
... TELL YOU WHAT, ANGELO... I GIVE YOU A JOB... A GUY NAME OF SHAFTSBURY LIVES IN THIS HOUSE, HE'S A RUNNER FOR SMITH & WHITE! ...YOU KNOW HIM??
HE LIVES ONNA 3RD FLOOR, BACK.
GET FRIENDLY WITH HIM... GET HIM TO TELL YOU WHENEVER HE DELIVERS NEGOTIABLE BONDS
WOT YOU GONNA DO?
IT'S NOT YOUR BUSINESS, ANGELO!
YOU GONNA DO LIKE HE SAYS ...RIGHT, PISAN? BE NICE !!

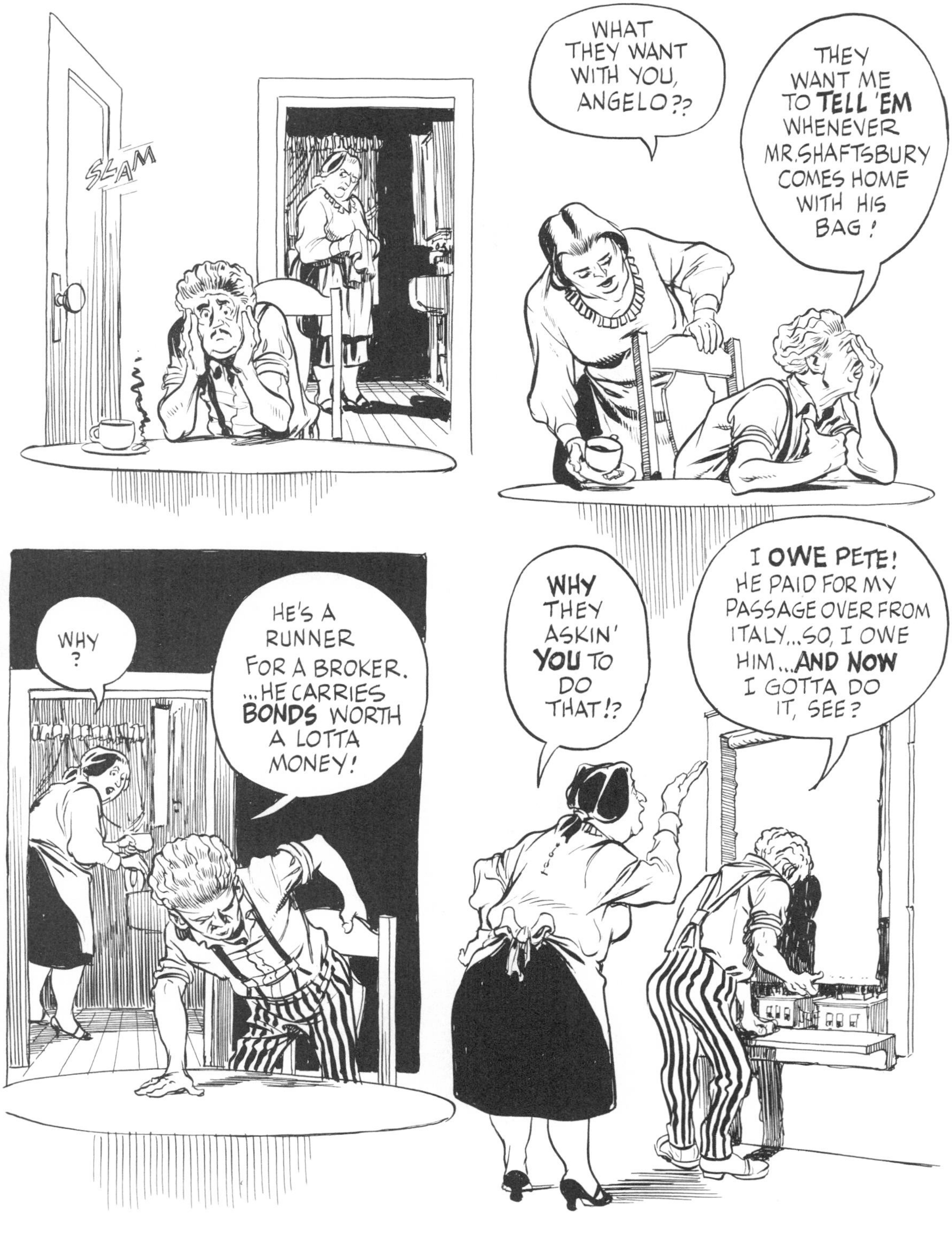
SLAM
WHAT THEY WANT WITH YOU, ANGELO??
THEY WANT ME TO TELL 'EM WHENEVER MR. SHAFTSBURY COMES HOME WITH HIS BAG!
WHY?
HE'S A RUNNER FOR A BROKER. ...HE CARRIES BONDS WORTH A LOTTA MONEY!
WHY THEY ASKIN' YOU TO DO THAT!?
I OWE PETE! HE PAID FOR MY PASSAGE OVER FROM ITALY...SO, I OWE HIM...AND NOW I GOTTA DO IT, SEE?

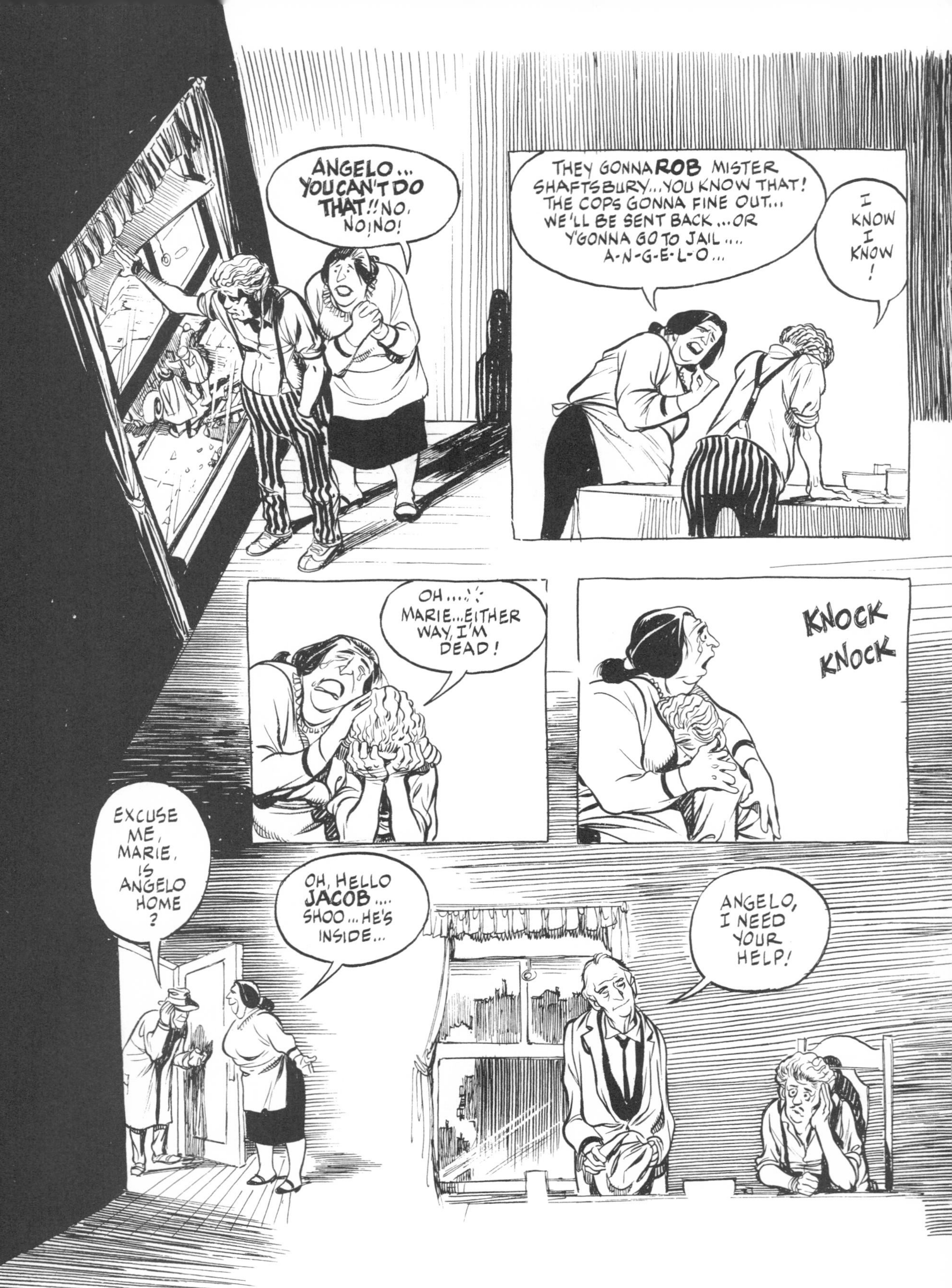
ANGELO... YOU CAN'T DO THAT!! NO, NO, NO!
THEY GONNA ROB MISTER SHAFTSBURY... YOU KNOW THAT! THE COPS GONNA FINE OUT... WE'LL BE SENT BACK... OR Y'GONNA GO TO JAIL.... A-N-G-E-L-O...
I KNOW I KNOW!
OH....!! MARIE... EITHER WAY, I'M DEAD!
KNOCK KNOCK
EXCUSE ME, MARIE, IS ANGELO HOME?
OH, HELLO JACOB.... SHOO... HE'S INSIDE...
ANGELO, I NEED YOUR HELP!

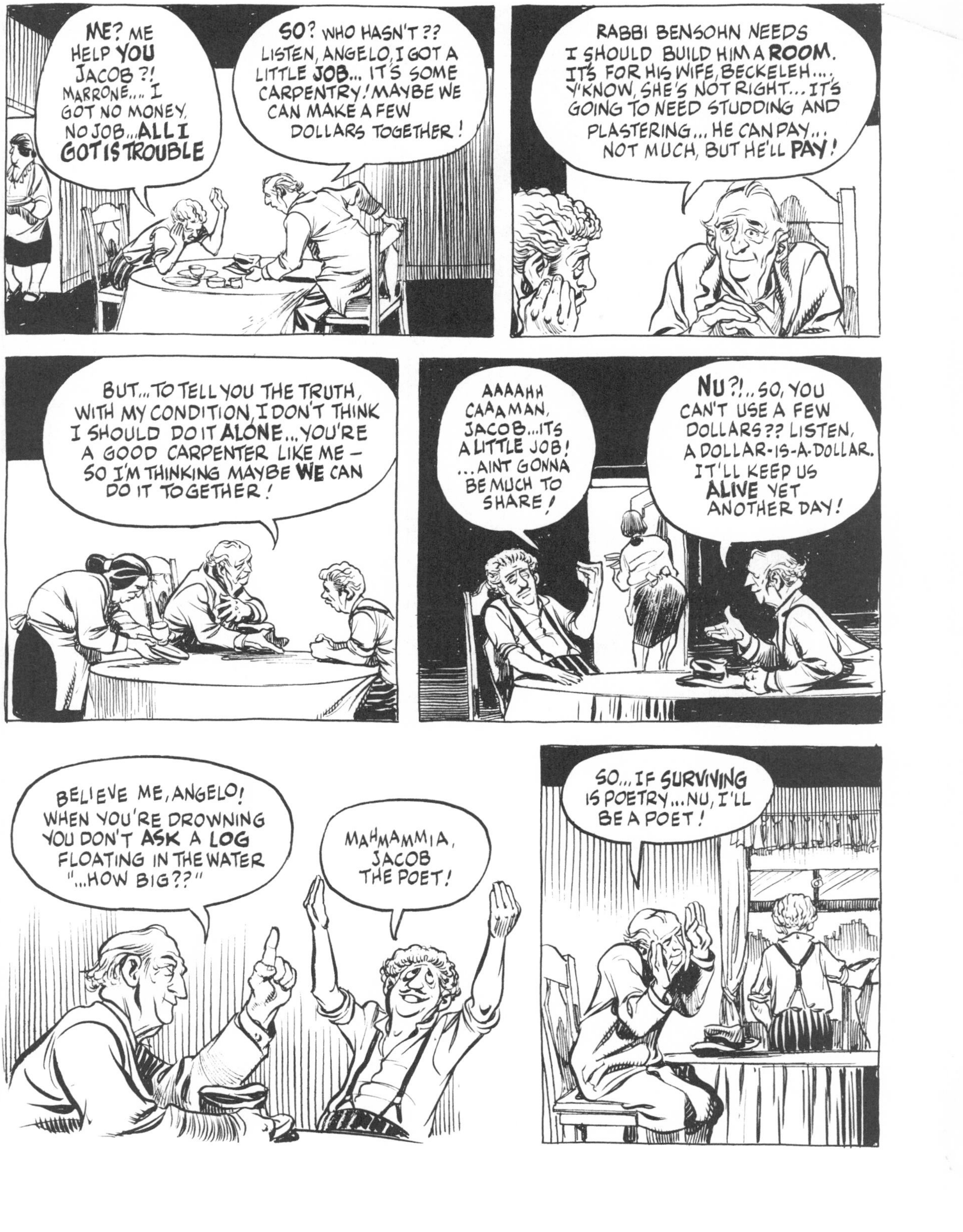
ME? ME HELP YOU JACOB?! MARRONE... I GOT NO MONEY, NO JOB... ALL I GOT IS TROUBLE
SO? WHO HASN'T?? LISTEN, ANGELO, I GOT A LITTLE JOB... IT'S SOME CARPENTRY! MAYBE WE CAN MAKE A FEW DOLLARS TOGETHER!
RABBI BENSOHN NEEDS I SHOULD BUILD HIM A ROOM. IT'S FOR HIS WIFE, BECKELEH..., Y'KNOW, SHE'S NOT RIGHT... IT'S GOING TO NEED STUDDING AND PLASTERING... HE CAN PAY... NOT MUCH, BUT HE'LL PAY!
BUT... TO TELL YOU THE TRUTH, WITH MY CONDITION, I DON'T THINK I SHOULD DO IT ALONE... YOU'RE A GOOD CARPENTER LIKE ME — SO I'M THINKING MAYBE WE CAN DO IT TOGETHER!
AAAAHH CAAAMAN, JACOB... ITS A LITTLE JOB! ...AINT GONNA BE MUCH TO SHARE!
NU?!.. SO, YOU CAN'T USE A FEW DOLLARS?? LISTEN, A DOLLAR-IS-A-DOLLAR. IT'LL KEEP US ALIVE YET ANOTHER DAY!
BELIEVE ME, ANGELO! WHEN YOU'RE DROWNING YOU DON'T ASK A LOG FLOATING IN THE WATER "...HOW BIG??"
MAHMAMMIA, JACOB THE POET!
SO... IF SURVIVING IS POETRY... NU, I'LL BE A POET!

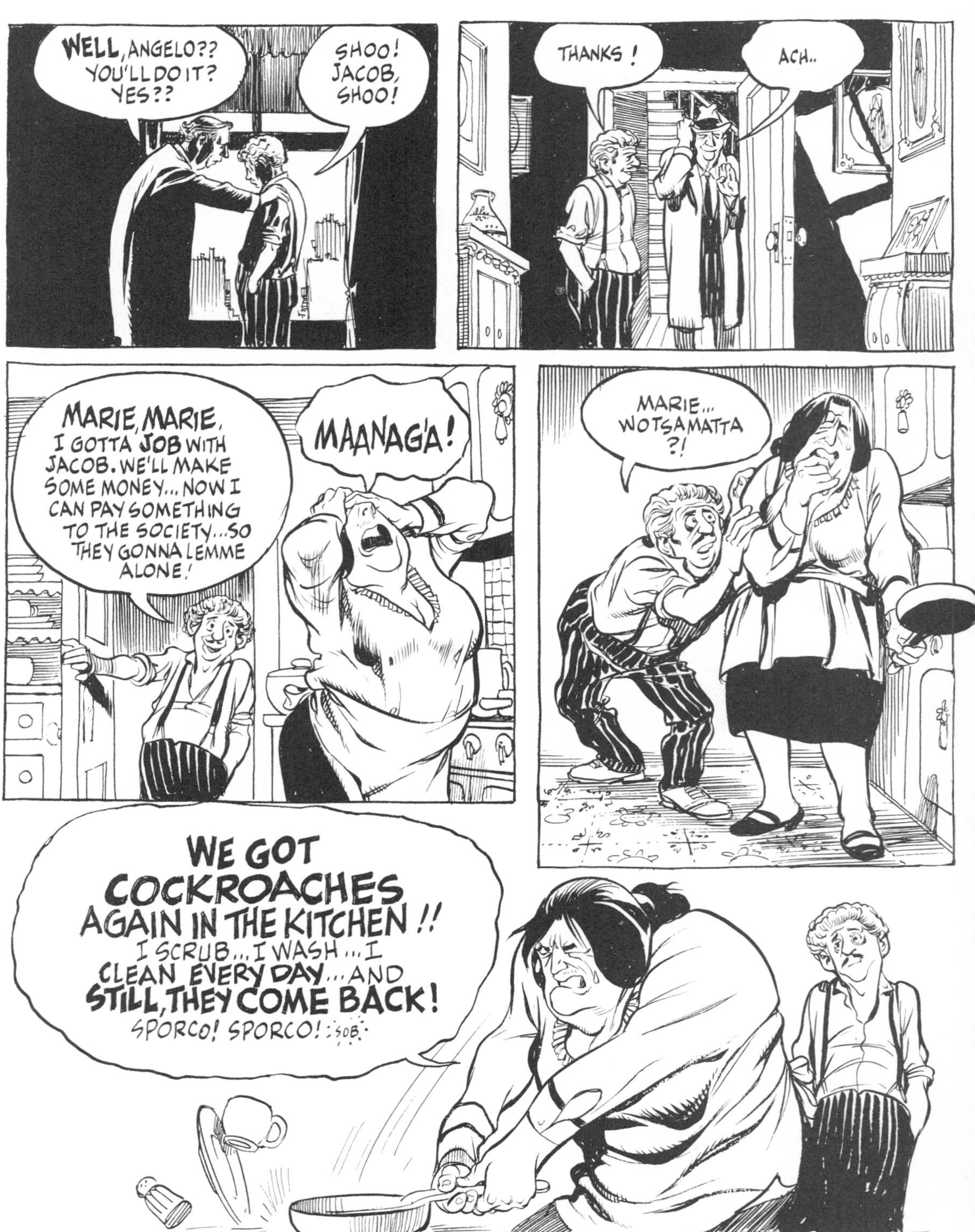
WELL, ANGELO?? YOU'LL DO IT? YES??
SHOO! JACOB, SHOO!
THANKS!
ACH..
MARIE, MARIE, I GOTTA JOB WITH JACOB. WE'LL MAKE SOME MONEY... NOW I CAN PAY SOMETHING TO THE SOCIETY... SO THEY GONNA LEMME ALONE!
MAANAG'A!
MARIE... WOTSAMATTA ?!
WE GOT COCKROACHES AGAIN IN THE KITCHEN!! I SCRUB... I WASH... I CLEAN EVERY DAY... AND STILL, THEY COME BACK! SPORCO! SPORCO! SOB

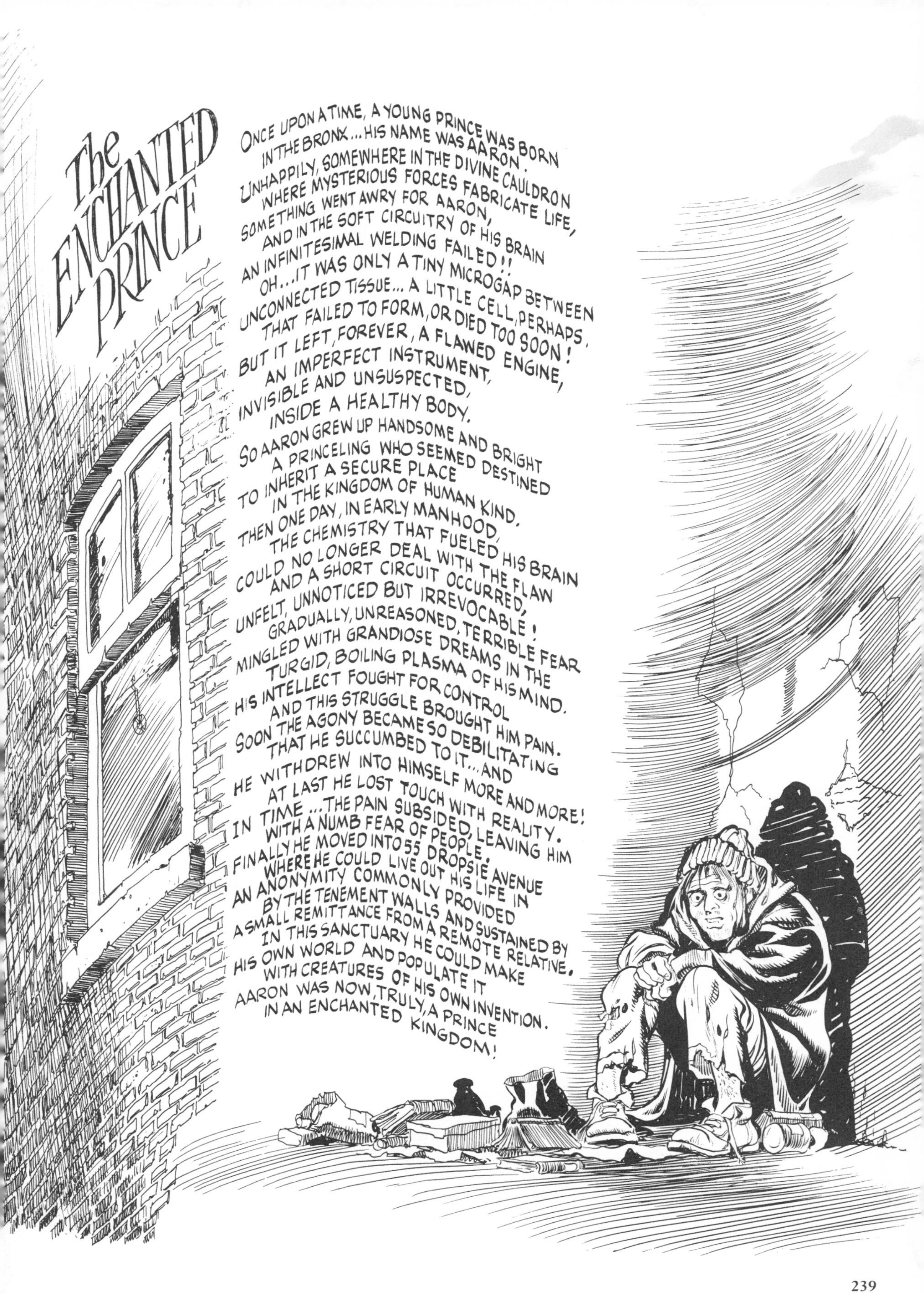
The Enchanted Prince
Once upon a time, a young prince was born
in the Bronx... his name was Aaron.
Unhappily, somewhere in the divine cauldron
where mysterious forces fabricate life,
something went awry for Aaron,
and in the soft circuitry of his brain
an infinitesimal welding failed!!
Oh... it was only a tiny microgap between
unconnected tissue... a little cell, perhaps,
that failed to form, or died too soon!
But it left, forever, a flawed engine,
an imperfect instrument,
invisible and unsuspected,
inside a healthy body.
So Aaron grew up handsome and bright
a princeling who seemed destined
to inherit a secure place
in the kingdom of human kind.
Then one day, in early manhood,
the chemistry that fueled his brain
could no longer deal with the flaw
and a short circuit occurred,
unfelt, unnoticed but irrevocable!
Gradually, unreasoned, terrible fear
mingled with grandiose dreams in the
turgid, boiling plasma of his mind.
His intellect fought for control
and this struggle brought him pain.
Soon the agony became so debilitating
that he succumbed to it... and
he withdrew into himself more and more!
At last he lost touch with reality.
In time... the pain subsided, leaving him
with a numb fear of people.
Finally he moved into 55 Dropsie Avenue
where he could live out his life in
an anonymity commonly provided
by the tenement walls and sustained by
a small remittance from a remote relative.
In this sanctuary he could make
his own world and populate it
with creatures of his own invention.
Aaron was now, truly, a prince
in an enchanted kingdom!

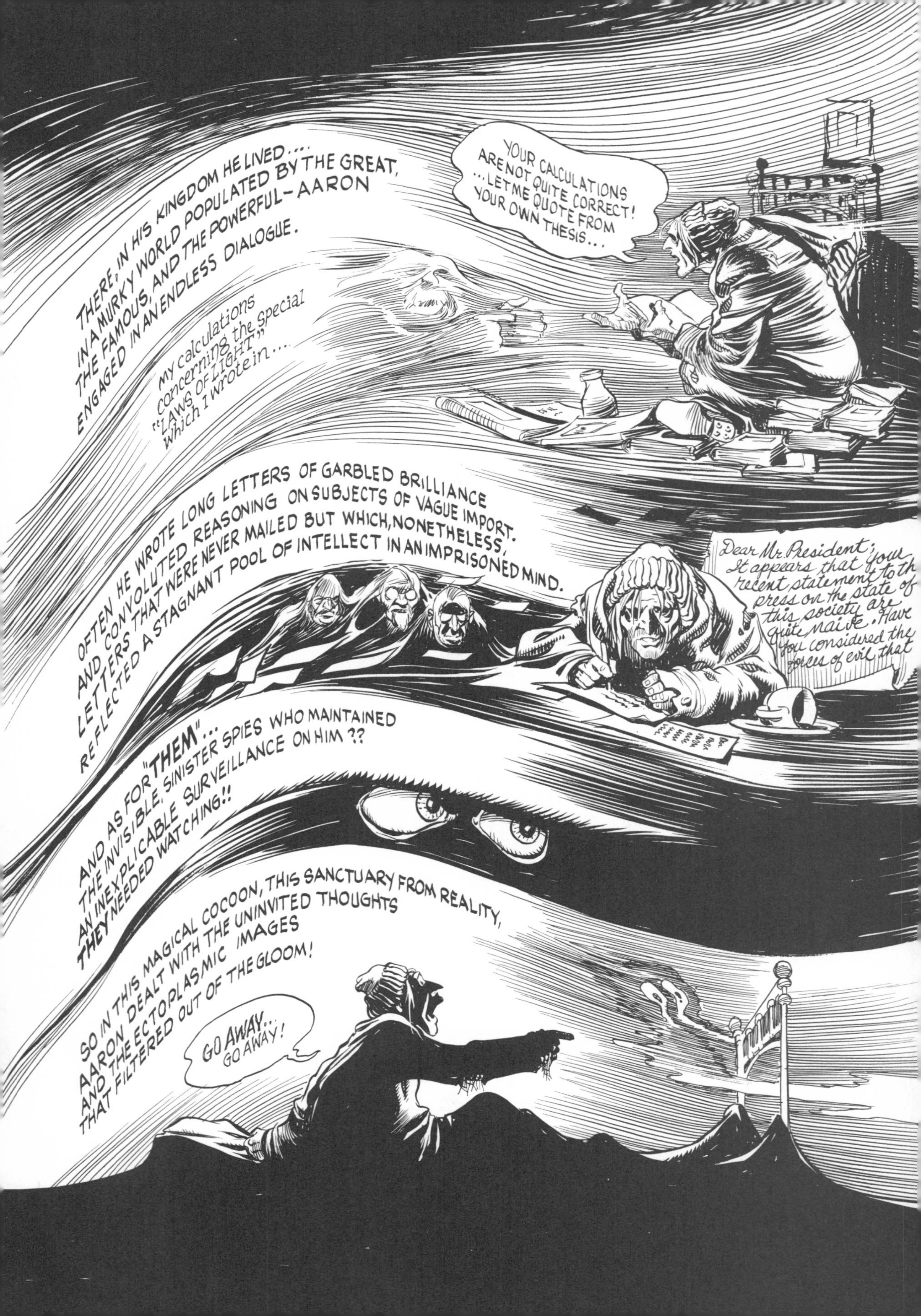
THERE, IN HIS KINGDOM HE LIVED.... IN A MURKY WORLD POPULATED BY THE GREAT, THE FAMOUS, AND THE POWERFUL-AARON ENGAGED IN AN ENDLESS DIALOGUE.
My calculations concerning the special "LAWS OF LIGHT" which I wrote in...
YOUR CALCULATIONS ARE NOT QUITE CORRECT! ...LET ME QUOTE FROM YOUR OWN THESIS...
OFTEN HE WROTE LONG LETTERS OF GARBLED BRILLIANCE AND CONVOLUTED REASONING ON SUBJECTS OF VAGUE IMPORT. LETTERS THAT WERE NEVER MAILED BUT WHICH, NONETHELESS, REFLECTED A STAGNANT POOL OF INTELLECT IN AN IMPRISONED MIND.
Dear Mr. President; It appears that your recent statement to th press on the state of this society are quite naive. Have you considered the forces of evil that
AND AS FOR "THEM"... THE INVISIBLE, SINISTER SPIES WHO MAINTAINED AN INEXPLICABLE SURVEILLANCE ON HIM ?? THEY NEEDED WATCHING!!
SO IN THIS MAGICAL COCOON, THIS SANCTUARY FROM REALITY, AARON DEALT WITH THE UNINVITED THOUGHTS AND THE ECTOPLASMIC IMAGES THAT FILTERED OUT OF THE GLOOM!
GO AWAY... GO AWAY!

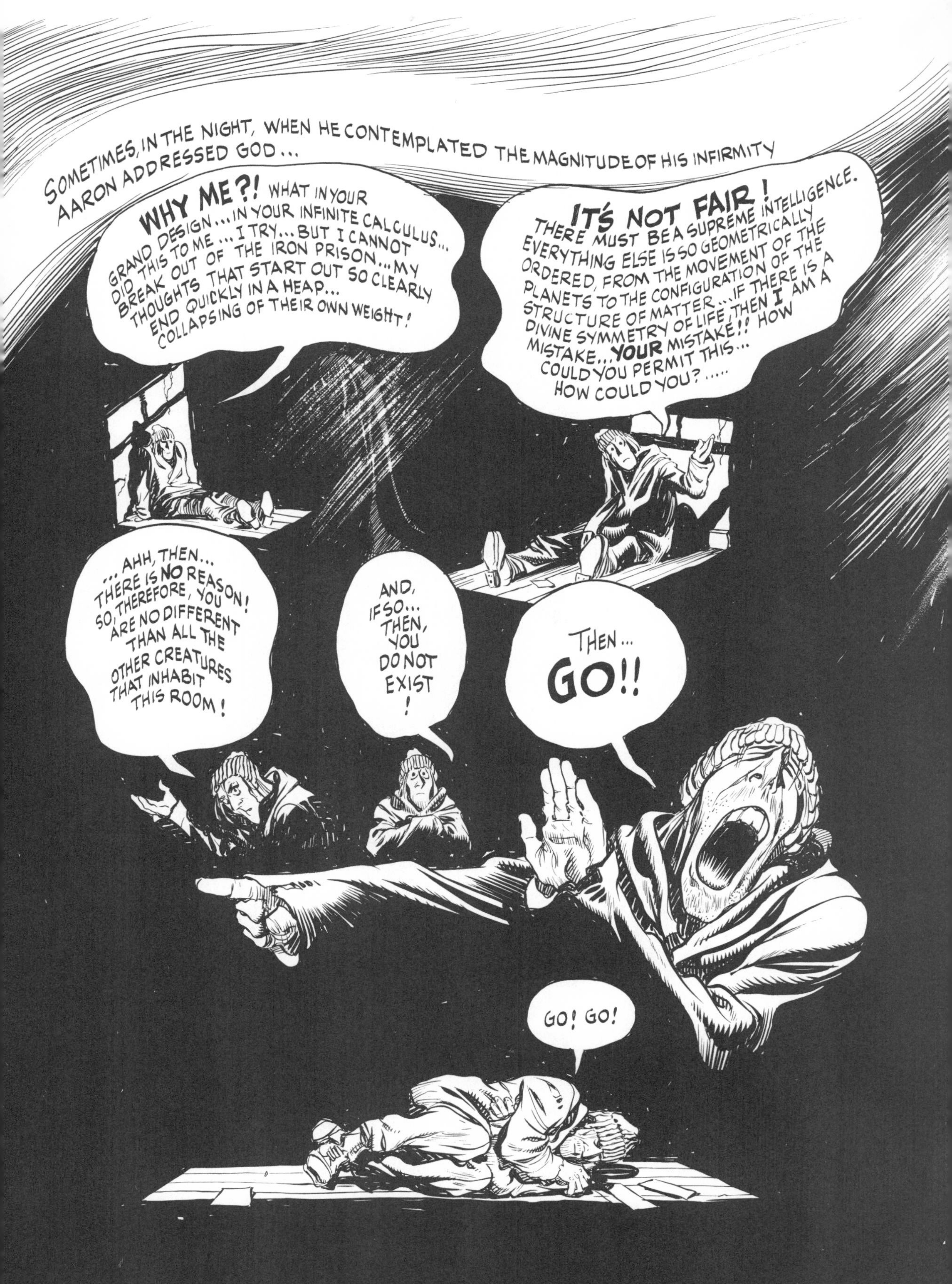

SOMETIMES, IN THE NIGHT, WHEN HE CONTEMPLATED THE MAGNITUDE OF HIS INFIRMITY AARON ADDRESSED GOD...
WHY ME?! WHAT IN YOUR GRAND DESIGN... IN YOUR INFINITE CALCULUS... DID THIS TO ME... I TRY... BUT I CANNOT BREAK OUT OF THE IRON PRISON... MY THOUGHTS THAT START OUT SO CLEARLY END QUICKLY IN A HEAP... COLLAPSING OF THEIR OWN WEIGHT!
IT'S NOT FAIR! THERE MUST BE A SUPREME INTELLIGENCE. EVERYTHING ELSE IS SO GEOMETRICALLY ORDERED, FROM THE MOVEMENT OF THE PLANETS TO THE CONFIGURATION OF THE STRUCTURE OF MATTER... IF THERE IS A DIVINE SYMMETRY OF LIFE, THEN I AM A MISTAKE... YOUR MISTAKE!! HOW COULD YOU PERMIT THIS... HOW COULD YOU?.....
... AHH, THEN... THERE IS NO REASON! SO, THEREFORE, YOU ARE NO DIFFERENT THAN ALL THE OTHER CREATURES THAT INHABIT THIS ROOM!
AND, IF SO... THEN, YOU DO NOT EXIST!
THEN... GO!!
GO! GO!

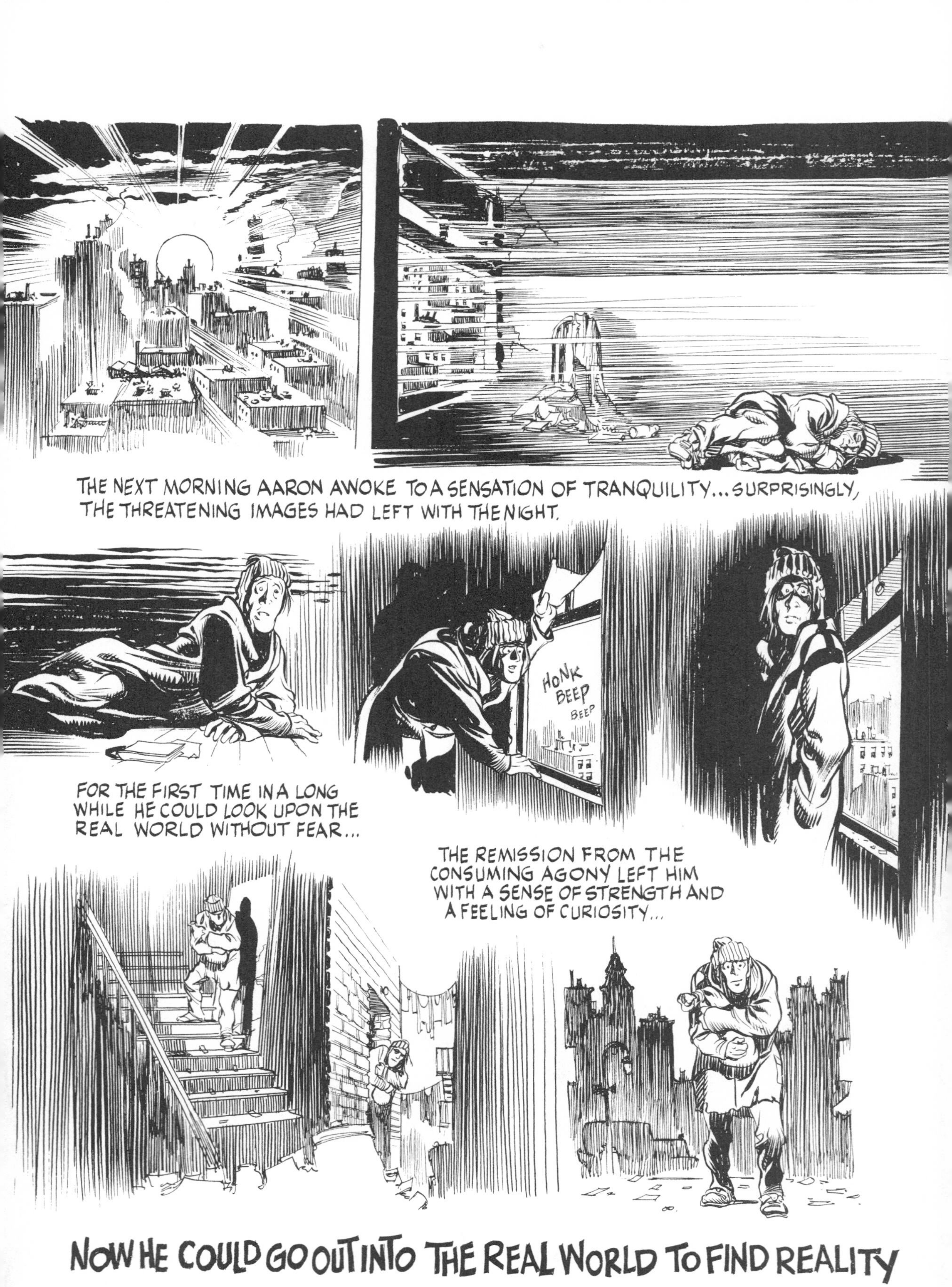
THE NEXT MORNING AARON AWOKE TO A SENSATION OF TRANQUILITY... SURPRISINGLY, THE THREATENING IMAGES HAD LEFT WITH THE NIGHT.
HONK
BEEP
BEEP
FOR THE FIRST TIME IN A LONG WHILE HE COULD LOOK UPON THE REAL WORLD WITHOUT FEAR...
THE REMISSION FROM THE CONSUMING AGONY LEFT HIM WITH A SENSE OF STRENGTH AND A FEELING OF CURIOSITY...
NOW HE COULD GO OUT INTO THE REAL WORLD TO FIND REALITY

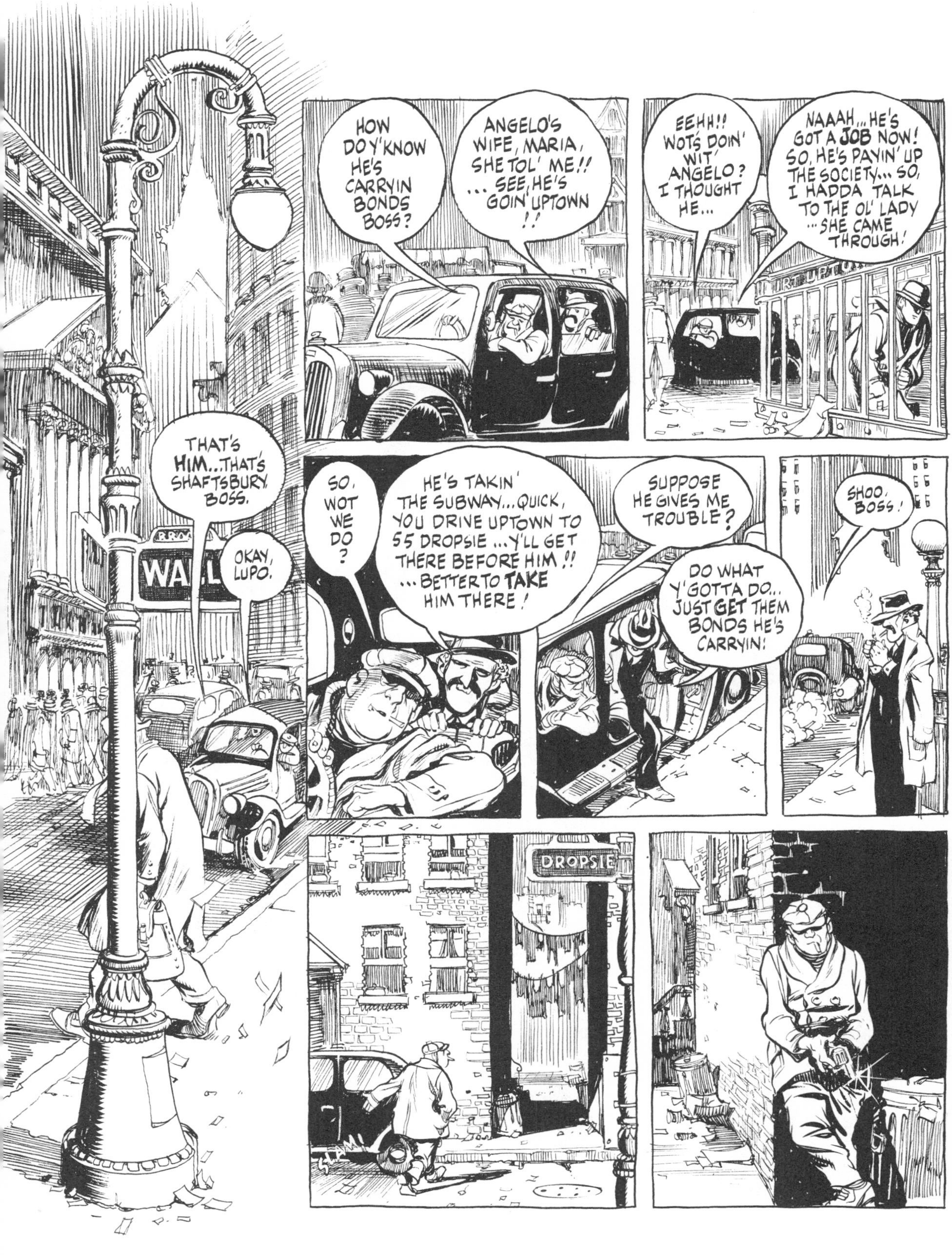
HOW DO Y'KNOW HE'S CARRYIN BONDS BOSS?
ANGELO'S WIFE, MARIA, SHE TOL' ME!! ... SEE, HE'S GOIN' UPTOWN!!
EEHH!! WOT'S DOIN' WIT' ANGELO? I THOUGHT HE...
NAAAH... HE'S GOT A JOB NOW! SO, HE'S PAYIN' UP THE SOCIETY... SO, I HADDA TALK TO THE OL' LADY ...SHE CAME THROUGH!
THAT'S HIM...THAT'S SHAFTSBURY, BOSS.
OKAY, LUPO.
WALL
SO, WOT WE DO?
HE'S TAKIN' THE SUBWAY... QUICK, YOU DRIVE UPTOWN TO 55 DROPSIE ...Y'LL GET THERE BEFORE HIM!! ... BETTER TO TAKE HIM THERE!
SUPPOSE HE GIVES ME TROUBLE?
DO WHAT Y'GOTTA DO... JUST GET THEM BONDS HE'S CARRYIN!
SHOO, BOSS!
DROPSIE

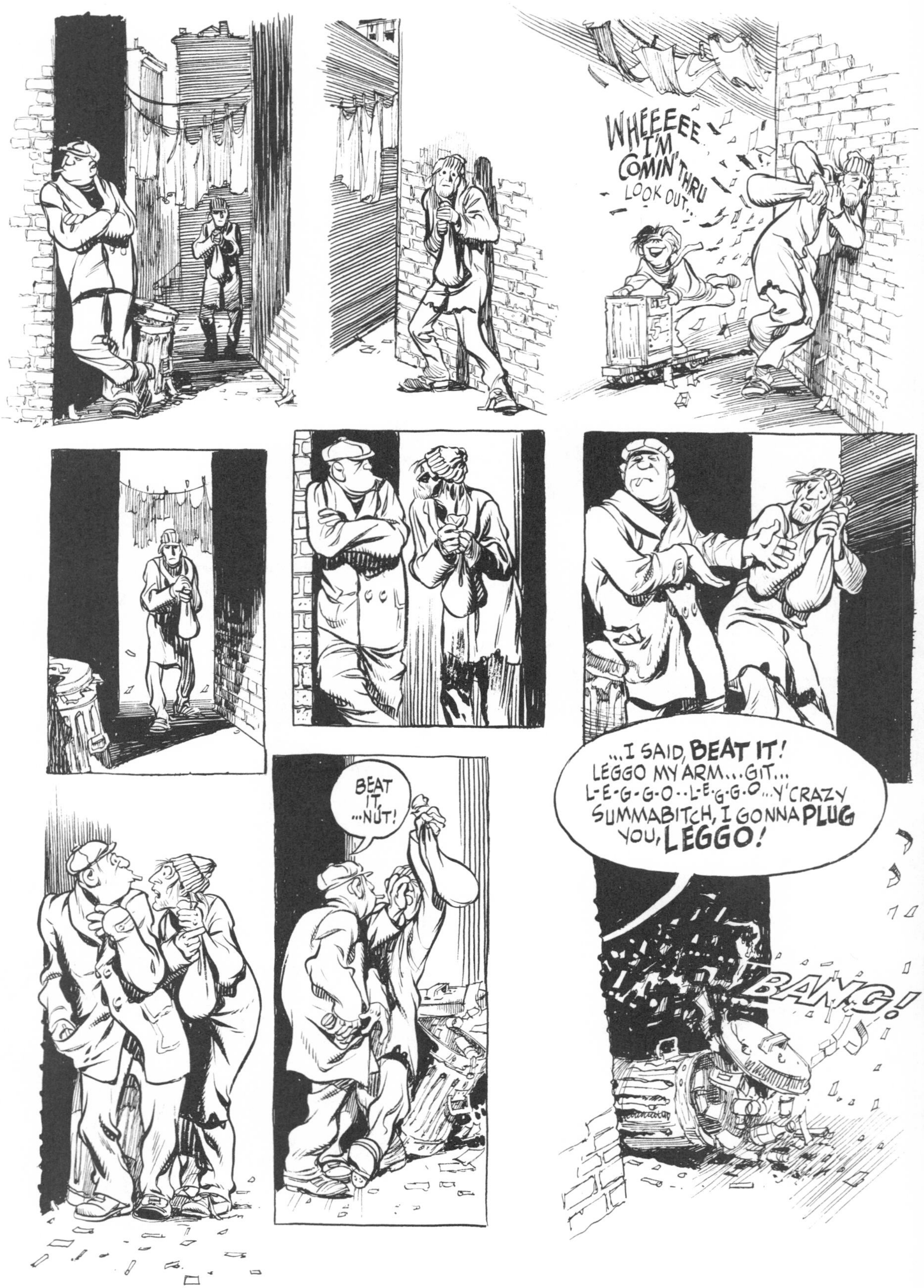

WHEEEEE I'M COMIN' THRU LOOK OUT..
BEAT IT, ...NUT!
...I SAID, BEAT IT! LEGGO MY ARM...GIT... L-E-G-G-O..L-E-G-G-O...Y'CRAZY SUMMABITCH, I GONNA PLUG YOU, LEGGO!
BANG!

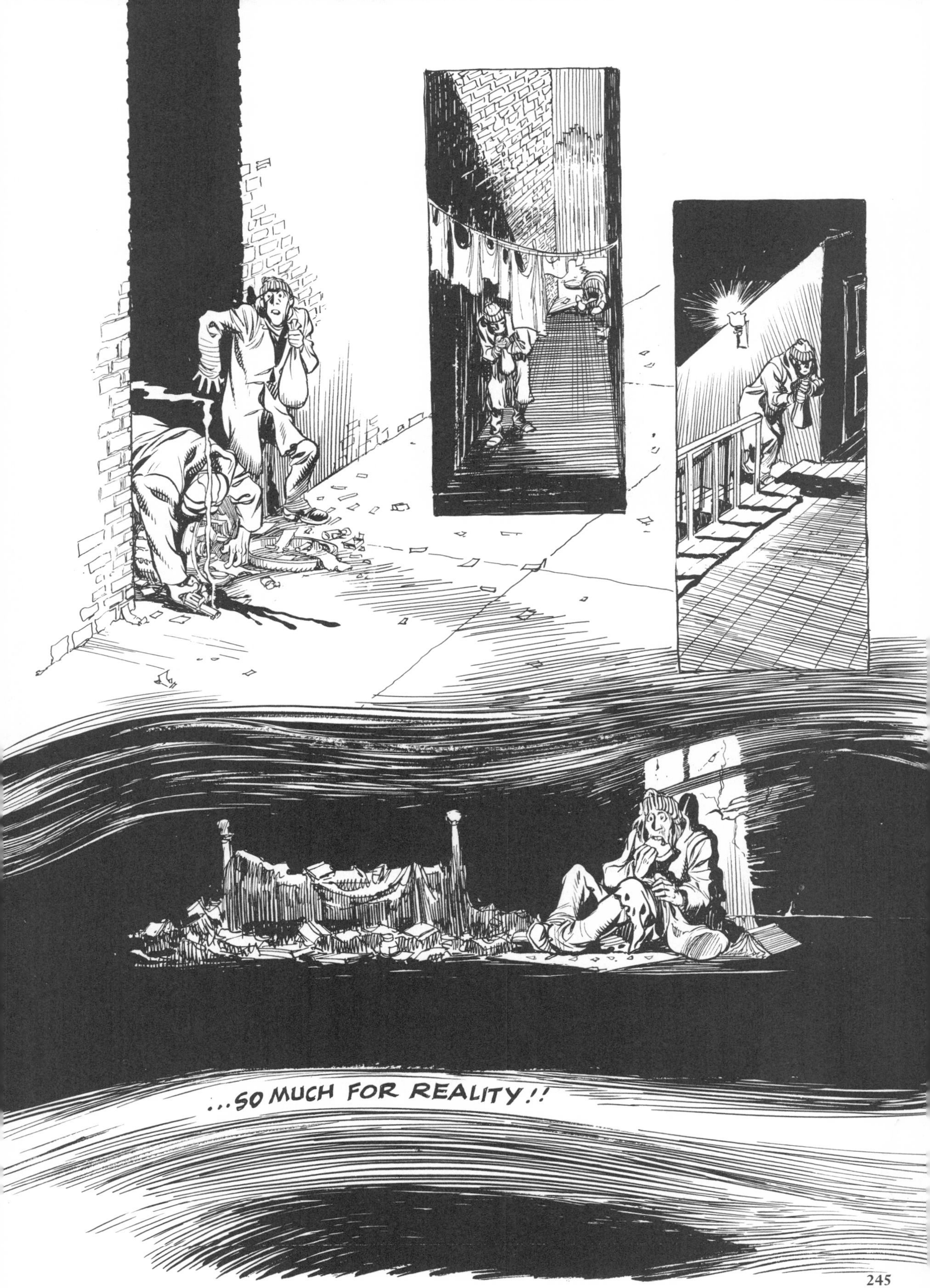
...SO MUCH FOR REALITY!!

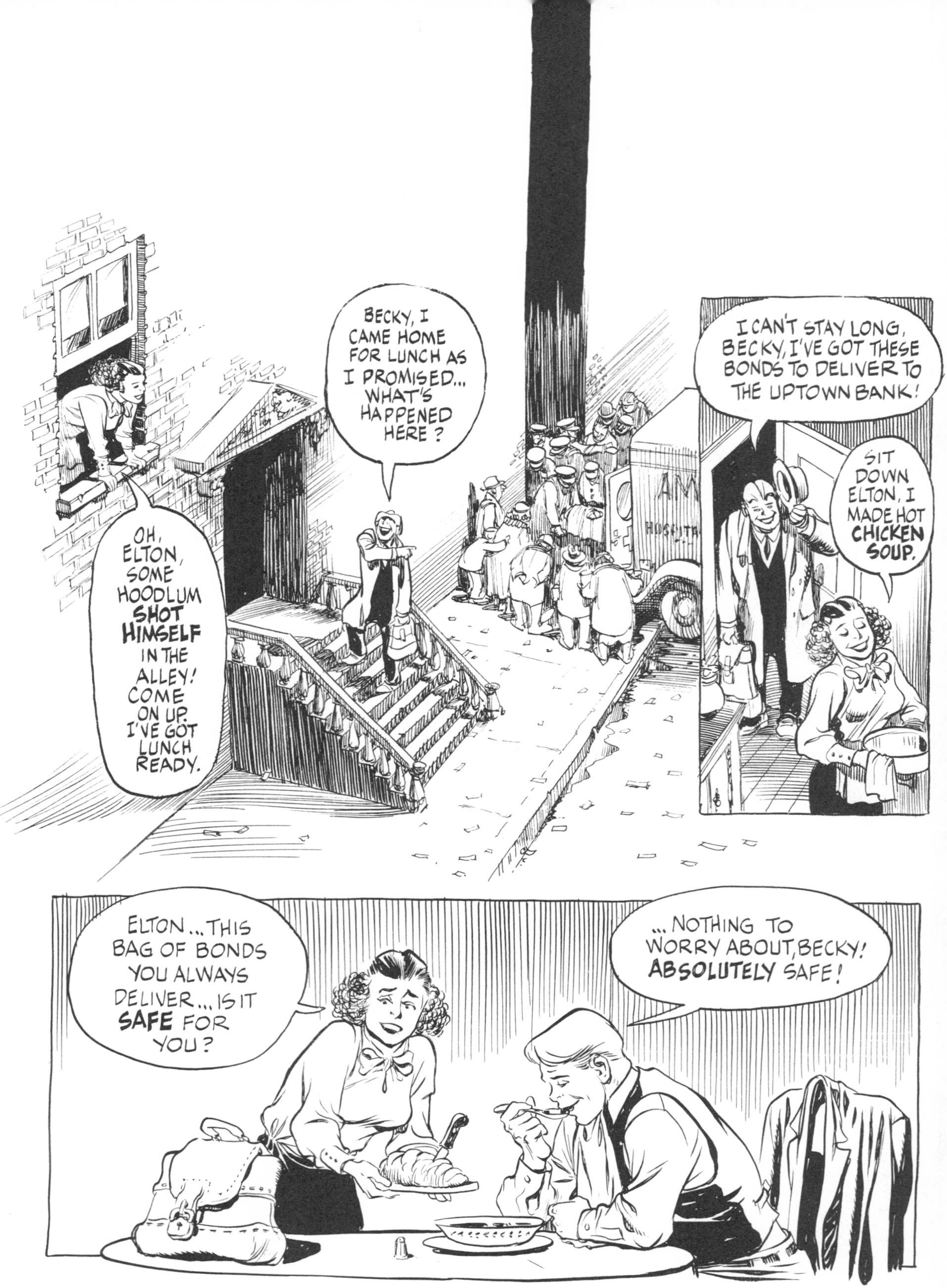

BECKY, I CAME HOME FOR LUNCH AS I PROMISED... WHAT'S HAPPENED HERE?
OH, ELTON, SOME HOODLUM **SHOT HIMSELF** IN THE ALLEY! COME ON UP. I'VE GOT LUNCH READY.
I CAN'T STAY LONG, BECKY, I'VE GOT THESE BONDS TO DELIVER TO THE UPTOWN BANK!
SIT DOWN ELTON, I MADE HOT **CHICKEN SOUP**.
ELTON... THIS BAG OF BONDS YOU ALWAYS DELIVER... IS IT **SAFE** FOR YOU?
... NOTHING TO WORRY ABOUT, BECKY! **ABSOLUTELY** SAFE!

THE REVOLUTIONARY

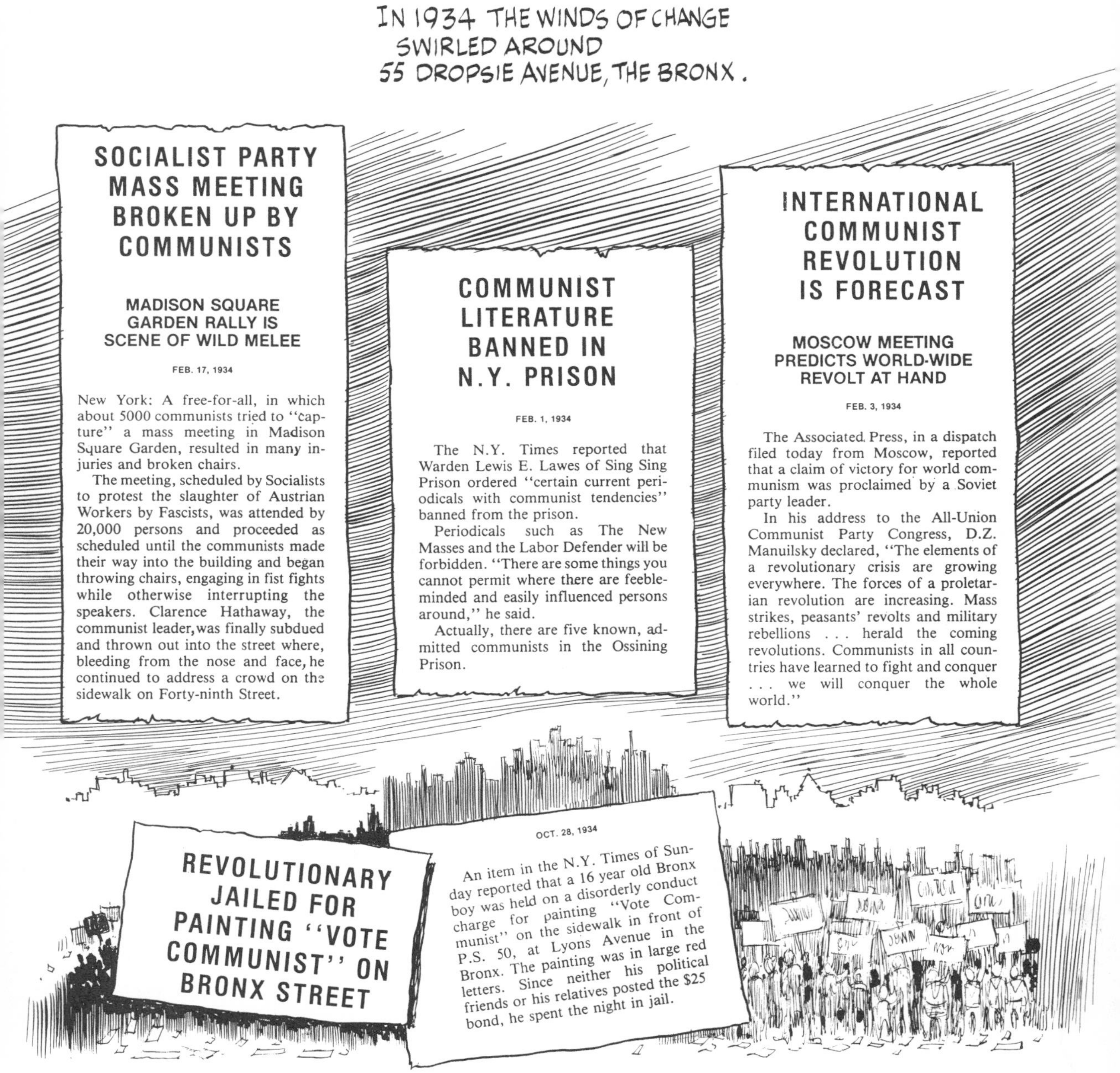
IN 1934 THE WINDS OF CHANGE SWIRLED AROUND 55 DROPSIE AVENUE, THE BRONX.
SOCIALIST PARTY MASS MEETING BROKEN UP BY COMMUNISTS
MADISON SQUARE GARDEN RALLY IS SCENE OF WILD MELEE
FEB. 17, 1934
New York: A free-for-all, in which about 5000 communists tried to "capture" a mass meeting in Madison Square Garden, resulted in many injuries and broken chairs.
The meeting, scheduled by Socialists to protest the slaughter of Austrian Workers by Fascists, was attended by 20,000 persons and proceeded as scheduled until the communists made their way into the building and began throwing chairs, engaging in fist fights while otherwise interrupting the speakers. Clarence Hathaway, the communist leader, was finally subdued and thrown out into the street where, bleeding from the nose and face, he continued to address a crowd on the sidewalk on Forty-ninth Street.
COMMUNIST LITERATURE BANNED IN N.Y. PRISON
FEB. 1, 1934
The N.Y. Times reported that Warden Lewis E. Lawes of Sing Sing Prison ordered "certain current periodicals with communist tendencies" banned from the prison.
Periodicals such as The New Masses and the Labor Defender will be forbidden. "There are some things you cannot permit where there are feeble-minded and easily influenced persons around," he said.
Actually, there are five known, admitted communists in the Ossining Prison.
INTERNATIONAL COMMUNIST REVOLUTION IS FORECAST
MOSCOW MEETING PREDICTS WORLD-WIDE REVOLT AT HAND
FEB. 3, 1934
The Associated Press, in a dispatch filed today from Moscow, reported that a claim of victory for world communism was proclaimed by a Soviet party leader.
In his address to the All-Union Communist Party Congress, D.Z. Manuilsky declared, "The elements of a revolutionary crisis are growing everywhere. The forces of a proletarian revolution are increasing. Mass strikes, peasants' revolts and military rebellions . . . herald the coming revolutions. Communists in all countries have learned to fight and conquer . . . we will conquer the whole world."
REVOLUTIONARY JAILED FOR PAINTING "VOTE COMMUNIST" ON BRONX STREET
OCT. 28, 1934
An item in the N.Y. Times of Sunday reported that a 16 year old Bronx boy was held on a disorderly conduct charge for painting "Vote Communist" on the sidewalk in front of P.S. 50, at Lyons Avenue in the Bronx. The painting was in large red letters. Since neither his political friends or his relatives posted the $25 bond, he spent the night in jail.

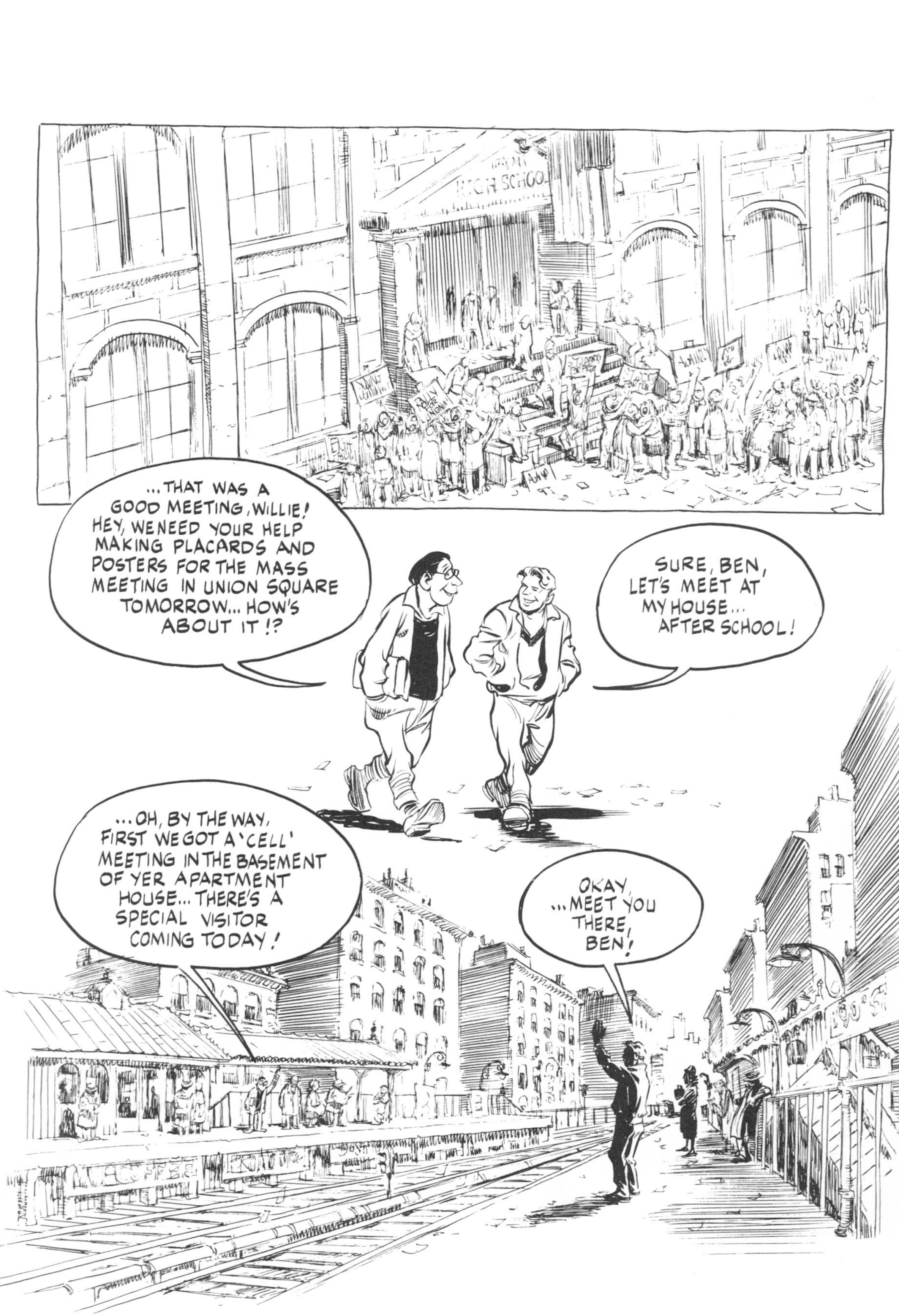
HIGH SCHOOL
...THAT WAS A GOOD MEETING, WILLIE! HEY, WE NEED YOUR HELP MAKING PLACARDS AND POSTERS FOR THE MASS MEETING IN UNION SQUARE TOMORROW... HOW'S ABOUT IT!?
SURE, BEN, LET'S MEET AT MY HOUSE... AFTER SCHOOL!
...OH, BY THE WAY, FIRST WE GOT A 'CELL' MEETING IN THE BASEMENT OF YER APARTMENT HOUSE... THERE'S A SPECIAL VISITOR COMING TODAY!
OKAY, ...MEET YOU THERE, BEN!

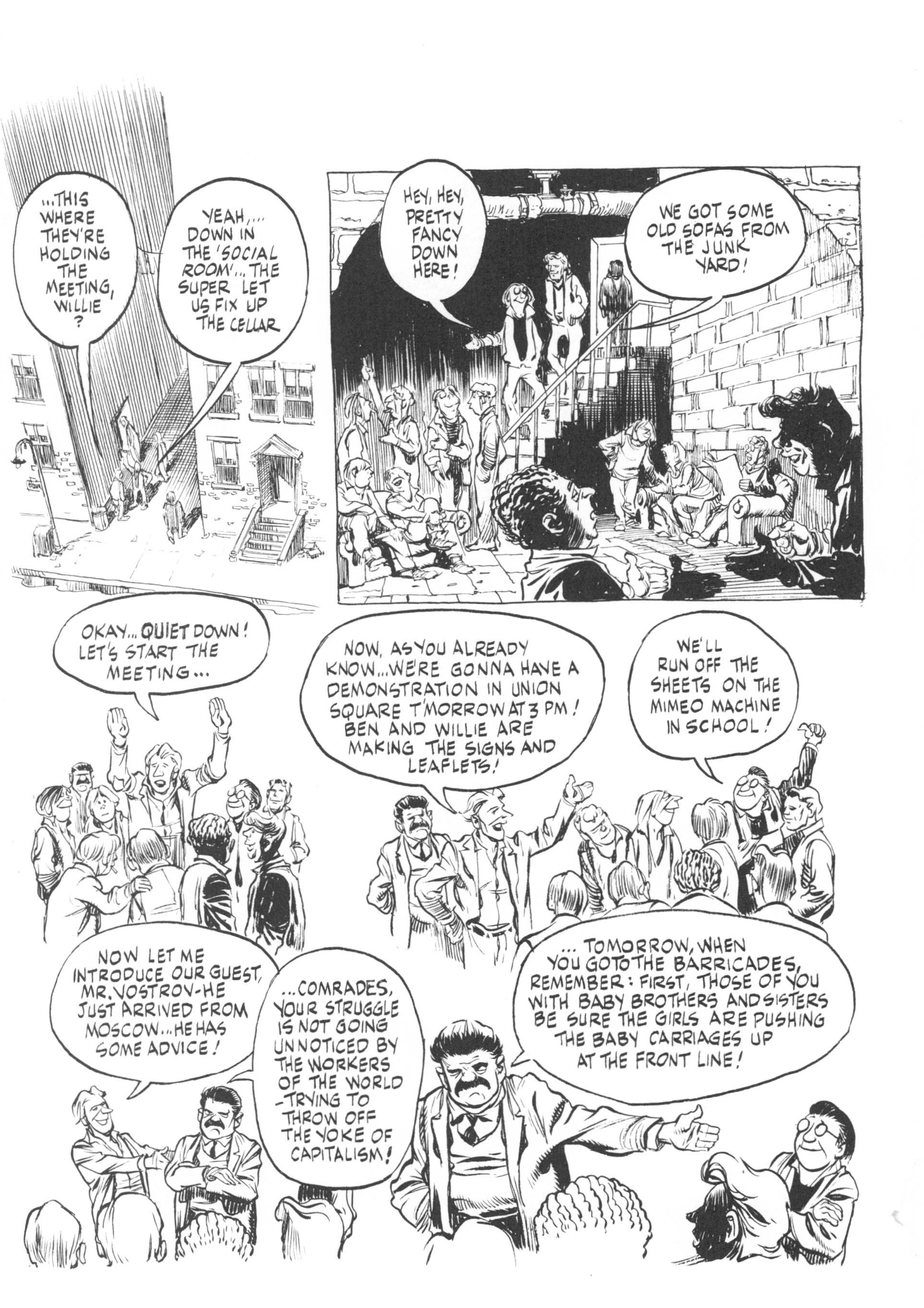
...THIS WHERE THEY'RE HOLDING THE MEETING, WILLIE ?
YEAH,... DOWN IN THE 'SOCIAL ROOM'... THE SUPER LET US FIX UP THE CELLAR
HEY, HEY, PRETTY FANCY DOWN HERE!
WE GOT SOME OLD SOFAS FROM THE JUNK YARD!
OKAY... QUIET DOWN! LET'S START THE MEETING...
NOW, AS YOU ALREADY KNOW... WE'RE GONNA HAVE A DEMONSTRATION IN UNION SQUARE T'MORROW AT 3 PM! BEN AND WILLIE ARE MAKING THE SIGNS AND LEAFLETS!
WE'LL RUN OFF THE SHEETS ON THE MIMEO MACHINE IN SCHOOL!
NOW LET ME INTRODUCE OUR GUEST, MR. VOSTROV-HE JUST ARRIVED FROM MOSCOW... HE HAS SOME ADVICE!
...COMRADES, YOUR STRUGGLE IS NOT GOING UNNOTICED BY THE WORKERS OF THE WORLD -TRYING TO THROW OFF THE YOKE OF CAPITALISM!
... TOMORROW, WHEN YOU GO TO THE BARRICADES, REMEMBER: FIRST, THOSE OF YOU WITH BABY BROTHERS AND SISTERS BE SURE THE GIRLS ARE PUSHING THE BABY CARRIAGES UP AT THE FRONT LINE!

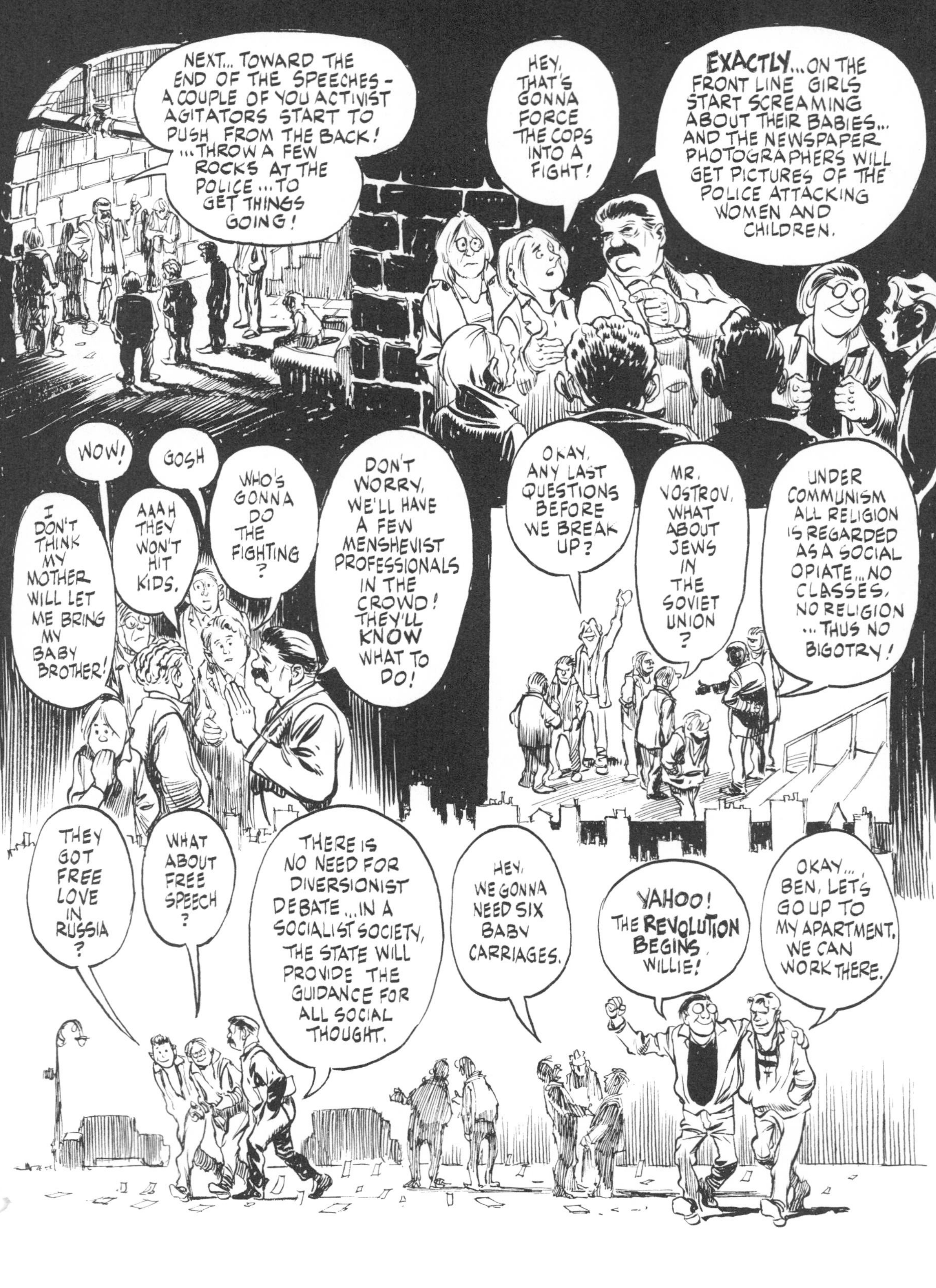
NEXT... TOWARD THE END OF THE SPEECHES - A COUPLE OF YOU ACTIVIST AGITATORS START TO PUSH FROM THE BACK! ...THROW A FEW ROCKS AT THE POLICE ...TO GET THINGS GOING!
HEY, THAT'S GONNA FORCE THE COPS INTO A FIGHT!
EXACTLY... ON THE FRONT LINE GIRLS START SCREAMING ABOUT THEIR BABIES... AND THE NEWSPAPER PHOTOGRAPHERS WILL GET PICTURES OF THE POLICE ATTACKING WOMEN AND CHILDREN.
WOW!
GOSH
I DON'T THINK MY MOTHER WILL LET ME BRING MY BABY BROTHER!
AAAH THEY WON'T HIT KIDS.
WHO'S GONNA DO THE FIGHTING?
DON'T WORRY, WE'LL HAVE A FEW MENSHEVIST PROFESSIONALS IN THE CROWD! THEY'LL KNOW WHAT TO DO!
OKAY, ANY LAST QUESTIONS BEFORE WE BREAK UP?
MR. VOSTROV, WHAT ABOUT JEWS IN THE SOVIET UNION?
UNDER COMMUNISM ALL RELIGION IS REGARDED AS A SOCIAL OPIATE... NO CLASSES, NO RELIGION ... THUS NO BIGOTRY!
THEY GOT FREE LOVE IN RUSSIA?
WHAT ABOUT FREE SPEECH?
THERE IS NO NEED FOR DIVERSIONIST DEBATE ... IN A SOCIALIST SOCIETY, THE STATE WILL PROVIDE THE GUIDANCE FOR ALL SOCIAL THOUGHT.
HEY, WE GONNA NEED SIX BABY CARRIAGES.
YAHOO! THE REVOLUTION BEGINS, WILLIE!
OKAY..., BEN, LET'S GO UP TO MY APARTMENT. WE CAN WORK THERE.

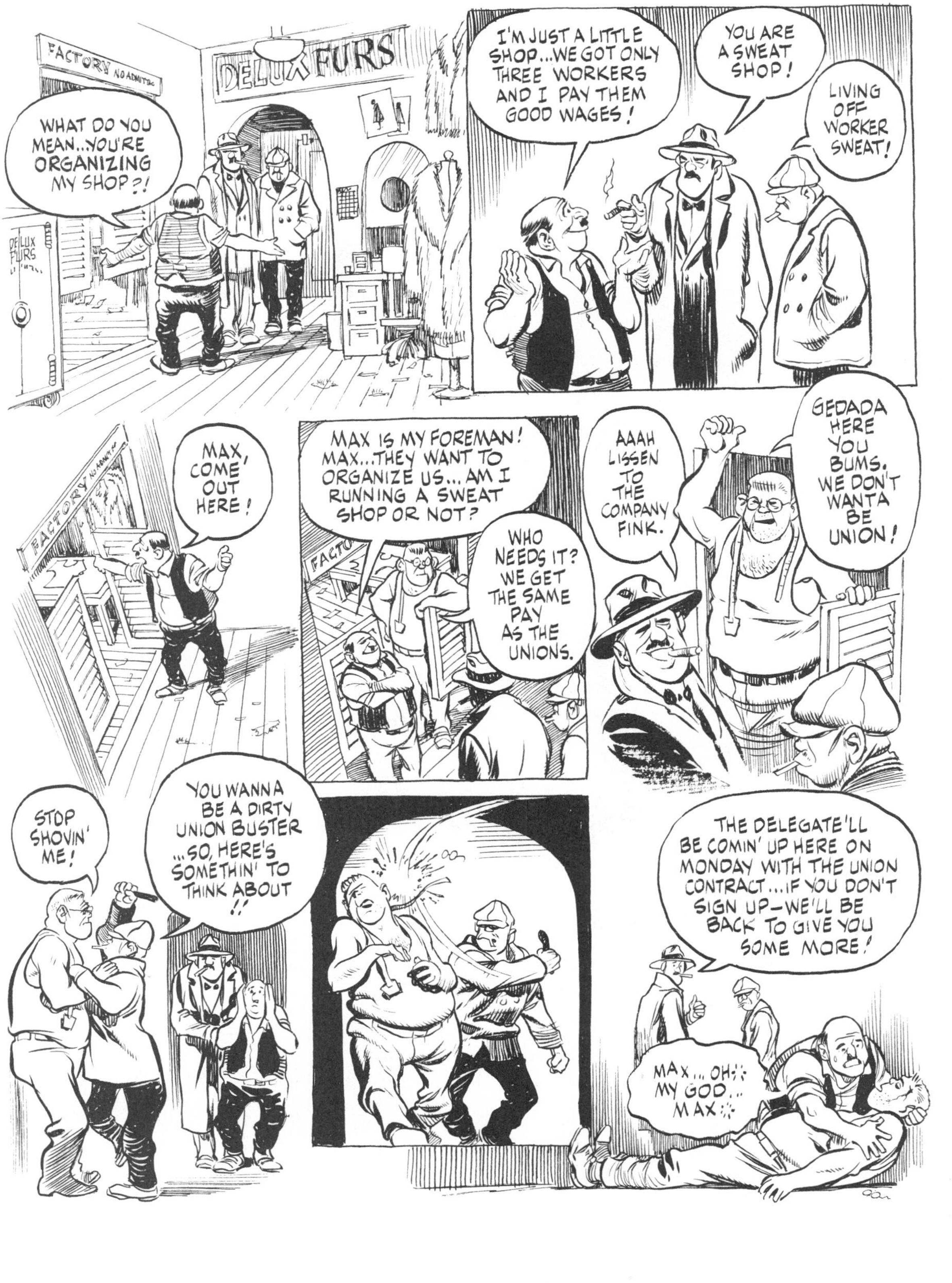
FACTORY NO ADMITTANCE
DELUX FURS
WHAT DO YOU MEAN...YOU'RE ORGANIZING MY SHOP?!
DELUX FURS
I'M JUST A LITTLE SHOP...WE GOT ONLY THREE WORKERS AND I PAY THEM GOOD WAGES!
YOU ARE A SWEAT SHOP!
LIVING OFF WORKER SWEAT!
FACTORY NO ADMITTANCE
MAX, COME OUT HERE!
MAX IS MY FOREMAN! MAX...THEY WANT TO ORGANIZE US...AM I RUNNING A SWEAT SHOP OR NOT?
WHO NEEDS IT? WE GET THE SAME PAY AS THE UNIONS.
AAAH LISSEN TO THE COMPANY FINK.
GEDADA HERE YOU BUMS. WE DON'T WANTA BE UNION!
STOP SHOVIN' ME!
YOU WANNA BE A DIRTY UNION BUSTER ...SO, HERE'S SOMETHIN' TO THINK ABOUT!!
THE DELEGATE'LL BE COMIN' UP HERE ON MONDAY WITH THE UNION CONTRACT...IF YOU DON'T SIGN UP—WE'LL BE BACK TO GIVE YOU SOME MORE!
MAX...OH! MY GOD... MAX

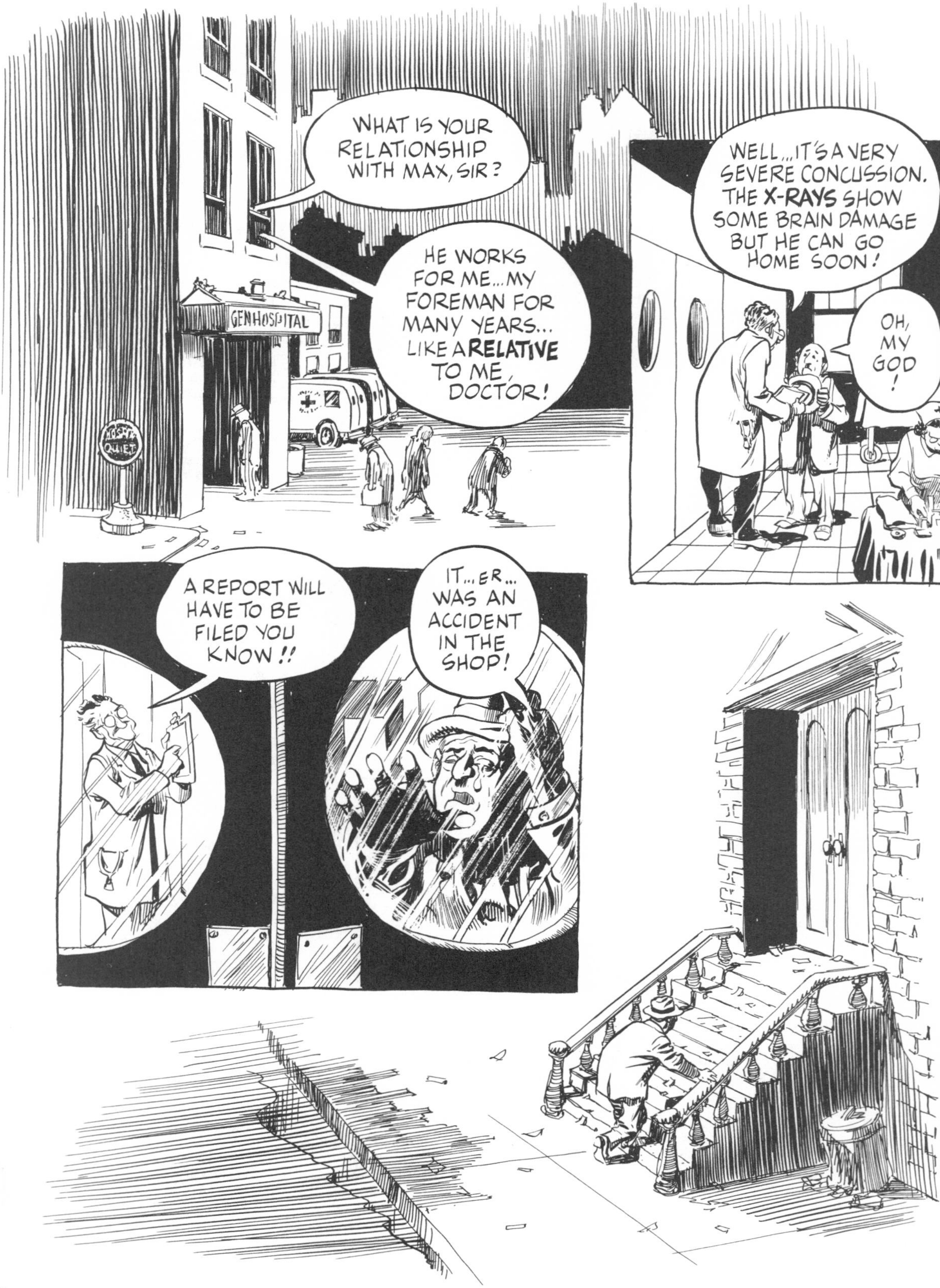

WHAT IS YOUR RELATIONSHIP WITH MAX, SIR?
HE WORKS FOR ME...MY FOREMAN FOR MANY YEARS... LIKE A **RELATIVE** TO ME, DOCTOR!
GEN HOSPITAL
WELL...IT'S A VERY SEVERE CONCUSSION. THE **X-RAYS** SHOW SOME BRAIN DAMAGE BUT HE CAN GO HOME SOON!
OH, MY GOD!
A REPORT WILL HAVE TO BE FILED YOU KNOW!!
IT...ER... WAS AN ACCIDENT IN THE SHOP!

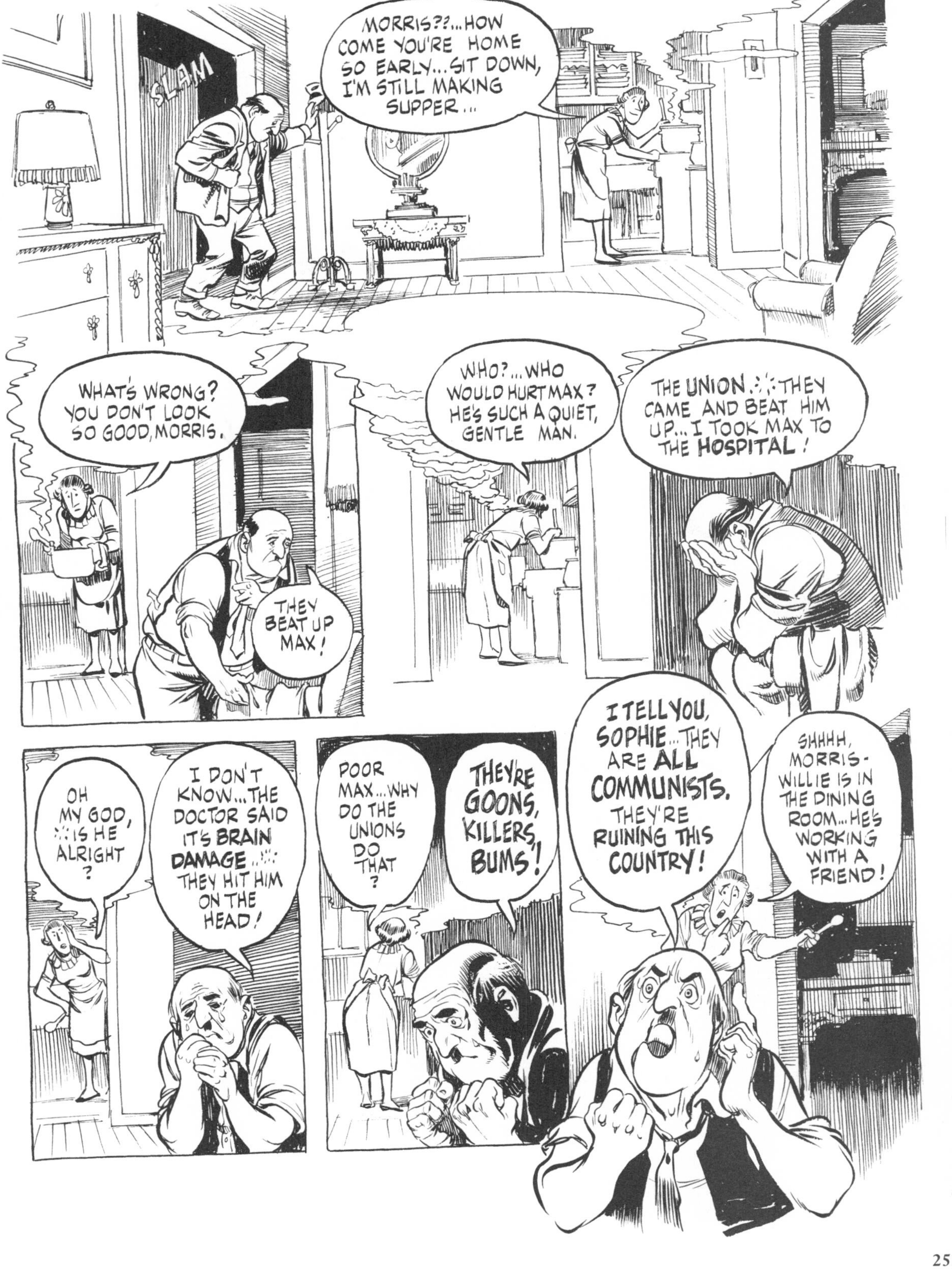
SLAM
MORRIS??... HOW COME YOU'RE HOME SO EARLY... SIT DOWN, I'M STILL MAKING SUPPER...
WHAT'S WRONG? YOU DON'T LOOK SO GOOD, MORRIS.
THEY BEAT UP MAX!
WHO?... WHO WOULD HURT MAX? HE'S SUCH A QUIET, GENTLE MAN.
THE UNION... THEY CAME AND BEAT HIM UP... I TOOK MAX TO THE HOSPITAL!
OH MY GOD, IS HE ALRIGHT?
I DON'T KNOW... THE DOCTOR SAID IT'S BRAIN DAMAGE... THEY HIT HIM ON THE HEAD!
POOR MAX... WHY DO THE UNIONS DO THAT?
THEY'RE GOONS, KILLERS, BUMS!
I TELL YOU, SOPHIE... THEY ARE ALL COMMUNISTS. THEY'RE RUINING THIS COUNTRY!
SHHHH, MORRIS- WILLIE IS IN THE DINING ROOM... HE'S WORKING WITH A FRIEND!

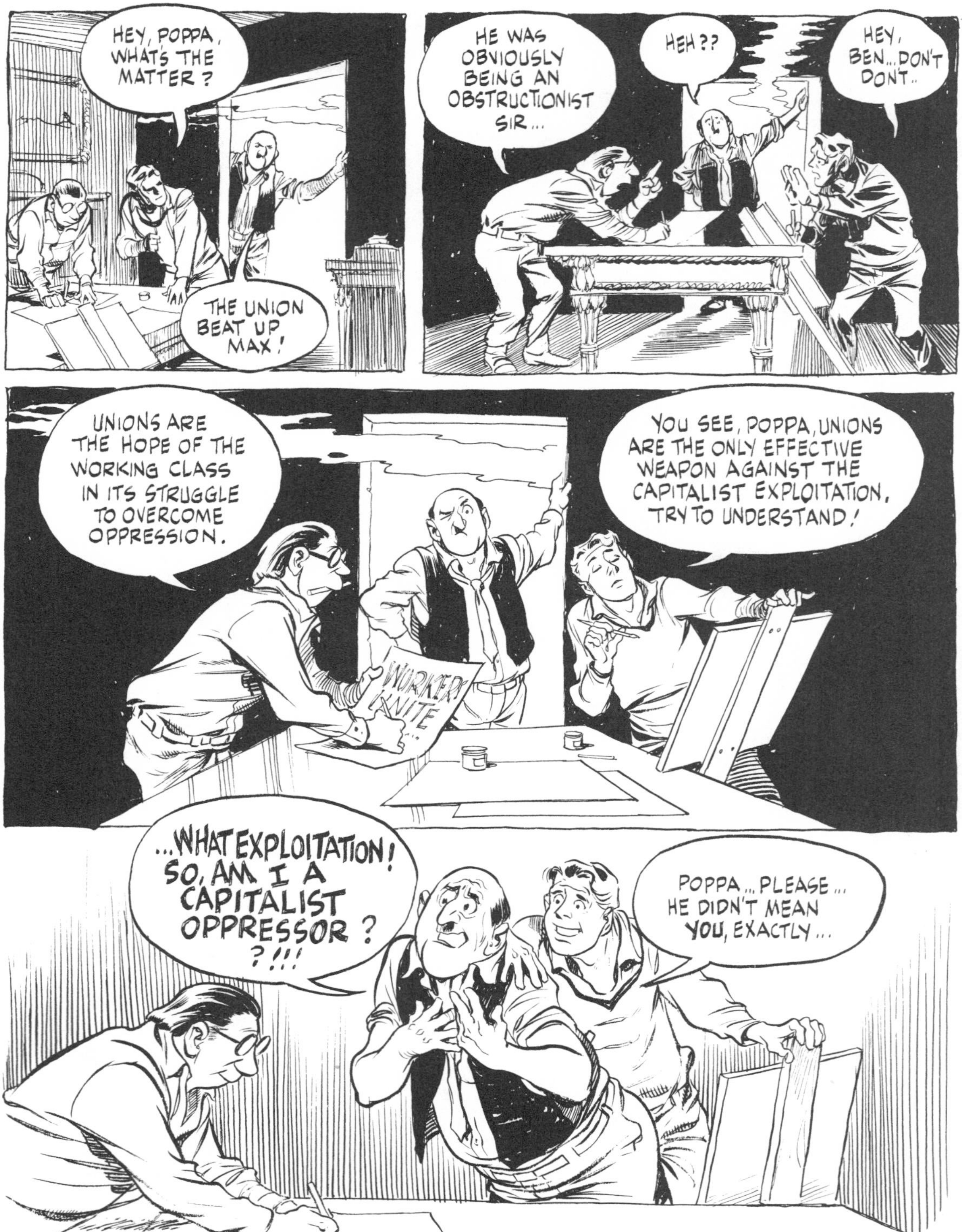
HEY, POPPA, WHAT'S THE MATTER?
THE UNION BEAT UP MAX!
HE WAS OBVIOUSLY BEING AN OBSTRUCTIONIST SIR...
HEH??
HEY, BEN...DON'T DON'T..
UNIONS ARE THE HOPE OF THE WORKING CLASS IN ITS STRUGGLE TO OVERCOME OPPRESSION.
YOU SEE, POPPA, UNIONS ARE THE ONLY EFFECTIVE WEAPON AGAINST THE CAPITALIST EXPLOITATION, TRY TO UNDERSTAND!
WORKERS UNITE
...WHAT EXPLOITATION! SO, AM I A CAPITALIST OPPRESSOR? ?!!!
POPPA... PLEASE... HE DIDN'T MEAN YOU, EXACTLY...

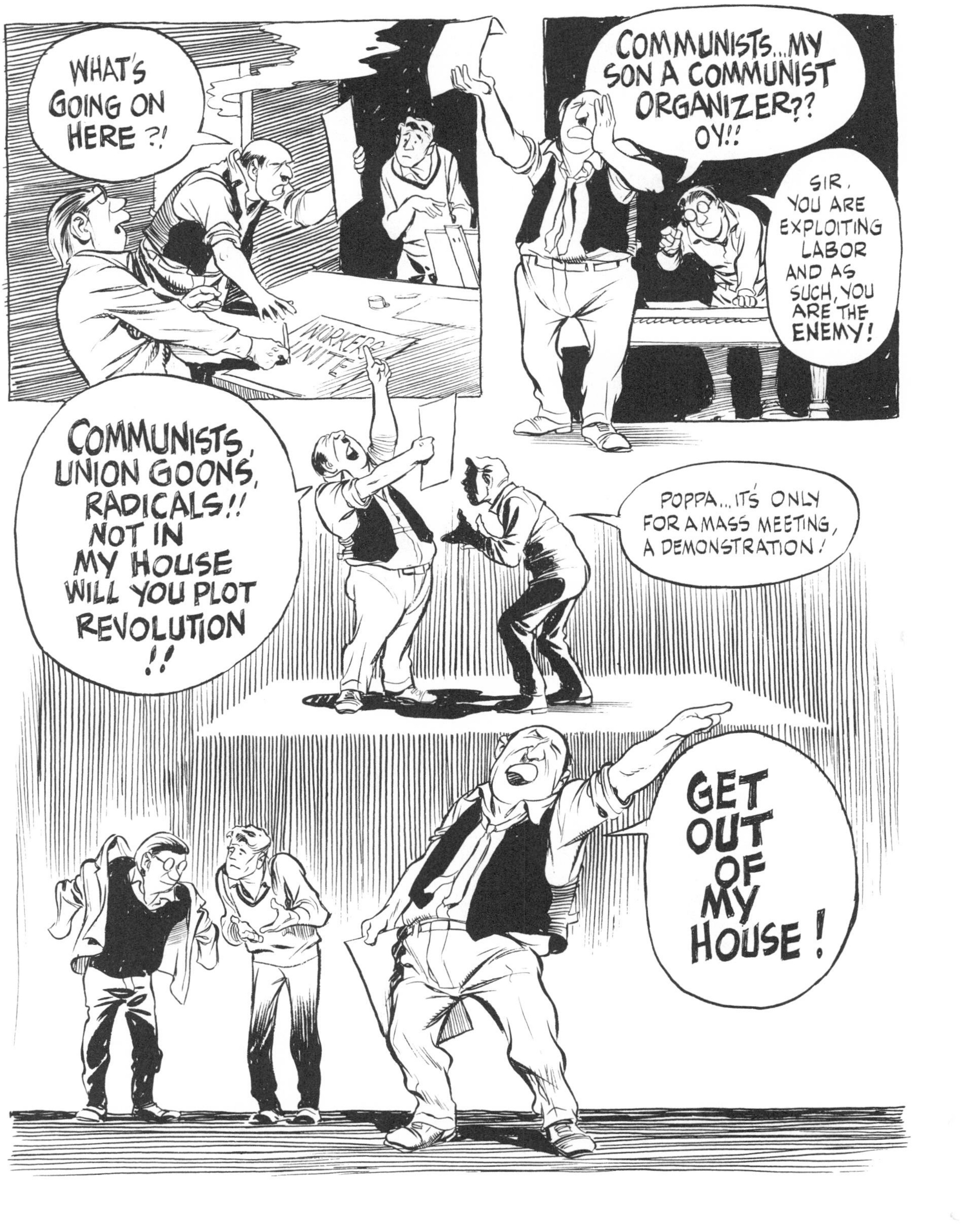
WHAT'S GOING ON HERE ?!
WORKERS UNITE
COMMUNISTS...MY SON A COMMUNIST ORGANIZER?? OY!!
SIR, YOU ARE EXPLOITING LABOR AND AS SUCH, YOU ARE THE ENEMY!
COMMUNISTS, UNION GOONS, RADICALS!! NOT IN MY HOUSE WILL YOU PLOT REVOLUTION !!
POPPA...IT'S ONLY FOR A MASS MEETING, A DEMONSTRATION!
GET OUT OF MY HOUSE!

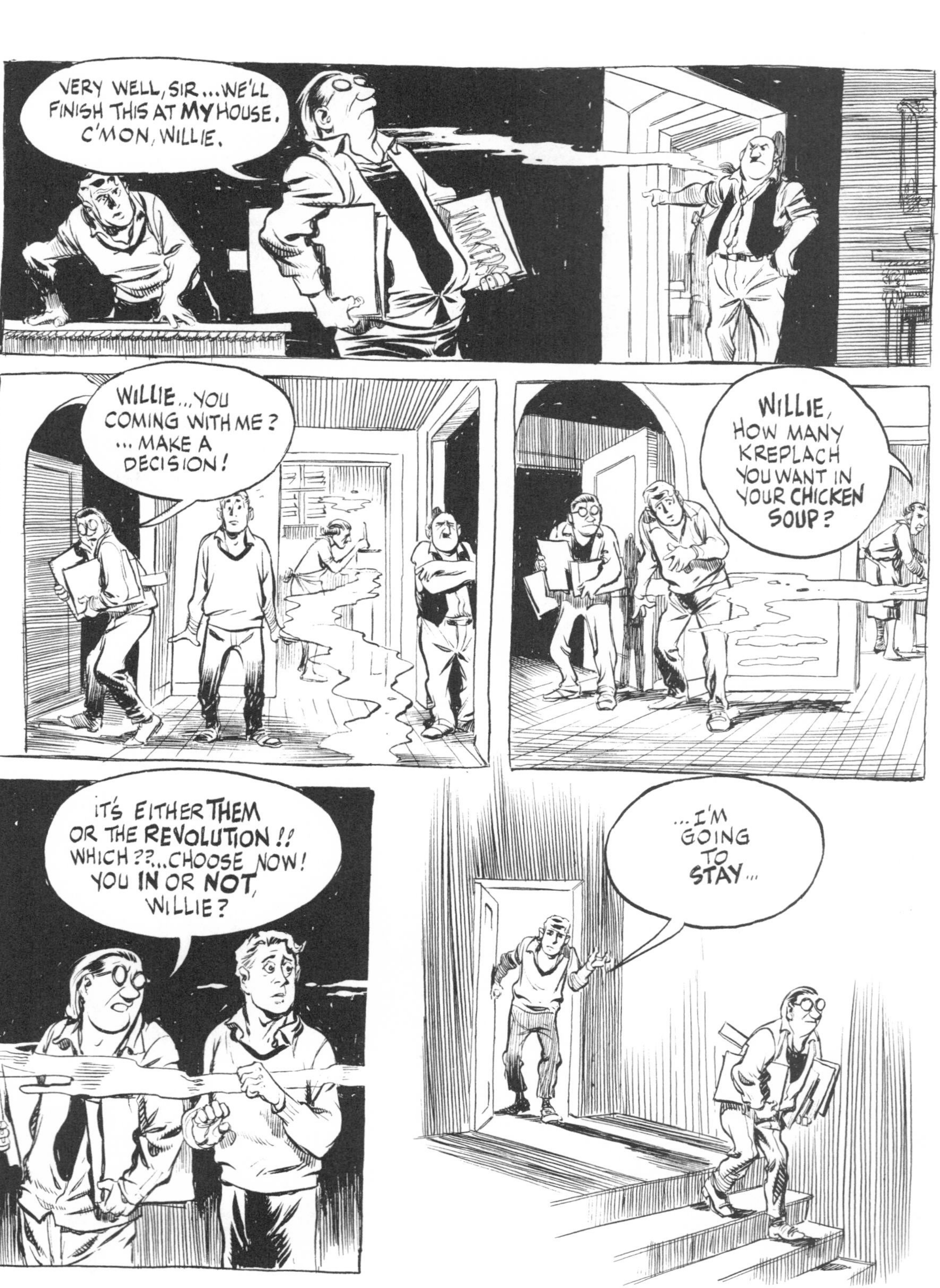
VERY WELL, SIR... WE'LL FINISH THIS AT MY HOUSE. C'MON, WILLIE.
WILLIE... YOU COMING WITH ME? ... MAKE A DECISION!
WILLIE, HOW MANY KREPLACH YOU WANT IN YOUR CHICKEN SOUP?
IT'S EITHER THEM OR THE REVOLUTION!! WHICH??... CHOOSE NOW! YOU IN OR NOT, WILLIE?
... I'M GOING TO STAY...

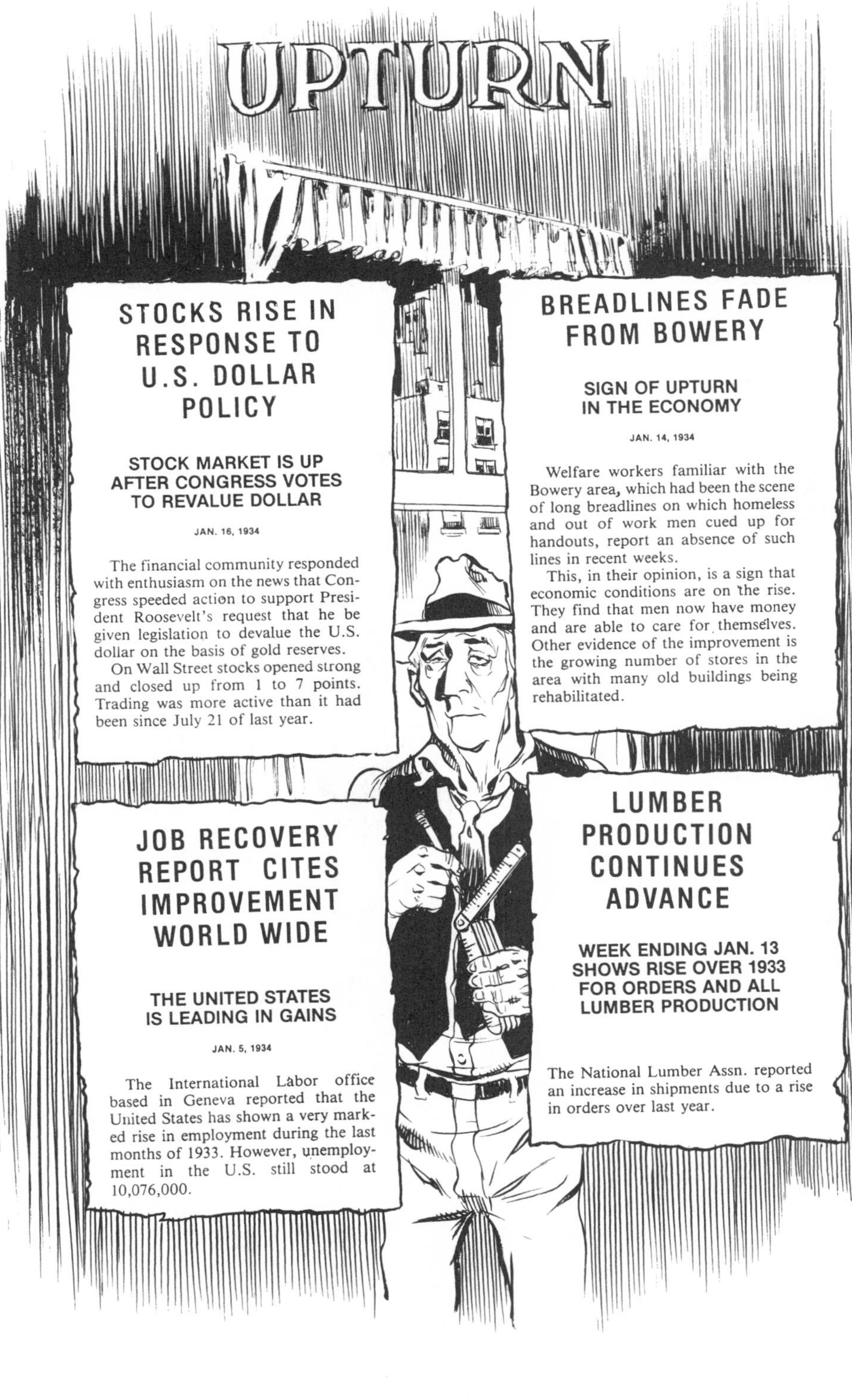
UPTURN

STOCKS RISE IN RESPONSE TO U.S. DOLLAR POLICY

STOCK MARKET IS UP AFTER CONGRESS VOTES TO REVALUE DOLLAR

JAN. 16, 1934

The financial community responded with enthusiasm on the news that Congress speeded action to support President Roosevelt's request that he be given legislation to devalue the U.S. dollar on the basis of gold reserves.

On Wall Street stocks opened strong and closed up from 1 to 7 points. Trading was more active than it had been since July 21 of last year.

BREADLINES FADE FROM BOWERY

SIGN OF UPTURN IN THE ECONOMY

JAN. 14, 1934

Welfare workers familiar with the Bowery area, which had been the scene of long breadlines on which homeless and out of work men cued up for handouts, report an absence of such lines in recent weeks.

This, in their opinion, is a sign that economic conditions are on the rise. They find that men now have money and are able to care for themselves. Other evidence of the improvement is the growing number of stores in the area with many old buildings being rehabilitated.

JOB RECOVERY REPORT CITES IMPROVEMENT WORLD WIDE

THE UNITED STATES IS LEADING IN GAINS

JAN. 5, 1934

The International Labor office based in Geneva reported that the United States has shown a very marked rise in employment during the last months of 1933. However, unemployment in the U.S. still stood at 10,076,000.

LUMBER PRODUCTION CONTINUES ADVANCE

WEEK ENDING JAN. 13 SHOWS RISE OVER 1933 FOR ORDERS AND ALL LUMBER PRODUCTION

The National Lumber Assn. reported an increase in shipments due to a rise in orders over last year.

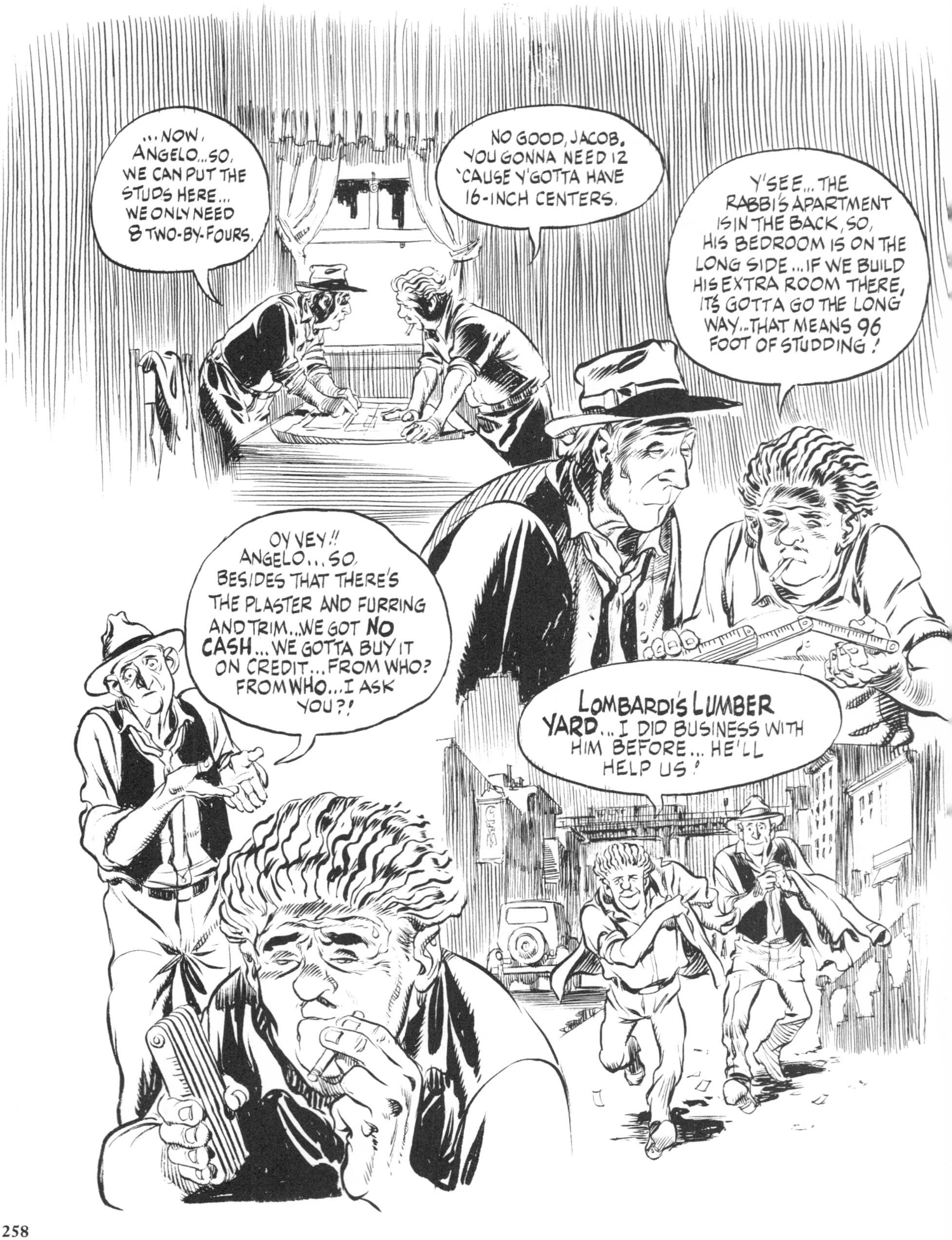
...NOW, ANGELO...SO, WE CAN PUT THE STUDS HERE... WE ONLY NEED 8 TWO-BY-FOURS.
NO GOOD, JACOB. YOU GONNA NEED 12 'CAUSE Y'GOTTA HAVE 16-INCH CENTERS.
Y'SEE... THE RABBI'S APARTMENT IS IN THE BACK, SO, HIS BEDROOM IS ON THE LONG SIDE... IF WE BUILD HIS EXTRA ROOM THERE, IT'S GOTTA GO THE LONG WAY...THAT MEANS 96 FOOT OF STUDDING!
OY VEY!! ANGELO...SO, BESIDES THAT THERE'S THE PLASTER AND FURRING AND TRIM...WE GOT NO CASH... WE GOTTA BUY IT ON CREDIT...FROM WHO? FROM WHO...I ASK YOU?!
LOMBARDI'S LUMBER YARD... I DID BUSINESS WITH HIM BEFORE... HE'LL HELP US!

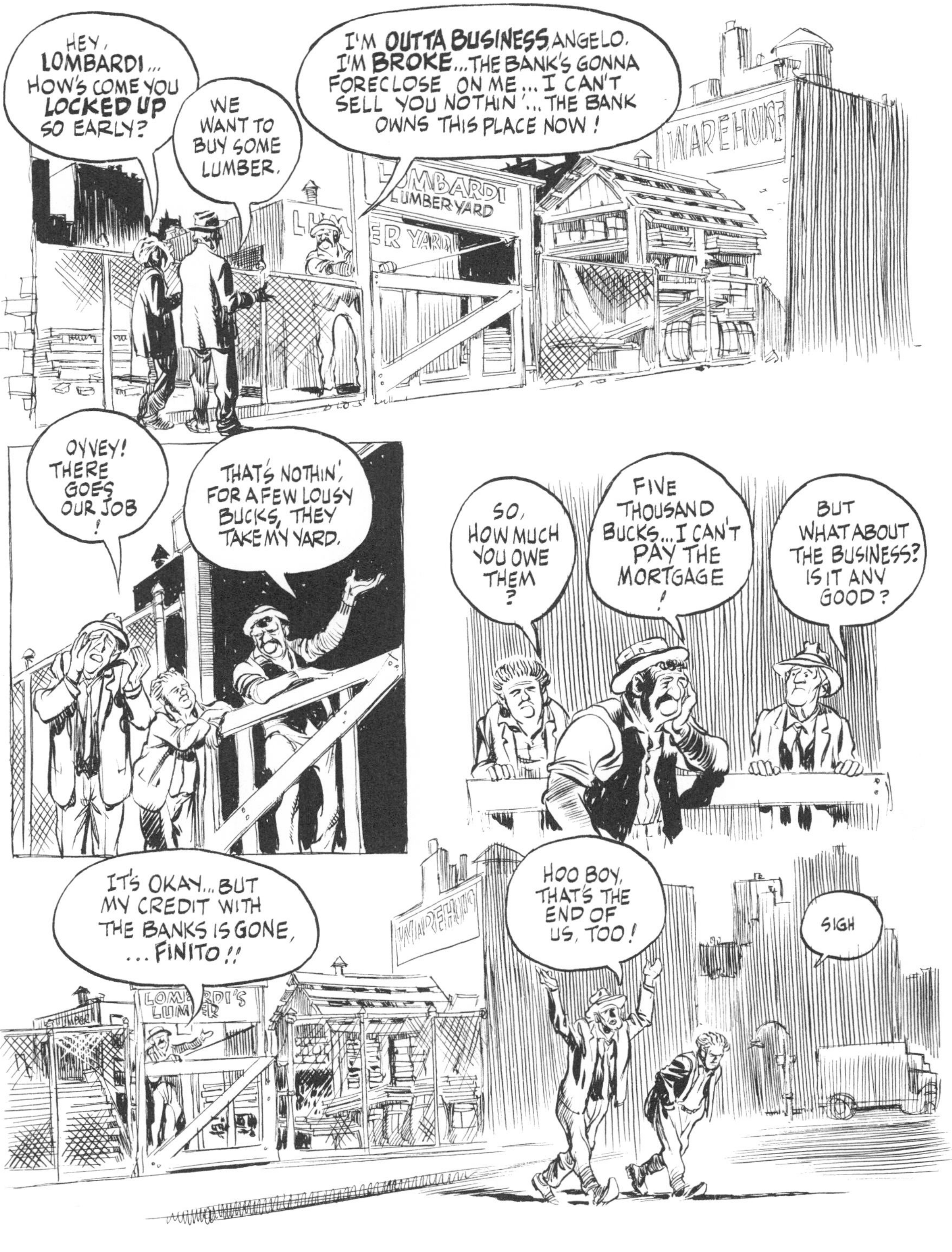
HEY, LOMBARDI... HOW'S COME YOU LOCKED UP SO EARLY?
WE WANT TO BUY SOME LUMBER.
I'M OUTTA BUSINESS, ANGELO. I'M BROKE... THE BANK'S GONNA FORECLOSE ON ME... I CAN'T SELL YOU NOTHIN'... THE BANK OWNS THIS PLACE NOW!
WAREHOUSE
LOMBARDI LUMBER YARD
LUMBER YARD
OY VEY! THERE GOES OUR JOB!
THAT'S NOTHIN', FOR A FEW LOUSY BUCKS, THEY TAKE MY YARD.
SO, HOW MUCH YOU OWE THEM?
FIVE THOUSAND BUCKS... I CAN'T PAY THE MORTGAGE!
BUT WHAT ABOUT THE BUSINESS? IS IT ANY GOOD?
IT'S OKAY... BUT MY CREDIT WITH THE BANKS IS GONE, ... FINITO!!
LOMBARDI'S LUMBER
HOO BOY, THAT'S THE END OF US, TOO!
SIGH

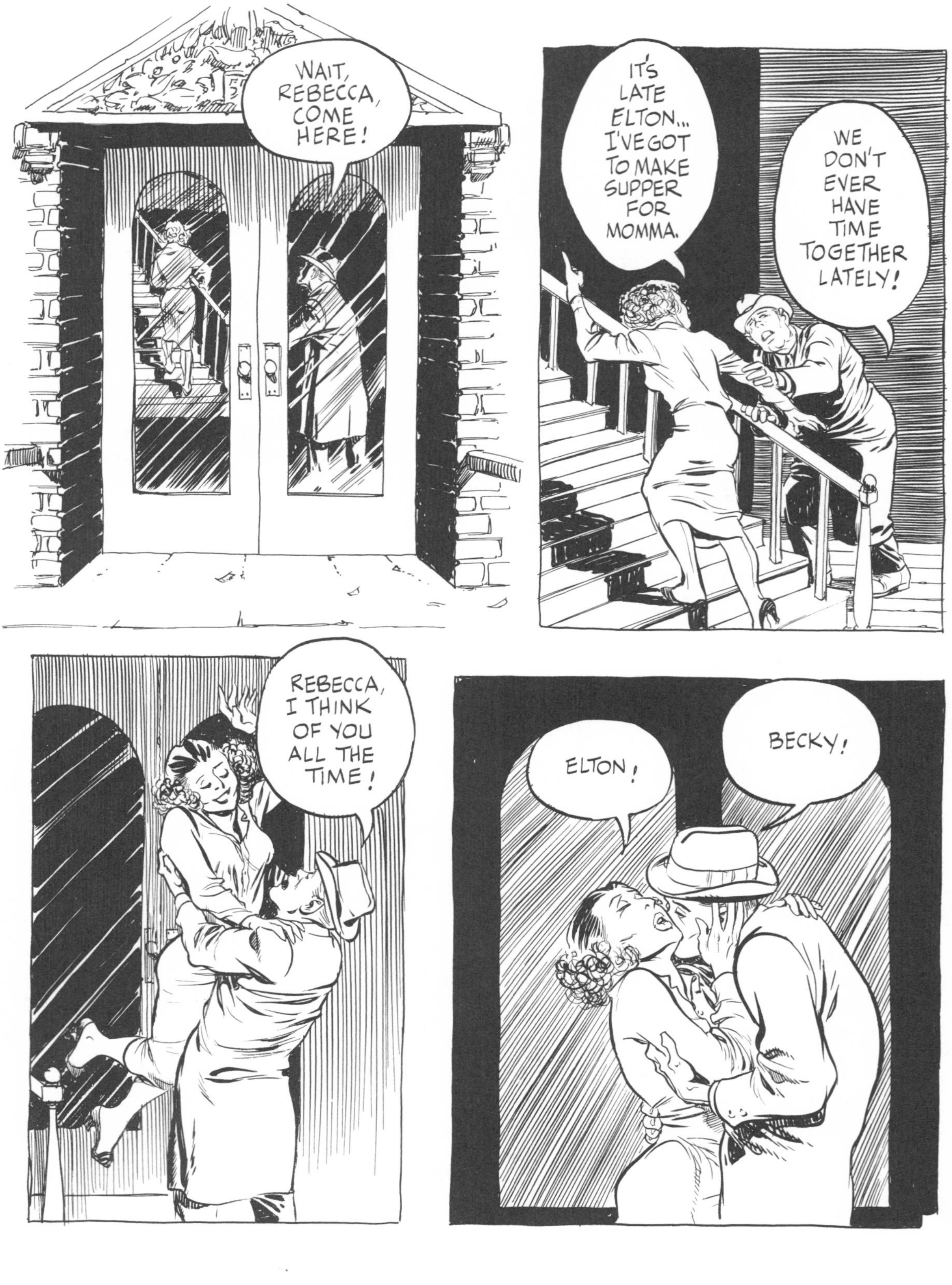
WAIT, REBECCA, COME HERE!
IT'S LATE ELTON... I'VE GOT TO MAKE SUPPER FOR MOMMA.
WE DON'T EVER HAVE TIME TOGETHER LATELY!
REBECCA, I THINK OF YOU ALL THE TIME!
ELTON!
BECKY!

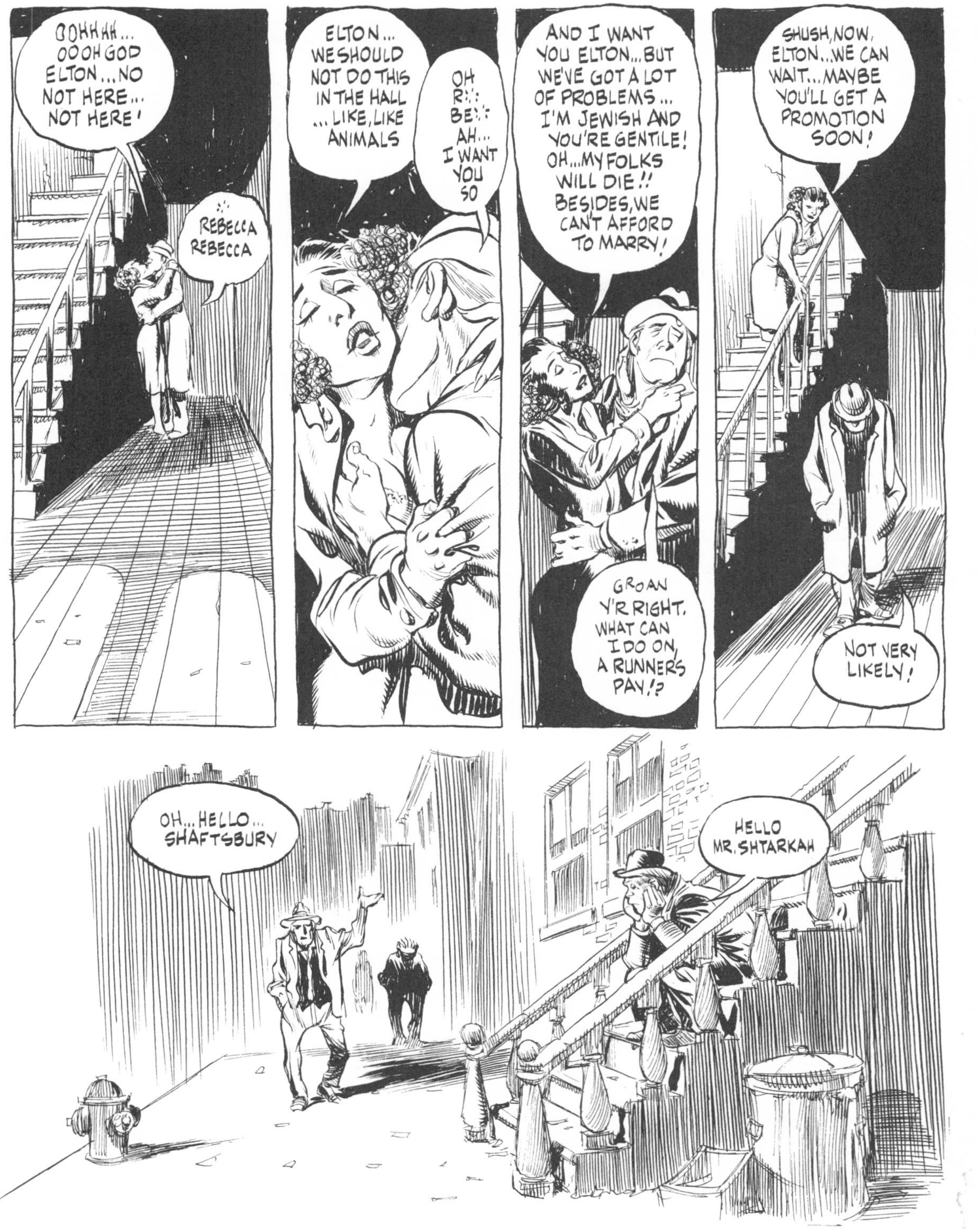
OOHHHH... OOOH GOD ELTON... NO NOT HERE... NOT HERE!
REBECCA REBECCA
ELTON... WE SHOULD NOT DO THIS IN THE HALL ...LIKE, LIKE ANIMALS
OH R... BE... AH... I WANT YOU SO
AND I WANT YOU ELTON... BUT WE'VE GOT A LOT OF PROBLEMS... I'M JEWISH AND YOU'RE GENTILE! OH... MY FOLKS WILL DIE!! BESIDES, WE CAN'T AFFORD TO MARRY!
GROAN
Y'R RIGHT. WHAT CAN I DO ON, A RUNNER'S PAY!?
SHUSH, NOW, ELTON... WE CAN WAIT... MAYBE YOU'LL GET A PROMOTION SOON!
NOT VERY LIKELY!
OH... HELLO... SHAFTSBURY
HELLO MR. SHTARKAH

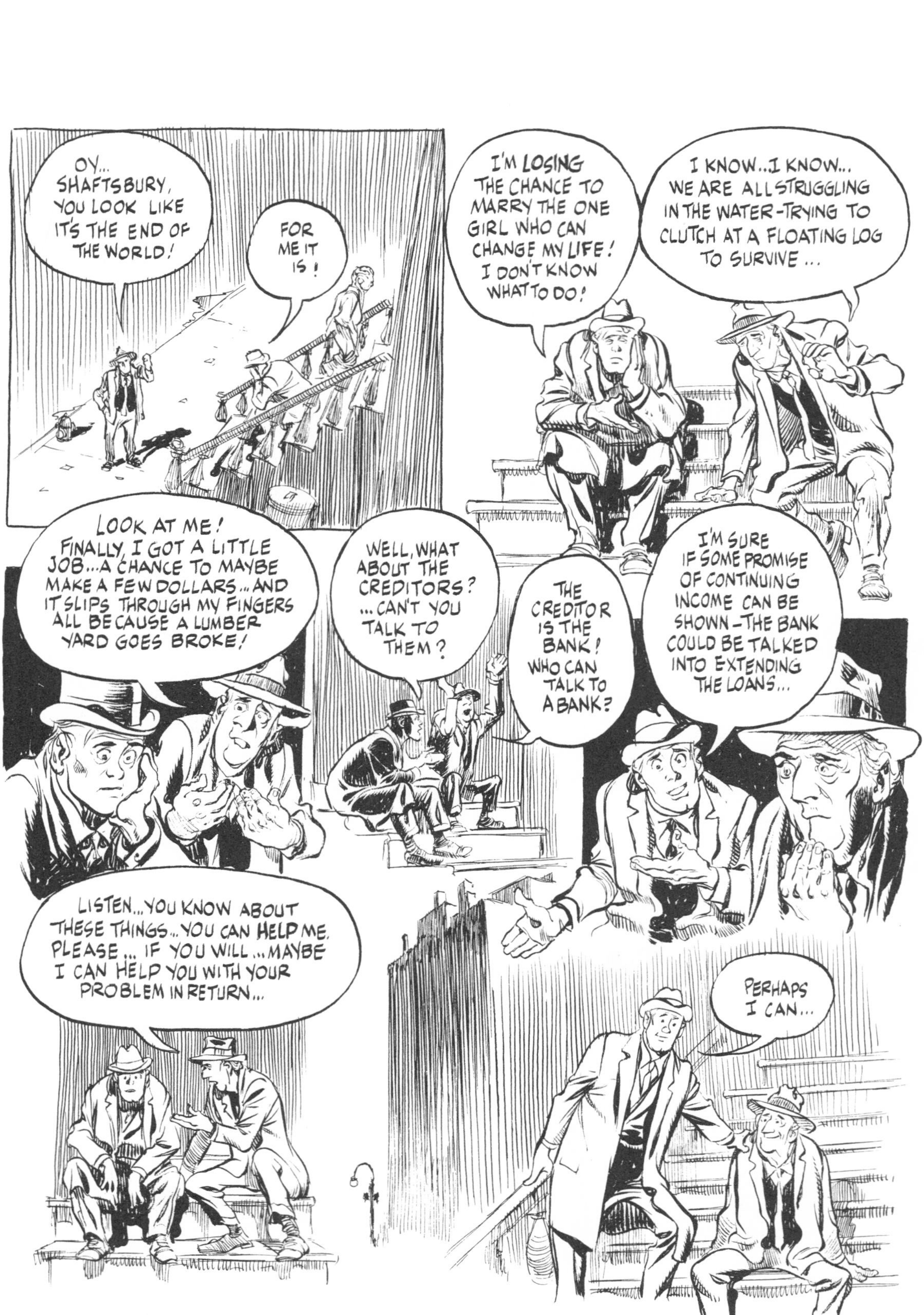
OY... SHAFTSBURY, YOU LOOK LIKE IT'S THE END OF THE WORLD!
FOR ME IT IS!
I'M LOSING THE CHANCE TO MARRY THE ONE GIRL WHO CAN CHANGE MY LIFE! I DON'T KNOW WHAT TO DO!
I KNOW...I KNOW... WE ARE ALL STRUGGLING IN THE WATER-TRYING TO CLUTCH AT A FLOATING LOG TO SURVIVE...
LOOK AT ME! FINALLY, I GOT A LITTLE JOB...A CHANCE TO MAYBE MAKE A FEW DOLLARS...AND IT SLIPS THROUGH MY FINGERS ALL BECAUSE A LUMBER YARD GOES BROKE!
WELL, WHAT ABOUT THE CREDITORS? ...CAN'T YOU TALK TO THEM?
THE CREDITOR IS THE BANK! WHO CAN TALK TO A BANK?
I'M SURE IF SOME PROMISE OF CONTINUING INCOME CAN BE SHOWN-THE BANK COULD BE TALKED INTO EXTENDING THE LOANS...
LISTEN...YOU KNOW ABOUT THESE THINGS...YOU CAN HELP ME. PLEASE... IF YOU WILL...MAYBE I CAN HELP YOU WITH YOUR PROBLEM IN RETURN...
PERHAPS I CAN...

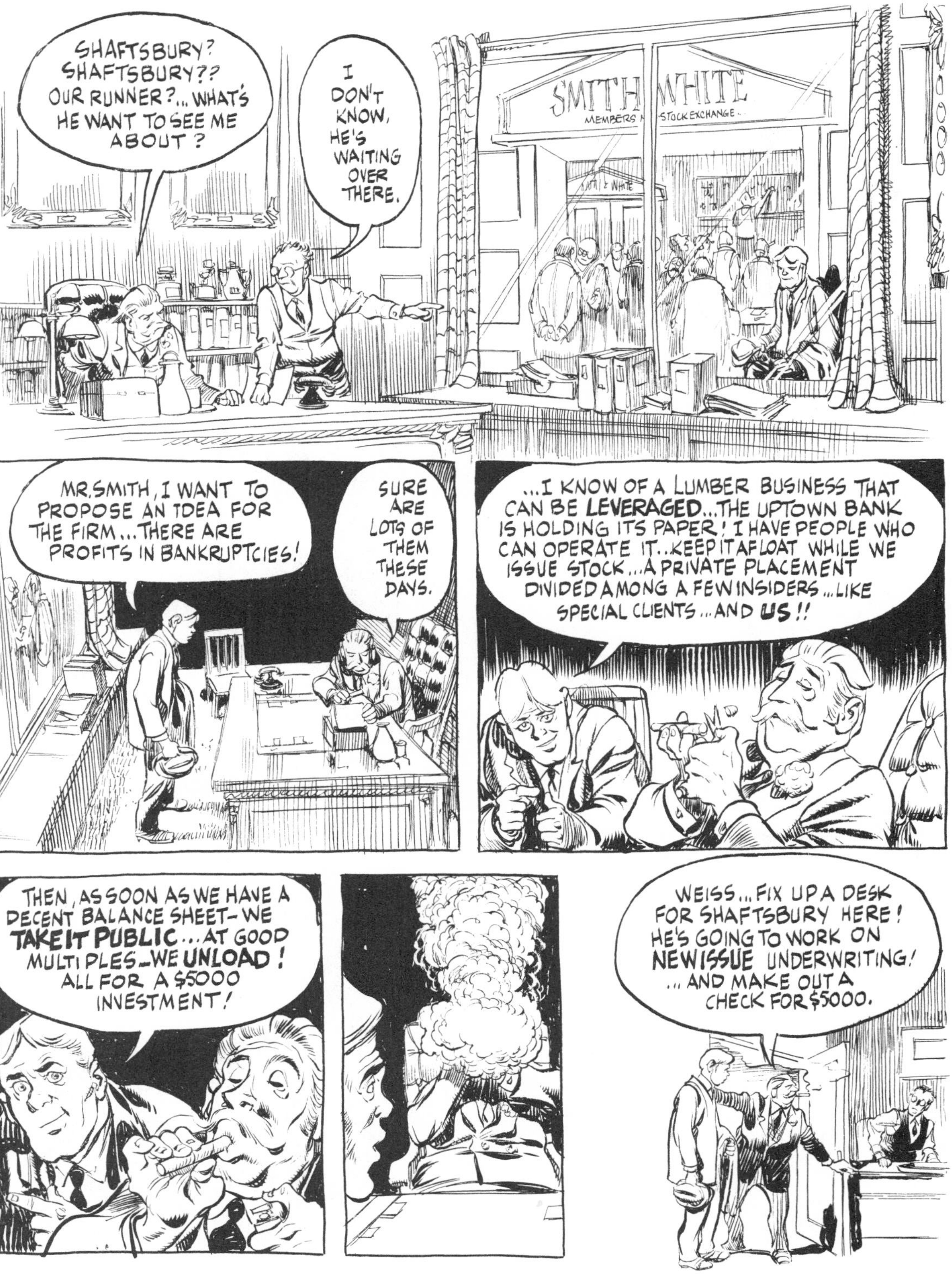
SHAFTSBURY? SHAFTSBURY?? OUR RUNNER?... WHAT'S HE WANT TO SEE ME ABOUT?
I DON'T KNOW, HE'S WAITING OVER THERE.
SMITH WHITE
MR. SMITH, I WANT TO PROPOSE AN IDEA FOR THE FIRM... THERE ARE PROFITS IN BANKRUPTCIES!
SURE ARE LOTS OF THEM THESE DAYS.
...I KNOW OF A LUMBER BUSINESS THAT CAN BE **LEVERAGED**... THE UPTOWN BANK IS HOLDING ITS PAPER! I HAVE PEOPLE WHO CAN OPERATE IT... KEEP IT AFLOAT WHILE WE ISSUE STOCK... A PRIVATE PLACEMENT DIVIDED AMONG A FEW INSIDERS... LIKE SPECIAL CLIENTS... AND **US**!!
THEN, AS SOON AS WE HAVE A DECENT BALANCE SHEET– WE **TAKE IT PUBLIC**... AT GOOD MULTIPLES– WE **UNLOAD**! ALL FOR A $5000 INVESTMENT!
WEISS... FIX UP A DESK FOR SHAFTSBURY HERE! HE'S GOING TO WORK ON **NEW ISSUE** UNDERWRITING! ... AND MAKE OUT A CHECK FOR $5000.

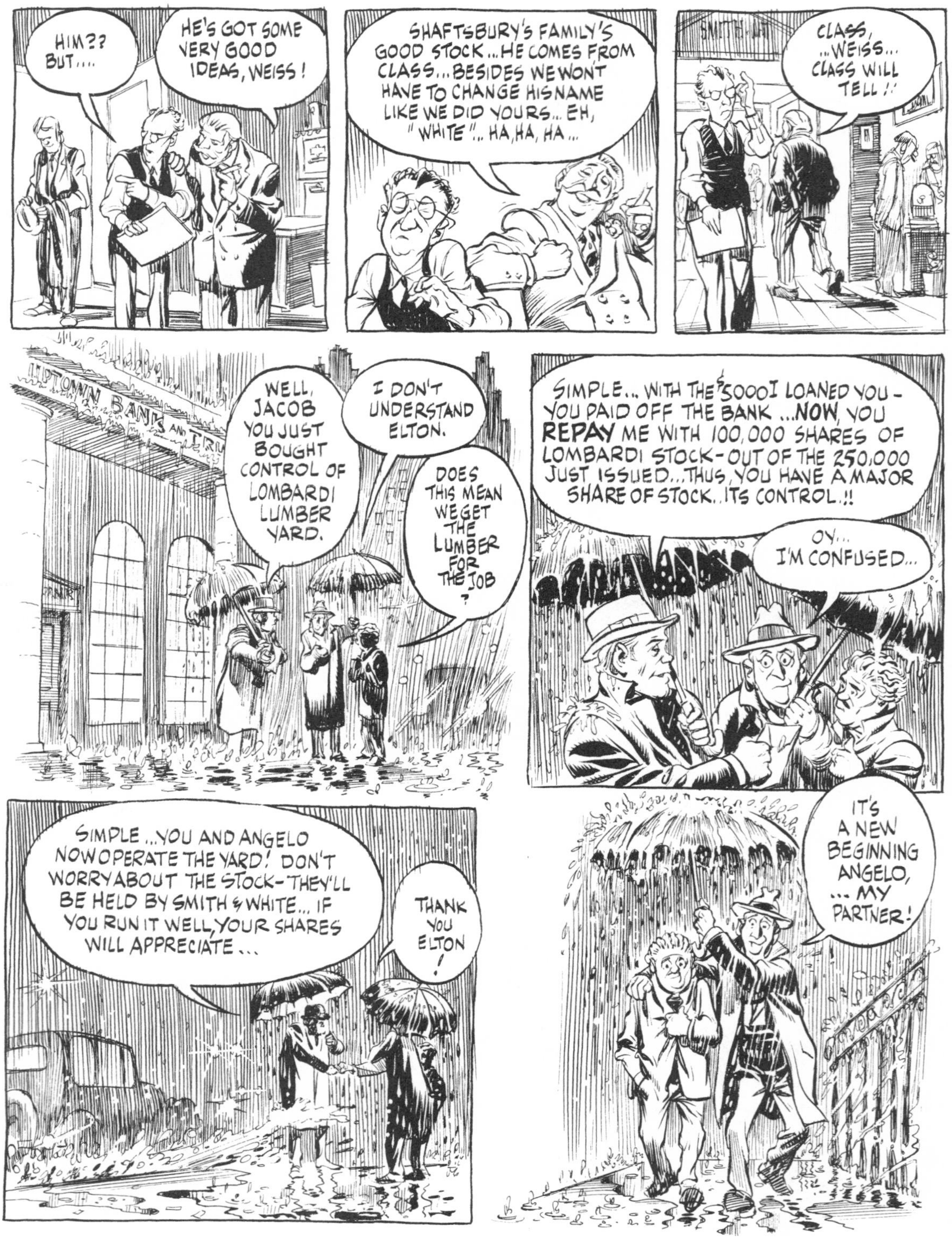
HIM?? BUT....
HE'S GOT SOME VERY GOOD IDEAS, WEISS!
SHAFTSBURY'S FAMILY'S GOOD STOCK...HE COMES FROM CLASS...BESIDES WE WON'T HAVE TO CHANGE HIS NAME LIKE WE DID YOURS...EH, "WHITE"... HA, HA, HA...
SMITH & WHITE
CLASS, ...WEISS... CLASS WILL TELL!
UPTOWN BANK AND TRUST
WELL, JACOB YOU JUST BOUGHT CONTROL OF LOMBARDI LUMBER YARD.
I DON'T UNDERSTAND ELTON.
DOES THIS MEAN WE GET THE LUMBER FOR THE JOB?
SIMPLE... WITH THE $5000 I LOANED YOU - YOU PAID OFF THE BANK ...NOW, YOU REPAY ME WITH 100,000 SHARES OF LOMBARDI STOCK - OUT OF THE 250,000 JUST ISSUED...THUS, YOU HAVE A MAJOR SHARE OF STOCK.. ITS CONTROL.!!
OY... I'M CONFUSED...
SIMPLE ...YOU AND ANGELO NOW OPERATE THE YARD! DON'T WORRY ABOUT THE STOCK - THEY'LL BE HELD BY SMITH & WHITE... IF YOU RUN IT WELL, YOUR SHARES WILL APPRECIATE...
THANK YOU ELTON!
IT'S A NEW BEGINNING ANGELO, ... MY PARTNER!

SANCTUARY

GERMANY RESTRICTS EMIGRATION & TRAVEL

JUNE 28, 1934

In a decree, the German government has restricted travellers to 50 marks in silver — a sum virtually worthless on the foreign exchange. In a second decree it reduced the amount emigrants may take with them to 2000 marks, equal to about $650 . . . U.S. currency. In the case of Jews who want to go to Palestine, they may take out a little more — enough to meet the British Mandate regulations. They could also get a little more if they agree to buy German goods when in Palestine.

This, according to a N.Y. Times correspondent, has the effect of stopping all travel outside of Germany for those without funds abroad.

GOEBBELS PUBLISHES CALL TO DISMISS ALL JEWS IN EXPORT FIELD

URGES REPLACEMENT OF "NON-ARYANS" BY MEN OF "GERMAN RACE"

JAN. 15, 1934

The Nazi anti-semitic program was pushed farther by Dr. Joseph Goebbels, Minister of Propaganda in his newspaper, "Der Angriff." The article said, "It seems intolerable to us that German firms still permit Jews to represent them abroad." He added that those concerned know this and will now make the necessary changes.

REICH TAKES ACTION TO DISCOURAGE ALL MIXED MARRIAGES

MARCH 26, 1934

Berlin: Aryans who married "non-Aryans" after the Nazi revolution may not use the divorce courts. The journal, German Justice, announced today that unless those who seek to annul such marriages by legal proceedings may do so only if they file during a six month period under the new law. It said, "All those who contracted mixed-marriages after their condemnation by National Socialism placed themselves in opposition to public opinion and will have to bear the consequences of their acts."

NAZIS NOW BAN JEWISH ACTORS

MARCH 7, 1934

Berlin: Anti-Jewish boycotts are now being encouraged officially in Germany. The Nazi organ, "Der Deutsche" has called on all places of entertainment to bar Jewish performers. This follows an order by Dr. Joseph Goebbels to remove all "non-Aryans" from the German stage. S.A. (Storm Troopers) have been stationed at cabaret entrances to enforce the boycott.

U.S. SECRETARY OF LABOR SAYS INCREASED IMMIGRATION NOW WOULD COMPLICATE U.S. UNEMPLOYMENT PROBLEMS

JAN. 30, 1934

Frances Perkins, Secretary of Labor, said in a speech today that her Department has been making efforts to "humanize the immigration service." She added that she perceived no sentiment in the country to increase present immigration.

THE N.J. STATE JEWISH WAR VETERANS ASSN. ASKS U.S. TO LOWER IMMIGRATION BARRIERS FOR ALL REFUGEES

MAR. 12, 1934

In a resolution at its annual convention, today, the group called on the United States to permit more German refugees to enter the country.

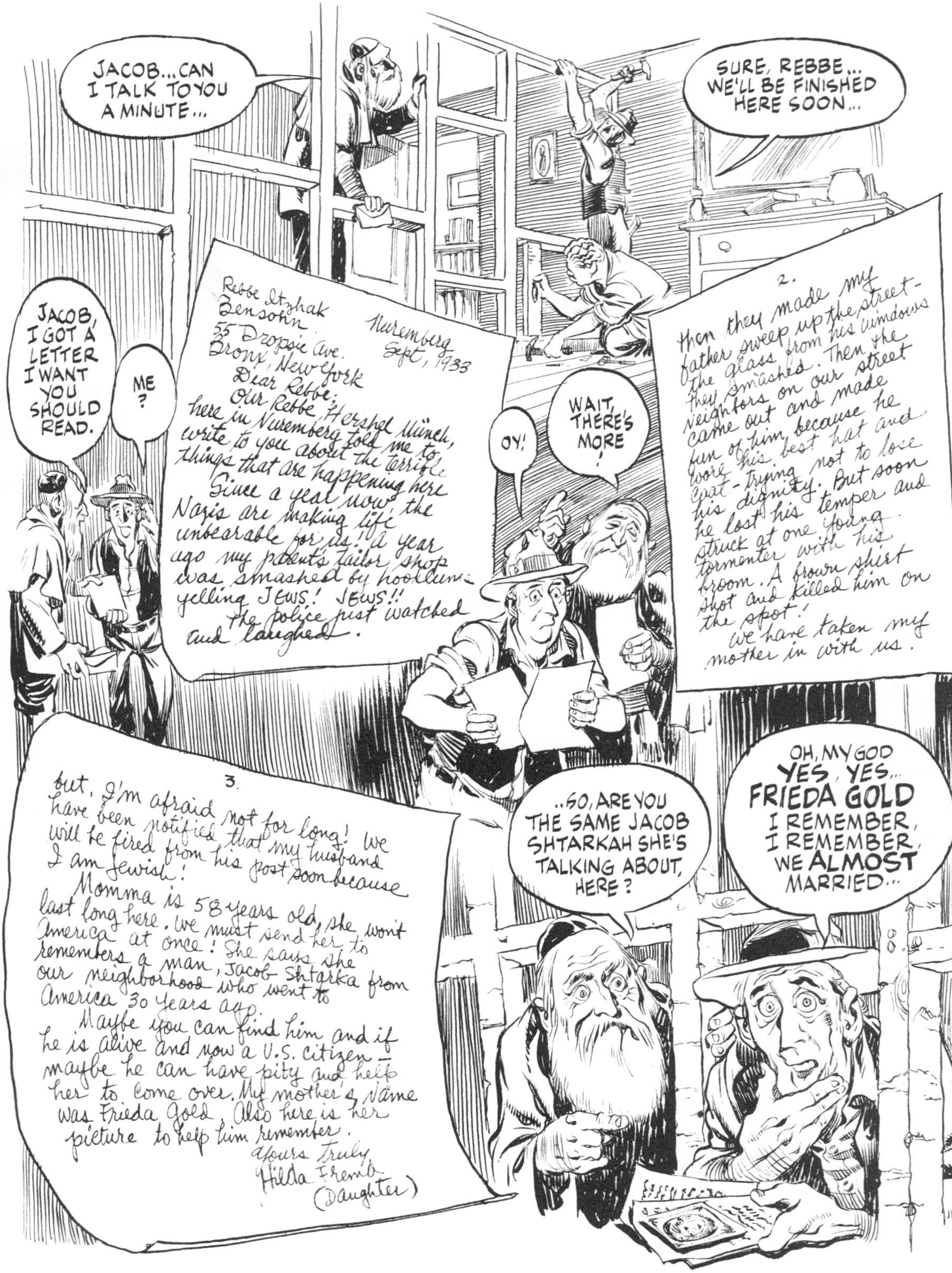
JACOB...CAN I TALK TO YOU A MINUTE...
SURE, REBBE... WE'LL BE FINISHED HERE SOON...
JACOB, I GOT A LETTER I WANT YOU SHOULD READ.
ME?
Rebbe Itzhak Bensohn
55 Dropsie Ave.
Bronx, New York
Nuremberg Sept, 1933
Dear Rebbe,
Our Rebbe, Hershel Münch,
here in Nuremberg told me to
write to you about the terrible
things that are happening here
Since a year now the
Nazis are making life
unbearable for us!! A year
ago my parent's tailor shop
was smashed by hoodlums
yelling JEWS! JEWS!!
The police just watched
and laughed.
OY!
WAIT, THERE'S MORE!
2.
then they made my
father sweep up the street-
the glass from his windows
they smashed. Then the
neighbors on our street
came out and made
fun of him because he
wore his best hat and
coat - trying not to lose
his dignity. But soon
he lost his temper and
struck at one young
tormenter with his
broom. A brown shirt
shot and killed him on
the spot!
We have taken my
mother in with us.
3.
but, I'm afraid not for long! We
have been notified that my husband
will be fired from his post soon because
I am Jewish!
Momma is 58 years old, she won't
last long here. We must send her to
America at once! She says she
remembers a man, Jacob Shtarka from
our neighborhood who went to
America 30 years ago.
Maybe you can find him and if
he is alive and now a U.S. citizen -
maybe he can have pity and help
her to come over. My mother's name
was Frieda Gold. Also here is her
picture to help him remember.
Yours truly
Hilda Fremd
(Daughter)
..SO, ARE YOU THE SAME JACOB SHTARKAH SHE'S TALKING ABOUT, HERE?
OH, MY GOD YES, YES... FRIEDA GOLD I REMEMBER, I REMEMBER, WE ALMOST MARRIED...

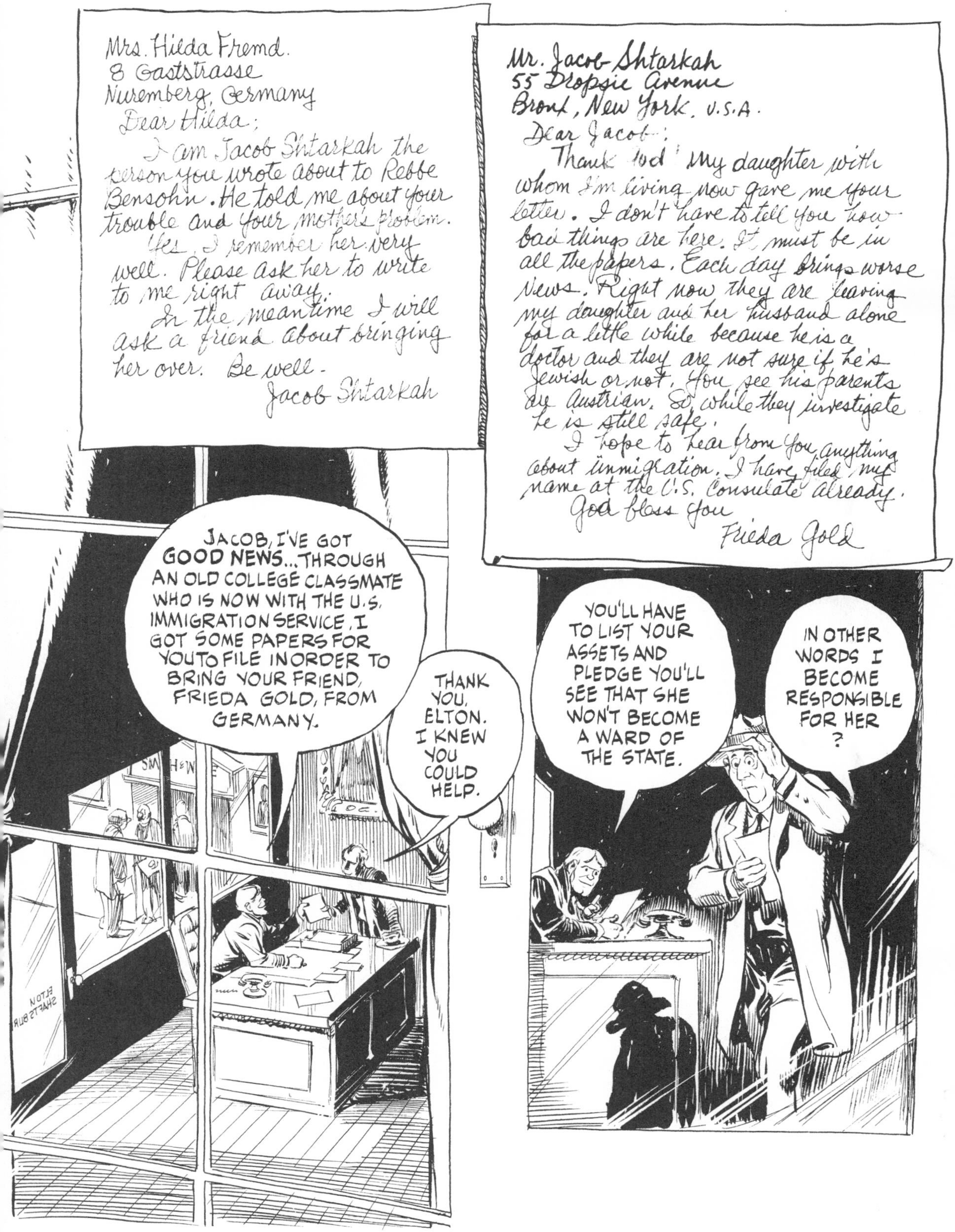
Mrs. Hilda Fremd.
8 Gaststrasse
Nuremberg, Germany
Dear Hilda;
I am Jacob Shtarkah the person you wrote about to Rebbe Bensohn. He told me about your trouble and your mother's problem.
Yes, I remember her very well. Please ask her to write to me right away.
In the meantime I will ask a friend about bringing her over. Be well.
Jacob Shtarkah
Mr. Jacob Shtarkah
55 Dropsie Avenue
Bronx, New York. U.S.A.
Dear Jacob:
Thank God! My daughter with whom I'm living now gave me your letter. I don't have to tell you how bad things are here. It must be in all the papers. Each day brings worse News. Right now they are leaving my daughter and her husband alone for a little while because he is a doctor and they are not sure if he's Jewish or not. You see his parents are Austrian. So, while they investigate he is still safe.
I hope to hear from you anything about immigration. I have filed my name at the U.S. Consulate already.
God bless you
Frieda Gold
JACOB, I'VE GOT GOOD NEWS... THROUGH AN OLD COLLEGE CLASSMATE WHO IS NOW WITH THE U.S. IMMIGRATION SERVICE, I GOT SOME PAPERS FOR YOU TO FILE IN ORDER TO BRING YOUR FRIEND, FRIEDA GOLD, FROM GERMANY.
THANK YOU, ELTON. I KNEW YOU COULD HELP.
YOU'LL HAVE TO LIST YOUR ASSETS AND PLEDGE YOU'LL SEE THAT SHE WON'T BECOME A WARD OF THE STATE.
IN OTHER WORDS I BECOME RESPONSIBLE FOR HER?

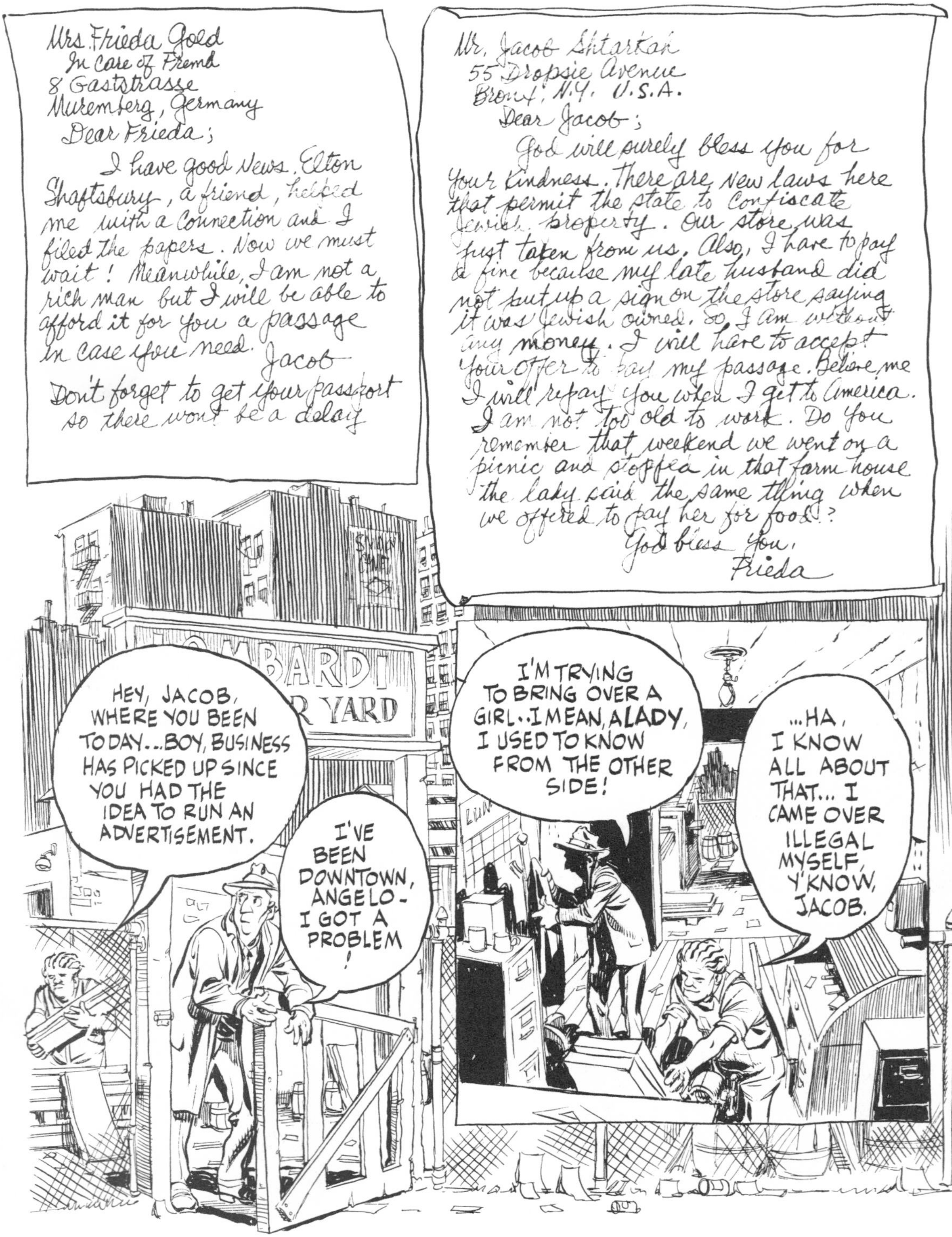

Mrs. Frieda Gold
In Care of Fremd
8 Gaststrasse
Nuremberg, Germany
Dear Frieda;
I have good News. Elton Shaftsbury, a friend, helped me with a Connection and I filed the papers. Now we must wait! Meanwhile, I am not a rich man but I will be able to afford it for you a passage in case you need.
Jacob
Don't forget to get your passport so there wont be a delay
Mr. Jacob Shtarkah
55 Dropsie Avenue
Bronx, N.Y. U.S.A.
Dear Jacob;
God will surely bless you for Your kindness. There are New laws here that permit the state to Confiscate Jewish property. Our store was just taken from us. Also, I have to pay a fine because my late husband did not put up a sign on the store saying it was Jewish owned. So, I am without any money. I will have to accept Your offer to pay my passage. Believe me I will repay You when I get to America. I am not too old to work. Do You remember that weekend we went on a picnic and stopped in that farm house the lady said the same thing when we offered to pay her for food!?
God bless You,
Frieda
HEY, JACOB, WHERE YOU BEEN TODAY...BOY, BUSINESS HAS PICKED UP SINCE YOU HAD THE IDEA TO RUN AN ADVERTISEMENT.
I'VE BEEN DOWNTOWN, ANGELO - I GOT A PROBLEM!
I'M TRYING TO BRING OVER A GIRL..I MEAN, A LADY, I USED TO KNOW FROM THE OTHER SIDE!
...HA, I KNOW ALL ABOUT THAT... I CAME OVER ILLEGAL MYSELF, Y'KNOW, JACOB.

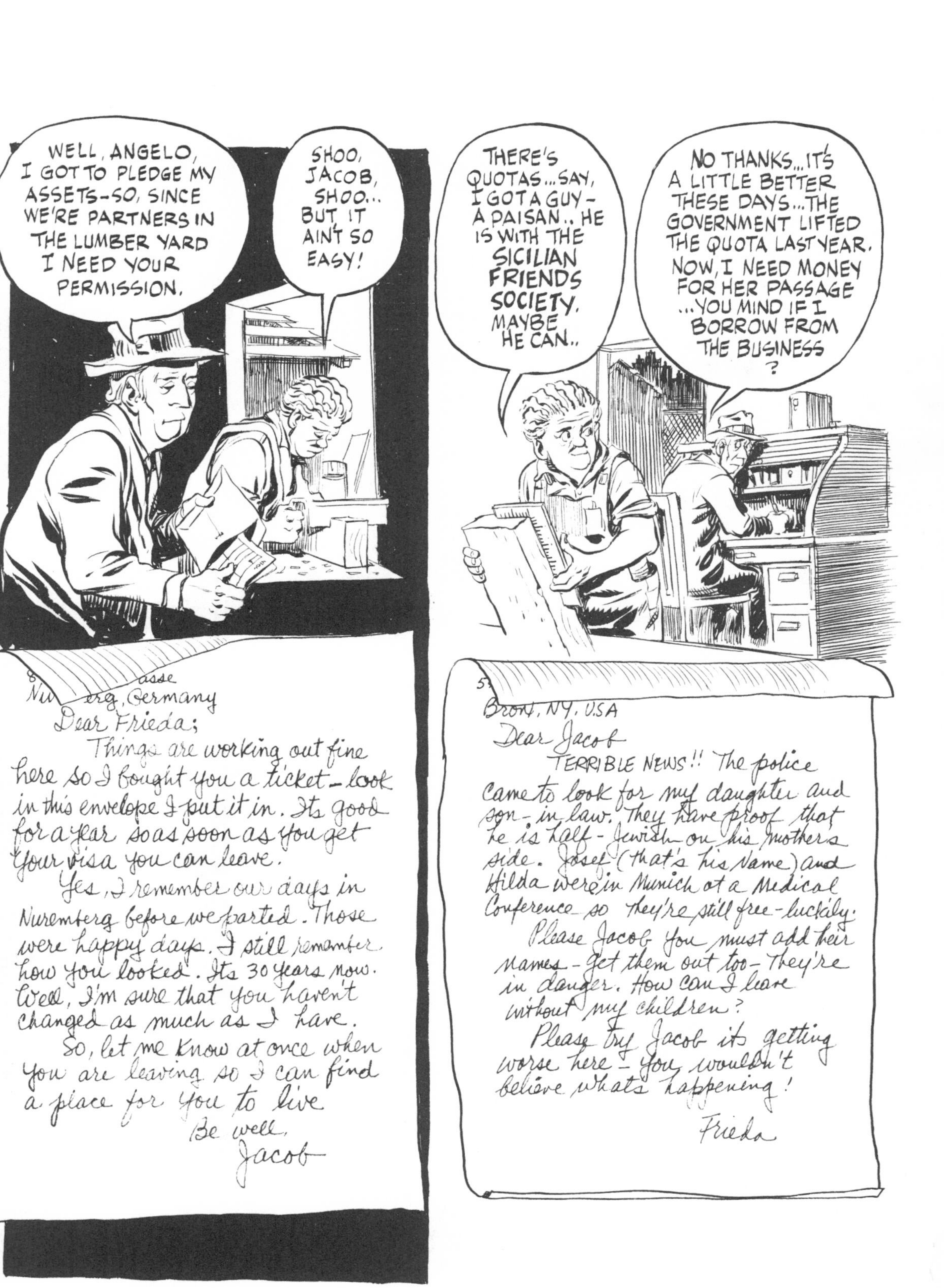
WELL, ANGELO, I GOT TO PLEDGE MY ASSETS-SO, SINCE WE'RE PARTNERS IN THE LUMBER YARD I NEED YOUR PERMISSION.
SHOO, JACOB, SHOO... BUT IT AIN'T SO EASY!
THERE'S QUOTAS...SAY, I GOT A GUY - A PAISAN.. HE IS WITH THE SICILIAN FRIENDS SOCIETY. MAYBE HE CAN..
NO THANKS...IT'S A LITTLE BETTER THESE DAYS...THE GOVERNMENT LIFTED THE QUOTA LAST YEAR. NOW, I NEED MONEY FOR HER PASSAGE ...YOU MIND IF I BORROW FROM THE BUSINESS ?
asse
erg, Germany
Dear Frieda;
Things are working out fine here so I bought you a ticket - look in this envelope I put it in. Its good for a year so as soon as you get your visa you can leave.
Yes, I remember our days in Nuremberg before we parted. Those were happy days. I still remember how you looked. Its 30 years now. Well, I'm sure that you haven't changed as much as I have.
So, let me know at once when you are leaving so I can find a place for you to live.
Be well,
Jacob
Bronx, NY, USA
Dear Jacob
TERRIBLE NEWS!! The police came to look for my daughter and son-in law. They have proof that he is half - Jewish on his mother's side. Josef (that's his name) and Hilda were in Munich at a Medical Conference so they're still free - luckily.
Please Jacob you must add their names - get them out too - They're in danger. How can I leave without my children?
Please try Jacob its getting worse here - you wouldn't believe whats happening!
Frieda

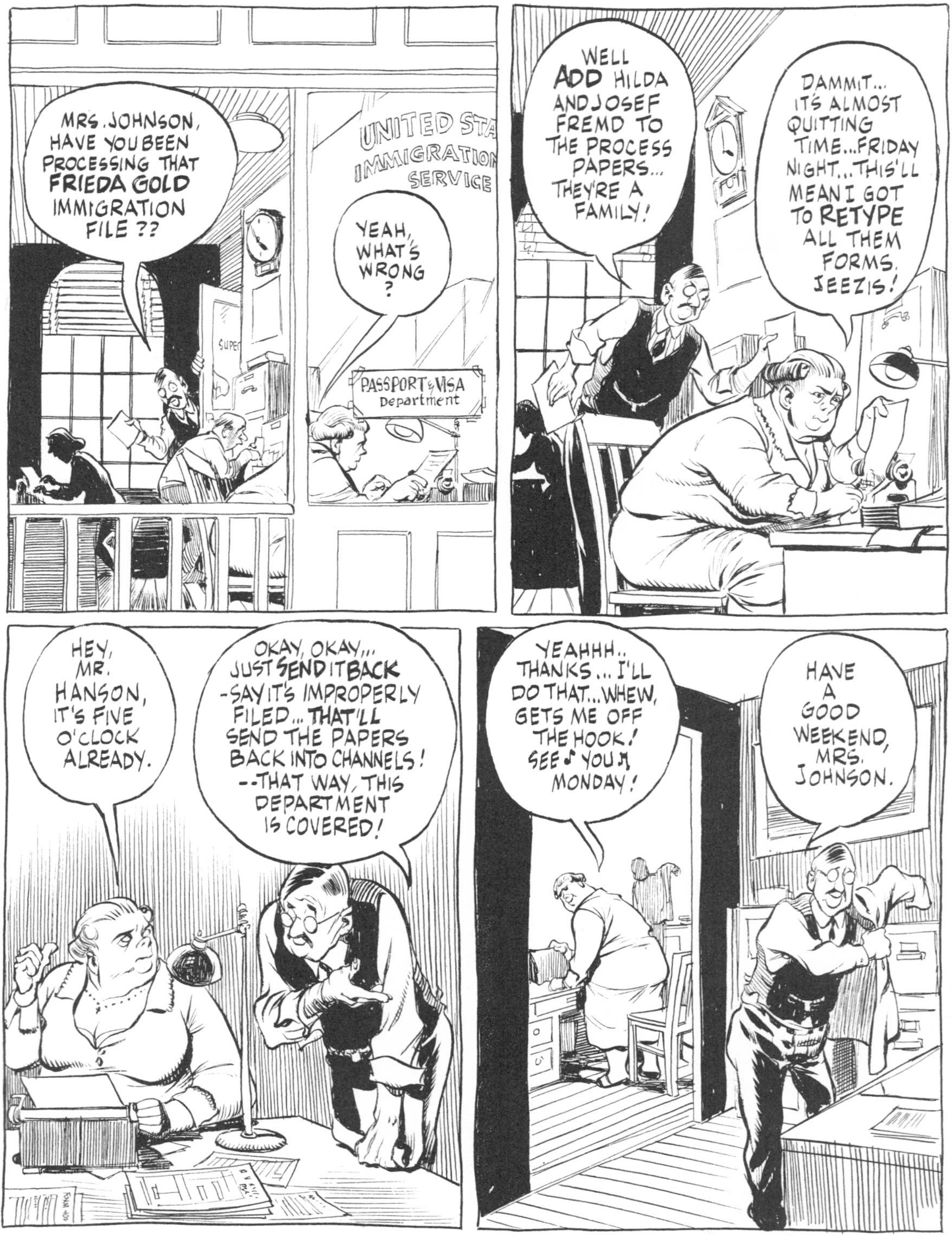

MRS. JOHNSON, HAVE YOU BEEN PROCESSING THAT FRIEDA GOLD IMMIGRATION FILE ??
UNITED STA IMMIGRATION SERVICE
YEAH, WHAT'S WRONG ?
PASSPORT & VISA Department
WELL ADD HILDA AND JOSEF FREMD TO THE PROCESS PAPERS... THEY'RE A FAMILY!
DAMMIT... IT'S ALMOST QUITTING TIME... FRIDAY NIGHT... THIS'LL MEAN I GOT TO RETYPE ALL THEM FORMS. JEEZIS!
HEY, MR. HANSON, IT'S FIVE O'CLOCK ALREADY.
OKAY, OKAY,,, JUST SEND IT BACK -SAY IT'S IMPROPERLY FILED... THAT'LL SEND THE PAPERS BACK INTO CHANNELS! --THAT WAY, THIS DEPARTMENT IS COVERED!
YEAHHH.. THANKS... I'LL DO THAT... WHEW, GETS ME OFF THE HOOK! SEE YOU MONDAY!
HAVE A GOOD WEEKEND, MRS. JOHNSON.

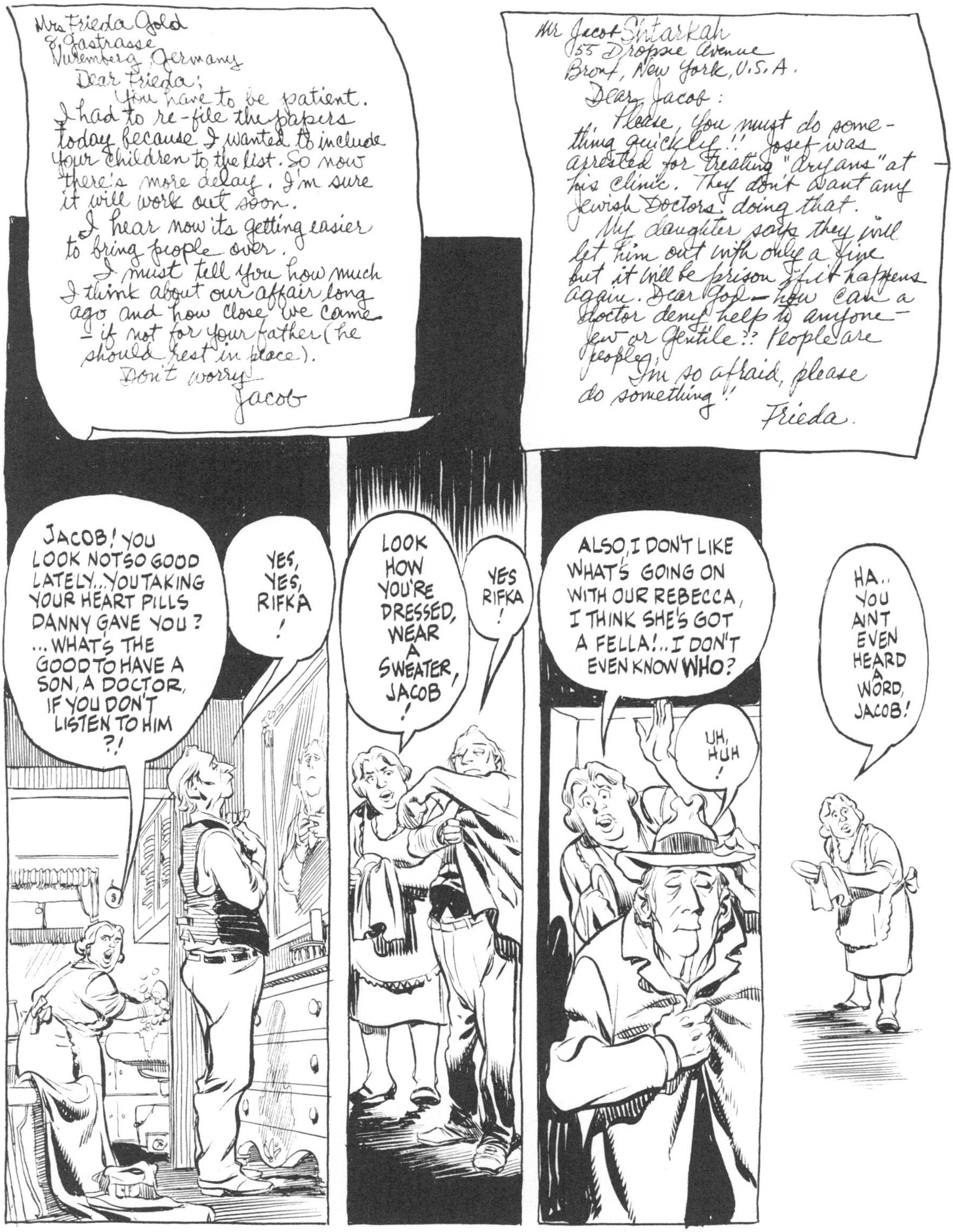
Mrs Frieda Gold
8 Gastrasse
Nuremberg Germany
Dear Frieda;
You have to be patient. I had to re-file the papers today because I wanted to include your children to the list. So now there's more delay. I'm sure it will work out soon.
I hear now its getting easier to bring people over.
I must tell you how much I think about our affair long ago and how close we came - if not for your father (he should rest in peace).
Don't worry
Jacob
Mr Jacob Shtarkah
55 Dropsie Avenue
Bronx, New York, U.S.A.
Dear Jacob:
Please, you must do something quickly!! Josef was arrested for treating "Aryans" at his clinic. They don't want any Jewish Doctors doing that.
My daughter says they will let him out with only a fine but it will be prison if it happens again. Dear God - how can a doctor deny help to anyone - Jew or Gentile?? People are people.
I'm so afraid, please do something!!
Frieda.
JACOB! YOU LOOK NOT SO GOOD LATELY... YOU TAKING YOUR HEART PILLS DANNY GAVE YOU? ... WHAT'S THE GOOD TO HAVE A SON, A DOCTOR, IF YOU DON'T LISTEN TO HIM ?!
YES, YES, RIFKA!
LOOK HOW YOU'RE DRESSED, WEAR A SWEATER, JACOB!
YES RIFKA!
ALSO, I DON'T LIKE WHAT'S GOING ON WITH OUR REBECCA, I THINK SHE'S GOT A FELLA!.. I DON'T EVEN KNOW WHO?
UH, HUH!
HA.. YOU AINT EVEN HEARD A WORD, JACOB!

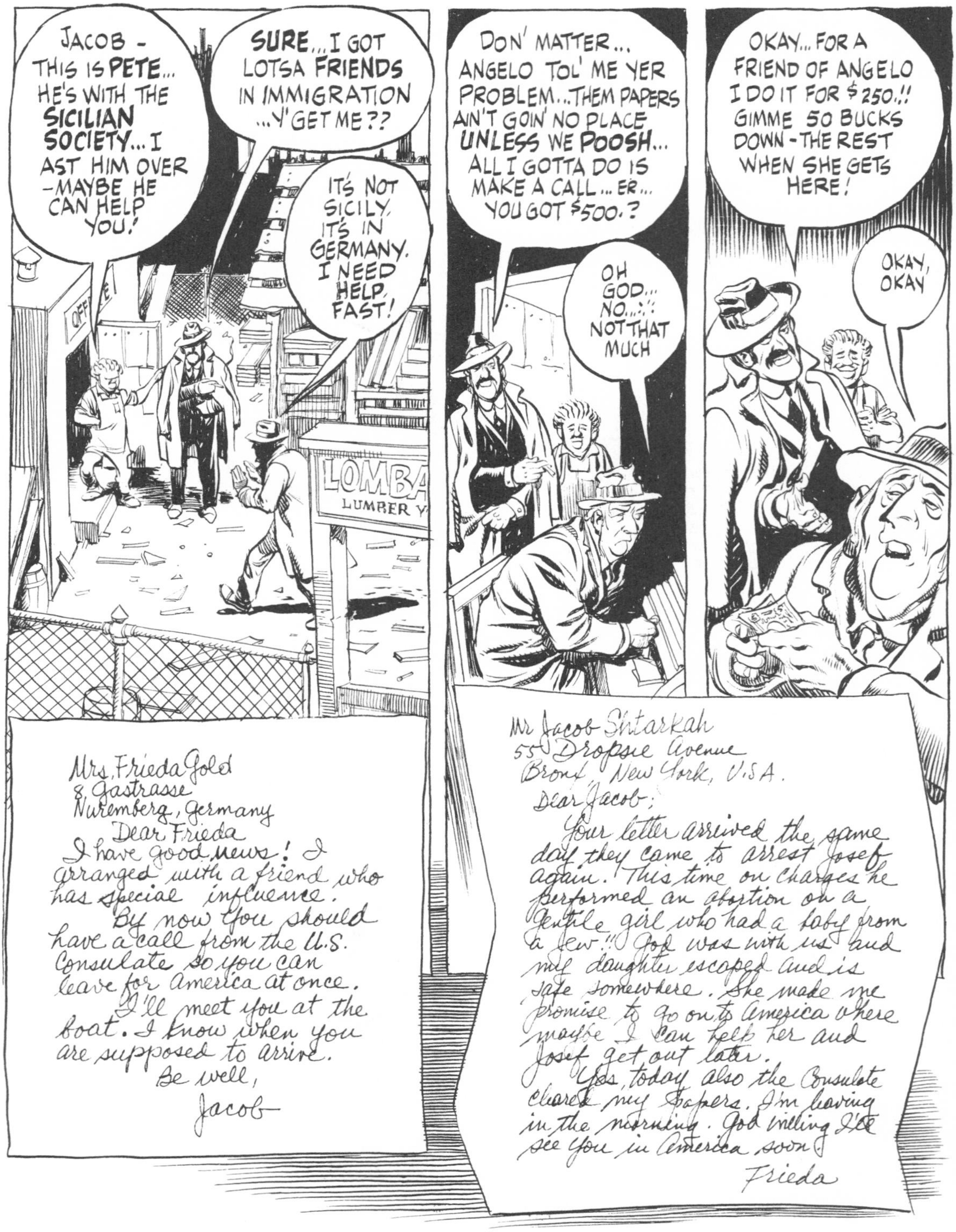
JACOB - THIS IS PETE... HE'S WITH THE SICILIAN SOCIETY... I AST HIM OVER -MAYBE HE CAN HELP YOU!
SURE... I GOT LOTSA FRIENDS IN IMMIGRATION ...Y'GET ME??
IT'S NOT SICILY, IT'S IN GERMANY. I NEED HELP, FAST!
OFFICE
LOMBA
LUMBER Y
DON' MATTER... ANGELO TOL' ME YER PROBLEM...THEM PAPERS AIN'T GOIN' NO PLACE UNLESS WE POOSH... ALL I GOTTA DO IS MAKE A CALL... ER... YOU GOT $500.?
OH GOD... NO... NOT THAT MUCH
OKAY... FOR A FRIEND OF ANGELO I DO IT FOR $250.!! GIMME 50 BUCKS DOWN - THE REST WHEN SHE GETS HERE!
OKAY, OKAY
Mrs. Frieda Gold
8 Gastrasse
Nuremberg, Germany
Dear Frieda
I have good news! I arranged with a friend who has special influence.
By now you should have a call from the U.S. Consulate so you can leave for America at once.
I'll meet you at the boat. I know when you are supposed to arrive.
Be well,
Jacob
Mr Jacob Shtarkah
55 Dropsie Avenue
Bronx, New York, U.S.A.
Dear Jacob;
Your letter arrived the same day they came to arrest Josef again. This time on charges he performed an abortion on a Gentile girl who had a baby from a Jew!! God was with us and my daughter escaped and is safe somewhere. She make me promise to go on to America where maybe I can help her and Josef get out later.
Yes, today also the Consulate cleared my papers. I'm leaving in the morning. God willing I'll see you in America soon
Frieda

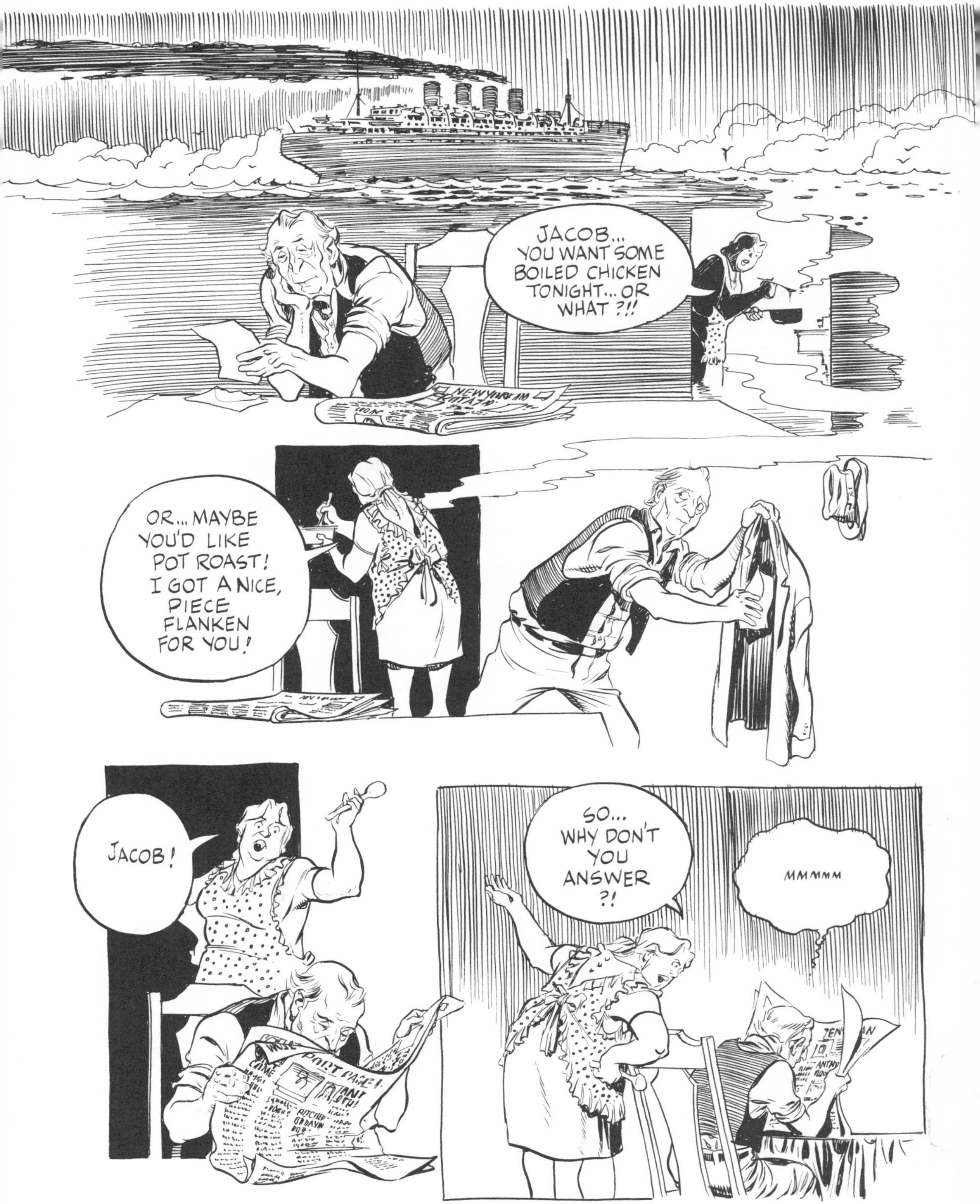
JACOB... YOU WANT SOME BOILED CHICKEN TONIGHT... OR WHAT ?!!
OR... MAYBE YOU'D LIKE POT ROAST! I GOT A NICE, PIECE FLANKEN FOR YOU!
JACOB!
SO... WHY DON'T YOU ANSWER ?!
MMMMM

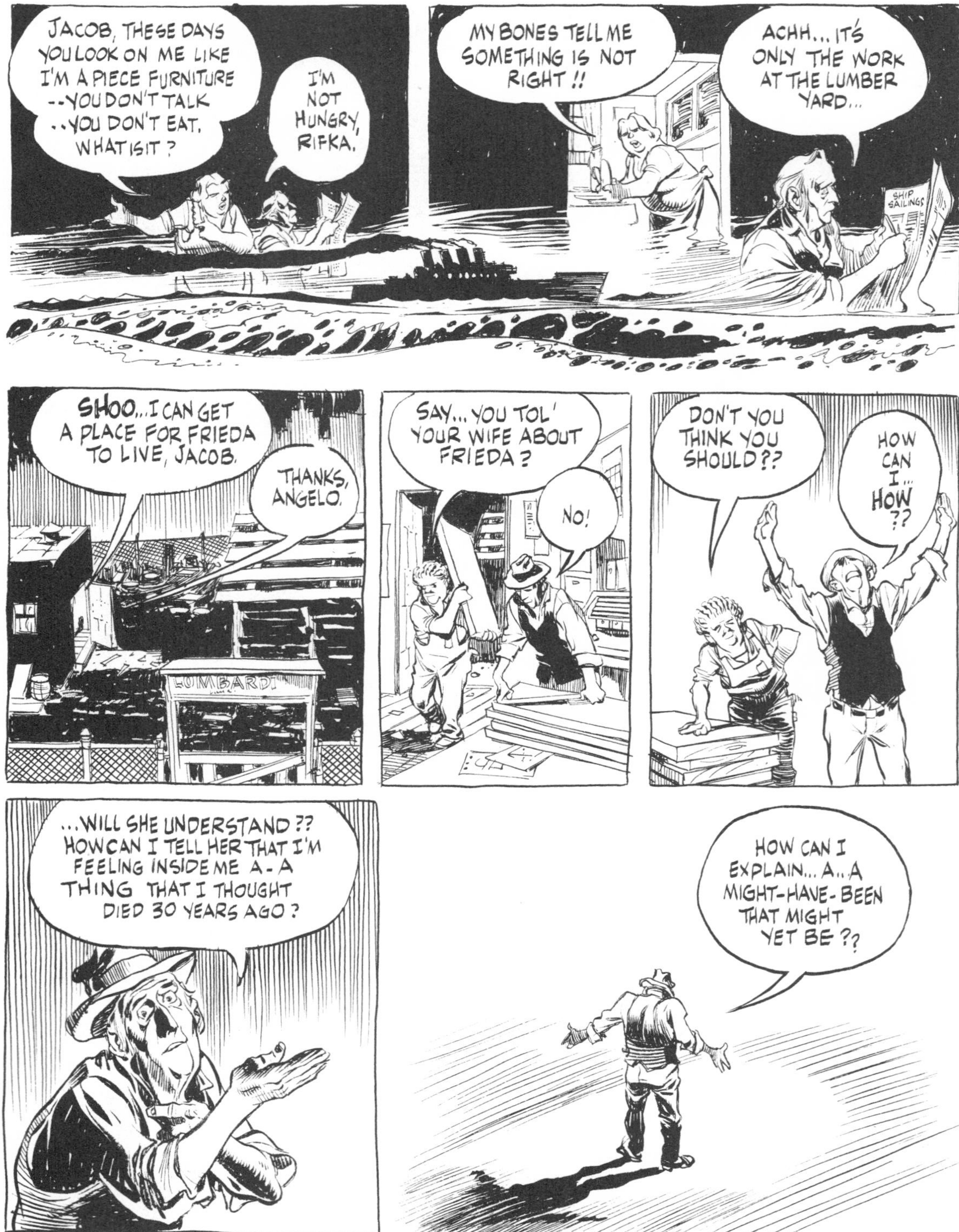
JACOB, THESE DAYS YOU LOOK ON ME LIKE I'M A PIECE FURNITURE --YOU DON'T TALK ..YOU DON'T EAT. WHAT IS IT?
I'M NOT HUNGRY, RIFKA.
MY BONES TELL ME SOMETHING IS NOT RIGHT!!
ACHH... IT'S ONLY THE WORK AT THE LUMBER YARD...
SHIP SAILINGS
SHOO... I CAN GET A PLACE FOR FRIEDA TO LIVE, JACOB.
THANKS, ANGELO.
LUMBARDI
SAY... YOU TOL' YOUR WIFE ABOUT FRIEDA?
NO!
DON'T YOU THINK YOU SHOULD??
HOW CAN I... HOW??
...WILL SHE UNDERSTAND?? HOW CAN I TELL HER THAT I'M FEELING INSIDE ME A-A THING THAT I THOUGHT DIED 30 YEARS AGO?
HOW CAN I EXPLAIN... A.. A MIGHT-HAVE-BEEN THAT MIGHT YET BE??

AMERICA, AMERICA

JEWISH REFUGEES GET LOCAL HELP

JUNE 15, 1934

The New York Times reported that 259 refugees of the 430 Jews who arrived in New York during May had fled from Nazi Germany. Of these a few came from other countries in Europe where they had fled earlier.

AMERICAN GROUP ASKS U.S. HAVEN FOR NAZI VICTIMS

PRESIDENT ROOSEVELT ASKED TO EASE CURB ON IMMIGRATION

MARCH 19, 1934

Mrs. Carrie Chapman Catt, chairman of a committee of outstanding American women, appealed to President Roosevelt for relief from an executive order issued by former President Herbert Hoover restricting immigration. Due to the rigid enforcement of the rules under Hoover beginning in 1930, definite proof that an alien applying for an immigration visa would not become a public charge was very strictly applied. The appeal pointed out that while legal German immigration quotas were 25,959, fewer than 600 had been admitted here in the period from July 1933 to date.

FEWER IMMIGRANTS AT ELLIS ISLAND NOW

JULY 8, 1934

Immigrants arriving in Ellis Island have dwindled in number from 5000 a day to only about 25 in the past 25 years. According to officials this reduced use of the depot is a result of the restrictions on immigration and that most of the aliens coming to settle here pass their technical requirements at the port of embarkation. This permits them to land at piers in this port with other passengers.

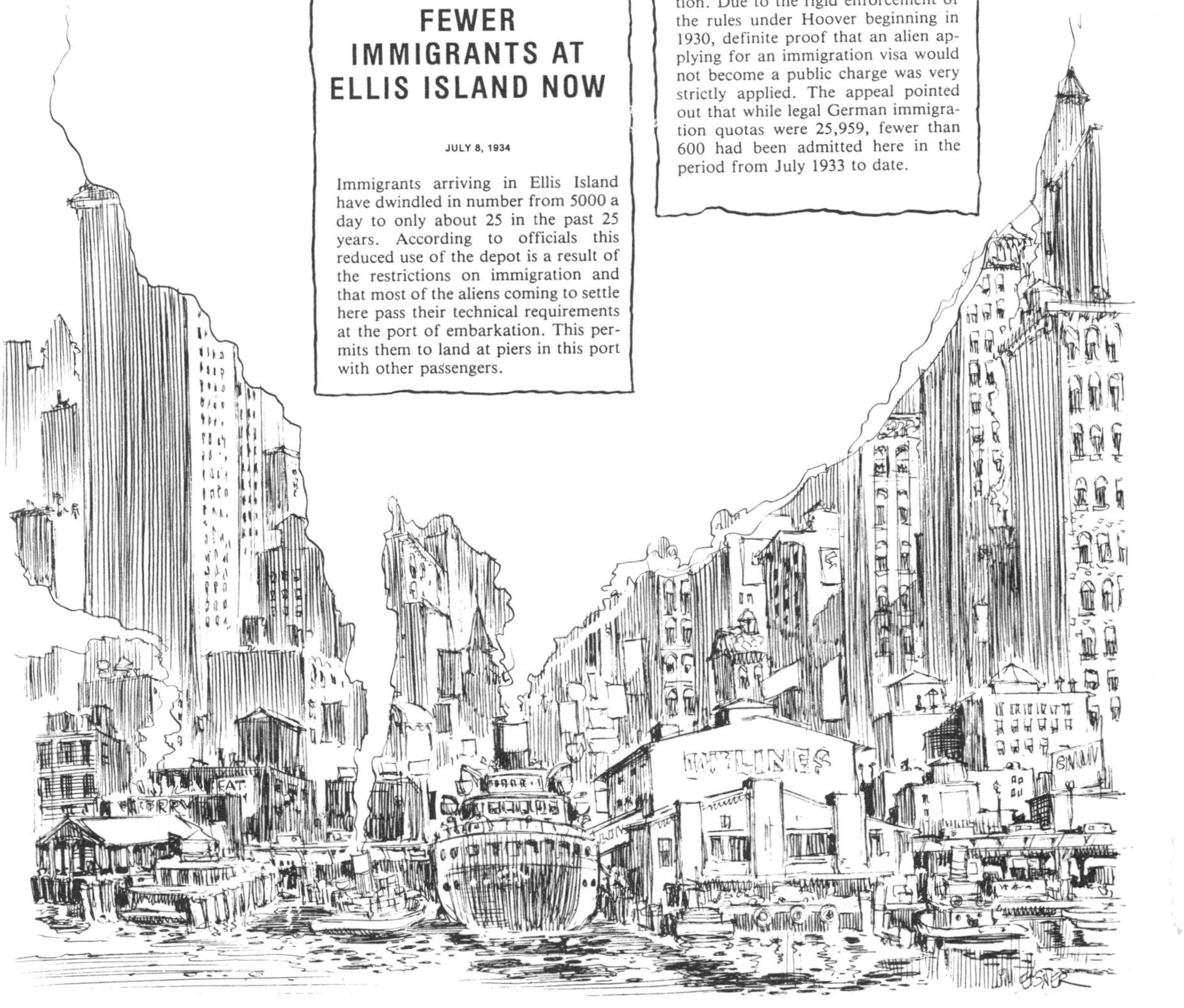

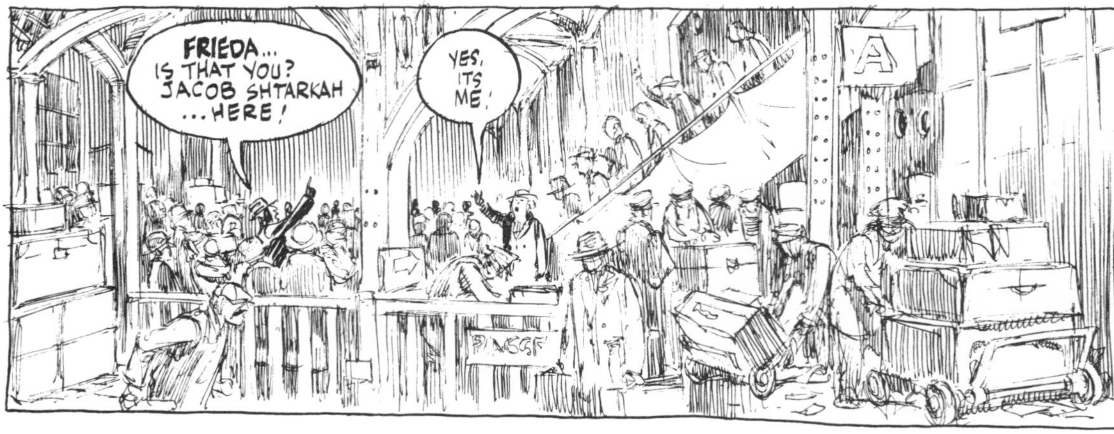
FRIEDA... IS THAT YOU? JACOB SHTARKAH ...HERE!
YES, ITS ME!

AT LONG LAST,
FRIEDA GOLD ARRIVED IN AMERICA.
BEHIND HER WERE THE ASHES OF
A ONCE-SECURE MIDDLE CLASS LIFE
WHERE SHE HAD TAKEN FOR GRANTED...
THE COMFORT OF BELONGING.

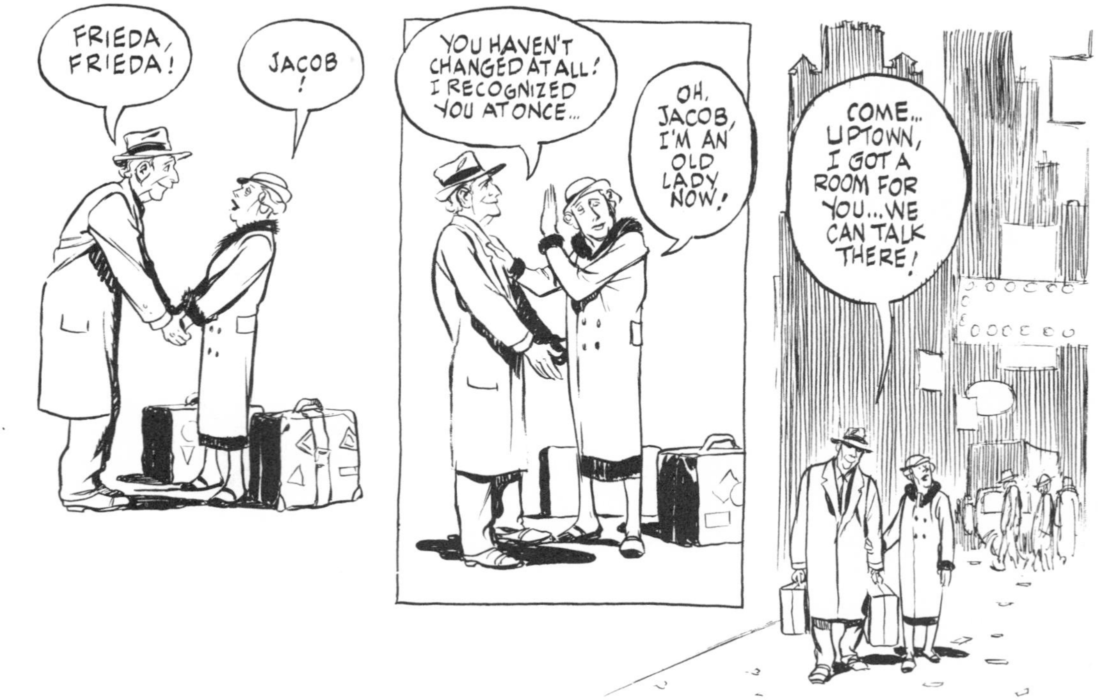
FRIEDA, FRIEDA!
JACOB!
YOU HAVEN'T CHANGED AT ALL! I RECOGNIZED YOU AT ONCE...
OH, JACOB, I'M AN OLD LADY NOW!
COME... UPTOWN, I GOT A ROOM FOR YOU... WE CAN TALK THERE!

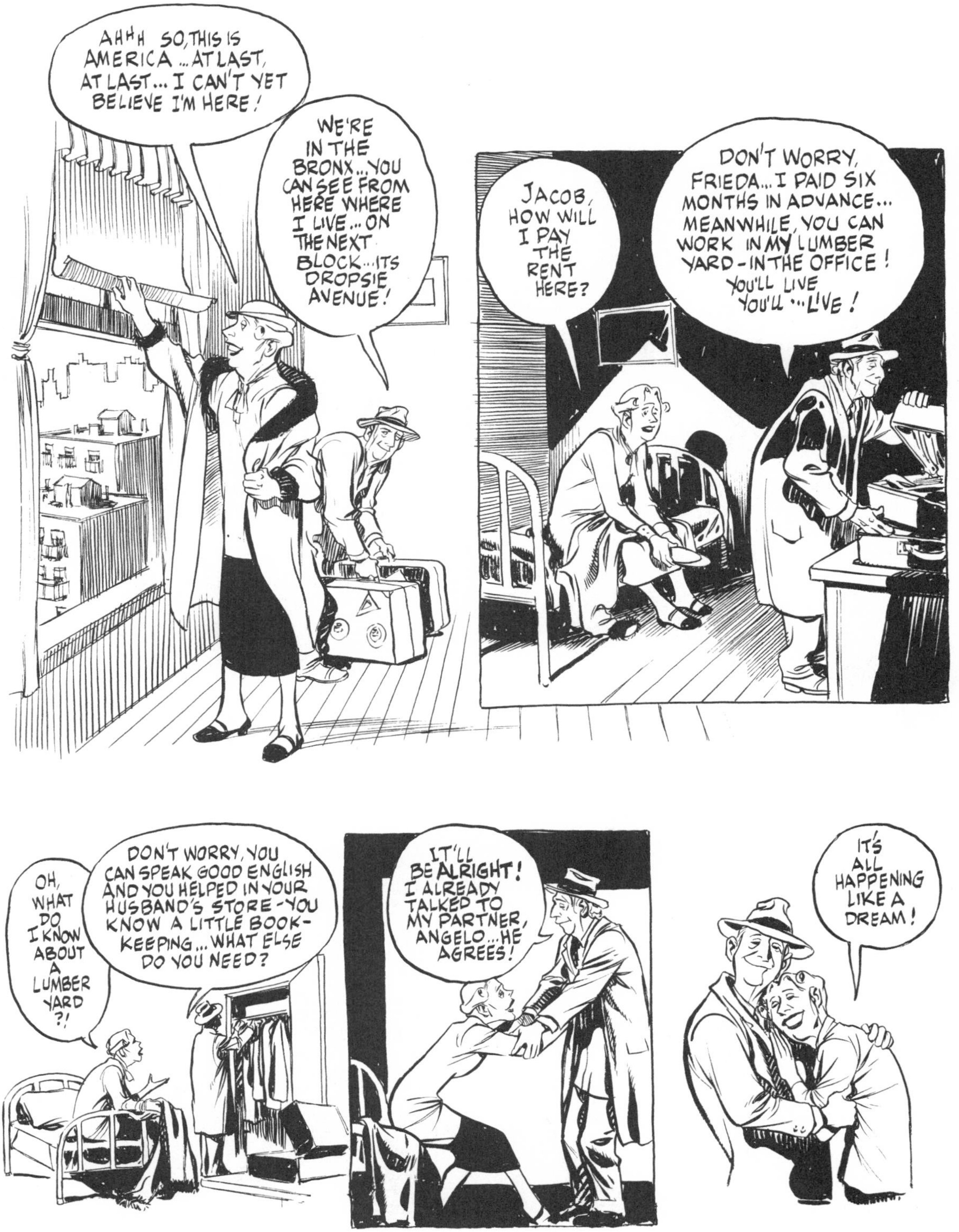
AHHH SO, THIS IS AMERICA ... AT LAST, AT LAST... I CAN'T YET BELIEVE I'M HERE!
WE'RE IN THE BRONX... YOU CAN SEE FROM HERE WHERE I LIVE... ON THE NEXT BLOCK... ITS DROPSIE AVENUE!
JACOB, HOW WILL I PAY THE RENT HERE?
DON'T WORRY, FRIEDA... I PAID SIX MONTHS IN ADVANCE... MEANWHILE, YOU CAN WORK IN MY LUMBER YARD - IN THE OFFICE! YOU'LL LIVE YOU'LL ...LIVE!
OH, WHAT DO I KNOW ABOUT A LUMBER YARD ?!
DON'T WORRY, YOU CAN SPEAK GOOD ENGLISH AND YOU HELPED IN YOUR HUSBAND'S STORE - YOU KNOW A LITTLE BOOK-KEEPING... WHAT ELSE DO YOU NEED?
IT'LL BE ALRIGHT! I ALREADY TALKED TO MY PARTNER, ANGELO... HE AGREES!
IT'S ALL HAPPENING LIKE A DREAM!

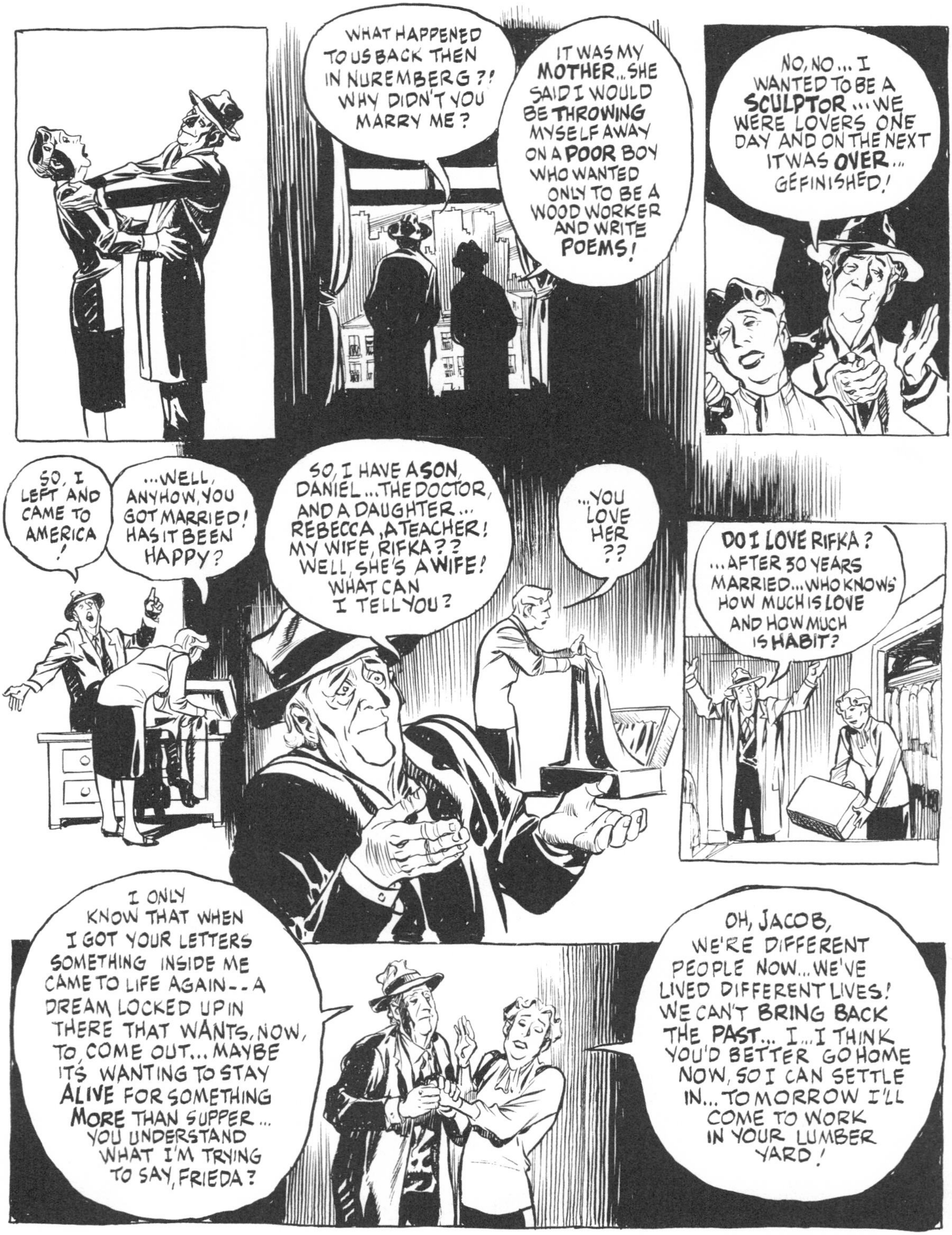
WHAT HAPPENED TO US BACK THEN IN NUREMBERG ?! WHY DIDN'T YOU MARRY ME?
IT WAS MY MOTHER... SHE SAID I WOULD BE THROWING MYSELF AWAY ON A POOR BOY WHO WANTED ONLY TO BE A WOOD WORKER AND WRITE POEMS!
NO, NO ... I WANTED TO BE A SCULPTOR ... WE WERE LOVERS ONE DAY AND ON THE NEXT IT WAS OVER ... GEFINISHED!
SO, I LEFT AND CAME TO AMERICA!
...WELL, ANYHOW, YOU GOT MARRIED! HAS IT BEEN HAPPY?
SO, I HAVE A SON, DANIEL... THE DOCTOR, AND A DAUGHTER... REBECCA, A TEACHER! MY WIFE, RIFKA?? WELL, SHE'S A WIFE! WHAT CAN I TELL YOU?
...YOU LOVE HER ??
DO I LOVE RIFKA? ...AFTER 30 YEARS MARRIED... WHO KNOWS HOW MUCH IS LOVE AND HOW MUCH IS HABIT?
I ONLY KNOW THAT WHEN I GOT YOUR LETTERS SOMETHING INSIDE ME CAME TO LIFE AGAIN -- A DREAM LOCKED UP IN THERE THAT WANTS, NOW, TO, COME OUT... MAYBE ITS WANTING TO STAY ALIVE FOR SOMETHING MORE THAN SUPPER... YOU UNDERSTAND WHAT I'M TRYING TO SAY, FRIEDA?
OH, JACOB, WE'RE DIFFERENT PEOPLE NOW... WE'VE LIVED DIFFERENT LIVES! WE CAN'T BRING BACK THE PAST... I...I THINK YOU'D BETTER GO HOME NOW, SO I CAN SETTLE IN... TOMORROW I'LL COME TO WORK IN YOUR LUMBER YARD!

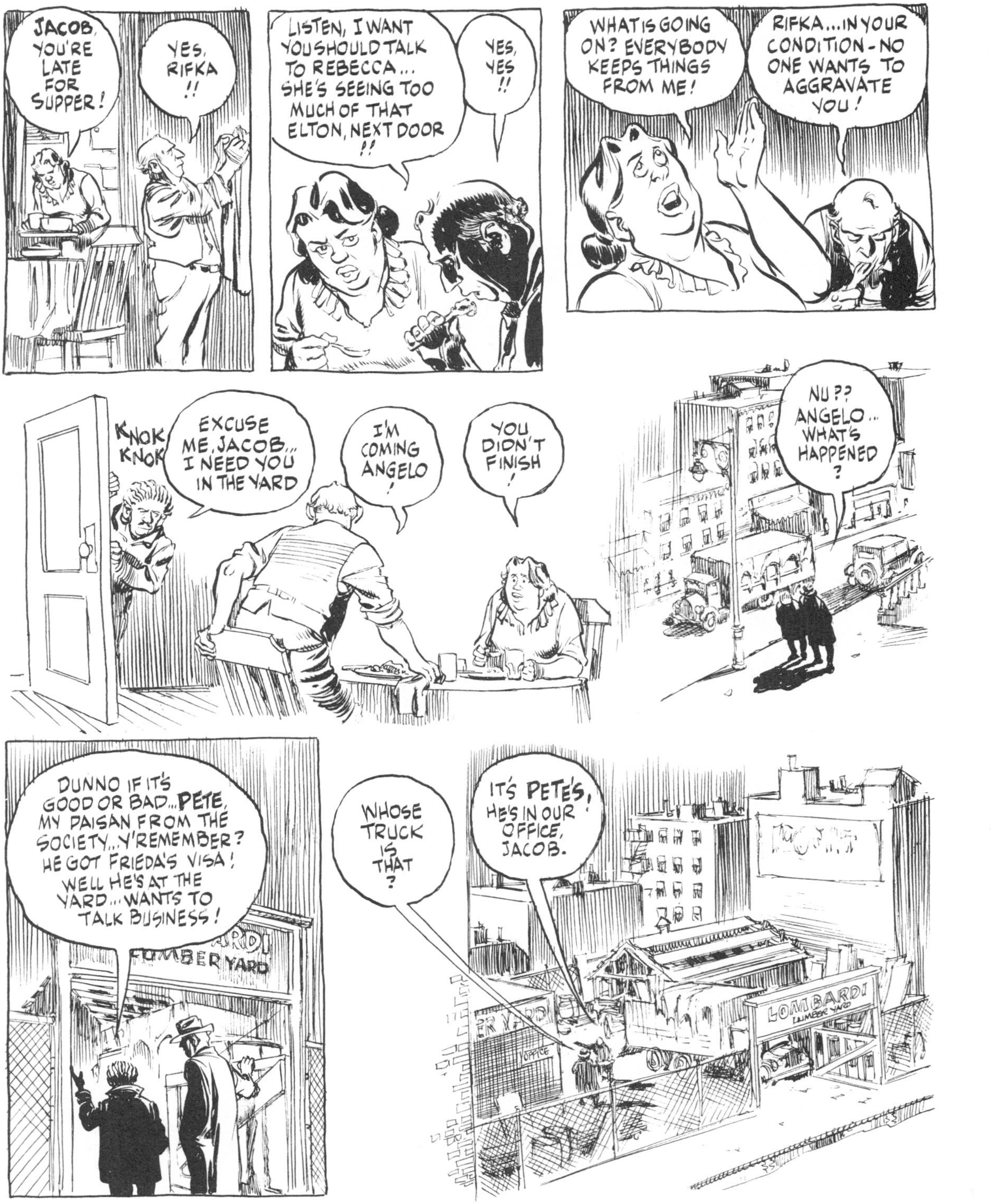
JACOB, YOU'RE LATE FOR SUPPER!
YES, RIFKA !!
LISTEN, I WANT YOU SHOULD TALK TO REBECCA... SHE'S SEEING TOO MUCH OF THAT ELTON, NEXT DOOR !!
YES, YES !!
WHAT IS GOING ON? EVERYBODY KEEPS THINGS FROM ME!
RIFKA... IN YOUR CONDITION - NO ONE WANTS TO AGGRAVATE YOU!
KNOK KNOK
EXCUSE ME, JACOB... I NEED YOU IN THE YARD
I'M COMING ANGELO!
YOU DIDN'T FINISH!
NU?? ANGELO... WHAT'S HAPPENED?
DUNNO IF IT'S GOOD OR BAD... PETE, MY PAISAN FROM THE SOCIETY... Y'REMEMBER? HE GOT FRIEDA'S VISA! WELL HE'S AT THE YARD... WANTS TO TALK BUSINESS!
LUMBER YARD
WHOSE TRUCK IS THAT?
IT'S PETE'S, HE'S IN OUR OFFICE, JACOB.
LOMBARDI LUMBER YARD
OFFICE

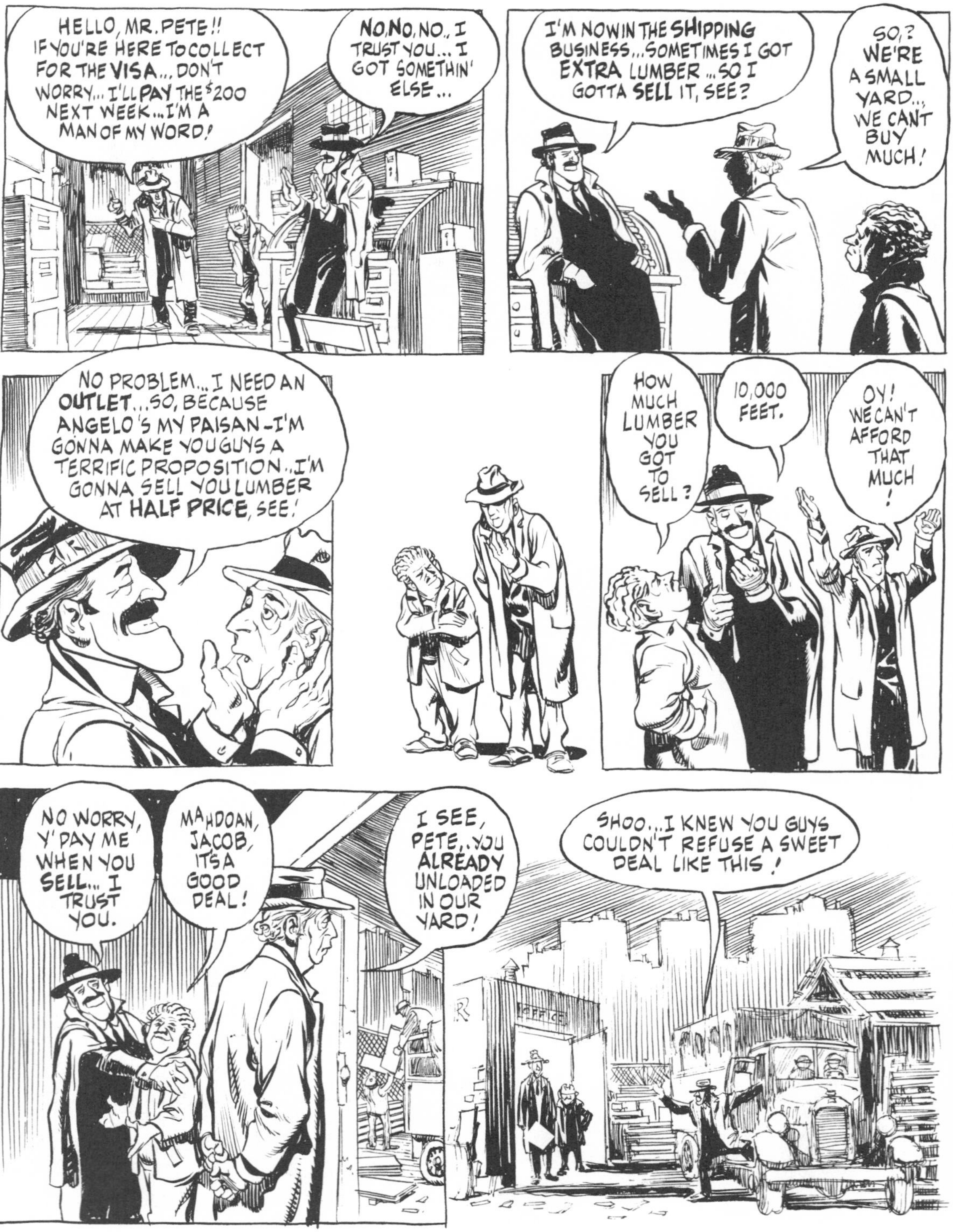
HELLO, MR. PETE!! IF YOU'RE HERE TO COLLECT FOR THE VISA... DON'T WORRY... I'LL PAY THE $200 NEXT WEEK... I'M A MAN OF MY WORD!
NO, NO, NO.. I TRUST YOU... I GOT SOMETHIN' ELSE...
I'M NOW IN THE SHIPPING BUSINESS... SOMETIMES I GOT EXTRA LUMBER... SO I GOTTA SELL IT, SEE?
SO? WE'RE A SMALL YARD... WE CAN'T BUY MUCH!
NO PROBLEM... I NEED AN OUTLET... SO, BECAUSE ANGELO'S MY PAISAN - I'M GONNA MAKE YOU GUYS A TERRIFIC PROPOSITION.. I'M GONNA SELL YOU LUMBER AT HALF PRICE, SEE!
HOW MUCH LUMBER YOU GOT TO SELL?
10,000 FEET.
OY! WE CAN'T AFFORD THAT MUCH!
NO WORRY, Y' PAY ME WHEN YOU SELL... I TRUST YOU.
MAHDOAN, JACOB, IT'S A GOOD DEAL!
I SEE, PETE.. YOU ALREADY UNLOADED IN OUR YARD!
SHOO... I KNEW YOU GUYS COULDN'T REFUSE A SWEET DEAL LIKE THIS!

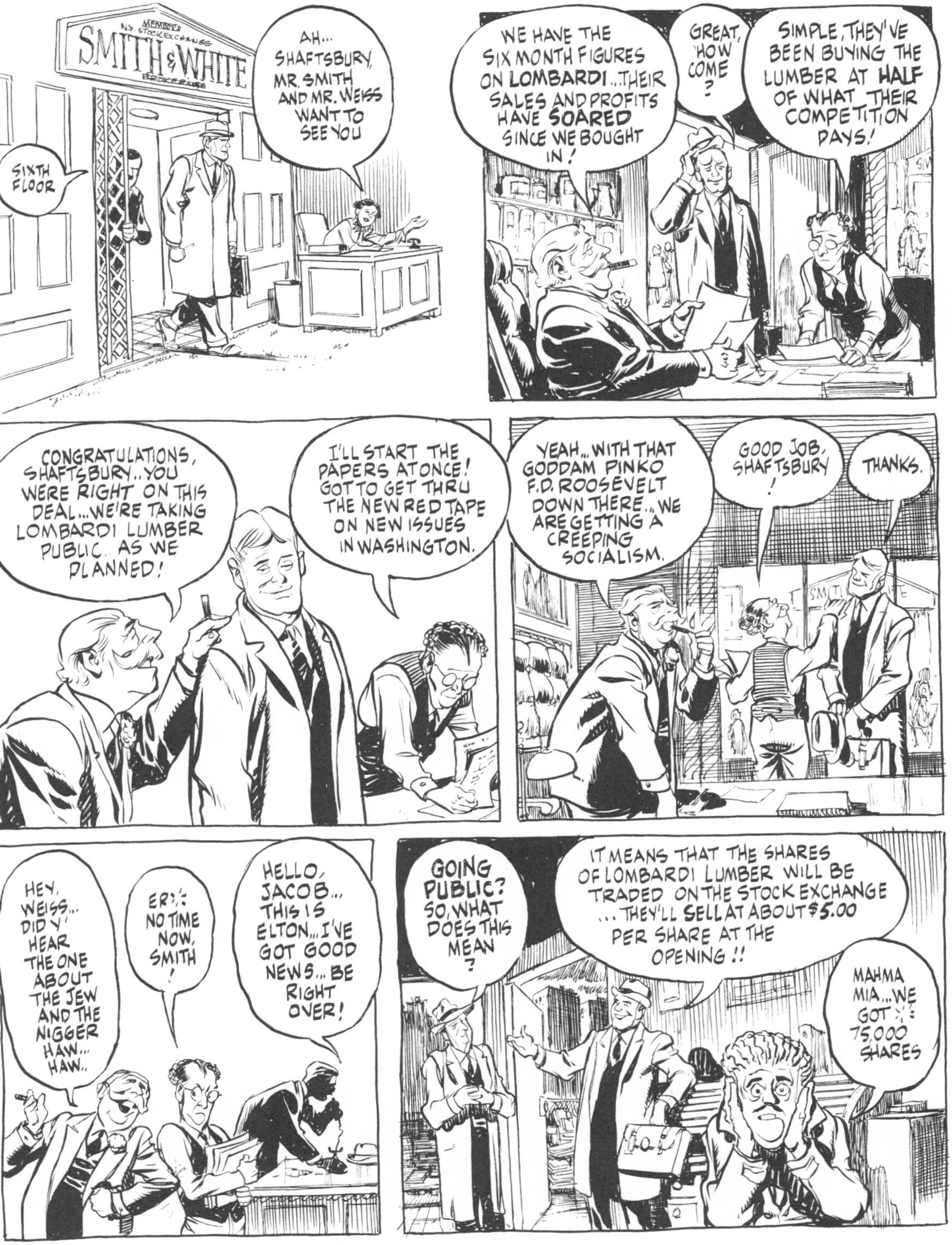
MEMBERS N.Y. STOCK EXCHANGE
SMITH & WHITE
BROKERAGE
SIXTH FLOOR
AH... SHAFTSBURY, MR. SMITH AND MR. WEISS WANT TO SEE YOU
WE HAVE THE SIX MONTH FIGURES ON LOMBARDI...THEIR SALES AND PROFITS HAVE SOARED SINCE WE BOUGHT IN!
GREAT, HOW COME?
SIMPLE, THEY'VE BEEN BUYING THE LUMBER AT HALF OF WHAT THEIR COMPETITION PAYS!
CONGRATULATIONS, SHAFTSBURY..YOU WERE RIGHT ON THIS DEAL...WE'RE TAKING LOMBARDI LUMBER PUBLIC.. AS WE PLANNED!
I'LL START THE PAPERS AT ONCE! GOT TO GET THRU THE NEW RED TAPE ON NEW ISSUES IN WASHINGTON.
YEAH... WITH THAT GODDAM PINKO F.D. ROOSEVELT DOWN THERE... WE ARE GETTING A CREEPING SOCIALISM.
GOOD JOB, SHAFTSBURY!
THANKS.
HEY, WEISS... DID Y' HEAR THE ONE ABOUT THE JEW AND THE NIGGER HAW... HAW..
ER... NO TIME NOW, SMITH!
HELLO, JACOB... THIS IS ELTON... I'VE GOT GOOD NEWS... BE RIGHT OVER!
GOING PUBLIC? SO, WHAT DOES THIS MEAN?
IT MEANS THAT THE SHARES OF LOMBARDI LUMBER WILL BE TRADED ON THE STOCK EXCHANGE ... THEY'LL SELL AT ABOUT $5.00 PER SHARE AT THE OPENING!!
MAHMA MIA... WE GOT... 75,000 SHARES

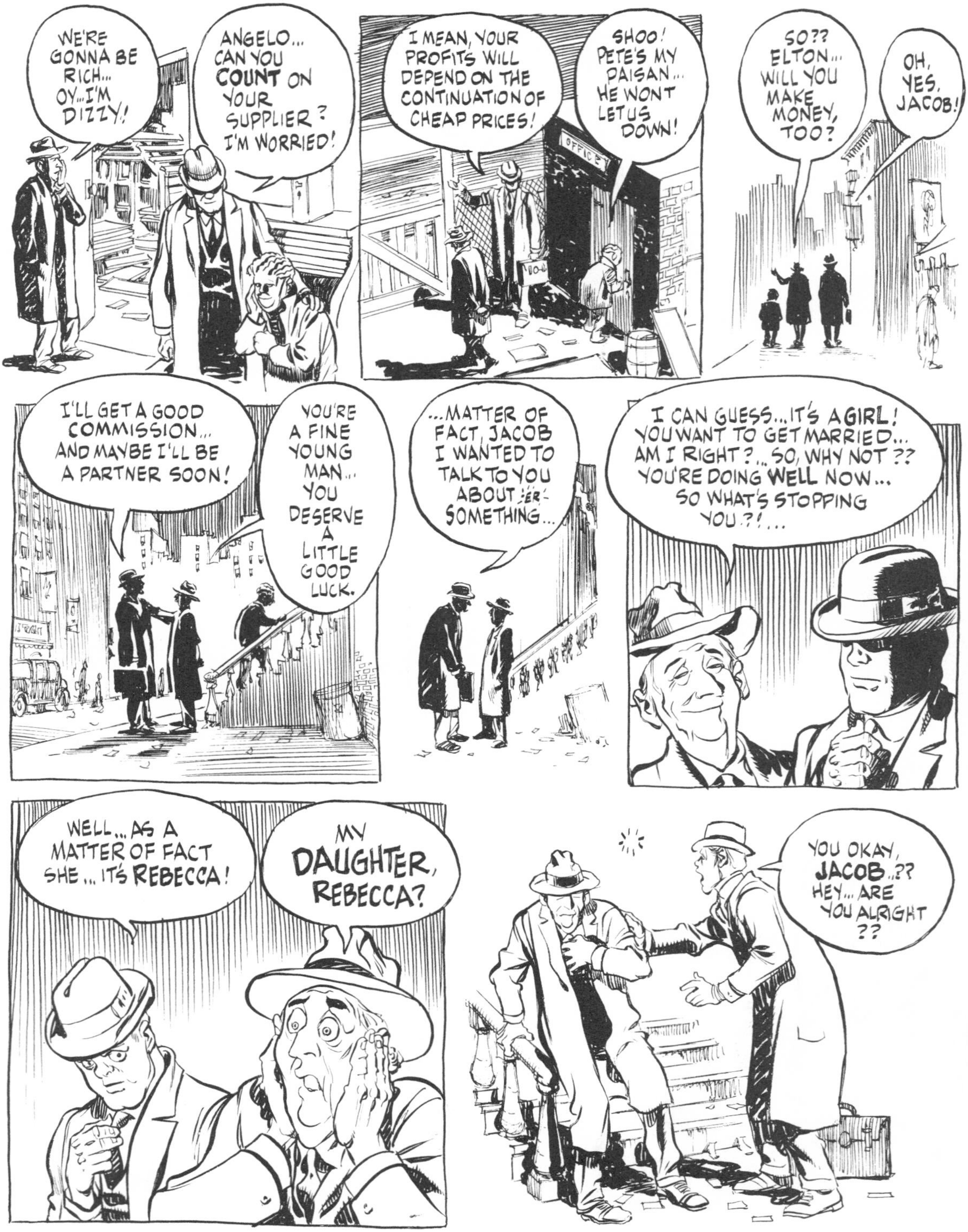
WE'RE GONNA BE RICH... OY...I'M DIZZY!
ANGELO... CAN YOU COUNT ON YOUR SUPPLIER? I'M WORRIED!
I MEAN, YOUR PROFITS WILL DEPEND ON THE CONTINUATION OF CHEAP PRICES!
SHOO! PETE'S MY PAISAN... HE WONT LET US DOWN!
OFFICE
SO?? ELTON... WILL YOU MAKE MONEY, TOO?
OH, YES, JACOB!
I'LL GET A GOOD COMMISSION... AND MAYBE I'LL BE A PARTNER SOON!
YOU'RE A FINE YOUNG MAN... YOU DESERVE A LITTLE GOOD LUCK.
...MATTER OF FACT, JACOB I WANTED TO TALK TO YOU ABOUT -ER- SOMETHING...
I CAN GUESS... IT'S A GIRL! YOU WANT TO GET MARRIED... AM I RIGHT?... SO, WHY NOT?? YOU'RE DOING WELL NOW... SO WHAT'S STOPPING YOU?!...
WELL... AS A MATTER OF FACT SHE... IT'S REBECCA!
MY DAUGHTER, REBECCA?
YOU OKAY, JACOB..?? HEY... ARE YOU ALRIGHT??

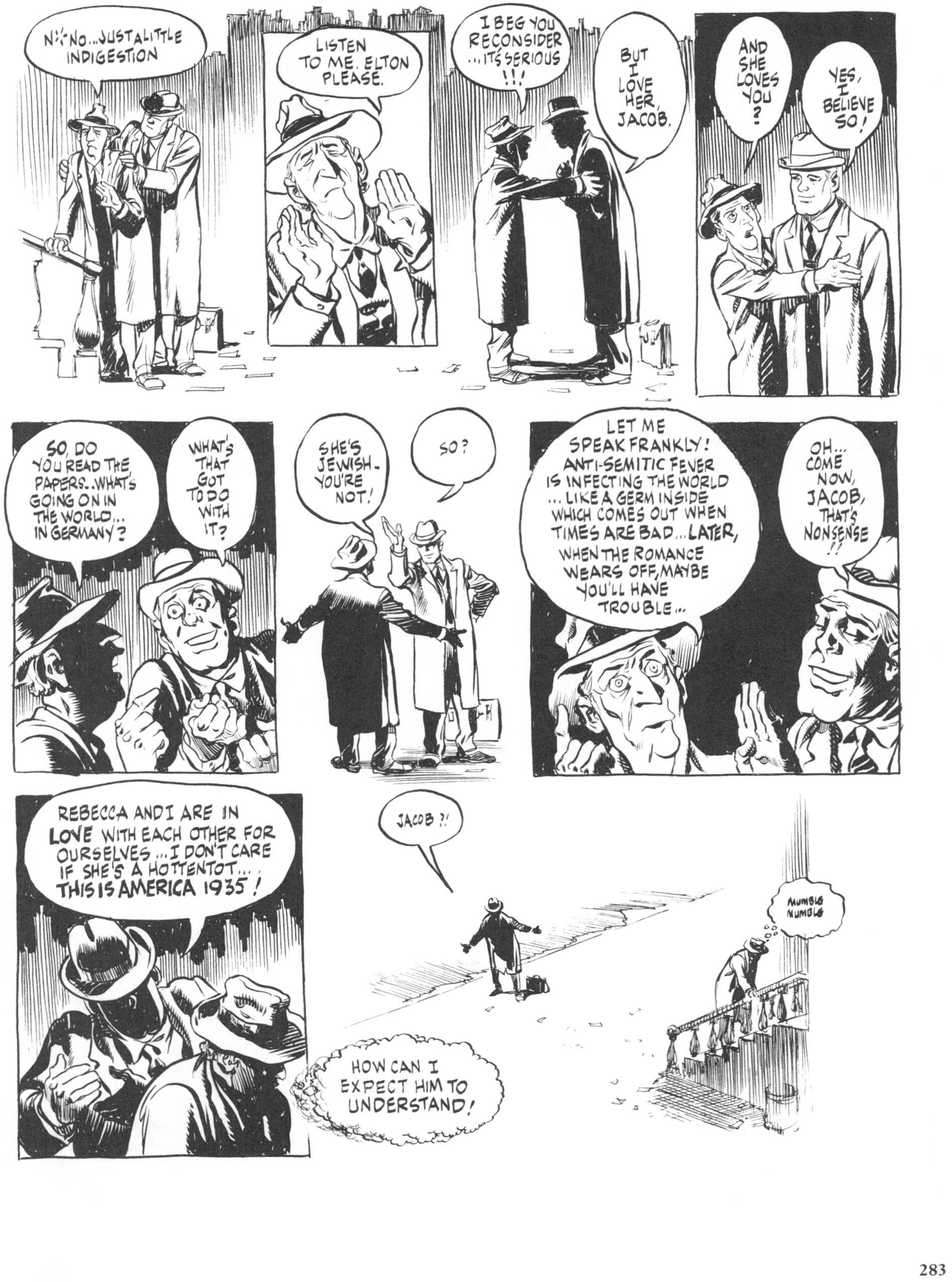
N-NO...JUST A LITTLE INDIGESTION
LISTEN TO ME, ELTON PLEASE.
I BEG YOU RECONSIDER ...IT'S SERIOUS !!!
BUT I LOVE HER, JACOB.
AND SHE LOVES YOU ?
YES, I BELIEVE SO!
SO, DO YOU READ THE PAPERS.. WHAT'S GOING ON IN THE WORLD... IN GERMANY?
WHAT'S THAT GOT TO DO WITH IT?
SHE'S JEWISH - YOU'RE NOT!
SO?
LET ME SPEAK FRANKLY! ANTI-SEMITIC FEVER IS INFECTING THE WORLD ... LIKE A GERM INSIDE WHICH COMES OUT WHEN TIMES ARE BAD... LATER, WHEN THE ROMANCE WEARS OFF, MAYBE YOU'LL HAVE TROUBLE...
OH... COME NOW, JACOB, THAT'S NONSENSE !!
REBECCA AND I ARE IN LOVE WITH EACH OTHER FOR OURSELVES ...I DON'T CARE IF SHE'S A HOTTENTOT... THIS IS AMERICA 1935!
JACOB ?!
MUMBLE MUMBLE
HOW CAN I EXPECT HIM TO UNDERSTAND!

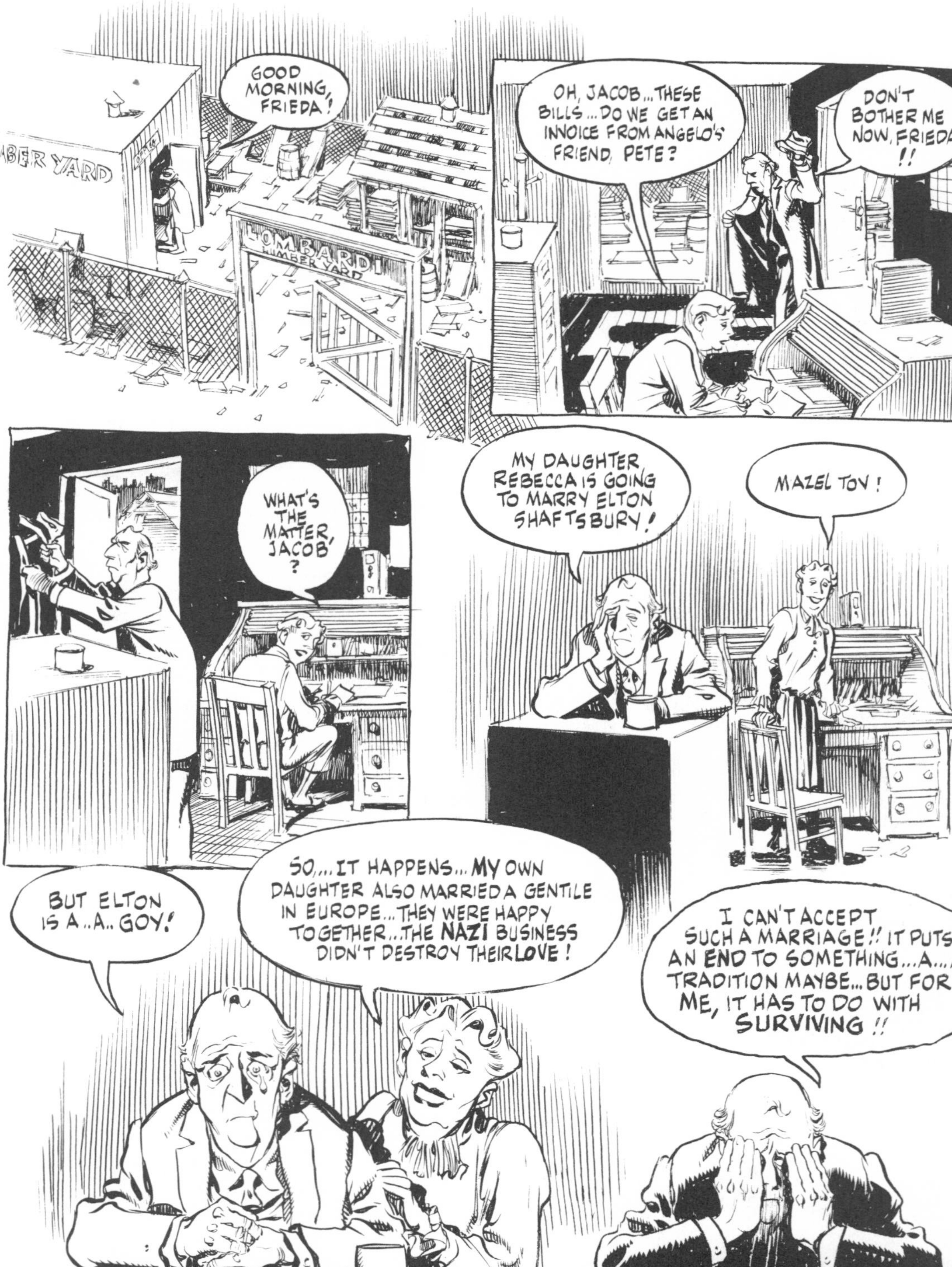

GOOD MORNING, FRIEDA!
BER YARD
LOMBARDI LUMBER YARD
OH, JACOB... THESE BILLS... DO WE GET AN INVOICE FROM ANGELO'S FRIEND, PETE?
DON'T BOTHER ME NOW, FRIEDA!!
WHAT'S THE MATTER, JACOB?
MY DAUGHTER REBECCA IS GOING TO MARRY ELTON SHAFTSBURY!
MAZEL TOV!
BUT ELTON IS A..A.. GOY!
SO,... IT HAPPENS... MY OWN DAUGHTER ALSO MARRIED A GENTILE IN EUROPE... THEY WERE HAPPY TOGETHER... THE NAZI BUSINESS DIDN'T DESTROY THEIR LOVE!
I CAN'T ACCEPT SUCH A MARRIAGE!! IT PUTS AN END TO SOMETHING... A... A TRADITION MAYBE... BUT FOR ME, IT HAS TO DO WITH SURVIVING!!

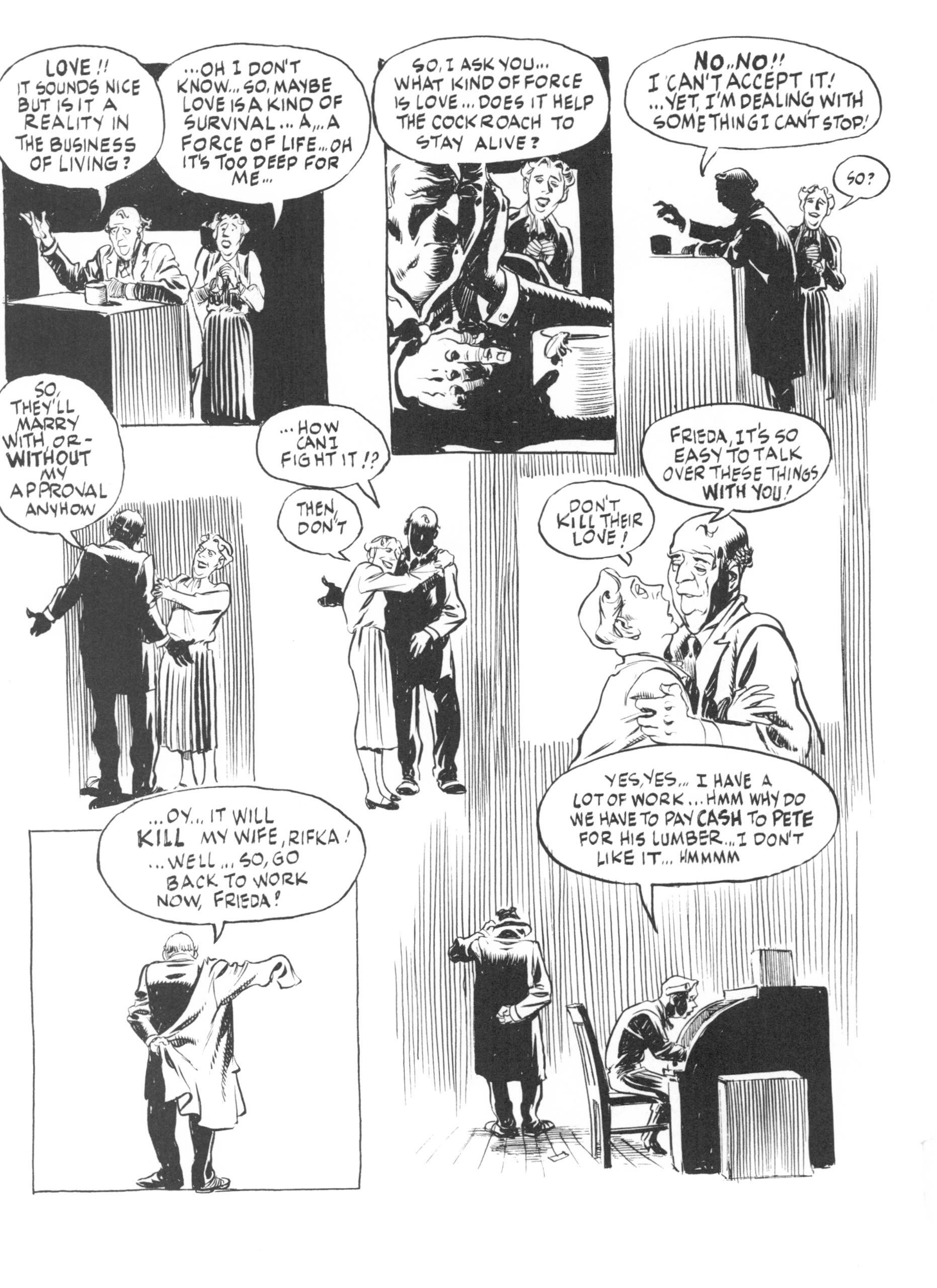
LOVE!! IT SOUNDS NICE BUT IS IT A REALITY IN THE BUSINESS OF LIVING?
...OH I DON'T KNOW... SO, MAYBE LOVE IS A KIND OF SURVIVAL... A,.. A FORCE OF LIFE... OH IT'S TOO DEEP FOR ME...
SO, I ASK YOU... WHAT KIND OF FORCE IS LOVE... DOES IT HELP THE COCKROACH TO STAY ALIVE?
NO..NO!! I CAN'T ACCEPT IT! ...YET, I'M DEALING WITH SOMETHING I CAN'T STOP!
SO?
SO, THEY'LL MARRY WITH, OR- WITHOUT MY APPROVAL ANYHOW
...HOW CAN I FIGHT IT!?
THEN, DON'T
FRIEDA, IT'S SO EASY TO TALK OVER THESE THINGS WITH YOU!
DON'T KILL THEIR LOVE!
...OY.. IT WILL KILL MY WIFE, RIFKA! ...WELL... SO, GO BACK TO WORK NOW, FRIEDA!
YES, YES... I HAVE A LOT OF WORK... HMM WHY DO WE HAVE TO PAY CASH TO PETE FOR HIS LUMBER... I DON'T LIKE IT... HMMMM

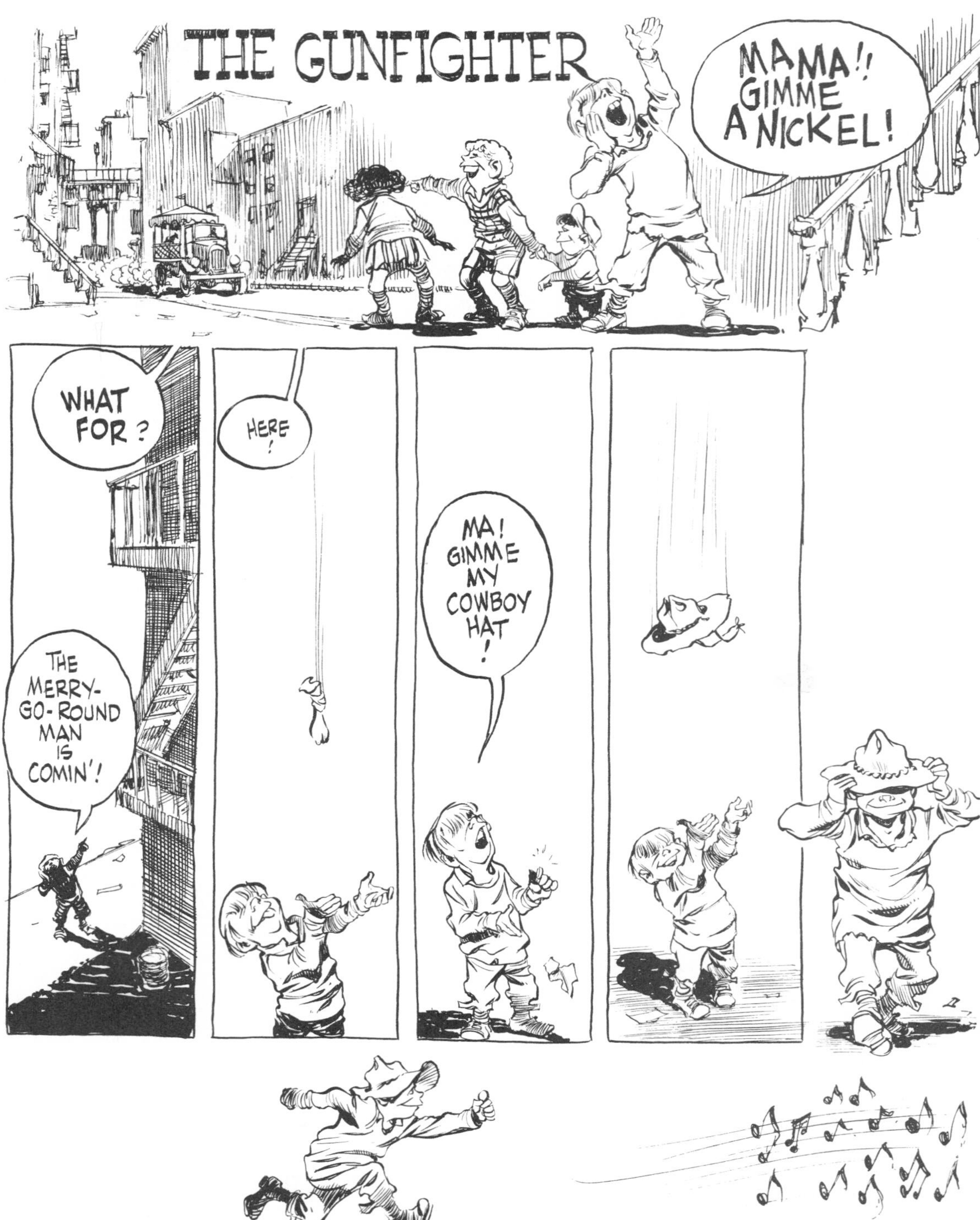
THE GUNFIGHTER
MAMA!! GIMME A NICKEL!
WHAT FOR?
THE MERRY-GO-ROUND MAN IS COMIN'!
HERE!
MA! GIMME MY COWBOY HAT!

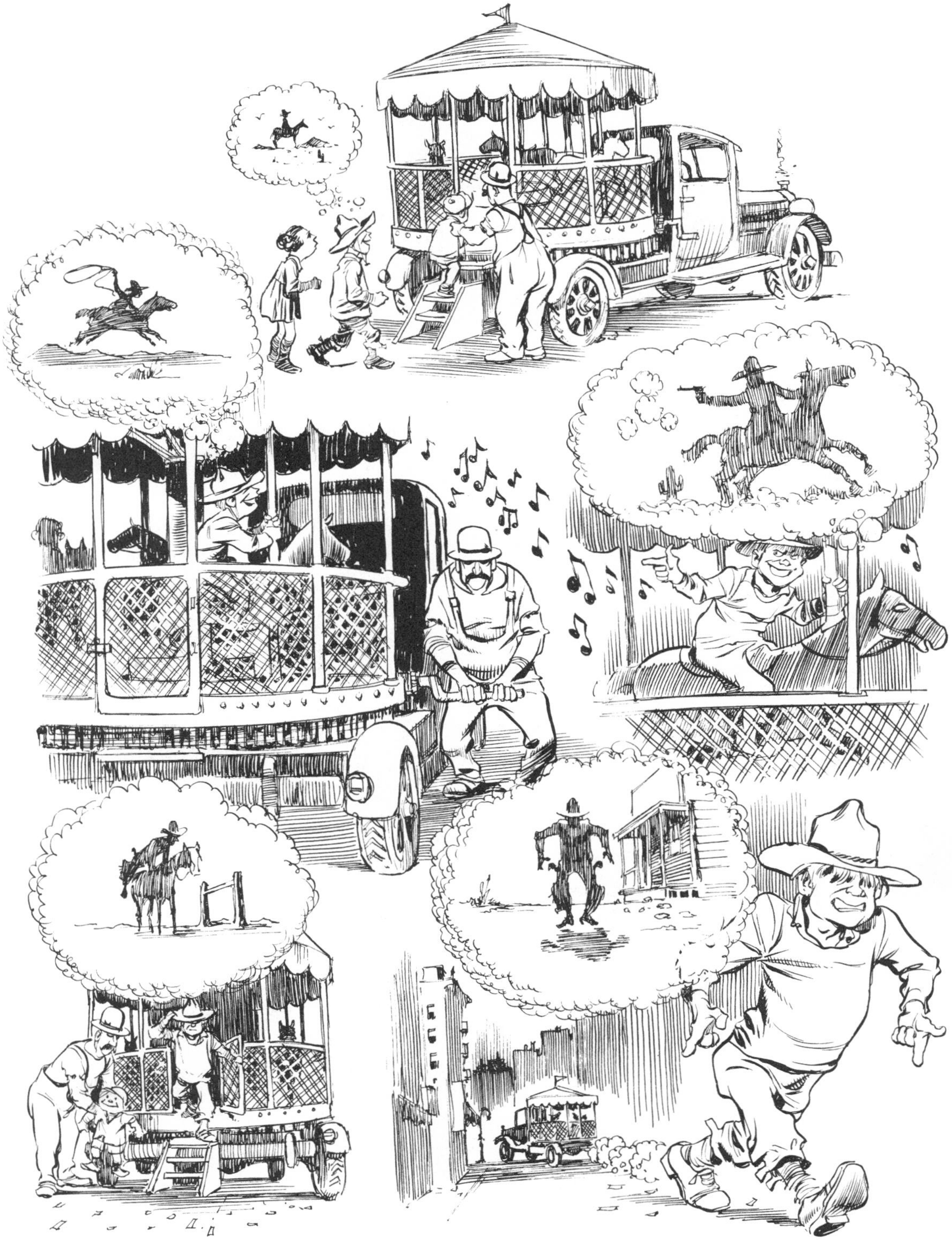

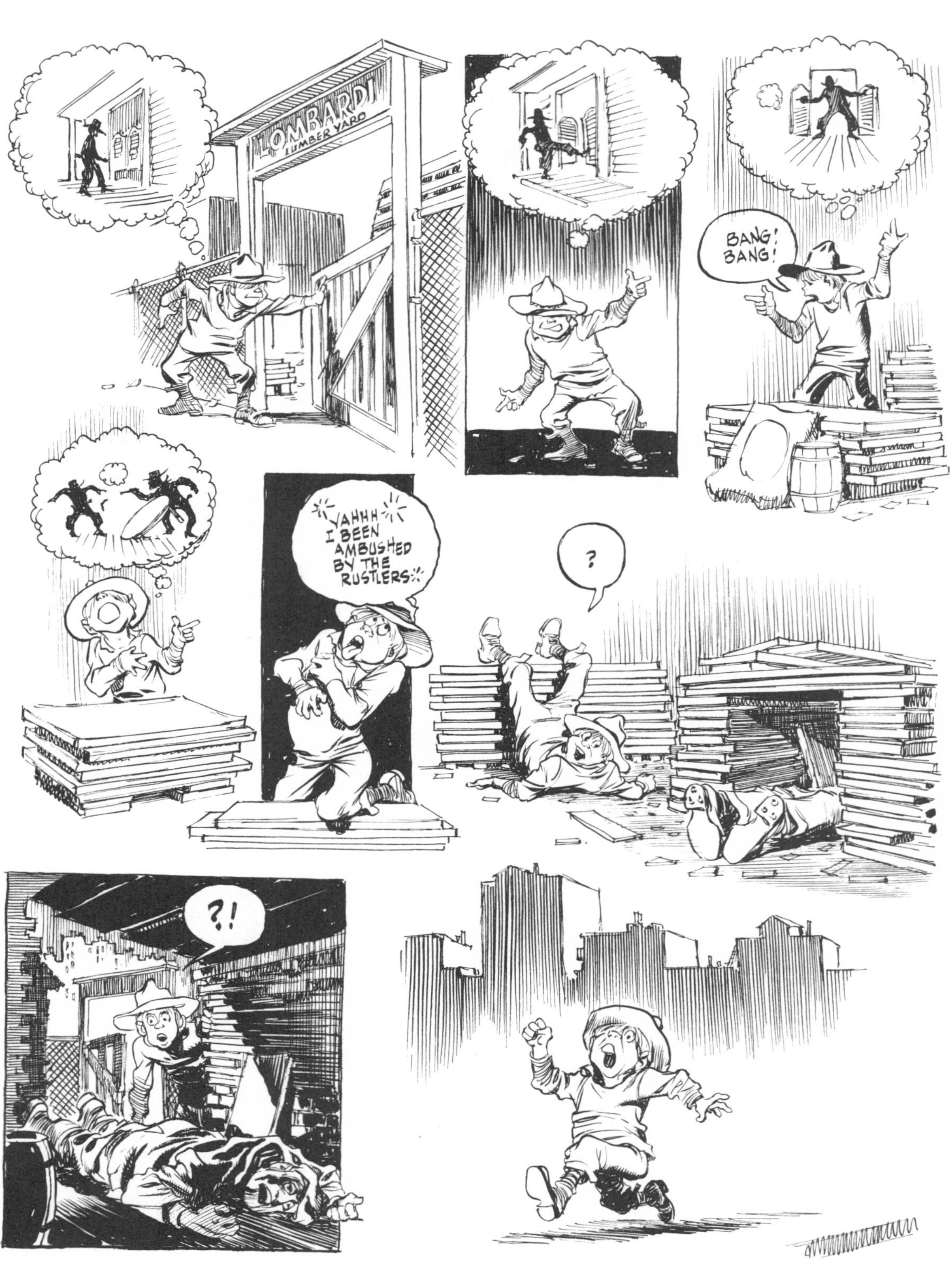
LOMBARDI
LUMBER YARD
BANG! BANG!
YAHHH I BEEN AMBUSHED BY THE RUSTLERS
?
?!

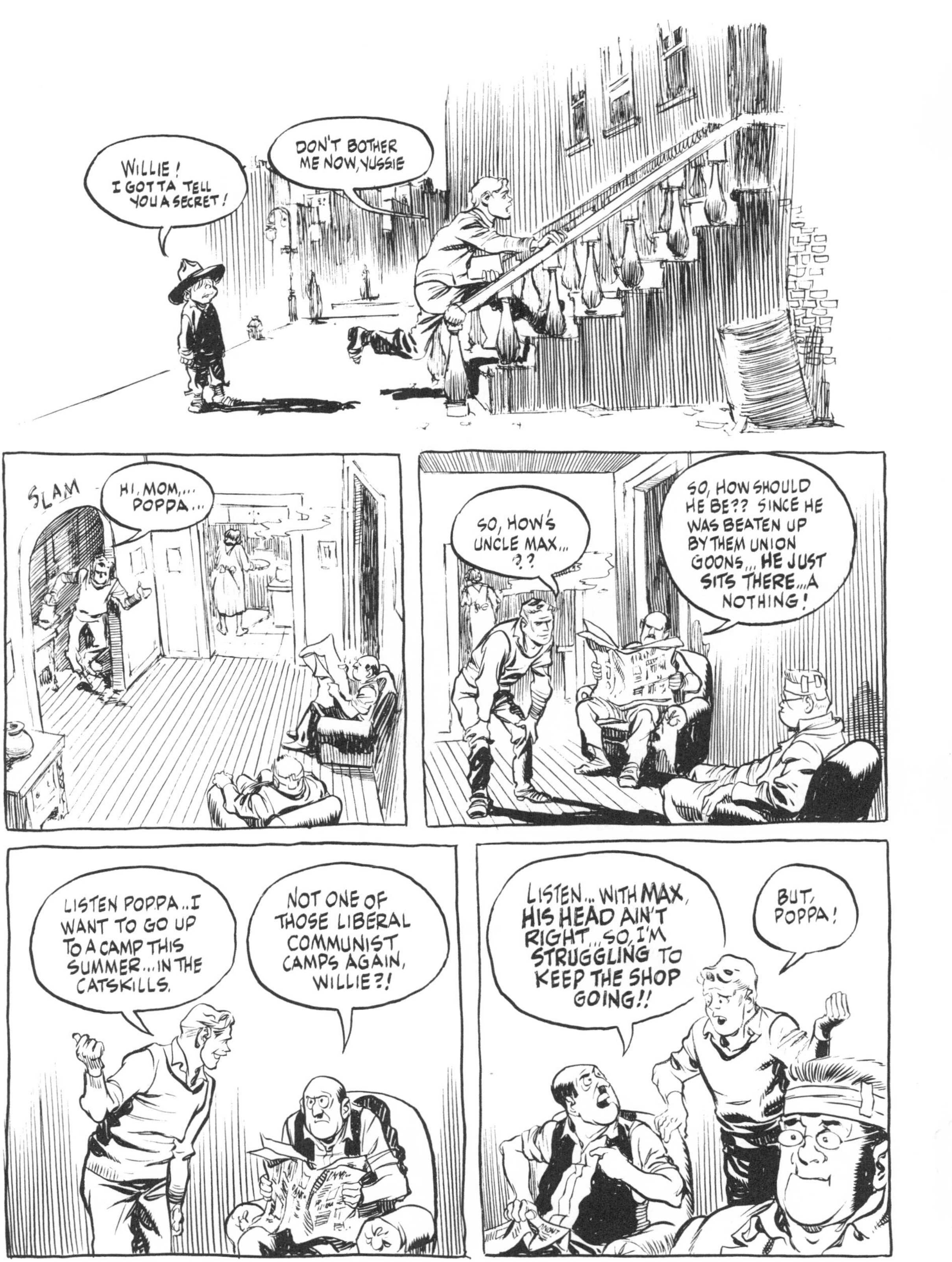
WILLIE! I GOTTA TELL YOU A SECRET!
DON'T BOTHER ME NOW, YUSSIE
SLAM
HI, MOM,... POPPA...
SO, HOW'S UNCLE MAX... ??
SO, HOW SHOULD HE BE?? SINCE HE WAS BEATEN UP BY THEM UNION GOONS... HE JUST SITS THERE...A NOTHING!
LISTEN POPPA..I WANT TO GO UP TO A CAMP THIS SUMMER...IN THE CATSKILLS.
NOT ONE OF THOSE LIBERAL COMMUNIST CAMPS AGAIN, WILLIE?!
LISTEN... WITH MAX, HIS HEAD AIN'T RIGHT...SO, I'M STRUGGLING TO KEEP THE SHOP GOING!!
BUT, POPPA!

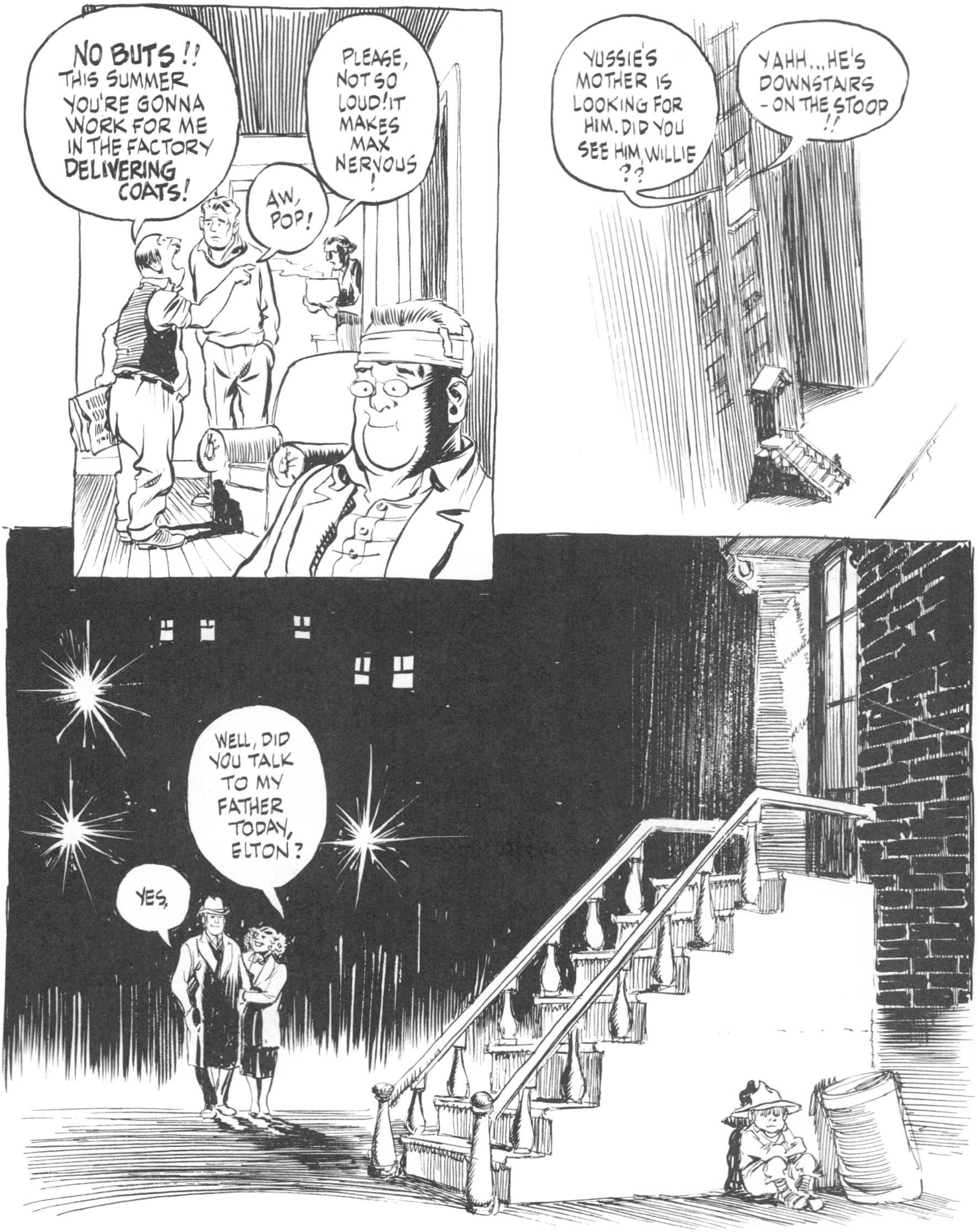
NO BUTS!! THIS SUMMER YOU'RE GONNA WORK FOR ME IN THE FACTORY DELIVERING COATS!
AW, POP!
PLEASE, NOT SO LOUD! IT MAKES MAX NERVOUS!
YUSSIE'S MOTHER IS LOOKING FOR HIM. DID YOU SEE HIM, WILLIE??
YAHH...HE'S DOWNSTAIRS - ON THE STOOP!!
WELL, DID YOU TALK TO MY FATHER TODAY, ELTON?
YES.

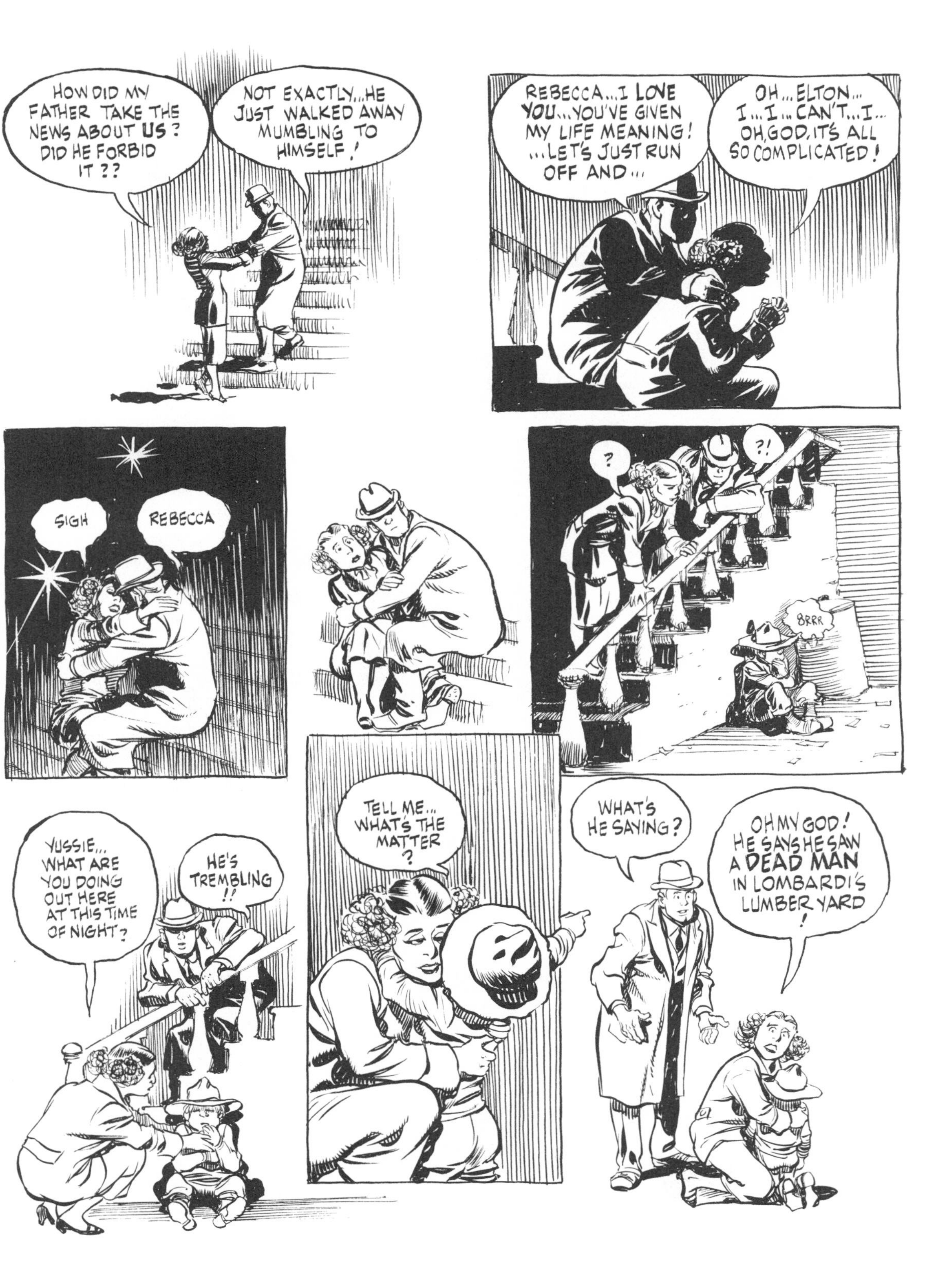
HOW DID MY FATHER TAKE THE NEWS ABOUT US? DID HE FORBID IT??
NOT EXACTLY...HE JUST WALKED AWAY MUMBLING TO HIMSELF!
REBECCA...I LOVE YOU...YOU'VE GIVEN MY LIFE MEANING! ...LET'S JUST RUN OFF AND...
OH...ELTON... I...I...CAN'T...I... OH,GOD,IT'S ALL SO COMPLICATED!
SIGH
REBECCA
?
?!
BRRR
YUSSIE... WHAT ARE YOU DOING OUT HERE AT THIS TIME OF NIGHT?
HE'S TREMBLING!!
TELL ME... WHAT'S THE MATTER?
WHAT'S HE SAYING?
OH MY GOD! HE SAYS HE SAW A DEAD MAN IN LOMBARDI'S LUMBER YARD!

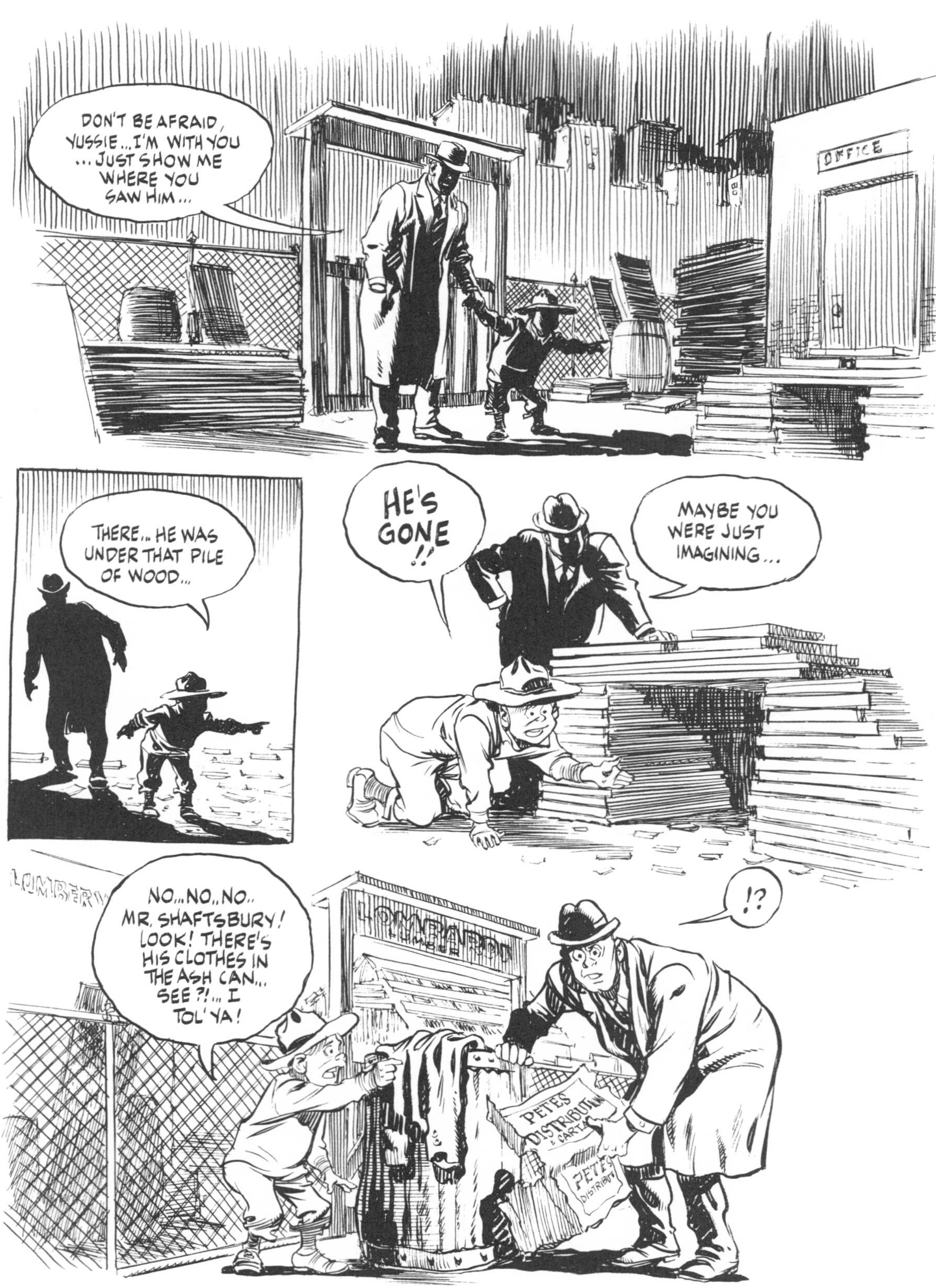
DON'T BE AFRAID, YUSSIE... I'M WITH YOU ... JUST SHOW ME WHERE YOU SAW HIM...
OFFICE
THERE.. HE WAS UNDER THAT PILE OF WOOD...
HE'S GONE !!
MAYBE YOU WERE JUST IMAGINING...
NO.. NO.. NO.. MR. SHAFTSBURY! LOOK! THERE'S HIS CLOTHES IN THE ASH CAN... SEE ?!... I TOL'YA!
!?

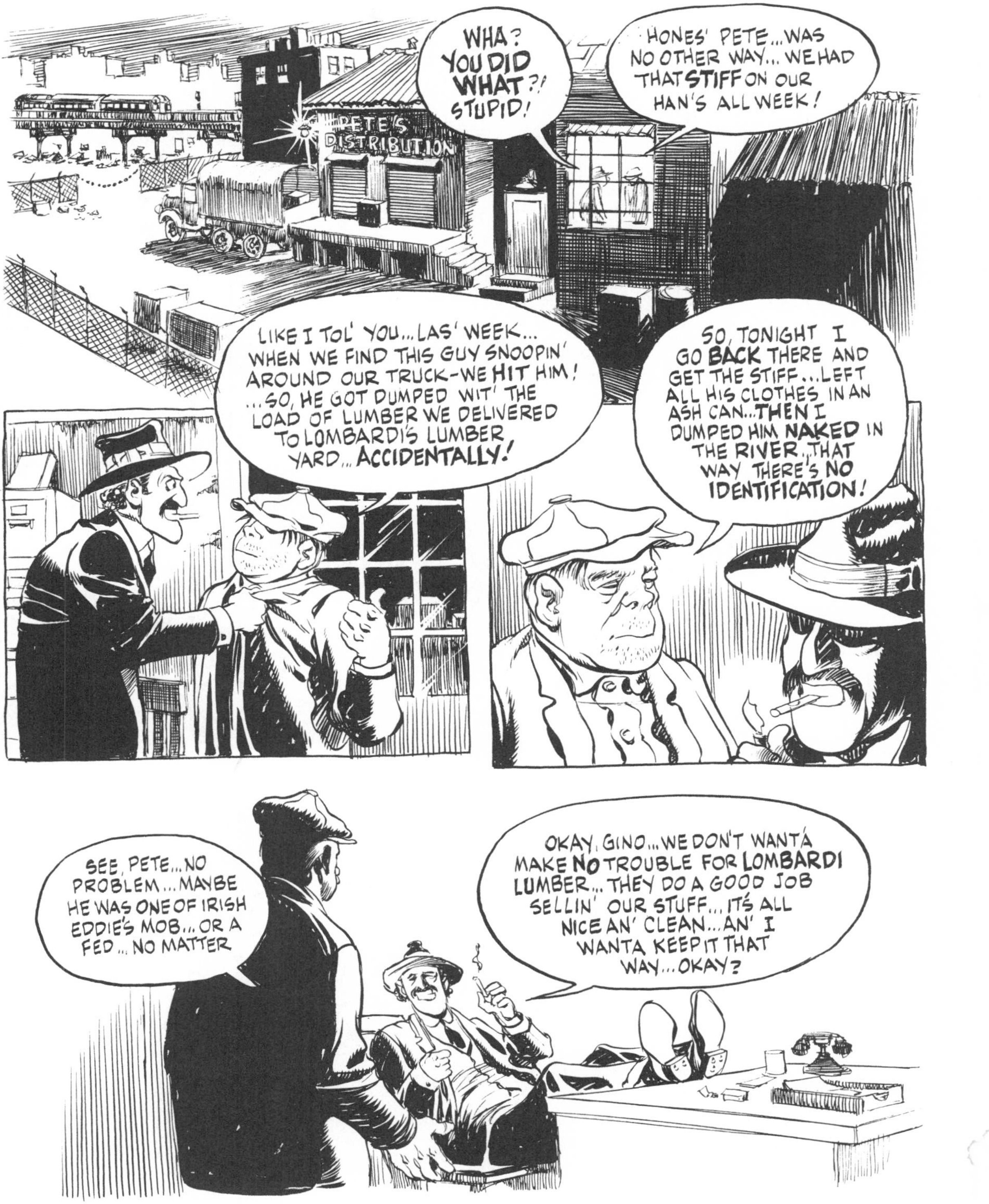
PETE'S DISTRIBUTION
WHA? YOU DID WHAT?! STUPID!
HONES' PETE...WAS NO OTHER WAY... WE HAD THAT STIFF ON OUR HAN'S ALL WEEK!
LIKE I TOL' YOU... LAS' WEEK... WHEN WE FIND THIS GUY SNOOPIN' AROUND OUR TRUCK-WE HIT HIM! ...SO, HE GOT DUMPED WIT' THE LOAD OF LUMBER WE DELIVERED TO LOMBARDI'S LUMBER YARD... ACCIDENTALLY!
SO, TONIGHT I GO BACK THERE AND GET THE STIFF...LEFT ALL HIS CLOTHES IN AN ASH CAN...THEN I DUMPED HIM NAKED IN THE RIVER, THAT WAY THERE'S NO IDENTIFICATION!
SEE, PETE...NO PROBLEM...MAYBE HE WAS ONE OF IRISH EDDIE'S MOB...OR A FED... NO MATTER
OKAY, GINO...WE DON'T WANT'A MAKE NO TROUBLE FOR LOMBARDI LUMBER... THEY DO A GOOD JOB SELLIN' OUR STUFF... IT'S ALL NICE AN' CLEAN... AN' I WANTA KEEP IT THAT WAY...OKAY?

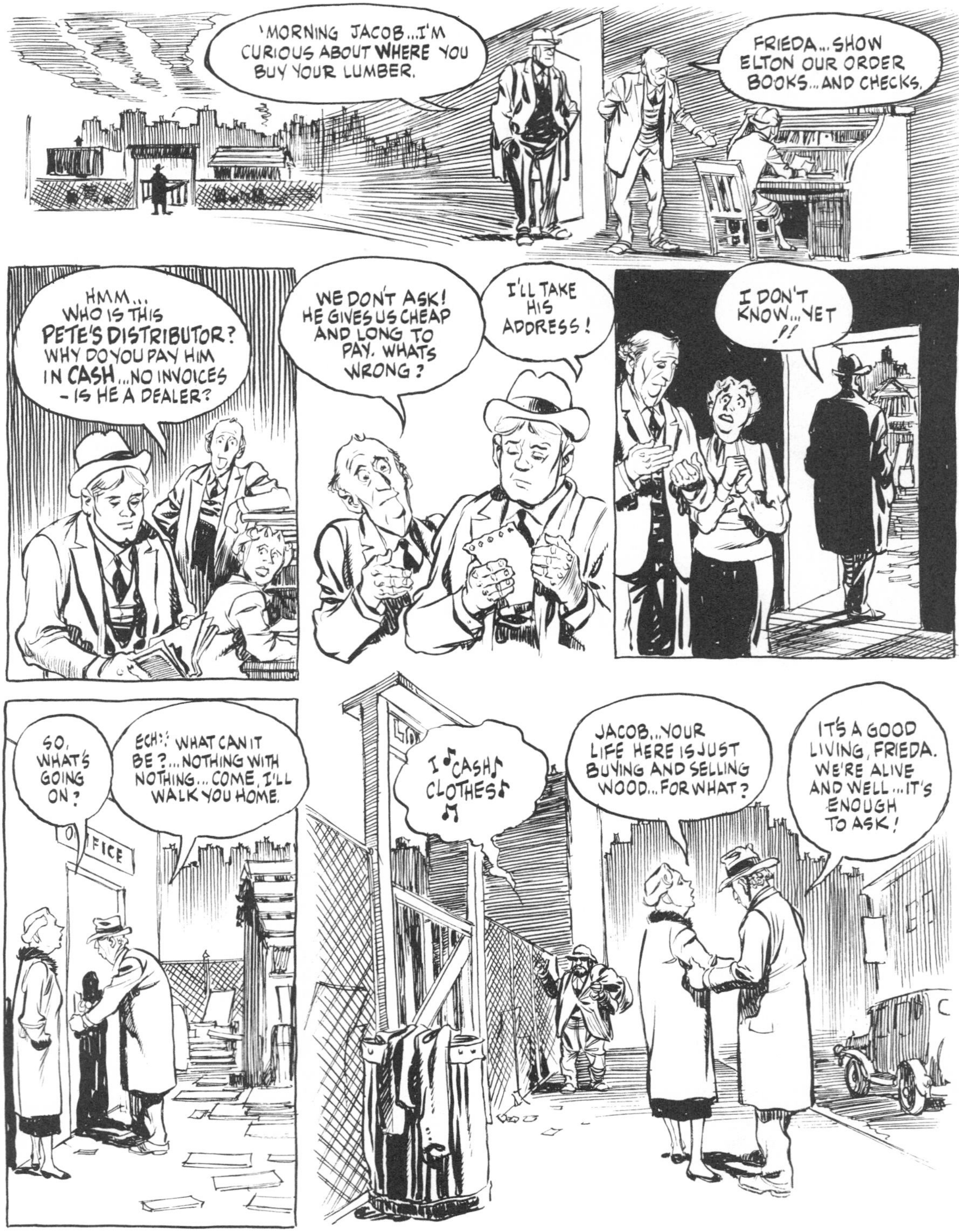
'MORNING JACOB...I'M CURIOUS ABOUT WHERE YOU BUY YOUR LUMBER.
FRIEDA...SHOW ELTON OUR ORDER BOOKS...AND CHECKS.
HMM... WHO IS THIS PETE'S DISTRIBUTOR? WHY DO YOU PAY HIM IN CASH...NO INVOICES – IS HE A DEALER?
WE DON'T ASK! HE GIVES US CHEAP AND LONG TO PAY. WHATS WRONG?
I'LL TAKE HIS ADDRESS!
I DON'T KNOW...YET
!!
SO, WHAT'S GOING ON?
ECH!! WHAT CAN IT BE?...NOTHING WITH NOTHING...COME, I'LL WALK YOU HOME.
OFFICE
I CASH CLOTHES
JACOB...YOUR LIFE HERE IS JUST BUYING AND SELLING WOOD...FOR WHAT?
IT'S A GOOD LIVING, FRIEDA. WE'RE ALIVE AND WELL...IT'S ENOUGH TO ASK!

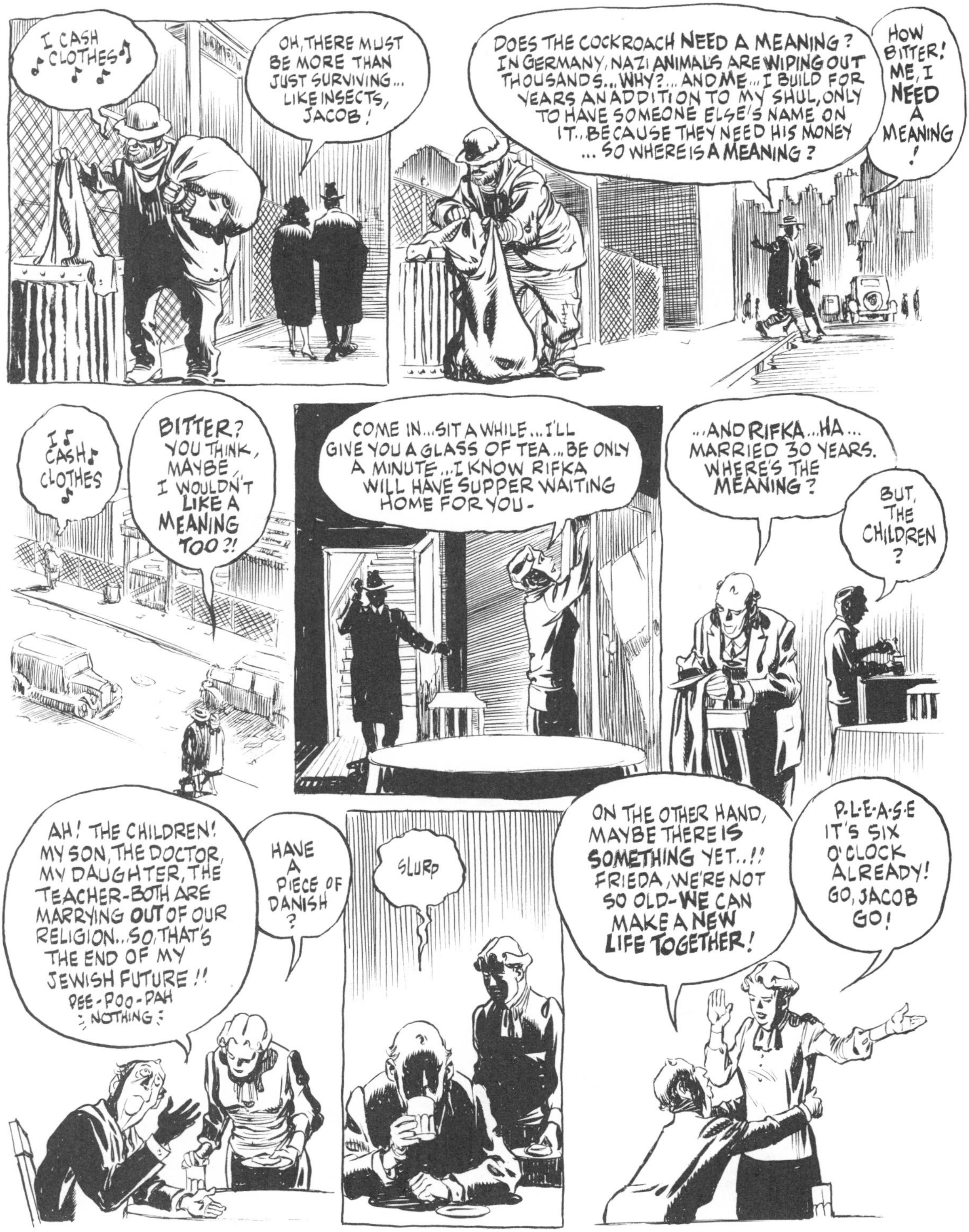

I CASH CLOTHES
OH, THERE MUST BE MORE THAN JUST SURVIVING... LIKE INSECTS, JACOB!
DOES THE COCKROACH NEED A MEANING? IN GERMANY, NAZI ANIMALS ARE WIPING OUT THOUSANDS... WHY?... AND ME... I BUILD FOR YEARS AN ADDITION TO MY SHUL, ONLY TO HAVE SOMEONE ELSE'S NAME ON IT.. BECAUSE THEY NEED HIS MONEY ... SO WHERE IS A MEANING?
HOW BITTER! ME, I NEED A MEANING!
I CASH CLOTHES
BITTER? YOU THINK, MAYBE, I WOULDN'T LIKE A MEANING TOO?!
COME IN... SIT A WHILE... I'LL GIVE YOU A GLASS OF TEA... BE ONLY A MINUTE... I KNOW RIFKA WILL HAVE SUPPER WAITING HOME FOR YOU -
...AND RIFKA... HA... MARRIED 30 YEARS. WHERE'S THE MEANING?
BUT, THE CHILDREN?
AH! THE CHILDREN! MY SON, THE DOCTOR, MY DAUGHTER, THE TEACHER-BOTH ARE MARRYING OUT OF OUR RELIGION.. SO, THAT'S THE END OF MY JEWISH FUTURE!! PEE-POO-PAH NOTHING
HAVE A PIECE OF DANISH?
SLURP
ON THE OTHER HAND, MAYBE THERE IS SOMETHING YET..!! FRIEDA, WE'RE NOT SO OLD-WE CAN MAKE A NEW LIFE TOGETHER!
P.L.E.A.S.E IT'S SIX O'CLOCK ALREADY! GO, JACOB GO!

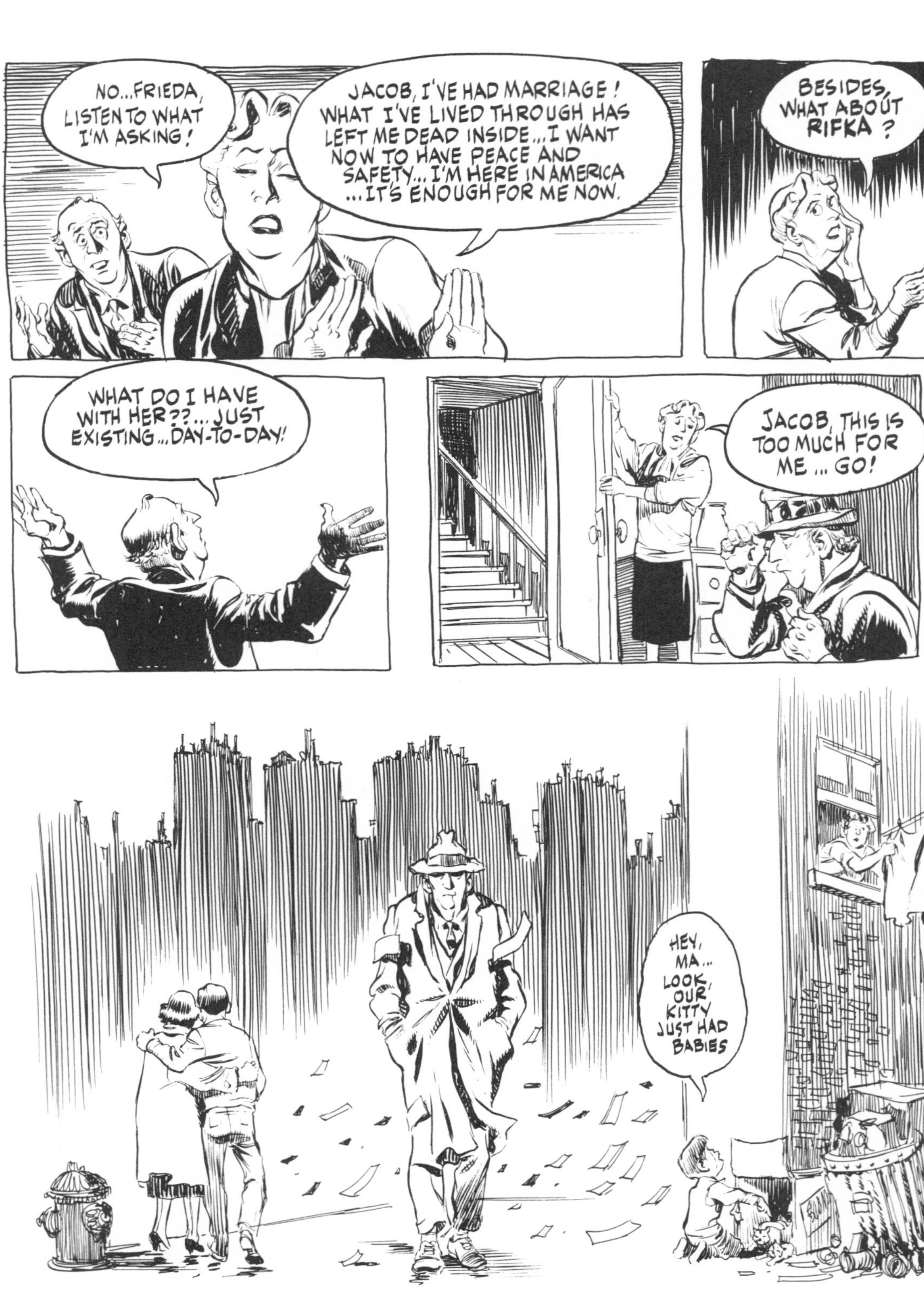
NO...FRIEDA, LISTEN TO WHAT I'M ASKING!
JACOB, I'VE HAD MARRIAGE! WHAT I'VE LIVED THROUGH HAS LEFT ME DEAD INSIDE... I WANT NOW TO HAVE PEACE AND SAFETY... I'M HERE IN AMERICA ... IT'S ENOUGH FOR ME NOW.
BESIDES, WHAT ABOUT RIFKA?
WHAT DO I HAVE WITH HER??... JUST EXISTING... DAY-TO-DAY!
JACOB, THIS IS TOO MUCH FOR ME ... GO!
HEY, MA... LOOK, OUR KITTY JUST HAD BABIES
114

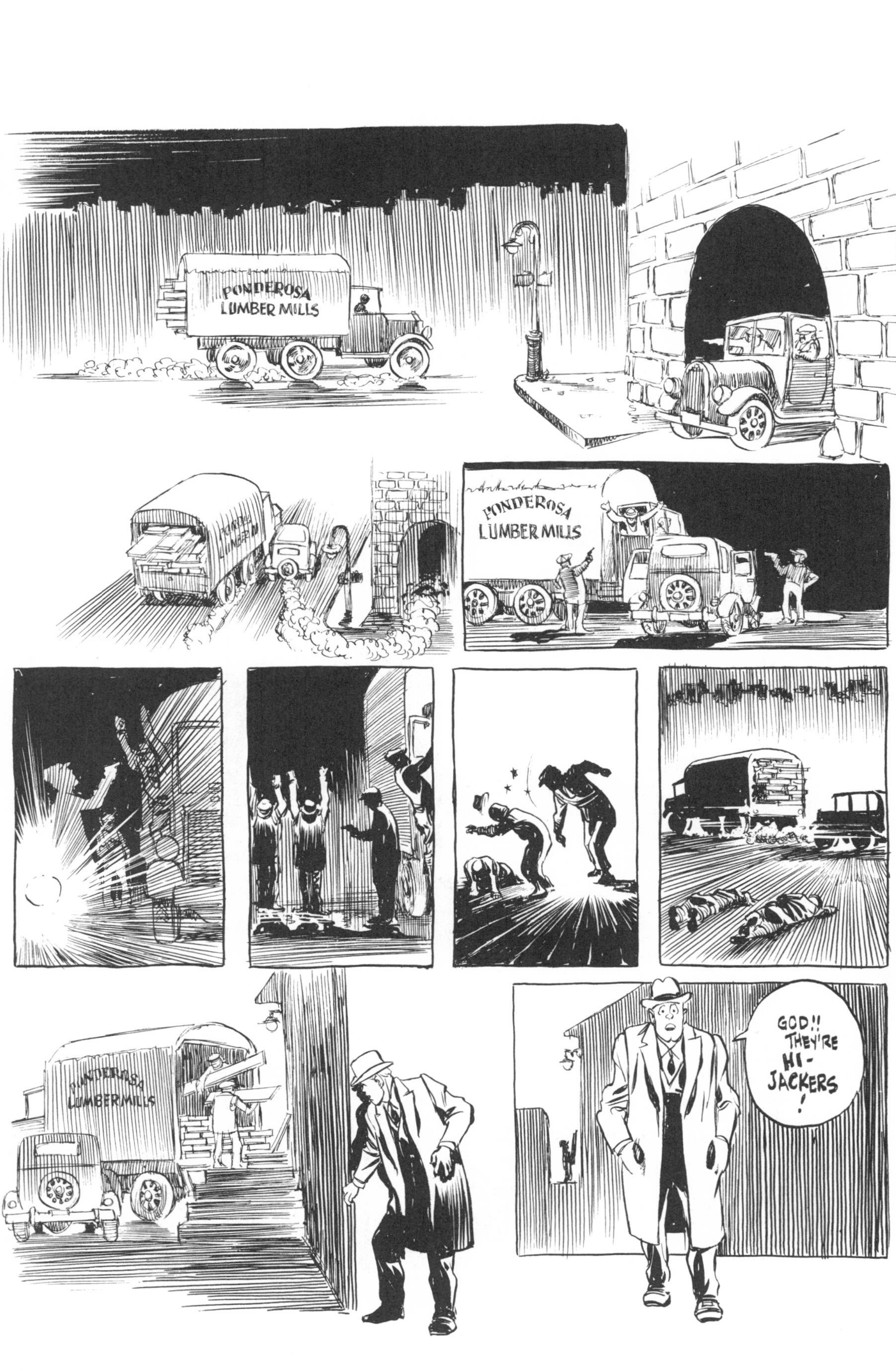
PONDEROSA
LUMBER MILLS
PONDEROSA
LUMBER MILLS
PONDEROSA
LUMBER MILLS
GOD!! THEY'RE HI-JACKERS!

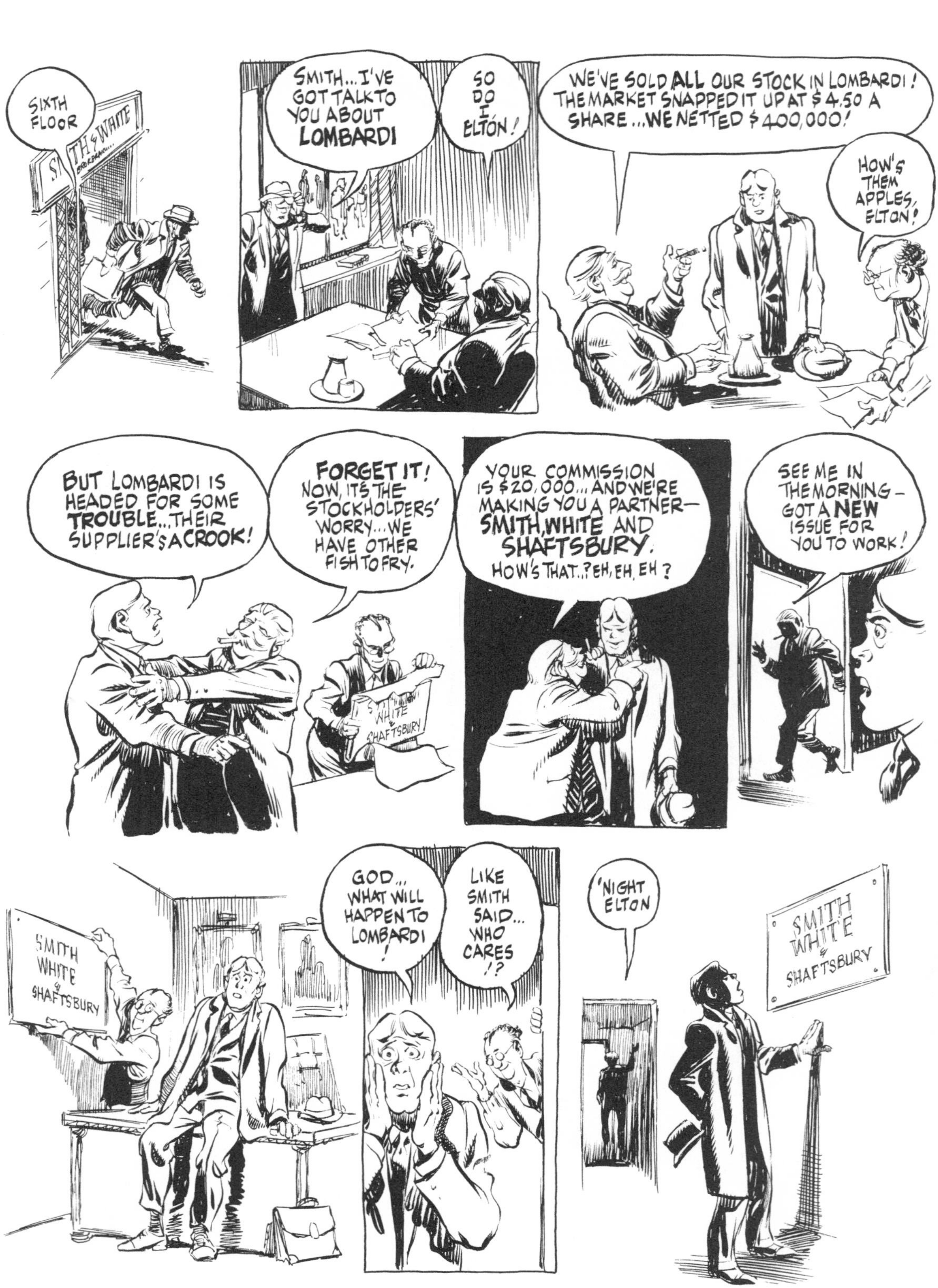

SIXTH FLOOR
SMITH & WHITE BROKERAGE
SMITH... I'VE GOT TALK TO YOU ABOUT LOMBARDI
SO DO I ELTON!
WE'VE SOLD ALL OUR STOCK IN LOMBARDI! THE MARKET SNAPPED IT UP AT $4.50 A SHARE... WE NETTED $400,000!
HOW'S THEM APPLES, ELTON!
BUT LOMBARDI IS HEADED FOR SOME TROUBLE... THEIR SUPPLIER'S A CROOK!
FORGET IT! NOW, IT'S THE STOCKHOLDERS' WORRY... WE HAVE OTHER FISH TO FRY.
SMITH WHITE & SHAFTSBURY
YOUR COMMISSION IS $20,000... AND WE'RE MAKING YOU A PARTNER— SMITH, WHITE AND SHAFTSBURY. HOW'S THAT..? EH, EH, EH?
SEE ME IN THE MORNING— GOT A NEW ISSUE FOR YOU TO WORK!
SMITH WHITE & SHAFTSBURY
GOD... WHAT WILL HAPPEN TO LOMBARDI!
LIKE SMITH SAID... WHO CARES!?
'NIGHT ELTON
SMITH WHITE & SHAFTSBURY

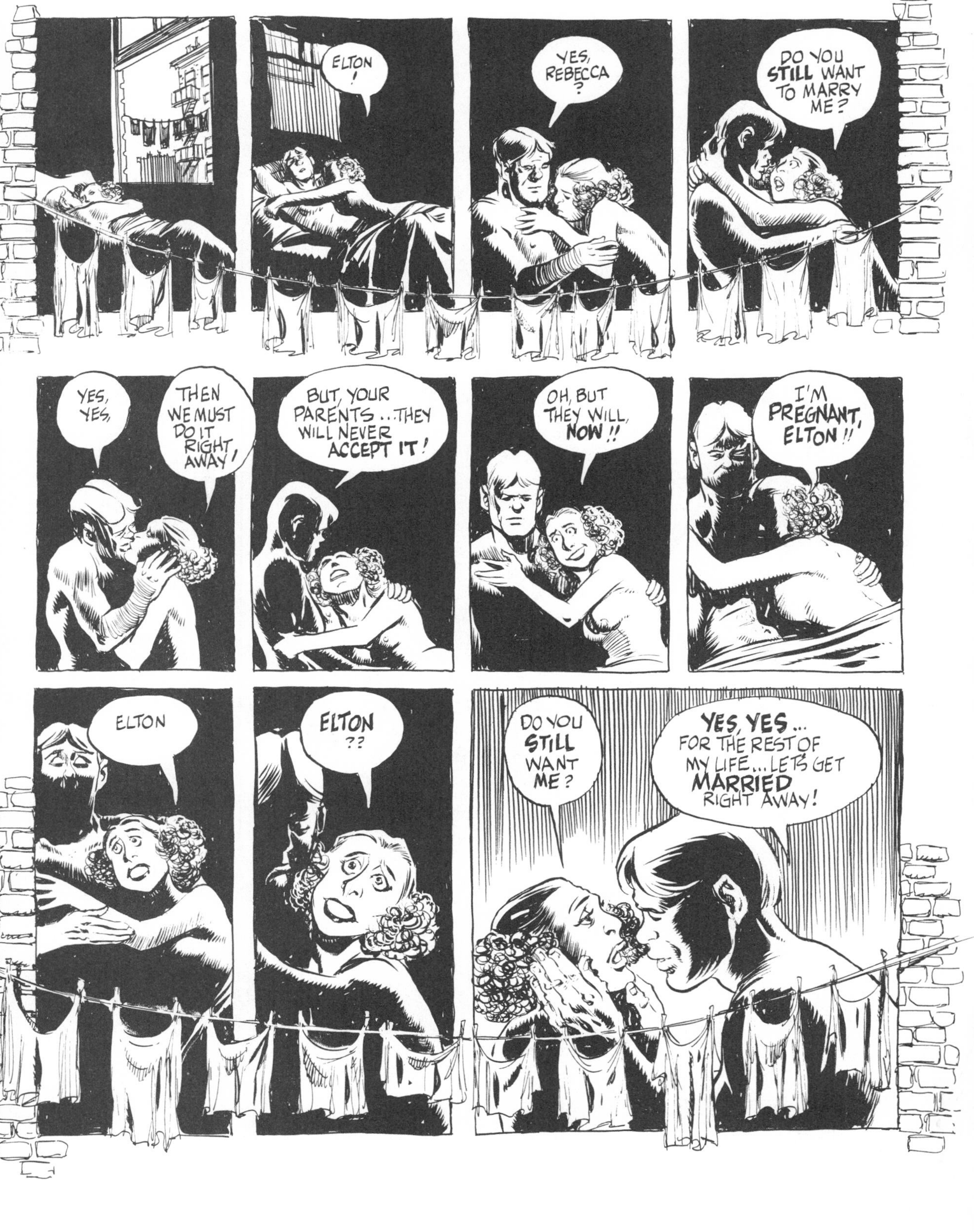
ELTON !
YES, REBECCA ?
DO YOU STILL WANT TO MARRY ME ?
YES, YES,
THEN WE MUST DO IT RIGHT AWAY !
BUT, YOUR PARENTS ... THEY WILL NEVER ACCEPT IT !
OH, BUT THEY WILL, NOW !!
I'M PREGNANT, ELTON !!
ELTON
ELTON ??
DO YOU STILL WANT ME ?
YES, YES ... FOR THE REST OF MY LIFE ... LET'S GET MARRIED RIGHT AWAY !

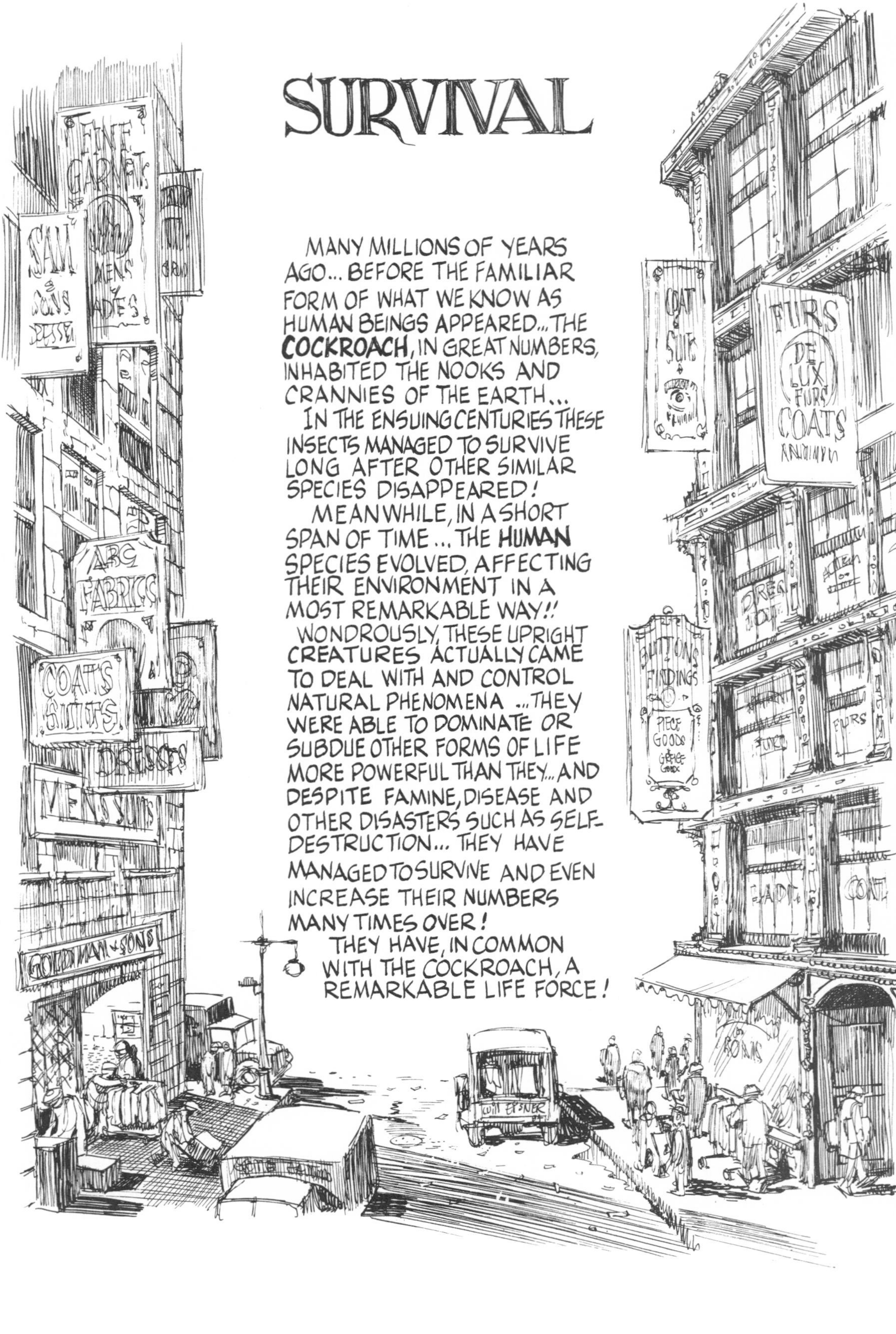
SURVIVAL
MANY MILLIONS OF YEARS AGO... BEFORE THE FAMILIAR FORM OF WHAT WE KNOW AS HUMAN BEINGS APPEARED... THE **COCKROACH**, IN GREAT NUMBERS, INHABITED THE NOOKS AND CRANNIES OF THE EARTH...
IN THE ENSUING CENTURIES THESE INSECTS MANAGED TO SURVIVE LONG AFTER OTHER SIMILAR SPECIES DISAPPEARED!
MEANWHILE, IN A SHORT SPAN OF TIME... THE **HUMAN** SPECIES EVOLVED, AFFECTING THEIR ENVIRONMENT IN A MOST REMARKABLE WAY!!
WONDROUSLY, THESE UPRIGHT CREATURES ACTUALLY CAME TO DEAL WITH AND CONTROL NATURAL PHENOMENA ...THEY WERE ABLE TO DOMINATE OR SUBDUE OTHER FORMS OF LIFE MORE POWERFUL THAN THEY... AND DESPITE FAMINE, DISEASE AND OTHER DISASTERS SUCH AS SELF-DESTRUCTION... THEY HAVE MANAGED TO SURVIVE AND EVEN INCREASE THEIR NUMBERS MANY TIMES OVER!
THEY HAVE, IN COMMON WITH THE COCKROACH, A REMARKABLE LIFE FORCE!
FINE GARMENTS
SAM & SONS
ABC FABRICS
COATS & SUITS
DRESSES
MENS SUITS
GOLDMAN & SONS
FURS DE LUX FURS COATS
COAT & SUITS
BUTTONS & FINDINGS
PIECE GOODS
FURS
WILL EISNER

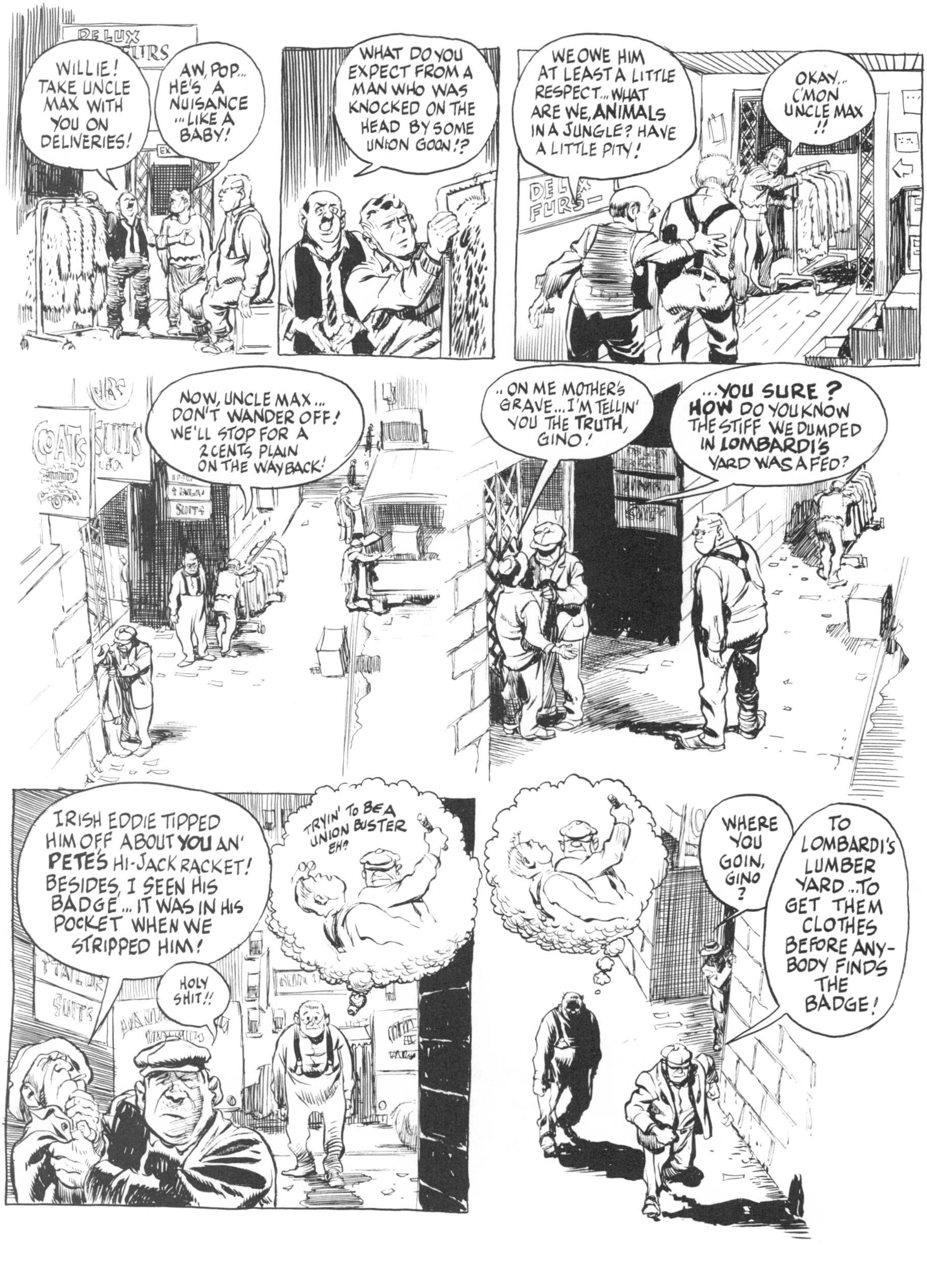
DE LUX FURS
WILLIE! TAKE UNCLE MAX WITH YOU ON DELIVERIES!
AW, POP... HE'S A NUISANCE ...LIKE A BABY!
WHAT DO YOU EXPECT FROM A MAN WHO WAS KNOCKED ON THE HEAD BY SOME UNION GOON!?
WE OWE HIM AT LEAST A LITTLE RESPECT... WHAT ARE WE, ANIMALS IN A JUNGLE? HAVE A LITTLE PITY!
DE LUX FURS
OKAY... C'MON UNCLE MAX!!
COATS
SUITS
NOW, UNCLE MAX... DON'T WANDER OFF! WE'LL STOP FOR A 2 CENTS PLAIN ON THE WAY BACK!
..ON ME MOTHER'S GRAVE... I'M TELLIN' YOU THE TRUTH, GINO!
...YOU SURE? HOW DO YOU KNOW THE STIFF WE DUMPED IN LOMBARDI'S YARD WAS A FED?
IRISH EDDIE TIPPED HIM OFF ABOUT YOU AN' PETE'S HI-JACK RACKET! BESIDES, I SEEN HIS BADGE... IT WAS IN HIS POCKET WHEN WE STRIPPED HIM!
TRYIN' TO BE A UNION BUSTER EH?
HOLY SHIT!!
TAILOR
SUITS
WHERE YOU GOIN, GINO?
TO LOMBARDI'S LUMBER YARD...TO GET THEM CLOTHES BEFORE ANYBODY FINDS THE BADGE!

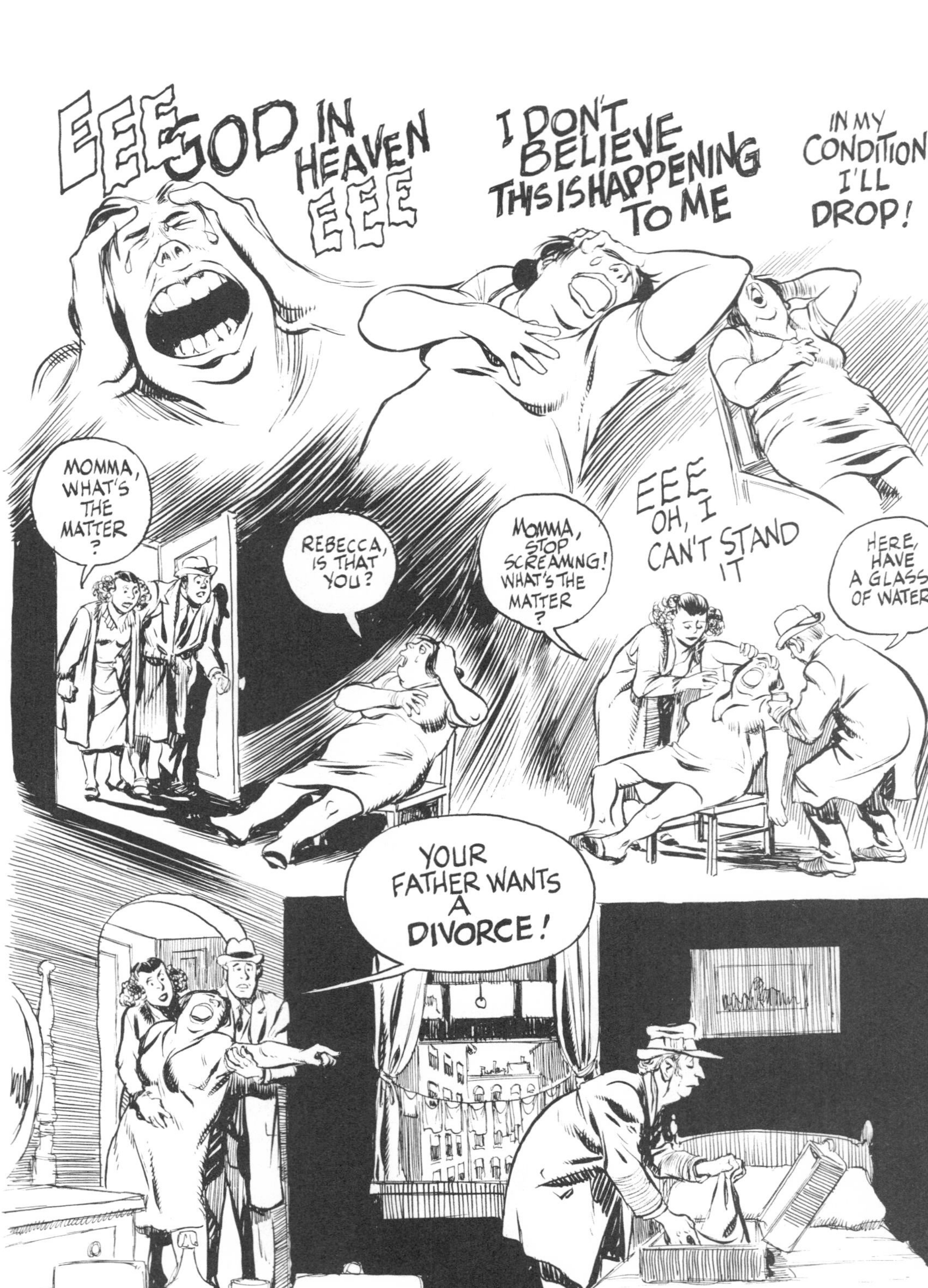
EEE GOD IN HEAVEN EEE
I DON'T BELIEVE THIS IS HAPPENING TO ME
IN MY CONDITION I'LL DROP!
MOMMA, WHAT'S THE MATTER?
REBECCA, IS THAT YOU?
MOMMA, STOP SCREAMING! WHAT'S THE MATTER?
EEE OH, I CAN'T STAND IT
HERE, HAVE A GLASS OF WATER!
YOUR FATHER WANTS A DIVORCE!

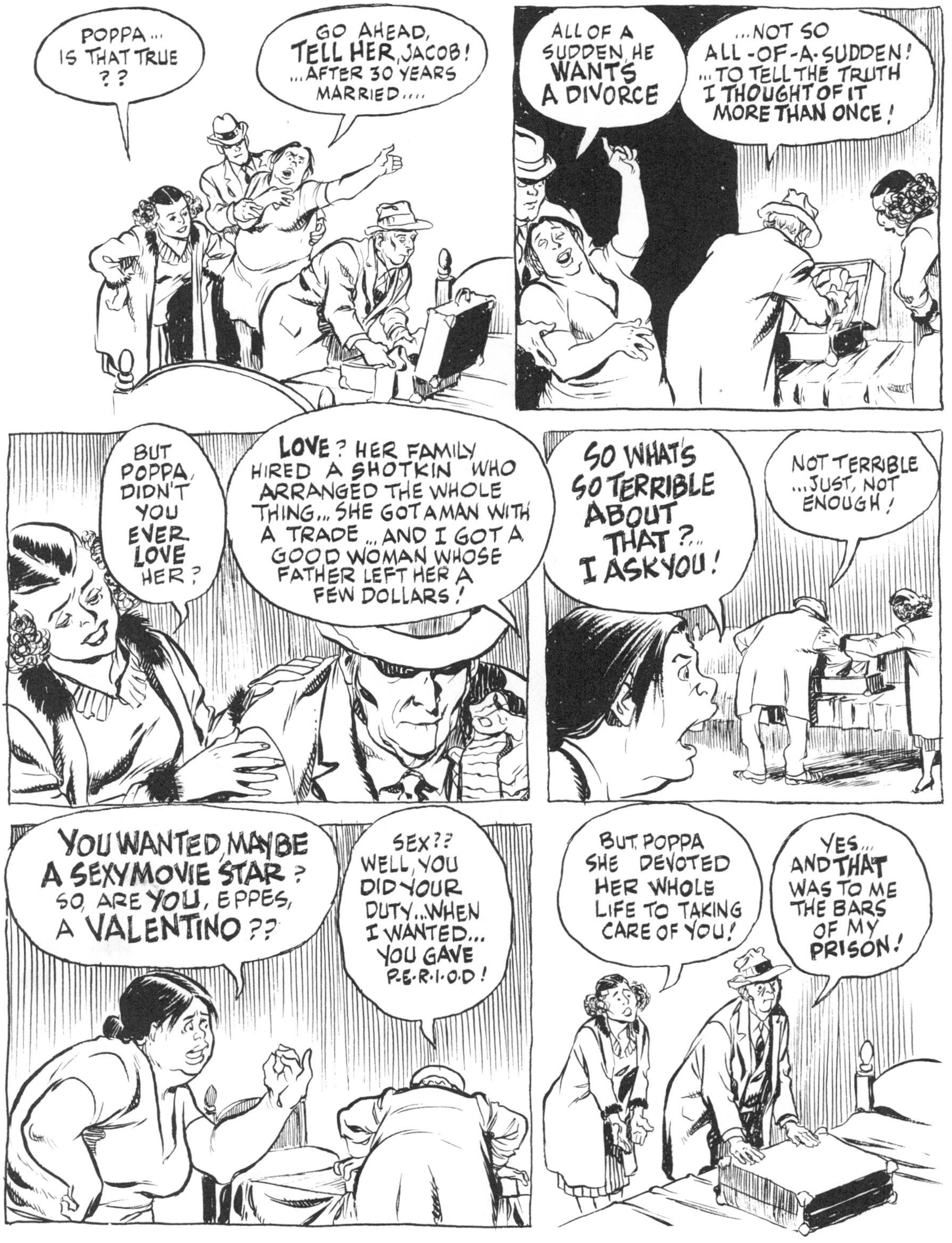
POPPA... IS THAT TRUE ??
GO AHEAD, TELL HER, JACOB! ...AFTER 30 YEARS MARRIED....
ALL OF A SUDDEN, HE WANTS A DIVORCE
...NOT SO ALL-OF-A-SUDDEN! ...TO TELL THE TRUTH I THOUGHT OF IT MORE THAN ONCE!
BUT POPPA, DIDN'T YOU EVER LOVE HER?
LOVE? HER FAMILY HIRED A SHOTKIN WHO ARRANGED THE WHOLE THING... SHE GOT A MAN WITH A TRADE ... AND I GOT A GOOD WOMAN WHOSE FATHER LEFT HER A FEW DOLLARS!
SO WHAT'S SO TERRIBLE ABOUT THAT?... I ASK YOU!
NOT TERRIBLE ...JUST, NOT ENOUGH!
YOU WANTED, MAYBE A SEXYMOVIE STAR? SO, ARE YOU, EPPES, A VALENTINO ??
SEX?? WELL, YOU DID YOUR DUTY...WHEN I WANTED... YOU GAVE P.E.R.I.O.D!
BUT, POPPA SHE DEVOTED HER WHOLE LIFE TO TAKING CARE OF YOU!
YES... AND THAT WAS TO ME THE BARS OF MY PRISON!

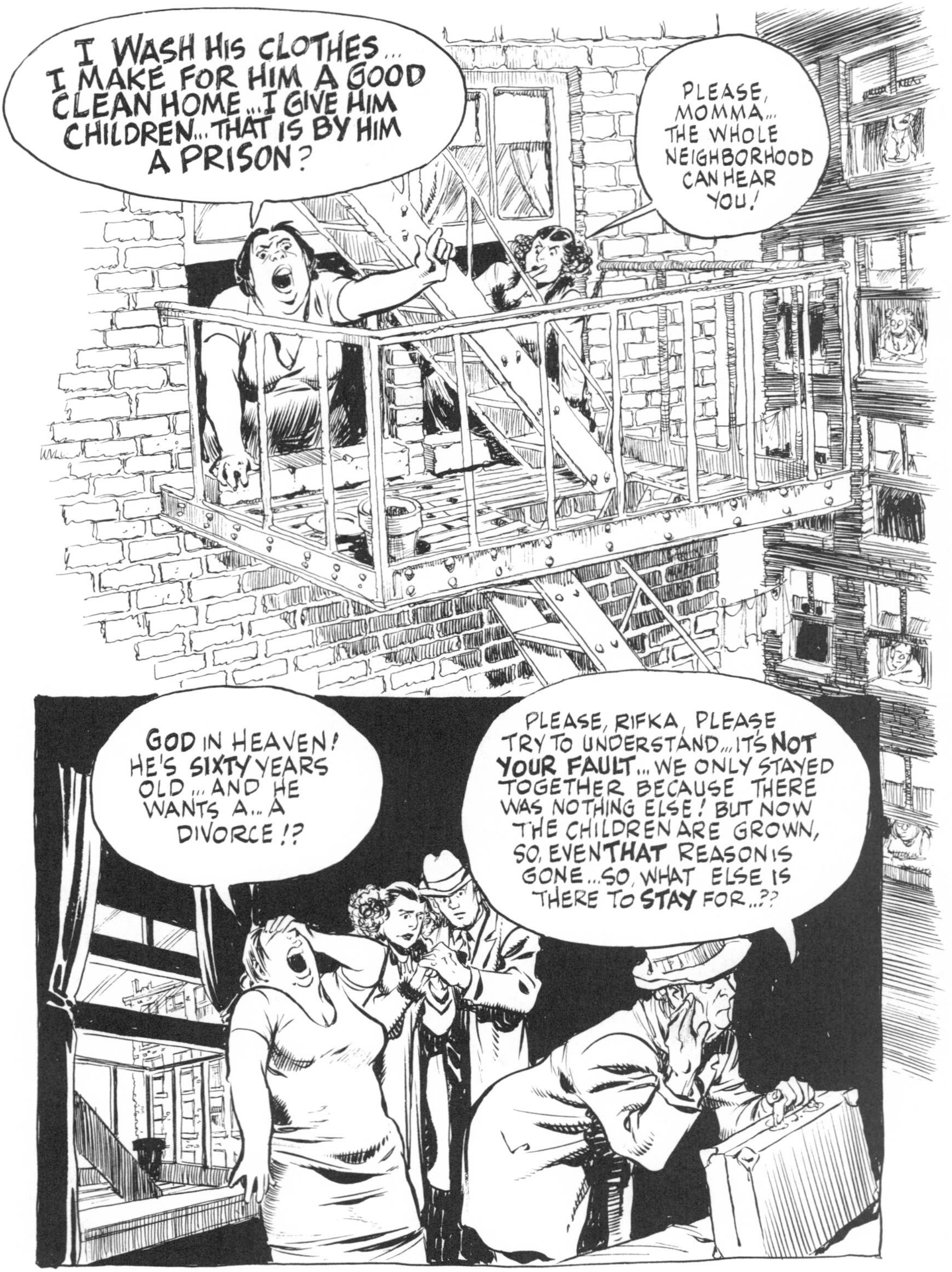
I WASH HIS CLOTHES... I MAKE FOR HIM A GOOD CLEAN HOME... I GIVE HIM CHILDREN... THAT IS BY HIM A PRISON?
PLEASE, MOMMA... THE WHOLE NEIGHBORHOOD CAN HEAR YOU!
GOD IN HEAVEN! HE'S SIXTY YEARS OLD... AND HE WANTS A... A DIVORCE!?
PLEASE, RIFKA, PLEASE TRY TO UNDERSTAND... IT'S NOT YOUR FAULT... WE ONLY STAYED TOGETHER BECAUSE THERE WAS NOTHING ELSE! BUT NOW THE CHILDREN ARE GROWN, SO, EVEN THAT REASON IS GONE... SO, WHAT ELSE IS THERE TO STAY FOR..??

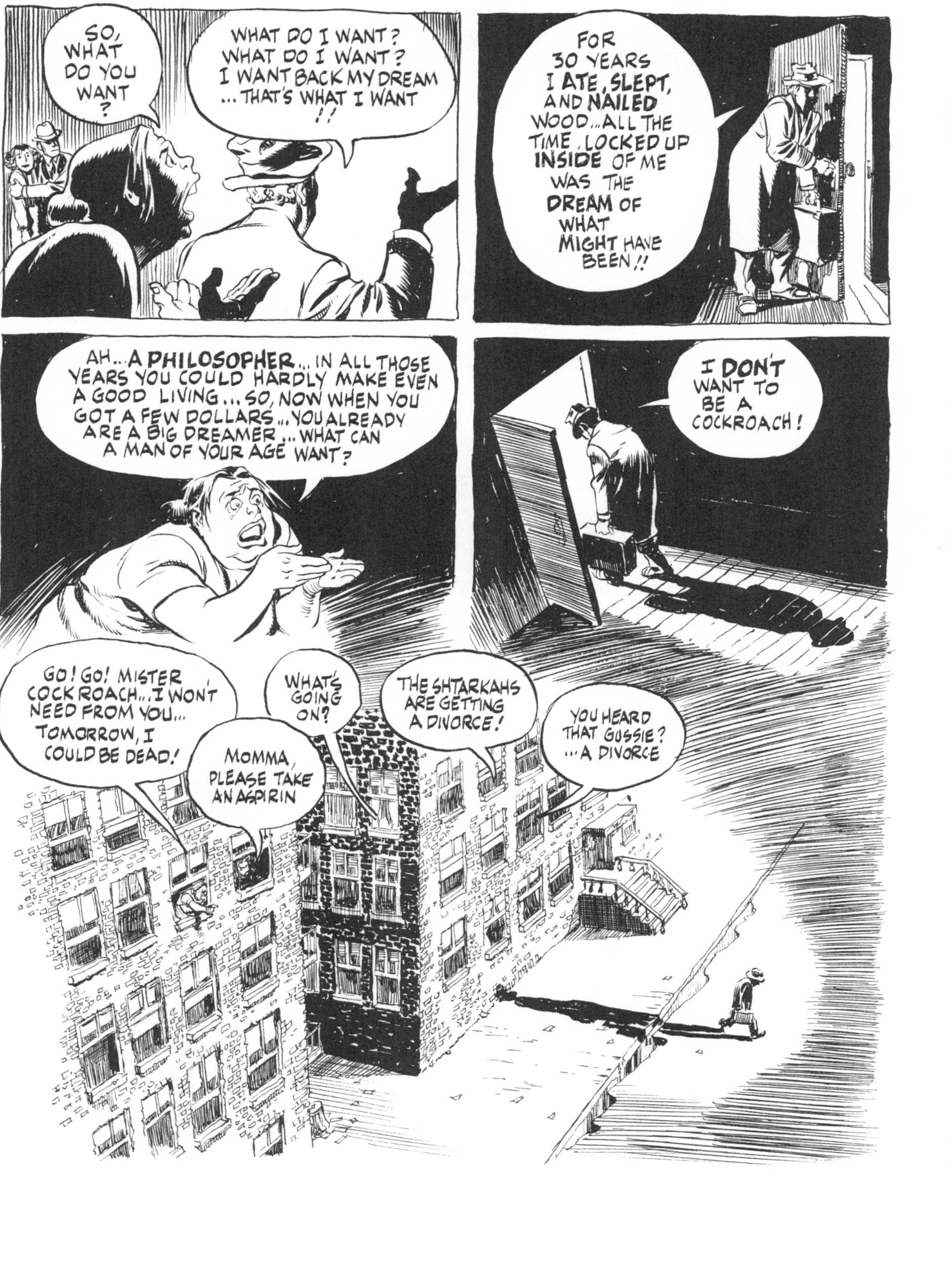
SO, WHAT DO YOU WANT ?
WHAT DO I WANT ? WHAT DO I WANT ? I WANT BACK MY DREAM ... THAT'S WHAT I WANT !!
FOR 30 YEARS I ATE, SLEPT, AND NAILED WOOD... ALL THE TIME, LOCKED UP INSIDE OF ME WAS THE DREAM OF WHAT MIGHT HAVE BEEN !!
AH... A PHILOSOPHER... IN ALL THOSE YEARS YOU COULD HARDLY MAKE EVEN A GOOD LIVING... SO, NOW WHEN YOU GOT A FEW DOLLARS... YOU ALREADY ARE A BIG DREAMER... WHAT CAN A MAN OF YOUR AGE WANT ?
I DON'T WANT TO BE A COCKROACH !
GO! GO! MISTER COCKROACH... I WON'T NEED FROM YOU... TOMORROW, I COULD BE DEAD!
MOMMA, PLEASE TAKE AN ASPIRIN
WHAT'S GOING ON?
THE SHTARKAHS ARE GETTING A DIVORCE!
YOU HEARD THAT GUSSIE? ... A DIVORCE

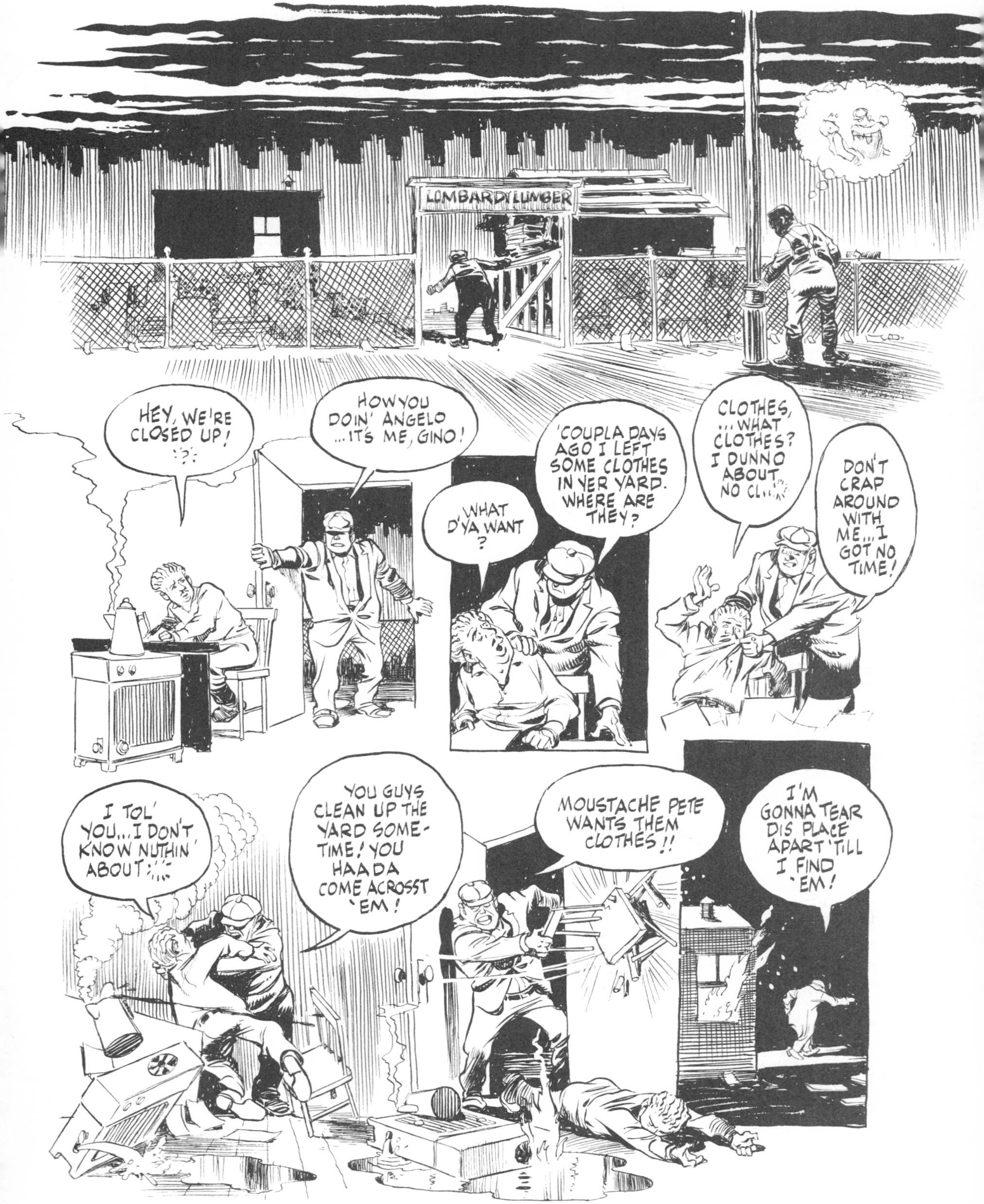
LOMBARDY LUMBER
HEY, WE'RE CLOSED UP!
HOW YOU DOIN' ANGELO ...IT'S ME, GINO!
WHAT D'YA WANT ?
'COUPLA DAYS AGO I LEFT SOME CLOTHES IN YER YARD. WHERE ARE THEY?
CLOTHES, ...WHAT CLOTHES? I DUNNO ABOUT NO CL...
DON'T CRAP AROUND WITH ME...I GOT NO TIME!
I TOL' YOU...I DON'T KNOW NUTHIN' ABOUT...
YOU GUYS CLEAN UP THE YARD SOME-TIME! YOU HAADA COME ACROSST 'EM!
MOUSTACHE PETE WANTS THEM CLOTHES!!
I'M GONNA TEAR DIS PLACE APART 'TILL I FIND 'EM!

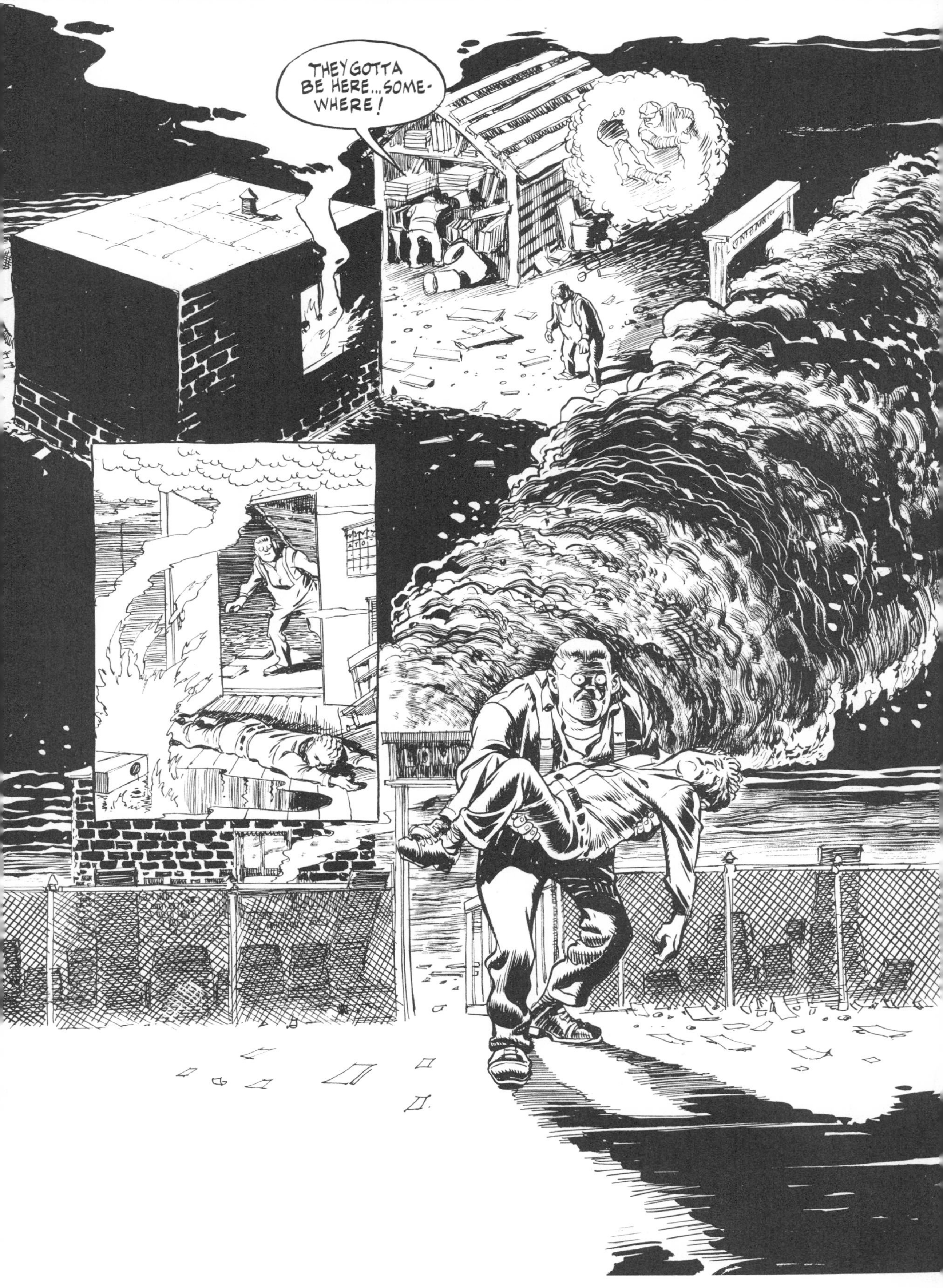
THEY GOTTA BE HERE... SOME-WHERE!

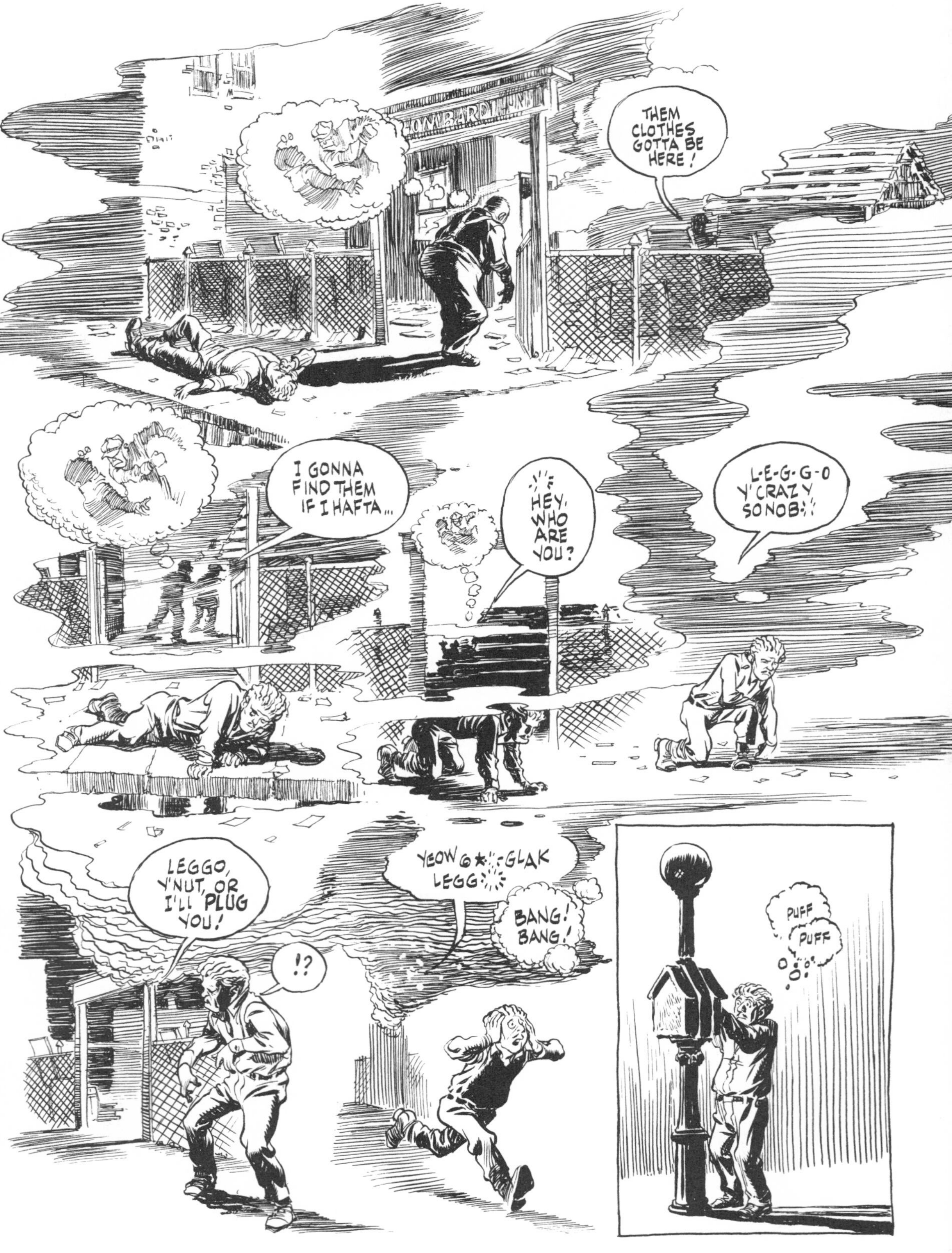
LOMBARDI
THEM CLOTHES GOTTA BE HERE!
I GONNA FIND THEM IF I HAFTA...
HEY, WHO ARE YOU?
L-E-G-G-O Y' CRAZY SONOB-
LEGGO, Y'NUT, OR I'LL PLUG YOU!
!?
YEOW-GLAK LEGG-
BANG! BANG!
PUFF
PUFF

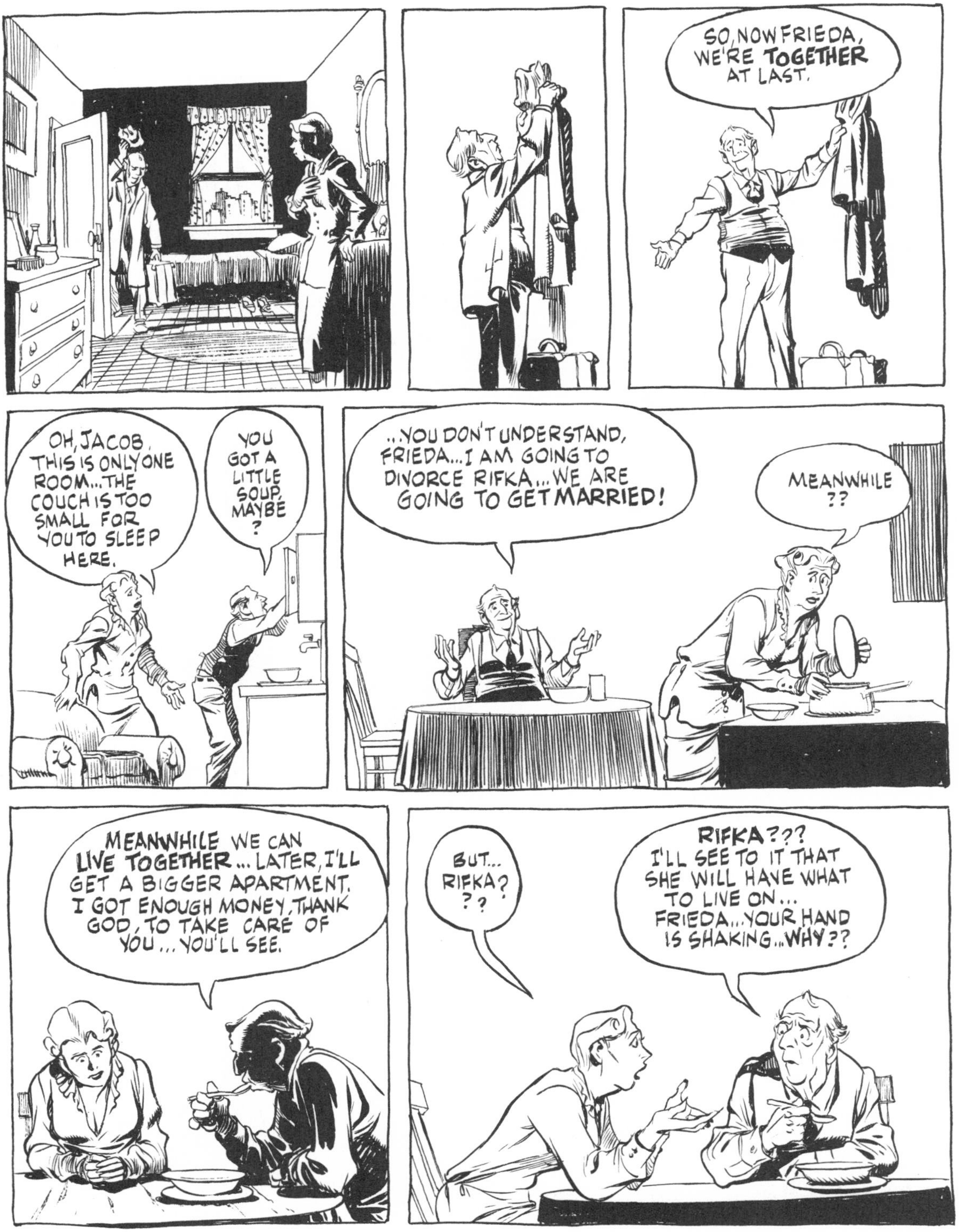
SO, NOW FRIEDA, WE'RE TOGETHER AT LAST.
OH, JACOB, THIS IS ONLY ONE ROOM... THE COUCH IS TOO SMALL FOR YOU TO SLEEP HERE.
YOU GOT A LITTLE SOUP, MAYBE ?
..YOU DON'T UNDERSTAND, FRIEDA...I AM GOING TO DIVORCE RIFKA...WE ARE GOING TO GET MARRIED!
MEANWHILE ??
MEANWHILE WE CAN LIVE TOGETHER... LATER, I'LL GET A BIGGER APARTMENT. I GOT ENOUGH MONEY, THANK GOD, TO TAKE CARE OF YOU... YOU'LL SEE.
BUT... RIFKA? ??
RIFKA??? I'LL SEE TO IT THAT SHE WILL HAVE WHAT TO LIVE ON... FRIEDA... YOUR HAND IS SHAKING...WHY??

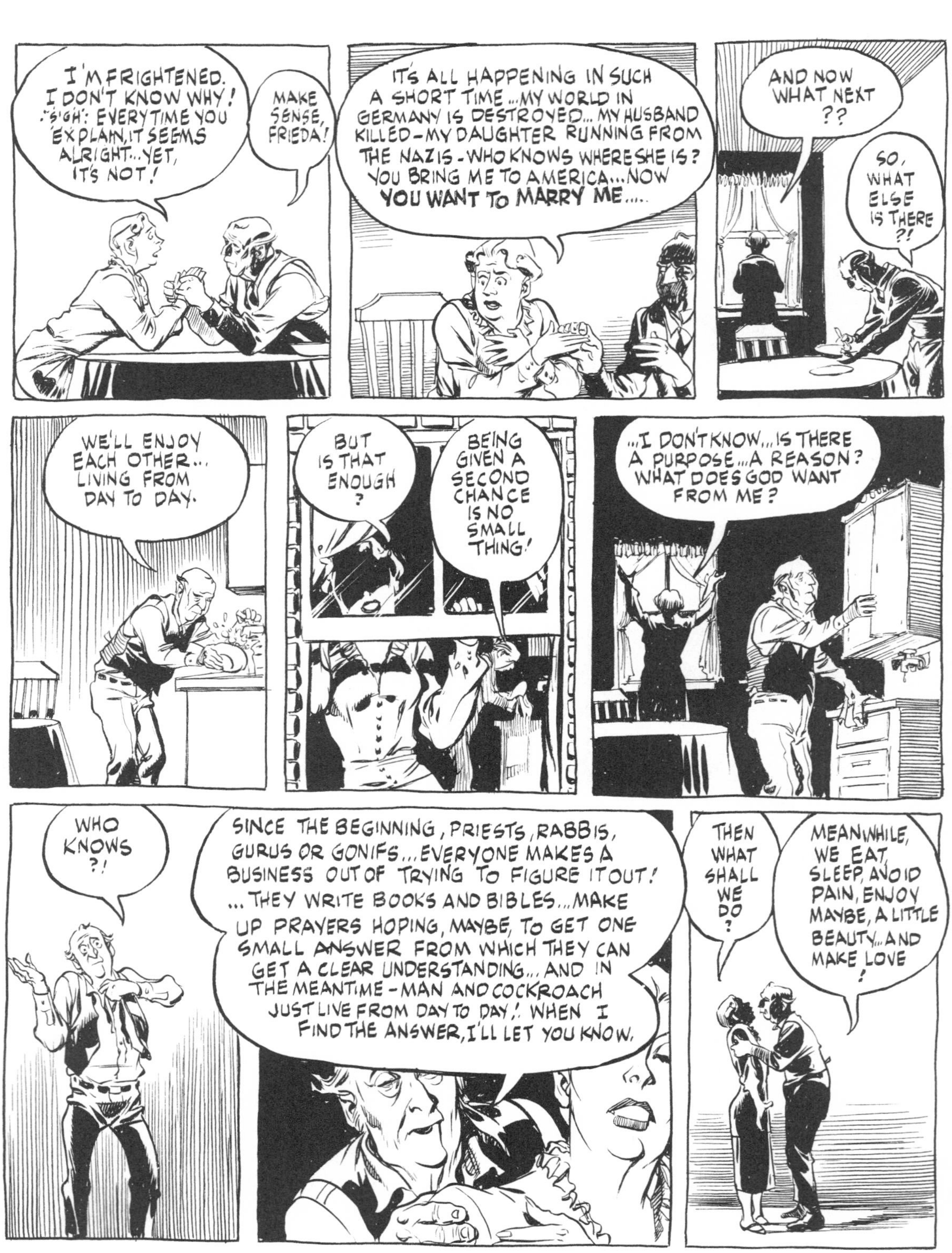
I'M FRIGHTENED. I DON'T KNOW WHY! :SIGH: EVERYTIME YOU EXPLAIN, IT SEEMS ALRIGHT... YET, IT'S NOT!
MAKE SENSE, FRIEDA!
IT'S ALL HAPPENING IN SUCH A SHORT TIME... MY WORLD IN GERMANY IS DESTROYED... MY HUSBAND KILLED - MY DAUGHTER RUNNING FROM THE NAZIS - WHO KNOWS WHERE SHE IS? YOU BRING ME TO AMERICA... NOW YOU WANT TO MARRY ME....
AND NOW WHAT NEXT ??
SO, WHAT ELSE IS THERE ?!
WE'LL ENJOY EACH OTHER... LIVING FROM DAY TO DAY.
BUT IS THAT ENOUGH ?
BEING GIVEN A SECOND CHANCE IS NO SMALL THING!
...I DON'T KNOW... IS THERE A PURPOSE... A REASON? WHAT DOES GOD WANT FROM ME?
WHO KNOWS ?!
SINCE THE BEGINNING, PRIESTS, RABBIS, GURUS OR GONIFS... EVERYONE MAKES A BUSINESS OUT OF TRYING TO FIGURE IT OUT! ... THEY WRITE BOOKS AND BIBLES... MAKE UP PRAYERS HOPING, MAYBE, TO GET ONE SMALL ANSWER FROM WHICH THEY CAN GET A CLEAR UNDERSTANDING... AND IN THE MEANTIME - MAN AND COCKROACH JUST LIVE FROM DAY TO DAY! WHEN I FIND THE ANSWER, I'LL LET YOU KNOW.
THEN WHAT SHALL WE DO ?
MEANWHILE, WE EAT, SLEEP, AVOID PAIN, ENJOY MAYBE, A LITTLE BEAUTY... AND MAKE LOVE !

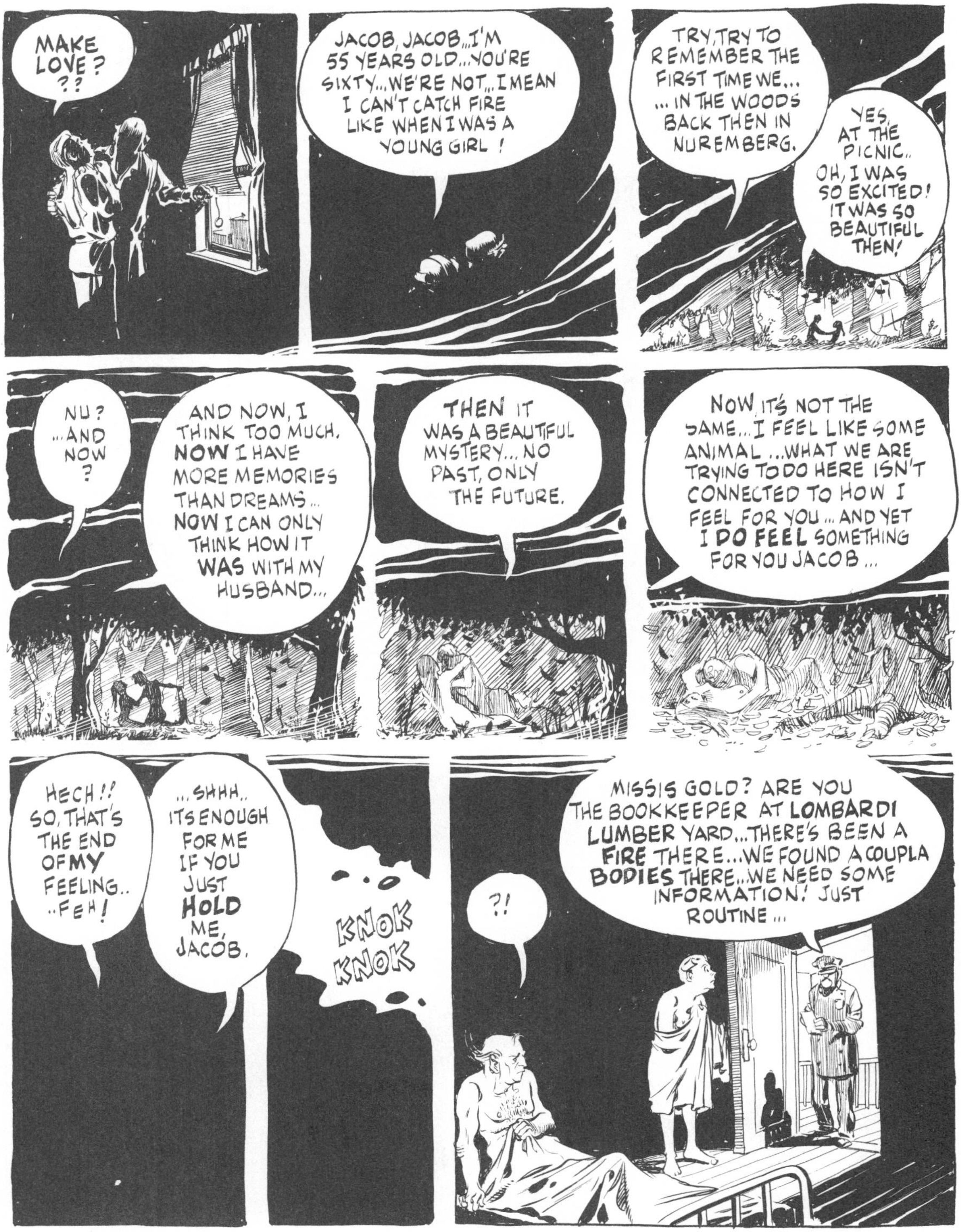
MAKE LOVE ? ??
JACOB, JACOB... I'M 55 YEARS OLD... YOU'RE SIXTY... WE'RE NOT... I MEAN I CAN'T CATCH FIRE LIKE WHEN I WAS A YOUNG GIRL !
TRY, TRY TO REMEMBER THE FIRST TIME WE... ...IN THE WOODS BACK THEN IN NUREMBERG.
YES, AT THE PICNIC.. OH, I WAS SO EXCITED! IT WAS SO BEAUTIFUL THEN!
NU? ...AND NOW ?
AND NOW, I THINK TOO MUCH. NOW I HAVE MORE MEMORIES THAN DREAMS... NOW I CAN ONLY THINK HOW IT WAS WITH MY HUSBAND...
THEN IT WAS A BEAUTIFUL MYSTERY... NO PAST, ONLY THE FUTURE.
NOW IT'S NOT THE SAME... I FEEL LIKE SOME ANIMAL ...WHAT WE ARE TRYING TO DO HERE ISN'T CONNECTED TO HOW I FEEL FOR YOU ... AND YET I DO FEEL SOMETHING FOR YOU JACOB ...
HECH !! SO, THAT'S THE END OF MY FEELING.. ..FEH!
...SHHH.. ITS ENOUGH FOR ME IF YOU JUST HOLD ME, JACOB.
KNOK KNOK
?!
MISSIS GOLD? ARE YOU THE BOOKKEEPER AT LOMBARDI LUMBER YARD... THERE'S BEEN A FIRE THERE... WE FOUND A COUPLA BODIES THERE... WE NEED SOME INFORMATION! JUST ROUTINE...

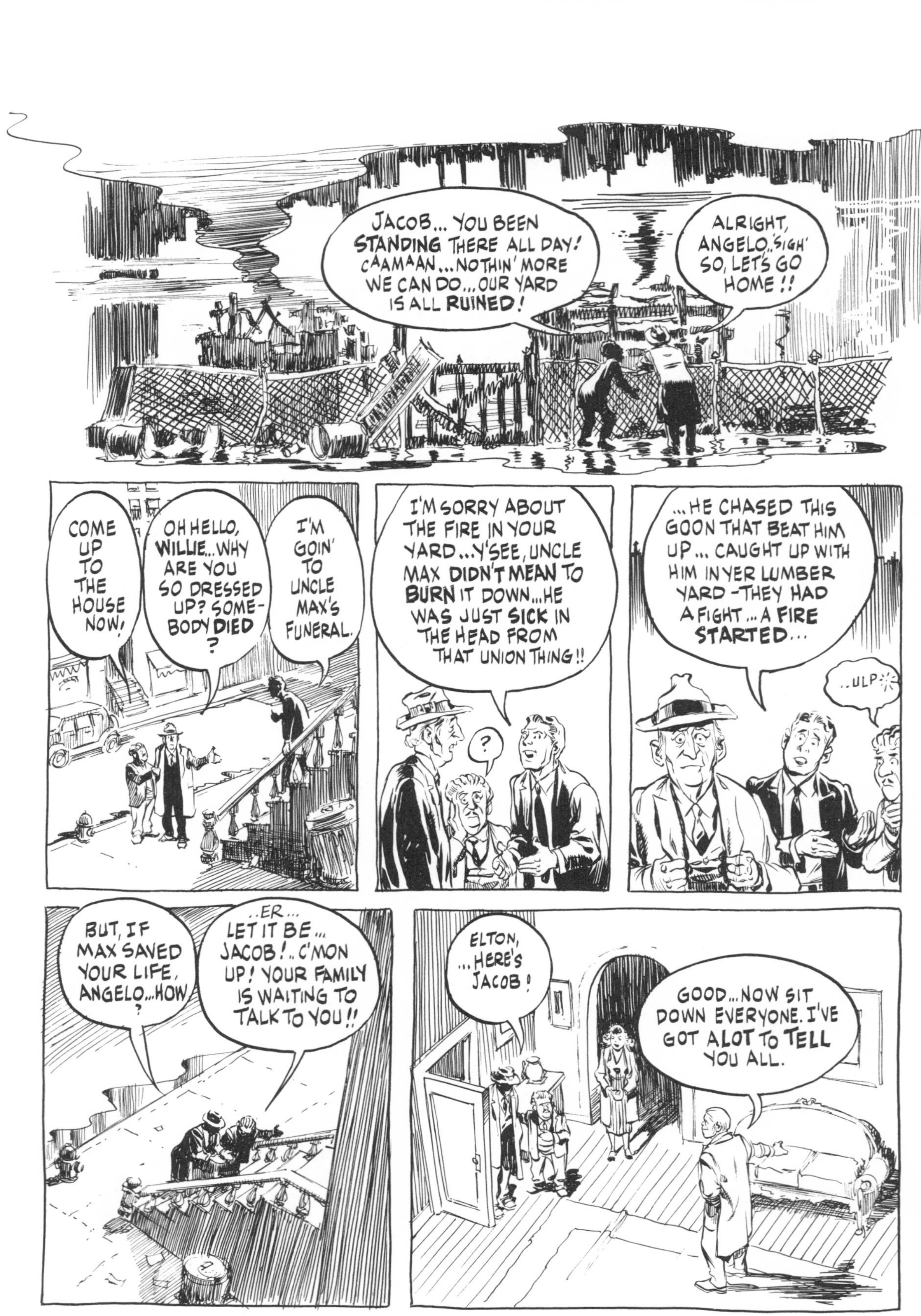

JACOB... YOU BEEN STANDING THERE ALL DAY! CAAMAAN...NOTHIN' MORE WE CAN DO...OUR YARD IS ALL RUINED!
ALRIGHT, ANGELO..'SIGH' SO, LET'S GO HOME!!
COME UP TO THE HOUSE NOW!
OH HELLO, WILLIE...WHY ARE YOU SO DRESSED UP? SOME-BODY DIED?
I'M GOIN' TO UNCLE MAX'S FUNERAL.
I'M SORRY ABOUT THE FIRE IN YOUR YARD...Y'SEE, UNCLE MAX DIDN'T MEAN TO BURN IT DOWN...HE WAS JUST SICK IN THE HEAD FROM THAT UNION THING!!
?
...HE CHASED THIS GOON THAT BEAT HIM UP... CAUGHT UP WITH HIM IN YER LUMBER YARD - THEY HAD A FIGHT... A FIRE STARTED...
..ULP
BUT, IF MAX SAVED YOUR LIFE, ANGELO...HOW?
..ER... LET IT BE... JACOB!.. C'MON UP! YOUR FAMILY IS WAITING TO TALK TO YOU!!
ELTON, ...HERE'S JACOB!
GOOD...NOW SIT DOWN EVERYONE. I'VE GOT ALOT TO TELL YOU ALL.

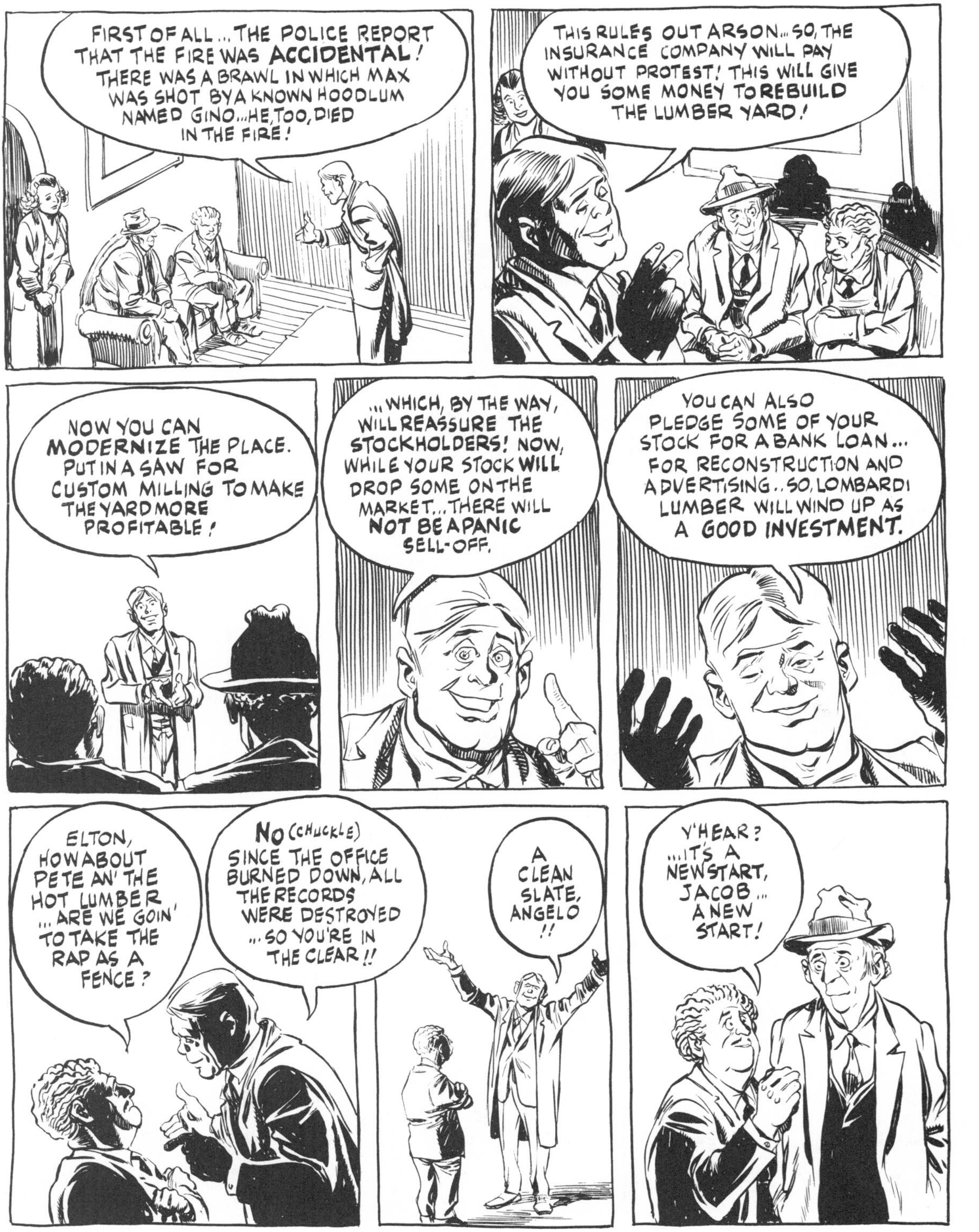
FIRST OF ALL ... THE POLICE REPORT THAT THE FIRE WAS ACCIDENTAL! THERE WAS A BRAWL IN WHICH MAX WAS SHOT BY A KNOWN HOODLUM NAMED GINO... HE, TOO, DIED IN THE FIRE!
THIS RULES OUT ARSON... SO, THE INSURANCE COMPANY WILL PAY WITHOUT PROTEST! THIS WILL GIVE YOU SOME MONEY TO REBUILD THE LUMBER YARD!
NOW YOU CAN MODERNIZE THE PLACE. PUT IN A SAW FOR CUSTOM MILLING TO MAKE THE YARD MORE PROFITABLE!
...WHICH, BY THE WAY, WILL REASSURE THE STOCKHOLDERS! NOW, WHILE YOUR STOCK WILL DROP SOME ON THE MARKET... THERE WILL NOT BE A PANIC SELL-OFF.
YOU CAN ALSO PLEDGE SOME OF YOUR STOCK FOR A BANK LOAN... FOR RECONSTRUCTION AND ADVERTISING.. SO, LOMBARDI LUMBER WILL WIND UP AS A GOOD INVESTMENT.
ELTON, HOW ABOUT PETE AN' THE HOT LUMBER ... ARE WE GOIN' TO TAKE THE RAP AS A FENCE?
NO (CHUCKLE) SINCE THE OFFICE BURNED DOWN, ALL THE RECORDS WERE DESTROYED ... SO YOU'RE IN THE CLEAR!!
A CLEAN SLATE, ANGELO!!
Y'HEAR? ...IT'S A NEW START, JACOB... A NEW START!

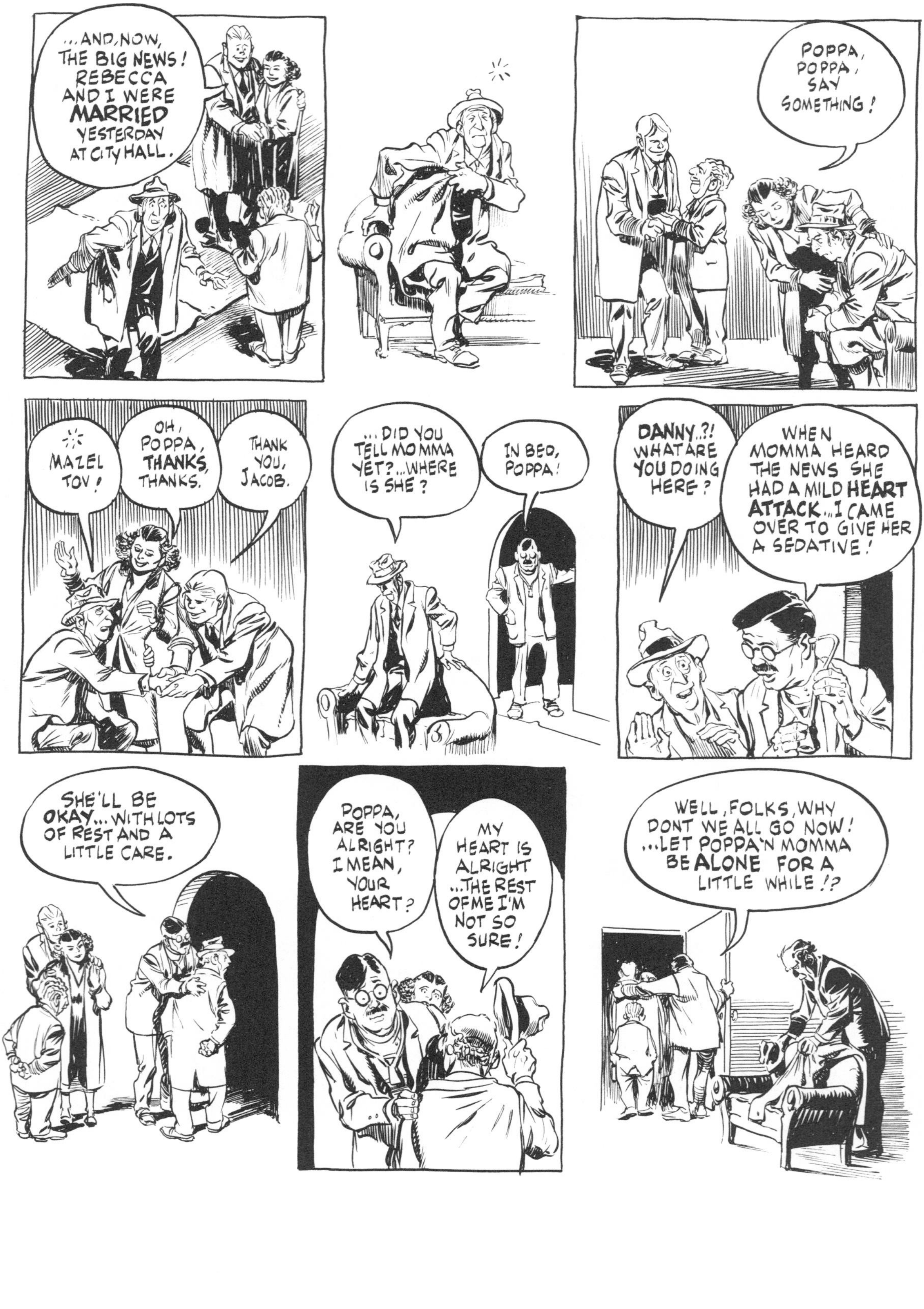
...AND, NOW, THE BIG NEWS! REBECCA AND I WERE MARRIED YESTERDAY AT CITY HALL.
POPPA, POPPA, SAY SOMETHING!
MAZEL TOV!
OH, POPPA, THANKS, THANKS.
THANK YOU, JACOB.
...DID YOU TELL MOMMA YET?...WHERE IS SHE?
IN BED, POPPA!
DANNY..?! WHAT ARE YOU DOING HERE?
WHEN MOMMA HEARD THE NEWS SHE HAD A MILD HEART ATTACK...I CAME OVER TO GIVE HER A SEDATIVE!
SHE'LL BE OKAY... WITH LOTS OF REST AND A LITTLE CARE.
POPPA, ARE YOU ALRIGHT? I MEAN, YOUR HEART?
MY HEART IS ALRIGHT ...THE REST OF ME I'M NOT SO SURE!
WELL, FOLKS, WHY DONT WE ALL GO NOW! ...LET POPPA 'N MOMMA BE ALONE FOR A LITTLE WHILE!?

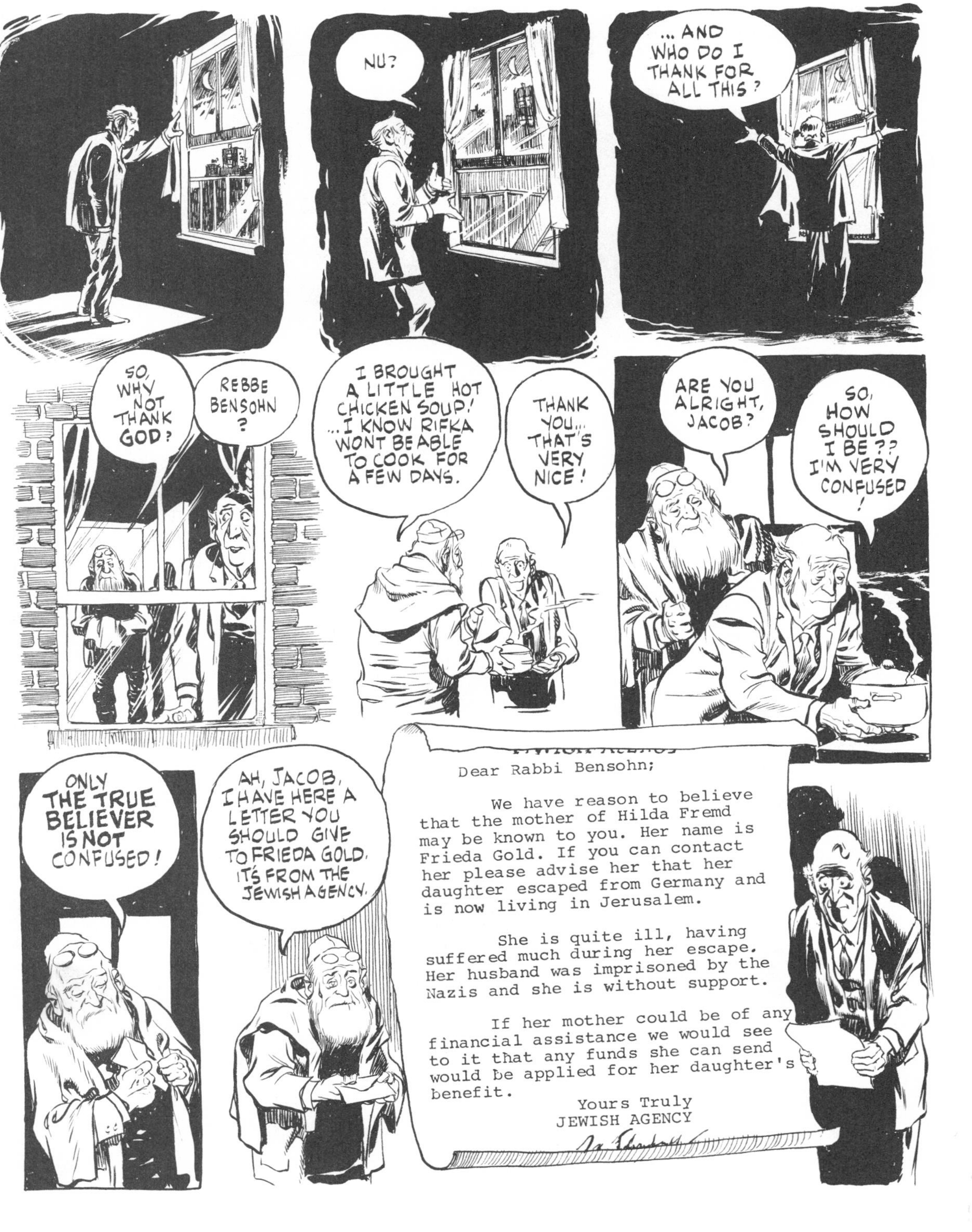
NU?
... AND WHO DO I THANK FOR ALL THIS?
SO, WHY NOT THANK GOD?
REBBE BENSOHN ?
I BROUGHT A LITTLE HOT CHICKEN SOUP! ...I KNOW RIFKA WONT BE ABLE TO COOK FOR A FEW DAYS.
THANK YOU... THAT'S VERY NICE!
ARE YOU ALRIGHT, JACOB?
SO, HOW SHOULD I BE ?? I'M VERY CONFUSED!
ONLY THE TRUE BELIEVER IS NOT CONFUSED!
AH, JACOB, I HAVE HERE A LETTER YOU SHOULD GIVE TO FRIEDA GOLD. IT'S FROM THE JEWISH AGENCY.
Dear Rabbi Bensohn;
We have reason to believe that the mother of Hilda Fremd may be known to you. Her name is Frieda Gold. If you can contact her please advise her that her daughter escaped from Germany and is now living in Jerusalem.
She is quite ill, having suffered much during her escape. Her husband was imprisoned by the Nazis and she is without support.
If her mother could be of any financial assistance we would see to it that any funds she can send would be applied for her daughter's benefit.
Yours Truly
JEWISH AGENCY

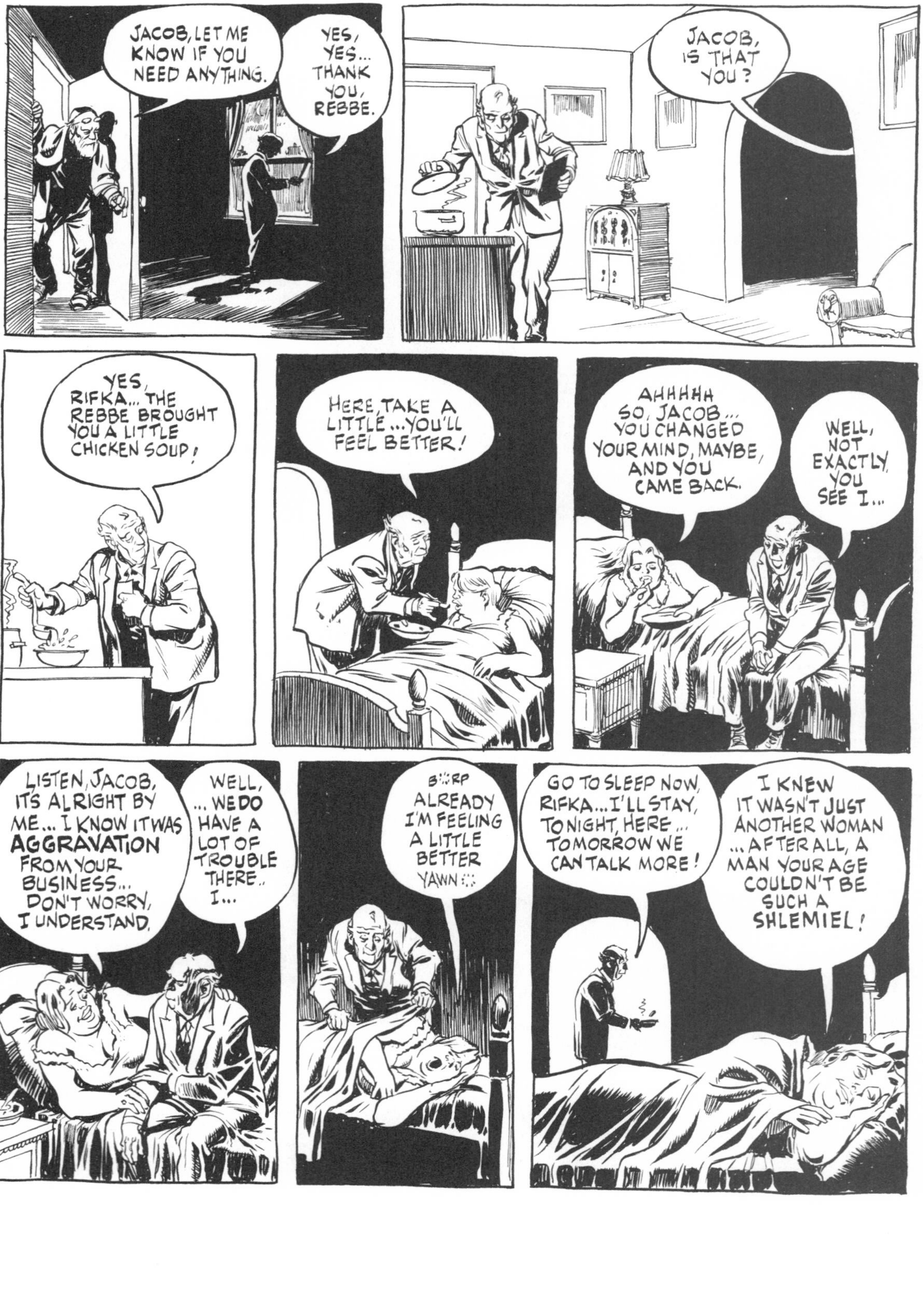
JACOB, LET ME KNOW IF YOU NEED ANYTHING.
YES, YES... THANK YOU, REBBE.
JACOB, IS THAT YOU?
YES, RIFKA... THE REBBE BROUGHT YOU A LITTLE CHICKEN SOUP!
HERE, TAKE A LITTLE ...YOU'LL FEEL BETTER!
AHHHHH SO, JACOB... YOU CHANGED YOUR MIND, MAYBE, AND YOU CAME BACK.
WELL, NOT EXACTLY, YOU SEE I...
LISTEN, JACOB, ITS ALRIGHT BY ME... I KNOW IT WAS AGGRAVATION FROM YOUR BUSINESS... DON'T WORRY, I UNDERSTAND.
WELL, ... WE DO HAVE A LOT OF TROUBLE THERE.. I...
ALREADY I'M FEELING A LITTLE BETTER
YAWN
GO TO SLEEP NOW, RIFKA... I'LL STAY, TONIGHT, HERE... TOMORROW WE CAN TALK MORE!
I KNEW IT WASN'T JUST ANOTHER WOMAN ...AFTER ALL, A MAN YOUR AGE COULDN'T BE SUCH A SHLEMIEL!

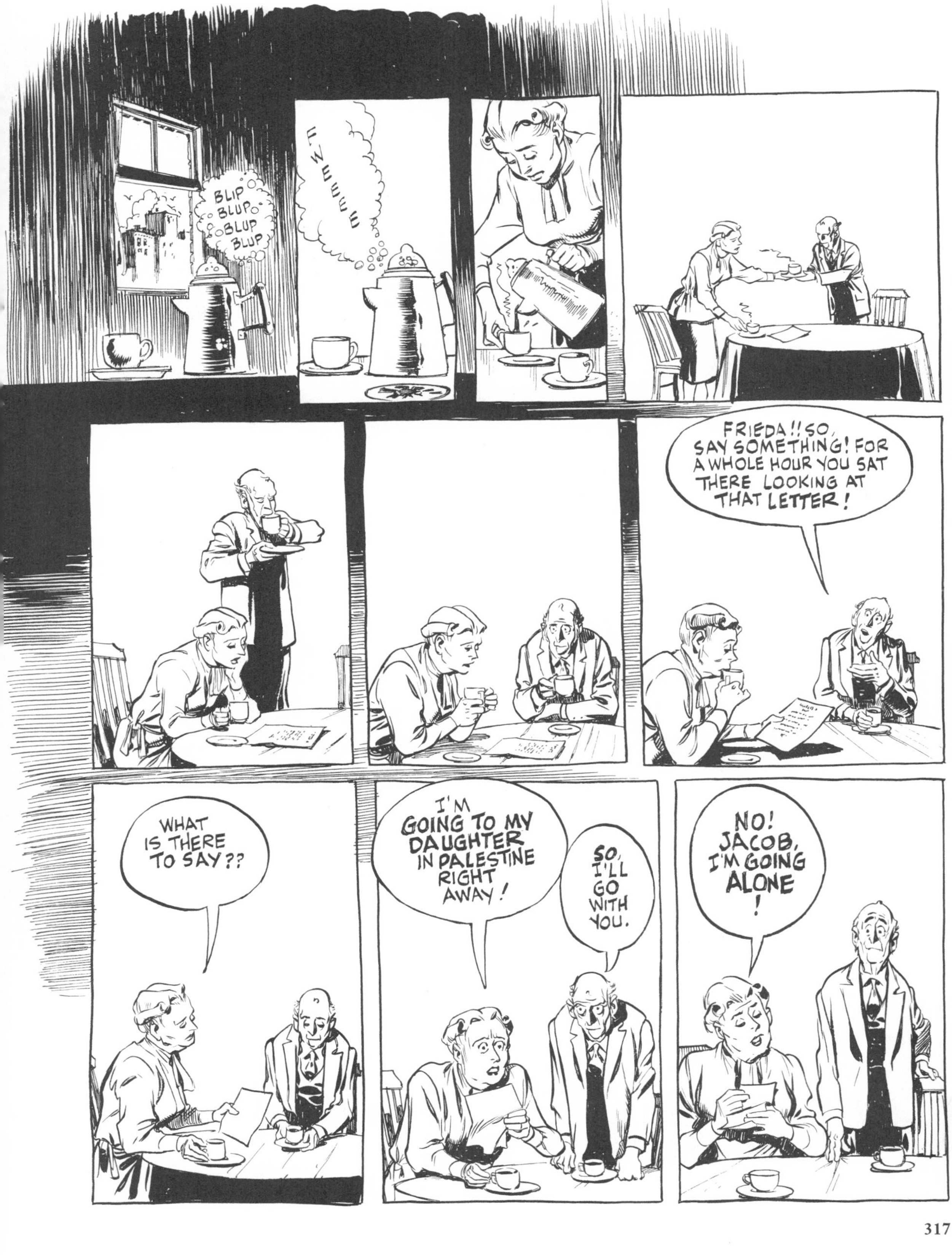
BLIP BLUP BLUP BLUP
FWEEEEE
FRIEDA!! SO, SAY SOMETHING! FOR A WHOLE HOUR YOU SAT THERE LOOKING AT THAT LETTER!
WHAT IS THERE TO SAY??
I'M GOING TO MY DAUGHTER IN PALESTINE RIGHT AWAY!
SO, I'LL GO WITH YOU.
NO! JACOB, I'M GOING ALONE!

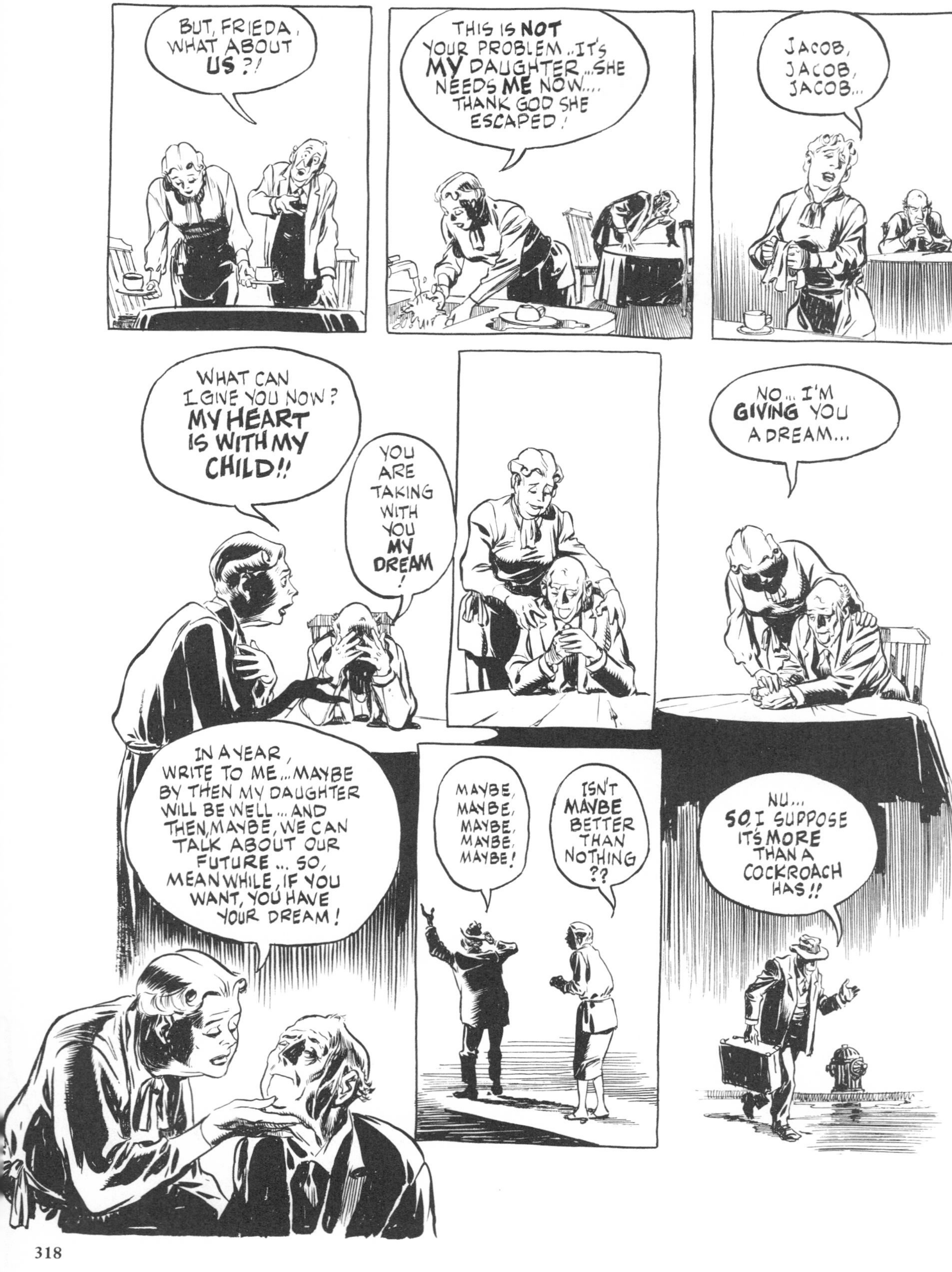
BUT, FRIEDA, WHAT ABOUT US ?!
THIS IS NOT YOUR PROBLEM .. IT'S MY DAUGHTER ... SHE NEEDS ME NOW.... THANK GOD SHE ESCAPED !
JACOB, JACOB, JACOB...
WHAT CAN I GIVE YOU NOW ? MY HEART IS WITH MY CHILD!!
YOU ARE TAKING WITH YOU MY DREAM !
NO... I'M GIVING YOU A DREAM...
IN A YEAR, WRITE TO ME... MAYBE BY THEN MY DAUGHTER WILL BE WELL ... AND THEN, MAYBE, WE CAN TALK ABOUT OUR FUTURE ... SO, MEANWHILE, IF YOU WANT, YOU HAVE YOUR DREAM !
MAYBE, MAYBE, MAYBE, MAYBE, MAYBE!
ISN'T MAYBE BETTER THAN NOTHING ??
NU... SO, I SUPPOSE IT'S MORE THAN A COCKROACH HAS !!

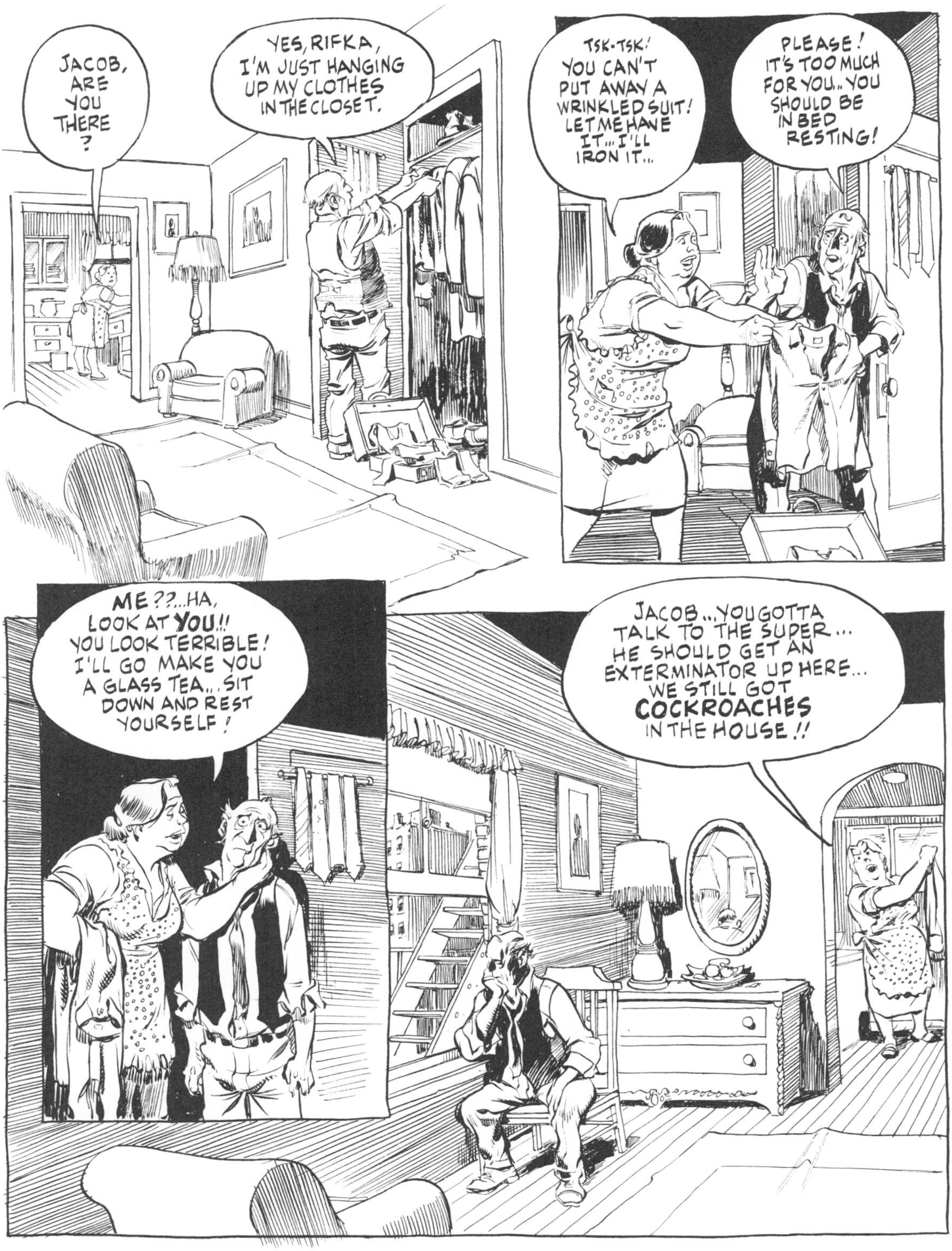
JACOB, ARE YOU THERE ?
YES, RIFKA, I'M JUST HANGING UP MY CLOTHES IN THE CLOSET.
TSK-TSK! YOU CAN'T PUT AWAY A WRINKLED SUIT! LET ME HAVE IT... I'LL IRON IT...
PLEASE! IT'S TOO MUCH FOR YOU.. YOU SHOULD BE IN BED RESTING!
ME??...HA, LOOK AT YOU!! YOU LOOK TERRIBLE! I'LL GO MAKE YOU A GLASS TEA... SIT DOWN AND REST YOURSELF!
JACOB... YOU GOTTA TALK TO THE SUPER... HE SHOULD GET AN EXTERMINATOR UP HERE... WE STILL GOT COCKROACHES IN THE HOUSE!!

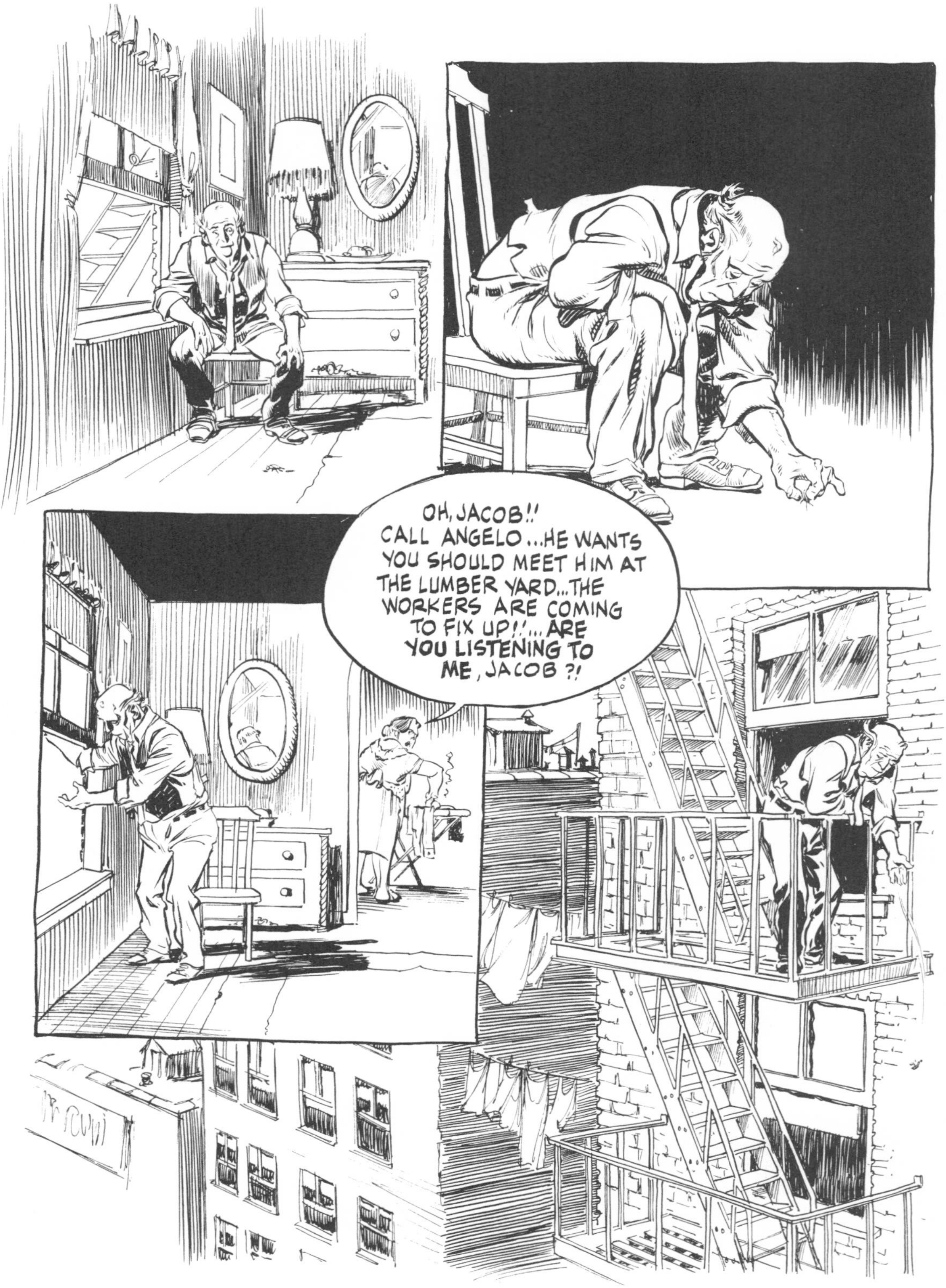
OH, JACOB!! CALL ANGELO...HE WANTS YOU SHOULD MEET HIM AT THE LUMBER YARD...THE WORKERS ARE COMING TO FIX UP!'...ARE YOU LISTENING TO ME, JACOB ?!

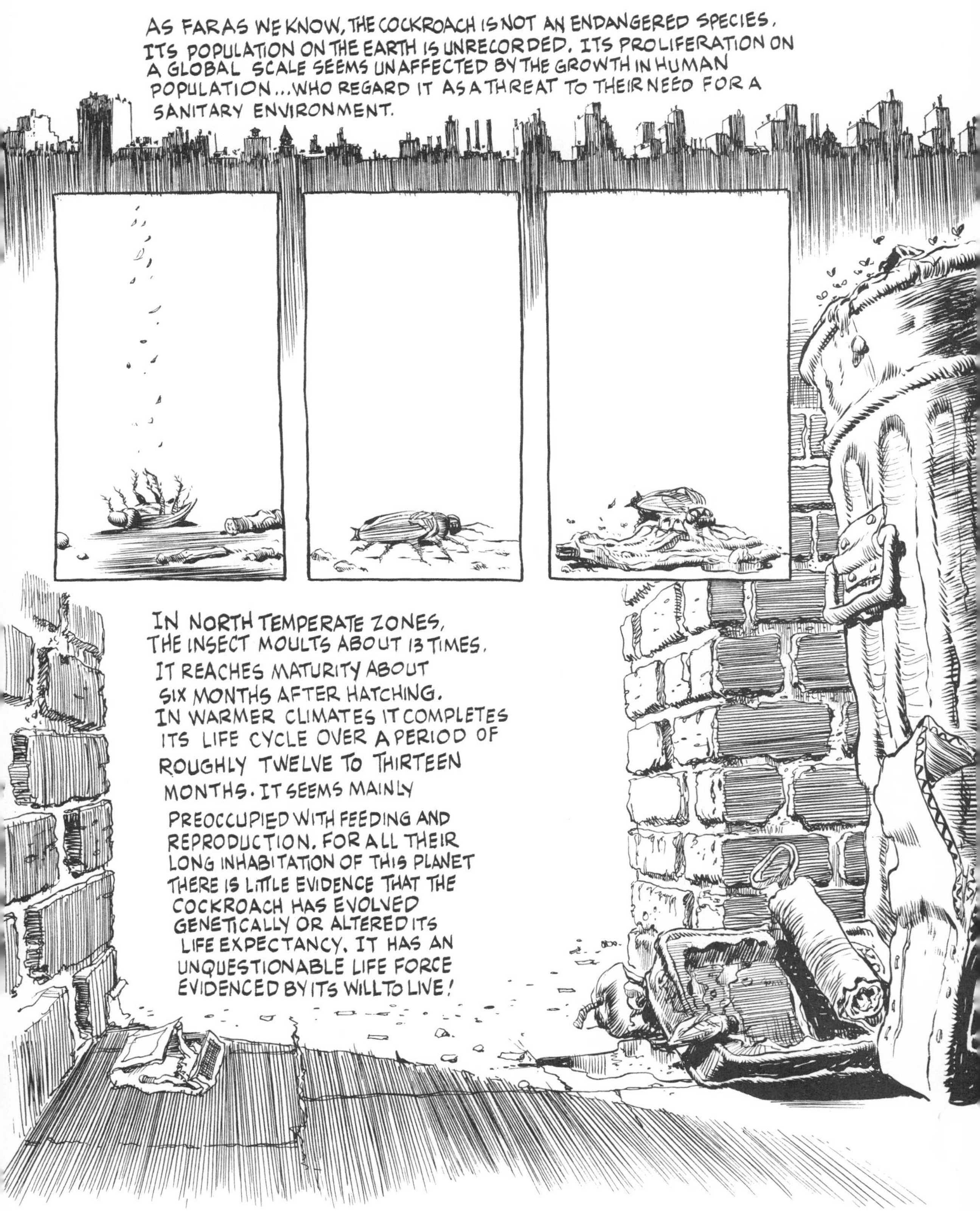
AS FARAS WE KNOW, THE COCKROACH IS NOT AN ENDANGERED SPECIES. ITS POPULATION ON THE EARTH IS UNRECORDED. ITS PROLIFERATION ON A GLOBAL SCALE SEEMS UNAFFECTED BY THE GROWTH IN HUMAN POPULATION...WHO REGARD IT AS A THREAT TO THEIR NEED FOR A SANITARY ENVIRONMENT.
IN NORTH TEMPERATE ZONES, THE INSECT MOULTS ABOUT 13 TIMES. IT REACHES MATURITY ABOUT SIX MONTHS AFTER HATCHING. IN WARMER CLIMATES IT COMPLETES ITS LIFE CYCLE OVER A PERIOD OF ROUGHLY TWELVE TO THIRTEEN MONTHS. IT SEEMS MAINLY PREOCCUPIED WITH FEEDING AND REPRODUCTION. FOR ALL THEIR LONG INHABITATION OF THIS PLANET THERE IS LITTLE EVIDENCE THAT THE COCKROACH HAS EVOLVED GENETICALLY OR ALTERED ITS LIFE EXPECTANCY. IT HAS AN UNQUESTIONABLE LIFE FORCE EVIDENCED BY ITS WILL TO LIVE!

..when the deep purple falls
over sleepy garden walls

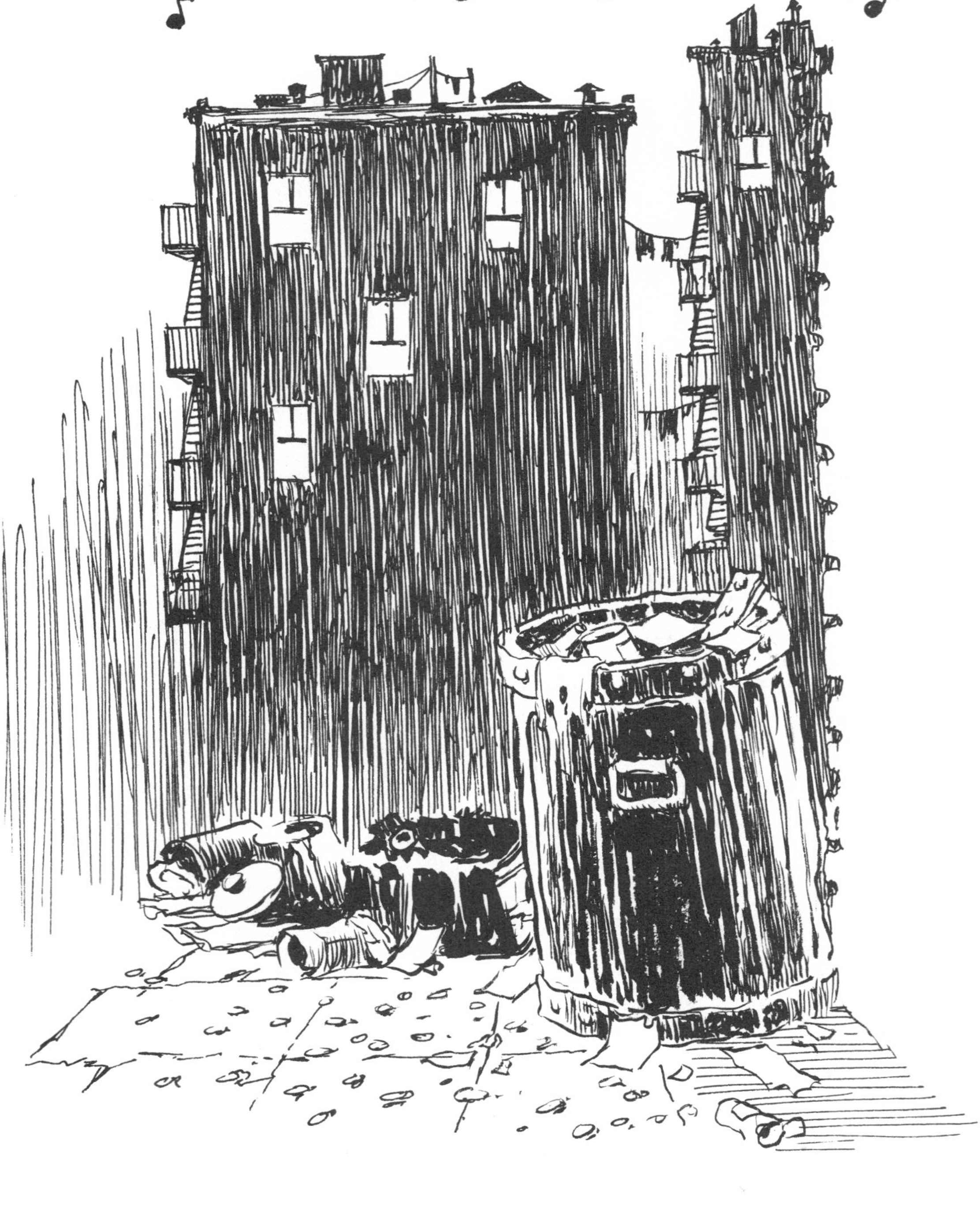

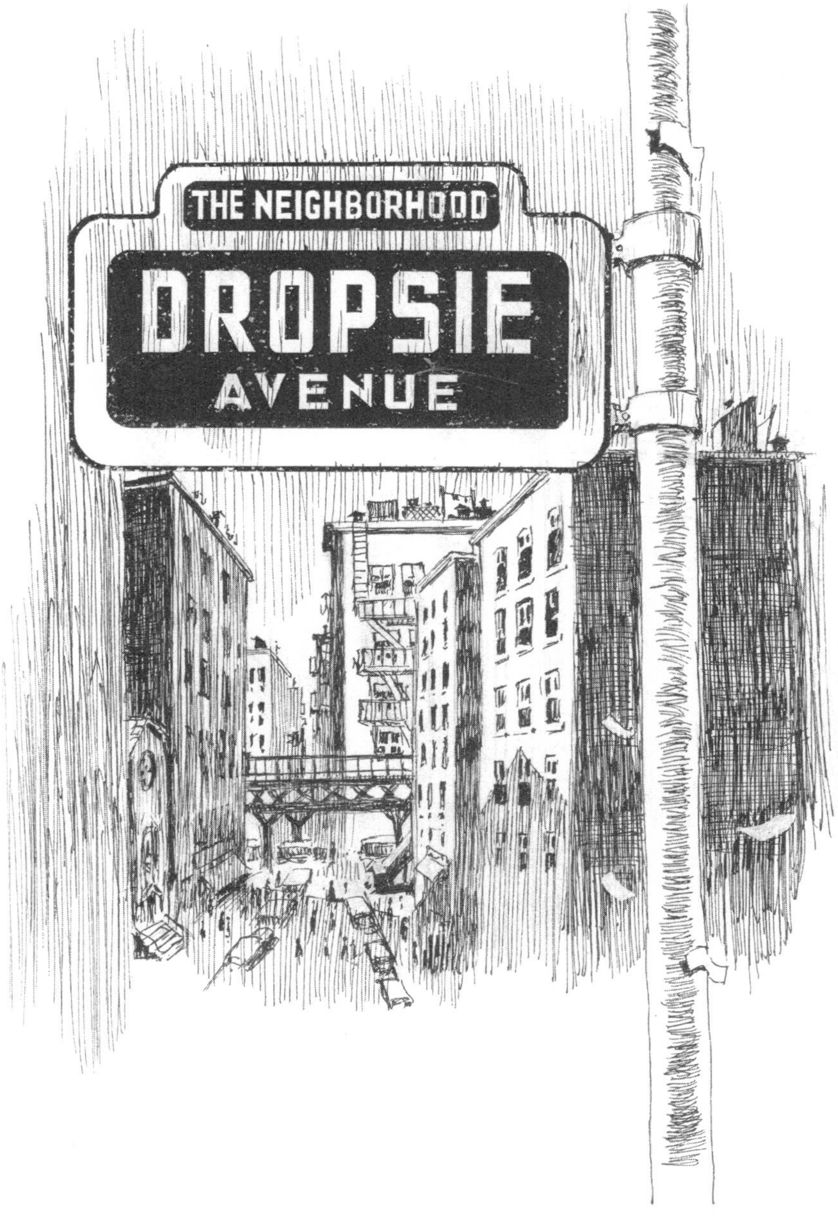
THE NEIGHBORHOOD
DROPSIE
AVENUE

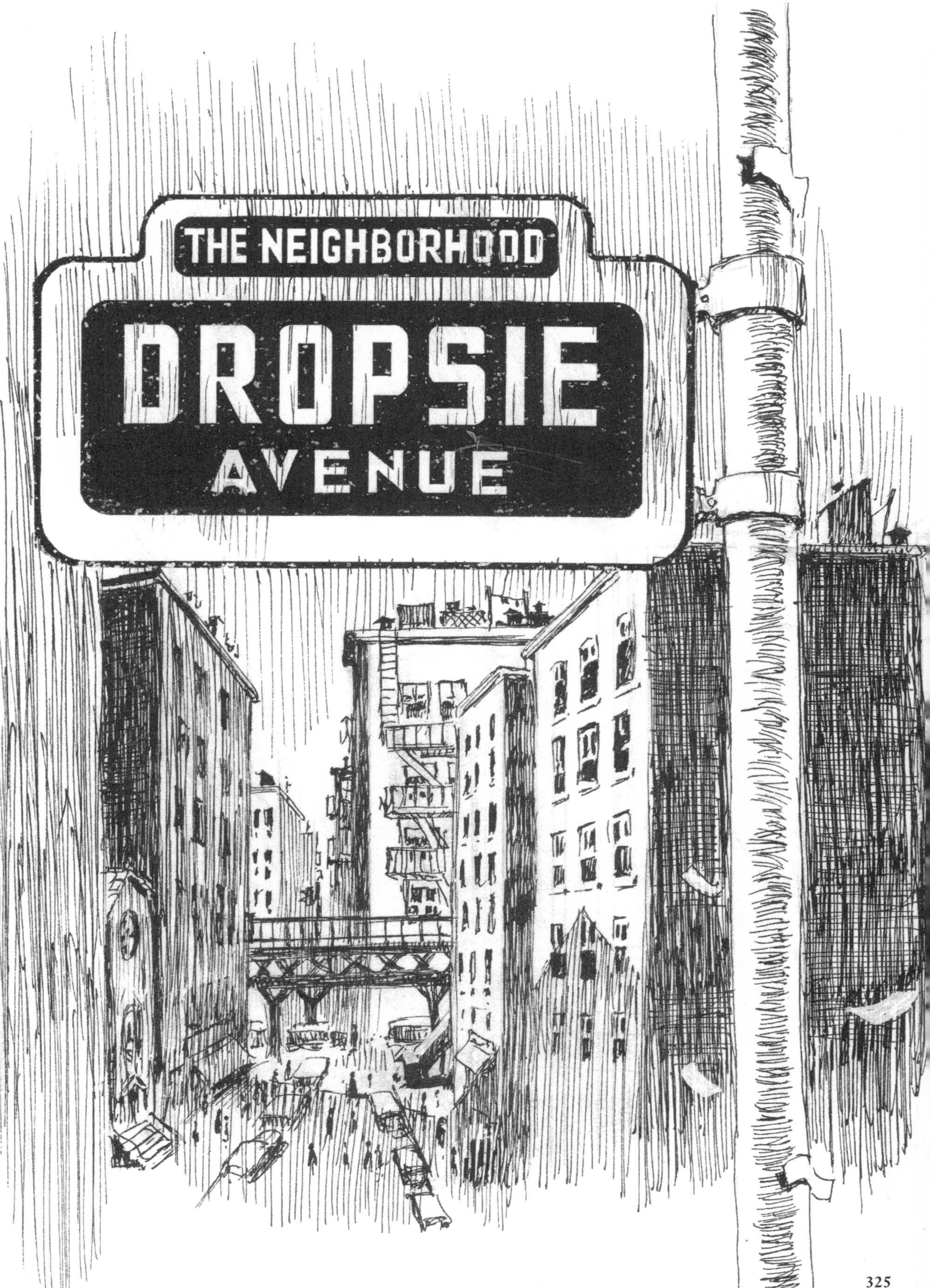
THE NEIGHBORHOOD
DROPSIE
AVENUE

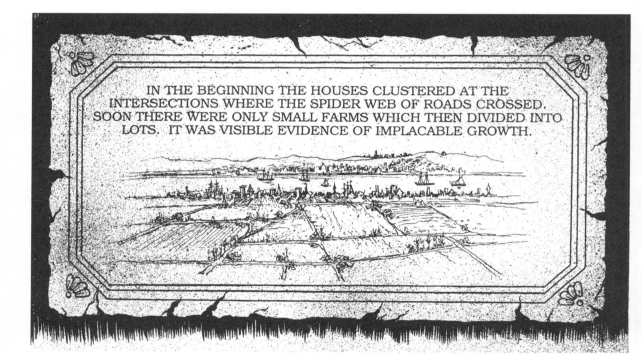

IN THE BEGINNING THE HOUSES CLUSTERED AT THE
INTERSECTIONS WHERE THE SPIDER WEB OF ROADS CROSSED.
SOON THERE WERE ONLY SMALL FARMS WHICH THEN DIVIDED INTO
LOTS. IT WAS VISIBLE EVIDENCE OF IMPLACABLE GROWTH.

THE NEIGHBORHOOD

BEGAN TO FORM EVEN WHILE A FEW OLD DUTCH FAMILIES STILL CLUNG TO THE HOLDINGS THEY INHERITED...

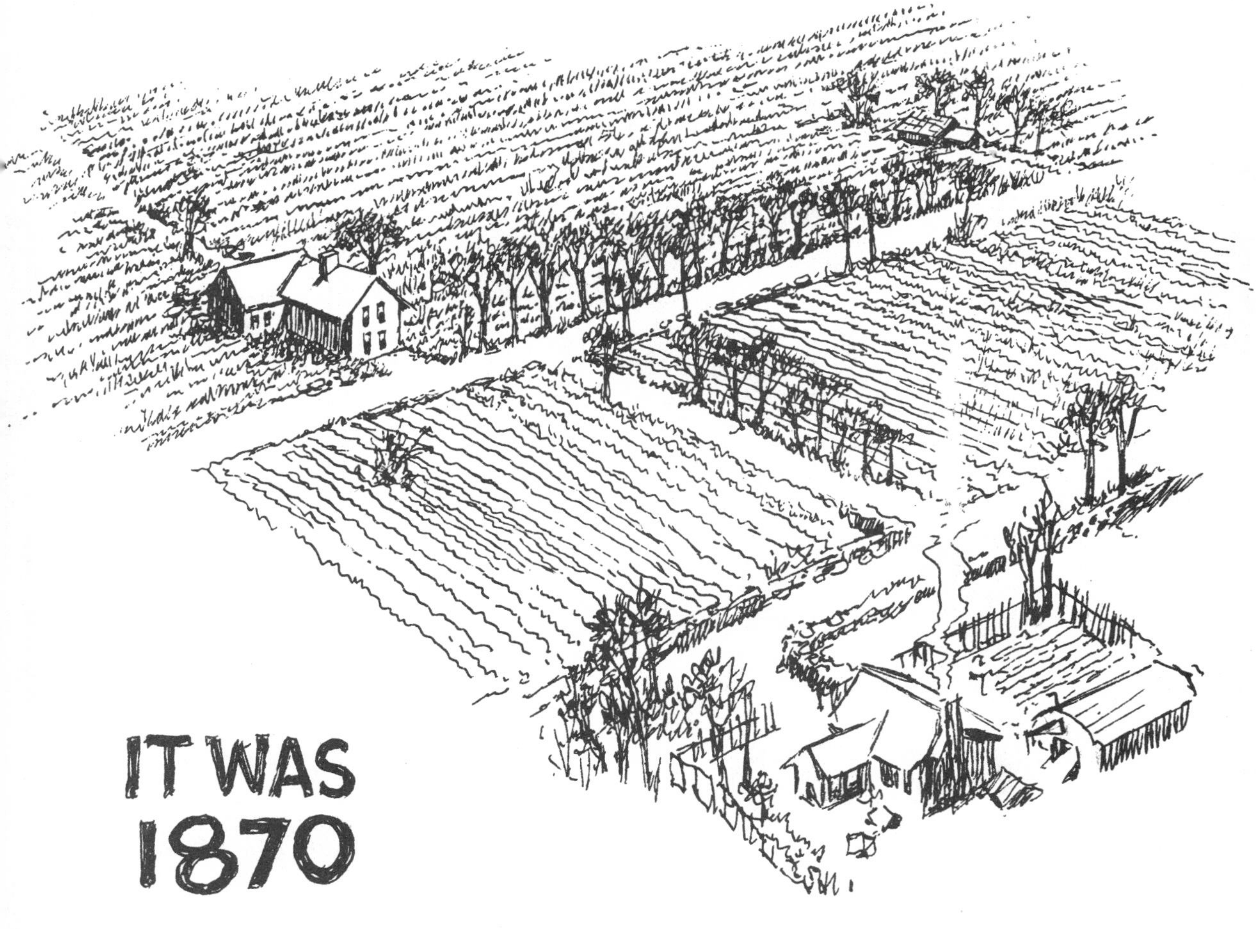

IT WAS 1870

AND STILL THERE WERE FARMS IN THE BRONX.

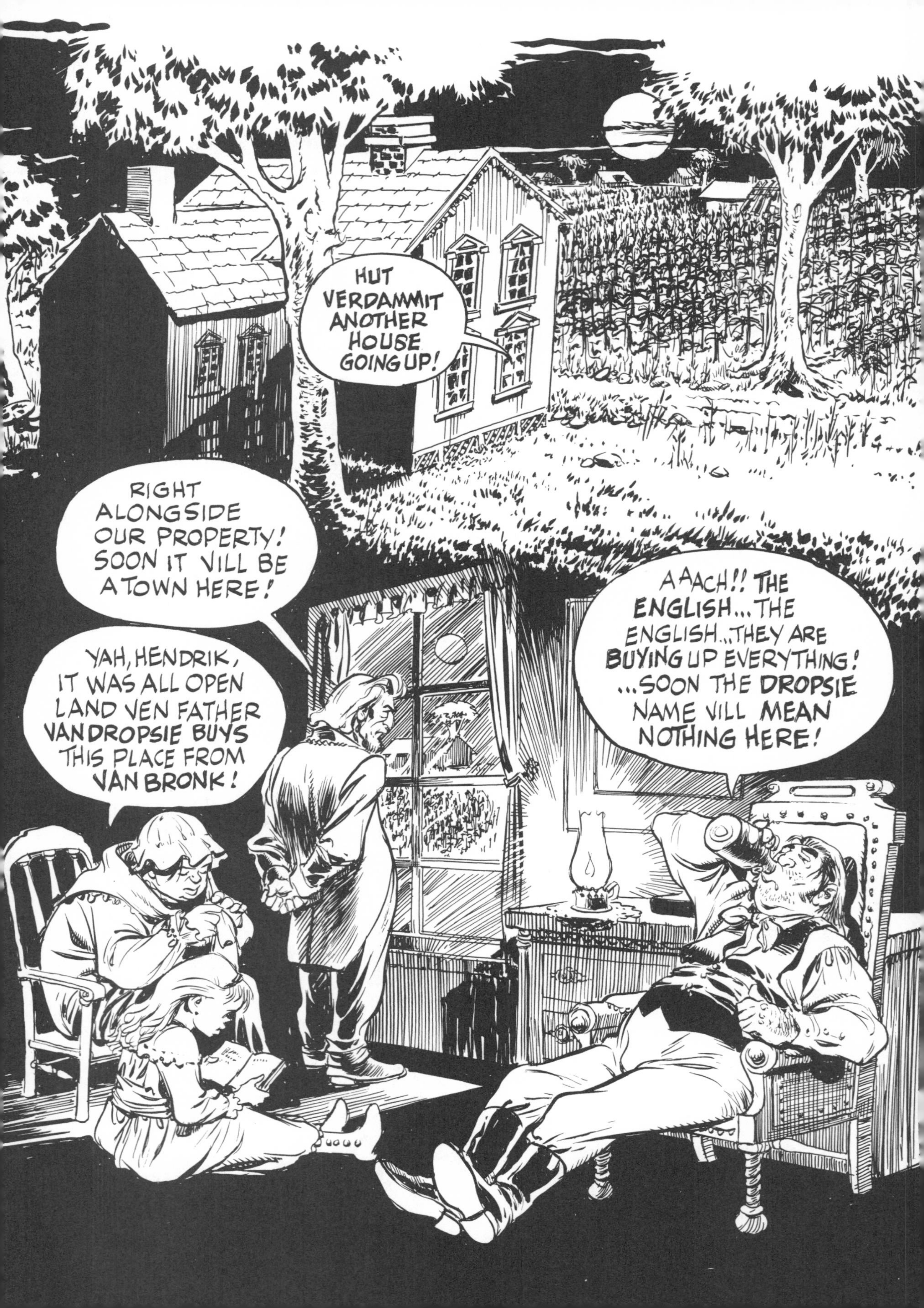
HUT VERDAMMIT ANOTHER HOUSE GOING UP!
RIGHT ALONGSIDE OUR PROPERTY! SOON IT VILL BE A TOWN HERE!
YAH, HENDRIK, IT WAS ALL OPEN LAND VEN FATHER VANDROPSIE BUYS THIS PLACE FROM VAN BRONK!
AAACH!! THE ENGLISH... THE ENGLISH.. THEY ARE BUYING UP EVERYTHING! ...SOON THE DROPSIE NAME VILL MEAN NOTHING HERE!

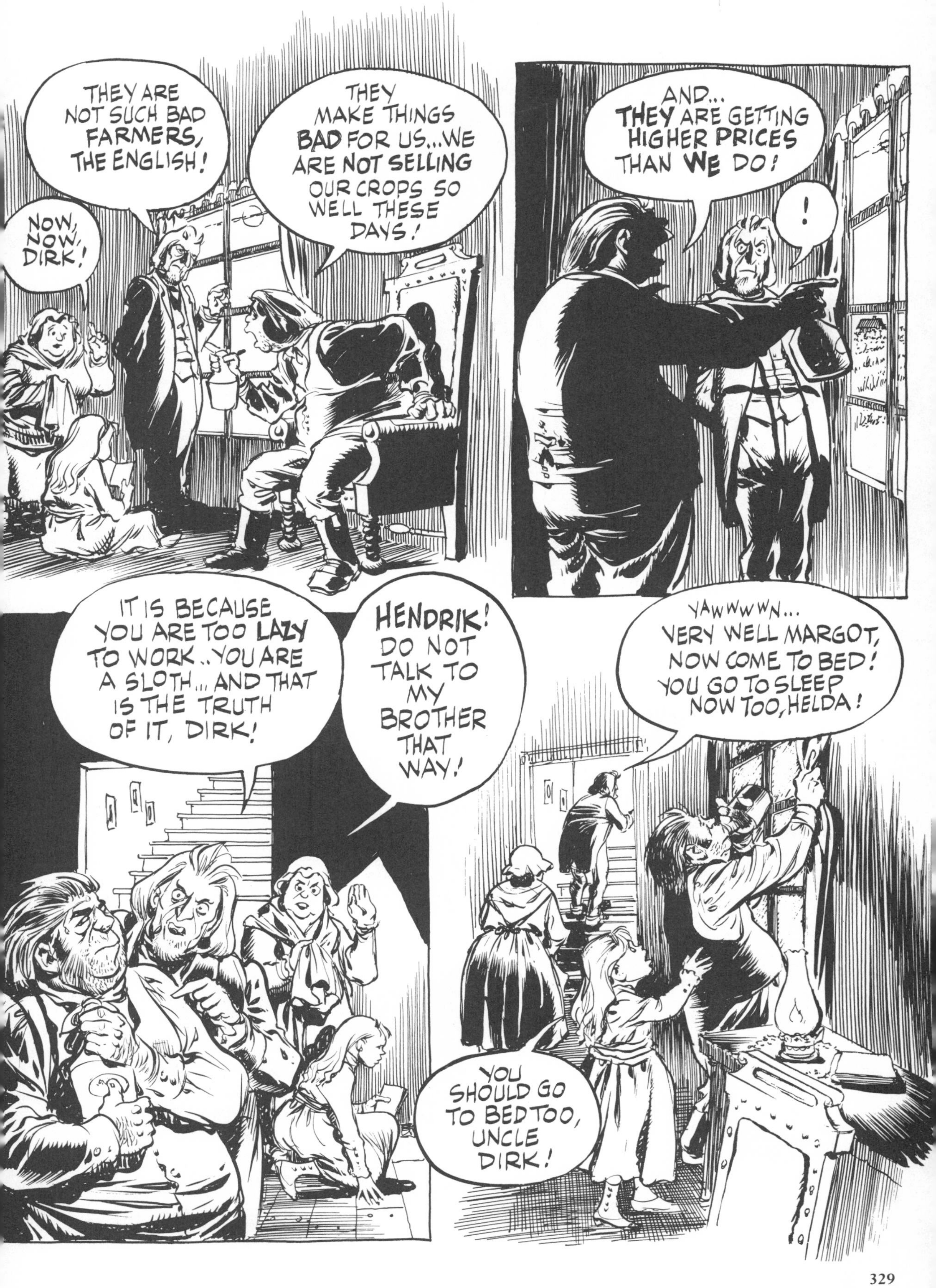
NOW, NOW, DIRK!
THEY ARE NOT SUCH BAD FARMERS, THE ENGLISH!
THEY MAKE THINGS BAD FOR US...WE ARE NOT SELLING OUR CROPS SO WELL THESE DAYS!
AND... THEY ARE GETTING HIGHER PRICES THAN WE DO!
!
IT IS BECAUSE YOU ARE TOO LAZY TO WORK..YOU ARE A SLOTH... AND THAT IS THE TRUTH OF IT, DIRK!
HENDRIK! DO NOT TALK TO MY BROTHER THAT WAY!
YAWWWWN... VERY WELL MARGOT, NOW COME TO BED! YOU GO TO SLEEP NOW TOO, HELDA!
YOU SHOULD GO TO BED TOO, UNCLE DIRK!

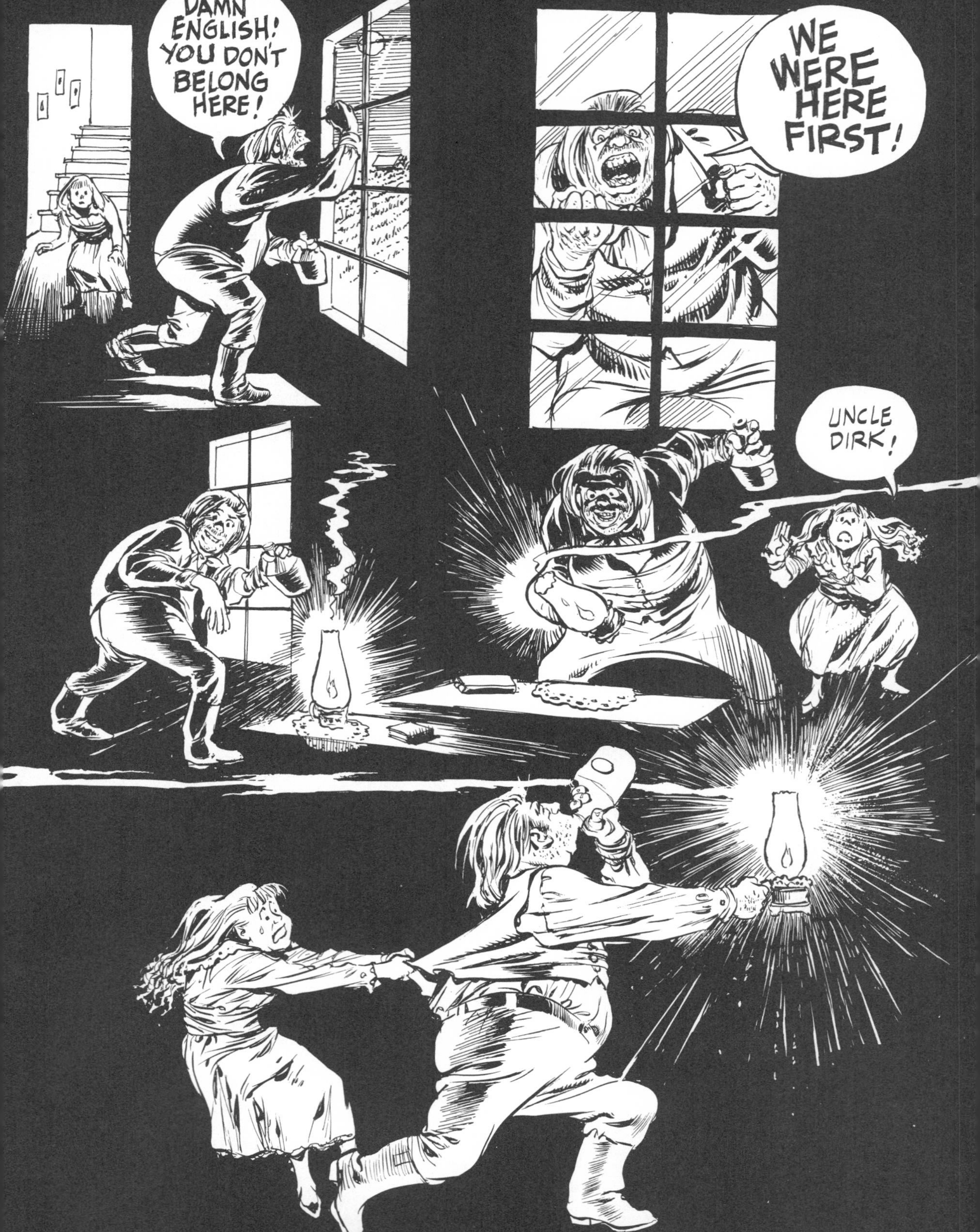
DAMN ENGLISH! YOU DON'T BELONG HERE!
WE WERE HERE FIRST!
UNCLE DIRK!

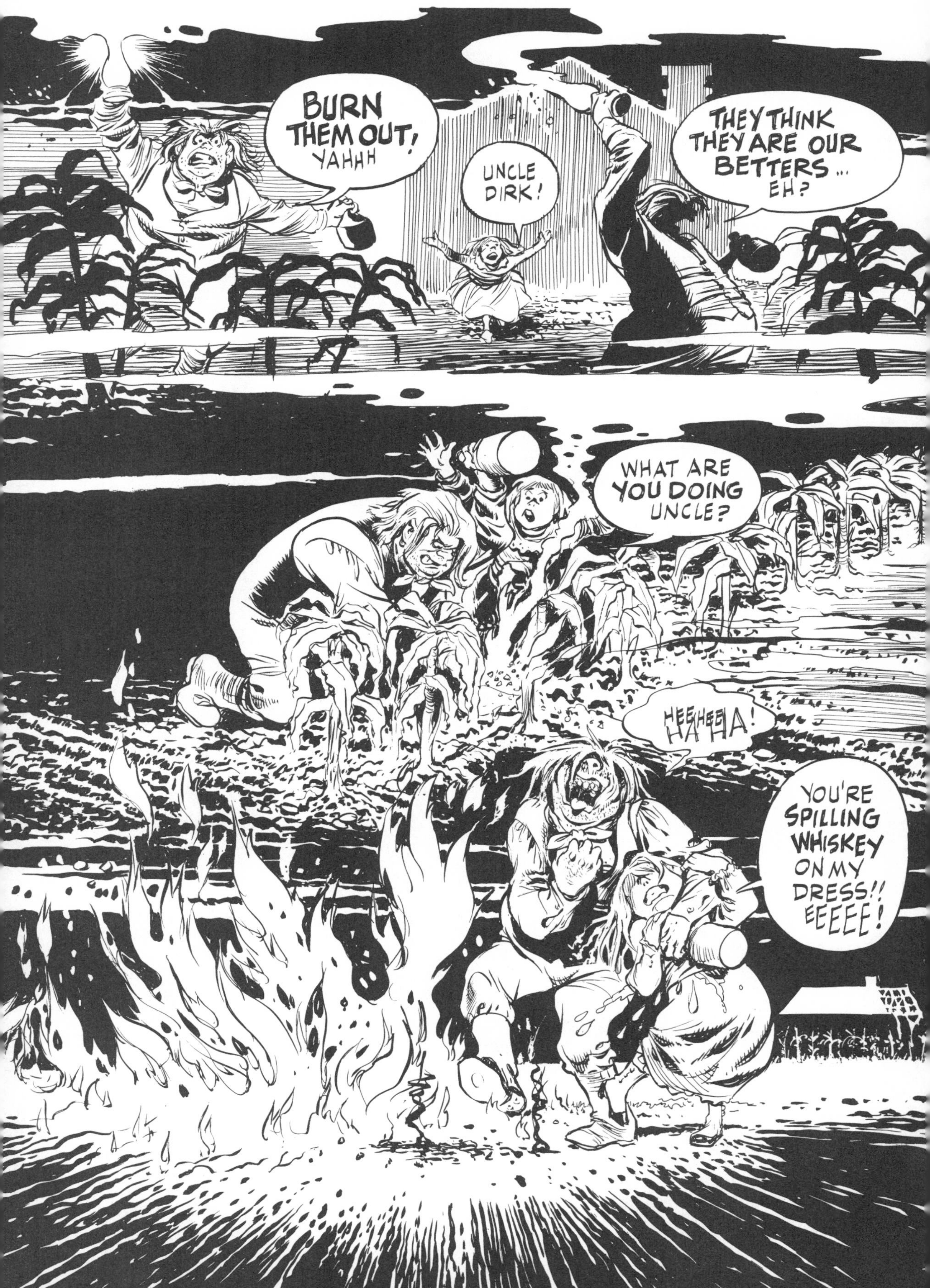

BURN THEM OUT! YAHHH
UNCLE DIRK!
THEY THINK THEY ARE OUR BETTERS... EH?
WHAT ARE YOU DOING UNCLE?
HEE HEE HA HA!
YOU'RE SPILLING WHISKEY ON MY DRESS!! EEEEE!

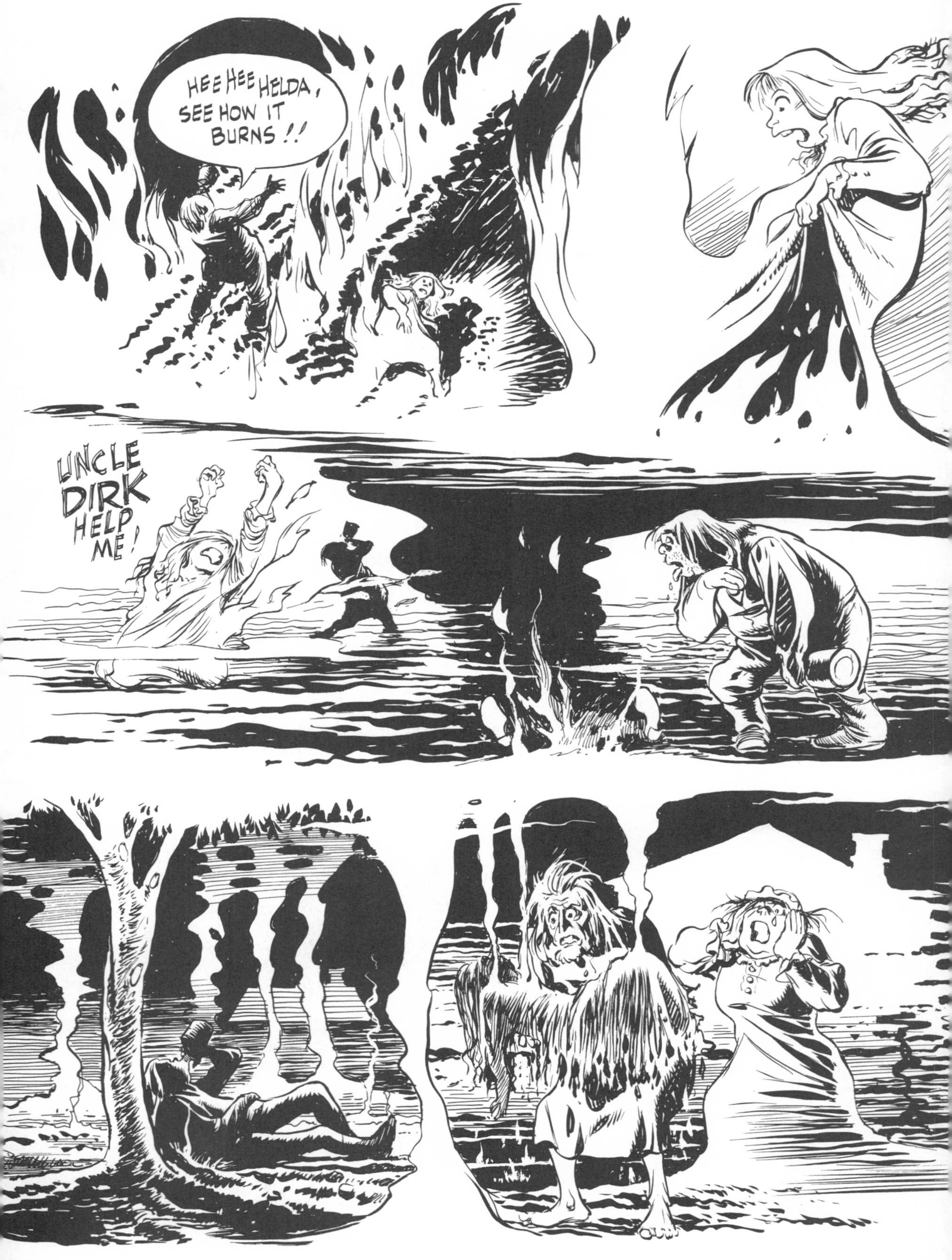
HEE HEE HELDA, SEE HOW IT BURNS!!
UNCLE DIRK HELP ME!

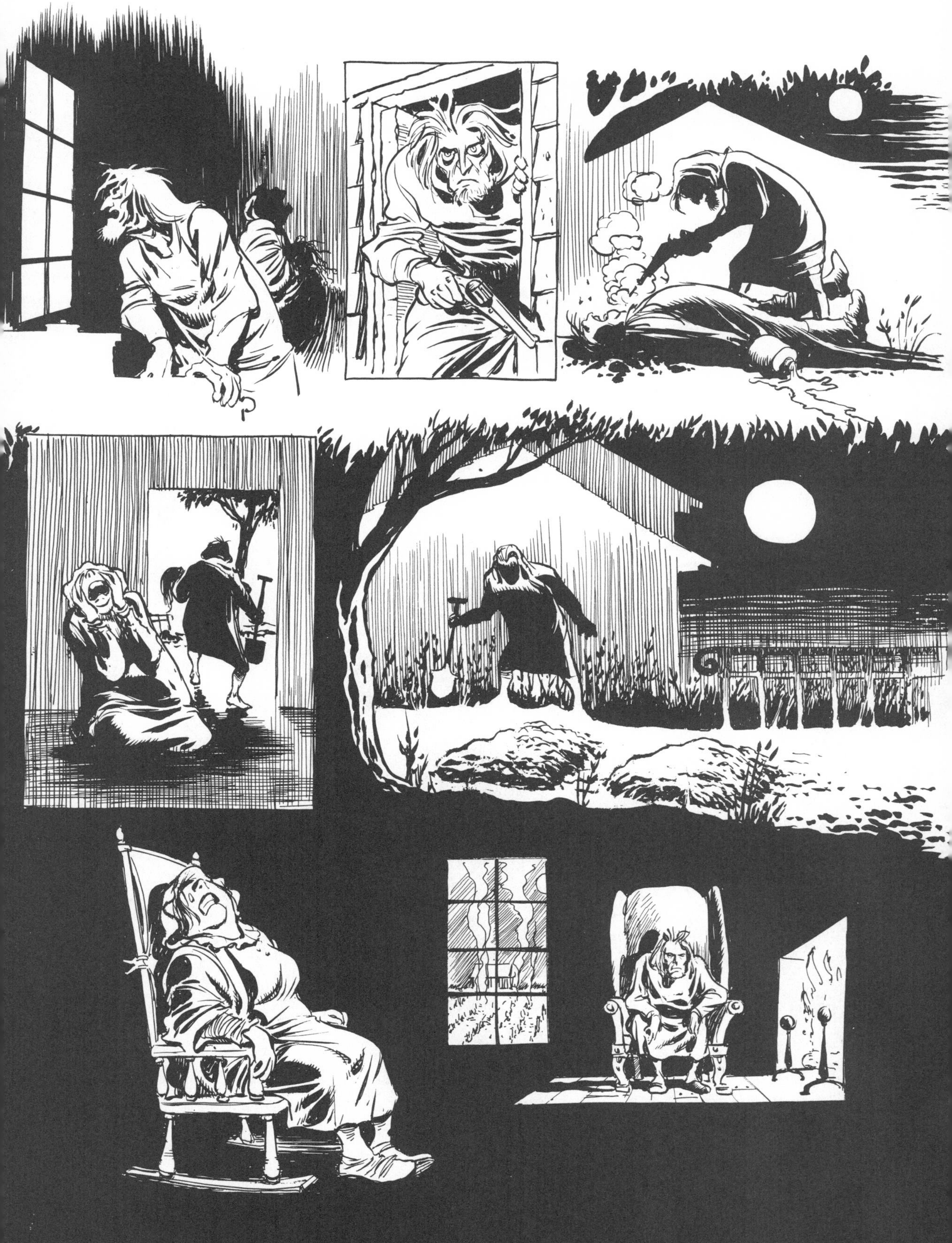

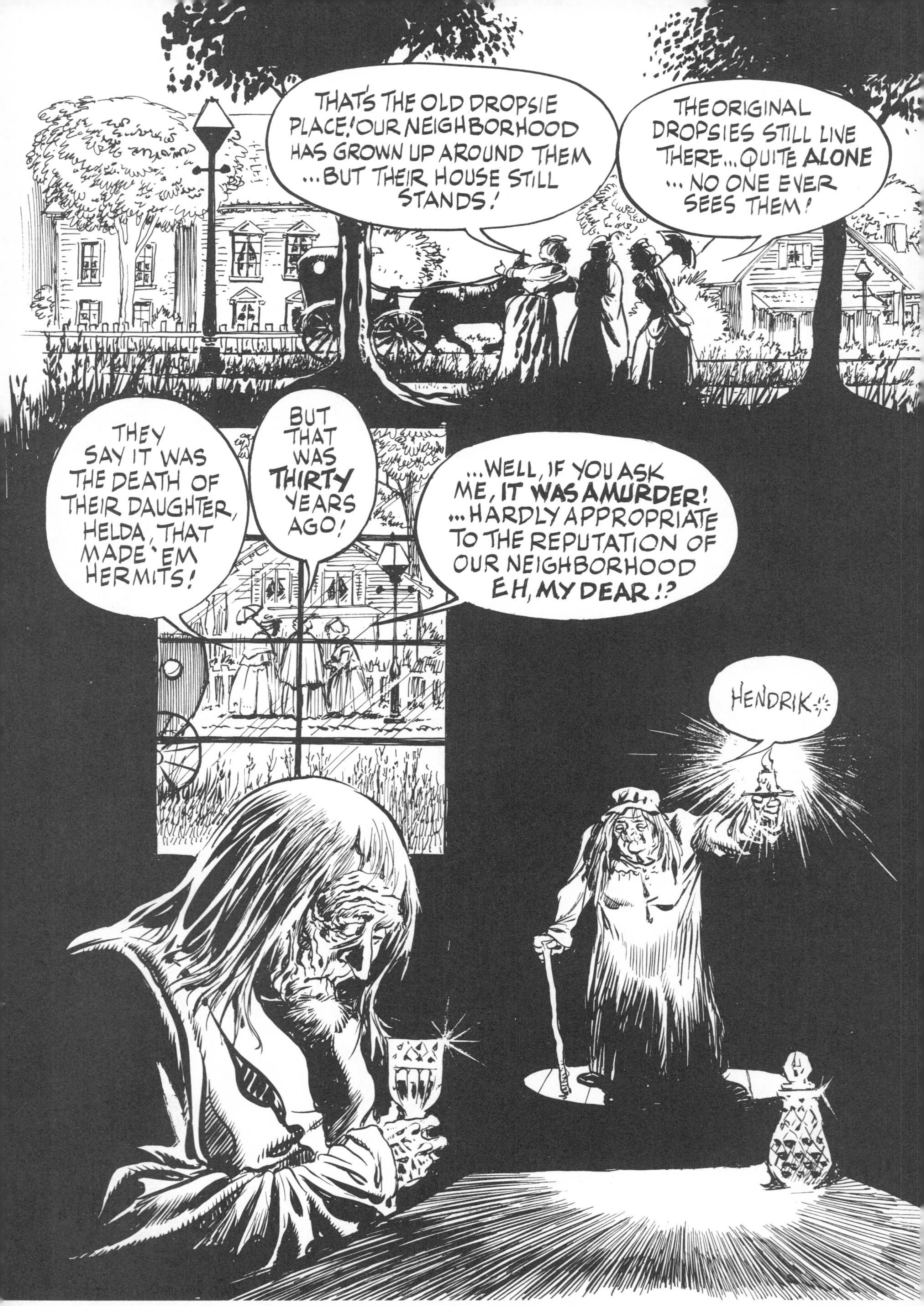
THAT'S THE OLD DROPSIE PLACE! OUR NEIGHBORHOOD HAS GROWN UP AROUND THEM ...BUT THEIR HOUSE STILL STANDS!
THE ORIGINAL DROPSIES STILL LIVE THERE... QUITE **ALONE** ...NO ONE EVER SEES THEM!
THEY SAY IT WAS THE DEATH OF THEIR DAUGHTER, HELDA, THAT MADE 'EM HERMITS!
BUT THAT WAS **THIRTY** YEARS AGO!
...WELL, IF YOU ASK ME, **IT WAS A MURDER!** ...HARDLY APPROPRIATE TO THE REPUTATION OF OUR NEIGHBORHOOD **EH, MY DEAR!?**
HENDRIK

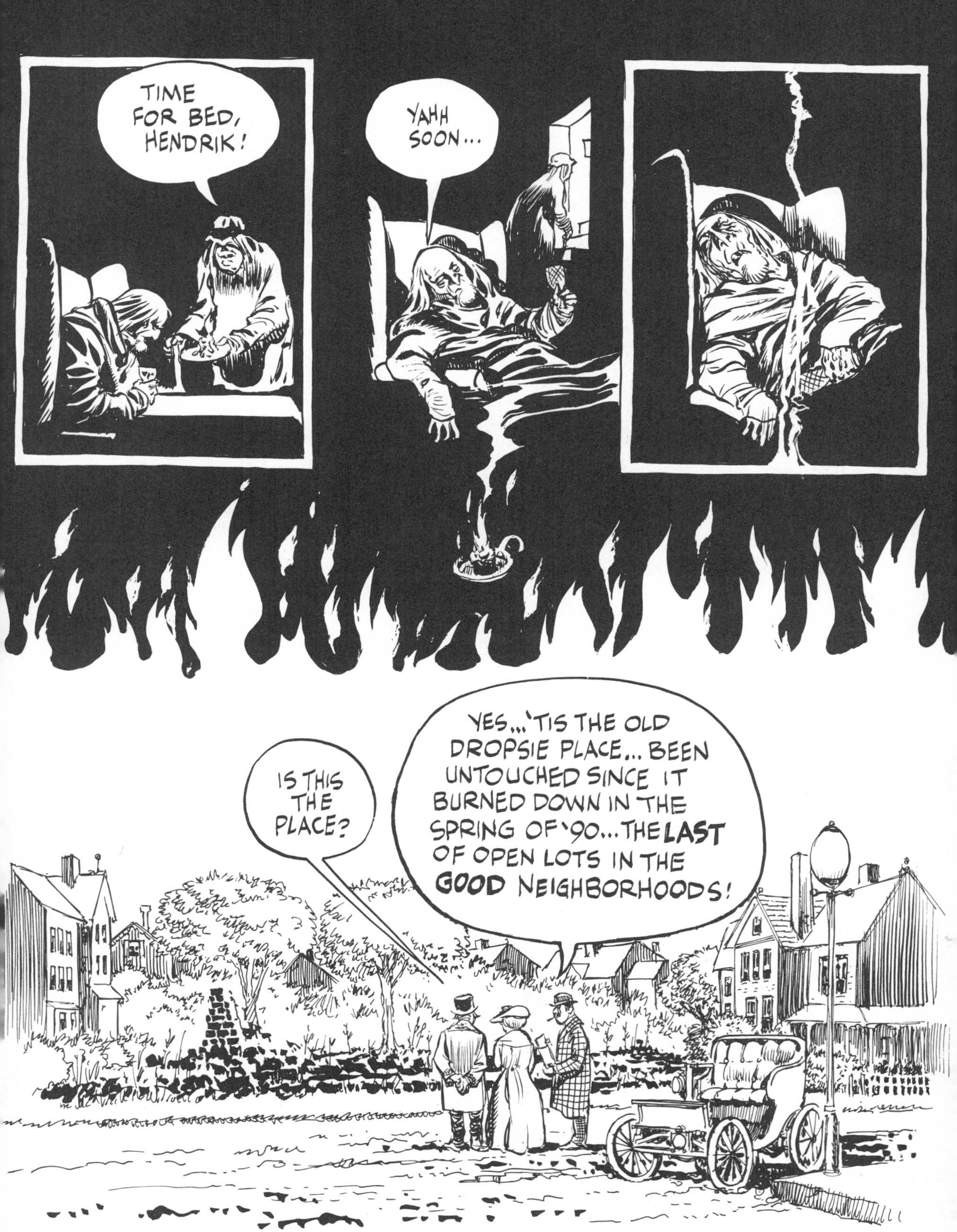
TIME FOR BED, HENDRIK!
YAHH SOON...
IS THIS THE PLACE?
YES...'TIS THE OLD DROPSIE PLACE... BEEN UNTOUCHED SINCE IT BURNED DOWN IN THE SPRING OF '90... THE LAST OF OPEN LOTS IN THE GOOD NEIGHBORHOODS!

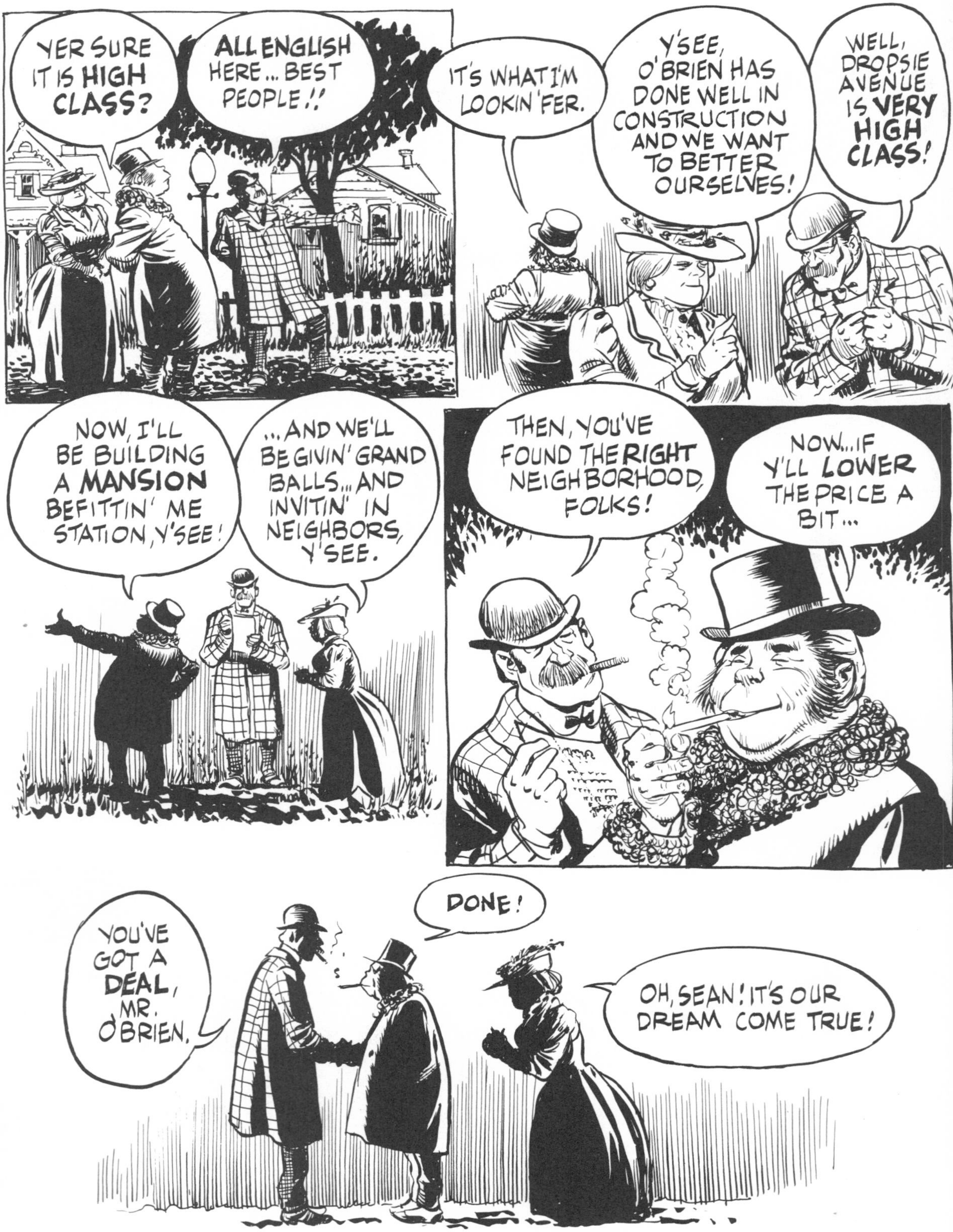
YER SURE IT IS **HIGH CLASS?**
ALL ENGLISH HERE ... BEST PEOPLE!!
IT'S WHAT I'M LOOKIN' FER.
Y'SEE, O'BRIEN HAS DONE WELL IN CONSTRUCTION AND WE WANT TO BETTER OURSELVES!
WELL, DROPSIE AVENUE IS **VERY HIGH CLASS!**
NOW, I'LL BE BUILDING A **MANSION** BEFITTIN' ME STATION, Y'SEE!
...AND WE'LL BE GIVIN' GRAND BALLS... AND INVITIN' IN NEIGHBORS, Y'SEE.
THEN, YOU'VE FOUND THE **RIGHT** NEIGHBORHOOD, FOLKS!
NOW...IF Y'LL **LOWER** THE PRICE A BIT...
YOU'VE GOT A **DEAL**, MR. O'BRIEN.
DONE!
OH, SEAN! IT'S OUR DREAM COME TRUE!

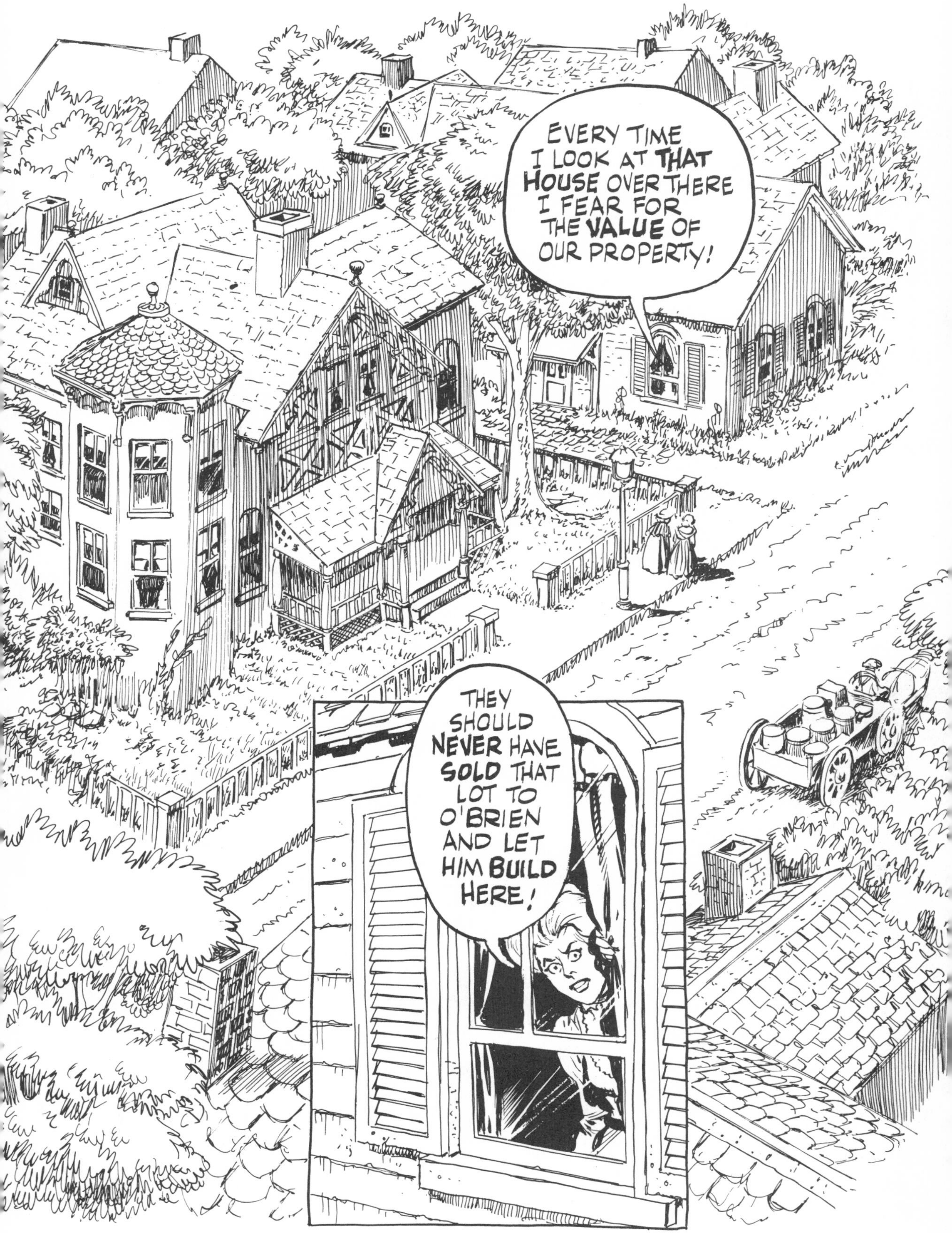
EVERY TIME I LOOK AT THAT HOUSE OVER THERE I FEAR FOR THE VALUE OF OUR PROPERTY!
THEY SHOULD NEVER HAVE SOLD THAT LOT TO O'BRIEN AND LET HIM BUILD HERE!

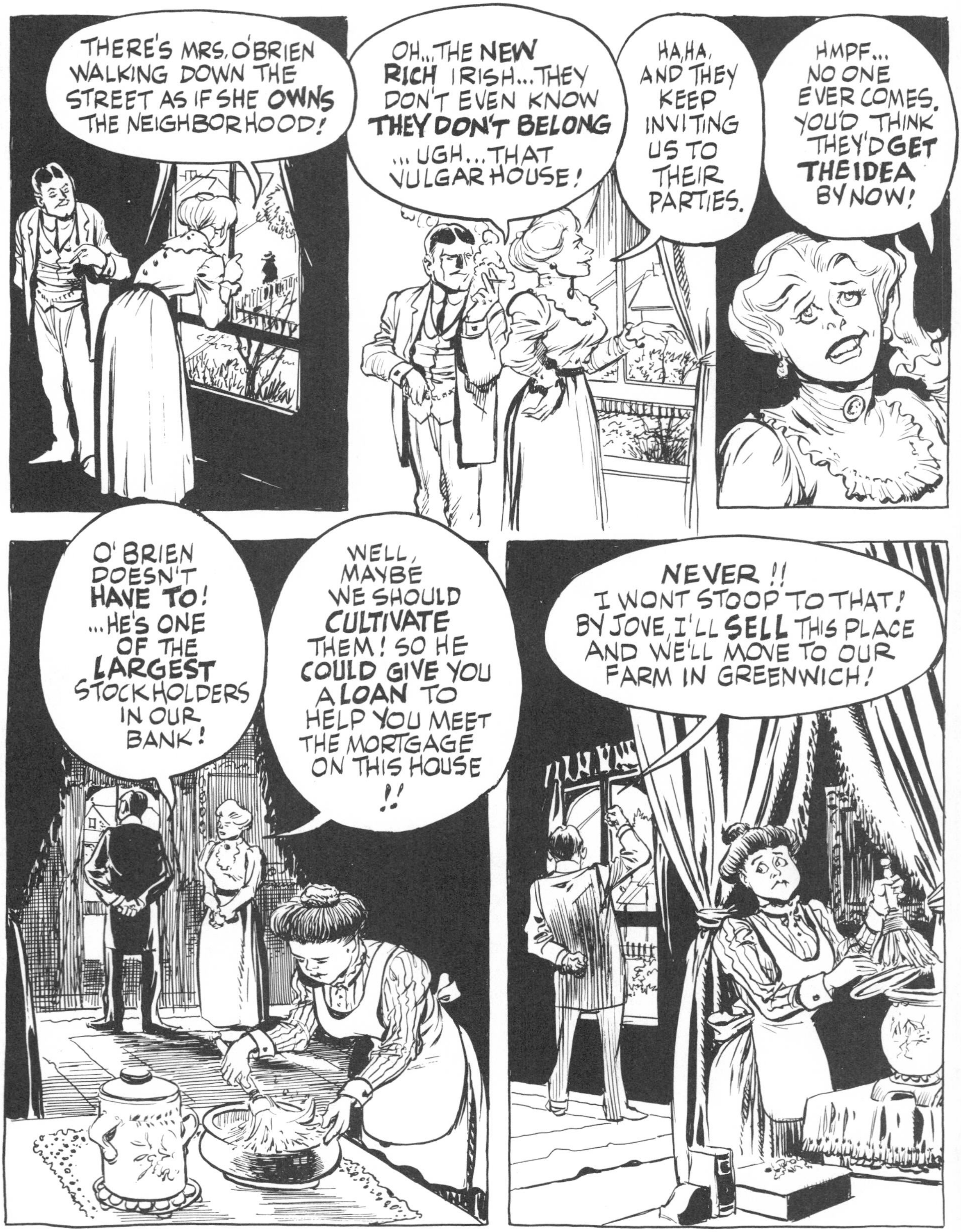
THERE'S MRS. O'BRIEN WALKING DOWN THE STREET AS IF SHE OWNS THE NEIGHBORHOOD!
OH... THE NEW RICH IRISH... THEY DON'T EVEN KNOW THEY DON'T BELONG ... UGH... THAT VULGAR HOUSE!
HA,HA, AND THEY KEEP INVITING US TO THEIR PARTIES.
HMPF... NO ONE EVER COMES. YOU'D THINK THEY'D GET THE IDEA BY NOW!
O'BRIEN DOESN'T HAVE TO! ...HE'S ONE OF THE LARGEST STOCKHOLDERS IN OUR BANK!
WELL, MAYBE WE SHOULD CULTIVATE THEM! SO HE COULD GIVE YOU A LOAN TO HELP YOU MEET THE MORTGAGE ON THIS HOUSE !!
NEVER !! I WONT STOOP TO THAT! BY JOVE, I'LL SELL THIS PLACE AND WE'LL MOVE TO OUR FARM IN GREENWICH!

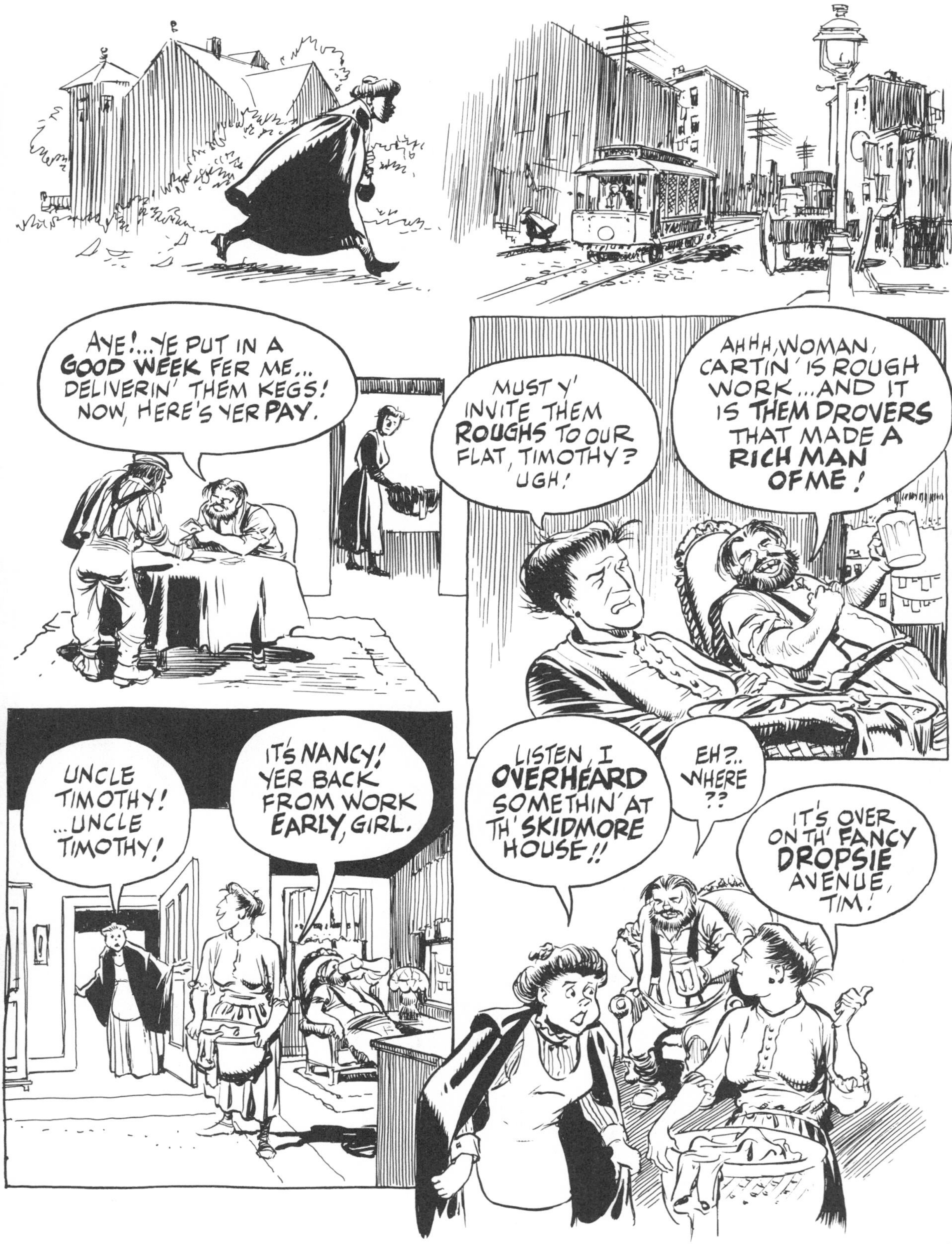
AYE!...YE PUT IN A GOOD WEEK FER ME... DELIVERIN' THEM KEGS! NOW, HERE'S YER PAY.
MUST Y' INVITE THEM ROUGHS TO OUR FLAT, TIMOTHY? UGH!
AHHH, WOMAN, CARTIN' IS ROUGH WORK...AND IT IS THEM DROVERS THAT MADE A RICH MAN OF ME!
UNCLE TIMOTHY! ...UNCLE TIMOTHY!
IT'S NANCY! YER BACK FROM WORK EARLY, GIRL.
LISTEN, I OVERHEARD SOMETHIN' AT TH' SKIDMORE HOUSE!!
EH?.. WHERE ??
IT'S OVER ON TH' FANCY DROPSIE AVENUE, TIM!

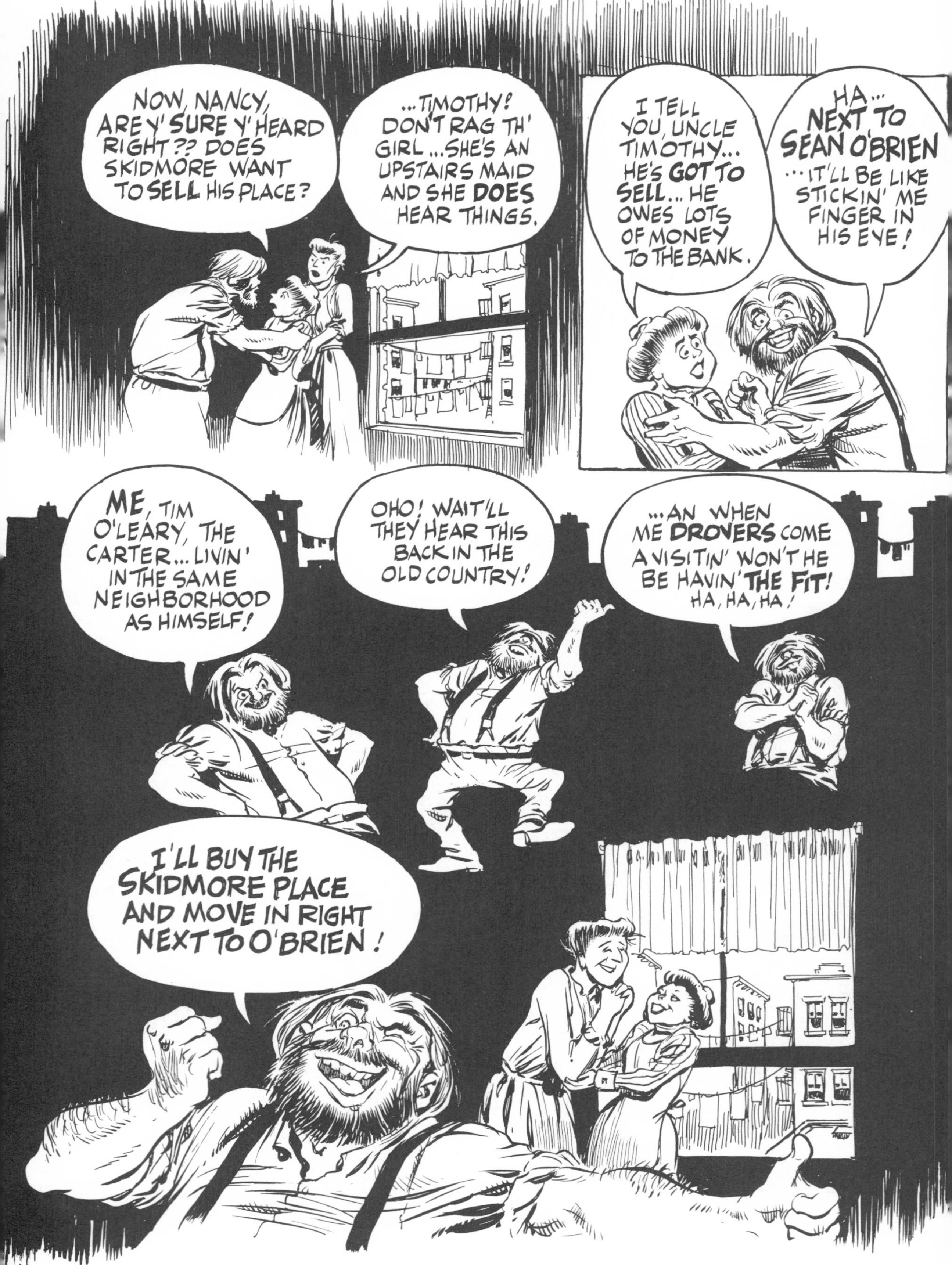
NOW, NANCY, ARE Y' SURE Y' HEARD RIGHT?? DOES SKIDMORE WANT TO SELL HIS PLACE?
...TIMOTHY! DON'T RAG TH' GIRL...SHE'S AN UPSTAIRS MAID AND SHE DOES HEAR THINGS.
I TELL YOU, UNCLE TIMOTHY... HE'S GOT TO SELL... HE OWES LOTS OF MONEY TO THE BANK.
HA... NEXT TO SEAN O'BRIEN ...IT'LL BE LIKE STICKIN' ME FINGER IN HIS EYE!
ME, TIM O'LEARY, THE CARTER...LIVIN' IN THE SAME NEIGHBORHOOD AS HIMSELF!
OHO! WAIT'LL THEY HEAR THIS BACK IN THE OLD COUNTRY!
...AN WHEN ME DROVERS COME A VISITIN' WON'T HE BE HAVIN' THE FIT! HA, HA, HA!
I'LL BUY THE SKIDMORE PLACE AND MOVE IN RIGHT NEXT TO O'BRIEN!

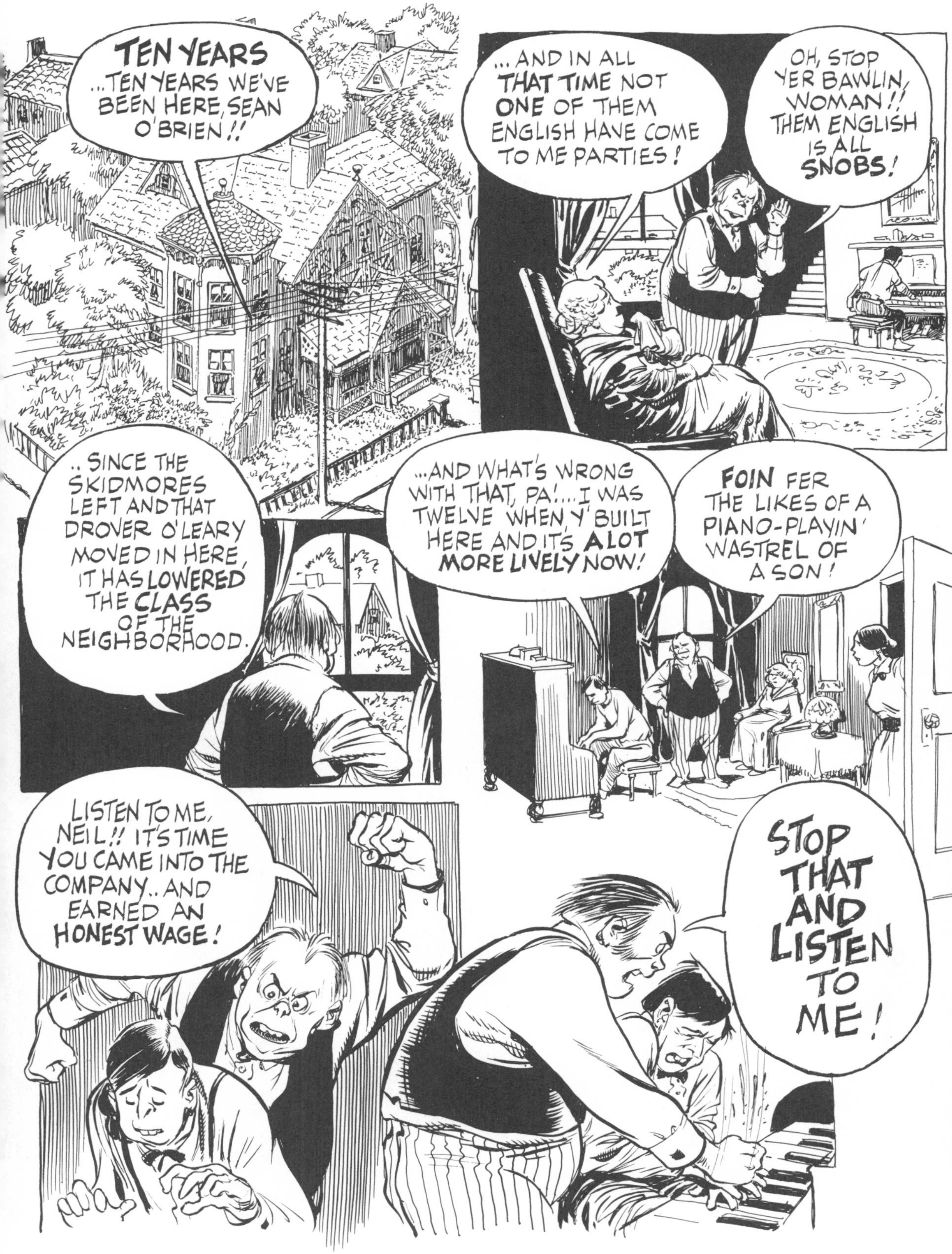
TEN YEARS ...TEN YEARS WE'VE BEEN HERE, SEAN O'BRIEN!!
...AND IN ALL THAT TIME NOT ONE OF THEM ENGLISH HAVE COME TO ME PARTIES!
OH, STOP YER BAWLIN, WOMAN!! THEM ENGLISH IS ALL SNOBS!
.. SINCE THE SKIDMORES LEFT AND THAT DROVER O'LEARY MOVED IN HERE, IT HAS LOWERED THE CLASS OF THE NEIGHBORHOOD.
...AND WHAT'S WRONG WITH THAT, PA!... I WAS TWELVE WHEN Y' BUILT HERE AND IT'S A LOT MORE LIVELY NOW!
FOIN FER THE LIKES OF A PIANO-PLAYIN' WASTREL OF A SON!
LISTEN TO ME, NEIL!! IT'S TIME YOU CAME INTO THE COMPANY.. AND EARNED AN HONEST WAGE!
STOP THAT AND LISTEN TO ME!

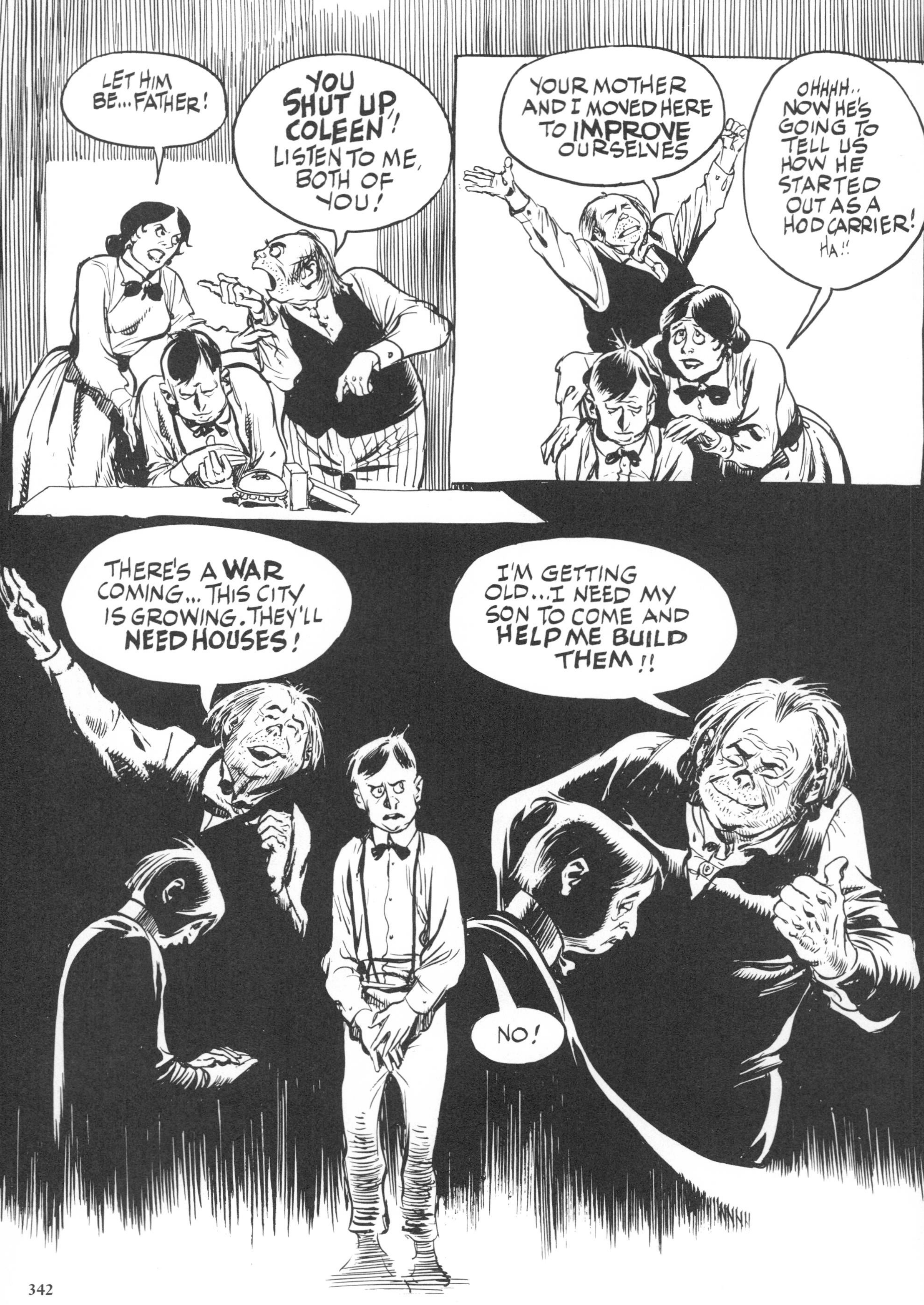

LET HIM BE...FATHER!
YOU SHUT UP, COLEEN! LISTEN TO ME, BOTH OF YOU!
YOUR MOTHER AND I MOVED HERE TO IMPROVE OURSELVES
OHHHH.. NOW HE'S GOING TO TELL US HOW HE STARTED OUT AS A HOD CARRIER! HA!!
THERE'S A WAR COMING... THIS CITY IS GROWING. THEY'LL NEED HOUSES!
I'M GETTING OLD...I NEED MY SON TO COME AND HELP ME BUILD THEM!!
NO!

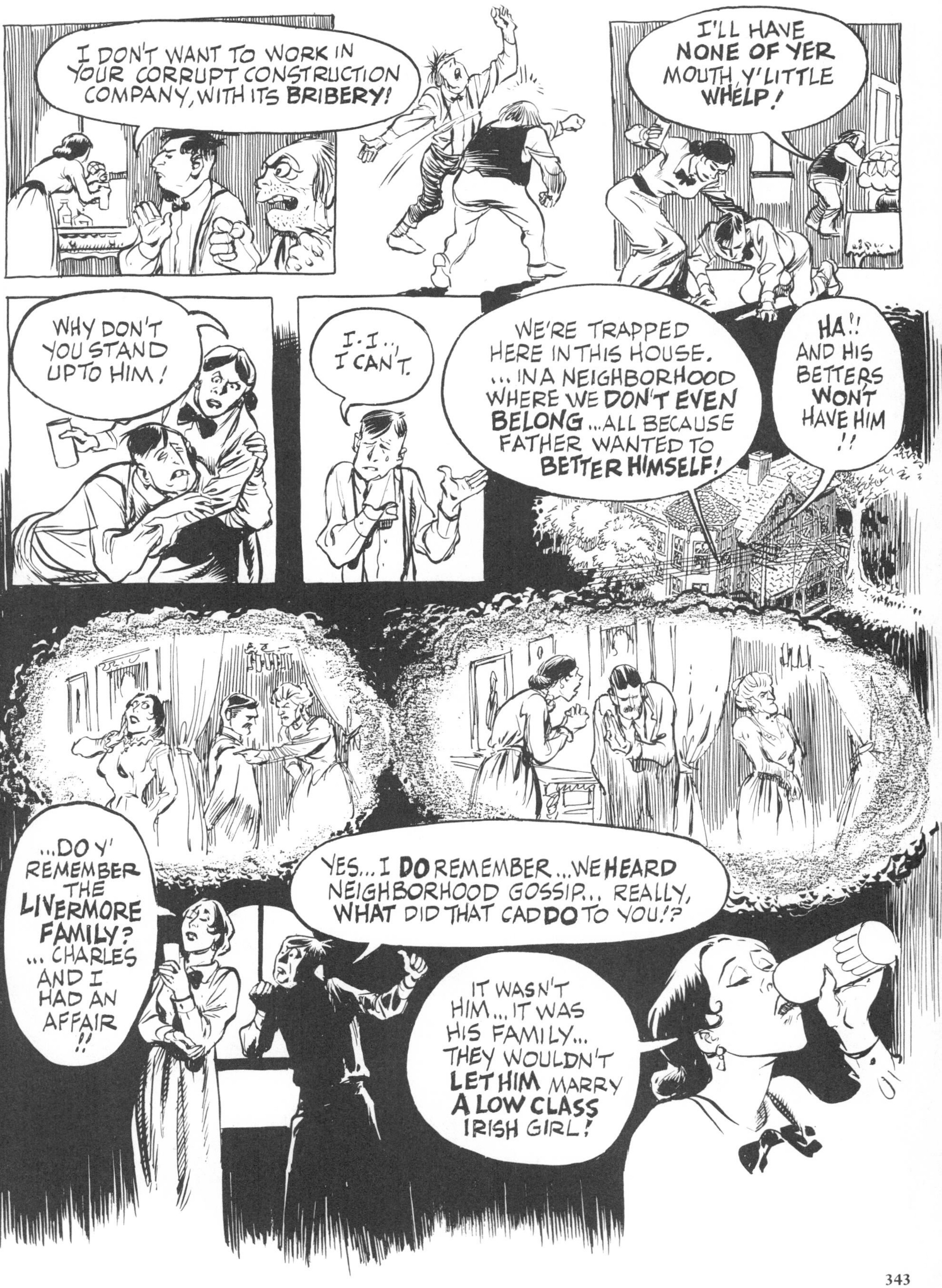
I DON'T WANT TO WORK IN YOUR CORRUPT CONSTRUCTION COMPANY, WITH ITS BRIBERY!
I'LL HAVE NONE OF YER MOUTH, Y'LITTLE WHELP!
WHY DON'T YOU STAND UP TO HIM!
I..I.. I CAN'T.
WE'RE TRAPPED HERE IN THIS HOUSE. ...IN A NEIGHBORHOOD WHERE WE DON'T EVEN BELONG ...ALL BECAUSE FATHER WANTED TO BETTER HIMSELF!
HA!! AND HIS BETTERS WON'T HAVE HIM!!
...DO Y' REMEMBER THE LIVERMORE FAMILY? ... CHARLES AND I HAD AN AFFAIR!!
YES... I DO REMEMBER ...WE HEARD NEIGHBORHOOD GOSSIP... REALLY, WHAT DID THAT CAD DO TO YOU!?
IT WASN'T HIM... IT WAS HIS FAMILY... THEY WOULDN'T LET HIM MARRY A LOW CLASS IRISH GIRL!

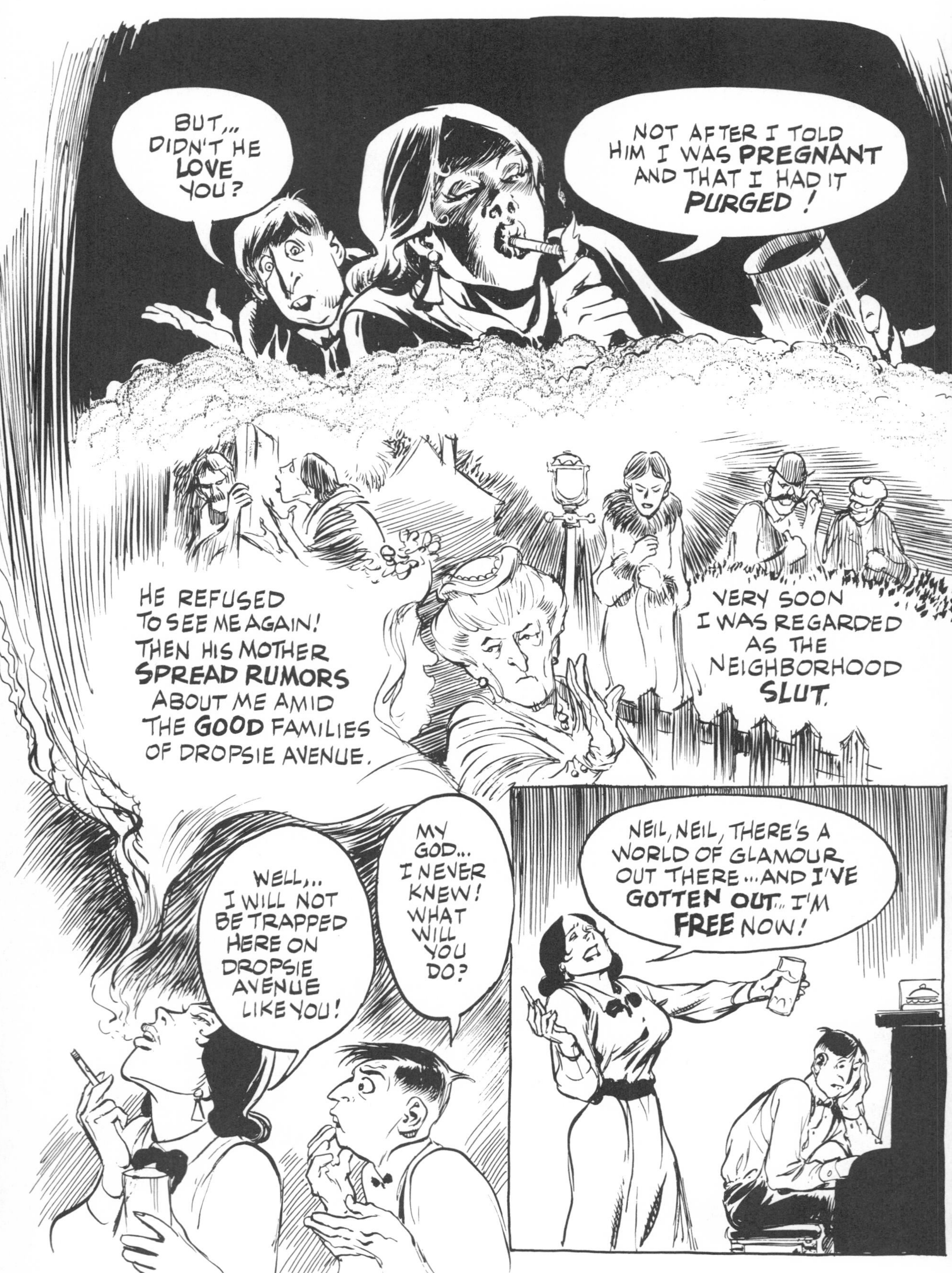
BUT,.. DIDN'T HE LOVE YOU?
NOT AFTER I TOLD HIM I WAS PREGNANT AND THAT I HAD IT PURGED!
HE REFUSED TO SEE ME AGAIN! THEN HIS MOTHER SPREAD RUMORS ABOUT ME AMID THE GOOD FAMILIES OF DROPSIE AVENUE.
VERY SOON I WAS REGARDED AS THE NEIGHBORHOOD SLUT.
WELL,.. I WILL NOT BE TRAPPED HERE ON DROPSIE AVENUE LIKE YOU!
MY GOD... I NEVER KNEW! WHAT WILL YOU DO?
NEIL, NEIL, THERE'S A WORLD OF GLAMOUR OUT THERE ... AND I'VE GOTTEN OUT.. I'M FREE NOW!

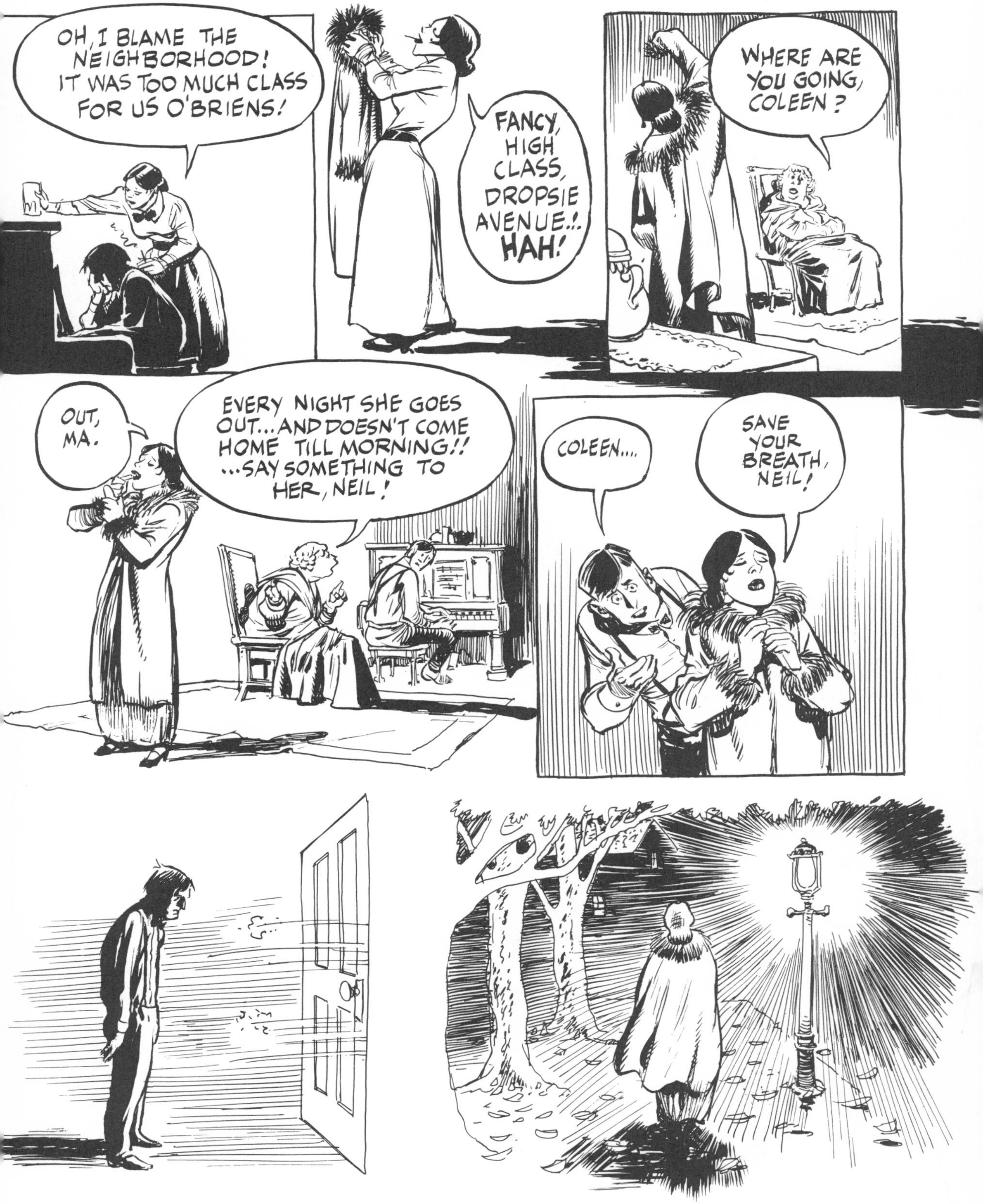
OH, I BLAME THE NEIGHBORHOOD! IT WAS TOO MUCH CLASS FOR US O'BRIENS!
FANCY, HIGH CLASS, DROPSIE AVENUE.!. HAH!
WHERE ARE YOU GOING, COLEEN ?
OUT, MA.
EVERY NIGHT SHE GOES OUT...AND DOESN'T COME HOME TILL MORNING!! ...SAY SOMETHING TO HER, NEIL!
COLEEN....
SAVE YOUR BREATH, NEIL!

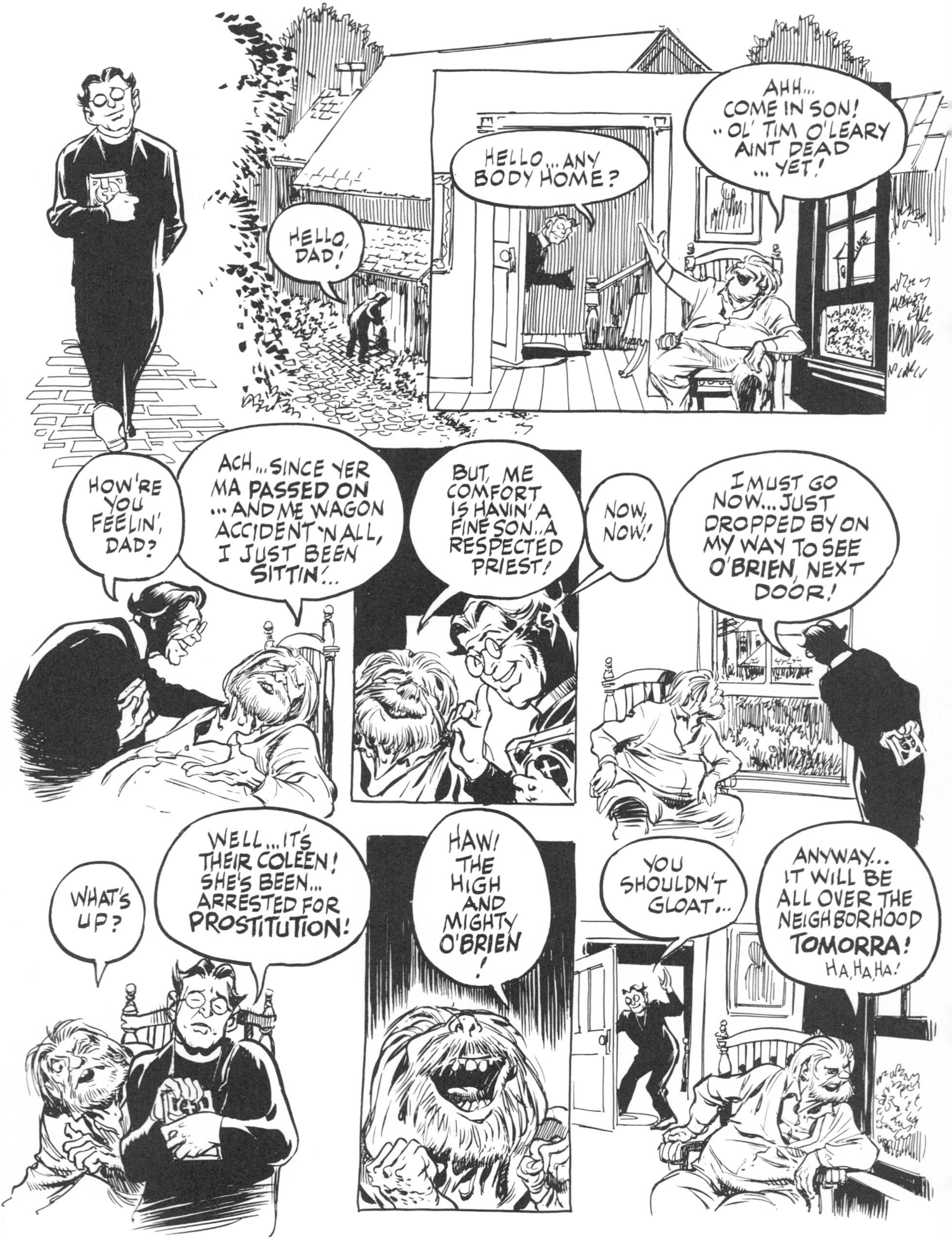
HELLO, DAD!
HELLO... ANY BODY HOME?
AHH... COME IN SON! ..OL' TIM O'LEARY AINT DEAD ... YET!
HOW'RE YOU FEELIN', DAD?
ACH... SINCE YER MA PASSED ON ...AND ME WAGON ACCIDENT 'N ALL, I JUST BEEN SITTIN'...
BUT, ME COMFORT IS HAVIN' A FINE SON.. A RESPECTED PRIEST!
NOW, NOW!
I MUST GO NOW... JUST DROPPED BY ON MY WAY TO SEE O'BRIEN, NEXT DOOR!
WHAT'S UP?
WELL... IT'S THEIR COLEEN! SHE'S BEEN... ARRESTED FOR PROSTITUTION!
HAW! THE HIGH AND MIGHTY O'BRIEN!
YOU SHOULDN'T GLOAT...
ANYWAY... IT WILL BE ALL OVER THE NEIGHBORHOOD TOMORRA! HA, HA, HA!

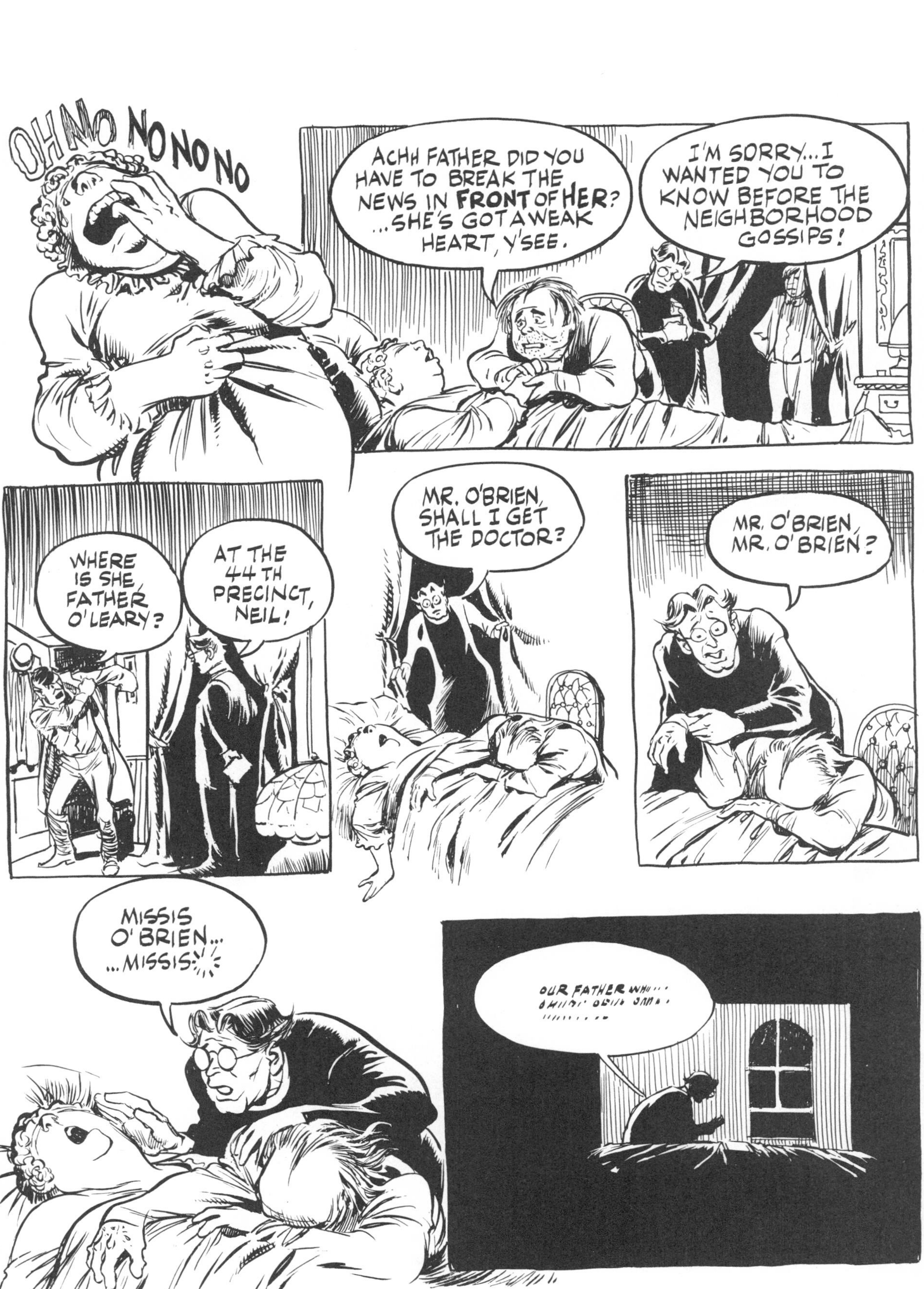
OH NO NO NO NO
ACHH FATHER DID YOU HAVE TO BREAK THE NEWS IN FRONT OF HER? ...SHE'S GOT A WEAK HEART, Y'SEE.
I'M SORRY...I WANTED YOU TO KNOW BEFORE THE NEIGHBORHOOD GOSSIPS!
WHERE IS SHE, FATHER O'LEARY?
AT THE 44TH PRECINCT, NEIL!
MR. O'BRIEN, SHALL I GET THE DOCTOR?
MR. O'BRIEN, MR. O'BRIEN?
MISSIS O'BRIEN... ...MISSIS!
OUR FATHER WH

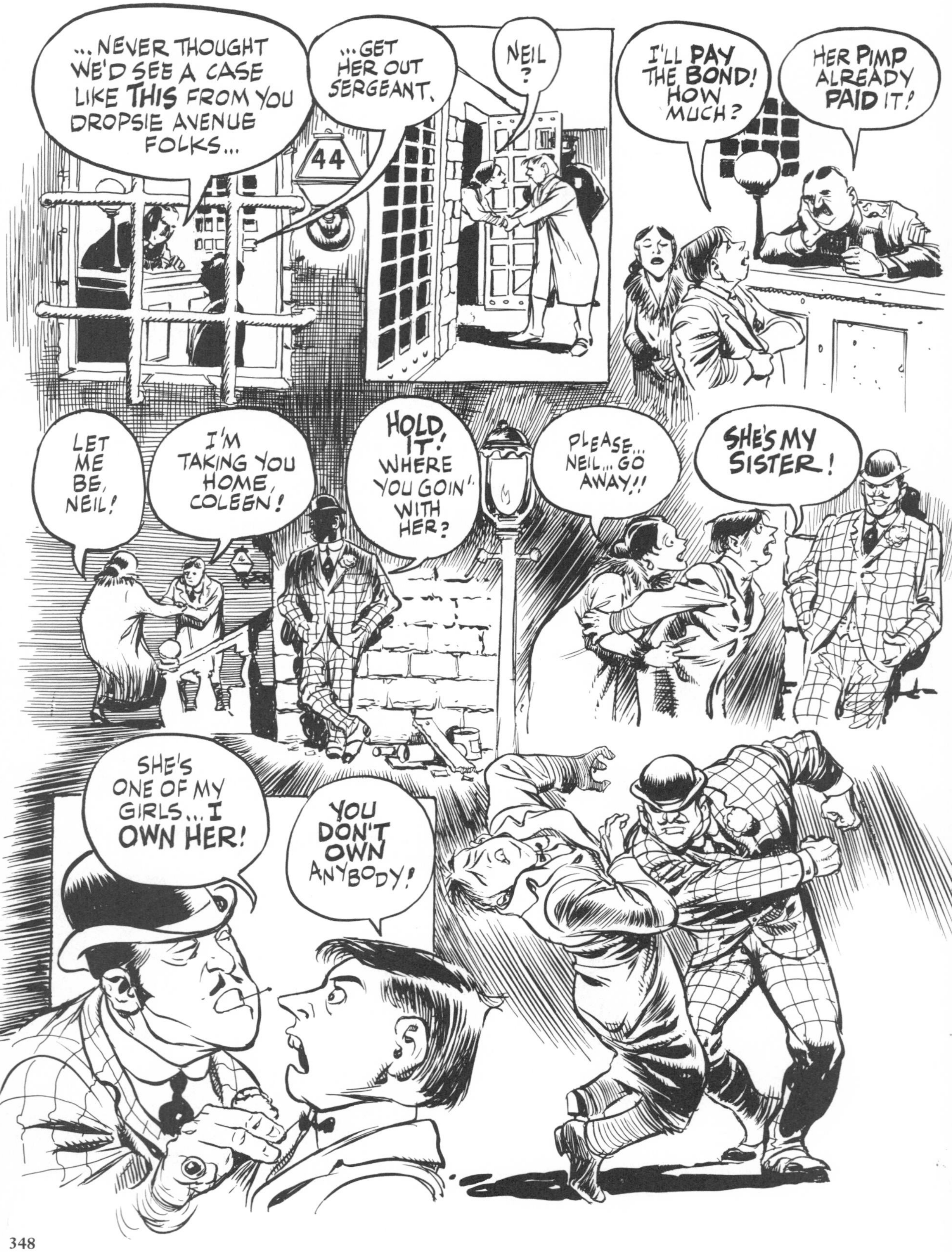
...NEVER THOUGHT WE'D SEE A CASE LIKE THIS FROM YOU DROPSIE AVENUE FOLKS...
...GET HER OUT SERGEANT.
44
NEIL ?
I'LL PAY THE BOND! HOW MUCH?
HER PIMP ALREADY PAID IT!
LET ME BE, NEIL!
I'M TAKING YOU HOME, COLEEN!
HOLD IT! WHERE YOU GOIN' WITH HER?
PLEASE... NEIL... GO AWAY!!
SHE'S MY SISTER!
SHE'S ONE OF MY GIRLS... I OWN HER!
YOU DON'T OWN ANYBODY!

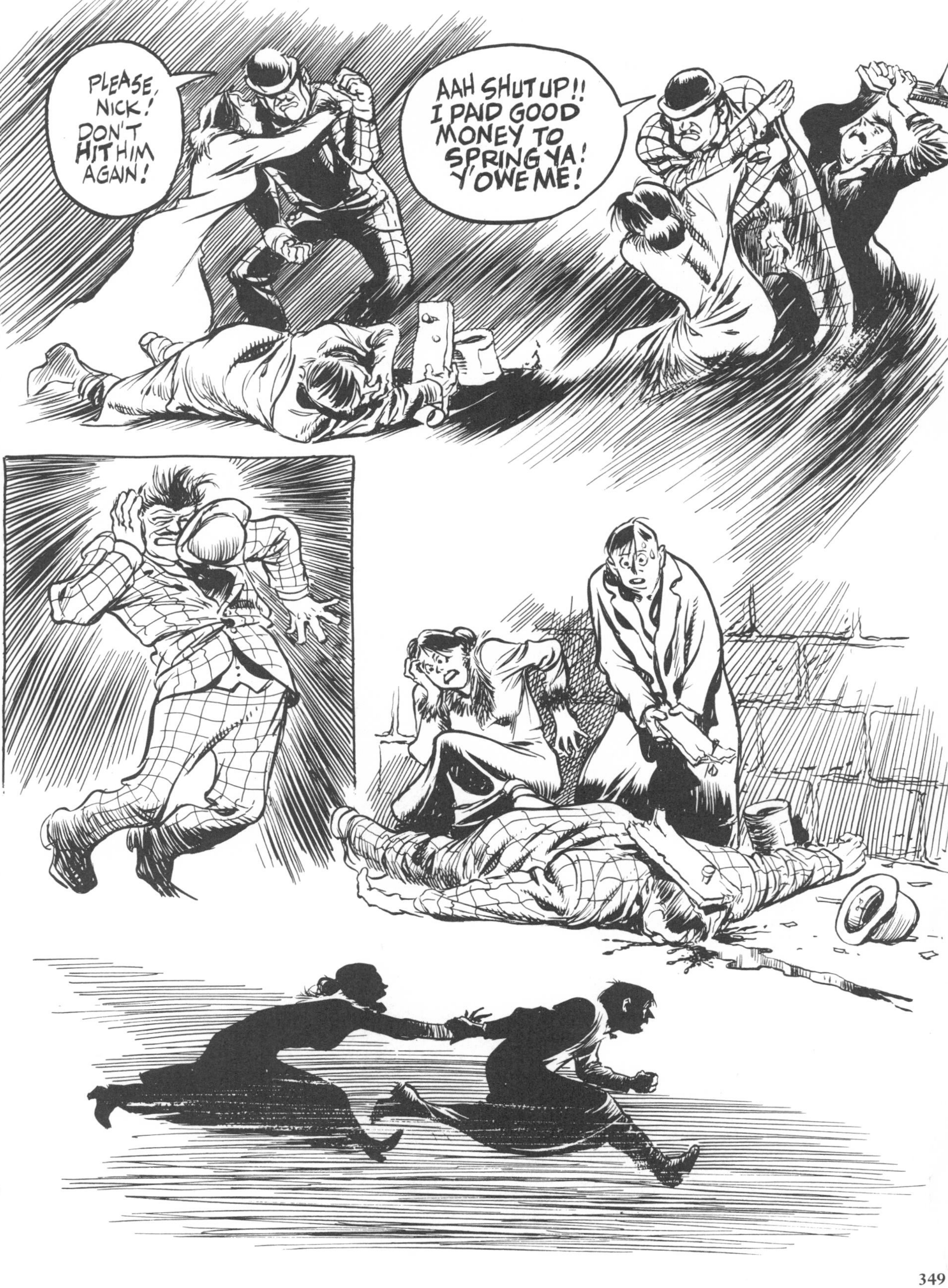
PLEASE, NICK! DON'T HIT HIM AGAIN!
AAH SHUT UP!! I PAID GOOD MONEY TO SPRING YA! Y'OWE ME!

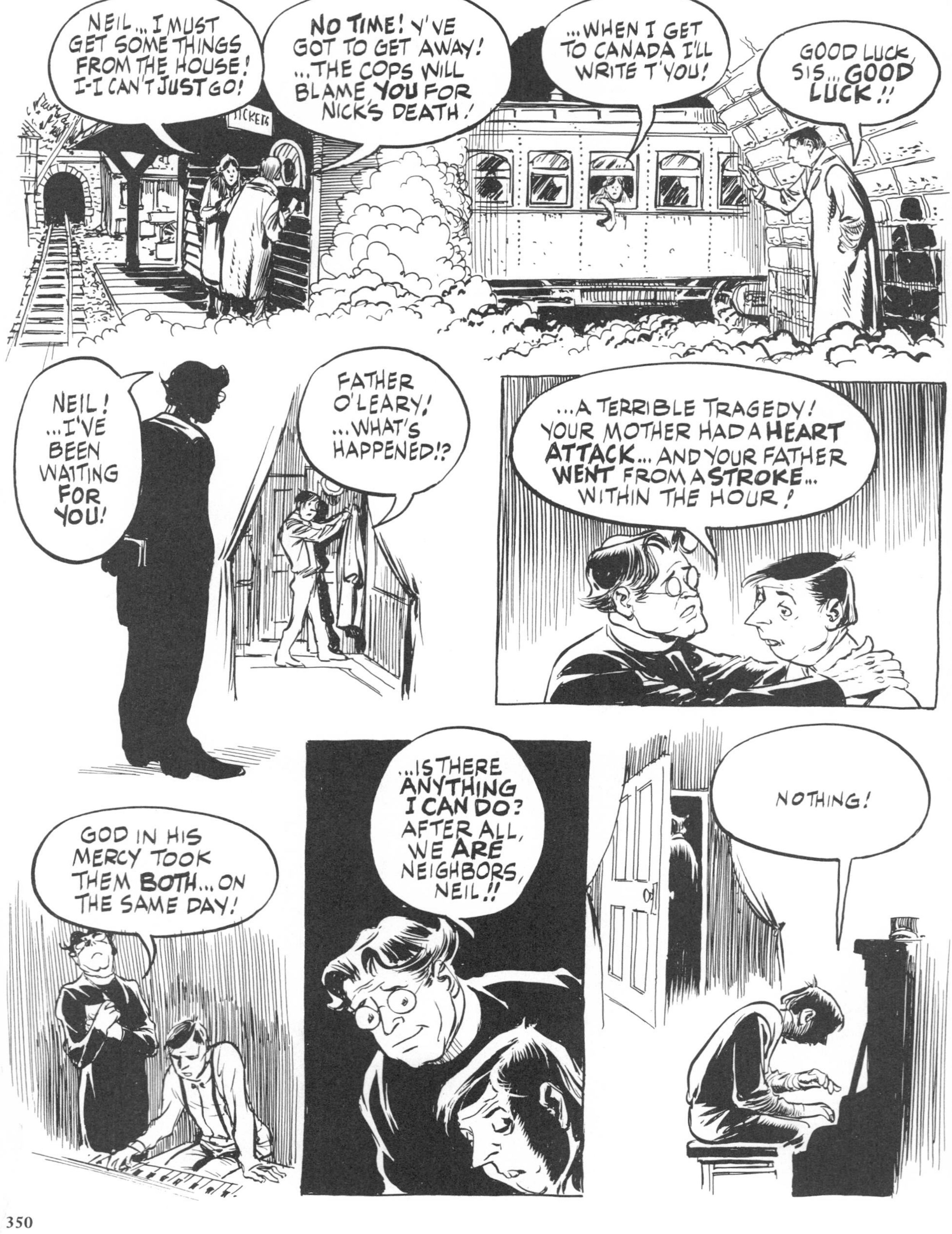
NEIL... I MUST GET SOME THINGS FROM THE HOUSE! I-I CAN'T JUST GO!
NO TIME! Y'VE GOT TO GET AWAY! ...THE COPS WILL BLAME YOU FOR NICK'S DEATH!
TICKETS
...WHEN I GET TO CANADA I'LL WRITE T'YOU!
GOOD LUCK, SIS... GOOD LUCK!!
NEIL! ...I'VE BEEN WAITING FOR YOU!
FATHER O'LEARY! ...WHAT'S HAPPENED!?
...A TERRIBLE TRAGEDY! YOUR MOTHER HAD A HEART ATTACK... AND YOUR FATHER WENT FROM A STROKE... WITHIN THE HOUR!
GOD IN HIS MERCY TOOK THEM BOTH... ON THE SAME DAY!
...IS THERE ANYTHING I CAN DO? AFTER ALL, WE ARE NEIGHBORS, NEIL!!
NOTHING!

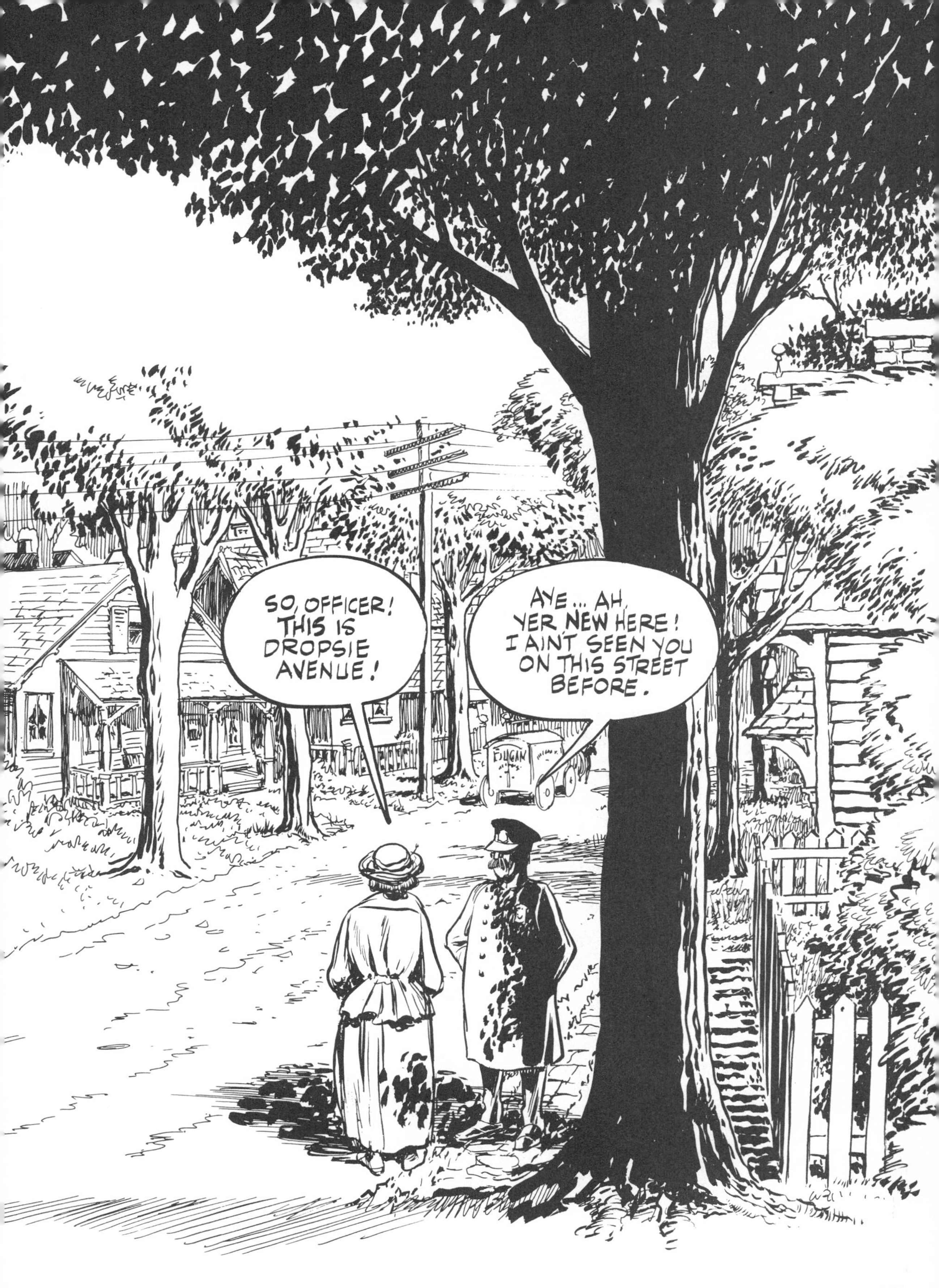
SO, OFFICER! THIS IS DROPSIE AVENUE!
AYE... AH, YER NEW HERE! I AINT SEEN YOU ON THIS STREET BEFORE.

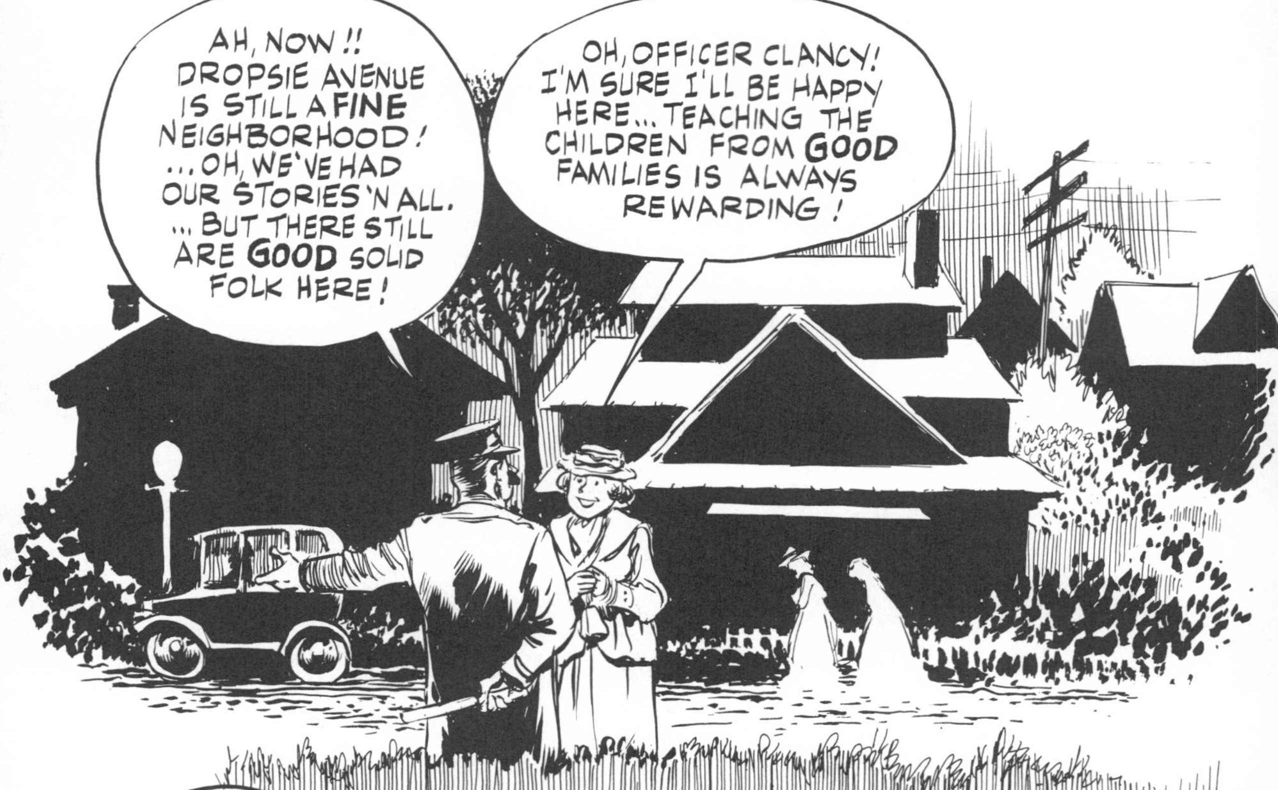
AH, NOW !! DROPSIE AVENUE IS STILL A FINE NEIGHBORHOOD! ... OH, WE'VE HAD OUR STORIES 'N ALL. ... BUT THERE STILL ARE GOOD SOLID FOLK HERE!
OH, OFFICER CLANCY! I'M SURE I'LL BE HAPPY HERE... TEACHING THE CHILDREN FROM GOOD FAMILIES IS ALWAYS REWARDING!

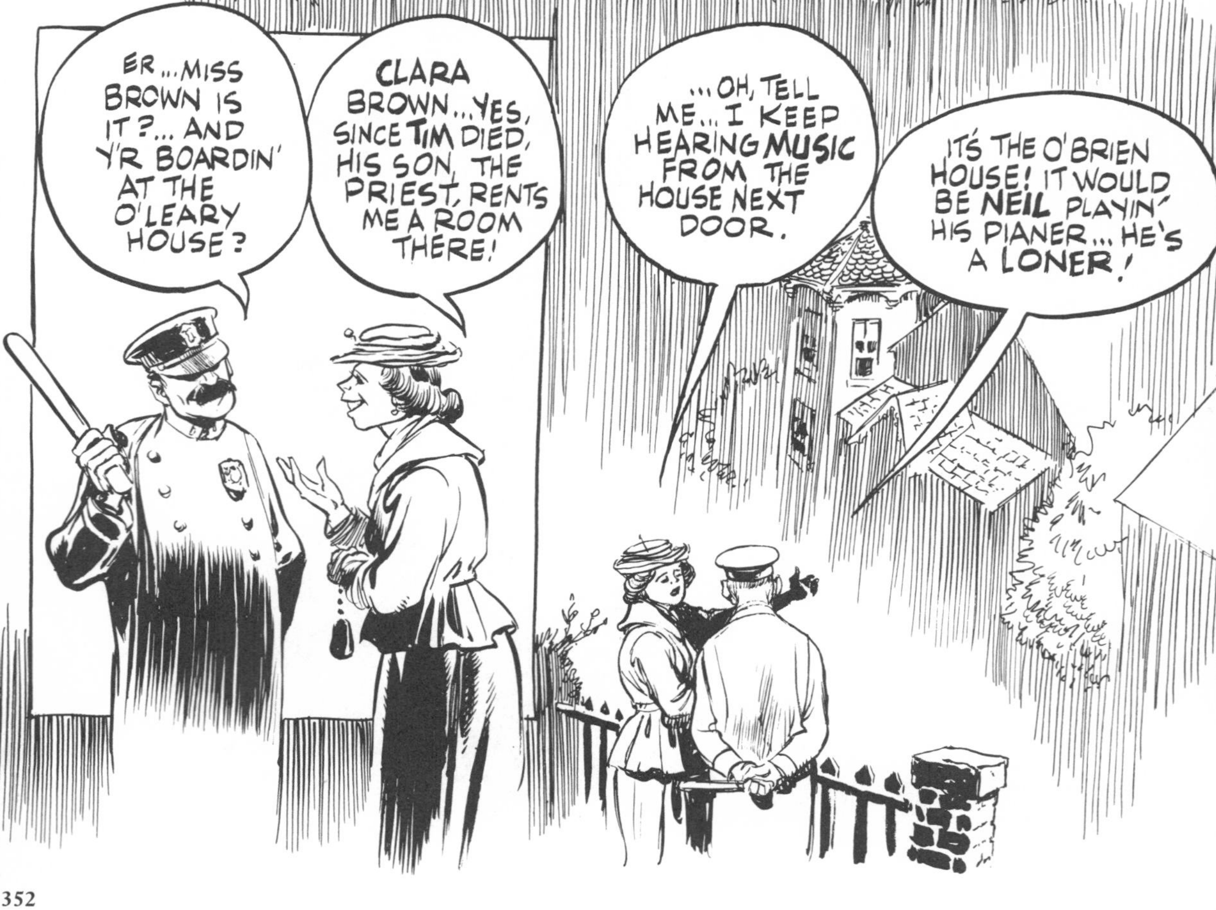
ER... MISS BROWN IS IT?... AND Y'R BOARDIN' AT THE O'LEARY HOUSE?
CLARA BROWN... YES, SINCE TIM DIED, HIS SON, THE PRIEST, RENTS ME A ROOM THERE!
... OH, TELL ME... I KEEP HEARING MUSIC FROM THE HOUSE NEXT DOOR.
IT'S THE O'BRIEN HOUSE! IT WOULD BE NEIL PLAYIN' HIS PIANER... HE'S A LONER!

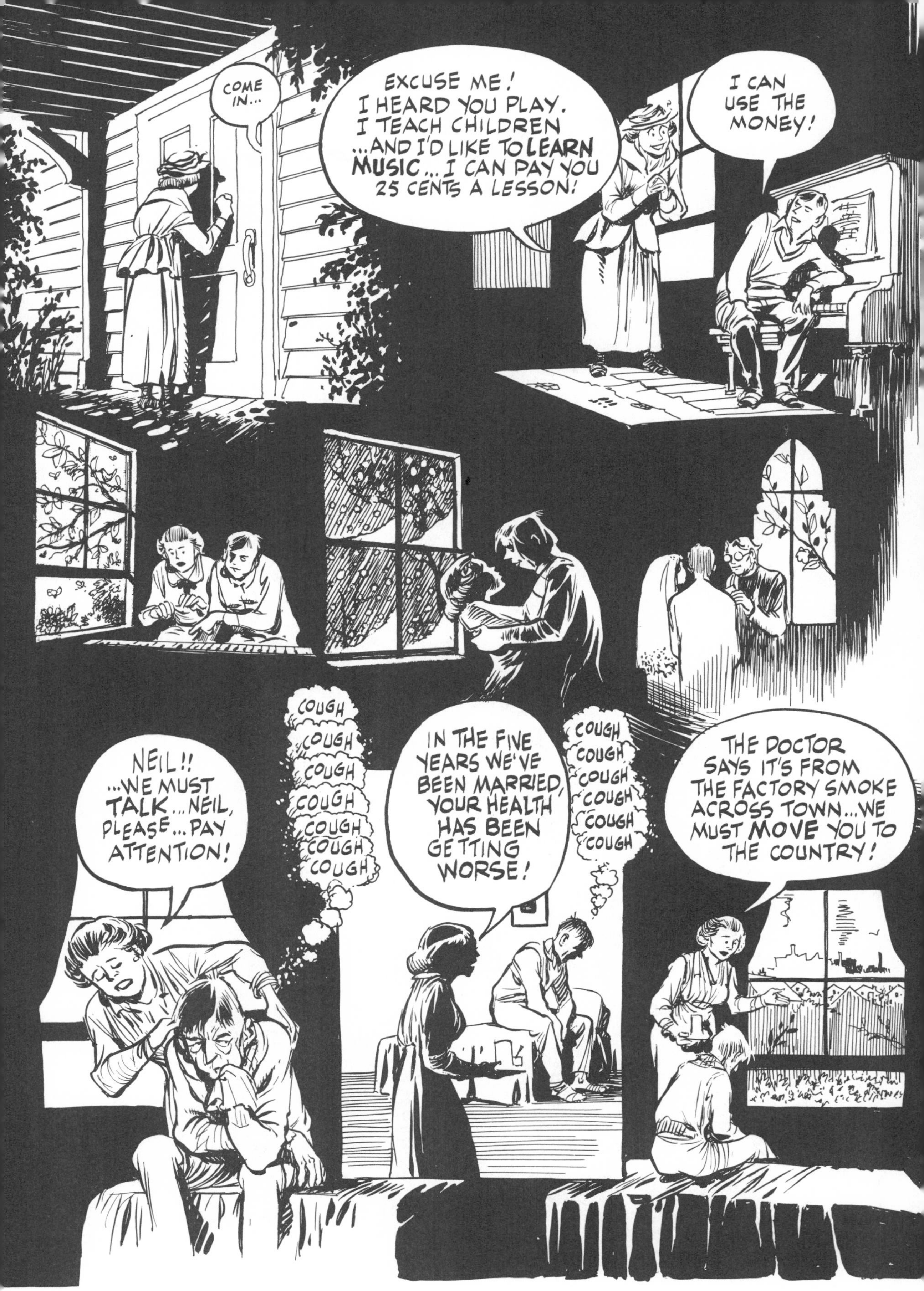
COME IN...
EXCUSE ME! I HEARD YOU PLAY. I TEACH CHILDREN ...AND I'D LIKE TO LEARN MUSIC... I CAN PAY YOU 25 CENTS A LESSON!
I CAN USE THE MONEY!
NEIL!! ...WE MUST TALK... NEIL, PLEASE... PAY ATTENTION!
COUGH COUGH COUGH COUGH COUGH COUGH COUGH
IN THE FIVE YEARS WE'VE BEEN MARRIED, YOUR HEALTH HAS BEEN GETTING WORSE!
COUGH COUGH COUGH COUGH COUGH COUGH
THE DOCTOR SAYS IT'S FROM THE FACTORY SMOKE ACROSS TOWN... WE MUST MOVE YOU TO THE COUNTRY!

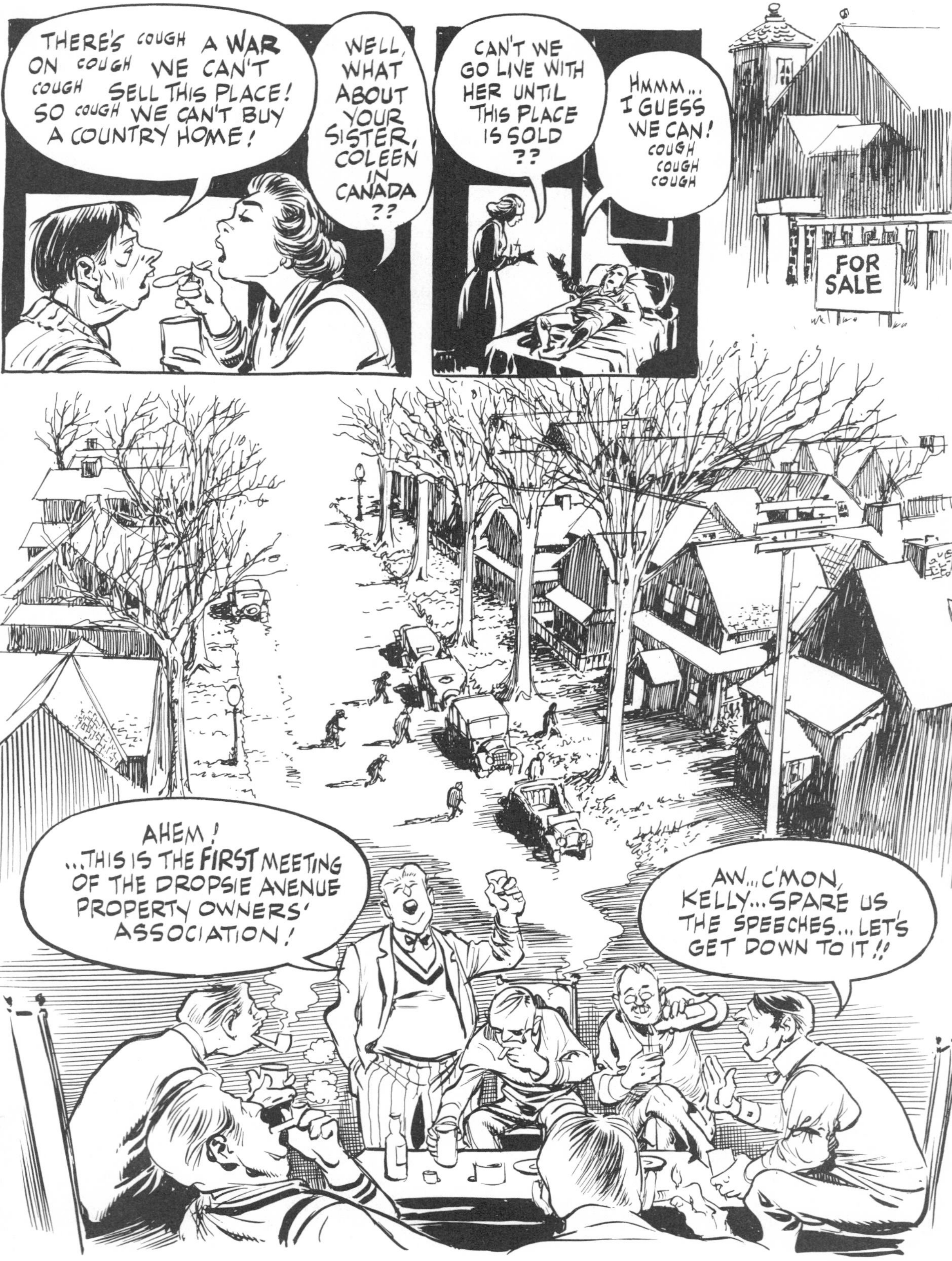
THERE'S cough A WAR ON cough WE CAN'T cough SELL THIS PLACE! SO cough WE CAN'T BUY A COUNTRY HOME!
WELL, WHAT ABOUT YOUR SISTER, COLEEN IN CANADA ??
CAN'T WE GO LIVE WITH HER UNTIL THIS PLACE IS SOLD ??
HMMM... I GUESS WE CAN! cough cough cough
FOR SALE
AHEM! ...THIS IS THE FIRST MEETING OF THE DROPSIE AVENUE PROPERTY OWNERS' ASSOCIATION!
AW... C'MON, KELLY... SPARE US THE SPEECHES... LET'S GET DOWN TO IT!!

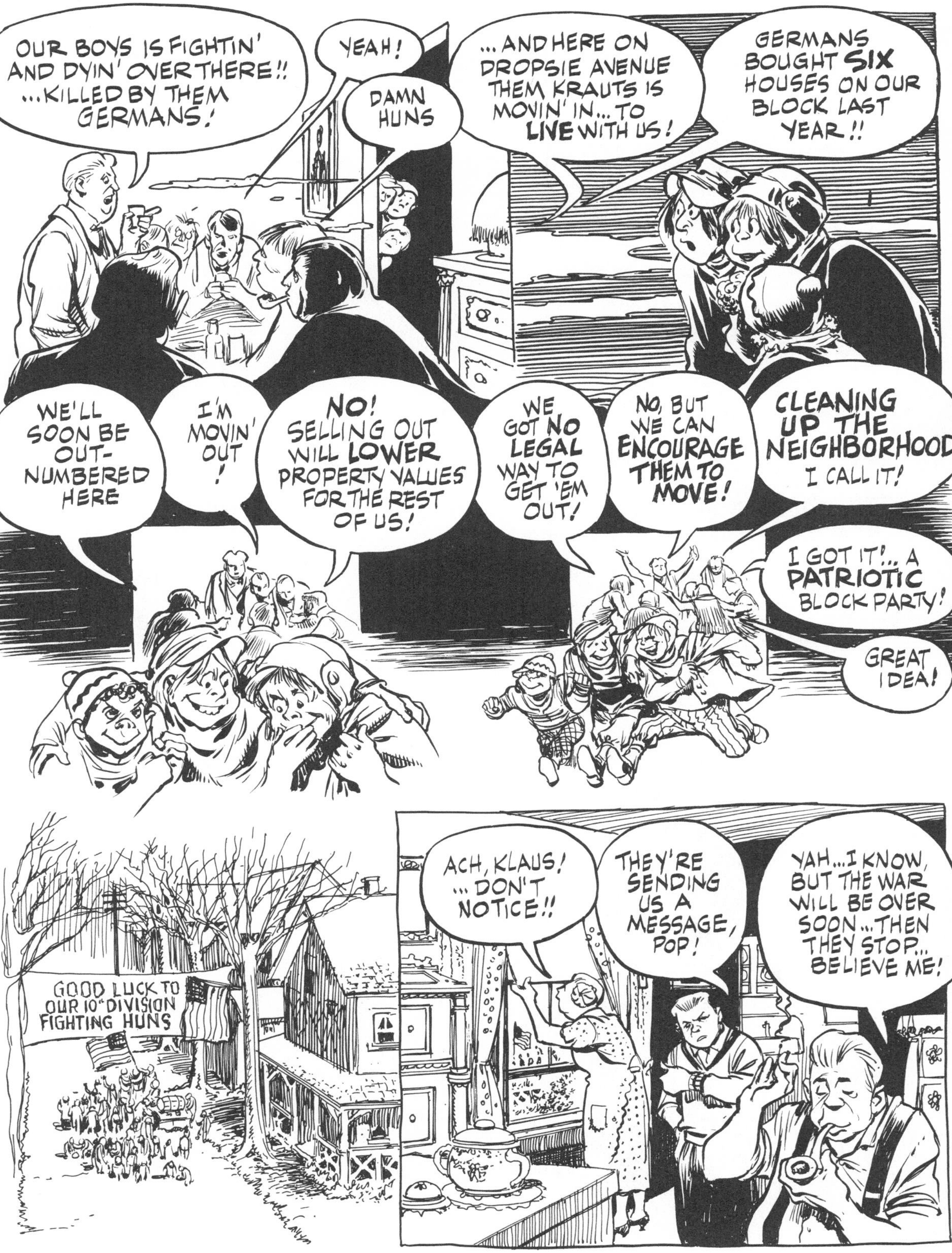
OUR BOYS IS FIGHTIN' AND DYIN' OVER THERE!! ...KILLED BY THEM GERMANS!
YEAH!
DAMN HUNS
...AND HERE ON DROPSIE AVENUE THEM KRAUTS IS MOVIN' IN... TO LIVE WITH US!
GERMANS BOUGHT SIX HOUSES ON OUR BLOCK LAST YEAR!!
WE'LL SOON BE OUT-NUMBERED HERE
I'M MOVIN' OUT!
NO! SELLING OUT WILL LOWER PROPERTY VALUES FOR THE REST OF US!
WE GOT NO LEGAL WAY TO GET 'EM OUT!
NO, BUT WE CAN ENCOURAGE THEM TO MOVE!
CLEANING UP THE NEIGHBORHOOD I CALL IT!
I GOT IT!... A PATRIOTIC BLOCK PARTY!
GREAT IDEA!
GOOD LUCK TO OUR 10th DIVISION FIGHTING HUNS
ACH, KLAUS! ...DON'T NOTICE!!
THEY'RE SENDING US A MESSAGE, POP!
YAH...I KNOW, BUT THE WAR WILL BE OVER SOON...THEN THEY STOP... BELIEVE ME!

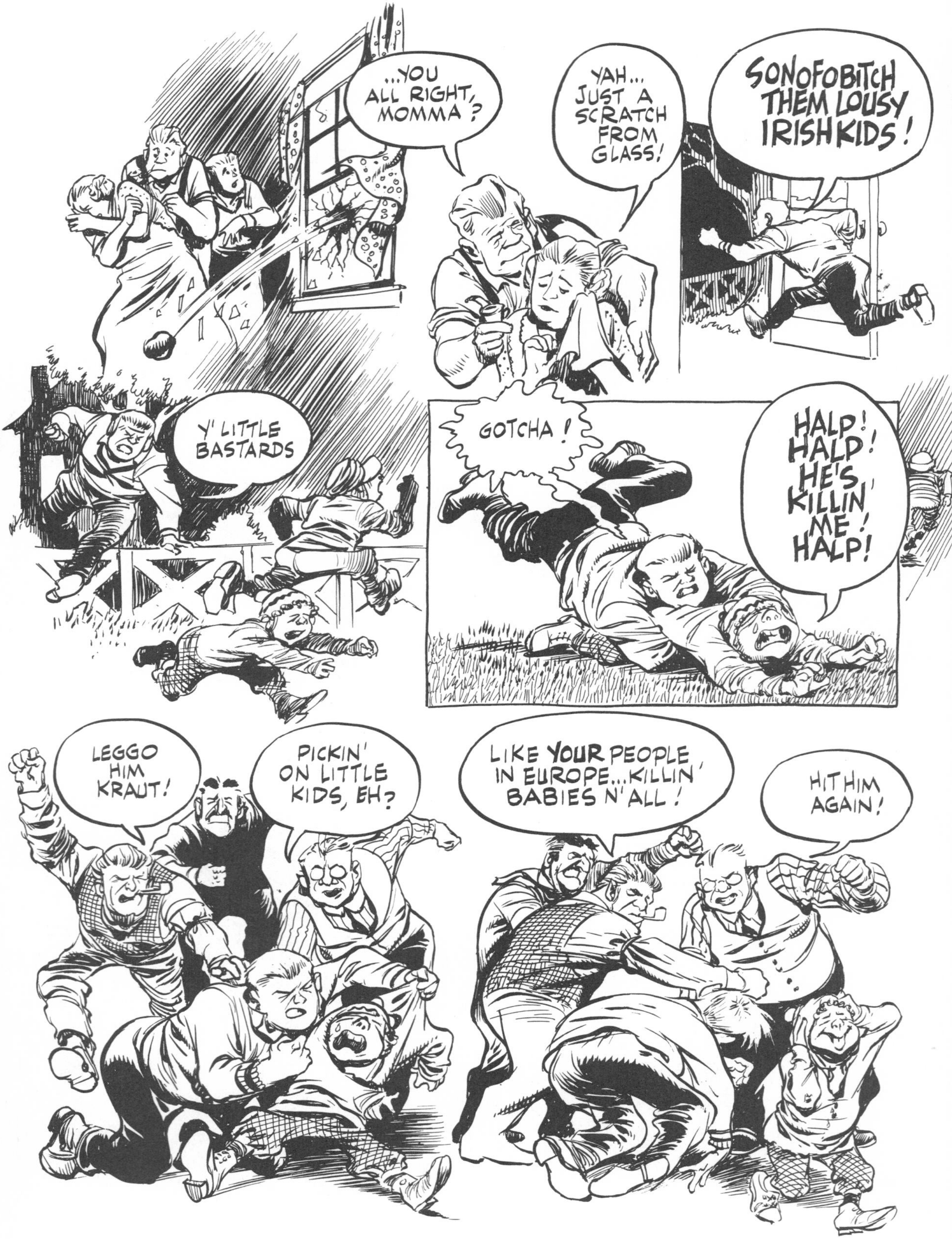
..YOU ALL RIGHT, MOMMA?
YAH... JUST A SCRATCH FROM GLASS!
SONOFOBITCH THEM LOUSY IRISH KIDS!
Y' LITTLE BASTARDS
GOTCHA!
HALP! HALP! HE'S KILLIN ME! HALP!
LEGGO HIM KRAUT!
PICKIN' ON LITTLE KIDS, EH?
LIKE YOUR PEOPLE IN EUROPE...KILLIN' BABIES N'ALL!
HIT HIM AGAIN!

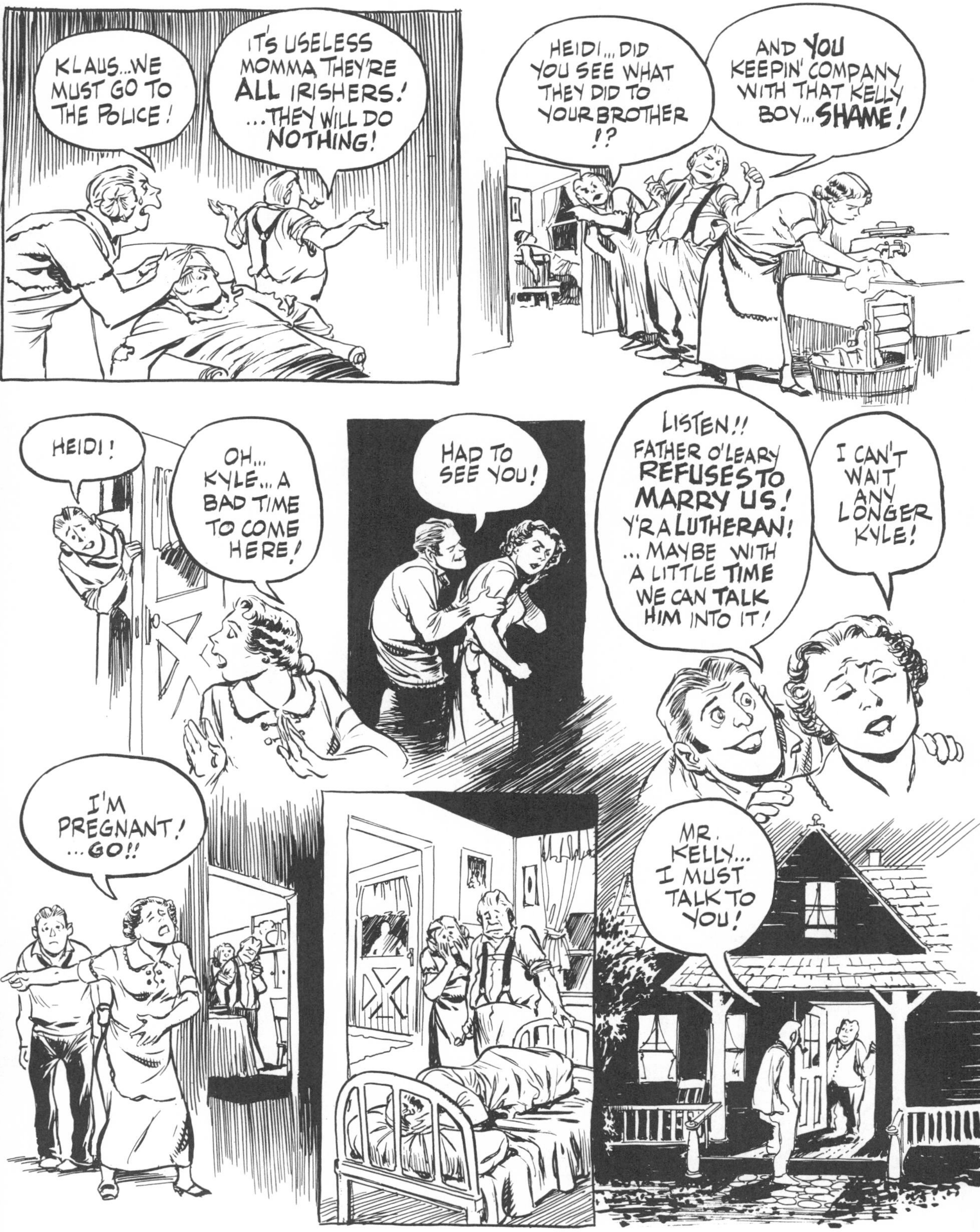
KLAUS...WE MUST GO TO THE POLICE!
IT'S USELESS MOMMA THEY'RE ALL IRISHERS! ...THEY WILL DO NOTHING!
HEIDI... DID YOU SEE WHAT THEY DID TO YOUR BROTHER !?
AND YOU KEEPIN' COMPANY WITH THAT KELLY BOY... SHAME!
HEIDI!
OH... KYLE... A BAD TIME TO COME HERE!
HAD TO SEE YOU!
LISTEN!! FATHER O'LEARY REFUSES TO MARRY US! Y'RA LUTHERAN! ... MAYBE WITH A LITTLE TIME WE CAN TALK HIM INTO IT!
I CAN'T WAIT ANY LONGER KYLE!
I'M PREGNANT! ...GO!!
MR. KELLY... I MUST TALK TO YOU!

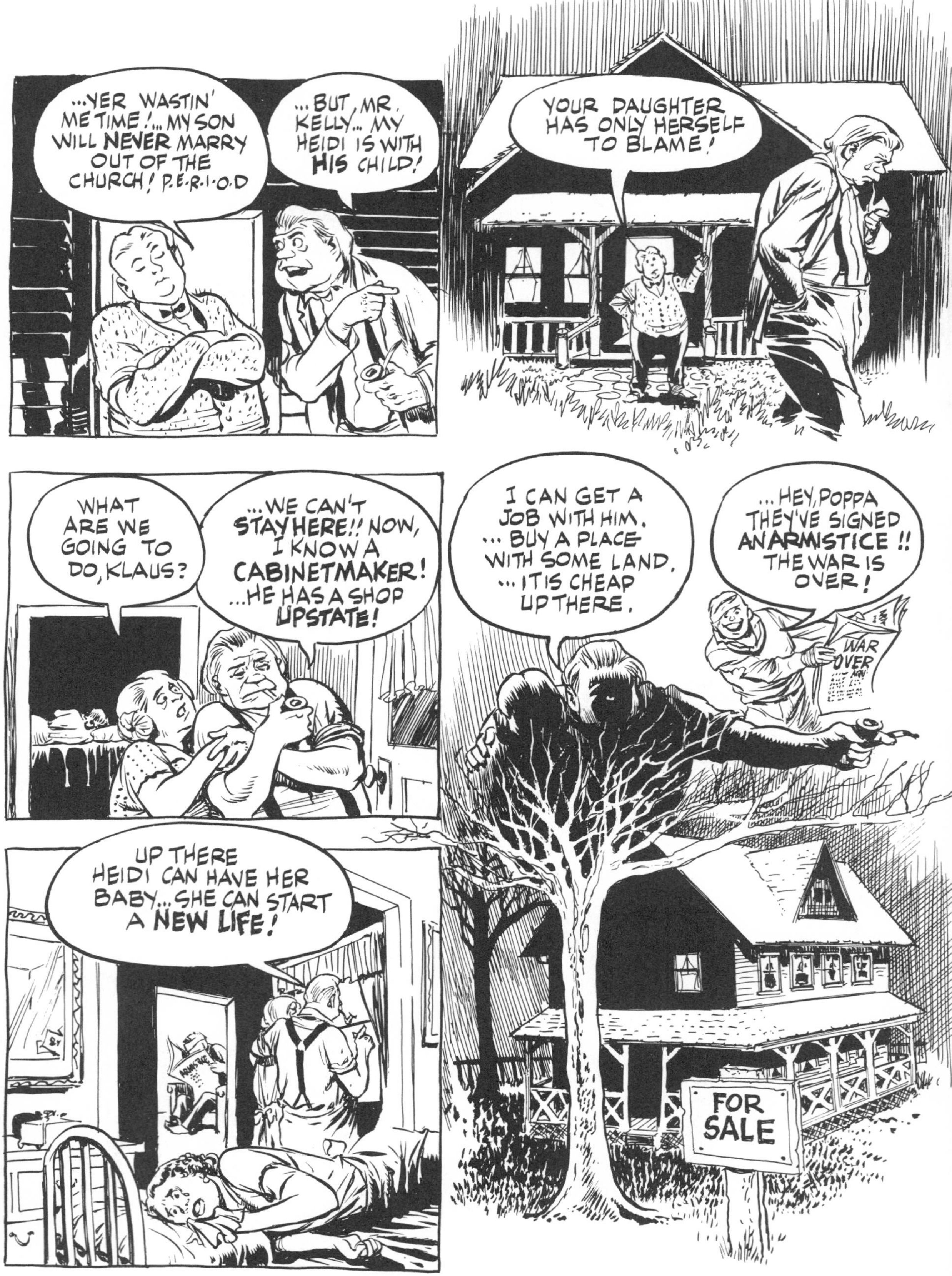
...YER WASTIN' ME TIME!... MY SON WILL NEVER MARRY OUT OF THE CHURCH! P.E.R.I.O.D
...BUT, MR. KELLY... MY HEIDI IS WITH HIS CHILD!
YOUR DAUGHTER HAS ONLY HERSELF TO BLAME!
WHAT ARE WE GOING TO DO, KLAUS?
...WE CAN'T STAY HERE!! NOW, I KNOW A CABINETMAKER! ...HE HAS A SHOP UPSTATE!
I CAN GET A JOB WITH HIM. ...BUY A PLACE WITH SOME LAND. ...IT IS CHEAP UP THERE.
...HEY, POPPA THEY'VE SIGNED AN ARMISTICE!! THE WAR IS OVER!
WAR OVER
UP THERE HEIDI CAN HAVE HER BABY... SHE CAN START A NEW LIFE!
FOR SALE

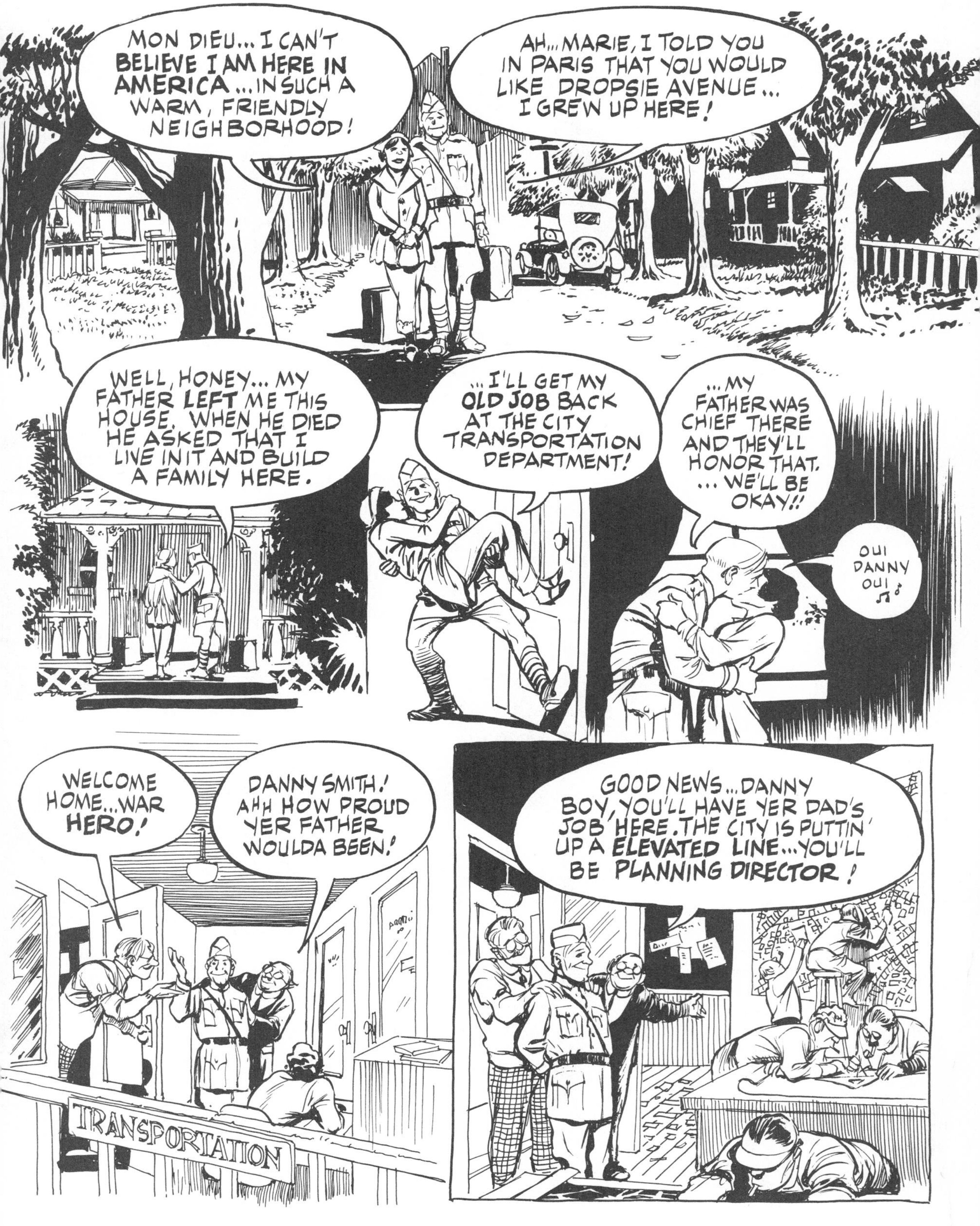
MON DIEU... I CAN'T BELIEVE I AM HERE IN AMERICA... IN SUCH A WARM, FRIENDLY NEIGHBORHOOD!
AH... MARIE, I TOLD YOU IN PARIS THAT YOU WOULD LIKE DROPSIE AVENUE... I GREW UP HERE!
WELL, HONEY... MY FATHER LEFT ME THIS HOUSE. WHEN HE DIED HE ASKED THAT I LIVE IN IT AND BUILD A FAMILY HERE.
... I'LL GET MY OLD JOB BACK AT THE CITY TRANSPORTATION DEPARTMENT!
... MY FATHER WAS CHIEF THERE AND THEY'LL HONOR THAT. ... WE'LL BE OKAY!!
OUI DANNY OUI
WELCOME HOME... WAR HERO!
DANNY SMITH! AHH HOW PROUD YER FATHER WOULDA BEEN!
TRANSPORTATION
GOOD NEWS... DANNY BOY, YOU'LL HAVE YER DAD'S JOB HERE. THE CITY IS PUTTIN' UP A ELEVATED LINE... YOU'LL BE PLANNING DIRECTOR!

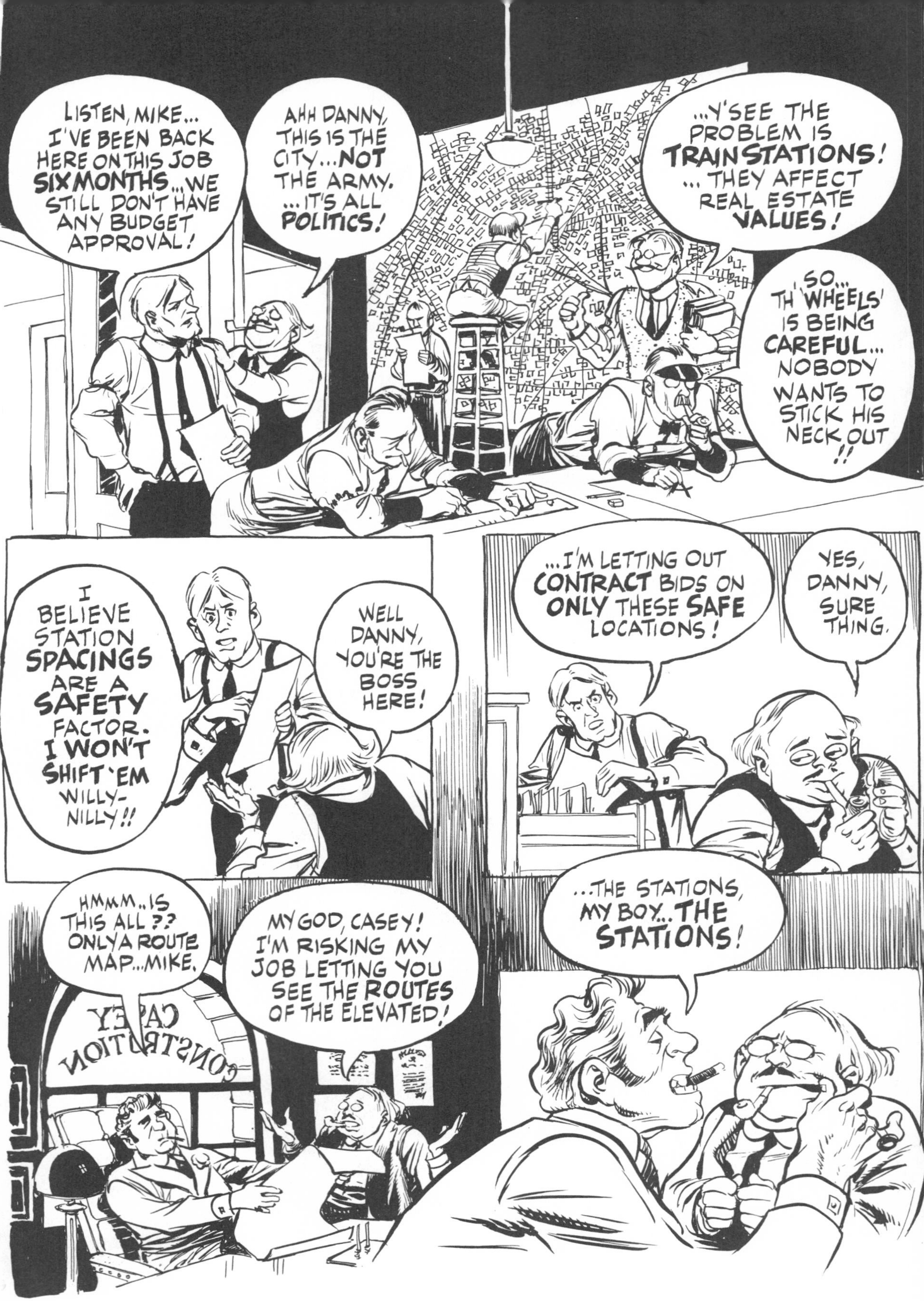
LISTEN, MIKE... I'VE BEEN BACK HERE ON THIS JOB SIX MONTHS... WE STILL DON'T HAVE ANY BUDGET APPROVAL!
AHH DANNY, THIS IS THE CITY... NOT THE ARMY. ...IT'S ALL POLITICS!
...Y'SEE THE PROBLEM IS TRAIN STATIONS! ...THEY AFFECT REAL ESTATE VALUES!
SO... TH' WHEELS' IS BEING CAREFUL... NOBODY WANTS TO STICK HIS NECK OUT!!
I BELIEVE STATION SPACINGS ARE A SAFETY FACTOR. I WON'T SHIFT 'EM WILLY-NILLY!!
WELL DANNY, YOU'RE THE BOSS HERE!
...I'M LETTING OUT CONTRACT BIDS ON ONLY THESE SAFE LOCATIONS!
YES, DANNY, SURE THING.
HMMM.. IS THIS ALL?? ONLY A ROUTE MAP... MIKE.
MY GOD, CASEY! I'M RISKING MY JOB LETTING YOU SEE THE ROUTES OF THE ELEVATED!
...THE STATIONS, MY BOY... THE STATIONS!

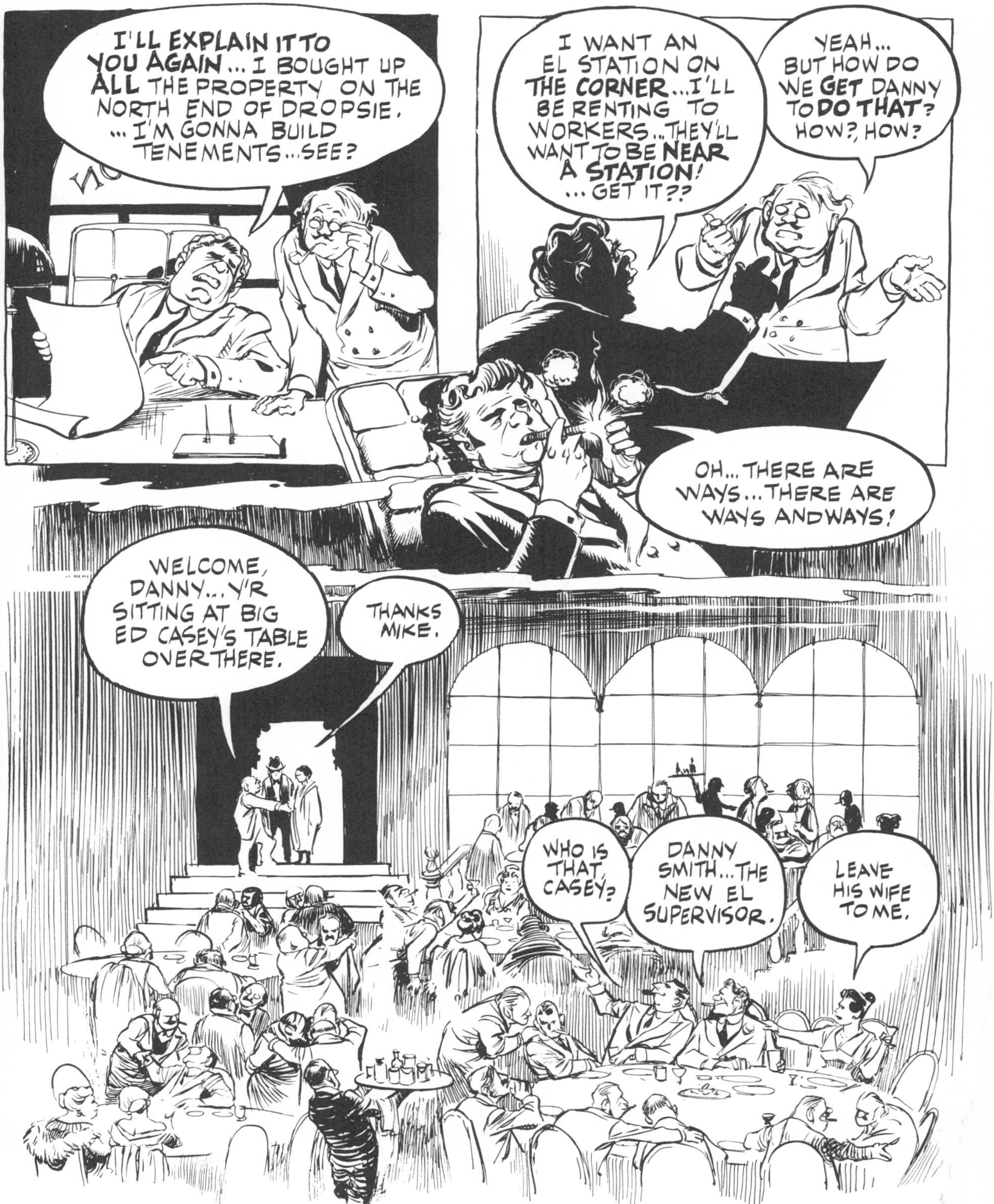

I'LL EXPLAIN IT TO YOU AGAIN... I BOUGHT UP ALL THE PROPERTY ON THE NORTH END OF DROPSIE. ... I'M GONNA BUILD TENEMENTS...SEE?
I WANT AN EL STATION ON THE CORNER...I'LL BE RENTING TO WORKERS...THEY'LL WANT TO BE NEAR A STATION! ...GET IT??
YEAH... BUT HOW DO WE GET DANNY TO DO THAT? HOW?, HOW?
OH...THERE ARE WAYS...THERE ARE WAYS AND WAYS!
WELCOME, DANNY...Y'R SITTING AT BIG ED CASEY'S TABLE OVER THERE.
THANKS MIKE.
WHO IS THAT, CASEY?
DANNY SMITH...THE NEW EL SUPERVISOR.
LEAVE HIS WIFE TO ME.

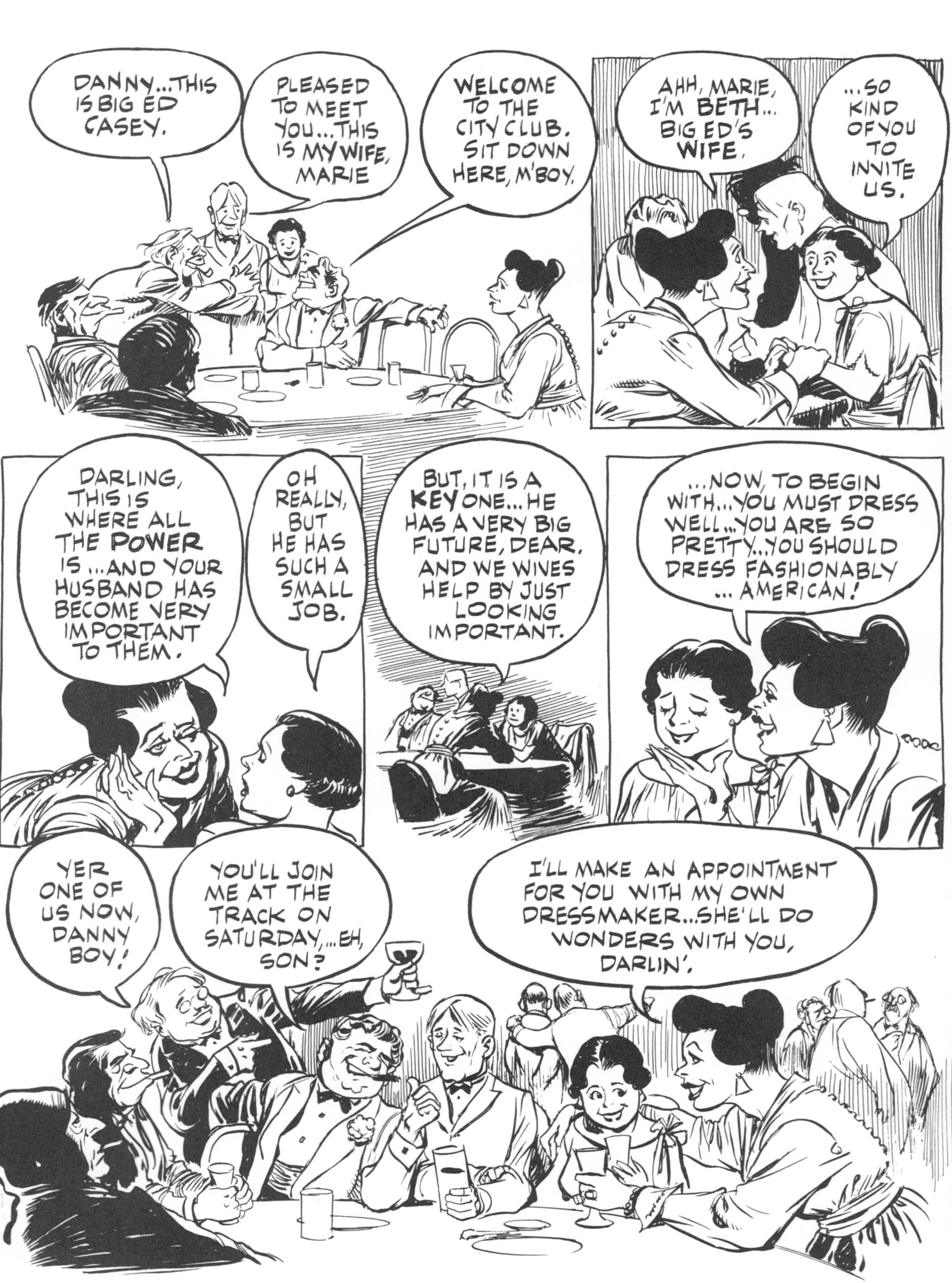
DANNY...THIS IS BIG ED CASEY.
PLEASED TO MEET YOU...THIS IS MY WIFE, MARIE
WELCOME TO THE CITY CLUB. SIT DOWN HERE, M'BOY.
AHH, MARIE, I'M BETH... BIG ED'S WIFE.
...SO KIND OF YOU TO INVITE US.
DARLING, THIS IS WHERE ALL THE POWER IS ...AND YOUR HUSBAND HAS BECOME VERY IMPORTANT TO THEM.
OH REALLY, BUT HE HAS SUCH A SMALL JOB.
BUT, IT IS A KEY ONE...HE HAS A VERY BIG FUTURE, DEAR. AND WE WIVES HELP BY JUST LOOKING IMPORTANT.
...NOW, TO BEGIN WITH...YOU MUST DRESS WELL...YOU ARE SO PRETTY...YOU SHOULD DRESS FASHIONABLY ... AMERICAN!
YER ONE OF US NOW, DANNY BOY!
YOU'LL JOIN ME AT THE TRACK ON SATURDAY,...EH, SON?
I'LL MAKE AN APPOINTMENT FOR YOU WITH MY OWN DRESSMAKER...SHE'LL DO WONDERS WITH YOU, DARLIN'.

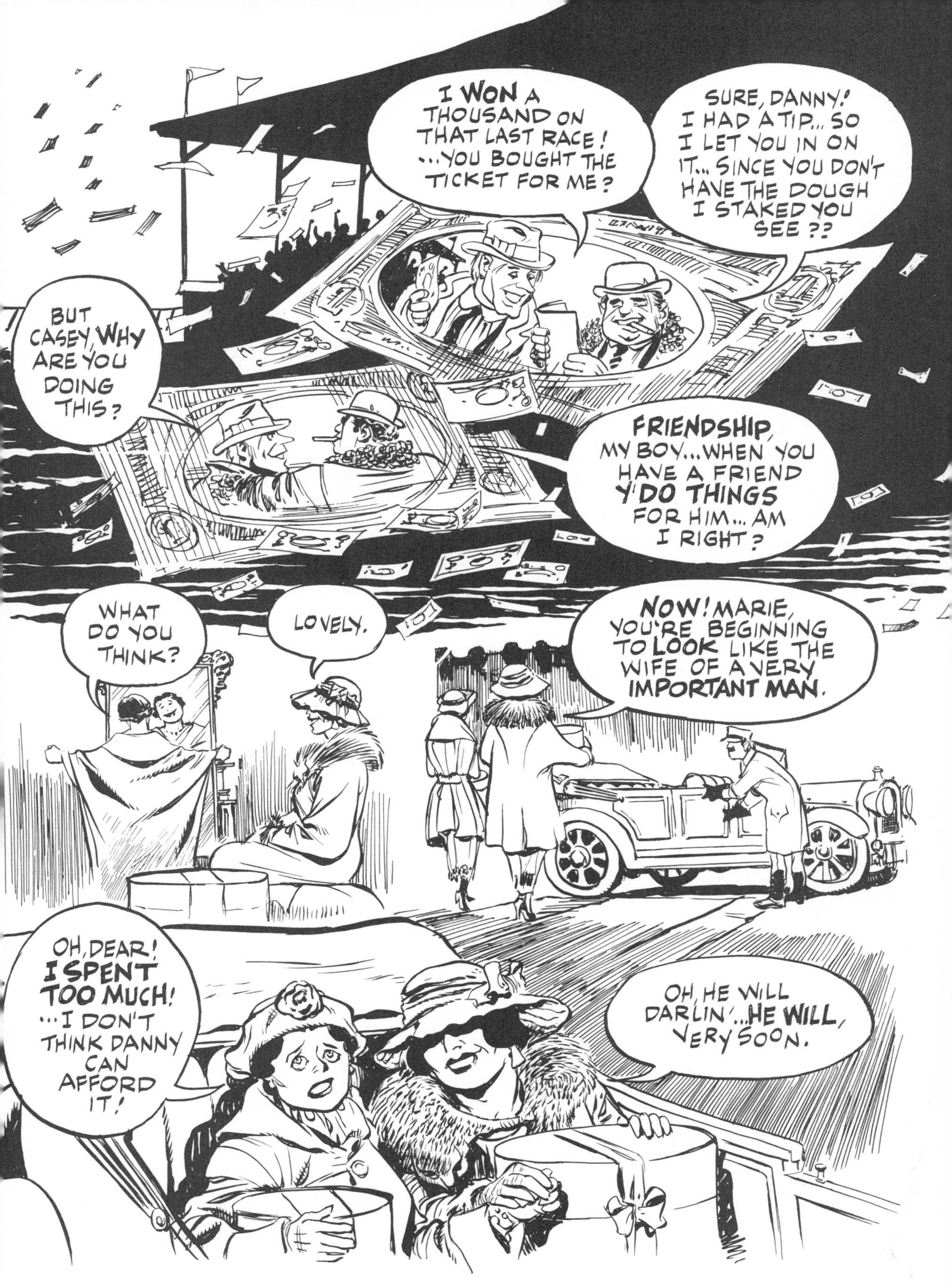
I WON A THOUSAND ON THAT LAST RACE! ...YOU BOUGHT THE TICKET FOR ME?
SURE, DANNY! I HAD A TIP... SO I LET YOU IN ON IT... SINCE YOU DON'T HAVE THE DOUGH I STAKED YOU SEE??
BUT CASEY, WHY ARE YOU DOING THIS?
FRIENDSHIP, MY BOY... WHEN YOU HAVE A FRIEND Y'DO THINGS FOR HIM... AM I RIGHT?
WHAT DO YOU THINK?
LOVELY.
NOW! MARIE, YOU'RE BEGINNING TO LOOK LIKE THE WIFE OF A VERY IMPORTANT MAN.
OH, DEAR! I SPENT TOO MUCH! ...I DON'T THINK DANNY CAN AFFORD IT!
OH HE WILL DARLIN'...HE WILL, VERY SOON.

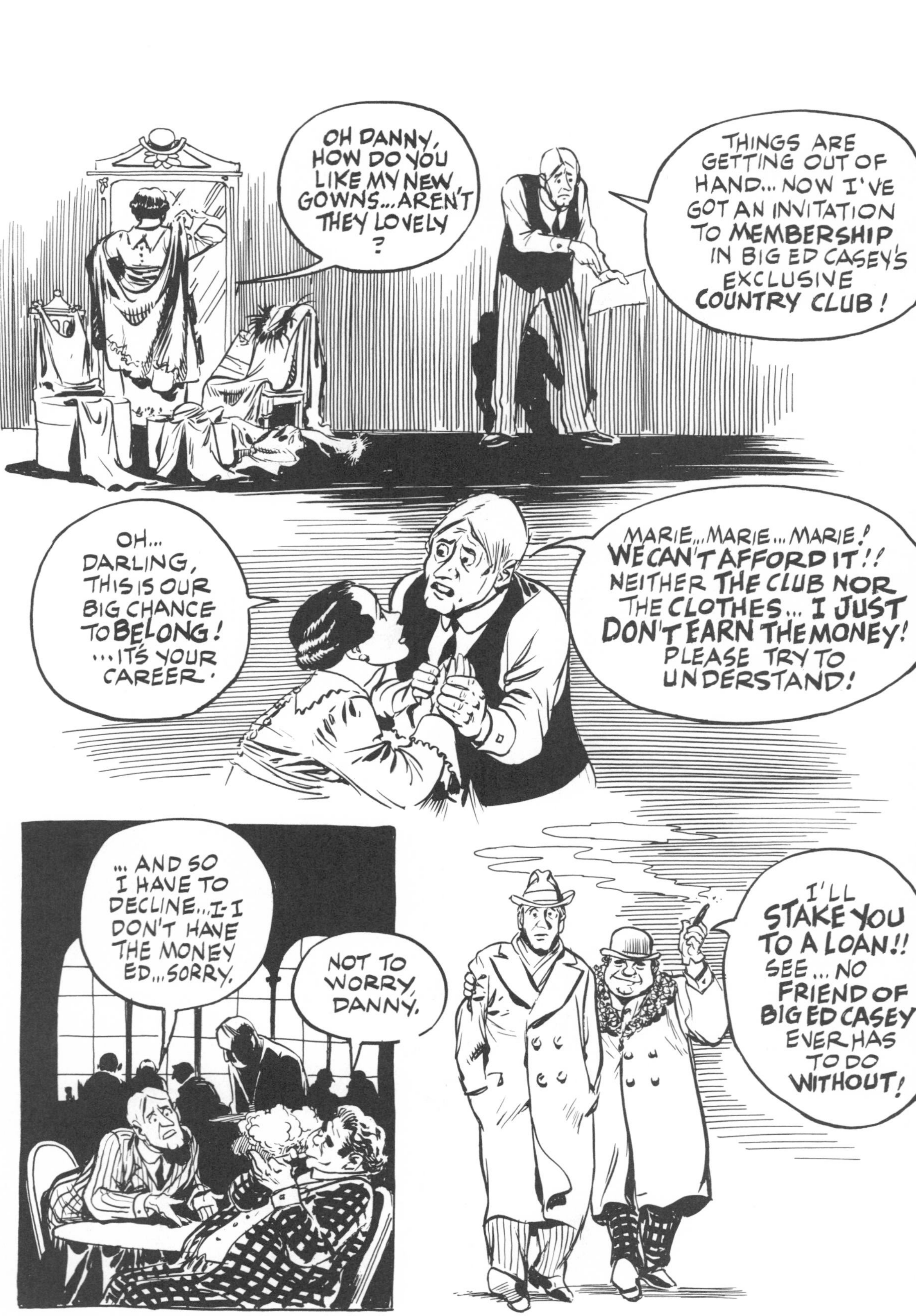
OH DANNY, HOW DO YOU LIKE MY NEW GOWNS...AREN'T THEY LOVELY ?
THINGS ARE GETTING OUT OF HAND... NOW I'VE GOT AN INVITATION TO MEMBERSHIP IN BIG ED CASEY'S EXCLUSIVE COUNTRY CLUB !
OH... DARLING, THIS IS OUR BIG CHANCE TO BELONG! ...IT'S YOUR CAREER.
MARIE...MARIE...MARIE! WE CAN'T AFFORD IT!! NEITHER THE CLUB NOR THE CLOTHES... I JUST DON'T EARN THE MONEY! PLEASE TRY TO UNDERSTAND!
... AND SO I HAVE TO DECLINE...I-I DON'T HAVE THE MONEY ED...SORRY.
NOT TO WORRY, DANNY.
I'LL STAKE YOU TO A LOAN!! SEE... NO FRIEND OF BIG ED CASEY EVER HAS TO DO WITHOUT!

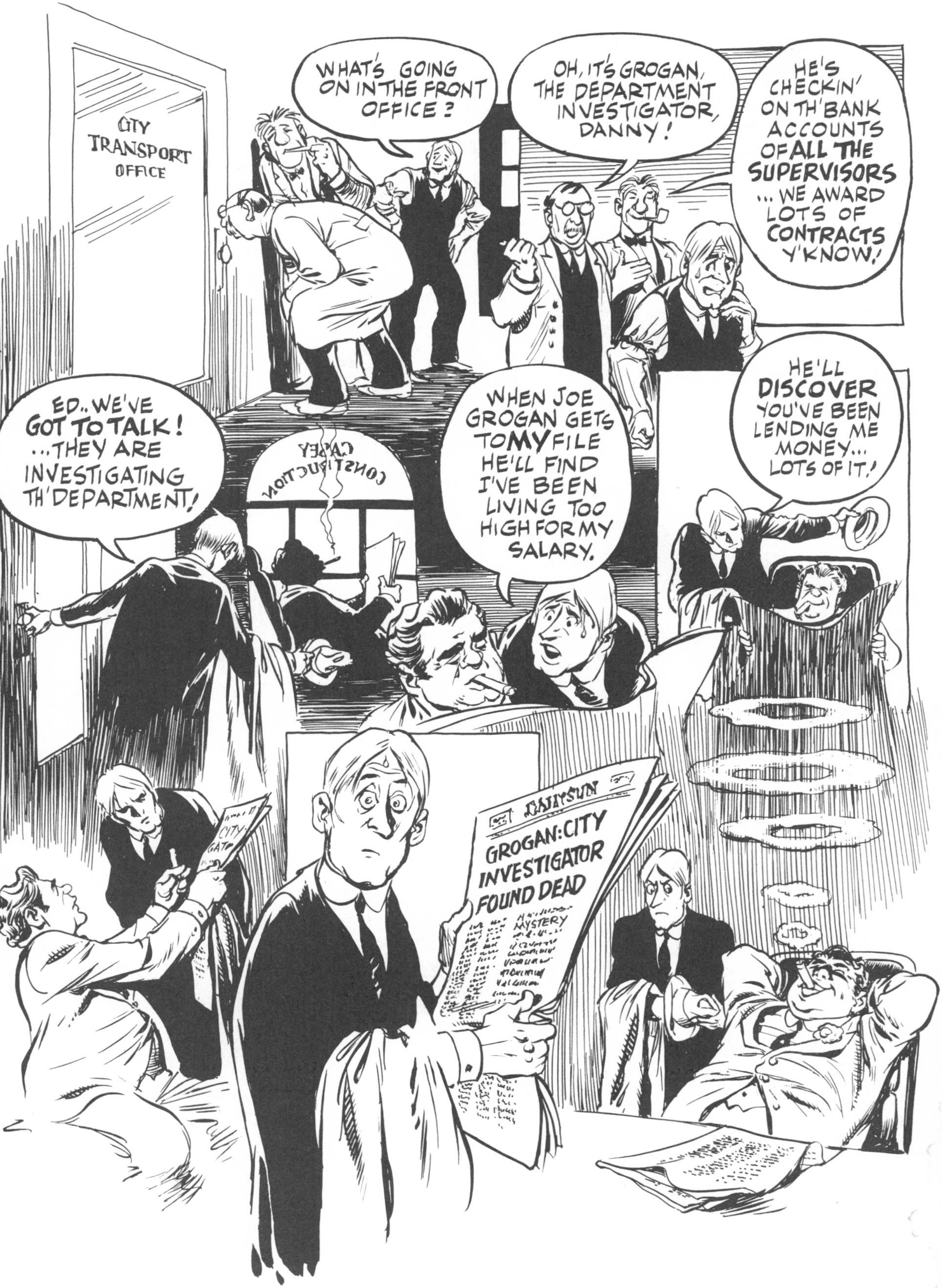
CITY TRANSPORT OFFICE
WHAT'S GOING ON IN THE FRONT OFFICE?
OH, IT'S GROGAN, THE DEPARTMENT INVESTIGATOR, DANNY!
HE'S CHECKIN' ON TH' BANK ACCOUNTS OF ALL THE SUPERVISORS ... WE AWARD LOTS OF CONTRACTS Y'KNOW!
ED.. WE'VE GOT TO TALK! ...THEY ARE INVESTIGATING TH' DEPARTMENT!
CASEY CONSTRUCTION
WHEN JOE GROGAN GETS TO MY FILE HE'LL FIND I'VE BEEN LIVING TOO HIGH FOR MY SALARY.
HE'LL DISCOVER YOU'VE BEEN LENDING ME MONEY... LOTS OF IT!
DAILY SUN
GROGAN: CITY INVESTIGATOR FOUND DEAD
MYSTERY
CITY

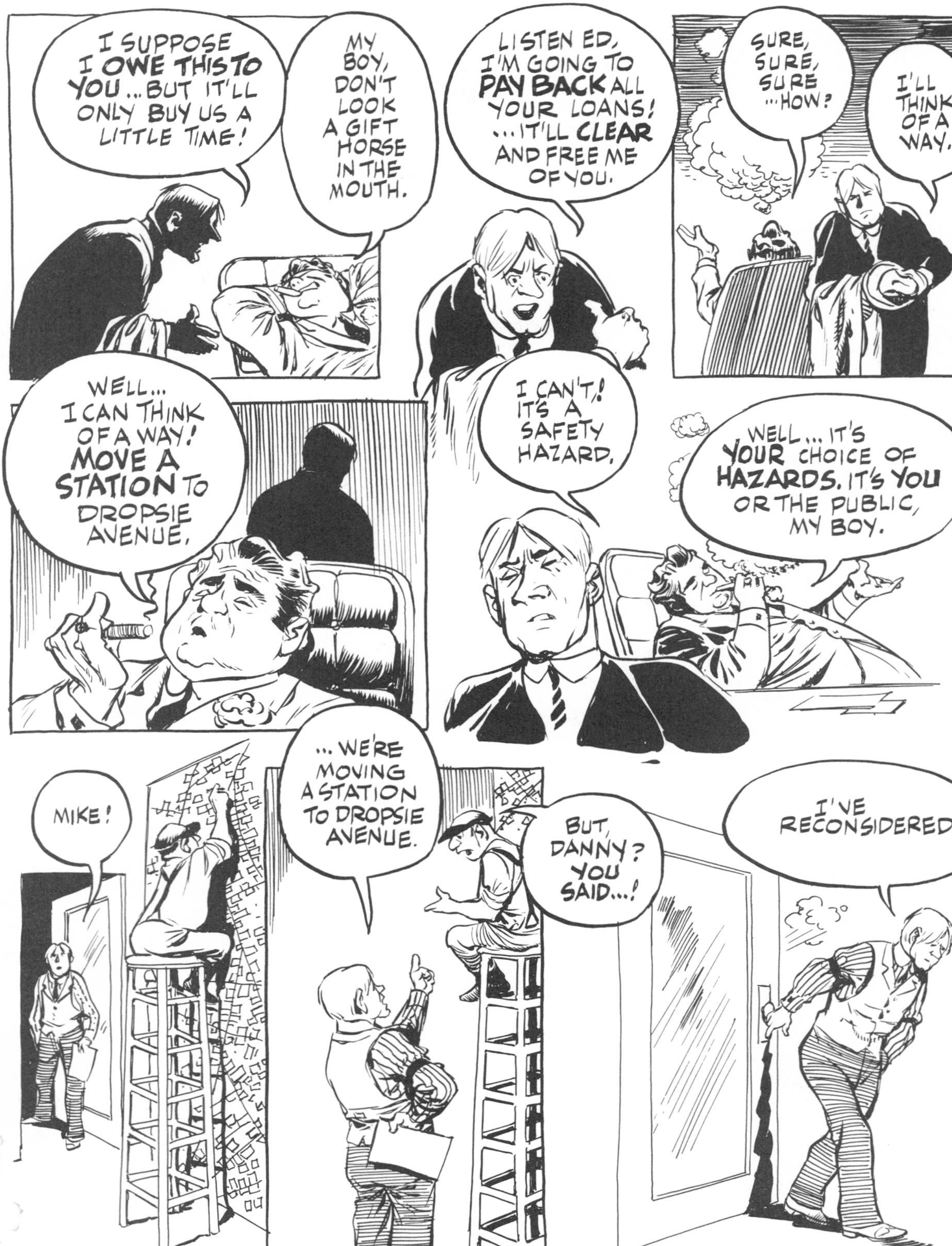
I SUPPOSE I OWE THIS TO YOU ... BUT IT'LL ONLY BUY US A LITTLE TIME!
MY BOY, DON'T LOOK A GIFT HORSE IN THE MOUTH.
LISTEN ED, I'M GOING TO PAY BACK ALL YOUR LOANS! ... IT'LL CLEAR AND FREE ME OF YOU.
SURE, SURE, SURE ... HOW?
I'LL THINK OF A WAY.
WELL... I CAN THINK OF A WAY! MOVE A STATION TO DROPSIE AVENUE.
I CAN'T! IT'S A SAFETY HAZARD.
WELL ... IT'S YOUR CHOICE OF HAZARDS. IT'S YOU OR THE PUBLIC, MY BOY.
MIKE!
... WE'RE MOVING A STATION TO DROPSIE AVENUE.
BUT, DANNY? YOU SAID...!
I'VE RECONSIDERED!

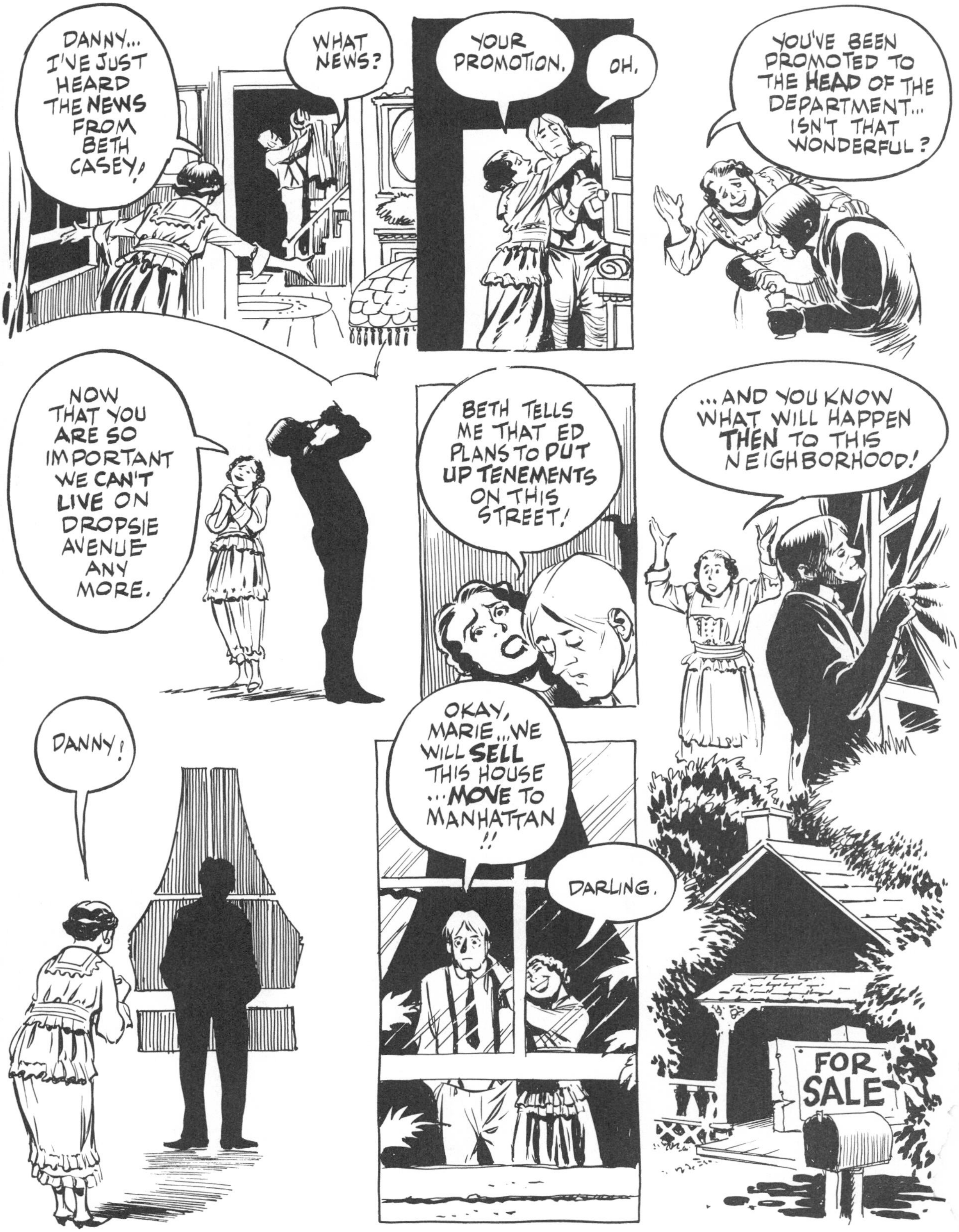
DANNY... I'VE JUST HEARD THE NEWS FROM BETH CASEY!
WHAT NEWS?
YOUR PROMOTION.
OH.
YOU'VE BEEN PROMOTED TO THE HEAD OF THE DEPARTMENT... ISN'T THAT WONDERFUL?
NOW THAT YOU ARE SO IMPORTANT WE CAN'T LIVE ON DROPSIE AVENUE ANY MORE.
BETH TELLS ME THAT ED PLANS TO PUT UP TENEMENTS ON THIS STREET!
...AND YOU KNOW WHAT WILL HAPPEN THEN TO THIS NEIGHBORHOOD!
DANNY!
OKAY, MARIE... WE WILL SELL THIS HOUSE ...MOVE TO MANHATTAN!!
DARLING.
FOR SALE

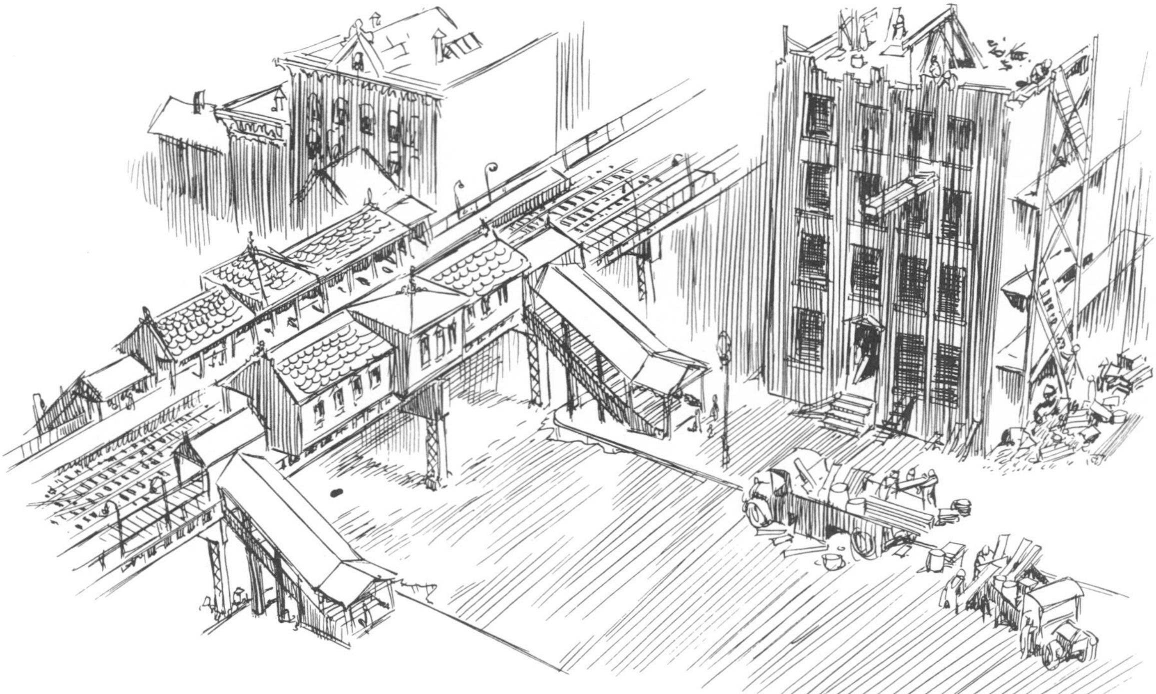

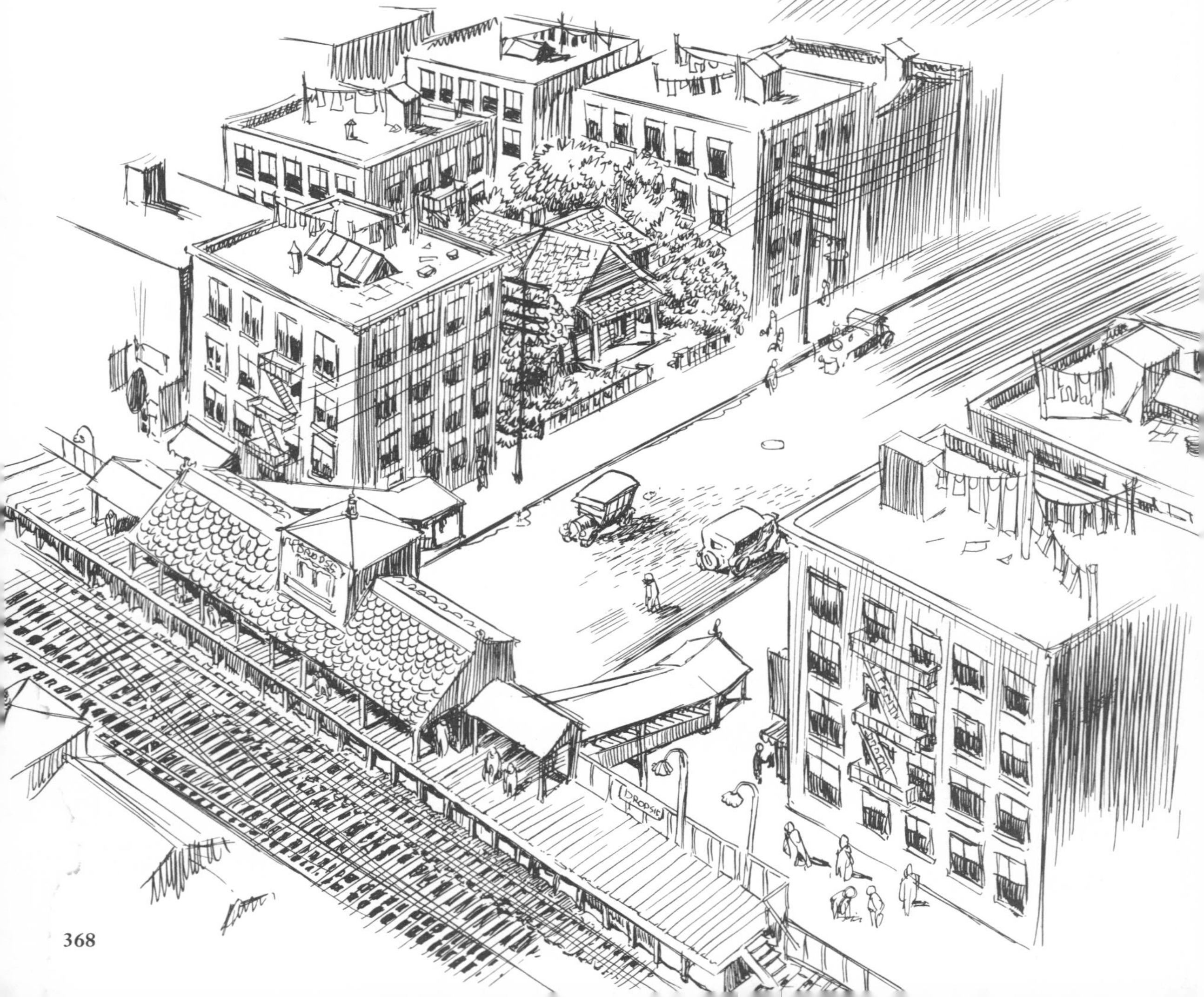

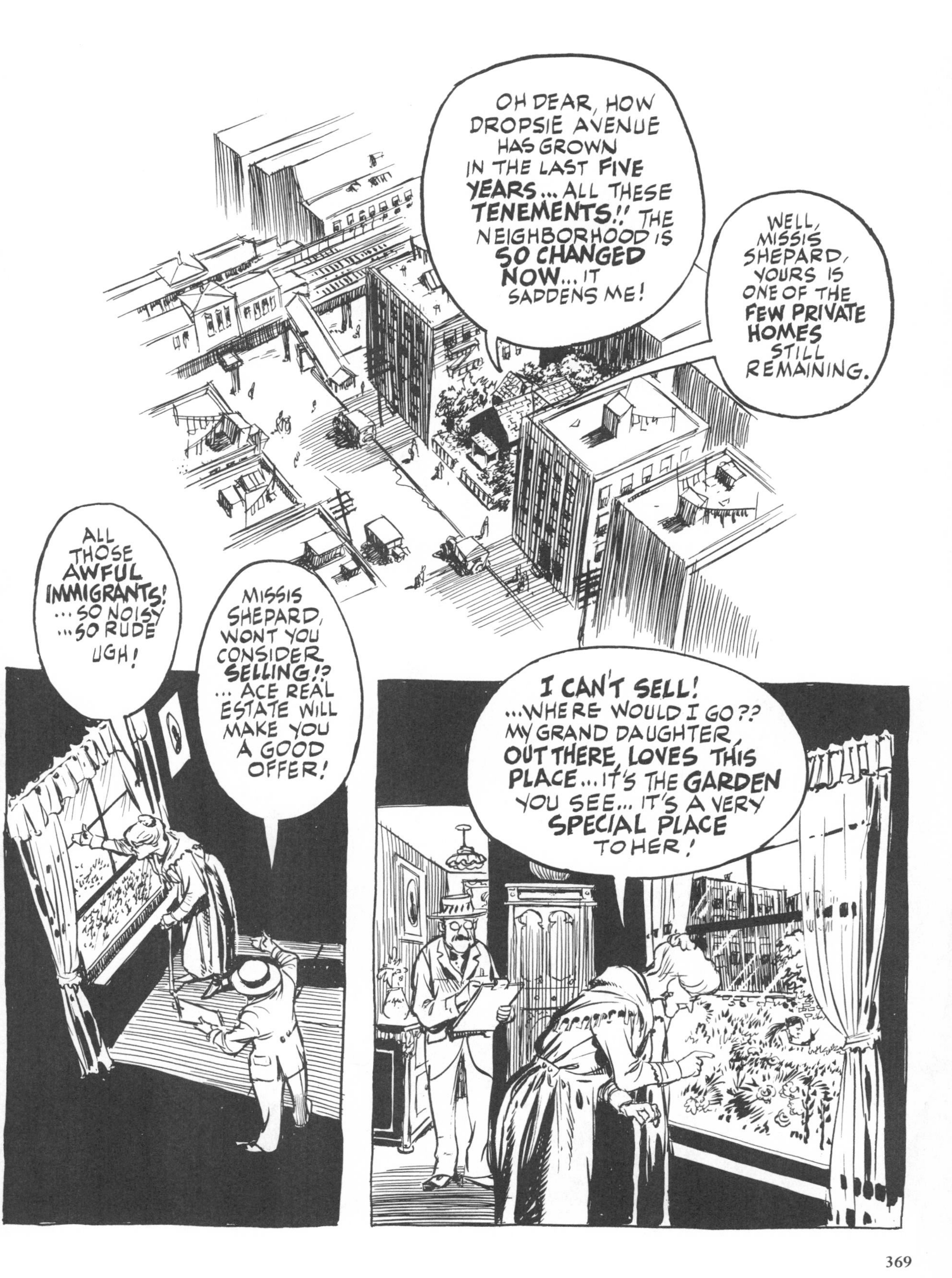

OH DEAR, HOW DROPSIE AVENUE HAS GROWN IN THE LAST FIVE YEARS... ALL THESE TENEMENTS!! THE NEIGHBORHOOD IS SO CHANGED NOW... IT SADDENS ME!
WELL, MISSIS SHEPARD, YOURS IS ONE OF THE FEW PRIVATE HOMES STILL REMAINING.
ALL THOSE AWFUL IMMIGRANTS! ...SO NOISY ...SO RUDE UGH!
MISSIS SHEPARD, WONT YOU CONSIDER SELLING!? ...ACE REAL ESTATE WILL MAKE YOU A GOOD OFFER!
I CAN'T SELL! ...WHERE WOULD I GO?? MY GRAND DAUGHTER, OUT THERE, LOVES THIS PLACE... IT'S THE GARDEN YOU SEE... IT'S A VERY SPECIAL PLACE TO HER!

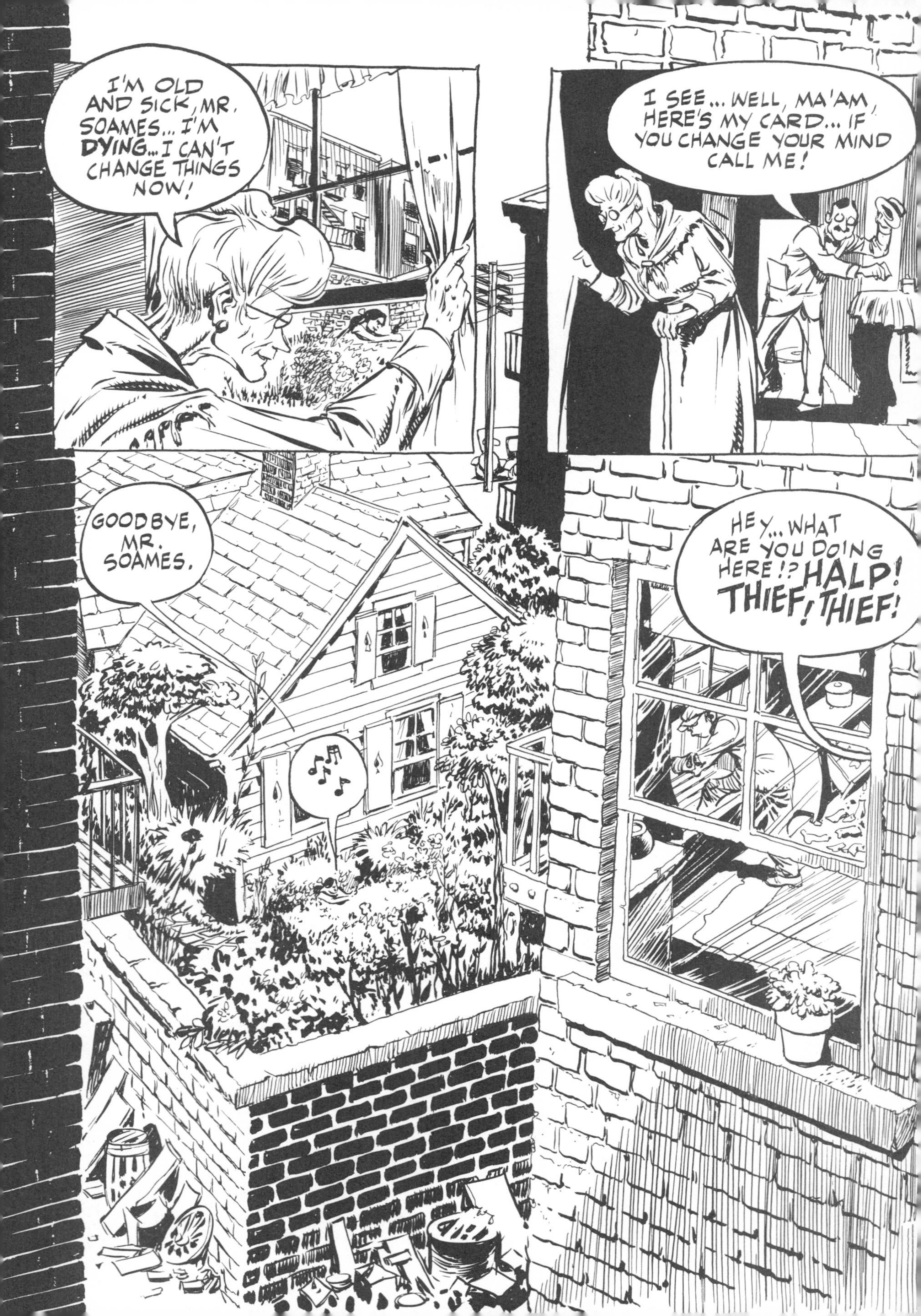
I'M OLD AND SICK, MR. SOAMES... I'M **DYING**... I CAN'T CHANGE THINGS NOW!
I SEE... WELL, MA'AM, HERE'S MY CARD... IF YOU CHANGE YOUR MIND CALL ME!
GOODBYE, MR. SOAMES.
HEY... WHAT ARE YOU DOING HERE!? **HALP! THIEF! THIEF!**

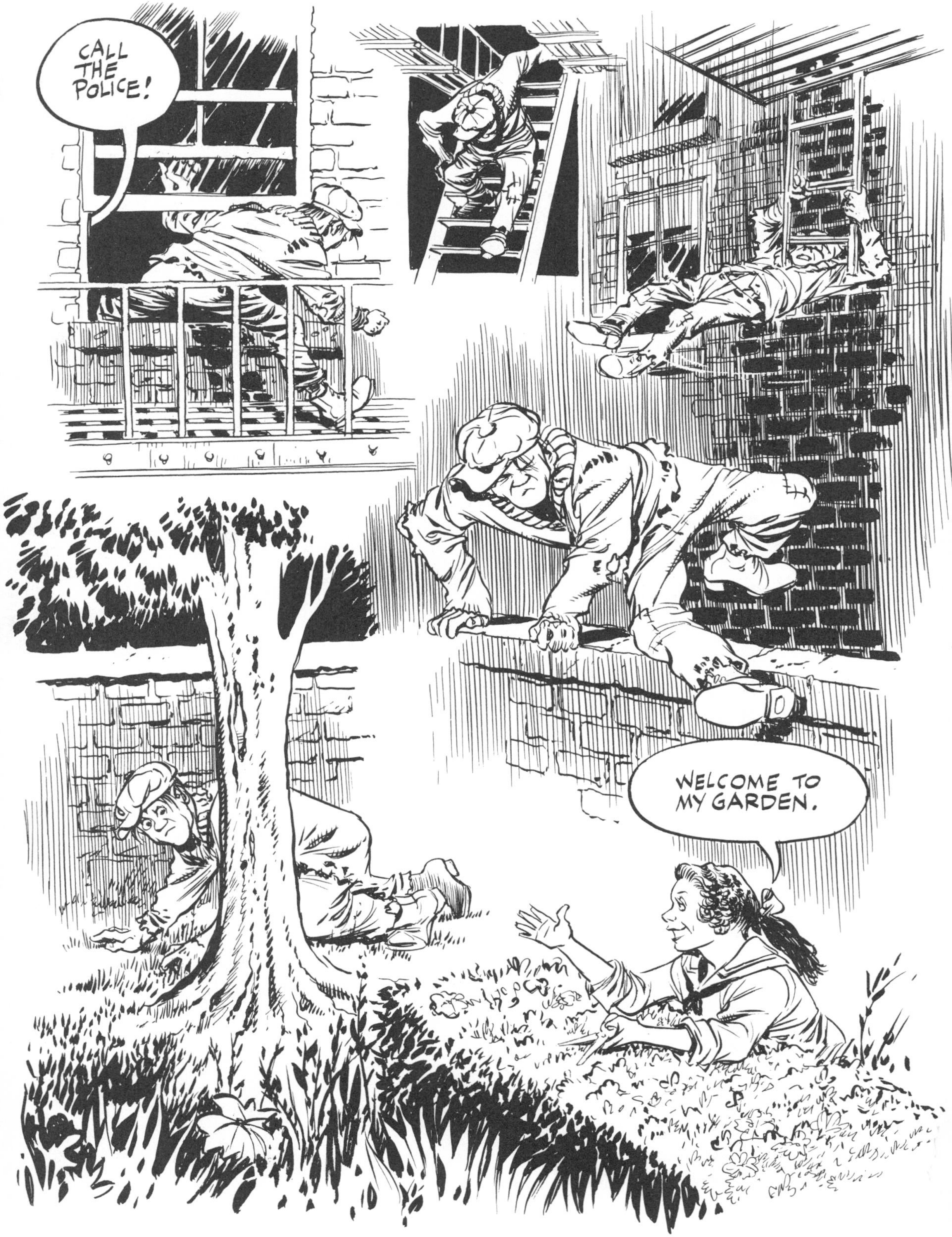
CALL THE POLICE!
WELCOME TO MY GARDEN.

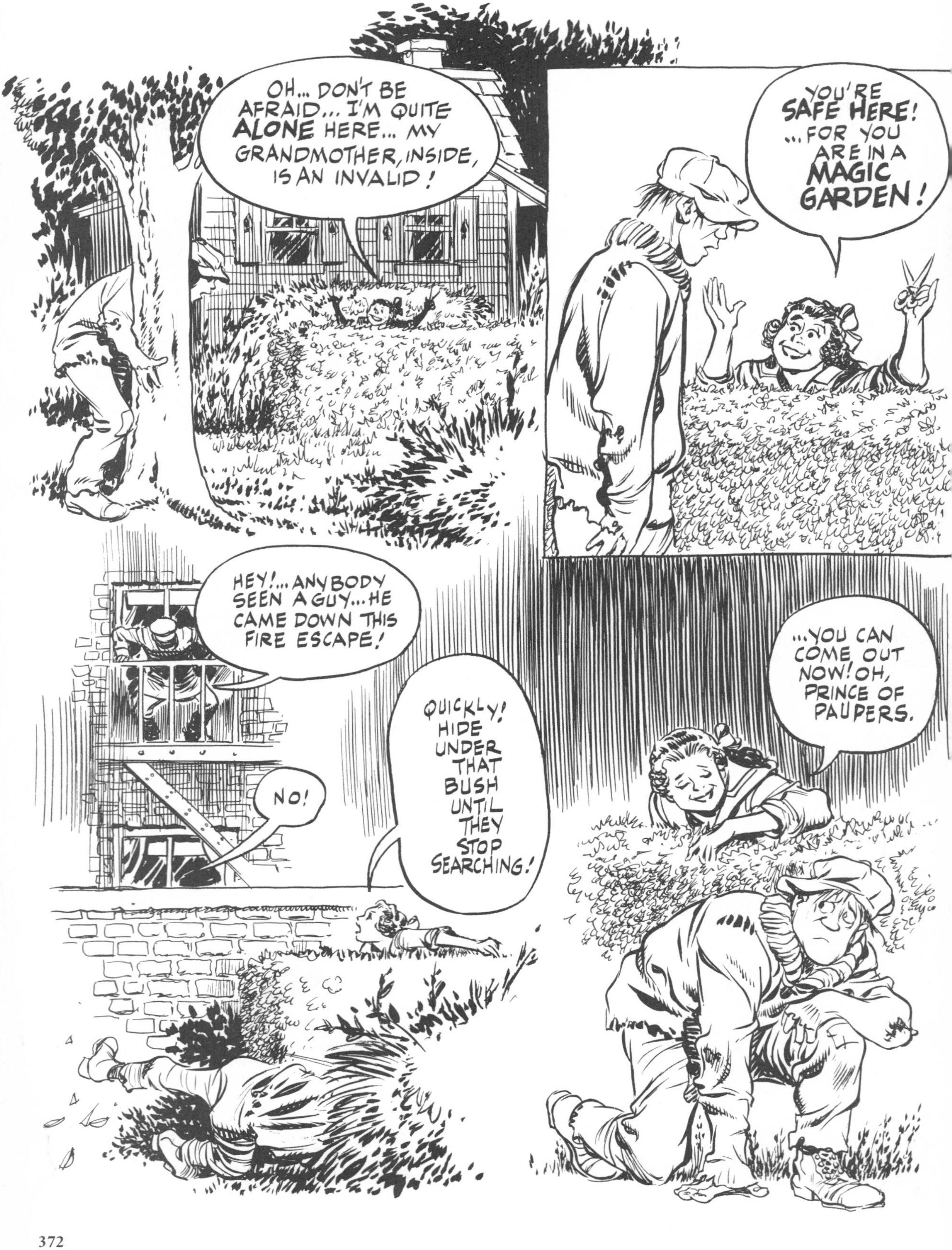
OH... DON'T BE AFRAID... I'M QUITE ALONE HERE... MY GRANDMOTHER, INSIDE, IS AN INVALID!
YOU'RE SAFE HERE! ...FOR YOU ARE IN A MAGIC GARDEN!
HEY!... ANYBODY SEEN A GUY... HE CAME DOWN THIS FIRE ESCAPE!
NO!
QUICKLY! HIDE UNDER THAT BUSH UNTIL THEY STOP SEARCHING!
...YOU CAN COME OUT NOW! OH, PRINCE OF PAUPERS.

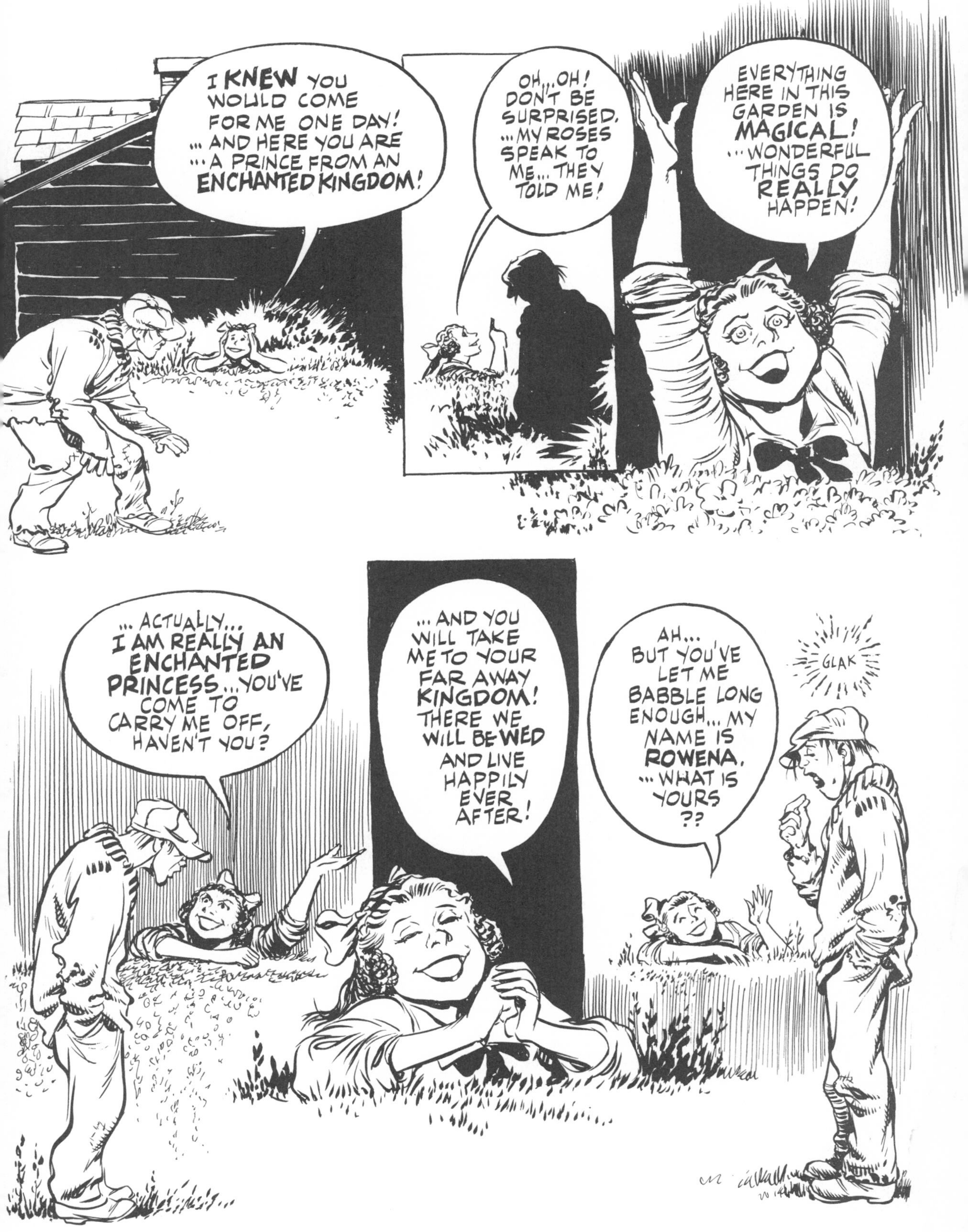
I KNEW YOU WOULD COME FOR ME ONE DAY! ... AND HERE YOU ARE ... A PRINCE FROM AN ENCHANTED KINGDOM!
OH,..OH! DON'T BE SURPRISED. ...MY ROSES SPEAK TO ME... THEY TOLD ME!
EVERYTHING HERE IN THIS GARDEN IS MAGICAL! ...WONDERFUL THINGS DO REALLY HAPPEN!
... ACTUALLY... I AM REALLY AN ENCHANTED PRINCESS... YOU'VE COME TO CARRY ME OFF, HAVEN'T YOU?
... AND YOU WILL TAKE ME TO YOUR FAR AWAY KINGDOM! THERE WE WILL BE WED AND LIVE HAPPILY EVER AFTER!
AH... BUT YOU'VE LET ME BABBLE LONG ENOUGH... MY NAME IS ROWENA. ... WHAT IS YOURS ??
GLAK

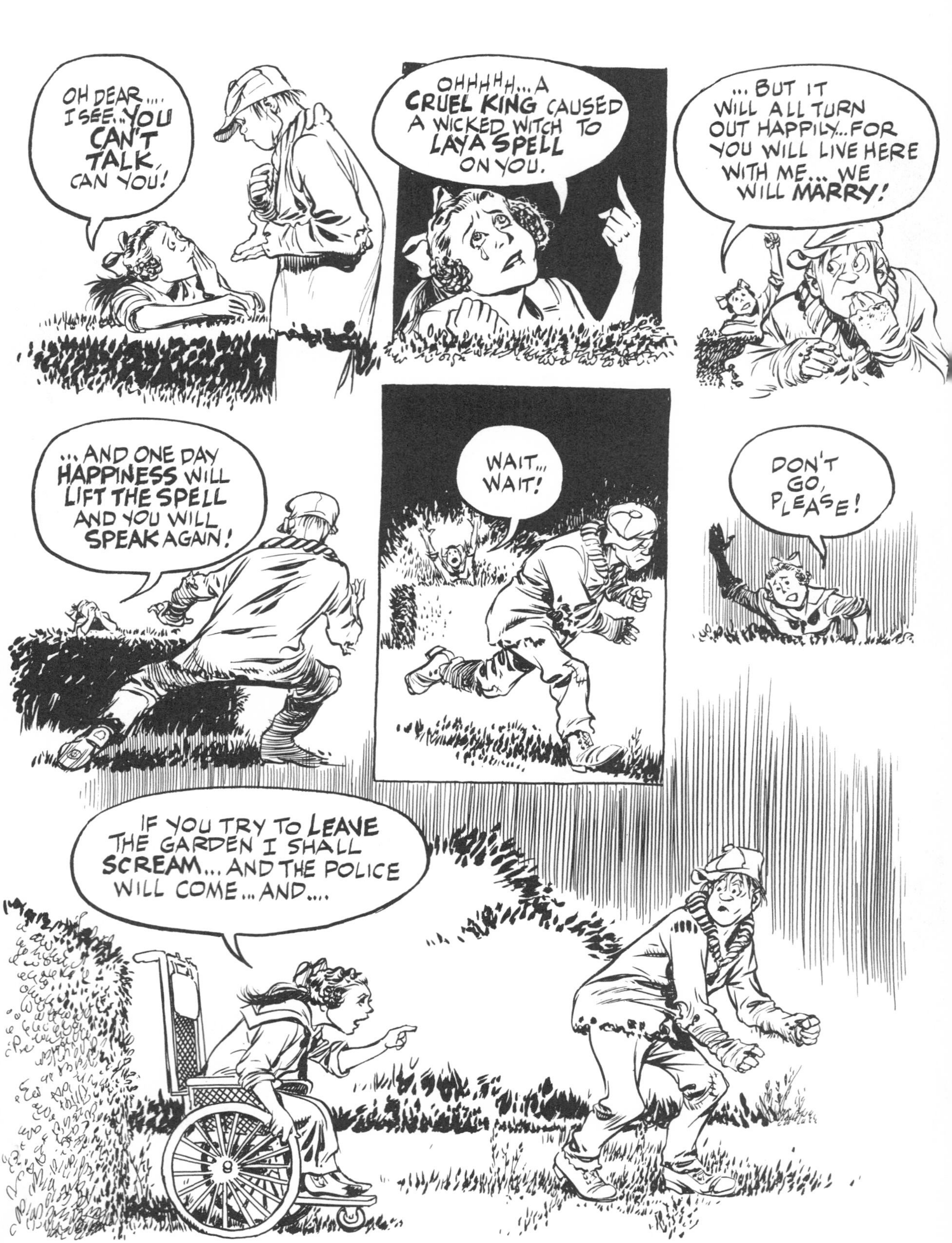
OH DEAR.... I SEE..YOU CAN'T TALK, CAN YOU!
OHHHHH...A CRUEL KING CAUSED A WICKED WITCH TO LAY A SPELL ON YOU.
...BUT IT WILL ALL TURN OUT HAPPILY...FOR YOU WILL LIVE HERE WITH ME... WE WILL MARRY!
...AND ONE DAY HAPPINESS WILL LIFT THE SPELL AND YOU WILL SPEAK AGAIN!
WAIT... WAIT!
DON'T GO, PLEASE!
IF YOU TRY TO LEAVE THE GARDEN I SHALL SCREAM... AND THE POLICE WILL COME...AND....

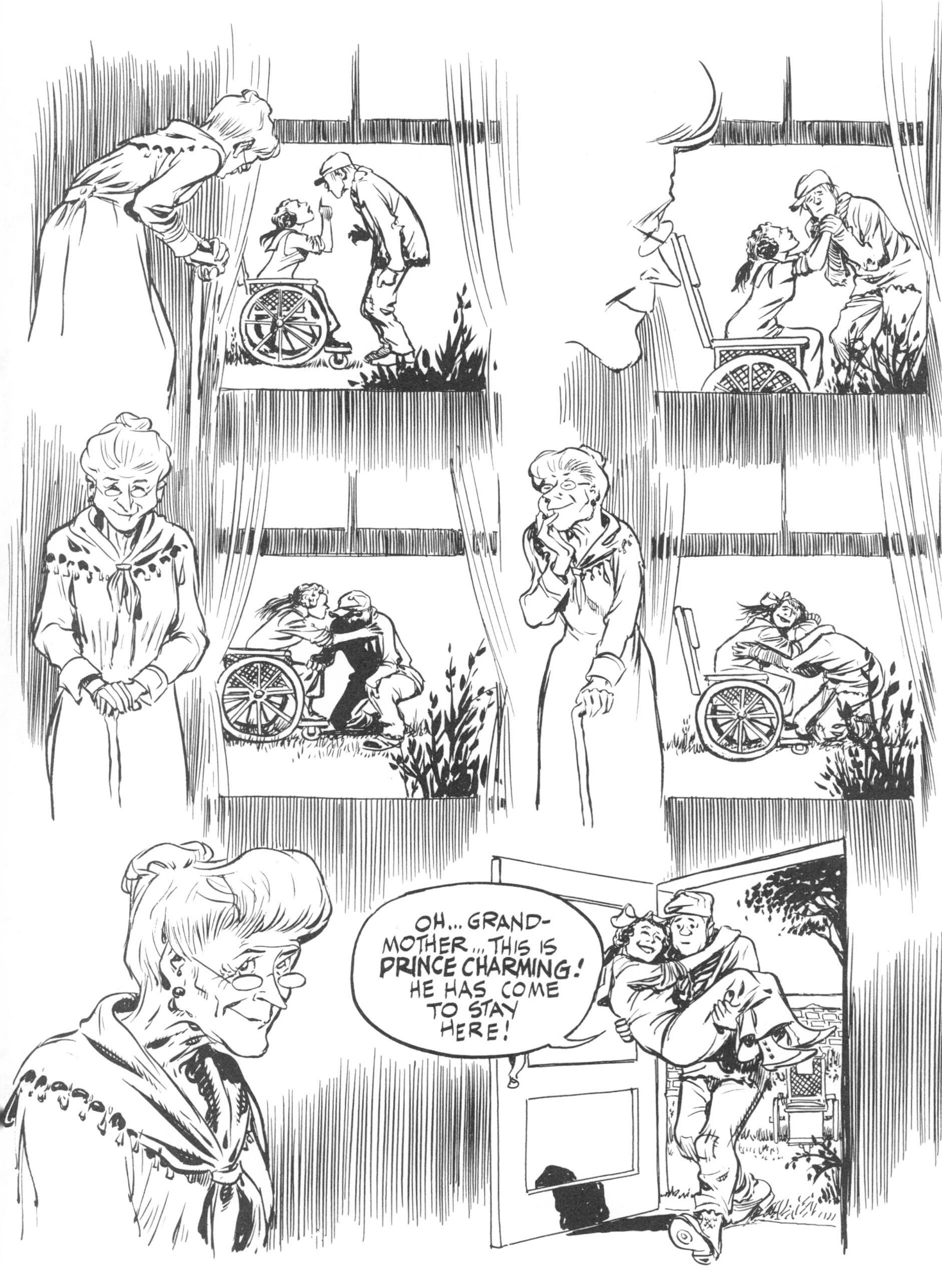
OH... GRAND-MOTHER... THIS IS PRINCE CHARMING! HE HAS COME TO STAY HERE!

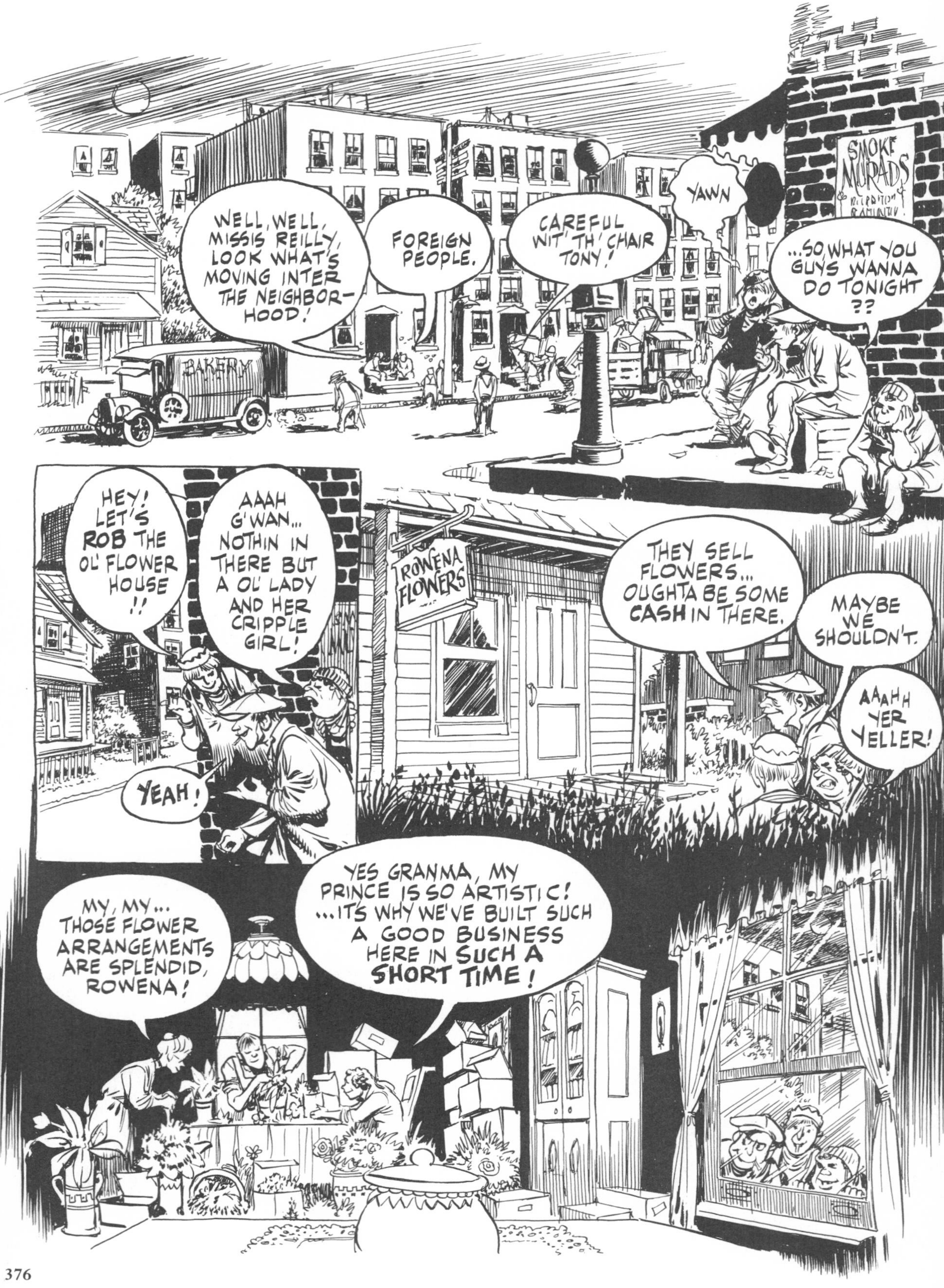
BAKERY
WELL, WELL, MISSIS REILLY, LOOK WHAT'S MOVING INTER THE NEIGHBOR-HOOD!
FOREIGN PEOPLE.
CAREFUL WIT' TH' CHAIR TONY!
YAWN
SMOKE MURADS
...SO, WHAT YOU GUYS WANNA DO TONIGHT ??
HEY! LET'S **ROB** THE OL' FLOWER HOUSE !!
AAAH G'WAN... NOTHIN IN THERE BUT A OL' LADY AND HER CRIPPLE GIRL!
YEAH!
ROWENA FLOWERS
THEY SELL FLOWERS... OUGHTA BE SOME **CASH** IN THERE.
MAYBE WE SHOULDN'T.
AAAHH YER YELLER!
MY, MY... THOSE FLOWER ARRANGEMENTS ARE SPLENDID, ROWENA!
YES GRANMA, MY PRINCE IS SO ARTISTIC! ...IT'S WHY WE'VE BUILT SUCH A GOOD BUSINESS HERE IN **SUCH A SHORT TIME**!

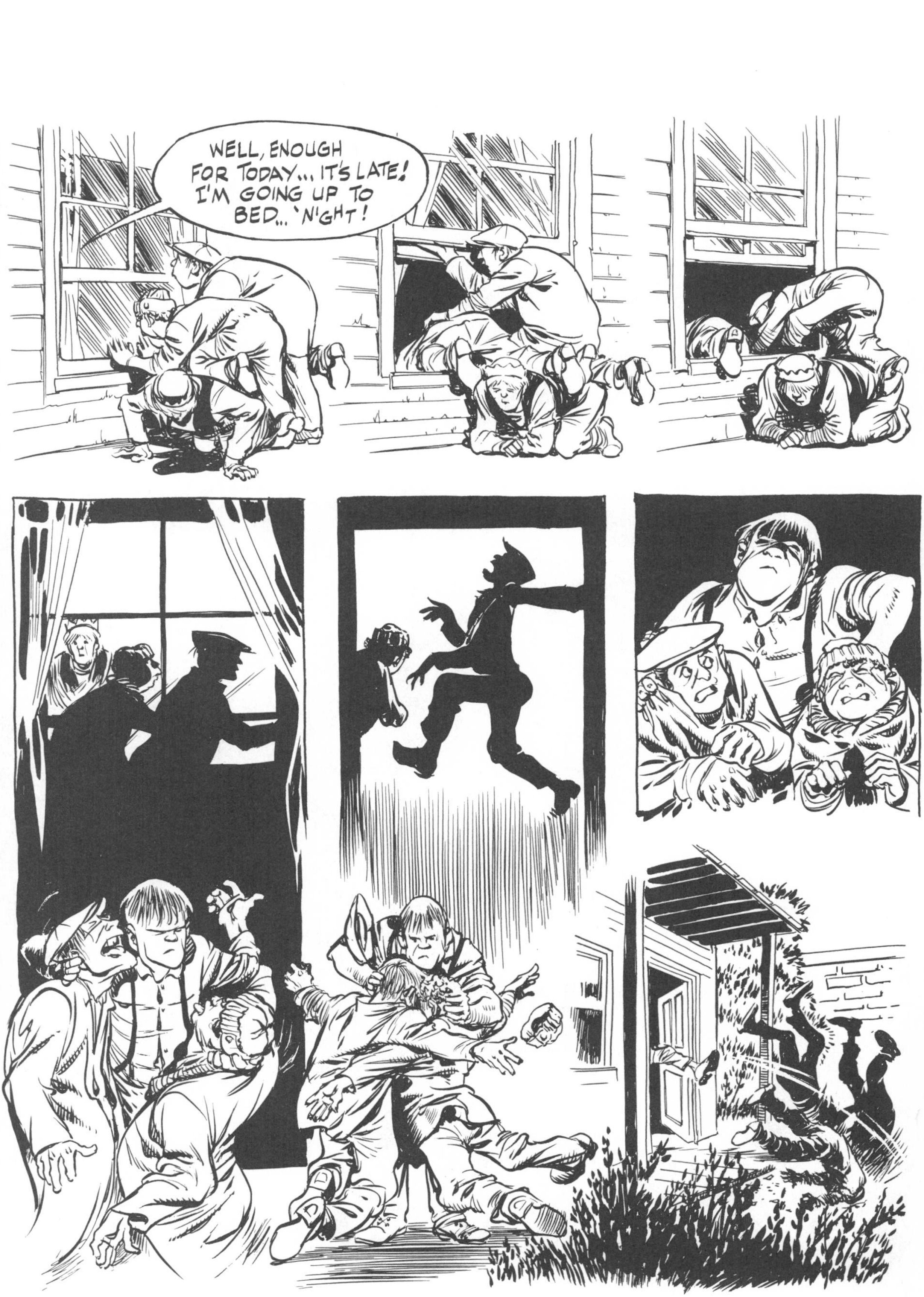
WELL, ENOUGH FOR TODAY... IT'S LATE! I'M GOING UP TO BED... 'NIGHT!

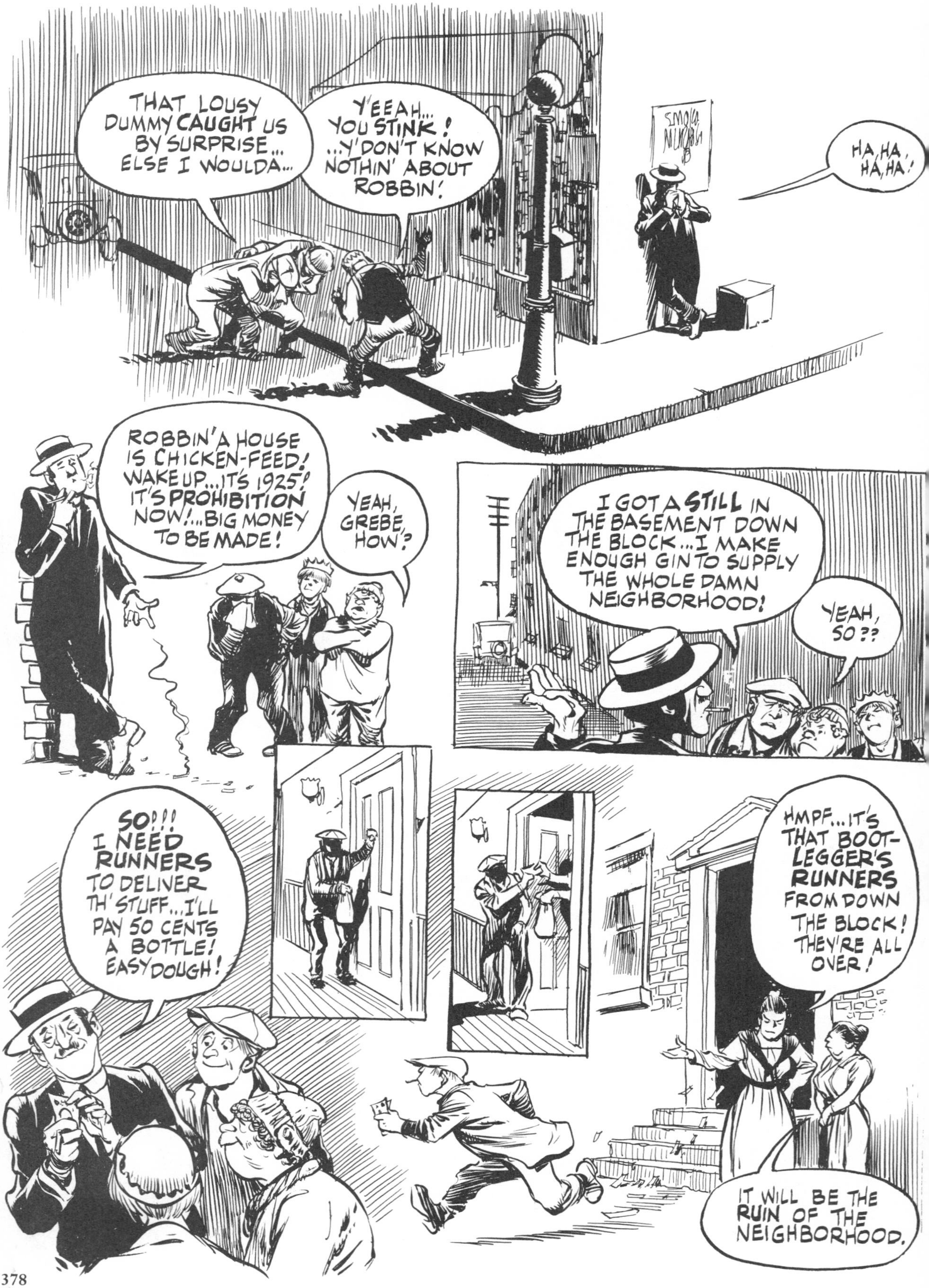

THAT LOUSY DUMMY CAUGHT US BY SURPRISE... ELSE I WOULDA...
Y'EEAH... YOU STINK! ...Y'DON'T KNOW NOTHIN' ABOUT ROBBIN'!
HA, HA, HA, HA!
ROBBIN' A HOUSE IS CHICKEN-FEED! WAKE UP... IT'S 1925! IT'S PROHIBITION NOW!... BIG MONEY TO BE MADE!
YEAH, GREBE, HOW?
I GOT A STILL IN THE BASEMENT DOWN THE BLOCK... I MAKE ENOUGH GIN TO SUPPLY THE WHOLE DAMN NEIGHBORHOOD!
YEAH, SO??
SO!!! I NEED RUNNERS TO DELIVER TH' STUFF... I'LL PAY 50 CENTS A BOTTLE! EASY DOUGH!
HMPF... IT'S THAT BOOT-LEGGER'S RUNNERS FROM DOWN THE BLOCK! THEY'RE ALL OVER!
IT WILL BE THE RUIN OF THE NEIGHBORHOOD.

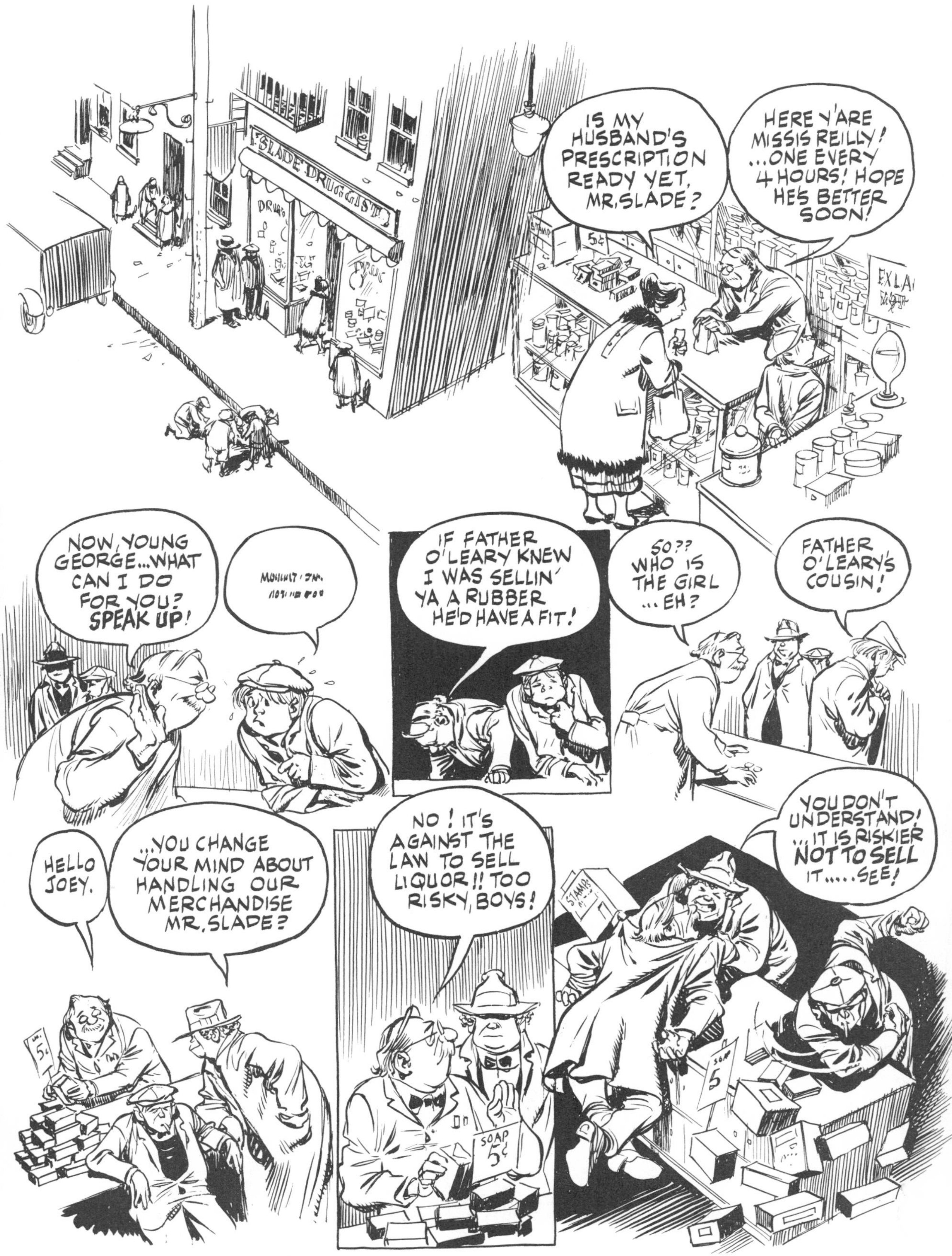
SLADE DRUGGIST
IS MY HUSBAND'S PRESCRIPTION READY YET, MR. SLADE?
HERE Y'ARE MISSIS REILLY! ...ONE EVERY 4 HOURS! HOPE HE'S BETTER SOON!
NOW, YOUNG GEORGE...WHAT CAN I DO FOR YOU? SPEAK UP!
IF FATHER O'LEARY KNEW I WAS SELLIN' YA A RUBBER HE'D HAVE A FIT!
SO?? WHO IS THE GIRL ...EH?
FATHER O'LEARY'S COUSIN!
HELLO JOEY.
...YOU CHANGE YOUR MIND ABOUT HANDLING OUR MERCHANDISE MR. SLADE?
NO! IT'S AGAINST THE LAW TO SELL LIQUOR!! TOO RISKY, BOYS!
YOU DON'T UNDERSTAND! ...IT IS RISKIER NOT TO SELL IT.....SEE!
SOAP 5¢

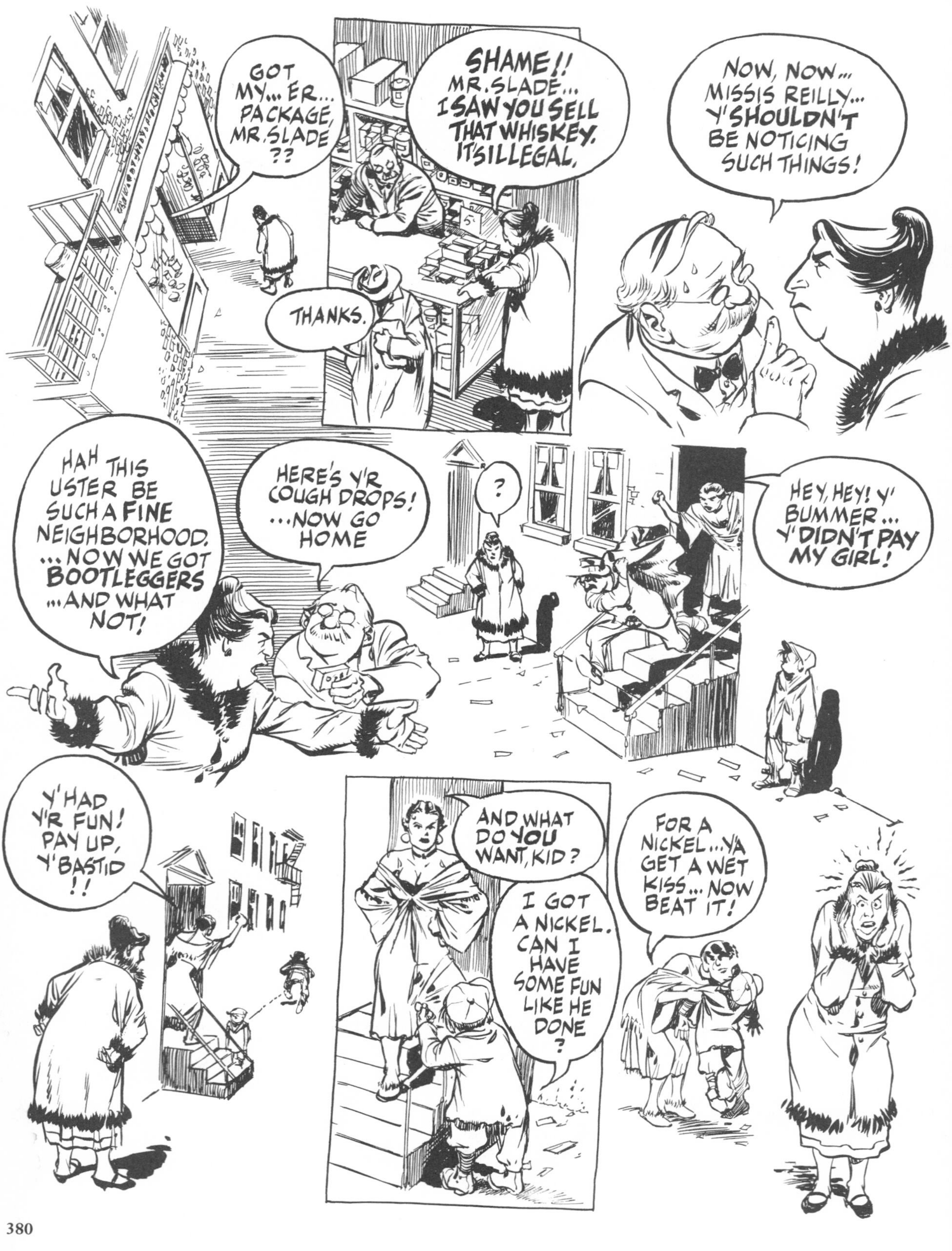
GOT MY... ER... PACKAGE, MR. SLADE ??
SHAME!! MR. SLADE... I SAW YOU SELL THAT WHISKEY. IT'S ILLEGAL.
THANKS.
NOW, NOW... MISSIS REILLY... Y'SHOULDN'T BE NOTICING SUCH THINGS!
HAH THIS USTER BE SUCH A FINE NEIGHBORHOOD. ...NOW WE GOT BOOTLEGGERS ...AND WHAT NOT!
HERE'S Y'R COUGH DROPS! ...NOW GO HOME
?
HEY, HEY! Y' BUMMER... Y' DIDN'T PAY MY GIRL!
Y'HAD Y'R FUN! PAY UP, Y'BASTID !!
AND WHAT DO YOU WANT, KID?
I GOT A NICKEL. CAN I HAVE SOME FUN LIKE HE DONE ?
FOR A NICKEL... YA GET A WET KISS... NOW BEAT IT!

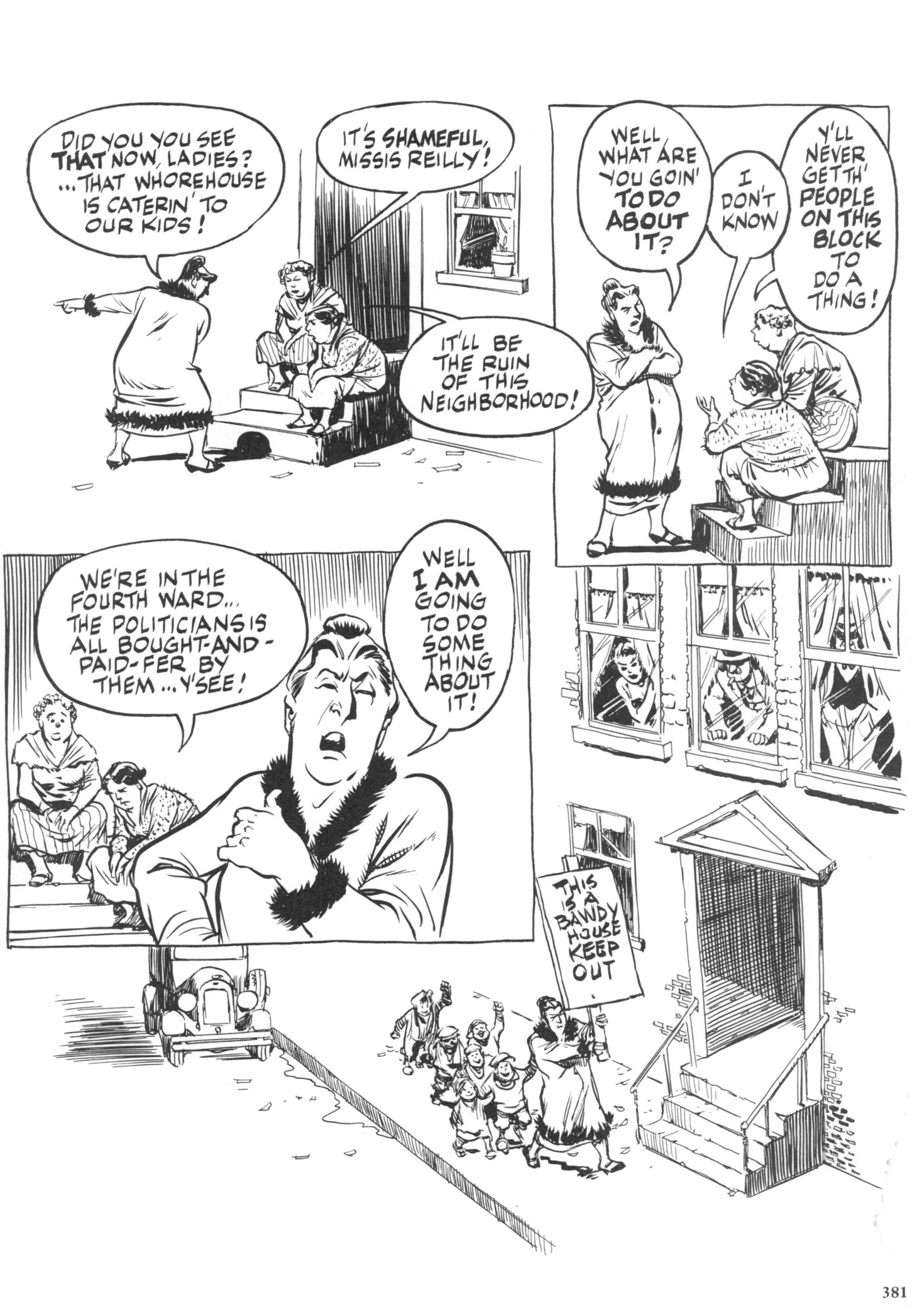
DID YOU YOU SEE THAT NOW, LADIES? ...THAT WHOREHOUSE IS CATERIN' TO OUR KIDS!
IT'S SHAMEFUL, MISSIS REILLY!
IT'LL BE THE RUIN OF THIS NEIGHBORHOOD!
WELL, WHAT ARE YOU GOIN' TO DO ABOUT IT?
I DON'T KNOW
Y'LL NEVER GET TH' PEOPLE ON THIS BLOCK TO DO A THING!
WE'RE IN THE FOURTH WARD... THE POLITICIANS IS ALL BOUGHT-AND-PAID-FER BY THEM... Y'SEE!
WELL I AM GOING TO DO SOME THING ABOUT IT!
THIS IS A BAWDY HOUSE KEEP OUT

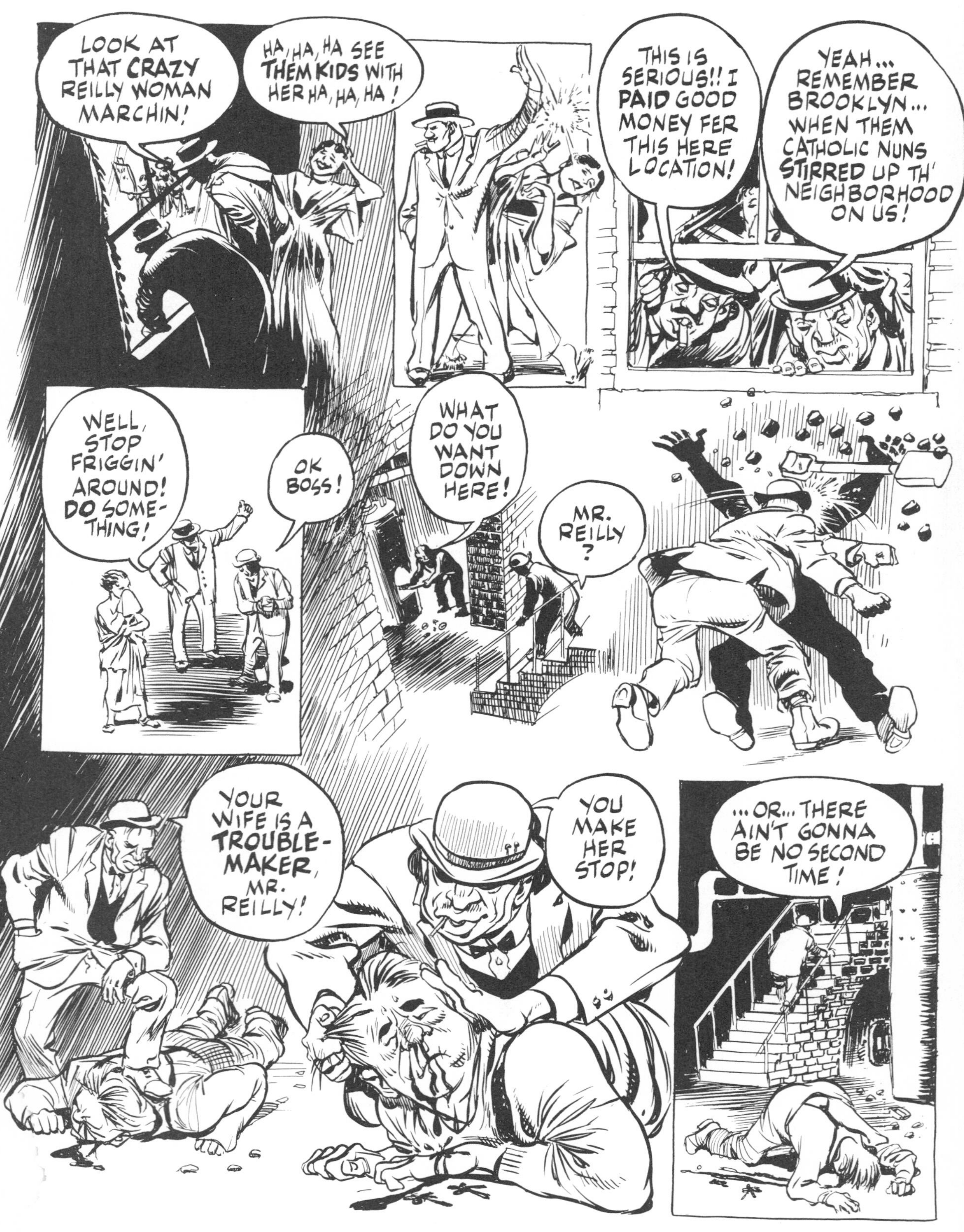
LOOK AT THAT CRAZY REILLY WOMAN MARCHIN'!
HA, HA, HA SEE THEM KIDS WITH HER HA, HA, HA!
THIS IS SERIOUS!! I PAID GOOD MONEY FER THIS HERE LOCATION!
YEAH... REMEMBER BROOKLYN... WHEN THEM CATHOLIC NUNS STIRRED UP TH' NEIGHBORHOOD ON US!
WELL, STOP FRIGGIN' AROUND! DO SOME-THING!
OK BOSS!
WHAT DO YOU WANT DOWN HERE!
MR. REILLY?
YOUR WIFE IS A TROUBLE-MAKER, MR. REILLY!
YOU MAKE HER STOP!
...OR... THERE AIN'T GONNA BE NO SECOND TIME!

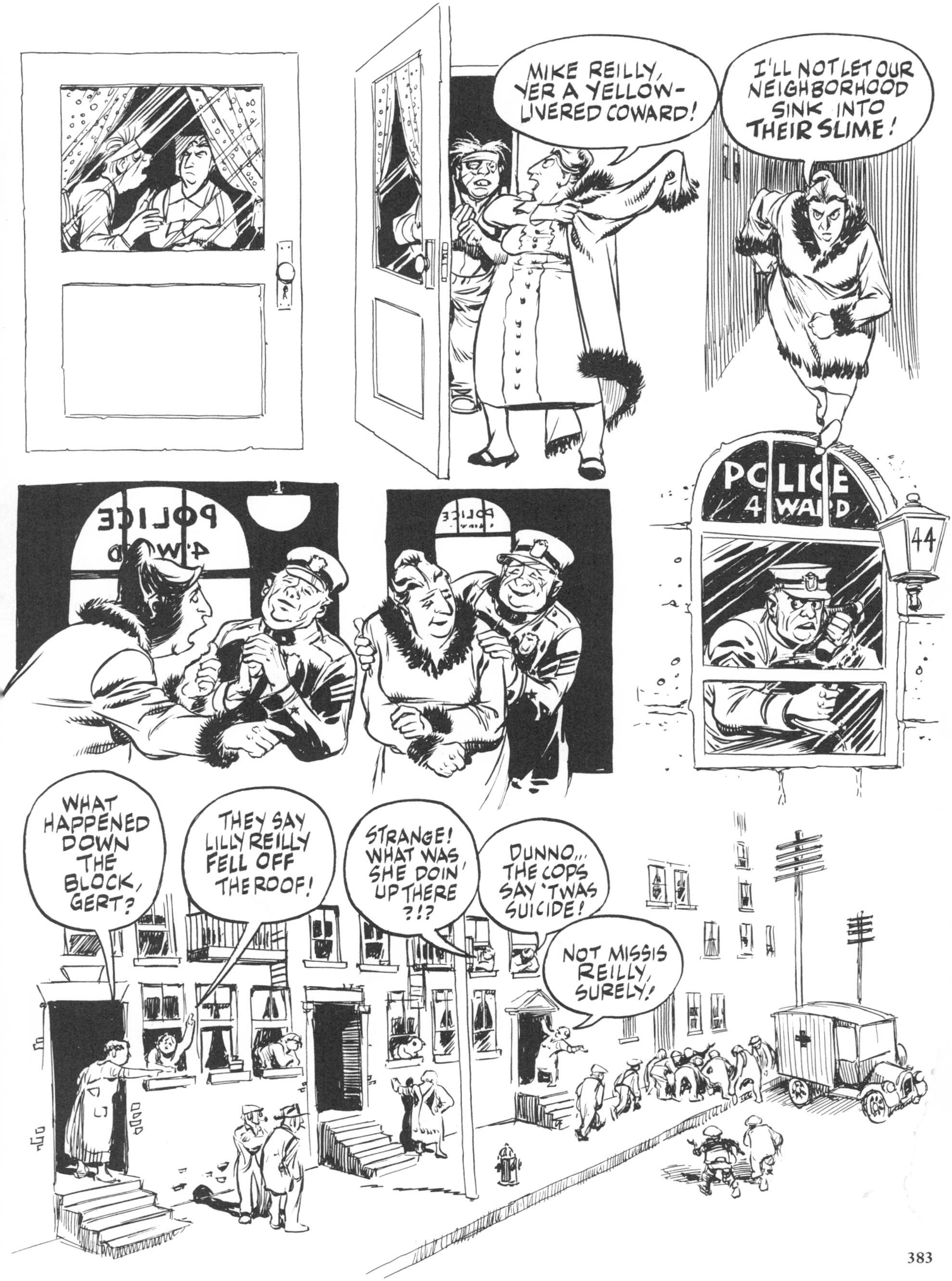
MIKE REILLY, YER A YELLOW-LIVERED COWARD!
I'LL NOT LET OUR NEIGHBORHOOD SINK INTO THEIR SLIME!
POLICE 4 WARD
44
WHAT HAPPENED DOWN THE BLOCK, GERT?
THEY SAY LILLY REILLY FELL OFF THE ROOF!
STRANGE! WHAT WAS SHE DOIN' UP THERE ?!?
DUNNO... THE COPS SAY 'TWAS SUICIDE!
NOT MISSIS REILLY, SURELY!

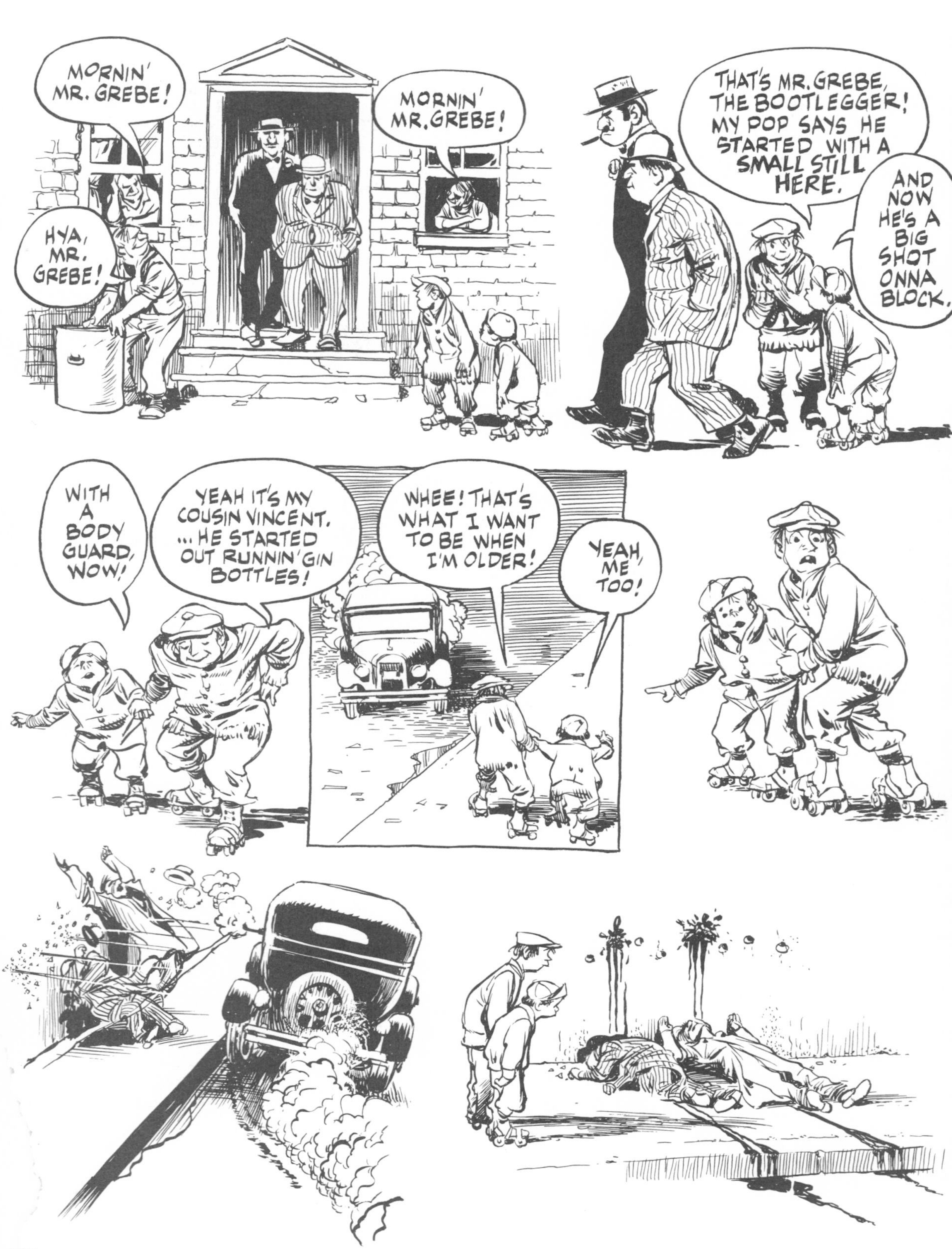
MORNIN' MR. GREBE!
MORNIN' MR. GREBE!
HYA, MR. GREBE!
THAT'S MR. GREBE, THE BOOTLEGGER! MY POP SAYS HE STARTED WITH A SMALL STILL HERE.
AND NOW HE'S A BIG SHOT ONNA BLOCK.
WITH A BODY GUARD, WOW!
YEAH IT'S MY COUSIN VINCENT. ... HE STARTED OUT RUNNIN' GIN BOTTLES!
WHEE! THAT'S WHAT I WANT TO BE WHEN I'M OLDER!
YEAH, ME TOO!

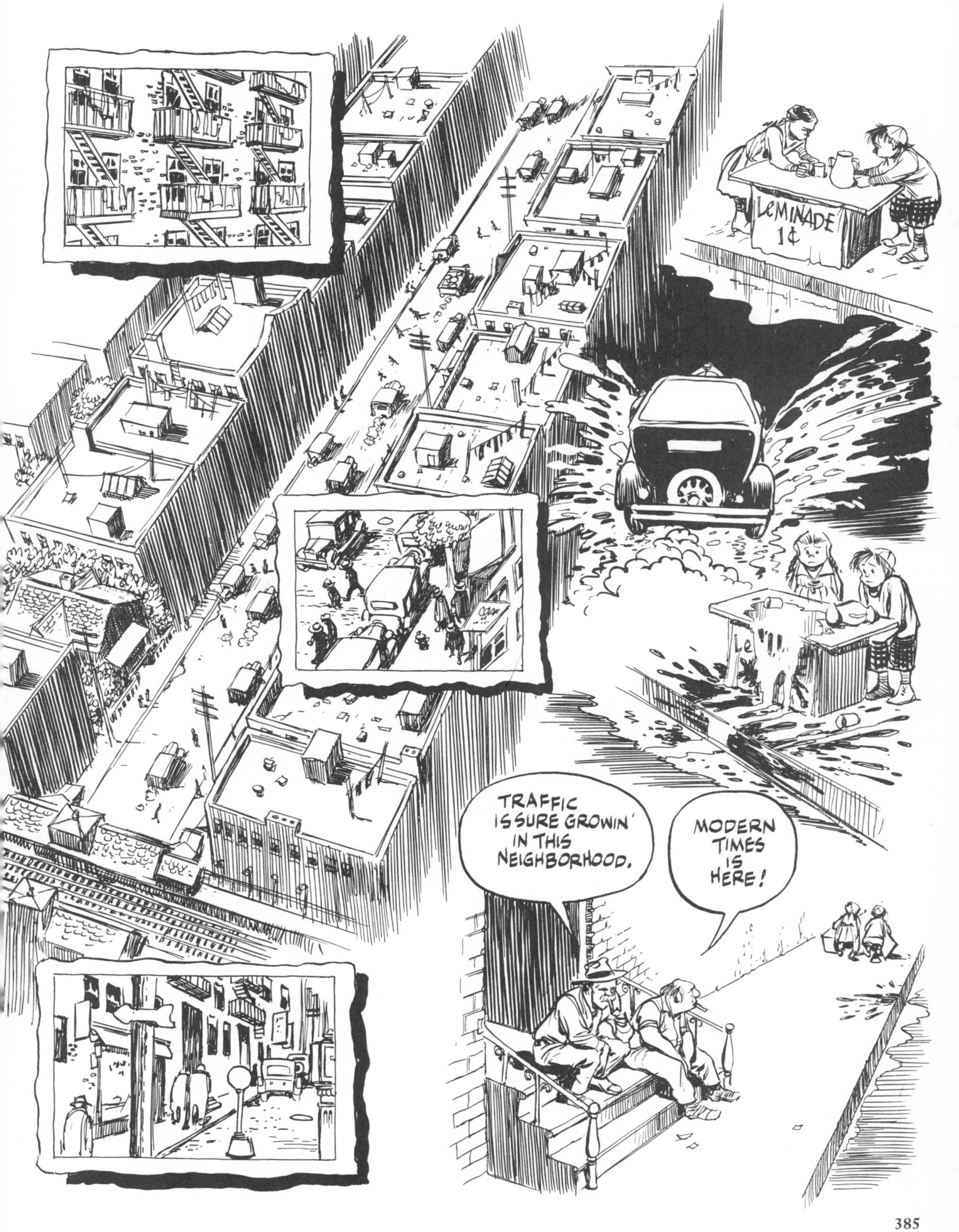

LEMINADE 1¢
TRAFFIC IS SURE GROWIN' IN THIS NEIGHBORHOOD.
MODERN TIMES IS HERE!

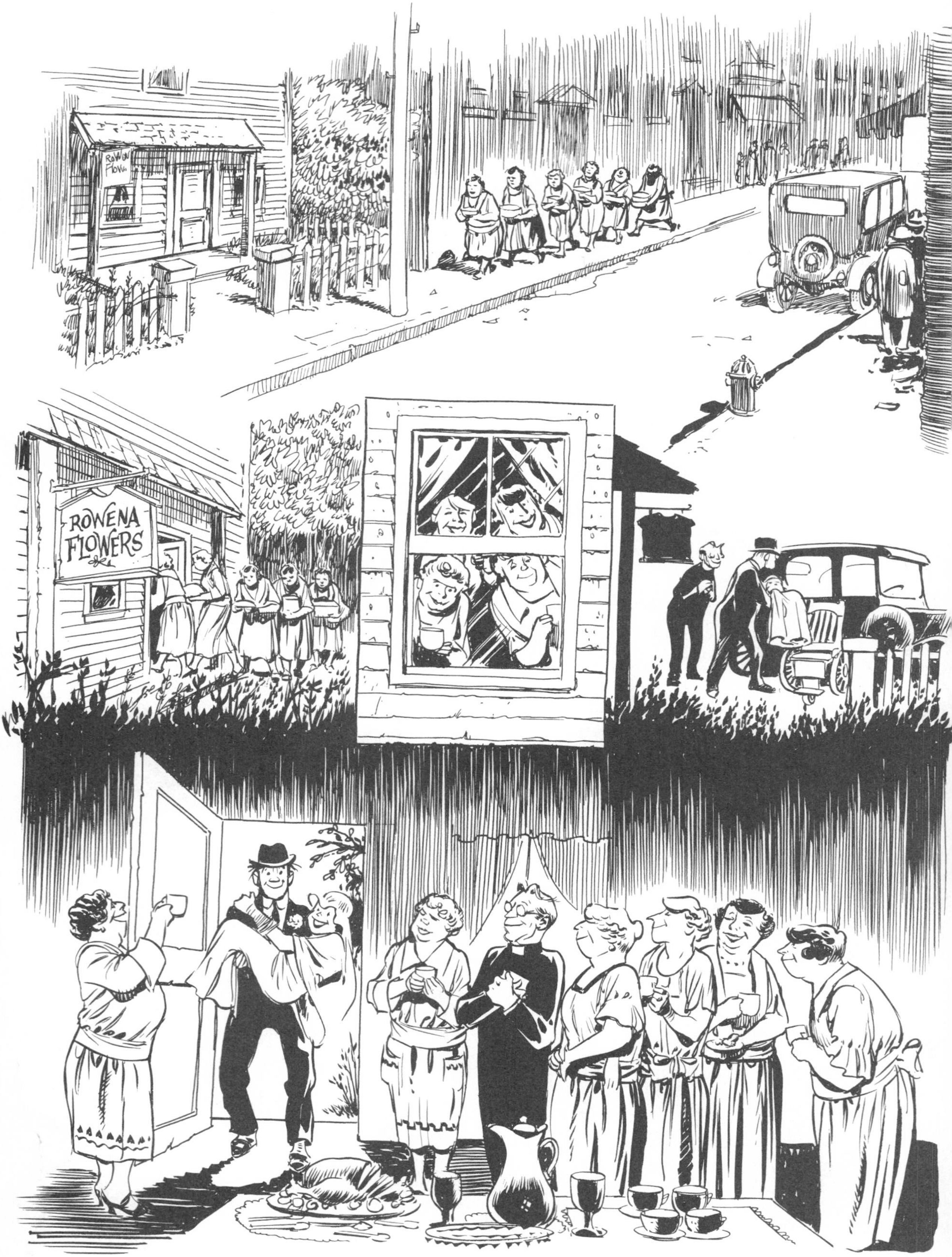
ROWENA FLOWERS

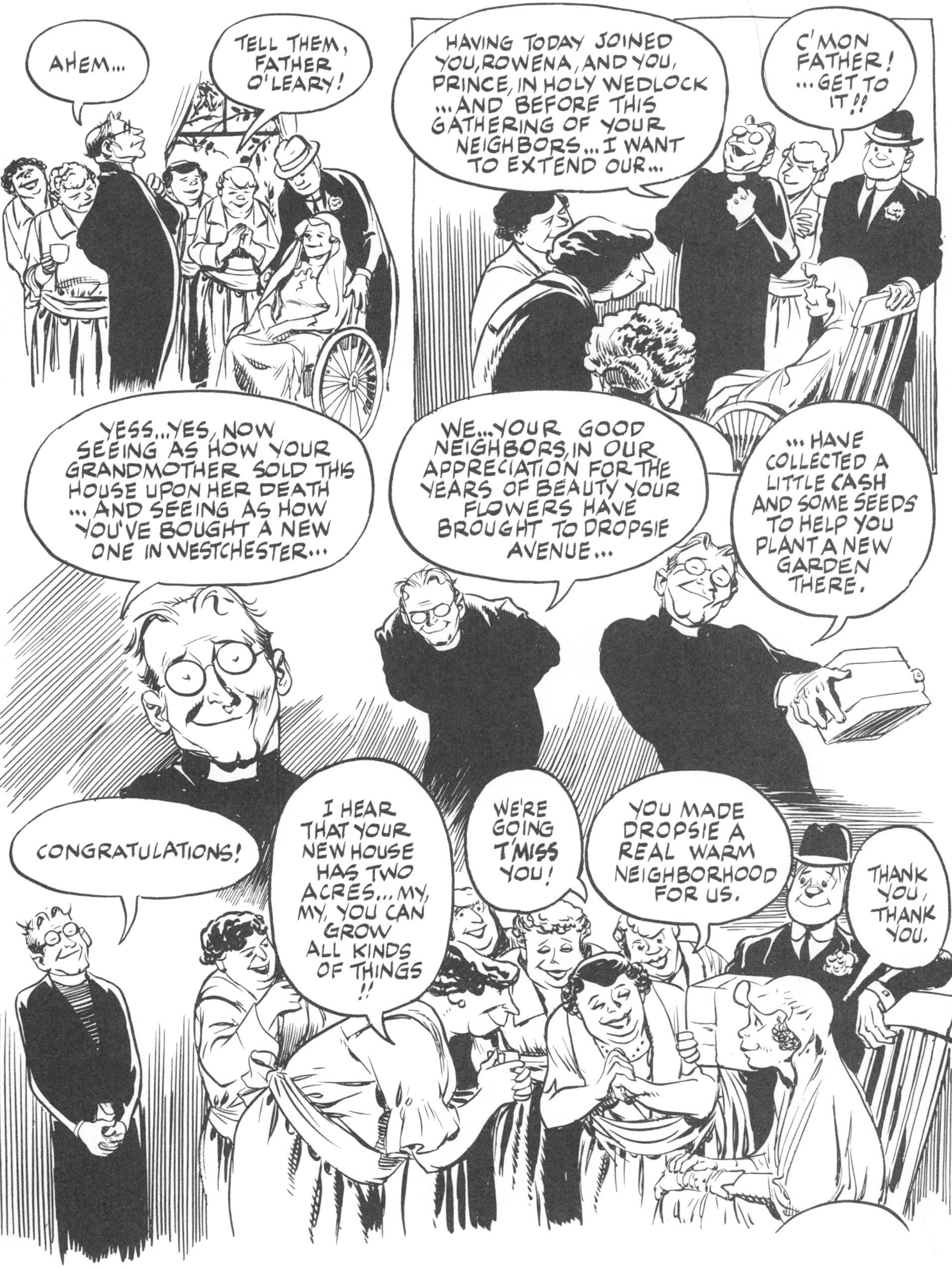
AHEM...
TELL THEM, FATHER O'LEARY!
HAVING TODAY JOINED YOU, ROWENA, AND YOU, PRINCE, IN HOLY WEDLOCK ...AND BEFORE THIS GATHERING OF YOUR NEIGHBORS... I WANT TO EXTEND OUR...
C'MON FATHER! ...GET TO IT!!
YESS...YES, NOW SEEING AS HOW YOUR GRANDMOTHER SOLD THIS HOUSE UPON HER DEATH ...AND SEEING AS HOW YOU'VE BOUGHT A NEW ONE IN WESTCHESTER...
WE...YOUR GOOD NEIGHBORS, IN OUR APPRECIATION FOR THE YEARS OF BEAUTY YOUR FLOWERS HAVE BROUGHT TO DROPSIE AVENUE...
...HAVE COLLECTED A LITTLE CASH AND SOME SEEDS TO HELP YOU PLANT A NEW GARDEN THERE.
CONGRATULATIONS!
I HEAR THAT YOUR NEW HOUSE HAS TWO ACRES... MY, MY, YOU CAN GROW ALL KINDS OF THINGS!!
WE'RE GOING T'MISS YOU!
YOU MADE DROPSIE A REAL WARM NEIGHBORHOOD FOR US.
THANK YOU, THANK YOU.

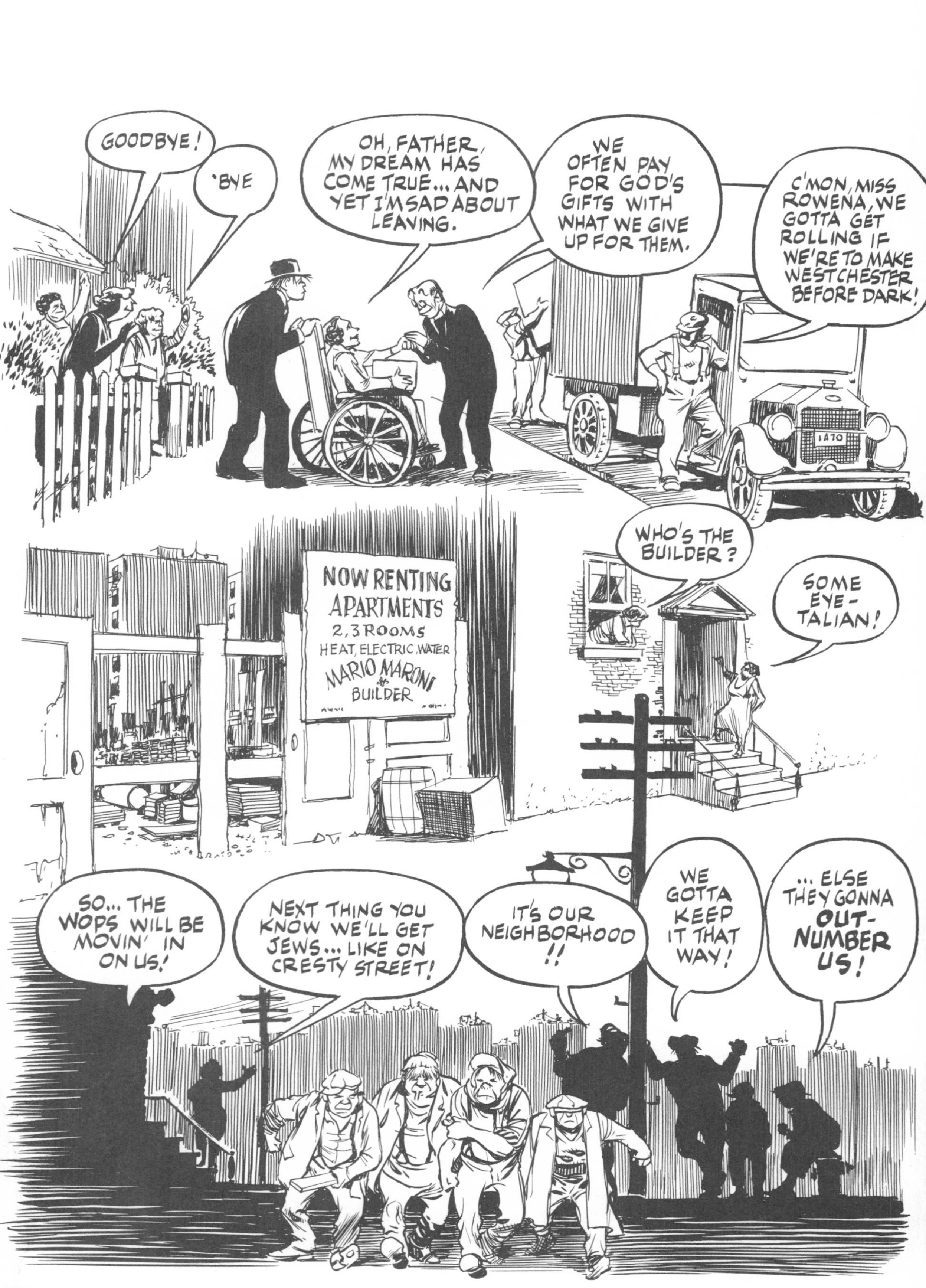
GOODBYE!
'BYE
OH, FATHER, MY DREAM HAS COME TRUE... AND YET I'M SAD ABOUT LEAVING.
WE OFTEN PAY FOR GOD'S GIFTS WITH WHAT WE GIVE UP FOR THEM.
C'MON, MISS ROWENA, WE GOTTA GET ROLLING IF WE'RE TO MAKE WESTCHESTER BEFORE DARK!
NOW RENTING APARTMENTS
2,3 ROOMS
HEAT, ELECTRIC, WATER
MARIO MARONI
BUILDER
WHO'S THE BUILDER?
SOME EYE-TALIAN!
SO... THE WOPS WILL BE MOVIN' IN ON US!
NEXT THING YOU KNOW WE'LL GET JEWS... LIKE ON CRESTY STREET!
IT'S OUR NEIGHBORHOOD!!
WE GOTTA KEEP IT THAT WAY!
... ELSE THEY GONNA **OUT-NUMBER US!**

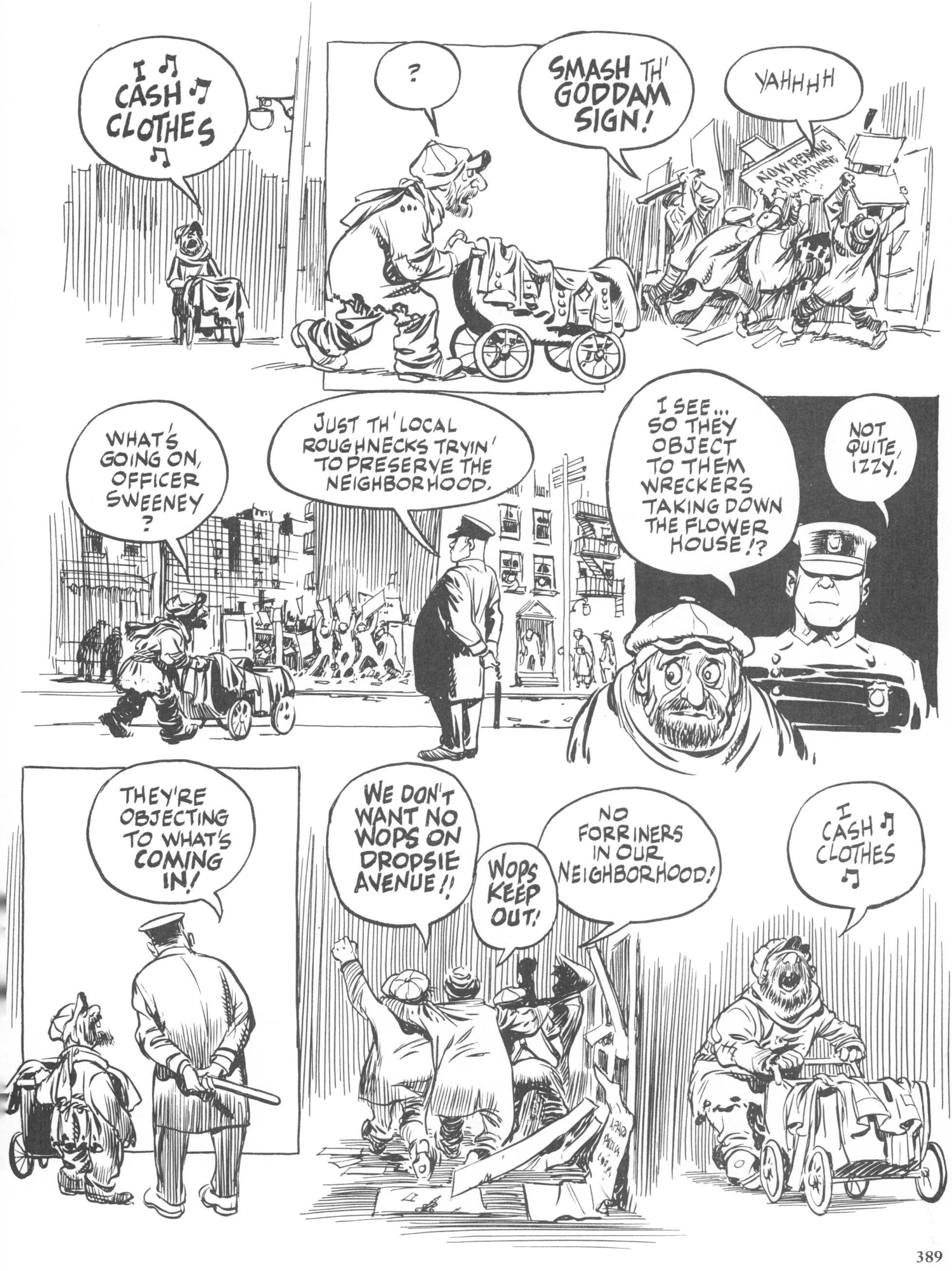
I ♫ CASH ♫ CLOTHES ♫
?
SMASH TH' GODDAM SIGN!
YAHHHH
NOW RENTING APARTMENT
WHAT'S GOING ON, OFFICER SWEENEY ?
JUST TH' LOCAL ROUGHNECKS TRYIN' TO PRESERVE THE NEIGHBORHOOD.
I SEE... SO THEY OBJECT TO THEM WRECKERS TAKING DOWN THE FLOWER HOUSE !?
NOT QUITE, IZZY.
THEY'RE OBJECTING TO WHAT'S COMING IN!
WE DON'T WANT NO WOPS ON DROPSIE AVENUE !!
WOPS KEEP OUT!
NO FORRINERS IN OUR NEIGHBORHOOD!
I CASH ♫ CLOTHES ♫

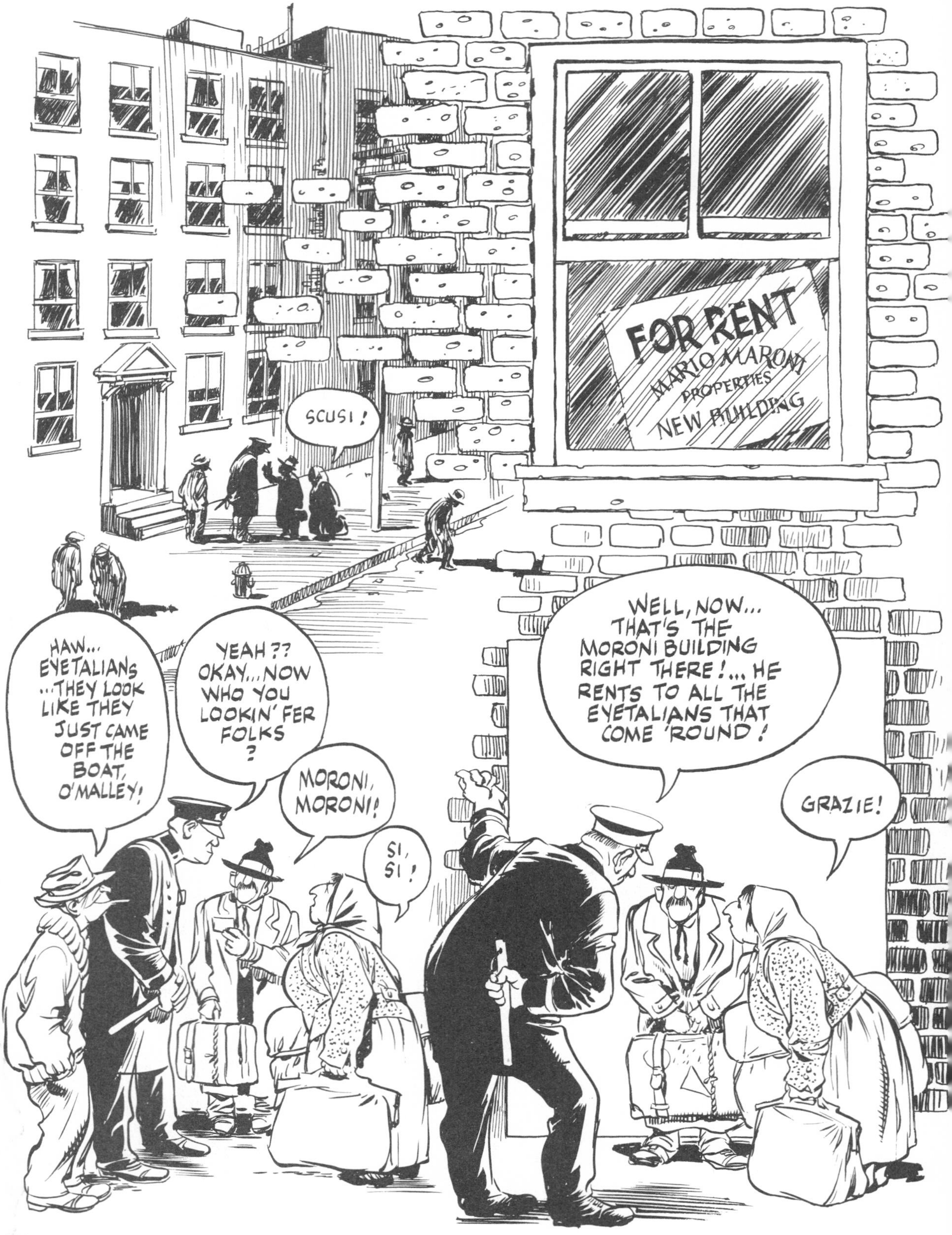
FOR RENT
MARIO MARONI PROPERTIES
NEW BUILDING
SCUSI!
HAW... EYETALIANS ...THEY LOOK LIKE THEY JUST CAME OFF THE BOAT, O'MALLEY!
YEAH?? OKAY...NOW WHO YOU LOOKIN' FER FOLKS?
MORONI, MORONI!
SI, SI!
WELL, NOW... THAT'S THE MORONI BUILDING RIGHT THERE!... HE RENTS TO ALL THE EYETALIANS THAT COME 'ROUND!
GRAZIE!

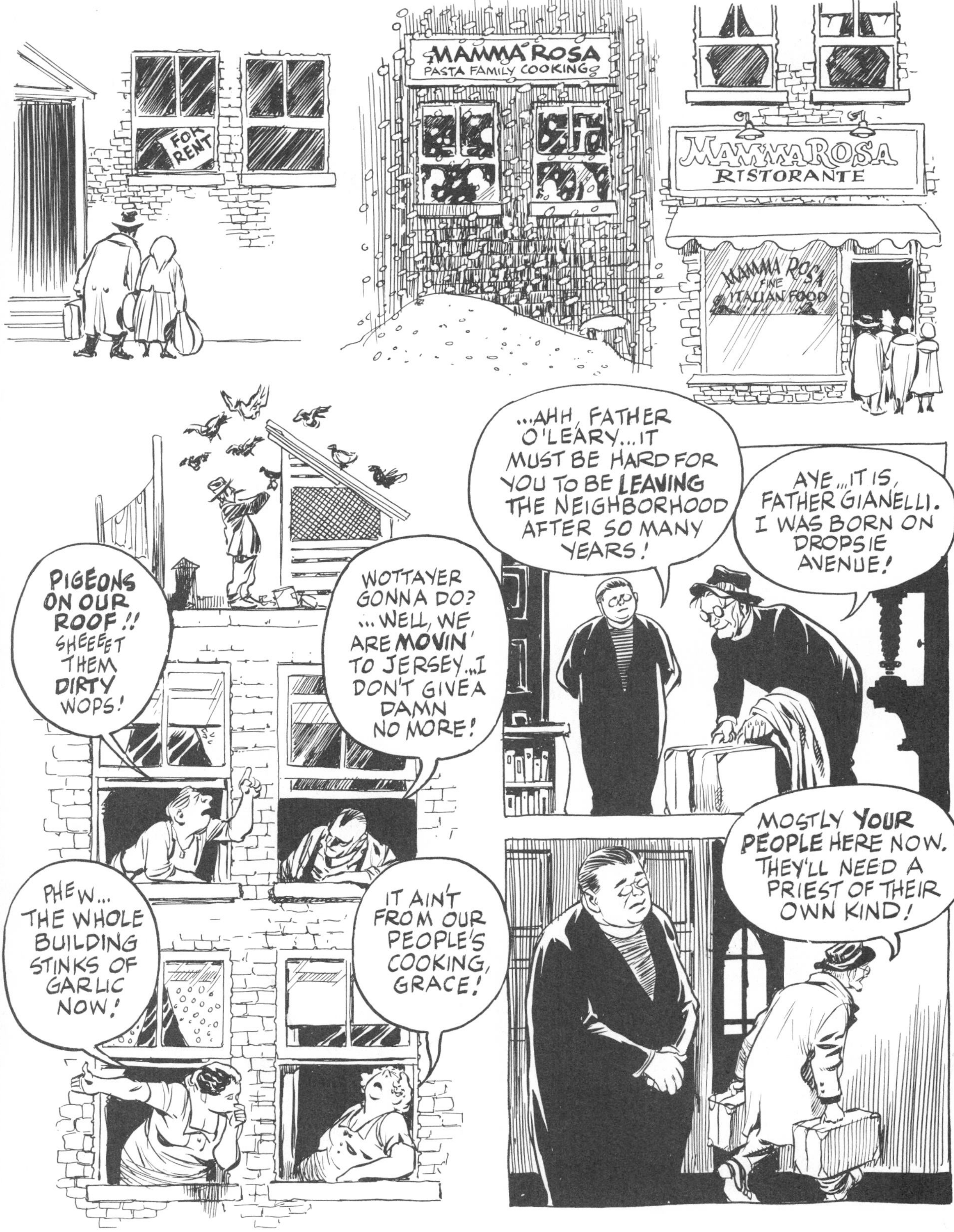
FOR RENT
MAMMA ROSA
PASTA FAMILY COOKING
MAMMA ROSA
RISTORANTE
MAMMA ROSA
FINE
ITALIAN FOOD
PIGEONS ON OUR ROOF!! SHEEEET THEM DIRTY WOPS!
WOTTAYER GONNA DO? ...WELL, WE ARE MOVIN' TO JERSEY...I DON'T GIVE A DAMN NO MORE!
PHEW... THE WHOLE BUILDING STINKS OF GARLIC NOW!
IT AIN'T FROM OUR PEOPLE'S COOKING, GRACE!
...AHH, FATHER O'LEARY...IT MUST BE HARD FOR YOU TO BE LEAVING THE NEIGHBORHOOD AFTER SO MANY YEARS!
AYE...IT IS, FATHER GIANELLI. I WAS BORN ON DROPSIE AVENUE!
MOSTLY YOUR PEOPLE HERE NOW. THEY'LL NEED A PRIEST OF THEIR OWN KIND!

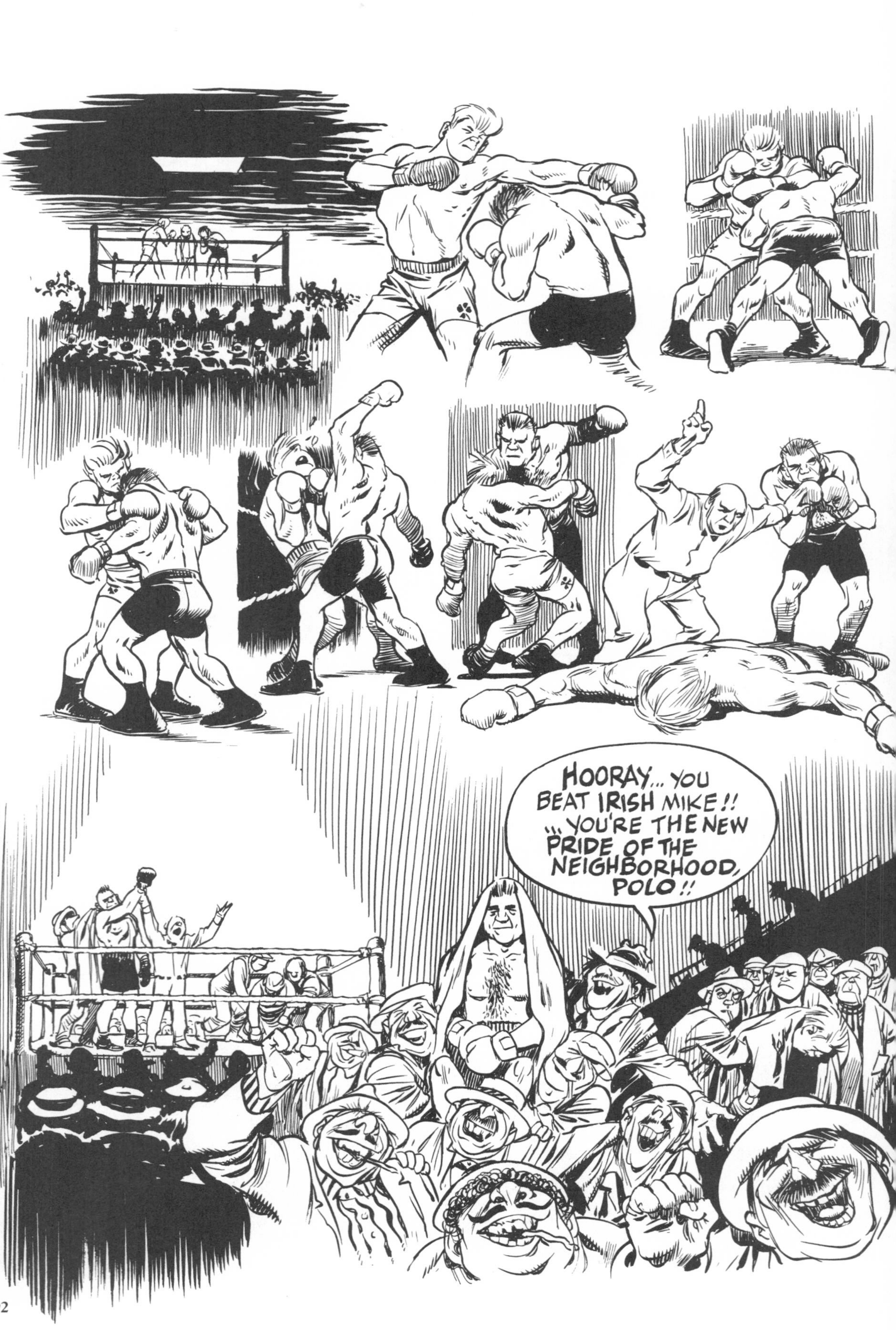
HOORAY... YOU BEAT IRISH MIKE!! ...YOU'RE THE NEW PRIDE OF THE NEIGHBORHOOD, POLO!!

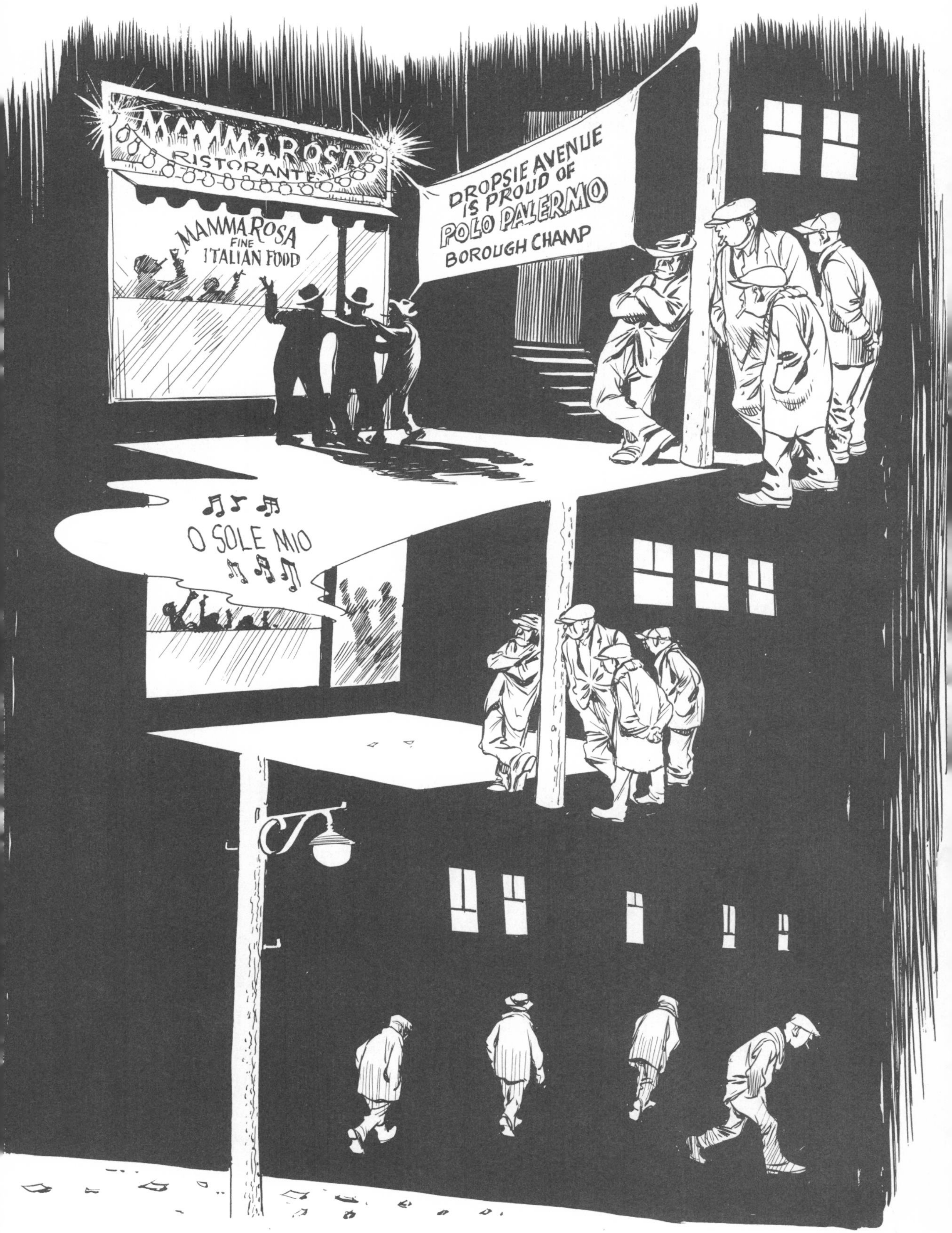
MAMMA ROSA
RISTORANTE
MAMMA ROSA
FINE
ITALIAN FOOD
DROPSIE AVENUE
IS PROUD OF
POLO PALERMO
BOROUGH CHAMP
O SOLE MIO

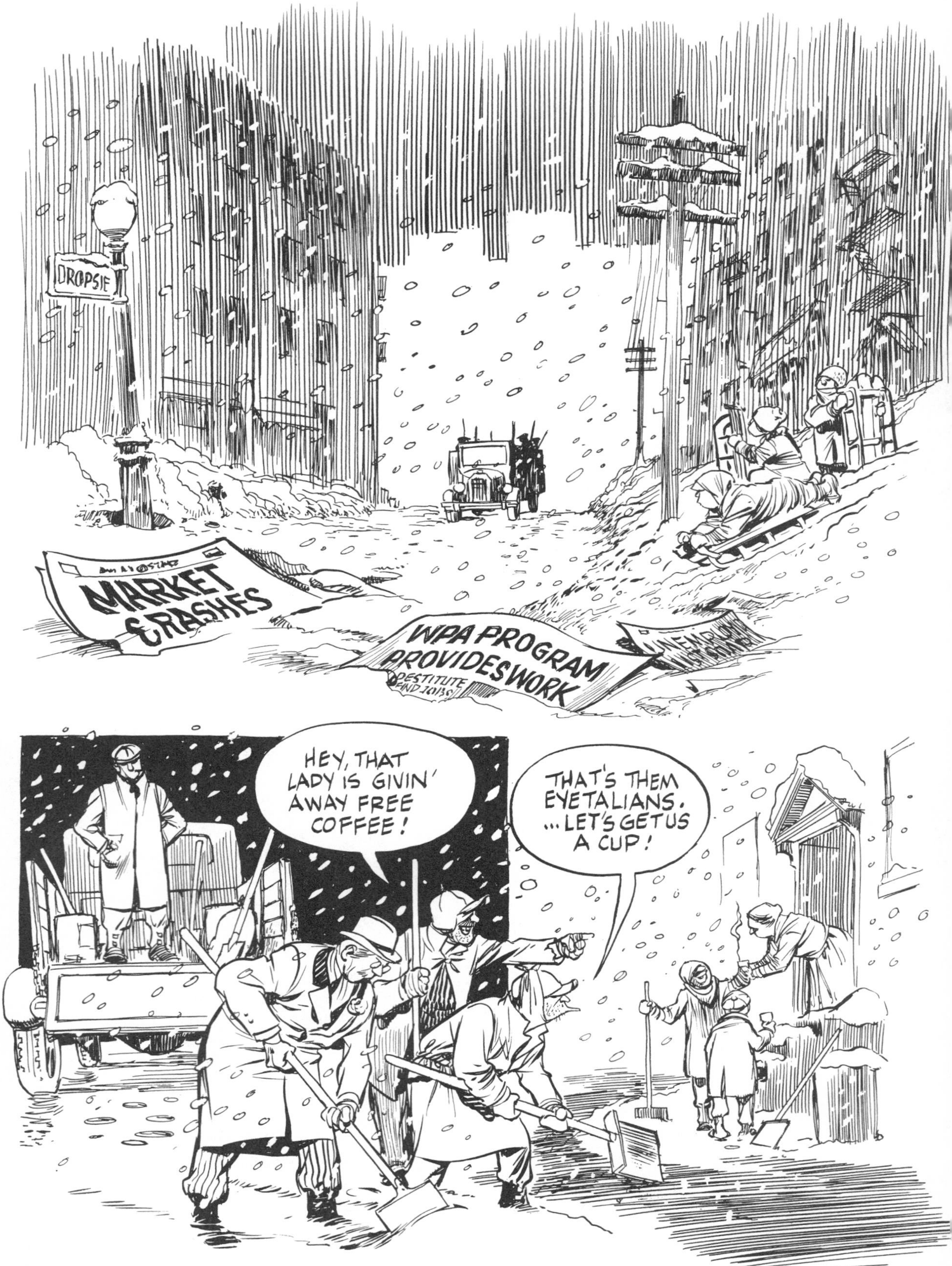
DROPSIE
MARKET CRASHES
WPA PROGRAM PROVIDES WORK
DESTITUTE FIND JOBS
HEY, THAT LADY IS GIVIN' AWAY FREE COFFEE!
THAT'S THEM EYETALIANS. ...LET'S GET US A CUP!

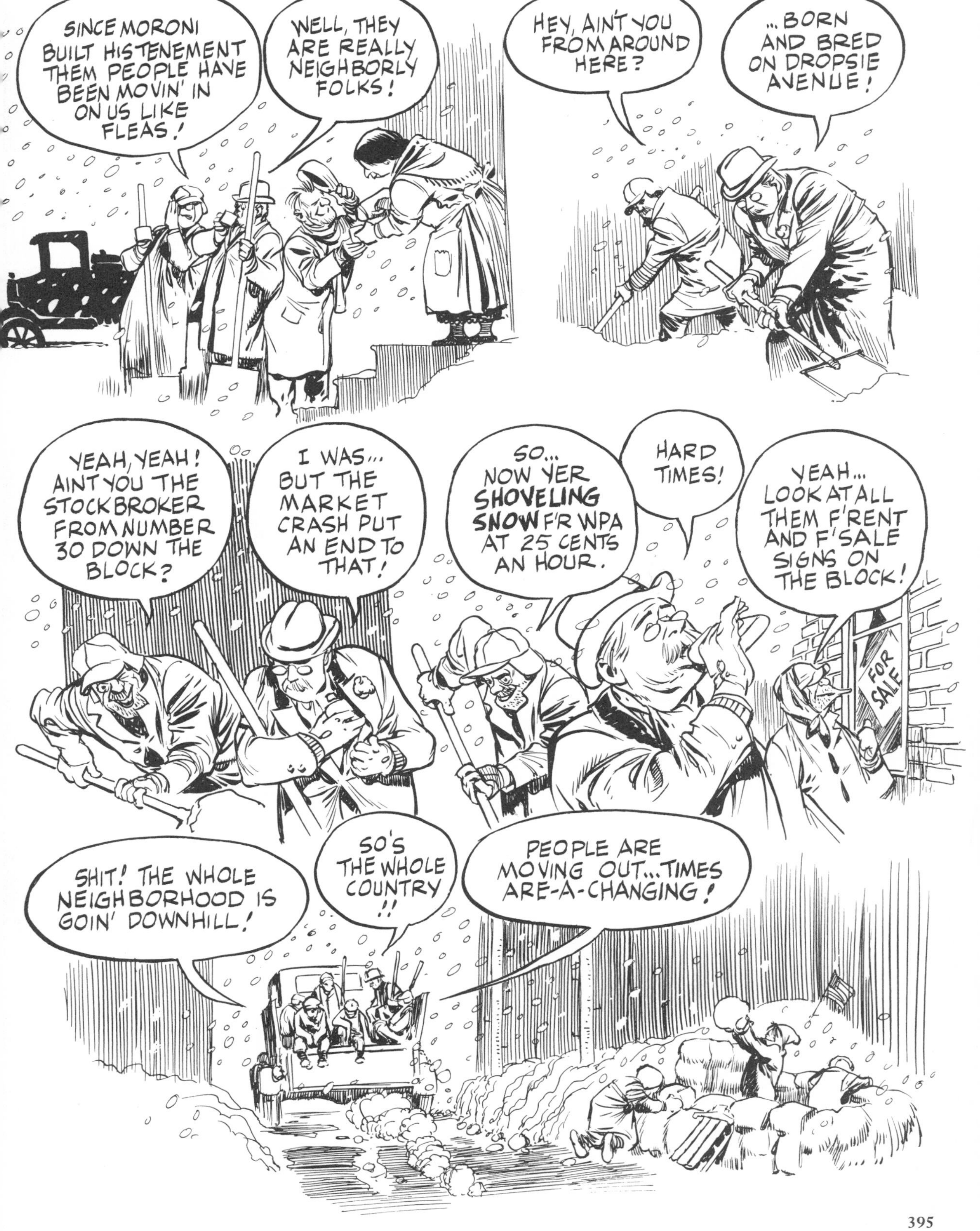
SINCE MORONI BUILT HIS TENEMENT THEM PEOPLE HAVE BEEN MOVIN' IN ON US LIKE FLEAS!
WELL, THEY ARE REALLY NEIGHBORLY FOLKS!
HEY, AIN'T YOU FROM AROUND HERE?
...BORN AND BRED ON DROPSIE AVENUE!
YEAH, YEAH! AINT YOU THE STOCKBROKER FROM NUMBER 30 DOWN THE BLOCK?
I WAS... BUT THE MARKET CRASH PUT AN END TO THAT!
SO... NOW YER **SHOVELING SNOW** F'R WPA AT 25 CENTS AN HOUR.
HARD TIMES!
YEAH... LOOK AT ALL THEM F'RENT AND F'SALE SIGNS ON THE BLOCK!
FOR SALE
SHIT! THE WHOLE NEIGHBORHOOD IS GOIN' DOWNHILL!
SO'S THE WHOLE COUNTRY!!
PEOPLE ARE MOVING OUT... TIMES ARE-A-CHANGING!

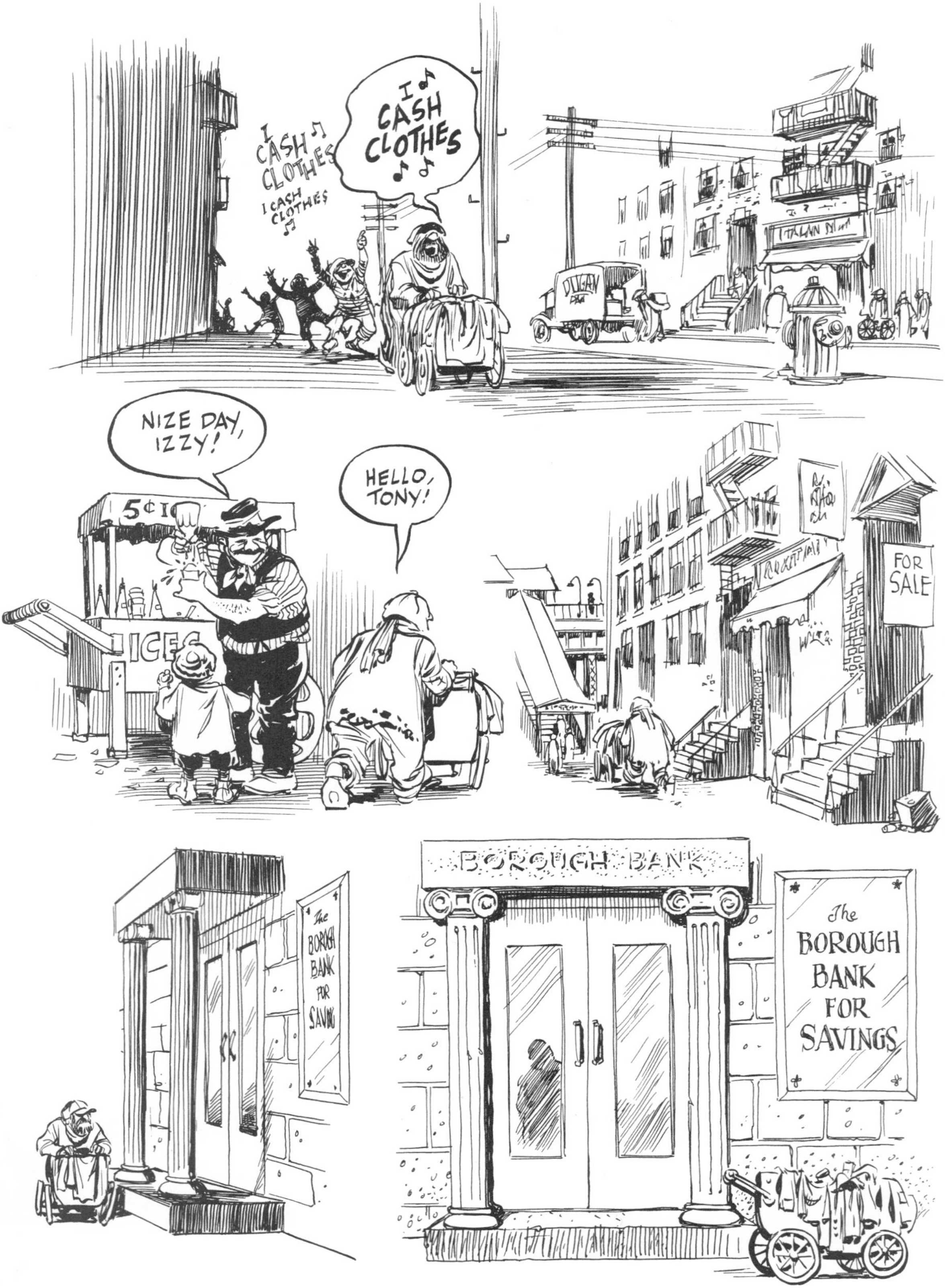
I CASH CLOTHES
I CASH CLOTHES
I CASH CLOTHES
ITALIAN
NIZE DAY, IZZY!
5¢ IC
ICES
HELLO, TONY!
FOR SALE
The BOROUGH BANK FOR SAVINGS
BOROUGH BANK
The BOROUGH BANK FOR SAVINGS

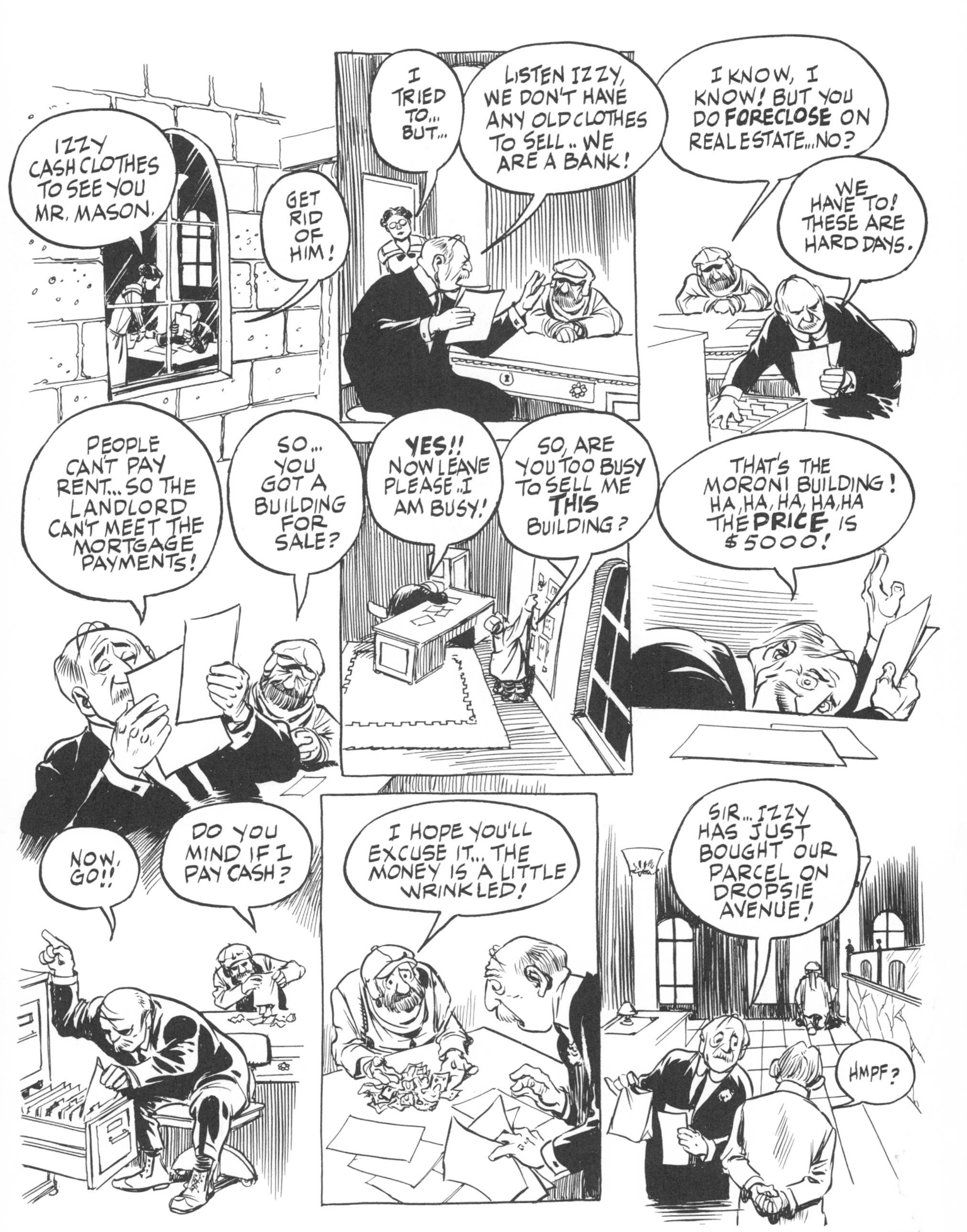
IZZY CASH CLOTHES TO SEE YOU MR. MASON.
GET RID OF HIM!
I TRIED TO... BUT...
LISTEN IZZY, WE DON'T HAVE ANY OLD CLOTHES TO SELL.. WE ARE A BANK!
I KNOW, I KNOW! BUT YOU DO FORECLOSE ON REAL ESTATE...NO?
WE HAVE TO! THESE ARE HARD DAYS.
PEOPLE CAN'T PAY RENT... SO THE LANDLORD CAN'T MEET THE MORTGAGE PAYMENTS!
SO... YOU GOT A BUILDING FOR SALE?
YES!! NOW LEAVE PLEASE..I AM BUSY!
SO, ARE YOU TOO BUSY TO SELL ME THIS BUILDING?
THAT'S THE MORONI BUILDING! HA, HA, HA, HA, HA THE PRICE IS $5000!
NOW, GO!!
DO YOU MIND IF I PAY CASH?
I HOPE YOU'LL EXCUSE IT... THE MONEY IS A LITTLE WRINKLED!
SIR... IZZY HAS JUST BOUGHT OUR PARCEL ON DROPSIE AVENUE!
HMPF?

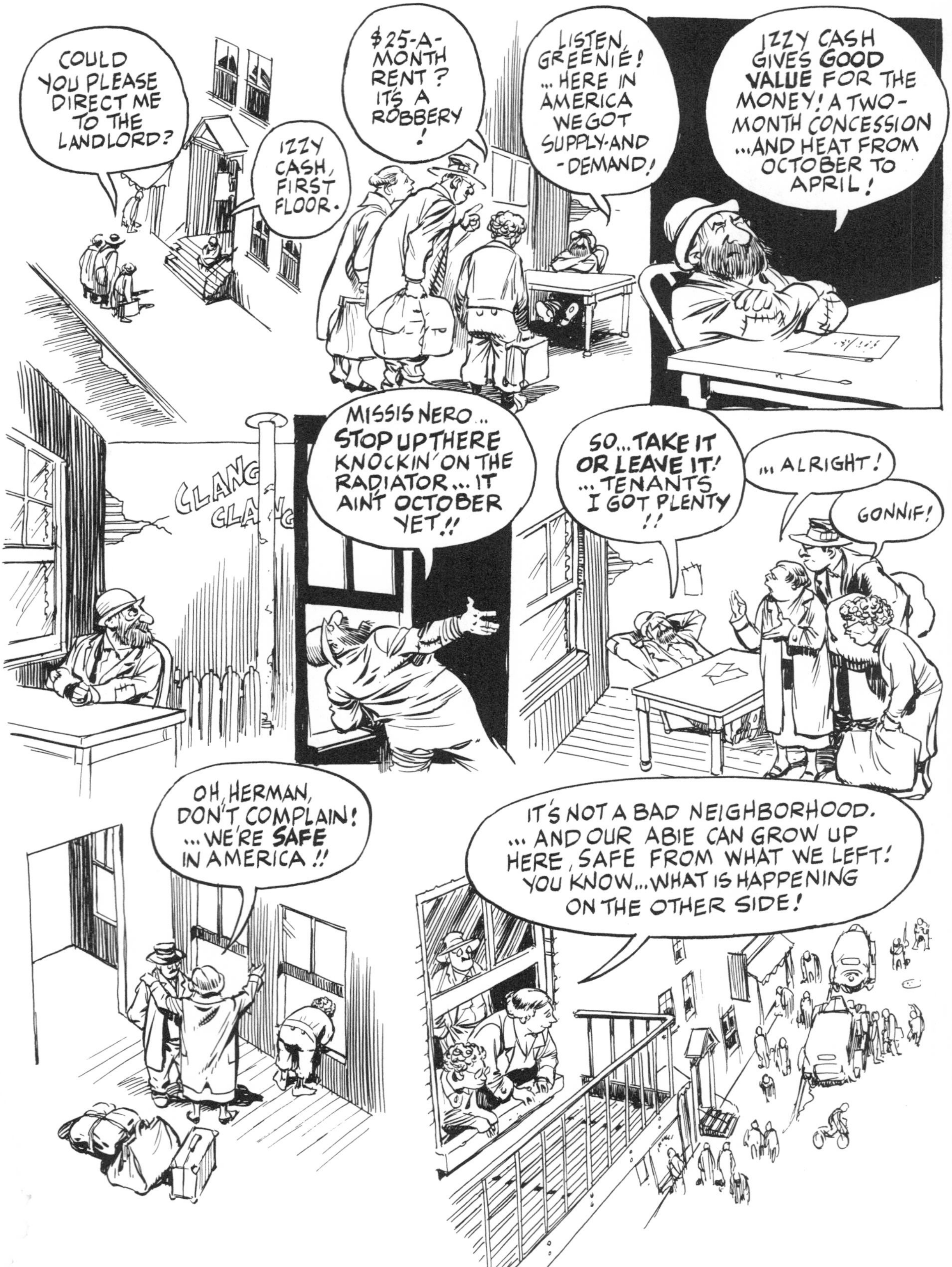
COULD YOU PLEASE DIRECT ME TO THE LANDLORD?
IZZY CASH, FIRST FLOOR.
$25-A-MONTH RENT? IT'S A ROBBERY!
LISTEN, GREENIE! ... HERE IN AMERICA WE GOT SUPPLY-AND-DEMAND!
IZZY CASH GIVES GOOD VALUE FOR THE MONEY! A TWO-MONTH CONCESSION ...AND HEAT FROM OCTOBER TO APRIL!
CLANG CLANG
MISSIS NERO... STOP UP THERE KNOCKIN' ON THE RADIATOR... IT AIN'T OCTOBER YET!!
SO... TAKE IT OR LEAVE IT! ... TENANTS I GOT PLENTY!!
... ALRIGHT!
GONNIF!
OH, HERMAN, DON'T COMPLAIN! ... WE'RE SAFE IN AMERICA!!
IT'S NOT A BAD NEIGHBORHOOD. ... AND OUR ABIE CAN GROW UP HERE, SAFE FROM WHAT WE LEFT! YOU KNOW... WHAT IS HAPPENING ON THE OTHER SIDE!

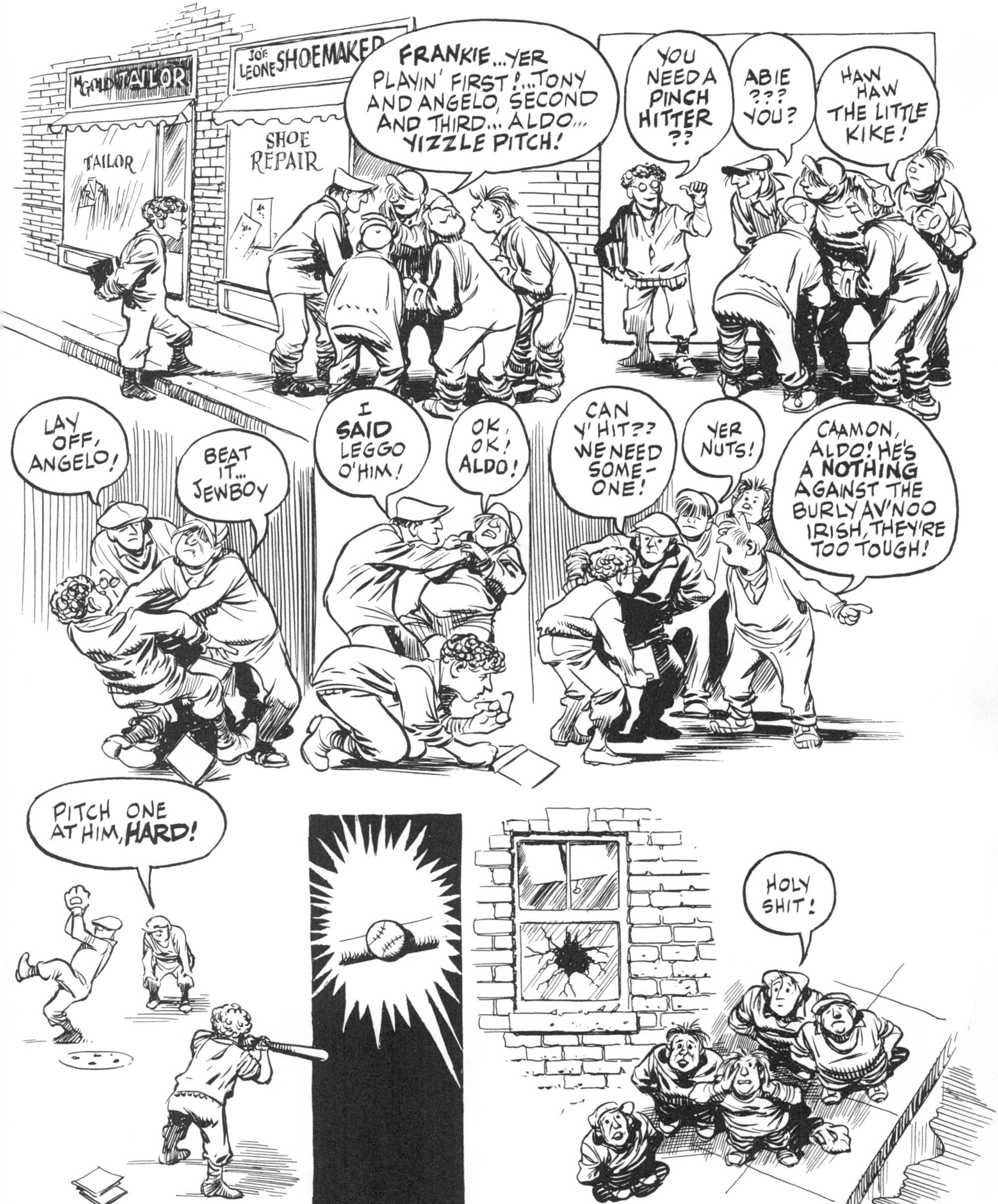
M GOLD TAILOR
JOE LEONE SHOEMAKER
TAILOR
SHOE REPAIR
FRANKIE...YER PLAYIN' FIRST!...TONY AND ANGELO, SECOND AND THIRD... ALDO... YIZZLE PITCH!
YOU NEED A PINCH HITTER ??
ABIE ??? YOU?
HAW HAW THE LITTLE KIKE!
LAY OFF, ANGELO!
BEAT IT... JEWBOY
I SAID LEGGO O'HIM!
OK, OK! ALDO!
CAN Y' HIT?? WE NEED SOME-ONE!
YER NUTS!
CAAMON, ALDO! HE'S A NOTHING AGAINST THE BURLY AV'NOO IRISH, THEY'RE TOO TOUGH!
PITCH ONE AT HIM, HARD!
HOLY SHIT!

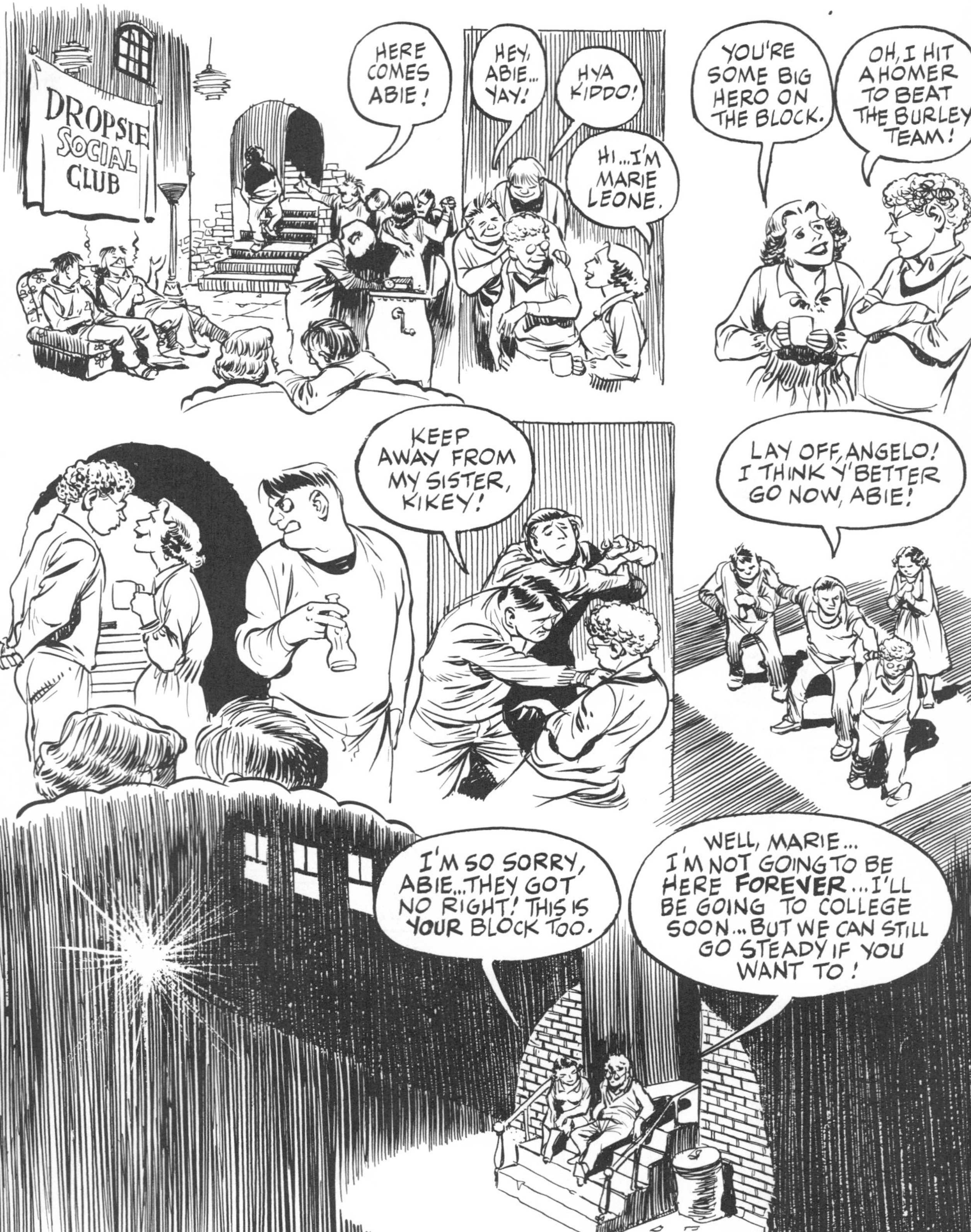
DROPSIE SOCIAL CLUB
HERE COMES ABIE!
HEY, ABIE... YAY!
HYA KIDDO!
HI...I'M MARIE LEONE.
YOU'RE SOME BIG HERO ON THE BLOCK.
OH, I HIT A HOMER TO BEAT THE BURLEY TEAM!
KEEP AWAY FROM MY SISTER, KIKEY!
LAY OFF, ANGELO! I THINK Y'BETTER GO NOW, ABIE!
I'M SO SORRY, ABIE...THEY GOT NO RIGHT! THIS IS YOUR BLOCK TOO.
WELL, MARIE... I'M NOT GOING TO BE HERE FOREVER...I'LL BE GOING TO COLLEGE SOON... BUT WE CAN STILL GO STEADY IF YOU WANT TO!

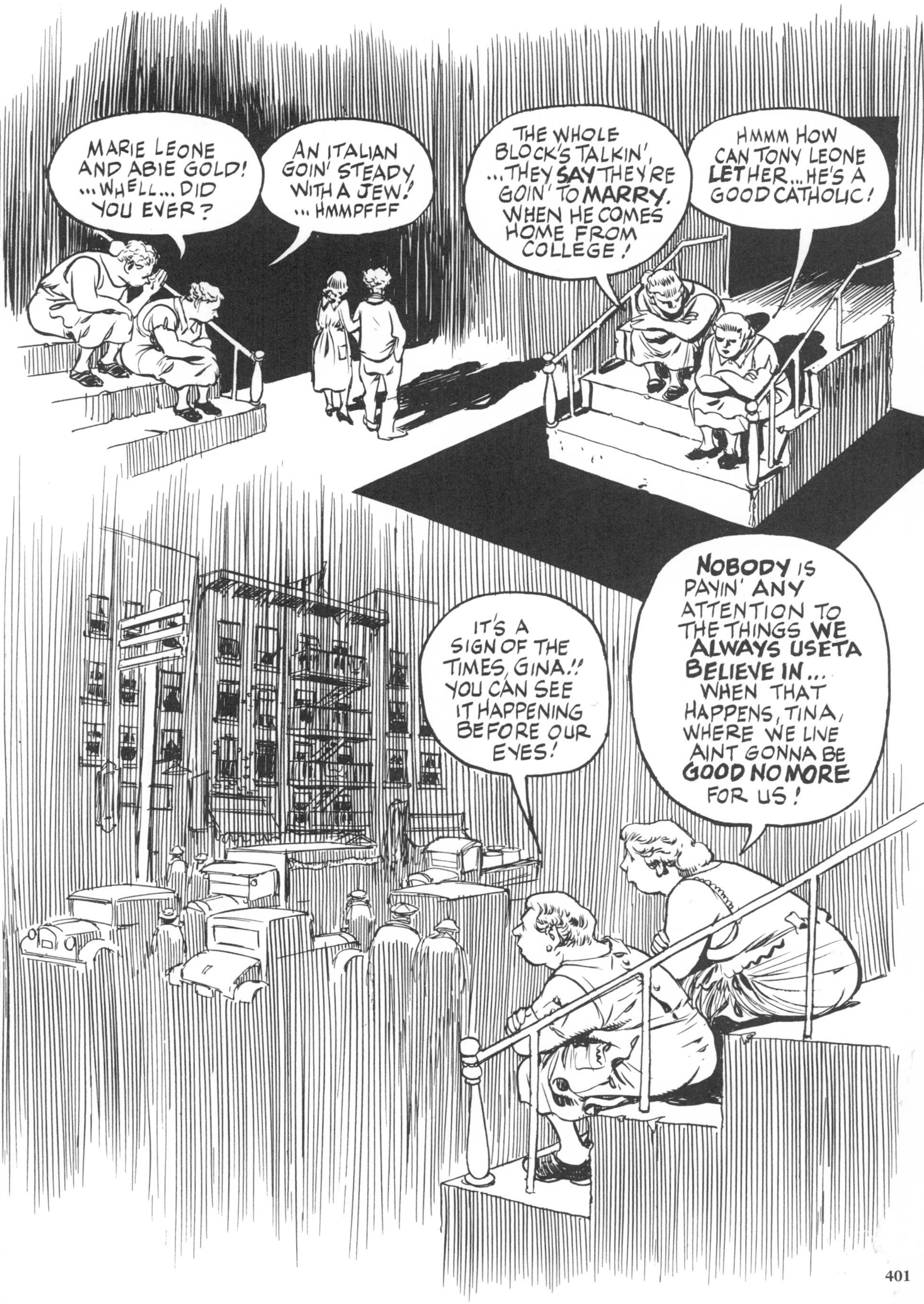
MARIE LEONE AND ABIE GOLD! ...WHELL... DID YOU EVER?
AN ITALIAN GOIN' STEADY WITH A JEW! ...HMMPFFF
THE WHOLE BLOCK'S TALKIN', ...THEY SAY THEY'RE GOIN' TO MARRY. WHEN HE COMES HOME FROM COLLEGE!
HMMM HOW CAN TONY LEONE LET HER... HE'S A GOOD CATHOLIC!
IT'S A SIGN OF THE TIMES, GINA!! YOU CAN SEE IT HAPPENING BEFORE OUR EYES!
NOBODY IS PAYIN' ANY ATTENTION TO THE THINGS WE ALWAYS USETA BELIEVE IN... WHEN THAT HAPPENS, TINA, WHERE WE LIVE AINT GONNA BE GOOD NO MORE FOR US!

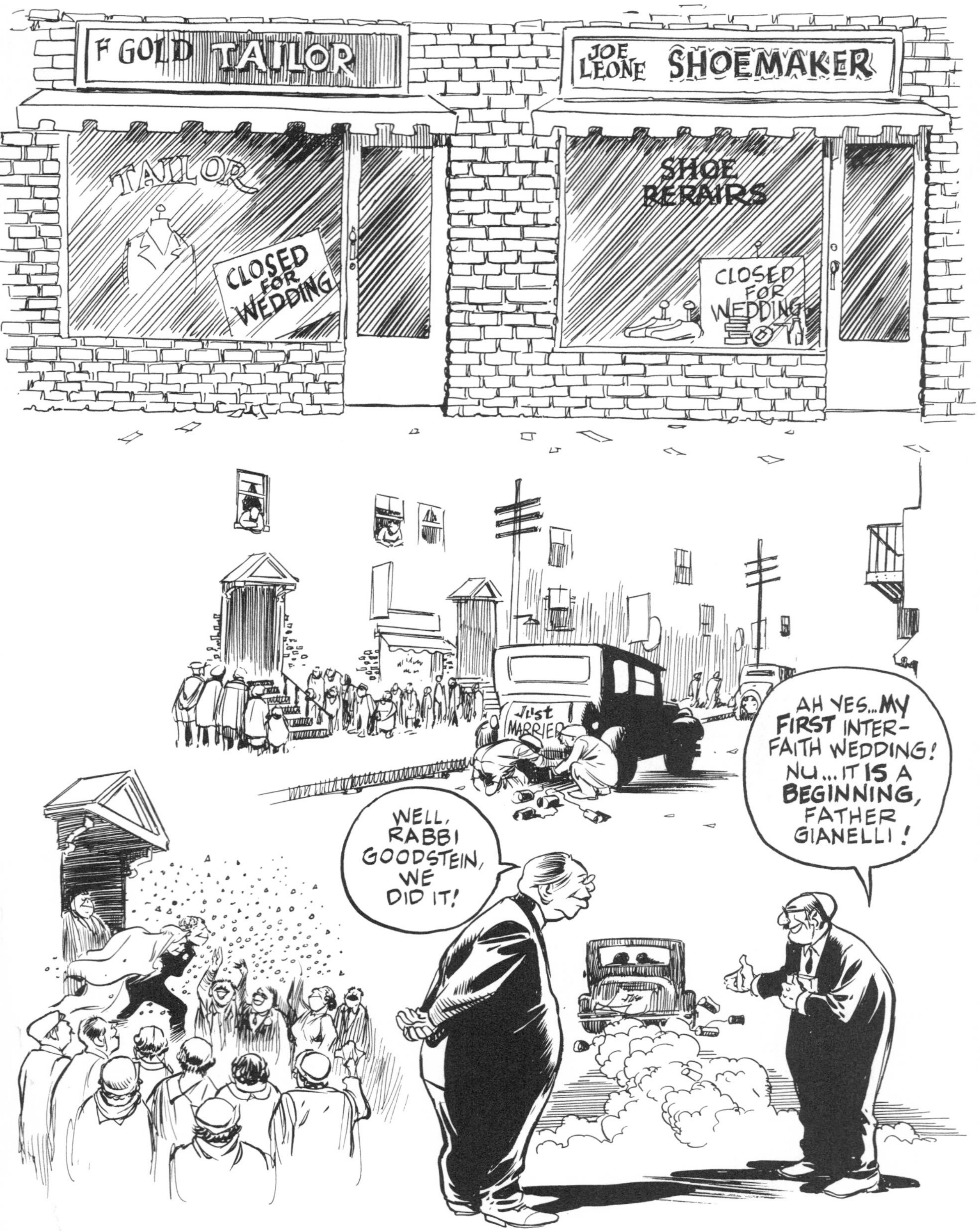
F GOLD TAILOR
JOE LEONE SHOEMAKER
TAILOR
CLOSED FOR WEDDING
SHOE REPAIRS
CLOSED FOR WEDDING
JUST MARRIED
WELL, RABBI GOODSTEIN, WE DID IT!
AH YES...MY FIRST INTER-FAITH WEDDING! NU...IT IS A BEGINNING, FATHER GIANELLI!

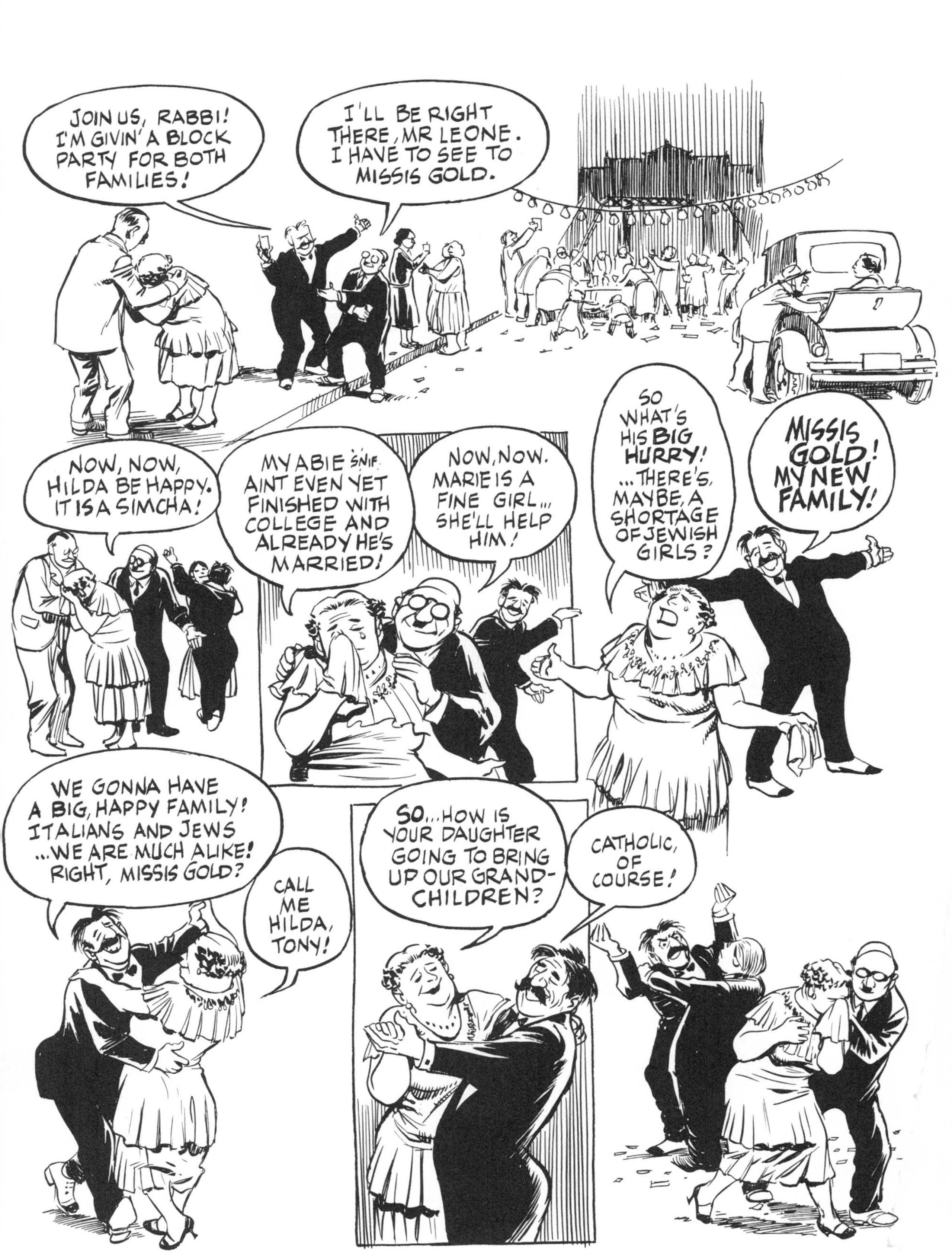
JOIN US, RABBI! I'M GIVIN' A BLOCK PARTY FOR BOTH FAMILIES!
I'LL BE RIGHT THERE, MR LEONE. I HAVE TO SEE TO MISSIS GOLD.
NOW, NOW, HILDA BE HAPPY. IT IS A SIMCHA!
MY ABIE SNIF AINT EVEN YET FINISHED WITH COLLEGE AND ALREADY HE'S MARRIED!
NOW, NOW. MARIE IS A FINE GIRL... SHE'LL HELP HIM!
SO WHAT'S HIS BIG HURRY! ...THERE'S, MAYBE, A SHORTAGE OF JEWISH GIRLS?
MISSIS GOLD! MY NEW FAMILY!
WE GONNA HAVE A BIG, HAPPY FAMILY! ITALIANS AND JEWS ...WE ARE MUCH ALIKE! RIGHT, MISSIS GOLD?
CALL ME HILDA, TONY!
SO... HOW IS YOUR DAUGHTER GOING TO BRING UP OUR GRAND-CHILDREN?
CATHOLIC, OF COURSE!

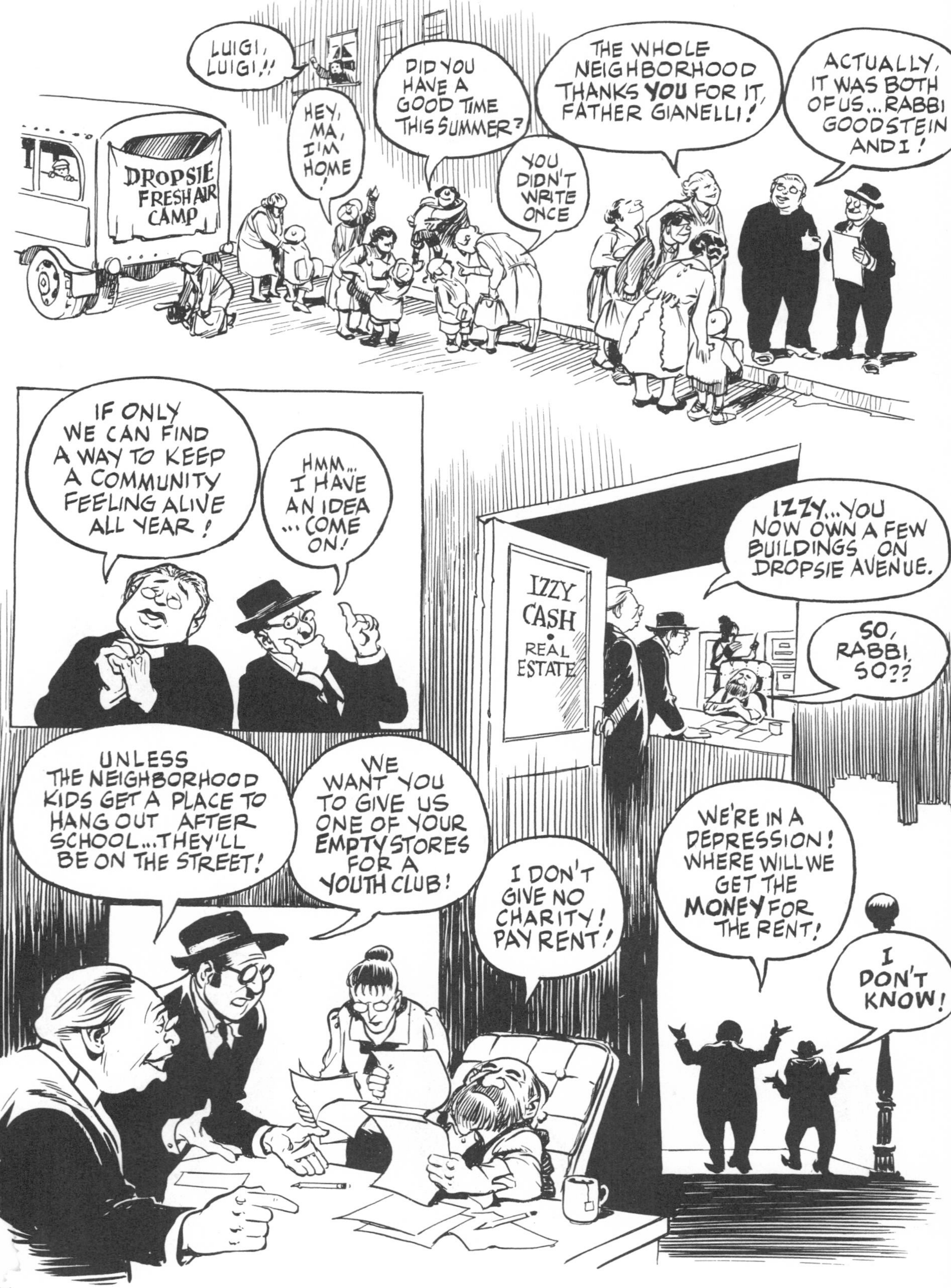
DROPSIE FRESH AIR CAMP
LUIGI, LUIGI,!!
HEY, MA, I'M HOME!
DID YOU HAVE A GOOD TIME THIS SUMMER?
YOU DIDN'T WRITE ONCE
THE WHOLE NEIGHBORHOOD THANKS YOU FOR IT, FATHER GIANELLI!
ACTUALLY, IT WAS BOTH OF US...RABBI GOODSTEIN AND I!
IF ONLY WE CAN FIND A WAY TO KEEP A COMMUNITY FEELING ALIVE ALL YEAR!
HMM... I HAVE AN IDEA ...COME ON!
IZZY CASH • REAL ESTATE
IZZY...YOU NOW OWN A FEW BUILDINGS ON DROPSIE AVENUE.
SO, RABBI, SO??
UNLESS THE NEIGHBORHOOD KIDS GET A PLACE TO HANG OUT AFTER SCHOOL...THEY'LL BE ON THE STREET!
WE WANT YOU TO GIVE US ONE OF YOUR EMPTY STORES FOR A YOUTH CLUB!
I DON'T GIVE NO CHARITY! PAY RENT!
WE'RE IN A DEPRESSION! WHERE WILL WE GET THE MONEY FOR THE RENT!
I DON'T KNOW!

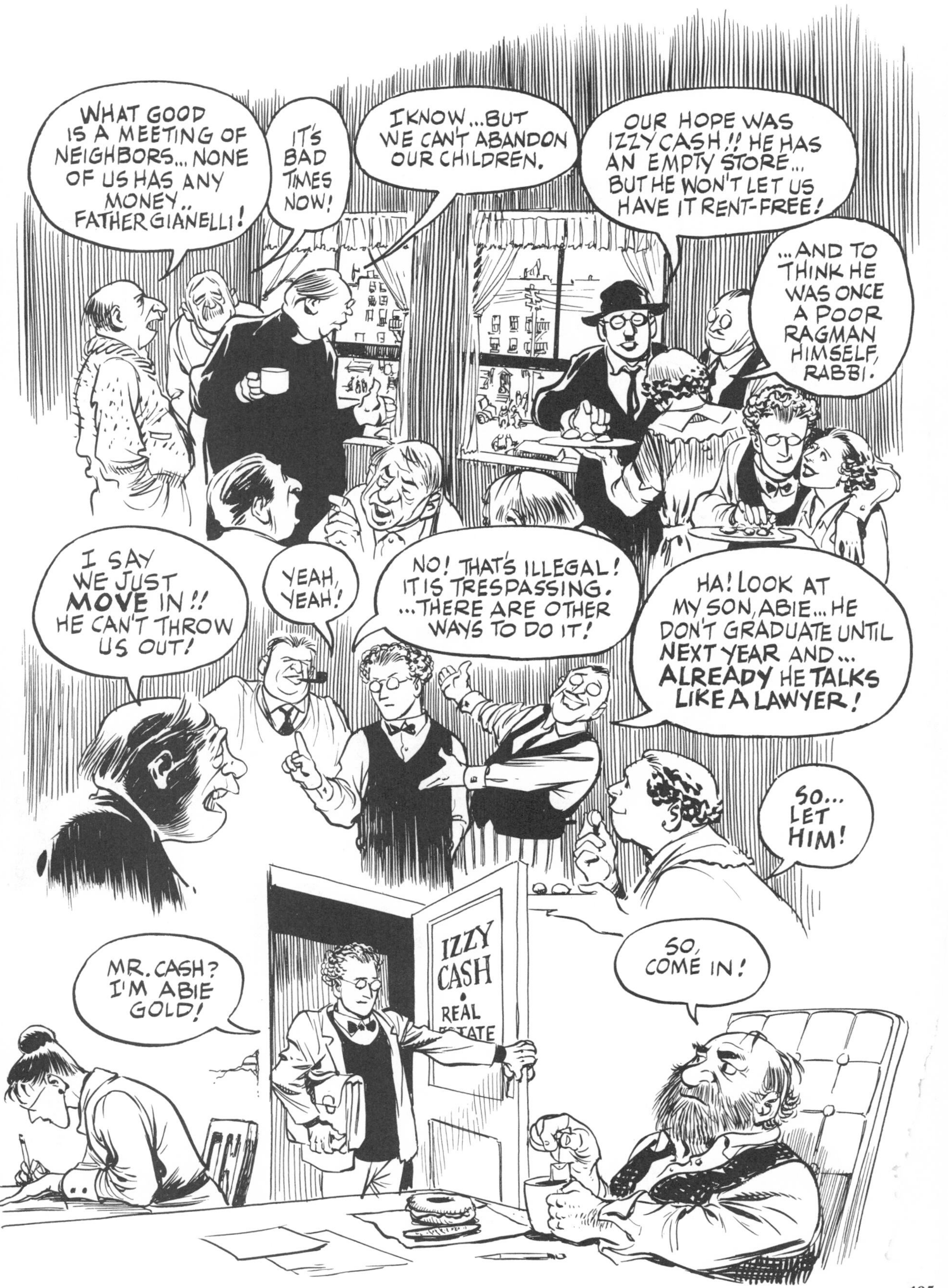
WHAT GOOD IS A MEETING OF NEIGHBORS... NONE OF US HAS ANY MONEY.. FATHER GIANELLI!
IT'S BAD TIMES NOW!
I KNOW ...BUT WE CAN'T ABANDON OUR CHILDREN.
OUR HOPE WAS IZZY CASH!! HE HAS AN EMPTY STORE... BUT HE WON'T LET US HAVE IT RENT-FREE!
...AND TO THINK HE WAS ONCE A POOR RAGMAN HIMSELF, RABBI.
I SAY WE JUST **MOVE** IN!! HE CAN'T THROW US OUT!
YEAH, YEAH!
NO! THAT'S ILLEGAL! IT IS TRESPASSING. ...THERE ARE OTHER WAYS TO DO IT!
HA! LOOK AT MY SON, ABIE... HE DON'T GRADUATE UNTIL **NEXT YEAR AND... ALREADY** HE **TALKS LIKE A LAWYER!**
SO... LET HIM!
IZZY CASH REAL ESTATE
MR. CASH? I'M ABIE GOLD!
SO, COME IN!

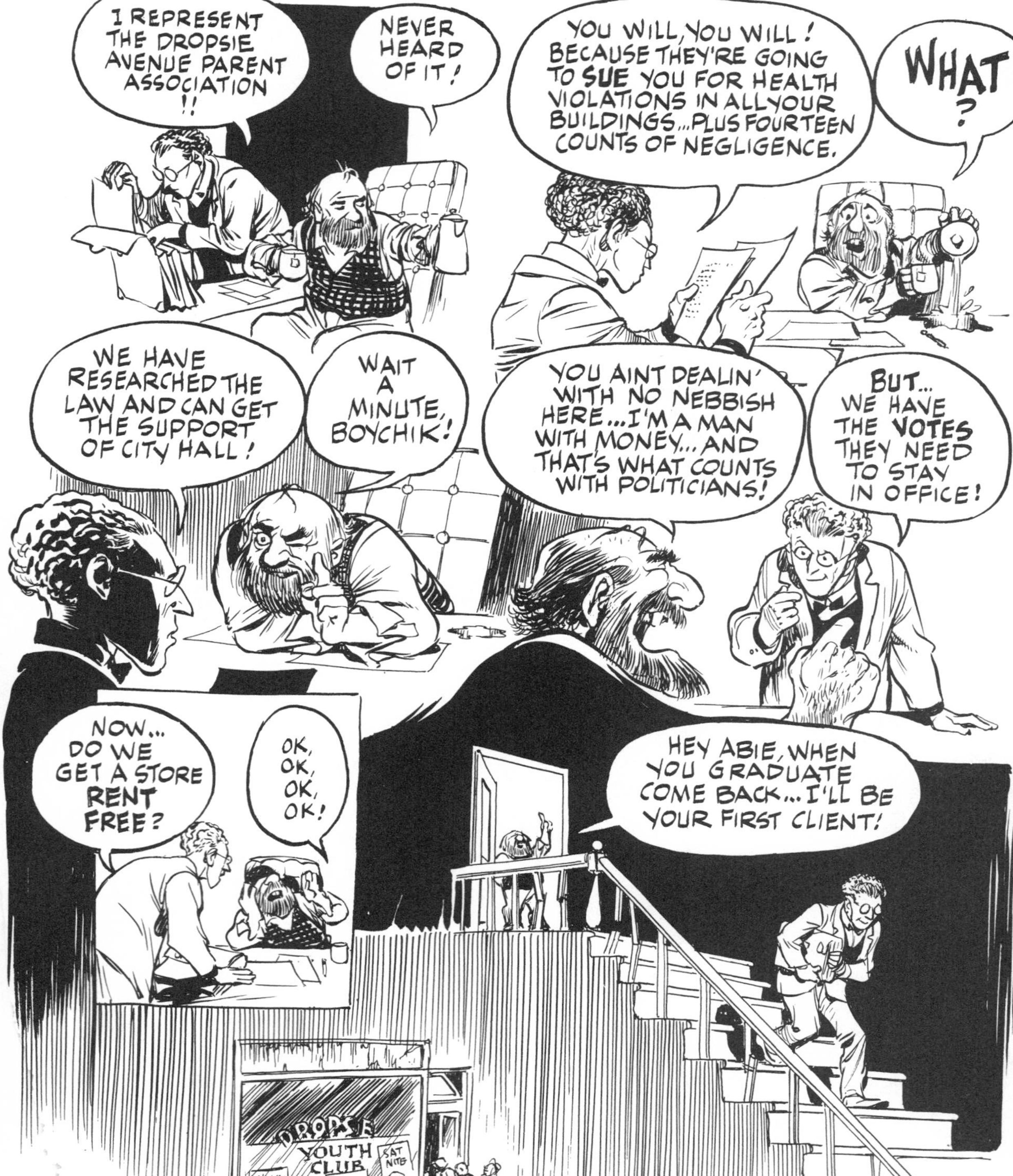
I REPRESENT THE DROPSIE AVENUE PARENT ASSOCIATION !!
NEVER HEARD OF IT!
YOU WILL, YOU WILL! BECAUSE THEY'RE GOING TO **SUE** YOU FOR HEALTH VIOLATIONS IN ALL YOUR BUILDINGS... PLUS FOURTEEN COUNTS OF NEGLIGENCE.
WHAT ?
WE HAVE RESEARCHED THE LAW AND CAN GET THE SUPPORT OF CITY HALL!
WAIT A MINUTE, BOYCHIK!
YOU AINT DEALIN' WITH NO NEBBISH HERE... I'M A MAN WITH MONEY... AND THAT'S WHAT COUNTS WITH POLITICIANS!
BUT... WE HAVE THE **VOTES** THEY NEED TO STAY IN OFFICE!
NOW... DO WE GET A STORE **RENT FREE**?
OK, OK, OK, OK!
HEY ABIE, WHEN YOU GRADUATE COME BACK... I'LL BE YOUR FIRST CLIENT!
DROPSIE YOUTH CLUB
SAT NITE
WELCOM

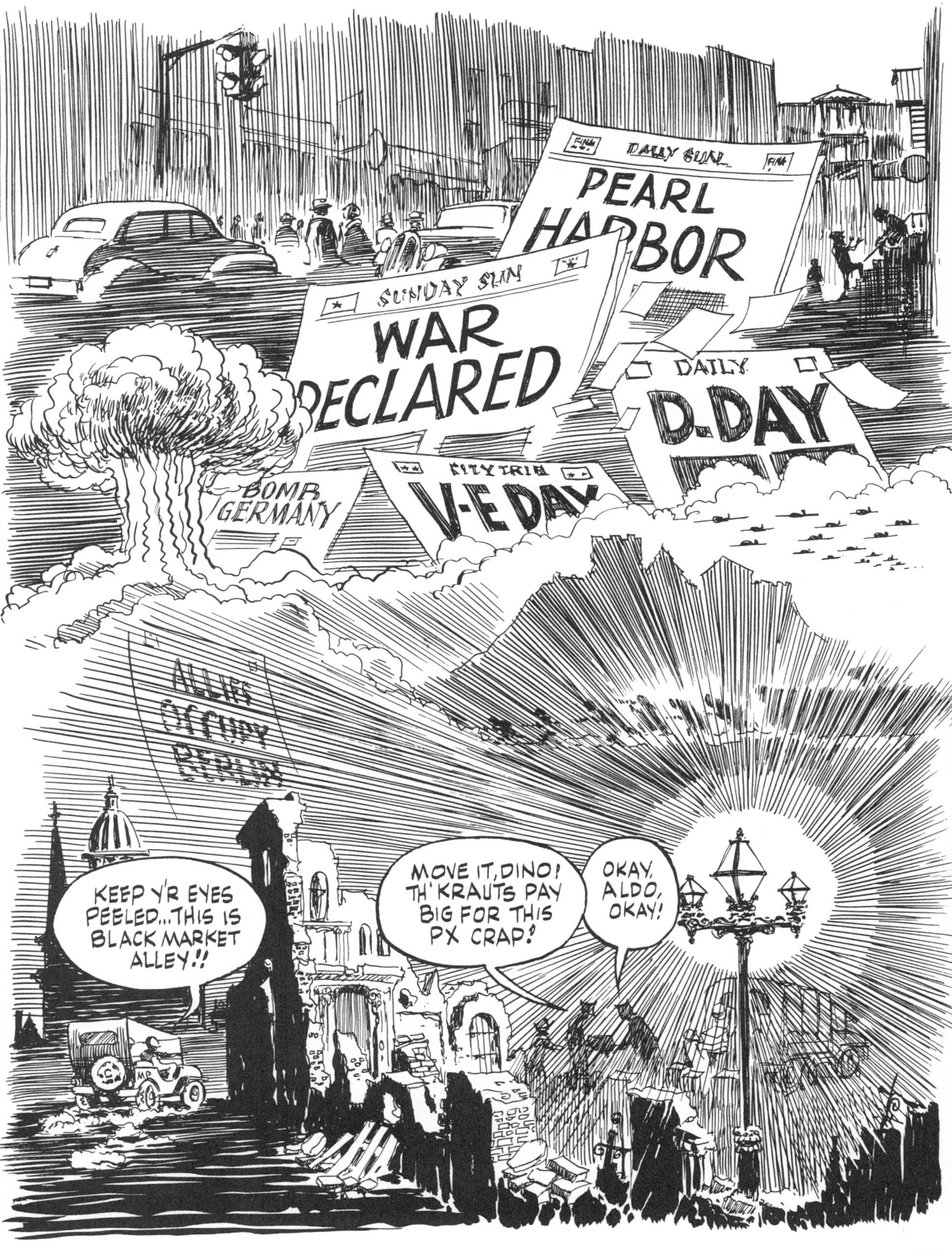
DAILY SUN
PEARL HARBOR
SUNDAY SUN
WAR DECLARED
DAILY
D-DAY
CITY TRIB
V-E DAY
BOMB GERMANY
ALLIES OCCUPY
KEEP Y'R EYES PEELED...THIS IS BLACK MARKET ALLEY!!
MOVE IT, DINO! TH' KRAUTS PAY BIG FOR THIS PX CRAP!
OKAY, ALDO, OKAY!

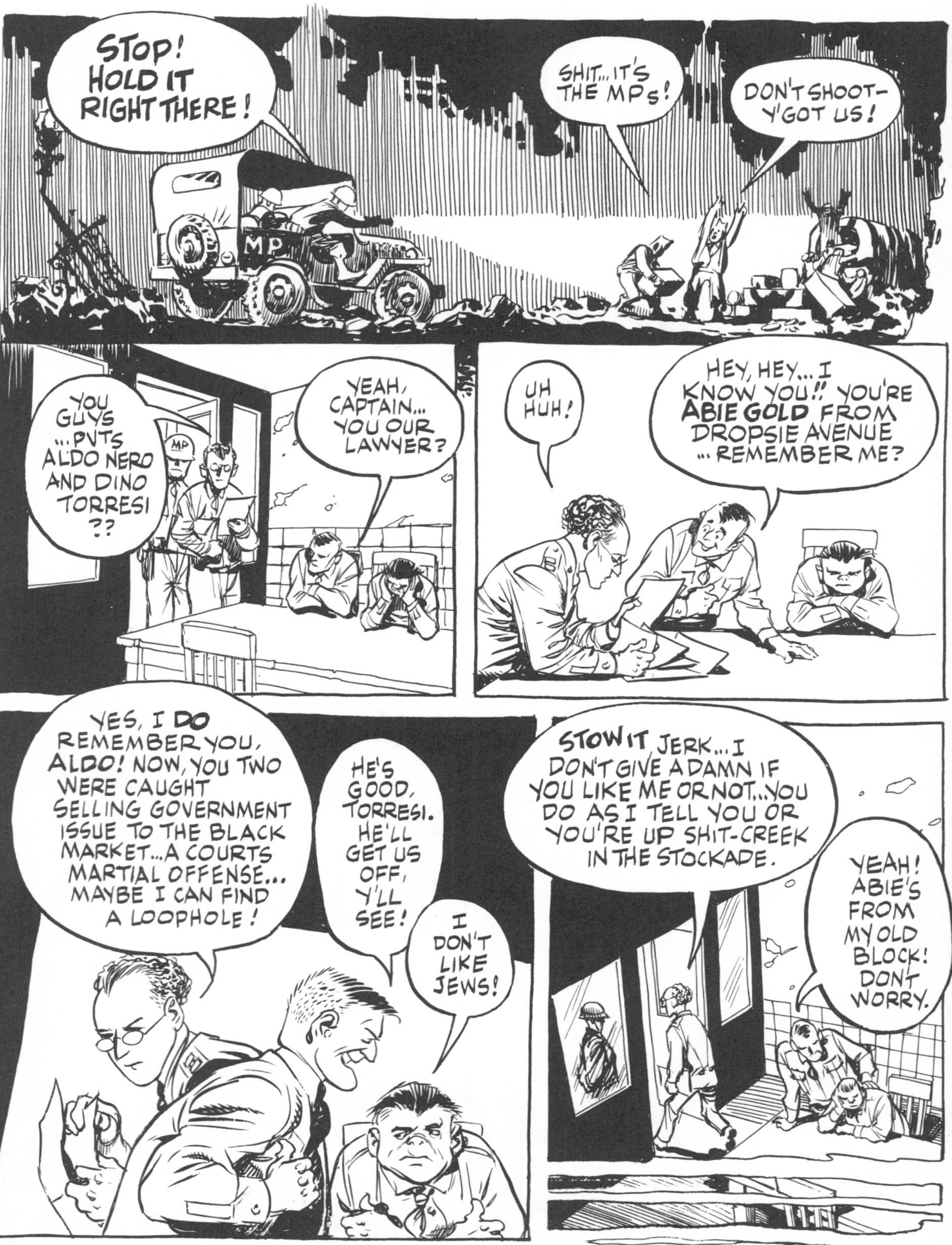
STOP! HOLD IT RIGHT THERE!
SHIT... IT'S THE MPs!
DON'T SHOOT- Y'GOT US!
MP
YOU GUYS ...PVTS ALDO NERO AND DINO TORRESI ??
YEAH, CAPTAIN... YOU OUR LAWYER?
UH HUH!
HEY, HEY... I KNOW YOU!! YOU'RE ABIE GOLD FROM DROPSIE AVENUE ...REMEMBER ME?
YES, I DO REMEMBER YOU, ALDO! NOW, YOU TWO WERE CAUGHT SELLING GOVERNMENT ISSUE TO THE BLACK MARKET...A COURTS MARTIAL OFFENSE... MAYBE I CAN FIND A LOOPHOLE!
HE'S GOOD, TORRESI. HE'LL GET US OFF, Y'LL SEE!
I DON'T LIKE JEWS!
STOW IT JERK... I DON'T GIVE A DAMN IF YOU LIKE ME OR NOT... YOU DO AS I TELL YOU OR YOU'RE UP SHIT-CREEK IN THE STOCKADE.
YEAH! ABIE'S FROM MY OLD BLOCK! DON'T WORRY.

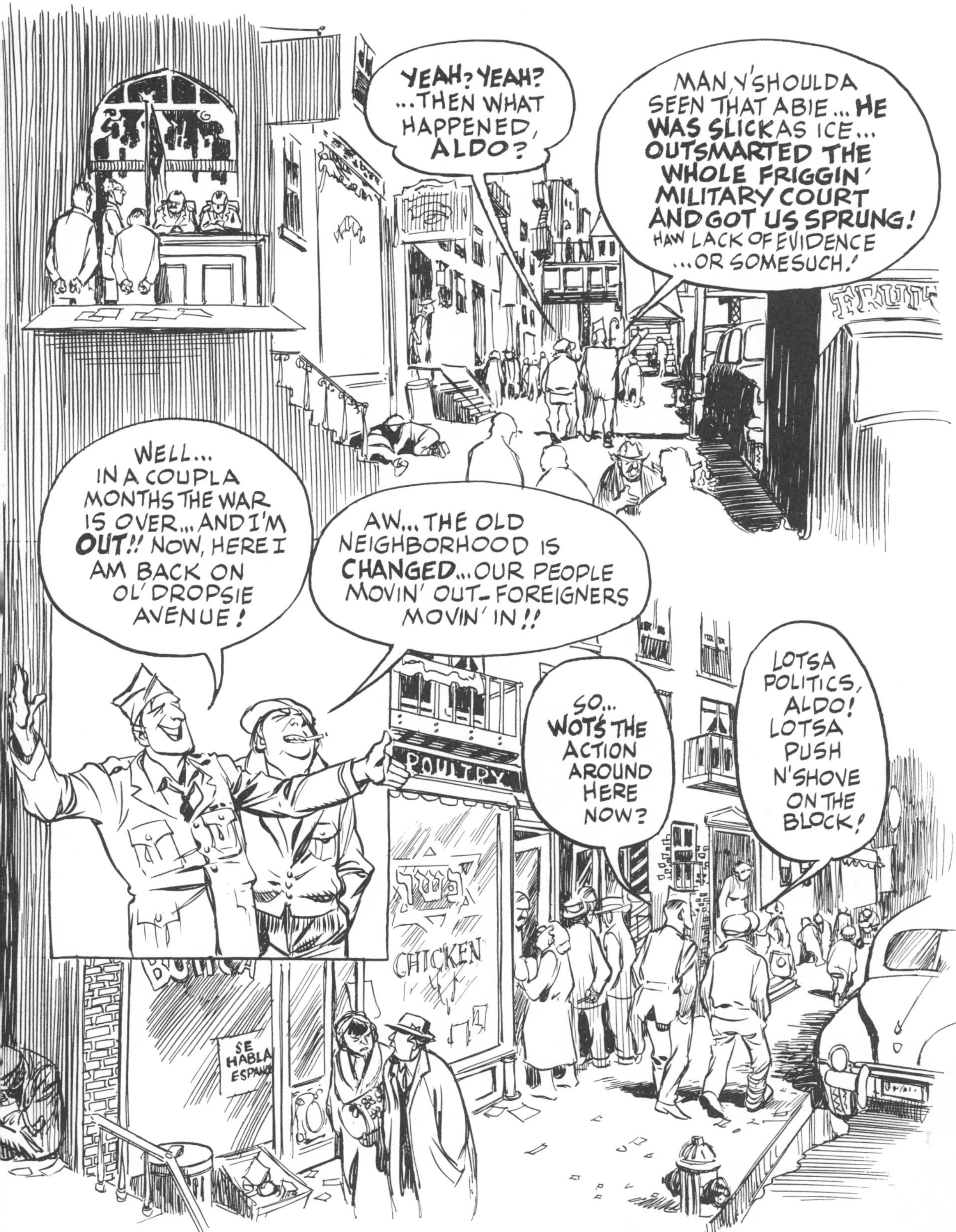
YEAH? YEAH? ...THEN WHAT HAPPENED, ALDO?
MAN, Y'SHOULDA SEEN THAT ABIE... HE WAS SLICK AS ICE... OUTSMARTED THE WHOLE FRIGGIN' MILITARY COURT AND GOT US SPRUNG! HAW LACK OF EVIDENCE ...OR SOMESUCH!
WELL... IN A COUPLA MONTHS THE WAR IS OVER... AND I'M OUT!! NOW, HERE I AM BACK ON OL' DROPSIE AVENUE!
AW... THE OLD NEIGHBORHOOD IS CHANGED... OUR PEOPLE MOVIN' OUT- FOREIGNERS MOVIN' IN!!
SO... WOT'S THE ACTION AROUND HERE NOW?
LOTSA POLITICS, ALDO! LOTSA PUSH N'SHOVE ON THE BLOCK!
POULTRY
CHICKEN
SE HABLA

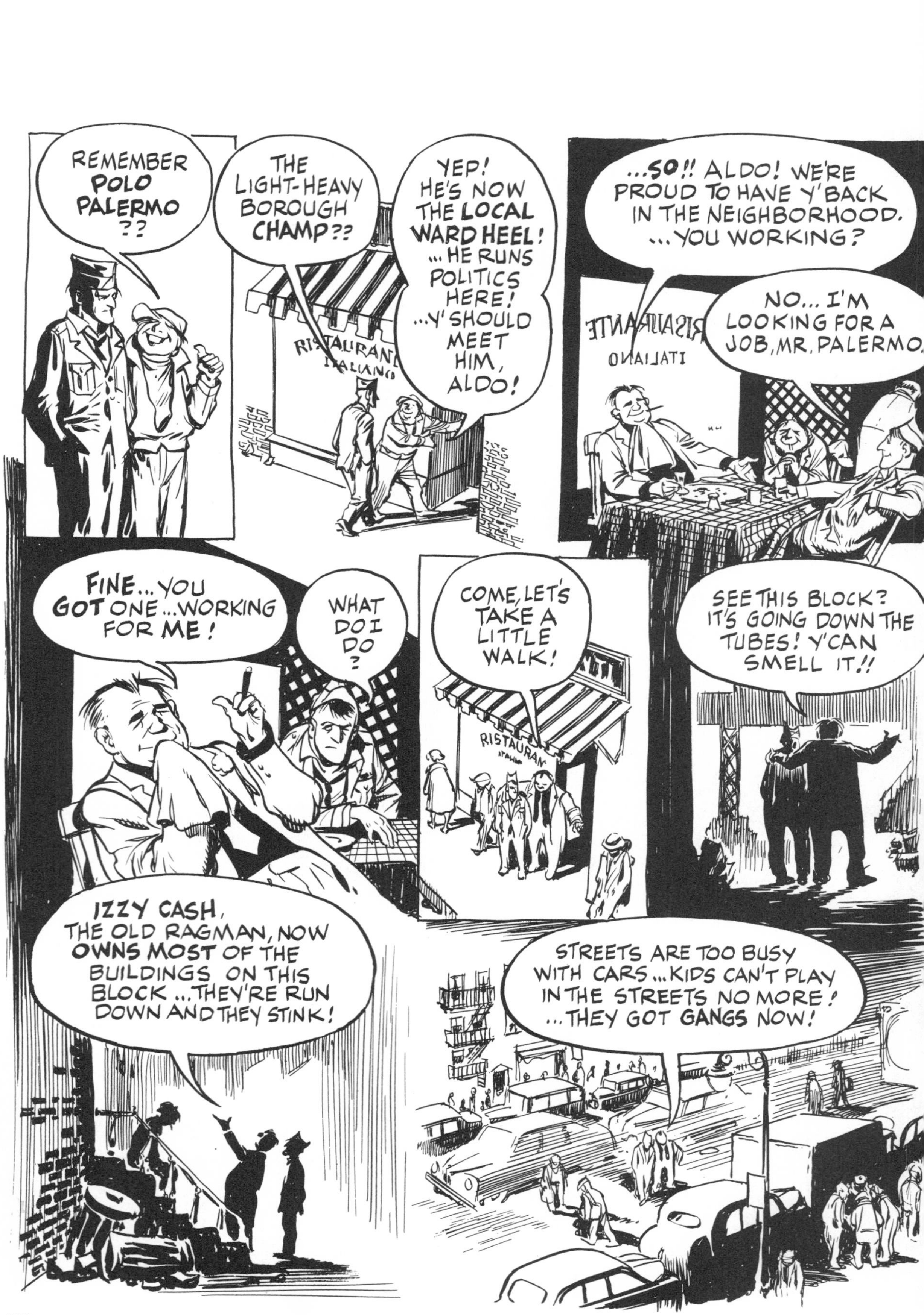
REMEMBER POLO PALERMO ??
THE LIGHT-HEAVY BOROUGH CHAMP??
YEP! HE'S NOW THE LOCAL WARD HEEL! ...HE RUNS POLITICS HERE! ...Y' SHOULD MEET HIM, ALDO!
RISTAURANT ITALIANO
...SO!! ALDO! WE'RE PROUD TO HAVE Y' BACK IN THE NEIGHBORHOOD. ...YOU WORKING?
NO... I'M LOOKING FOR A JOB, MR. PALERMO.
FINE... YOU GOT ONE... WORKING FOR ME!
WHAT DO I DO ?
COME, LET'S TAKE A LITTLE WALK!
RISTAURAN ITALIANO
SEE THIS BLOCK? IT'S GOING DOWN THE TUBES! Y'CAN SMELL IT!!
IZZY CASH, THE OLD RAGMAN, NOW OWNS MOST OF THE BUILDINGS ON THIS BLOCK ...THEY'RE RUN DOWN AND THEY STINK!
STREETS ARE TOO BUSY WITH CARS... KIDS CAN'T PLAY IN THE STREETS NO MORE! ...THEY GOT GANGS NOW!

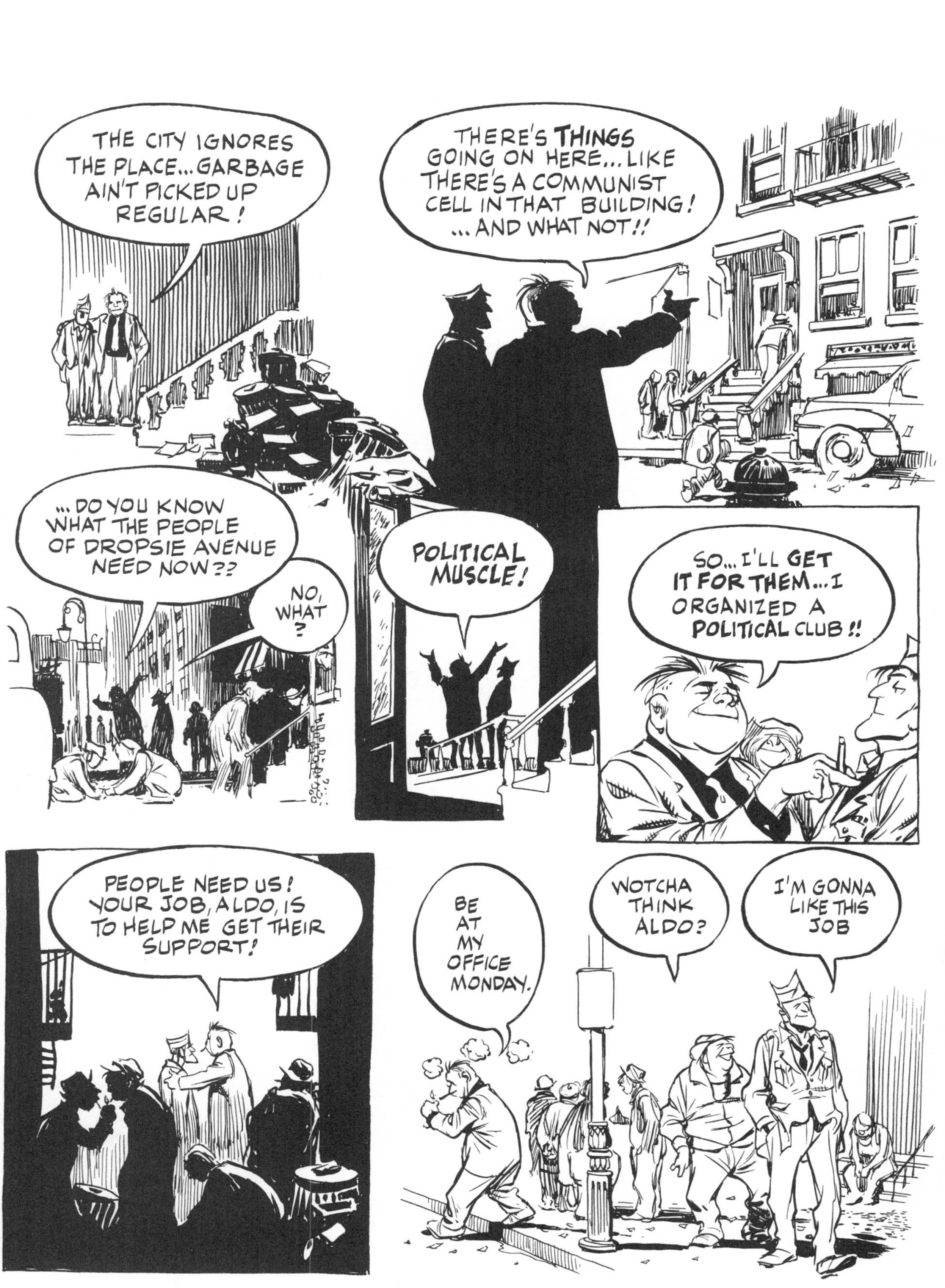
THE CITY IGNORES THE PLACE...GARBAGE AIN'T PICKED UP REGULAR!
THERE'S THINGS GOING ON HERE...LIKE THERE'S A COMMUNIST CELL IN THAT BUILDING! ...AND WHAT NOT!!
...DO YOU KNOW WHAT THE PEOPLE OF DROPSIE AVENUE NEED NOW??
NO, WHAT?
POLITICAL MUSCLE!
SO...I'LL GET IT FOR THEM...I ORGANIZED A POLITICAL CLUB!!
PEOPLE NEED US! YOUR JOB, ALDO, IS TO HELP ME GET THEIR SUPPORT!
BE AT MY OFFICE MONDAY.
WOTCHA THINK ALDO?
I'M GONNA LIKE THIS JOB

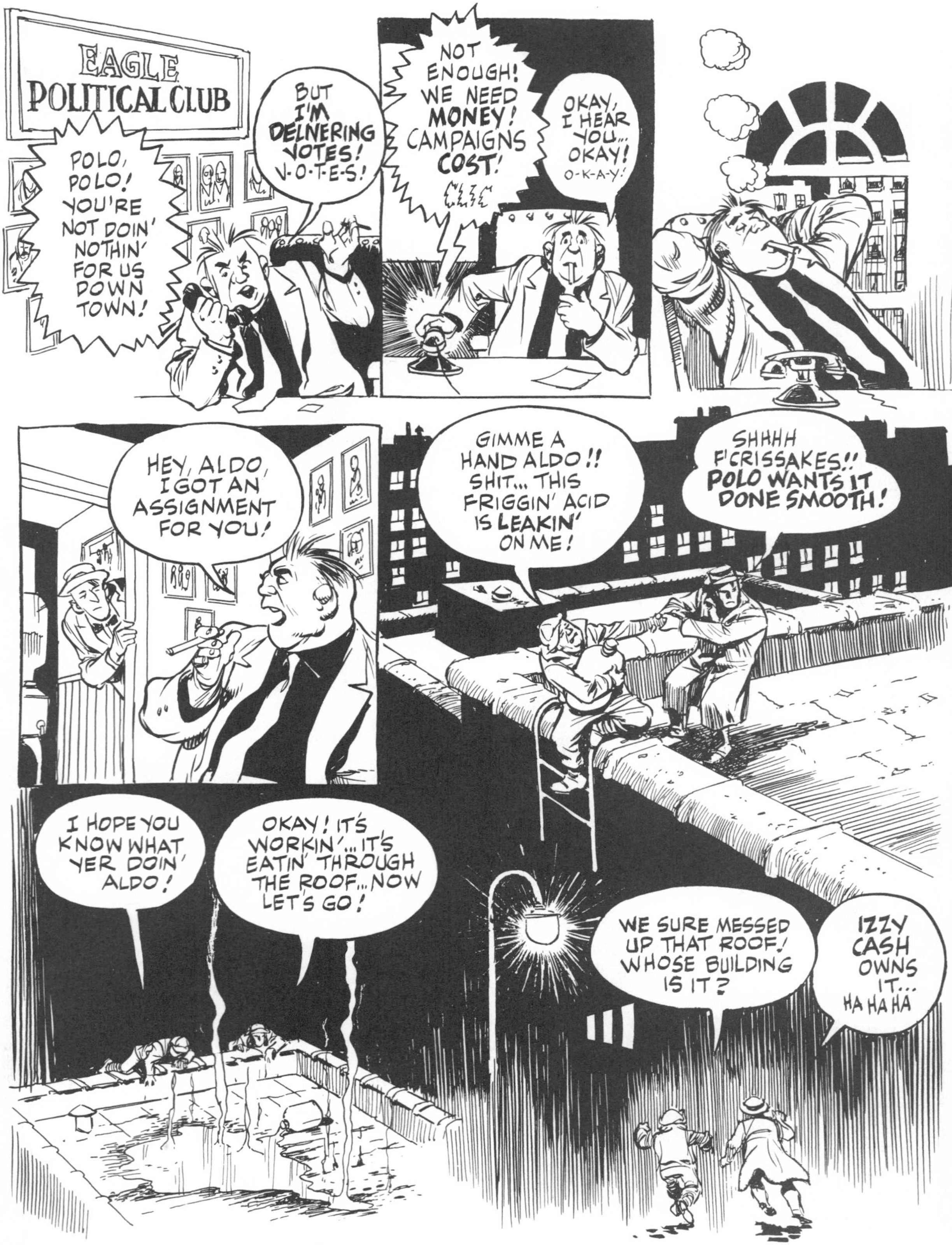

EAGLE POLITICAL CLUB
POLO, POLO! YOU'RE NOT DOIN' NOTHIN' FOR US DOWN TOWN!
BUT I'M DELIVERING VOTES! V-O-T-E-S!
NOT ENOUGH! WE NEED MONEY! CAMPAIGNS COST!
CLIC
OKAY, I HEAR YOU... OKAY! O-K-A-Y!
HEY, ALDO, I GOT AN ASSIGNMENT FOR YOU!
GIMME A HAND ALDO!! SHIT... THIS FRIGGIN' ACID IS LEAKIN' ON ME!
SHHHH F'CRISSAKES!! POLO WANTS IT DONE SMOOTH!
I HOPE YOU KNOW WHAT YER DOIN' ALDO!
OKAY! IT'S WORKIN'... IT'S EATIN' THROUGH THE ROOF... NOW LET'S GO!
WE SURE MESSED UP THAT ROOF! WHOSE BUILDING IS IT?
IZZY CASH OWNS IT... HA HA HA

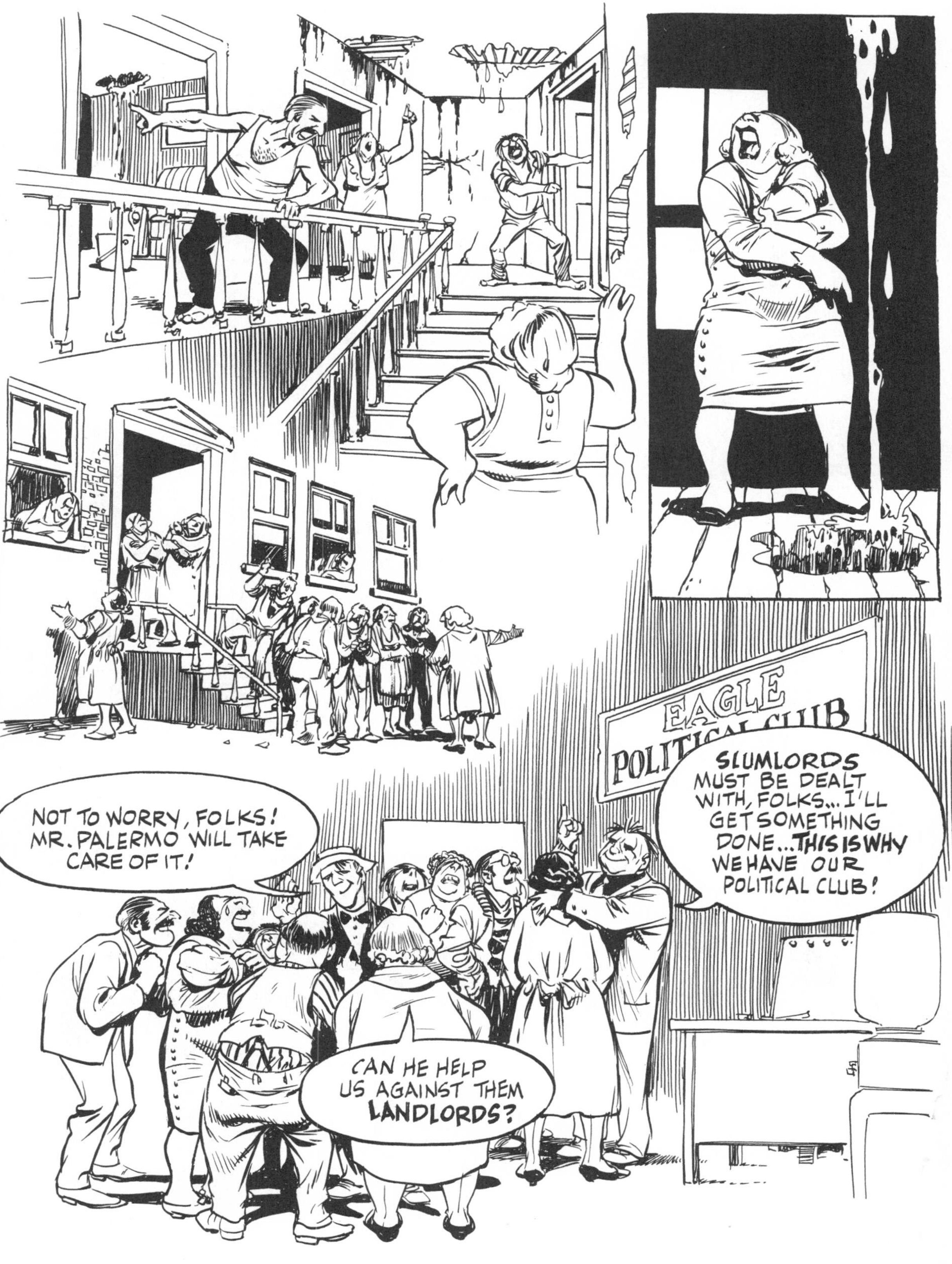
EAGLE POLITICAL CLUB
NOT TO WORRY, FOLKS! MR. PALERMO WILL TAKE CARE OF IT!
SLUMLORDS MUST BE DEALT WITH, FOLKS... I'LL GET SOMETHING DONE... THIS IS WHY WE HAVE OUR POLITICAL CLUB!
CAN HE HELP US AGAINST THEM LANDLORDS?

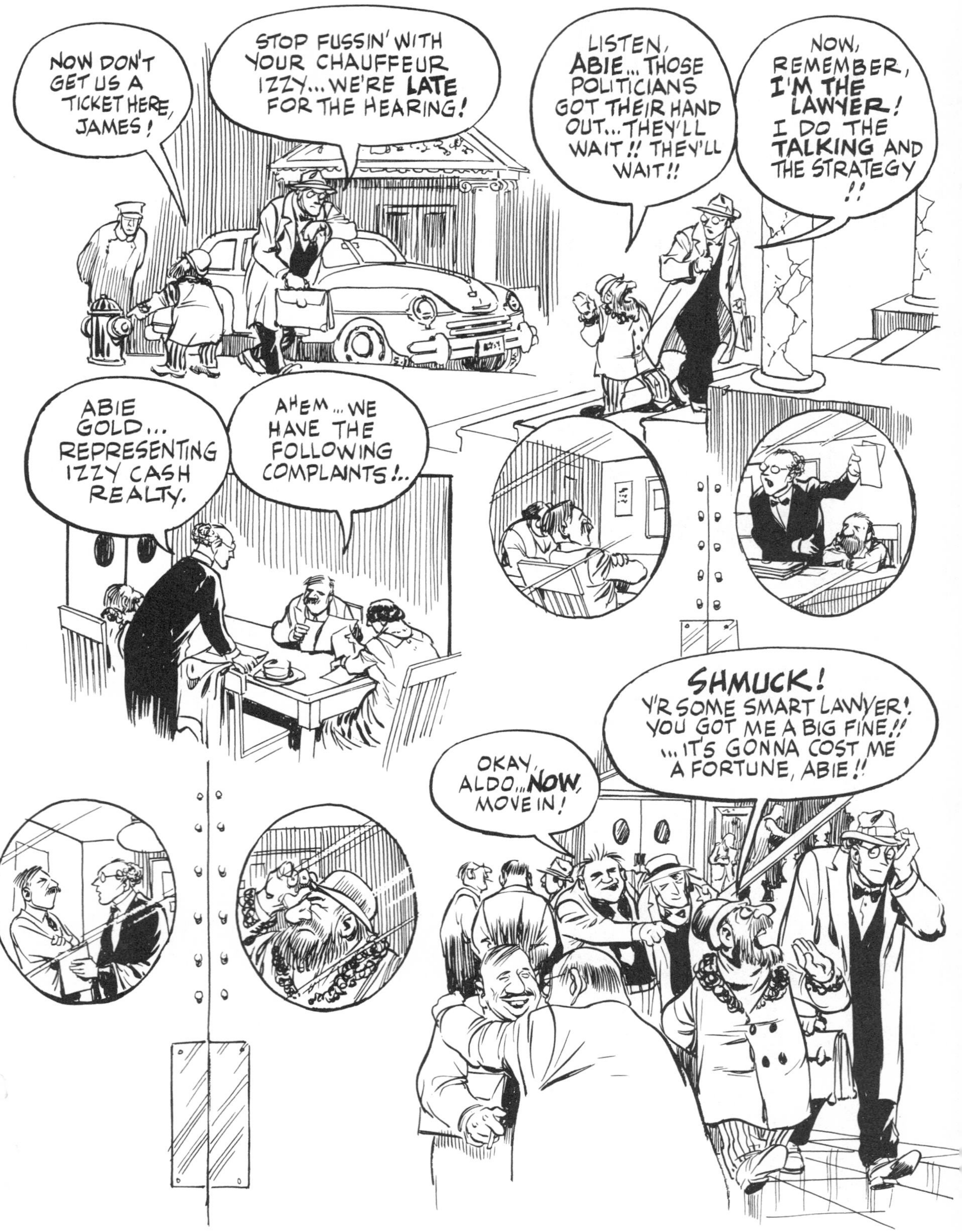

NOW DON'T GET US A TICKET HERE, JAMES!
STOP FUSSIN' WITH YOUR CHAUFFEUR IZZY... WE'RE **LATE** FOR THE HEARING!
LISTEN, **ABIE**... THOSE POLITICIANS GOT THEIR HAND OUT... THEY'LL WAIT!! THEY'LL WAIT!!
NOW, REMEMBER, **I'M THE LAWYER**! I DO THE **TALKING** AND THE STRATEGY!!
ABIE GOLD... REPRESENTING IZZY CASH REALTY.
AHEM... WE HAVE THE FOLLOWING COMPLAINTS!..
OKAY, ALDO... **NOW**, MOVE IN!
SHMUCK! Y'R SOME SMART LAWYER! YOU GOT ME A BIG FINE!! ...IT'S GONNA COST ME A FORTUNE, ABIE!!

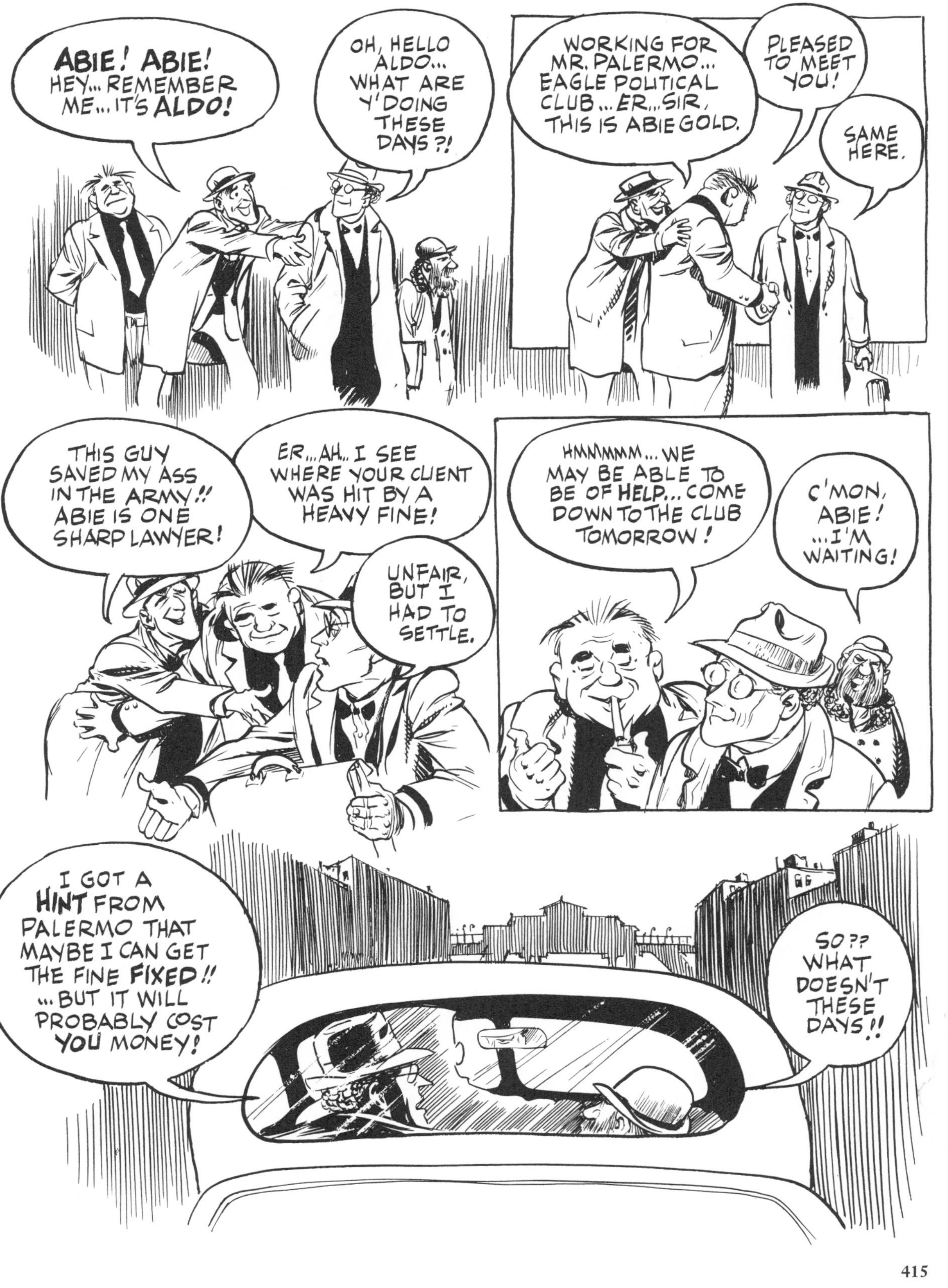
ABIE! ABIE! HEY... REMEMBER ME... IT'S ALDO!
OH, HELLO ALDO... WHAT ARE Y'DOING THESE DAYS ?!
WORKING FOR MR. PALERMO... EAGLE POLITICAL CLUB... ER... SIR, THIS IS ABIE GOLD.
PLEASED TO MEET YOU!
SAME HERE.
THIS GUY SAVED MY ASS IN THE ARMY!! ABIE IS ONE SHARP LAWYER!
ER... AH... I SEE WHERE YOUR CLIENT WAS HIT BY A HEAVY FINE!
UNFAIR, BUT I HAD TO SETTLE.
HMMMMM... WE MAY BE ABLE TO BE OF HELP... COME DOWN TO THE CLUB TOMORROW!
C'MON, ABIE! ...I'M WAITING!
I GOT A HINT FROM PALERMO THAT MAYBE I CAN GET THE FINE FIXED!! ...BUT IT WILL PROBABLY COST YOU MONEY!
SO?? WHAT DOESN'T THESE DAYS!!

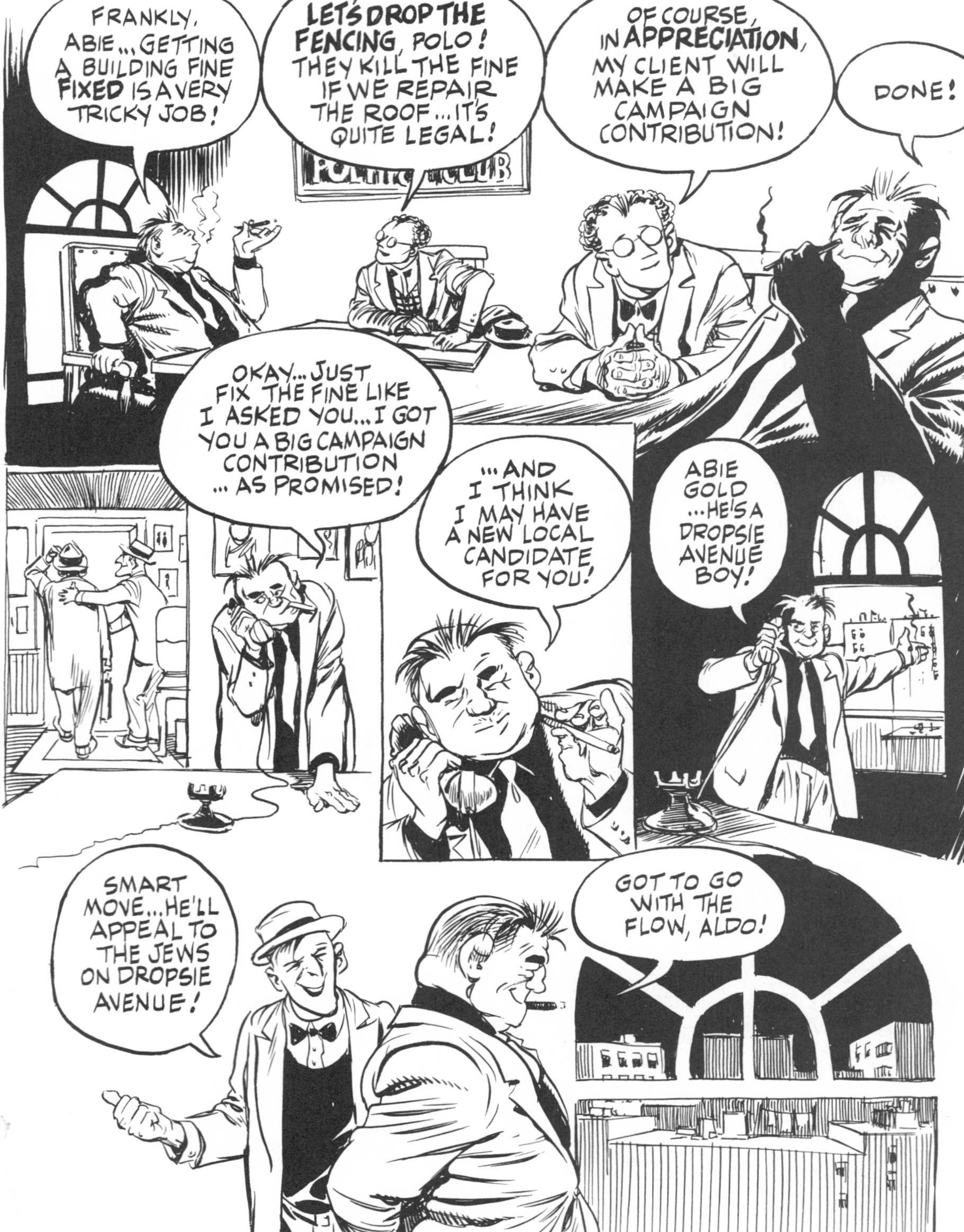
FRANKLY, ABIE... GETTING A BUILDING FINE FIXED IS A VERY TRICKY JOB!
LET'S DROP THE FENCING, POLO! THEY KILL THE FINE IF WE REPAIR THE ROOF... IT'S QUITE LEGAL!
OF COURSE, IN APPRECIATION, MY CLIENT WILL MAKE A BIG CAMPAIGN CONTRIBUTION!
DONE!
OKAY... JUST FIX THE FINE LIKE I ASKED YOU... I GOT YOU A BIG CAMPAIGN CONTRIBUTION ... AS PROMISED!
...AND I THINK I MAY HAVE A NEW LOCAL CANDIDATE FOR YOU!
ABIE GOLD ...HE'S A DROPSIE AVENUE BOY!
SMART MOVE... HE'LL APPEAL TO THE JEWS ON DROPSIE AVENUE!
GOT TO GO WITH THE FLOW, ALDO!

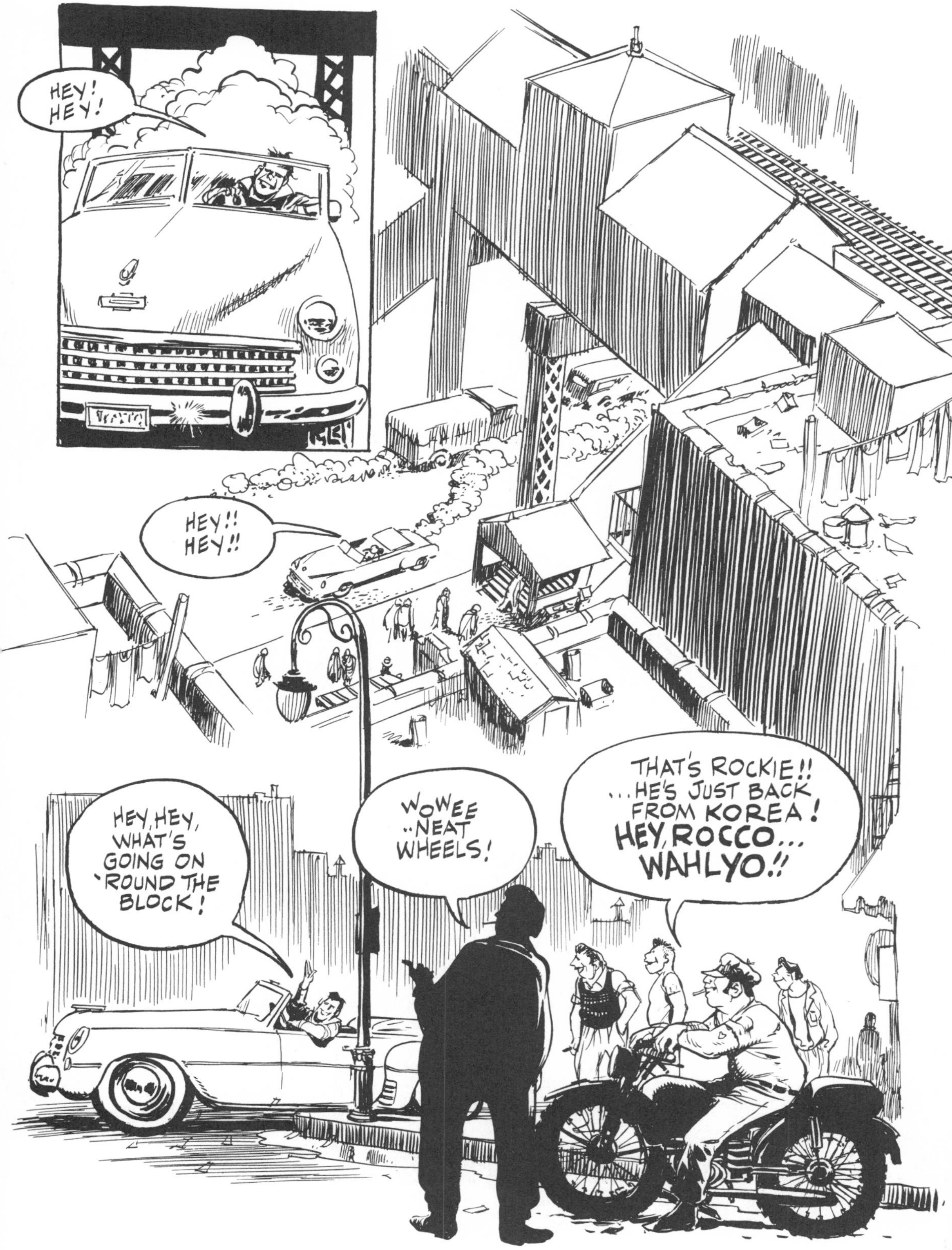
HEY! HEY!
HEY!! HEY!!
HEY, HEY, WHAT'S GOING ON 'ROUND THE BLOCK!
WOWEE ..NEAT WHEELS!
THAT'S ROCKIE!! ...HE'S JUST BACK FROM KOREA! HEY, ROCCO... WAHLYO.!!

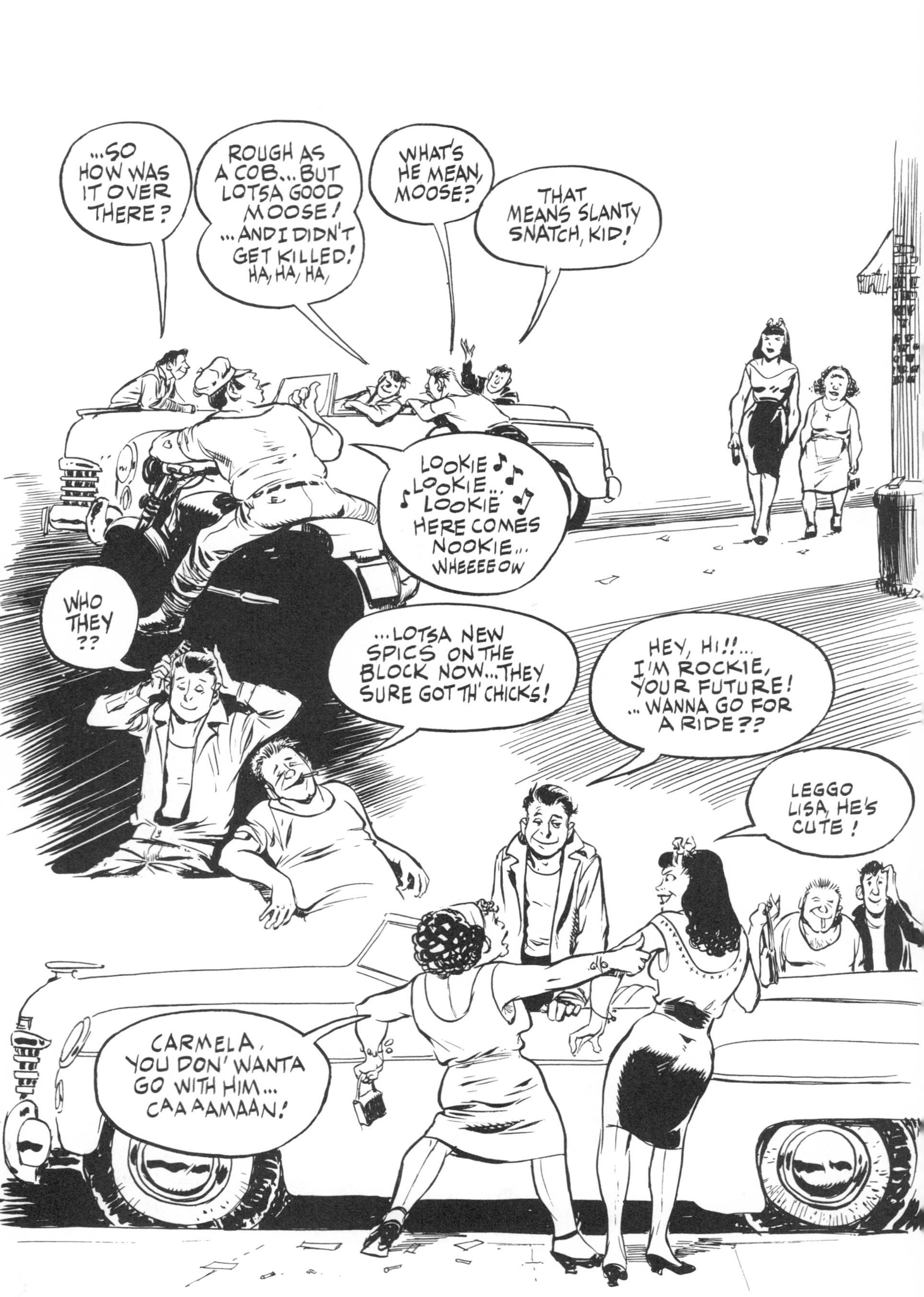
...SO HOW WAS IT OVER THERE?
ROUGH AS A COB... BUT LOTSA GOOD MOOSE! ...AND I DIDN'T GET KILLED! HA, HA, HA,
WHAT'S HE MEAN, MOOSE?
THAT MEANS SLANTY SNATCH, KID!
LOOKIE LOOKIE... LOOKIE HERE COMES NOOKIE... WHEEEEOW
WHO THEY??
...LOTSA NEW SPICS ON THE BLOCK NOW... THEY SURE GOT TH' CHICKS!
HEY, HI!!... I'M ROCKIE, YOUR FUTURE! ...WANNA GO FOR A RIDE??
LEGGO LISA, HE'S CUTE!
CARMELA, YOU DON' WANTA GO WITH HIM... CAAAAMAAN!

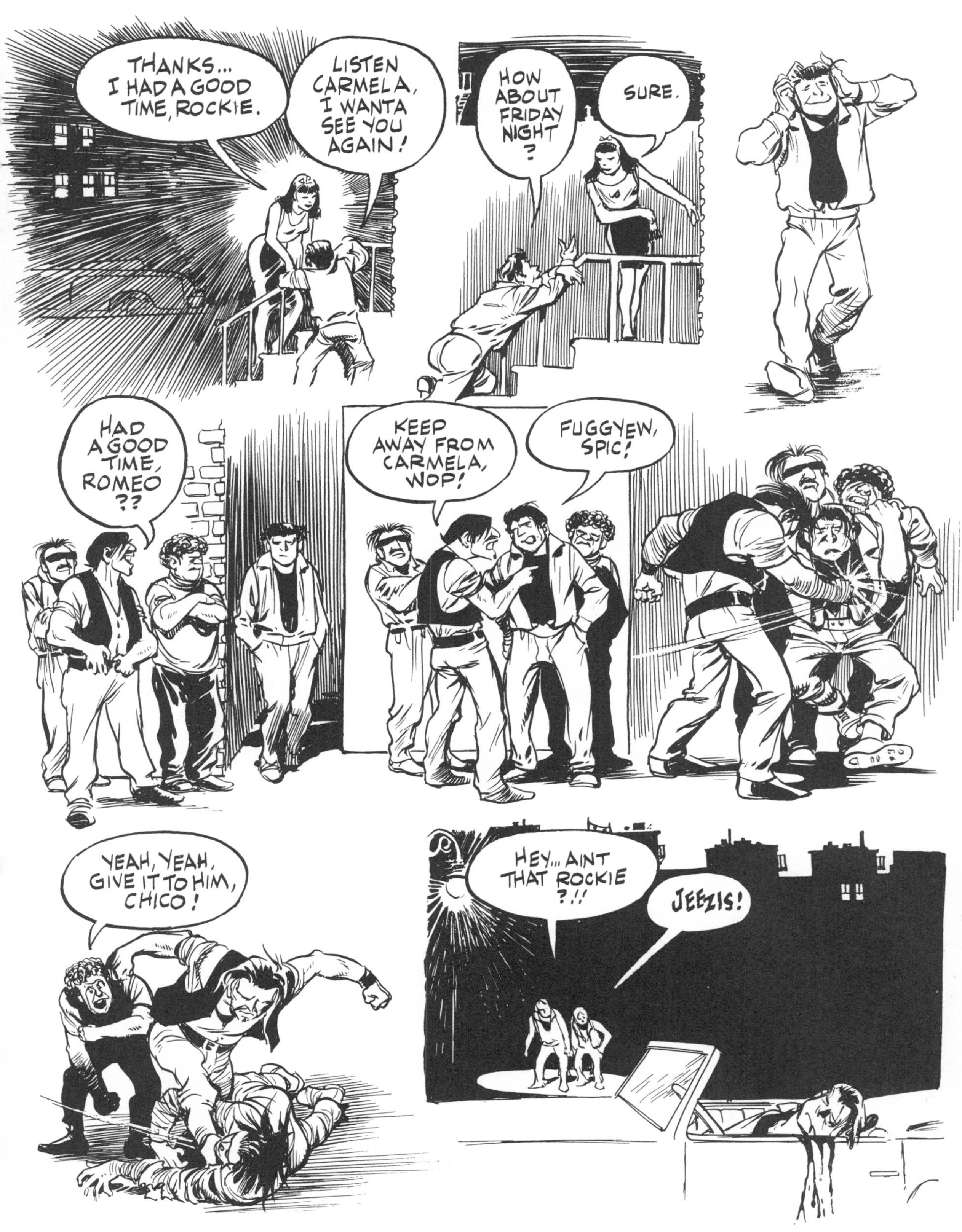

THANKS... I HAD A GOOD TIME, ROCKIE.
LISTEN CARMELA, I WANTA SEE YOU AGAIN!
HOW ABOUT FRIDAY NIGHT?
SURE.
HAD A GOOD TIME, ROMEO??
KEEP AWAY FROM CARMELA, WOP!
FUGGYEW, SPIC!
YEAH, YEAH, GIVE IT TO HIM, CHICO!
HEY... AINT THAT ROCKIE?!!
JEEZIS!

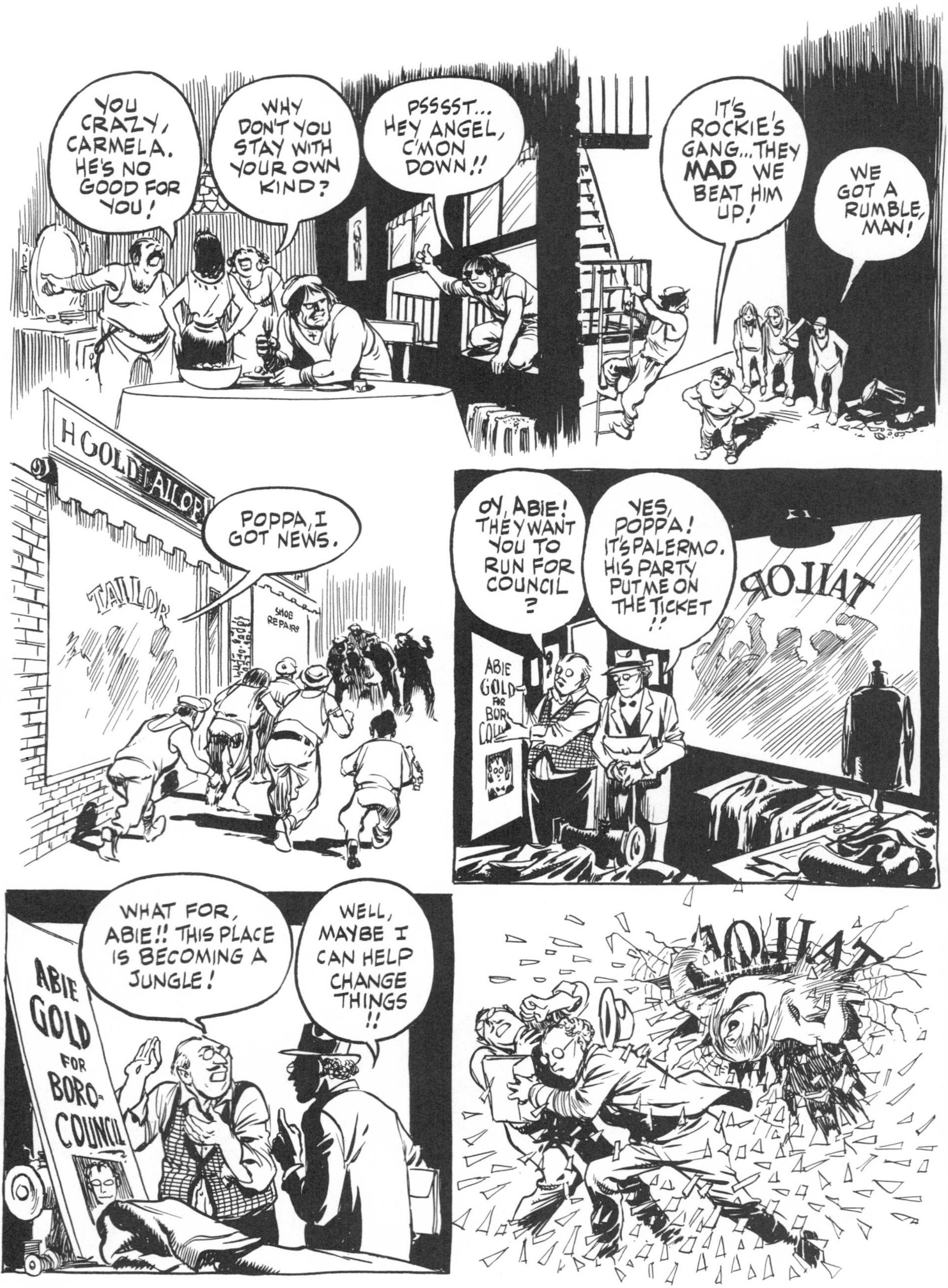
YOU CRAZY, CARMELA. HE'S NO GOOD FOR YOU!
WHY DON'T YOU STAY WITH YOUR OWN KIND?
PSSSST... HEY ANGEL, C'MON DOWN!!
IT'S ROCKIE'S GANG...THEY MAD WE BEAT HIM UP!
WE GOT A RUMBLE, MAN!
H GOLD TAILOR
TAILOR
SHOE REPAIRS
POPPA, I GOT NEWS.
OY, ABIE! THEY WANT YOU TO RUN FOR COUNCIL?
YES, POPPA! IT'S PALERMO. HIS PARTY PUT ME ON THE TICKET!!
ABIE GOLD FOR BORO COU
TAILOR
ABIE GOLD FOR BORO-COUNCIL
WHAT FOR, ABIE!! THIS PLACE IS BECOMING A JUNGLE!
WELL, MAYBE I CAN HELP CHANGE THINGS!!
TAILOR

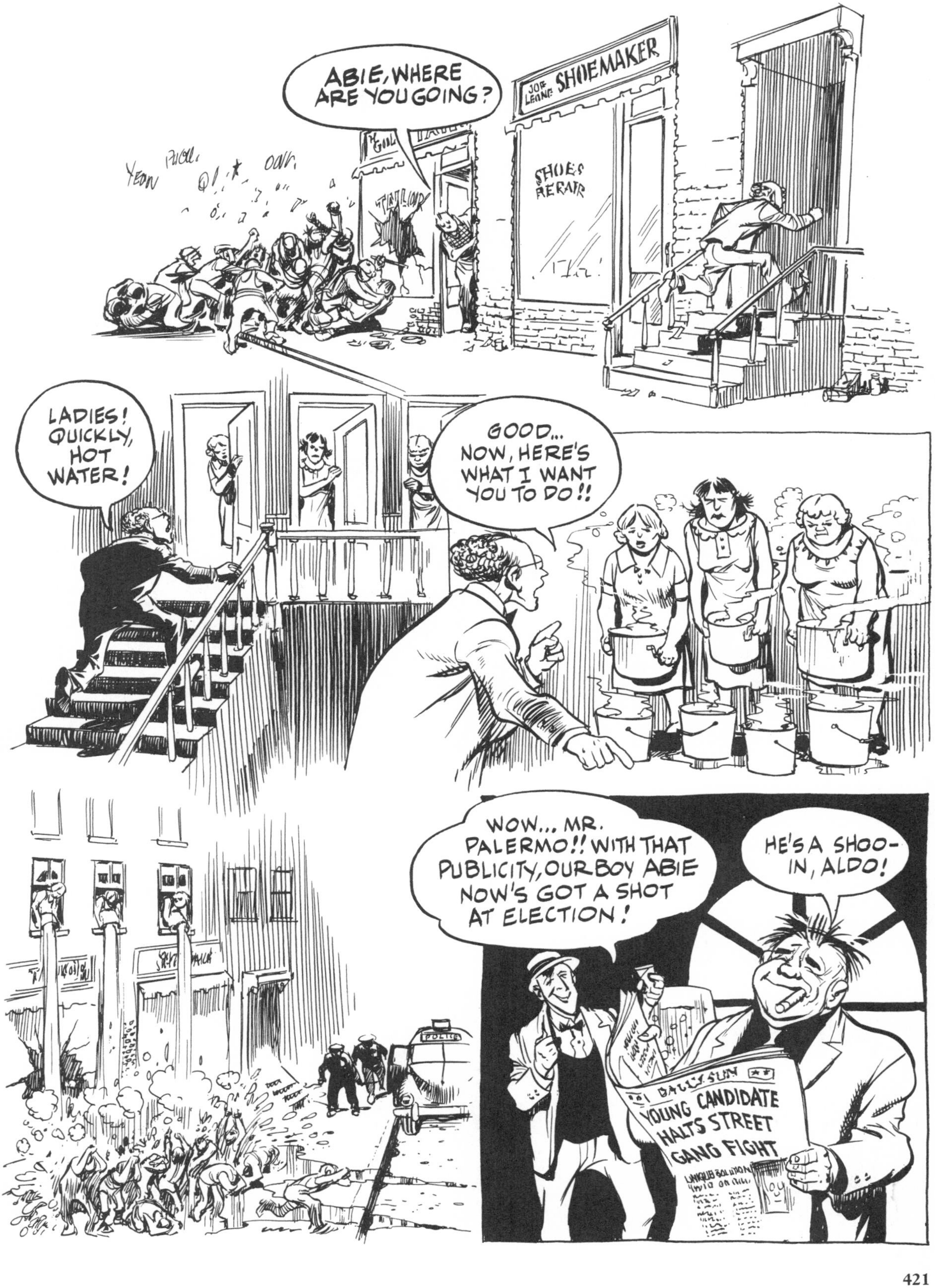
ABIE, WHERE ARE YOU GOING?
SHOEMAKER
SHOES REPAIR
LADIES! QUICKLY, HOT WATER!
GOOD... NOW, HERE'S WHAT I WANT YOU TO DO!!
WOW... MR. PALERMO!! WITH THAT PUBLICITY, OUR BOY ABIE NOW'S GOT A SHOT AT ELECTION!
HE'S A SHOO-IN, ALDO!
YOUNG CANDIDATE HALTS STREET GANG FIGHT

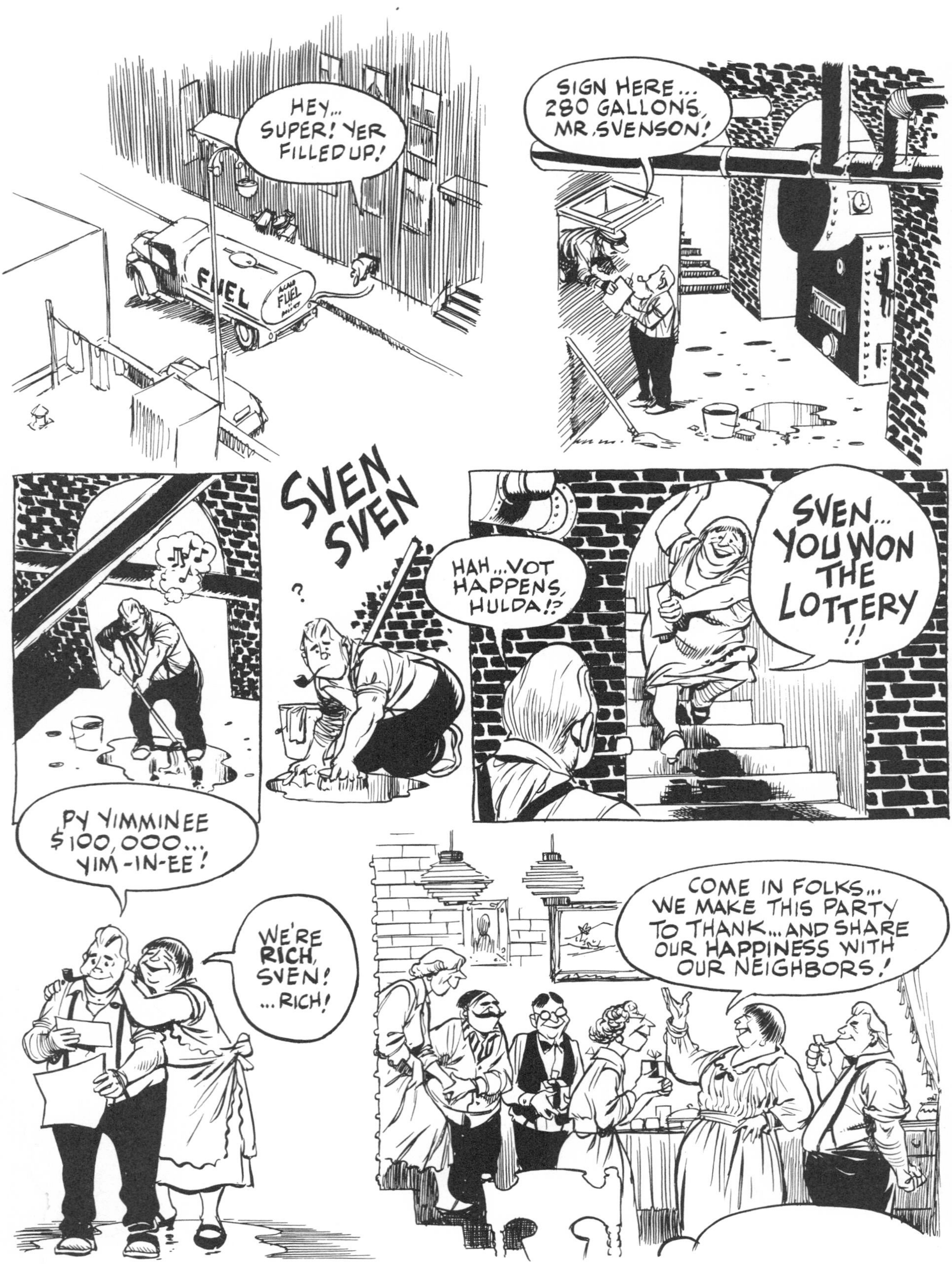
HEY... SUPER! YER FILLED UP!
FUEL
SIGN HERE... 280 GALLONS, MR. SVENSON!
SVEN SVEN
?
HAH... VOT HAPPENS, HULDA!?
SVEN... YOU WON THE LOTTERY !!
PY YIMMINEE $100,000..., YIM-IN-EE!
WE'RE RICH, SVEN! ...RICH!
COME IN FOLKS... WE MAKE THIS PARTY TO THANK... AND SHARE OUR HAPPINESS WITH OUR NEIGHBORS!

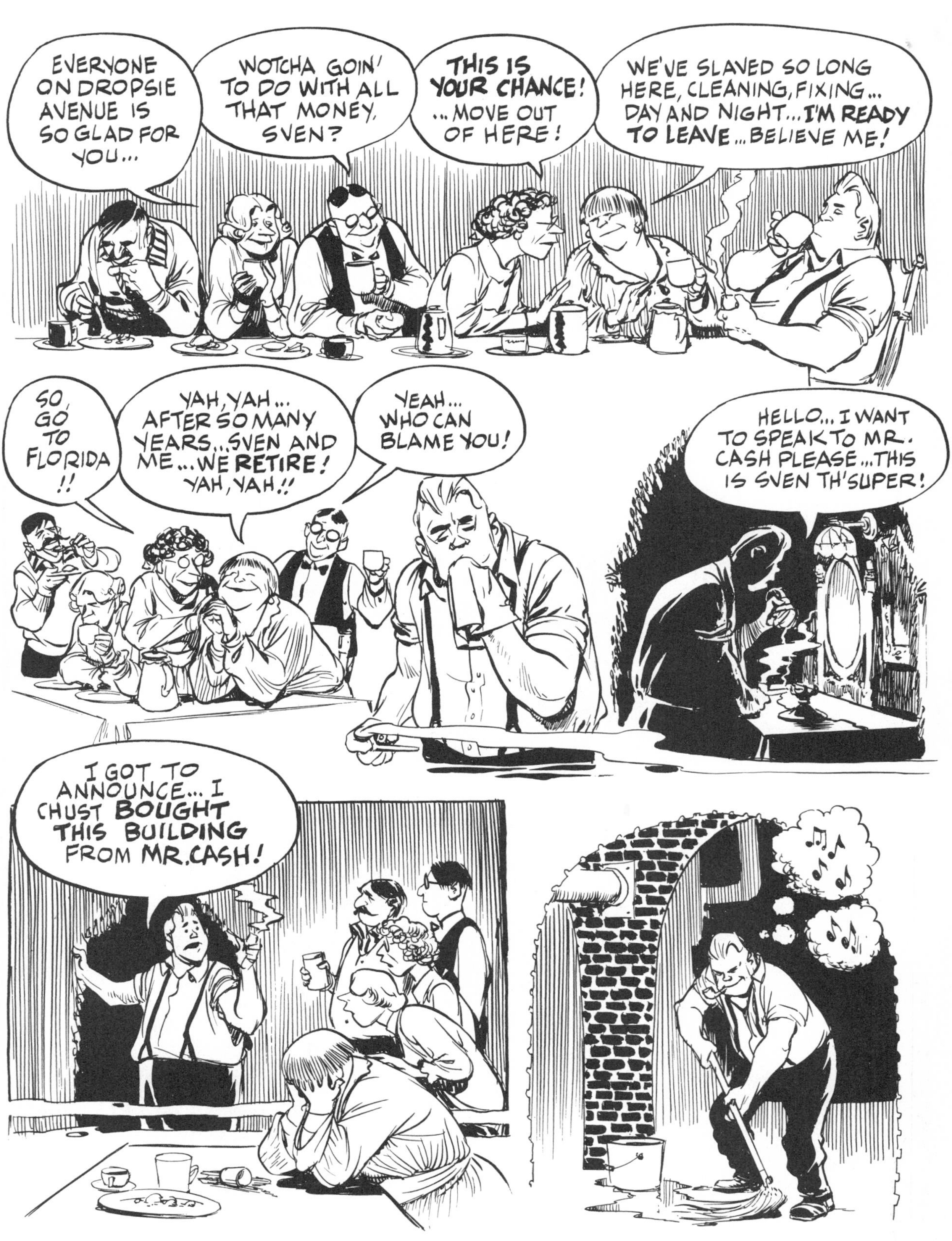
EVERYONE ON DROPSIE AVENUE IS SO GLAD FOR YOU...
WOTCHA GOIN' TO DO WITH ALL THAT MONEY, SVEN?
THIS IS YOUR CHANCE! ...MOVE OUT OF HERE!
WE'VE SLAVED SO LONG HERE, CLEANING, FIXING... DAY AND NIGHT... I'M READY TO LEAVE... BELIEVE ME!
SO, GO TO FLORIDA !!
YAH, YAH... AFTER SO MANY YEARS...SVEN AND ME... WE RETIRE! YAH, YAH!!
YEAH... WHO CAN BLAME YOU!
HELLO... I WANT TO SPEAK TO MR. CASH PLEASE... THIS IS SVEN TH'SUPER!
I GOT TO ANNOUNCE... I CHUST BOUGHT THIS BUILDING FROM MR.CASH!

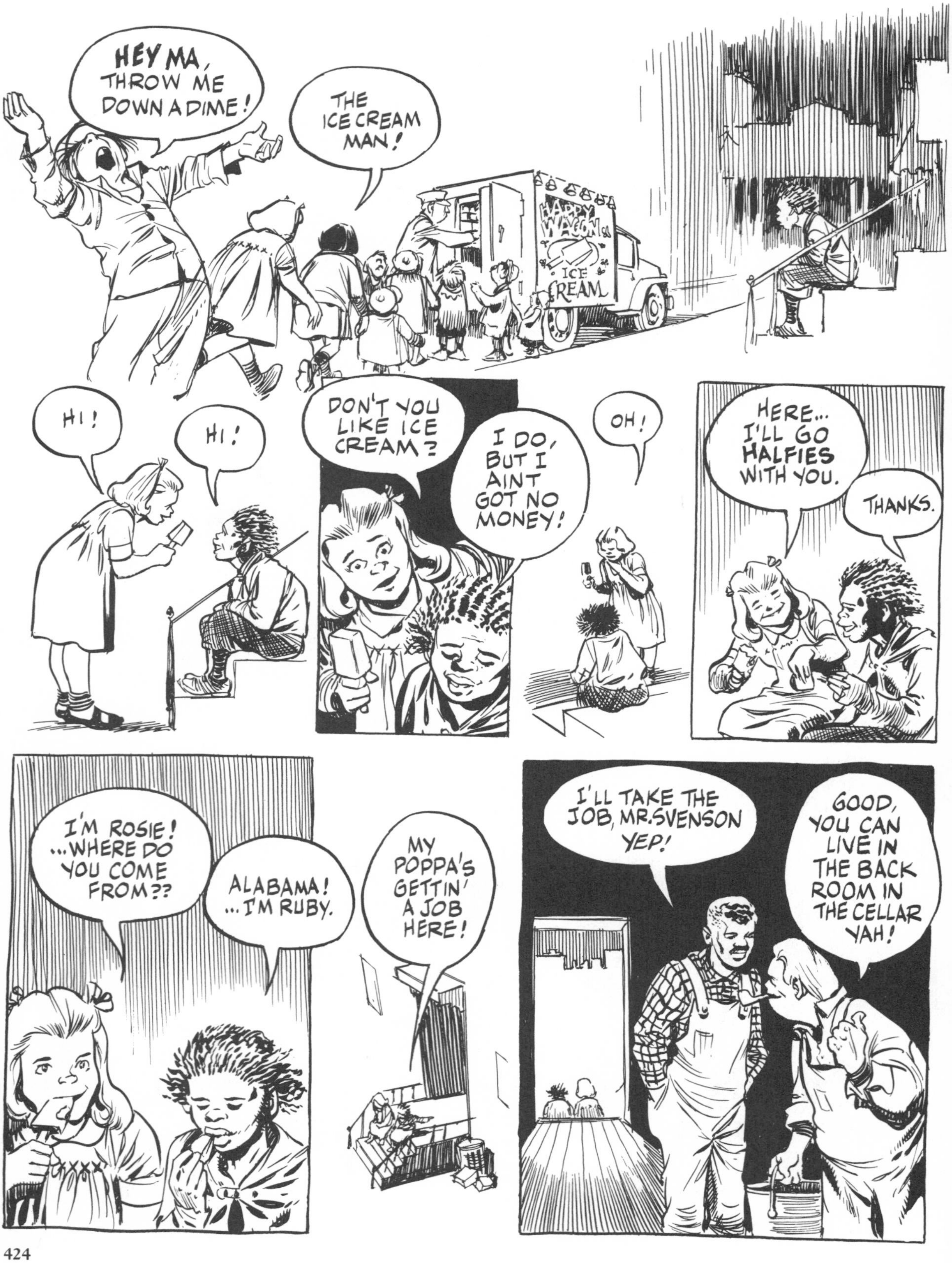
HEY MA, THROW ME DOWN A DIME!
THE ICE CREAM MAN!
HAPPY WAGON
ICE CREAM
HI!
HI!
DON'T YOU LIKE ICE CREAM?
I DO, BUT I AINT GOT NO MONEY!
OH!
HERE... I'LL GO HALFIES WITH YOU.
THANKS.
I'M ROSIE! ...WHERE DO YOU COME FROM??
ALABAMA! ...I'M RUBY.
MY POPPA'S GETTIN' A JOB HERE!
I'LL TAKE THE JOB, MR. SVENSON YEP!
GOOD, YOU CAN LIVE IN THE BACK ROOM IN THE CELLAR YAH!

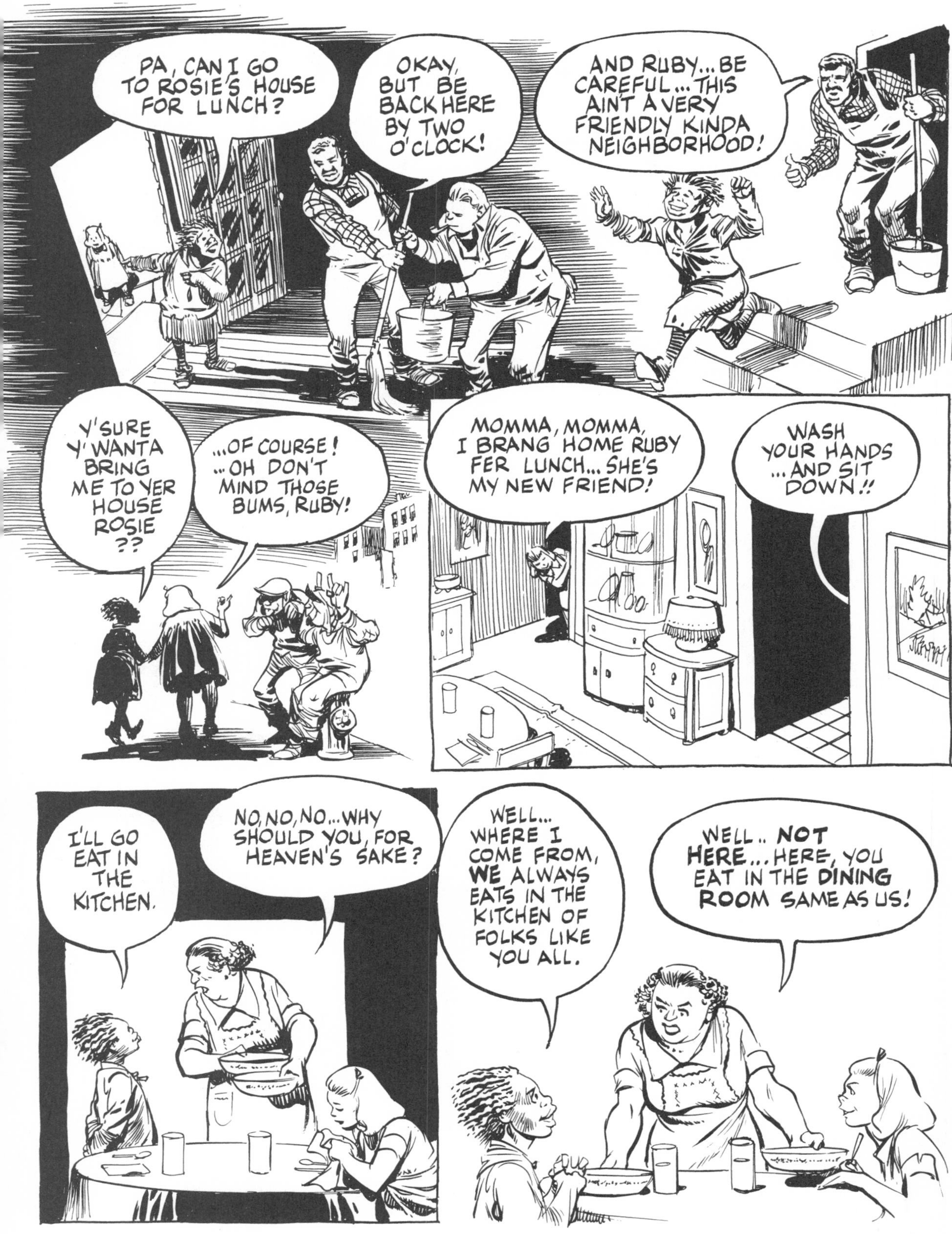

PA, CAN I GO TO ROSIE'S HOUSE FOR LUNCH?
OKAY, BUT BE BACK HERE BY TWO O'CLOCK!
AND RUBY... BE CAREFUL... THIS AIN'T A VERY FRIENDLY KINDA NEIGHBORHOOD!
Y'SURE Y'WANTA BRING ME TO YER HOUSE ROSIE ??
...OF COURSE! ...OH DON'T MIND THOSE BUMS, RUBY!
MOMMA, MOMMA, I BRANG HOME RUBY FER LUNCH... SHE'S MY NEW FRIEND!
WASH YOUR HANDS ...AND SIT DOWN.!!
I'LL GO EAT IN THE KITCHEN.
NO, NO, NO... WHY SHOULD YOU, FOR HEAVEN'S SAKE?
WELL... WHERE I COME FROM, WE ALWAYS EATS IN THE KITCHEN OF FOLKS LIKE YOU ALL.
WELL.. NOT HERE... HERE, YOU EAT IN THE DINING ROOM SAME AS US!

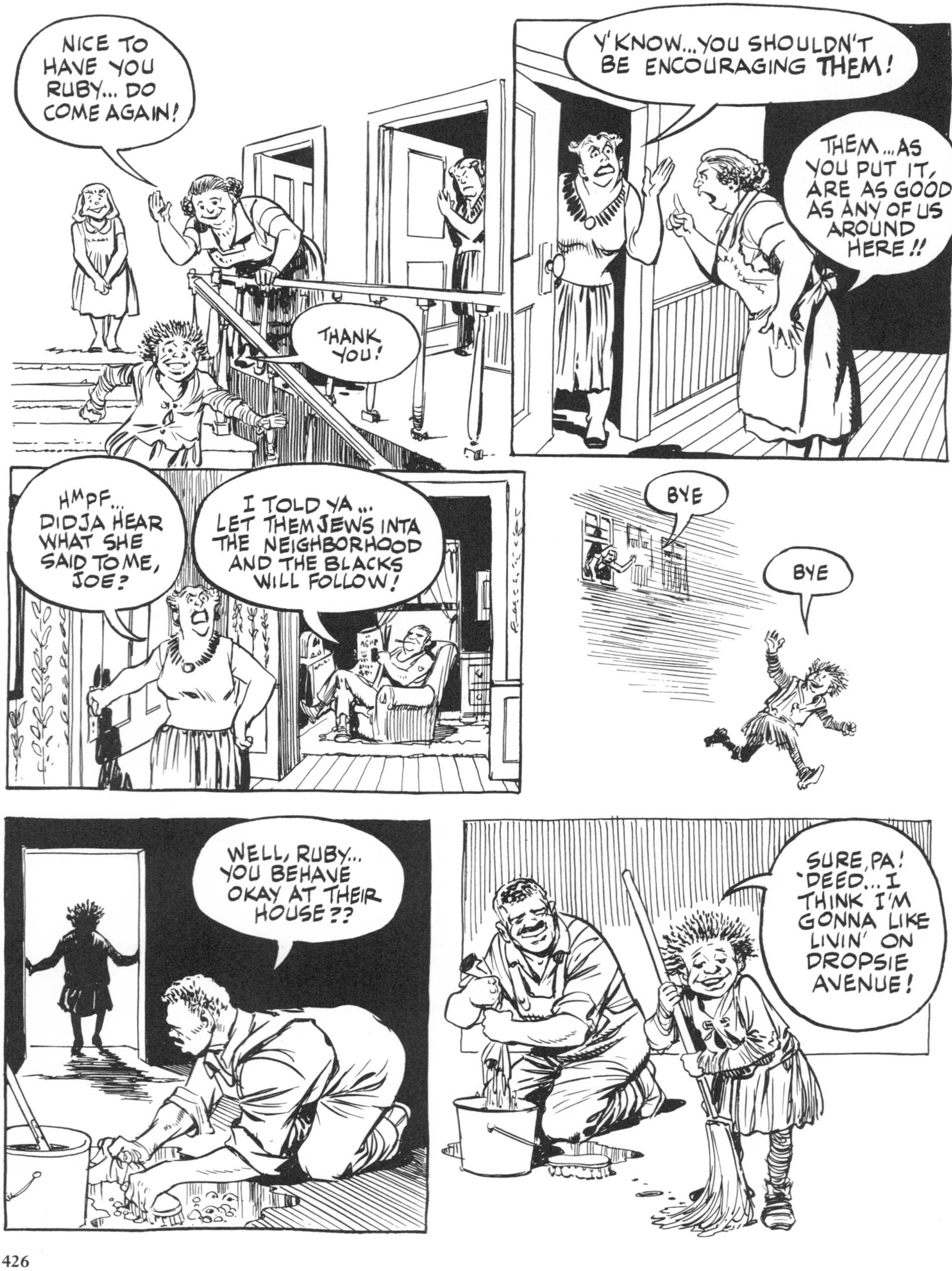

NICE TO HAVE YOU RUBY... DO COME AGAIN!
THANK YOU!
Y'KNOW...YOU SHOULDN'T BE ENCOURAGING THEM!
THEM...AS YOU PUT IT, ARE AS GOOD AS ANY OF US AROUND HERE!!
HMPF... DIDJA HEAR WHAT SHE SAID TO ME, JOE?
I TOLD YA... LET THEM JEWS INTA THE NEIGHBORHOOD AND THE BLACKS WILL FOLLOW!
BYE
BYE
WELL, RUBY... YOU BEHAVE OKAY AT THEIR HOUSE??
SURE, PA! 'DEED...I THINK I'M GONNA LIKE LIVIN' ON DROPSIE AVENUE!

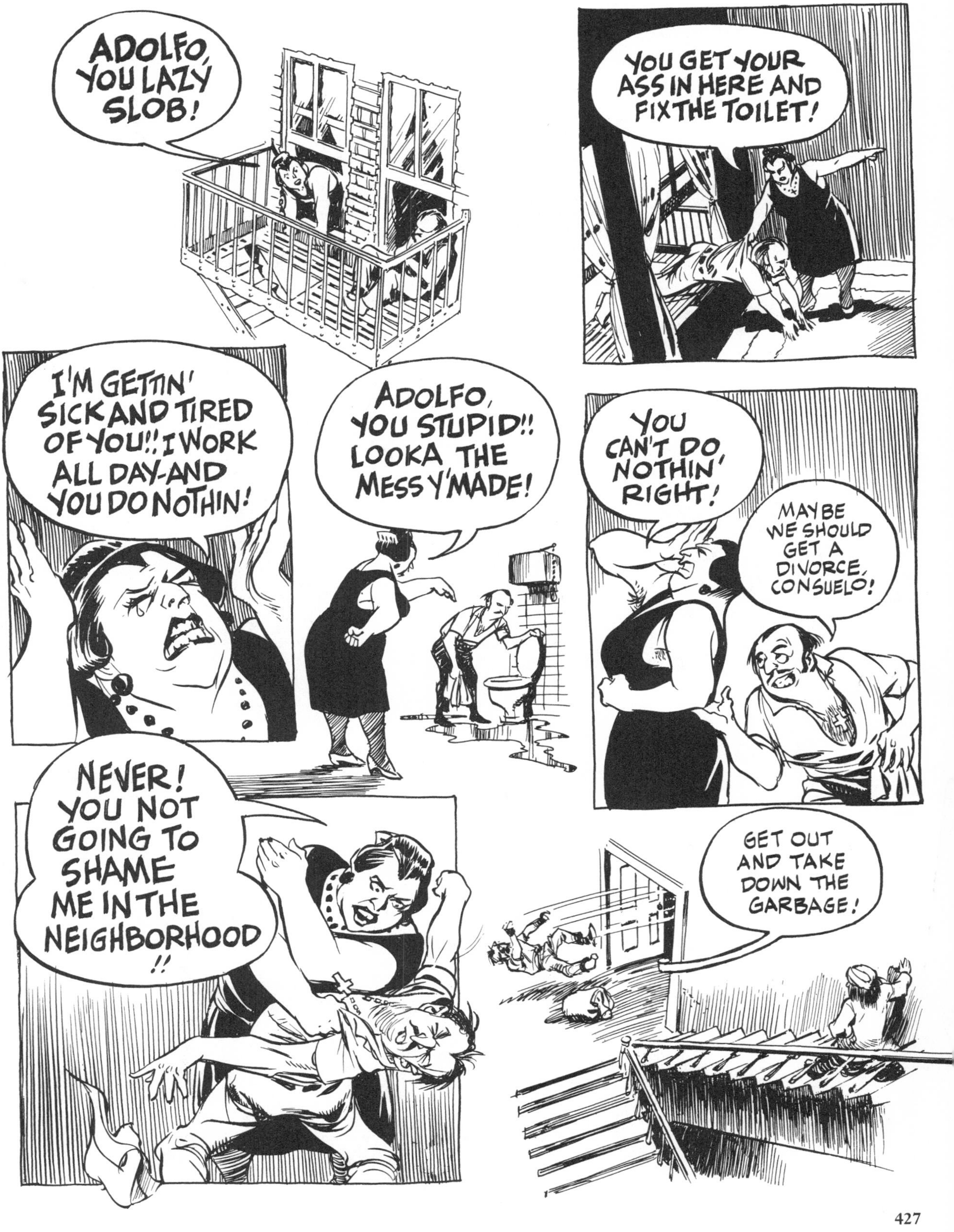
ADOLFO, YOU LAZY SLOB!
YOU GET YOUR ASS IN HERE AND FIX THE TOILET!
I'M GETTIN' SICK AND TIRED OF YOU!! I WORK ALL DAY-AND YOU DO NOTHIN!
ADOLFO, YOU STUPID!! LOOKA THE MESS Y'MADE!
YOU CAN'T DO NOTHIN' RIGHT!
MAYBE WE SHOULD GET A DIVORCE, CONSUELO!
NEVER! YOU NOT GOING TO SHAME ME IN THE NEIGHBORHOOD!!
GET OUT AND TAKE DOWN THE GARBAGE!

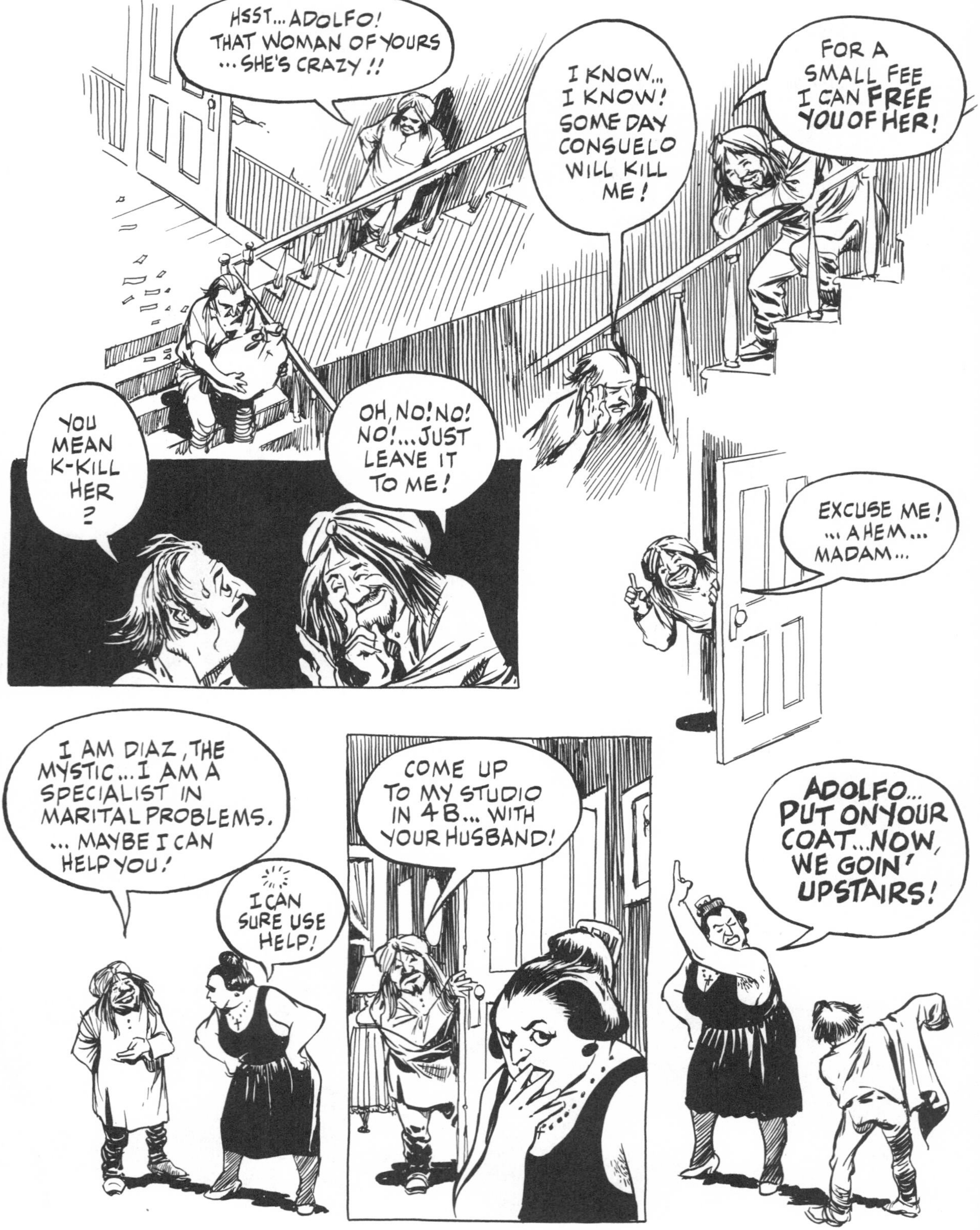
HSST... ADOLFO! THAT WOMAN OF YOURS ... SHE'S CRAZY !!
I KNOW... I KNOW! SOME DAY CONSUELO WILL KILL ME!
FOR A SMALL FEE I CAN FREE YOU OF HER!
YOU MEAN K-KILL HER ?
OH, NO! NO! NO!... JUST LEAVE IT TO ME!
EXCUSE ME! ... AHEM... MADAM...
I AM DIAZ, THE MYSTIC... I AM A SPECIALIST IN MARITAL PROBLEMS. ... MAYBE I CAN HELP YOU!
I CAN SURE USE HELP!
COME UP TO MY STUDIO IN 4B... WITH YOUR HUSBAND!
ADOLFO... PUT ON YOUR COAT... NOW, WE GOIN' UPSTAIRS!

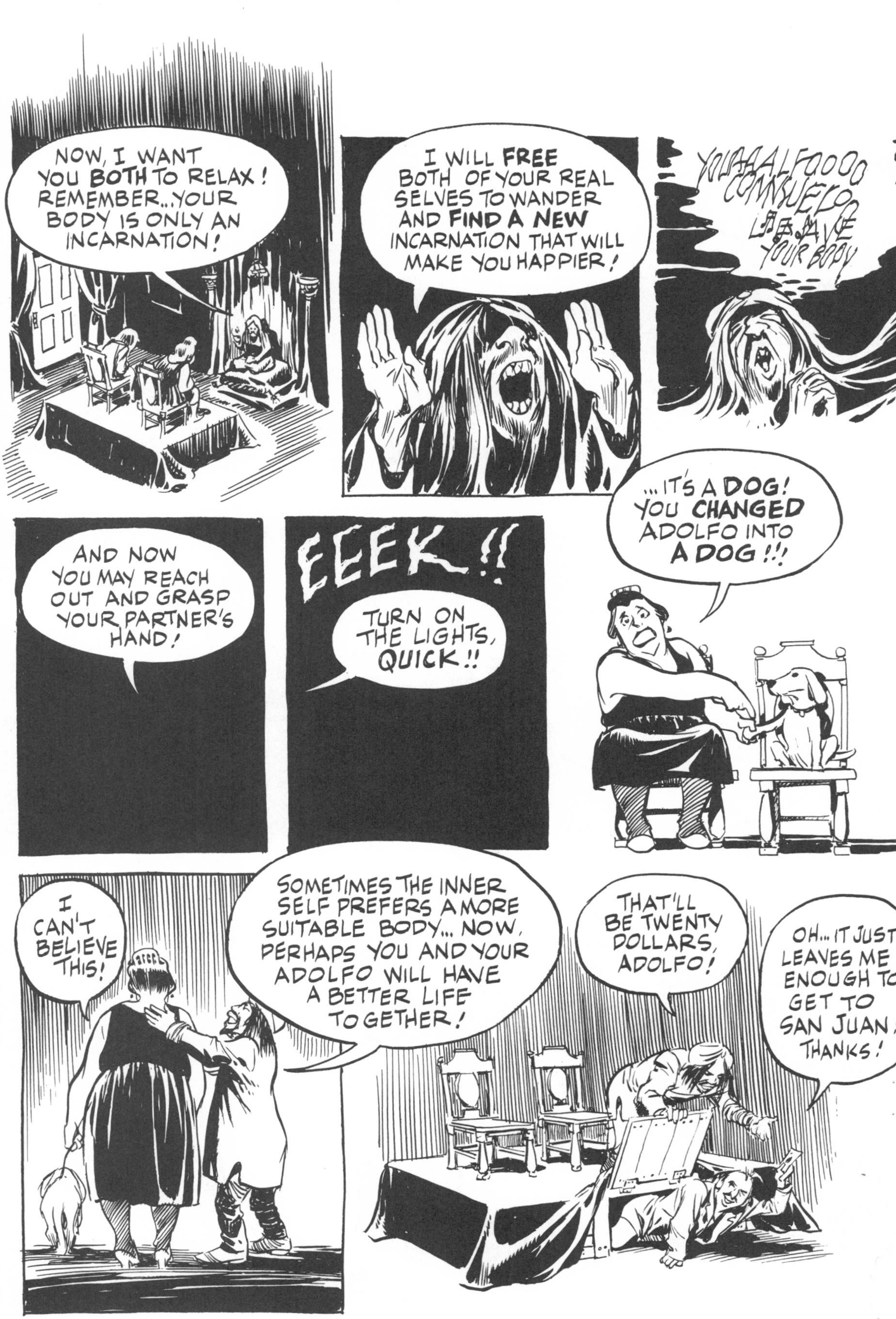
NOW, I WANT YOU BOTH TO RELAX! REMEMBER...YOUR BODY IS ONLY AN INCARNATION!
I WILL FREE BOTH OF YOUR REAL SELVES TO WANDER AND FIND A NEW INCARNATION THAT WILL MAKE YOU HAPPIER!
YOUAAALFOOOO CONNSUELOO LEAVE YOUR BODY
AND NOW YOU MAY REACH OUT AND GRASP YOUR PARTNER'S HAND!
EEEK!!
TURN ON THE LIGHTS, QUICK!!
...IT'S A DOG! YOU CHANGED ADOLFO INTO A DOG!!!
I CAN'T BELIEVE THIS!
SOMETIMES THE INNER SELF PREFERS A MORE SUITABLE BODY... NOW, PERHAPS YOU AND YOUR ADOLFO WILL HAVE A BETTER LIFE TOGETHER!
THAT'LL BE TWENTY DOLLARS, ADOLFO!
OH... IT JUST LEAVES ME ENOUGH TO GET TO SAN JUAN! THANKS!

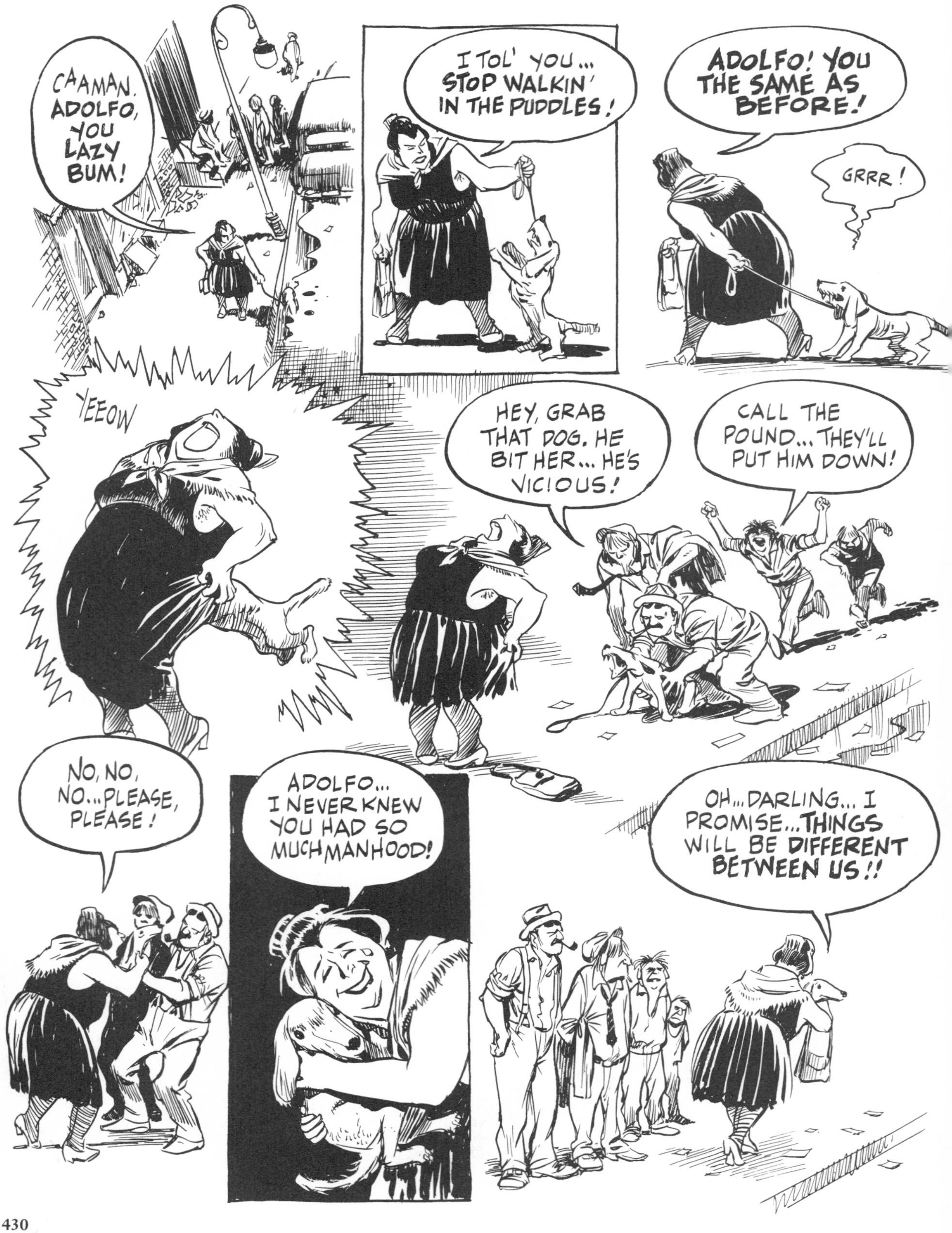
CAAMAN. ADOLFO, YOU LAZY BUM!
I TOL' YOU... STOP WALKIN' IN THE PUDDLES!
ADOLFO! YOU THE SAME AS BEFORE!
GRRR!
YEEOW
HEY, GRAB THAT DOG. HE BIT HER... HE'S VICIOUS!
CALL THE POUND... THEY'LL PUT HIM DOWN!
NO, NO, NO... PLEASE, PLEASE!
ADOLFO... I NEVER KNEW YOU HAD SO MUCH MANHOOD!
OH... DARLING... I PROMISE... THINGS WILL BE DIFFERENT BETWEEN US!!

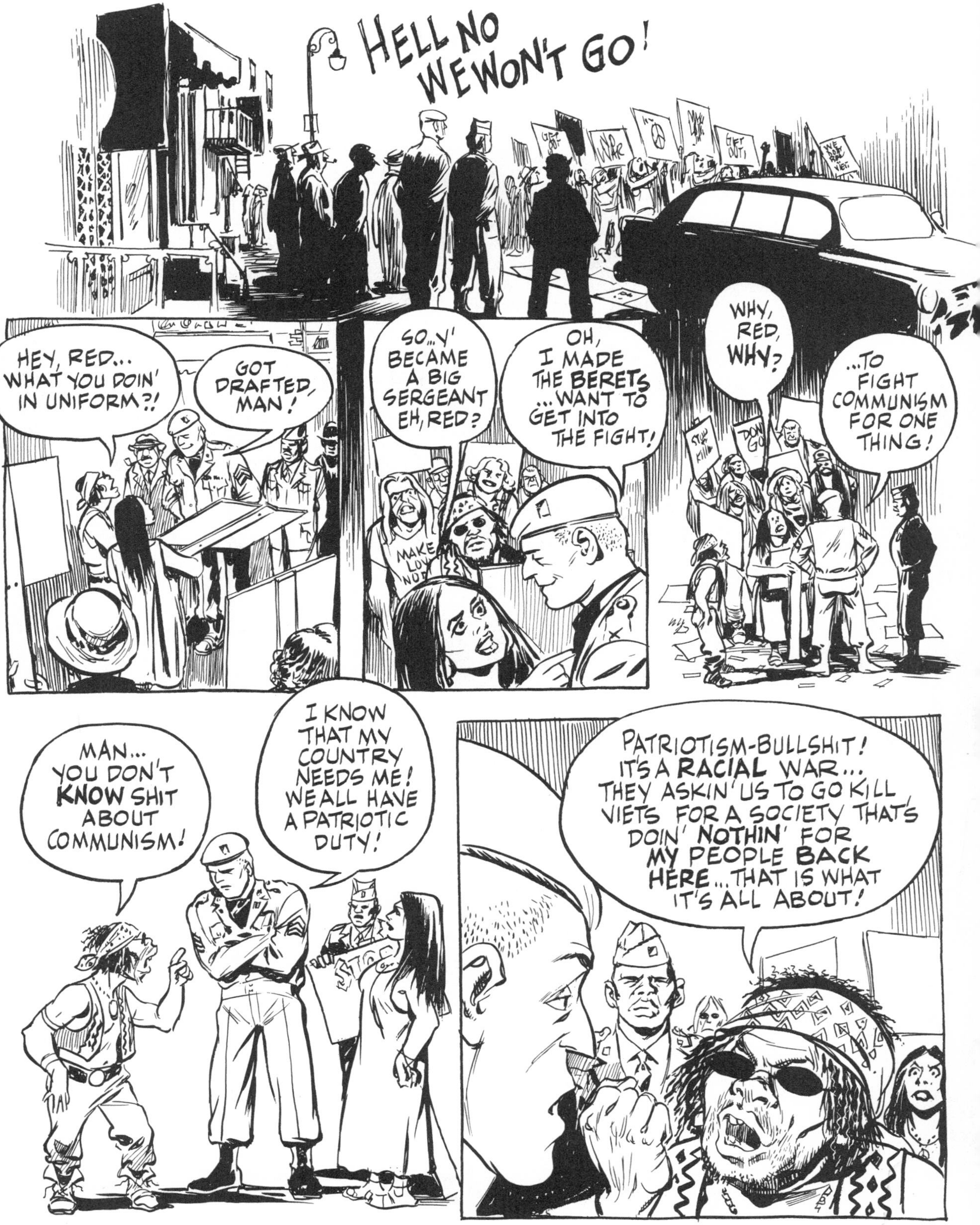
HELL NO WE WON'T GO!
HEY, RED... WHAT YOU DOIN' IN UNIFORM?!
GOT DRAFTED, MAN!
SO...Y' BECAME A BIG SERGEANT EH, RED?
OH, I MADE THE BERETS ...WANT TO GET INTO THE FIGHT!
WHY, RED, WHY?
...TO FIGHT COMMUNISM FOR ONE THING!
MAN... YOU DON'T KNOW SHIT ABOUT COMMUNISM!
I KNOW THAT MY COUNTRY NEEDS ME! WE ALL HAVE A PATRIOTIC DUTY!
PATRIOTISM-BULLSHIT! IT'S A RACIAL WAR... THEY ASKIN' US TO GO KILL VIETS FOR A SOCIETY THAT'S DOIN' NOTHIN' FOR MY PEOPLE BACK HERE... THAT IS WHAT IT'S ALL ABOUT!

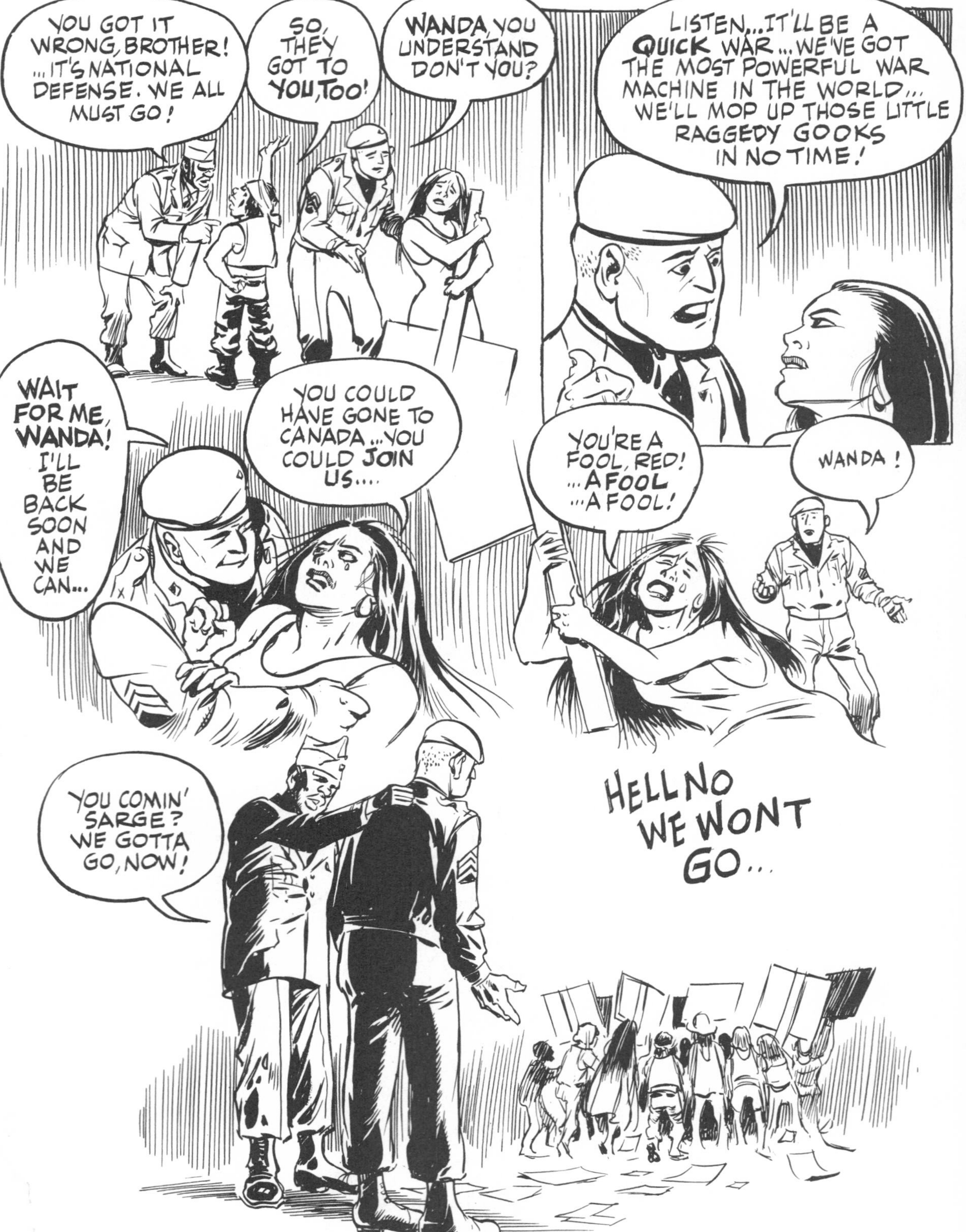
YOU GOT IT WRONG, BROTHER! ...IT'S NATIONAL DEFENSE. WE ALL MUST GO!
SO, THEY GOT TO YOU, TOO!
WANDA, YOU UNDERSTAND DON'T YOU?
LISTEN,..IT'LL BE A QUICK WAR...WE'VE GOT THE MOST POWERFUL WAR MACHINE IN THE WORLD... WE'LL MOP UP THOSE LITTLE RAGGEDY GOOKS IN NO TIME!
WAIT FOR ME, WANDA! I'LL BE BACK SOON AND WE CAN...
YOU COULD HAVE GONE TO CANADA...YOU COULD JOIN US....
YOU'RE A FOOL, RED! ...A FOOL ...A FOOL!
WANDA!
YOU COMIN' SARGE? WE GOTTA GO, NOW!
HELL NO WE WONT GO...

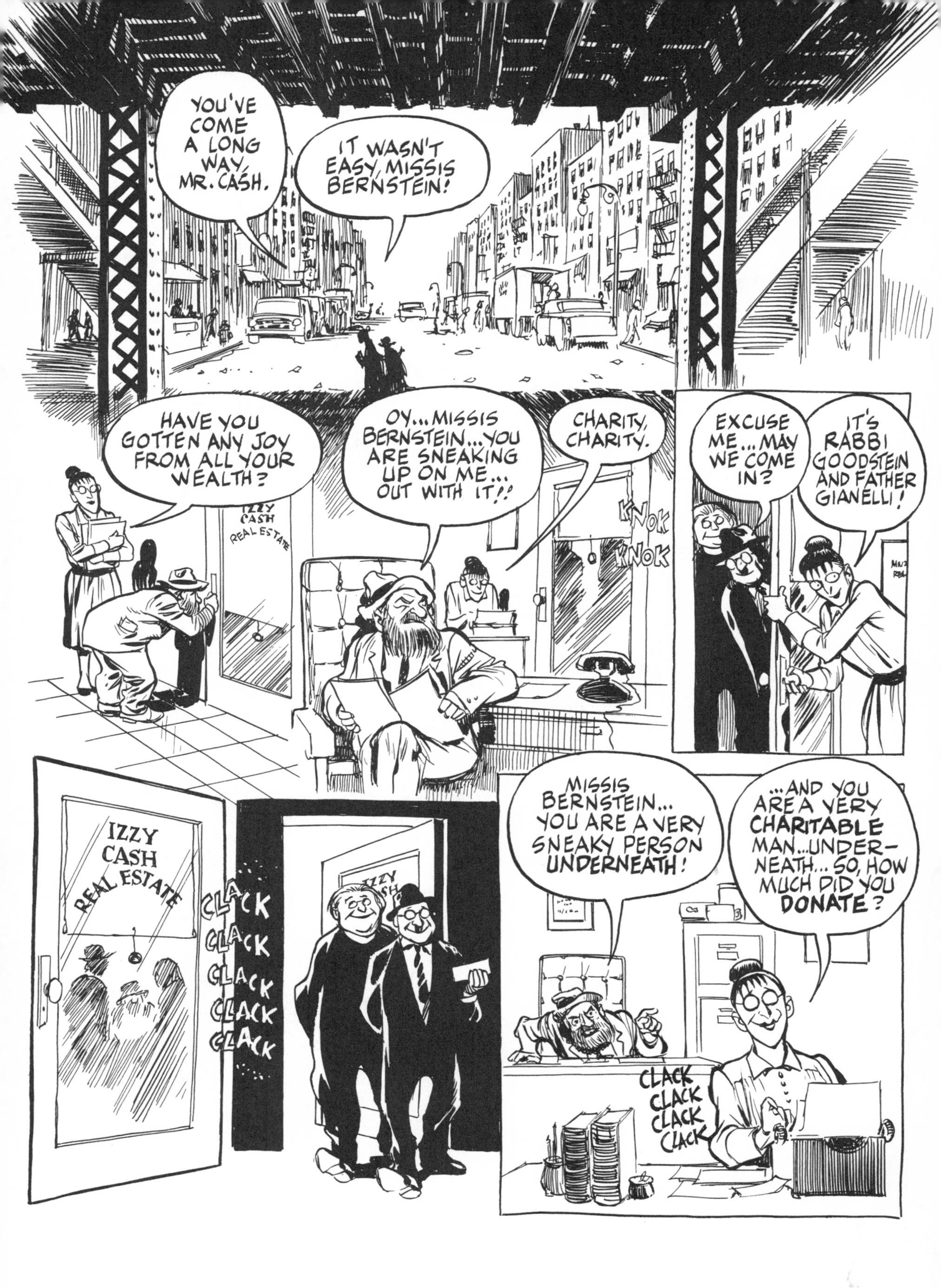

YOU'VE COME A LONG WAY, MR. CASH.
IT WASN'T EASY, MISSIS BERNSTEIN!
HAVE YOU GOTTEN ANY JOY FROM ALL YOUR WEALTH?
IZZY CASH REAL ESTATE
OY... MISSIS BERNSTEIN... YOU ARE SNEAKING UP ON ME... OUT WITH IT!?!
CHARITY, CHARITY.
KNOK KNOK
EXCUSE ME... MAY WE COME IN?
IT'S RABBI GOODSTEIN AND FATHER GIANELLI!
IZZY CASH REAL ESTATE
CLACK CLACK CLACK CLACK CLACK
MISSIS BERNSTEIN... YOU ARE A VERY SNEAKY PERSON UNDERNEATH!
...AND YOU ARE A VERY CHARITABLE MAN... UNDER-NEATH... SO, HOW MUCH DID YOU DONATE?
CLACK CLACK CLACK CLACK

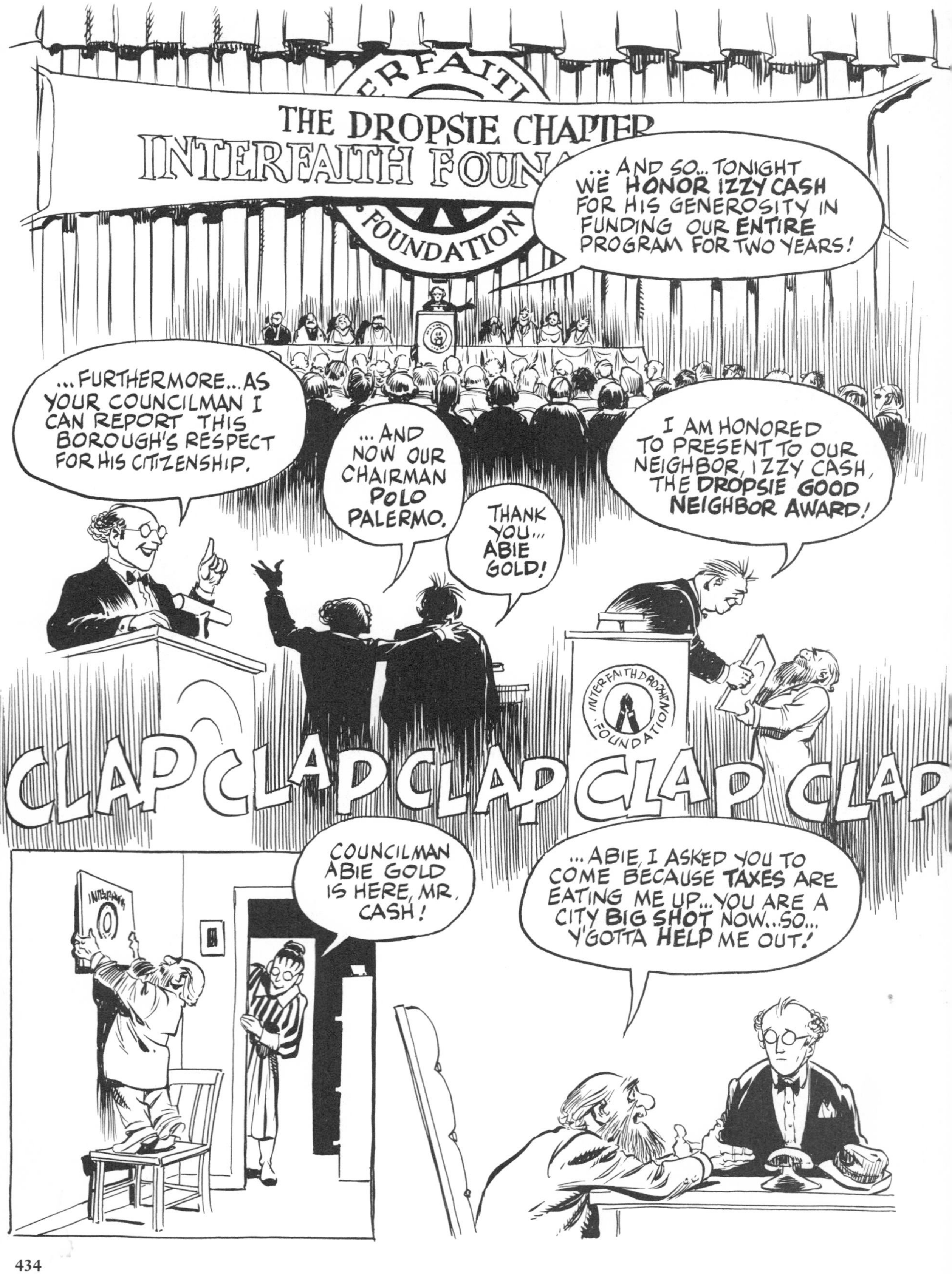
THE DROPSIE CHAPTER
INTERFAITH FOUN
ERFAITH
FOUNDATION
... AND SO... TONIGHT WE HONOR IZZY CASH FOR HIS GENEROSITY IN FUNDING OUR ENTIRE PROGRAM FOR TWO YEARS!
... FURTHERMORE... AS YOUR COUNCILMAN I CAN REPORT THIS BOROUGH'S RESPECT FOR HIS CITIZENSHIP.
... AND NOW OUR CHAIRMAN POLO PALERMO.
THANK YOU... ABIE GOLD!
I AM HONORED TO PRESENT TO OUR NEIGHBOR, IZZY CASH, THE DROPSIE GOOD NEIGHBOR AWARD!
INTERFAITH DROPSIE FOUNDATION
CLAP CLAP CLAP CLAP CLAP CLAP
COUNCILMAN ABIE GOLD IS HERE, MR. CASH!
... ABIE, I ASKED YOU TO COME BECAUSE TAXES ARE EATING ME UP... YOU ARE A CITY BIG SHOT NOW... SO... Y'GOTTA HELP ME OUT!

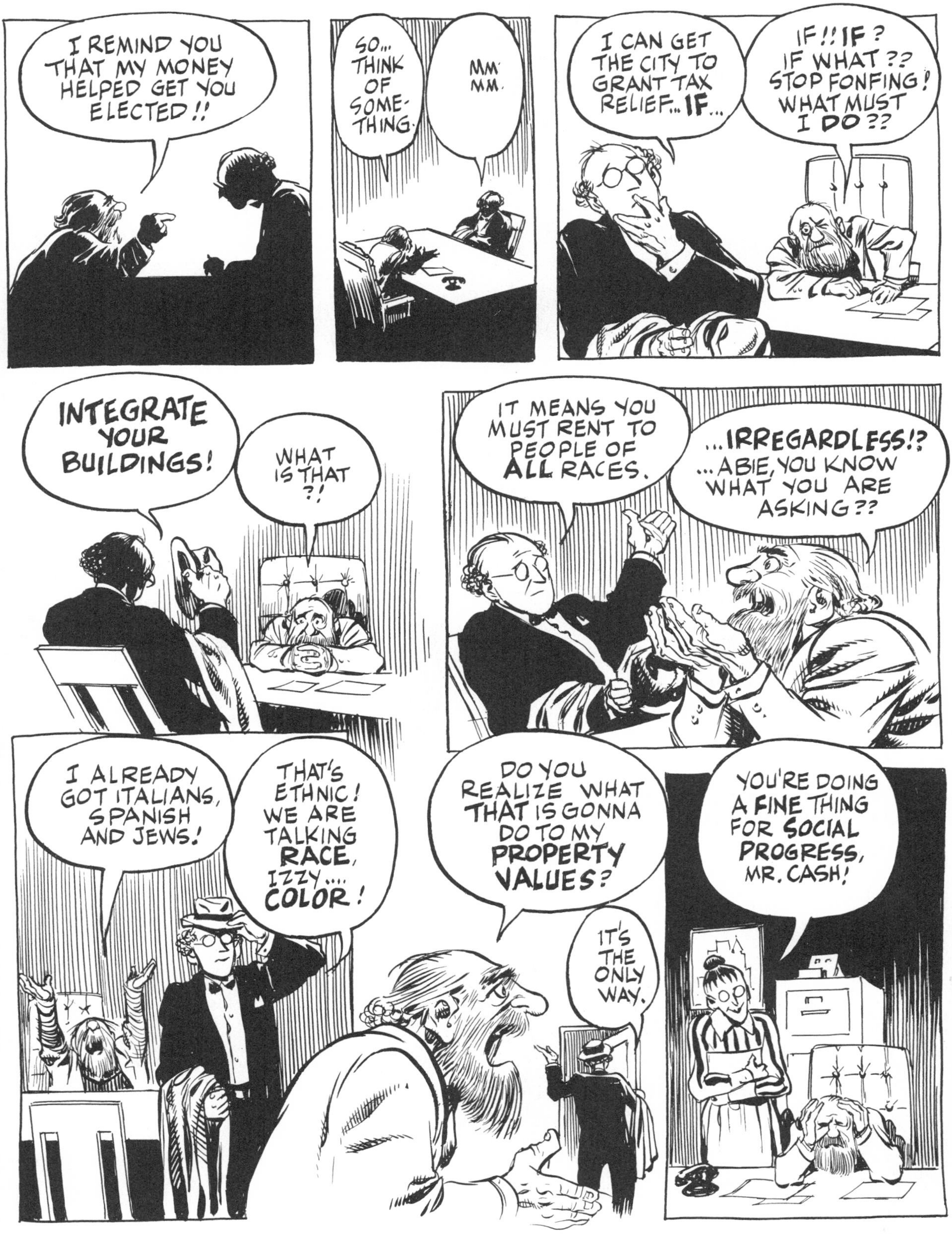
I REMIND YOU THAT MY MONEY HELPED GET YOU ELECTED!!
SO... THINK OF SOME-THING.
MM MM.
I CAN GET THE CITY TO GRANT TAX RELIEF... IF...
IF!! IF? IF WHAT?? STOP FONFING! WHAT MUST I DO??
INTEGRATE YOUR BUILDINGS!
WHAT IS THAT ?!
IT MEANS YOU MUST RENT TO PEOPLE OF ALL RACES.
...IRREGARDLESS!? ...ABIE, YOU KNOW WHAT YOU ARE ASKING??
I ALREADY GOT ITALIANS, SPANISH AND JEWS!
THAT'S ETHNIC! WE ARE TALKING RACE, IZZY.... COLOR!
DO YOU REALIZE WHAT THAT IS GONNA DO TO MY PROPERTY VALUES?
IT'S THE ONLY WAY.
YOU'RE DOING A FINE THING FOR SOCIAL PROGRESS, MR. CASH!

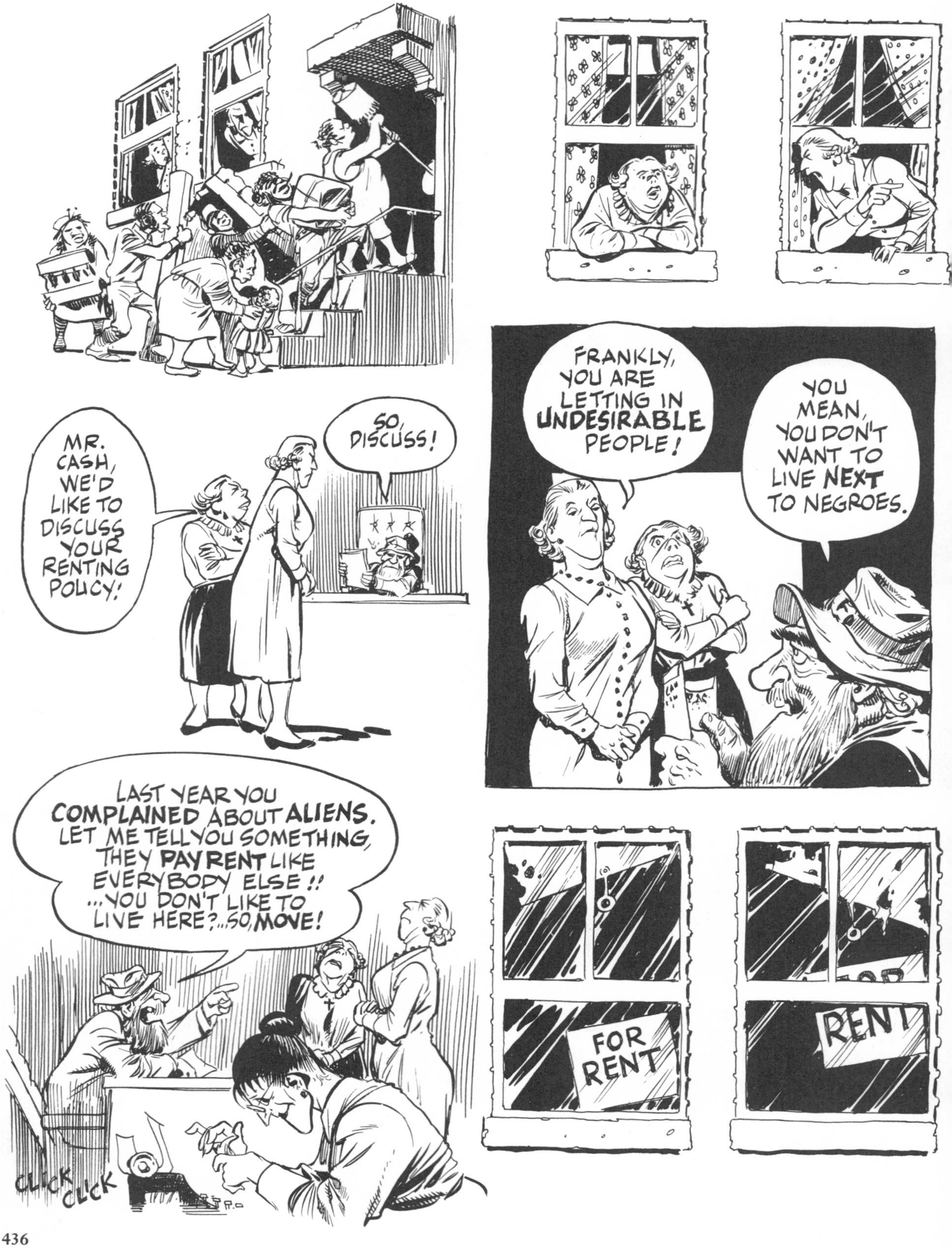
MR. CASH, WE'D LIKE TO DISCUSS YOUR RENTING POLICY!
SO, DISCUSS!
FRANKLY, YOU ARE LETTING IN UNDESIRABLE PEOPLE!
YOU MEAN, YOU DON'T WANT TO LIVE NEXT TO NEGROES.
LAST YEAR YOU COMPLAINED ABOUT ALIENS. LET ME TELL YOU SOMETHING, THEY PAY RENT LIKE EVERYBODY ELSE!! ...YOU DON'T LIKE TO LIVE HERE?...SO, MOVE!
CLICK CLICK
FOR RENT
RENT

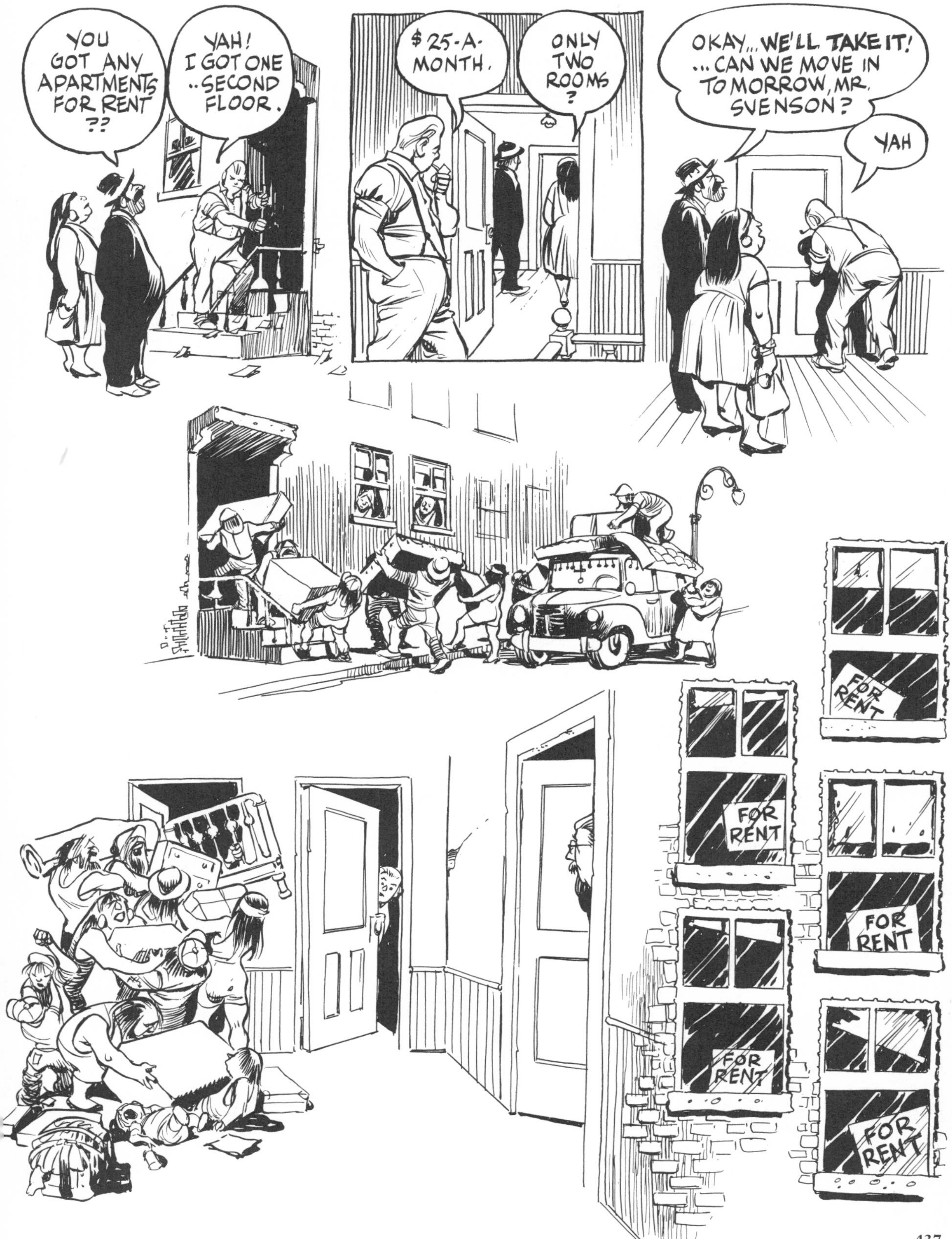
YOU GOT ANY APARTMENTS FOR RENT ??
YAH! I GOT ONE ..SECOND FLOOR.
$25-A-MONTH.
ONLY TWO ROOMS ?
OKAY... WE'LL TAKE IT! ...CAN WE MOVE IN TOMORROW, MR. SVENSON?
YAH
FOR RENT
FOR RENT
FOR RENT
FOR RENT
FOR RENT

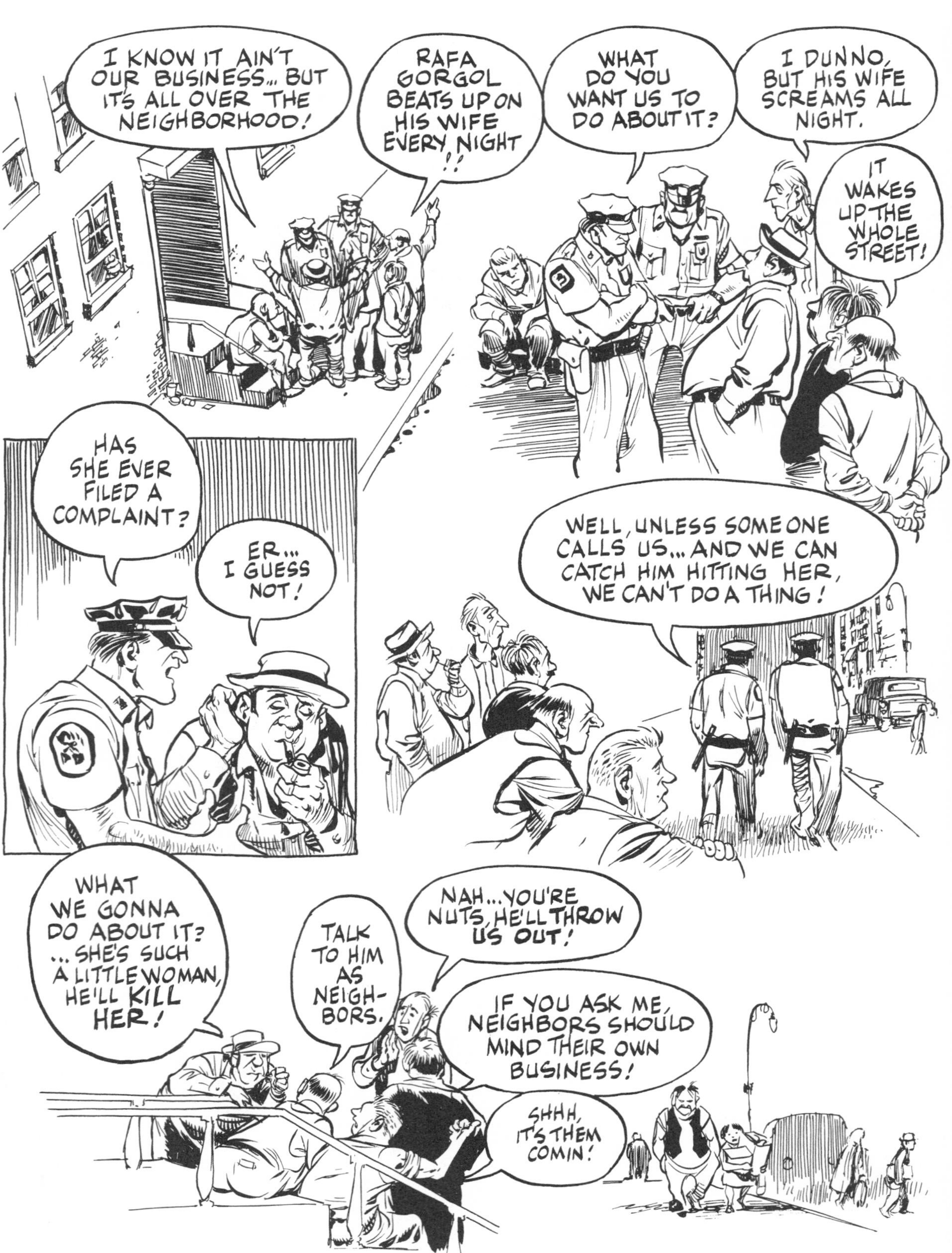
I KNOW IT AIN'T OUR BUSINESS... BUT IT'S ALL OVER THE NEIGHBORHOOD!
RAFA GORGOL BEATS UP ON HIS WIFE EVERY NIGHT!!
WHAT DO YOU WANT US TO DO ABOUT IT?
I DUNNO, BUT HIS WIFE SCREAMS ALL NIGHT.
IT WAKES UP THE WHOLE STREET!
HAS SHE EVER FILED A COMPLAINT?
ER... I GUESS NOT!
WELL, UNLESS SOME ONE CALLS US... AND WE CAN CATCH HIM HITTING HER, WE CAN'T DO A THING!
WHAT WE GONNA DO ABOUT IT? ... SHE'S SUCH A LITTLE WOMAN, HE'LL KILL HER!
TALK TO HIM AS NEIGH-BORS.
NAH... YOU'RE NUTS, HE'LL THROW US OUT!
IF YOU ASK ME, NEIGHBORS SHOULD MIND THEIR OWN BUSINESS!
SHHH, IT'S THEM COMIN!

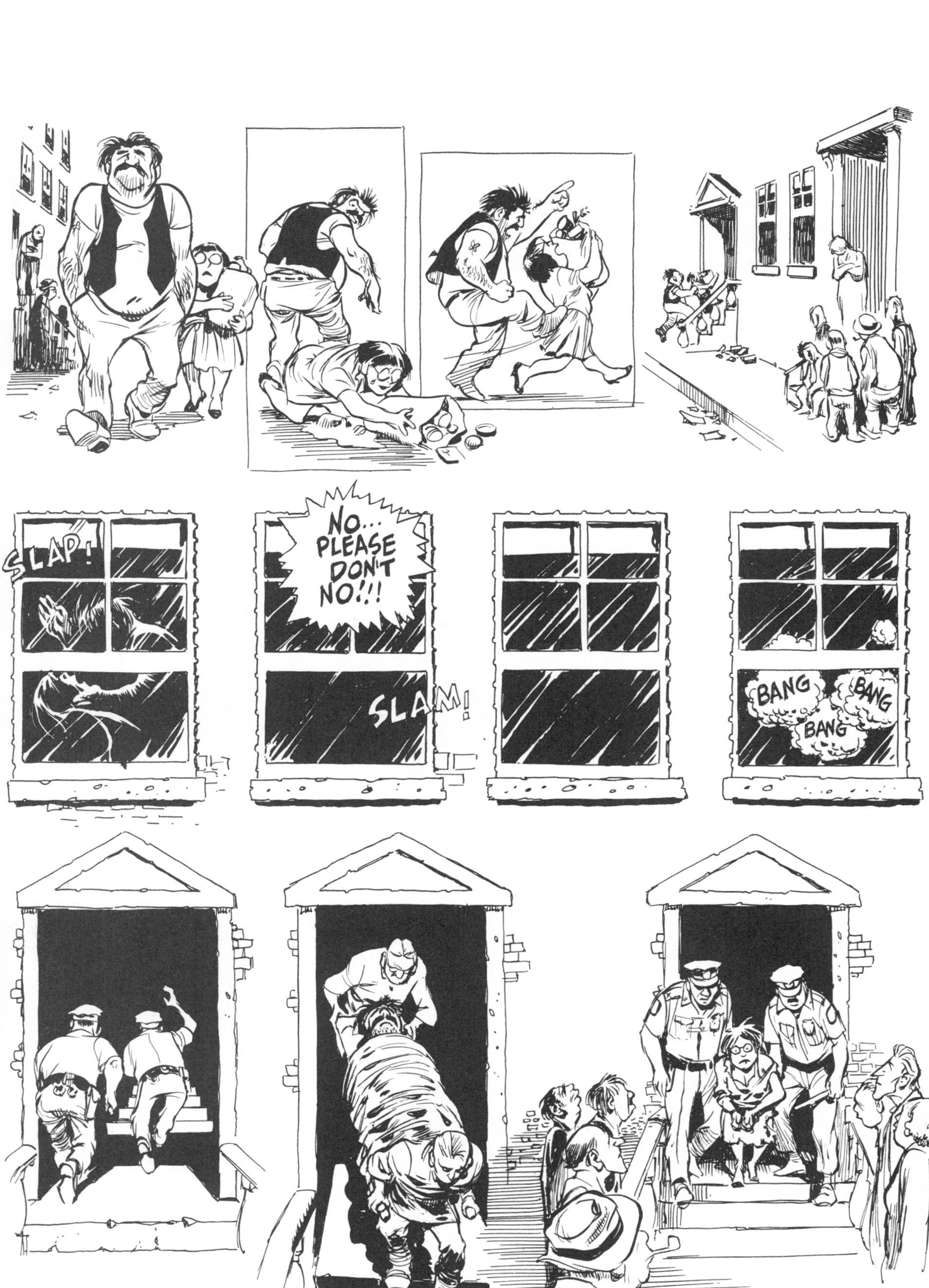

SLAP!
NO... PLEASE DON'T NO!!!
SLAM!
BANG
BANG
BANG

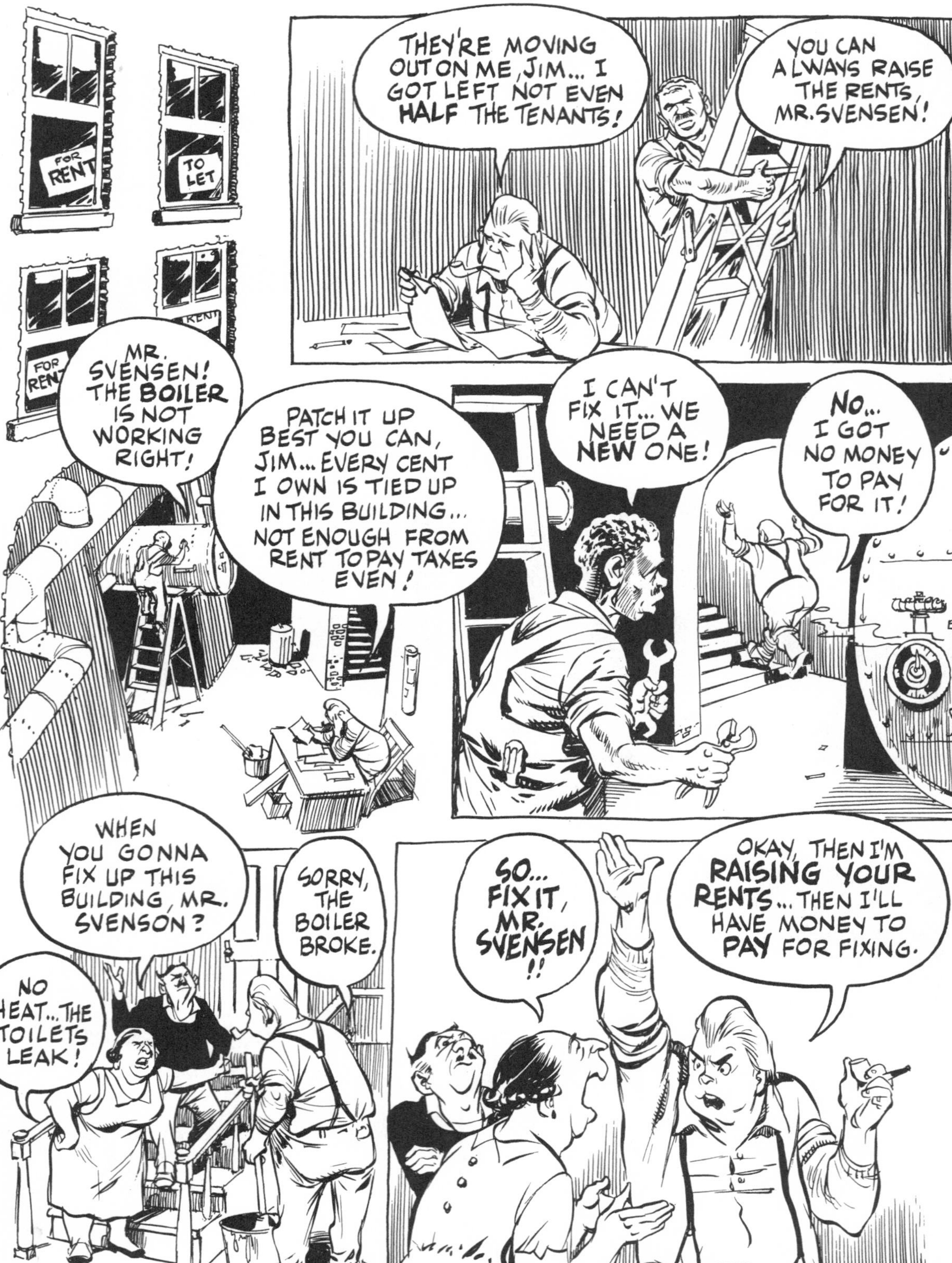
FOR RENT
TO LET
FOR RENT
THEY'RE MOVING OUT ON ME, JIM... I GOT LEFT NOT EVEN HALF THE TENANTS!
YOU CAN ALWAYS RAISE THE RENTS, MR. SVENSEN!
MR. SVENSEN! THE BOILER IS NOT WORKING RIGHT!
PATCH IT UP BEST YOU CAN, JIM... EVERY CENT I OWN IS TIED UP IN THIS BUILDING... NOT ENOUGH FROM RENT TO PAY TAXES EVEN!
I CAN'T FIX IT... WE NEED A NEW ONE!
NO... I GOT NO MONEY TO PAY FOR IT!
WHEN YOU GONNA FIX UP THIS BUILDING, MR. SVENSON?
SORRY, THE BOILER BROKE.
NO HEAT... THE TOILETS LEAK!
SO... FIX IT, MR. SVENSEN!!
OKAY, THEN I'M RAISING YOUR RENTS... THEN I'LL HAVE MONEY TO PAY FOR FIXING.

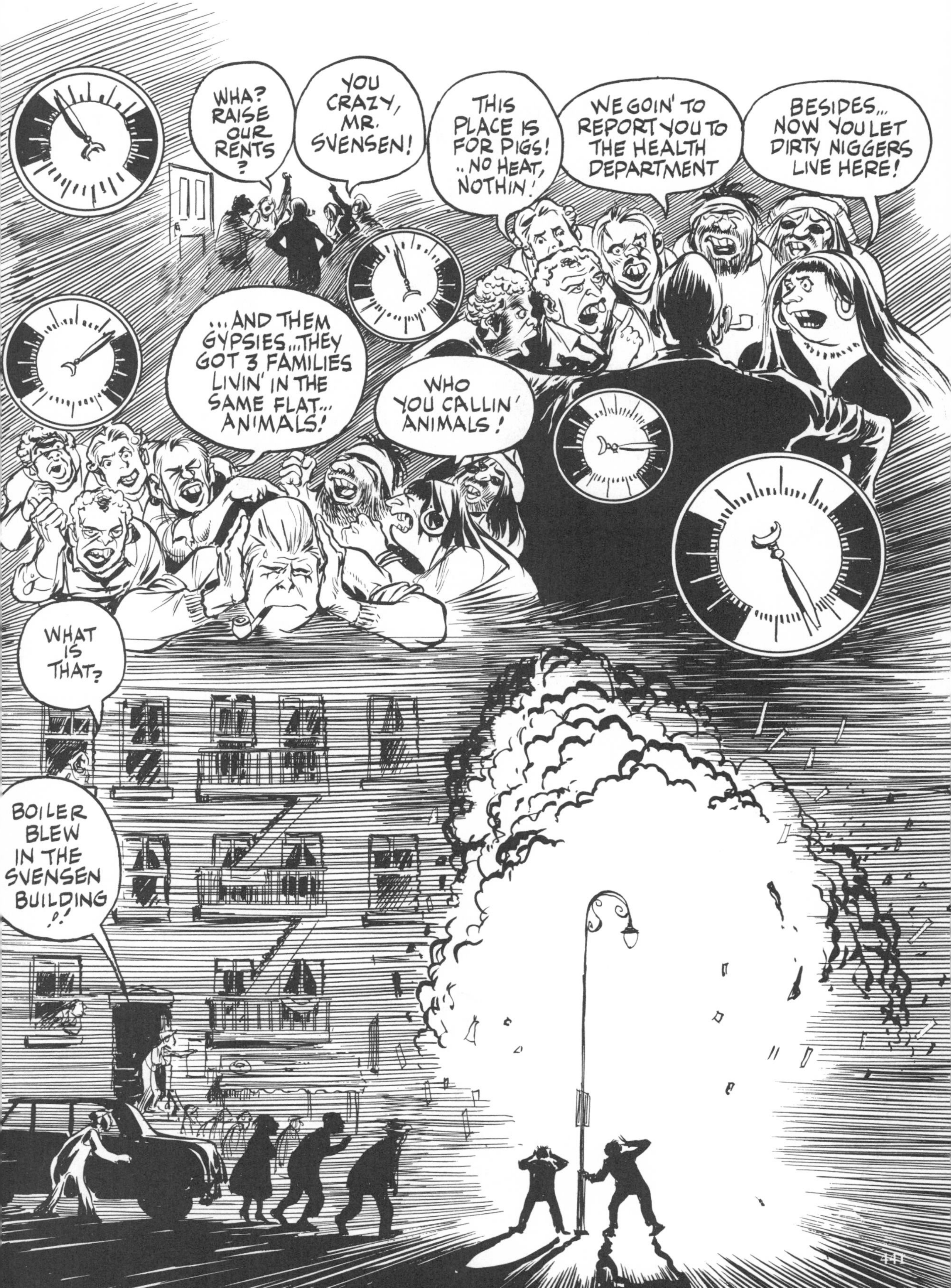
WHA? RAISE OUR RENTS ?
YOU CRAZY, MR. SVENSEN!
THIS PLACE IS FOR PIGS! ..NO HEAT, NOTHIN'!
WE GOIN' TO REPORT YOU TO THE HEALTH DEPARTMENT
BESIDES... NOW YOU LET DIRTY NIGGERS LIVE HERE!
...AND THEM GYPSIES...THEY GOT 3 FAMILIES LIVIN' IN THE SAME FLAT... ANIMALS!
WHO YOU CALLIN' ANIMALS!
WHAT IS THAT?
BOILER BLEW IN THE SVENSEN BUILDING !.!

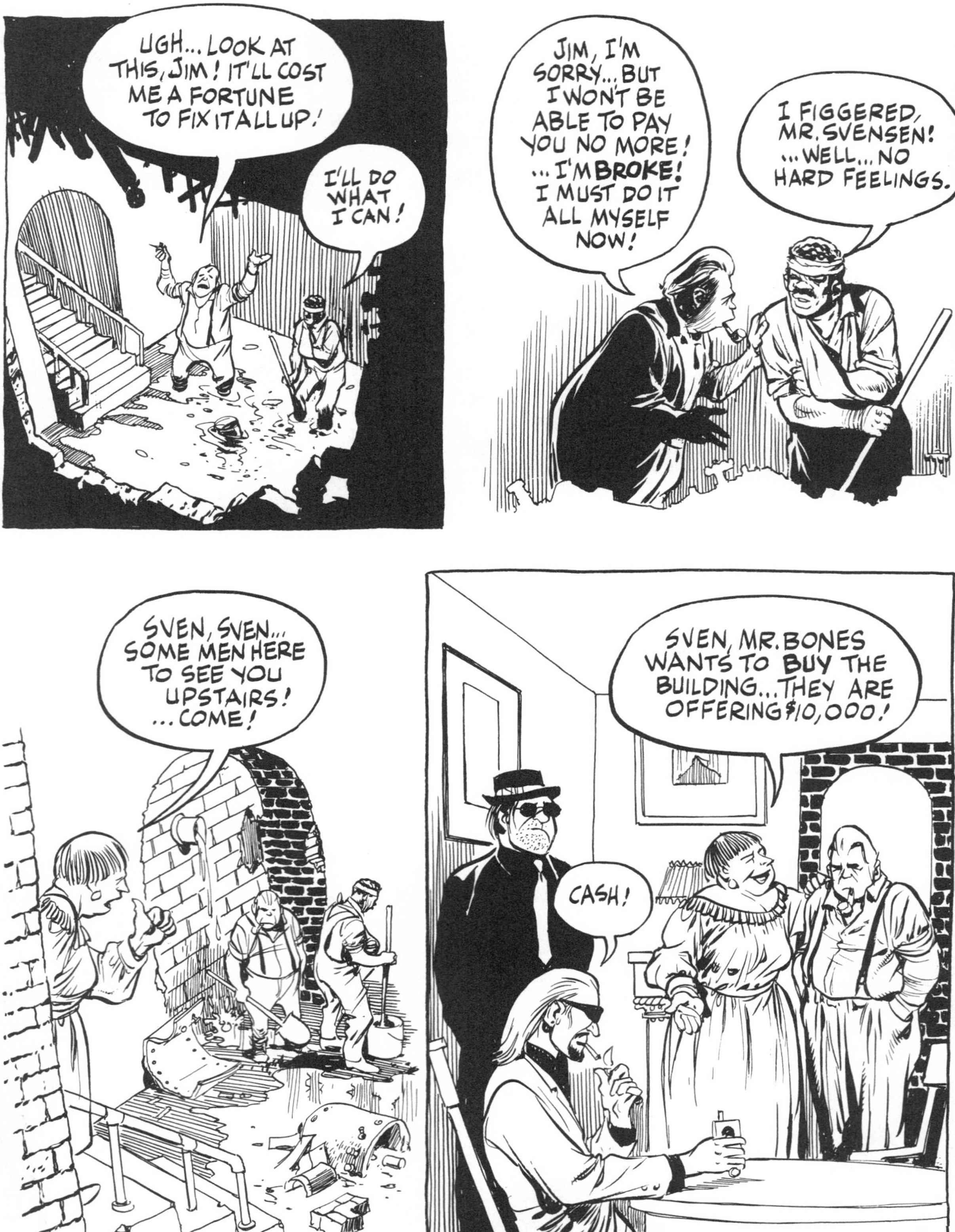
UGH... LOOK AT THIS, JIM! IT'LL COST ME A FORTUNE TO FIX IT ALL UP!
I'LL DO WHAT I CAN!
JIM, I'M SORRY... BUT I WON'T BE ABLE TO PAY YOU NO MORE! ... I'M BROKE! I MUST DO IT ALL MYSELF NOW!
I FIGGERED, MR. SVENSEN! ...WELL... NO HARD FEELINGS.
SVEN, SVEN... SOME MEN HERE TO SEE YOU UPSTAIRS! ...COME!
SVEN, MR. BONES WANTS TO BUY THE BUILDING... THEY ARE OFFERING $10,000!
CASH!

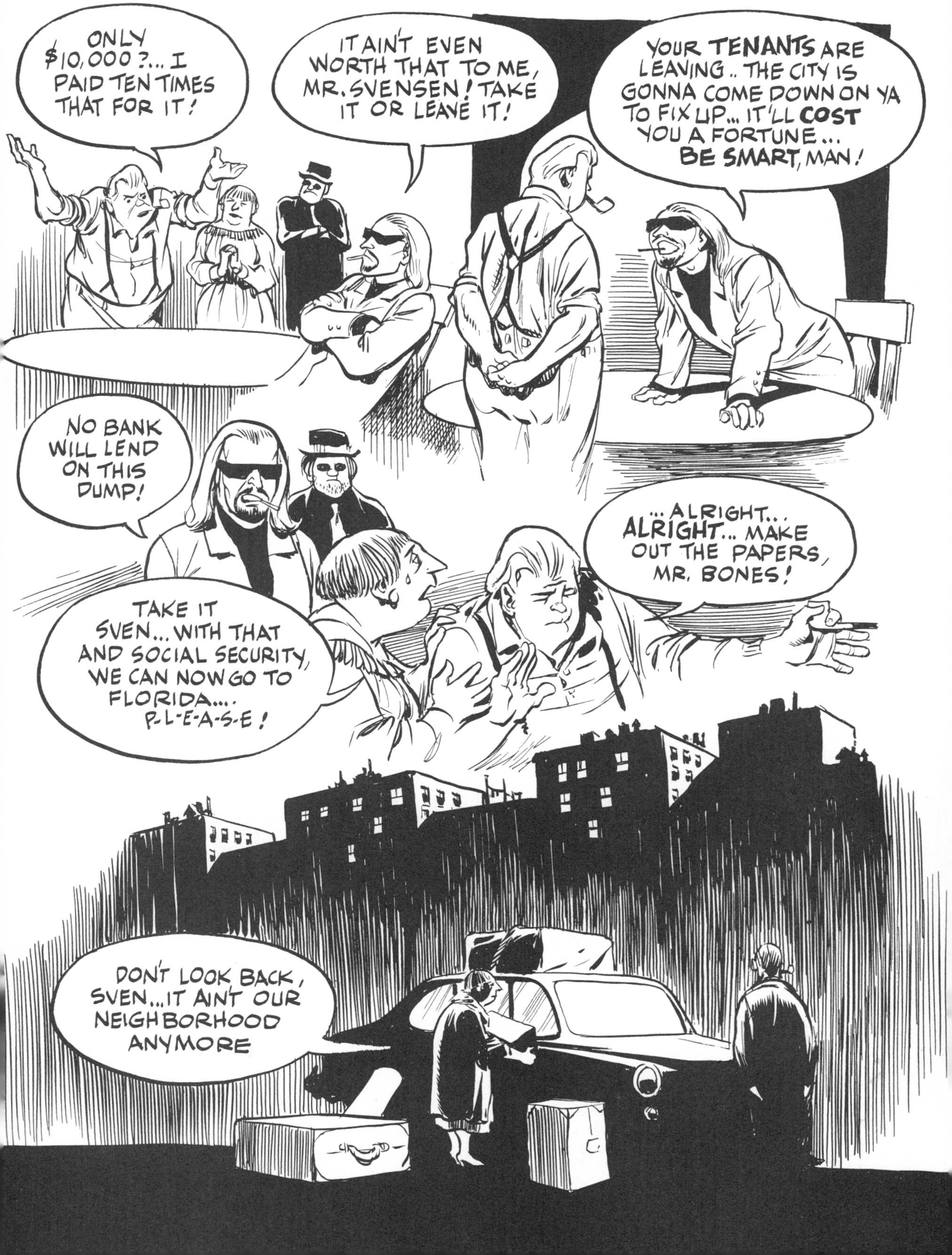
ONLY $10,000 ?... I PAID TEN TIMES THAT FOR IT!
IT AIN'T EVEN WORTH THAT TO ME, MR. SVENSEN! TAKE IT OR LEAVE IT!
YOUR TENANTS ARE LEAVING.. THE CITY IS GONNA COME DOWN ON YA TO FIX UP... IT'LL COST YOU A FORTUNE... BE SMART, MAN!
NO BANK WILL LEND ON THIS DUMP!
...ALRIGHT... ALRIGHT... MAKE OUT THE PAPERS, MR. BONES!
TAKE IT SVEN... WITH THAT AND SOCIAL SECURITY, WE CAN NOW GO TO FLORIDA.... P-L-E-A-S-E!
DON'T LOOK BACK, SVEN... IT AIN'T OUR NEIGHBORHOOD ANYMORE

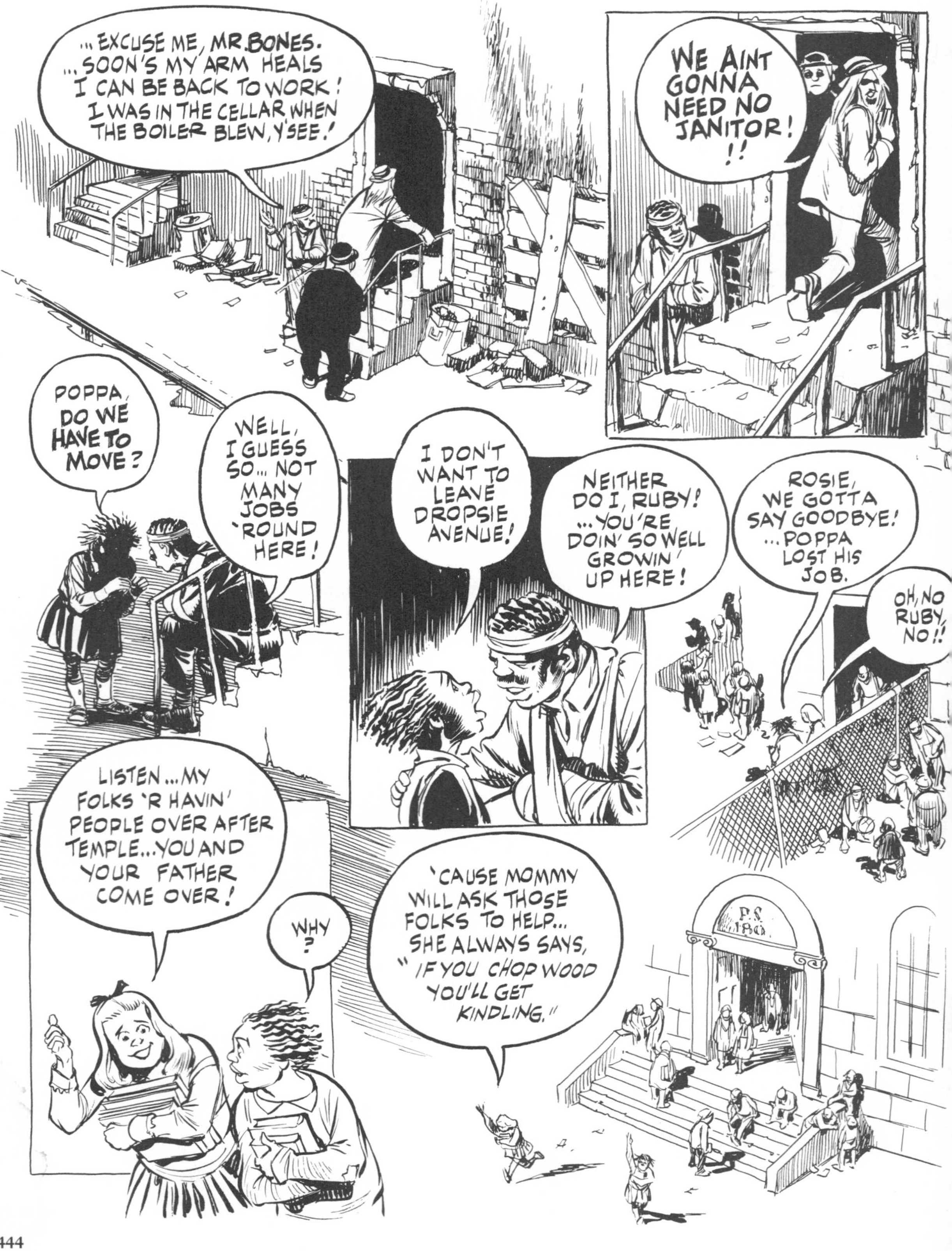
...EXCUSE ME, MR. BONES. ...SOON'S MY ARM HEALS I CAN BE BACK TO WORK! I WAS IN THE CELLAR WHEN THE BOILER BLEW, Y'SEE!
WE AINT GONNA NEED NO JANITOR!!!
POPPA, DO WE HAVE TO MOVE?
WELL, I GUESS SO... NOT MANY JOBS 'ROUND HERE!
I DON'T WANT TO LEAVE DROPSIE AVENUE!
NEITHER DO I, RUBY! ...YOU'RE DOIN' SO WELL GROWIN' UP HERE!
ROSIE, WE GOTTA SAY GOODBYE! ...POPPA LOST HIS JOB.
OH, NO RUBY, NO!!
LISTEN... MY FOLKS 'R HAVIN' PEOPLE OVER AFTER TEMPLE... YOU AND YOUR FATHER COME OVER!
WHY?
'CAUSE MOMMY WILL ASK THOSE FOLKS TO HELP... SHE ALWAYS SAYS, "IF YOU CHOP WOOD YOU'LL GET KINDLING."

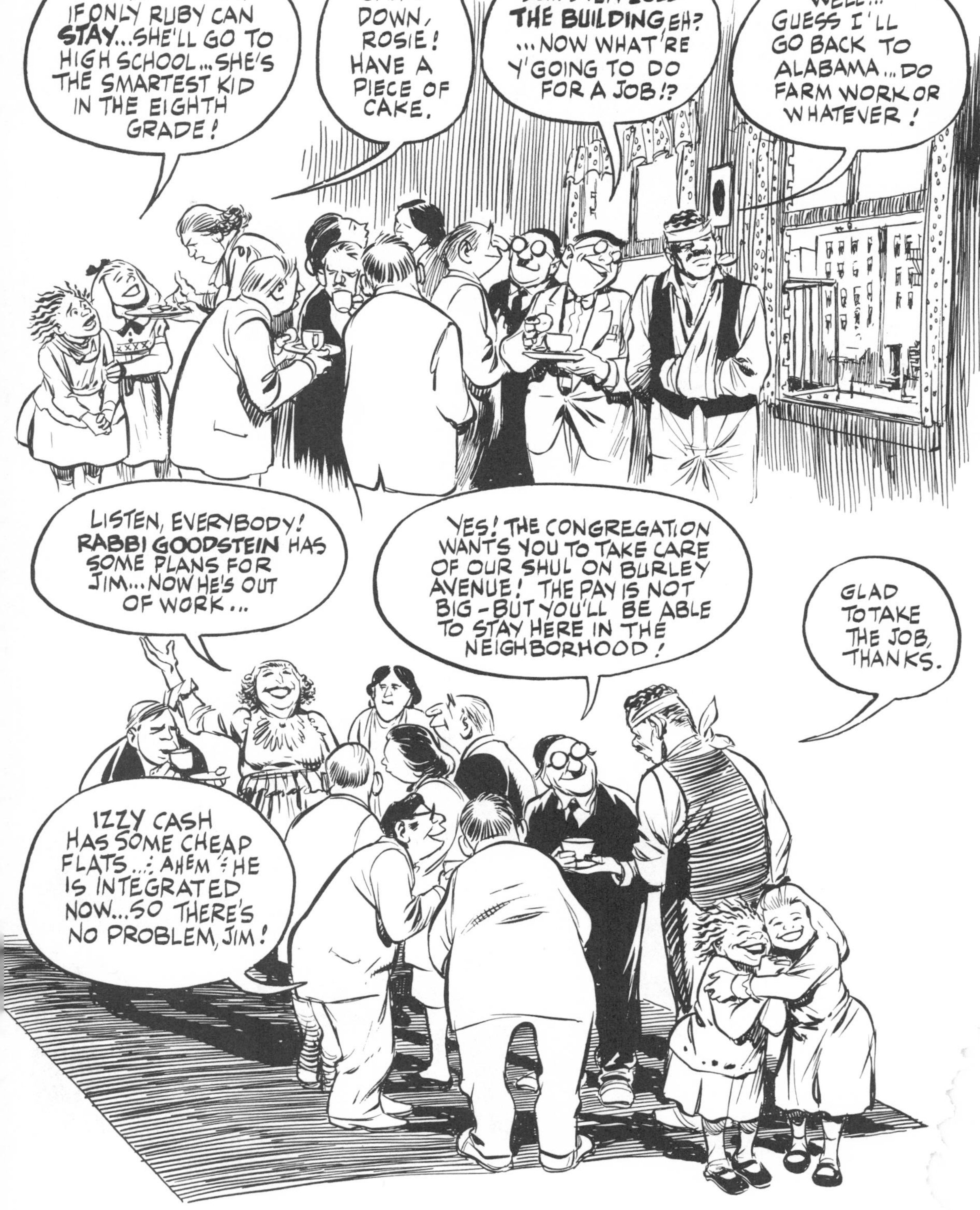
OH, MOMMA, IF ONLY RUBY CAN STAY...SHE'LL GO TO HIGH SCHOOL...SHE'S THE SMARTEST KID IN THE EIGHTH GRADE!
CALM DOWN, ROSIE! HAVE A PIECE OF CAKE.
SO...SVEN SOLD THE BUILDING, EH? ...NOW WHAT'RE Y'GOING TO DO FOR A JOB!?
WELL... GUESS I'LL GO BACK TO ALABAMA...DO FARM WORK OR WHATEVER!
LISTEN, EVERYBODY! RABBI GOODSTEIN HAS SOME PLANS FOR JIM...NOW HE'S OUT OF WORK...
YES! THE CONGREGATION WANTS YOU TO TAKE CARE OF OUR SHUL ON BURLEY AVENUE! THE PAY IS NOT BIG-BUT YOU'LL BE ABLE TO STAY HERE IN THE NEIGHBORHOOD!
GLAD TO TAKE THE JOB, THANKS.
IZZY CASH HAS SOME CHEAP FLATS...: AHEM : HE IS INTEGRATED NOW...SO THERE'S NO PROBLEM, JIM!

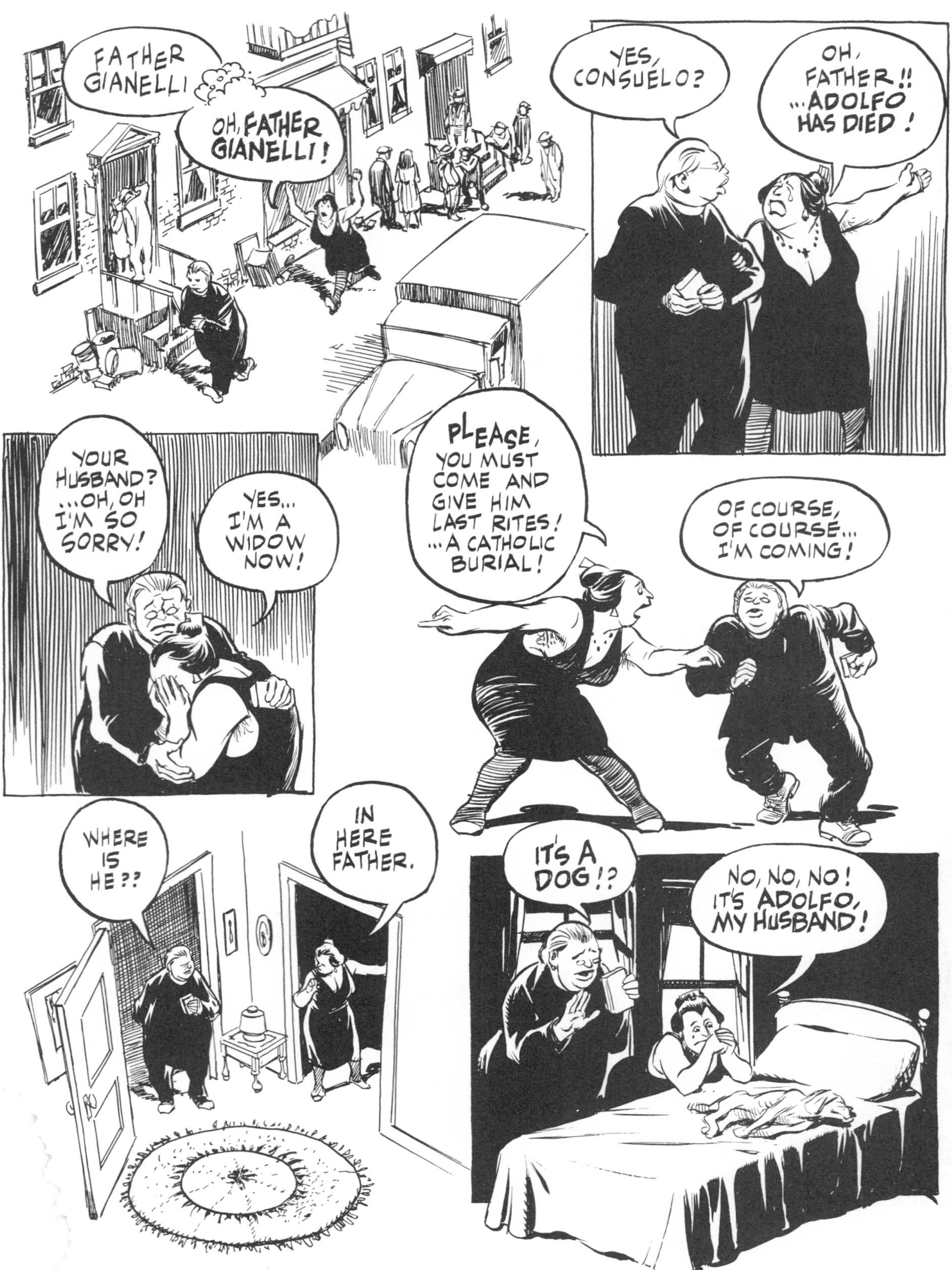
FATHER GIANELLI
OH, FATHER GIANELLI!
YES, CONSUELO?
OH, FATHER!! ...ADOLFO HAS DIED!
YOUR HUSBAND? ...OH, OH I'M SO SORRY!
YES... I'M A WIDOW NOW!
PLEASE, YOU MUST COME AND GIVE HIM LAST RITES! ...A CATHOLIC BURIAL!
OF COURSE, OF COURSE... I'M COMING!
WHERE IS HE??
IN HERE FATHER.
IT'S A DOG!?
NO, NO, NO! IT'S ADOLFO, MY HUSBAND!

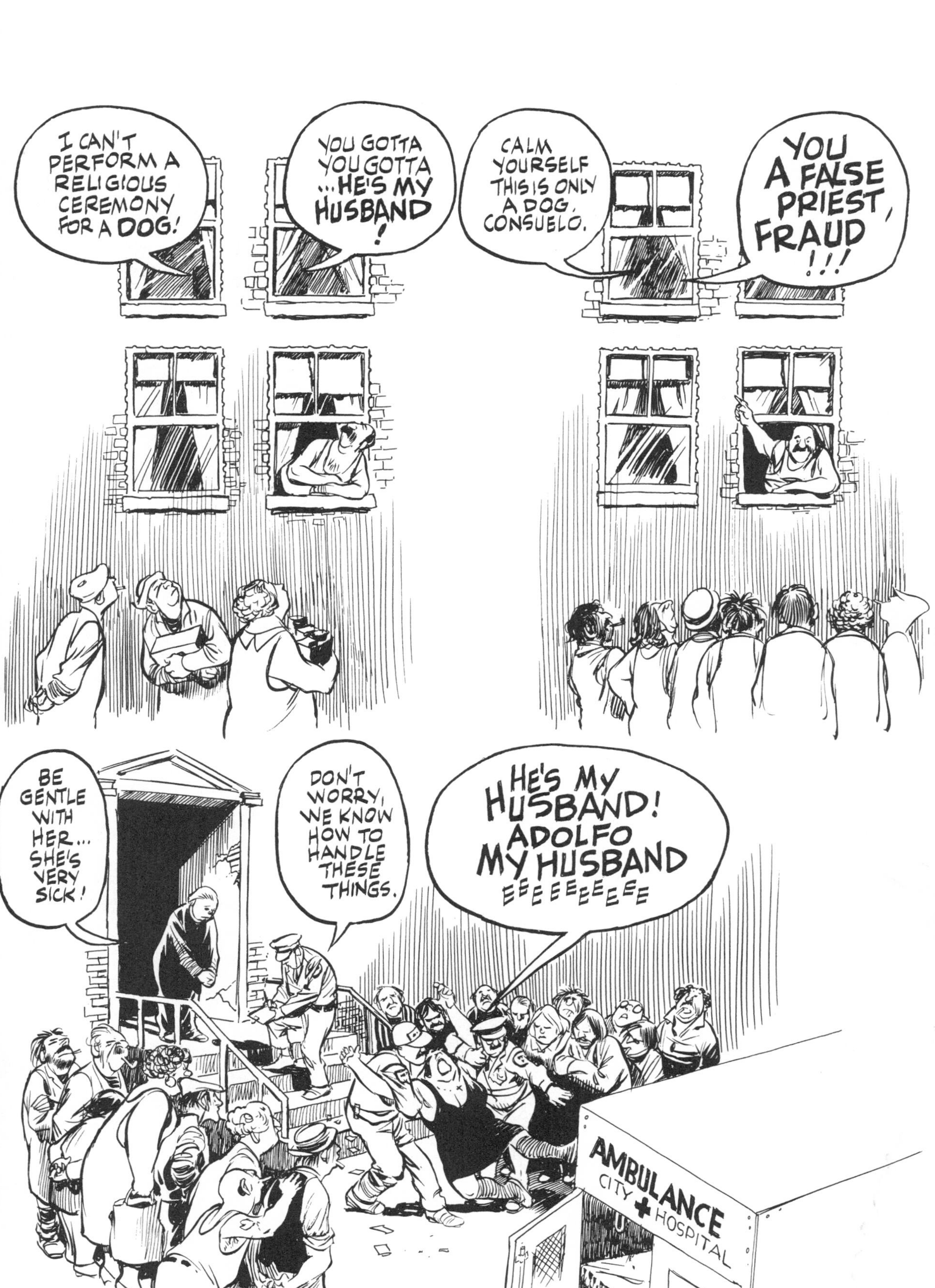
I CAN'T PERFORM A RELIGIOUS CEREMONY FOR A DOG!
YOU GOTTA YOU GOTTA ...HE'S MY HUSBAND!
CALM YOURSELF THIS IS ONLY A DOG, CONSUELO.
YOU A FALSE PRIEST, FRAUD!!!
BE GENTLE WITH HER... SHE'S VERY SICK!
DON'T WORRY, WE KNOW HOW TO HANDLE THESE THINGS.
HE'S MY HUSBAND! ADOLFO MY HUSBAND EEEEEEEEE
AMBULANCE
CITY HOSPITAL

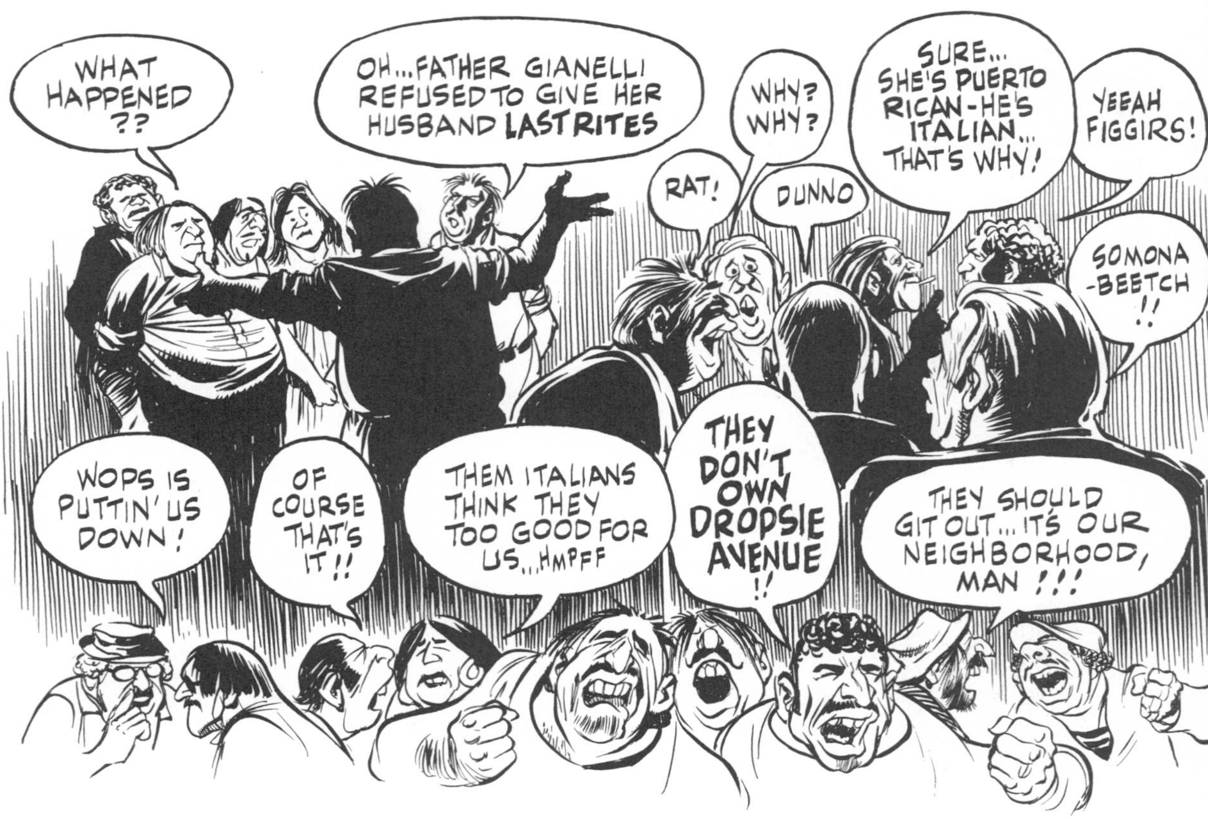
WHAT HAPPENED ??
OH...FATHER GIANELLI REFUSED TO GIVE HER HUSBAND LAST RITES
RAT!
WHY? WHY?
DUNNO
SURE... SHE'S PUERTO RICAN-HE'S ITALIAN... THAT'S WHY!
YEEAH FIGGIRS!
SOMONA-BEETCH !!
WOPS IS PUTTIN' US DOWN!
OF COURSE THAT'S IT!!
THEM ITALIANS THINK THEY TOO GOOD FOR US...HMPFF
THEY DON'T OWN DROPSIE AVENUE !!
THEY SHOULD GIT OUT...IT'S OUR NEIGHBORHOOD, MAN!!!

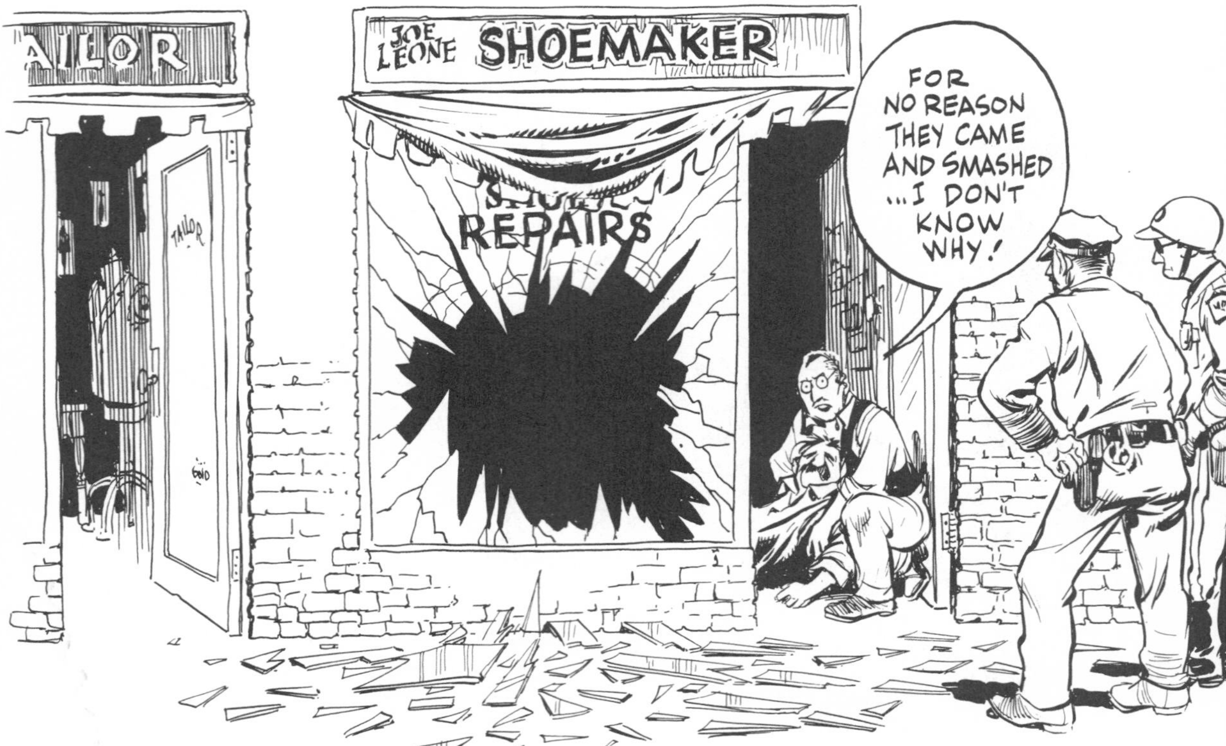
JOE LEONE SHOEMAKER
REPAIRS
FOR NO REASON THEY CAME AND SMASHED ...I DON'T KNOW WHY!

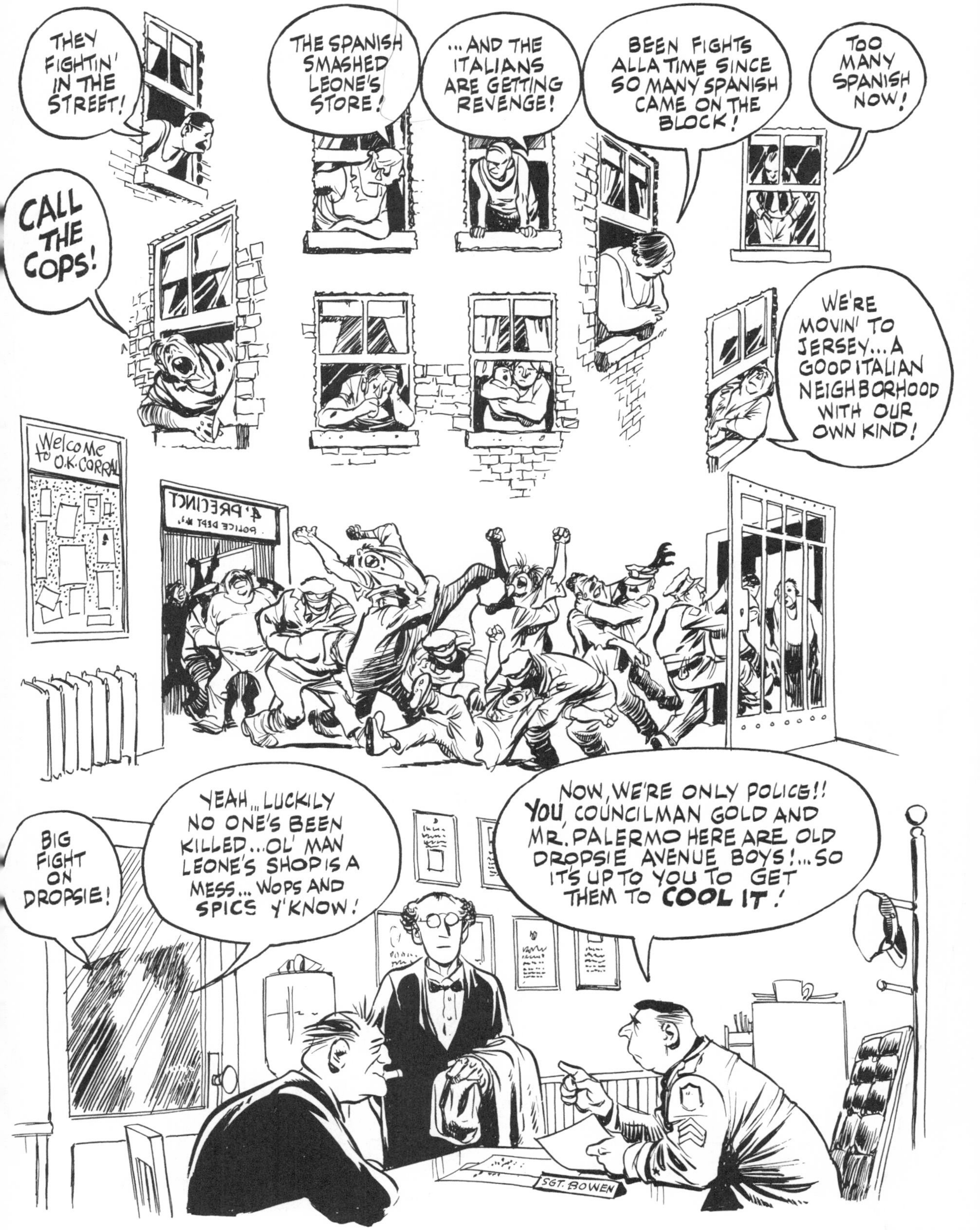

THEY FIGHTIN' IN THE STREET!
THE SPANISH SMASHED LEONE'S STORE!
...AND THE ITALIANS ARE GETTING REVENGE!
BEEN FIGHTS ALLA TIME SINCE SO MANY SPANISH CAME ON THE BLOCK!
TOO MANY SPANISH NOW!
CALL THE COPS!
WE'RE MOVIN' TO JERSEY... A GOOD ITALIAN NEIGHBORHOOD WITH OUR OWN KIND!
Welcome to O.K. CORRAL
BIG FIGHT ON DROPSIE!
YEAH... LUCKILY NO ONE'S BEEN KILLED...OL' MAN LEONE'S SHOP IS A MESS... WOPS AND SPICS Y'KNOW!
NOW, WE'RE ONLY POLICE!! YOU, COUNCILMAN GOLD AND MR. PALERMO HERE ARE OLD DROPSIE AVENUE BOYS!...SO IT'S UP TO YOU TO GET THEM TO COOL IT!
SGT. BOWEN

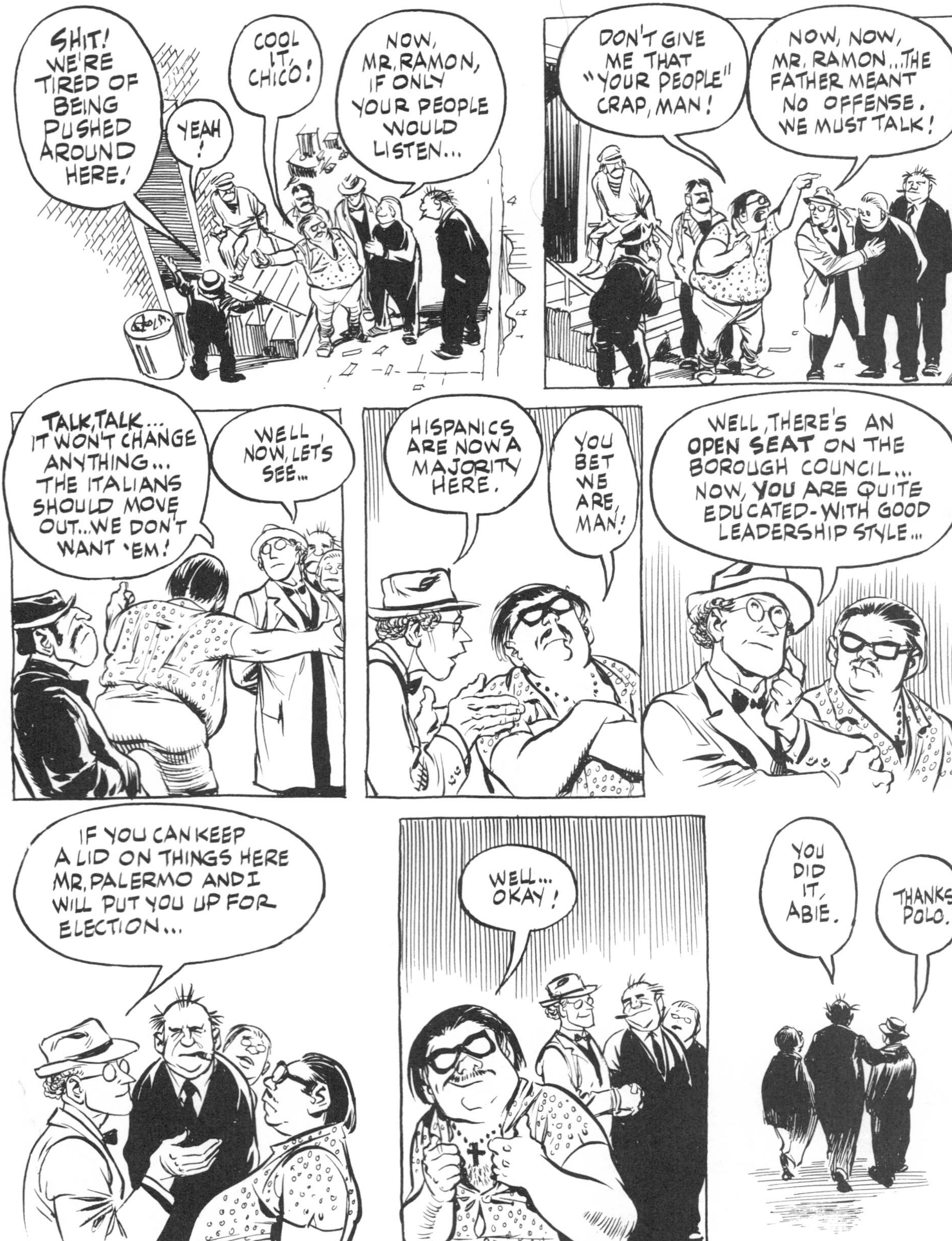
SHIT! WE'RE TIRED OF BEING PUSHED AROUND HERE!
YEAH!
COOL IT, CHICO!
NOW, MR. RAMON, IF ONLY YOUR PEOPLE WOULD LISTEN...
DON'T GIVE ME THAT "YOUR PEOPLE" CRAP, MAN!
NOW, NOW, MR. RAMON...THE FATHER MEANT NO OFFENSE. WE MUST TALK!
TALK, TALK... IT WON'T CHANGE ANYTHING... THE ITALIANS SHOULD MOVE OUT...WE DON'T WANT 'EM!
WELL NOW, LET'S SEE...
HISPANICS ARE NOW A MAJORITY HERE.
YOU BET WE ARE, MAN!
WELL, THERE'S AN OPEN SEAT ON THE BOROUGH COUNCIL... NOW, YOU ARE QUITE EDUCATED-WITH GOOD LEADERSHIP STYLE...
IF YOU CAN KEEP A LID ON THINGS HERE MR. PALERMO AND I WILL PUT YOU UP FOR ELECTION...
WELL... OKAY!
YOU DID IT, ABIE.
THANKS, POLO.

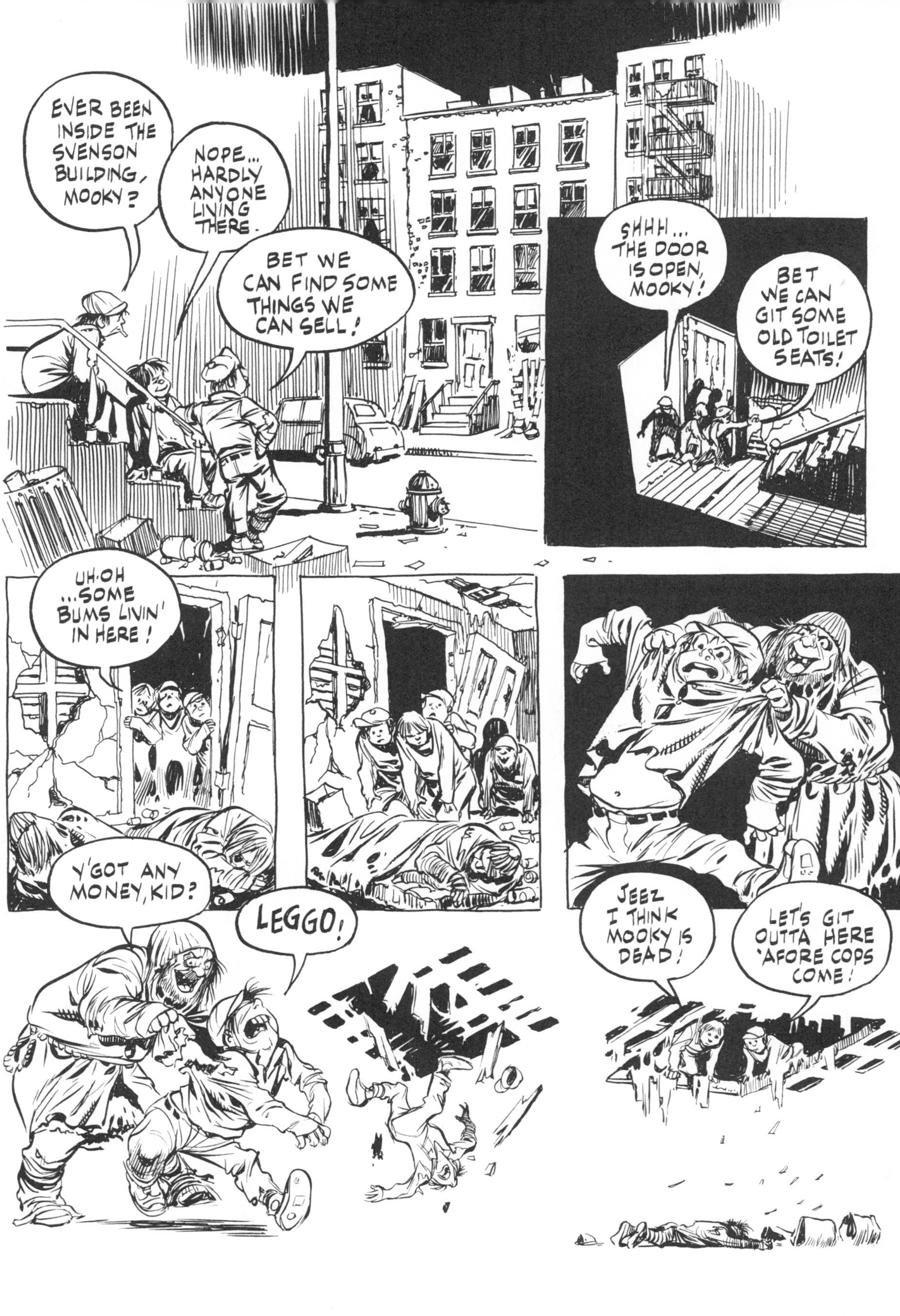
EVER BEEN INSIDE THE SVENSON BUILDING, MOOKY?
NOPE... HARDLY ANYONE LIVING THERE.
BET WE CAN FIND SOME THINGS WE CAN SELL!
SHHH... THE DOOR IS OPEN, MOOKY!
BET WE CAN GIT SOME OLD TOILET SEATS!
UH-OH ...SOME BUMS LIVIN' IN HERE!
Y'GOT ANY MONEY, KID?
LEGGO!
JEEZ I THINK MOOKY IS DEAD!
LET'S GIT OUTTA HERE 'AFORE COPS COME!

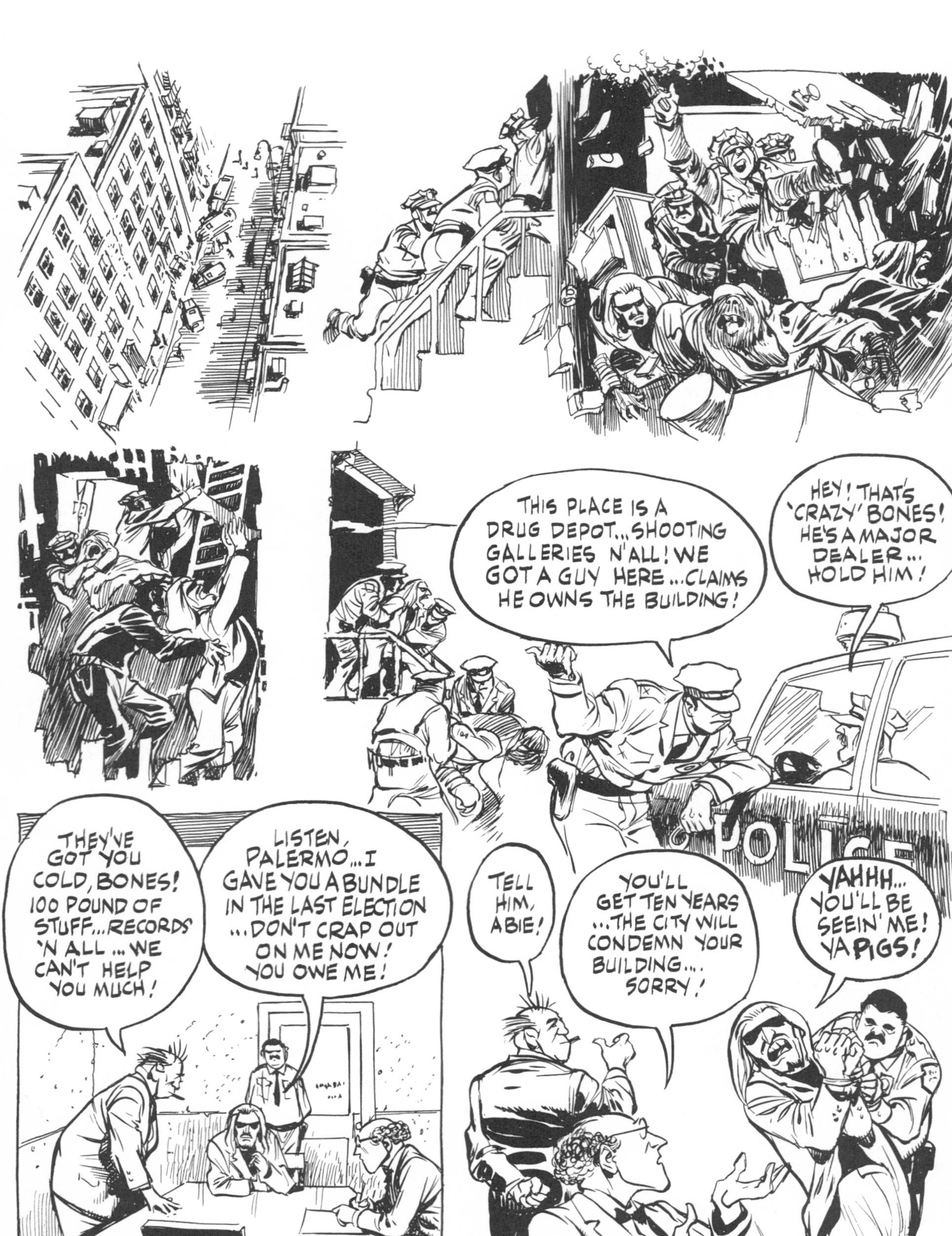
THIS PLACE IS A DRUG DEPOT...SHOOTING GALLERIES N'ALL! WE GOT A GUY HERE...CLAIMS HE OWNS THE BUILDING!
HEY! THAT'S 'CRAZY' BONES! HE'S A MAJOR DEALER... HOLD HIM!
POLICE
THEY'VE GOT YOU COLD, BONES! 100 POUND OF STUFF...RECORDS 'N ALL...WE CAN'T HELP YOU MUCH!
LISTEN, PALERMO...I GAVE YOU A BUNDLE IN THE LAST ELECTION ...DON'T CRAP OUT ON ME NOW! YOU OWE ME!
TELL HIM, ABIE!
YOU'LL GET TEN YEARS ...THE CITY WILL CONDEMN YOUR BUILDING.... SORRY!
YAHHH... YOU'LL BE SEEIN' ME! YA PIGS!

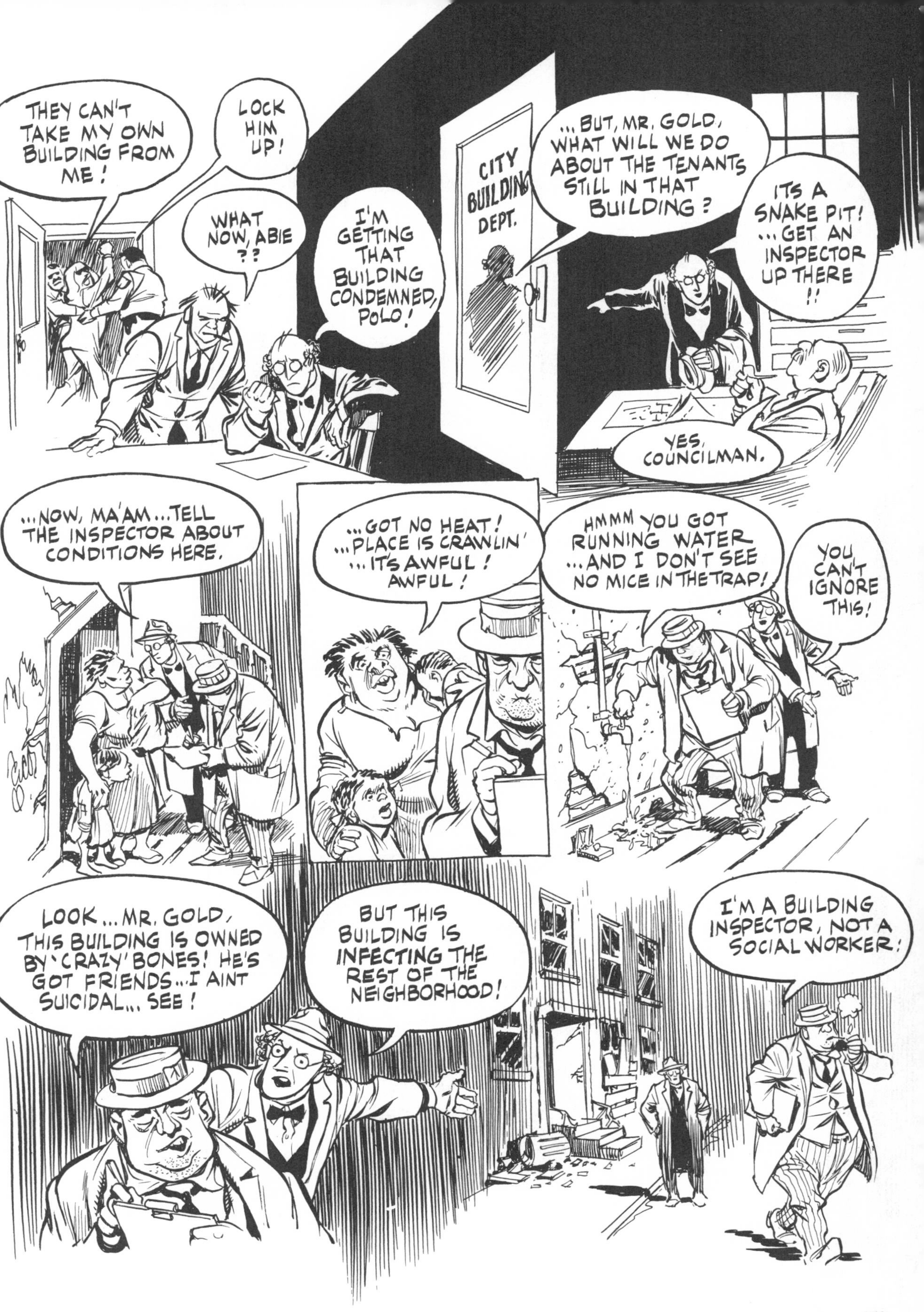
THEY CAN'T TAKE MY OWN BUILDING FROM ME!
LOCK HIM UP!
WHAT NOW, ABIE ??
I'M GETTING THAT BUILDING CONDEMNED, POLO!
CITY BUILDING DEPT.
... BUT, MR. GOLD, WHAT WILL WE DO ABOUT THE TENANTS STILL IN THAT BUILDING?
ITS A SNAKE PIT! ... GET AN INSPECTOR UP THERE !!
YES, COUNCILMAN.
... NOW, MA'AM ... TELL THE INSPECTOR ABOUT CONDITIONS HERE.
... GOT NO HEAT! ... PLACE IS CRAWLIN' ... IT'S AWFUL! AWFUL!
HMMM YOU GOT RUNNING WATER ... AND I DON'T SEE NO MICE IN THE TRAP!
YOU CAN'T IGNORE THIS!
LOOK ... MR. GOLD, THIS BUILDING IS OWNED BY 'CRAZY' BONES! HE'S GOT FRIENDS ... I AINT SUICIDAL ... SEE!
BUT THIS BUILDING IS INFECTING THE REST OF THE NEIGHBORHOOD!
I'M A BUILDING INSPECTOR, NOT A SOCIAL WORKER!

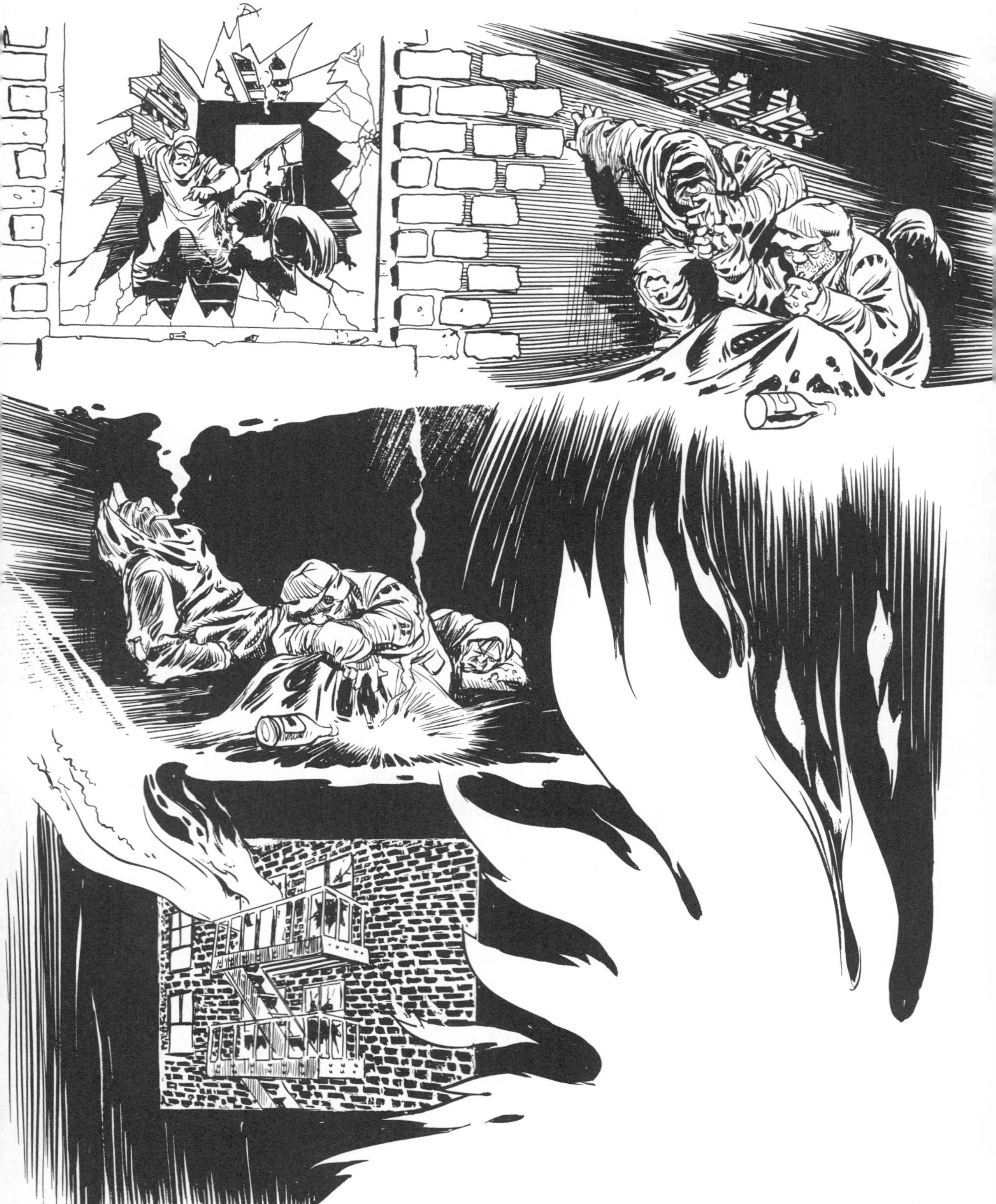

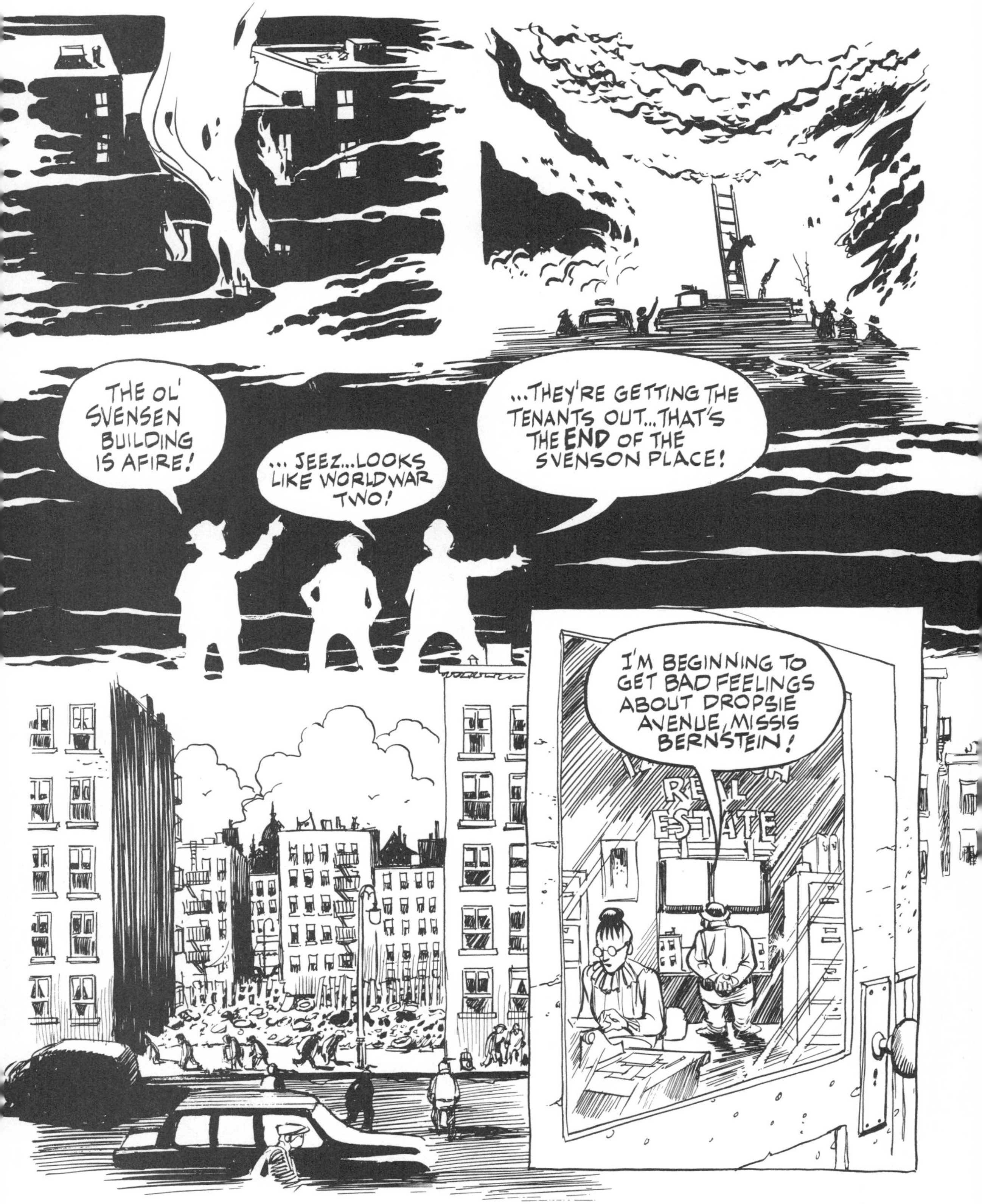
THE OL' SVENSEN BUILDING IS AFIRE!
... JEEZ...LOOKS LIKE WORLDWAR TWO!
...THEY'RE GETTING THE TENANTS OUT...THAT'S THE END OF THE SVENSON PLACE!
I'M BEGINNING TO GET BAD FEELINGS ABOUT DROPSIE AVENUE, MISSIS BERNSTEIN!
REAL ESTATE

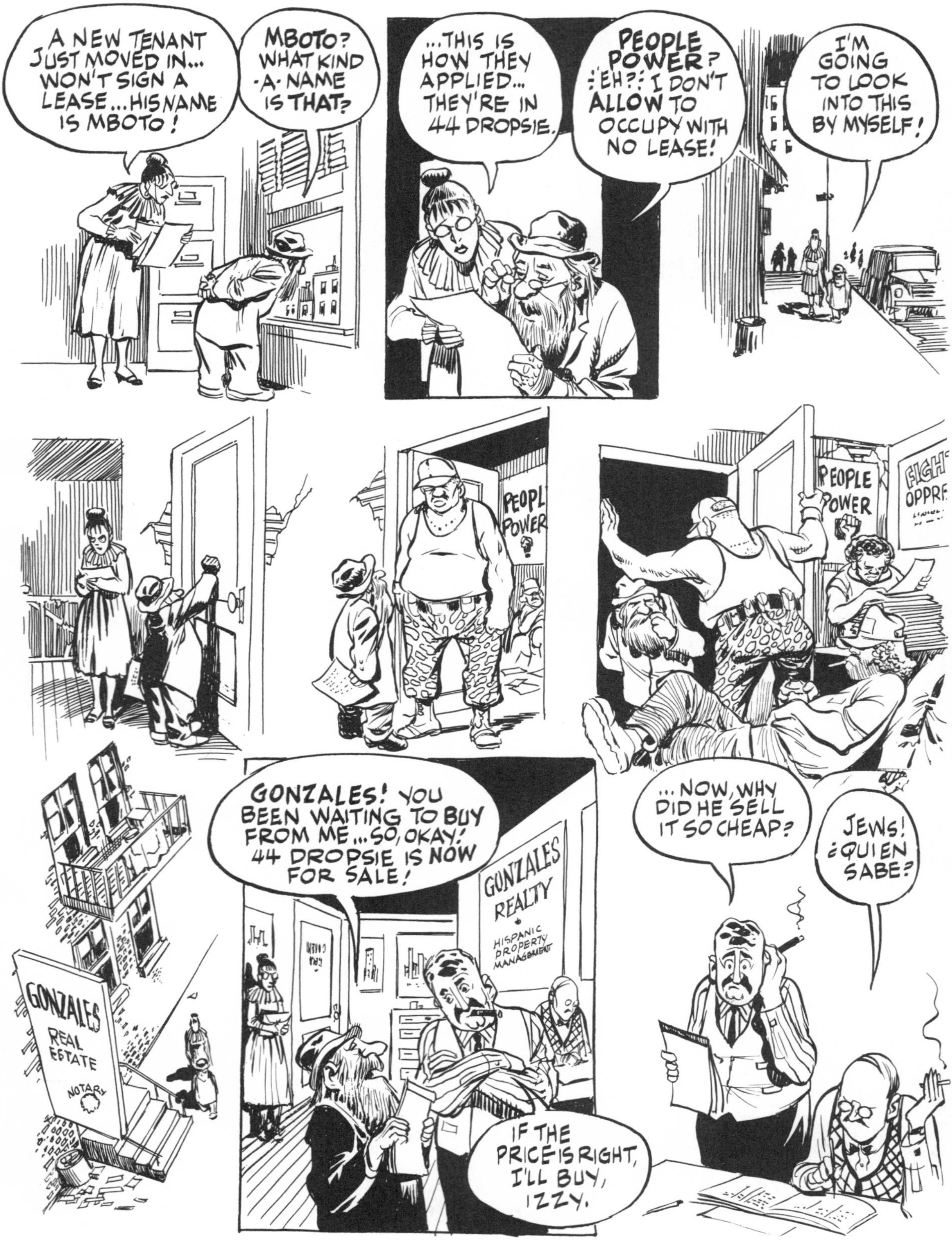
A NEW TENANT JUST MOVED IN... WON'T SIGN A LEASE...HIS NAME IS MBOTO!
MBOTO? WHAT KIND -A- NAME IS THAT?
...THIS IS HOW THEY APPLIED... THEY'RE IN 44 DROPSIE.
PEOPLE POWER? ¿EH?¿ I DON'T ALLOW TO OCCUPY WITH NO LEASE!
I'M GOING TO LOOK INTO THIS BY MYSELF!
PEOPLE POWER
GONZALES REAL ESTATE
NOTARY
GONZALES! YOU BEEN WAITING TO BUY FROM ME...SO, OKAY! 44 DROPSIE IS NOW FOR SALE!
GONZALES REALTY
HISPANIC PROPERTY MANAGEMENT
IF THE PRICE IS RIGHT, I'LL BUY, IZZY.
...NOW, WHY DID HE SELL IT SO CHEAP?
JEWS! ¿QUIEN SABE?

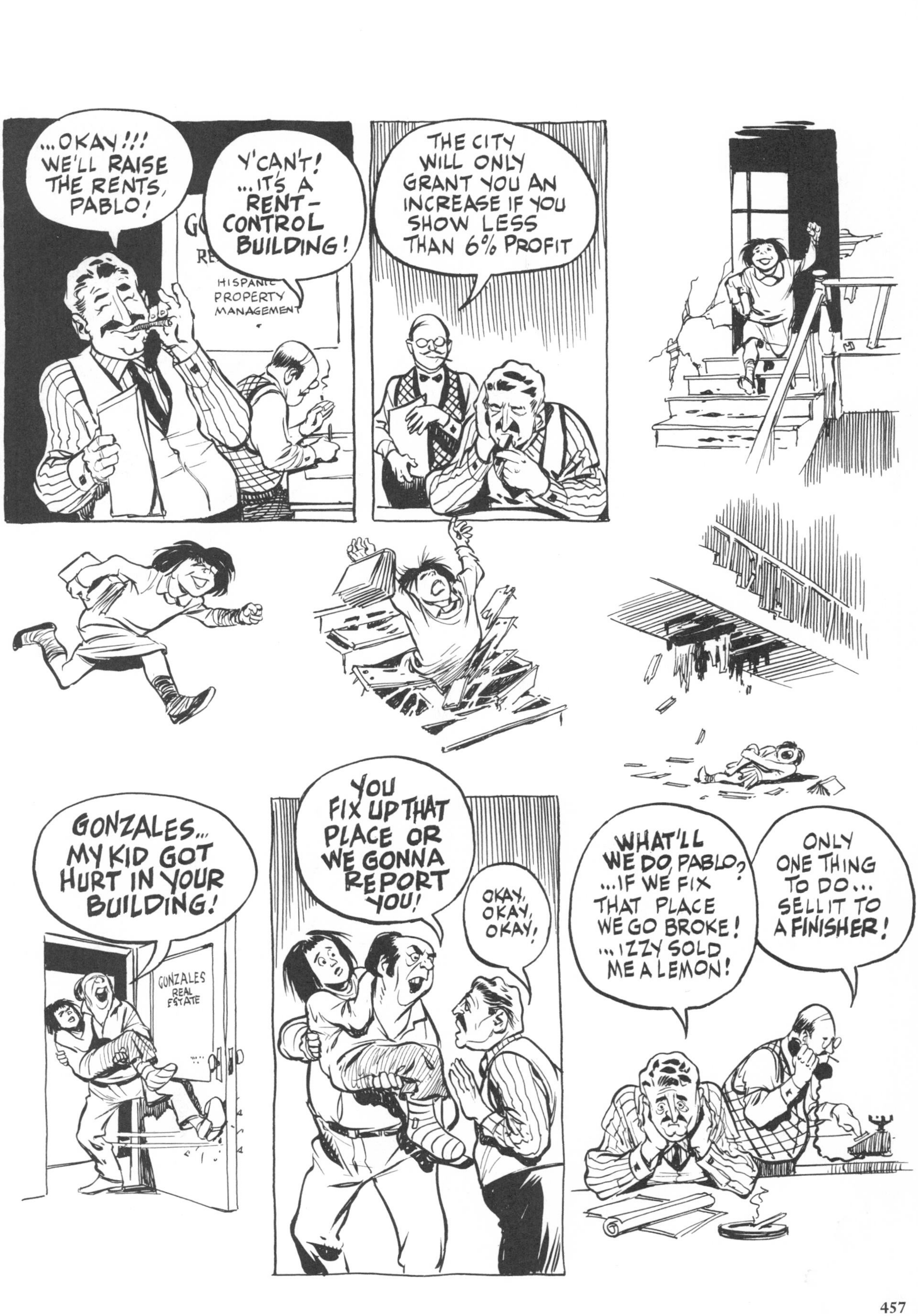
...OKAY!!! WE'LL RAISE THE RENTS, PABLO!
Y'CAN'T! ...IT'S A RENT-CONTROL BUILDING!
HISPANIC PROPERTY MANAGEMENT
THE CITY WILL ONLY GRANT YOU AN INCREASE IF YOU SHOW LESS THAN 6% PROFIT
GONZALES... MY KID GOT HURT IN YOUR BUILDING!
GONZALES REAL ESTATE
YOU FIX UP THAT PLACE OR WE GONNA REPORT YOU!
OKAY, OKAY, OKAY!
WHAT'LL WE DO, PABLO? ...IF WE FIX THAT PLACE WE GO BROKE! ...IZZY SOLD ME A LEMON!
ONLY ONE THING TO DO... SELL IT TO A FINISHER!

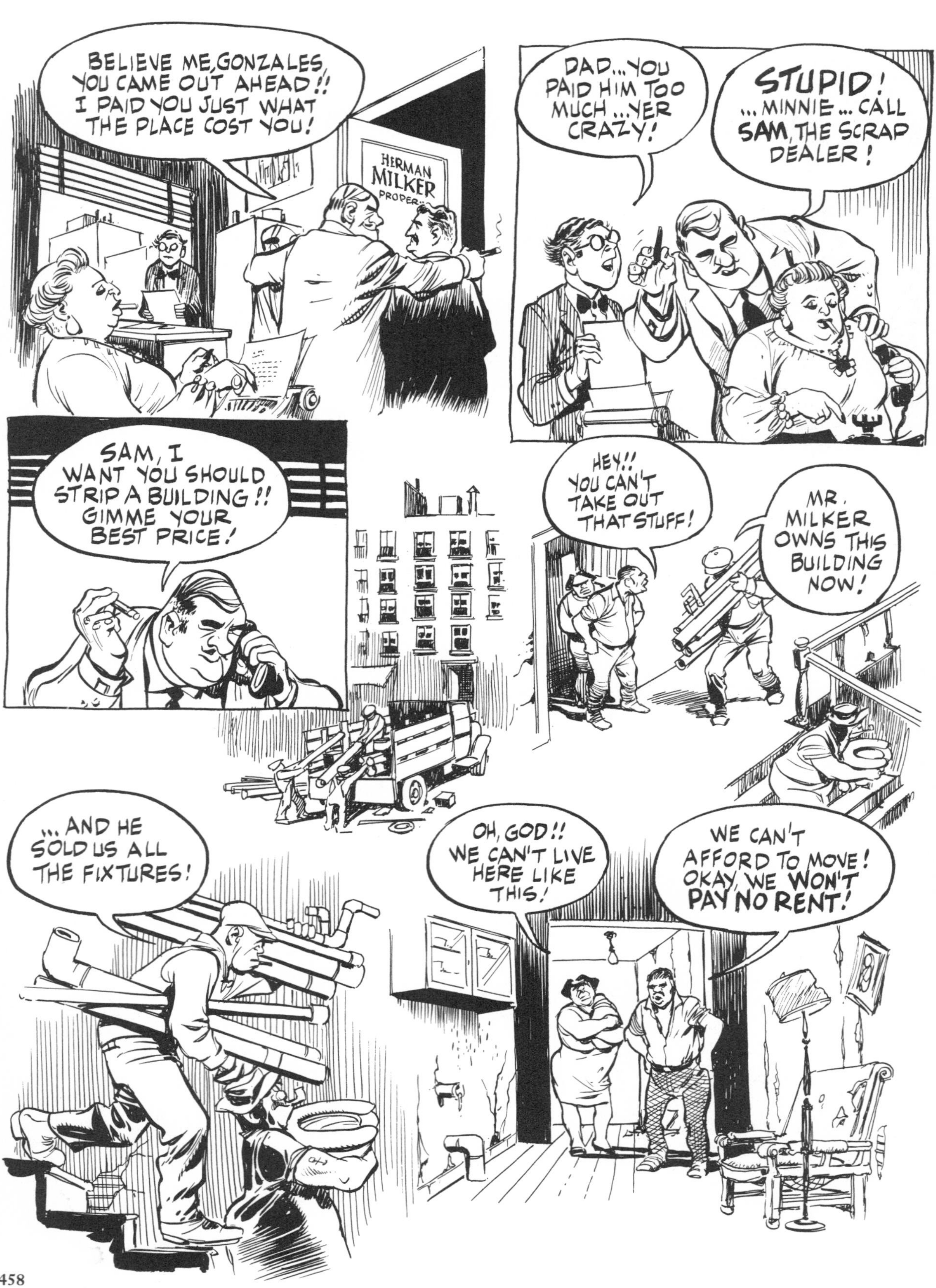
BELIEVE ME, GONZALES, YOU CAME OUT AHEAD!! I PAID YOU JUST WHAT THE PLACE COST YOU!
HERMAN MILKER PROPER..
DAD...YOU PAID HIM TOO MUCH...YER CRAZY!
STUPID! ... MINNIE ... CALL SAM, THE SCRAP DEALER!
SAM, I WANT YOU SHOULD STRIP A BUILDING!! GIMME YOUR BEST PRICE!
HEY!! YOU CAN'T TAKE OUT THAT STUFF!
MR. MILKER OWNS THIS BUILDING NOW!
... AND HE SOLD US ALL THE FIXTURES!
OH, GOD!! WE CAN'T LIVE HERE LIKE THIS!
WE CAN'T AFFORD TO MOVE! OKAY, WE WON'T PAY NO RENT!

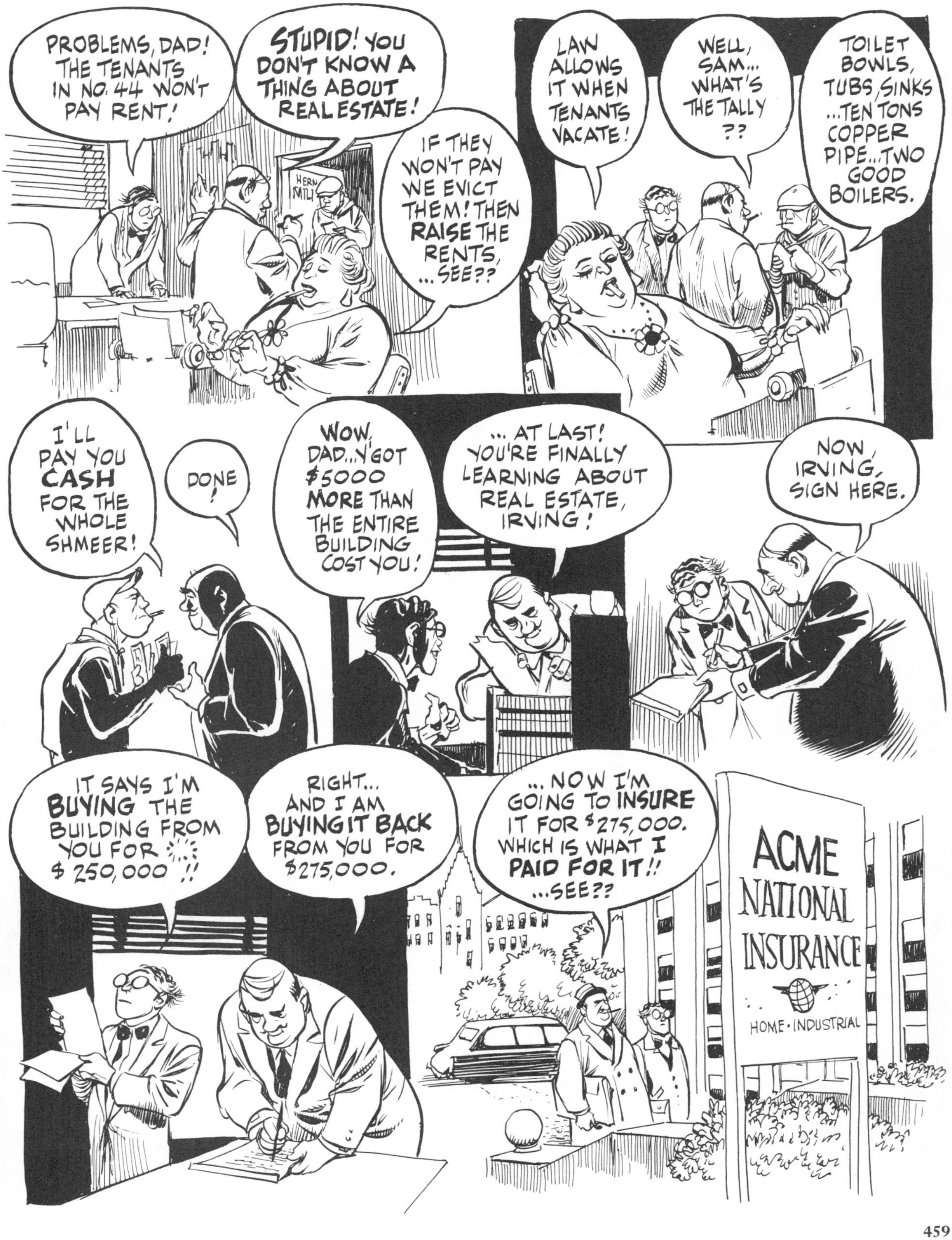
PROBLEMS, DAD! THE TENANTS IN NO. 44 WON'T PAY RENT!
STUPID! YOU DON'T KNOW A THING ABOUT REAL ESTATE!
IF THEY WON'T PAY WE EVICT THEM! THEN RAISE THE RENTS, ... SEE??
LAW ALLOWS IT WHEN TENANTS VACATE!
WELL, SAM... WHAT'S THE TALLY ??
TOILET BOWLS, TUBS, SINKS ...TEN TONS COPPER PIPE...TWO GOOD BOILERS.
I'LL PAY YOU CASH FOR THE WHOLE SHMEER!
DONE!
WOW, DAD...Y'GOT $5000 MORE THAN THE ENTIRE BUILDING COST YOU!
... AT LAST! YOU'RE FINALLY LEARNING ABOUT REAL ESTATE, IRVING!
NOW, IRVING, SIGN HERE.
IT SAYS I'M BUYING THE BUILDING FROM YOU FOR $ 250,000 !!
RIGHT... AND I AM BUYING IT BACK FROM YOU FOR $275,000.
... NOW I'M GOING TO INSURE IT FOR $275,000. WHICH IS WHAT I PAID FOR IT!! ...SEE??
ACME NATIONAL INSURANCE
HOME · INDUSTRIAL

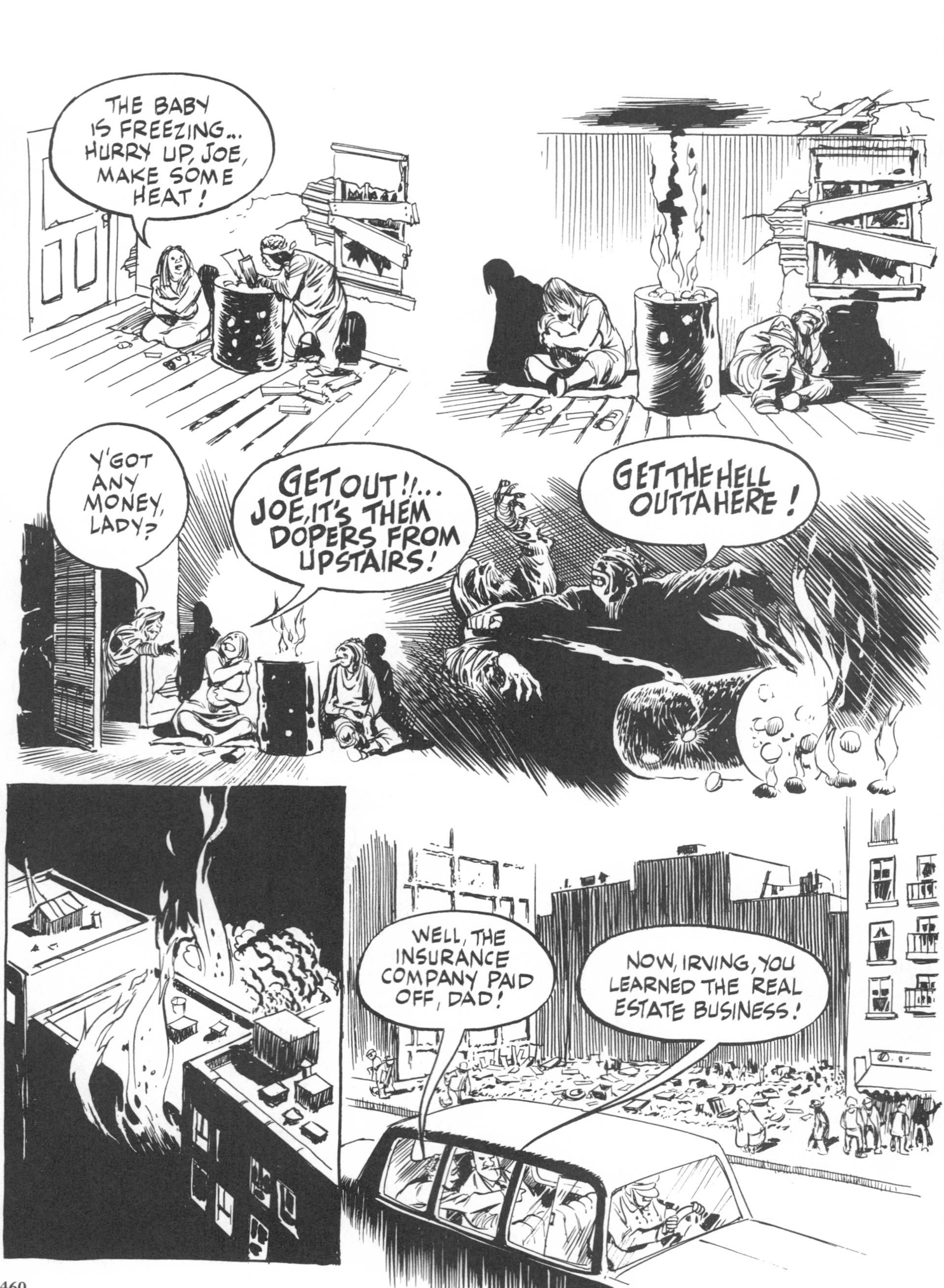
THE BABY IS FREEZING... HURRY UP, JOE, MAKE SOME HEAT!
Y'GOT ANY MONEY, LADY?
GET OUT!!... JOE, IT'S THEM DOPERS FROM UPSTAIRS!
GET THE HELL OUTTA HERE!
WELL, THE INSURANCE COMPANY PAID OFF, DAD!
NOW, IRVING, YOU LEARNED THE REAL ESTATE BUSINESS!

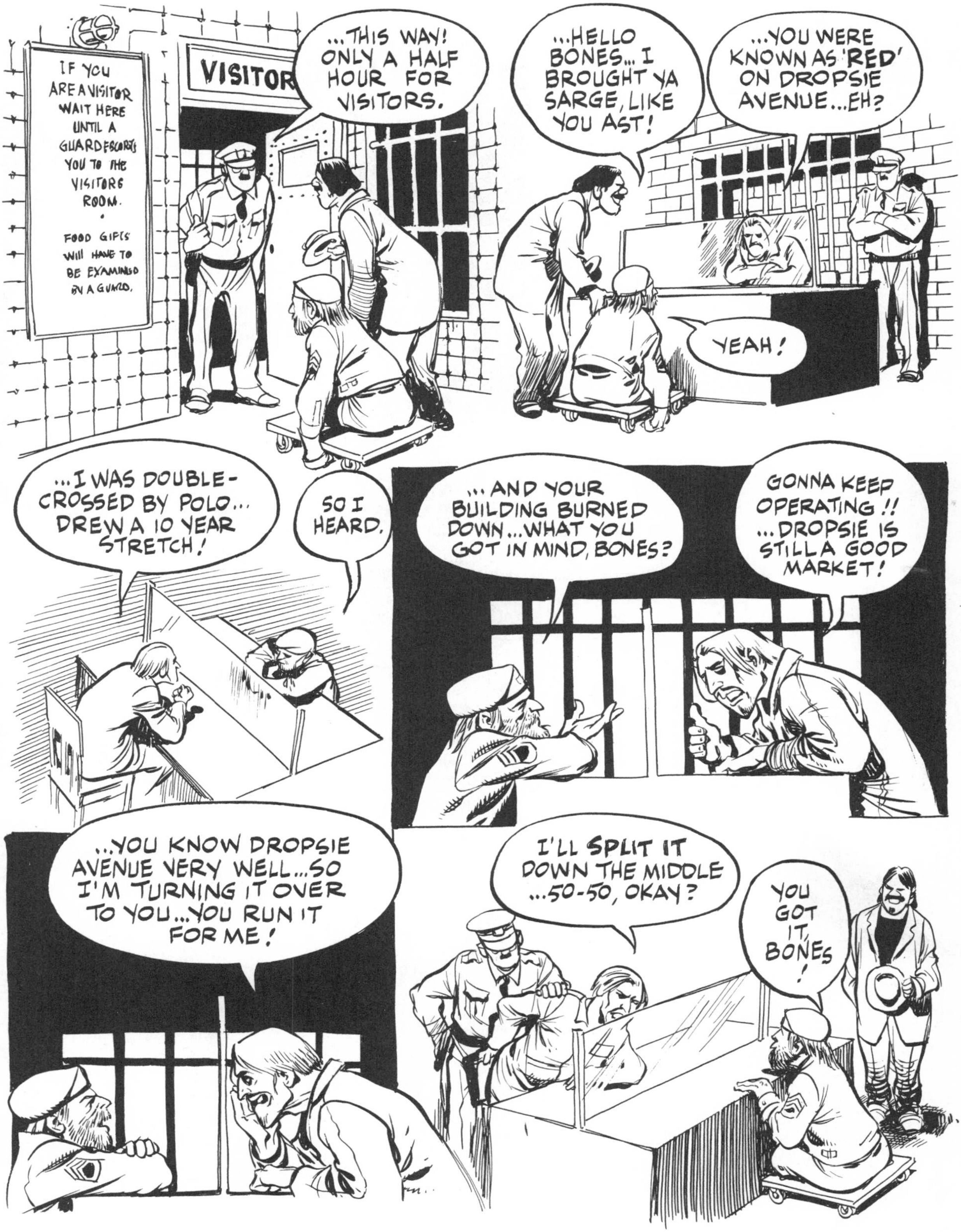
IF YOU ARE A VISITOR WAIT HERE UNTIL A GUARD ESCORTS YOU TO THE VISITORS ROOM.
FOOD GIFTS WILL HAVE TO BE EXAMINED BY A GUARD.
VISITOR
...THIS WAY! ONLY A HALF HOUR FOR VISITORS.
...HELLO BONES... I BROUGHT YA SARGE, LIKE YOU AST!
...YOU WERE KNOWN AS 'RED' ON DROPSIE AVENUE...EH?
YEAH!
...I WAS DOUBLE-CROSSED BY POLO... DREW A 10 YEAR STRETCH!
SO I HEARD.
...AND YOUR BUILDING BURNED DOWN...WHAT YOU GOT IN MIND, BONES?
GONNA KEEP OPERATING!! ...DROPSIE IS STILL A GOOD MARKET!
...YOU KNOW DROPSIE AVENUE VERY WELL...SO I'M TURNING IT OVER TO YOU...YOU RUN IT FOR ME!
I'LL SPLIT IT DOWN THE MIDDLE ...50-50, OKAY?
YOU GOT IT, BONES!

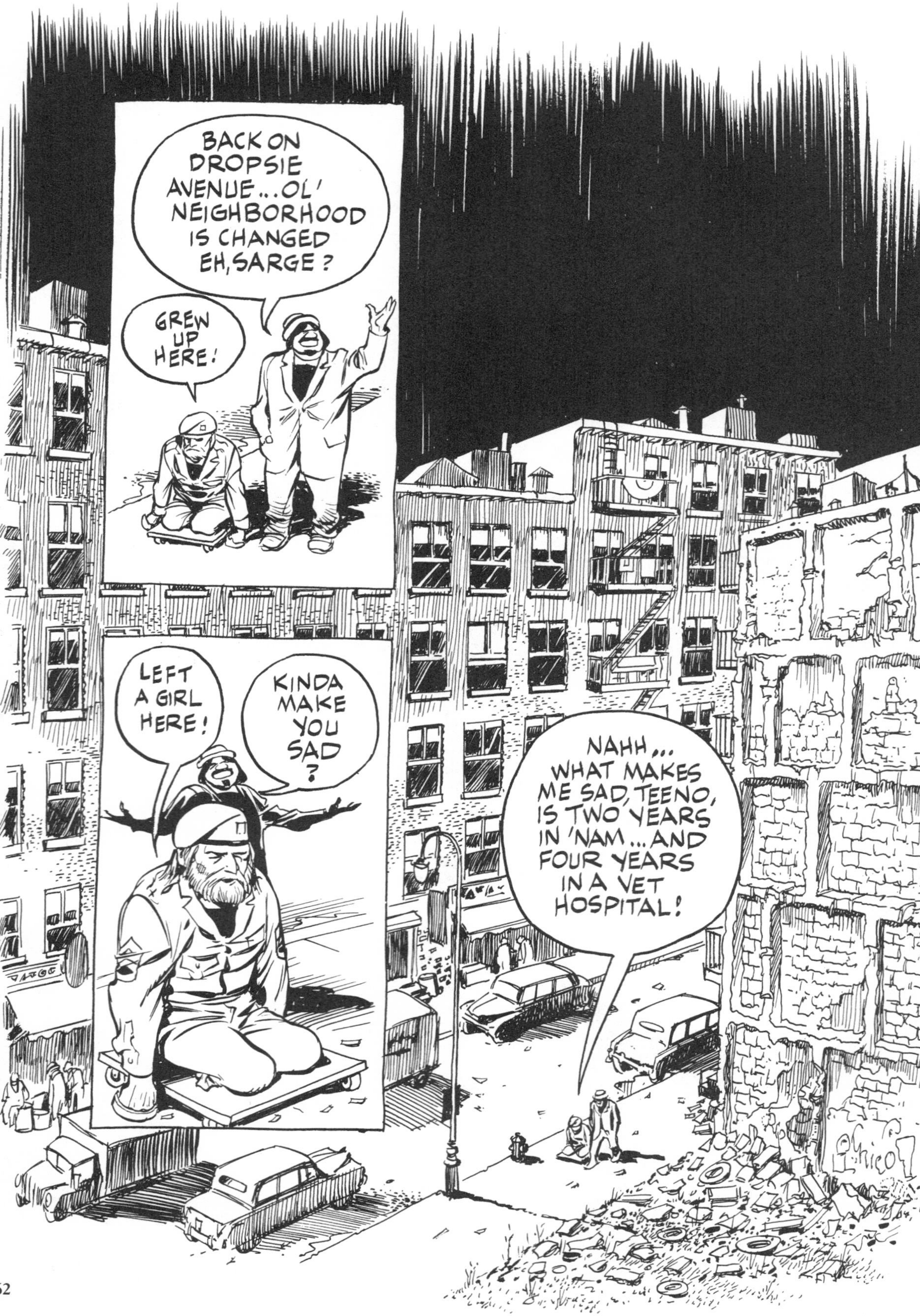
BACK ON DROPSIE AVENUE...OL' NEIGHBORHOOD IS CHANGED EH, SARGE?
GREW UP HERE!
LEFT A GIRL HERE!
KINDA MAKE YOU SAD?
NAHH... WHAT MAKES ME SAD, TEENO, IS TWO YEARS IN 'NAM...AND FOUR YEARS IN A VET HOSPITAL!

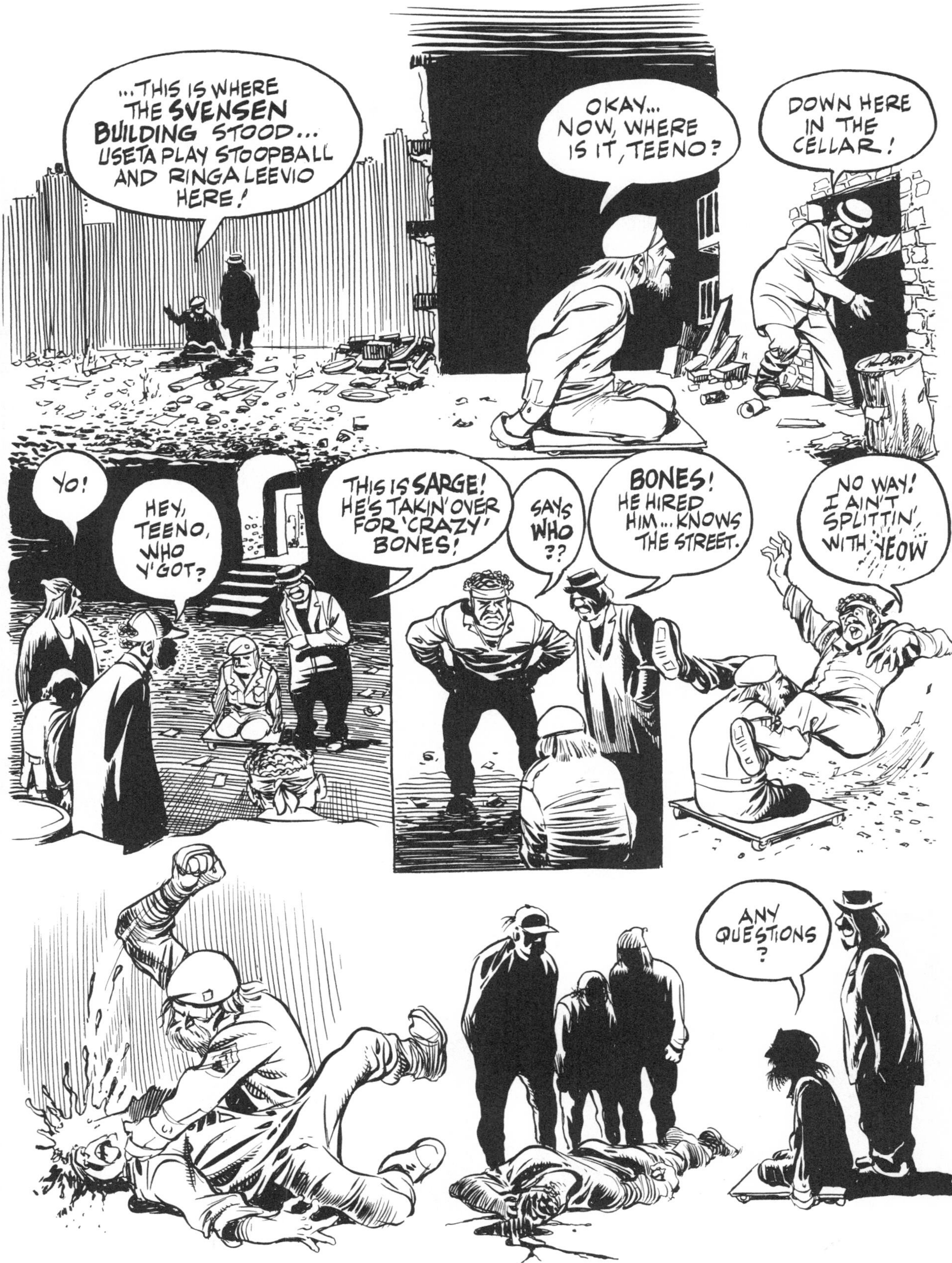
...THIS IS WHERE THE SVENSEN BUILDING STOOD... USETA PLAY STOOPBALL AND RINGALEEVIO HERE!
OKAY... NOW, WHERE IS IT, TEENO?
DOWN HERE IN THE CELLAR!
YO!
HEY, TEENO, WHO Y'GOT?
THIS IS SARGE! HE'S TAKIN' OVER FOR 'CRAZY' BONES!
SAYS WHO ??
BONES! HE HIRED HIM... KNOWS THE STREET.
NO WAY! I AIN'T SPLITTIN' WITH... YEOW
ANY QUESTIONS ?

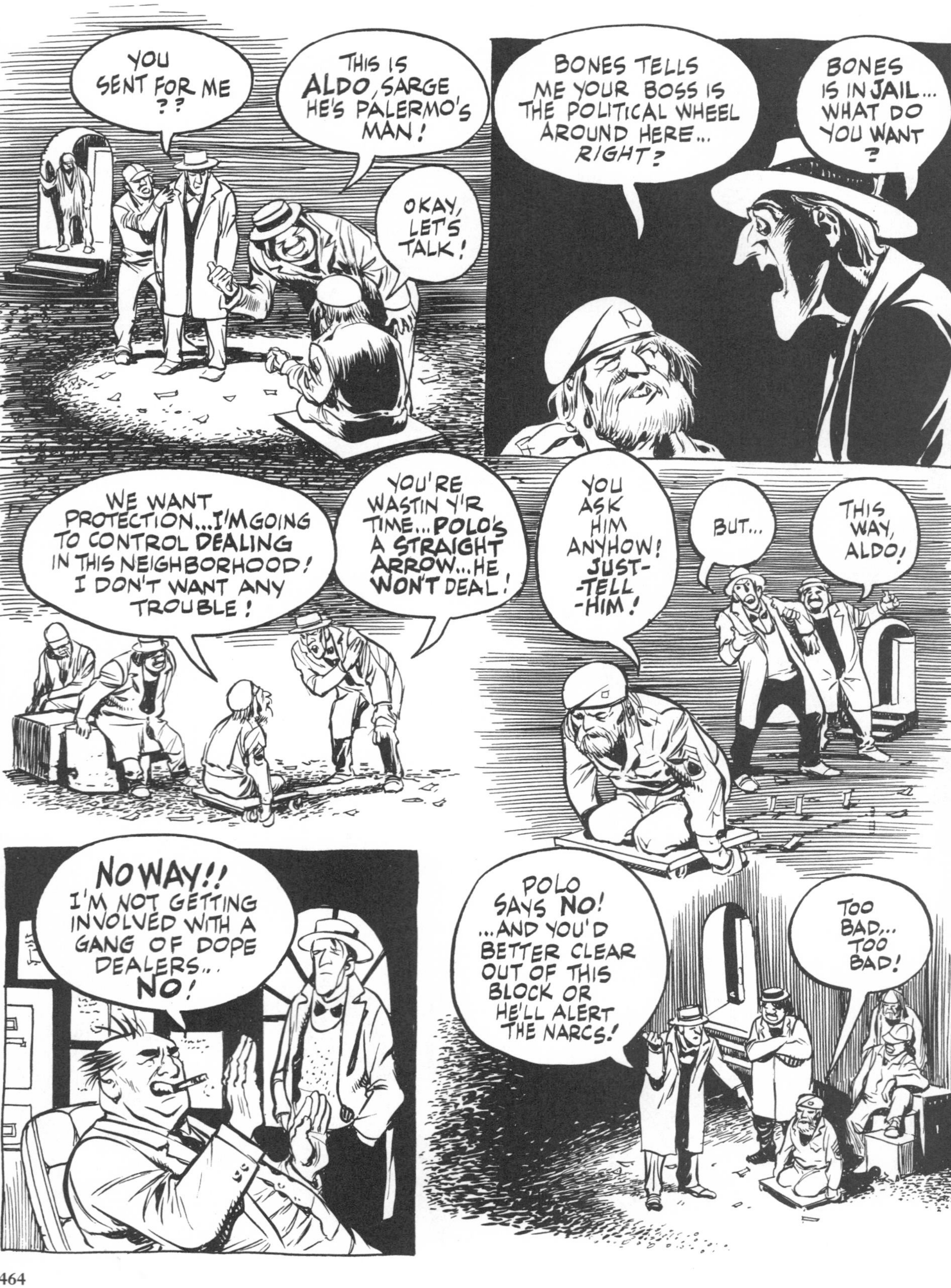
YOU SENT FOR ME ??
THIS IS ALDO, SARGE HE'S PALERMO'S MAN!
OKAY, LET'S TALK!
BONES TELLS ME YOUR BOSS IS THE POLITICAL WHEEL AROUND HERE... RIGHT?
BONES IS IN JAIL... WHAT DO YOU WANT ?
WE WANT PROTECTION...I'M GOING TO CONTROL DEALING IN THIS NEIGHBORHOOD! I DON'T WANT ANY TROUBLE!
YOU'RE WASTIN Y'R TIME...POLO'S A STRAIGHT ARROW...HE WON'T DEAL!
YOU ASK HIM ANYHOW! JUST- -TELL -HIM!
BUT...
THIS WAY, ALDO!
NO WAY!! I'M NOT GETTING INVOLVED WITH A GANG OF DOPE DEALERS... NO!
POLO SAYS NO! ...AND YOU'D BETTER CLEAR OUT OF THIS BLOCK OR HE'LL ALERT THE NARCS!
TOO BAD... TOO BAD!

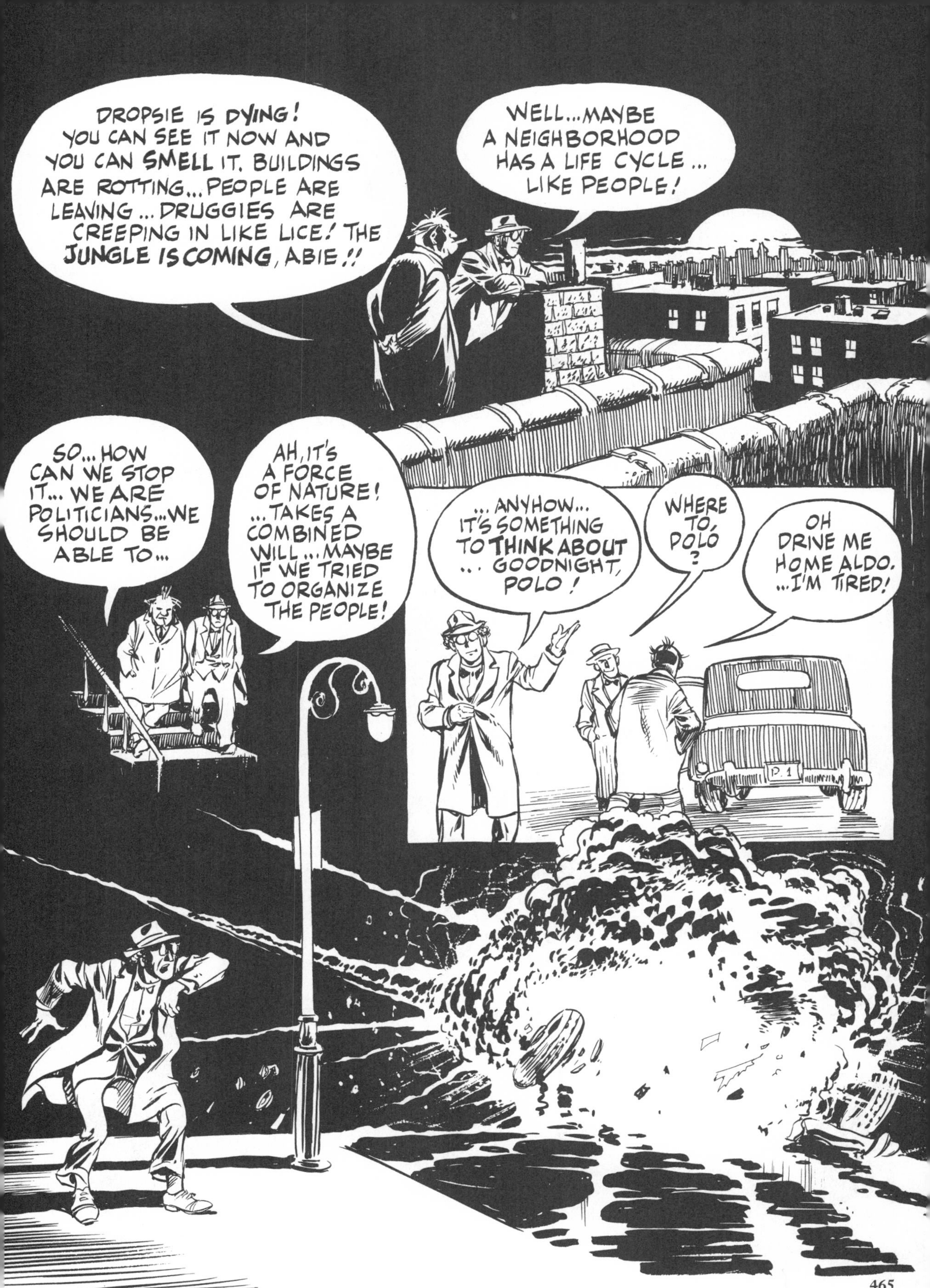
DROPSIE IS DYING! YOU CAN SEE IT NOW AND YOU CAN SMELL IT. BUILDINGS ARE ROTTING... PEOPLE ARE LEAVING... DRUGGIES ARE CREEPING IN LIKE LICE! THE JUNGLE IS COMING, ABIE!!
WELL... MAYBE A NEIGHBORHOOD HAS A LIFE CYCLE... LIKE PEOPLE!
SO... HOW CAN WE STOP IT... WE ARE POLITICIANS... WE SHOULD BE ABLE TO...
AH, IT'S A FORCE OF NATURE! ...TAKES A COMBINED WILL... MAYBE IF WE TRIED TO ORGANIZE THE PEOPLE!
... ANYHOW... IT'S SOMETHING TO THINK ABOUT ... GOODNIGHT, POLO!
WHERE TO, POLO?
OH DRIVE ME HOME ALDO. ...I'M TIRED!
P. 1

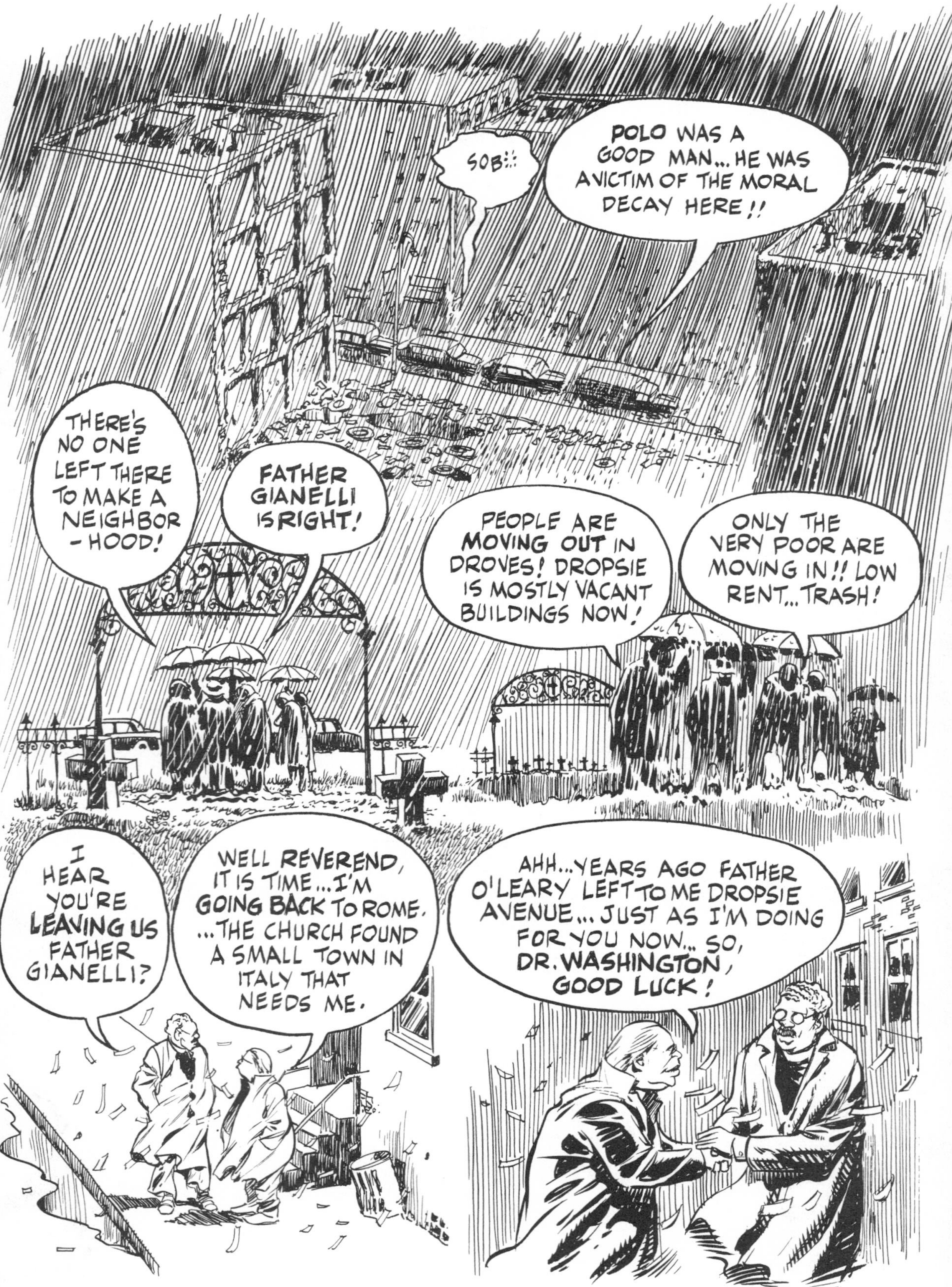
SOB!!
POLO WAS A GOOD MAN... HE WAS A VICTIM OF THE MORAL DECAY HERE!!
THERE'S NO ONE LEFT THERE TO MAKE A NEIGHBOR-HOOD!
FATHER GIANELLI IS RIGHT!
PEOPLE ARE MOVING OUT IN DROVES! DROPSIE IS MOSTLY VACANT BUILDINGS NOW!
ONLY THE VERY POOR ARE MOVING IN!! LOW RENT... TRASH!
I HEAR YOU'RE LEAVING US FATHER GIANELLI?
WELL REVEREND, IT IS TIME... I'M GOING BACK TO ROME. ...THE CHURCH FOUND A SMALL TOWN IN ITALY THAT NEEDS ME.
AHH... YEARS AGO FATHER O'LEARY LEFT TO ME DROPSIE AVENUE... JUST AS I'M DOING FOR YOU NOW... SO, DR. WASHINGTON, GOOD LUCK!

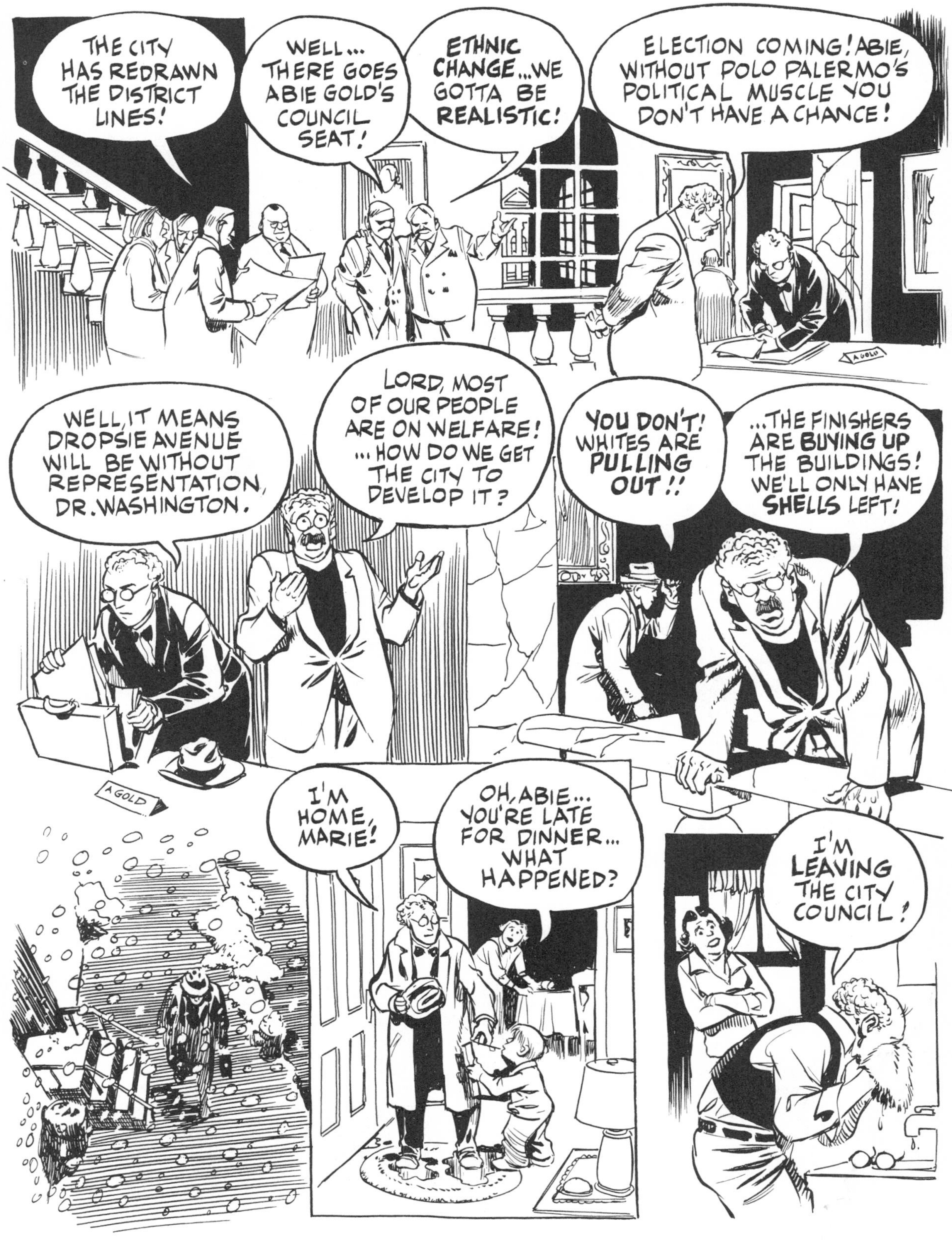
THE CITY HAS REDRAWN THE DISTRICT LINES!
WELL... THERE GOES ABIE GOLD'S COUNCIL SEAT!
ETHNIC CHANGE... WE GOTTA BE REALISTIC!
ELECTION COMING! ABIE, WITHOUT POLO PALERMO'S POLITICAL MUSCLE YOU DON'T HAVE A CHANCE!
A GOLD
WELL, IT MEANS DROPSIE AVENUE WILL BE WITHOUT REPRESENTATION, DR. WASHINGTON.
LORD, MOST OF OUR PEOPLE ARE ON WELFARE! ...HOW DO WE GET THE CITY TO DEVELOP IT?
YOU DON'T! WHITES ARE PULLING OUT!!
...THE FINISHERS ARE BUYING UP THE BUILDINGS! WE'LL ONLY HAVE SHELLS LEFT!
A GOLD
I'M HOME, MARIE!
OH, ABIE... YOU'RE LATE FOR DINNER... WHAT HAPPENED?
I'M LEAVING THE CITY COUNCIL!

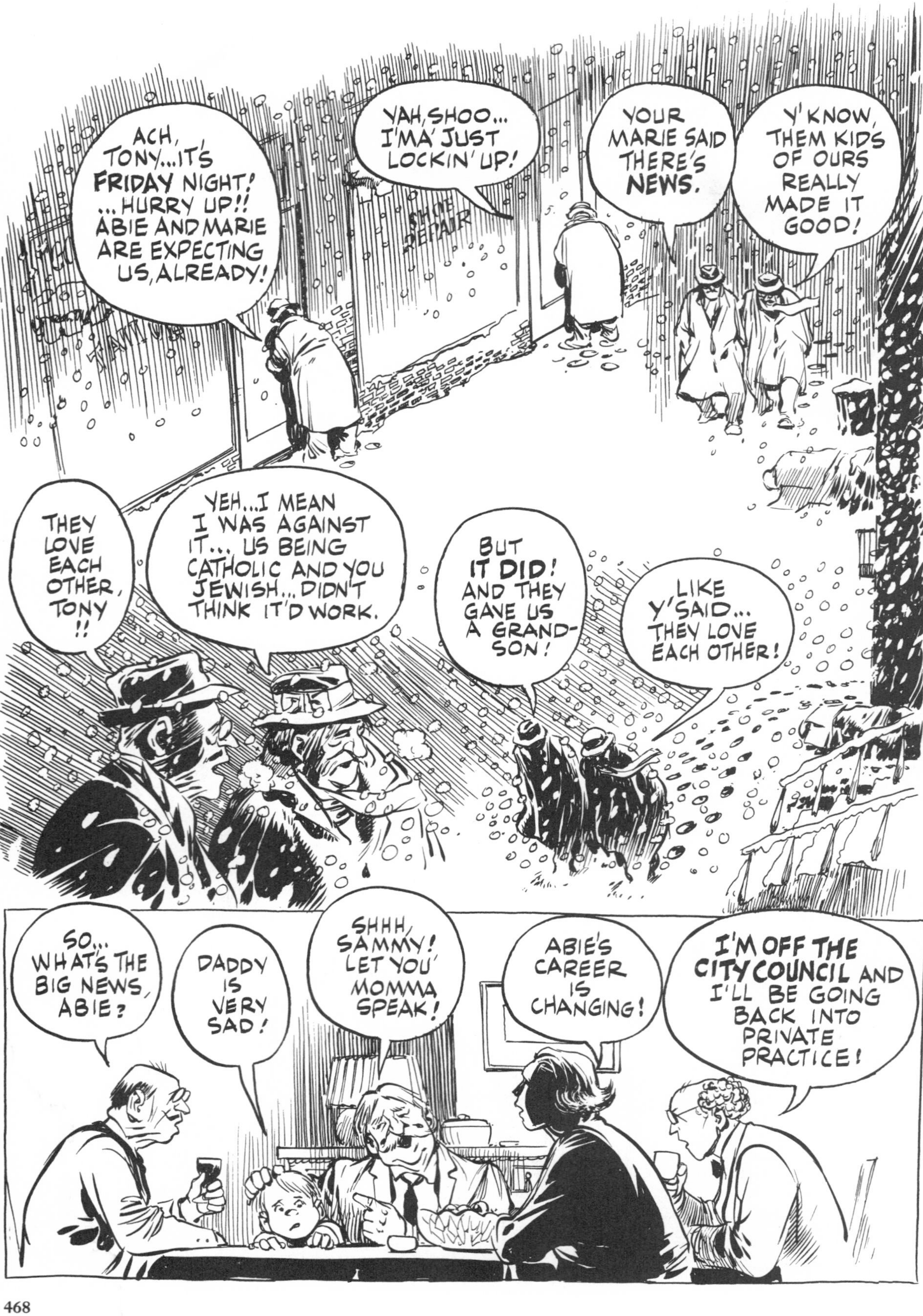

ACH, TONY...IT'S FRIDAY NIGHT! ...HURRY UP!! ABIE AND MARIE ARE EXPECTING US, ALREADY!
YAH, SHOO... I'MA' JUST LOCKIN' UP!
SHOE REPAIR
YOUR MARIE SAID THERE'S NEWS.
Y'KNOW, THEM KIDS OF OURS REALLY MADE IT GOOD!
THEY LOVE EACH OTHER, TONY!!
YEH...I MEAN I WAS AGAINST IT... US BEING CATHOLIC AND YOU JEWISH... DIDN'T THINK IT'D WORK.
BUT IT DID! AND THEY GAVE US A GRAND-SON!
LIKE Y'SAID... THEY LOVE EACH OTHER!
SO... WHAT'S THE BIG NEWS, ABIE?
DADDY IS VERY SAD!
SHHH, SAMMY! LET YOU' MOMMA SPEAK!
ABIE'S CAREER IS CHANGING!
I'M OFF THE CITY COUNCIL AND I'LL BE GOING BACK INTO PRIVATE PRACTICE!

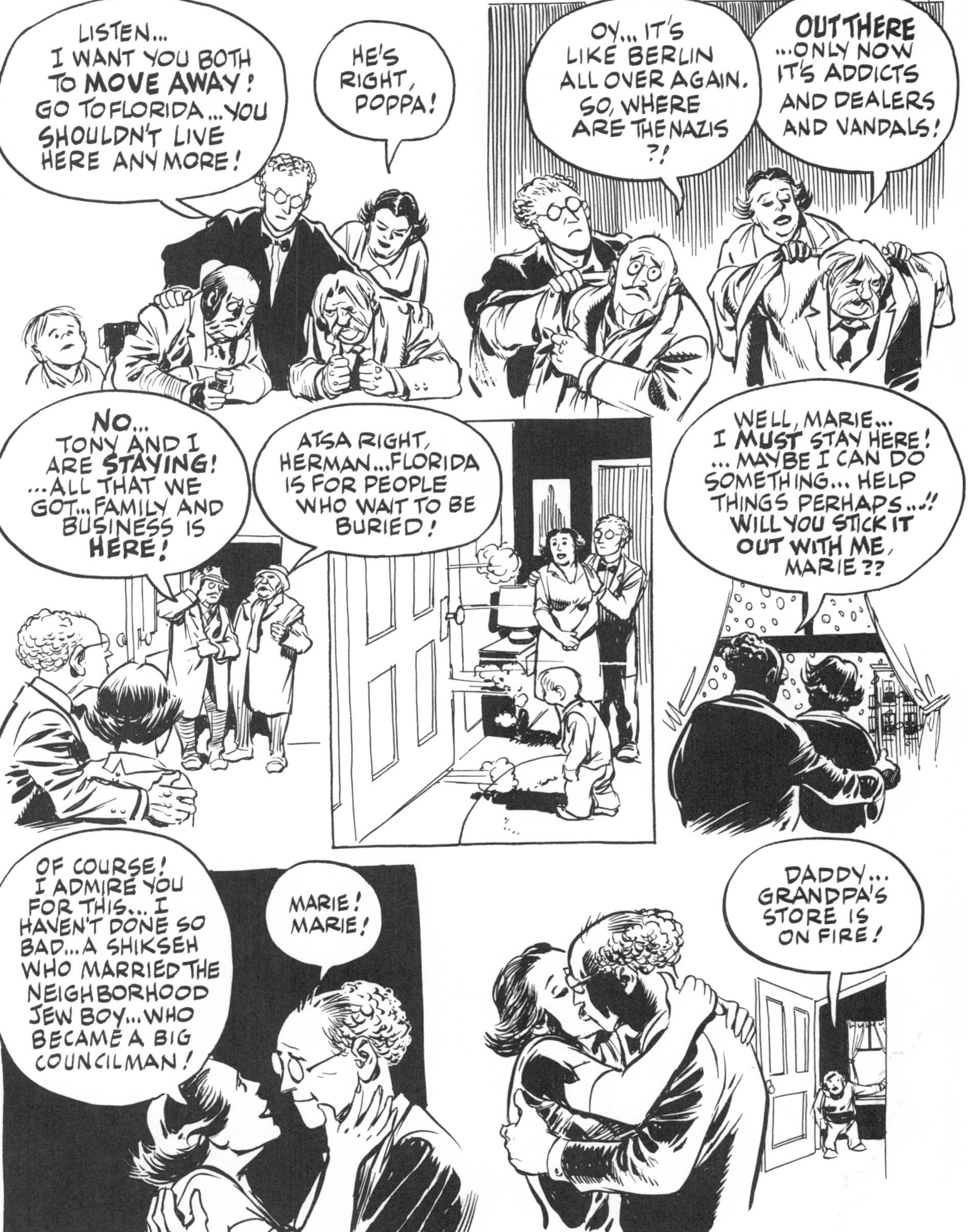
LISTEN... I WANT YOU BOTH TO MOVE AWAY! GO TO FLORIDA... YOU SHOULDN'T LIVE HERE ANYMORE!
HE'S RIGHT, POPPA!
OY... IT'S LIKE BERLIN ALL OVER AGAIN. SO, WHERE ARE THE NAZIS ?!
OUT THERE ...ONLY NOW IT'S ADDICTS AND DEALERS AND VANDALS!
NO... TONY AND I ARE STAYING! ...ALL THAT WE GOT... FAMILY AND BUSINESS IS HERE!
ATSA RIGHT, HERMAN... FLORIDA IS FOR PEOPLE WHO WAIT TO BE BURIED!
WELL, MARIE... I MUST STAY HERE! ... MAYBE I CAN DO SOMETHING... HELP THINGS PERHAPS...! WILL YOU STICK IT OUT WITH ME, MARIE??
OF COURSE! I ADMIRE YOU FOR THIS... I HAVEN'T DONE SO BAD... A SHIKSEH WHO MARRIED THE NEIGHBORHOOD JEW BOY... WHO BECAME A BIG COUNCILMAN!
MARIE! MARIE!
DADDY... GRANDPA'S STORE IS ON FIRE!

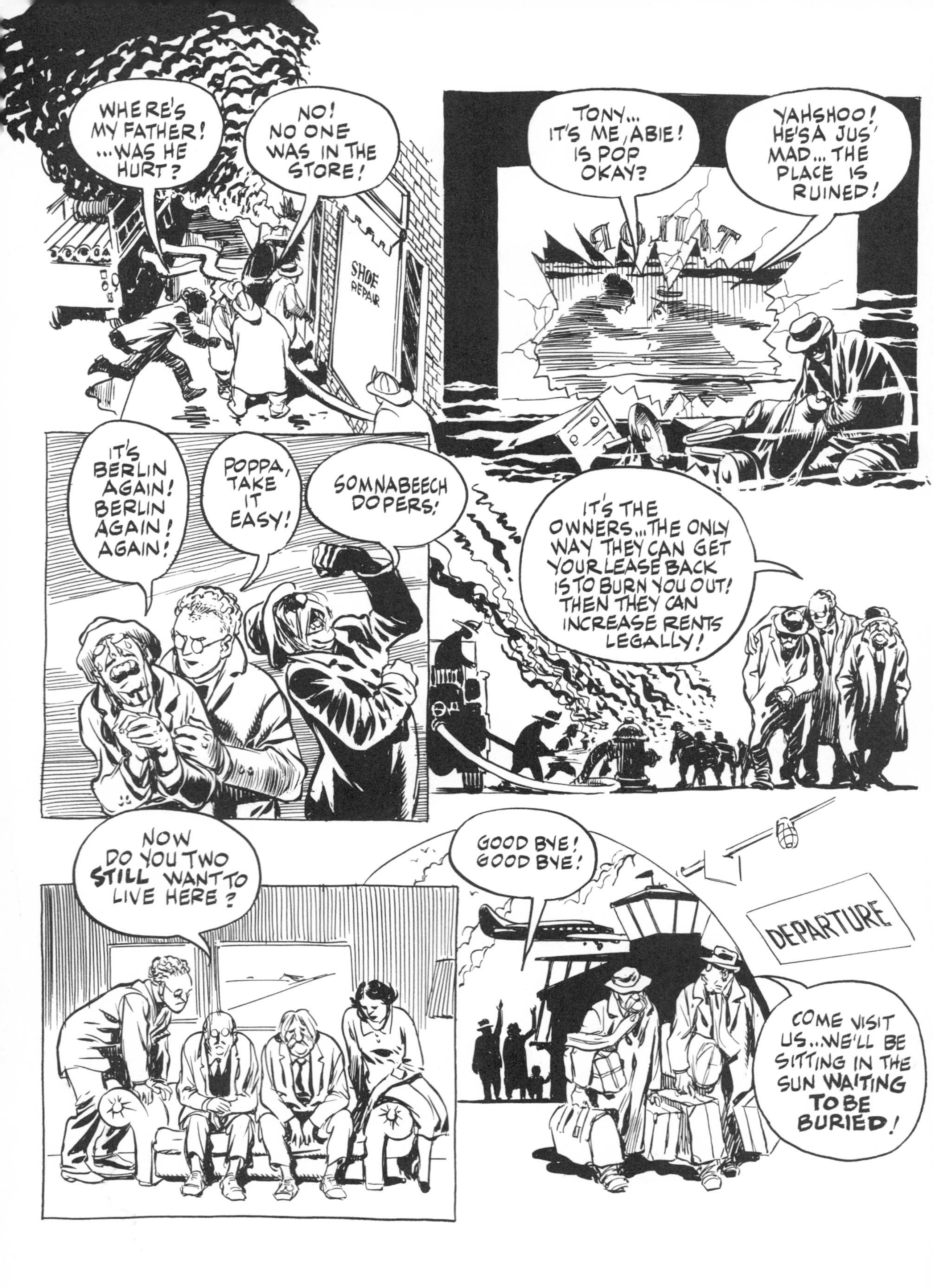
WHERE'S MY FATHER! ...WAS HE HURT?
NO! NO ONE WAS IN THE STORE!
SHOE REPAIR
TONY... IT'S ME, ABIE! IS POP OKAY?
YAHSHOO! HE'SA JUS' MAD... THE PLACE IS RUINED!
IT'S BERLIN AGAIN! BERLIN AGAIN! AGAIN!
POPPA, TAKE IT EASY!
SOMNABEECH DOPERS!
IT'S THE OWNERS... THE ONLY WAY THEY CAN GET YOUR LEASE BACK IS TO BURN YOU OUT! THEN THEY CAN INCREASE RENTS LEGALLY!
NOW DO YOU TWO STILL WANT TO LIVE HERE?
GOOD BYE! GOOD BYE!
DEPARTURE
COME VISIT US... WE'LL BE SITTING IN THE SUN WAITING TO BE BURIED!

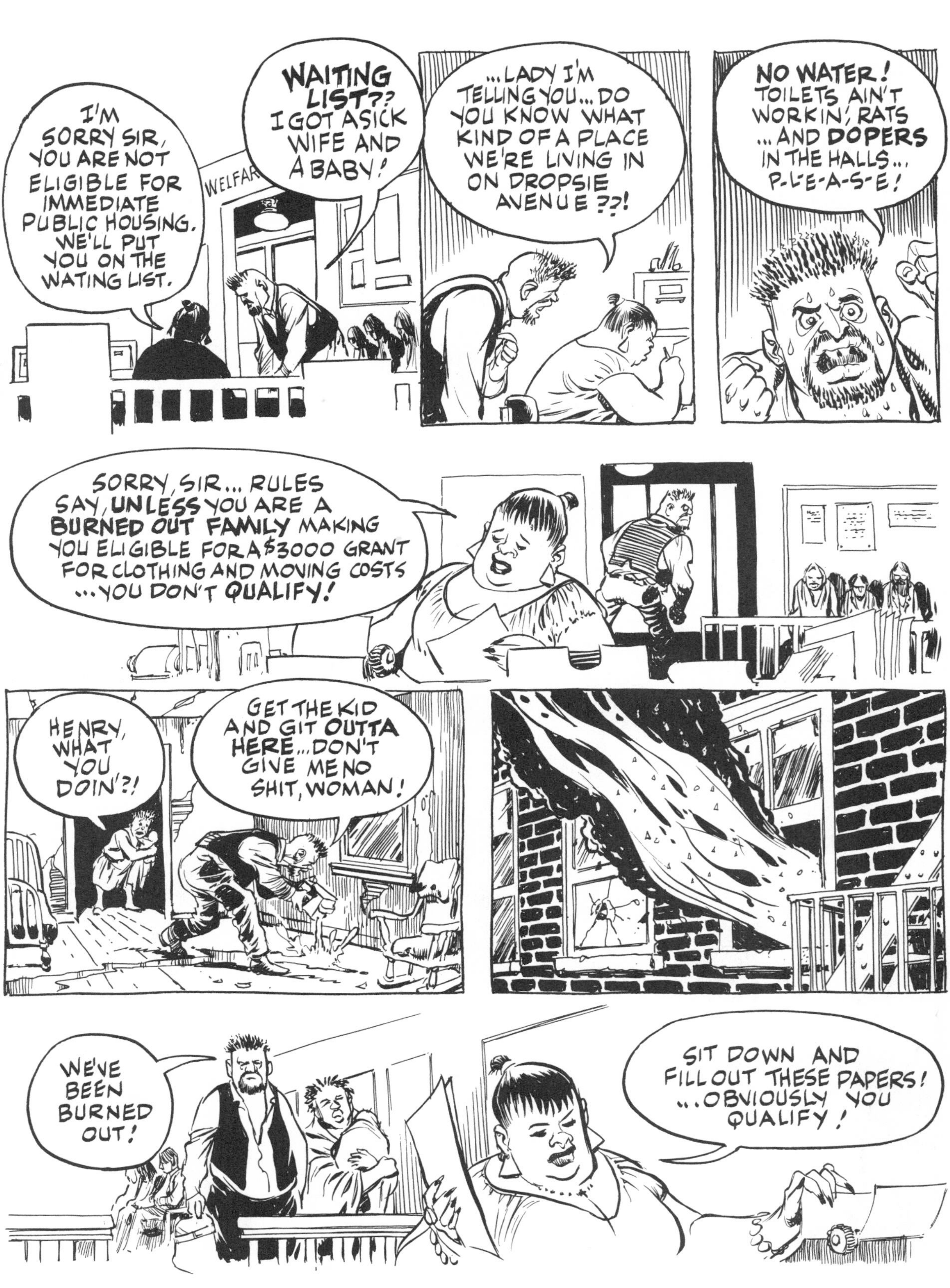
I'M SORRY SIR, YOU ARE NOT ELIGIBLE FOR IMMEDIATE PUBLIC HOUSING. WE'LL PUT YOU ON THE WATING LIST.
WELFAR
WAITING LIST?? I GOT A SICK WIFE AND A BABY!
...LADY I'M TELLING YOU... DO YOU KNOW WHAT KIND OF A PLACE WE'RE LIVING IN ON DROPSIE AVENUE??!
NO WATER! TOILETS AIN'T WORKIN', RATS ...AND DOPERS IN THE HALLS... P-L-E-A-S-E!
SORRY, SIR... RULES SAY, UNLESS YOU ARE A BURNED OUT FAMILY MAKING YOU ELIGIBLE FOR A $3000 GRANT FOR CLOTHING AND MOVING COSTS ...YOU DON'T QUALIFY!
HENRY, WHAT YOU DOIN'?!
GET THE KID AND GIT OUTTA HERE...DON'T GIVE ME NO SHIT, WOMAN!
WE'VE BEEN BURNED OUT!
SIT DOWN AND FILL OUT THESE PAPERS! ..OBVIOUSLY YOU QUALIFY!

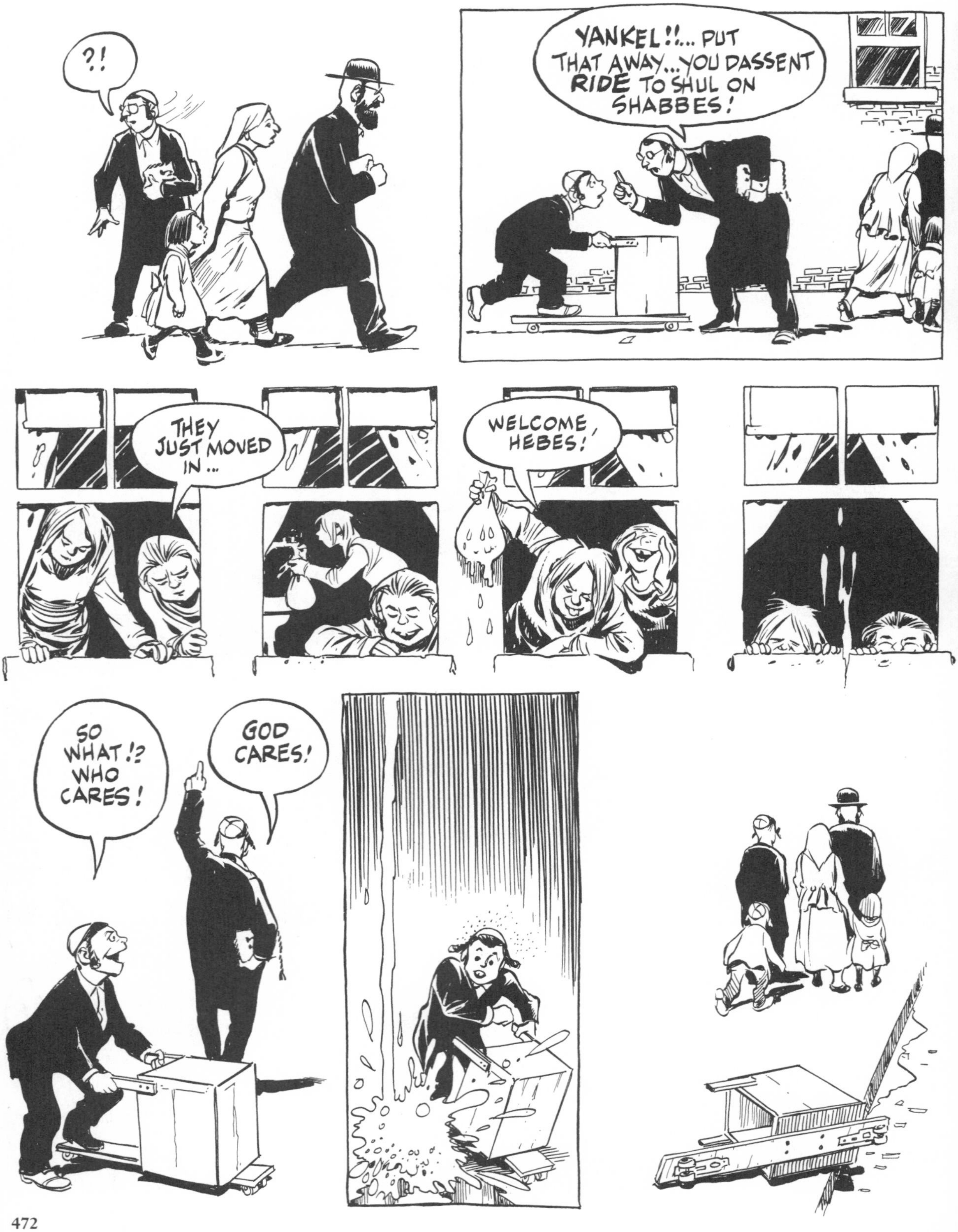
?!
YANKEL!!... PUT THAT AWAY... YOU DASSENT RIDE TO SHUL ON SHABBES!
THEY JUST MOVED IN...
WELCOME, HEBES!
SO WHAT!? WHO CARES!
GOD CARES!

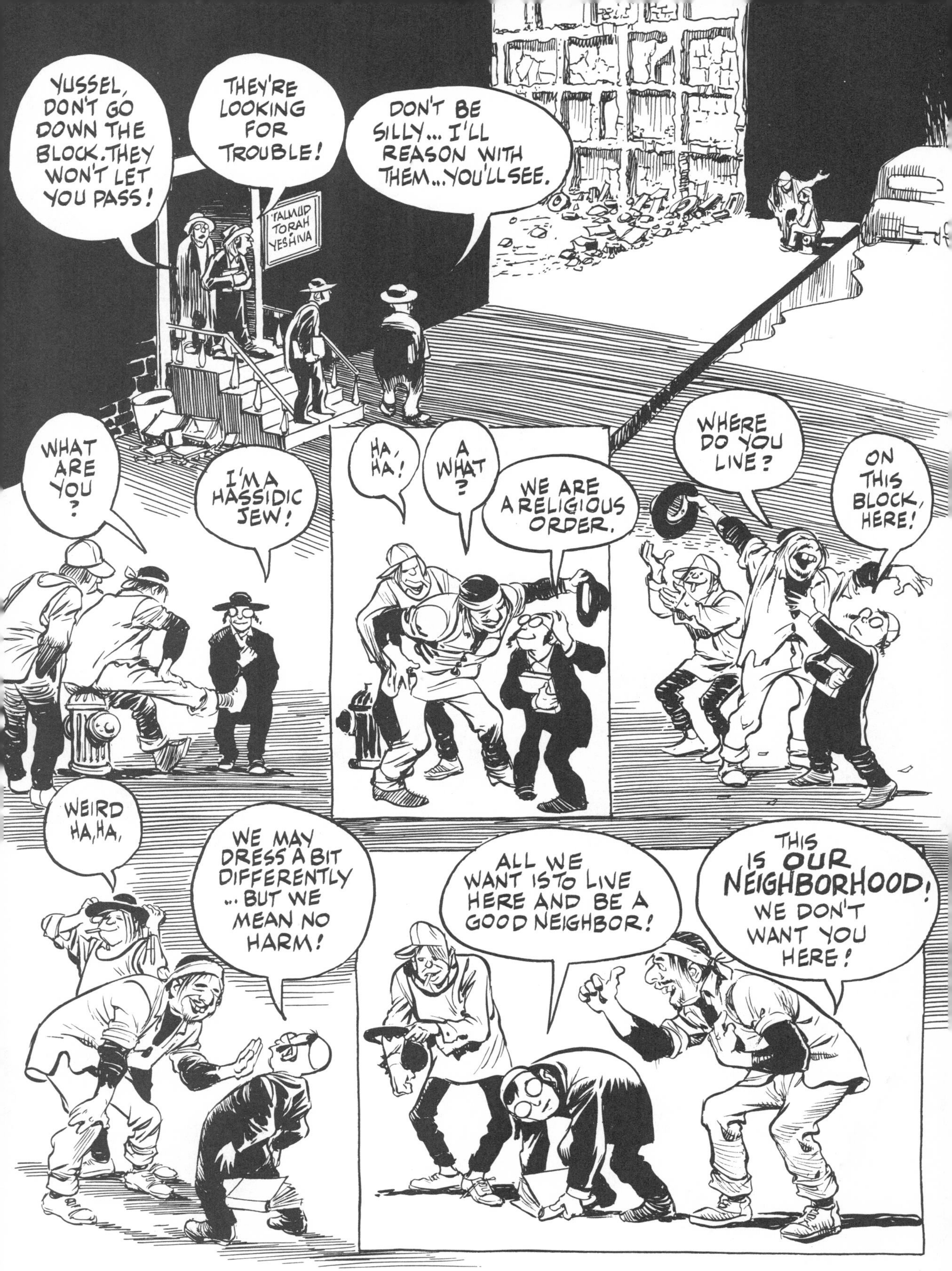
YUSSEL, DON'T GO DOWN THE BLOCK. THEY WON'T LET YOU PASS!
THEY'RE LOOKING FOR TROUBLE!
TALMUD TORAH YESHIVA
DON'T BE SILLY... I'LL REASON WITH THEM... YOU'LL SEE.
WHAT ARE YOU ?
I'M A HASSIDIC JEW!
HA, HA!
A WHAT ?
WE ARE A RELIGIOUS ORDER.
WHERE DO YOU LIVE?
ON THIS BLOCK, HERE!
WEIRD HA, HA,
WE MAY DRESS A BIT DIFFERENTLY ... BUT WE MEAN NO HARM!
ALL WE WANT IS TO LIVE HERE AND BE A GOOD NEIGHBOR!
THIS IS OUR NEIGHBORHOOD! WE DON'T WANT YOU HERE!

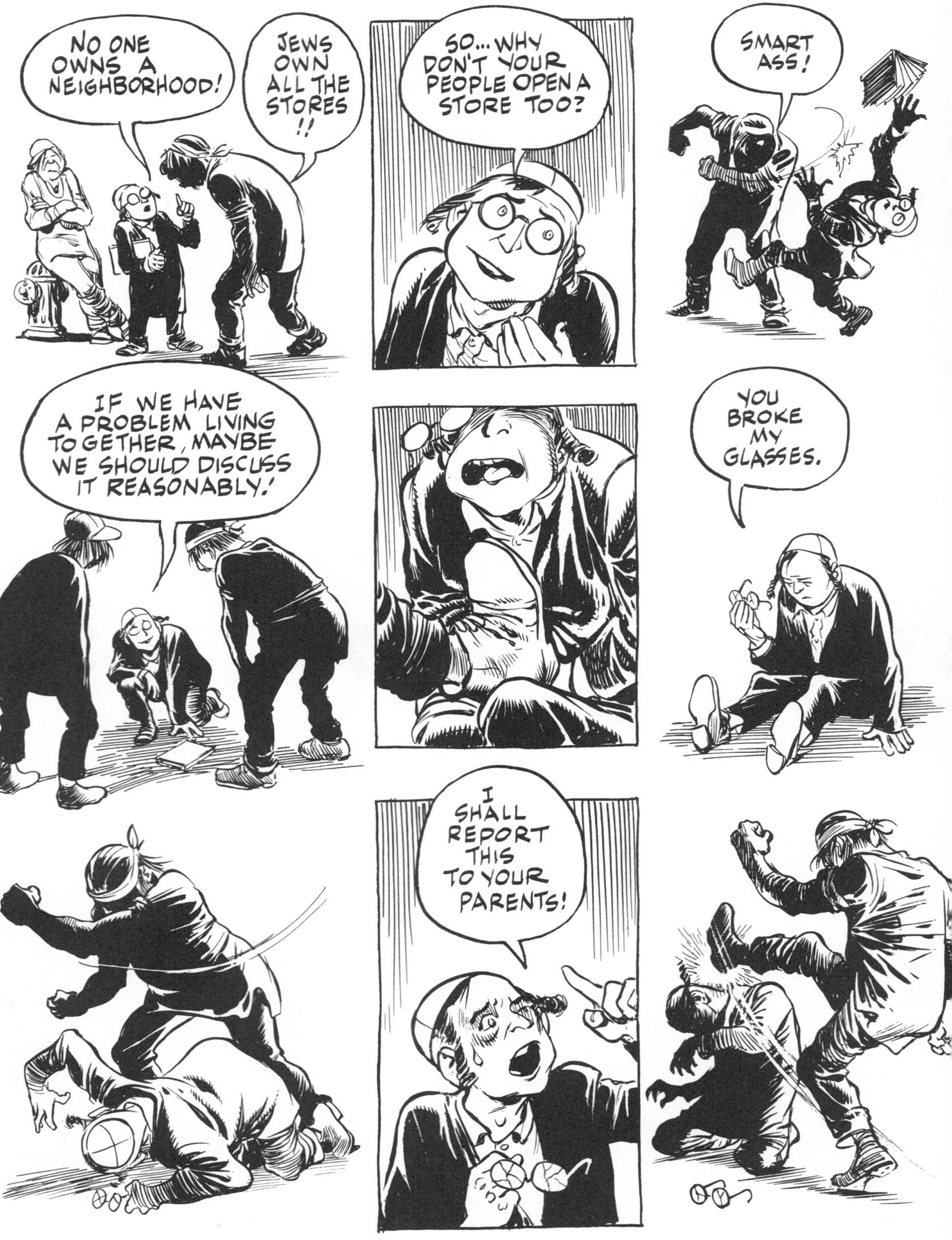
NO ONE OWNS A NEIGHBORHOOD!
JEWS OWN ALL THE STORES !!
SO... WHY DON'T YOUR PEOPLE OPEN A STORE TOO?
SMART ASS!
IF WE HAVE A PROBLEM LIVING TOGETHER, MAYBE WE SHOULD DISCUSS IT REASONABLY!
YOU BROKE MY GLASSES.
I SHALL REPORT THIS TO YOUR PARENTS!

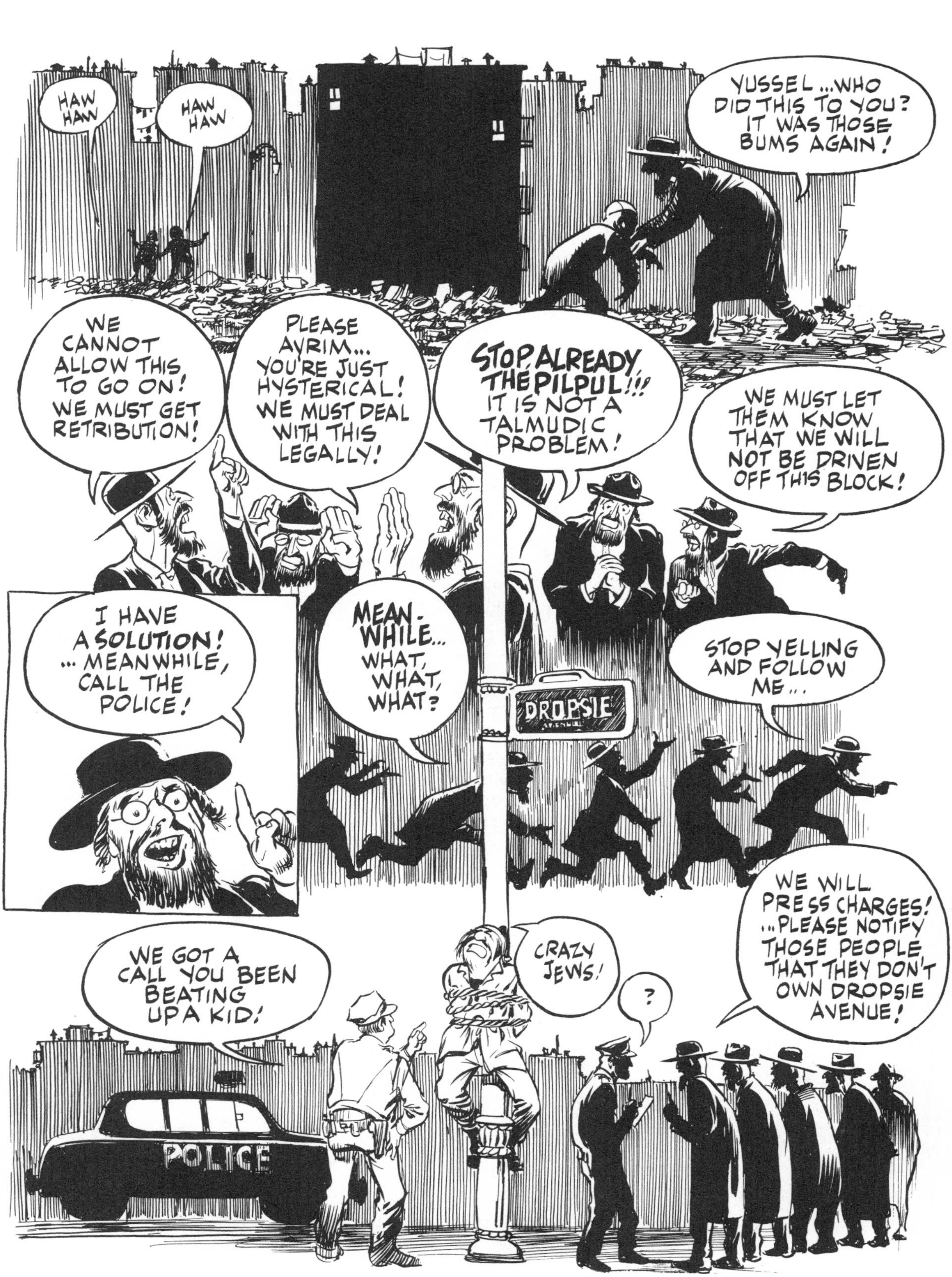

HAW HAW
HAW HAW
YUSSEL ...WHO DID THIS TO YOU? IT WAS THOSE BUMS AGAIN!
WE CANNOT ALLOW THIS TO GO ON! WE MUST GET RETRIBUTION!
PLEASE AVRIM... YOU'RE JUST HYSTERICAL! WE MUST DEAL WITH THIS LEGALLY!
STOP ALREADY THE PILPUL!!! IT IS NOT A TALMUDIC PROBLEM!
WE MUST LET THEM KNOW THAT WE WILL NOT BE DRIVEN OFF THIS BLOCK!
I HAVE A SOLUTION! ... MEANWHILE, CALL THE POLICE!
MEAN-WHILE... WHAT, WHAT, WHAT?
DROPSIE
STOP YELLING AND FOLLOW ME...
WE GOT A CALL YOU BEEN BEATING UP A KID!
CRAZY JEWS!
?
WE WILL PRESS CHARGES! ...PLEASE NOTIFY THOSE PEOPLE THAT THEY DON'T OWN DROPSIE AVENUE!
POLICE

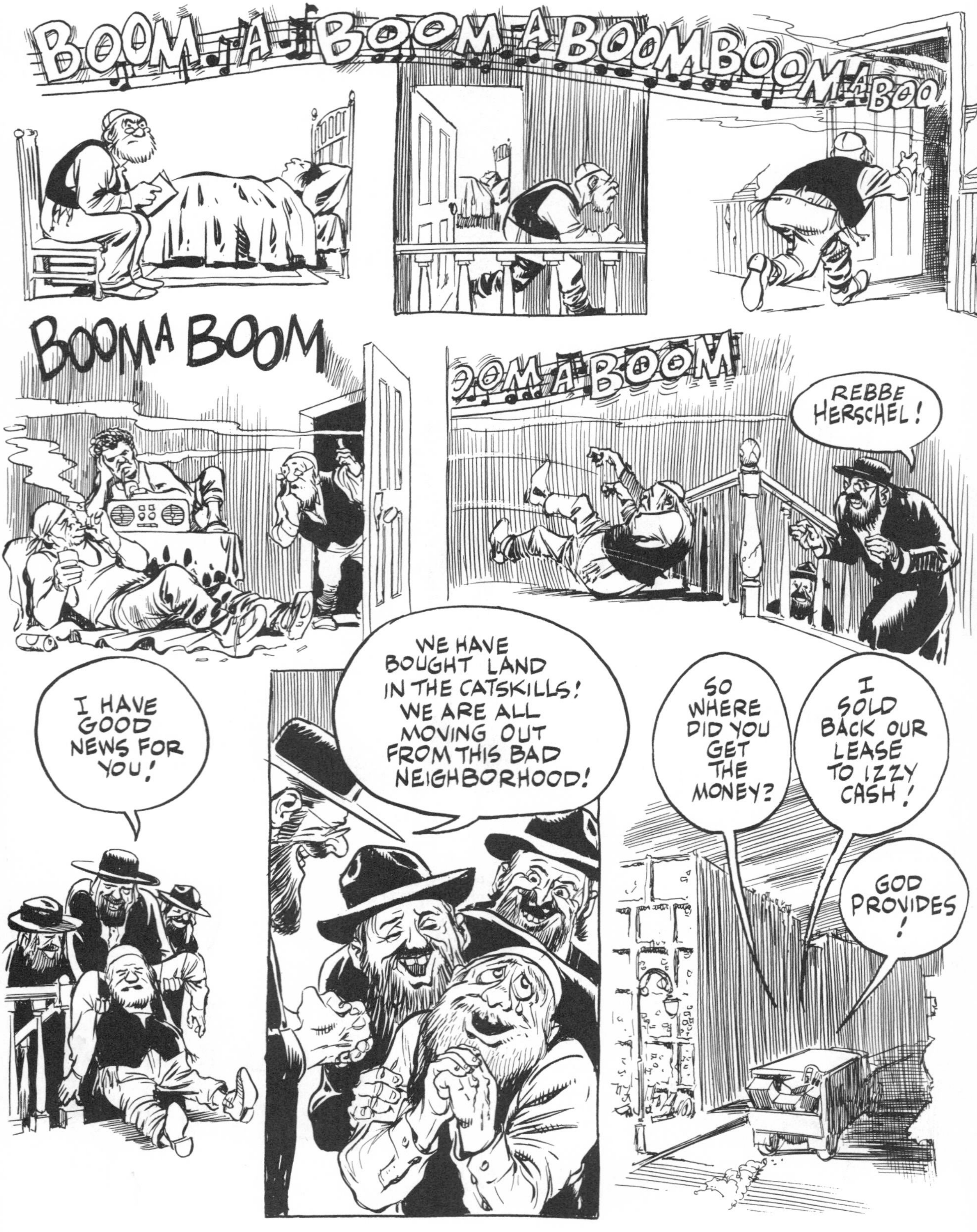
BOOM A BOOM A BOOM BOOM A BOO
BOOM A BOOM
OOM A BOOM
REBBE HERSCHEL!
I HAVE GOOD NEWS FOR YOU!
WE HAVE BOUGHT LAND IN THE CATSKILLS! WE ARE ALL MOVING OUT FROM THIS BAD NEIGHBORHOOD!
SO WHERE DID YOU GET THE MONEY?
I SOLD BACK OUR LEASE TO IZZY CASH!
GOD PROVIDES!

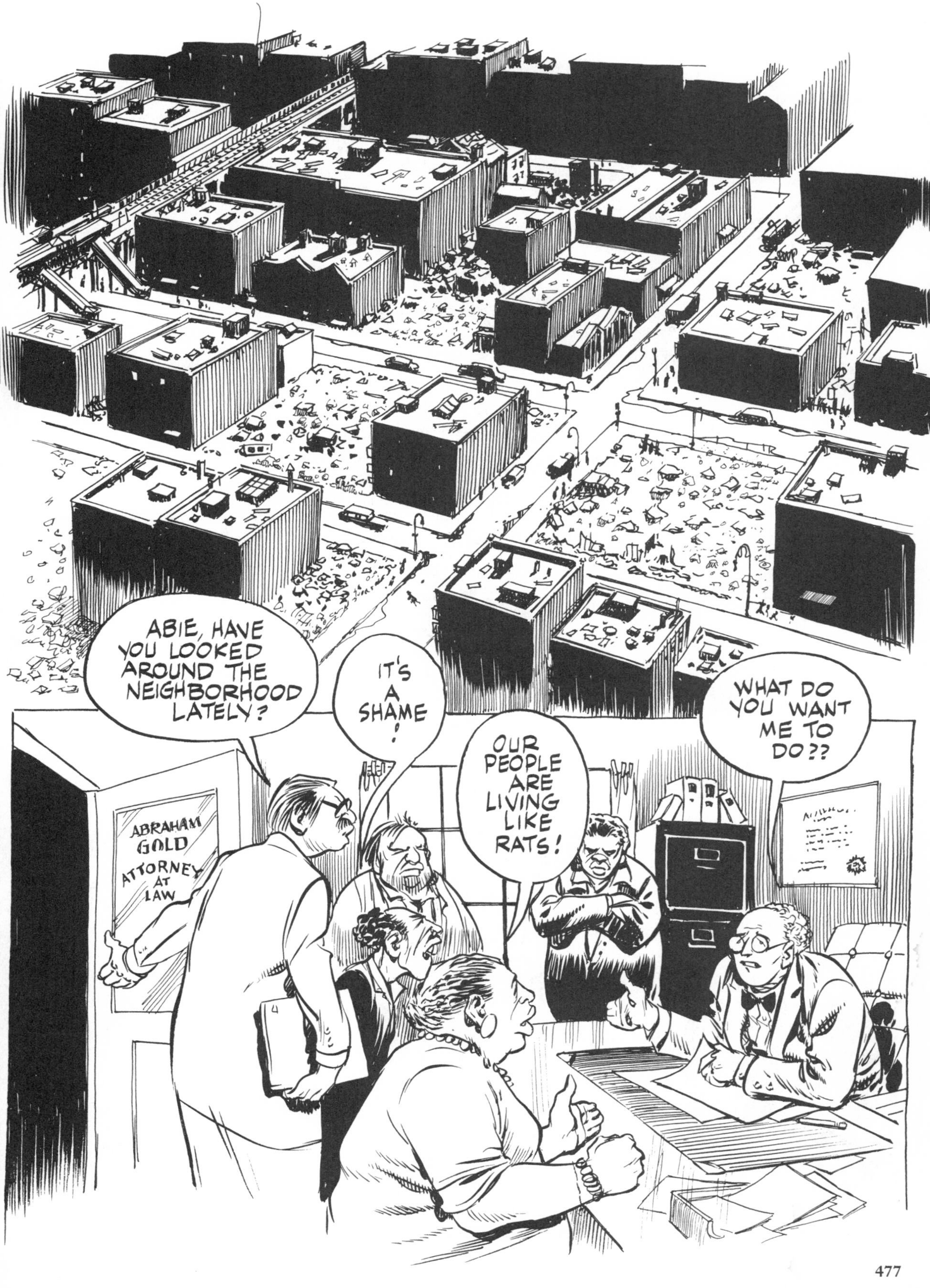
ABIE, HAVE YOU LOOKED AROUND THE NEIGHBORHOOD LATELY?
IT'S A SHAME!
OUR PEOPLE ARE LIVING LIKE RATS!
WHAT DO YOU WANT ME TO DO??
ABRAHAM GOLD ATTORNEY AT LAW

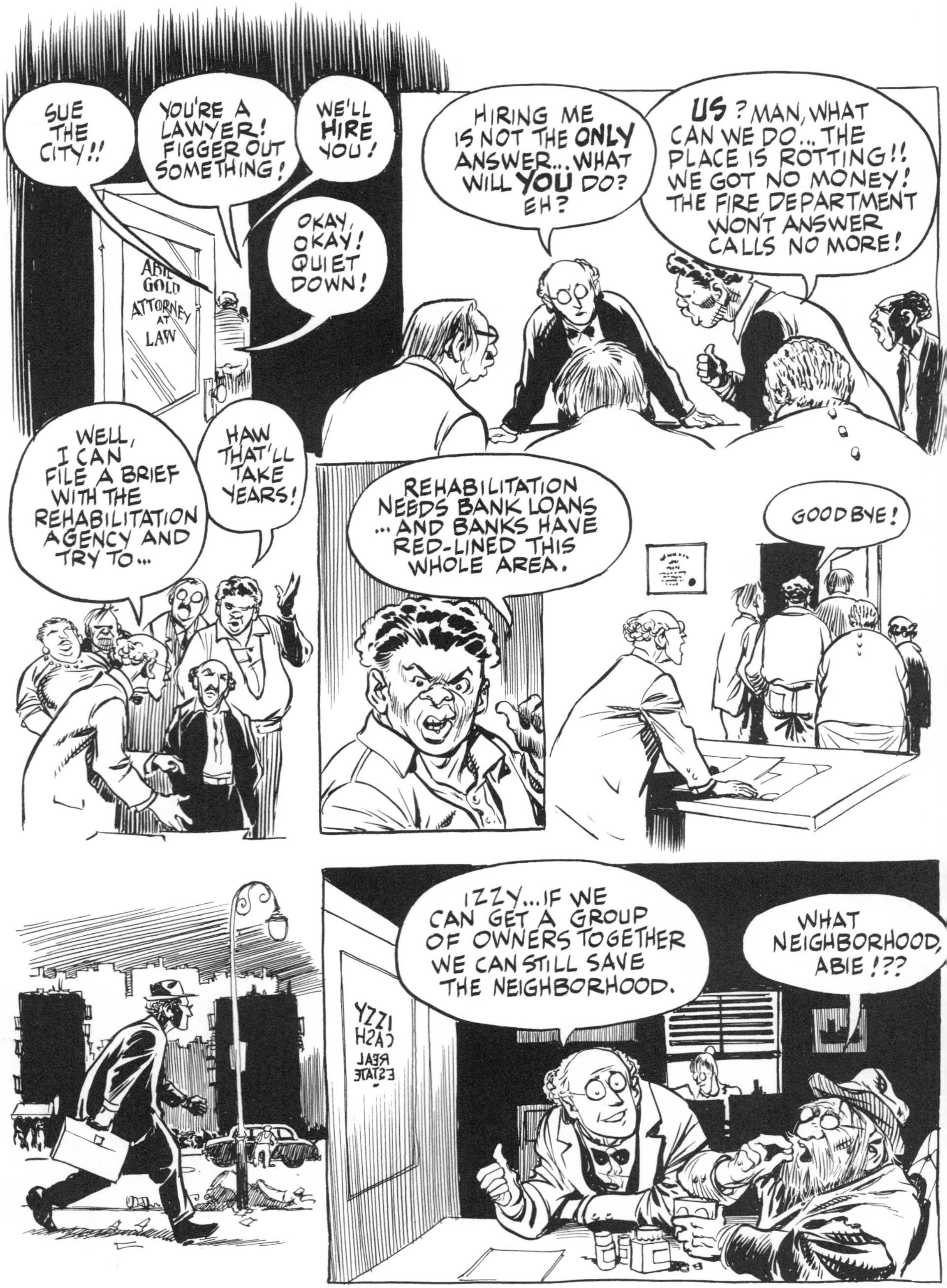
SUE THE CITY!!
YOU'RE A LAWYER! FIGGER OUT SOMETHING!
WE'LL HIRE YOU!
ABIE GOLD ATTORNEY AT LAW
OKAY, OKAY! QUIET DOWN!
HIRING ME IS NOT THE ONLY ANSWER... WHAT WILL YOU DO? EH?
US? MAN, WHAT CAN WE DO... THE PLACE IS ROTTING!! WE GOT NO MONEY! THE FIRE DEPARTMENT WON'T ANSWER CALLS NO MORE!
WELL, I CAN FILE A BRIEF WITH THE REHABILITATION AGENCY AND TRY TO...
HAW THAT'LL TAKE YEARS!
REHABILITATION NEEDS BANK LOANS ... AND BANKS HAVE RED-LINED THIS WHOLE AREA.
GOODBYE!
IZZY... IF WE CAN GET A GROUP OF OWNERS TOGETHER WE CAN STILL SAVE THE NEIGHBORHOOD.
WHAT NEIGHBORHOOD, ABIE!??

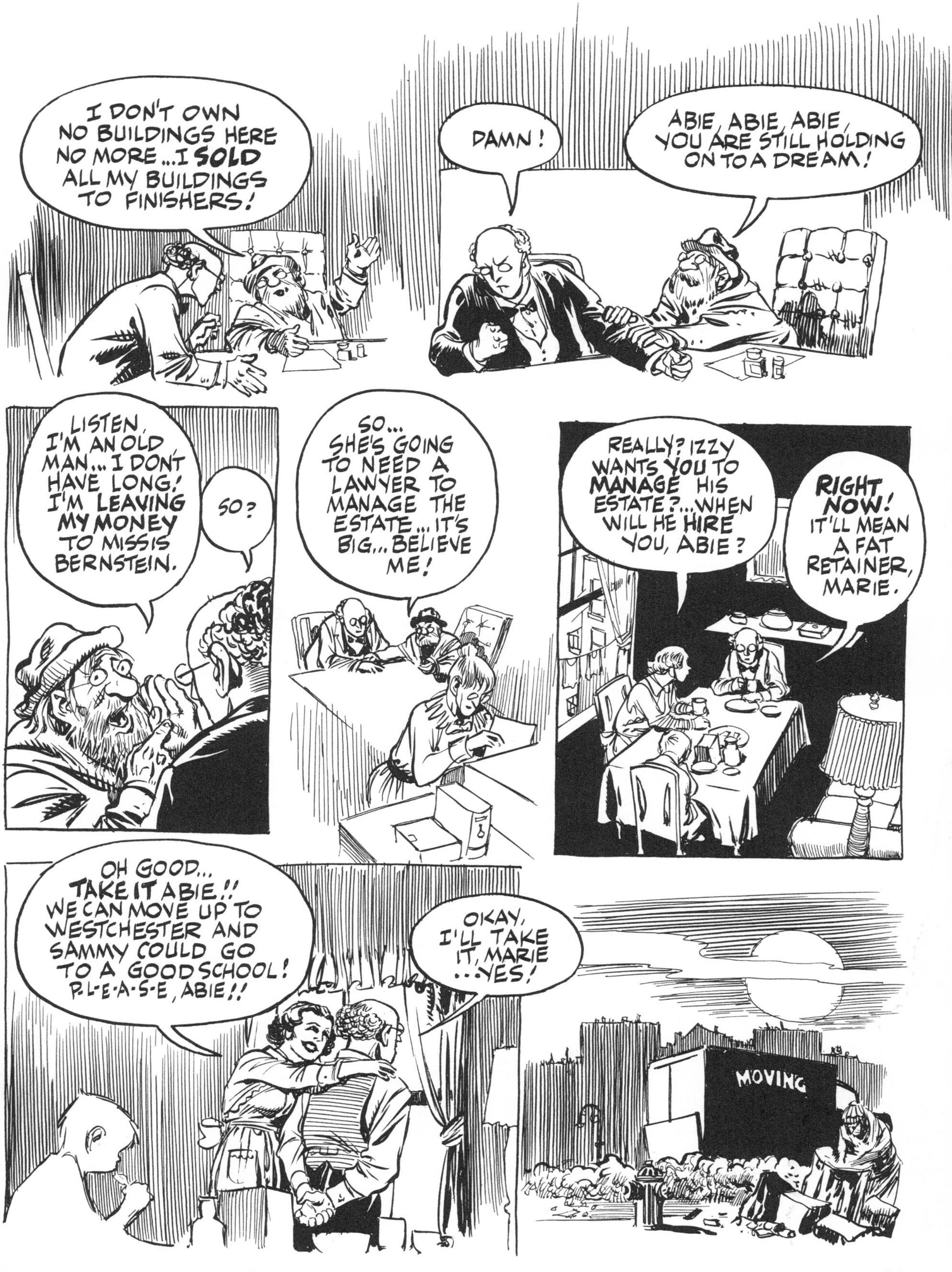
I DON'T OWN NO BUILDINGS HERE NO MORE ...I **SOLD** ALL MY BUILDINGS TO FINISHERS!
DAMN!
ABIE, ABIE, ABIE, YOU ARE STILL HOLDING ON TO A DREAM!
LISTEN, I'M AN OLD MAN... I DON'T HAVE LONG! I'M **LEAVING MY MONEY** TO MISSIS BERNSTEIN.
SO?
SO... SHE'S GOING TO NEED A LAWYER TO MANAGE THE ESTATE... IT'S BIG... BELIEVE ME!
REALLY? IZZY WANTS **YOU** TO **MANAGE** HIS ESTATE?... WHEN WILL HE **HIRE** YOU, ABIE?
RIGHT NOW! IT'LL MEAN A FAT RETAINER, MARIE.
OH GOOD... **TAKE IT** ABIE!! WE CAN MOVE UP TO WESTCHESTER AND SAMMY COULD GO TO A GOOD SCHOOL! P-L-E-A-S-E, ABIE!!
OKAY, I'LL TAKE IT, MARIE ... YES!
MOVING

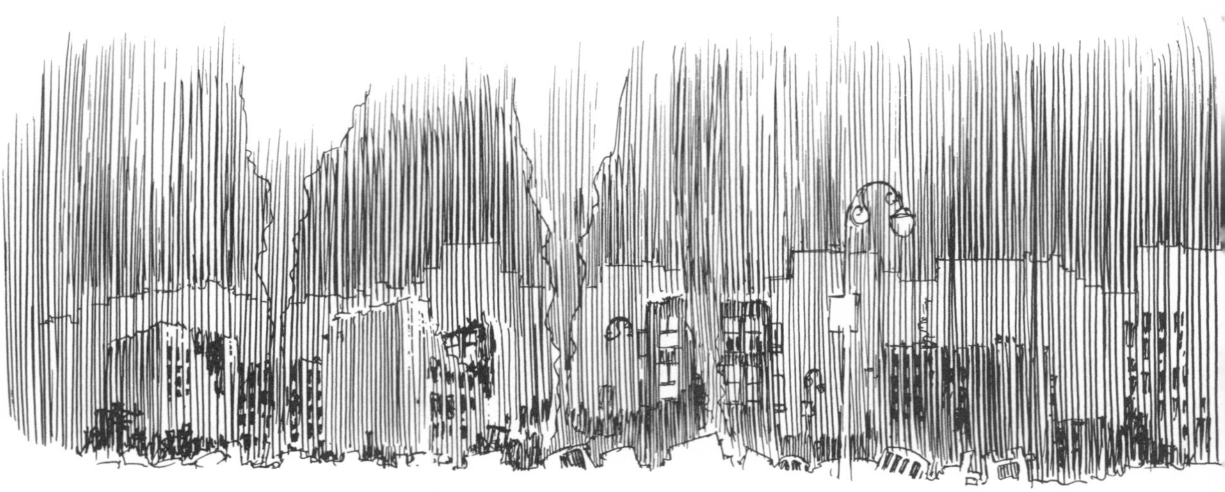

IN THE ONE HUNDRETH YEAR OF DROPSIE AVENUE EIGHT BUILDINGS WERE BURNED TO THE GROUND. IN THAT PART OF THE BOROUGH OVER 10,000 FIRES WERE REPORTED DURING THE YEAR.

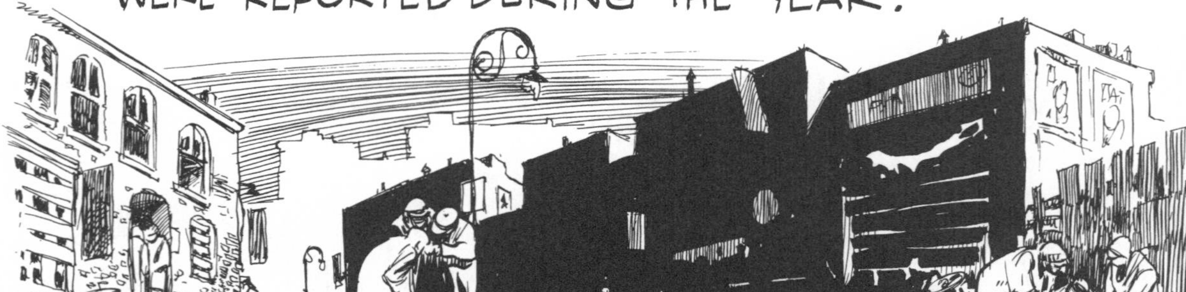

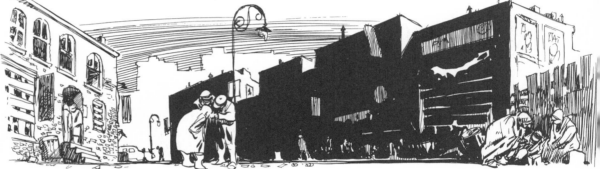

HUNDREDS OF SMALL BUSINESSES AND RETAIL SHOPS LEFT THE AREA AND OVER 17,000 JOBS DISAPPEARED. CRIME INCREASED.

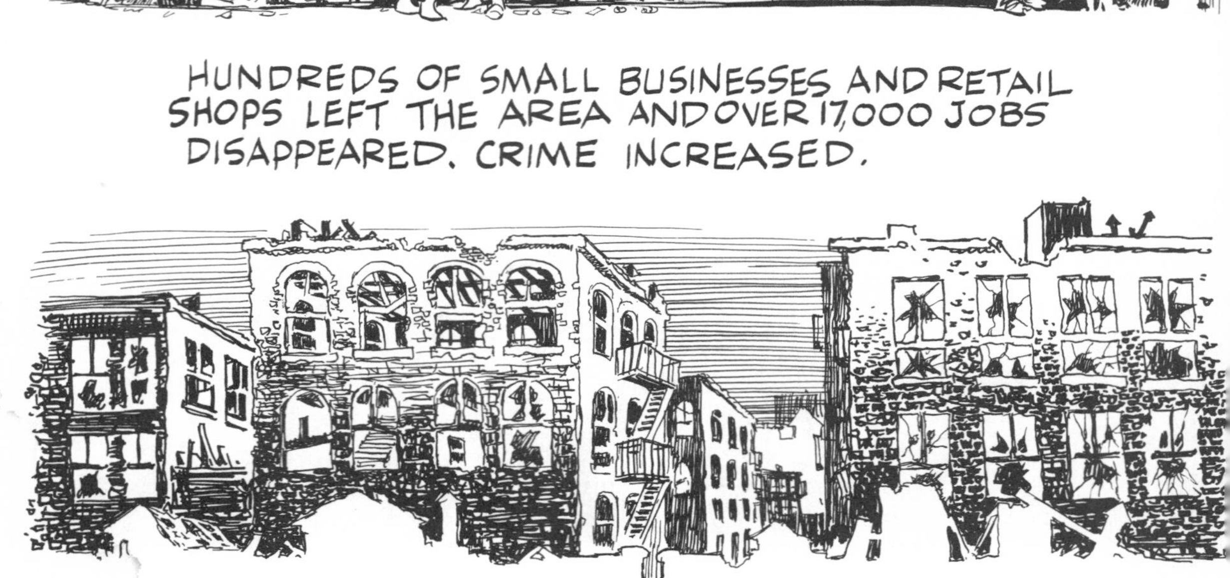

15,000 BUILDINGS BECAME VACANT IN THE SURROUNDING NEIGHBORHOOD AND OVER 60,000 PEOPLE MOVED OUT OF THE AREA.

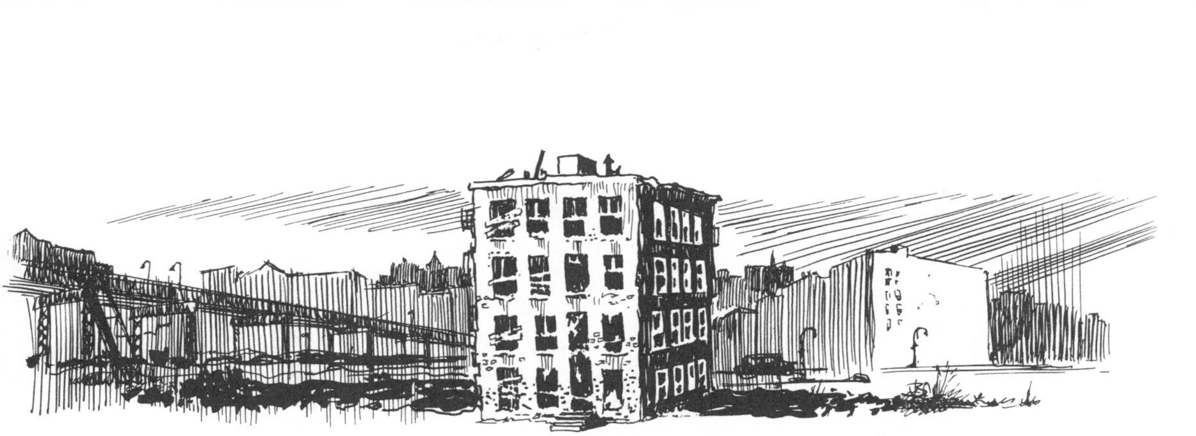

NOW...DROPSIE AVENUE WAS *"BOMBED OUT."* ONLY ONE BUILDING REMAINED STANDING.

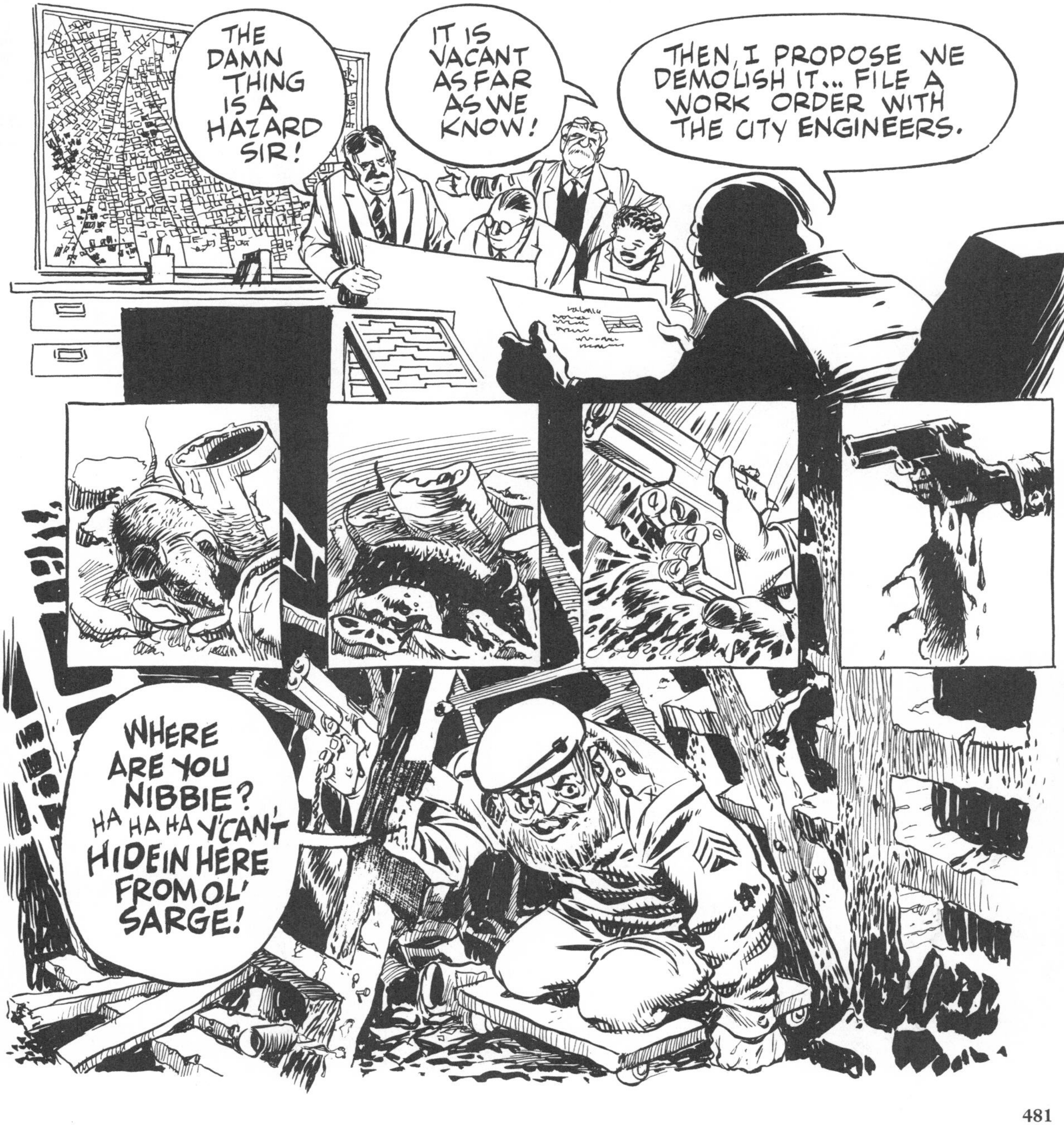
THE DAMN THING IS A HAZARD SIR!
IT IS VACANT AS FAR AS WE KNOW!
THEN, I PROPOSE WE DEMOLISH IT... FILE A WORK ORDER WITH THE CITY ENGINEERS.
WHERE ARE YOU NIBBIE? HA HA HA Y'CAN'T HIDE IN HERE FROM OL' SARGE!

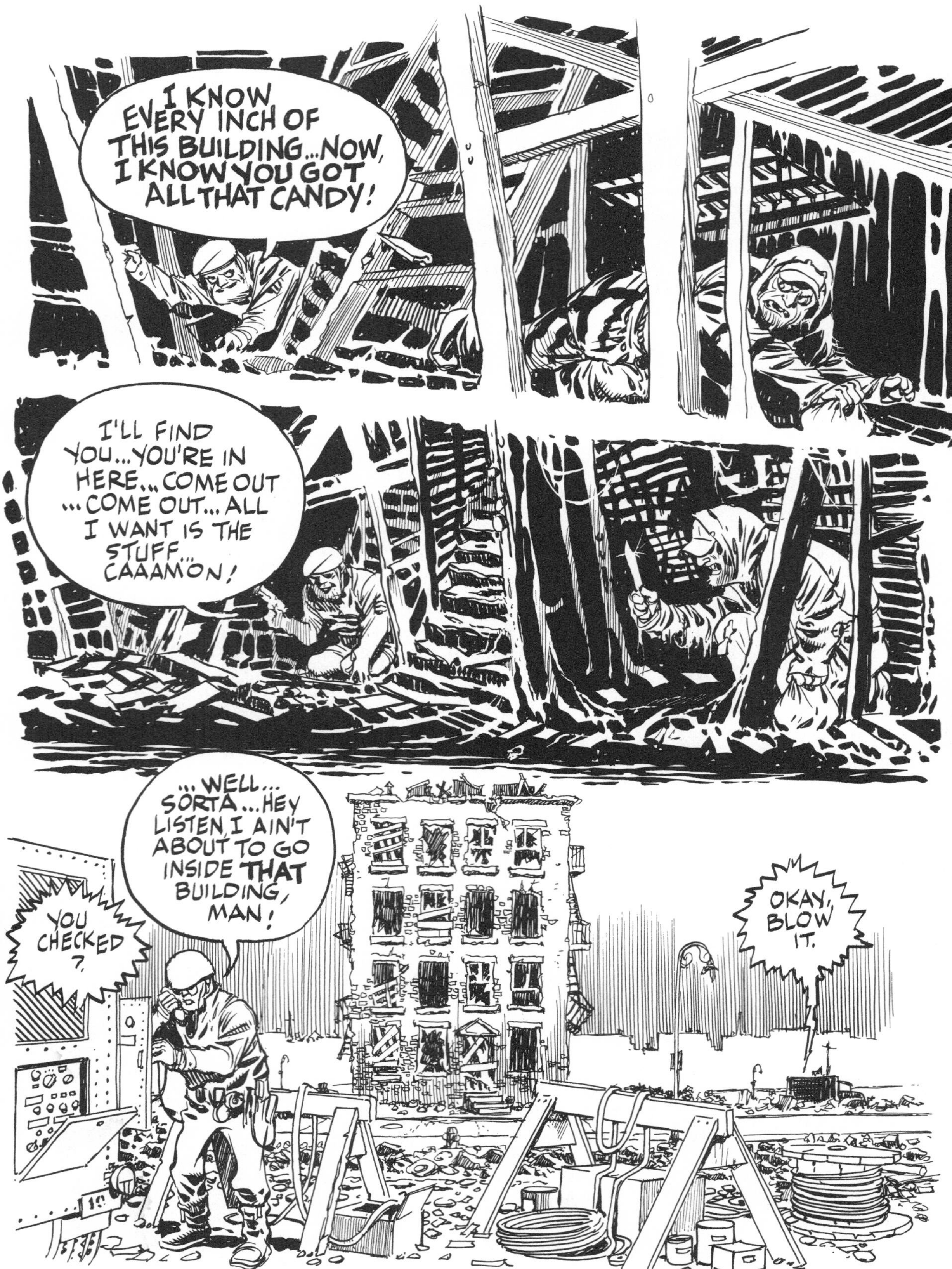
I KNOW EVERY INCH OF THIS BUILDING...NOW, I KNOW YOU GOT ALL THAT CANDY!
I'LL FIND YOU...YOU'RE IN HERE...COME OUT ...COME OUT...ALL I WANT IS THE STUFF... CAAAM'ON!
YOU CHECKED ?
...WELL... SORTA...HEY LISTEN, I AIN'T ABOUT TO GO INSIDE THAT BUILDING, MAN!
OKAY, BLOW IT.

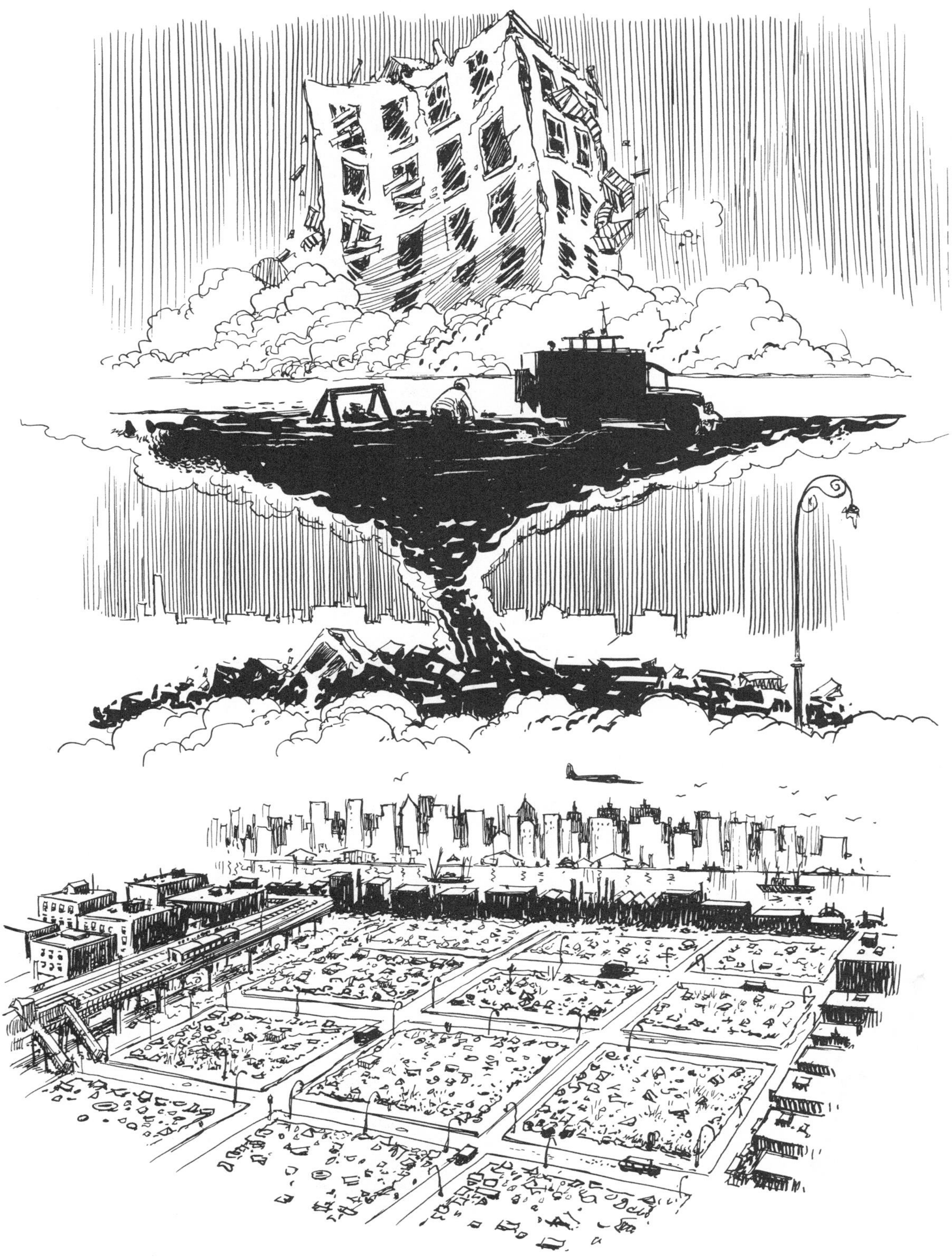

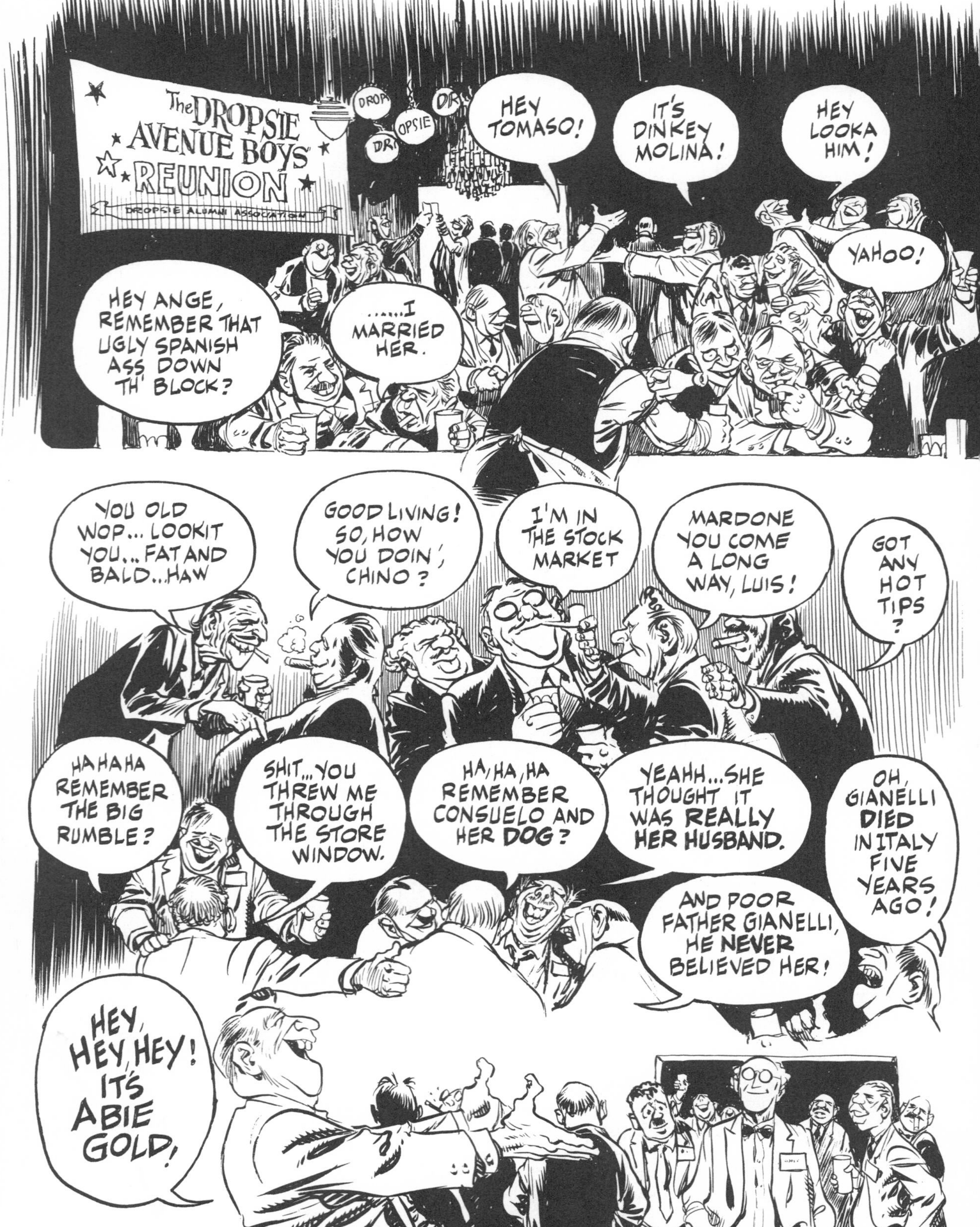
The DROPSIE AVENUE BOYS' REUNION
DROPSIE ALUMNI ASSOCIATION
HEY TOMASO!
IT'S DINKEY MOLINA!
HEY LOOKA HIM!
YAHOO!
HEY ANGE, REMEMBER THAT UGLY SPANISH ASS DOWN TH' BLOCK?
......I MARRIED HER.
YOU OLD WOP... LOOKIT YOU... FAT AND BALD...HAW
GOOD LIVING! SO, HOW YOU DOIN', CHINO?
I'M IN THE STOCK MARKET
MARDONE YOU COME A LONG WAY, LUIS!
GOT ANY HOT TIPS?
HAHAHA REMEMBER THE BIG RUMBLE?
SHIT...YOU THREW ME THROUGH THE STORE WINDOW.
HA, HA, HA REMEMBER CONSUELO AND HER **DOG**?
YEAHH...SHE THOUGHT IT WAS **REALLY HER HUSBAND.**
OH, GIANELLI **DIED** IN ITALY FIVE YEARS AGO!
AND POOR FATHER GIANELLI, HE **NEVER** BELIEVED HER!
HEY, HEY, HEY! IT'S ABIE GOLD!

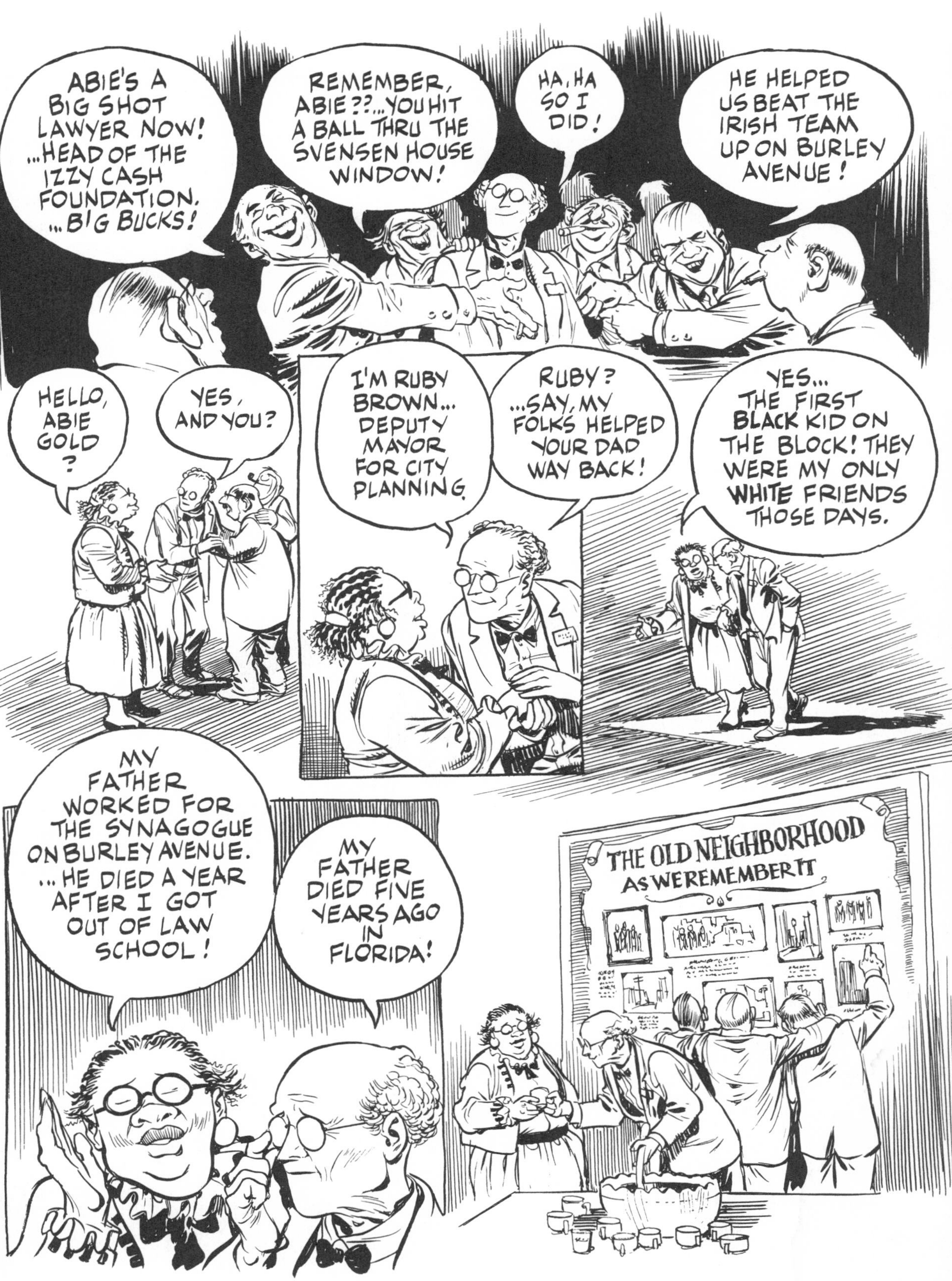

ABIE'S A BIG SHOT LAWYER NOW! ...HEAD OF THE IZZY CASH FOUNDATION. ...BIG BUCKS!
REMEMBER, ABIE??...YOU HIT A BALL THRU THE SVENSEN HOUSE WINDOW!
HA, HA SO I DID!
HE HELPED US BEAT THE IRISH TEAM UP ON BURLEY AVENUE!
HELLO, ABIE GOLD ?
YES, AND YOU?
I'M RUBY BROWN... DEPUTY MAYOR FOR CITY PLANNING.
RUBY? ...SAY, MY FOLKS HELPED YOUR DAD WAY BACK!
YES... THE FIRST BLACK KID ON THE BLOCK! THEY WERE MY ONLY WHITE FRIENDS THOSE DAYS.
MY FATHER WORKED FOR THE SYNAGOGUE ON BURLEY AVENUE. ...HE DIED A YEAR AFTER I GOT OUT OF LAW SCHOOL!
MY FATHER DIED FIVE YEARS AGO IN FLORIDA!
THE OLD NEIGHBORHOOD
AS WE REMEMBER IT

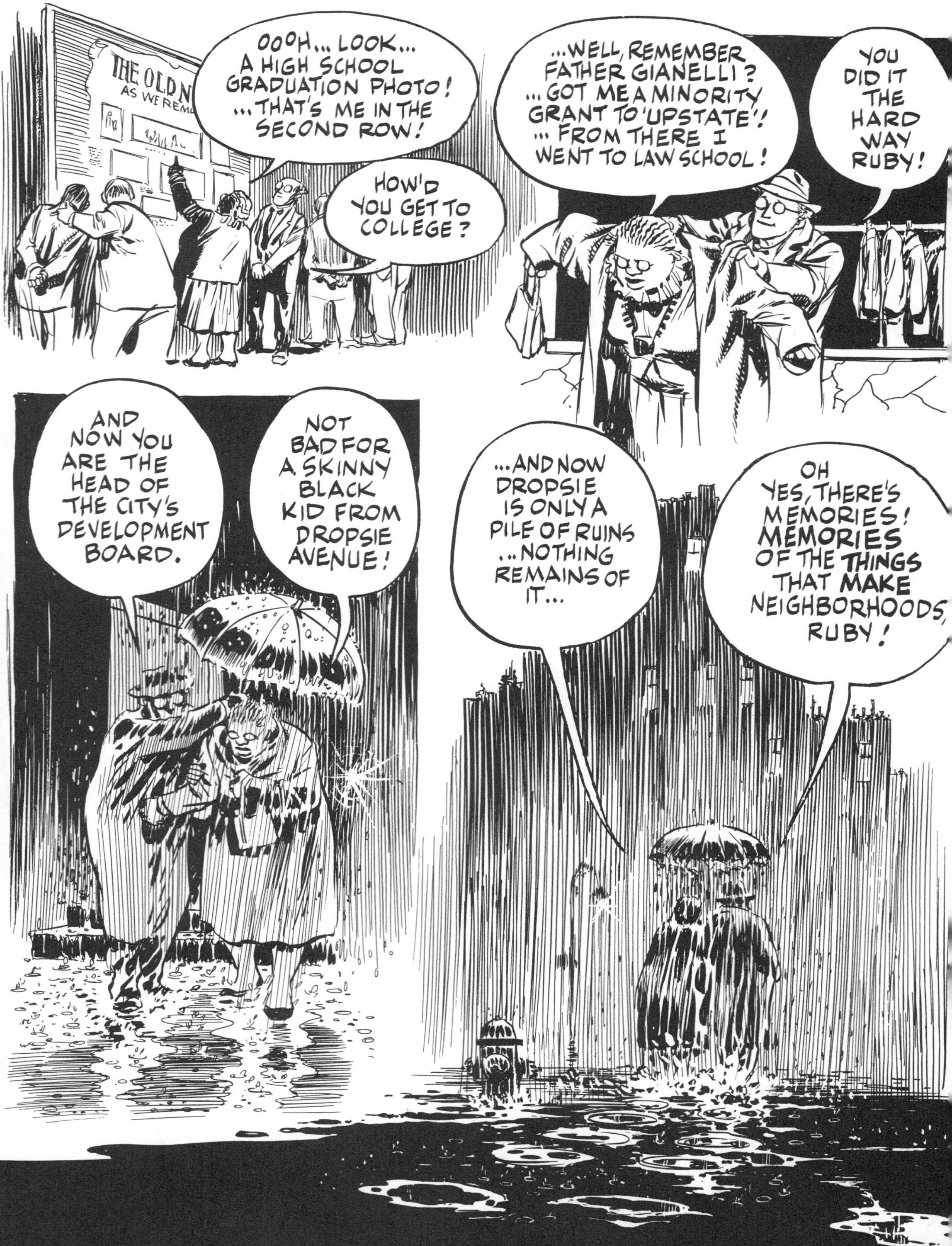
OOOH... LOOK... A HIGH SCHOOL GRADUATION PHOTO! ...THAT'S ME IN THE SECOND ROW!
HOW'D YOU GET TO COLLEGE?
...WELL, REMEMBER FATHER GIANELLI? ...GOT ME A MINORITY GRANT TO 'UPSTATE'! ...FROM THERE I WENT TO LAW SCHOOL!
YOU DID IT THE HARD WAY RUBY!
AND NOW YOU ARE THE HEAD OF THE CITY'S DEVELOPMENT BOARD.
NOT BAD FOR A SKINNY BLACK KID FROM DROPSIE AVENUE!
...AND NOW DROPSIE IS ONLY A PILE OF RUINS ...NOTHING REMAINS OF IT...
OH YES, THERE'S MEMORIES! MEMORIES OF THE THINGS THAT MAKE NEIGHBORHOODS, RUBY!

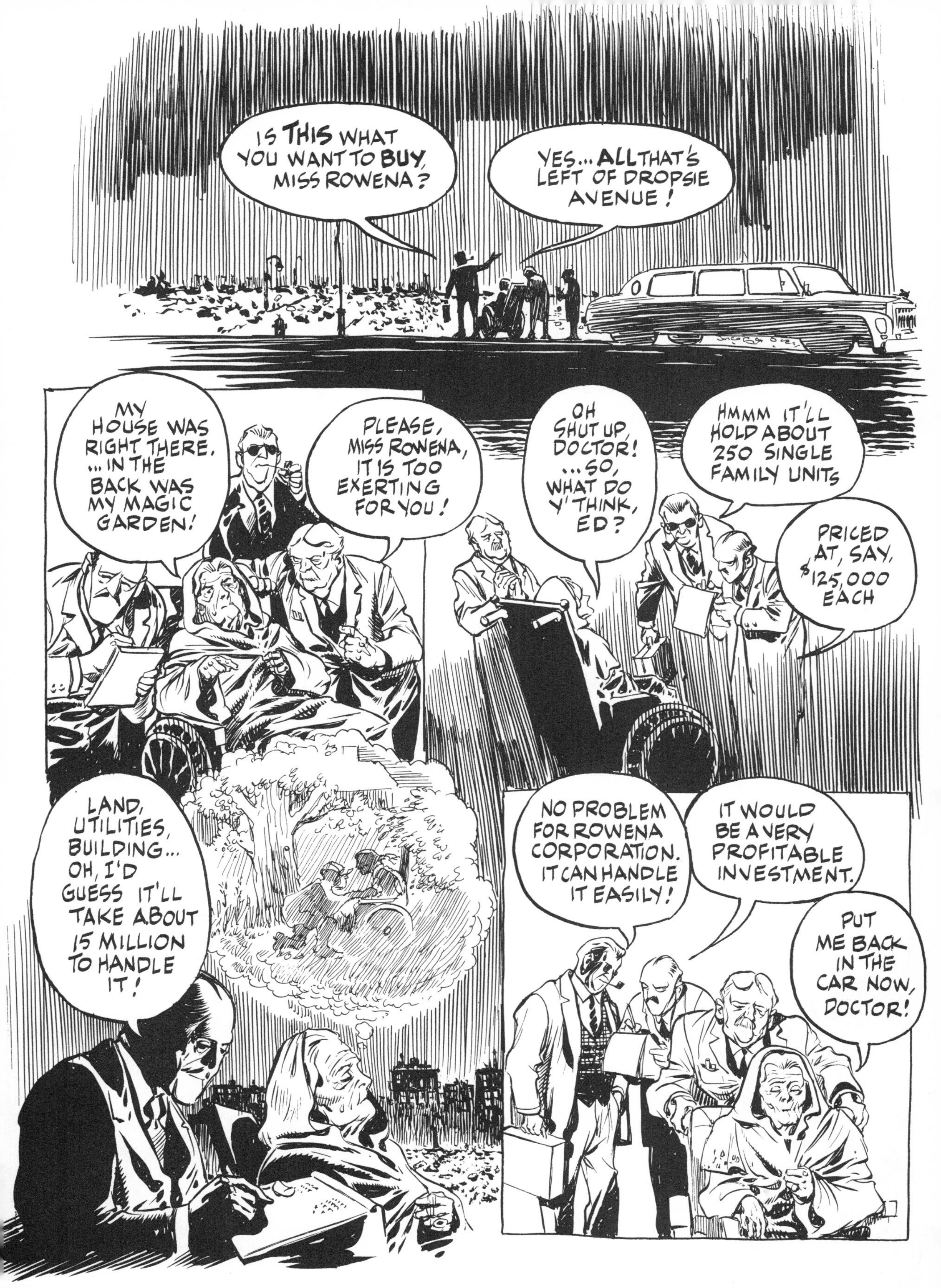
IS THIS WHAT YOU WANT TO BUY, MISS ROWENA?
YES... ALL THAT'S LEFT OF DROPSIE AVENUE!
MY HOUSE WAS RIGHT THERE. ...IN THE BACK WAS MY MAGIC GARDEN!
PLEASE, MISS ROWENA, IT IS TOO EXERTING FOR YOU!
OH SHUT UP, DOCTOR! ...SO, WHAT DO Y'THINK, ED?
HMMM IT'LL HOLD ABOUT 250 SINGLE FAMILY UNITS
PRICED AT, SAY, $125,000 EACH
LAND, UTILITIES, BUILDING... OH, I'D GUESS IT'LL TAKE ABOUT 15 MILLION TO HANDLE IT!
NO PROBLEM FOR ROWENA CORPORATION. IT CAN HANDLE IT EASILY!
IT WOULD BE A VERY PROFITABLE INVESTMENT.
PUT ME BACK IN THE CAR NOW, DOCTOR!

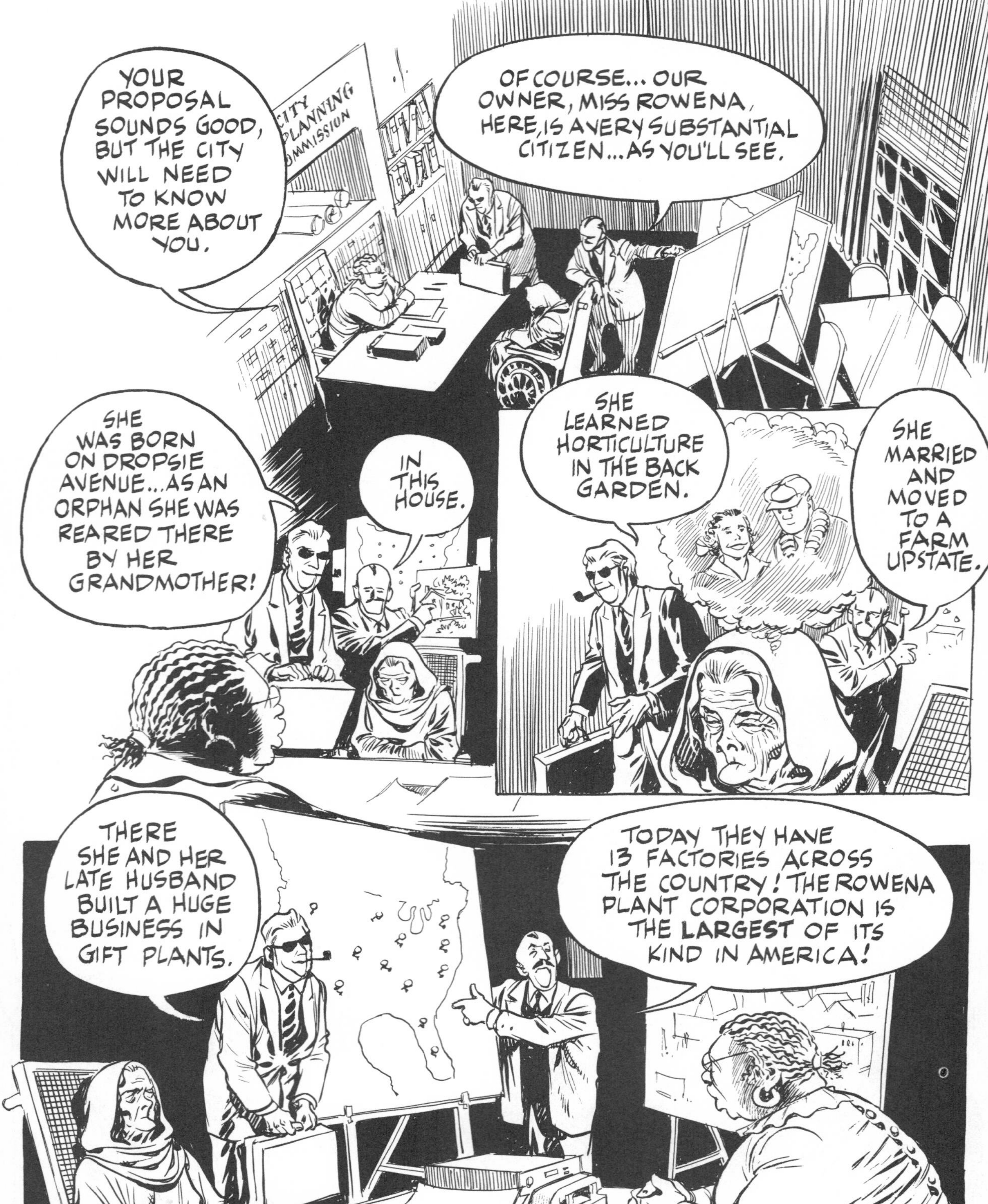
YOUR PROPOSAL SOUNDS GOOD, BUT THE CITY WILL NEED TO KNOW MORE ABOUT YOU.
CITY PLANNING COMMISSION
OF COURSE... OUR OWNER, MISS ROWENA, HERE, IS A VERY SUBSTANTIAL CITIZEN... AS YOU'LL SEE.
SHE WAS BORN ON DROPSIE AVENUE... AS AN ORPHAN SHE WAS REARED THERE BY HER GRANDMOTHER!
IN THIS HOUSE.
SHE LEARNED HORTICULTURE IN THE BACK GARDEN.
SHE MARRIED AND MOVED TO A FARM UPSTATE.
THERE SHE AND HER LATE HUSBAND BUILT A HUGE BUSINESS IN GIFT PLANTS.
TODAY THEY HAVE 13 FACTORIES ACROSS THE COUNTRY! THE ROWENA PLANT CORPORATION IS THE **LARGEST** OF ITS KIND IN AMERICA!

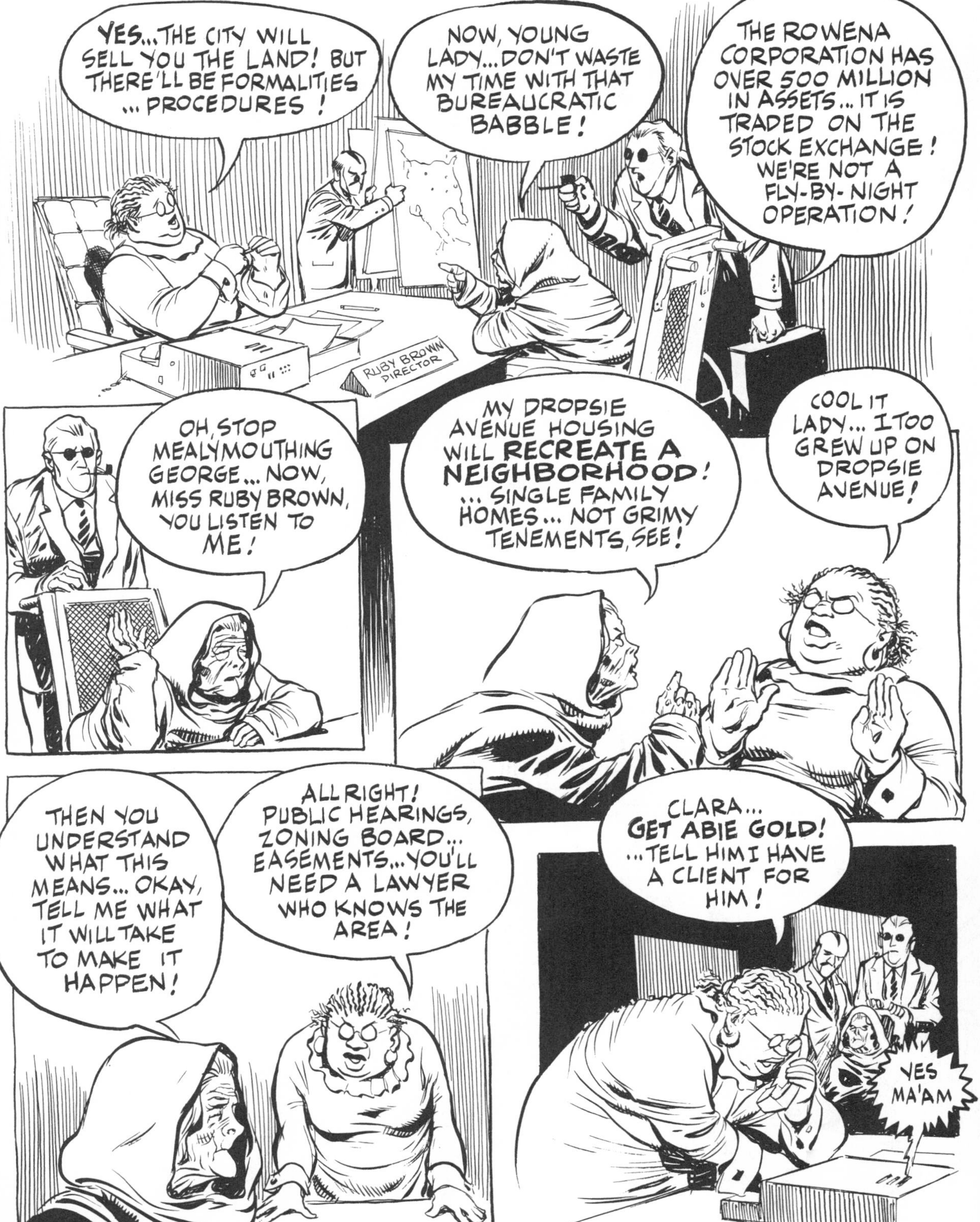
YES... THE CITY WILL SELL YOU THE LAND! BUT THERE'LL BE FORMALITIES ... PROCEDURES!
NOW, YOUNG LADY... DON'T WASTE MY TIME WITH THAT BUREAUCRATIC BABBLE!
THE ROWENA CORPORATION HAS OVER 500 MILLION IN ASSETS... IT IS TRADED ON THE STOCK EXCHANGE! WE'RE NOT A FLY-BY-NIGHT OPERATION!
RUBY BROWN DIRECTOR
OH, STOP MEALYMOUTHING GEORGE... NOW, MISS RUBY BROWN, YOU LISTEN TO ME!
MY DROPSIE AVENUE HOUSING WILL RECREATE A NEIGHBORHOOD! ... SINGLE FAMILY HOMES... NOT GRIMY TENEMENTS, SEE!
COOL IT LADY... I TOO GREW UP ON DROPSIE AVENUE!
THEN YOU UNDERSTAND WHAT THIS MEANS... OKAY, TELL ME WHAT IT WILL TAKE TO MAKE IT HAPPEN!
ALL RIGHT! PUBLIC HEARINGS, ZONING BOARD... EASEMENTS... YOU'LL NEED A LAWYER WHO KNOWS THE AREA!
CLARA... GET ABIE GOLD! ...TELL HIM I HAVE A CLIENT FOR HIM!
YES MA'AM

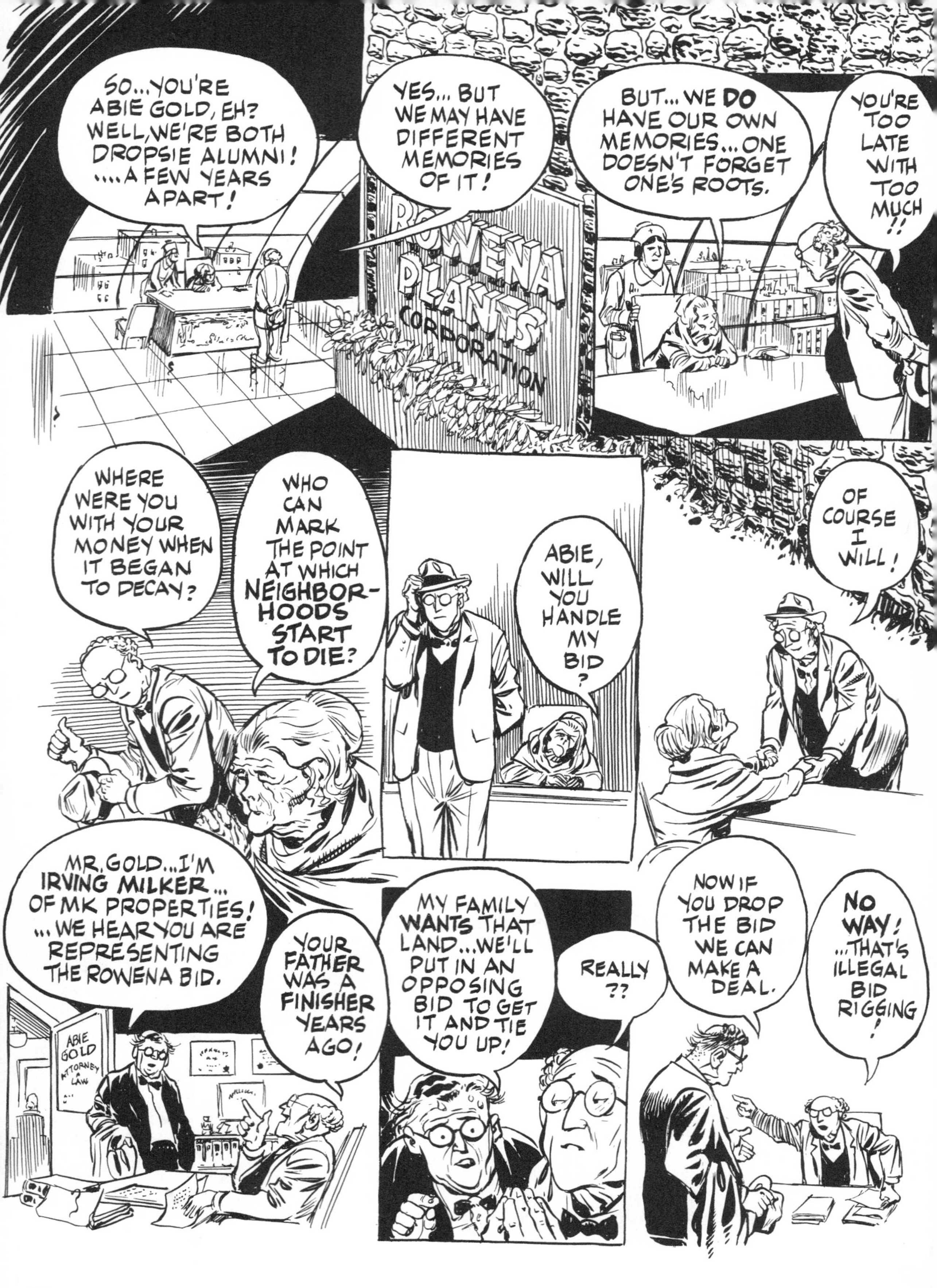

SO...YOU'RE ABIE GOLD, EH? WELL, WE'RE BOTH DROPSIE ALUMNI! ....A FEW YEARS APART!
YES... BUT WE MAY HAVE DIFFERENT MEMORIES OF IT!
ROWENA PLANTS CORPORATION
BUT... WE DO HAVE OUR OWN MEMORIES... ONE DOESN'T FORGET ONE'S ROOTS.
YOU'RE TOO LATE WITH TOO MUCH!!
WHERE WERE YOU WITH YOUR MONEY WHEN IT BEGAN TO DECAY?
WHO CAN MARK THE POINT AT WHICH NEIGHBORHOODS START TO DIE?
ABIE, WILL YOU HANDLE MY BID?
OF COURSE I WILL!
MR. GOLD...I'M IRVING MILKER... OF MK PROPERTIES! ...WE HEAR YOU ARE REPRESENTING THE ROWENA BID.
ABIE GOLD ATTORNEY AT LAW
YOUR FATHER WAS A FINISHER YEARS AGO!
MY FAMILY WANTS THAT LAND...WE'LL PUT IN AN OPPOSING BID TO GET IT AND TIE YOU UP!
REALLY??
NOW IF YOU DROP THE BID WE CAN MAKE A DEAL.
NO WAY! ...THAT'S ILLEGAL BID RIGGING!

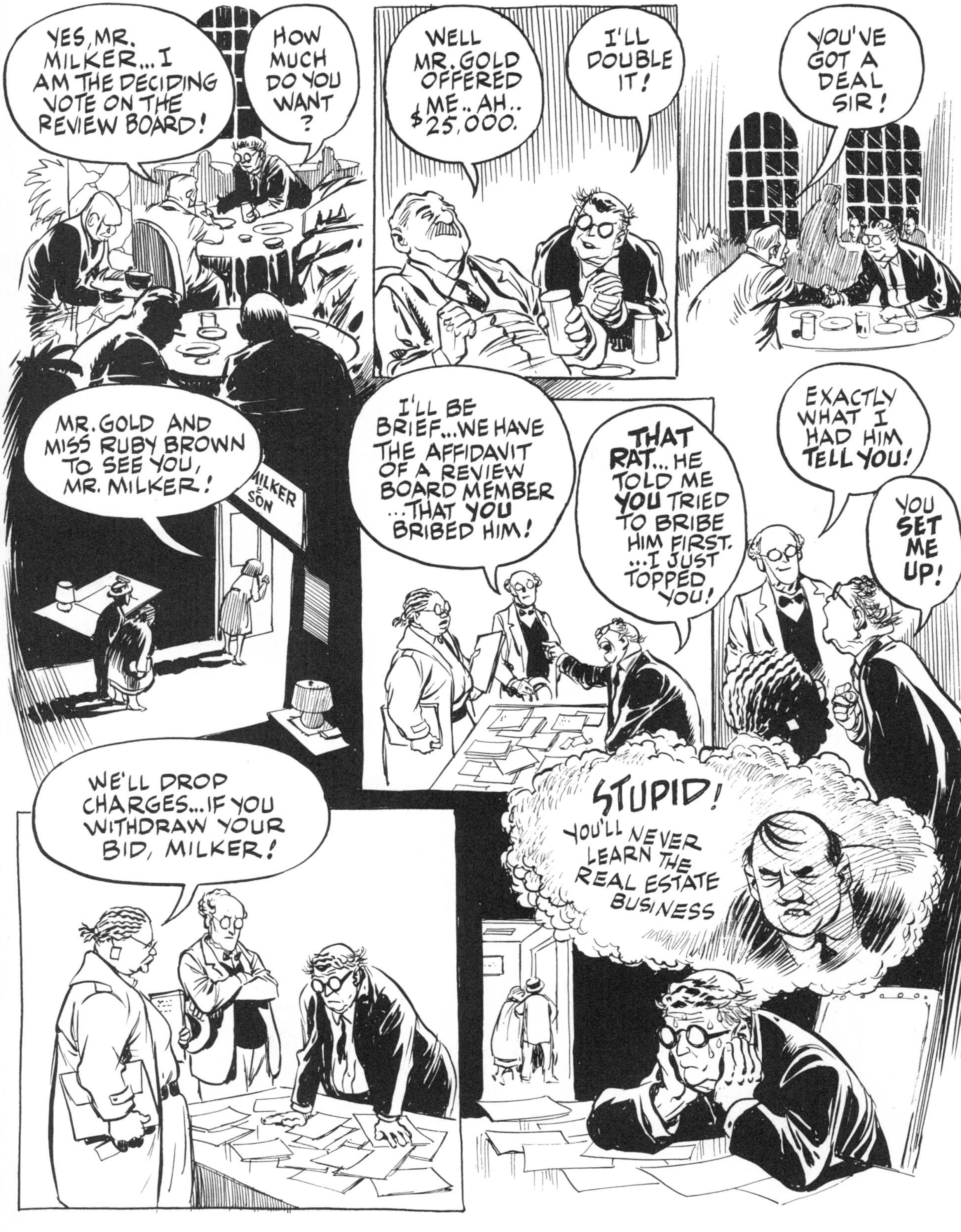
YES, MR. MILKER... I AM THE DECIDING VOTE ON THE REVIEW BOARD!
HOW MUCH DO YOU WANT?
WELL MR. GOLD OFFERED ME.. AH.. $25,000.
I'LL DOUBLE IT!
YOU'VE GOT A DEAL SIR!
MR. GOLD AND MISS RUBY BROWN TO SEE YOU, MR. MILKER!
MILKER & SON
I'LL BE BRIEF...WE HAVE THE AFFIDAVIT OF A REVIEW BOARD MEMBER ...THAT YOU BRIBED HIM!
THAT RAT... HE TOLD ME YOU TRIED TO BRIBE HIM FIRST. ...I JUST TOPPED YOU!
EXACTLY WHAT I HAD HIM TELL YOU!
YOU SET ME UP!
WE'LL DROP CHARGES...IF YOU WITHDRAW YOUR BID, MILKER!
STUPID!
YOU'LL NEVER LEARN THE REAL ESTATE BUSINESS

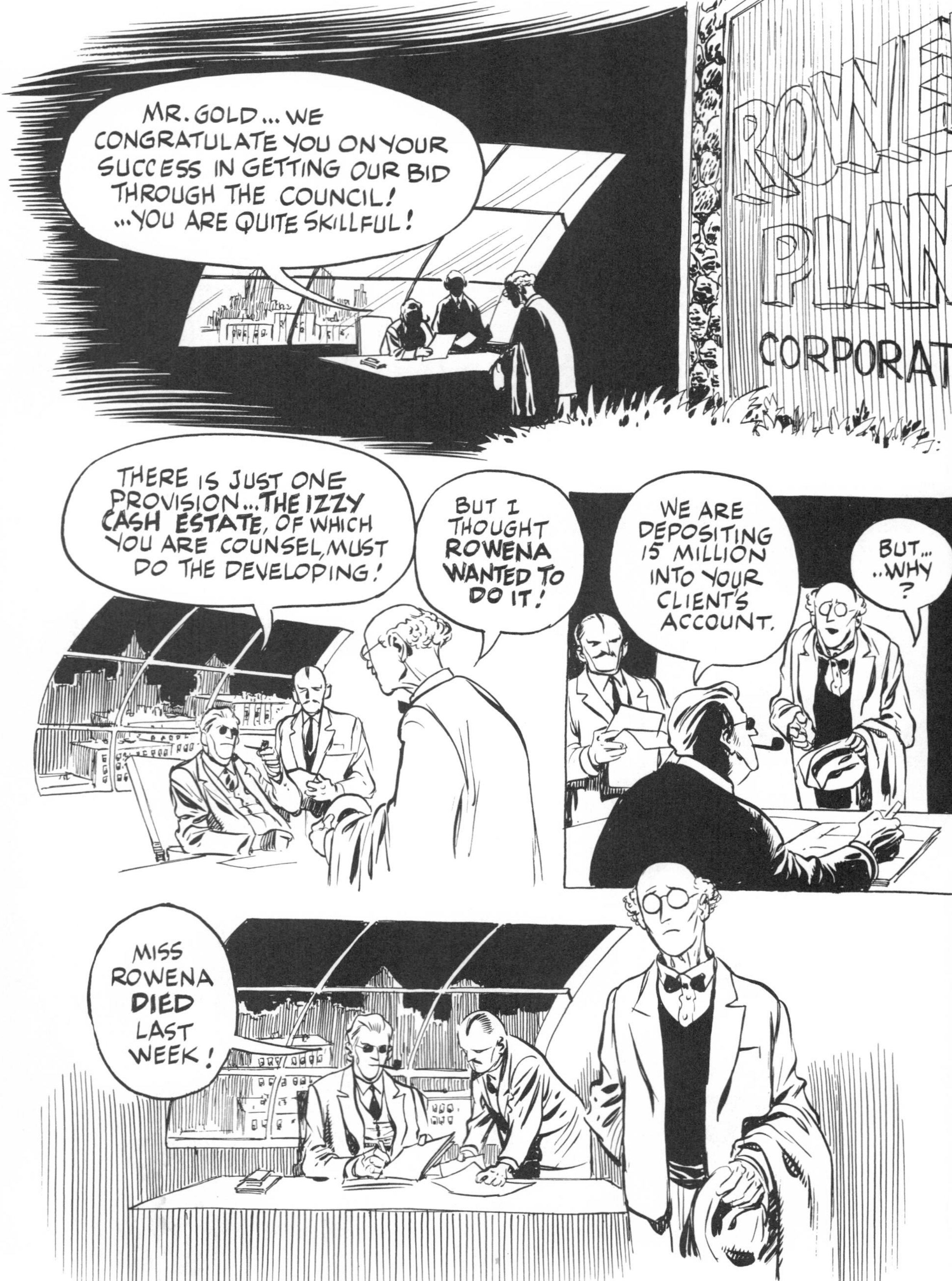
MR. GOLD... WE CONGRATULATE YOU ON YOUR SUCCESS IN GETTING OUR BID THROUGH THE COUNCIL! ...YOU ARE QUITE SKILLFUL!
CORPORAT
THERE IS JUST ONE PROVISION... THE IZZY CASH ESTATE, OF WHICH YOU ARE COUNSEL, MUST DO THE DEVELOPING!
BUT I THOUGHT ROWENA WANTED TO DO IT!
WE ARE DEPOSITING 15 MILLION INTO YOUR CLIENT'S ACCOUNT.
BUT... ..WHY ?
MISS ROWENA DIED LAST WEEK!

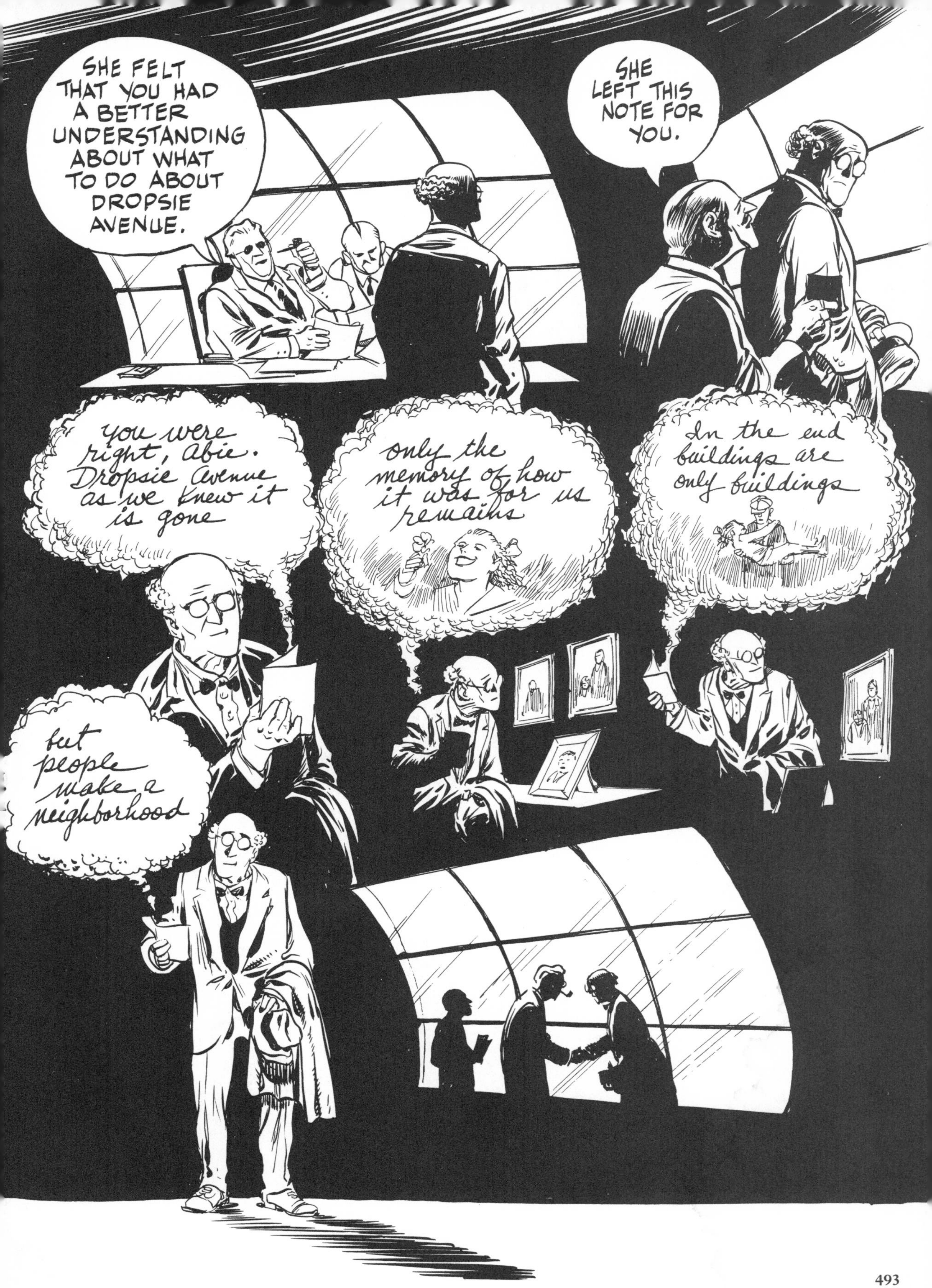
SHE FELT THAT YOU HAD A BETTER UNDERSTANDING ABOUT WHAT TO DO ABOUT DROPSIE AVENUE.
SHE LEFT THIS NOTE FOR YOU.
you were right, Abie. Dropsie Avenue as we knew it is gone
only the memory of how it was for us remains
In the end buildings are only buildings
but people make a neighborhood

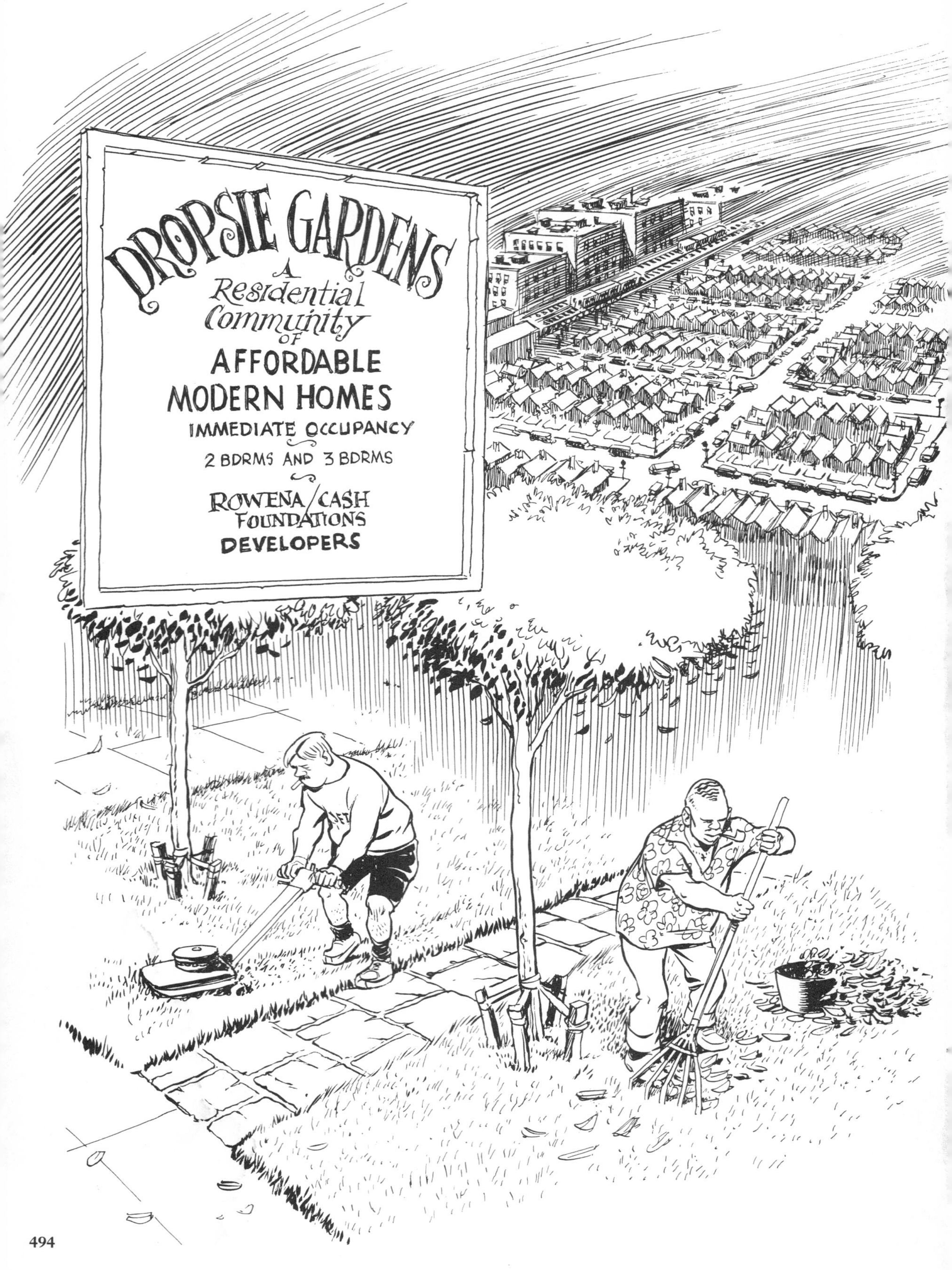
DROPSIE GARDENS
A
Residential
Community
OF
AFFORDABLE
MODERN HOMES
IMMEDIATE OCCUPANCY
2 BDRMS AND 3 BDRMS
ROWENA/CASH
FOUNDATIONS
DEVELOPERS

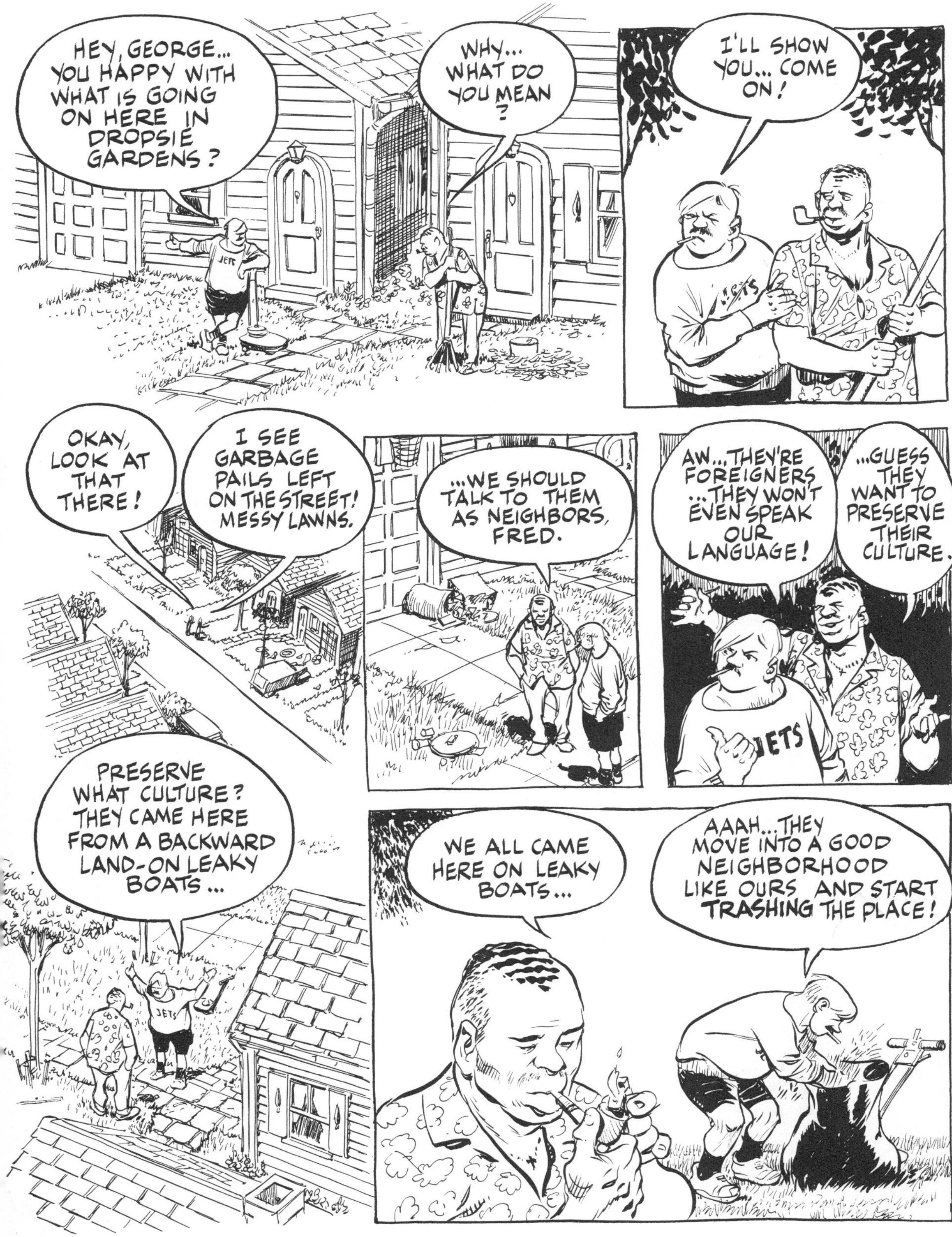
HEY, GEORGE... YOU HAPPY WITH WHAT IS GOING ON HERE IN DROPSIE GARDENS?
WHY... WHAT DO YOU MEAN?
I'LL SHOW YOU... COME ON!
OKAY, LOOK AT THAT THERE!
I SEE GARBAGE PAILS LEFT ON THE STREET! MESSY LAWNS.
...WE SHOULD TALK TO THEM AS NEIGHBORS, FRED.
AW... THEY'RE FOREIGNERS ...THEY WON'T EVEN SPEAK OUR LANGUAGE!
...GUESS THEY WANT TO PRESERVE THEIR CULTURE.
PRESERVE WHAT CULTURE? THEY CAME HERE FROM A BACKWARD LAND-ON LEAKY BOATS...
WE ALL CAME HERE ON LEAKY BOATS...
AAAH... THEY MOVE INTO A GOOD NEIGHBORHOOD LIKE OURS AND START TRASHING THE PLACE!
JETS

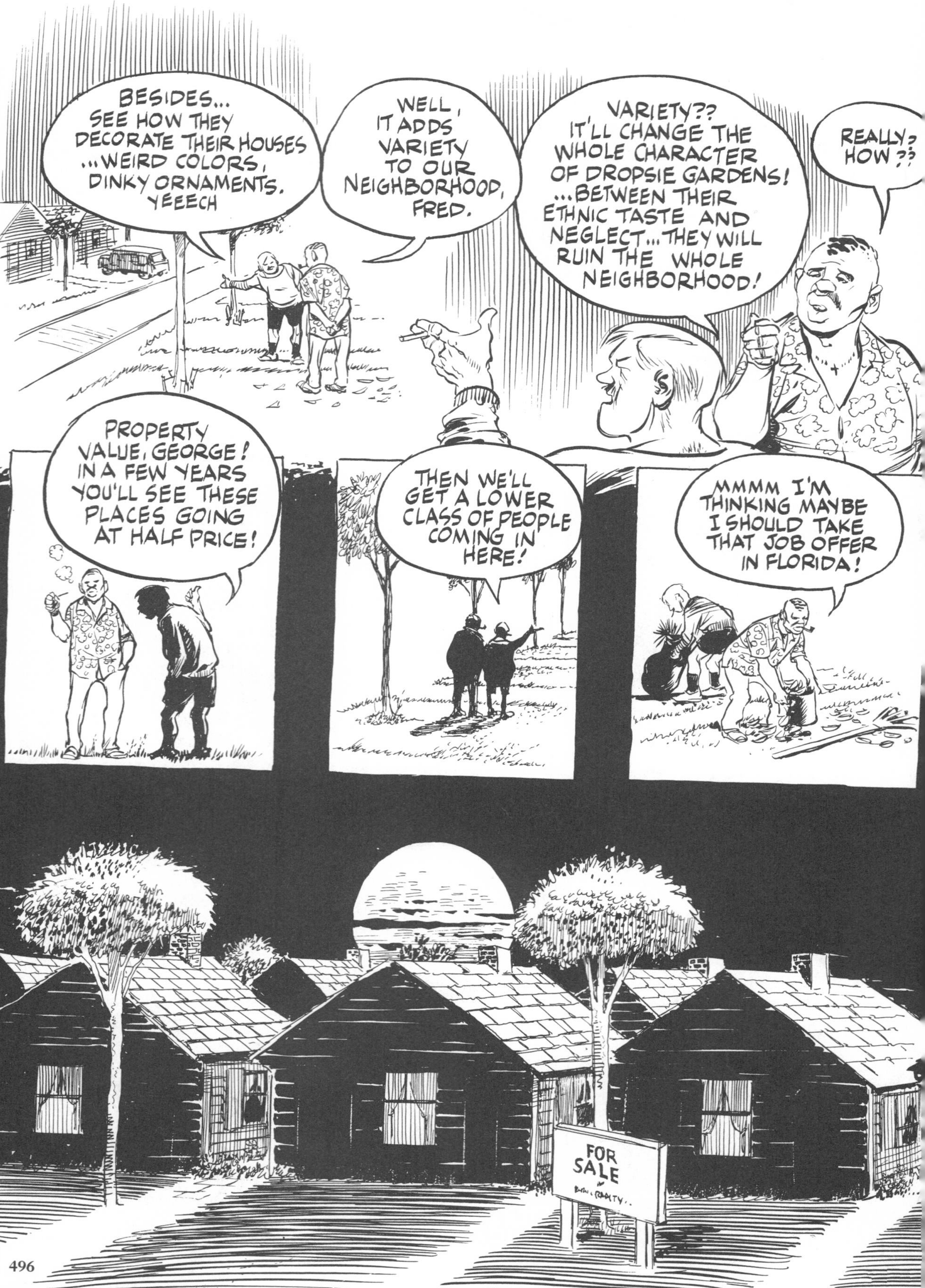
BESIDES... SEE HOW THEY DECORATE THEIR HOUSES ...WEIRD COLORS, DINKY ORNAMENTS. YEEECH
WELL, IT ADDS VARIETY TO OUR NEIGHBORHOOD, FRED.
VARIETY?? IT'LL CHANGE THE WHOLE CHARACTER OF DROPSIE GARDENS! ...BETWEEN THEIR ETHNIC TASTE AND NEGLECT... THEY WILL RUIN THE WHOLE NEIGHBORHOOD!
REALLY? HOW??
PROPERTY VALUE, GEORGE! IN A FEW YEARS YOU'LL SEE THESE PLACES GOING AT HALF PRICE!
THEN WE'LL GET A LOWER CLASS OF PEOPLE COMING IN HERE!
MMMM I'M THINKING MAYBE I SHOULD TAKE THAT JOB OFFER IN FLORIDA!
FOR SALE

AS IT OFTEN HAPPENS TO NEIGHBORHOODS DROPSIE AVENUE'S ETHNIC MIX BEGAN TO CHANGE. THE SIMPLE INEXPENSIVE HOME ATTRACTED A NEW GROUP OF PEOPLE. POORER AND IMMIGRANT, THEY CAME WITH DIFFERENT CULTURAL TASTES AND A LESS RESPONSIBLE ATTUTUDE TOWARD OWNERSHIP AND COMMUNITY. SOON THEY ADDED BRIGHTLY COLORED IMPROVISED STRUCTURES TO ACCOMMODATE THEIR LARGE FAMILIES. AS EARLIER RESIDENTS MOVED OUT, ITS CHARACTER CHANGED.... VISIBLE EVIDENCE OF IMPLACABLE GROWTH.

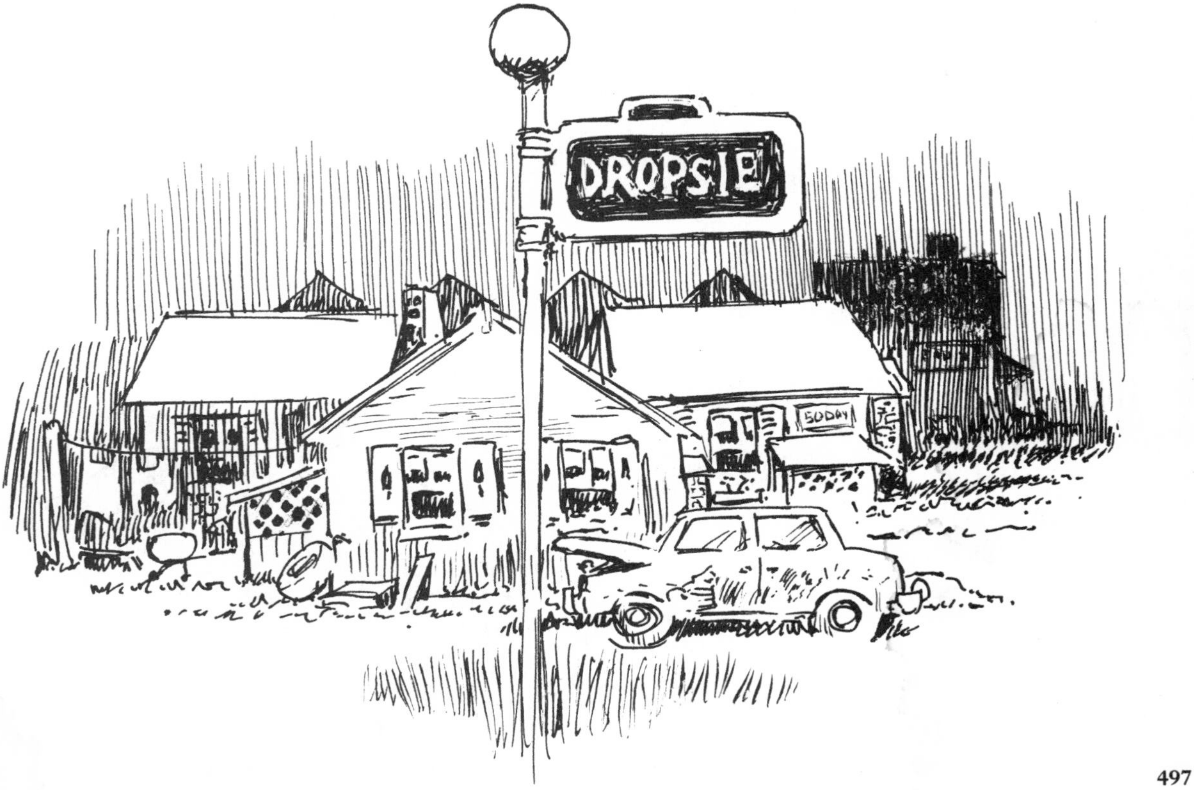
DROPSIE

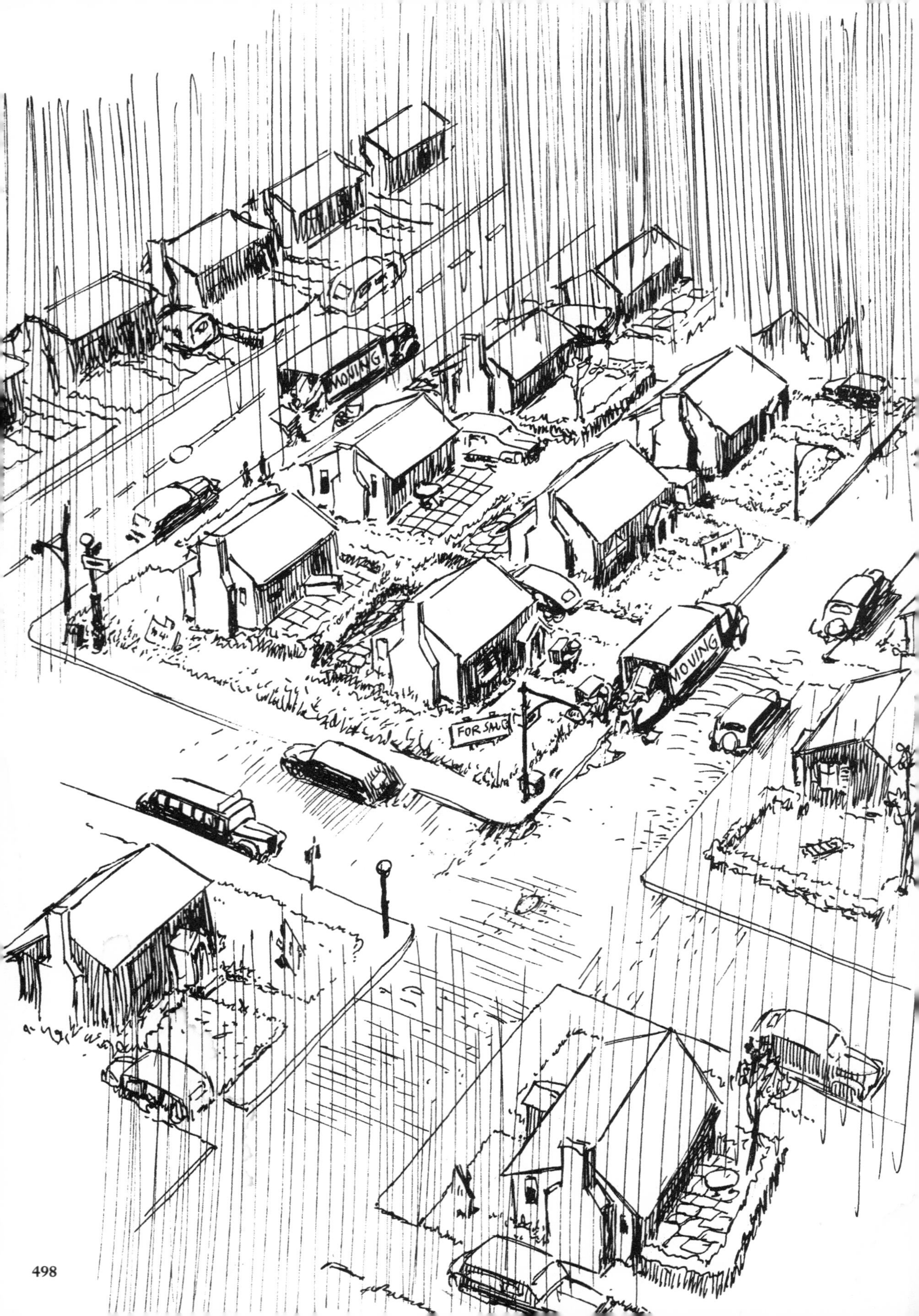

MOVING
MOVING
FOR SALE

DATE DUE

GAYLORD			PRINTED IN U.S.A.